F. SCOTT FITZGERALD

F. Scott Fitzgerald

NOVELS AND STORIES 1920–1922

This Side of Paradise
Flappers and Philosophers
The Beautiful and Damned
Tales of the Jazz Age

THE LIBRARY OF AMERICA

The paper used in this publication meets the
minimum requirements of the American National Standard for
Information Sciences—Permanence of Paper for Printed
Library Materials, ANSI Z39.48—1984.

Distributed to the trade in the United States
by Penguin Putnam Inc.
and in Canada by Penguin Books Canada Ltd.

Library of Congress Catalog Number: 00-024287

For cataloging information, see end of Notes.
ISBN 1-883011-84-1

First Printing
The Library of America—117

Manufactured in the United States of America

Jackson R. Bryer
wrote the chronology and notes
for this volume

Contents

This Side of Paradise 1

Flappers and Philosophers
- The Offshore Pirate 253
- The Ice Palace 284
- Head and Shoulders 310
- The Cut-Glass Bowl 335
- Bernice Bobs Her Hair 356
- Benediction 382
- Dalyrimple Goes Wrong 399
- The Four Fists 417

The Beautiful and Damned 435

Tales of the Jazz Age
- The Jelly Bean 803
- The Camel's Back 823
- May Day 850
- Porcelain and Pink 903
- The Diamond as Big as the Ritz 913
- The Curious Case of Benjamin Button 954
- Tarquin of Cheapside 980
- "O Russet Witch!" 988
- The Lees of Happiness 1019
- Mr. Icky 1041
- Jemina, the Mountain Girl 1049

Chronology 1057
Note on the Texts 1068
Notes 1072

THIS SIDE OF PARADISE

. . . Well this side of Paradise! . . .
There's little comfort in the wise.
—*Rupert Brooke.*

Experience is the name so many people give to their mistakes.
—*Oscar Wilde.*

TO

SIGOURNEY FAY

CONTENTS

BOOK ONE: THE ROMANTIC EGOTIST

CHAPTER		PAGE
I.	Amory, Son of Beatrice	5
II.	Spires and Gargoyles	35
III.	The Egotist Considers	82
IV.	Narcissus Off Duty	108

[Interlude: May, 1917—February, 1919.]

BOOK TWO: THE EDUCATION OF A PERSONAGE

CHAPTER		PAGE
I.	The Débutante	145
II.	Experiments in Convalescence	172
III.	Young Irony	193
IV.	The Supercilious Sacrifice	212
V.	The Egotist Becomes a Personage	222

BOOK ONE

THE ROMANTIC EGOTIST

CHAPTER I

Amory, Son of Beatrice

AMORY BLAINE inherited from his mother every trait, except the stray inexpressible few, that made him worth while. His father, an ineffectual, inarticulate man with a taste for Byron and a habit of drowsing over the *Encyclopædia Britannica*, grew wealthy at thirty through the death of two elder brothers, successful Chicago brokers, and in the first flush of feeling that the world was his, went to Bar Harbor and met Beatrice O'Hara. In consequence, Stephen Blaine handed down to posterity his height of just under six feet and his tendency to waver at crucial moments, these two abstractions appearing in his son Amory. For many years he hovered in the background of his family's life, an unassertive figure with a face half-obliterated by lifeless, silky hair, continually occupied in "taking care" of his wife, continually harassed by the idea that he didn't and couldn't understand her.

But Beatrice Blaine! There was a woman! Early pictures taken on her father's estate at Lake Geneva, Wisconsin, or in Rome at the Sacred Heart Convent—an educational extravagance that in her youth was only for the daughters of the exceptionally wealthy—showed the exquisite delicacy of her features, the consummate art and simplicity of her clothes. A brilliant education she had—her youth passed in renaissance glory, she was versed in the latest gossip of the Older Roman Families; known by name as a fabulously wealthy American girl to Cardinal Vitori and Queen Margherita and more subtle celebrities that one must have had some culture even to have heard of. She learned in England to prefer whiskey and soda to wine, and her small talk was broadened in two senses during a winter in Vienna. All in all Beatrice O'Hara absorbed the sort of education that will be quite impossible ever again; a tutelage measured by the number of things and people one could be contemptuous of and charming about; a culture rich in all arts and traditions, barren of all ideas, in the last of those days when the great gardener clipped the inferior roses to produce one perfect bud.

In her less important moments she returned to America, met Stephen Blaine and married him—this almost entirely because she was a little bit weary, a little bit sad. Her only child was carried through a tiresome season and brought into the world on a spring day in ninety-six.

When Amory was five he was already a delightful companion for her. He was an auburn-haired boy, with great, handsome eyes which he would grow up to in time, a facile imaginative mind and a taste for fancy dress. From his fourth to his tenth year he *did* the country with his mother in her father's private car, from Coronado, where his mother became so bored that she had a nervous breakdown in a fashionable hotel, down to Mexico City, where she took a mild, almost epidemic consumption. This trouble pleased her, and later she made use of it as an intrinsic part of her atmosphere—especially after several astounding bracers.

So, while more or less fortunate little rich boys were defying governesses on the beach at Newport, or being spanked or tutored or read to from "Do and Dare," or "Frank on the Mississippi," Amory was biting acquiescent bell-boys in the Waldorf, outgrowing a natural repugnance to chamber music and symphonies, and deriving a highly specialized education from his mother.

"Amory."

"Yes, Beatrice." (Such a quaint name for his mother; she encouraged it.)

"Dear, don't *think* of getting out of bed yet. I've always suspected that early rising in early life makes one nervous. Clothilde is having your breakfast brought up."

"All right."

"I am feeling very old to-day, Amory," she would sigh, her face a rare cameo of pathos, her voice exquisitely modulated, her hands as facile as Bernhardt's. "My nerves are on edge—on edge. We must leave this terrifying place to-morrow and go searching for sunshine."

Amory's penetrating green eyes would look out through

tangled hair at his mother. Even at this age he had no illusions about her.

"Amory."

"Oh, *yes.*"

"I want you to take a red-hot bath—as hot as you can bear it, and just relax your nerves. You can read in the tub if you wish."

She fed him sections of the "Fêtes Galantes" before he was ten; at eleven he could talk glibly, if rather reminiscently, of Brahms and Mozart and Beethoven. One afternoon, when left alone in the hotel at Hot Springs, he sampled his mother's apricot cordial, and as the taste pleased him, he became quite tipsy. This was fun for a while, but he essayed a cigarette in his exaltation, and succumbed to a vulgar, plebeian reaction. Though this incident horrified Beatrice, it also secretly amused her and became part of what in a later generation would have been termed her "line."

"This son of mine," he heard her tell a room full of awe-struck, admiring women one day, "is entirely sophisticated and quite charming—but delicate—we're all delicate; *here*, you know." Her hand was radiantly outlined against her beautiful bosom; then sinking her voice to a whisper, she told them of the apricot cordial. They rejoiced, for she was a brave raconteuse, but many were the keys turned in sideboard locks that night against the possible defection of little Bobby or Barbara. . . . .

These domestic pilgrimages were invariably in state; two maids, the private car, or Mr. Blaine when available, and very often a physician. When Amory had the whooping-cough four disgusted specialists glared at each other hunched around his bed; when he took scarlet fever the number of attendants, including physicians and nurses, totalled fourteen. However, blood being thicker than broth, he was pulled through.

The Blaines were attached to no city. They were the Blaines of Lake Geneva; they had quite enough relatives to serve in place of friends, and an enviable standing from Pasadena to Cape Cod. But Beatrice grew more and more prone to like only new acquaintances, as there were certain stories, such as the history of her constitution and its many amendments, memories of her years abroad, that it was necessary for her to repeat at regular intervals. Like Freudian dreams, they must be thrown off, else they would sweep in and lay siege to her nerves. But Beatrice was critical about American women, especially the floating population of ex-Westerners.

"They have accents, my dear," she told Amory, "not Southern accents or Boston accents, not an accent attached to any locality, just an accent"—she became dreamy. "They pick up old, moth-eaten London accents that are down on their luck and have to be used by some one. They talk as an English butler might after several years in a Chicago grand-opera company." She became almost incoherent— "Suppose—time in every Western woman's life—she feels her husband is prosperous enough for her to have—accent—they try to impress *me*, my dear——"

Though she thought of her body as a mass of frailties, she considered her soul quite as ill, and therefore important in her life. She had once been a Catholic, but discovering that priests were infinitely more attentive when she was in process of losing or regaining faith in Mother Church, she maintained an enchantingly wavering attitude. Often she deplored the bourgeois quality of the American Catholic clergy, and was quite sure that had she lived in the shadow of the great Continental cathedrals her soul would still be a thin flame on the mighty altar of Rome. Still, next to doctors, priests were her favorite sport.

"Ah, Bishop Wiston," she would declare, "I do not *want* to talk of myself. I can imagine the stream of hysterical women fluttering at your doors, beseeching you to be sim*pati*co"—then after an interlude filled by the clergyman—"but my mood—is—oddly dissimilar."

Only to bishops and above did she divulge her clerical romance. When she had first returned to her country there had been a pagan, Swinburnian young man in Asheville, for whose passionate kisses and unsentimental conversations she had taken a decided penchant—they had discussed the matter pro and con with an intellectual romancing quite devoid of soppiness. Eventually she had decided to marry for background, and the young pagan from Asheville had gone through a spiritual crisis, joined the Catholic Church, and was now—Monsignor Darcy.

"Indeed, Mrs. Blaine, he is still delightful company—quite the cardinal's right-hand man."

"Amory will go to him one day, I know," breathed the beautiful lady, "and Monsignor Darcy will understand him as he understood me."

Amory became thirteen, rather tall and slender, and more than ever on to his Celtic mother. He had tutored occasionally—the idea being that he was to "keep up," at each place "taking up the work where he left off," yet as no tutor ever found the place he left off, his mind was still in very good shape. What a few more years of this life would have made of him is problematical. However, four hours out from land, Italy bound, with Beatrice, his appendix burst, probably from too many meals in bed, and after a series of frantic telegrams to Europe and America, to the amazement of the passengers the great ship slowly wheeled around and returned to New York to deposit Amory at the pier. You will admit that if it was not life it was magnificent.

After the operation Beatrice had a nervous breakdown that bore a suspicious resemblance to delirium tremens, and Amory was left in Minneapolis, destined to spend the ensuing two years with his aunt and uncle. There the crude, vulgar air of Western civilization first catches him—in his underwear, so to speak.

A Kiss For Amory

His lip curled when he read it.

"I am going to have a bobbing party," it said, *"on Thursday, December the seventeenth, at five o'clock, and I would like it very much if you could come.*

Yours truly,

R.S.V.P. *Myra St. Claire."*

He had been two months in Minneapolis, and his chief struggle had been the concealing from "the other guys at school" how particularly superior he felt himself to be, yet this conviction was built upon shifting sands. He had shown off one day in French class (he was in senior French class) to the utter confusion of Mr. Reardon, whose accent Amory damned contemptuously, and to the delight of the class. Mr. Reardon, who had spent several weeks in Paris ten years before, took his revenge on the verbs, whenever he had his book open. But another time Amory showed off in history class, with quite disastrous results, for the boys there were his own age, and they shrilled innuendoes at each other all the following week:

"Aw—I b'lieve, doncherknow, the Umuricun revolution was *lawgely* an affair of the middul *clawses*," or

"Washington came of very good blood—aw, quite good—I b'lieve."

Amory ingeniously tried to retrieve himself by blundering on purpose. Two years before he had commenced a history of the United States which, though it only got as far as the Colonial Wars, had been pronounced by his mother completely enchanting.

His chief disadvantage lay in athletics, but as soon as he discovered that it was the touchstone of power and popularity at school, he began to make furious, persistent efforts to excel in the winter sports, and with his ankles aching and bending in spite of his efforts, he skated valiantly around the Lorelie rink every afternoon, wondering how soon he would be able to carry a hockey-stick without getting it inexplicably tangled in his skates.

The invitation to Miss Myra St. Claire's bobbing party spent the morning in his coat pocket, where it had an intense physical affair with a dusty piece of peanut brittle. During the afternoon he brought it to light with a sigh, and after some consideration and a preliminary draft in the back of Collar and Daniel's "First-Year Latin," composed an answer:

My dear Miss St. Claire:

Your truly charming envitation for the evening of next Thursday evening was truly delightful to receive this morning. I will be charm and inchanted indeed to present my compliments on next Thursday evening.

Faithfully,

Amory Blaine.

On Thursday, therefore, he walked pensively along the slippery, shovel-scraped sidewalks, and came in sight of Myra's house, on the half-hour after five, a lateness which he fancied his mother would have favored. He waited on the door-step with his eyes nonchalantly half-closed, and planned his entrance with precision. He would cross the floor, not too hastily, to Mrs. St. Claire, and say with exactly the correct modulation:

"My *dear* Mrs. St. Claire, I'm *frightfully* sorry to be late, but my maid"—he paused there and realized he would be quoting—"but my uncle and I had to see a fella— Yes, I've met your enchanting daughter at dancing-school."

Then he would shake hands, using that slight, half-foreign bow, with all the starchy little females, and nod to the fellas who would be standing 'round, paralyzed into rigid groups for mutual protection.

A butler (one of the three in Minneapolis) swung open the door. Amory stepped inside and divested himself of cap and coat. He was mildly surprised not to hear the shrill squawk of conversation from the next room, and he decided it must be quite formal. He approved of that—as he approved of the butler.

"Miss Myra," he said.

To his surprise the butler grinned horribly.

"Oh, yeah," he declared, "she's here." He was unaware that his failure to be cockney was ruining his standing. Amory considered him coldly.

"But," continued the butler, his voice rising unnecessarily, "she's the only one what *is* here. The party's gone."

Amory gasped in sudden horror.

"What?"

"She's been waitin' for Amory Blaine. That's you, ain't it? Her mother says that if you showed up by five-thirty you two was to go after 'em in the Packard."

Amory's despair was crystallized by the appearance of Myra herself, bundled to the ears in a polo coat, her face plainly sulky, her voice pleasant only with difficulty.

" 'Lo, Amory."

" 'Lo, Myra." He had described the state of his vitality.

"Well—you *got* here, *any*ways."

"Well—I'll tell you. I guess you don't know about the auto accident," he romanced.

Myra's eyes opened wide.

"Who was it to?"

"Well," he continued desperately, "uncle 'n aunt 'n I."

"Was any one *killed*?"

Amory paused and then nodded.

"Your uncle?"—alarm.

"Oh, no—just a horse—a sorta gray horse."

At this point the Erse butler snickered.

"Probably killed the engine," he suggested. Amory would have put him on the rack without a scruple.

"We'll go now," said Myra coolly. "You see, Amory, the bobs were ordered for five and everybody was here, so we couldn't wait——"

"Well, I couldn't help it, could I?"

"So mama said for me to wait till ha'past five. We'll catch the bob before it gets to the Minnehaha Club, Amory."

Amory's shredded poise dropped from him. He pictured the happy party jingling along snowy streets, the appearance of the limousine, the horrible public descent of him and Myra before sixty reproachful eyes, his apology—a real one this time. He sighed aloud.

"What?" inquired Myra.

"Nothing. I was just yawning. Are we going to *surely* catch up with 'em before they get there?" He was encouraging a faint hope that they might slip into the Minnehaha Club and meet the others there, be found in blasé seclusion before the fire and quite regain his lost attitude.

"Oh, sure Mike, we'll catch 'em all right—let's hurry."

He became conscious of his stomach. As they stepped into the machine he hurriedly slapped the paint of diplomacy over a rather box-like plan he had conceived. It was based upon some "trade-lasts" gleaned at dancing-school, to the effect that he was "awful good-looking and *English*, sort of."

"Myra," he said, lowering his voice and choosing his words carefully, "I beg a thousand pardons. Can you ever forgive me?"

She regarded him gravely, his intent green eyes, his mouth, that to her thirteen-year-old, arrow-collar taste was the quintessence of romance. Yes, Myra could forgive him very easily.

"Why—yes—sure."

He looked at her again, and then dropped his eyes. He had lashes.

"I'm awful," he said sadly. "I'm diff'runt. I don't know why I make faux pas. 'Cause I don't care, I s'pose." Then, recklessly: "I been smoking too much. I've got t'bacca heart."

Myra pictured an all-night tobacco debauch, with Amory pale and reeling from the effect of nicotined lungs. She gave a little gasp.

"Oh, *Amory*, don't smoke. You'll stunt your *growth*!"

"I don't care," he persisted gloomily. "I gotta. I got the habit. I've done a lot of things that if my fambly knew"—he hesitated, giving her imagination time to picture dark horrors—"I went to the burlesque show last week."

Myra was quite overcome. He turned the green eyes on her again.

"You're the only girl in town I like much," he exclaimed in a rush of sentiment. "You're simpatico."

Myra was not sure that she was, but it sounded stylish though vaguely improper.

Thick dusk had descended outside, and as the limousine made a sudden turn she was jolted against him; their hands touched.

"You shouldn't smoke, Amory," she whispered. "Don't you know that?"

He shook his head.

"Nobody cares."

Myra hesitated.

"*I* care."

Something stirred within Amory.

"Oh, yes, you do! You got a crush on Froggy Parker. I guess everybody knows that."

"No, I haven't," very slowly.

A silence, while Amory thrilled. There was something fascinating about Myra, shut away here cosily from the dim, chill air. Myra, a little bundle of clothes, with strands of yellow hair curling out from under her skating cap.

"Because I've got a crush, too—" He paused, for he heard in the distance the sound of young laughter, and, peering through the frosted glass along the lamp-lit street, he made out the dark outline of the bobbing party. He must act quickly. He reached over with a violent, jerky effort, and clutched Myra's hand—her thumb, to be exact.

"Tell him to go to the Minnehaha straight," he whispered. "I wanta talk to you—I *got* to talk to you."

Myra made out the party ahead, had an instant vision of her mother, and then—alas for convention—glanced into the eyes beside.

"Turn down this side street, Richard, and drive straight to the Minnehaha Club!" she cried through the speaking tube. Amory sank back against the cushions with a sigh of relief.

"I can kiss her," he thought. "I'll bet I can. I'll *bet* I can!"

Overhead the sky was half crystalline, half misty, and the night around was chill and vibrant with rich tension. From the Country Club steps the roads stretched away, dark creases on the white blanket; huge heaps of snow lining the sides like the tracks of giant moles. They lingered for a moment on the steps, and watched the white holiday moon.

"Pale moons like that one"—Amory made a vague gesture—"make people mysterieuse. You look like a young witch with her cap off and her hair sorta mussed"—her hands clutched at her hair— "Oh, leave it, it looks *good*."

They drifted up the stairs and Myra led the way into the little den of his dreams, where a cosy fire was burning before a big sink-down couch. A few years later this was to be a great stage for Amory, a cradle for many an emotional crisis. Now they talked for a moment about bobbing parties.

"There's always a bunch of shy fellas," he commented, "sitting at the tail of the bob, sorta lurkin' an' whisperin' an' pushin' each other off. Then there's always some crazy cross-eyed girl"—he gave a terrifying imitation—"she's always talkin' *hard*, sorta, to the chaperon."

"You're such a funny boy," puzzled Myra.

"How d'y' mean?" Amory gave immediate attention, on his own ground at last.

"Oh—always talking about crazy things. Why don't you come ski-ing with Marylyn and I to-morrow?"

"I don't like girls in the daytime," he said shortly, and then, thinking this a bit abrupt, he added: "But I like you." He cleared his throat. "I like you first and second and third."

Myra's eyes became dreamy. What a story this would make to tell Marylyn! Here on the couch with this *wonderful*-looking boy—the little fire—the sense that they were alone in the great building——

Myra capitulated. The atmosphere was too appropriate.

"I like you the first twenty-five," she confessed, her voice trembling, "and Froggy Parker twenty-sixth."

Froggy had fallen twenty-five places in one hour. As yet he had not even noticed it.

But Amory, being on the spot, leaned over quickly and kissed Myra's cheek. He had never kissed a girl before, and he tasted his lips curiously, as if he had munched some new fruit. Then their lips brushed like young wild flowers in the wind.

"We're awful," rejoiced Myra gently. She slipped her hand into his, her head drooped against his shoulder. Sudden revulsion seized Amory, disgust, loathing for the whole incident. He desired frantically to be away, never to see Myra again, never to kiss any one; he became conscious of his face and hers, of their clinging hands, and he wanted to creep out of his body and hide somewhere safe out of sight, up in the corner of his mind.

"Kiss me again." Her voice came out of a great void.

"I don't want to," he heard himself saying. There was another pause.

"I don't want to!" he repeated passionately.

Myra sprang up, her cheeks pink with bruised vanity, the great bow on the back of her head trembling sympathetically.

"I hate you!" she cried. "Don't you ever dare to speak to me again!"

"What?" stammered Amory.

"I'll tell mama you kissed me! I will too! I will too! I'll tell mama, and she won't let me play with you!"

Amory rose and stared at her helplessly, as though she were a new animal of whose presence on the earth he had not heretofore been aware.

The door opened suddenly, and Myra's mother appeared on the threshold, fumbling with her lorgnette.

"Well," she began, adjusting it benignantly, "the man at the desk told me you two children were up here— How do you do, Amory."

Amory watched Myra and waited for the crash—but none came. The pout faded, the high pink subsided, and Myra's voice was placid as a summer lake when she answered her mother.

"Oh, we started so late, mama, that I thought we might as *well*——"

He heard from below the shrieks of laughter, and smelled the vapid odor of hot chocolate and tea-cakes as he silently followed mother and daughter down-stairs. The sound of the graphophone mingled with the voices of many girls humming the air, and a faint glow was born and spread over him:

"Casey-Jones—mounted to the cab-un
Casey-Jones—'th his orders in his hand.
Casey-Jones—mounted to the cab-un
Took his farewell journey to the prom-ised land."

Snapshots of the Young Egotist

Amory spent nearly two years in Minneapolis. The first winter he wore moccasins that were born yellow, but after many applications of oil and dirt assumed their mature color, a dirty, greenish brown; he wore a gray plaid mackinaw coat, and a red toboggan cap. His dog, Count Del Monte, ate the red cap, so his uncle gave him a gray one that pulled down over his face. The trouble with this one was that you breathed into it and your breath froze; one day the darn thing froze his cheek. He rubbed snow on his cheek, but it turned bluish-black just the same.

The Count Del Monte ate a box of bluing once, but it didn't hurt him. Later, however, he lost his mind and ran madly up the street, bumping into fences, rolling in gutters, and pursuing his eccentric course out of Amory's life. Amory cried on his bed.

"Poor little Count," he cried. "Oh, *poor* little *Count*!"

After several months he suspected Count of a fine piece of emotional acting.

Amory and Frog Parker considered that the greatest line in literature occurred in Act III of "Arsene Lupin."

They sat in the first row at the Wednesday and Saturday matinées. The line was:

"If one can't be a great artist or a great soldier, the next best thing is to be a great criminal."

Amory fell in love again, and wrote a poem. This was it:

"Marylyn and Sall*ee*,
Those are the girls for me.
Marylyn stands above
Sall*ee* in that sweet, deep love."

He was interested in whether McGovern of Minnesota would make the first or second All-American, how to do the card-pass, how to do the coin-pass, chameleon ties, how babies were born, and whether Three-fingered Brown was really a better pitcher than Christie Mathewson.

Among other things he read: "For the Honor of the School," "Little Women" (twice), "The Common Law," "Sapho," "Dangerous Dan McGrew," "The Broad Highway" (three times), "The Fall of the House of Usher," "Three Weeks," "Mary Ware, the Little Colonel's Chum," "Gunga Dhin," *The Police Gazette*, and *Jim-Jam Jems.*

He had all the Henty biasses in history, and was particularly fond of the cheerful murder stories of Mary Roberts Rineheart.

School ruined his French and gave him a distaste for standard authors. His masters considered him idle, unreliable and superficially clever.

He collected locks of hair from many girls. He wore the rings of several. Finally he could borrow no more rings, owing to his nervous habit of chewing them out of shape. This, it seemed, usually aroused the jealous suspicions of the next borrower.

All through the summer months Amory and Frog Parker went each week to the Stock Company. Afterward they would stroll home in the balmy air of August night, dreaming along

Hennepin and Nicollet Avenues, through the gay crowd. Amory wondered how people could fail to notice that he was a boy marked for glory, and when faces of the throng turned toward him and ambiguous eyes stared into his, he assumed the most romantic of expressions and walked on the air cushions that lie on the asphalts of fourteen.

Always, after he was in bed, there were voices—indefinite, fading, enchanting—just outside his window, and before he fell asleep he would dream one of his favorite waking dreams, the one about becoming a great half-back, or the one about the Japanese invasion, when he was rewarded by being made the youngest general in the world. It was always the becoming he dreamed of, never the being. This, too, was quite characteristic of Amory.

Code of the Young Egotist

Before he was summoned back to Lake Geneva, he had appeared, shy but inwardly glowing, in his first long trousers, set off by a purple accordion tie and a "Belmont" collar with the edges unassailably meeting, purple socks, and handkerchief with a purple border peeping from his breast pocket. But more than that, he had formulated his first philosophy, a code to live by, which, as near as it can be named, was a sort of aristocratic egotism.

He had realized that his best interests were bound up with those of a certain variant, changing person, whose label, in order that his past might always be identified with him, was Amory Blaine. Amory marked himself a fortunate youth, capable of infinite expansion for good or evil. He did not consider himself a "strong char'c'ter," but relied on his facility (learn things sorta quick) and his superior mentality (read a lotta deep books). He was proud of the fact that he could never become a mechanical or scientific genius. From no other heights was he debarred.

Physically.—Amory thought that he was exceedingly handsome. He was. He fancied himself an athlete of possibilities and a supple dancer.

Socially.—Here his condition was, perhaps, most dangerous. He granted himself personality, charm, magnetism, poise, the power of dominating all contemporary males, the gift of fascinating all women.

Mentally.—Complete, unquestioned superiority.

Now a confession will have to be made. Amory had rather a Puritan conscience. Not that he yielded to it—later in life he almost completely slew it—but at fifteen it made him consider himself a great deal worse than other boys . . . unscrupulousness . . . the desire to influence people in almost every way, even for evil . . . a certain coldness and lack of affection, amounting sometimes to cruelty . . . a shifting sense of honor . . . an unholy selfishness . . . a puzzled, furtive interest in everything concerning sex.

There was, also, a curious strain of weakness running crosswise through his make-up . . . a harsh phrase from the lips of an older boy (older boys usually detested him) was liable to sweep him off his poise into surly sensitiveness, or timid stupidity . . . he was a slave to his own moods and he felt that though he was capable of recklessness and audacity, he possessed neither courage, perseverance, nor self-respect.

Vanity, tempered with self-suspicion if not self-knowledge, a sense of people as automatons to his will, a desire to "pass" as many boys as possible and get to a vague top of the world . . . with this background did Amory drift into adolescence.

Preparatory to the Great Adventure

The train slowed up with midsummer languor at Lake Geneva, and Amory caught sight of his mother waiting in her electric on the gravelled station drive. It was an ancient electric, one of the early types, and painted gray. The sight of her sitting there, slenderly erect, and of her face, where beauty and dignity combined, melting to a dreamy recollected smile, filled him with a sudden great pride of her. As they kissed coolly and he stepped into the electric, he felt a quick fear lest he had lost the requisite charm to measure up to her.

"Dear boy—you're *so* tall . . . look behind and see if there's anything coming . . ."

She looked left and right, she slipped cautiously into a speed of two miles an hour, beseeching Amory to act as sentinel; and at one busy crossing she made him get out and run ahead to signal her forward like a traffic policeman. Beatrice was what might be termed a careful driver.

"You *are* tall—but you're still very handsome—you've skipped the awkward age, or is that sixteen; perhaps it's fourteen or fifteen; I can never remember; but you've skipped it."

"Don't embarrass me," murmured Amory.

"But, my dear boy, what odd clothes! They look as if they were a *set*—don't they? Is your underwear purple, too?"

Amory grunted impolitely.

"You must go to Brooks' and get some really nice suits. Oh, we'll have a talk to-night or perhaps to-morrow night. I want to tell you about your heart—you've probably been neglecting your heart—and you don't *know*."

Amory thought how superficial was the recent overlay of his own generation. Aside from a minute shyness, he felt that the old cynical kinship with his mother had not been one bit broken. Yet for the first few days he wandered about the gardens and along the shore in a state of superloneliness, finding a lethargic content in smoking "Bull" at the garage with one of the chauffeurs.

The sixty acres of the estate were dotted with old and new summer houses and many fountains and white benches that came suddenly into sight from foliage-hung hiding-places; there was a great and constantly increasing family of white cats that prowled the many flower-beds and were silhouetted suddenly at night against the darkening trees. It was on one of the shadowy paths that Beatrice at last captured Amory, after Mr. Blaine had, as usual, retired for the evening to his private library. After reproving him for avoiding her, she took him for a long tête-à-tête in the moonlight. He could not reconcile himself to her beauty, that was mother to his own, the exquisite neck and shoulders, the grace of a fortunate woman of thirty.

"Amory, dear," she crooned softly, "I had such a strange, weird time after I left you."

"Did you, Beatrice?"

"When I had my last breakdown"—she spoke of it as a sturdy, gallant feat.

"The doctors told me"—her voice sang on a confidential

note—"that if any man alive had done the consistent drinking that I have, he would have been physically *shattered*, my dear, and in his *grave*—long in his grave."

Amory winced, and wondered how this would have sounded to Froggy Parker.

"Yes," continued Beatrice tragically, "I had dreams—wonderful visions." She pressed the palms of her hands into her eyes. "I saw bronze rivers lapping marble shores, and great birds that soared through the air, parti-colored birds with iridescent plumage. I heard strange music and the flare of barbaric trumpets—what?"

Amory had snickered.

"What, Amory?"

"I said go on, Beatrice."

"That was all—it merely recurred and recurred—gardens that flaunted coloring against which this would be quite dull, moons that whirled and swayed, paler than winter moons, more golden than harvest moons——"

"Are you quite well now, Beatrice?"

"Quite well—as well as I will ever be. I am not understood, Amory. I know that can't express it to you, Amory, but—I am not understood."

Amory was quite moved. He put his arm around his mother, rubbing his head gently against her shoulder.

"Poor Beatrice—poor Beatrice."

"Tell me about *you*, Amory. Did you have two *horrible* years?"

Amory considered lying, and then decided against it.

"No, Beatrice. I enjoyed them. I adapted myself to the bourgeoisie. I became conventional." He surprised himself by saying that, and he pictured how Froggy would have gaped.

"Beatrice," he said suddenly, "I want to go away to school. Everybody in Minneapolis is going to go away to school."

Beatrice showed some alarm.

"But you're only fifteen."

"Yes, but everybody goes away to school at fifteen, and I *want* to, Beatrice."

On Beatrice's suggestion the subject was dropped for the rest of the walk, but a week later she delighted him by saying:

"Amory, I have decided to let you have your way. If you still want to, you can go to school."

"Yes?"

"To St. Regis's in Connecticut."

Amory felt a quick excitement.

"It's being arranged," continued Beatrice. "It's better that you should go away. I'd have preferred you to have gone to Eton, and then to Christ Church, Oxford, but it seems impracticable now—and for the present we'll let the university question take care of itself."

"What are you going to do, Beatrice?"

"Heaven knows. It seems my fate to fret away my years in this country. Not for a second do I regret being American—indeed, I think that a regret typical of very vulgar people, and I feel sure we are the great coming nation—yet"—and she sighed—"I feel my life should have drowsed away close to an older, mellower civilization, a land of greens and autumnal browns——"

Amory did not answer, so his mother continued:

"My regret is that you haven't been abroad, but still, as you are a man, it's better that you should grow up here under the snarling eagle—is that the right term?"

Amory agreed that it was. She would not have appreciated the Japanese invasion.

"When do I go to school?"

"Next month. You'll have to start East a little early to take your examinations. After that you'll have a free week, so I want you to go up the Hudson and pay a visit."

"To who?"

"To Monsignor Darcy, Amory. He wants to see you. He went to Harrow and then to Yale—became a Catholic. I want him to talk to you—I feel he can be such a help—" She stroked his auburn hair gently. "Dear Amory, dear Amory——"

"Dear Beatrice——"

So early in September Amory, provided with "six suits summer underwear, six suits winter underwear, one sweater or T shirt, one jersey, one overcoat, winter, etc.," set out for New England, the land of schools.

There were Andover and Exeter with their memories of New England dead—large, college-like democracies; St. Mark's, Groton, St. Regis'—recruited from Boston and the Knickerbocker families of New York; St. Paul's, with its great rinks; Pomfret and St. George's, prosperous and well-dressed; Taft and Hotchkiss, which prepared the wealth of the Middle West for social success at Yale; Pawling, Westminster, Choate, Kent, and a hundred others; all milling out their well-set-up, conventional, impressive type, year after year; their mental stimulus the college entrance exams; their vague purpose set forth in a hundred circulars as "To impart a Thorough Mental, Moral, and Physical Training as a Christian Gentleman, to fit the boy *for meeting the problems of his day and generation*, and to give a solid foundation in the Arts and Sciences."

At St. Regis' Amory stayed three days and took his exams with a scoffing confidence, then doubling back to New York to pay his tutelary visit. The metropolis, barely glimpsed, made little impression on him, except for the sense of cleanliness he drew from the tall white buildings seen from a Hudson River steamboat in the early morning. Indeed, his mind was so crowded with dreams of athletic prowess at school that he considered this visit only as a rather tiresome prelude to the great adventure. This, however, it did not prove to be.

Monsignor Darcy's house was an ancient, rambling structure set on a hill overlooking the river, and there lived its owner, between his trips to all parts of the Roman-Catholic world, rather like an exiled Stuart king waiting to be called to the rule of his land. Monsignor was forty-four then, and bustling—a trifle too stout for symmetry, with hair the color of spun gold, and a brilliant, enveloping personality. When he came into a room clad in his full purple regalia from thatch to toe, he resembled a Turner sunset, and attracted both admiration and attention. He had written two novels: one of them violently anti-Catholic, just before his conversion, and five years later another, in which he had attempted to turn all his clever jibes against Catholics into even cleverer innuendoes against Episcopalians. He was intensely ritualistic, startlingly dramatic, loved the idea of God enough to be a celibate, and rather liked his neighbor.

Children adored him because he was like a child; youth revelled in his company because he was still a youth, and couldn't be shocked. In the proper land and century he might have been a Richelieu—at present he was a very moral, very religious (if not particularly pious) clergyman, making a great mystery about pulling rusty wires, and appreciating life to the fullest, if not entirely enjoying it.

He and Amory took to each other at first sight—the jovial, impressive prelate who could dazzle an embassy ball, and the green-eyed, intent youth, in his first long trousers, accepted in their own minds a relation of father and son within a half-hour's conversation.

"My dear boy, I've been waiting to see you for years. Take a big chair and we'll have a chat."

"I've just come from school—St. Regis's, you know."

"So your mother says—a remarkable woman; have a cigarette—I'm sure you smoke. Well, if you're like me, you loathe all science and mathematics——"

Amory nodded vehemently.

"Hate 'em all. Like English and history."

"Of course. You'll hate school for a while, too, but I'm glad you're going to St. Regis's."

"Why?"

"Because it's a gentleman's school, and democracy won't hit you so early. You'll find plenty of that in college."

"I want to go to Princeton," said Amory. "I don't know why, but I think of all Harvard men as sissies, like I used to be, and all Yale men as wearing big blue sweaters and smoking pipes."

Monsignor chuckled.

"I'm one, you know."

"Oh, you're different—I think of Princeton as being lazy and good-looking and aristocratic—you know, like a spring day. Harvard seems sort of indoors——"

"And Yale is November, crisp and energetic," finished Monsignor.

"That's it."

They slipped briskly into an intimacy from which they never recovered.

"I was for Bonnie Prince Charlie," announced Amory.

"Of course you were—and for Hannibal——"

"Yes, and for the Southern Confederacy." He was rather sceptical about being an Irish patriot—he suspected that being Irish was being somewhat common—but Monsignor assured him that Ireland was a romantic lost cause and Irish people quite charming, and that it should, by all means, be one of his principal biasses.

After a crowded hour which included several more cigarettes, and during which Monsignor learned, to his surprise but not to his horror, that Amory had not been brought up a Catholic, he announced that he had another guest. This turned out to be the Honorable Thornton Hancock, of Boston, ex-minister to The Hague, author of an erudite history of the Middle Ages and the last of a distinguished, patriotic, and brilliant family.

"He comes here for a rest," said Monsignor confidentially, treating Amory as a contemporary. "I act as an escape from the weariness of agnosticism, and I think I'm the only man who knows how his staid old mind is really at sea and longs for a sturdy spar like the Church to cling to."

Their first luncheon was one of the memorable events of Amory's early life. He was quite radiant and gave off a peculiar brightness and charm. Monsignor called out the best that he had thought by question and suggestion, and Amory talked with an ingenious brilliance of a thousand impulses and desires and repulsions and faiths and fears. He and Monsignor held the floor, and the older man, with his less receptive, less accepting, yet certainly not colder mentality, seemed content to listen and bask in the mellow sunshine that played between these two. Monsignor gave the effect of sunlight to many people; Amory gave it in his youth and, to some extent, when he was very much older, but never again was it quite so mutually spontaneous.

"He's a radiant boy," thought Thornton Hancock, who had seen the splendor of two continents and talked with Parnell and Gladstone and Bismarck—and afterward he added to Monsignor: "But his education ought not to be intrusted to a school or college."

But for the next four years the best of Amory's intellect was concentrated on matters of popularity, the intricacies of a university social system and American Society as represented by Biltmore Teas and Hot Springs golf-links.

. . . In all, a wonderful week, that saw Amory's mind turned inside out, a hundred of his theories confirmed, and his joy of life crystallized to a thousand ambitions. Not that the conversation was scholastic—heaven forbid! Amory had only the vaguest idea as to what Bernard Shaw was—but Monsignor made quite as much out of "The Beloved Vagabond" and "Sir Nigel," taking good care that Amory never once felt out of his depth.

But the trumpets were sounding for Amory's preliminary skirmish with his own generation.

"You're not sorry to go, of course. With people like us our home is where we are not," said Monsignor.

"I *am* sorry——"

"No, you're not. No one person in the world is necessary to you or to me."

"Well——"

"Good-by."

The Egotist Down

Amory's two years at St. Regis', though in turn painful and triumphant, had as little real significance in his own life as the American "prep" school, crushed as it is under the heel of the universities, has to American life in general. We have no Eton to create the self-consciousness of a governing class; we have, instead, clean, flaccid and innocuous preparatory schools.

He went all wrong at the start, was generally considered both conceited and arrogant, and universally detested. He played football intensely, alternating a reckless brilliancy with a tendency to keep himself as safe from hazard as decency would permit. In a wild panic he backed out of a fight with a boy his own size, to a chorus of scorn, and a week later, in desperation, picked a battle with another boy very much bigger, from which he emerged badly beaten, but rather proud of himself.

He was resentful against all those in authority over him, and this, combined with a lazy indifference toward his work, exasperated every master in school. He grew discouraged and imagined himself a pariah; took to sulking in corners and reading after lights. With a dread of being alone he attached a few friends, but since they were not among the élite of the school, he used them simply as mirrors of himself, audiences before which he might do that posing absolutely essential to him. He was unbearably lonely, desperately unhappy.

There were some few grains of comfort. Whenever Amory was submerged, his vanity was the last part to go below the surface, so he could still enjoy a comfortable glow when "Wookey-wookey," the deaf old housekeeper, told him that he was the best-looking boy she had ever seen. It had pleased him to be the lightest and youngest man on the first football squad; it pleased him when Doctor Dougall told him at the end of a heated conference that he could, if he wished, get the best marks in school. But Doctor Dougall was wrong. It was temperamentally impossible for Amory to get the best marks in school.

Miserable, confined to bounds, unpopular with both faculty and students—that was Amory's first term. But at Christmas he had returned to Minneapolis, tight-lipped and strangely jubilant.

"Oh, I was sort of fresh at first," he told Frog Parker patronizingly, "but I got along fine—lightest man on the squad. You ought to go away to school, Froggy. It's great stuff."

Incident of the Well-Meaning Professor

On the last night of his first term, Mr. Margotson, the senior master, sent word to study hall that Amory was to come to his room at nine. Amory suspected that advice was forthcoming, but he determined to be courteous, because this Mr. Margotson had been kindly disposed toward him.

His summoner received him gravely, and motioned him to a chair. He hemmed several times and looked consciously kind, as a man will when he knows he's on delicate ground.

"Amory," he began. "I've sent for you on a personal matter."

"Yes, sir."

"I've noticed you this year and I—I like you. I think you have in you the makings of a—a very good man."

"Yes, sir," Amory managed to articulate. He hated having people talk as if he were an admitted failure.

"But I've noticed," continued the older man blindly, "that you're not very popular with the boys."

"No, sir." Amory licked his lips.

"Ah—I thought you might not understand exactly what it was they—ah—objected to. I'm going to tell you, because I believe—ah—that when a boy knows his difficulties he's better able to cope with them—to conform to what others expect of him." He a-hemmed again with delicate reticence, and continued: "They seem to think that you're—ah—rather too fresh——"

Amory could stand no more. He rose from his chair, scarcely controlling his voice when he spoke.

"I know—oh, *don't* you s'pose I know." His voice rose. "I know what they think; do you s'pose you have to *tell* me!" He paused. "I'm—I've got to go back now—hope I'm not rude——"

He left the room hurriedly. In the cool air outside, as he walked to his house, he exulted in his refusal to be helped.

"That *damn* old fool!" he cried wildly. "As if I didn't *know*!"

He decided, however, that this was a good excuse not to go back to study hall that night, so, comfortably couched up in his room, he munched nabiscos and finished "The White Company."

Incident of the Wonderful Girl

There was a bright star in February. New York burst upon him on Washington's Birthday with the brilliance of a long-anticipated event. His glimpse of it as a vivid whiteness against a deep-blue sky had left a picture of splendor that rivalled the dream cities in the Arabian Nights; but this time he saw it by electric light, and romance gleamed from the chariot-race sign on Broadway and from the women's eyes at the Astor, where he and young Paskert from St. Regis' had dinner. When they walked down the aisle of the theatre, greeted by the nervous twanging and discord of untuned violins and the sensuous, heavy fragrance of paint and powder, he moved in a sphere of epicurean delight. Everything enchanted him. The play was "The Little Millionaire," with George M. Cohan, and there was one stunning young brunette who made him sit with brimming eyes in the ecstasy of watching her dance.

"Oh—you—wonderful girl,
What a wonderful girl you are—"

sang the tenor, and Amory agreed silently, but passionately.

"All—your—wonderful words
Thrill me through—"

The violins swelled and quavered on the last notes, the girl sank to a crumpled butterfly on the stage, a great burst of clapping filled the house. Oh, to fall in love like that, to the languorous magic melody of such a tune!

The last scene was laid on a roof-garden, and the 'cellos sighed to the musical moon, while light adventure and facile froth-like comedy flitted back and forth in the calcium. Amory was on fire to be an habitué of roof-gardens, to meet a girl who should look like that—better, that very girl; whose hair would be drenched with golden moonlight, while at his elbow sparkling wine was poured by an unintelligible waiter. When the curtain fell for the last time he gave such a long sigh that the people in front of him twisted around and stared and said loud enough for him to hear:

"What a *remarkable*-looking boy!"

This took his mind off the play, and he wondered if he really did seem handsome to the population of New York.

Paskert and he walked in silence toward their hotel. The former was the first to speak. His uncertain fifteen-year-old voice broke in in a melancholy strain on Amory's musings:

"I'd marry that girl to-night."

There was no need to ask what girl he referred to.

"I'd be proud to take her home and introduce her to my people," continued Paskert.

Amory was distinctly impressed. He wished he had said it instead of Paskert. It sounded so mature.

"I wonder about actresses; are they all pretty bad?"

"No, *sir*, not by a darn sight," said the worldly youth with emphasis, "and I know that girl's as good as gold. I can tell."

They wandered on, mixing in the Broadway crowd, dreaming on the music that eddied out of the cafés. New faces flashed on and off like myriad lights, pale or rouged faces, tired, yet sustained by a weary excitement. Amory watched them in fascination. He was planning his life. He was going to live in New York, and be known at every restaurant and café, wearing a dress-suit from early evening to early morning, sleeping away the dull hours of the forenoon.

"Yes, *sir*, I'd marry that girl to-night!"

Heroic in General Tone

October of his second and last year at St. Regis' was a high point in Amory's memory. The game with Groton was played from three of a snappy, exhilarating afternoon far into the crisp autumnal twilight, and Amory at quarter-back, exhorting in wild despair, making impossible tackles, calling signals in a voice that had diminished to a hoarse, furious whisper, yet found time to revel in the blood-stained bandage around his head, and the straining, glorious heroism of plunging, crashing bodies and aching limbs. For those minutes courage flowed like wine out of the November dusk, and he was the eternal hero, one with the sea-rover on the prow of a Norse galley, one with Roland and Horatius, Sir Nigel and Ted Coy, scraped and stripped into trim and then flung by his own will into the breach, beating back the tide, hearing from afar the thunder of cheers . . . finally bruised and weary, but still elusive, circling an end, twisting, changing pace, straight-arming . . . falling behind the Groton goal with two men on his legs, in the only touchdown of the game.

The Philosophy of the Slicker

From the scoffing superiority of sixth-form year and success Amory looked back with cynical wonder on his status of the year before. He was changed as completely as Amory Blaine could ever be changed. Amory plus Beatrice plus two years in Minneapolis—these had been his ingredients when he entered

St. Regis'. But the Minneapolis years were not a thick enough overlay to conceal the "Amory plus Beatrice" from the ferreting eyes of a boarding-school, so St. Regis' had very painfully drilled Beatrice out of him, and begun to lay down new and more conventional planking on the fundamental Amory. But both St. Regis' and Amory were unconscious of the fact that this fundamental Amory had not in himself changed. Those qualities for which he had suffered, his moodiness, his tendency to pose, his laziness, and his love of playing the fool, were now taken as a matter of course, recognized eccentricities in a star quarter-back, a clever actor, and the editor of the *St. Regis Tattler*: it puzzled him to see impressionable small boys imitating the very vanities that had not long ago been contemptible weaknesses.

After the football season he slumped into dreamy content. The night of the pre-holiday dance he slipped away and went early to bed for the pleasure of hearing the violin music cross the grass and come surging in at his window. Many nights he lay there dreaming awake of secret cafés in Mont Martre, where ivory women delved in romantic mysteries with diplomats and soldiers of fortune, while orchestras played Hungarian waltzes and the air was thick and exotic with intrigue and moonlight and adventure. In the spring he read "L'Allegro," by request, and was inspired to lyrical outpourings on the subject of Arcady and the pipes of Pan. He moved his bed so that the sun would wake him at dawn that he might dress and go out to the archaic swing that hung from an apple-tree near the sixth-form house. Seating himself in this he would pump higher and higher until he got the effect of swinging into the wide air, into a fairy-land of piping satyrs and nymphs with the faces of fair-haired girls he passed in the streets of Eastchester. As the swing reached its highest point, Arcady really lay just over the brow of a certain hill, where the brown road dwindled out of sight in a golden dot.

He read voluminously all spring, the beginning of his eighteenth year: "The Gentleman from Indiana," "The New Arabian Nights," "The Morals of Marcus Ordeyne," "The Man Who Was Thursday," which he liked without understanding; "Stover at Yale," that became somewhat of a textbook; "Dombey and Son," because he thought he really should read better stuff; Robert Chambers, David Graham Phillips, and E. Phillips Oppenheim complete, and a scattering of Tennyson and Kipling. Of all his class work only "L'Allegro" and some quality of rigid clarity in solid geometry stirred his languid interest.

As June drew near, he felt the need of conversation to formulate his own ideas, and, to his surprise, found a co-philosopher in Rahill, the president of the sixth form. In many a talk, on the highroad or lying belly-down along the edge of the baseball diamond, or late at night with their cigarettes glowing in the dark, they threshed out the questions of school, and there was developed the term "slicker."

"Got tobacco?" whispered Rahill one night, putting his head inside the door five minutes after lights.

"Sure."

"I'm coming in."

"Take a couple of pillows and lie in the window-seat, why don't you."

Amory sat up in bed and lit a cigarette while Rahill settled for a conversation. Rahill's favorite subject was the respective futures of the sixth form, and Amory never tired of outlining them for his benefit.

"Ted Converse? 'At's easy. He'll fail his exams, tutor all summer at Harstrum's, get into Sheff with about four conditions, and flunk out in the middle of the freshman year. Then he'll go back West and raise hell for a year or so; finally his father will make him go into the paint business. He'll marry and have four sons, all bone heads. He'll always think St. Regis's spoiled him, so he'll send his sons to day school in Portland. He'll die of locomotor ataxia when he's forty-one, and his wife will give a baptizing stand or whatever you call it to the Presbyterian Church, with his name on it——"

"Hold up, Amory. That's too darned gloomy. How about yourself?"

"I'm in a superior class. You are, too. We're philosophers."

"I'm not."

"Sure you are. You've got a darn good head on you." But Amory knew that nothing in the abstract, no theory or generality, ever moved Rahill until he stubbed his toe upon the concrete minutiæ of it.

"Haven't," insisted Rahill. "I let people impose on me here and don't get anything out of it. I'm the prey of my friends, damn it—do their lessons, get 'em out of trouble, pay 'em stupid summer visits, and always entertain their kid sisters; keep my temper when they get selfish and *then* they think they pay me back by voting for me and telling me I'm the 'big man' of St. Regis's. I want to get where everybody does their own work and I can tell people where to go. I'm tired of being nice to every poor fish in school."

"You're not a slicker," said Amory suddenly.

"A what?"

"A slicker."

"What the devil's that?"

"Well, it's something that—that—there's a lot of them. You're not one, and neither am I, though I am more than you are."

"Who is one? What makes you one?"

Amory considered.

"Why—why, I suppose that the *sign* of it is when a fellow slicks his hair back with water."

"Like Carstairs?"

"Yes—sure. He's a slicker."

They spent two evenings getting an exact definition. The slicker was good-looking or *clean*-looking; he had brains, social brains, that is, and he used all means on the broad path of honesty to get ahead, be popular, admired, and never in trouble. He dressed well, was particularly neat in appearance, and derived his name from the fact that his hair was inevitably worn short, soaked in water or tonic, parted in the middle, and slicked back as the current of fashion dictated. The slickers of that year had adopted tortoise-shell spectacles as badges of their slickerhood, and this made them so easy to recognize that Amory and Rahill never missed one. The slicker seemed distributed through school, always a little wiser and shrewder than his contemporaries, managing some team or other, and keeping his cleverness carefully concealed.

Amory found the slicker a most valuable classification until his junior year in college, when the outline became so blurred and indeterminate that it had to be subdivided many times, and became only a quality. Amory's secret ideal had all the slicker qualifications, but, in addition, courage and tremendous brains and talents—also Amory conceded him a bizarre streak that was quite irreconcilable to the slicker proper.

This was a first real break from the hypocrisy of school tradition. The slicker was a definite element of success, differing intrinsically from the prep school "big man."

"The Slicker"	"The Big Man"
1. Clever sense of social values.	1. Inclined to stupidity and unconscious of social values.
2. Dresses well. Pretends that dress is superficial—but knows that it isn't.	2. Thinks dress is superficial, and is inclined to be careless about it.
3. Goes into such activities as he can shine in.	3. Goes out for everything from a sense of duty.
4. Gets to college and is, in a worldly way, successful.	4. Gets to college and has a problematical future. Feels lost without his circle, and always says that school days were happiest, after all. Goes back to school and makes speeches about what St. Regis's boys are doing.
5. Hair slicked.	5. Hair not slicked.

Amory had decided definitely on Princeton, even though he would be the only boy entering that year from St. Regis'. Yale had a romance and glamour from the tales of Minneapolis, and St. Regis' men who had been "tapped for Skull and Bones," but Princeton drew him most, with its atmosphere of bright colors and its alluring reputation as the pleasantest country club in America. Dwarfed by the menacing college exams, Amory's school days drifted into the past. Years afterward, when he went back to St. Regis', he seemed to have forgotten the successes of sixth-form year, and to be able to picture himself only as the unadjustable boy who had hurried down corridors, jeered at by his rabid contemporaries mad with common sense.

CHAPTER II

Spires and Gargoyles

AT FIRST Amory noticed only the wealth of sunshine creeping across the long, green swards, dancing on the leaded window-panes, and swimming around the tops of spires and towers and battlemented walls. Gradually he realized that he was really walking up University Place, self-conscious about his suitcase, developing a new tendency to glare straight ahead when he passed any one. Several times he could have sworn that men turned to look at him critically. He wondered vaguely if there was something the matter with his clothes, and wished he had shaved that morning on the train. He felt unnecessarily stiff and awkward among these white-flannelled, bareheaded youths, who must be juniors and seniors, judging from the savoir faire with which they strolled.

He found that 12 University Place was a large, dilapidated mansion, at present apparently uninhabited, though he knew it housed usually a dozen freshmen. After a hurried skirmish with his landlady he sallied out on a tour of exploration, but he had gone scarcely a block when he became horribly conscious that he must be the only man in town who was wearing a hat. He returned hurriedly to 12 University, left his derby, and, emerging bareheaded, loitered down Nassau Street, stopping to investigate a display of athletic photographs in a store window, including a large one of Allenby, the football captain, and next attracted by the sign "Jigger Shop" over a confectionary window. This sounded familiar, so he sauntered in and took a seat on a high stool.

"Chocolate sundae," he told a colored person.

"Double chocolate jiggah? Anything else?"

"Why—yes."

"Bacon bun?"

"Why—yes."

He munched four of these, finding them of pleasing savor, and then consumed another double-chocolate jigger before ease descended upon him. After a cursory inspection of the pillow-cases, leather pennants, and Gibson Girls that lined the walls, he left, and continued along Nassau Street with his hands in his pockets. Gradually he was learning to distinguish between upper classmen and entering men, even though the freshman cap would not appear until the following Monday. Those who were too obviously, too nervously at home were freshmen, for as each train brought a new contingent it was immediately absorbed into the hatless, white-shod, book-laden throng, whose function seemed to be to drift endlessly up and down the street, emitting great clouds of smoke from brand-new pipes. By afternoon Amory realized that now the newest arrivals were taking him for an upper classman, and he tried conscientiously to look both pleasantly blasé and casually critical, which was as near as he could analyze the prevalent facial expression.

At five o'clock he felt the need of hearing his own voice, so he retreated to his house to see if any one else had arrived. Having climbed the rickety stairs he scrutinized his room resignedly, concluding that it was hopeless to attempt any more inspired decoration than class banners and tiger pictures. There was a tap at the door.

"Come in!"

A slim face with gray eyes and a humorous smile appeared in the doorway.

"Got a hammer?"

"No—sorry. Maybe Mrs. Twelve, or whatever she goes by, has one."

The stranger advanced into the room.

"You an inmate of this asylum?"

Amory nodded.

"Awful barn for the rent we pay."

Amory had to agree that it was.

"I thought of the campus," he said, "but they say there's so few freshmen that they're lost. Have to sit around and study for something to do."

The gray-eyed man decided to introduce himself.

"My name's Holiday."

"Blaine's my name."

They shook hands with the fashionable low swoop. Amory grinned.

"Where'd you prep?"

"Andover—where did you?"

"St. Regis's."

"Oh, did you? I had a cousin there."

They discussed the cousin thoroughly, and then Holiday announced that he was to meet his brother for dinner at six.

"Come along and have a bite with us."

"All right."

At the Kenilworth Amory met Burne Holiday—he of the gray eyes was Kerry—and during a limpid meal of thin soup and anæmic vegetables they stared at the other freshmen, who sat either in small groups looking very ill at ease, or in large groups seeming very much at home.

"I hear Commons is pretty bad," said Amory.

"That's the rumor. But you've got to eat there—or pay anyways."

"Crime!"

"Imposition!"

"Oh, at Princeton you've got to swallow everything the first year. It's like a damned prep school."

Amory agreed.

"Lot of pep, though," he insisted. "I wouldn't have gone to Yale for a million."

"Me either."

"You going out for anything?" inquired Amory of the elder brother.

"Not me—Burne here is going out for the Prince—the Daily Princetonian, you know."

"Yes, I know."

"You going out for anything?"

"Why—yes. I'm going to take a whack at freshman football."

"Play at St. Regis's?"

"Some," admitted Amory depreciatingly, "but I'm getting so damned thin."

"You're not thin."

"Well, I used to be stocky last fall."

"Oh!"

After supper they attended the movies, where Amory was fascinated by the glib comments of a man in front of him, as well as by the wild yelling and shouting.

"*Yoho!*"

"Oh, honey-*baby*—you're so big and strong, but oh, so *gentle*!"

"Clinch!"

"Oh, *Clinch!*"

"Kiss her, kiss 'at lady, *quick!*"

"Oh-h-h——!"

A group began whistling "By the Sea," and the audience took it up noisily. This was followed by an indistinguishable song that included much stamping and then by an endless, incoherent dirge.

"Oh-h-h-h-h
She works in a Jam Factoree
And—that-may-be-all-right
But you can't-fool-me
For I know—DAMN—WELL
That she DON'T-make-jam-all-night!
Oh-h-h-h!"

As they pushed out, giving and receiving curious impersonal glances, Amory decided that he liked the movies, wanted to enjoy them as the row of upper classmen in front had enjoyed them, with their arms along the backs of the seats, their comments Gaelic and caustic, their attitude a mixture of critical wit and tolerant amusement.

"Want a sundae—I mean a jigger?" asked Kerry.

"Sure."

They suppered heavily and then, still sauntering, eased back to 12.

"Wonderful night."

"It's a whiz."

"You men going to unpack?"

"Guess so. Come on, Burne."

Amory decided to sit for a while on the front steps, so he bade them good night.

The great tapestries of trees had darkened to ghosts back at the last edge of twilight. The early moon had drenched the arches with pale blue, and, weaving over the night, in and out of the gossamer rifts of moon, swept a song, a song with more than a hint of sadness, infinitely transient, infinitely regretful.

He remembered that an alumnus of the nineties had told him of one of Booth Tarkington's amusements: standing in mid-campus in the small hours and singing tenor songs to the stars, arousing mingled emotions in the couched undergraduates according to the sentiment of their moods.

Now, far down the shadowy line of University Place a white-clad phalanx broke the gloom, and marching figures, white-shirted, white-trousered, swung rhythmically up the street, with linked arms and heads thrown back:

"Going back—going back,
Going—back—to—Nas-sau—Hall,
Going back—going back—
To the—Best—Old—Place—of—All.
Going back—going back,
From all—this—earth-ly—ball,
We'll—clear—the—track—as—we—go—back—
Going—back—to—Nas-sau—Hall!"

Amory closed his eyes as the ghostly procession drew near. The song soared so high that all dropped out except the tenors, who bore the melody triumphantly past the danger-point and relinquished it to the fantastic chorus. Then Amory opened his eyes, half afraid that sight would spoil the rich illusion of harmony.

He sighed eagerly. There at the head of the white platoon marched Allenby, the football captain, slim and defiant, as if aware that this year the hopes of the college rested on him, that his hundred-and-sixty pounds were expected to dodge to victory through the heavy blue and crimson lines.

Fascinated, Amory watched each rank of linked arms as it came abreast, the faces indistinct above the polo shirts, the voices blent in a pæan of triumph—and then the procession passed through shadowy Campbell Arch, and the voices grew fainter as it wound eastward over the campus.

The minutes passed and Amory sat there very quietly. He regretted the rule that would forbid freshmen to be outdoors after curfew, for he wanted to ramble through the shadowy scented lanes, where Witherspoon brooded like a dark mother over Whig and Clio, her Attic children, where the black Gothic snake of Little curled down to Cuyler and Patton, these in turn flinging the mystery out over the placid slope rolling to the lake.

Princeton of the daytime filtered slowly into his consciousness—West and Reunion, redolent of the sixties, Seventy-nine Hall, brick-red and arrogant, Upper and Lower Pyne, aristocratic Elizabethan ladies not quite content to live among shopkeepers, and, topping all, climbing with clear blue aspiration, the great dreaming spires of Holder and Cleveland towers.

From the first he loved Princeton—its lazy beauty, its half-grasped significance, the wild moonlight revel of the rushes, the handsome, prosperous big-game crowds, and under it all the air of struggle that pervaded his class. From the day when, wild-eyed and exhausted, the jerseyed freshmen sat in the gymnasium and elected some one from Hill School class president, a Lawrenceville celebrity vice-president, a hockey star from St. Paul's secretary, up until the end of sophomore year it never ceased, that breathless social system, that worship, seldom named, never really admitted, of the bogey "Big Man."

First it was schools, and Amory, alone from St. Regis', watched the crowds form and widen and form again; St. Paul's, Hill, Pomfret, eating at certain tacitly reserved tables in Commons, dressing in their own corners of the gymnasium, and drawing unconsciously about them a barrier of the slightly less important but socially ambitious to protect them from the friendly, rather puzzled high-school element. From the moment he realized this Amory resented social barriers as artificial distinctions made by the strong to bolster up their weak retainers and keep out the almost strong.

Having decided to be one of the gods of the class, he reported for freshman football practice, but in the second week, playing quarter-back, already paragraphed in corners of the *Princetonian*, he wrenched his knee seriously enough to put him out for the rest of the season. This forced him to retire and consider the situation.

"12 Univee" housed a dozen miscellaneous question-marks. There were three or four inconspicuous and quite startled boys from Lawrenceville, two amateur wild men from a New York private school (Kerry Holiday christened them the "plebeian drunks"), a Jewish youth, also from New York, and, as compensation for Amory, the two Holidays, to whom he took an instant fancy.

The Holidays were rumored twins, but really the dark-haired one, Kerry, was a year older than his blond brother, Burne. Kerry was tall, with humorous gray eyes, and a sudden, attractive smile; he became at once the mentor of the house, reaper of ears that grew too high, censor of conceit, vendor of rare, satirical humor. Amory spread the table of their future friendship with all his ideas of what college should and did mean. Kerry, not inclined as yet to take things seriously, chided him gently for being curious at this inopportune time about the intricacies of the social system, but liked him and was both interested and amused.

Burne, fair-haired, silent, and intent, appeared in the house only as a busy apparition, gliding in quietly at night and off again in the early morning to get up his work in the library—he was out for the *Princetonian*, competing furiously against forty others for the coveted first place. In December he came down with diphtheria, and some one else won the competition, but, returning to college in February, he dauntlessly went after the prize again. Necessarily, Amory's acquaintance with him was in the way of three-minute chats, walking to and from lectures, so he failed to penetrate Burne's one absorbing interest and find what lay beneath it.

Amory was far from contented. He missed the place he had won at St. Regis', the being known and admired, yet Princeton stimulated him, and there were many things ahead calculated to arouse the Machiavelli latent in him, could he but insert a wedge. The upper-class clubs, concerning which he had pumped a reluctant graduate during the previous summer, excited his curiosity: Ivy, detached and breathlessly aristocratic; Cottage, an impressive mélange of brilliant adventurers and well-dressed philanderers; Tiger Inn, broad-shouldered and athletic, vitalized by an honest elaboration of prep-school standards; Cap and Gown, anti-alcoholic, faintly religious and politically powerful; flamboyant Colonial; literary Quadrangle; and the dozen others, varying in age and position.

Anything which brought an under classman into too glaring a light was labelled with the damning brand of "running it out." The movies thrived on caustic comments, but the men who made them were generally running it out; talking of clubs was running it out; standing for anything very strongly, as, for instance, drinking parties or teetotalling, was running it out; in short, being personally conspicuous was not tolerated, and the influential man was the non-committal man, until at club elections in sophomore year every one should be sewed up in some bag for the rest of his college career.

Amory found that writing for the *Nassau Literary Magazine* would get him nothing, but that being on the board of the *Daily Princetonian* would get any one a good deal. His vague desire to do immortal acting with the English Dramatic Association faded out when he found that the most ingenious brains and talents were concentrated upon the Triangle Club, a musical comedy organization that every year took a great Christmas trip. In the meanwhile, feeling strangely alone and restless in Commons, with new desires and ambitions stirring in his mind, he let the first term go by between an envy of the embryo successes and a puzzled fretting with Kerry as to why they were not accepted immediately among the élite of the class.

Many afternoons they lounged in the windows of 12 Univee and watched the class pass to and from Commons, noting satellites already attaching themselves to the more prominent, watching the lonely grind with his hurried step and downcast eye, envying the happy security of the big school groups.

"We're the damned middle class, that's what!" he complained to Kerry one day as he lay stretched out on the sofa, consuming a family of Fatimas with contemplative precision.

"Well, why not? We came to Princeton so we could feel that way toward the small colleges—have it on 'em, more self-confidence, dress better, cut a swathe——"

"Oh, it isn't that I mind the glittering caste system," admitted Amory. "I like having a bunch of hot cats on top, but gosh, Kerry, I've got to be one of them."

"But just now, Amory, you're only a sweaty bourgeois."

Amory lay for a moment without speaking.

"I won't be—long," he said finally. "But I hate to get anywhere by working for it. I'll show the marks, don't you know."

"Honorable scars." Kerry craned his neck suddenly at the street. "There's Langueduc, if you want to see what he looks like—and Humbird just behind."

Amory rose dynamically and sought the windows.

"Oh," he said, scrutinizing these worthies, "Humbird looks like a knockout, but this Langueduc—he's the rugged type, isn't he? I distrust that sort. All diamonds look big in the rough."

"Well," said Kerry, as the excitement subsided, "you're a literary genius. It's up to you."

"I wonder"—Amory paused—"if I could be. I honestly think so sometimes. That sounds like the devil, and I wouldn't say it to anybody except you."

"Well—go ahead. Let your hair grow and write poems like this guy D'Invilliers in the Lit."

Amory reached lazily at a pile of magazines on the table.

"Read his latest effort?"

"Never miss 'em. They're rare."

Amory glanced through the issue.

"Hello!" he said in surprise, "he's a freshman, isn't he?"

"Yeah."

"Listen to this! My God!

" '*A serving lady speaks:*
Black velvet trails its folds over the day,
White tapers, prisoned in their silver frames,
Wave their thin flames like shadows in the wind,
Pia, Pompia, come—come away——'

"Now, what the devil does that mean?"

"It's a pantry scene."

" '*Her toes are stiffened like a stork's in flight;*
She's laid upon her bed, on the white sheets,
Her hands pressed on her smooth bust like a saint,
Bella Cunizza, come into the light!'

"My gosh, Kerry, what in hell is it all about? I swear I don't get him at all, and I'm a literary bird myself."

"It's pretty tricky," said Kerry, "only you've got to think of hearses and stale milk when you read it. That isn't as pash as some of them."

Amory tossed the magazine on the table.

"Well," he sighed, "I sure am up in the air. I know I'm not a regular fellow, yet I loathe anybody else that isn't. I can't decide whether to cultivate my mind and be a great dramatist, or to thumb my nose at the Golden Treasury and be a Princeton slicker."

"Why decide?" suggested Kerry. "Better drift, like me. I'm going to sail into prominence on Burne's coat-tails."

"I can't drift—I want to be interested. I want to pull strings, even for somebody else, or be Princetonian chairman or Triangle president. I want to be admired, Kerry."

"You're thinking too much about yourself."

Amory sat up at this.

"No. I'm thinking about you, too. We've got to get out and mix around the class right now, when it's fun to be a snob. I'd like to bring a sardine to the prom in June, for instance, but I wouldn't do it unless I could be damn debonaire about it—introduce her to all the prize parlor-snakes, and the football captain, and all that simple stuff."

"Amory," said Kerry impatiently, "you're just going around in a circle. If you want to be prominent, get out and try for something; if you don't, just take it easy." He yawned. "Come on, let's let the smoke drift off. We'll go down and watch football practice."

Amory gradually accepted this point of view, decided that next fall would inaugurate his career, and relinquished himself to watching Kerry extract joy from 12 Univee.

They filled the Jewish youth's bed with lemon pie; they put out the gas all over the house every night by blowing into the jet in Amory's room, to the bewilderment of Mrs. Twelve and the local plumber; they set up the effects of the plebeian drunks—pictures, books, and furniture—in the bathroom, to the confusion of the pair, who hazily discovered the transposition on their return from a Trenton spree; they were disappointed beyond measure when the plebeian drunks decided to take it as a joke; they played red-dog and twenty-one and jack-pot from dinner to dawn, and on the occasion of one man's birthday persuaded him to buy sufficient champagne for a hilarious celebration. The donor of the party having remained sober, Kerry and Amory accidently dropped him down two flights of stairs and called, shame-faced and penitent, at the infirmary all the following week.

"Say, who are all these women?" demanded Kerry one day, protesting at the size of Amory's mail. "I've been looking at the postmarks lately—Farmington and Dobbs and Westover and Dana Hall—what's the idea?"

Amory grinned.

"All from the Twin Cities." He named them off. "There's Marylyn De Witt—she's pretty, got a car of her own and that's damn convenient; there's Sally Weatherby—she's getting too fat; there's Myra St. Claire, she's an old flame, easy to kiss if you like it——"

"What line do you throw 'em?" demanded Kerry. "I've tried everything, and the mad wags aren't even afraid of me."

"You're the 'nice boy' type," suggested Amory.

"That's just it. Mother always feels the girl is safe if she's with me. Honestly, it's annoying. If I start to hold somebody's hand, they laugh at me, and *let* me, just as if it wasn't part of them. As soon as I get hold of a hand they sort of disconnect it from the rest of them."

"Sulk," suggested Amory. "Tell 'em you're wild and have 'em reform you—go home furious—come back in half an hour—startle 'em."

Kerry shook his head.

"No chance. I wrote a St. Timothy girl a really loving letter last year. In one place I got rattled and said: 'My God, how I love you!' She took a nail scissors, clipped out the 'My God' and showed the rest of the letter all over school. Doesn't work at all. I'm just 'good old Kerry' and all that rot."

Amory smiled and tried to picture himself as "good old Amory." He failed completely.

February dripped snow and rain, the cyclonic freshman mid-years passed, and life in 12 Univee continued interesting if not purposeful. Once a day Amory indulged in a club sandwich, cornflakes, and Julienne potatoes at "Joe's," accompanied usually by Kerry or Alec Connage. The latter was a quiet, rather aloof slicker from Hotchkiss, who lived next door and shared the same enforced singleness as Amory, due to the fact that his entire class had gone to Yale. "Joe's" was unæsthetic and faintly unsanitary, but a limitless charge account could be opened there, a convenience that Amory appreciated. His father had been experimenting with mining stocks and, in consequence, his allowance, while liberal, was not at all what he had expected.

"Joe's" had the additional advantage of seclusion from curious upper-class eyes, so at four each afternoon Amory, accompanied by friend or book, went up to experiment with his digestion. One day in March, finding that all the tables were occupied, he slipped into a chair opposite a freshman who bent intently over a book at the last table. They nodded briefly. For twenty minutes Amory sat consuming bacon buns and reading "Mrs. Warren's Profession" (he had discovered Shaw quite by accident while browsing in the library during mid-years); the other freshman, also intent on his volume, meanwhile did away with a trio of chocolate malted milks.

By and by Amory's eyes wandered curiously to his fellow-luncher's book. He spelled out the name and title upside down—"Marpessa," by Stephen Phillips. This meant nothing to him, his metrical education having been confined to such Sunday classics as "Come into the Garden, Maude," and what morsels of Shakespeare and Milton had been recently forced upon him.

Moved to address his vis-à-vis, he simulated interest in his book for a moment, and then exclaimed aloud as if involuntarily:

"Ha! Great stuff!"

The other freshman looked up and Amory registered artificial embarrassment.

"Are you referring to your bacon buns?" His cracked, kindly voice went well with the large spectacles and the impression of a voluminous keenness that he gave.

"No," Amory answered. "I was referring to Bernard Shaw." He turned the book around in explanation.

"I've never read any Shaw. I've always meant to." The boy paused and then continued: "Did you ever read Stephen Phillips, or do you like poetry?"

"Yes, indeed," Amory affirmed eagerly. "I've never read much of Phillips, though." (He had never heard of any Phillips except the late David Graham.)

"It's pretty fair, I think. Of course he's a Victorian." They sallied into a discussion of poetry, in the course of which they introduced themselves, and Amory's companion proved to be none other than "that awful highbrow, Thomas Parke D'Invilliers," who signed the passionate love-poems in the *Lit.* He was, perhaps, nineteen, with stooped shoulders, pale blue eyes, and, as Amory could tell from his general appearance, without much conception of social competition and such phenomena of absorbing interest. Still, he liked books, and it seemed forever since Amory had met any one who did; if only that St. Paul's crowd at the next table would not mistake *him* for a bird, too, he would enjoy the encounter tremendously. They didn't seem to be noticing, so he let himself go, discussed books by the dozens—books he had read, read about, books he had never heard of, rattling off lists of titles with the facility of a Brentano's clerk. D'Invilliers was partially taken in and wholly delighted. In a good-natured way he had almost decided that Princeton was one part deadly Philistines and one part deadly grinds, and to find a person who could mention Keats without stammering, yet evidently washed his hands, was rather a treat.

"Ever read any Oscar Wilde?" he asked.

"No. Who wrote it?"

"It's a man—don't you know?"

"Oh, surely." A faint chord was struck in Amory's memory. "Wasn't the comic opera, 'Patience,' written about him?"

"Yes, that's the fella. I've just finished a book of his, 'The Picture of Dorian Gray,' and I certainly wish you'd read it. You'd like it. You can borrow it if you want to."

"Why, I'd like it a lot—thanks."

"Don't you want to come up to the room? I've got a few other books."

Amory hesitated, glanced at the St. Paul's group—one of them was the magnificent, exquisite Humbird—and he considered how determinate the addition of this friend would be. He never got to the stage of making them and getting rid of them—he was not hard enough for that—so he measured Thomas Parke D'Invilliers' undoubted attractions and value against the menace of cold eyes behind tortoise-rimmed spectacles that he fancied glared from the next table.

"Yes, I'll go."

So he found "Dorian Gray" and the "Mystic and Somber Dolores" and the "Belle Dame sans Merci"; for a month was keen on naught else. The world became pale and interesting, and he tried hard to look at Princeton through the satiated eyes of Oscar Wilde and Swinburne—or "Fingal O'Flaherty" and "Algernon Charles," as he called them in précieuse jest. He read enormously every night—Shaw, Chesterton, Barrie, Pinero, Yeats, Synge, Ernest Dowson, Arthur Symons, Keats, Sudermann, Robert Hugh Benson, the Savoy Operas—just a heterogeneous mixture, for he suddenly discovered that he had read nothing for years.

Tom D'Invilliers became at first an occasion rather than a friend. Amory saw him about once a week, and together they gilded the ceiling of Tom's room and decorated the walls with imitation tapestry, bought at an auction, tall candlesticks and figured curtains. Amory liked him for being clever and literary without effeminacy or affectation. In fact, Amory did most of the strutting and tried painfully to make every remark an epigram, than which, if one is content with ostensible epigrams, there are many feats harder. 12 Univee was amused. Kerry read "Dorian Gray" and simulated Lord Henry, following Amory about, addressing him as "Dorian" and pretending to encourage in him wicked fancies and attenuated tendencies to ennui. When he carried it into commons, to the amazement of the others at table, Amory became furiously embarrassed, and after that made epigrams only before D'Invilliers or a convenient mirror.

One day Tom and Amory tried reciting their own and Lord Dunsany's poems to the music of Kerry's graphophone.

"Chant!" cried Tom. "Don't recite! *Chant!*"

Amory, who was performing, looked annoyed, and claimed that he needed a record with less piano in it. Kerry thereupon rolled on the floor in stifled laughter.

"Put on 'Hearts and Flowers'!" he howled. "Oh, my Lord, I'm going to cast a kitten."

"Shut off the damn graphophone," Amory cried, rather red in the face. "I'm not giving an exhibition."

In the meanwhile Amory delicately kept trying to awaken a sense of the social system in D'Invilliers, for he knew that this poet was really more conventional than he, and needed merely watered hair, a smaller range of conversation, and a darker brown hat to become quite regular. But the liturgy of Livingstone collars and dark ties fell on heedless ears; in fact D'Invilliers faintly resented his efforts; so Amory confined himself to calls once a week, and brought him occasionally to 12 Univee. This caused mild titters among the other freshmen, who called them "Doctor Johnson and Boswell."

Alec Connage, another frequent visitor, liked him in a vague way, but was afraid of him as a highbrow. Kerry, who saw through his poetic patter to the solid, almost respectable depths within, was immensely amused and would have him recite poetry by the hour, while he lay with closed eyes on Amory's sofa and listened:

"Asleep or waking is it? for her neck
Kissed over close, wears yet a purple speck
Wherein the pained blood falters and goes out;
Soft and stung softly—fairer for a fleck . . ."

"That's good," Kerry would say softly. "It pleases the elder Holiday. That's a great poet, I guess." Tom, delighted at an audience, would ramble through the "Poems and Ballades" until Kerry and Amory knew them almost as well as he.

Amory took to writing poetry on spring afternoons, in the gardens of the big estates near Princeton, while swans made effective atmosphere in the artificial pools, and slow clouds sailed harmoniously above the willows. May came too soon, and suddenly unable to bear walls, he wandered the campus at all hours through starlight and rain.

A Damp Symbolic Interlude

The night mist fell. From the moon it rolled, clustered about the spires and towers, and then settled below them, so that the dreaming peaks were still in lofty aspiration toward the sky. Figures that dotted the day like ants now brushed along as shadowy ghosts, in and out of the foreground. The Gothic halls and cloisters were infinitely more mysterious as they loomed suddenly out of the darkness, outlined each by myriad faint squares of yellow light. Indefinitely from somewhere a bell boomed the quarter-hour, and Amory, pausing by the sun-dial, stretched himself out full length on the damp grass. The cool bathed his eyes and slowed the flight of time—time that had crept so insidiously through the lazy April afternoons, seemed so intangible in the long spring twilights. Evening after evening the senior singing had drifted over the campus in melancholy beauty, and through the shell of his undergraduate consciousness had broken a deep and reverent devotion to the gray walls and Gothic peaks and all they symbolized as warehouses of dead ages.

The tower that in view of his window sprang upward, grew into a spire, yearning higher until its uppermost tip was half invisible against the morning skies, gave him the first sense of the transiency and unimportance of the campus figures except as holders of the apostolic succession. He liked knowing that Gothic architecture, with its upward trend, was peculiarly appropriate to universities, and the idea became personal to him. The silent stretches of green, the quiet halls with an occasional late-burning scholastic light held his imagination in a strong grasp, and the chastity of the spire became a symbol of this perception.

"Damn it all," he whispered aloud, wetting his hands in the damp and running them through his hair. "Next year I work!" Yet he knew that where now the spirit of spires and towers made him dreamily acquiescent, it would then overawe him. Where now he realized only his own inconsequence, effort would make him aware of his own impotency and insufficiency.

The college dreamed on—awake. He felt a nervous excitement that might have been the very throb of its slow heart. It was a stream where he was to throw a stone whose faint ripple would be vanishing almost as it left his hand. As yet he had given nothing, he had taken nothing.

A belated freshman, his oilskin slicker rasping loudly,

slushed along the soft path. A voice from somewhere called the inevitable formula, "Stick out your head!" below an unseen window. A hundred little sounds of the current drifting on under the fog pressed in finally on his consciousness.

"Oh, *God!*" he cried suddenly, and started at the sound of his voice in the stillness. The rain dripped on. A minute longer he lay without moving, his hands clinched. Then he sprang to his feet and gave his clothes a tentative pat.

"I'm very damn wet!" he said aloud to the sun-dial.

Historical

The war began in the summer following his freshman year. Beyond a sporting interest in the German dash for Paris the whole affair failed either to thrill or interest him. With the attitude he might have held toward an amusing melodrama he hoped it would be long and bloody. If it had not continued he would have felt like an irate ticket-holder at a prize-fight where the principals refused to mix it up.

That was his total reaction.

"Ha-Ha Hortense!"

"All right, po*nies!*"

"Shake it up!"

"Hey, ponies—how about easing up on that crap game and shaking a mean hip?"

"Hey, *ponies!*"

The coach fumed helplessly, the Triangle Club president, glowering with anxiety, varied between furious bursts of authority and fits of temperamental lassitude, when he sat spiritless and wondered how the devil the show was ever going on tour by Christmas.

"All right. We'll take the pirate song."

The ponies took last drags at their cigarettes and slumped into place; the leading lady rushed into the foreground, setting his hands and feet in an atmospheric mince; and as the coach clapped and stamped and tumped and da-da'd, they hashed out a dance.

A great, seething ant-hill was the Triangle Club. It gave a

musical comedy every year, travelling with cast, chorus, orchestra, and scenery all through Christmas vacation. The play and music were the work of undergraduates, and the club itself was the most influential of institutions, over three hundred men competing for it every year.

Amory, after an easy victory in the first sophomore *Princetonian* competition, stepped into a vacancy of the cast as *Boiling Oil, a Pirate Lieutenant.* Every night for the last week they had rehearsed "Ha-Ha Hortense!" in the Casino, from two in the afternoon until eight in the morning, sustained by dark and powerful coffee, and sleeping in lectures through the interim. A rare scene, the Casino. A big, barnlike auditorium, dotted with boys as girls, boys as pirates, boys as babies; the scenery in course of being violently set up; the spotlight man rehearsing by throwing weird shafts into angry eyes; over all the constant tuning of the orchestra or the cheerful tumpty-tump of a Triangle tune. The boy who writes the lyrics stands in the corner, biting a pencil, with twenty minutes to think of an encore; the business manager argues with the secretary as to how much money can be spent on "those damn milkmaid costumes"; the old graduate, president in ninety-eight, perches on a box and thinks how much simpler it was in his day.

How a Triangle show ever got off was a mystery, but it was a riotous mystery, anyway, whether or not one did enough service to wear a little gold Triangle on his watch-chain. "Ha-Ha Hortense!" was written over six times and had the names of nine collaborators on the programme. All Triangle shows started by being "something different—not just a regular musical comedy," but when the several authors, the president, the coach and the faculty committee finished with it, there remained just the old reliable Triangle show with the old reliable jokes and the star comedian who got expelled or sick or something just before the trip, and the dark-whiskered man in the pony-ballet, who "absolutely won't shave twice a day, dog-gone it!"

There was one brilliant place in "Ha-Ha Hortense!" It is a Princeton tradition that whenever a Yale man who is a member of the widely advertised "Skull and Bones" hears the sacred name mentioned, he must leave the room. It is also a

but she will serve only to make things more secretive and brilliant as she sits in solitary state at the deserted table and thinks such entertainments as this are not half so bad as they are painted, only rather wearying. But the P. D. is in love again . . . it was odd, wasn't it?—that though there was so much room left in the taxi the P. D. and the boy from Williams were somehow crowded out and had to go in a separate car. Odd! Didn't you notice how flushed the P. D. was when she arrived just seven minutes late? But the P. D. "gets away with it."

The "belle" had become the "flirt," the "flirt" had become the "baby vamp." The "belle" had five or six callers every afternoon. If the P. D., by some strange accident, has two, it is made pretty uncomfortable for the one who hasn't a date with her. The "belle" was surrounded by a dozen men in the intermissions between dances. Try to find the P. D. between dances, just *try* to find her.

The same girl . . . deep in an atmosphere of jungle music and the questioning of moral codes. Amory found it rather fascinating to feel that any popular girl he met before eight he might quite possibly kiss before twelve.

"Why on earth are we here?" he asked the girl with the green combs one night as they sat in some one's limousine, outside the Country Club in Louisville.

"I don't know. I'm just full of the devil."

"Let's be frank—we'll never see each other again. I wanted to come out here with you because I thought you were the best-looking girl in sight. You really don't care whether you ever see me again, do you?"

"No—but is this your line for every girl? What have I done to deserve it?"

"And you didn't feel tired dancing or want a cigarette or any of the things you said? You just wanted to be——"

"Oh, let's go in," she interrupted, "if you want to *analyze*. Let's not *talk* about it."

When the hand-knit, sleeveless jerseys were stylish, Amory, in a burst of inspiration, named them "petting shirts." The name travelled from coast to coast on the lips of parlor-snakes and P. D.'s.

Descriptive

Amory was now eighteen years old, just under six feet tall and exceptionally, but not conventionally, handsome. He had rather a young face, the ingenuousness of which was marred by the penetrating green eyes, fringed with long dark eyelashes. He lacked somehow that intense animal magnetism that so often accompanies beauty in men or women; his personality seemed rather a mental thing, and it was not in his power to turn it on and off like a water-faucet. But people never forgot his face.

Isabelle

She paused at the top of the staircase. The sensations attributed to divers on spring-boards, leading ladies on opening nights, and lumpy, husky young men on the day of the Big Game, crowded through her. She should have descended to a burst of drums or a discordant blend of themes from "Thais" and "Carmen." She had never been so curious about her appearance, she had never been so satisfied with it. She had been sixteen years old for six months.

"Isabelle!" called her cousin Sally from the doorway of the dressing-room.

"I'm ready." She caught a slight lump of nervousness in her throat.

"I had to send back to the house for another pair of slippers. It'll be just a minute."

Isabelle started toward the dressing-room for a last peek in the mirror, but something decided her to stand there and gaze down the broad stairs of the Minnehaha Club. They curved tantalizingly, and she could catch just a glimpse of two pairs of masculine feet in the hall below. Pump-shod in uniform black, they gave no hint of identity, but she wondered eagerly if one pair were attached to Amory Blaine. This young man, not as yet encountered, had nevertheless taken up a considerable part of her day—the first day of her arrival. Coming up in the machine from the station, Sally had volunteered, amid a rain of question, comment, revelation, and exaggeration:

"You remember Amory Blaine, of *course*. Well, he's simply mad to see you again. He's stayed over a day from college, and he's coming to-night. He's heard so much about you—says he remembers your eyes."

This had pleased Isabelle. It put them on equal terms, although she was quite capable of staging her own romances, with or without advance advertising. But following her happy tremble of anticipation, came a sinking sensation that made her ask:

"How do you mean he's heard about me? What sort of things?"

Sally smiled. She felt rather in the capacity of a showman with her more exotic cousin.

"He knows you're—you're considered beautiful and all that"—she paused—"and I guess he knows you've been kissed."

At this Isabelle's little fist had clinched suddenly under the fur robe. She was accustomed to be thus followed by her desperate past, and it never failed to rouse in her the same feeling of resentment; yet—in a strange town it was an advantageous reputation. She was a "Speed," was she? Well—let them find out.

Out of the window Isabelle watched the snow glide by in the frosty morning. It was ever so much colder here than in Baltimore; she had not remembered; the glass of the side door was iced, the windows were shirred with snow in the corners. Her mind played still with one subject. Did *he* dress like that boy there, who walked calmly down a bustling business street, in moccasins and winter-carnival costume? How very *Western*! Of course he wasn't that way: he went to Princeton, was a sophomore or something. Really she had no distinct idea of him. An ancient snap-shot she had preserved in an old kodak book had impressed her by the big eyes (which he had probably grown up to by now). However, in the last month, when her winter visit to Sally had been decided on, he had assumed the proportions of a worthy adversary. Children, most astute of match-makers, plot their campaigns quickly, and Sally had played a clever correspondence sonata to Isabelle's excitable temperament. Isabelle had been for some time capable of very strong, if very transient emotions. . . .

They drew up at a spreading, white-stone building, set back from the snowy street. Mrs. Weatherby greeted her warmly and her various younger cousins were produced from the corners where they skulked politely. Isabelle met them tactfully. At her best she allied all with whom she came in contact—except older girls and some women. All the impressions she made were conscious. The half-dozen girls she renewed acquaintance with that morning were all rather impressed and as much by her direct personality as by her reputation. Amory Blaine was an open subject. Evidently a bit light of love, neither popular nor unpopular—every girl there seemed to have had an affair with him at some time or other, but no one volunteered any really useful information. He was going to fall for her. . . . Sally had published that information to her young set and they were retailing it back to Sally as fast as they set eyes on Isabelle. Isabelle resolved secretly that she would, if necessary, *force* herself to like him—she owed it to Sally. Suppose she were terribly disappointed. Sally had painted him in such glowing colors—he was good-looking, "sort of distinguished, when he wants to be," had a line, and was properly inconstant. In fact, he summed up all the romance that her age and environment led her to desire. She wondered if those were his dancing-shoes that fox-trotted tentatively around the soft rug below.

All impressions and, in fact, all ideas were extremely kaleidoscopic to Isabelle. She had that curious mixture of the social and the artistic temperaments found often in two classes, society women and actresses. Her education or, rather, her sophistication, had been absorbed from the boys who had dangled on her favor; her tact was instinctive, and her capacity for love-affairs was limited only by the number of the susceptible within telephone distance. Flirt smiled from her large black-brown eyes and shone through her intense physical magnetism.

So she waited at the head of the stairs that evening while slippers were fetched. Just as she was growing impatient, Sally came out of the dressing-room, beaming with her accustomed good nature and high spirits, and together they descended to the floor below, while the shifting search-light of Isabelle's mind flashed on two ideas: she was glad she had high color to-night, and she wondered if he danced well.

Down-stairs, in the club's great room, she was surrounded for a moment by the girls she had met in the afternoon, then she heard Sally's voice repeating a cycle of names, and found herself bowing to a sextet of black and white, terribly stiff, vaguely familiar figures. The name Blaine figured somewhere, but at first she could not place him. A very confused, very juvenile moment of awkward backings and bumpings followed, and every one found himself talking to the person he least desired to. Isabelle manœuvred herself and Froggy Parker, freshman at Harvard, with whom she had once played hop-scotch, to a seat on the stairs. A humorous reference to the past was all she needed. The things Isabelle could do socially with one idea were remarkable. First, she repeated it rapturously in an enthusiastic contralto with a soupçon of Southern accent; then she held it off at a distance and smiled at it—her wonderful smile; then she delivered it in variations and played a sort of mental catch with it, all this in the nominal form of dialogue. Froggy was fascinated and quite unconscious that this was being done, not for him, but for the green eyes that glistened under the shining carefully watered hair, a little to her left, for Isabelle had discovered Amory. As an actress even in the fullest flush of her own conscious magnetism gets a deep impression of most of the people in the front row, so Isabelle sized up her antagonist. First, he had auburn hair, and from her feeling of disappointment she knew that she had expected him to be dark and of garter-advertisement slenderness. . . . For the rest, a faint flush and a straight, romantic profile; the effect set off by a close-fitting dress suit and a silk ruffled shirt of the kind that women still delight to see men wear, but men were just beginning to get tired of.

During this inspection Amory was quietly watching.

"Don't *you* think so?" she said suddenly, turning to him, innocent-eyed.

There was a stir, and Sally led the way over to their table. Amory struggled to Isabelle's side, and whispered:

"You're my dinner partner, you know. We're all coached for each other."

Isabelle gasped—this was rather right in line. But really she felt as if a good speech had been taken from the star and given to a minor character. . . . She mustn't lose the leadership a bit. The dinner-table glittered with laughter at the confusion of getting places, and then curious eyes were turned on her, sitting near the head. She was enjoying this immensely, and Froggy Parker was so engrossed with the added sparkle of her rising color that he forgot to pull out Sally's chair, and fell into a dim confusion. Amory was on the other side, full of confidence and vanity, gazing at her in open admiration. He began directly, and so did Froggy:

"I've heard a lot about you since you wore braids——"

"Wasn't it funny this afternoon——"

Both stopped. Isabelle turned to Amory shyly. Her face was always enough answer for any one, but she decided to speak.

"How—from whom?"

"From everybody—for all the years since you've been away." She blushed appropriately. On her right Froggy was *hors de combat* already, although he hadn't quite realized it.

"I'll tell you what I remembered about you all these years," Amory continued. She leaned slightly toward him and looked modestly at the celery before her. Froggy sighed—he knew Amory, and the situations that Amory seemed born to handle. He turned to Sally and asked her if she was going away to school next year. Amory opened with grape-shot.

"I've got an adjective that just fits you." This was one of his favorite starts—he seldom had a word in mind, but it was a curiosity provoker, and he could always produce something complimentary if he got in a tight corner.

"Oh—what?" Isabelle's face was a study in enraptured curiosity.

Amory shook his head.

"I don't know you very well yet."

"Will you tell me—afterward?" she half whispered.

He nodded.

"We'll sit out."

Isabelle nodded.

"Did any one ever tell you, you have keen eyes?" she said.

Amory attempted to make them look even keener. He fancied, but he was not sure, that her foot had just touched his under the table. But it might possibly have been only the table leg. It was so hard to tell. Still it thrilled him. He wondered quickly if there would be any difficulty in securing the little den up-stairs.

Babes in the Woods

Isabelle and Amory were distinctly not innocent, nor were they particularly brazen. Moreover, amateur standing had very little value in the game they were playing, a game that would presumably be her principal study for years to come. She had begun as he had, with good looks and an excitable temperament, and the rest was the result of accessible popular novels and dressing-room conversation culled from a slightly older set. Isabelle had walked with an artificial gait at nine and a half, and when her eyes, wide and starry, proclaimed the ingenue most, Amory was proportionately less deceived. He waited for the mask to drop off, but at the same time he did not question her right to wear it. She, on her part, was not impressed by his studied air of blasé sophistication. She had lived in a larger city and had slightly an advantage in range. But she accepted his pose—it was one of the dozen little conventions of this kind of affair. He was aware that he was getting this particular favor now because she had been coached; he knew that he stood for merely the best game in sight, and that he would have to improve his opportunity before he lost his advantage. So they proceeded with an infinite guile that would have horrified her parents.

After the dinner the dance began . . . smoothly. Smoothly?—boys cut in on Isabelle every few feet and then squabbled in the corners with: "You might let me get more than an inch!" and "She didn't like it either—she told me so next time I cut in." It was true—she told every one so, and gave every hand a parting pressure that said: "You know that your dances are *making* my evening."

But time passed, two hours of it, and the less subtle beaux had better learned to focus their pseudo-passionate glances elsewhere, for eleven o'clock found Isabelle and Amory sitting on the couch in the little den off the reading-room upstairs. She was conscious that they were a handsome pair, and seemed to belong distinctively in this seclusion, while lesser lights fluttered and chattered down-stairs.

Boys who passed the door looked in enviously—girls who passed only laughed and frowned and grew wise within themselves.

They had now reached a very definite stage. They had traded accounts of their progress since they had met last, and she had listened to much she had heard before. He was a sophomore, was on the *Princetonian* board, hoped to be chairman in senior year. He learned that some of the boys she went with in Baltimore were "terrible speeds" and came to dances in states of artificial stimulation; most of them were twenty or so, and drove alluring red Stutzes. A good half seemed to have already flunked out of various schools and colleges, but some of them bore athletic names that made him look at her admiringly. As a matter of fact, Isabelle's closer acquaintance with the universities was just commencing. She had bowing acquaintance with a lot of young men who thought she was a "pretty kid—worth keeping an eye on." But Isabelle strung the names into a fabrication of gayety that would have dazzled a Viennese nobleman. Such is the power of young contralto voices on sink-down sofas.

He asked her if she thought he was conceited. She said there was a difference between conceit and self-confidence. She adored self-confidence in men.

"Is Froggy a good friend of yours?" she asked.

"Rather—why?"

"He's a bum dancer."

Amory laughed.

"He dances as if the girl were on his back instead of in his arms."

She appreciated this.

"You're awfully good at sizing people up."

Amory denied this painfully. However, he sized up several people for her. Then they talked about hands.

"You've got awfully nice hands," she said. "They look as if you played the piano. Do you?"

I have said they had reached a very definite stage—nay, more, a very critical stage. Amory had stayed over a day to see her, and his train left at twelve-eighteen that night. His trunk and suitcase awaited him at the station; his watch was beginning to hang heavy in his pocket.

"Isabelle," he said suddenly, "I want to tell you something." They had been talking lightly about "that funny look in her eyes," and Isabelle knew from the change in his manner what was coming—indeed, she had been wondering how soon it would come. Amory reached above their heads and turned out the electric light, so that they were in the dark, except for the red glow that fell through the door from the reading-room lamps. Then he began:

"I don't know whether or not you know what you—what I'm going to say. Lordy, Isabelle—this *sounds* like a line, but it isn't."

"I know," said Isabelle softly.

"Maybe we'll never meet again like this—I have darned hard luck sometimes." He was leaning away from her on the other arm of the lounge, but she could see his eyes plainly in the dark.

"You'll meet me again—silly." There was just the slightest emphasis on the last word—so that it became almost a term of endearment. He continued a bit huskily:

"I've fallen for a lot of people—girls—and I guess you have, too—boys, I mean, but, honestly, you—" he broke off suddenly and leaned forward, chin on his hands: "Oh, what's the use—you'll go your way and I suppose I'll go mine."

Silence for a moment. Isabelle was quite stirred; she wound her handkerchief into a tight ball, and by the faint light that streamed over her, dropped it deliberately on the floor. Their hands touched for an instant, but neither spoke. Silences were becoming more frequent and more delicious. Outside another stray couple had come up and were experimenting on the piano in the next room. After the usual preliminary of "chopsticks," one of them started "Babes in the Woods" and a light tenor carried the words into the den:

"Give me your hand—
I'll understand
We're off to slumberland."

Isabelle hummed it softly and trembled as she felt Amory's hand close over hers.

"Isabelle," he whispered. "You know I'm mad about you. You *do* give a darn about me."

"Yes."

"How much do you care—do you like any one better?"

"No." He could scarcely hear her, although he bent so near that he felt her breath against his cheek.

"Isabelle, I'm going back to college for six long months, and why shouldn't we—if I could only just have one thing to remember you by——"

"Close the door. . . ." Her voice had just stirred so that he half wondered whether she had spoken at all. As he swung the door softly shut, the music seemed quivering just outside.

"Moonlight is bright,
Kiss me good night."

What a wonderful song, she thought—everything was wonderful to-night, most of all this romantic scene in the den, with their hands clinging and the inevitable looming charmingly close. The future vista of her life seemed an unending succession of scenes like this: under moonlight and pale starlight, and in the backs of warm limousines and in low, cosey roadsters stopped under sheltering trees—only the boy might change, and this one was *so* nice. He took her hand softly. With a sudden movement he turned it and, holding it to his lips, kissed the palm.

"Isabelle!" His whisper blended in the music, and they seemed to float nearer together. Her breath came faster. "Can't I kiss you, Isabelle—Isabelle?" Lips half parted, she turned her head to him in the dark. Suddenly the ring of voices, the sound of running footsteps surged toward them. Quick as a flash Amory reached up and turned on the light, and when the door opened and three boys, the wrathy and dance-craving Froggy among them, rushed in, he was turning over the magazines on the table, while she sat without moving, serene and unembarrassed, and even greeted them with a welcoming smile. But her heart was beating wildly, and she felt somehow as if she had been deprived.

It was evidently over. There was a clamor for a dance, there was a glance that passed between them—on his side despair, on hers regret, and then the evening went on, with the reassured beaux and the eternal cutting in.

At quarter to twelve Amory shook hands with her gravely, in the midst of a small crowd assembled to wish him good-speed. For an instant he lost his poise, and she felt a bit rattled when a satirical voice from a concealed wit cried:

"Take her outside, Amory!" As he took her hand he pressed it a little, and she returned the pressure as she had done to twenty hands that evening—that was all.

At two o'clock back at the Weatherbys' Sally asked her if she and Amory had had a "time" in the den. Isabelle turned to her quietly. In her eyes was the light of the idealist, the inviolate dreamer of Joan-like dreams.

"No," she answered. "I don't do that sort of thing any more; he asked me to, but I said no."

As she crept in bed she wondered what he'd say in his special delivery to-morrow. He had such a good-looking mouth —would she ever——?

"Fourteen angels were watching o'er them," sang Sally sleepily from the next room.

"Damn!" muttered Isabelle, punching the pillow into a luxurious lump and exploring the cold sheets cautiously. "Damn!"

Carnival

Amory, by way of the *Princetonian*, had arrived. The minor snobs, finely balanced thermometers of success, warmed to him as the club elections grew nigh, and he and Tom were visited by groups of upper classmen who arrived awkwardly, balanced on the edge of the furniture and talked of all subjects except the one of absorbing interest. Amory was amused at the intent eyes upon him, and, in case the visitors represented some club in which he was not interested, took great pleasure in shocking them with unorthodox remarks.

"Oh, let me see—" he said one night to a flabbergasted delegation, "what club do you represent?"

With visitors from Ivy and Cottage and Tiger Inn he played the "nice, unspoilt, ingenuous boy" very much at ease and quite unaware of the object of the call.

When the fatal morning arrived, early in March, and the campus became a document in hysteria, he slid smoothly into Cottage with Alec Connage and watched his suddenly neurotic class with much wonder.

There were fickle groups that jumped from club to club; there were friends of two or three days who announced tearfully and wildly that they must join the same club, nothing should separate them; there were snarling disclosures of long-hidden grudges as the Suddenly Prominent remembered snubs of freshman year. Unknown men were elevated into importance when they received certain coveted bids; others who were considered "all set" found that they had made unexpected enemies, felt themselves stranded and deserted, talked wildly of leaving college.

In his own crowd Amory saw men kept out for wearing green hats, for being "a damn tailor's dummy," for having "too much pull in heaven," for getting drunk one night "not like a gentleman, by God," or for unfathomable secret reasons known to no one but the wielders of the black balls.

This orgy of sociability culminated in a gigantic party at the Nassau Inn, where punch was dispensed from immense bowls, and the whole down-stairs became a delirious, circulating, shouting pattern of faces and voices.

"Hi, Dibby—'gratulations!"

"Goo' boy, Tom, you got a good bunch in Cap."

"Say, Kerry——"

"Oh, Kerry—I hear you went Tiger with all the weight-lifters!"

"Well, I didn't go Cottage—the parlor-snakes' delight."

"They say Overton fainted when he got his Ivy bid— Did he sign up the first day?—oh, *no.* Tore over to Murray-Dodge on a bicycle—afraid it was a mistake."

"How'd you get into Cap—you old roué?"

" 'Gratulations!"

" 'Gratulations yourself. Hear you got a good crowd."

When the bar closed, the party broke up into groups and streamed, singing, over the snow-clad campus, in a weird delusion that snobbishness and strain were over at last, and that they could do what they pleased for the next two years.

Long afterward Amory thought of sophomore spring as the

happiest time of his life. His ideas were in tune with life as he found it; he wanted no more than to drift and dream and enjoy a dozen new-found friendships through the April afternoons.

Alec Connage came into his room one morning and woke him up into the sunshine and peculiar glory of Campbell Hall shining in the window.

"Wake up, Original Sin, and scrape yourself together. Be in front of Renwick's in half an hour. Somebody's got a car." He took the bureau cover and carefully deposited it, with its load of small articles, upon the bed.

"Where'd you get the car?" demanded Amory cynically.

"Sacred trust, but don't be a critical goopher or you can't go!"

"I think I'll sleep," Amory said calmly, resettling himself and reaching beside the bed for a cigarette.

"Sleep!"

"Why not? I've got a class at eleven-thirty."

"You damned gloom! Of course, if you don't want to go to the coast——"

With a bound Amory was out of bed, scattering the bureau cover's burden on the floor. The coast . . . he hadn't seen it for years, since he and his mother were on their pilgrimage.

"Who's going?" he demanded as he wriggled into his B.V.D.'s.

"Oh, Dick Humbird and Kerry Holiday and Jesse Ferrenby and—oh about five or six. Speed it up, kid!"

In ten minutes Amory was devouring cornflakes in Renwick's, and at nine-thirty they bowled happily out of town, headed for the sands of Deal Beach.

"You see," said Kerry, "the car belongs down there. In fact, it was stolen from Asbury Park by persons unknown, who deserted it in Princeton and left for the West. Heartless Humbird here got permission from the city council to deliver it."

"Anybody got any money?" suggested Ferrenby, turning around from the front seat.

There was an emphatic negative chorus.

"That makes it interesting."

"Money—what's money? We can sell the car."

"Charge him salvage or something."

"How're we going to get food?" asked Amory.

"Honestly," answered Kerry, eying him reprovingly, "do you doubt Kerry's ability for three short days? Some people have lived on nothing for years at a time. Read the Boy Scout Monthly."

"Three days," Amory mused, "and I've got classes."

"One of the days is the Sabbath."

"Just the same, I can only cut six more classes, with over a month and a half to go."

"Throw him out!"

"It's a long walk back."

"Amory, you're running it out, if I may coin a new phrase."

"Hadn't you better get some dope on yourself, Amory?"

Amory subsided resignedly and drooped into a contemplation of the scenery. Swinburne seemed to fit in somehow.

"Oh, winter's rains and ruins are over,
And all the seasons of snows and sins;
The days dividing lover and lover,
The light that loses, the night that wins;
And time remembered is grief forgotten,
And frosts are slain and flowers begotten,
And in green underwood and cover,
Blossom by blossom the spring begins.

"The full streams feed on flower of——"

"What's the matter, Amory? Amory's thinking about poetry, about the pretty birds and flowers. I can see it in his eye."

"No, I'm not," he lied. "I'm thinking about the Princetonian. I ought to make up to-night; but I can telephone back, I suppose."

"Oh," said Kerry respectfully, "these important men——"

Amory flushed and it seemed to him that Ferrenby, a defeated competitor, winced a little. Of course, Kerry was only kidding, but he really mustn't mention the *Princetonian.*

It was a halcyon day, and as they neared the shore and the salt breezes scurried by, he began to picture the ocean and long, level stretches of sand and red roofs over blue sea. Then they hurried through the little town and it all flashed upon his consciousness to a mighty pæan of emotion. . . .

"Oh, good Lord! *Look* at it!" he cried.

"What?"

"Let me out, quick—I haven't seen it for eight years! Oh, gentlefolk, stop the car!"

"What an odd child!" remarked Alec.

"I do believe he's a bit eccentric."

The car was obligingly drawn up at a curb, and Amory ran for the boardwalk. First, he realized that the sea was blue and that there was an enormous quantity of it, and that it roared and roared—really all the banalities about the ocean that one could realize, but if any one had told him then that these things were banalities, he would have gaped in wonder.

"Now we'll get lunch," ordered Kerry, wandering up with the crowd. "Come on, Amory, tear yourself away and get practical."

"We'll try the best hotel first," he went on, "and thence and so forth."

They strolled along the boardwalk to the most imposing hostelry in sight, and, entering the dining-room, scattered about a table.

"Eight Bronxes," commanded Alec, "and a club sandwich and Juliennes. The food for one. Hand the rest around."

Amory ate little, having seized a chair where he could watch the sea and feel the rock of it. When luncheon was over they sat and smoked quietly.

"What's the bill?"

Some one scanned it.

"Eight twenty-five."

"Rotten overcharge. We'll give them two dollars and one for the waiter. Kerry, collect the small change."

The waiter approached, and Kerry gravely handed him a dollar, tossed two dollars on the check, and turned away. They sauntered leisurely toward the door, pursued in a moment by the suspicious Ganymede.

"Some mistake, sir."

Kerry took the bill and examined it critically.

"No mistake!" he said, shaking his head gravely, and, tearing it into four pieces, he handed the scraps to the waiter, who was so dumfounded that he stood motionless and expressionless while they walked out.

"Won't he send after us?"

"No," said Kerry; "for a minute he'll think we're the proprietor's sons or something; then he'll look at the check again and call the manager, and in the meantime——"

They left the car at Asbury and street-car'd to Allenhurst, where they investigated the crowded pavilions for beauty. At four there were refreshments in a lunch-room, and this time they paid an even smaller per cent on the total cost; something about the appearance and savoir-faire of the crowd made the thing go, and they were not pursued.

"You see, Amory, we're Marxian Socialists," explained Kerry. "We don't believe in property and we're putting it to the great test."

"Night will descend," Amory suggested.

"Watch, and put your trust in Holiday."

They became jovial about five-thirty and, linking arms, strolled up and down the boardwalk in a row, chanting a monotonous ditty about the sad sea waves. Then Kerry saw a face in the crowd that attracted him and, rushing off, reappeared in a moment with one of the homeliest girls Amory had ever set eyes on. Her pale mouth extended from ear to ear, her teeth projected in a solid wedge, and she had little, squinty eyes that peeped ingratiatingly over the side sweep of her nose. Kerry presented them formally.

"Name of Kaluka, Hawaiian queen! Let me present Messrs. Connage, Sloane, Humbird, Ferrenby, and Blaine."

The girl bobbed courtesies all around. Poor creature; Amory supposed she had never before been noticed in her life—possibly she was half-witted. While she accompanied them (Kerry had invited her to supper) she said nothing which could discountenance such a belief.

"She prefers her native dishes," said Alec gravely to the waiter, "but any coarse food will do."

All through supper he addressed her in the most respectful language, while Kerry made idiotic love to her on the other side, and she giggled and grinned. Amory was content to sit and watch the by-play, thinking what a light touch Kerry had, and how he could transform the barest incident into a thing of curve and contour. They all seemed to have the spirit of it more or less, and it was a relaxation to be with them. Amory usually liked men individually, yet feared them in crowds unless the crowd was around *him*. He wondered how much each one contributed to the party, for there was somewhat of a spiritual tax levied. Alec and Kerry were the life of it, but not quite the centre. Somehow the quiet Humbird, and Sloane, with his impatient superciliousness, were the centre.

Dick Humbird had, ever since freshman year, seemed to Amory a perfect type of aristocrat. He was slender but well-built—black curly hair, straight features, and rather a dark skin. Everything he said sounded intangibly appropriate. He possessed infinite courage, an averagely good mind, and a sense of honor with a clear charm and noblesse oblige that varied it from righteousness. He could dissipate without going to pieces, and even his most bohemian adventures never seemed "running it out." People dressed like him, tried to talk as he did. . . . Amory decided that he probably held the world back, but he wouldn't have changed him. . . .

He differed from the healthy type that was essentially middle-class—he never seemed to perspire. Some people couldn't be familiar with a chauffeur without having it returned; Humbird could have lunched at Sherry's with a colored man, yet people would have somehow known that it was all right. He was not a snob, though he knew only half his class. His friends ranged from the highest to the lowest, but it was impossible to "cultivate" him. Servants worshipped him, and treated him like a god. He seemed the eternal example of what the upper class tries to be.

"He's like those pictures in the Illustrated London News of the English officers who have been killed," Amory had said to Alec.

"Well," Alec had answered, "if you want to know the shocking truth, his father was a grocery clerk who made a fortune in Tacoma real estate and came to New York ten years ago."

Amory had felt a curious sinking sensation.

This present type of party was made possible by the surging together of the class after club elections—as if to make a last desperate attempt to know itself, to keep together, to fight off the tightening spirit of the clubs. It was a let-down from the conventional heights they had all walked so rigidly.

After supper they saw Kaluka to the boardwalk, and then strolled back along the beach to Asbury. The evening sea was a new sensation, for all its color and mellow age was gone, and it seemed the bleak waste that made the Norse sagas sad; Amory thought of Kipling's

"Beaches of Lukanon before the sealers came."

It was still a music, though, infinitely sorrowful.

Ten o'clock found them penniless. They had suppered greatly on their last eleven cents and, singing, strolled up through the casinos and lighted arches on the boardwalk, stopping to listen approvingly to all band concerts. In one place Kerry took up a collection for the French War Orphans which netted a dollar and twenty cents, and with this they bought some brandy in case they caught cold in the night. They finished the day in a moving-picture show and went into solemn systematic roars of laughter at an ancient comedy, to the startled annoyance of the rest of the audience. Their entrance was distinctly strategic, for each man as he entered pointed reproachfully at the one just behind him. Sloane, bringing up the rear, disclaimed all knowledge and responsibility as soon as the others were scattered inside; then as the irate ticket-taker rushed in he followed nonchalantly.

They reassembled later by the Casino and made arrangements for the night. Kerry wormed permission from the watchman to sleep on the platform and, having collected a huge pile of rugs from the booths to serve as mattresses and blankets, they talked until midnight, and then fell into a dreamless sleep, though Amory tried hard to stay awake and watch that marvellous moon settle on the sea.

So they progressed for two happy days, up and down the shore by street-car or machine, or by shoe-leather on the crowded boardwalk; sometimes eating with the wealthy, more frequently dining frugally at the expense of an unsuspecting restaurateur. They had their photos taken, eight poses, in a quick-development store. Kerry insisted on grouping them as a "varsity" football team, and then as a tough gang from the East Side, with their coats inside out, and himself sitting in the middle on a cardboard moon. The photographer probably has them yet—at least, they never called for them. The weather was perfect, and again they slept outside, and again Amory fell unwillingly asleep.

Sunday broke stolid and respectable, and even the sea seemed to mumble and complain, so they returned to Princeton via the Fords of transient farmers, and broke up with colds in their heads, but otherwise none the worse for wandering.

Even more than in the year before, Amory neglected his work, not deliberately but lazily and through a multitude of other interests. Co-ordinate geometry and the melancholy hexameters of Corneille and Racine held forth small allurements, and even psychology, which he had eagerly awaited, proved to be a dull subject full of muscular reactions and biological phrases rather than the study of personality and influence. That was a noon class, and it always sent him dozing. Having found that "subjective and objective, sir," answered most of the questions, he used the phrase on all occasions, and it became the class joke when, on a query being levelled at him, he was nudged awake by Ferrenby or Sloane to gasp it out.

Mostly there were parties—to Orange or the Shore, more rarely to New York and Philadelphia, though one night they marshalled fourteen waitresses out of Childs' and took them to ride down Fifth Avenue on top of an auto bus. They all cut more classes than were allowed, which meant an additional course the following year, but spring was too rare to let anything interfere with their colorful ramblings. In May Amory was elected to the Sophomore Prom Committee, and when after a long evening's discussion with Alec they made out a tentative list of class probabilities for the senior council, they placed themselves among the surest. The senior council was composed presumably of the eighteen most representative seniors, and in view of Alec's football managership and Amory's chance of nosing out Burne Holiday as *Princetonian* chairman, they seemed fairly justified in this presumption. Oddly enough, they both placed D'Invilliers as among the possibilities, a guess that a year before the class would have gaped at.

All through the spring Amory had kept up an intermittent correspondence with Isabelle Borgé, punctuated by violent squabbles and chiefly enlivened by his attempts to find new words for love. He discovered Isabelle to be discreetly and aggravatingly unsentimental in letters, but he hoped against hope that she would prove not too exotic a bloom to fit the large spaces of spring as she had fitted the den in the Minnehaha Club. During May he wrote thirty-page documents almost nightly, and sent them to her in bulky envelopes exteriorly labelled "Part I" and "Part II."

"Oh, Alec, I believe I'm tired of college," he said sadly, as they walked the dusk together.

"I think I am, too, in a way."

"All I'd like would be a little home in the country, some warm country, and a wife, and just enough to do to keep from rotting."

"Me, too."

"I'd like to quit."

"What does your girl say?"

"Oh!" Amory gasped in horror. "She wouldn't *think* of marrying . . . that is, not now. I mean the future, you know."

"My girl would. I'm engaged."

"Are you really?"

"Yes. Don't say a word to anybody, please, but I am. I may not come back next year."

"But you're only twenty! Give up college?"

"Why, Amory, you were saying a minute ago——"

"Yes," Amory interrupted, "but I was just wishing. I wouldn't think of leaving college. It's just that I feel so sad these wonderful nights. I sort of feel they're never coming again, and I'm not really getting all I could out of them. I wish my girl lived here. But marry—not a chance. Especially as father says the money isn't forthcoming as it used to be."

"What a waste these nights are!" agreed Alec.

But Amory sighed and made use of the nights. He had a snap-shot of Isabelle, enshrined in an old watch, and at eight almost every night he would turn off all the lights except the desk lamp and, sitting by the open windows with the picture before him, write her rapturous letters.

. . . Oh, it's so hard to write you what I really *feel* when I think about you so much; you've gotten to mean to me a *dream* that I can't put on paper any more. Your last letter came and it was wonderful! I read it over about six times, especially the *last* part, but I do wish, sometimes, you'd be more *frank* and tell me what you really do think of me, yet your last letter was too good to be true, and I can hardly wait until June! Be sure and be able to come to the prom. It'll be fine, I think, and I want to bring *you* just at the end of a wonderful year. I often think over what you said on that night and wonder how much you meant. If it were any one but you—but you see I *thought* you were fickle the first time I saw you and you are so popular and everything that I can't imagine your really liking me *best*.

Oh, Isabelle, dear—it's a wonderful night. Somebody is playing "Love Moon" on a mandolin far across the campus, and the music seems to bring you into the window. Now he's playing "Good-by, Boys, I'm Through," and how well it suits me. For I *am* through with everything. I have decided never to take a cocktail again, and I know I'll never again fall in love—I couldn't—you've been too much a part of my days and nights to ever let me think of another girl. I meet them all the time and they don't interest me. I'm not pretending to be blasé, because it's not that. It's just that I'm in love. Oh, *dearest* Isabelle (somehow I can't call you just Isabelle, and I'm afraid I'll come out with the "dearest" before your family this June), you've *got* to come to the prom, and then I'll come up to your house for a day and everything'll be perfect. . . .

And so on in an eternal monotone that seemed to both of them infinitely charming, infinitely new.

June came and the days grew so hot and lazy that they could not worry even about exams, but spent dreamy evenings on the court of Cottage, talking of long subjects until the sweep of country toward Stony Brook became a blue haze and the lilacs were white around tennis-courts, and words gave way to silent cigarettes. . . . Then down deserted Prospect and along McCosh with song everywhere around them, up to the hot joviality of Nassau Street.

Tom D'Invilliers and Amory walked late in those days. A gambling fever swept through the sophomore class and they bent over the bones till three o'clock many a sultry night. After one session they came out of Sloane's room to find the dew fallen and the stars old in the sky.

"Let's borrow bicycles and take a ride," Amory suggested.

"All right. I'm not a bit tired and this is almost the last

night of the year, really, because the prom stuff starts Monday."

They found two unlocked bicycles in Holder Court and rode out about half-past three along the Lawrenceville Road.

"What are you going to do this summer, Amory?"

"Don't ask me—same old things, I suppose. A month or two in Lake Geneva—I'm counting on you to be there in July, you know—then there'll be Minneapolis, and that means hundreds of summer hops, parlor-snaking, getting bored—But oh, Tom," he added suddenly, "hasn't this year been slick!"

"No," declared Tom emphatically, a new Tom, clothed by Brooks, shod by Franks, "I've won this game, but I feel as if I never want to play another. You're all right—you're a rubber ball, and somehow it suits you, but I'm sick of adapting myself to the local snobbishness of this corner of the world. I want to go where people aren't barred because of the color of their neckties and the roll of their coats."

"You can't, Tom," argued Amory, as they rolled along through the scattering night; "wherever you go now you'll always unconsciously apply these standards of 'having it' or 'lacking it.' For better or worse we've stamped you; you're a Princeton type!"

"Well, then," complained Tom, his cracked voice rising plaintively, "why do I have to come back at all? I've learned all that Princeton has to offer. Two years more of mere pedantry and lying around a club aren't going to help. They're just going to disorganize me, conventionalize me completely. Even now I'm so spineless that I wonder how I get away with it."

"Oh, but you're missing the real point, Tom," Amory interrupted. "You've just had your eyes opened to the snobbishness of the world in a rather abrupt manner. Princeton invariably gives the thoughtful man a social sense."

"You consider you taught me that, don't you?" he asked quizzically, eying Amory in the half dark.

Amory laughed quietly.

"Didn't I?"

"Sometimes," he said slowly, "I think you're my bad angel. I might have been a pretty fair poet."

"Come on, that's rather hard. You chose to come to an Eastern college. Either your eyes were opened to the mean scrambling quality of people, or you'd have gone through blind, and you'd hate to have done that—been like Marty Kaye."

"Yes," he agreed, "you're right. I wouldn't have liked it. Still, it's hard to be made a cynic at twenty."

"I was born one," Amory murmured. "I'm a cynical idealist." He paused and wondered if that meant anything.

They reached the sleeping school of Lawrenceville, and turned to ride back.

"It's good, this ride, isn't it?" Tom said presently.

"Yes; it's a good finish, it's knock-out; everything's good to-night. Oh, for a hot, languorous summer and Isabelle!"

"Oh, you and your Isabelle! I'll bet she's a simple one . . . let's say some poetry."

So Amory declaimed "The Ode to a Nightingale" to the bushes they passed.

"I'll never be a poet," said Amory as he finished. "I'm not enough of a sensualist really; there are only a few obvious things that I notice as primarily beautiful: women, spring evenings, music at night, the sea; I don't catch the subtle things like 'silver-snarling trumpets.' I may turn out an intellectual, but I'll never write anything but mediocre poetry."

They rode into Princeton as the sun was making colored maps of the sky behind the graduate school, and hurried to the refreshment of a shower that would have to serve in place of sleep. By noon the bright-costumed alumni crowded the streets with their bands and choruses, and in the tents there was great reunion under the orange-and-black banners that curled and strained in the wind. Amory looked long at one house which bore the legend "Sixty-nine." There a few gray-haired men sat and talked quietly while the classes swept by in panorama of life.

Under the Arc-Light

Then tragedy's emerald eyes glared suddenly at Amory over the edge of June. On the night after his ride to Lawrenceville a crowd sallied to New York in quest of adventure, and started back to Princeton about twelve o'clock in two machines. It had been a gay party and different stages of sobriety were represented. Amory was in the car behind; they had taken the wrong road and lost the way, and so were hurrying to catch up.

It was a clear night and the exhilaration of the road went to Amory's head. He had the ghost of two stanzas of a poem forming in his mind. . . .

So the gray car crept nightward in the dark and there was no life stirred as it went by. . . . As the still ocean paths before the shark in starred and glittering waterways, beauty-high, the moon-swathed trees divided, pair on pair, while flapping nightbirds cried across the air. . . .

A moment by an inn of lamps and shades, a yellow inn under a yellow moon—then silence, where crescendo laughter fades . . . the car swung out again to the winds of June, mellowed the shadows where the distance grew, then crushed the yellow shadows into blue. . . .

They jolted to a stop, and Amory peered up, startled. A woman was standing beside the road, talking to Alec at the wheel. Afterward he remembered the harpy effect that her old kimono gave her, and the cracked hollowness of her voice as she spoke:

"You Princeton boys?"

"Yes."

"Well, there's one of you killed here, and two others about dead."

"*My God!*"

"Look!" She pointed and they gazed in horror. Under the full light of a roadside arc-light lay a form, face downward in a widening circle of blood.

They sprang from the car. Amory thought of the back of that head—that hair—that hair . . . and then they turned the form over.

"It's Dick—Dick Humbird!"

"Oh, Christ!"

"Feel his heart!"

Then the insistent voice of the old crone in a sort of croaking triumph:

"He's quite dead, all right. The car turned over. Two of the men that weren't hurt just carried the others in, but this one's no use."

Amory rushed into the house and the rest followed with a limp mass that they laid on the sofa in the shoddy little front parlor. Sloane, with his shoulder punctured, was on another lounge. He was half delirious, and kept calling something about a chemistry lecture at 8:10.

"I don't know what happened," said Ferrenby in a strained voice. "Dick was driving and he wouldn't give up the wheel; we told him he'd been drinking too much—then there was this damn curve—oh, my *God!* . . ." He threw himself face downward on the floor and broke into dry sobs.

The doctor had arrived, and Amory went over to the couch, where some one handed him a sheet to put over the body. With a sudden hardness, he raised one of the hands and let it fall back inertly. The brow was cold but the face not expressionless. He looked at the shoe-laces—Dick had tied them that morning. *He* had tied them—and now he was this heavy white mass. All that remained of the charm and personality of the Dick Humbird he had known—oh, it was all so horrible and unaristocratic and close to the earth. All tragedy has that strain of the grotesque and squalid—so useless, futile . . . the way animals die. . . . Amory was reminded of a cat that had lain horribly mangled in some alley of his childhood.

"Some one go to Princeton with Ferrenby."

Amory stepped outside the door and shivered slightly at the late night wind—a wind that stirred a broken fender on the mass of bent metal to a plaintive, tinny sound.

CRESCENDO!

Next day, by a merciful chance, passed in a whirl. When Amory was by himself his thoughts zigzagged inevitably to the picture of that red mouth yawning incongruously in the white face, but with a determined effort he piled present excitement upon the memory of it and shut it coldly away from his mind.

Isabelle and her mother drove into town at four, and they rode up smiling Prospect Avenue, through the gay crowd, to have tea at Cottage. The clubs had their annual dinners that night, so at seven he loaned her to a freshman and arranged to meet her in the gymnasium at eleven, when the upper classmen were admitted to the freshman dance. She was all he had expected, and he was happy and eager to make that night the centre of every dream. At nine the upper classes stood in front of the clubs as the freshman torchlight parade rioted past, and Amory wondered if the dress-suited groups against the dark, stately backgrounds and under the flare of the torches made the night as brilliant to the staring, cheering freshman as it had been to him the year before.

The next day was another whirl. They lunched in a gay party of six in a private dining-room at the club, while Isabelle and Amory looked at each other tenderly over the fried chicken and knew that their love was to be eternal. They danced away the prom until five, and the stags cut in on Isabelle with joyous abandon, which grew more and more enthusiastic as the hour grew late, and their wines, stored in overcoat pockets in the coat room, made old weariness wait until another day. The stag line is a most homogeneous mass of men. It fairly sways with a single soul. A dark-haired beauty dances by and there is a half-gasping sound as the ripple surges forward and some one sleeker than the rest darts out and cuts in. Then when the six-foot girl (brought by Kaye in your class, and to whom he has been trying to introduce you all evening) gallops by, the line surges back and the groups face about and become intent on far corners of the hall, for Kaye, anxious and perspiring, appears elbowing through the crowd in search of familiar faces.

"I say, old man, I've got an awfully nice——"

"Sorry, Kaye, but I'm set for this one. I've got to cut in on a fella."

"Well, the next one?"

"What—ah—er—I swear I've got to go cut in—look me up when she's got a dance free."

It delighted Amory when Isabelle suggested that they leave for a while and drive around in her car. For a delicious hour that passed too soon they glided the silent roads about Princeton and talked from the surface of their hearts in shy excitement. Amory felt strangely ingenuous and made no attempt to kiss her.

Next day they rode up through the Jersey country, had luncheon in New York, and in the afternoon went to see a problem play at which Isabelle wept all through the second act, rather to Amory's embarrassment—though it filled him with tenderness to watch her. He was tempted to lean over and kiss away her tears, and she slipped her hand into his under cover of darkness to be pressed softly.

Then at six they arrived at the Borgés' summer place on Long Island, and Amory rushed up-stairs to change into a dinner coat. As he put in his studs he realized that he was enjoying life as he would probably never enjoy it again. Everything was hallowed by the haze of his own youth. He had arrived, abreast of the best in his generation at Princeton. He was in love and his love was returned. Turning on all the lights, he looked at himself in the mirror, trying to find in his own face the qualities that made him see clearer than the great crowd of people, that made him decide firmly, and able to influence and follow his own will. There was little in his life now that he would have changed. . . . Oxford might have been a bigger field.

Silently he admired himself. How conveniently well he looked, and how well a dinner coat became him. He stepped into the hall and then waited at the top of the stairs, for he heard footsteps coming. It was Isabelle, and from the top of her shining hair to her little golden slippers she had never seemed so beautiful.

"Isabelle!" he cried, half involuntarily, and held out his arms. As in the story-books, she ran into them, and on that half-minute, as their lips first touched, rested the high point of vanity, the crest of his young egotism.

CHAPTER III

The Egotist Considers

"OUCH! Let me go!"

He dropped his arms to his sides.

"What's the matter?"

"Your shirt stud—it hurt me—look!" She was looking down at her neck, where a little blue spot about the size of a pea marred its pallor.

"Oh, Isabelle," he reproached himself, "I'm a goopher. Really, I'm sorry—I shouldn't have held you so close."

She looked up impatiently.

"Oh, Amory, of course you couldn't help it, and it didn't hurt much; but what *are* we going to do about it?"

"*Do* about it?" he asked. "Oh—that spot; it'll disappear in a second."

"It isn't," she said, after a moment of concentrated gazing, "it's still there—and it looks like Old Nick—oh, Amory, what'll we do! It's *just* the height of your shoulder."

"Massage it," he suggested, repressing the faintest inclination to laugh.

She rubbed it delicately with the tips of her fingers, and then a tear gathered in the corner of her eye, and slid down her cheek.

"Oh, Amory," she said despairingly, lifting up a most pathetic face, "I'll just make my whole neck *flame* if I rub it. What'll I do?"

A quotation sailed into his head and he couldn't resist repeating it aloud.

"All the perfumes of Arabia will not whiten this little hand."

She looked up and the sparkle of the tear in her eye was like ice.

"You're not very sympathetic."

Amory mistook her meaning.

"Isabelle, darling, I think it'll——"

"Don't touch me!" she cried. "Haven't I enough on my mind and you stand there and *laugh*!"

Then he slipped again.

"Well, it *is* funny, Isabelle, and we were talking the other day about a sense of humor being——"

She was looking at him with something that was not a smile, rather the faint, mirthless echo of a smile, in the corners of her mouth.

"Oh, shut up!" she cried suddenly, and fled down the hallway toward her room. Amory stood there, covered with remorseful confusion.

"Damn!"

When Isabelle reappeared she had thrown a light wrap about her shoulders, and they descended the stairs in a silence that endured through dinner.

"Isabelle," he began rather testily, as they arranged themselves in the car, bound for a dance at the Greenwich Country Club, "you're angry, and I'll be, too, in a minute. Let's kiss and make up."

Isabelle considered glumly.

"I hate to be laughed at," she said finally.

"I won't laugh any more. I'm not laughing now, am I?"

"You did."

"Oh, don't be so darned feminine."

Her lips curled slightly.

"I'll be anything I want."

Amory kept his temper with difficulty. He became aware that he had not an ounce of real affection for Isabelle, but her coldness piqued him. He wanted to kiss her, kiss her a lot, because then he knew he could leave in the morning and not care. On the contrary, if he didn't kiss her, it would worry him. . . . It would interfere vaguely with his idea of himself as a conqueror. It wasn't dignified to come off second best, *pleading*, with a doughty warrior like Isabelle.

Perhaps she suspected this. At any rate, Amory watched the night that should have been the consummation of romance glide by with great moths overhead and the heavy fragrance of roadside gardens, but without those broken words, those little sighs. . . .

Afterward they suppered on ginger ale and devil's food in the pantry, and Amory announced a decision.

"I'm leaving early in the morning."

"Why?"

"Why not?" he countered.

"There's no need."

"However, I'm going."

"Well, if you insist on being ridiculous——"

"Oh, don't put it that way," he objected.

"—just because I won't let you kiss me. Do you think——"

"Now, Isabelle," he interrupted, "you know it's not that—even suppose it is. We've reached the stage where we either ought to kiss—or—or—nothing. It isn't as if you were refusing on moral grounds."

She hesitated.

"I really don't know what to think about you," she began, in a feeble, perverse attempt at conciliation. "You're so funny."

"How?"

"Well, I thought you had a lot of self-confidence and all that; remember you told me the other day that you could do anything you wanted, or get anything you wanted?"

Amory flushed. He *had* told her a lot of things.

"Yes."

"Well, you didn't seem to feel so self-confident to-night. Maybe you're just plain conceited."

"No, I'm not," he hesitated. "At Princeton——"

"Oh, you and Princeton! You'd think that was the world, the way you talk! Perhaps you *can* write better than anybody else on your old Princetonian; maybe the freshmen *do* think you're important——"

"You don't understand——"

"Yes, I do," she interrupted. "I *do*, because you're always talking about yourself and I used to like it; now I don't."

"Have I to-night?"

"That's just the point," insisted Isabelle. "You got all upset to-night. You just sat and watched my eyes. Besides, I have to think all the time I'm talking to you—you're so critical."

"I make you think, do I?" Amory repeated with a touch of vanity.

"You're a nervous strain"—this emphatically—"and when you analyze every little emotion and instinct I just don't have 'em."

"I know." Amory admitted her point and shook his head helplessly.

"Let's go." She stood up.

He rose abstractedly and they walked to the foot of the stairs.

"What train can I get?"

"There's one about 9:11 if you really must go."

"Yes, I've got to go, really. Good night."

"Good night."

They were at the head of the stairs, and as Amory turned into his room he thought he caught just the faintest cloud of discontent in her face. He lay awake in the darkness and wondered how much he cared—how much of his sudden unhappiness was hurt vanity—whether he was, after all, temperamentally unfitted for romance.

When he awoke, it was with a glad flood of consciousness. The early wind stirred the chintz curtains at the windows and he was idly puzzled not to be in his room at Princeton with his school football picture over the bureau and the Triangle Club on the wall opposite. Then the grandfather's clock in the hall outside struck eight, and the memory of the night before came to him. He was out of bed, dressing, like the wind; he must get out of the house before he saw Isabelle. What had seemed a melancholy happening, now seemed a tiresome anticlimax. He was dressed at half past, so he sat down by the window; felt that the sinews of his heart were twisted somewhat more than he had thought. What an ironic mockery the morning seemed!—bright and sunny, and full of the smell of the garden; hearing Mrs. Borgé's voice in the sun-parlor below, he wondered where was Isabelle.

There was a knock at the door.

"The car will be around at ten minutes of nine, sir."

He returned to his contemplation of the outdoors, and began repeating over and over, mechanically, a verse from Browning, which he had once quoted to Isabelle in a letter:

"Each life unfulfilled, you see,
It hangs still, patchy and scrappy;
We have not sighed deep, laughed free,
Starved, feasted, despaired—been happy."

But his life would not be unfulfilled. He took a sombre satisfaction in thinking that perhaps all along she had been nothing except what he had read into her; that this was her high point, that no one else would ever make her think. Yet that was what she had objected to in him; and Amory was suddenly tired of thinking, thinking!

"Damn her!" he said bitterly, "she's spoiled my year!"

THE SUPERMAN GROWS CARELESS

On a dusty day in September Amory arrived in Princeton and joined the sweltering crowd of conditioned men who thronged the streets. It seemed a stupid way to commence his upper-class years, to spend four hours a morning in the stuffy room of a tutoring school, imbibing the infinite boredom of conic sections. Mr. Rooney, pander to the dull, conducted the class and smoked innumerable Pall Malls as he drew diagrams and worked equations from six in the morning until midnight.

"Now, Langueduc, if I used that formula, where would my *A* point be?"

Langueduc lazily shifts his six-foot-three of football material and tries to concentrate.

"Oh—ah—I'm damned if I know, Mr. Rooney."

"Oh, why of course, of course you can't *use* that formula. *That's* what I wanted you to say."

"Why, sure, of course."

"Do you see why?"

"You bet—I suppose so."

"If you don't see, tell me. I'm here to show you."

"Well, Mr. Rooney, if you don't mind, I wish you'd go over that again."

"Gladly. Now here's '*A*' . . ."

The room was a study in stupidity—two huge stands for paper, Mr. Rooney in his shirt-sleeves in front of them, and slouched around on chairs, a dozen men: Fred Sloane, the pitcher, who absolutely *had* to get eligible; "Slim" Langueduc, who would beat Yale this fall, if only he could muster a poor fifty per cent; McDowell, gay young sophomore, who thought it was quite a sporting thing to be tutoring here with all these prominent athletes.

"Those poor birds who haven't a cent to tutor, and have to study during the term are the ones I pity," he announced to Amory one day, with a flaccid camaraderie in the droop of the cigarette from his pale lips. "I should think it would be such a bore, there's so much else to do in New York during the term. I suppose they don't know what they miss, anyhow." There was such an air of "you and I" about Mr. McDowell that Amory very nearly pushed him out of the open window when he said this. . . . Next February his mother would wonder why he didn't make a club and increase his allowance . . . simple little nut. . . .

Through the smoke and the air of solemn, dense earnestness that filled the room would come the inevitable helpless cry:

"I don't get it! Repeat that, Mr. Rooney!" Most of them were so stupid or careless that they wouldn't admit when they didn't understand, and Amory was of the latter. He found it impossible to study conic sections; something in their calm and tantalizing respectability breathing defiantly through Mr. Rooney's fetid parlors distorted their equations into insoluble anagrams. He made a last night's effort with the proverbial wet towel, and then blissfully took the exam, wondering unhappily why all the color and ambition of the spring before had faded out. Somehow, with the defection of Isabelle the idea of undergraduate success had loosed its grasp on his imagination, and he contemplated a possible failure to pass off his condition with equanimity, even though it would arbitrarily mean his removal from the *Princetonian* board and the slaughter of his chances for the Senior Council.

There was always his luck.

He yawned, scribbled his honor pledge on the cover, and sauntered from the room.

"If you don't pass it," said the newly arrived Alec as they sat on the window-seat of Amory's room and mused upon a scheme of wall decoration, "you're the world's worst goopher. Your stock will go down like an elevator at the club and on the campus."

"Oh, hell, I know it. Why rub it in?"

"'Cause you deserve it. Anybody that'd risk what you were in line for *ought* to be ineligible for Princetonian chairman."

"Oh, drop the subject," Amory protested. "Watch and wait and shut up. I don't want every one at the club asking me about it, as if I were a prize potato being fattened for a vegetable show."

One evening a week later Amory stopped below his own window on the way to Renwick's, and, seeing a light, called up:

"Oh, Tom, any mail?"

Alec's head appeared against the yellow square of light.

"Yes, your result's here."

His heart clamored violently.

"What is it, blue or pink?"

"Don't know. Better come up."

He walked into the room and straight over to the table, and then suddenly noticed that there were other people in the room.

"'Lo, Kerry." He was most polite. "Ah, men of Princeton." They seemed to be mostly friends, so he picked up the envelope marked "Registrar's Office," and weighed it nervously.

"We have here quite a slip of paper."

"Open it, Amory."

"Just to be dramatic, I'll let you know that if it's blue, my name is withdrawn from the editorial board of the Prince, and my short career is over."

He paused, and then saw for the first time Ferrenby's eyes, wearing a hungry look and watching him eagerly. Amory returned the gaze pointedly.

"Watch my face, gentlemen, for the primitive emotions."

He tore it open and held the slip up to the light.

"Well?"

"Pink or blue?"

"Say what it is."

"We're all ears, Amory."

"Smile or swear—or something."

There was a pause . . . a small crowd of seconds swept by . . . then he looked again and another crowd went on into time.

"Blue as the sky, gentlemen . . . ."

Aftermath

What Amory did that year from early September to late in the spring was so purposeless and inconsecutive that it seems scarcely worth recording. He was, of course, immediately sorry for what he had lost. His philosophy of success had tumbled down upon him, and he looked for the reasons.

"Your own laziness," said Alec later.

"No—something deeper than that. I've begun to feel that I was meant to lose this chance."

"They're rather off you at the club, you know; every man that doesn't come through makes our crowd just so much weaker."

"I hate that point of view."

"Of course, with a little effort you could still stage a come-back."

"No—I'm through—as far as ever being a power in college is concerned."

"But, Amory, honestly, what makes me the angriest isn't the fact that you won't be chairman of the Prince and on the Senior Council, but just that you didn't get down and pass that exam."

"Not me," said Amory slowly; "I'm mad at the concrete thing. My own idleness was quite in accord with my system, but the luck broke."

"Your system broke, you mean."

"Maybe."

"Well, what are you going to do? Get a better one quick, or just bum around for two more years as a has-been?"

"I don't know yet . . ."

"Oh, Amory, buck up!"

"Maybe."

Amory's point of view, though dangerous, was not far from the true one. If his reactions to his environment could be tabulated, the chart would have appeared like this, beginning with his earliest years:

1. The fundamental Amory.
2. Amory plus Beatrice.
3. Amory plus Beatrice plus Minneapolis.

Then St. Regis' had pulled him to pieces and started him over again:

4. Amory plus St. Regis'.

5. Amory plus St. Regis' plus Princeton.

That had been his nearest approach to success through conformity. The fundamental Amory, idle, imaginative, rebellious, had been nearly snowed under. He had conformed, he had succeeded, but as his imagination was neither satisfied nor grasped by his own success, he had listlessly, half-accidentally chucked the whole thing and become again:

6. The fundamental Amory.

Financial

His father died quietly and inconspicuously at Thanksgiving. The incongruity of death with either the beauties of Lake Geneva or with his mother's dignified, reticent attitude diverted him, and he looked at the funeral with an amused tolerance. He decided that burial was after all preferable to cremation, and he smiled at his old boyhood choice, slow oxidation in the top of a tree. The day after the ceremony he was amusing himself in the great library by sinking back on a couch in graceful mortuary attitudes, trying to determine whether he would, when his day came, be found with his arms crossed piously over his chest (Monsignor Darcy had once advocated this posture as being the most distinguished), or with his hands clasped behind his head, a more pagan and Byronic attitude.

What interested him much more than the final departure of his father from things mundane was a tri-cornered conversation between Beatrice, Mr. Barton, of Barton and Krogman, their lawyers, and himself, that took place several days after the funeral. For the first time he came into actual cognizance of the family finances, and realized what a tidy fortune had once been under his father's management. He took a ledger labelled "1906" and ran through it rather carefully. The total expenditure that year had come to something over one hundred and ten thousand dollars. Forty thousand of this had been Beatrice's own income, and there had been no attempt to account for it: it was all under the heading, "Drafts, checks, and letters of credit forwarded to Beatrice Blaine." The dispersal of the rest was rather minutely itemized: the taxes and improvements on the Lake Geneva estate had come to almost nine thousand dollars; the general up-keep, including Beatrice's electric and a French car, bought that year, was over thirty-five thousand dollars. The rest was fully taken care of, and there were invariably items which failed to balance on the right side of the ledger.

In the volume for 1912 Amory was shocked to discover the decrease in the number of bond holdings and the great drop in the income. In the case of Beatrice's money this was not so pronounced, but it was obvious that his father had devoted the previous year to several unfortunate gambles in oil. Very little of the oil had been burned, but Stephen Blaine had been rather badly singed. The next year and the next and the next showed similar decreases, and Beatrice had for the first time begun using her own money for keeping up the house. Yet her doctor's bill for 1913 had been over nine thousand dollars.

About the exact state of things Mr. Barton was quite vague and confused. There had been recent investments, the outcome of which was for the present problematical, and he had an idea there were further speculations and exchanges concerning which he had not been consulted.

It was not for several months that Beatrice wrote Amory the full situation. The entire residue of the Blaine and O'Hara fortunes consisted of the place at Lake Geneva and approximately a half million dollars, invested now in fairly conservative six-per-cent holdings. In fact, Beatrice wrote that she was putting the money into railroad and street-car bonds as fast as she could conveniently transfer it.

"I am quite sure," she wrote to Amory, "that if there is one thing we can be positive of, it is that people will not stay in one place. This Ford person has certainly made the most of that idea. So I am instructing Mr. Barton to specialize on such things as Northern Pacific and these Rapid Transit Companies, as they call the street-cars. I shall never forgive myself for not buying Bethlehem Steel. I've heard the most *fascinating* stories. You must go into finance, Amory. I'm sure you would revel in it. You start as a messenger or a teller, I believe, and from that you go up—almost indefinitely. I'm sure if I were a man I'd love the handling of money; it has become quite a senile passion with me. Before I get any farther I want to discuss something. A Mrs. Bispam, an overcordial little lady whom I met at a tea the other day, told me that her son, he is at Yale, wrote her that all the boys there wore their summer underwear *all during the winter*, and also went about with their heads wet and in low shoes on the *coldest days*. Now, Amory, I don't know whether that is a fad at Princeton too, but I don't want you to be so foolish. It not only inclines a young man to *pneumonia* and *infantile paralysis*, but to all forms of lung trouble, to which you are particularly *inclined*. You cannot experiment with your health. I have found that out. I will not make myself ridiculous as some mothers no doubt do, by insisting that you wear overshoes, though I remember one Christmas you wore them around *constantly* without a single buckle latched, making such a curious swishing sound, and you refused to buckle them because it was not the thing to do. The very *next* Christmas you would not wear even *rubbers*, though I begged you. You are nearly twenty years old now, dear, and I can't be with you constantly to find whether you are doing the sensible thing.

"This has been a very *practical* letter. I warned you in my last that the lack of money to do the things one wants to makes one quite prosy and domestic, but there is still plenty for everything if we are not too extravagant. Take care of yourself, my dear boy, and do try to write at least *once* a week, because I imagine all sorts of horrible things if I don't hear from you.

Affectionately, MOTHER."

FIRST APPEARANCE OF THE TERM "PERSONAGE"

Monsignor Darcy invited Amory up to the Stuart palace on the Hudson for a week at Christmas, and they had enormous conversations around the open fire. Monsignor was growing a trifle stouter and his personality had expanded even with that, and Amory felt both rest and security in sinking into a squat, cushioned chair and joining him in the middle-aged sanity of a cigar.

"I've felt like leaving college, Monsignor."

"Why?"

"All my career's gone up in smoke; you think it's petty and all that, but——"

"Not at all petty. I think it's most important. I want to hear the whole thing. Everything you've been doing since I saw you last."

Amory talked; he went thoroughly into the destruction of his egotistic highways, and in a half-hour the listless quality had left his voice.

"What would you do if you left college?" asked Monsignor.

"Don't know. I'd like to travel, but of course this tiresome war prevents that. Anyways, mother would hate not having me graduate. I'm just at sea. Kerry Holiday wants me to go over with him and join the Lafayette Esquadrille."

"You know you wouldn't like to go."

"Sometimes I would—to-night I'd go in a second."

"Well, you'd have to be very much more tired of life than I think you are. I know you."

"I'm afraid you do," agreed Amory reluctantly. "It just seemed an easy way out of everything—when I think of another useless, draggy year."

"Yes, I know; but to tell you the truth, I'm not worried about you; you seem to me to be progressing perfectly naturally."

"No," Amory objected. "I've lost half my personality in a year."

"Not a bit of it!" scoffed Monsignor. "You've lost a great amount of vanity and that's all."

"Lordy! I feel, anyway, as if I'd gone through another fifth form at St. Regis's."

"No." Monsignor shook his head. "That was a misfortune; this has been a good thing. Whatever worth while comes to you, won't be through the channels you were searching last year."

"What could be more unprofitable than my present lack of pep?"

"Perhaps in itself . . . but you're developing. This has given you time to think and you're casting off a lot of your old luggage about success and the superman and all. People like us can't adopt whole theories, as you did. If we can do the next thing, and have an hour a day to think in, we can accomplish marvels, but as far as any high-handed scheme of blind dominance is concerned—we'd just make asses of ourselves."

"But, Monsignor, I can't do the next thing."

"Amory, between you and me, I have only just learned to do it myself. I can do the one hundred things beyond the next thing, but I stub my toe on that, just as you stubbed your toe on mathematics this fall."

"Why do we have to do the next thing? It never seems the sort of thing I should do."

"We have to do it because we're not personalities, but personages."

"That's a good line—what do you mean?"

"A personality is what you thought you were, what this Kerry and Sloane you tell me of evidently are. Personality is a physical matter almost entirely; it lowers the people it acts on—I've seen it vanish in a long sickness. But while a personality is active, it overrides 'the next thing.' Now a personage, on the other hand, gathers. He is never thought of apart from what he's done. He's a bar on which a thousand things have been hung—glittering things sometimes, as ours are; but he uses those things with a cold mentality back of them."

"And several of my most glittering possessions had fallen off when I needed them." Amory continued the simile eagerly.

"Yes, that's it; when you feel that your garnered prestige and talents and all that are hung out, you need never bother about anybody; you can cope with them without difficulty."

"But, on the other hand, if I haven't my possessions, I'm helpless!"

"Absolutely."

"That's certainly an idea."

"Now you've a clean start—a start Kerry or Sloane can constitutionally never have. You brushed three or four ornaments down, and, in a fit of pique, knocked off the rest of them. The thing now is to collect some new ones, and the farther you look ahead in the collecting the better. But remember, do the next thing!"

"How clear you can make things!"

So they talked, often about themselves, sometimes of philosophy and religion, and life as respectively a game or a mystery. The priest seemed to guess Amory's thoughts before they were clear in his own head, so closely related were their minds in form and groove.

"Why do I make lists?" Amory asked him one night. "Lists of all sorts of things?"

"Because you're a mediævalist," Monsignor answered. "We both are. It's the passion for classifying and finding a type."

"It's a desire to get something definite."

"It's the nucleus of scholastic philosophy."

"I was beginning to think I was growing eccentric till I came up here. It was a pose, I guess."

"Don't worry about that; for you not posing may be the biggest pose of all. Pose——"

"Yes?"

"But do the next thing."

After Amory returned to college he received several letters from Monsignor which gave him more egotistic food for consumption.

I am afraid that I gave you too much assurance of your inevitable safety, and you must remember that I did that through faith in your springs of effort; not in the silly conviction that you will arrive without struggle. Some nuances of character you will have to take for granted in yourself, though you must be careful in confessing them to others. You are unsentimental, almost incapable of affection, astute without being cunning and vain without being proud.

Don't let yourself feel worthless; often through life you will really be at your worst when you seem to think best of yourself; and don't worry about losing your "personality," as you persist in calling it; at fifteen you had the radiance of early morning, at twenty you will begin to have the melancholy brilliance of the moon, and when you are my age you will give out, as I do, the genial golden warmth of 4 P.M.

If you write me letters, please let them be natural ones. Your last, that dissertation on architecture, was perfectly awful—so "high-brow" that I picture you living in an intellectual and emotional vacuum; and beware of trying to classify people too definitely into types; you will find that all through their youth they will persist annoyingly in jumping from class to class, and by pasting a supercilious label on every one you meet you are merely packing a Jack-in-the-box that will spring up and leer at you when you begin to come into really antagonistic contact with the world. An idealization of some such a man as Leonardo da Vinci would be a more valuable beacon to you at present.

You are bound to go up and down, just as I did in my youth, but do keep your clarity of mind, and if fools or sages dare to criticise don't blame yourself too much.

You say that convention is all that really keeps you straight in this "woman proposition"; but it's more than that, Amory; it's the fear that what you begin you can't stop; you would run amuck, and I know whereof I speak; it's that half-miraculous sixth sense by which you detect evil, it's the half-realized fear of God in your heart.

Whatever your metier proves to be—religion, architecture, literature—I'm sure you would be much safer anchored to the Church, but I won't risk my influence by arguing with you even though I am secretly sure that the "black chasm of Romanism" yawns beneath you. Do write me soon.

With affectionate regards,

THAYER DARCY.

Even Amory's reading paled during this period; he delved further into the misty side streets of literature: Huysmans, Walter Pater, Theophile Gautier, and the racier sections of Rabelais, Boccaccio, Petronius, and Suetonius. One week, through general curiosity, he inspected the private libraries of his classmates and found Sloane's as typical as any: sets of Kipling, O. Henry, John Fox, Jr., and Richard Harding Davis; "What Every Middle-Aged Woman Ought to Know," "The Spell of the Yukon"; a "gift" copy of James Whitcomb Riley, an assortment of battered, annotated school-books, and, finally, to his surprise, one of his own late discoveries, the collected poems of Rupert Brooke.

Together with Tom D'Invilliers, he sought among the lights of Princeton for some one who might found the Great American Poetic Tradition.

The undergraduate body itself was rather more interesting that year than had been the entirely Philistine Princeton of two years before. Things had livened surprisingly, though at the sacrifice of much of the spontaneous charm of freshman year. In the old Princeton they would never have discovered Tanaduke Wylie. Tanaduke was a sophomore, with tremendous ears and a way of saying, "The earth swirls down through the ominous moons of preconsidered generations!" that made them vaguely wonder why it did not sound quite clear, but never question that it was the utterance of a super-soul. At least so Tom and Amory took him. They told him in all earnestness that he had a mind like Shelley's, and featured his ultrafree free verse and prose poetry in the *Nassau Literary Magazine*. But Tanaduke's genius absorbed the many colors of the age, and he took to the Bohemian life, to their great disappointment. He talked of Greenwich Village now instead of "noon-swirled moons," and met winter muses, unacademic, and cloistered by Forty-second Street and Broadway, instead of the Shelleyan dream-children with whom he had regaled their expectant appreciation. So they surrendered Tanaduke to the futurists, deciding that he and his flaming ties would do better there. Tom gave him the final advice that he should stop writing for two years and read the complete works of Alexander Pope four times, but on Amory's suggestion that Pope for Tanaduke was like foot-ease for stomach trouble, they withdrew in laughter, and called it a coin's toss whether this genius was too big or too petty for them.

Amory rather scornfully avoided the popular professors who dispensed easy epigrams and thimblefuls of Chartreuse to groups of admirers every night. He was disappointed, too, at the air of general uncertainty on every subject that seemed linked with the pedantic temperament; his opinions took shape in a miniature satire called "In a Lecture-Room," which he persuaded Tom to print in the *Nassau Lit.*

"Good-morning, Fool . . .
Three times a week
You hold us helpless while you speak,
Teasing our thirsty souls with the
Sleek 'yeas' of your philosophy . . .
Well, here we are, your hundred sheep,
Tune up, play on, pour forth . . . we sleep . . .
You are a student, so they say;
You hammered out the other day
A syllabus, from what we know
Of some forgotten folio;
You'd sniffled through an era's must,
Filling your nostrils up with dust,
And then, arising from your knees,
Published, in one gigantic sneeze . . .
But here's a neighbor on my right,
An *Eager Ass*, considered bright;
Asker of questions. . . . How he'll stand,
With earnest air and fidgy hand,

After this hour, telling you
He sat all night and burrowed through
Your book. . . . Oh, you'll be coy and he
Will simulate precosity,
And pedants both, you'll smile and smirk,
And leer, and hasten back to work. . . .

'Twas this day week, sir, you returned
A theme of mine, from which I learned
(Through various comment on the side
Which you had scrawled) that I defied
The *highest rules of criticism*
For *cheap* and *careless* witticism. . . .
'Are you quite sure that this could be?'
And
'Shaw is no authority!'
But *Eager Ass*, with what he's sent,
Plays havoc with your best per cent.

Still—still I meet you here and there . . .
When Shakespeare's played you hold a chair,
And some defunct, moth-eaten star
Enchants the mental prig you are . . .
A radical comes down and shocks
The *atheistic orthodox*?—
You're representing *Common Sense*,
Mouth open, in the audience.
And, sometimes, even chapel lures
That conscious tolerance of yours,
That broad and beaming view of truth
(Including *Kant* and *General Booth* . . .)
And so from shock to shock you live,
A hollow, pale affirmative . . .

The hour's up . . . and roused from rest
One hundred children of the blest
Cheat you a word or two with feet
That down the noisy aisle-ways beat . . .
Forget on *narrow-minded earth*
The Mighty Yawn that gave you birth."

In April, Kerry Holiday left college and sailed for France to enroll in the Lafayette Esquadrille. Amory's envy and admiration of this step was drowned in an experience of his own to which he never succeeded in giving an appropriate value, but which, nevertheless, haunted him for three years afterward.

THE DEVIL

Healy's they left at twelve and taxied to Bistolary's. There were Axia Marlowe and Phœbe Column, from the Summer Garden show, Fred Sloane and Amory. The evening was so very young that they felt ridiculous with surplus energy, and burst into the café like Dionysian revellers.

"Table for four in the middle of the floor," yelled Phœbe. "Hurry, old dear, tell 'em we're here!"

"Tell 'em to play 'Admiration'!" shouted Sloane. "You two order; Phœbe and I are going to shake a wicked calf," and they sailed off in the muddled crowd. Axia and Amory, acquaintances of an hour, jostled behind a waiter to a table at a point of vantage; there they took seats and watched.

"There's Findle Margotson, from New Haven!" she cried above the uproar. "'Lo, Findle! Whoo-ee!"

"Oh, Axia!" he shouted in salutation. "C'mon over to our table."

"No!" Amory whispered.

"Can't do it, Findle; I'm with somebody else! Call me up to-morrow about one o'clock!"

Findle, a nondescript man-about-Bisty's, answered incoherently and turned back to the brilliant blonde whom he was endeavoring to steer around the room.

"There's a natural damn fool," commented Amory.

"Oh, he's all right. Here's the old jitney waiter. If you ask me, I want a double Daiquiri."

"Make it four."

The crowd whirled and changed and shifted. They were mostly from the colleges, with a scattering of the male refuse of Broadway, and women of two types, the higher of which was the chorus girl. On the whole it was a typical crowd, and their party as typical as any. About three-fourths of the whole business was for effect and therefore harmless, ended at the door of the café, soon enough for the five-o'clock train back to Yale or Princeton; about one-fourth continued on into the dimmer hours and gathered strange dust from strange places. Their party was scheduled to be one of the harmless kind. Fred Sloane and Phœbe Column were old friends; Axia and Amory new ones. But strange things are prepared even in the dead of night, and the unusual, which lurks least in the café, home of the prosaic and inevitable, was preparing to spoil for him the waning romance of Broadway. The way it took was so inexpressibly terrible, so unbelievable, that afterward he never thought of it as experience; but it was a scene from a misty tragedy, played far behind the veil, and that it meant something definite he knew.

About one o'clock they moved to Maxim's, and two found them in Devinière's. Sloane had been drinking consecutively and was in a state of unsteady exhilaration, but Amory was quite tiresomely sober; they had run across none of those ancient, corrupt buyers of champagne who usually assisted their New York parties.

They were just through dancing and were making their way back to their chairs when Amory became aware that some one at a near-by table was looking at him. He turned and glanced casually . . . a middle-aged man dressed in a brown sack suit, it was, sitting a little apart at a table by himself and watching their party intently. At Amory's glance he smiled faintly. Amory turned to Fred, who was just sitting down.

"Who's that pale fool watching us?" he complained indignantly.

"Where?" cried Sloane. "We'll have him thrown out!" He rose to his feet and swayed back and forth, clinging to his chair. "Where is he?"

Axia and Phœbe suddenly leaned and whispered to each other across the table, and before Amory realized it they found themselves on their way to the door.

"Where now?"

"Up to the flat," suggested Phœbe. "We've got brandy and fizz—and everything's slow down here to-night."

Amory considered quickly. He hadn't been drinking, and decided that if he took no more, it would be reasonably discreet for him to trot along in the party. In fact, it would be, perhaps, the thing to do in order to keep an eye on Sloane, who was not in a state to do his own thinking. So he took Axia's arm and, piling intimately into a taxicab, they drove out over the hundreds and drew up at a tall, white-stone apartment-house. . . . Never would he forget that street. . . . It was a broad street, lined on both sides with just such tall, white-stone buildings, dotted with dark windows; they stretched along as far as the eye could see, flooded with a bright moonlight that gave them a calcium pallor. He imagined each one to have an elevator and a colored hall-boy and a key-rack; each one to be eight stories high and full of three and four room suites. He was rather glad to walk into the cheeriness of Phœbe's living-room and sink onto a sofa, while the girls went rummaging for food.

"Phœbe's great stuff," confided Sloane, sotto voce.

"I'm only going to stay half an hour," Amory said sternly. He wondered if it sounded priggish.

"Hell y' say," protested Sloane. "We're here now—don't le's rush."

"I don't like this place," Amory said sulkily, "and I don't want any food."

Phœbe reappeared with sandwiches, brandy bottle, siphon, and four glasses.

"Amory, pour 'em out," she said, "and we'll drink to Fred Sloane, who has a rare, distinguished edge."

"Yes," said Axia, coming in, "and Amory. I like Amory." She sat down beside him and laid her yellow head on his shoulder.

"I'll pour," said Sloane; "you use siphon, Phœbe."

They filled the tray with glasses.

"Ready, here she goes!"

Amory hesitated, glass in hand.

There was a minute while temptation crept over him like a warm wind, and his imagination turned to fire, and he took the glass from Phœbe's hand. That was all; for at the second that his decision came, he looked up and saw, ten yards from him, the man who had been in the café, and with his jump of astonishment the glass fell from his uplifted hand. There the man half sat, half leaned against a pile of pillows on the corner divan. His face was cast in the same yellow wax as in the café, neither the dull, pasty color of a dead man—rather a sort of virile pallor—nor unhealthy, you'd have called it; but like a strong man who'd worked in a mine or done night shifts in a damp climate. Amory looked him over carefully and later he could have drawn him after a fashion, down to the merest details. His mouth was the kind that is called frank, and he had steady gray eyes that moved slowly from one to the other of their group, with just the shade of a questioning expression. Amory noticed his hands; they weren't fine at all, but they had versatility and a tenuous strength . . . they were nervous hands that sat lightly along the cushions and moved constantly with little jerky openings and closings. Then, suddenly, Amory perceived the feet, and with a rush of blood to the head he realized he was afraid. The feet were all wrong . . . with a sort of wrongness that he felt rather than knew. . . . It was like weakness in a good woman, or blood on satin; one of those terrible incongruities that shake little things in the back of the brain. He wore no shoes, but, instead, a sort of half moccasin, pointed, though, like the shoes they wore in the fourteenth century, and with the little ends curling up. They were a darkish brown and his toes seemed to fill them to the end. . . . They were unutterably terrible. . . .

He must have said something, or looked something, for Axia's voice came out of the void with a strange goodness.

"Well, look at Amory! Poor old Amory's sick—old head going 'round?"

"Look at that man!" cried Amory, pointing toward the corner divan.

"You mean that purple zebra!" shrieked Axia facetiously. "Ooo-ee! Amory's got a purple zebra watching him!"

Sloane laughed vacantly.

"Ole zebra gotcha, Amory?"

There was a silence. . . . The man regarded Amory quizzically. . . . Then the human voices fell faintly on his ear:

"Thought you weren't drinking," remarked Axia sardonically, but her voice was good to hear; the whole divan that held the man was alive; alive like heat waves over asphalt, like wriggling worms. . . .

"Come back! Come back!" Axia's arm fell on his. "Amory, dear, you aren't going, Amory!" He was half-way to the door.

"Come on, Amory, stick 'th us!"
"Sick, are you?"
"Sit down a second!"
"Take some water."
"Take a little brandy. . . ."

The elevator was close, and the colored boy was half asleep, paled to a livid bronze . . . Axia's beseeching voice floated down the shaft. Those feet . . . those feet . . .

As they settled to the lower floor the feet came into view in the sickly electric light of the paved hall.

In the Alley

Down the long street came the moon, and Amory turned his back on it and walked. Ten, fifteen steps away sounded the footsteps. They were like a slow dripping, with just the slightest insistence in their fall. Amory's shadow lay, perhaps, ten feet ahead of him, and soft shoes was presumably that far behind. With the instinct of a child Amory edged in under the blue darkness of the white buildings, cleaving the moonlight for haggard seconds, once bursting into a slow run with clumsy stumblings. After that he stopped suddenly; he must keep hold, he thought. His lips were dry and he licked them.

If he met any one good—were there any good people left in the world or did they all live in white apartment-houses now? Was every one followed in the moonlight? But if he met some one good who'd know what he meant and hear this damned scuffle . . . then the scuffling grew suddenly nearer, and a black cloud settled over the moon. When again the pale sheen skimmed the cornices, it was almost beside him, and Amory thought he heard a quiet breathing. Suddenly he realized that the footsteps were not behind, had never been behind, they were ahead and he was not eluding but following . . . following. He began to run, blindly, his heart knocking heavily, his hands clinched. Far ahead a black dot showed itself, resolved slowly into a human shape. But Amory was beyond that now; he turned off the street and darted into an alley, narrow and dark and smelling of old rottenness. He twisted down a long, sinuous blackness, where the moonlight was shut away except for tiny glints and patches . . . then suddenly sank panting into a corner by a fence, exhausted. The steps ahead stopped, and he could hear them shift slightly with a continuous motion, like waves around a dock.

He put his face in his hands and covered eyes and ears as well as he could. During all this time it never occurred to him that he was delirious or drunk. He had a sense of reality such as material things could never give him. His intellectual content seemed to submit passively to it, and it fitted like a glove everything that had ever preceded it in his life. It did not muddle him. It was like a problem whose answer he knew on paper, yet whose solution he was unable to grasp. He was far beyond horror. He had sunk through the thin surface of that, now moved in a region where the feet and the fear of white walls were real, living things, things he must accept. Only far inside his soul a little fire leaped and cried that something was pulling him down, trying to get him inside a door and slam it behind him. After that door was slammed there would be only footfalls and white buildings in the moonlight, and perhaps he would be one of the footfalls.

During the five or ten minutes he waited in the shadow of the fence, there was somehow this fire . . . that was as near as he could name it afterward. He remembered calling aloud:

"I want some one stupid. Oh, send some one stupid!" This to the black fence opposite him, in whose shadows the footsteps shuffled . . . shuffled. He supposed "stupid" and "good" had become somehow intermingled through previous association. When he called thus it was not an act of will at all—will had turned him away from the moving figure in the street; it was almost instinct that called, just the pile on pile of inherent tradition or some wild prayer from way over the night. Then something clanged like a low gong struck at a distance, and before his eyes a face flashed over the two feet, a face pale and distorted with a sort of infinite evil that twisted it like flame in the wind; *but he knew, for the half instant that the gong tanged and hummed, that it was the face of Dick Humbird.*

Minutes later he sprang to his feet, realizing dimly that there was no more sound, and that he was alone in the graying alley. It was cold, and he started on a steady run for the light that showed the street at the other end.

At the Window

It was late morning when he woke and found the telephone beside his bed in the hotel tolling frantically, and remembered that he had left word to be called at eleven. Sloane was snoring heavily, his clothes in a pile by his bed. They dressed and ate breakfast in silence, and then sauntered out to get some air. Amory's mind was working slowly, trying to assimilate what had happened and separate from the chaotic imagery that stacked his memory the bare shreds of truth. If the morning had been cold and gray he could have grasped the reins of the past in an instant, but it was one of those days that New York gets sometimes in May, when the air on Fifth Avenue is a soft, light wine. How much or how little Sloane remembered Amory did not care to know; he apparently had none of the nervous tension that was gripping Amory and forcing his mind back and forth like a shrieking saw.

Then Broadway broke upon them, and with the babel of noise and the painted faces a sudden sickness rushed over Amory.

"For God's sake, let's go back! Let's get off of this—this place!"

Sloane looked at him in amazement.

"What do you mean?"

"This street, it's ghastly! Come on! let's get back to the Avenue!"

"Do you mean to say," said Sloane stolidly, "that 'cause you had some sort of indigestion that made you act like a maniac last night, you're never coming on Broadway again?"

Simultaneously Amory classed him with the crowd, and he seemed no longer Sloane of the debonair humor and the happy personality, but only one of the evil faces that whirled along the turbid stream.

"Man!" he shouted so loud that the people on the corner turned and followed them with their eyes, "it's filthy, and if you can't see it, you're filthy, too!"

"I can't help it," said Sloane doggedly. "What's the matter with you? Old remorse getting you? You'd be in a fine state if you'd gone through with our little party."

"I'm going, Fred," said Amory slowly. His knees were

shaking under him, and he knew that if he stayed another minute on this street he would keel over where he stood. "I'll be at the Vanderbilt for lunch." And he strode rapidly off and turned over to Fifth Avenue. Back at the hotel he felt better, but as he walked into the barber-shop, intending to get a head massage, the smell of the powders and tonics brought back Axia's sidelong, suggestive smile, and he left hurriedly. In the doorway of his room a sudden blackness flowed around him like a divided river.

When he came to himself he knew that several hours had passed. He pitched onto the bed and rolled over on his face with a deadly fear that he was going mad. He wanted people, people, some one sane and stupid and good. He lay for he knew not how long without moving. He could feel the little hot veins on his forehead standing out, and his terror had hardened on him like plaster. He felt he was passing up again through the thin crust of horror, and now only could he distinguish the shadowy twilight he was leaving. He must have fallen asleep again, for when he next recollected himself he had paid the hotel bill and was stepping into a taxi at the door. It was raining torrents.

On the train for Princeton he saw no one he knew, only a crowd of fagged-looking Philadelphians. The presence of a painted woman across the aisle filled him with a fresh burst of sickness and he changed to another car, tried to concentrate on an article in a popular magazine. He found himself reading the same paragraphs over and over, so he abandoned this attempt and leaning over wearily pressed his hot forehead against the damp window-pane. The car, a smoker, was hot and stuffy with most of the smells of the state's alien population; he opened a window and shivered against the cloud of fog that drifted in over him. The two hours' ride were like days, and he nearly cried aloud with joy when the towers of Princeton loomed up beside him and the yellow squares of light filtered through the blue rain.

Tom was standing in the centre of the room, pensively relighting a cigar-stub. Amory fancied he looked rather relieved on seeing him.

"Had a hell of a dream about you last night," came in the

cracked voice through the cigar smoke. "I had an idea you were in some trouble."

"Don't tell me about it!" Amory almost shrieked. "Don't say a word; I'm tired and pepped out."

Tom looked at him queerly and then sank into a chair and opened his Italian note-book. Amory threw his coat and hat on the floor, loosened his collar, and took a Wells novel at random from the shelf. "Wells is sane," he thought, "and if he won't do I'll read Rupert Brooke."

Half an hour passed. Outside the wind came up, and Amory started as the wet branches moved and clawed with their finger-nails at the window-pane. Tom was deep in his work, and inside the room only the occasional scratch of a match or the rustle of leather as they shifted in their chairs broke the stillness. Then like a zigzag of lightning came the change. Amory sat bolt upright, frozen cold in his chair. Tom was looking at him with his mouth drooping, eyes fixed.

"God help us!" Amory cried.

"Oh, my heavens!" shouted Tom, "look behind!" Quick as a flash Amory whirled around. He saw nothing but the dark window-pane.

"It's gone now," came Tom's voice after a second in a still terror. "Something was looking at you."

Trembling violently, Amory dropped into his chair again.

"I've got to tell you," he said. "I've had one hell of an experience. I think I've—I've seen the devil or—something like him. What face did you just see?—or no," he added quickly, "don't tell me!"

And he gave Tom the story. It was midnight when he finished, and after that, with all lights burning, two sleepy, shivering boys read to each other from "The New Machiavelli," until dawn came up out of Witherspoon Hall, and the *Princetonian* fell against the door, and the May birds hailed the sun on last night's rain.

CHAPTER IV

Narcissus Off Duty

DURING Princeton's transition period, that is, during Amory's last two years there, while he saw it change and broaden and live up to its Gothic beauty by better means than night parades, certain individuals arrived who stirred it to its plethoric depths. Some of them had been freshmen, and wild freshmen, with Amory; some were in the class below; and it was in the beginning of his last year and around small tables at the Nassau Inn that they began questioning aloud the institutions that Amory and countless others before him had questioned so long in secret. First, and partly by accident, they struck on certain books, a definite type of biographical novel that Amory christened "quest" books. In the "quest" book the hero set off in life armed with the best weapons and avowedly intending to use them as such weapons are usually used, to push their possessors ahead as selfishly and blindly as possible, but the heroes of the "quest" books discovered that there might be a more magnificent use for them. "None Other Gods," "Sinister Street," and "The Research Magnificent" were examples of such books; it was the latter of these three that gripped Burne Holiday and made him wonder in the beginning of senior year how much it was worth while being a diplomatic autocrat around his club on Prospect Avenue and basking in the high lights of class office. It was distinctly through the channels of aristocracy that Burne found his way. Amory, through Kerry, had had a vague drifting acquaintance with him, but not until January of senior year did their friendship commence.

"Heard the latest?" said Tom, coming in late one drizzly evening with that triumphant air he always wore after a successful conversational bout.

"No. Somebody flunked out? Or another ship sunk?"

"Worse than that. About one-third of the junior class are going to resign from their clubs."

"What?"

"Actual fact!"

"Why?"

"Spirit of reform and all that. Burne Holiday is behind it. The club presidents are holding a meeting to-night to see if they can find a joint means of combating it."

"Well, what's the idea of the thing?"

"Oh, clubs injurious to Princeton democracy; cost a lot; draw social lines, take time; the regular line you get sometimes from disappointed sophomores. Woodrow thought they should be abolished and all that."

"But this is the real thing?"

"Absolutely. I think it'll go through."

"For Pete's sake, tell me more about it."

"Well," began Tom, "it seems that the idea developed simultaneously in several heads. I was talking to Burne awhile ago, and he claims that it's a logical result if an intelligent person thinks long enough about the social system. They had a 'discussion crowd' and the point of abolishing the clubs was brought up by some one—everybody there leaped at it—it had been in each one's mind, more or less, and it just needed a spark to bring it out."

"Fine! I swear I think it'll be most entertaining. How do they feel up at Cap and Gown?"

"Wild, of course. Every one's been sitting and arguing and swearing and getting mad and getting sentimental and getting brutal. It's the same at all the clubs; I've been the rounds. They get one of the radicals in the corner and fire questions at him."

"How do the radicals stand up?"

"Oh, moderately well. Burne's a damn good talker, and so obviously sincere that you can't get anywhere with him. It's so evident that resigning from his club means so much more to him than preventing it does to us that I felt futile when I argued; finally took a position that was brilliantly neutral. In fact, I believe Burne thought for a while that he'd converted me."

"And you say almost a third of the junior class are going to resign?"

"Call it a fourth and be safe."

"Lord—who'd have thought it possible!"

There was a brisk knock at the door, and Burne himself came in.

"Hello, Amory—hello, Tom."

Amory rose.

"'Evening, Burne. Don't mind if I seem to rush; I'm going to Renwick's."

Burne turned to him quickly.

"You probably know what I want to talk to Tom about, and it isn't a bit private. I wish you'd stay."

"I'd be glad to." Amory sat down again, and as Burne perched on a table and launched into argument with Tom, he looked at this revolutionary more carefully than he ever had before. Broad-browed and strong-chinned, with a fineness in the honest gray eyes that were like Kerry's, Burne was a man who gave an immediate impression of bigness and security—stubborn, that was evident, but his stubbornness wore no stolidity, and when he had talked for five minutes Amory knew that this keen enthusiasm had in it no quality of dilettantism.

The intense power Amory felt later in Burne Holiday differed from the admiration he had had for Humbird. This time it began as purely a mental interest. With other men of whom he had thought as primarily first-class, he had been attracted first by their personalities, and in Burne he missed that immediate magnetism to which he usually swore allegiance. But that night Amory was struck by Burne's intense earnestness, a quality he was accustomed to associate only with the dread stupidity, and by the great enthusiasm that struck dead chords in his heart. Burne stood vaguely for a land Amory hoped he was drifting toward—and it was almost time that land was in sight. Tom and Amory and Alec had reached an impasse; never did they seem to have new experiences in common, for Tom and Alec had been as blindly busy with their committees and boards as Amory had been blindly idling, and the things they had for dissection—college, contemporary personality and the like—they had hashed and rehashed for many a frugal conversational meal.

That night they discussed the clubs until twelve, and, in the main, they agreed with Burne. To the roommates it did not seem such a vital subject as it had in the two years before, but the logic of Burne's objections to the social system dovetailed so completely with everything they had thought, that they questioned rather than argued, and envied the sanity that enabled this man to stand out so against all traditions.

Then Amory branched off and found that Burne was deep in other things as well. Economics had interested him and he was turning socialist. Pacifism played in the back of his mind, and he read the *Masses* and Lyoff Tolstoi faithfully.

"How about religion?" Amory asked him.

"Don't know. I'm in a muddle about a lot of things—I've just discovered that I've a mind, and I'm starting to read."

"Read what?"

"Everything. I have to pick and choose, of course, but mostly things to make me think. I'm reading the four gospels now, and the 'Varieties of Religious Experience.' "

"What chiefly started you?"

"Wells, I guess, and Tolstoi, and a man named Edward Carpenter. I've been reading for over a year now—on a few lines, on what I consider the essential lines."

"Poetry?"

"Well, frankly, not what you call poetry, or for your reasons—you two write, of course, and look at things differently. Whitman is the man that attracts me."

"Whitman?"

"Yes; he's a definite ethical force."

"Well, I'm ashamed to say that I'm a blank on the subject of Whitman. How about you, Tom?"

Tom nodded sheepishly.

"Well," continued Burne, "you may strike a few poems that are tiresome, but I mean the mass of his work. He's tremendous—like Tolstoi. They both look things in the face, and, somehow, different as they are, stand for somewhat the same things."

"You have me stumped, Burne," Amory admitted. "I've read 'Anna Karénina' and the 'Kreutzer Sonata' of course, but Tolstoi is mostly in the original Russian as far as I'm concerned."

"He's the greatest man in hundreds of years," cried Burne enthusiastically. "Did you ever see a picture of that shaggy old head of his?"

They talked until three, from biology to organized religion, and when Amory crept shivering into bed it was with his mind aglow with ideas and a sense of shock that some one else had discovered the path he might have followed. Burne Holiday was so evidently developing—and Amory had considered that he was doing the same. He had fallen into a deep cynicism over what had crossed his path, plotted the imperfectability of man and read Shaw and Chesterton enough to keep his mind from the edges of decadence—now suddenly all his mental processes of the last year and a half seemed stale and futile—a petty consummation of himself . . . and like a sombre background lay that incident of the spring before, that filled half his nights with a dreary terror and made him unable to pray. He was not even a Catholic, yet that was the only ghost of a code that he had, the gaudy, ritualistic, paradoxical Catholicism whose prophet was Chesterton, whose claqueurs were such reformed rakes of literature as Huysmans and Bourget, whose American sponsor was Ralph Adams Cram, with his adulation of thirteenth-century cathedrals—a Catholicism which Amory found convenient and ready-made, without priest or sacraments or sacrifice.

He could not sleep, so he turned on his reading-lamp and, taking down the "Kreutzer Sonata," searched it carefully for the germs of Burne's enthusiasm. Being Burne was suddenly so much realler than being clever. Yet he sighed . . . here were other possible clay feet.

He thought back through two years, of Burne as a hurried, nervous freshman, quite submerged in his brother's personality. Then he remembered an incident of sophomore year, in which Burne had been suspected of the leading rôle.

Dean Hollister had been heard by a large group arguing with a taxi-driver, who had driven him from the junction. In the course of the altercation the dean remarked that he "might as well buy the taxicab." He paid and walked off, but next morning he entered his private office to find the taxicab itself in the space usually occupied by his desk, bearing a sign which read "Property of Dean Hollister. Bought and Paid for." . . . It took two expert mechanics half a day to dissemble it into its minutest parts and remove it, which only goes to prove the rare energy of sophomore humor under efficient leadership.

Then again, that very fall, Burne had caused a sensation. A certain Phyllis Styles, an intercollegiate prom-trotter, had failed to get her yearly invitation to the Harvard-Princeton game.

Jesse Ferrenby had brought her to a smaller game a few weeks before, and had pressed Burne into service—to the ruination of the latter's misogyny.

"Are you coming to the Harvard game?" Burne had asked indiscreetly, merely to make conversation.

"If you ask me," cried Phyllis quickly.

"Of course I do," said Burne feebly. He was unversed in the arts of Phyllis, and was sure that this was merely a vapid form of kidding. Before an hour had passed he knew that he was indeed involved. Phyllis had pinned him down and served him up, informed him the train she was arriving by, and depressed him thoroughly. Aside from loathing Phyllis, he had particularly wanted to stag that game and entertain some Harvard friends.

"She'll see," he informed a delegation who arrived in his room to josh him. "This will be the last game she ever persuades any young innocent to take her to!"

"But, Burne—why did you *invite* her if you didn't want her?"

"Burne, you *know* you're secretly mad about her—that's the *real* trouble."

"What can *you* do, Burne? What can *you* do against Phyllis?"

But Burne only shook his head and muttered threats which consisted largely of the phrase: "She'll see, she'll see!"

The blithesome Phyllis bore her twenty-five summers gayly from the train, but on the platform a ghastly sight met her eyes. There were Burne and Fred Sloane arrayed to the last dot like the lurid figures on college posters. They had bought flaring suits with huge peg-top trousers and gigantic padded shoulders. On their heads were rakish college hats, pinned up in front and sporting bright orange-and-black bands, while from their celluloid collars blossomed flaming orange ties. They wore black arm-bands with orange "P's," and carried canes flying Princeton pennants, the effect completed by socks and peeping handkerchiefs in the same color motifs. On a clanking chain they led a large, angry tom-cat, painted to represent a tiger.

A good half of the station crowd was already staring at them, torn between horrified pity and riotous mirth, and as Phyllis, with her svelte jaw dropping, approached, the pair bent over and emitted a college cheer in loud, far-carrying voices, thoughtfully adding the name "Phyllis" to the end. She was vociferously greeted and escorted enthusiastically across the campus, followed by half a hundred village urchins—to the stifled laughter of hundreds of alumni and visitors, half of whom had no idea that this was a practical joke, but thought that Burne and Fred were two varsity sports showing their girl a collegiate time.

Phyllis's feelings as she was paraded by the Harvard and Princeton stands, where sat dozens of her former devotees, can be imagined. She tried to walk a little ahead, she tried to walk a little behind—but they stayed close, that there should be no doubt whom she was with, talking in loud voices of their friends on the football team, until she could almost hear her acquaintances whispering:

"Phyllis Styles must be *awfully hard up* to have to come with *those two.*"

That had been Burne, dynamically humorous, fundamentally serious. From that root had blossomed the energy that he was now trying to orient with progress. . . .

So the weeks passed and March came and the clay feet that Amory looked for failed to appear. About a hundred juniors and seniors resigned from their clubs in a final fury of righteousness, and the clubs in helplessness turned upon Burne their finest weapon: ridicule. Every one who knew him liked him—but what he stood for (and he began to stand for more all the time) came under the lash of many tongues, until a frailer man than he would have been snowed under.

"Don't you mind losing prestige?" asked Amory one night. They had taken to exchanging calls several time a week.

"Of course I don't. What's prestige, at best?"

"Some people say that you're just a rather original politician."

He roared with laughter.

"That's what Fred Sloane told me to-day. I suppose I have it coming."

One afternoon they dipped into a subject that had interested Amory for a long time—the matter of the bearing of physical attributes on a man's make-up. Burne had gone into the biology of this, and then:

"Of course health counts—a healthy man has twice the chance of being good," he said.

"I don't agree with you—I don't believe in 'muscular Christianity.' "

"I do—I believe Christ had great physical vigor."

"Oh, no," Amory protested. "He worked too hard for that. I imagine that when he died he was a broken-down man—and the great saints haven't been strong."

"Half of them have."

"Well, even granting that, I don't think health has anything to do with goodness; of course, it's valuable to a great saint to be able to stand enormous strains, but this fad of popular preachers rising on their toes in simulated virility, bellowing that calisthenics will save the world—no, Burne, I can't go that."

"Well, let's waive it—we won't get anywhere, and besides I haven't quite made up my mind about it myself. Now, here's something I *do* know—personal appearance has a lot to do with it."

"Coloring?" Amory asked eagerly.

"Yes."

"That's what Tom and I figured," Amory agreed. "We took the year-books for the last ten years and looked at the pictures of the senior council. I know you don't think much of that august body, but it does represent success here in a general way. Well, I suppose only about thirty-five per cent of every class here are blonds, are really light—yet *two-thirds* of every senior council are light. We looked at pictures of ten years of them, mind you; that means that out of every *fifteen* light-haired men in the senior class *one* is on the senior council, and of the dark-haired men it's only one in *fifty*."

"It's true," Burne agreed. "The light-haired man *is* a higher type, generally speaking. I worked the thing out with the Presidents of the United States once, and found that way over half of them were light-haired—yet think of the preponderant number of brunettes in the race."

"People unconsciously admit it," said Amory. "You'll notice a blond person is *expected* to talk. If a blond girl doesn't talk we call her a 'doll'; if a light-haired man is silent he's considered stupid. Yet the world is full of 'dark silent men' and 'languorous brunettes' who haven't a brain in their heads, but somehow are never accused of the dearth."

"And the large mouth and broad chin and rather big nose undoubtedly make the superior face."

"I'm not so sure." Amory was all for classical features.

"Oh, yes—I'll show you," and Burne pulled out of his desk a photographic collection of heavily bearded, shaggy celebrities—Tolstoi, Whitman, Carpenter, and others.

"Aren't they wonderful?"

Amory tried politely to appreciate them, and gave up laughingly.

"Burne, I think they're the ugliest-looking crowd I ever came across. They look like an old man's home."

"Oh, Amory, look at that forehead on Emerson; look at Tolstoi's eyes." His tone was reproachful.

Amory shook his head.

"No! Call them remarkable-looking or anything you want—but ugly they certainly are."

Unabashed, Burne ran his hand lovingly across the spacious foreheads, and piling up the pictures put them back in his desk.

Walking at night was one of his favorite pursuits, and one night he persuaded Amory to accompany him.

"I hate the dark," Amory objected. "I didn't use to—except when I was particularly imaginative, but now, I really do—I'm a regular fool about it."

"That's useless, you know."

"Quite possibly."

"We'll go east," Burne suggested, "and down that string of roads through the woods."

"Doesn't sound very appealing to me," admitted Amory reluctantly, "but let's go."

They set off at a good gait, and for an hour swung along in

a brisk argument until the lights of Princeton were luminous white blots behind them.

"Any person with any imagination is bound to be afraid," said Burne earnestly. "And this very walking at night is one of the things I was afraid about. I'm going to tell you why I can walk anywhere now and not be afraid."

"Go on," Amory urged eagerly. They were striding toward the woods, Burne's nervous, enthusiastic voice warming to his subject.

"I used to come out here alone at night, oh, three months ago, and I always stopped at that cross-road we just passed. There were the woods looming up ahead, just as they do now, there were dogs howling and the shadows and no human sound. Of course, I peopled the woods with everything ghastly, just like you do; don't you?"

"I do," Amory admitted.

"Well, I began analyzing it—my imagination persisted in sticking horrors into the dark—so I stuck my imagination into the dark instead, and let it look out at me—I let it play stray dog or escaped convict or ghost, and then saw myself coming along the road. That made it all right—as it always makes everything all right to project yourself completely into another's place. I knew that if I were the dog or the convict or the ghost I wouldn't be a menace to Burne Holiday any more than he was a menace to me. Then I thought of my watch. I'd better go back and leave it and then essay the woods. No; I decided, it's better on the whole that I should lose a watch than that I should turn back—and I did go into them—not only followed the road through them, but walked into them until I wasn't frightened any more—did it until one night I sat down and dozed off in there; then I knew I was through being afraid of the dark."

"Lordy," Amory breathed. "I couldn't have done that. I'd have come out half-way, and the first time an automobile passed and made the dark thicker when its lamps disappeared, I'd have come in."

"Well," Burne said suddenly, after a few moments' silence, "we're half-way through, let's turn back."

On the return he launched into a discussion of will.

"It's the whole thing," he asserted. "It's the one dividing

line between good and evil. I've never met a man who led a rotten life and didn't have a weak will."

"How about great criminals?"

"They're usually insane. If not, they're weak. There is no such thing as a strong, sane criminal."

"Burne, I disagree with you altogether; how about the superman?"

"Well?"

"He's evil, I think, yet he's strong and sane."

"I've never met him. I'll bet, though, that he's stupid or insane."

"I've met him over and over and he's neither. That's why I think you're wrong."

"I'm sure I'm not—and so I don't believe in imprisonment except for the insane."

On this point Amory could not agree. It seemed to him that life and history were rife with the strong criminal, keen, but often self-deluding; in politics and business one found him and among the old statesmen and kings and generals; but Burne never agreed and their courses began to split on that point.

Burne was drawing farther and farther away from the world about him. He resigned the vice-presidency of the senior class and took to reading and walking as almost his only pursuits. He voluntarily attended graduate lectures in philosophy and biology, and sat in all of them with a rather pathetically intent look in his eyes, as if waiting for something the lecturer would never quite come to. Sometimes Amory would see him squirm in his seat; and his face would light up; he was on fire to debate a point.

He grew more abstracted on the street and was even accused of becoming a snob, but Amory knew it was nothing of the sort, and once when Burne passed him four feet off, absolutely unseeingly, his mind a thousand miles away, Amory almost choked with the romantic joy of watching him. Burne seemed to be climbing heights where others would be forever unable to get a foothold.

"I tell you," Amory declared to Tom, "he's the first contemporary I've ever met whom I'll admit is my superior in mental capacity."

"It's a bad time to admit it—people are beginning to think he's odd."

"He's way over their heads—you know you think so yourself when you talk to him— Good Lord, Tom, you *used* to stand out against 'people.' Success has completely conventionalized you."

Tom grew rather annoyed.

"What's he trying to do—be excessively holy?"

"No! not like anybody you've ever seen. Never enters the Philadelphian Society. He has no faith in that rot. He doesn't believe that public swimming-pools and a kind word in time will right the wrongs of the world; moreover, he takes a drink whenever he feels like it."

"He certainly is getting in wrong."

"Have you talked to him lately?"

"No."

"Then you haven't any conception of him."

The argument ended nowhere, but Amory noticed more than ever how the sentiment toward Burne had changed on the campus.

"It's odd," Amory said to Tom one night when they had grown more amicable on the subject, "that the people who violently disapprove of Burne's radicalism are distinctly the Pharisee class—I mean they're the best-educated men in college—the editors of the papers, like yourself and Ferrenby, the younger professors. . . . The illiterate athletes like Langueduc think he's getting eccentric, but they just say, 'Good old Burne has got some queer ideas in his head,' and pass on—the Pharisee class—Gee! they ridicule him unmercifully."

The next morning he met Burne hurrying along McCosh walk after a recitation.

"Whither bound, Tsar?"

"Over to the Prince office to see Ferrenby," he waved a copy of the morning's *Princetonian* at Amory. "He wrote this editorial."

"Going to flay him alive?"

"No—but he's got me all balled up. Either I've misjudged him or he's suddenly become the world's worst radical."

Burne hurried on, and it was several days before Amory

heard an account of the ensuing conversation. Burne had come into the editor's sanctum displaying the paper cheerfully.

"Hello, Jesse."

"Hello there, Savonarola."

"I just read your editorial."

"Good boy—didn't know you stooped that low."

"Jesse, you startled me."

"How so?"

"Aren't you afraid the faculty'll get after you if you pull this irreligious stuff?"

"What?"

"Like this morning."

"What the devil—that editorial was on the coaching system."

"Yes, but that quotation——"

Jesse sat up.

"What quotation?"

"You know: 'He who is not with me is against me.' "

"Well—what about it?"

Jesse was puzzled but not alarmed.

"Well, you say here—let me see." Burne opened the paper and read: " '*He who is not with me is against me,* as that gentleman said who was notoriously capable of only coarse distinctions and puerile generalities.' "

"What of it?" Ferrenby began to look alarmed. "Oliver Cromwell said it, didn't he? or was it Washington, or one of the saints? Good Lord, I've forgotten."

Burne roared with laughter.

"Oh, Jesse, oh, good, kind Jesse."

"Who said it, for Pete's sake?"

"Well," said Burne, recovering his voice, "St. Matthew attributes it to Christ."

"My God!" cried Jesse, and collapsed backward into the waste-basket.

Amory Writes a Poem

The weeks tore by. Amory wandered occasionally to New York on the chance of finding a new shining green auto-bus, that its stick-of-candy glamour might penetrate his disposition. One day he ventured into a stock-company revival of a play whose name was faintly familiar. The curtain rose—he watched casually as a girl entered. A few phrases rang in his ear and touched a faint chord of memory. Where—? When—?

Then he seemed to hear a voice whispering beside him, a very soft, vibrant voice: "Oh, I'm such a poor little fool; *do* tell me when I do wrong."

The solution came in a flash and he had a quick, glad memory of Isabelle.

He found a blank space on his programme, and began to scribble rapidly:

"Here in the figured dark I watch once more,
There, with the curtain, roll the years away;
Two years of years—there was an idle day
Of ours, when happy endings didn't bore
Our unfermented souls; I could adore
Your eager face beside me, wide-eyed, gay,
Smiling a repertoire while the poor play
Reached me as a faint ripple reaches shore.

Yawning and wondering an evening through,
I watch alone . . . and chatterings, of course,
Spoil the one scene which, somehow, *did* have charms;
You wept a bit, and I grew sad for you
Right here! Where Mr. X defends divorce
And What's-Her-Name falls fainting in his arms."

Still Calm

"Ghosts are such dumb things," said Alec, "they're slow-witted. I can always outguess a ghost."

"How?" asked Tom.

"Well, it depends where. Take a bedroom, for example. If you use *any* discretion a ghost can never get you in a bedroom."

"Go on, s'pose you think there's maybe a ghost in your bedroom—what measures do you take on getting home at night?" demanded Amory, interested.

"Take a stick," answered Alec, with ponderous reverence,

"one about the length of a broom-handle. Now, the first thing to do is to get the room *cleared*—to do this you rush with your eyes closed into your study and turn on the lights—next, approaching the closet, carefully run the stick in the door three or four times. Then, if nothing happens, you can look in. *Always, always* run the stick in viciously first—*never* look first!"

"Of course, that's the ancient Celtic school," said Tom gravely.

"Yes—but they usually pray first. Anyway, you use this method to clear the closets and also for behind all doors——"

"And the bed," Amory suggested.

"Oh, Amory, no!" cried Alec in horror. "That isn't the way—the bed requires different tactics—let the bed alone, as you value your reason—if there is a ghost in the room and that's only about a third of the time, it is *almost always* under the bed."

"Well—" Amory began.

Alec waved him into silence.

"Of *course* you never look. You stand in the middle of the floor and before he knows what you're going to do make a sudden leap for the bed—never walk near the bed; to a ghost your ankle is your most vulnerable part—once in bed, you're safe; he may lie around under the bed all night, but you're safe as daylight. If you still have doubts pull the blanket over your head."

"All that's very interesting, Tom."

"Isn't it?" Alec beamed proudly. "All my own, too—the Sir Oliver Lodge of the new world."

Amory was enjoying college immensely again. The sense of going forward in a direct, determined line had come back; youth was stirring and shaking out a few new feathers. He had even stored enough surplus energy to sally into a new pose.

"What's the idea of all this 'distracted' stuff, Amory?" asked Alec one day, and then as Amory pretended to be cramped over his book in a daze: "Oh, don't try to act Burne, the mystic, to me."

Amory looked up innocently.

"What?"

"What?" mimicked Alec. "Are you trying to read yourself into a rhapsody with—let's see the book."

He snatched it; regarded it derisively.

"Well?" said Amory a little stiffly.

" 'The Life of St. Teresa,' " read Alec aloud. "Oh, my gosh!"

"Say, Alec."

"What?"

"Does it bother you?"

"Does what bother me?"

"My acting dazed and all that?"

"Why, no—of course it doesn't *bother* me."

"Well, then, don't spoil it. If I enjoy going around telling people guilelessly that I think I'm a genius, let me do it."

"You're getting a reputation for being eccentric," said Alec, laughing, "if that's what you mean."

Amory finally prevailed, and Alec agreed to accept his face value in the presence of others if he was allowed rest periods when they were alone; so Amory "ran it out" at a great rate, bringing the most eccentric characters to dinner, wild-eyed grad students, preceptors with strange theories of God and government, to the cynical amazement of the supercilious Cottage Club.

As February became slashed by sun and moved cheerfully into March, Amory went several times to spend week-ends with Monsignor; once he took Burne, with great success, for he took equal pride and delight in displaying them to each other. Monsignor took him several times to see Thornton Hancock, and once or twice to the house of a Mrs. Lawrence, a type of Rome-haunting American whom Amory liked immediately.

Then one day came a letter from Monsignor, which appended an interesting P.S.:

"Do you know," it ran, "that your third cousin, Clara Page, widowed six months and very poor, is living in Philadelphia? I don't think you've ever met her, but I wish, as a favor to me, you'd go to see her. To my mind, she's rather a remarkable woman, and just about your age."

Amory sighed and decided to go, as a favor. . . .

Clara

She was immemorial. . . . Amory wasn't good enough for Clara, Clara of ripply golden hair, but then no man was. Her goodness was above the prosy morals of the husband-seeker, apart from the dull literature of female virtue.

Sorrow lay lightly around her, and when Amory found her in Philadelphia he thought her steely blue eyes held only happiness; a latent strength, a realism, was brought to its fullest development by the facts that she was compelled to face. She was alone in the world, with two small children, little money, and, worst of all, a host of friends. He saw her that winter in Philadelphia entertaining a houseful of men for an evening, when he knew she had not a servant in the house except the little colored girl guarding the babies overhead. He saw one of the greatest libertines in that city, a man who was habitually drunk and notorious at home and abroad, sitting opposite her for an evening, discussing *girls' boarding-schools* with a sort of innocent excitement. What a twist Clara had to her mind! She could make fascinating and almost brilliant conversation out of the thinnest air that ever floated through a drawing-room.

The idea that the girl was poverty-stricken had appealed to Amory's sense of situation. He arrived in Philadelphia expecting to be told that 921 Ark Street was in a miserable lane of hovels. He was even disappointed when it proved to be nothing of the sort. It was an old house that had been in her husband's family for years. An elderly aunt, who objected to having it sold, had put ten years' taxes with a lawyer and pranced off to Honolulu, leaving Clara to struggle with the heating-problem as best she could. So no wild-haired woman with a hungry baby at her breast and a sad Amelia-like look greeted him. Instead, Amory would have thought from his reception that she had not a care in the world.

A calm virility and a dreamy humor, marked contrasts to her level-headedness—into these moods she slipped sometimes as a refuge. She could do the most prosy things (though she was wise enough never to stultify herself with such "household arts" as *knitting* and *embroidery*), yet immediately afterward pick up a book and let her imagination rove as a formless cloud with the wind. Deepest of all in her personality was the golden radiance that she diffused around her. As an open fire in a dark room throws romance and pathos into the quiet faces at its edge, so she cast her lights and shadows around the rooms that held her, until she made of her prosy old uncle a man of quaint and meditative charm, metamorphosed the stray telegraph boy into a Puck-like creature of delightful originality. At first this quality of hers somehow irritated Amory. He considered his own uniqueness sufficient, and it rather embarrassed him when she tried to read new interests into him for the benefit of what other adorers were present. He felt as if a polite but insistent stage-manager were attempting to make him give a new interpretation of a part he had conned for years.

But Clara talking, Clara telling a slender tale of a hat-pin and an inebriated man and herself. . . . People tried afterward to repeat her anecdotes but for the life of them they could make them sound like nothing whatever. They gave her a sort of innocent attention and the best smiles many of them had smiled for long; there were few tears in Clara, but people smiled misty-eyed at her.

Very occasionally Amory stayed for little half-hours after the rest of the court had gone, and they would have bread and jam and tea late in the afternoon or "maple-sugar lunches," as she called them, at night.

"You *are* remarkable, aren't you!" Amory was becoming trite from where he perched in the centre of the dining-room table one six o'clock.

"Not a bit," she answered. She was searching out napkins in the sideboard. "I'm really most humdrum and commonplace. One of those people who have no interest in anything but their children."

"Tell that to somebody else," scoffed Amory. "You know you're perfectly effulgent." He asked her the one thing that he knew might embarrass her. It was the remark that the first bore made to Adam.

"Tell me about yourself." And she gave the answer that Adam must have given.

"There's nothing to tell."

But eventually Adam probably told the bore all the things

he thought about at night when the locusts sang in the sandy grass, and he must have remarked patronizingly how *different* he was from Eve, forgetting how different she was from him . . . . at any rate, Clara told Amory much about herself that evening. She had had a harried life from sixteen on, and her education had stopped sharply with her leisure. Browsing in her library, Amory found a tattered gray book out of which fell a yellow sheet that he impudently opened. It was a poem that she had written at school about a gray convent wall on a gray day, and a girl with her cloak blown by the wind sitting atop of it and thinking about the many-colored world. As a rule such sentiment bored him, but this was done with so much simplicity and atmosphere, that it brought a picture of Clara to his mind, of Clara on such a cool, gray day with her keen blue eyes staring out, trying to see her tragedies come marching over the gardens outside. He envied that poem. How he would have loved to have come along and seen her on the wall and talked nonsense or romance to her, perched above him in the air. He began to be frightfully jealous of everything about Clara: of her past, of her babies, of the men and women who flocked to drink deep of her cool kindness and rest their tired minds as at an absorbing play.

"*Nobody* seems to bore you," he objected.

"About half the world do," she admitted, "but I think that's a pretty good average, don't you?" and she turned to find something in Browning that bore on the subject. She was the only person he ever met who could look up passages and quotations to show him in the middle of the conversation, and yet not be irritating to distraction. She did it constantly, with such a serious enthusiasm that he grew fond of watching her golden hair bent over a book, brow wrinkled ever so little at hunting her sentence.

Through early March he took to going to Philadelphia for week-ends. Almost always there was some one else there and she seemed not anxious to see him alone, for many occasions presented themselves when a word from her would have given him another delicious half-hour of adoration. But he fell gradually in love and began to speculate wildly on marriage. Though this design flowed through his brain even to his lips, still he knew afterward that the desire had not been deeply rooted. Once he dreamt that it had come true and woke up in a cold panic, for in his dream she had been a silly, flaxen Clara, with the gold gone out of her hair and platitudes falling insipidly from her changeling tongue. But she was the first fine woman he ever knew and one of the few good people who ever interested him. She made her goodness such an asset. Amory had decided that most good people either dragged theirs after them as a liability, or else distorted it to artificial geniality, and of course there were the ever-present prig and Pharisee—(but Amory never included *them* as being among the saved).

St. Cecilia

"Over her gray and velvet dress,
Under her molten, beaten hair,
Color of rose in mock distress
Flushes and fades and makes her fair;
Fills the air from her to him
With light and languor and little sighs,
Just so subtly he scarcely knows . . .
Laughing lightning, color of rose."

"Do you like me?"

"Of course I do," said Clara seriously.

"Why?"

"Well, we have some qualities in common. Things that are spontaneous in each of us—or were originally."

"You're implying that I haven't used myself very well?"

Clara hesitated.

"Well, I can't judge. A man, of course, has to go through a lot more, and I've been sheltered."

"Oh, don't stall, please, Clara," Amory interrupted; "but do talk about me a little, won't you?"

"Surely, I'd adore to." She didn't smile.

"That's sweet of you. First answer some questions. Am I painfully conceited?"

"Well—no, you have tremendous vanity, but it'll amuse the people who notice its preponderance."

"I see."

"You're really humble at heart. You sink to the third hell of depression when you think you've been slighted. In fact, you haven't much self-respect."

"Centre of target twice, Clara. How do you do it? You never let me say a word."

"Of course not—I can never judge a man while he's talking. But I'm not through; the reason you have so little real self-confidence, even though you gravely announce to the occasional philistine that you think you're a genius, is that you've attributed all sorts of atrocious faults to yourself and are trying to live up to them. For instance, you're always saying that you are a slave to high-balls."

"But I am, potentially."

"And you say you're a weak character, that you've no will."

"Not a bit of will—I'm a slave to my emotions, to my likes, to my hatred of boredom, to most of my desires——"

"You are not!" She brought one little fist down onto the other. "You're a slave, a bound helpless slave to one thing in the world, your imagination."

"You certainly interest me. If this isn't boring you, go on."

"I notice that when you want to stay over an extra day from college you go about it in a sure way. You never decide at first while the merits of going or staying are fairly clear in your mind. You let your imagination shinny on the side of your desires for a few hours, and then you decide. Naturally your imagination, after a little freedom, thinks up a million reasons why you should stay, so your decision when it comes isn't true. It's biassed."

"Yes," objected Amory, "but isn't it lack of will-power to let my imagination shinny on the wrong side?"

"My dear boy, there's your big mistake. This has nothing to do with will-power; that's a crazy, useless word, anyway; you lack judgment—the judgment to decide at once when you know your imagination will play you false, given half a chance."

"Well, I'll be darned!" exclaimed Amory in surprise, "that's the last thing I expected."

Clara didn't gloat. She changed the subject immediately. But she had started him thinking and he believed she was partly right. He felt like a factory-owner who after accusing a clerk of dishonesty finds that his own son, in the office, is changing the books once a week. His poor, mistreated will that he had been holding up to the scorn of himself and his friends, stood before him innocent, and his judgment walked off to prison with the unconfineable imp, imagination, dancing in mocking glee beside him. Clara's was the only advice he ever asked without dictating the answer himself—except, perhaps, in his talks with Monsignor Darcy.

How he loved to do any sort of thing with Clara! Shopping with her was a rare, epicurean dream. In every store where she had ever traded she was whispered about as the beautiful Mrs. Page.

"I'll bet she won't stay single long."

"Well, don't scream it out. She ain't lookin' for no advice."

"*Ain't* she beautiful!"

(Enter a floor-walker—silence till he moves forward, smirking.)

"Society person, ain't she?"

"Yeah, but poor now, I guess; so they say."

"Gee! girls, *ain't* she some kid!"

And Clara beamed on all alike. Amory believed that tradespeople gave her discounts, sometimes to her knowledge and sometimes without it. He knew she dressed very well, had always the best of everything in the house, and was inevitably waited upon by the head floor-walker at the very least.

Sometimes they would go to church together on Sunday and he would walk beside her and revel in her cheeks moist from the soft water in the new air. She was very devout, always had been, and God knows what heights she attained and what strength she drew down to herself when she knelt and bent her golden hair into the stained-glass light.

"St. Cecilia," he cried aloud one day, quite involuntarily, and the people turned and peered, and the priest paused in his sermon and Clara and Amory turned to fiery red.

That was the last Sunday they had, for he spoiled it all that night. He couldn't help it.

They were walking through the March twilight where it was as warm as June, and the joy of youth filled his soul so that he felt he must speak.

"I think," he said and his voice trembled, "that if I lost faith in you I'd lose faith in God."

She looked at him with such a startled face that he asked her the matter.

"Nothing," she said slowly, "only this: five men have said that to me before, and it frightens me."

"Oh, Clara, is that your fate!"

She did not answer.

"I suppose love to you is—" he began.

She turned like a flash.

"I have never been in love."

They walked along, and he realized slowly how much she had told him . . . never in love. . . . She seemed suddenly a daughter of light alone. His entity dropped out of her plane and he longed only to touch her dress with almost the realization that Joseph must have had of Mary's eternal significance. But quite mechanically he heard himself saying:

"And I love you—any latent greatness that I've got is . . . oh, I can't talk, but Clara, if I come back in two years in a position to marry you——"

She shook her head.

"No," she said; "I'd never marry again. I've got my two children and I want myself for them. I like you—I like all clever men, you more than any—but you know me well enough to know that I'd never marry a clever man—" She broke off suddenly.

"Amory."

"What?"

"You're not in love with me. You never wanted to marry me, did you?"

"It was the twilight," he said wonderingly. "I didn't feel as though I were speaking aloud. But I love you—or adore you—or worship you——"

"There you go—running through your catalogue of emotions in five seconds."

He smiled unwillingly.

"Don't make me out such a light-weight, Clara; you *are* depressing sometimes."

"You're not a light-weight, of all things," she said intently, taking his arm and opening wide her eyes—he could see their kindliness in the fading dusk. "A light-weight is an eternal nay."

"There's so much spring in the air—there's so much lazy sweetness in your heart."

She dropped his arm.

"You're all fine now, and I feel glorious. Give me a cigarette. You've never seen me smoke, have you? Well, I do, about once a month."

And then that wonderful girl and Amory raced to the corner like two mad children gone wild with pale-blue twilight.

"I'm going to the country for to-morrow," she announced, as she stood panting, safe beyond the flare of the corner lamp-post. "These days are too magnificent to miss, though perhaps I feel them more in the city."

"Oh, Clara!" Amory said; "what a devil you could have been if the Lord had just bent your soul a little the other way!"

"Maybe," she answered; "but I think not. I'm never really wild and never have been. That little outburst was pure spring."

"And you are, too," said he.

They were walking along now.

"No—you're wrong again, how can a person of your own self-reputed brains be so constantly wrong about me? I'm the opposite of everything spring ever stood for. It's unfortunate, if I happen to look like what pleased some soppy old Greek sculptor, but I assure you that if it weren't for my face I'd be a quiet nun in the convent without"—then she broke into a run and her raised voice floated back to him as he followed—"my precious babies, which I must go back and see."

She was the only girl he ever knew with whom he could understand how another man might be preferred. Often Amory met wives whom he had known as débutantes, and looking intently at them imagined that he found something in their faces which said:

"Oh, if I could only have gotten *you*!" Oh, the enormous conceit of the man!

But that night seemed a night of stars and singing and Clara's bright soul still gleamed on the ways they had trod.

"Golden, golden is the air—" he chanted to the little pools

of water. . . . *"Golden is the air, golden notes from golden mandolins, golden frets of golden violins, fair, oh, wearily fair. . . . Skeins from braided basket, mortals may not hold; oh, what young extravagant God, who would know or ask it? . . . who could give such gold . . ."*

Amory is Resentful

Slowly and inevitably, yet with a sudden surge at the last, while Amory talked and dreamed, war rolled swiftly up the beach and washed the sands where Princeton played. Every night the gymnasium echoed as platoon after platoon swept over the floor and shuffled out the basket-ball markings. When Amory went to Washington the next week-end he caught some of the spirit of crisis which changed to repulsion in the Pullman car coming back, for the berths across from him were occupied by stinking aliens—Greeks, he guessed, or Russians. He thought how much easier patriotism had been to a homogeneous race, how much easier it would have been to fight as the Colonies fought, or as the Confederacy fought. And he did no sleeping that night, but listened to the aliens guffaw and snore while they filled the car with the heavy scent of latest America.

In Princeton every one bantered in public and told themselves privately that their deaths at least would be heroic. The literary students read Rupert Brooke passionately; the lounge-lizards worried over whether the government would permit the English-cut uniform for officers; a few of the hopelessly lazy wrote to the obscure branches of the War Department, seeking an easy commission and a soft berth.

Then, after a week, Amory saw Burne and knew at once that argument would be futile—Burne had come out as a pacifist. The socialist magazines, a great smattering of Tolstoi, and his own intense longing for a cause that would bring out whatever strength lay in him, had finally decided him to preach peace as a subjective ideal.

"When the German army entered Belgium," he began, "if the inhabitants had gone peaceably about their business, the German army would have been disorganized in——"

"I know," Amory interrupted, "I've heard it all. But I'm not going to talk propaganda with you. There's a chance that you're right—but even so we're hundreds of years before the time when non-resistance can touch us as a reality."

"But, Amory, listen——"

"Burne, we'd just argue——"

"Very well."

"Just one thing—I don't ask you to think of your family or friends, because I know they don't count a picayune with you beside your sense of duty—but, Burne, how do you know that the magazines you read and the societies you join and these idealists you meet aren't just plain *German*?"

"Some of them are, of course."

"How do you know they aren't *all* pro-German—just a lot of weak ones—with German-Jewish names."

"That's the chance, of course," he said slowly. "How much or how little I'm taking this stand because of propaganda I've heard, I don't know; naturally I think that it's my most innermost conviction—it seems a path spread before me just now."

Amory's heart sank.

"But think of the cheapness of it—no one's really going to martyr you for being a pacifist—it's just going to throw you in with the worst——"

"I doubt it," he interrupted.

"Well, it all smells of Bohemian New York to me."

"I know what you mean, and that's why I'm not sure I'll agitate."

"You're one man, Burne—going to talk to people who won't listen—with all God's given you."

"That's what Stephen must have thought many years ago. But he preached his sermon and they killed him. He probably thought as he was dying what a waste it all was. But you see, I've always felt that Stephen's death was the thing that occurred to Paul on the road to Damascus, and sent him to preach the word of Christ all over the world."

"Go on."

"That's all—this is my particular duty. Even if right now I'm just a pawn—just sacrificed. God! Amory—you don't think *I* like the Germans!"

"Well, I can't say anything else—I get to the end of all the logic about non-resistance, and there, like an excluded middle, stands the huge spectre of man as he is and always will be. And this spectre stands right beside the one logical necessity of Tolstoi's, and the other logical necessity of Nietzsche's—" Amory broke off suddenly. "When are you going?"

"I'm going next week."

"I'll see you, of course."

As he walked away it seemed to Amory that the look in his face bore a great resemblance to that in Kerry's when he had said good-by under Blair Arch two years before. Amory wondered unhappily why he could never go into anything with the primal honesty of those two.

"Burne's a fanatic," he said to Tom, "and he's dead wrong and, I'm inclined to think, just an unconscious pawn in the hands of anarchistic publishers and German-paid rag wavers—but he haunts me—just leaving everything worth while——"

Burne left in a quietly dramatic manner a week later. He sold all his possessions and came down to the room to say good-by, with a battered old bicycle, on which he intended to ride to his home in Pennsylvania.

"Peter the Hermit bidding farewell to Cardinal Richelieu," suggested Alec, who was lounging in the window-seat as Burne and Amory shook hands.

But Amory was not in a mood for that, and as he saw Burne's long legs propel his ridiculous bicycle out of sight beyond Alexander Hall, he knew he was going to have a bad week. Not that he doubted the war—Germany stood for everything repugnant to him; for materialism and the direction of tremendous licentious force; it was just that Burne's face stayed in his memory and he was sick of the hysteria he was beginning to hear.

"What on earth is the use of suddenly running down Goethe," he declared to Alec and Tom. "Why write books to prove he started the war—or that that stupid, overestimated Schiller is a demon in disguise?"

"Have you ever read anything of theirs?" asked Tom shrewdly.

"No," Amory admitted.

"Neither have I," he said laughing.

"People will shout," said Alec quietly, "but Goethe's on his same old shelf in the library—to bore any one that wants to read him!"

Amory subsided, and the subject dropped.

"What are you going to do, Amory?"

"Infantry or aviation, I can't make up my mind—I hate mechanics, but then of course aviation's the thing for me——"

"I feel as Amory does," said Tom. "Infantry or aviation—aviation sounds like the romantic side of the war, of course—like cavalry used to be, you know; but like Amory I don't know a horse-power from a piston-rod."

Somehow Amory's dissatisfaction with his lack of enthusiasm culminated in an attempt to put the blame for the whole war on the ancestors of his generation . . . all the people who cheered for Germany in 1870. . . . All the materialists rampant, all the idolizers of German science and efficiency. So he sat one day in an English lecture and heard "Locksley Hall" quoted and fell into a brown study with contempt for Tennyson and all he stood for—for he took him as a representative of the Victorians.

"Victorians, Victorians, who never learned to weep
Who sowed the bitter harvest that your children go to reap——"

scribbled Amory in his note-book. The lecturer was saying something about Tennyson's solidity and fifty heads were bent to take notes. Amory turned over to a fresh page and began scrawling again.

"They shuddered when they found what Mr. Darwin was about,
They shuddered when the waltz came in and Newman hurried out——"

But the waltz came in much earlier; he crossed that out.

"And entitled *A Song in the Time of Order*," came the professor's voice, droning far away. "Time of Order"—Good Lord! Everything crammed in the box and the Victorians sitting on the lid smiling serenely. . . . With Browning in his Italian villa crying bravely: "All's for the best." Amory scribbled again.

"You knelt up in the temple and he bent to hear you pray,
You thanked him for your 'glorious gains'—reproached him for 'Cathay.' "

Why could he never get more than a couplet at a time? Now he needed something to rhyme with:

"You would keep Him straight with science, tho He had gone wrong before . . ."

Well, anyway. . . .

"You met your children in your home—'I've fixed it up!' you cried,
Took your fifty years of Europe, and then virtuously—died."

"That was to a great extent Tennyson's idea," came the lecturer's voice. "Swinburne's *Song in the Time of Order* might well have been Tennyson's title. He idealized order against chaos, against waste."

At last Amory had it. He turned over another page and scrawled vigorously for the twenty minutes that was left of the hour. Then he walked up to the desk and deposited a page torn out of his note-book.

"Here's a poem to the Victorians, sir," he said coldly.

The professor picked it up curiously while Amory backed rapidly through the door.

Here is what he had written:

"Songs in the time of order
You left for us to sing,
Proofs with excluded middles,
Answers to life in rhyme,
Keys of the prison warder
And ancient bells to ring,
Time was the end of riddles,
We were the end of time . . .

Here were domestic oceans
And a sky that we might reach,
Guns and a guarded border,
Gantlets—but not to fling,
Thousands of old emotions

INTERLUDE

May, 1917—February, 1919

A letter dated January, 1918, written by Monsignor Darcy to Amory, who is a second lieutenant in the 171st Infantry, Port of Embarkation, Camp Mills, Long Island.

My dear Boy:—

All you need tell me of yourself is that you still are; for the rest I merely search back in a restive memory, a thermometer that records only fevers, and match you with what I was at your age. But men will chatter and you and I will still shout our futilities to each other across the stage until the last silly curtain falls *plump!* upon our bobbing heads. But you are starting the spluttering magic-lantern show of life with much the same array of slides as I had, so I need to write you if only to shriek the colossal stupidity of *people*. . . .

This is the end of one thing: for better or worse you will never again be quite the Amory Blaine that I knew, never again will we meet as we have met, because your generation is growing hard, much harder than mine ever grew, nourished as they were on the stuff of the nineties.

Amory, lately I reread Æschylus and there in the divine irony of the "Agamemnon" I find the only answer to this bitter age—all the world tumbled about our ears, and the closest parallel ages back in that hopeless resignation. There are times when I think of the men out there as Roman legionaries, miles from their corrupt city, stemming back the hordes . . . hordes a little more menacing, after all, than the corrupt city . . . another blind blow at the race, furies that we passed with ovations years ago, over whose corpses we bleated triumphantly all through the Victorian era. . . .

And afterward an out-and-out materialistic world—and the Catholic Church. I wonder where you'll fit in. Of one thing I'm sure—Celtic you'll live and Celtic you'll die; so if you don't use heaven as a continual referendum for your ideas you'll find earth a continual recall to your ambitions.

Amory, I've discovered suddenly that I'm an old man. Like all old men, I've had dreams sometimes and I'm going to tell you of them. I've enjoyed imagining that you were my son, that perhaps when I was young I went into a state of coma and begat you, and when I came to, had no recollection of it . . . it's the paternal instinct, Amory—celibacy goes deeper than the flesh. . . .

Sometimes I think that the explanation of our deep resemblance is some common ancestor, and I find that the only blood that the Darcys and the O'Haras have in common is that of the O'Donahues . . . Stephen was his name, I think. . . .

When the lightning strikes one of us it strikes both: you had hardly arrived at the port of embarkation when I got my papers to start for Rome, and I am waiting every moment to be told where to take ship. Even before you get this letter I shall be on the ocean; then will come your turn. You went to war as a gentleman should, just as you went to school and college, because it was the thing to do. It's better to leave the blustering and tremulo-heroism to the middle classes; they do it so much better.

Do you remember that week-end last March when you brought Burne Holiday from Princeton to see me? What a magnificent boy he is! It gave me a frightful shock afterward when you wrote that he thought me splendid; how could he be so deceived? Splendid is the one thing that neither you nor I are. We are many other things—we're extraordinary, we're clever, we could be said, I suppose, to be brilliant. We can attract people, we can make atmosphere, we can almost lose our Celtic souls in Celtic subtleties, we can almost always have our own way; but splendid—rather not!

I am going to Rome with a wonderful dossier and letters of introduction that cover every capital in Europe, and there will be "no small stir" when I get there. How I wish you were with me! This sounds like a rather cynical paragraph, not at all the sort of thing that a middle-aged clergyman should write to a youth about to depart for the war; the only excuse is that the middle-aged clergyman is talking to himself. There are deep things in us and you know what they are as well as I do. We have great faith, though yours at present is uncrystallized; we have a terrible honesty that all our sophistry cannot destroy and, above all, a childlike simplicity that keeps us from ever being really malicious.

I have written a keen for you which follows. I am sorry your cheeks are not up to the description I have written of them, but you *will* smoke and read all night——

At any rate here it is:

A Lament for a Foster Son, and He going to the War Against the King of Foreign.

"Ochone
He is gone from me the son of my mind
And he in his golden youth like Angus Oge
Angus of the bright birds
And his mind strong and subtle like the mind of Cuchulin on Muirtheme.

Awirra sthrue
His brow is as white as the milk of the cows of Maeve
  And his cheeks like the cherries of the tree
And it bending down to Mary and she feeding the Son of God.

Aveelia Vrone
His hair is like the golden collar of the Kings at Tara
  And his eyes like the four gray seas of Erin.
And they swept with the mists of rain.

Mavrone go Gudyo
He to be in the joyful and red battle
  Amongst the chieftains and they doing great deeds of valor
His life to go from him
  It is the chords of my own soul would be loosed.

A Vich Deelish
My heart is in the heart of my son
  And my life is in his life surely
A man can be twice young
  In the life of his sons only.

Jia du Vaha Alanav
May the Son of God be above him and beneath him, before him and behind him
  May the King of the elements cast a mist over the eyes of the King of Foreign,
May the Queen of the Graces lead him by the hand the way he can go through the midst of his enemies and they not seeing him
  May Patrick of the Gael and Collumb of the Churches and the five thousand Saints of Erin be better than a shield to him
And he go into the fight.
  Och Ochone."

Amory—Amory—I feel, somehow, that this is all; one or both of us is not going to last out this war. . . . I've been trying to tell you how much this reincarnation of myself in you has meant in the last few years . . . curiously alike we are . . . curiously unlike.

Good-by, dear boy, and God be with you.

THAYER DARCY.

EMBARKING AT NIGHT

Amory moved forward on the deck until he found a stool under an electric light. He searched in his pocket for note-book and pencil and then began to write, slowly, laboriously:

"We leave to-night . . .
Silent, we filled the still, deserted street,
A column of dim gray,
And ghosts rose startled at the muffled beat
Along the moonless way;
The shadowy shipyards echoed to the feet
That turned from night and day.

And so we linger on the windless decks,
See on the spectre shore
Shades of a thousand days, poor gray-ribbed wrecks . . . .
Oh, shall we then deplore
These futile years!
See how the sea is white!
The clouds have broken and the heavens burn
To hollow highways, paved with gravelled light
The churning of the waves about the stern
Rises to one voluminous nocturne,
. . . We leave to-night."

A letter from Amory, headed "Brest, March 11th, 1919," to Lieutenant T. P. D'Invilliers, Camp Gordon, Ga.

DEAR BAUDELAIRE:—

We meet in Manhattan on the 30th of this very mo.; we then proceed to take a very sporty apartment, you and I and Alec, who is at me elbow as I write. I don't know what I'm going to do but I have a vague dream of going into politics. Why is it that the pick of the young Englishmen from Oxford and Cambridge go into politics and in the U. S. A. we leave it to the muckers?—raised in the ward, educated in the assembly and sent to Congress, fat-paunched bundles of corruption, devoid of "both ideas and ideals" as the debaters used to say. Even forty years ago we had good men in politics, but *we*, we are brought up to pile up a million and "show what we are made of." Sometimes I wish I'd been an Englishman; American life is so damned dumb and stupid and healthy.

Since poor Beatrice died I'll probably have a little money, but very darn little. I can forgive mother almost everything except the fact that in a sudden burst of religiosity toward the end, she left half of what remained to be spent in stained-glass windows and seminary endowments. Mr. Barton, my lawyer, writes me that my thousands are mostly in street railways and that the said Street R.R.s are losing money because of the five-cent fares. Imagine a salary list that gives $350 a month to a man that can't read and write!—yet I believe in it, even though I've seen what was once a sizable fortune melt away between speculation, extravagance, the democratic administration, and the income tax—modern, that's me all over, Mabel.

At any rate we'll have really knock-out rooms—you can get a job on some fashion magazine, and Alec can go into the Zinc Company or whatever it is that his people own—he's looking over my shoulder and he says it's a brass company, but I don't think it matters much, do you? There's probably as much corruption in zinc-made money as brass-made money. As for the well-known Amory, he would write immortal literature if he were sure enough about anything to risk telling any one else about it. There is no more dangerous gift to posterity than a few cleverly turned platitudes.

Tom, why don't you become a Catholic? Of course to be a good one you'd have to give up those violent intrigues you used to tell me about, but you'd write better poetry if you were linked up to tall golden candlesticks and long, even chants, and even if the American priests are rather burgeois, as Beatrice used to say, still you need only go to the sporty churches, and I'll introduce you to Monsignor Darcy who really is a wonder.

Kerry's death was a blow, so was Jesse's to a certain extent. And I have a great curiosity to know what queer corner of the world has swallowed Burne. Do you suppose he's in prison under some false name? I confess that the war instead of making me orthodox, which is the correct reaction, has made me a passionate agnostic. The Catholic Church has had its wings clipped so often lately that its part was timidly negligible, and they haven't any good writers any more. I'm sick of Chesterton.

I've only discovered one soldier who passed through the much-advertised spiritual crisis, like this fellow, Donald Hankey, and the one I knew was already studying for the ministry, so he was ripe for it. I honestly think that's all pretty much rot, though it seemed to give sentimental comfort to those at home; and may make fathers and mothers appreciate their children. This crisis-inspired religion is rather valueless and fleeting at best. I think four men have discovered Paris to one that discovered God.

But *us*—you and me and Alec—oh, we'll get a Jap butler and dress for dinner and have wine on the table and lead a contemplative, emotionless life until we decide to use machine-guns with the property owners—or throw bombs with the Bolshevik. God! Tom, I hope something happens. I'm restless as the devil and have a horror of getting fat or falling in love and growing domestic.

The place at Lake Geneva is now for rent but when I land I'm going West to see Mr. Barton and get some details. Write me care of the Blackstone, Chicago.

S'ever, dear Boswell,

SAMUEL JOHNSON.

BOOK TWO

THE EDUCATION OF A PERSONAGE

CHAPTER I

The Débutante

The time is February. The place is a large, dainty bedroom in the Connage house on Sixty-eighth Street, New York. A girl's room: pink walls and curtains and a pink bedspread on a cream-colored bed. Pink and cream are the motifs of the room, but the only article of furniture in full view is a luxurious dressing-table with a glass top and a three-sided mirror. On the walls there is an expensive print of "Cherry Ripe," a few polite dogs by Landseer, and the "King of the Black Isles," by Maxfield Parrish.

Great disorder consisting of the following items: (1) seven or eight empty cardboard boxes, with tissue-paper tongues hanging panting from their mouths; (2) an assortment of street dresses mingled with their sisters of the evening, all upon the table, all evidently new; (3) a roll of tulle, which has lost its dignity and wound itself tortuously around everything in sight, and (4) upon the two small chairs, a collection of lingerie that beggars description. One would enjoy seeing the bill called forth by the finery displayed and one is possessed by a desire to see the princess for whose benefit— Look! There's some one! Disappointment! This is only a maid hunting for something—she lifts a heap from a chair— Not there; another heap, the dressing-table, the chiffonier drawers. She brings to light several beautiful chemises and an amazing pajama but this does not satisfy her—she goes out.

An indistinguishable mumble from the next room.

Now, we are getting warm. This is Alec's mother, Mrs. Connage, ample, dignified, rouged to the dowager point and quite worn out. Her lips move significantly as she looks for IT. Her search is less thorough than the maid's but there is a touch of fury in it, that quite makes up for its sketchiness.

She stumbles on the tulle and her "damn" is quite audible. She retires, empty-handed.

More chatter outside and a girl's voice, a very spoiled voice, says: "Of all the stupid people——"

After a pause a third seeker enters, not she of the spoiled voice, but a younger edition. This is Cecelia Connage, sixteen, pretty, shrewd, and constitutionally good-humored. She is dressed for the evening in a gown the obvious simplicity of which probably bores her. She goes to the nearest pile, selects a small pink garment and holds it up appraisingly.

CECELIA: Pink?

ROSALIND: (*Outside*) Yes!

CECELIA: *Very* snappy?

ROSALIND: Yes!

CECELIA: I've got it!

(*She sees herself in the mirror of the dressing-table and commences to shimmy enthusiastically.*)

ROSALIND: (*Outside*) What are you doing—trying it on?

(CECELIA *ceases and goes out carrying the garment at the right shoulder.*

From the other door, enters ALEC CONNAGE. *He looks around quickly and in a huge voice shouts:* Mama! *There is a chorus of protest from next door and encouraged he starts toward it, but is repelled by another chorus.*)

ALEC: So *that's* where you all are! Amory Blaine is here.

CECELIA: (*Quickly*) Take him down-stairs.

ALEC: Oh, he *is* down-stairs.

MRS. CONNAGE: Well, you can show him where his room is. Tell him I'm sorry that I can't meet him now.

ALEC: He's heard a lot about you all. I wish you'd hurry. Father's telling him all about the war and he's restless. He's sort of temperamental.

(*This last suffices to draw* CECELIA *into the room.*)

CECELIA: (*Seating herself high upon lingerie*) How do you mean—temperamental? You used to say that about him in letters.

ALEC: Oh, he writes stuff.

CECELIA: Does he play the piano?

ALEC: Don't think so.

CECELIA: (*Speculatively*) Drink?

ALEC: Yes—nothing queer about him.

CECELIA: Money?

ALEC: Good Lord—ask him, he used to have a lot, and he's got some income now.

(MRS. CONNAGE *appears.*)

MRS. CONNAGE: Alec, of course we're glad to have any friend of yours——

ALEC: You certainly ought to meet Amory.

MRS. CONNAGE: Of course, I want to. But I think it's so childish of you to leave a perfectly good home to go and live with two other boys in some impossible apartment. I hope it isn't in order that you can all drink as much as you want. (*She pauses.*) He'll be a little neglected to-night. This is Rosalind's week, you see. When a girl comes out, she needs *all* the attention.

ROSALIND: (*Outside*) Well, then, prove it by coming here and hooking me.

(MRS. CONNAGE *goes.*)

ALEC: Rosalind hasn't changed a bit.

CECELIA: (*In a lower tone*) She's awfully spoiled.

ALEC: She'll meet her match to-night.

CECELIA: Who—Mr. Amory Blaine?

(ALEC *nods.*)

CECELIA: Well, Rosalind has still to meet the man she can't outdistance. Honestly, Alec, she treats men terribly. She abuses them and cuts them and breaks dates with them and yawns in their faces—and they come back for more.

ALEC: They love it.

CECELIA: They hate it. She's a—she's a sort of vampire, I think—and she can make girls do what she wants usually—only she hates girls.

ALEC: Personality runs in our family.

CECELIA: (*Resignedly*) I guess it ran out before it got to me.

ALEC: Does Rosalind behave herself?

CECELIA: Not particularly well. Oh, she's average—smokes sometimes, drinks punch, frequently kissed— Oh, yes—common knowledge—one of the effects of the war, you know.

(*Emerges* MRS. CONNAGE.)

MRS. CONNAGE: Rosalind's almost finished so I can go down and meet your friend.

(ALEC *and his mother go out.*)

ROSALIND: (*Outside*) Oh, mother——

CECELIA: Mother's gone down.

(*And now* ROSALIND *enters.* ROSALIND *is—utterly* ROSALIND. *She is one of those girls who need never make the slightest effort to have men fall in love with them. Two types of men seldom do: dull men are usually afraid of her cleverness and intellectual men are usually afraid of her beauty. All others are hers by natural prerogative.*

If ROSALIND *could be spoiled the process would have been complete by this time, and as a matter of fact, her disposition is not all it should be; she wants what she wants when she wants it and she is prone to make every one around her pretty miserable when she doesn't get it—but in the true sense she is not spoiled. Her fresh enthusiasm, her will to grow and learn, her endless faith in the inexhaustibility of romance, her courage and fundamental honesty—these things are not spoiled.*

There are long periods when she cordially loathes her whole family. She is quite unprincipled; her philosophy is carpe diem for herself and laissez faire for others. She loves shocking stories: she has that coarse streak that usually goes with natures that are both fine and big. She wants people to like her, but if they do not it never worries her or changes her.

She is by no means a model character.

The education of all beautiful women is the knowledge of men. ROSALIND *had been disappointed in man after man as individuals, but she had great faith in man as a sex. Women she detested. They represented qualities that she felt and despised in herself—incipient meanness, conceit, cowardice, and petty dishonesty. She once told a roomful of her mother's friends that the only excuse for women was the necessity for a disturbing element among men. She danced exceptionally well, drew cleverly but hastily, and had a startling facility with words, which she used only in love-letters.*

But all criticism of ROSALIND *ends in her beauty. There was that shade of glorious yellow hair, the desire to imitate which supports the dye industry. There was the eternal kissable mouth, small, slightly sensual, and utterly disturbing. There were gray eyes and an unimpeachable skin with two spots of vanishing color. She was slender and athletic, without underdevelopment, and it was a delight to watch her move about a room, walk along a street, swing a golf club, or turn a "cartwheel."*

A last qualification—her vivid, instant personality escaped that conscious, theatrical quality that AMORY *had found in* ISABELLE. MONSIGNOR DARCY *would have been quite up a tree whether to call her a personality or a personage. She was perhaps the delicious, inexpressible, once-in-a-century blend.*

On the night of her début she is, for all her strange, stray wisdom, quite like a happy little girl. Her mother's maid has just done her hair, but she has decided impatiently that she can do a better job herself. She is too nervous just now to stay in one place. To that we owe her presence in this littered room. She is going to speak. ISABELLE'S *alto tones had been like a violin, but if you could hear* ROSALIND, *you would say her voice was musical as a waterfall.*

ROSALIND: Honestly, there are only two costumes in the world that I really enjoy being in— (*Combing her hair at the dressing-table.*) One's a hoop skirt with pantaloons; the other's a one-piece bathing-suit. I'm quite charming in both of them.

CECELIA: Glad you're coming out?

ROSALIND: Yes; aren't you?

CECELIA: (*Cynically*) You're glad so you can get married and live on Long Island with the *fast younger married set.* You want life to be a chain of flirtation with a man for every link.

ROSALIND: *Want* it to be one! You mean I've *found* it one.

CECELIA: Ha!

ROSALIND: Cecelia, darling, you don't know what a trial it is to be—like me. I've got to keep my face like steel in the street to keep men from winking at me. If I laugh hard from a front row in the theatre, the comedian plays to me for the rest of the evening. If I drop my voice, my eyes, my handkerchief at a dance, my partner calls me up on the 'phone every day for a week.

CECELIA: It must be an awful strain.

ROSALIND: The unfortunate part is that the only men who interest me at all are the totally ineligible ones. Now—if I were poor I'd go on the stage.

CECELIA: Yes, you might as well get paid for the amount of acting you do.

ROSALIND: Sometimes when I've felt particularly radiant I've thought, why should this be wasted on one man?

CECELIA: Often when you're particularly sulky, I've wondered why it should all be wasted on just one family. (*Getting up.*) I think I'll go down and meet Mr. Amory Blaine. I like temperamental men.

ROSALIND: There aren't any. Men don't know how to be really angry or really happy—and the ones that do, go to pieces.

CECELIA: Well, I'm glad I don't have all your worries. I'm engaged.

ROSALIND: (*With a scornful smile*) Engaged? Why, you little lunatic! If mother heard you talking like that she'd send you off to boarding-school, where you belong.

CECELIA: You won't tell her, though, because I know things I could tell—and you're too selfish!

ROSALIND: (*A little annoyed*) Run along, little girl! Who are you engaged to, the Iceman? the man that keeps the candy-store?

CECELIA: Cheap wit—good-by, darling, I'll see you later.

ROSALIND: Oh, be *sure* and do that—you're *such* a help.

(*Exit* CECELIA. ROSALIND *finishes her hair and rises, humming. She goes up to the mirror and starts to dance in front of it on the soft carpet. She watches not her feet, but her eyes—never casually but always intently, even when she smiles. The door suddenly opens and then slams behind* AMORY, *very cool and handsome as usual. He melts into instant confusion.*)

HE: Oh, I'm sorry. I thought——

SHE: (*Smiling radiantly*) Oh, you're Amory Blaine, aren't you?

HE: (*Regarding her closely*) And you're Rosalind?

SHE: I'm going to call you Amory—oh, come in—it's all right—mother'll be right in—(*under her breath*) unfortunately.

HE: (*Gazing around*) This is sort of a new wrinkle for me.

SHE: This is No Man's Land.

HE: This is where you—you—(*pause*)

SHE: Yes—all those things. (*She crosses to the bureau.*) See, here's my rouge—eye pencils.

HE: I didn't know you were that way.

SHE: What did you expect?

HE: I thought you'd be sort of—sort of—sexless, you know, swim and play golf.

SHE: Oh, I do—but not in business hours.

HE: Business?

SHE: Six to two—strictly.

HE: I'd like to have some stock in the corporation.

SHE: Oh, it's not a corporation—it's just "Rosalind, Unlimited." Fifty-one shares, name, good-will, and everything goes at $25,000 a year.

HE: (*Disapprovingly*) Sort of a chilly proposition.

SHE: Well, Amory, you don't mind—do you? When I meet a man that doesn't bore me to death after two weeks, perhaps it'll be different.

HE: Odd, you have the same point of view on men that I have on women.

SHE: I'm not really feminine, you know—in my mind.

HE: (*Interested*) Go on.

SHE: No, you—you go on—you've made me talk about myself. That's against the rules.

HE: Rules?

SHE: My own rules—but you— Oh, Amory, I hear you're brilliant. The family expects *so* much of you.

HE: How encouraging!

SHE: Alec said you'd taught him to think. Did you? I didn't believe any one could.

HE: No. I'm really quite dull.

(*He evidently doesn't intend this to be taken seriously.*)

SHE: Liar.

HE: I'm—I'm religious—I'm literary. I've—I've even written poems.

SHE: Vers libre—splendid! (*She declaims.*)

"The trees are green,
The birds are singing in the trees,
The girl sips her poison
The bird flies away the girl dies."

HE: (*Laughing*) No, not that kind.

SHE: (*Suddenly*) I like you.

HE: Don't.

SHE: Modest too——

HE: I'm afraid of you. I'm always afraid of a girl—until I've kissed her.

SHE: (*Emphatically*) My dear boy, the war is over.

HE: So I'll always be afraid of you.

SHE: (*Rather sadly*) I suppose you will.

(*A slight hesitation on both their parts.*)

HE: (*After due consideration*) Listen. This is a frightful thing to ask.

SHE: (*Knowing what's coming*) After five minutes.

HE: But will you—kiss me? Or are you afraid?

SHE: I'm never afraid—but your reasons are so poor.

HE: Rosalind, I really *want* to kiss you.

SHE: So do I.

(*They kiss—definitely and thoroughly.*)

HE: (*After a breathless second*) Well, is your curiosity satisfied?

SHE: Is yours?

HE: No, it's only aroused.

(*He looks it.*)

SHE: (*Dreamily*) I've kissed dozens of men. I suppose I'll kiss dozens more.

HE: (*Abstractedly*) Yes, I suppose you could—like that.

SHE: Most people like the way I kiss.

conservatory exchanging silliness with any one—or listening to it.

ROSALIND: (*Sarcastically*) Yes, listening to it *is* better.

MRS. CONNAGE: And don't waste a lot of time with the college set—little boys nineteen and twenty years old. I don't mind a prom or a football game, but staying away from advantageous parties to eat in little café down-town with Tom, Dick, and Harry——

ROSALIND: (*Offering her code, which is, in its way, quite as high as her mother's*) Mother, it's done—you can't run everything now the way you did in the early nineties.

MRS. CONNAGE: (*Paying no attention*) There are several bachelor friends of your father's that I want you to meet to-night—youngish men.

ROSALIND: (*Nodding wisely*) About forty-five?

MRS. CONNAGE: (*Sharply*) Why not?

ROSALIND: Oh, *quite* all right—they know life and are so adorably tired looking (*shakes her head*)—but they *will* dance.

MRS. CONNAGE: I haven't met Mr. Blaine—but I don't think you'll care for him. He doesn't sound like a money-maker.

ROSALIND: Mother, I never *think* about money.

MRS. CONNAGE: You never keep it long enough to think about it

ROSALIND: (*Sighs*) Yes, I suppose some day I'll marry a ton of it—out of sheer boredom.

MRS. CONNAGE: (*Referring to note-book*) I had a wire from Hartford. Dawson Ryder is coming up. Now there's a young man I like, and he's floating in money. It seems to me that since you seem tired of Howard Gillespie you might give Mr. Ryder some encouragement. This is the third time he's been up in a month.

ROSALIND: How did you know I was tired of Howard Gillespie?

MRS. CONNAGE: The poor boy looks so miserable every time he comes.

ROSALIND: That was one of those romantic, pre-battle affairs. They're all wrong.

MRS. CONNAGE: (*Her say said*) At any rate, make us proud of you to-night.

ROSALIND: Don't you think I'm beautiful?

MRS. CONNAGE: You know you are.

(*From down-stairs is heard the moan of a violin being tuned, the roll of a drum.* MRS. CONNAGE *turns quickly to her daughter.*)

MRS. CONNAGE: Come!

ROSALIND: One minute!

(*Her mother leaves.* ROSALIND *goes to the glass where she gazes at herself with great satisfaction. She kisses her hand and touches her mirrored mouth with it. Then she turns out the lights and leaves the room. Silence for a moment. A few chords from the piano, the discreet patter of faint drums, the rustle of new silk, all blend on the staircase outside and drift in through the partly opened door. Bundled figures pass in the lighted hall. The laughter heard below becomes doubled and multiplied. Then some one comes in, closes the door, and switches on the lights. It is* CECELIA. *She goes to the chiffonier, looks in the drawers, hesitates—then to the desk whence she takes the cigarette-case and extracts one. She lights it and then, puffing and blowing, walks toward the mirror.*)

CECELIA: (*In tremendously sophisticated accents*) Oh, yes, coming out is *such* a farce nowadays, you know. One really plays around so much before one is seventeen, that it's positively anticlimax. (*Shaking hands with a visionary middle-aged nobleman.*) Yes, your grace—I b'lieve I've heard my sister speak of you. Have a puff—they're very good. They're—they're Coronas. You don't smoke? What a pity! The king doesn't allow it, I suppose. Yes, I'll dance.

(*So she dances around the room to a tune from downstairs, her arms outstretched to an imaginary partner, the cigarette waving in her hand.*)

SEVERAL HOURS LATER

The corner of a den down-stairs, filled by a very comfortable leather lounge. A small light is on each side above, and in the middle, over the couch hangs a painting of a very old, very dignified gentleman, period 1860. Outside the music is heard in a fox-trot.

ROSALIND *is seated on the lounge and on her left is* HOWARD

GILLESPIE, *a vapid youth of about twenty-four. He is obviously very unhappy, and she is quite bored.*

GILLESPIE: (*Feebly*) What do you mean I've changed. I feel the same toward you.

ROSALIND: But you don't look the same to me.

GILLESPIE: Three weeks ago you used to say that you liked me because I was so blasé, so indifferent—I still am.

ROSALIND: But not about me. I used to like you because you had brown eyes and thin legs.

GILLESPIE: (*Helplessly*) They're still thin and brown. You're a vampire, that's all.

ROSALIND: The only thing I know about vamping is what's on the piano score. What confuses men is that I'm perfectly natural. I used to think you were never jealous. Now you follow me with your eyes wherever I go.

GILLESPIE: I love you.

ROSALIND: (*Coldly*) I know it.

GILLESPIE: And you haven't kissed me for two weeks. I had an idea that after a girl was kissed she was—was—won.

ROSALIND: Those days are over. I have to be won all over again every time you see me.

GILLESPIE: Are you serious?

ROSALIND: About as usual. There used to be two kinds of kisses: First when girls were kissed and deserted; second, when they were engaged. Now there's a third kind, where the man is kissed and deserted. If Mr. Jones of the nineties bragged he'd kissed a girl, every one knew he was through with her. If Mr. Jones of 1919 brags the same every one knows it's because he can't kiss her any more. Given a decent start any girl can beat a man nowadays.

GILLESPIE: Then why do you play with men?

ROSALIND: (*Leaning forward confidentially*) For that first moment, when he's interested. There is a moment— Oh, just before the first kiss, a whispered word—something that makes it worth while.

GILLESPIE: And then?

ROSALIND: Then after that you make him talk about himself. Pretty soon he thinks of nothing but being alone with you—he sulks, he won't fight, he doesn't want to play—Victory!

(*Enter* DAWSON RYDER, *twenty-six, handsome, wealthy, faithful to his own, a bore perhaps, but steady and sure of success.*)

RYDER: I believe this is my dance, Rosalind.

ROSALIND: Well, Dawson, so you recognize me. Now I know I haven't got too much paint on. Mr. Ryder, this is Mr. Gillespie.

(*They shake hands and* GILLESPIE *leaves, tremendously downcast.*)

RYDER: Your party is certainly a success.

ROSALIND: Is it— I haven't seen it lately. I'm weary— Do you mind sitting out a minute?

RYDER: Mind—I'm delighted. You know I loathe this "rushing" idea. See a girl yesterday, to-day, to-morrow.

ROSALIND: Dawson!

RYDER: What?

ROSALIND: I wonder if you know you love me.

RYDER: (*Startled*) What— Oh—you know you're remarkable!

ROSALIND: Because you know I'm an awful proposition. Any one who marries me will have his hands full. I'm mean—mighty mean.

RYDER: Oh, I wouldn't say that.

ROSALIND: Oh, yes, I am—especially to the people nearest to me. (*She rises.*) Come, let's go. I've changed my mind and I want to dance. Mother is probably having a fit.

(*Exeunt. Enter* ALEC *and* CECELIA.)

CECELIA: Just my luck to get my own brother for an intermission.

ALEC: (*Gloomily*) I'll go if you want me to.

CECELIA: Good heavens, no—with whom would I begin the next dance? (*Sighs.*) There's no color in a dance since the French officers went back.

ALEC: (*Thoughtfully*) I don't want Amory to fall in love with Rosalind.

CECELIA: Why, I had an idea that that was just what you did want.

ALEC: I did, but since seeing these girls—I don't know. I'm awfully attached to Amory. He's sensitive and I don't want him to break his heart over somebody who doesn't care about him.

CECELIA: He's very good looking.

ALEC: (*Still thoughtfully*) She won't marry him, but a girl doesn't have to marry a man to break his heart.

CECELIA: What does it? I wish I knew the secret.

ALEC: Why, you cold-blooded little kitty. It's lucky for some that the Lord gave you a pug nose.

(*Enter* MRS. CONNAGE.)

MRS. CONNAGE: Where on earth is Rosalind?

ALEC: (*Brilliantly*) Of course you've come to the best people to find out. She'd naturally be with us.

MRS. CONNAGE: Her father has marshalled eight bachelor millionaires to meet her.

ALEC: You might form a squad and march through the halls.

MRS. CONNAGE: I'm perfectly serious—for all I know she may be at the Cocoanut Grove with some football player on the night of her début. You look left and I'll——

ALEC: (*Flippantly*) Hadn't you better send the butler through the cellar?

MRS. CONNAGE: (*Perfectly serious*) Oh, you don't think she'd be there?

CECELIA: He's only joking, mother.

ALEC: Mother had a picture of her tapping a keg of beer with some high hurdler.

MRS. CONNAGE: Let's look right away.

(*They go out.* ROSALIND *comes in with* GILLESPIE.)

GILLESPIE: Rosalind— Once more I ask you. Don't you care a blessed thing about me?

(AMORY *walks in briskly.*)

AMORY: My dance.

ROSALIND: Mr. Gillespie, this is Mr. Blaine.

GILLESPIE: I've met Mr. Blaine. From Lake Geneva, aren't you?

AMORY: Yes.

GILLESPIE: (*Desperately*) I've been there. It's in the—the Middle West, isn't it?

AMORY: (*Spicily*) Approximately. But I always felt that I'd rather be provincial hot-tamale than soup without seasoning.

GILLESPIE: What!

AMORY: Oh, no offense.

(GILLESPIE *bows and leaves.*)

ROSALIND: He's too much *people.*

AMORY: I was in love with a *people* once.

ROSALIND: So?

AMORY: Oh, yes—her name was Isabelle—nothing at all to her except what I read into her.

ROSALIND: What happened?

AMORY: Finally I convinced her that she was smarter than I was—then she threw me over. Said I was critical and impractical, you know.

ROSALIND: What do you mean impractical?

AMORY: Oh—drive a car, but can't change a tire.

ROSALIND: What are you going to do?

AMORY: Can't say—run for President, write——

ROSALIND: Greenwich Village?

AMORY: Good heavens, no—I said write—not drink.

ROSALIND: I like business men. Clever men are usually so homely.

AMORY: I feel as if I'd known you for ages.

ROSALIND: Oh, are you going to commence the "pyramid" story?

AMORY: No—I was going to make it French. I was Louis XIV and you were one of my—my— (*Changing his tone.*) Suppose—we fell in love.

ROSALIND: I've suggested pretending.

AMORY: If we did it would be very big.

ROSALIND: Why?

AMORY: Because selfish people are in a way terribly capable of great loves.

ROSALIND: (*Turning her lips up*) Pretend.

(*Very deliberately they kiss.*)

AMORY: I can't say sweet things. But you *are* beautiful.

ROSALIND: Not that.

AMORY: What then?

ROSALIND: (*Sadly*) Oh, nothing—only I want sentiment, real sentiment—and I never find it.

AMORY: I never find anything else in the world—and I loathe it.

ROSALIND: It's so hard to find a male to gratify one's artistic taste.

(*Some one has opened a door and the music of a waltz surges into the room.* ROSALIND *rises.*)

ROSALIND: Listen! they're playing "Kiss Me Again."

(*He looks at her.*)

AMORY: Well?

ROSALIND: Well?

AMORY: (*Softly—the battle lost*) I love you.

ROSALIND: I love you—now.

(*They kiss.*)

AMORY: Oh, God, what have I done?

ROSALIND: Nothing. Oh, don't talk. Kiss me again.

AMORY: I don't know why or how, but I love you—from the moment I saw you.

ROSALIND: Me too—I—I—oh, to-night's to-night.

(*Her brother strolls in, starts and then in a loud voice says:* "Oh, excuse me," *and goes.*)

ROSALIND: (*Her lips scarcely stirring*) Don't let me go—I don't care who knows what I do.

AMORY: Say it!

ROSALIND: I love you—now. (*They part.*) Oh—I am very youthful, thank God—and rather beautiful, thank God—and happy, thank God, thank God— (*She pauses and then, in an odd burst of prophecy, adds*) Poor Amory!

(*He kisses her again.*)

KISMET

Within two weeks Amory and Rosalind were deeply and passionately in love. The critical qualities which had spoiled for each of them a dozen romances were dulled by the great wave of emotion that washed over them.

"It may be an insane love-affair," she told her anxious mother, "but it's not inane."

The wave swept Amory into an advertising agency early in March, where he alternated between astonishing bursts of rather exceptional work and wild dreams of becoming suddenly rich and touring Italy with Rosalind.

They were together constantly, for lunch, for dinner, and nearly every evening—always in a sort of breathless hush, as if they feared that any minute the spell would break and drop them out of this paradise of rose and flame. But the spell became a trance, seemed to increase from day to day; they began to talk of marrying in July—in June. All life was transmitted into terms of their love, all experience, all desires, all ambitions, were nullified—their senses of humor crawled into corners to sleep; their former love-affairs seemed faintly laughable and scarcely regretted juvenilia.

For the second time in his life Amory had had a complete bouleversement and was hurrying into line with his generation.

A Little Interlude

Amory wandered slowly up the avenue and thought of the night as inevitably his—the pageantry and carnival of rich dusk and dim streets . . . it seemed that he had closed the book of fading harmonies at last and stepped into the sensuous vibrant walks of life. Everywhere these countless lights, this promise of a night of streets and singing—he moved in a half-dream through the crowd as if expecting to meet Rosalind hurrying toward him with eager feet from every corner. . . . How the unforgettable faces of dusk would blend to her, the myriad footsteps, a thousand overtures, would blend to her footsteps; and there would be more drunkenness than wine in the softness of her eyes on his. Even his dreams now were faint violins drifting like summer sounds upon the summer air.

The room was in darkness except for the faint glow of Tom's cigarette where he lounged by the open window. As the door shut behind him, Amory stood a moment with his back against it.

"Hello, Benvenuto Blaine. How went the advertising business to-day?"

Amory sprawled on a couch.

"I loathed it as usual!" The momentary vision of the bustling agency was displaced quickly by another picture.

"My God! She's wonderful!"

Tom sighed.

"I can't tell you," repeated Amory, "just how wonderful she is. I don't want you to know. I don't want any one to know."

Another sigh came from the window—quite a resigned sigh.

"She's life and hope and happiness, my whole world now."

He felt the quiver of a tear on his eyelid.

"Oh, *Golly*, Tom!"

Bitter Sweet

"Sit like we do," she whispered.

He sat in the big chair and held out his arms so that she could nestle inside them.

"I knew you'd come to-night," she said softly, "like summer, just when I needed you most . . . darling . . . darling . . ."

His lips moved lazily over her face.

"You *taste* so good," he sighed.

"How do you mean, lover?"

"Oh, just sweet, just sweet . . ." he held her closer.

"Amory," she whispered, "when you're ready for me I'll marry you."

"We won't have much at first."

"Don't!" she cried. "It hurts when you reproach yourself for what you can't give me. I've got your precious self—and that's enough for me."

"Tell me . . ."

"You know, don't you? Oh, you know."

"Yes, but I want to hear you say it."

"I love you, Amory, with all my heart."

"Always, will you?"

"All my life— Oh, Amory——"

"What?"

"I want to belong to you. I want your people to be my people. I want to have your babies."

"But I haven't any people."

"Don't laugh at me, Amory. Just kiss me."

"I'll do what you want," he said.

"No, I'll do what *you* want. We're *you*—not me. Oh, you're so much a part, so much all of me . . ."

He closed his eyes.

"I'm so happy that I'm frightened. Wouldn't it be awful if this was—was the high point? . . ."

She looked at him dreamily.

"Beauty and love pass, I know. . . . Oh, there's sadness, too. I suppose all great happiness is a little sad. Beauty means the scent of roses and then the death of roses——"

"Beauty means the agony of sacrifice and the end of agony. . . ."

"And, Amory, we're beautiful, I know. I'm sure God loves us——"

"He loves you. You're his most precious possession."

"I'm not his, I'm yours. Amory, I belong to you. For the first time I regret all the other kisses; now I know how much a kiss can mean."

Then they would smoke and he would tell her about his day at the office—and where they might live. Sometimes, when he was particularly loquacious, she went to sleep in his arms, but he loved that Rosalind—all Rosalinds as he had never in the world loved any one else. Intangibly fleeting, unrememberable hours.

Aquatic Incident

One day Amory and Howard Gillespie meeting by accident down-town took lunch together, and Amory heard a story that delighted him. Gillespie after several cocktails was in a talkative mood; he began by telling Amory that he was sure Rosalind was slightly eccentric.

He had gone with her on a swimming party up in Westchester County, and some one mentioned that Annette Kellerman had been there one day on a visit and had dived from the top of a rickety, thirty-foot summer-house. Immediately Rosalind insisted that Howard should climb up with her to see what it looked like.

A minute later, as he sat and dangled his feet on the edge, a form shot by him; Rosalind, her arms spread in a beautiful swan dive, had sailed through the air into the clear water.

"Of course *I* had to go, after that—and I nearly killed myself. I thought I was pretty good to even try it. Nobody else in the party tried it. Well, afterward Rosalind had the nerve to ask me why I stooped over when I dove. 'It didn't make it any easier,' she said, 'it just took all the courage out of it.' I ask you, what can a man do with a girl like that? Unnecessary, I call it."

Gillespie failed to understand why Amory was smiling delightedly all through lunch. He thought perhaps he was one of these hollow optimists.

FIVE WEEKS LATER

Again the library of the Connage house. ROSALIND *is alone, sitting on the lounge staring very moodily and unhappily at nothing. She has changed perceptibly—she is a trifle thinner for one thing; the light in her eyes is not so bright; she looks easily a year older.*

Her mother comes in, muffled in an opera-cloak. She takes in ROSALIND *with a nervous glance.*

MRS. CONNAGE: Who is coming to-night?

(ROSALIND *fails to hear her, at least takes no notice.*)

MRS. CONNAGE: Alec is coming up to take me to this Barrie play, "Et tu, Brutus." (*She perceives that she is talking to herself.*) Rosalind! I asked you who is coming to-night?

ROSALIND: (*Starting*) Oh—what—oh—Amory——

MRS. CONNAGE: (*Sarcastically*) You have so *many* admirers lately that I couldn't imagine *which* one. (ROSALIND *doesn't answer.*) Dawson Ryder is more patient than I thought he'd be. You haven't given him an evening this week.

ROSALIND: (*With a very weary expression that is quite new to her face.*) Mother—please——

MRS. CONNAGE: Oh, *I* won't interfere. You've already wasted over two months on a theoretical genius who hasn't a penny to his name, but *go* ahead, waste your life on him. *I* won't interfere.

ROSALIND: (*As if repeating a tiresome lesson*) You know he has a little income—and you know he's earning thirty-five dollars a week in advertising——

MRS. CONNAGE: And it wouldn't buy your clothes. (*She pauses but* ROSALIND *makes no reply.*) I have your best interests at heart when I tell you not to take a step you'll spend your days regretting. It's not as if your father could help you. Things have been hard for him lately and he's an old man. You'd be dependent absolutely on a dreamer, a nice, well-born boy, but a dreamer—merely *clever.* (*She implies that this quality in itself is rather vicious.*)

ROSALIND: For heaven's sake, mother——

(*A maid appears, announces Mr. Blaine who follows immediately.* AMORY'S *friends have been telling him for ten days that he "looks like the wrath of God," and he does. As a matter of fact he has not been able to eat a mouthful in the last thirty-six hours.*)

AMORY: Good evening, Mrs. Connage.

MRS. CONNAGE: (*Not unkindly*) Good evening, Amory.

(AMORY *and* ROSALIND *exchange glances—and* ALEC *comes in.* ALEC'S *attitude throughout has been neutral. He believes in his heart that the marriage would make* AMORY *mediocre and* ROSALIND *miserable, but he feels a great sympathy for both of them.*)

ALEC: Hi, Amory!

AMORY: Hi, Alec! Tom said he'd meet you at the theatre.

ALEC: Yeah, just saw him. How's the advertising to-day? Write some brilliant copy?

AMORY: Oh, it's about the same. I got a raise—(*Every one looks at him rather eagerly*)—of two dollars a week. (*General collapse.*)

MRS. CONNAGE: Come, Alec, I hear the car.

(*A good night, rather chilly in sections. After* MRS. CONNAGE *and* ALEC *go out there is a pause.* ROSALIND *still stares moodily at the fireplace.* AMORY *goes to her and puts his arm around her.*)

AMORY: Darling girl.

(*They kiss. Another pause and then she seizes his hand, covers it with kisses and holds it to her breast.*)

ROSALIND: (*Sadly*) I love your hands, more than anything. I see them often when you're away from me—so tired; I know every line of them. Dear hands!

(*Their eyes meet for a second and then she begins to cry—a tearless sobbing.*)

AMORY: Rosalind!

ROSALIND: Oh, we're so darned pitiful!

AMORY: Rosalind!

ROSALIND: Oh, I want to die!

AMORY: Rosalind, another night of this and I'll go to

pieces. You've been this way four days now. You've got to be more encouraging or I can't work or eat or sleep. (*He looks around helplessly as if searching for new words to clothe an old, shop-worn phrase.*) We'll have to make a start. I *like* having to make a start together. (*His forced hopefulness fades as he sees her unresponsive.*) What's the matter? (*He gets up suddenly and starts to pace the floor.*) It's Dawson Ryder, that's what it is. He's been working on your nerves. You've been with him every afternoon for a week. People come and tell me they've seen you together, and I have to smile and nod and pretend it hasn't the slightest significance for me. And you won't tell me anything as it develops.

ROSALIND: Amory, if you don't sit down I'll scream.

AMORY: (*Sitting down suddenly beside her*) Oh, Lord.

ROSALIND: (*Taking his hand gently*) You know I love you, don't you?

AMORY: Yes.

ROSALIND: You know I'll always love you——

AMORY: Don't talk that way; you frighten me. It sounds as if we weren't going to have each other. (*She cries a little and rising from the couch goes to the armchair.*) I've felt all afternoon that things were worse. I nearly went wild down at the office—couldn't write a line. Tell me everything.

ROSALIND: There's nothing to tell, I say. I'm just nervous.

AMORY: Rosalind, you're playing with the idea of marrying Dawson Ryder.

ROSALIND: (*After a pause*) He's been asking me to all day.

AMORY: Well, he's got his nerve!

ROSALIND: (*After another pause*) I like him.

AMORY: Don't say that. It hurts me.

ROSALIND: Don't be a silly idiot. You know you're the only man I've ever loved, ever will love.

AMORY: (*Quickly*) Rosalind, let's get married—next week.

ROSALIND: We can't.

AMORY: Why not?

ROSALIND: Oh, we can't. I'd be your squaw—in some horrible place.

AMORY: We'll have two hundred and seventy-five dollars a month all told.

ROSALIND: Darling, I don't even do my own hair, usually.

AMORY: I'll do it for you.

ROSALIND: (*Between a laugh and a sob*) Thanks.

AMORY: Rosalind, you *can't* be thinking of marrying some one else. Tell me! You leave me in the dark. I can help you fight it out if you'll only tell me.

ROSALIND: It's just—us. We're pitiful, that's all. The very qualities I love you for are the ones that will always make you a failure.

AMORY: (*Grimly*) Go on.

ROSALIND: Oh—it *is* Dawson Ryder. He's so reliable, I almost feel that he'd be a—a background.

AMORY: You don't love him.

ROSALIND: I know, but I respect him, and he's a good man and a strong one.

AMORY: (*Grudgingly*) Yes—he's that.

ROSALIND: Well—here's one little thing. There was a little poor boy we met in Rye Tuesday afternoon—and, oh, Dawson took him on his lap and talked to him and promised him an Indian suit—and next day he remembered and bought it—and, oh, it was so sweet and I couldn't help thinking he'd be so nice to—to our children—take care of them—and I wouldn't have to worry.

AMORY: (*In despair*) Rosalind! Rosalind!

ROSALIND: (*With a faint roguishness*) Don't look so consciously suffering.

AMORY: What power we have of hurting each other!

ROSALIND: (*Commencing to sob again*) It's been so perfect—you and I. So like a dream that I'd longed for and never thought I'd find. The first real unselfishness I've ever felt in my life. And I can't see it fade out in a colorless atmosphere!

AMORY: It won't—it won't!

ROSALIND: I'd rather keep it as a beautiful memory—tucked away in my heart.

AMORY: Yes, women can do that—but not men. I'd remember always, not the beauty of it while it lasted, but just the bitterness, the long bitterness.

ROSALIND: Don't!

AMORY: All the years never to see you, never to kiss you, just a gate shut and barred—you don't dare be my wife.

ROSALIND: No—no—I'm taking the hardest course, the

strongest course. Marrying you would be a failure and I never fail—if you don't stop walking up and down I'll scream!

(*Again he sinks despairingly onto the lounge.*)

AMORY: Come over here and kiss me.

ROSALIND: No.

AMORY: Don't you *want* to kiss me?

ROSALIND: To-night I want you to love me calmly and coolly.

AMORY: The beginning of the end.

ROSALIND: (*With a burst of insight*) Amory, you're young. I'm young. People excuse us now for our poses and vanities, for treating people like Sancho and yet getting away with it. They excuse us now. But you've got a lot of knocks coming to you——

AMORY: And you're afraid to take them with me.

ROSALIND: No, not that. There was a poem I read somewhere—you'll say Ella Wheeler Wilcox and laugh—but listen:

"For this is wisdom—to love and live,
To take what fate or the gods may give,
To ask no question, to make no prayer,
To kiss the lips and caress the hair,
Speed passion's ebb as we greet its flow,
To have and to hold, and, in time—let go."

AMORY: But we haven't had.

ROSALIND: Amory, I'm yours—you know it. There have been times in the last month I'd have been completely yours if you'd said so. But I can't marry you and ruin both our lives.

AMORY: We've got to take our chance for happiness.

ROSALIND: Dawson says I'd learn to love him.

(AMORY *with his head sunk in his hands does not move. The life seems suddenly gone out of him.*)

ROSALIND: Lover! Lover! I can't do with you, and I can't imagine life without you.

AMORY: Rosalind, we're on each other's nerves. It's just that we're both high-strung, and this week——

(*His voice is curiously old. She crosses to him and taking his face in her hands, kisses him.*)

ROSALIND: I can't, Amory. I can't be shut away from the

trees and flowers, cooped up in a little flat, waiting for you. You'd hate me in a narrow atmosphere. I'd make you hate me.

(*Again she is blinded by sudden uncontrolled tears.*)

AMORY: Rosalind——

ROSALIND: Oh, darling, go— Don't make it harder! I can't stand it——

AMORY: (*His face drawn, his voice strained*) Do you know what you're saying? Do you mean forever?

(*There is a difference somehow in the quality of their suffering.*)

ROSALIND: Can't you see——

AMORY: I'm afraid I can't if you love me. You're afraid of taking two years' knocks with me.

ROSALIND: I wouldn't be the Rosalind you love.

AMORY: (*A little hysterically*) I can't give you up! I can't, that's all! I've got to have you!

ROSALIND: (*A hard note in her voice*) You're being a baby now.

AMORY: (*Wildly*) I don't care! You're spoiling our lives!

ROSALIND: I'm doing the wise thing, the only thing.

AMORY: Are you going to marry Dawson Ryder?

ROSALIND: Oh, don't ask me. You know I'm old in some ways—in others—well, I'm just a little girl. I like sunshine and pretty things and cheerfulness—and I dread responsibility. I don't want to think about pots and kitchens and brooms. I want to worry whether my legs will get slick and brown when I swim in the summer.

AMORY: And you love me.

ROSALIND: That's just why it has to end. Drifting hurts too much. We can't have any more scenes like this.

(*She draws his ring from her finger and hands it to him. Their eyes blind again with tears.*)

AMORY: (*His lips against her wet cheek*) Don't! Keep it, please—oh, don't break my heart!

(*She presses the ring softly into his hand*)

ROSALIND: (*Brokenly*) You'd better go.

AMORY: Good-by——

(*She looks at him once more, with infinite longing, infinite sadness.*)

ROSALIND: Don't ever forget me, Amory——

AMORY: Good-by——

(*He goes to the door, fumbles for the knob, finds it—she sees him throw back his head—and he is gone. Gone—she half starts from the lounge and then sinks forward on her face into the pillows.*)

ROSALIND: Oh, God, I want to die! (*After a moment she rises and with her eyes closed feels her way to the door. Then she turns and looks once more at the room. Here they had sat and dreamed: that tray she had so often filled with matches for him; that shade that they had discreetly lowered one long Sunday afternoon. Misty-eyed she stands and remembers; she speaks aloud.*) Oh, Amory, what have I done to you?

(*And deep under the aching sadness that will pass in time, Rosalind feels that she has lost something, she knows not what, she knows not why.*)

CHAPTER II

Experiments in Convalescence

THE Knickerbocker Bar, beamed upon by Maxfield Parrish's jovial, colorful "Old King Cole," was well crowded. Amory stopped in the entrance and looked at his wrist-watch; he wanted particularly to know the time, for something in his mind that catalogued and classified liked to chip things off cleanly. Later it would satisfy him in a vague way to be able to think "that thing ended at exactly twenty minutes after eight on Thursday, June 10, 1919." This was allowing for the walk from her house—a walk concerning which he had afterward not the faintest recollection.

He was in rather grotesque condition: two days of worry and nervousness, of sleepless nights, of untouched meals, culminating in the emotional crisis and Rosalind's abrupt decision—the strain of it had drugged the foreground of his mind into a merciful coma. As he fumbled clumsily with the olives at the free-lunch table, a man approached and spoke to him, and the olives dropped from his nervous hands.

"Well, Amory . . ."

It was some one he had known at Princeton; he had no idea of the name.

"Hello, old boy—" he heard himself saying.

"Name's Jim Wilson—you've forgotten."

"Sure, you bet, Jim. I remember."

"Going to reunion?"

"You know!" Simultaneously he realized that he was not going to reunion.

"Get overseas?"

Amory nodded, his eyes staring oddly. Stepping back to let some one pass, he knocked the dish of olives to a crash on the floor.

"Too bad," he muttered. "Have a drink?"

Wilson, ponderously diplomatic, reached over and slapped him on the back.

"You've had plenty, old boy."

Amory eyed him dumbly until Wilson grew embarrassed under the scrutiny.

"Plenty, hell!" said Amory finally. "I haven't had a drink today."

Wilson looked incredulous.

"Have a drink or not?" cried Amory rudely.

Together they sought the bar.

"Rye high."

"I'll just take a Bronx."

Wilson had another; Amory had several more. They decided to sit down. At ten o'clock Wilson was displaced by Carling, class of '15. Amory, his head spinning gorgeously, layer upon layer of soft satisfaction setting over the bruised spots of his spirit, was discoursing volubly on the war.

"'S a mental was'e," he insisted with owl-like wisdom. "Two years my life spent inalleshual vacuity. Los' idealism, got be physcal anmal," he shook his fist expressively at Old King Cole, "got be Prussian 'bout ev'thing, women 'specially. Use' be straight 'bout women college. Now don'givadam." He expressed his lack of principle by sweeping a seltzer bottle with a broad gesture to noisy extinction on the floor, but this did not interrupt his speech. "Seek pleasure where find it for to-morrow die. 'At's philos'phy for me now on."

Carling yawned, but Amory, waxing brilliant, continued:

"Use' wonder 'bout things—people satisfied compromise, fif'y-fif'y att'tude on life. Now don' wonder, don' wonder—" He became so emphatic in impressing on Carling the fact that he didn't wonder that he lost the thread of his discourse and concluded by announcing to the bar at large that he was a "physcal anmal."

"What are you celebrating, Amory?"

Amory leaned forward confidentially.

"Cel'brating blowmylife. Great moment blow my life. Can't tell you 'bout it——"

He heard Carling addressing a remark to the bartender:

"Give him a bromo-seltzer."

Amory shook his head indignantly.

"None that stuff!"

"But listen, Amory, you're making yourself sick. You're white as a ghost."

Amory considered the question. He tried to look at himself in the mirror but even by squinting up one eye could only see as far as the row of bottles behind the bar.

"Like som'n solid. We go get some—some salad."

He settled his coat with an attempt at nonchalance, but letting go of the bar was too much for him, and he slumped against a chair.

"We'll go over to Shanley's," suggested Carling, offering an elbow.

With this assistance Amory managed to get his legs in motion enough to propel him across Forty-second Street.

Shanley's was very dim. He was conscious that he was talking in a loud voice, very succinctly and convincingly, he thought, about a desire to crush people under his heel. He consumed three club sandwiches, devouring each as though it were no larger than a chocolate-drop. Then Rosalind began popping into his mind again, and he found his lips forming her name over and over. Next he was sleepy, and he had a hazy, listless sense of people in dress suits, probably waiters, gathering around the table. . . .

. . . He was in a room and Carling was saying something about a knot in his shoe-lace.

"Nemmine," he managed to articulate drowsily. "Sleep in 'em. . . ."

Still Alcoholic

He awoke laughing and his eyes lazily roamed his surroundings, evidently a bedroom and bath in a good hotel. His head was whirring and picture after picture was forming and blurring and melting before his eyes, but beyond the desire to laugh he had no entirely conscious reaction. He reached for the 'phone beside his bed.

"Hello—what hotel is this—?

"Knickerbocker? All right, send up two rye high-balls——"

He lay for a moment and wondered idly whether they'd send up a bottle or just two of those little glass containers. Then, with an effort, he struggled out of bed and ambled into the bathroom.

When he emerged, rubbing himself lazily with a towel, he found the bar boy with the drinks and had a sudden desire to kid him. On reflection he decided that this would be undignified, so he waved him away.

As the new alcohol tumbled into his stomach and warmed him, the isolated pictures began slowly to form a cinema reel of the day before. Again he saw Rosalind curled weeping among the pillows, again he felt her tears against his cheek. Her words began ringing in his ears: "Don't ever forget me, Amory—don't ever forget me——"

"Hell!" he faltered aloud, and then he choked and collapsed on the bed in a shaken spasm of grief. After a minute he opened his eyes and regarded the ceiling.

"Damned fool!" he exclaimed in disgust, and with a voluminous sigh rose and approached the bottle. After another glass he gave way loosely to the luxury of tears. Purposely he called up into his mind little incidents of the vanished spring, phrased to himself emotions that would make him react even more strongly to sorrow.

"We were so happy," he intoned dramatically, "so very happy." Then he gave way again and knelt beside the bed, his head half-buried in the pillow.

"My own girl—my own— Oh——"

He clenched his teeth so that the tears streamed in a flood from his eyes.

"Oh . . . my baby girl, all I had, all I wanted! . . . Oh, my girl, come back, come back! I need you . . . need you . . . we're so pitiful . . . just misery we brought each other. . . . She'll be shut away from me. . . . I can't see her; I can't be her friend. It's got to be that way—it's got to be——"

And then again:

"We've been so happy, so very happy. . . ."

He rose to his feet and threw himself on the bed in an ecstasy of sentiment, and then lay exhausted while he realized slowly that he had been very drunk the night before, and that his head was spinning again wildly. He laughed, rose, and crossed again to Lethe. . . .

At noon he ran into a crowd in the Biltmore bar, and the riot began again. He had a vague recollection afterward of discussing French poetry with a British officer who was introduced to him as "Captain Corn, of his Majesty's Foot," and he remembered attempting to recite "Clair de Lune" at luncheon; then he slept in a big, soft chair until almost five o'clock when another crowd found and woke him; there followed an alcoholic dressing of several temperaments for the ordeal of dinner. They selected theatre tickets at Tyson's for a play that had a four-drink programme—a play with two monotonous voices, with turbid, gloomy scenes, and lighting effects that were hard to follow when his eyes behaved so amazingly. He imagined afterward that it must have been "The Jest." . . .

. . . Then the Cocoanut Grove, where Amory slept again on a little balcony outside. Out in Shanley's, Yonkers, he became almost logical, and by a careful control of the number of high-balls he drank, grew quite lucid and garrulous. He found that the party consisted of five men, two of whom he knew slightly; he became righteous about paying his share of the expense and insisted in a loud voice on arranging everything then and there to the amusement of the tables around him. . . .

Some one mentioned that a famous cabaret star was at the next table, so Amory rose and, approaching gallantly, introduced himself . . . this involved him in an argument, first with her escort and then with the head-waiter—Amory's attitude being a lofty and exaggerated courtesy . . . he consented, after being confronted with irrefutable logic, to being led back to his own table.

"Decided to commit suicide," he announced suddenly.

"When? Next year?"

"Now. To-morrow morning. Going to take a room at the Commodore, get into a hot bath and open a vein."

"He's getting morbid!"

"You need another rye, old boy!"

"We'll all talk it over to-morrow."

But Amory was not to be dissuaded, from argument at least.

"Did you ever get that way?" he demanded confidentially fortaccio.

"Sure!"

"Often?"

"My chronic state."

This provoked discussion. One man said that he got so depressed sometimes that he seriously considered it. Another agreed that there was nothing to live for. "Captain Corn," who had somehow rejoined the party, said that in his opinion it was when one's health was bad that one felt that way most. Amory's suggestion was that they should each order a Bronx, mix broken glass in it, and drink it off. To his relief no one applauded the idea, so having finished his high-ball, he balanced his chin in his hand and his elbow on the table—a most delicate, scarcely noticeable sleeping position, he assured himself—and went into a deep stupor. . . .

He was awakened by a woman clinging to him, a pretty woman, with brown, disarranged hair and dark blue eyes.

"Take me home!" she cried.

"Hello!" said Amory, blinking.

"I like you," she announced tenderly.

"I like you too."

He noticed that there was a noisy man in the background and that one of his party was arguing with him.

"Fella I was with's a damn fool," confided the blue-eyed woman. "I hate him. I want to go home with you."

"You drunk?" queried Amory with intense wisdom.

She nodded coyly.

"Go home with him," he advised gravely. "He brought you."

At this point the noisy man in the background broke away from his detainers and approached.

"Say!" he said fiercely. "I brought this girl out here and you're butting in!"

Amory regarded him coldly, while the girl clung to him closer.

"You let go that girl!" cried the noisy man.

Amory tried to make his eyes threatening.

"You go to hell!" he directed finally, and turned his attention to the girl.

"Love first sight," he suggested.

"I love you," she breathed and nestled close to him. She *did* have beautiful eyes.

Some one leaned over and spoke in Amory's ear.

"That's just Margaret Diamond. She's drunk and this fellow here brought her. Better let her go."

"Let him take care of her, then!" shouted Amory furiously. "I'm no W.Y.C.A. worker, am I?—am I?"

"Let her go!"

"It's *her* hanging on, damn it! Let her hang!"

The crowd around the table thickened. For an instant a brawl threatened, but a sleek waiter bent back Margaret Diamond's fingers until she released her hold on Amory, whereupon she slapped the waiter furiously in the face and flung her arms about her raging original escort.

"Oh, Lord!" cried Amory.

"Let's go!"

"Come on, the taxis are getting scarce!"

"Check, waiter."

"C'mon, Amory. Your romance is over."

Amory laughed.

"You don't know how true you spoke. No idea. 'At's the whole trouble."

Amory on the Labor Question

Two mornings later he knocked at the president's door at Bascome and Barlow's advertising agency.

"Come in!"

Amory entered unsteadily.

"'Morning, Mr. Barlow."

Mr. Barlow brought his glasses to the inspection and set his mouth slightly ajar that he might better listen.

"Well, Mr. Blaine. We haven't seen you for several days."

"No," said Amory. "I'm quitting."

"Well—well—this is——"

"I don't like it here."

"I'm sorry. I thought our relations had been quite—ah—pleasant. You seemed to be a hard worker—a little inclined perhaps to write fancy copy——"

"I just got tired of it," interrupted Amory rudely. "It didn't matter a damn to me whether Harebell's flour was any better than any one else's. In fact, I never ate any of it. So I got tired of telling people about it—oh, I know I've been drinking——"

Mr. Barlow's face steeled by several ingots of expression.

"You asked for a position——"

Amory waved him to silence.

"And I think I was rottenly underpaid. Thirty-five dollars a week—less than a good carpenter."

"You had just started. You'd never worked before," said Mr. Barlow coolly.

"But it took about ten thousand dollars to educate me where I could write your darned stuff for you. Anyway, as far as length of service goes, you've got stenographers here you've paid fifteen a week for five years."

"I'm not going to argue with you, sir," said Mr. Barlow rising.

"Neither am I. I just wanted to tell you I'm quitting."

They stood for a moment looking at each other impassively and then Amory turned and left the office.

A Little Lull

Four days after that he returned at last to the apartment. Tom was engaged on a book review for *The New Democracy* on the staff of which he was employed. They regarded each other for a moment in silence.

"Well?"

"Well?"

"Good Lord, Amory, where'd you get the black eye—and the jaw?"

Amory laughed.

"That's a mere nothing."

He peeled off his coat and bared his shoulders.

"Look here!"

Tom emitted a low whistle.

"What hit you?"

Amory laughed again.

"Oh, a lot of people. I got beaten up. Fact." He slowly replaced his shirt. "It was bound to come sooner or later and I wouldn't have missed it for anything."

"Who was it?"

"Well, there were some waiters and a couple of sailors and a few stray pedestrians, I guess. It's the strangest feeling. You ought to get beaten up just for the experience of it. You fall down after a while and everybody sort of slashes in at you before you hit the ground—then they kick you."

Tom lighted a cigarette.

"I spent a day chasing you all over town, Amory. But you always kept a little ahead of me. I'd say you've been on some party."

Amory tumbled into a chair and asked for a cigarette.

"You sober now?" asked Tom quizzically.

"Pretty sober. Why?"

"Well, Alec has left. His family had been after him to go home and live, so he——"

A spasm of pain shook Amory.

"Too bad."

"Yes, it is too bad. We'll have to get some one else if we're going to stay here. The rent's going up."

"Sure. Get anybody. I'll leave it to you, Tom."

Amory walked into his bedroom. The first thing that met his glance was a photograph of Rosalind that he had intended to have framed, propped up against a mirror on his dresser. He looked at it unmoved. After the vivid mental pictures of her that were his portion at present, the portrait was curiously unreal. He went back into the study.

"Got a cardboard box?"

"No," answered Tom, puzzled. "Why should I have? Oh, yes—there may be one in Alec's room."

Eventually Amory found what he was looking for and, returning to his dresser, opened a drawer full of letters, notes, part of a chain, two little handkerchiefs, and some snap-shots. As he transferred them carefully to the box his mind wandered to some place in a book where the hero, after preserving for a year a cake of his lost love's soap, finally washed his hands with it. He laughed and began to hum "After you've gone" . . . ceased abruptly . . .

The string broke twice, and then he managed to secure it, dropped the package into the bottom of his trunk, and having slammed the lid returned to the study.

"Going out?" Tom's voice held an undertone of anxiety.

"Uh-huh."

"Where?"

"Couldn't say, old keed."

"Let's have dinner together."

"Sorry. I told Sukey Brett I'd eat with him."

"Oh."

"By-by."

Amory crossed the street and had a high-ball; then he walked to Washington Square and found a top seat on a bus. He disembarked at Forty-third Street and strolled to the Biltmore bar.

"Hi, Amory!"

"What'll you have?"

"Yoho! Waiter!"

Temperature Normal

The advent of prohibition with the "thirsty-first" put a sudden stop to the submerging of Amory's sorrows, and when he awoke one morning to find that the old bar-to-bar days were over, he had neither remorse for the past three weeks nor regret that their repetition was impossible. He had taken the most violent, if the weakest, method to shield himself from the stabs of memory, and while it was not a course he would have prescribed for others, he found in the end that it had done its business: he was over the first flush of pain.

Don't misunderstand! Amory had loved Rosalind as he would never love another living person. She had taken the first flush of his youth and brought from his unplumbed depths tenderness that had surprised him, gentleness and unselfishness that he had never given to another creature. He had later love-affairs, but of a different sort: in those he went back to that, perhaps, more typical frame of mind, in which the girl became the mirror of a mood in him. Rosalind had drawn out what was more than passionate admiration; he had a deep, undying affection for Rosalind.

But there had been, near the end, so much dramatic tragedy, culminating in the arabesque nightmare of his three weeks' spree, that he was emotionally worn out. The people and surroundings that he remembered as being cool or delicately artificial, seemed to promise him a refuge. He wrote a cynical story which featured his father's funeral and despatched it to a magazine, receiving in return a check for sixty dollars and a request for more of the same tone. This tickled his vanity, but inspired him to no further effort.

He read enormously. He was puzzled and depressed by "A Portrait of the Artist as a Young Man"; intensely interested by "Joan and Peter" and "The Undying Fire," and rather surprised by his discovery through a critic named Mencken of several excellent American novels: "Vandover and the Brute," "The Damnation of Theron Ware," and "Jennie Gerhardt." Mackenzie, Chesterton, Galsworthy, Bennet, had sunk in his appreciation from sagacious, life-saturated geniuses to merely diverting contemporaries. Shaw's aloof clarity and brilliant consistency and the gloriously intoxicated efforts of H. G. Wells to fit the key of romantic symmetry into the elusive lock of truth, alone won his rapt attention.

He wanted to see Monsignor Darcy, to whom he had written when he landed, but he had not heard from him; besides he knew that a visit to Monsignor would entail the story of Rosalind, and the thought of repeating it turned him cold with horror.

In his search for cool people he remembered Mrs. Lawrence, a very intelligent, very dignified lady, a convert to the church, and a great devotee of Monsignor's.

He called her on the 'phone one day. Yes, she remembered him perfectly; no, Monsignor wasn't in town, was in Boston she thought; he'd promised to come to dinner when he returned. Couldn't Amory take luncheon with her?

"I thought I'd better catch up, Mrs. Lawrence," he said rather ambiguously when he arrived.

"Monsignor was here just last week," said Mrs. Lawrence regretfully. "He was very anxious to see you, but he'd left your address at home."

"Did he think I'd plunged into Bolshevism?" asked Amory, interested.

"Oh, he's having a frightful time."

"Why?"

"About the Irish Republic. He thinks it lacks dignity."

"So?"

"He went to Boston when the Irish President arrived and he was greatly distressed because the receiving committee, when they rode in an automobile, *would* put their arms around the President."

"I don't blame him."

"Well, what impressed you more than anything while you were in the army? You look a great deal older."

"That's from another, more disastrous battle," he answered, smiling in spite of himself. "But the army—let me see—well, I discovered that physical courage depends to a great extent on the physical shape a man is in. I found that I was as brave as the next man—it used to worry me before."

"What else?"

"Well, the idea that men can stand anything if they get used to it, and the fact that I got a high mark in the psychological examination."

Mrs. Lawrence laughed. Amory was finding it a great relief to be in this cool house on Riverside Drive, away from more condensed New York and the sense of people expelling great quantities of breath into a little space. Mrs. Lawrence reminded him vaguely of Beatrice, not in temperament, but in her perfect grace and dignity. The house, its furnishings, the manner in which dinner was served, were in immense contrast to what he had met in the great places on Long Island, where the servants were so obtrusive that they had positively to be bumped out of the way, or even in the houses of more conservative "Union Club" families. He wondered if this air of symmetrical restraint, this grace, which he felt was continental, was distilled through Mrs. Lawrence's New England ancestry or acquired in long residence in Italy and Spain.

Two glasses of sauterne at luncheon loosened his tongue, and he talked, with what he felt was something of his old charm, of religion and literature and the menacing phenomena of the social order. Mrs. Lawrence was ostensibly pleased with him, and her interest was especially in his mind; he wanted people to like his mind again—after a while it might be such a nice place in which to live.

"Monsignor Darcy still thinks that you're his reincarnation, that your faith will eventually clarify."

"Perhaps," he assented. "I'm rather pagan at present. It's just that religion doesn't seem to have the slightest bearing on life at my age."

When he left her house he walked down Riverside Drive with a feeling of satisfaction. It was amusing to discuss again such subjects as this young poet, Stephen Vincent Benét, or the Irish Republic. Between the rancid accusations of Edward Carson and Justice Cohalan he had completely tired of the Irish question; yet there had been a time when his own Celtic traits were pillars of his personal philosophy.

There seemed suddenly to be much left in life, if only this revival of old interests did not mean that he was backing away from it again—backing away from life itself.

Restlessness

"I'm tres old and tres bored, Tom," said Amory one day, stretching himself at ease in the comfortable window-seat. He always felt most natural in a recumbent position.

"You used to be entertaining before you started to write," he continued. "Now you save any idea that you think would do to print."

Existence had settled back to an ambitionless normality. They had decided that with economy they could still afford the apartment, which Tom, with the domesticity of an elderly cat, had grown fond of. The old English hunting prints on the wall were Tom's, and the large tapestry by courtesy, a relic of decadent days in college, and the great profusion of orphaned candlesticks and the carved Louis XV chair in which no one could sit more than a minute without acute spinal disorders—Tom claimed that this was because one was sitting in the lap of Montespan's wraith—at any rate, it was Tom's furniture that decided them to stay.

They went out very little: to an occasional play, or to dinner at the Ritz or the Princeton Club. With prohibition the great rendezvous had received their death wounds; no longer could one wander to the Biltmore bar at twelve or five and find congenial spirits, and both Tom and Amory had outgrown the passion for dancing with mid-Western or New

Jersey debbies at the Club-de-Vingt (surnamed the "Club de Gink") or the Plaza Rose Room—besides even that required several cocktails "to come down to the intellectual level of the women present," as Amory had once put it to a horrified matron.

Amory had lately received several alarming letters from Mr. Barton—the Lake Geneva house was too large to be easily rented; the best rent obtainable at present would serve this year to little more than pay for the taxes and necessary improvements; in fact, the lawyer suggested that the whole property was simply a white elephant on Amory's hands. Nevertheless, even though it might not yield a cent for the next three years, Amory decided with a vague sentimentality that for the present, at any rate, he would not sell the house.

This particular day on which he announced his ennui to Tom had been quite typical. He had risen at noon, lunched with Mrs. Lawrence, and then ridden abstractedly homeward atop one of his beloved buses.

"Why shouldn't you be bored," yawned Tom. "Isn't that the conventional frame of mind for the young man of your age and condition?"

"Yes," said Amory speculatively, "but I'm more than bored; I am restless."

"Love and war did for you."

"Well," Amory considered, "I'm not sure that the war itself had any great effect on either you or me—but it certainly ruined the old backgrounds, sort of killed individualism out of our generation."

Tom looked up in surprise.

"Yes it did," insisted Amory. "I'm not sure it didn't kill it out of the whole world. Oh, Lord, what a pleasure it used to be to dream I might be a really great dictator or writer or religious or political leader—and now even a Leonardo da Vinci or Lorenzo de Medici couldn't be a real old-fashioned bolt in the world. Life is too huge and complex. The world is so overgrown that it can't lift its own fingers, and I was planning to be such an important finger——"

"I don't agree with you," Tom interrupted. "There never were men placed in such egotistic positions since—oh, since the French Revolution."

Amory disagreed violently.

"You're mistaking this period when every nut is an individualist for a period of individualism. Wilson has only been powerful when he has represented; he's had to compromise over and over again. Just as soon as Trotsky and Lenine take a definite, consistent stand they'll become merely two-minute figures like Kerensky. Even Foch hasn't half the significance of Stonewall Jackson. War used to be the most individualistic pursuit of man, and yet the popular heroes of the war had neither authority nor responsibility: Guynemer and Sergeant York. How could a schoolboy make a hero of Pershing? A big man has no time really to do anything but just sit and be big."

"Then you don't think there will be any more permanent world heroes?"

"Yes—in history—not in life. Carlyle would have difficulty getting material for a new chapter on 'The Hero as a Big Man.' "

"Go on. I'm a good listener to-day."

"People try so hard to believe in leaders now, pitifully hard. But we no sooner get a popular reformer or politician or soldier or writer or philosopher—a Roosevelt, a Tolstoi, a Wood, a Shaw, a Nietzsche, than the cross-currents of criticism wash him away. My Lord, no man can stand prominence these days. It's the surest path to obscurity. People get sick of hearing the same name over and over."

"Then you blame it on the press?"

"Absolutely. Look at you; you're on The New Democracy, considered the most brilliant weekly in the country, read by the men who do things and all that. What's your business? Why, to be as clever, as interesting, and as brilliantly cynical as possible about every man, doctrine, book, or policy that is assigned you to deal with. The more strong lights, the more spiritual scandal you can throw on the matter, the more money they pay you, the more the people buy the issue. You, Tom d'Invilliers, a blighted Shelley, changing, shifting, clever, unscrupulous, represent the critical consciousness of the race— Oh, don't protest, I know the stuff. I used to write book reviews in college; I considered it rare sport to refer to the latest honest, conscientious effort to propound a theory or a remedy as a 'welcome addition to our light summer reading.' Come on now, admit it."

Tom laughed, and Amory continued triumphantly.

"We *want* to believe. Young students try to believe in older authors, constituents try to believe in their Congressmen, countries try to believe in their statesmen, but they *can't*. Too many voices, too much scattered, illogical, ill-considered criticism. It's worse in the case of newspapers. Any rich, unprogressive old party with that particularly grasping, acquisitive form of mentality known as financial genius can own a paper that is the intellectual meat and drink of thousands of tired, hurried men, men too involved in the business of modern living to swallow anything but predigested food. For two cents the voter buys his politics, prejudices, and philosophy. A year later there is a new political ring or a change in the paper's ownership, consequence: more confusion, more contradiction, a sudden inrush of new ideas, their tempering, their distillation, the reaction against them——"

He paused only to get his breath.

"And that is why I have sworn not to put pen to paper until my ideas either clarify or depart entirely; I have quite enough sins on my soul without putting dangerous, shallow epigrams into people's heads; I might cause a poor, inoffensive capitalist to have a vulgar liaison with a bomb, or get some innocent little Bolshevik tangled up with a machine-gun bullet——"

Tom was growing restless under this lampooning of his connection with *The New Democracy*.

"What's all this got to do with your being bored?"

Amory considered that it had much to do with it.

"How'll I fit in?" he demanded. "What am I for? To propagate the race? According to the American novels we are led to believe that the 'healthy American boy' from nineteen to twenty-five is an entirely sexless animal. As a matter of fact, the healthier he is the less that's true. The only alternative to letting it get you is some violent interest. Well, the war is over; I believe too much in the responsibilities of authorship to write just now; and business, well, business speaks for itself. It has no connection with anything in the world that I've ever been interested in, except a slim, utilitarian connection with economics. What I'd see of it, lost in a clerkship, for the next and best ten years of my life would have the intellectual content of an industrial movie."

"Try fiction," suggested Tom.

"Trouble is I get distracted when I start to write stories—get afraid I'm doing it instead of living—get thinking maybe life is waiting for me in the Japanese gardens at the Ritz or at Atlantic City or on the lower East Side.

"Anyway," he continued, "I haven't the vital urge. I wanted to be a regular human being but the girl couldn't see it that way."

"You'll find another."

"God! Banish the thought. Why don't you tell me that 'if the girl had been worth having she'd have waited for you'? No, sir, the girl really worth having won't wait for anybody. If I thought there'd be another I'd lose my remaining faith in human nature. Maybe I'll play—but Rosalind was the only girl in the wide world that could have held me."

"Well," yawned Tom, "I've played confidant a good hour by the clock. Still, I'm glad to see you're beginning to have violent views again on something."

"I am," agreed Amory reluctantly. "Yet when I see a happy family it makes me sick at my stomach——"

"Happy families try to make people feel that way," said Tom cynically.

Tom the Censor

There were days when Amory listened. These were when Tom, wreathed in smoke, indulged in the slaughter of American literature. Words failed him.

"Fifty thousand dollars a year," he would cry. "My God! Look at them, look at them—Edna Ferber, Gouverneur Morris, Fanny Hurst, Mary Roberts Rinehart—not producing among 'em one story or novel that will last ten years. This man Cobb—I don't think he's either clever or amusing—and what's more, I don't think very many people do, except the editors. He's just groggy with advertising. And—oh Harold Bell Wright oh Zane Grey——"

"They try."

"No, they don't even try. Some of them *can* write, but they won't sit down and do one honest novel. Most of them *can't* write, I'll admit. I believe Rupert Hughes tries to give a real, comprehensive picture of American life, but his style and perspective are barbarous. Ernest Poole and Dorothy Canfield try but they're hindered by their absolute lack of any sense of humor; but at least they crowd their work instead of spreading it thin. Every author ought to write every book as if he were going to be beheaded the day he finished it."

"Is that double entente?"

"Don't slow me up! Now there's a few of 'em that seem to have some cultural background, some intelligence and a good deal of literary felicity but they just simply won't write honestly; they'd all claim there was no public for good stuff. Then why the devil is it that Wells, Conrad, Galsworthy, Shaw, Bennett, and the rest depend on America for over half their sales?"

"How does little Tommy like the poets?"

Tom was overcome. He dropped his arms until they swung loosely beside the chair and emitted faint grunts.

"I'm writing a satire on 'em now, calling it 'Boston Bards and Hearst Reviewers.' "

"Let's hear it," said Amory eagerly.

"I've only got the last few lines done."

"That's very modern. Let's hear 'em, if they're funny."

Tom produced a folded paper from his pocket and read aloud, pausing at intervals so that Amory could see that it was free verse:

"So
Walter Arensberg,
Alfred Kreymborg,
Carl Sandburg,
Louis Untermeyer,
Eunice Tietjens,
Clara Shanafelt,
James Oppenheim,
Maxwell Bodenheim,
Richard Glaenzer,
Scharmel Iris,

Conrad Aiken,
I place your names here
So that you may live
If only as names,
Sinuous, mauve-colored names,
In the Juvenilia
Of my collected editions."

Amory roared.

"You win the iron pansy. I'll buy you a meal on the arrogance of the last two lines."

Amory did not entirely agree with Tom's sweeping damnation of American novelists and poets. He enjoyed both Vachel Lindsay and Booth Tarkington, and admired the conscientious, if slender, artistry of Edgar Lee Masters.

"What I hate is this idiotic drivel about 'I am God—I am man—I ride the winds—I look through the smoke—I am the life sense.' "

"It's ghastly!"

"And I wish American novelists would give up trying to make business romantically interesting. Nobody wants to read about it, unless it's crooked business. If it was an entertaining subject they'd buy the life of James J. Hill and not one of these long office tragedies that harp along on the significance of smoke——"

"And gloom," said Tom. "That's another favorite, though I'll admit the Russians have the monopoly. Our specialty is stories about little girls who break their spines and get adopted by grouchy old men because they smile so much. You'd think we were a race of cheerful cripples and that the common end of the Russian peasant was suicide——"

"Six o'clock," said Amory, glancing at his wrist-watch. "I'll buy you a grea' big dinner on the strength of the Juvenilia of your collected editions."

Looking Backward

July sweltered out with a last hot week, and Amory in another surge of unrest realized that it was just five months since he and Rosalind had met. Yet it was already hard for him to visualize the heart-whole boy who had stepped off the transport, passionately desiring the adventure of life. One night while the heat, overpowering and enervating, poured into the windows of his room he struggled for several hours in a vague effort to immortalize the poignancy of that time.

The February streets, wind-washed by night, blow full of strange half-intermittent damps, bearing on wasted walks in shining sight wet snow plashed into gleams under the lamps, like golden oil from some divine machine, in an hour of thaw and stars.

Strange damps—full of the eyes of many men, crowded with life borne in upon a lull. . . . Oh, I was young, for I could turn again to you, most finite and most beautiful, and taste the stuff of half-remembered dreams, sweet and new on your mouth.

. . . There was a tanging in the midnight air—silence was dead and sound not yet awoken— Life cracked like ice!—one brilliant note and there, radiant and pale, you stood . . . and spring had broken. (The icicles were short upon the roofs and the changeling city swooned.)

Our thoughts were frosty mist along the eaves; our two ghosts kissed, high on the long, mazed wires—eerie half-laughter echoes here and leaves only a fatuous sigh for young desires; regret has followed after things she loved, leaving the great husk.

Another Ending

In mid-August came a letter from Monsignor Darcy, who had evidently just stumbled on his address:

My dear Boy:—

Your last letter was quite enough to make me worry about you. It was not a bit like yourself. Reading between the lines I should imagine that your engagement to this girl is making you rather unhappy, and I see you have lost all the feeling of romance that you had before the war. You make a great mistake if you think you can be romantic without religion. Sometimes I think that with both of us the secret of success, when we find it, is the mystical element in us: something flows into us that enlarges our personalities, and when it ebbs out our personalities shrink; I should call your last two letters rather shrivelled. Beware of losing yourself in the personality of another being, man or woman.

His Eminence Cardinal O'Neill and the Bishop of Boston are staying with me at present, so it is hard for me to get a moment to write, but I wish you would come up here later if only for a week-end. I go to Washington this week.

What I shall do in the future is hanging in the balance. Absolutely between ourselves I should not be surprised to see the red hat of a cardinal descend upon my unworthy head within the next eight months. In any event, I should like to have a house in New York or Washington where you could drop in for week-ends.

Amory, I'm very glad we're both alive; this war could easily have been the end of a brilliant family. But in regard to matrimony, you are now at the most dangerous period of your life. You might marry in haste and repent at leisure, but I think you won't. From what you write me about the present calamitous state of your finances, what you want is naturally impossible. However, if I judge you by the means I usually choose, I should say that there will be something of an emotional crisis within the next year.

Do write me. I feel annoyingly out of date on you.

With greatest affection,

THAYER DARCY.

Within a week after the receipt of this letter their little household fell precipitously to pieces. The immediate cause was the serious and probably chronic illness of Tom's mother. So they stored the furniture, gave instructions to sublet and shook hands gloomily in the Pennsylvania Station. Amory and Tom seemed always to be saying good-by.

Feeling very much alone, Amory yielded to an impulse and set off southward, intending to join Monsignor in Washington. They missed connections by two hours, and, deciding to spend a few days with an ancient, remembered uncle, Amory journeyed up through the luxuriant fields of Maryland into Ramilly County. But instead of two days his stay lasted from mid-August nearly through September, for in Maryland he met Eleanor.

CHAPTER III

Young Irony

FOR YEARS afterward when Amory thought of Eleanor he seemed still to hear the wind sobbing around him and sending little chills into the places beside his heart. The night when they rode up the slope and watched the cold moon float through the clouds, he lost a further part of him that nothing could restore; and when he lost it he lost also the power of regretting it. Eleanor was, say, the last time that evil crept close to Amory under the mask of beauty, the last weird mystery that held him with wild fascination and pounded his soul to flakes.

With her his imagination ran riot and that is why they rode to the highest hill and watched an evil moon ride high, for they knew then that they could see the devil in each other. But Eleanor—did Amory dream her? Afterward their ghosts played, yet both of them hoped from their souls never to meet. Was it the infinite sadness of her eyes that drew him or the mirror of himself that he found in the gorgeous clarity of her mind? She will have no other adventure like Amory, and if she reads this she will say:

"And Amory will have no other adventure like me."

Nor will she sigh, any more than he would sigh.

Eleanor tried to put it on paper once:

"The fading things we only know
  We'll have forgotten . . .
    Put away . . .
Desires that melted with the snow,
  And dreams begotten
    This to-day:
The sudden dawns we laughed to greet,
  That all could see, that none could share,
Will be but dawns . . . and if we meet
  We shall not care.

Dear . . . not one tear will rise for this . . .
A little while hence
No regret
Will stir for a remembered kiss—
Not even silence,
When we've met,
Will give old ghosts a waste to roam,
Or stir the surface of the sea . . .
If gray shapes drift beneath the foam
We shall not see."

They quarrelled dangerously because Amory maintained that *sea* and *see* couldn't possibly be used as a rhyme. And then Eleanor had part of another verse that she couldn't find a beginning for:

". . . But wisdom passes . . . still the years
Will feed us wisdom. . . . Age will go
Back to the old— For all our tears
We shall not know."

Eleanor hated Maryland passionately. She belonged to the oldest of the old families of Ramilly County and lived in a big, gloomy house with her grandfather. She had been born and brought up in France. . . . I see I am starting wrong. Let me begin again.

Amory was bored, as he usually was in the country. He used to go for far walks by himself—and wander along reciting "Ulalume" to the corn-fields, and congratulating Poe for drinking himself to death in that atmosphere of smiling complacency. One afternoon he had strolled for several miles along a road that was new to him, and then through a wood on bad advice from a colored woman . . . losing himself entirely. A passing storm decided to break out, and to his great impatience the sky grew black as pitch and the rain began to splatter down through the trees, become suddenly furtive and ghostly. Thunder rolled with menacing crashes up the valley and scattered through the woods in intermittent batteries. He stumbled blindly on, hunting for a way out, and finally, through webs of twisted branches, caught sight of a rift in the trees where the unbroken lightning showed open country. He rushed to the edge of the woods and then hesitated whether or not to cross the fields and try to reach the shelter of the little house marked by a light far down the valley. It was only half past five, but he could see scarcely ten steps before him, except when the lightning made everything vivid and grotesque for great sweeps around.

Suddenly a strange sound fell on his ears. It was a song, in a low, husky voice, a girl's voice, and whoever was singing was very close to him. A year before he might have laughed, or trembled; but in his restless mood he only stood and listened while the words sank into his consciousness:

"Les sanglots longs
Des violons
De l'automne
Blessent mon cœur
D'une langueur
Monotone."

The lightning split the sky, but the song went on without a quaver. The girl was evidently in the field and the voice seemed to come vaguely from a haystack about twenty feet in front of him.

Then it ceased; ceased and began again in a weird chant that soared and hung and fell and blended with the rain:

"Tout suffocant
Et blême quand
Sonne l'heure
Je me souviens
Des jours anciens
Et je pleure. . . ."

"Who the devil is there in Ramilly County," muttered Amory aloud, "who would deliver Verlaine in an extemporaneous tune to a soaking haystack?"

"Somebody's there!" cried the voice unalarmed. "Who are you?—Manfred, St. Christopher, or Queen Victoria?"

"I'm Don Juan!" Amory shouted on impulse, raising his voice above the noise of the rain and the wind.

A delighted shriek came from the haystack.

"I know who you are—you're the blond boy that likes 'Ulalume'—I recognize your voice."

"How do I get up?" he cried from the foot of the haystack, whither he had arrived, dripping wet. A head appeared over the edge—it was so dark that Amory could just make out a patch of damp hair and two eyes that gleamed like a cat's.

"Run back!" came the voice, "and jump and I'll catch your hand—no, not there—on the other side."

He followed directions and as he sprawled up the side, knee-deep in hay, a small, white hand reached out, gripped his, and helped him onto the top.

"Here you are, Juan," cried she of the damp hair. "Do you mind if I drop the Don?"

"You've got a thumb like mine!" he exclaimed.

"And you're holding my hand, which is dangerous without seeing my face." He dropped it quickly.

As if in answer to his prayers came a flash of lightning and he looked eagerly at her who stood beside him on the soggy haystack, ten feet above the ground. But she had covered her face and he saw nothing but a slender figure, dark, damp, bobbed hair, and the small white hands with the thumbs that bent back like his.

"Sit down," she suggested politely, as the dark closed in on them. "If you'll sit opposite me in this hollow you can have half of the raincoat, which I was using as a water-proof tent until you so rudely interrupted me."

"I was asked," Amory said joyfully; "you asked me—you know you did."

"Don Juan always manages that," she said, laughing, "but I shan't call you that any more, because you've got reddish hair. Instead you can recite 'Ulalume' and I'll be Psyche, your soul."

Amory flushed, happily invisible under the curtain of wind and rain. They were sitting opposite each other in a slight hollow in the hay with the raincoat spread over most of them, and the rain doing for the rest. Amory was trying desperately to see Psyche, but the lightning refused to flash again, and he waited impatiently. Good Lord! supposing she wasn't beautiful—supposing she was forty and pedantic—heavens! Suppose, only suppose, she was mad. But he knew the last was unworthy. Here had Providence sent a girl to amuse him just as it sent Benvenuto Cellini men to murder, and he was wondering if she was mad, just because she exactly filled his mood.

"I'm not," she said.

"Not what?"

"Not mad. I didn't think you were mad when I first saw you, so it isn't fair that you should think so of me."

"How on earth——"

As long as they knew each other Eleanor and Amory could be "on a subject" and stop talking with the definite thought of it in their heads, yet ten minutes later speak aloud and find that their minds had followed the same channels and led them each to a parallel idea, an idea that others would have found absolutely unconnected with the first.

"Tell me," he demanded, leaning forward eagerly, "how do you know about 'Ulalume'—how did you know the color of my hair? What's your name? What were you doing here? Tell me all at once!"

Suddenly the lightning flashed in with a leap of overreaching light and he saw Eleanor, and looked for the first time into those eyes of hers. Oh, she was magnificent—pale skin, the color of marble in starlight, slender brows, and eyes that glittered green as emeralds in the blinding glare. She was a witch, of perhaps nineteen, he judged, alert and dreamy and with the tell-tale white line over her upper lip that was a weakness and a delight. He sank back with a gasp against the wall of hay.

"Now you've seen me," she said calmly, "and I suppose you're about to say that my green eyes are burning into your brain."

"What color is your hair?" he asked intently. "It's bobbed, isn't it?"

"Yes, it's bobbed. I don't know what color it is," she answered, musing, "so many men have asked me. It's medium, I suppose— No one ever looks long at my hair. I've got beautiful eyes, though, haven't I. I don't care what you say, I have beautiful eyes."

"Answer my question, Madeline."

"Don't remember them all—besides my name isn't Madeline, it's Eleanor."

"I might have guessed it. You *look* like Eleanor—you have that Eleanor look. You know what I mean."

There was a silence as they listened to the rain.

"It's going down my neck, fellow lunatic," she offered finally.

"Answer my questions."

"Well—name of Savage, Eleanor; live in big old house mile down road; nearest living relation to be notified, grandfather—Ramilly Savage; height, five feet four inches; number on watch-case, 3077 W; nose, delicate aquiline; temperament, uncanny——"

"And me," Amory interrupted, "where did you see me?"

"Oh, you're one of *those* men," she answered haughtily, "must lug old self into conversation. Well, my boy, I was behind a hedge sunning myself one day last week, and along comes a man saying in a pleasant, conceited way of talking:

" 'And now when the night was senescent'
(says he)
'And the star dials pointed to morn
At the end of the path a liquescent'
(says he)
'And nebulous lustre was born.'

So I poked my eyes up over the hedge, but you had started to run, for some unknown reason, and so I saw but the back of your beautiful head. 'Oh!' says I, 'there's a man for whom many of us might sigh,' and I continued in my best Irish——"

"All right," Amory interrupted. "Now go back to yourself."

"Well, I will. I'm one of those people who go through the world giving other people thrills, but getting few myself except those I read into men on such nights as these. I have the social courage to go on the stage, but not the energy; I haven't the patience to write books; and I never met a man I'd marry. However, I'm only eighteen."

The storm was dying down softly and only the wind kept

up its ghostly surge and made the stack lean and gravely settle from side to side. Amory was in a trance. He felt that every moment was precious. He had never met a girl like this before—she would never seem quite the same again. He didn't at all feel like a character in a play, the appropriate feeling in an unconventional situation—instead, he had a sense of coming home.

"I have just made a great decision," said Eleanor after another pause, "and that is why I'm here, to answer another of your questions. I have just decided that I don't believe in immortality."

"Really! how banal!"

"Frightfully so," she answered, "but depressing with a stale, sickly depression, nevertheless. I came out here to get wet—like a wet hen; wet hens always have great clarity of mind," she concluded.

"Go on," Amory said politely.

"Well—I'm not afraid of the dark, so I put on my slicker and rubber boots and came out. You see I was always afraid, before, to say I didn't believe in God—because the lightning might strike me—but here I am and it hasn't, of course, but the main point is that this time I wasn't any more afraid of it than I had been when I was a Christian Scientist, like I was last year. So now I know I'm a materialist and I was fraternizing with the hay when you came out and stood by the woods, scared to death."

"Why, you little wretch—" cried Amory indignantly. "Scared of what?"

"*Yourself!*" she shouted, and he jumped. She clapped her hands and laughed. "See—see! Conscience—kill it like me! Eleanor Savage, materiologist—no jumping, no starting, come early——"

"But I *have* to have a soul," he objected. "I can't be rational—and I won't be molecular."

She leaned toward him, her burning eyes never leaving his own and whispered with a sort of romantic finality:

"I thought so, Juan, I feared so—you're sentimental. You're not like me. I'm a romantic little materialist."

"I'm not sentimental—I'm as romantic as you are. The idea, you know, is that the sentimental person thinks things will last—the romantic person has a desperate confidence that they won't." (This was an ancient distinction of Amory's.)

"Epigrams. I'm going home," she said sadly. "Let's get off the haystack and walk to the cross-roads."

They slowly descended from their perch. She would not let him help her down and motioning him away arrived in a graceful lump in the soft mud where she sat for an instant, laughing at herself. Then she jumped to her feet and slipped her hand into his, and they tiptoed across the fields, jumping and swinging from dry spot to dry spot. A transcendent delight seemed to sparkle in every pool of water, for the moon had risen and the storm had scurried away into western Maryland. When Eleanor's arm touched his he felt his hands grow cold with deadly fear lest he should lose the shadow brush with which his imagination was painting wonders of her. He watched her from the corners of his eyes as ever he did when he walked with her—she was a feast and a folly and he wished it had been his destiny to sit forever on a haystack and see life through her green eyes. His paganism soared that night and when she faded out like a gray ghost down the road, a deep singing came out of the fields and filled his way homeward. All night the summer moths flitted in and out of Amory's window; all night large looming sounds swayed in mystic revery through the silver grain—and he lay awake in the clear darkness.

September

Amory selected a blade of grass and nibbled at it scientifically.

"I never fall in love in August or September," he proffered.

"When then?"

"Christmas or Easter. I'm a liturgist."

"Easter!" She turned up her nose. "Huh! Spring in corsets!"

"Easter *would* bore spring, wouldn't she? Easter has her hair braided, wears a tailored suit."

> "Bind on thy sandals, oh, thou most fleet.
> Over the splendor and speed of thy feet——"

quoted Eleanor softly, and then added: "I suppose Hallowe'en is a better day for autumn than Thanksgiving."

"Much better—and Christmas eve does very well for winter, but summer . . ."

"Summer has no day," she said. "We can't possibly have a summer love. So many people have tried that the name's become proverbial. Summer is only the unfulfilled promise of spring, a charlatan in place of the warm balmy nights I dream of in April. It's a sad season of life without growth. . . . It has no day."

"Fourth of July," Amory suggested facetiously.

"Don't be funny!" she said, raking him with her eyes.

"Well, what could fulfil the promise of spring?"

She thought a moment.

"Oh, I suppose heaven would, if there was one," she said finally, "a sort of pagan heaven—you ought to be a materialist," she continued irrelevantly.

"Why?"

"Because you look a good deal like the pictures of Rupert Brooke."

To some extent Amory tried to play Rupert Brooke as long as he knew Eleanor. What he said, his attitude toward life, toward her, toward himself, were all reflexes of the dead Englishman's literary moods. Often she sat in the grass, a lazy wind playing with her short hair, her voice husky as she ran up and down the scale from Grantchester to Waikiki. There was something most passionate in Eleanor's reading aloud. They seemed nearer, not only mentally, but physically, when they read, than when she was in his arms, and this was often, for they fell half into love almost from the first. Yet was Amory capable of love now? He could, as always, run through the emotions in a half hour, but even while they revelled in their imaginations, he knew that neither of them could care as he had cared once before—I suppose that was why they turned to Brooke, and Swinburne, and Shelley. Their chance was to make everything fine and finished and rich and imaginative; they must bend tiny golden tentacles from his imagination to hers, that would take the place of the great, deep love that was never so near, yet never so much of a dream.

One poem they read over and over; Swinburne's "Triumph

of Time," and four lines of it rang in his memory afterward on warm nights when he saw the fireflies among dusky tree trunks and heard the low drone of many frogs. Then Eleanor seemed to come out of the night and stand by him, and he heard her throaty voice, with its tone of a fleecy-headed drum, repeating:

> *"Is it worth a tear, is it worth an hour,*
> *To think of things that are well outworn;*
> *Of fruitless husk and fugitive flower,*
> *The dream foregone and the deed foreborne?"*

They were formally introduced two days later, and his aunt told him her history. The Ramillys were two: old Mr. Ramilly and his granddaughter, Eleanor. She had lived in France with a restless mother whom Amory imagined to have been very like his own, on whose death she had come to America, to live in Maryland. She had gone to Baltimore first to stay with a bachelor uncle, and there she insisted on being a débutante at the age of seventeen. She had a wild winter and arrived in the country in March, having quarrelled frantically with all her Baltimore relatives, and shocked them into fiery protest. A rather fast crowd had come out, who drank cocktails in limousines and were promiscuously condescending and patronizing toward older people, and Eleanor with an esprit that hinted strongly of the boulevards, led many innocents still redolent of St. Timothy's and Farmington, into paths of Bohemian naughtiness. When the story came to her uncle, a forgetful cavalier of a more hypocritical era, there was a scene, from which Eleanor emerged, subdued but rebellious and indignant, to seek haven with her grandfather who hovered in the country on the near side of senility. That's as far as her story went; she told him the rest herself, but that was later.

Often they swam and as Amory floated lazily in the water he shut his mind to all thoughts except those of hazy soap-bubble lands where the sun splattered through wind-drunk trees. How could any one possibly think or worry, or do anything except splash and dive and loll there on the edge of time while the flower months failed. Let the days move over—sadness and memory and pain recurred outside, and here, once more, before he went on to meet them he wanted to drift and be young.

There were days when Amory resented that life had changed from an even progress along a road stretching ever in sight, with the scenery merging and blending, into a succession of quick, unrelated scenes—two years of sweat and blood, that sudden absurd instinct for paternity that Rosalind had stirred; the half-sensual, half-neurotic quality of this autumn with Eleanor. He felt that it would take all time, more than he could ever spare, to glue these strange cumbersome pictures into the scrap-book of his life. It was all like a banquet where he sat for this half-hour of his youth and tried to enjoy brilliant epicurean courses.

Dimly he promised himself a time where all should be welded together. For months it seemed that he had alternated between being borne along a stream of love or fascination, or left in an eddy, and in the eddies he had not desired to think, rather to be picked up on a wave's top and swept along again.

"The despairing, dying autumn and our love—how well they harmonize!" said Eleanor sadly one day as they lay dripping by the water.

"The Indian summer of our hearts—" he ceased.

"Tell me," she said finally, "was she light or dark?"

"Light."

"Was she more beautiful than I am?"

"I don't know," said Amory shortly.

One night they walked while the moon rose and poured a great burden of glory over the garden until it seemed fairyland with Amory and Eleanor, dim phantasmal shapes, expressing eternal beauty in curious elfin love moods. Then they turned out of the moonlight into the trellised darkness of a vine-hung pagoda, where there were scents so plaintive as to be nearly musical.

"Light a match," she whispered. "I want to see you."

Scratch! Flare!

The night and the scarred trees were like scenery in a play, and to be there with Eleanor, shadowy and unreal, seemed somehow oddly familiar. Amory thought how it was only the past that ever seemed strange and unbelievable. The match went out.

"It's black as pitch."

"We're just voices now," murmured Eleanor, "little lonesome voices. Light another."

"That was my last match."

Suddenly he caught her in his arms.

"You *are* mine—you know you're mine!" he cried wildly . . . the moonlight twisted in through the vines and listened . . . the fireflies hung upon their whispers as if to win his glance from the glory of their eyes.

THE END OF SUMMER

"No wind is stirring in the grass; not one wind stirs . . . the water in the hidden pools, as glass, fronts the full moon and so inters the golden token in its icy mass," chanted Eleanor to the trees that skeletoned the body of the night. "Isn't it ghostly here? If you can hold your horse's feet up, let's cut through the woods and find the hidden pools."

"It's after one, and you'll get the devil," he objected, "and I don't know enough about horses to put one away in the pitch dark."

"Shut up, you old fool," she whispered irrelevantly, and, leaning over, she patted him lazily with her riding-crop. "You can leave your old plug in our stable and I'll send him over to-morrow."

"But my uncle has got to drive me to the station with this old plug at seven o'clock."

"Don't be a spoil-sport—remember, you have a tendency toward wavering that prevents you from being the entire light of my life."

Amory drew his horse up close beside, and, leaning toward her, grasped her hand.

"Say I am—*quick*, or I'll pull you over and make you ride behind me."

She looked up and smiled and shook her head excitedly.

"Oh, do!—or rather, don't! Why are all the exciting things so uncomfortable, like fighting and exploring and ski-ing in Canada? By the way, we're going to ride up Harper's Hill. I think that comes in our programme about five o'clock."

"You little devil," Amory growled. "You're going to make

me stay up all night and sleep in the train like an immigrant all day to-morrow, going back to New York."

"Hush! some one's coming along the road—let's go! *Whoo-ee-oop!*" And with a shout that probably gave the belated traveller a series of shivers, she turned her horse into the woods and Amory followed slowly, as he had followed her all day for three weeks.

The summer was over, but he had spent the days in watching Eleanor, a graceful, facile Manfred, build herself intellectual and imaginative pyramids while she revelled in the artificialities of the temperamental teens and they wrote poetry at the dinner-table.

When Vanity kissed Vanity, a hundred happy Junes ago, he pondered o'er her breathlessly, and, that all men might ever know, he rhymed her eyes with life and death:

"Thru Time I'll save my love!" he said . . . yet Beauty vanished with his breath, and, with her lovers, she was dead . . .

—Ever his wit and not her eyes, ever his art and not her hair:

"Who'd learn a trick in rhyme, be wise and pause before his sonnet there" . . . So all my words, however true, might sing you to a thousandth June, and no one ever *know* that you were Beauty for an afternoon.

So he wrote one day, when he pondered how coldly we thought of the "Dark Lady of the Sonnets," and how little we remembered her as the great man wanted her remembered. For what Shakespeare *must* have desired, to have been able to write with such divine despair, was that the lady should live . . . and now we have no real interest in her. . . . The irony of it is that if he had cared *more* for the poem than for the lady the sonnet would be only obvious, imitative rhetoric and no one would ever have read it after twenty years. . . .

This was the last night Amory ever saw Eleanor. He was leaving in the morning and they had agreed to take a long farewell trot by the cold moonlight. She wanted to talk, she said—perhaps the last time in her life that she could be rational (she meant pose with comfort). So they had turned into the woods and rode for half an hour with scarcely a word, except when she whispered "Damn!" at a bothersome branch—whispered it as no other girl was ever able to whisper it. Then they started up Harper's Hill, walking their tired horses.

"Good Lord! It's quiet here!" whispered Eleanor; "much more lonesome than the woods."

"I hate woods," Amory said, shuddering. "Any kind of foliage or underbrush at night. Out here it's so broad and easy on the spirit."

"The long slope of a long hill."

"And the cold moon rolling moonlight down it."

"And thee and me, last and most important."

It was quiet that night—the straight road they followed up to the edge of the cliff knew few footsteps at any time. Only an occasional negro cabin, silver-gray in the rock-ribbed moonlight, broke the long line of bare ground; behind lay the black edge of the woods like a dark frosting on white cake, and ahead the sharp, high horizon. It was much colder—so cold that it settled on them and drove all the warm nights from their minds.

"The end of summer," said Eleanor softly. "Listen to the beat of our horses' hoofs—'tump-tump-tump-a-tump.' Have you ever been feverish and had all noises divide into 'tump-tump-tump' until you could swear eternity was divisible into so many tumps? That's the way I feel—old horses go tump-tump. . . . I guess that's the only thing that separates horses and clocks from us. Human beings can't go 'tump-tump-tump' without going crazy."

The breeze freshened and Eleanor pulled her cape around her and shivered.

"Are you very cold?" asked Amory.

"No, I'm thinking about myself—my black old inside self, the real one, with the fundamental honesty that keeps me from being absolutely wicked by making me realize my own sins."

They were riding up close by the cliff and Amory gazed over. Where the fall met the ground a hundred feet below, a black stream made a sharp line, broken by tiny glints in the swift water.

"Rotten, rotten old world," broke out Eleanor suddenly, "and the wretchedest thing of all is me—oh, *why* am I a girl? Why am I not a stupid—? Look at you; you're stupider than I am, not much, but some, and you can lope about and get bored and then lope somewhere else, and you can play around with girls without being involved in meshes of sentiment, and you can do anything and be justified—and here am I with the brains to do everything, yet tied to the sinking ship of future matrimony. If I were born a hundred years from now, well and good, but now what's in store for me—I have to marry, that goes without saying. Who? I'm too bright for most men, and yet I have to descend to their level and let them patronize my intellect in order to get their attention. Every year that I don't marry I've got less chance for a first-class man. At the best I can have my choice from one or two cities and, of course, I have to marry into a dinner-coat.

"Listen," she leaned close again, "I like clever men and good-looking men, and, of course, no one cares more for personality than I do. Oh, just one person in fifty has any glimmer of what sex is. I'm hipped on Freud and all that, but it's rotten that every bit of *real* love in the world is ninety-nine per cent passion and one little soupçon of jealousy." She finished as suddenly as she began.

"Of course, you're right," Amory agreed. "It's a rather unpleasant overpowering force that's part of the machinery under everything. It's like an actor that lets you see his mechanics! Wait a minute till I think this out. . . ."

He paused and tried to get a metaphor. They had turned the cliff and were riding along the road about fifty feet to the left.

"You see every one's got to have some cloak to throw around it. The mediocre intellects, Plato's second class, use the remnants of romantic chivalry diluted with Victorian sentiment—and we who consider ourselves the intellectuals cover it up by pretending that it's another side of us, has nothing to do with our shining brains; we pretend that the fact that we realize it is really absolving us from being a prey to it. But the truth is that sex is right in the middle of our purest abstractions, so close that it obscures vision. . . . I can kiss you now and will. . . ." He leaned toward her in his saddle, but she drew away.

"I can't—I can't kiss you now—I'm more sensitive."

"You're more stupid then," he declared rather impatiently. "Intellect is no protection from sex any more than convention is . . ."

"What is?" she fired up. "The Catholic Church or the maxims of Confucius?"

Amory looked up, rather taken aback.

"That's your panacea, isn't it?" she cried. "Oh, you're just an old hypocrite, too. Thousands of scowling priests keeping the degenerate Italians and illiterate Irish repentant with gabble-gabble about the sixth and ninth commandments. It's just all cloaks, sentiment and spiritual rouge and panaceas. I'll tell you there *is* no God, not even a definite abstract goodness; so it's all got to be worked out for the individual by the individual here in high white foreheads like mine, and you're too much the prig to admit it." She let go her reins and shook her little fists at the stars.

"If there's a God let him strike me—strike me!"

"Talking about God again after the manner of atheists," Amory said sharply. His materialism, always a thin cloak, was torn to shreds by Eleanor's blasphemy. . . . She knew it and it angered him that she knew it.

"And like most intellectuals who don't find faith convenient," he continued coldly, "like Napoleon and Oscar Wilde and the rest of your type, you'll yell loudly for a priest on your death-bed."

Eleanor drew her horse up sharply and he reined in beside her.

"Will I?" she said in a queer voice that scared him. "Will I? Watch! *I'm going over the cliff!*" And before he could interfere she had turned and was riding breakneck for the end of the plateau.

He wheeled and started after her, his body like ice, his nerves in a vast clangor. There was no chance of stopping her. The moon was under a cloud and her horse would step blindly over. Then some ten feet from the edge of the cliff she gave a sudden shriek and flung herself sideways—plunged from her horse and, rolling over twice, landed in a pile of brush five feet from the edge. The horse went over with a frantic whinny. In a minute he was by Eleanor's side and saw that her eyes were open.

"Eleanor!" he cried.

She did not answer, but her lips moved and her eyes filled with sudden tears.

"Eleanor, are you hurt?"

"No; I don't think so," she said faintly, and then began weeping.

"My horse dead?"

"Good God— Yes!"

"Oh!" she wailed. "I thought I was going over. I didn't know——"

He helped her gently to her feet and boosted her onto his saddle. So they started homeward; Amory walking and she bent forward on the pommel, sobbing bitterly.

"I've got a crazy streak," she faltered, "twice before I've done things like that. When I was eleven mother went—went mad—stark raving crazy. We were in Vienna——"

All the way back she talked haltingly about herself, and Amory's love waned slowly with the moon. At her door they started from habit to kiss good night, but she could not run into his arms, nor were they stretched to meet her as in the week before. For a minute they stood there, hating each other with a bitter sadness. But as Amory had loved himself in Eleanor, so now what he hated was only a mirror. Their poses were strewn about the pale dawn like broken glass. The stars were long gone and there were left only the little sighing gusts of wind and the silences between . . . but naked souls are poor things ever, and soon he turned homeward and let new lights come in with the sun.

A Poem that Eleanor Sent Amory Several Years Later

"Here, Earth-born, over the lilt of the water,
   Lisping its music and bearing a burden of light,
Bosoming day as a laughing and radiant daughter . . .
   Here we may whisper unheard, unafraid of the night.
Walking alone . . . was it splendor, or what, we were bound
      with,
   Deep in the time when summer lets down her hair?
Shadows we loved and the patterns they covered the ground
      with
   Tapestries, mystical, faint in the breathless air.

That was the day . . . and the night for another story,
Pale as a dream and shadowed with pencilled trees—
Ghosts of the stars came by who had sought for glory,
Whispered to us of peace in the plaintive breeze,
Whispered of old dead faiths that the day had shattered,
Youth the penny that bought delight of the moon;
That was the urge that we knew and the language that mattered
That was the debt that we paid to the usurer June.

Here, deepest of dreams, by the waters that bring not
Anything back of the past that we need not know,
What if the light is but sun and the little streams sing not,
We are together, it seems . . . I have loved you so . . .
What did the last night hold, with the summer over,
Drawing us back to the home in the changing glade?
What leered out of the dark in the ghostly clover?
God! . . . till you stirred in your sleep . . . and were wild afraid . . .

Well . . . we have passed . . . we are chronicle now to the eerie.
Curious metal from meteors that failed in the sky;
Earth-born the tireless is stretched by the water, quite weary,
Close to this ununderstandable changeling that's I . . .
Fear is an echo we traced to Security's daughter;
Now we are faces and voices . . . and less, too soon,
Whispering half-love over the lilt of the water . . .
Youth the penny that bought delight of the moon."

A Poem Amory Sent to Eleanor and Which He Called "Summer Storm"

"Faint winds, and a song fading and leaves falling,
Faint winds, and far away a fading laughter . . .
And the rain and over the fields a voice calling . . .

Our gray blown cloud scurries and lifts above,
Slides on the sun and flutters there to waft her
Sisters on. The shadow of a dove

Falls on the cote, the trees are filled with wings;
And down the valley through the crying trees
The body of the darker storm flies; brings
With its new air the breath of sunken seas
And slender tenuous thunder . . .
                                        But I wait . . .
Wait for the mists and for the blacker rain—
Heavier winds that stir the veil of fate,
Happier winds that pile her hair;
                                        Again
They tear me, teach me, strew the heavy air
Upon me, winds that I know, and storm.

There was a summer every rain was rare;
There was a season every wind was warm. . . .
And now *you* pass me in the mist . . . your hair
Rain-blown about you, damp lips curved once more
In that wild irony, that gay despair
That made you old when we have met before;
Wraith-like you drift on out before the rain,
Across the fields, blown with the stemless flowers,
With your old hopes, dead leaves and loves again—
Dim as a dream and wan with all old hours
(Whispers will creep into the growing dark . . .
Tumult will die over the trees)
                                        Now night
Tears from her wetted breast the splattered blouse
Of day, glides down the dreaming hills, tear-bright,
To cover with her hair the eerie green . . .
Love for the dusk . . . Love for the glistening after;
Quiet the trees to their last tops . . . serene . . .

Faint winds, and far away a fading laughter . . ."

CHAPTER IV

The Supercilious Sacrifice

ATLANTIC CITY. Amory paced the board walk at day's end, lulled by the everlasting surge of changing waves, smelling the half-mournful odor of the salt breeze. The sea, he thought, had treasured its memories deeper than the faithless land. It seemed still to whisper of Norse galleys ploughing the water world under raven-figured flags, of the British dreadnoughts, gray bulwarks of civilization steaming up through the fog of one dark July into the North Sea.

"Well—Amory Blaine!"

Amory looked down into the street below. A low racing car had drawn to a stop and a familiar cheerful face protruded from the driver's seat.

"Come on down, goopher!" cried Alec.

Amory called a greeting and descending a flight of wooden steps approached the car. He and Alec had been meeting intermittently, but the barrier of Rosalind lay always between them. He was sorry for this; he hated to lose Alec.

"Mr. Blaine, this is Miss Waterson, Miss Wayne, and Mr. Tully."

"How d'y do?"

"Amory," said Alec exuberantly, "if you'll jump in we'll take you to some secluded nook and give you a wee jolt of Bourbon."

Amory considered.

"That's an idea."

"Step in—move over, Jill, and Amory will smile very handsomely at you."

Amory squeezed into the back seat beside a gaudy, vermilion-lipped blonde.

"Hello, Doug Fairbanks," she said flippantly. "Walking for exercise or hunting for company?"

"I was counting the waves," replied Amory gravely. "I'm going in for statistics."

"Don't kid me, Doug."

When they reached an unfrequented side street Alec stopped the car among deep shadows.

"What you doing down here these cold days, Amory?" he demanded, as he produced a quart of Bourbon from under the fur rug.

Amory avoided the question. Indeed, he had had no definite reason for coming to the coast.

"Do you remember that party of ours, sophomore year?" he asked instead.

"Do I? When we slept in the pavilions up in Asbury Park——"

"Lord, Alec! It's hard to think that Jesse and Dick and Kerry are all three dead."

Alec shivered.

"Don't talk about it. These dreary fall days depress me enough."

Jill seemed to agree.

"Doug here is sorta gloomy anyways," she commented. "Tell him to drink deep—it's good and scarce these days."

"What I really want to ask you, Amory, is where you are——"

"Why, New York, I suppose——"

"I mean to-night, because if you haven't got a room yet you'd better help me out."

"Glad to."

"You see, Tully and I have two rooms with bath between at the Ranier, and he's got to go back to New York. I don't want to have to move. Question is, will you occupy one of the rooms?"

Amory was willing, if he could get in right away.

"You'll find the key in the office; the rooms are in my name."

Declining further locomotion or further stimulation, Amory left the car and sauntered back along the board walk to the hotel.

He was in an eddy again, a deep, lethargic gulf, without desire to work or write, love or dissipate. For the first time in his life he rather longed for death to roll over his generation, obliterating their petty fevers and struggles and exultations. His youth seemed never so vanished as now in the contrast between the utter loneliness of this visit and that riotous, joyful party of four years before. Things that had been the merest commonplaces of his life then, deep sleep, the sense of beauty around him, all desire, had flown away and the gaps they left were filled only with the great listlessness of his disillusion.

"To hold a man a woman has to appeal to the worst in him." This sentence was the thesis of most of his bad nights, of which he felt this was to be one. His mind had already started to play variations on the subject. Tireless passion, fierce jealousy, longing to possess and crush—these alone were left of all his love for Rosalind; these remained to him as payment for the loss of his youth—bitter calomel under the thin sugar of love's exaltation.

In his room he undressed and wrapping himself in blankets to keep out the chill October air drowsed in an armchair by the open window.

He remembered a poem he had read months before:

"Oh staunch old heart who toiled so long for me,
I waste my years sailing along the sea——"

Yet he had no sense of waste, no sense of the present hope that waste implied. He felt that life had rejected him.

"Rosalind! Rosalind!" He poured the words softly into the half-darkness until she seemed to permeate the room; the wet salt breeze filled his hair with moisture, the rim of a moon seared the sky and made the curtains dim and ghostly. He fell asleep.

When he awoke it was very late and quiet. The blanket had slipped partly off his shoulders and he touched his skin to find it damp and cold.

Then he became aware of a tense whispering not ten feet away.

He became rigid.

"Don't make a sound!" It was Alec's voice. *"Jill—do you hear me?"*

"Yes—" breathed very low, very frightened. They were in the bathroom.

Then his ears caught a louder sound from somewhere along the corridor outside. It was a mumbling of men's voices and a repeated muffled rapping. Amory threw off the blankets and moved close to the bathroom door.

"My God!" came the girl's voice again. "You'll have to let them in."

"Sh!"

Suddenly a steady, insistent knocking began at Amory's hall door and simultaneously out of the bathroom came Alec, followed by the vermilion-lipped girl. They were both clad in pajamas.

"Amory!" an anxious whisper.

"What's the trouble?"

"It's house detectives. My God, Amory—they're just looking for a test-case——"

"Well, better let them in."

"You don't understand. They can get me under the Mann Act."

The girl followed him slowly, a rather miserable, pathetic figure in the darkness.

Amory tried to plan quickly.

"You make a racket and let them in your room," he suggested anxiously, "and I'll get her out by this door."

"They're here too, though. They'll watch this door."

"Can't you give a wrong name?"

"No chance. I registered under my own name; besides, they'd trail the auto license number."

"Say you're married."

"Jill says one of the house detectives knows her."

The girl had stolen to the bed and tumbled upon it; lay there listening wretchedly to the knocking which had grown gradually to a pounding. Then came a man's voice, angry and imperative:

"Open up or we'll break the door in!"

In the silence when this voice ceased Amory realized that there were other things in the room besides people . . . over and around the figure crouched on the bed there hung an aura, gossamer as a moonbeam, tainted as stale, weak wine, yet a horror, diffusively brooding already over the three of them . . . and over by the window among the stirring curtains stood something else, featureless and indistinguishable, yet strangely familiar. . . . Simultaneously two great cases presented themselves side by side to Amory; all that took place in his mind, then, occupied in actual time less than ten seconds.

The first fact that flashed radiantly on his comprehension was the great impersonality of sacrifice—he perceived that what we call love and hate, reward and punishment, had no more to do with it than the date of the month. He quickly recapitulated the story of a sacrifice he had heard of in college: a man had cheated in an examination; his roommate in a gust of sentiment had taken the entire blame—due to the shame of it the innocent one's entire future seemed shrouded in regret and failure, capped by the ingratitude of the real culprit. He had finally taken his own life—years afterward the facts had come out. At the time the story had both puzzled and worried Amory. Now he realized the truth; that sacrifice was no purchase of freedom. It was like a great elective office, it was like an inheritance of power—to certain people at certain times an essential luxury, carrying with it not a guarantee but a responsibility, not a security but an infinite risk. Its very momentum might drag him down to ruin—the passing of the emotional wave that made it possible might leave the one who made it high and dry forever on an island of despair.

. . . Amory knew that afterward Alec would secretly hate him for having done so much for him. . . .

. . . All this was flung before Amory like an opened scroll, while ulterior to him and speculating upon him were those two breathless, listening forces: the gossamer aura that hung over and about the girl and that familiar thing by the window.

Sacrifice by its very nature was arrogant and impersonal; sacrifice should be eternally supercilious.

Weep not for me but for thy children.

That—thought Amory—would be somehow the way God would talk to me.

Amory felt a sudden surge of joy and then like a face in a motion-picture the aura over the bed faded out; the dynamic shadow by the window, that was as near as he could name it, remained for the fraction of a moment and then the breeze seemed to lift it swiftly out of the room. He clinched his hands in quick ecstatic excitement . . . the ten seconds were up. . . .

"Do what I say, Alec—do what I say. Do you understand?"

Alec looked at him dumbly—his face a tableau of anguish.

"You have a family," continued Amory slowly. "You have a family and it's important that you should get out of this. Do you hear me?" He repeated clearly what he had said. "Do you hear me?"

"I hear you." The voice was curiously strained, the eyes never for a second left Amory's.

"Alec, you're going to lie down here. If any one comes in you act drunk. You do what I say—if you don't I'll probably kill you."

There was another moment while they stared at each other. Then Amory went briskly to the bureau and, taking his pocket-book, beckoned peremptorily to the girl. He heard one word from Alec that sounded like "penitentiary," then he and Jill were in the bathroom with the door bolted behind them.

"You're here with me," he said sternly. "You've been with me all evening."

She nodded, gave a little half cry.

In a second he had the door of the other room open and three men entered. There was an immediate flood of electric light and he stood there blinking.

"You've been playing a little too dangerous a game, young man!"

Amory laughed.

"Well?"

The leader of the trio nodded authoritatively at a burly man in a check suit.

"All right, Olson."

"I got you, Mr. O'May," said Olson, nodding. The other two took a curious glance at their quarry and then withdrew, closing the door angrily behind them.

The burly man regarded Amory contemptuously.

"Didn't you ever hear of the Mann Act? Coming down here with her," he indicated the girl with his thumb, "with a New York license on your car—to a hotel like *this*." He shook his head implying that he had struggled over Amory but now gave him up.

"Well," said Amory rather impatiently, "what do you want us to do?"

"Get dressed, quick—and tell your friend not to make such a racket." Jill was sobbing noisily on the bed, but at these words she subsided sulkily and, gathering up her clothes, retired to the bathroom. As Amory slipped into Alec's B.V.D.'s he found that his attitude toward the situation was agreeably humorous. The aggrieved virtue of the burly man made him want to laugh.

"Anybody else here?" demanded Olson, trying to look keen and ferret-like.

"Fellow who had the rooms," said Amory carelessly. "He's drunk as an owl, though. Been in there asleep since six o'clock."

"I'll take a look at him presently."

"How did you find out?" asked Amory curiously.

"Night clerk saw you go up-stairs with this woman."

Amory nodded; Jill reappeared from the bathroom, completely if rather untidily arrayed.

"Now then," began Olson, producing a note-book, "I want your real names—no damn John Smith or Mary Brown."

"Wait a minute," said Amory quietly. "Just drop that big-bully stuff. We merely got caught, that's all."

Olson glared at him.

"Name?" he snapped.

Amory gave his name and New York address.

"And the lady?"

"Miss Jill——"

"Say," cried Olson indignantly, "just ease up on the nursery rhymes. What's your name? Sarah Murphy? Minnie Jackson?"

"Oh, my God!" cried the girl cupping her tear-stained face in her hands. "I don't want my mother to know. I don't want my mother to know."

"Come on now!"

"Shut up!" cried Amory at Olson.

An instant's pause.

"Stella Robbins," she faltered finally. "General Delivery, Rugway, New Hampshire."

Olson snapped his note-book shut and looked at them very ponderously.

"By rights the hotel could turn the evidence over to the

police and you'd go to penitentiary, you would, for bringin' a girl from one State to 'nother f'r immoral purp'ses"—he paused to let the majesty of his words sink in. "But—the hotel is going to let you off."

"It doesn't want to get in the papers," cried Jill fiercely. "Let us off! Huh!"

A great lightness surrounded Amory. He realized that he was safe and only then did he appreciate the full enormity of what he might have incurred.

"However," continued Olson, "there's a protective association among the hotels. There's been too much of this stuff, and we got a 'rangement with the newspapers so that you get a little free publicity. Not the name of the hotel, but just a line sayin' that you had a little trouble in 'lantic City. See?"

"I see."

"You're gettin' off light—damn light—but——"

"Come on," said Amory briskly. "Let's get out of here. We don't need a valedictory."

Olson walked through the bathroom and took a cursory glance at Alec's still form. Then he extinguished the lights and motioned them to follow him. As they walked into the elevator Amory considered a piece of bravado—yielded finally. He reached out and tapped Olson on the arm.

"Would you mind taking off your hat? There's a lady in the elevator."

Olson's hat came off slowly. There was a rather embarrassing two minutes under the lights of the lobby while the night clerk and a few belated guests stared at them curiously; the loudly dressed girl with bent head, the handsome young man with his chin several points aloft; the inference was quite obvious. Then the chill outdoors—where the salt air was fresher and keener still with the first hints of morning.

"You can get one of those taxis and beat it," said Olson, pointing to the blurred outline of two machines whose drivers were presumably asleep inside.

"Good-by," said Olson. He reached in his pocket suggestively, but Amory snorted, and, taking the girl's arm, turned away.

"Where did you tell the driver to go?" she asked as they whirled along the dim street.

"The station."

"If that guy writes my mother——"

"He won't. Nobody'll ever know about this—except our friends and enemies."

Dawn was breaking over the sea.

"It's getting blue," she said.

"It does very well," agreed Amory critically, and then as an after-thought: "It's almost breakfast-time—do you want something to eat?"

"Food—" she said with a cheerful laugh. "Food is what queered the party. We ordered a big supper to be sent up to the room about two o'clock. Alec didn't give the waiter a tip, so I guess the little bastard snitched."

Jill's low spirits seemed to have gone faster than the scattering night. "Let me tell you," she said emphatically, "when you want to stage that sorta party stay away from liquor, and when you want to get tight stay away from bedrooms."

"I'll remember."

He tapped suddenly at the glass and they drew up at the door of an all-night restaurant.

"Is Alec a great friend of yours?" asked Jill as they perched themselves on high stools inside, and set their elbows on the dingy counter.

"He used to be. He probably won't want to be any more—and never understand why."

"It was sorta crazy you takin' all that blame. Is he pretty important? Kinda more important than you are?"

Amory laughed.

"That remains to be seen," he answered. "That's the question."

THE COLLAPSE OF SEVERAL PILLARS

Two days later back in New York Amory found in a newspaper what he had been searching for—a dozen lines which announced to whom it might concern that Mr. Amory Blaine, who "gave his address" as, etc., had been requested to leave his hotel in Atlantic City because of entertaining in his room a lady *not* his wife.

Then he started, and his fingers trembled, for directly above was a longer paragraph of which the first words were:

"Mr. and Mrs. Leland R. Connage are announcing the engagement of their daughter, Rosalind, to Mr. J. Dawson Ryder, of Hartford, Connecticut——"

He dropped the paper and lay down on his bed with a frightened, sinking sensation in the pit of his stomach. She was gone, definitely, finally gone. Until now he had half unconsciously cherished the hope deep in his heart that some day she would need him and send for him, cry that it had been a mistake, that her heart ached only for the pain she had caused him. Never again could he find even the sombre luxury of wanting her—not this Rosalind, harder, older—nor any beaten, broken woman that his imagination brought to the door of his forties— Amory had wanted her youth, the fresh radiance of her mind and body, the stuff that she was selling now once and for all. So far as he was concerned, young Rosalind was dead.

A day later came a crisp, terse letter from Mr. Barton in Chicago, which informed him that as three more street-car companies had gone into the hands of receivers he could expect for the present no further remittances. Last of all, on a dazed Sunday night, a telegram told him of Monsignor Darcy's sudden death in Philadelphia five days before.

He knew then what it was that he had perceived among the curtains of the room in Atlantic City.

CHAPTER V

The Egotist Becomes a Personage

"A fathom deep in sleep I lie
With old desires, restrained before,
To clamor lifeward with a cry,
As dark flies out the greying door;
And so in quest of creeds to share
I seek assertive day again . . .
But old monotony is there:
Endless avenues of rain.

Oh, might I rise again! Might I
Throw off the heat of that old wine,
See the new morning mass the sky
With fairy towers, line on line;
Find each mirage in the high air
A symbol, not a dream again . . .
But old monotony is there:
Endless avenues of rain."

Under the glass portcullis of a theatre Amory stood, watching the first great drops of rain splatter down and flatten to dark stains on the sidewalk. The air became gray and opalescent; a solitary light suddenly outlined a window over the way; then another light; then a hundred more danced and glimmered into vision. Under his feet a thick, iron-studded skylight turned yellow; in the street the lamps of the taxi-cabs sent out glistening sheens along the already black pavement. The unwelcome November rain had perversely stolen the day's last hour and pawned it with that ancient fence, the night.

The silence of the theatre behind him ended with a curious snapping sound, followed by the heavy roaring of a rising crowd and the interlaced clatter of many voices. The matinée was over.

He stood aside, edged a little into the rain to let the throng pass. A small boy rushed out, sniffed in the damp, fresh air and turned up the collar of his coat; came three or four couples in a great hurry; came a further scattering of people whose eyes as they emerged glanced invariably, first at the wet street, then at the rain-filled air, finally at the dismal sky; last a dense, strolling mass that depressed him with its heavy odor compounded of the tobacco smell of the men and the fetid sensuousness of stale powder on women. After the thick crowd came another scattering; a stray half-dozen; a man on crutches; finally the rattling bang of folding seats inside announced that the ushers were at work.

New York seemed not so much awakening as turning over in its bed. Pallid men rushed by, pinching together their coat-collars; a great swarm of tired, magpie girls from a department-store crowded along with shrieks of strident laughter, three to an umbrella; a squad of marching policemen passed, already miraculously protected by oilskin capes.

The rain gave Amory a feeling of detachment, and the numerous unpleasant aspects of city life without money occurred to him in threatening procession. There was the ghastly, stinking crush of the subway—the car cards thrusting themselves at one, leering out like dull bores who grab your arm with another story; the querulous worry as to whether some one isn't leaning on you; a man deciding not to give his seat to a woman, hating her for it; the woman hating him for not doing it; at worst a squalid phantasmagoria of breath, and old cloth on human bodies and the smells of the food men ate—at best just people—too hot or too cold, tired, worried.

He pictured the rooms where these people lived—where the patterns of the blistered wall-papers were heavy reiterated sunflowers on green and yellow backgrounds, where there were tin bathtubs and gloomy hallways and verdureless, unnamable spaces in back of the buildings; where even love dressed as seduction—a sordid murder around the corner, illicit motherhood in the flat above. And always there was the economical stuffiness of indoor winter, and the long summers, nightmares of perspiration between sticky enveloping walls . . . dirty restaurants where careless, tired people helped themselves to sugar with their own used coffee-spoons, leaving hard brown deposits in the bowl.

It was not so bad where there were only men or else only women; it was when they were vilely herded that it all seemed so rotten. It was some shame that women gave off at having men see them tired and poor—it was some disgust that men had for women who were tired and poor. It was dirtier than any battle-field he had seen, harder to contemplate than any actual hardship moulded of mire and sweat and danger, it was an atmosphere wherein birth and marriage and death were loathsome, secret things.

He remembered one day in the subway when a delivery boy had brought in a great funeral wreath of fresh flowers, how the smell of it had suddenly cleared the air and given every one in the car a momentary glow.

"I detest poor people," thought Amory suddenly. "I hate them for being poor. Poverty may have been beautiful once, but it's rotten now. It's the ugliest thing in the world. It's essentially cleaner to be corrupt and rich than it is to be innocent and poor." He seemed to see again a figure whose significance had once impressed him—a well-dressed young man gazing from a club window on Fifth Avenue and saying something to his companion with a look of utter disgust. Probably, thought Amory, what he said was: "My God! Aren't people horrible!"

Never before in his life had Amory considered poor people. He thought cynically how completely he was lacking in all human sympathy. O. Henry had found in these people romance, pathos, love, hate—Amory saw only coarseness, physical filth, and stupidity. He made no self-accusations: never any more did he reproach himself for feelings that were natural and sincere. He accepted all his reactions as a part of him, unchangeable, unmoral. This problem of poverty transformed, magnified, attached to some grander, more dignified attitude might some day even be his problem; at present it roused only his profound distaste.

He walked over to Fifth Avenue, dodging the blind, black menace of umbrellas, and standing in front of Delmonico's hailed an auto-bus. Buttoning his coat closely around him he climbed to the roof, where he rode in solitary state through the thin, persistent rain, stung into alertness by the cool moisture perpetually reborn on his cheek. Somewhere in his mind a conversation began, rather resumed its place in his attention. It was composed not of two voices, but of one, which acted alike as questioner and answerer:

Question.—Well—what's the situation?

Answer.—That I have about twenty-four dollars to my name.

Q.—You have the Lake Geneva estate.

A.—But I intend to keep it.

Q.—Can you live?

A.—I can't imagine not being able to. People make money in books and I've found that I can always do the things that people do in books. Really they are the only things I can do.

Q.—Be definite.

A.—I don't know what I'll do—nor have I much curiosity. To-morrow I'm going to leave New York for good. It's a bad town unless you're on top of it.

Q.—Do you want a lot of money?

A.—No. I am merely afraid of being poor.

Q.—Very afraid?

A.—Just passively afraid.

Q.—Where are you drifting?

A.—Don't ask *me*!

Q.—Don't you care?

A.—Rather. I don't want to commit moral suicide.

Q.—Have you no interests left?

A.—None. I've no more virtue to lose. Just as a cooling pot gives off heat, so all through youth and adolescence we give off calories of virtue. That's what's called ingenuousness.

Q.—An interesting idea.

A.—That's why a "good man going wrong" attracts people. They stand around and literally *warm themselves* at the calories of virtue he gives off. Sarah makes an unsophisticated remark and the faces simper in delight—"How *innocent* the poor child is!" They're warming themselves at her virtue. But Sarah sees the simper and never makes that remark again. Only she feels a little colder after that.

Q.—All your calories gone?

A.—All of them. I'm beginning to warm myself at other people's virtue.

Q.—Are you corrupt?

A.—I think so. I'm not sure. I'm not sure about good and evil at all any more.

Q.—Is that a bad sign in itself?

A.—Not necessarily.

Q.—What would be the test of corruption?

A.—Becoming really insincere—calling myself "not such a bad fellow," thinking I regretted my lost youth when I only envy the delights of losing it. Youth is like having a big plate of candy. Sentimentalists think they want to be in the pure, simple state they were in before they ate the candy. They don't. They just want the fun of eating it all over again. The matron doesn't want to repeat her girlhood—she wants to repeat her honeymoon. I don't want to repeat my innocence. I want the pleasure of losing it again.

Q.—Where are you drifting?

This dialogue merged grotesquely into his mind's most familiar state—a grotesque blending of desires, worries, exterior impressions and physical reactions.

One Hundred and Twenty-seventh Street—or One Hundred and Thirty-seventh Street. . . . Two and three look alike—no, not much. Seat damp . . . are clothes absorbing wetness from seat, or seat absorbing dryness from clothes? . . . Sitting on wet substance gave appendicitis, so Froggy Parker's mother said. Well, he'd had it—I'll sue the steamboat company, Beatrice said, and my uncle has a quarter interest—did Beatrice go to heaven? . . . probably not— He represented Beatrice's immortality, also love-affairs of numerous dead men who surely had never thought of him . . . if it wasn't appendicitis, influenza maybe. What? One Hundred and Twentieth Street? That must have been One Hundred and Twelfth back there. One O Two instead of One Two Seven. Rosalind not like Beatrice, Eleanor like Beatrice, only wilder and brainier. Apartments along here expensive—probably hundred and fifty a month—maybe two hundred. Uncle had only paid hundred a month for whole great big house in Minneapolis. Question—were the stairs on the left or right as you came in? Anyway, in 12 Univee they were straight back and to the left. What a dirty river—want to go down there and see if it's dirty—French rivers all brown or black, so were Southern rivers. Twenty-four dollars meant four hundred and eighty doughnuts. He could live on it three months and sleep in the park. Wonder where Jill was—Jill Bayne, Fayne, Sayne—what the devil—neck hurts, darned uncomfortable seat. No desire to sleep with Jill, what could Alec see in her? Alec had a coarse taste in women. Own taste the best; Isabelle, Clara, Rosalind, Eleanor, were all-American. Eleanor would pitch, probably southpaw. Rosalind was outfield, wonderful hitter, Clara first base, maybe. Wonder what Humbird's body looked like now. If he himself hadn't been bayonet instructor he'd have gone up to line three months sooner, probably been killed. Where's the darned bell——

The street numbers of Riverside Drive were obscured by the mist and dripping trees from anything but the swiftest scrutiny, but Amory had finally caught sight of one—One Hundred and Twenty-seventh Street. He got off and with no distinct destination followed a winding, descending sidewalk and came out facing the river, in particular a long pier and a partitioned litter of shipyards for miniature craft: small launches, canoes, rowboats, and catboats. He turned northward and followed the shore, jumped a small wire fence and found himself in a great disorderly yard adjoining a dock. The hulls of many boats in various stages of repair were around him; he smelled sawdust and paint and the scarcely distinguishable flat odor of the Hudson. A man approached through the heavy gloom.

"Hello," said Amory.

"Got a pass?"

"No. Is this private?"

"This is the Hudson River Sporting and Yacht Club."

"Oh! I didn't know. I'm just resting."

"Well—" began the man dubiously.

"I'll go if you want me to."

The man made non-committal noises in his throat and passed on. Amory seated himself on an overturned boat and leaned forward thoughtfully until his chin rested in his hand.

"Misfortune is liable to make me a damn bad man," he said slowly.

In the Drooping Hours

While the rain drizzled on Amory looked futilely back at the stream of his life, all its glitterings and dirty shallows. To begin with, he was still afraid—not physically afraid any more, but afraid of people and prejudice and misery and monotony. Yet, deep in his bitter heart, he wondered if he was after all worse than this man or the next. He knew that he could sophisticate himself finally into saying that his own weakness was just the result of circumstances and environment; that often when he raged at himself as an egotist something would whisper ingratiatingly: "No. Genius!" That was one manifestation of fear, that voice which whispered that he could not be both great and good, that genius was the exact combination of those inexplicable grooves and twists in his mind, that any discipline would curb it to mediocrity. Probably more than any concrete vice or failing Amory despised his own personality—he loathed knowing that to-morrow and the thousand days after he would swell pompously at a compliment and sulk at an ill word like a third-rate musician or a first-class actor. He was ashamed of the fact that very simple and honest people usually distrusted him; that he had been cruel, often, to those who had sunk their personalities in him—several girls, and a man here and there through college, that he had been an evil influence on; people who had followed him here and there into mental adventures from which he alone rebounded unscathed.

Usually, on nights like this, for there had been many lately, he could escape from this consuming introspection by thinking of children and the infinite possibilities of children—he leaned and listened and he heard a startled baby awake in a house across the street and lend a tiny whimper to the still night. Quick as a flash he turned away, wondering with a touch of panic whether something in the brooding despair of his mood had made a darkness in its tiny soul. He shivered. What if some day the balance was overturned, and he became a thing that frightened children and crept into rooms in the dark, approached dim communion with those phantoms who whispered shadowy secrets to the mad of that dark continent upon the moon. . . .

*

Amory smiled a bit.

"You're too much wrapped up in yourself," he heard some one say. And again——

"Get out and do some real work——"

"Stop worrying——"

He fancied a possible future comment of his own.

"Yes—I was perhaps an egotist in youth, but I soon found it made me morbid to think too much about myself."

Suddenly he felt an overwhelming desire to let himself go to the devil—not to go violently as a gentleman should, but to sink safely and sensuously out of sight. He pictured himself in an adobe house in Mexico, half-reclining on a rug-covered couch, his slender, artistic fingers closed on a cigarette while he listened to guitars strumming melancholy undertones to an age-old dirge of Castile and an olive-skinned, carmine-lipped girl caressed his hair. Here he might live a strange litany, delivered from right and wrong and from the hound of heaven and from every God (except the exotic Mexican one who was pretty slack himself and rather addicted to Oriental scents)—delivered from success and hope and poverty into that long chute of indulgence which led, after all, only to the artificial lake of death.

There were so many places where one might deteriorate pleasantly: Port Said, Shanghai, parts of Turkestan, Constantinople, the South Seas—all lands of sad, haunting music and many odors, where lust could be a mode and expression of life, where the shades of night skies and sunsets would seem to reflect only moods of passion: the colors of lips and poppies.

Still Weeding

Once he had been miraculously able to scent evil as a horse detects a broken bridge at night, but the man with the queer feet in Phœbe's room had diminished to the aura over Jill. His instinct perceived the fetidness of poverty, but no longer ferreted out the deeper evils in pride and sensuality.

There were no more wise men; there were no more heroes;

Burne Holiday was sunk from sight as though he had never lived; Monsignor was dead. Amory had grown up to a thousand books, a thousand lies; he had listened eagerly to people who pretended to know, who knew nothing. The mystical reveries of saints that had once filled him with awe in the still hours of night, now vaguely repelled him. The Byrons and Brookes who had defied life from mountain tops were in the end but flaneurs and poseurs, at best mistaking the shadow of courage for the substance of wisdom. The pageantry of his disillusion took shape in a world-old procession of Prophets, Athenians, Martyrs, Saints, Scientists, Don Juans, Jesuits, Puritans, Fausts, Poets, Pacifists; like costumed alumni at a college reunion they streamed before him as their dreams, personalities, and creeds had in turn thrown colored lights on his soul; each had tried to express the glory of life and the tremendous significance of man; each had boasted of synchronizing what had gone before into his own rickety generalities; each had depended after all on the set stage and the convention of the theatre, which is that man in his hunger for faith will feed his mind with the nearest and most convenient food.

Women—of whom he had expected so much; whose beauty he had hoped to transmute into modes of art; whose unfathomable instincts, marvellously incoherent and inarticulate, he had thought to perpetuate in terms of experience—had become merely consecrations to their own posterity. Isabelle, Clara, Rosalind, Eleanor, were all removed by their very beauty, around which men had swarmed, from the possibility of contributing anything but a sick heart and a page of puzzled words to write.

Amory based his loss of faith in help from others on several sweeping syllogisms. Granted that his generation, however bruised and decimated from this Victorian war, were the heirs of progress. Waving aside petty differences of conclusions which, although they might occasionally cause the deaths of several millions of young men, might be explained away—supposing that after all Bernard Shaw and Bernhardi, Bonar Law and Bethmann-Hollweg were mutual heirs of progress if only in agreeing against the ducking of witches—waiving the antitheses and approaching individually these men who seemed to be the leaders, he was repelled by the discrepancies and contradictions in the men themselves.

There was, for example, Thornton Hancock, respected by half the intellectual world as an authority on life, a man who had verified and believed the code he lived by, an educator of educators, an adviser to Presidents—yet Amory knew that this man had, in his heart, leaned on the priest of another religion.

And Monsignor, upon whom a cardinal rested, had moments of strange and horrible insecurity—inexplicable in a religion that explained even disbelief in terms of its own faith: if you doubted the devil it was the devil that made you doubt him. Amory had seen Monsignor go to the houses of stolid philistines, read popular novels furiously, saturate himself in routine, to escape from that horror.

And this priest, a little wiser, somewhat purer, had been, Amory knew, not essentially older than he.

Amory was alone—he had escaped from a small enclosure into a great labyrinth. He was where Goethe was when he began "Faust"; he was where Conrad was when he wrote "Almayer's Folly."

Amory said to himself that there were essentially two sorts of people who through natural clarity or disillusion left the enclosure and sought the labyrinth. There were men like Wells and Plato, who had, half unconsciously, a strange, hidden orthodoxy, who would accept for themselves only what could be accepted for all men—incurable romanticists who never, for all their efforts, could enter the labyrinth as stark souls; there were on the other hand sword-like pioneering personalities, Samuel Butler, Renan, Voltaire, who progressed much slower, yet eventually much further, not in the direct pessimistic line of speculative philosophy but concerned in the eternal attempt to attach a positive value to life. . . .

Amory stopped. He began for the first time in his life to have a strong distrust of all generalities and epigrams. They were too easy, too dangerous to the public mind. Yet all thought usually reached the public after thirty years in some such form: Benson and Chesterton had popularized Huysmans and Newman; Shaw had sugar-coated Nietzsche and Ibsen and Schopenhauer. The man in the street heard the conclusions of dead genius through some one else's clever paradoxes and didactic epigrams.

Life was a damned muddle . . . a football game with every one off-side and the referee gotten rid of—every one claiming the referee would have been on his side. . . .

Progress was a labyrinth . . . people plunging blindly in and then rushing wildly back, shouting that they had found it . . . the invisible king—the élan vital—the principle of evolution . . . writing a book, starting a war, founding a school. . . .

Amory, even had he not been a selfish man, would have started all inquiries with himself. He was his own best example—sitting in the rain, a human creature of sex and pride, foiled by chance and his own temperament of the balm of love and children, preserved to help in building up the living consciousness of the race.

In self-reproach and loneliness and disillusion he came to the entrance of the labyrinth.

Another dawn flung itself across the river; a belated taxi hurried along the street, its lamps still shining like burning eyes in a face white from a night's carouse. A melancholy siren sounded far down the river.

Monsignor

Amory kept thinking how Monsignor would have enjoyed his own funeral. It was magnificently Catholic and liturgical. Bishop O'Neill sang solemn high mass and the cardinal gave the final absolutions. Thornton Hancock, Mrs. Lawrence, the British and Italian ambassadors, the papal delegate, and a host of friends and priests were there—yet the inexorable shears had cut through all these threads that Monsignor had gathered into his hands. To Amory it was a haunting grief to see him lying in his coffin, with closed hands upon his purple vestments. His face had not changed, and, as he never knew he was dying, it showed no pain or fear. It was Amory's dear old friend, his and the others'—for the church was full of people with daft, staring faces, the most exalted seeming the most stricken.

The cardinal, like an archangel in cope and mitre, sprinkled the holy water; the organ broke into sound; the choir began to sing the *Requiem Eternam*.

All these people grieved because they had to some extent depended upon Monsignor. Their grief was more than sentiment for the "crack in his voice or a certain break in his walk," as Wells put it. These people had leaned on Monsignor's faith, his way of finding cheer, of making religion a thing of lights and shadows, making all light and shadow merely aspects of God. People felt safe when he was near.

Of Amory's attempted sacrifice had been born merely the full realization of his disillusion, but of Monsignor's funeral was born the romantic elf who was to enter the labyrinth with him. He found something that he wanted, had always wanted and always would want—not to be admired, as he had feared; not to be loved, as he had made himself believe; but to be necessary to people, to be indispensable; he remembered the sense of security he had found in Burne.

Life opened up in one of its amazing bursts of radiance and Amory suddenly and permanently rejected an old epigram that had been playing listlessly in his mind: "Very few things matter and nothing matters very much."

On the contrary, Amory felt an immense desire to give people a sense of security.

The Big Man with Goggles

On the day that Amory started on his walk to Princeton the sky was a colorless vault, cool, high and barren of the threat of rain. It was a gray day, that least fleshly of all weathers; a day of dreams and far hopes and clear visions. It was a day easily associated with those abstract truths and purities that dissolve in the sunshine or fade out in mocking laughter by the light of the moon. The trees and clouds were carved in classical severity; the sounds of the countryside had harmonized to a monotone, metallic as a trumpet, breathless as the Grecian urn.

The day had put Amory in such a contemplative mood that he caused much annoyance to several motorists who were forced to slow up considerably or else run him down. So engrossed in his thoughts was he that he was scarcely surprised at that strange phenomenon—cordiality manifested within fifty miles of Manhattan—when a passing car slowed down beside him and a voice hailed him. He looked up and saw a magnificent Locomobile in which sat two middle-aged men, one of them small and anxious looking, apparently an artificial growth on the other who was large and begoggled and imposing.

"Do you want a lift?" asked the apparently artificial growth, glancing from the corner of his eye at the imposing man as if for some habitual, silent corroboration.

"You bet I do. Thanks."

The chauffeur swung open the door, and, climbing in, Amory settled himself in the middle of the back seat. He took in his companions curiously. The chief characteristic of the big man seemed to be a great confidence in himself set off against a tremendous boredom with everything around him. That part of his face which protruded under the goggles was what is generally termed "strong"; rolls of not undignified fat had collected near his chin; somewhere above was a wide thin mouth and the rough model for a Roman nose, and, below, his shoulders collapsed without a struggle into the powerful bulk of his chest and belly. He was excellently and quietly dressed. Amory noticed that he was inclined to stare straight at the back of the chauffeur's head as if speculating steadily but hopelessly some baffling hirsute problem.

The smaller man was remarkable only for his complete submersion in the personality of the other. He was of that lower secretarial type who at forty have engraved upon their business cards: "Assistant to the President," and without a sigh consecrate the rest of their lives to second-hand mannerisms.

"Going far?" asked the smaller man in a pleasant disinterested way.

"Quite a stretch."

"Hiking for exercise?"

"No," responded Amory succinctly, "I'm walking because I can't afford to ride."

"Oh."

Then again:

"Are you looking for work? Because there's lots of work," he continued rather testily. "All this talk of lack of work. The West is especially short of labor." He expressed the West with a sweeping, lateral gesture. Amory nodded politely.

"Have you a trade?"

No—Amory had no trade.

"Clerk, eh?"

No—Amory was not a clerk.

"Whatever your line is," said the little man, seeming to agree wisely with something Amory had said, "now is the time of opportunity and business openings." He glanced again toward the big man, as a lawyer grilling a witness glances involuntarily at the jury.

Amory decided that he must say something and for the life of him could think of only one thing to say.

"Of course I want a great lot of money——"

The little man laughed mirthlessly but conscientiously.

"That's what every one wants nowadays, but they don't want to work for it."

"A very natural, healthy desire. Almost all normal people want to be rich without great effort—except the financiers in problem plays, who want to 'crash their way through.' Don't you want easy money?"

"Of course not," said the secretary indignantly.

"But," continued Amory disregarding him, "being very poor at present I am contemplating socialism as possibly my forte."

Both men glanced at him curiously.

"These bomb throwers—" The little man ceased as words lurched ponderously from the big man's chest.

"If I thought you were a bomb thrower I'd run you over to the Newark jail. That's what I think of Socialists."

Amory laughed.

"What are you," asked the big man, "one of these parlor Bolsheviks, one of these idealists? I must say I fail to see the difference. The idealists loaf around and write the stuff that stirs up the poor immigrants."

"Well," said Amory, "if being an idealist is both safe and lucrative, I might try it."

"What's your difficulty? Lost your job?"

"Not exactly, but—well, call it that."

"What was it?"

"Writing copy for an advertising agency."

"Lots of money in advertising."

Amory smiled discreetly.

"Oh, I'll admit there's money in it eventually. Talent doesn't starve any more. Even art gets enough to eat these days. Artists draw your magazine covers, write your advertisements, hash out rag-time for your theatres. By the great commercializing of printing you've found a harmless, polite occupation for every genius who might have carved his own niche. But beware the artist who's an intellectual also. The artist who doesn't fit—the Rousseau, the Tolstoi, the Samuel Butler, the Amory Blaine——"

"Who's he?" demanded the little man suspiciously.

"Well," said Amory, "he's a—he's an intellectual personage not very well known at present."

The little man laughed his conscientious laugh, and stopped rather suddenly as Amory's burning eyes turned on him.

"What are you laughing at?"

"These *intellectual* people——"

"Do you know what it means?"

The little man's eyes twitched nervously.

"Why, it *usually* means——"

"It *always* means brainy and well-educated," interrupted Amory. "It means having an active knowledge of the race's experience." Amory decided to be very rude. He turned to the big man. "The young man," he indicated the secretary with his thumb, and said young man as one says bell-boy, with no implication of youth, "has the usual muddled connotation of all popular words."

"You object to the fact that capital controls printing?" said the big man, fixing him with his goggles.

"Yes—and I object to doing their mental work for them. It seemed to me that the root of all the business I saw around me consisted in overworking and underpaying a bunch of dubs who submitted to it."

"Here now," said the big man, "you'll have to admit that the laboring man is certainly highly paid—five and six hour days—it's ridiculous. You can't buy an honest day's work from a man in the trades-unions."

"You've brought it on yourselves," insisted Amory. "You people never make concessions until they're wrung out of you."

"What people?"

"Your class; the class I belonged to until recently; those who by inheritance or industry or brains or dishonesty have become the moneyed class."

"Do you imagine that if that road-mender over there had the money he'd be any more willing to give it up?"

"No, but what's that got to do with it?"

The older man considered.

"No, I'll admit it hasn't. It rather sounds as if it had though."

"In fact," continued Amory, "he'd be worse. The lower classes are narrower, less pleasant and personally more selfish—certainly more stupid. But all that has nothing to do with the question."

"Just exactly what is the question?"

Here Amory had to pause to consider exactly what the question was.

Amory Coins a Phrase

"When life gets hold of a brainy man of fair education," began Amory slowly, "that is, when he marries he becomes, nine times out of ten, a conservative as far as existing social conditions are concerned. He may be unselfish, kind-hearted, even just in his own way, but his first job is to provide and to hold fast. His wife shoos him on, from ten thousand a year to twenty thousand a year, on and on, in an enclosed treadmill that hasn't any windows. He's done! Life's got him! He's no help! He's a spiritually married man."

Amory paused and decided that it wasn't such a bad phrase.

"Some men," he continued, "escape the grip. Maybe their wives have no social ambitions; maybe they've hit a sentence or two in a 'dangerous book' that pleased them; maybe they started on the treadmill as I did and were knocked off.

Anyway, they're the congressmen you can't bribe, the Presidents who aren't politicians, the writers, speakers, scientists, statesmen who aren't just popular grab-bags for a half-dozen women and children."

"He's the natural radical?"

"Yes," said Amory. "He may vary from the disillusioned critic like old Thornton Hancock, all the way to Trotsky. Now this spiritually unmarried man hasn't direct power, for unfortunately the spiritually married man, as a by-product of his money chase, has garnered in the great newspaper, the popular magazine, the influential weekly—so that Mrs. Newspaper, Mrs. Magazine, Mrs. Weekly can have a better limousine than those oil people across the street or those cement people 'round the corner."

"Why not?"

"It makes wealthy men the keepers of the world's intellectual conscience and, of course, a man who has money under one set of social institutions quite naturally can't risk his family's happiness by letting the clamor for another appear in his newspaper."

"But it appears," said the big man.

"Where?—in the discredited mediums. Rotten cheap-papered weeklies."

"All right—go on."

"Well, my first point is that through a mixture of conditions of which the family is the first, there are these two sorts of brains. One sort takes human nature as it finds it, uses its timidity, its weakness, and its strength for its own ends. Opposed is the man who, being spiritually unmarried, continually seeks for new systems that will control or counteract human nature. His problem is harder. It is not life that's complicated, it's the struggle to guide and control life. That is his struggle. He is a part of progress—the spiritually married man is not."

The big man produced three big cigars, and proffered them on his huge palm. The little man took one, Amory shook his head and reached for a cigarette.

"Go on talking," said the big man. "I've been wanting to hear one of you fellows."

Going Faster

"Modern life," began Amory again, "changes no longer century by century, but year by year, ten times faster than it ever has before—populations doubling, civilizations unified more closely with other civilizations, economic interdependence, racial questions, and—we're *dawdling* along. My idea is that we've got to go very much faster." He slightly emphasized the last words and the chauffeur unconsciously increased the speed of the car. Amory and the big man laughed; the little man laughed, too, after a pause.

"Every child," said Amory, "should have an equal start. If his father can endow him with a good physique and his mother with some common sense in his early education, that should be his heritage. If the father can't give him a good physique, if the mother has spent in chasing men the years in which she should have been preparing herself to educate her children, so much the worse for the child. He shouldn't be artificially bolstered up with money, sent to these horrible tutoring schools, dragged through college . . . . Every boy ought to have an equal start."

"All right," said the big man, his goggles indicating neither approval nor objection.

"Next I'd have a fair trial of government ownership of all industries."

"That's been proven a failure."

"No—it merely failed. If we had government ownership we'd have the best analytical business minds in the government working for something besides themselves. We'd have Mackays instead of Burlesons; we'd have Morgans in the Treasury Department; we'd have Hills running interstate commerce. We'd have the best lawyers in the Senate."

"They wouldn't give their best efforts for nothing. McAdoo——"

"No," said Amory, shaking his head. "Money isn't the only stimulous that brings out the best that's in a man, even in America."

"You said a while ago that it was."

"It is, right now. But if it were made illegal to have more

than a certain amount the best men would all flock for the one other reward which attracts humanity—honor."

The big man made a sound that was very like *boo.*

"That's the silliest thing you've said yet."

"No, it isn't silly. It's quite plausible. If you'd gone to college you'd have been struck by the fact that the men there would work twice as hard for any one of a hundred petty honors as those other men did who were earning their way through."

"Kids—child's play!" scoffed his antagonist.

"Not by a darned sight—unless we're all children. Did you ever see a grown man when he's trying for a secret society—or a rising family whose name is up at some club? They'll jump when they hear the sound of the word. The idea that to make a man work you've got to hold gold in front of his eyes is a growth, not an axiom. We've done that for so long that we've forgotten there's any other way. We've made a world where that's necessary. Let me tell you"—Amory became emphatic—"if there were ten men insured against either wealth or starvation, and offered a green ribbon for five hours' work a day and a blue ribbon for ten hours' work a day, nine out of ten of them would be trying for the blue ribbon. That competitive instinct only wants a badge. If the size of their house is the badge they'll sweat their heads off for that. If it's only a blue ribbon, I damn near believe they'll work just as hard. They have in other ages."

"I don't agree with you."

"I know it," said Amory nodding sadly. "It doesn't matter any more though. I think these people are going to come and take what they want pretty soon."

A fierce hiss came from the little man.

"Machine-guns!"

"Ah, but you've taught them their use."

The big man shook his head.

"In this country there are enough property owners not to permit that sort of thing."

Amory wished he knew the statistics of property owners and non-property owners; he decided to change the subject.

But the big man was aroused.

"When you talk of 'taking things away,' you're on dangerous ground."

"How can they get it without taking it? For years people have been stalled off with promises. Socialism may not be progress, but the threat of the red flag is certainly the inspiring force of all reform. You've got to be sensational to get attention."

"Russia is your example of a beneficent violence, I suppose?"

"Quite possibly," admitted Amory. "Of course, it's overflowing just as the French Revolution did, but I've no doubt that it's really a great experiment and well worth while."

"Don't you believe in moderation?"

"You won't listen to the moderates, and it's almost too late. The truth is that the public has done one of those startling and amazing things that they do about once in a hundred years. They've seized an idea."

"What is it?"

"That however the brains and abilities of men may differ, their stomachs are essentially the same."

The Little Man Gets His

"If you took all the money in the world," said the little man with much profundity, "and divided it up in equ——"

"Oh, shut up!" said Amory briskly and, paying no attention to the little man's enraged stare, he went on with his argument.

"The human stomach—" he began; but the big man interrupted rather impatiently.

"I'm letting you talk, you know," he said, "but please avoid stomachs. I've been feeling mine all day. Anyway, I don't agree with one-half you've said. Government ownership is the basis of your whole argument, and it's invariably a beehive of corruption. Men won't work for blue ribbons, that's all rot."

When he ceased the little man spoke up with a determined nod, as if resolved this time to have his say out.

"There are certain things which are human nature," he asserted with an owl-like look, "which always have been and always will be, which can't be changed."

Amory looked from the small man to the big man helplessly.

"Listen to that! *That's* what makes me discouraged with progress. *Listen* to that! I can name offhand over one hundred natural phenomena that have been changed by the will of man—a hundred instincts in man that have been wiped out or are now held in check by civilization. What this man here just said has been for thousands of years the last refuge of the associated mutton-heads of the world. It negates the efforts of every scientist, statesman, moralist, reformer, doctor, and philosopher that ever gave his life to humanity's service. It's a flat impeachment of all that's worth while in human nature. Every person over twenty-five years old who makes that statement in cold blood ought to be deprived of the franchise."

The little man leaned back against the seat, his face purple with rage. Amory continued, addressing his remarks to the big man.

"These quarter-educated, stale-minded men such as your friend here, who *think* they think; every question that comes up, you'll find his type in the usual ghastly muddle. One minute it's 'the brutality and inhumanity of these Prussians'—the next it's 'we ought to exterminate the whole German people.' They always believe that 'things are in a bad way now,' but they 'haven't any faith in these idealists.' One minute they call Wilson 'just a dreamer, not practical'—a year later they rail at him for making his dreams realities. They haven't clear logical ideas on one single subject except a sturdy, stolid opposition to all change. They don't think uneducated people should be highly paid, but they won't see that if they don't pay the uneducated people their children are going to be uneducated too, and we're going round and round in a circle. That—is the great middle class!"

The big man with a broad grin on his face leaned over and smiled at the little man.

"You're catching it pretty heavy, Garvin; how do you feel?"

The little man made an attempt to smile and act as if the whole matter were so ridiculous as to be beneath notice. But Amory was not through.

"The theory that people are fit to govern themselves rests on this man. If he can be educated to think clearly, concisely, and logically, freed of his habit of taking refuge in platitudes and prejudices and sentimentalisms, then I'm a militant Socialist. If he can't, then I don't think it matters much what happens to man or his systems, now or hereafter."

"I am both interested and amused," said the big man. "You are very young."

"Which may only mean that I have neither been corrupted nor made timid by contemporary experience. I possess the most valuable experience, the experience of the race, for in spite of going to college I've managed to pick up a good education."

"You talk glibly."

"It's not all rubbish," cried Amory passionately. "This is the first time in my life I've argued Socialism. It's the only panacea I know. I'm restless. My whole generation is restless. I'm sick of a system where the richest man gets the most beautiful girl if he wants her, where the artist without an income has to sell his talents to a button manufacturer. Even if I had no talents I'd not be content to work ten years, condemned either to celibacy or a furtive indulgence, to give some man's son an automobile."

"But, if you're not sure——"

"That doesn't matter," exclaimed Amory. "My position couldn't be worse. A social revolution might land me on top. Of course I'm selfish. It seems to me I've been a fish out of water in too many outworn systems. I was probably one of the two dozen men in my class at college who got a decent education; still they'd let any well-tutored flathead play football and *I* was ineligible, because some silly old men thought we should *all* profit by conic sections. I loathed the army. I loathed business. I'm in love with change and I've killed my conscience——"

"So you'll go along crying that we must go faster."

"That, at least, is true," Amory insisted. "Reform won't catch up to the needs of civilization unless it's made to. A laissez-faire policy is like spoiling a child by saying he'll turn out all right in the end. He will—if he's made to."

"But you don't believe all this Socialist patter you talk."

"I don't know. Until I talked to you I hadn't thought seriously about it. I wasn't sure of half of what I said."

"You puzzle me," said the big man, "but you're all alike. They say Bernard Shaw, in spite of his doctrines, is the most exacting of all dramatists about his royalties. To the last farthing."

"Well," said Amory, "I simply state that I'm a product of a versatile mind in a restless generation—with every reason to throw my mind and pen in with the radicals. Even if, deep in my heart, I thought we were all blind atoms in a world as limited as a stroke of a pendulum, I and my sort would struggle against tradition; try, at least, to displace old cants with new ones. I've thought I was right about life at various times, but faith is difficult. One thing I know. If living isn't a seeking for the grail it may be a damned amusing game."

For a minute neither spoke and then the big man asked:

"What was your university?"

"Princeton."

The big man became suddenly interested; the expression of his goggles altered slightly.

"I sent my son to Princeton."

"Did you?"

"Perhaps you knew him. His name was Jesse Ferrenby. He was killed last year in France."

"I knew him very well. In fact, he was one of my particular friends."

"He was—a—quite a fine boy. We were very close."

Amory began to perceive a resemblance between the father and the dead son and he told himself that there had been all along a sense of familiarity. Jesse Ferrenby, the man who in college had borne off the crown that he had aspired to. It was all so far away. What little boys they had been, working for blue ribbons——

The car slowed up at the entrance to a great estate, ringed around by a huge hedge and a tall iron fence.

"Won't you come in for lunch?"

Amory shook his head.

"Thank you, Mr. Ferrenby, but I've got to get on."

The big man held out his hand. Amory saw that the fact that he had known Jesse more than outweighed any disfavor he had created by his opinions. What ghosts were people with which to work! Even the little man insisted on shaking hands.

"Good-by!" shouted Mr. Ferrenby, as the car turned the corner and started up the drive. "Good luck to you and bad luck to your theories."

"Same to you, sir," cried Amory, smiling and waving his hand.

"Out of the Fire, Out of the Little Room"

Eight hours from Princeton Amory sat down by the Jersey roadside and looked at the frost-bitten country. Nature as a rather coarse phenomenon composed largely of flowers that, when closely inspected, appeared moth-eaten, and of ants that endlessly traversed blades of grass, was always disillusioning; nature represented by skies and waters and far horizons was more likable. Frost and the promise of winter thrilled him now, made him think of a wild battle between St. Regis and Groton, ages ago, seven years ago—and of an autumn day in France twelve months before when he had lain in tall grass, his platoon flattened down close around him, waiting to tap the shoulders of a Lewis gunner. He saw the two pictures together with somewhat the same primitive exaltation—two games he had played, differing in quality of acerbity, linked in a way that differed them from Rosalind or the subject of labyrinths which were, after all, the business of life.

"I am selfish," he thought.

"This is not a quality that will change when I 'see human suffering' or 'lose my parents' or 'help others.'

"This selfishness is not only part of me. It is the most living part.

"It is by somehow transcending rather than by avoiding that selfishness that I can bring poise and balance into my life.

"There is no virtue of unselfishness that I cannot use. I can make sacrifices, be charitable, give to a friend, endure for a friend, lay down my life for a friend—all because these things may be the best possible expression of myself; yet I have not one drop of the milk of human kindness."

The problem of evil had solidified for Amory into the problem of sex. He was beginning to identify evil with the strong phallic worship in Brooke and the early Wells. Inseparably linked with evil was beauty—beauty, still a constant rising tumult; soft in Eleanor's voice, in an old song at night, rioting deliriously through life like superimposed waterfalls, half rhythm, half darkness. Amory knew that every time he had reached toward it longingly it had leered out at him with the grotesque face of evil. Beauty of great art, beauty of all joy, most of all the beauty of women.

After all, it had too many associations with license and indulgence. Weak things were often beautiful, weak things were never good. And in this new loneness of his that had been selected for what greatness he might achieve, beauty must be relative or, itself a harmony, it would make only a discord.

In a sense this gradual renunciation of beauty was the second step after his disillusion had been made complete. He felt that he was leaving behind him his chance of being a certain type of artist. It seemed so much more important to be a certain sort of man.

His mind turned a corner suddenly and he found himself thinking of the Catholic Church. The idea was strong in him that there was a certain intrinsic lack in those to whom orthodox religion was necessary, and religion to Amory meant the Church of Rome. Quite conceivably it was an empty ritual but it was seemingly the only assimilative, traditionary bulwark against the decay of morals. Until the great mobs could be educated into a moral sense some one must cry: "Thou shalt not!" Yet any acceptance was, for the present, impossible. He wanted time and the absence of ulterior pressure. He wanted to keep the tree without ornaments, realize fully the direction and momentum of this new start.

The afternoon waned from the purging good of three o'clock to the golden beauty of four. Afterward he walked through the dull ache of a setting sun when even the clouds seemed bleeding and at twilight he came to a graveyard. There was a dusky, dreamy smell of flowers and the ghost of a new moon in the sky and shadows everywhere. On an impulse he considered trying to open the door of a rusty iron vault built into the side of a hill; a vault washed clean and covered with late-blooming, weepy watery-blue flowers that might have grown from dead eyes, sticky to the touch with a sickening odor.

Amory wanted to *feel* "William Dayfield, 1864."

He wondered that graves ever made people consider life in vain. Somehow he could find nothing hopeless in having lived. All the broken columns and clasped hands and doves and angels meant romances. He fancied that in a hundred years he would like having young people speculate as to whether his eyes were brown or blue, and he hoped quite passionately that his grave would have about it an air of many, many years ago. It seemed strange that out of a row of Union soldiers two or three made him think of dead loves and dead lovers, when they were exactly like the rest, even to the yellowish moss.

Long after midnight the towers and spires of Princeton were visible, with here and there a late-burning light—and suddenly out of the clear darkness the sound of bells. As an endless dream it went on; the spirit of the past brooding over a new generation, the chosen youth from the muddled, unchastened world, still fed romantically on the mistakes and half-forgotten dreams of dead statesmen and poets. Here was a new generation, shouting the old cries, learning the old creeds, through a revery of long days and nights; destined finally to go out into that dirty gray turmoil to follow love and pride; a new generation dedicated more than the last to the fear of poverty and the worship of success; grown up to find all Gods dead, all wars fought, all faiths in man shaken. . . .

Amory, sorry for them, was still not sorry for himself—art, politics, religion, whatever his medium should be, he knew he was safe now, free from all hysteria—he could accept what was acceptable, roam, grow, rebel, sleep deep through many nights. . . .

There was no God in his heart, he knew; his ideas were still in riot; there was ever the pain of memory; the regret for his lost youth—yet the waters of disillusion had left a deposit on his soul, responsibility and a love of life, the faint stirring of old ambitions and unrealized dreams. But—oh, Rosalind! Rosalind! . . .

"It's all a poor substitute at best," he said sadly.

And he could not tell why the struggle was worth while, why he had determined to use to the utmost himself and his heritage from the personalities he had passed. . . .

He stretched out his arms to the crystalline, radiant sky.

"I know myself," he cried, "but that is all."

FLAPPERS AND PHILOSOPHERS

TO ZELDA

Contents

The Offshore Pirate ... 253

The Ice Palace ... 284

Head and Shoulders ... 310

The Cut-Glass Bowl ... 335

Bernice Bobs Her Hair ... 356

Benediction ... 382

Dalyrimple Goes Wrong ... 399

The Four Fists ... 417

The Offshore Pirate

THIS unlikely story begins on a sea that was a blue dream, as colorful as blue-silk stockings, and beneath a sky as blue as the irises of children's eyes. From the western half of the sky the sun was shying little golden disks at the sea—if you gazed intently enough you could see them skip from wave tip to wave tip until they joined a broad collar of golden coin that was collecting half a mile out and would eventually be a dazzling sunset. About half-way between the Florida shore and the golden collar a white steam-yacht, very young and graceful, was riding at anchor and under a blue-and-white awning aft a yellow-haired girl reclined in a wicker settee reading The Revolt of the Angels, by Anatole France.

She was about nineteen, slender and supple, with a spoiled alluring mouth and quick gray eyes full of a radiant curiosity. Her feet, stockingless, and adorned rather than clad in blue-satin slippers which swung nonchalantly from her toes, were perched on the arm of a settee adjoining the one she occupied. And as she read she intermittently regaled herself by a faint application to her tongue of a half-lemon that she held in her hand. The other half, sucked dry, lay on the deck at her feet and rocked very gently to and fro at the almost imperceptible motion of the tide.

The second half-lemon was well-nigh pulpless and the golden collar had grown astonishing in width, when suddenly the drowsy silence which enveloped the yacht was broken by the sound of heavy footsteps and an elderly man topped with orderly gray hair and clad in a white-flannel suit appeared at the head of the companionway. There he paused for a moment until his eyes became accustomed to the sun, and then seeing the girl under the awning he uttered a long even grunt of disapproval.

If he had intended thereby to obtain a rise of any sort he was doomed to disappointment. The girl calmly turned over two pages, turned back one, raised the lemon mechanically to tasting distance, and then very faintly but quite unmistakably yawned.

"Ardita!" said the gray-haired man sternly.

Ardita uttered a small sound indicating nothing.

"Ardita!" he repeated. "Ardita!"

Ardita raised the lemon languidly, allowing three words to slip out before it reached her tongue.

"Oh, shut up."

"Ardita!"

"What?"

"Will you listen to me—or will I have to get a servant to hold you while I talk to you?"

The lemon descended slowly and scornfully.

"Put it in writing."

"Will you have the decency to close that abominable book and discard that damn lemon for two minutes?"

"Oh, can't you lemme alone for a second?"

"Ardita, I have just received a telephone message from the shore——"

"Telephone?" She showed for the first time a faint interest.

"Yes, it was——"

"Do you mean to say," she interrupted wonderingly, " 'at they let you run a wire out here?"

"Yes, and just now——"

"Won't other boats bump into it?"

"No. It's run along the bottom. Five min——"

"Well, I'll be darned! Gosh! Science is golden or something—isn't it?"

"Will you let me say what I started to?"

"Shoot!"

"Well, it seems—well, I am up here—" He paused and swallowed several times distractedly. "Oh, yes. Young woman, Colonel Moreland has called up again to ask me to be sure to bring you in to dinner. His son Toby has come all the way from New York to meet you and he's invited several other young people. For the last time, will you——"

"No," said Ardita shortly, "I won't. I came along on this darn cruise with the one idea of going to Palm Beach, and you knew it, and I absolutely refuse to meet any darn old colonel or any darn young Toby or any darn old young people or to set foot in any other darn old town in this crazy state. So you either take me to Palm Beach or else shut up and go away."

"Very well. This is the last straw. In your infatuation for this man—a man who is notorious for his excesses, a man your father would not have allowed to so much as mention your name—you have reflected the demi-monde rather than the circles in which you have presumably grown up. From now on——"

"I know," interrupted Ardita ironically, "from now on you go your way and I go mine. I've heard that story before. You know I'd like nothing better."

"From now on," he announced grandiloquently, "you are no niece of mine. I——"

"O-o-o-oh!" The cry was wrung from Ardita with the agony of a lost soul. "Will you stop boring me! Will you go 'way! Will you jump overboard and drown! Do you want me to throw this book at you!"

"If you dare do any——"

Smack! The Revolt of the Angels sailed through the air, missed its target by the length of a short nose, and bumped cheerfully down the companionway.

The gray-haired man made an instinctive step backward and then two cautious steps forward. Ardita jumped to her five feet four and stared at him defiantly, her gray eyes blazing.

"Keep off!"

"How dare you!" he cried.

"Because I darn please!"

"You've grown unbearable! Your disposition——"

"You've made me that way! No child ever has a bad disposition unless it's her family's fault! Whatever I am, you did it."

Muttering something under his breath her uncle turned and, walking forward, called in a loud voice for the launch. Then he returned to the awning, where Ardita had again seated herself and resumed her attention to the lemon.

"I am going ashore," he said slowly. "I will be out again at nine o'clock to-night. When I return we will start back to New York, where I shall turn you over to your aunt for the rest of your natural, or rather unnatural, life."

He paused and looked at her, and then all at once something in the utter childishness of her beauty seemed to puncture his anger like an inflated tire, and render him helpless, uncertain, utterly fatuous.

"Ardita," he said not unkindly, "I'm no fool. I've been round. I know men. And, child, confirmed libertines don't reform until they're tired—and then they're not themselves—they're husks of themselves." He looked at her as if expecting agreement, but receiving no sight or sound of it he continued. "Perhaps the man loves you—that's possible. He's loved many women and he'll love many more. Less than a month ago, one month, Ardita, he was involved in a notorious affair with that red-haired woman, Mimi Merril; promised to give her the diamond bracelet that the Czar of Russia gave his mother. You know—you read the papers."

"Thrilling scandals by an anxious uncle," yawned Ardita. "Have it filmed. Wicked clubman making eyes at virtuous flapper. Virtuous flapper conclusively vamped by his lurid past. Plans to meet him at Palm Beach. Foiled by anxious uncle."

"Will you tell me why the devil you want to marry him?"

"I'm sure I couldn't say," said Ardita shortly. "Maybe because he's the only man I know, good or bad, who has an imagination and the courage of his convictions. Maybe it's to get away from the young fools that spend their vacuous hours pursuing me around the country. But as for the famous Russian bracelet, you can set your mind at rest on that score. He's going to give it to me at Palm Beach—if you'll show a little intelligence."

"How about the—red-haired woman?"

"He hasn't seen her for six months," she said angrily. "Don't you suppose I have enough pride to see to that? Don't you know by this time that I can do any darn thing with any darn man I want to?"

She put her chin in the air like the statue of France Aroused, and then spoiled the pose somewhat by raising the lemon for action.

"Is it the Russian bracelet that fascinates you?"

"No, I'm merely trying to give you the sort of argument that would appeal to your intelligence. And I wish you'd go 'way," she said, her temper rising again. "You know I never change my mind. You've been boring me for three days until I'm about to go crazy. I won't go ashore! Won't! Do you hear? Won't!"

"Very well," he said, "and you won't go to Palm Beach either. Of all the selfish, spoiled, uncontrolled, disagreeable, impossible girls I have——"

Splush! The half-lemon caught him in the neck. Simultaneously came a hail from over the side.

"The launch is ready, Mr. Farnam."

Too full of words and rage to speak, Mr. Farnam cast one utterly condemning glance at his niece and, turning, ran swiftly down the ladder.

II

Five o'clock rolled down from the sun and plumped soundlessly into the sea. The golden collar widened into a glittering island; and a faint breeze that had been playing with the edges of the awning and swaying one of the dangling blue slippers became suddenly freighted with song. It was a chorus of men in close harmony and in perfect rhythm to an accompanying sound of oars cleaving the blue waters. Ardita lifted her head and listened.

"Carrots and peas,
Beans on their knees,
Pigs in the seas,
    Lucky fellows!
Blow us a breeze,
Blow us a breeze,
Blow us a breeze,
    With your bellows."

Ardita's brow wrinkled in astonishment. Sitting very still she listened eagerly as the chorus took up a second verse.

"Onions and beans,
Marshalls and Deans,
Goldbergs and Greens
    And Costellos.

Blow us a breeze,
Blow us a breeze,
Blow us a breeze,
With your bellows."

With an exclamation she tossed her book to the deck, where it sprawled at a straddle, and hurried to the rail. Fifty feet away a large rowboat was approaching containing seven men, six of them rowing and one standing up in the stern keeping time to their song with an orchestra leader's baton.

"Oysters and rocks,
Sawdust and socks,
Who could make clocks
Out of cellos?—"

The leader's eyes suddenly rested on Ardita, who was leaning over the rail spellbound with curiosity. He made a quick movement with his baton and the singing instantly ceased. She saw that he was the only white man in the boat—the six rowers were negroes.

"Narcissus ahoy!" he called politely.

"What's the idea of all the discord?" demanded Ardita cheerfully. "Is this the varsity crew from the county nut farm?"

By this time the boat was scraping the side of the yacht and a great hulking negro in the bow turned round and grasped the ladder. Thereupon the leader left his position in the stern and before Ardita had realized his intention he ran up the ladder and stood breathless before her on the deck.

"The women and children will be spared!" he said briskly. "All crying babies will be immediately drowned and all males put in double irons!"

Digging her hands excitedly down into the pockets of her dress Ardita stared at him, speechless with astonishment.

He was a young man with a scornful mouth and the bright blue eyes of a healthy baby set in a dark sensitive face. His hair was pitch black, damp and curly—the hair of a Grecian statue gone brunette. He was trimly built, trimly dressed, and graceful as an agile quarter-back.

"Well, I'll be a son of a gun!" she said dazedly.

They eyed each other coolly.

"Do you surrender the ship?"

"Is this an outburst of wit?" demanded Ardita. "Are you an idiot—or just being initiated to some fraternity?"

"I asked you if you surrendered the ship."

"I thought the country was dry," said Ardita disdainfully. "Have you been drinking finger-nail enamel? You better get off this yacht!"

"What?" The young man's voice expressed incredulity.

"Get off the yacht! You heard me!"

He looked at her for a moment as if considering what she had said.

"No," said his scornful mouth slowly; "no, I won't get off the yacht. You can get off if you wish."

Going to the rail he gave a curt command and immediately the crew of the rowboat scrambled up the ladder and ranged themselves in line before him, a coal-black and burly darky at one end and a miniature mulatto of four feet nine at the other. They seemed to be uniformly dressed in some sort of blue costume ornamented with dust, mud, and tatters; over the shoulder of each was slung a small, heavy-looking white sack, and under their arms they carried large black cases apparently containing musical instruments.

"'Ten-*shun*!" commanded the young man, snapping his own heels together crisply. "Right *driss*! Front! Step out here, Babe!"

The smallest negro took a quick step forward and saluted.

"Yas-suh!"

"Take command, go down below, catch the crew and tie 'em up—all except the engineer. Bring him up to me. Oh, and pile those bags by the rail there."

"Yas-suh!"

Babe saluted again and wheeling about motioned for the five others to gather about him. Then after a short whispered consultation they all filed noiselessly down the companionway.

"Now," said the young man cheerfully to Ardita, who had witnessed this last scene in withering silence, "if you will swear on your honor as a flapper—which probably isn't worth much—that you'll keep that spoiled little mouth of yours tight shut for forty-eight hours, you can row yourself ashore in our rowboat."

"Otherwise what?"

"Otherwise you're going to sea in a ship."

With a little sigh as for a crisis well passed, the young man sank into the settee Ardita had lately vacated and stretched his arms lazily. The corners of his mouth relaxed appreciatively as he looked round at the rich striped awning, the polished brass, and the luxurious fittings of the deck. His eye fell on the book, and then on the exhausted lemon.

"Hm," he said, "Stonewall Jackson claimed that lemon-juice cleared his head. Your head feel pretty clear?"

Ardita disdained to answer.

"Because inside of five minutes you'll have to make a clear decision whether it's go or stay."

He picked up the book and opened it curiously.

"The Revolt of the Angels. Sounds pretty good. French, eh?" He stared at her with new interest. "You French?"

"No."

"What's your name?"

"Farnam."

"Farnam what?"

"Ardita Farnam."

"Well, Ardita, no use standing up there and chewing out the insides of your mouth. You ought to break those nervous habits while you're young. Come over here and sit down."

Ardita took a carved jade case from her pocket, extracted a cigarette and lit it with a conscious coolness, though she knew her hand was trembling a little; then she crossed over with her supple, swinging walk, and sitting down in the other settee blew a mouthful of smoke at the awning.

"You can't get me off this yacht," she said steadily; "and you haven't got very much sense if you think you'll get far with it. My uncle'll have wirelesses zigzagging all over this ocean by half past six."

"Hm."

She looked quickly at his face, caught anxiety stamped there plainly in the faintest depression of the mouth's corners.

"It's all the same to me," she said, shrugging her shoulders.

" 'Tisn't my yacht. I don't mind going for a coupla hours' cruise. I'll even lend you that book so you'll have something to read on the revenue boat that takes you up to Sing Sing."

He laughed scornfully.

"If that's advice you needn't bother. This is part of a plan arranged before I ever knew this yacht existed. If it hadn't been this one it'd have been the next one we passed anchored along the coast."

"Who are you?" demanded Ardita suddenly. "And what are you?"

"You've decided not to go ashore?"

"I never even faintly considered it."

"We're generally known," he said, "all seven of us, as Curtis Carlyle and his Six Black Buddies, late of the Winter Garden and the Midnight Frolic."

"You're singers?"

"We were until to-day. At present, due to those white bags you see there, we're fugitives from justice, and if the reward offered for our capture hasn't by this time reached twenty thousand dollars I miss my guess."

"What's in the bags?" asked Ardita curiously.

"Well," he said, "for the present we'll call it—mud—Florida mud."

III

Within ten minutes after Curtis Carlyle's interview with a very frightened engineer the yacht Narcissus was under way, steaming south through a balmy tropical twilight. The little mulatto, Babe, who seemed to have Carlyle's implicit confidence, took full command of the situation. Mr. Farnam's valet and the chef, the only members of the crew on board except the engineer, having shown fight, were now reconsidering, strapped securely to their bunks below. Trombone Mose, the biggest negro, was set busy with a can of paint obliterating the name Narcissus from the bow, and substituting the name Hula Hula, and the others congregated aft and became intently involved in a game of craps.

Having given orders for a meal to be prepared and served on deck at seven-thirty, Carlyle rejoined Ardita, and, sinking back into his settee, half closed his eyes and fell into a state of profound abstraction.

Ardita scrutinized him carefully—and classed him immediately as a romantic figure. He gave the effect of towering self-confidence erected on a slight foundation—just under the surface of each of his decisions she discerned a hesitancy that was in decided contrast to the arrogant curl of his lips.

"He's not like me," she thought. "There's a difference somewhere."

Being a supreme egotist Ardita frequently thought about herself; never having had her egotism disputed she did it entirely naturally and with no detraction from her unquestioned charm. Though she was nineteen she gave the effect of a high-spirited precocious child, and in the present glow of her youth and beauty all the men and women she had known were but driftwood on the ripples of her temperament. She had met other egotists—in fact she found that selfish people bored her rather less than unselfish people—but as yet there had not been one she had not eventually defeated and brought to her feet.

But though she recognized an egotist in the settee next to her, she felt none of that usual shutting of doors in her mind which meant clearing ship for action; on the contrary her instinct told her that this man was somehow completely pregnable and quite defenseless. When Ardita defied convention—and of late it had been her chief amusement—it was from an intense desire to be herself, and she felt that this man, on the contrary, was preoccupied with his own defiance.

She was much more interested in him than she was in her own situation, which affected her as the prospect of a matinée might affect a ten-year-old child. She had implicit confidence in her ability to take care of herself under any and all circumstances.

The night deepened. A pale new moon smiled misty-eyed upon the sea, and as the shore faded dimly out and dark clouds were blown like leaves along the far horizon a great haze of moonshine suddenly bathed the yacht and spread an avenue of glittering mail in her swift path. From time to time there was the bright flare of a match as one of them lighted a cigarette, but except for the low undertone of the throbbing engines and the even wash of the waves about the stern the yacht was quiet as a dream boat star-bound through the heavens. Round them flowed the smell of the night sea, bringing with it an infinite languor.

Carlyle broke the silence at last.

"Lucky girl," he sighed, "I've always wanted to be rich—and buy all this beauty."

Ardita yawned.

"I'd rather be you," she said frankly.

"You would—for about a day. But you do seem to possess a lot of nerve for a flapper."

"I wish you wouldn't call me that."

"Beg your pardon."

"As to nerve," she continued slowly, "it's my one redeeming feature. I'm not afraid of anything in heaven or earth."

"Hm, I am."

"To be afraid," said Ardita, "a person has either to be very great and strong—or else a coward. I'm neither." She paused for a moment, and eagerness crept into her tone. "But I want to talk about you. What on earth have you done—and how did you do it?"

"Why?" he demanded cynically. "Going to write a movie about me?"

"Go on," she urged. "Lie to me by the moonlight. Do a fabulous story."

A negro appeared, switched on a string of small lights under the awning, and began setting the wicker table for supper. And while they ate cold sliced chicken, salad, artichokes, and strawberry jam from the plentiful larder below, Carlyle began to talk, hesitatingly at first, but eagerly as he saw she was interested. Ardita scarcely touched her food as she watched his dark young face—handsome, ironic, faintly ineffectual.

He began life as a poor kid in a Tennessee town, he said, so poor that his people were the only white family in their street. He never remembered any white children—but there were inevitably a dozen pickaninnies streaming in his trail, passionate admirers whom he kept in tow by the vividness of his imagination and the amount of trouble he was always getting them in and out of. And it seemed that this association diverted a rather unusual musical gift into a strange channel.

There had been a colored woman named Belle Pope Calhoun who played the piano at parties given for white children—nice white children that would have passed Curtis Carlyle with a sniff. But the ragged little "poh white" used to sit beside her piano by the hour and try to get in an alto with one of those kazoos that boys hum through. Before he was thirteen he was picking up a living teasing ragtime out of a battered violin in little cafés round Nashville. Eight years later the ragtime craze hit the country, and he took six darkies on the Orpheum circuit. Five of them were boys he had grown up with; the other was the little mulatto, Babe Divine, who was a wharf nigger round New York, and long before that a plantation hand in Bermuda, until he stuck an eight-inch stiletto in his master's back. Almost before Carlyle realized his good fortune he was on Broadway, with offers of engagements on all sides, and more money than he had ever dreamed of.

It was about then that a change began in his whole attitude, a rather curious, embittering change. It was when he realized that he was spending the golden years of his life gibbering round a stage with a lot of black men. His act was good of its kind—three trombones, three saxaphones, and Carlyle's flute—and it was his own peculiar sense of rhythm that made all the difference; but he began to grow strangely sensitive about it, began to hate the thought of appearing, dreaded it from day to day.

They were making money—each contract he signed called for more—but when he went to managers and told them that he wanted to separate from his sextet and go on as a regular pianist, they laughed at him and told him he was crazy—it would be an artistic suicide. He used to laugh afterward at the phrase "artistic suicide." They all used it.

Half a dozen times they played at private dances at three thousand dollars a night, and it seemed as if these crystallized all his distaste for his mode of livelihood. They took place in clubs and houses that he couldn't have gone into in the daytime. After all, he was merely playing the rôle of the eternal monkey, a sort of sublimated chorus man. He was sick of the very smell of the theatre, of powder and rouge and the chatter of the greenroom, and the patronizing approval of the boxes. He couldn't put his heart into it any more. The idea of a slow approach to the luxury of leisure drove him wild. He was, of course, progressing toward it, but, like a child, eating his ice-cream so slowly that he couldn't taste it at all.

He wanted to have a lot of money and time, and opportunity to read and play, and the sort of men and women round him that he could never have—the kind who, if they thought of him at all, would have considered him rather contemptible; in short he wanted all those things which he was beginning to lump under the general head of aristocracy, an aristocracy which it seemed almost any money could buy except money made as he was making it. He was twenty-five then, without family or education or any promise that he would succeed in a business career. He began speculating wildly, and within three weeks he had lost every cent he had saved.

Then the war came. He went to Plattsburg, and even there his profession followed him. A brigadier-general called him up to headquarters and told him he could serve the country better as a band leader—so he spent the war entertaining celebrities behind the line with a headquarters band. It was not so bad—except that when the infantry came limping back from the trenches he wanted to be one of them. The sweat and mud they wore seemed only one of those ineffable symbols of aristocracy that were forever eluding him.

"It was the private dances that did it. After I came back from the war the old routine started. We had an offer from a syndicate of Florida hotels. It was only a question of time then."

He broke off and Ardita looked at him expectantly, but he shook his head.

"No," he said, "I'm not going to tell you about it. I'm enjoying it too much, and I'm afraid I'd lose a little of that enjoyment if I shared it with any one else. I want to hang on to those few breathless, heroic moments when I stood out before them all and let them know I was more than a damn bobbing, squawking clown."

From up forward came suddenly the low sound of singing. The negroes had gathered together on the deck and their voices rose together in a haunting melody that soared in poignant harmonics toward the moon. And Ardita listened in enchantment.

"Oh down—
   Oh down,
Mammy wanna take me downa milky way,
Oh down—
   Oh down,
Pappy say to-morra-a-a-ah!
But mammy say to-day,
Yes—mammy say to-day!"

Carlyle sighed and was silent for a moment, looking up at the gathered host of stars blinking like arc-lights in the warm sky. The negroes' song had died away to a plaintive humming and it seemed as if minute by minute the brightness and the great silence were increasing until he could almost hear the midnight toilet of the mermaids as they combed their silver dripping curls under the moon and gossiped to each other of the fine wrecks they lived in on the green opalescent avenues below.

"You see," said Carlyle softly, "this is the beauty I want. Beauty has got to be astonishing, astounding—it's got to burst in on you like a dream, like the exquisite eyes of a girl."

He turned to her, but she was silent.

"You see, don't you, Anita—I mean, Ardita?"

Again she made no answer. She had been sound asleep for some time.

IV

In the dense sun-flooded noon of next day a spot in the sea before them resolved casually into a green-and-gray islet, apparently composed of a great granite cliff at its northern end which slanted south through a mile of vivid coppice and grass to a sandy beach melting lazily into the surf. When Ardita, reading in her favorite seat, came to the last page of The Revolt of the Angels, and slamming the book shut looked up and saw it, she gave a little cry of delight, and called to Carlyle, who was standing moodily by the rail.

"Is this it? Is this where you're going?"

Carlyle shrugged his shoulders carelessly.

"You've got me." He raised his voice and called up to the acting skipper: "Oh, Babe, is this your island?"

The mulatto's miniature head appeared from round the corner of the deck-house.

"Yas-suh! This yeah's it."

Carlyle joined Ardita.

"Looks sort of sporting, doesn't it?"

"Yes," she agreed; "but it doesn't look big enough to be much of a hiding-place."

"You still putting your faith in those wirelesses your uncle was going to have zigzagging round?"

"No," said Ardita frankly. "I'm all for you. I'd really like to see you make a get-away."

He laughed.

"You're our Lady Luck. Guess we'll have to keep you with us as a mascot—for the present, anyway."

"You couldn't very well ask me to swim back," she said coolly. "If you do I'm going to start writing dime novels founded on that interminable history of your life you gave me last night."

He flushed and stiffened slightly.

"I'm very sorry I bored you."

"Oh, you didn't—until just at the end with some story about how furious you were because you couldn't dance with the ladies you played music for."

He rose angrily.

"You have got a darn mean little tongue."

"Excuse me," she said, melting into laughter, "but I'm not used to having men regale me with the story of their life ambitions—especially if they've lived such deathly platonic lives."

"Why? What do men usually regale you with?"

"Oh, they talk about me," she yawned. "They tell me I'm the spirit of youth and beauty."

"What do you tell them?"

"Oh, I agree quietly."

"Does every man you meet tell you he loves you?"

Ardita nodded.

"Why shouldn't he? All life is just a progression toward, and then a recession from, one phrase—'I love you.' "

Carlyle laughed and sat down.

"That's very true. That's—that's not bad. Did you make that up?"

"Yes—or rather I found it out. It doesn't mean anything especially. It's just clever."

"It's the sort of remark," he said gravely, "that's typical of your class."

"Oh," she interrupted impatiently, "don't start that lecture on aristocracy again! I distrust people who can be intense at this hour in the morning. It's a mild form of insanity—a sort of breakfast-food jag. Morning's the time to sleep, swim, and be careless."

Ten minutes later they had swung round in a wide circle as if to approach the island from the north.

"There's a trick somewhere," commented Ardita thoughtfully. "He can't mean just to anchor up against this cliff."

They were heading straight in now toward the solid rock, which must have been well over a hundred feet tall, and not until they were within fifty yards of it did Ardita see their objective. Then she clapped her hands in delight. There was a break in the cliff entirely hidden by a curious overlapping of rock, and through this break the yacht entered and very slowly traversed a narrow channel of crystal-clear water between high gray walls. Then they were riding at anchor in a miniature world of green and gold, a gilded bay smooth as glass and set round with tiny palms, the whole resembling the mirror lakes and twig trees that children set up in sand piles.

"Not so darned bad!" cried Carlyle excitedly. "I guess that little coon knows his way round this corner of the Atlantic."

His exuberance was contagious, and Ardita became quite jubilant.

"It's an absolutely sure-fire hiding-place!"

"Lordy, yes! It's the sort of island you read about."

The rowboat was lowered into the golden lake and they pulled ashore.

"Come on," said Carlyle as they landed in the slushy sand, "we'll go exploring."

The fringe of palms was in turn ringed in by a round mile of flat, sandy country. They followed it south and brushing through a farther rim of tropical vegetation came out on a pearl-gray virgin beach where Ardita kicked off her brown golf shoes—she seemed to have permanently abandoned stockings—and went wading. Then they sauntered back to the yacht, where the indefatigable Babe had luncheon ready for them. He had posted a lookout on the high cliff to the north to watch the sea on both sides, though he doubted if the entrance to the cliff was generally known—he had never even seen a map on which the island was marked.

"What's its name," asked Ardita—"the island, I mean?"

"No name 'tall," chuckled Babe. "Reckin she jus' island, 'at's all."

In the late afternoon they sat with their backs against great boulders on the highest part of the cliff and Carlyle sketched for her his vague plans. He was sure they were hot after him by this time. The total proceeds of the coup he had pulled off, and concerning which he still refused to enlighten her, he estimated as just under a million dollars. He counted on lying up here several weeks and then setting off southward, keeping well outside the usual channels of travel, rounding the Horn and heading for Callao, in Peru. The details of coaling and provisioning he was leaving entirely to Babe, who, it seemed, had sailed these seas in every capacity from cabin-boy aboard a coffee trader to virtual first mate on a Brazilian pirate craft, whose skipper had long since been hung.

"If he'd been white he'd have been king of South America long ago," said Carlyle emphatically. "When it comes to intelligence he makes Booker T. Washington look like a moron. He's got the guile of every race and nationality whose blood is in his veins, and that's half a dozen or I'm a liar. He worships me because I'm the only man in the world who can play better ragtime than he can. We used to sit together on the wharfs down on the New York water-front, he with a bassoon and me with an oboe, and we'd blend minor keys in African harmonics a thousand years old until the rats would crawl up the posts and sit round groaning and squeaking like dogs will in front of a phonograph."

Ardita roared.

"How you can tell 'em!"

Carlyle grinned.

"I swear that's the gos——"

"What you going to do when you get to Callao?" she interrupted.

"Take ship for India. I want to be a rajah. I mean it. My idea is to go up into Afghanistan somewhere, buy up a palace and a reputation, and then after about five years appear in England with a foreign accent and a mysterious past. But India first. Do you know, they say that all the gold in the world drifts very gradually back to India. Something fascinating about that to me. And I want leisure to read—an immense amount."

"How about after that?"

"Then," he answered defiantly, "comes aristocracy. Laugh if you want to—but at least you'll have to admit that I know what I want—which I imagine is more than you do."

"On the contrary," contradicted Ardita, reaching in her pocket for her cigarette case, "when I met you I was in the midst of a great uproar of all my friends and relatives because I did know what I wanted."

"What was it?"

"A man."

He started.

"You mean you were engaged?"

"After a fashion. If you hadn't come aboard I had every intention of slipping ashore yesterday evening—how long ago it seems—and meeting him in Palm Beach. He's waiting there for me with a bracelet that once belonged to Catharine of Russia. Now don't mutter anything about aristocracy," she put in quickly. "I liked him simply because he had had an imagination and the utter courage of his convictions."

"But your family disapproved, eh?"

"What there is of it—only a silly uncle and a sillier aunt. It seems he got into some scandal with a red-haired woman named Mimi something—it was frightfully exaggerated, he said, and men don't lie to me—and anyway I didn't care what he'd done; it was the future that counted. And I'd see to that. When a man's in love with me he doesn't care for other amusements. I told him to drop her like a hot cake, and he did."

"I feel rather jealous," said Carlyle, frowning—and then he laughed. "I guess I'll just keep you along with us until we get to Callao. Then I'll lend you enough money to get back to the States. By that time you'll have had a chance to think that gentleman over a little more."

"Don't talk to me like that!" fired up Ardita. "I won't tolerate the parental attitude from anybody! Do you understand me?"

He chuckled and then stopped, rather abashed, as her cold anger seemed to fold him about and chill him.

"I'm sorry," he offered uncertainly.

"Oh, don't apologize! I can't stand men who say 'I'm sorry' in that manly, reserved tone. Just shut up!"

A pause ensued, a pause which Carlyle found rather awkward, but which Ardita seemed not to notice at all as she sat contentedly enjoying her cigarette and gazing out at the shining sea. After a minute she crawled out on the rock and lay with her face over the edge looking down. Carlyle, watching her, reflected how it seemed impossible for her to assume an ungraceful attitude.

"Oh, look!" she cried. "There's a lot of sort of ledges down there. Wide ones of all different heights."

He joined her and together they gazed down the dizzy height.

"We'll go swimming to-night!" she said excitedly. "By moonlight."

"Wouldn't you rather go in at the beach on the other end?"

"Not a chance. I like to dive. You can use my uncle's bathing-suit, only it'll fit you like a gunny sack, because he's a very flabby man. I've got a one-piece affair that's shocked the natives all along the Atlantic coast from Biddeford Pool to St. Augustine."

"I suppose you're a shark."

"Yes, I'm pretty good. And I look cute too. A sculptor up at Rye last summer told me my calves were worth five hundred dollars."

There didn't seem to be any answer to this, so Carlyle was silent, permitting himself only a discreet interior smile.

V

When the night crept down in shadowy blue and silver they threaded the shimmering channel in the rowboat and, tying it to a jutting rock, began climbing the cliff together. The first shelf was ten feet up, wide, and furnishing a natural diving platform. There they sat down in the bright moonlight and watched the faint incessant surge of the waters, almost stilled now as the tide set seaward.

"Are you happy?" he asked suddenly.

She nodded.

"Always happy near the sea. You know," she went on, "I've been thinking all day that you and I are somewhat alike. We're both rebels—only for different reasons. Two years ago, when I was just eighteen, and you were——"

"Twenty-five."

"—well, we were both conventional successes. I was an utterly devastating débutante and you were a prosperous musician just commissioned in the army——"

"Gentleman by act of Congress," he put in ironically.

"Well, at any rate, we both fitted. If our corners were not rubbed off they were at least pulled in. But deep in us both was something that made us require more for happiness. I didn't know what I wanted. I went from man to man, restless, impatient, month by month getting less acquiescent and more dissatisfied. I used to sit sometimes chewing at the insides of my mouth and thinking I was going crazy—I had a frightful sense of transiency. I wanted things now—now—now! Here I was—beautiful—I am, aren't I?"

"Yes," agreed Carlyle tentatively.

Ardita rose suddenly.

"Wait a second. I want to try this delightful-looking sea."

She walked to the end of the ledge and shot out over the sea, doubling up in mid-air and then straightening out and entering the water straight as a blade in a perfect jack-knife dive.

In a minute her voice floated up to him.

"You see, I used to read all day and most of the night. I began to resent society——"

"Come on up here," he interrupted. "What on earth are you doing?"

"Just floating round on my back. I'll be up in a minute. Let me tell you. The only thing I enjoyed was shocking people; wearing something quite impossible and quite charming to a fancy-dress party, going round with the fastest men in New York, and getting into some of the most hellish scrapes imaginable."

The sounds of splashing mingled with her words, and then he heard her hurried breathing as she began climbing up the side to the ledge.

"Go on in!" she called.

Obediently he rose and dived. When he emerged, dripping, and made the climb he found that she was no longer on the ledge, but after a frightened second he heard her light laughter from another shelf ten feet up. There he joined her and they both sat quietly for a moment, their arms clasped round their knees, panting a little from the climb.

"The family were wild," she said suddenly. "They tried to marry me off. And then when I'd begun to feel that after all life was scarcely worth living I found something"—her eyes went skyward exultantly—"I found something!"

Carlyle waited and her words came with a rush.

"Courage—just that; courage as a rule of life, and something to cling to always. I began to build up this enormous faith in myself. I began to see that in all my idols in the past some manifestation of courage had unconsciously been the thing that attracted me. I began separating courage from the other things of life. All sorts of courage—the beaten, bloody prize-fighter coming up for more—I used to make men take me to prize-fights; the déclassé woman sailing through a nest of cats and looking at them as if they were mud under her feet; the liking what you like always; the utter disregard for other people's opinions—just to live as I liked always and to die in my own way— Did you bring up the cigarettes?"

He handed one over and held a match for her silently.

"Still," Ardita continued, "the men kept gathering—old men and young men, my mental and physical inferiors, most of them, but all intensely desiring to have me—to own this rather magnificent proud tradition I'd built up round me. Do you see?"

"Sort of. You never were beaten and you never apologized."

"Never!"

She sprang to the edge, poised for a moment like a crucified figure against the sky; then describing a dark parabola plunked without a slash between two silver ripples twenty feet below.

Her voice floated up to him again.

"And courage to me meant ploughing through that dull gray mist that comes down on life—not only overriding people and circumstances but overriding the bleakness of living. A sort of insistence on the value of life and the worth of transient things."

She was climbing up now, and at her last words her head, with the damp yellow hair slicked symmetrically back, appeared on his level.

"All very well," objected Carlyle. "You can call it courage, but your courage is really built, after all, on a pride of birth. You were bred to that defiant attitude. On my gray days even courage is one of the things that's gray and lifeless."

She was sitting near the edge, hugging her knees and gazing abstractedly at the white moon; he was farther back, crammed like a grotesque god into a niche in the rock.

"I don't want to sound like Pollyanna," she began, "but you haven't grasped me yet. My courage is faith—faith in the eternal resilience of me—that joy'll come back, and hope and spontaneity. And I feel that till it does I've got to keep my lips shut and my chin high, and my eyes wide—not necessarily any silly smiling. Oh, I've been through hell without a whine quite often—and the female hell is deadlier than the male."

"But supposing," suggested Carlyle, "that before joy and hope and all that came back the curtain was drawn on you for good?"

Ardita rose, and going to the wall climbed with some difficulty to the next ledge, another ten or fifteen feet above.

"Why," she called back, "then I'd have won!"

He edged out till he could see her.

"Better not dive from there! You'll break your back," he said quickly.

She laughed.

"Not I!"

Slowly she spread her arms and stood there swan-like, radiating a pride in her young perfection that lit a warm glow in Carlyle's heart.

"We're going through the black air with our arms wide," she called, "and our feet straight out behind like a dolphin's tail, and we're going to think we'll never hit the silver down there till suddenly it'll be all warm round us and full of little kissing, caressing waves."

Then she was in the air, and Carlyle involuntarily held his breath. He had not realized that the dive was nearly forty feet. It seemed an eternity before he heard the swift compact sound as she reached the sea.

And it was with his glad sigh of relief when her light watery laughter curled up the side of the cliff and into his anxious ears that he knew he loved her.

VI

Time, having no axe to grind, showered down upon them three days of afternoons. When the sun cleared the port-hole of Ardita's cabin an hour after dawn she rose cheerily, donned her bathing-suit, and went up on deck. The negroes would leave their work when they saw her, and crowd, chuckling and chattering, to the rail as she floated, an agile minnow, on and under the surface of the clear water. Again in the cool of the afternoon she would swim—and loll and smoke with Carlyle upon the cliff; or else they would lie on their sides in the sands of the southern beach, talking little, but watching the day fade colorfully and tragically into the infinite languor of a tropical evening.

And with the long, sunny hours Ardita's idea of the episode as incidental, madcap, a sprig of romance in a desert of reality, gradually left her. She dreaded the time when he would strike off southward; she dreaded all the eventualities that presented themselves to her; thoughts were suddenly troublesome and decisions odious. Had prayers found place in the pagan rituals of her soul she would have asked of life only to be unmolested for a while, lazily acquiescent to the ready, naïf flow of Carlyle's ideas, his vivid boyish imagination, and the vein of monomania that seemed to run crosswise through his temperament and colored his every action.

But this is not a story of two on an island, nor concerned primarily with love bred of isolation. It is merely the presentation of two personalities, and its idyllic setting among the palms of the Gulf Stream is quite incidental. Most of us are content to exist and breed and fight for the right to do both, and the dominant idea, the foredoomed attempt to control one's destiny, is reserved for the fortunate or unfortunate few. To me the interesting thing about Ardita is the courage that will tarnish with her beauty and youth.

"Take me with you," she said late one night as they sat lazily in the grass under the shadowy spreading palms. The negroes had brought ashore their musical instruments, and the sound of weird ragtime was drifting softly over on the warm breath of the night. "I'd love to reappear in ten years as a fabulously wealthy high-caste Indian lady," she continued.

Carlyle looked at her quickly.

"You can, you know."

She laughed.

"Is it a proposal of marriage? Extra! Ardita Farnam becomes pirate's bride. Society girl kidnapped by ragtime bank robber."

"It wasn't a bank."

"What was it? Why won't you tell me?"

"I don't want to break down your illusions."

"My dear man, I have no illusions about you."

"I mean your illusions about yourself."

She looked up in surprise.

"About myself! What on earth have I got to do with whatever stray felonies you've committed?"

"That remains to be seen."

She reached over and patted his hand.

"Dear Mr. Curtis Carlyle," she said softly, "are you in love with me?"

"As if it mattered."

"But it does—because I think I'm in love with you."

He looked at her ironically.

"Thus swelling your January total to half a dozen," he suggested. "Suppose I call your bluff and ask you to come to India with me?"

"Shall I?"

He shrugged his shoulders.

"We can get married in Callao."

"What sort of life can you offer me? I don't mean that unkindly, but seriously; what would become of me if the people who want that twenty-thousand-dollar reward ever catch up with you?"

"I thought you weren't afraid."

"I never am—but I won't throw my life away just to show one man I'm not."

"I wish you'd been poor. Just a little poor girl dreaming over a fence in a warm cow country."

"Wouldn't it have been nice?"

"I'd have enjoyed astonishing you—watching your eyes open on things. If you only wanted things! Don't you see?"

"I know—like girls who stare into the windows of jewelry-stores."

"Yes—and want the big oblong watch that's platinum and has diamonds all round the edge. Only you'd decide it was too expensive and choose one of white gold for a hundred dollars. Then I'd say: 'Expensive? I should say not!' And we'd go into the store and pretty soon the platinum one would be gleaming on your wrist."

"That sounds so nice and vulgar—and fun, doesn't it?" murmured Ardita.

"Doesn't it? Can't you see us travelling round and spending money right and left, and being worshipped by bell-boys and waiters? Oh, blessed are the simple rich, for they inherit the earth!"

"I honestly wish we were that way."

"I love you, Ardita," he said gently.

Her face lost its childish look for a moment and became oddly grave.

"I love to be with you," she said, "more than with any man I've ever met. And I like your looks and your dark old hair, and the way you go over the side of the rail when we come ashore. In fact, Curtis Carlyle, I like all the things you do when you're perfectly natural. I think you've got nerve, and you know how I feel about that. Sometimes when you're around I've been tempted to kiss you suddenly and tell you that you were just an idealistic boy with a lot of caste nonsense in his head. Perhaps if I were just a little bit older and a little more bored I'd go with you. As it is, I think I'll go back and marry—that other man."

Over across the silver lake the figures of the negroes writhed and squirmed in the moonlight, like acrobats who, having been too long inactive, must go through their tricks from sheer surplus energy. In single file they marched, weaving in concentric circles, now with their heads thrown back, now bent over their instruments like piping fauns. And from trombone and saxaphone ceaselessly whined a blended melody, sometimes riotous and jubilant, sometimes haunting and plaintive as a death-dance from the Congo's heart.

"Let's dance!" cried Ardita. "I can't sit still with that perfect jazz going on."

Taking her hand he led her out into a broad stretch of hard sandy soil that the moon flooded with great splendor. They floated out like drifting moths under the rich hazy light, and as the fantastic symphony wept and exulted and wavered and despaired Ardita's last sense of reality dropped away, and she abandoned her imagination to the dreamy summer scents of tropical flowers and the infinite starry spaces overhead, feeling that if she opened her eyes it would be to find herself dancing with a ghost in a land created by her own fancy.

"This is what I should call an exclusive private dance," he whispered.

"I feel quite mad—but delightfully mad!"

"We're enchanted. The shades of unnumbered generations of cannibals are watching us from high up on the side of the cliff there."

"And I'll bet the cannibal women are saying that we dance too close, and that it was immodest of me to come without my nose-ring."

They both laughed softly—and then their laughter died as over across the lake they heard the trombones stop in the middle of a bar, and the saxaphones give a startled moan and fade out.

"What's the matter?" called Carlyle.

After a moment's silence they made out the dark figure of a man rounding the silver lake at a run. As he came closer they saw it was Babe in a state of unusual excitement. He drew up before them and gasped out his news in a breath.

"Ship stan'in' off sho' 'bout half a mile, suh. Mose, he uz on watch, he say look's if she's done ancho'd."

"A ship—what kind of a ship?" demanded Carlyle anxiously.

Dismay was in his voice, and Ardita's heart gave a sudden wrench as she saw his whole face suddenly droop.

"He say he don't know, suh."

"Are they landing a boat?"

"No, suh."

"We'll go up," said Carlyle.

They ascended the hill in silence, Ardita's hand still resting in Carlyle's as it had when they finished dancing. She felt it clinch nervously from time to time as though he were unaware of the contact, but though he hurt her she made no attempt to remove it. It seemed an hour's climb before they reached the top and crept cautiously across the silhouetted plateau to the edge of the cliff. After one short look Carlyle involuntarily gave a little cry. It was a revenue boat with six-inch guns mounted fore and aft.

"They know!" he said with a short intake of breath. "They know! They picked up the trail somewhere."

"Are you sure they know about the channel? They may be only standing by to take a look at the island in the morning. From where they are they couldn't see the opening in the cliff."

"They could with field-glasses," he said hopelessly. He looked at his wrist-watch. "It's nearly two now. They won't do anything until dawn, that's certain. Of course there's always the faint possibility that they're waiting for some other ship to join; or for a coaler."

"I suppose we may as well stay right here."

The hours passed and they lay there side by side, very silently, their chins in their hands like dreaming children. In back of them squatted the negroes, patient, resigned, acquiescent, announcing now and then with sonorous snores that not even the presence of danger could subdue their unconquerable African craving for sleep.

Just before five o'clock Babe approached Carlyle. There were half a dozen rifles aboard the Narcissus he said. Had it been decided to offer no resistance? A pretty good fight might be made, he thought, if they worked out some plan.

Carlyle laughed and shook his head.

"That isn't a Spic army out there, Babe. That's a revenue boat. It'd be like a bow and arrow trying to fight a machine-gun. If you want to bury those bags somewhere and take a chance on recovering them later, go on and do it. But it won't work—they'd dig this island over from one end to the other. It's a lost battle all round, Babe."

Babe inclined his head silently and turned away, and Carlyle's voice was husky as he turned to Ardita.

"There's the best friend I ever had. He'd die for me, and be proud to, if I'd let him."

"You've given up?"

"I've no choice. Of course there's always one way out—the sure way—but that can wait. I wouldn't miss my trial for anything—it'll be an interesting experiment in notoriety. 'Miss Farnam testifies that the pirate's attitude to her was at all times that of a gentleman.' "

"Don't!" she said. "I'm awfully sorry."

When the color faded from the sky and lustreless blue changed to leaden gray a commotion was visible on the ship's deck, and they made out a group of officers clad in white duck, gathered near the rail. They had field-glasses in their hands and were attentively examining the islet.

"It's all up," said Carlyle grimly.

"Damn!" whispered Ardita. She felt tears gathering in her eyes.

"We'll go back to the yacht," he said. "I prefer that to being hunted out up here like a 'possum."

Leaving the plateau they descended the hill, and reaching the lake were rowed out to the yacht by the silent negroes. Then, pale and weary, they sank into the settees and waited.

Half an hour later in the dim gray light the nose of the revenue boat appeared in the channel and stopped, evidently fearing that the bay might be too shallow. From the peaceful look of the yacht, the man and the girl in the settees, and the negroes lounging curiously against the rail, they evidently judged that there would be no resistance, for two boats were lowered casually over the side, one containing an officer and six bluejackets, and the other, four rowers and in the stern two gray-haired men in yachting flannels. Ardita and Carlyle stood up, and half unconsciously started toward each other. Then he paused and putting his hand suddenly into his pocket he pulled out a round, glittering object and held it out to her.

"What is it?" she asked wonderingly.

"I'm not positive, but I think from the Russian inscription inside that it's your promised bracelet."

"Where—where on earth——"

"It came out of one of those bags. You see, Curtis Carlyle and his Six Black Buddies, in the middle of their performance in the tea-room of the hotel at Palm Beach, suddenly changed their instruments for automatics and held up the crowd. I took this bracelet from a pretty, overrouged woman with red hair."

Ardita frowned and then smiled.

"So that's what you did! You *have* got nerve!"

He bowed.

"A well-known bourgeois quality," he said.

And then dawn slanted dynamically across the deck and flung the shadows reeling into gray corners. The dew rose and turned to golden mist, thin as a dream, enveloping them until they seemed gossamer relics of the late night, infinitely transient and already fading. For a moment sea and sky were breathless, and dawn held a pink hand over the young mouth of life—then from out in the lake came the complaint of a rowboat and the swish of oars.

Suddenly against the golden furnace low in the east their two graceful figures melted into one, and he was kissing her spoiled young mouth.

"It's a sort of glory," he murmured after a second.

She smiled up at him.

"Happy, are you?"

Her sigh was a benediction—an ecstatic surety that she was youth and beauty now as much as she would ever know. For another instant life was radiant and time a phantom and their strength eternal—then there was a bumping, scraping sound as the rowboat scraped alongside.

Up the ladder scrambled the two gray-haired men, the officer and two of the sailors with their hands on their revolvers. Mr. Farnam folded his arms and stood looking at his niece.

"So," he said, nodding his head slowly.

With a sigh her arms unwound from Carlyle's neck, and her eyes, transfigured and far away, fell upon the boarding party. Her uncle saw her upper lip slowly swell into that arrogant pout he knew so well.

"So," he repeated savagely. "So this is your idea of—of romance. A runaway affair, with a high-seas pirate."

Ardita glanced at him carelessly.

"What an old fool you are!" she said quietly.

"Is that the best you can say for yourself?"

"No," she said as if considering. "No, there's something else. There's that well-known phrase with which I have ended most of our conversations for the past few years—'Shut up!'"

And with that she turned, included the two old men, the officer, and the two sailors in a curt glance of contempt, and walked proudly down the companionway.

But had she waited an instant longer she would have heard a sound from her uncle quite unfamiliar in most of their interviews. He gave vent to a whole-hearted amused chuckle, in which the second old man joined.

The latter turned briskly to Carlyle, who had been regarding this scene with an air of cryptic amusement.

"Well, Toby," he said genially, "you incurable, harebrained, romantic chaser of rainbows, did you find that she was the person you wanted?"

Carlyle smiled confidently.

"Why—naturally," he said. "I've been perfectly sure ever since I first heard tell of her wild career. That's why I had Babe send up the rocket last night."

"I'm glad you did," said Colonel Moreland gravely. "We've been keeping pretty close to you in case you should have trouble with those six strange niggers. And we hoped we'd find you two in some such compromising position," he sighed. "Well, set a crank to catch a crank!"

"Your father and I sat up all night hoping for the best—or perhaps it's the worst. Lord knows you're welcome to her, my boy. She's run me crazy. Did you give her the Russian bracelet my detective got from that Mimi woman?"

Carlyle nodded.

"Sh!" he said. "She's coming on deck."

Ardita appeared at the head of the companionway and gave a quick involuntary glance at Carlyle's wrists. A puzzled look passed across her face. Back aft the negroes had begun to sing, and the cool lake, fresh with dawn, echoed serenely to their low voices.

"Ardita," said Carlyle unsteadily.

She swayed a step toward him.

"Ardita," he repeated breathlessly, "I've got to tell you the—the truth. It was all a plant, Ardita. My name isn't Carlyle. It's Moreland, Toby Moreland. The story was invented, Ardita, invented out of thin Florida air."

She stared at him, bewildered amazement, disbelief, and anger flowing in quick waves across her face. The three men held their breaths. Moreland, Senior, took a step toward her; Mr. Farnam's mouth dropped a little open as he waited, panic-stricken, for the expected crash.

But it did not come. Ardita's face became suddenly radiant, and with a little laugh she went swiftly to young Moreland and looked up at him without a trace of wrath in her gray eyes.

"Will you swear," she said quietly, "that it was entirely a product of your own brain?"

"I swear," said young Moreland eagerly.

She drew his head down and kissed him gently.

"What an imagination!" she said softly and almost enviously. "I want you to lie to me just as sweetly as you know how for the rest of my life."

The negroes' voices floated drowsily back, mingled in an air that she had heard them sing before.

> "Time is a thief;
> Gladness and grief
> Cling to the leaf
> As it yellows——"

"What was in the bags?" she asked softly.

"Florida mud," he answered. "That was one of the two true things I told you."

"Perhaps I can guess the other one," she said; and reaching up on her tiptoes she kissed him softly in the illustration.

The Ice Palace

THE sunlight dripped over the house like golden paint over an art jar, and the freckling shadows here and there only intensified the rigor of the bath of light. The Butterworth and Larkin houses flanking were intrenched behind great stodgy trees; only the Happer house took the full sun, and all day long faced the dusty road-street with a tolerant kindly patience. This was the city of Tarleton in southernmost Georgia, September afternoon.

Up in her bedroom window Sally Carrol Happer rested her nineteen-year-old chin on a fifty-two-year-old sill and watched Clark Darrow's ancient Ford turn the corner. The car was hot—being partly metallic it retained all the heat it absorbed or evolved—and Clark Darrow sitting bolt upright at the wheel wore a pained, strained expression as though he considered himself a spare part, and rather likely to break. He laboriously crossed two dust ruts, the wheels squeaking indignantly at the encounter, and then with a terrifying expression he gave the steering-gear a final wrench and deposited self and car approximately in front of the Happer steps. There was a plaintive heaving sound, a death-rattle, followed by a short silence; and then the air was rent by a startling whistle.

Sally Carrol gazed down sleepily. She started to yawn, but finding this quite impossible unless she raised her chin from the window-sill, changed her mind and continued silently to regard the car, whose owner sat brilliantly if perfunctorily at attention as he waited for an answer to his signal. After a moment the whistle once more split the dusty air.

"Good mawnin'."

With difficulty Clark twisted his tall body round and bent a distorted glance on the window.

" 'Tain't mawnin', Sally Carrol."

"Isn't it, sure enough?"

"What you doin'?"

"Eatin' 'n apple."

"Come on go swimmin'—want to?"

"Reckon so."

"How 'bout hurryin' up?"

"Sure enough."

Sally Carrol sighed voluminously and raised herself with profound inertia from the floor, where she had been occupied in alternately destroying parts of a green apple and painting paper dolls for her younger sister. She approached a mirror, regarded her expression with a pleased and pleasant languor, dabbed two spots of rouge on her lips and a grain of powder on her nose, and covered her bobbed corn-colored hair with a rose-littered sunbonnet. Then she kicked over the painting water, said, "Oh, damn!"—but let it lay—and left the room.

"How you, Clark?" she inquired a minute later as she slipped nimbly over the side of the car.

"Mighty fine, Sally Carrol."

"Where we go swimmin'?"

"Out to Walley's Pool. Told Marylyn we'd call by an' get her an' Joe Ewing."

Clark was dark and lean, and when on foot was rather inclined to stoop. His eyes were ominous and his expression somewhat petulant except when startlingly illuminated by one of his frequent smiles. Clark had "a income"—just enough to keep himself in ease and his car in gasolene—and he had spent the two years since he graduated from Georgia Tech in dozing round the lazy streets of his home town, discussing how he could best invest his capital for an immediate fortune.

Hanging round he found not at all difficult; a crowd of little girls had grown up beautifully, the amazing Sally Carrol foremost among them; and they enjoyed being swum with and danced with and made love to in the flower-filled summery evenings—and they all liked Clark immensely. When feminine company palled there were half a dozen other youths who were always just about to do something, and meanwhile were quite willing to join him in a few holes of golf, or a game of billiards, or the consumption of a quart of "hard yella licker." Every once in a while one of these contemporaries made a farewell round of calls before going up to New York or Philadelphia or Pittsburgh to go into business, but mostly they just stayed round in this languid paradise of dreamy skies and firefly evenings and noisy niggery street fairs—and especially of gracious, soft-voiced girls, who were brought up on memories instead of money.

The Ford having been excited into a sort of restless resentful life Clark and Sally Carrol rolled and rattled down Valley Avenue into Jefferson Street, where the dust road became a pavement; along opiate Millicent Place, where there were half a dozen prosperous, substantial mansions; and on into the down-town section. Driving was perilous here, for it was shopping time; the population idled casually across the streets and a drove of low-moaning oxen were being urged along in front of a placid street-car; even the shops seemed only yawning their doors and blinking their windows in the sunshine before retiring into a state of utter and finite coma.

"Sally Carrol," said Clark suddenly, "it a fact that you're engaged?"

She looked at him quickly.

"Where'd you hear that?"

"Sure enough, you engaged?"

" 'At's a nice question!"

"Girl told me you were engaged to a Yankee you met up in Asheville last summer."

Sally Carrol sighed.

"Never saw such an old town for rumors."

"Don't marry a Yankee, Sally Carrol. We need you round here."

Sally Carrol was silent a moment.

"Clark," she demanded suddenly, "who on earth shall I marry?"

"I offer my services."

"Honey, you couldn't support a wife," she answered cheerfully. "Anyway, I know you too well to fall in love with you."

" 'At doesn't mean you ought to marry a Yankee," he persisted.

"S'pose I love him?"

He shook his head.

"You couldn't. He'd be a lot different from us, every way."

He broke off as he halted the car in front of a rambling, dilapidated house. Marylyn Wade and Joe Ewing appeared in the doorway.

" 'Lo, Sally Carrol."

"Hi!"

"How you-all?"

"Sally Carrol," demanded Marylyn as they started off again, "you engaged?"

"Lawdy, where'd all this start? Can't I look at a man 'thout everybody in town engagin' me to him?"

Clark stared straight in front of him at a bolt on the clattering wind-shield.

"Sally Carrol," he said with a curious intensity, "don't you like us?"

"What?"

"Us down here?"

"Why, Clark, you know I do. I adore all you boys."

"Then why you gettin' engaged to a Yankee?"

"Clark, I don't know. I'm not sure what I'll do, but—well, I want to go places and see people. I want my mind to grow. I want to live where things happen on a big scale."

"What you mean?"

"Oh, Clark, I love you, and I love Joe here, and Ben Arrot, and you-all, but you'll—you'll——"

"We'll all be failures?"

"Yes. I don't mean only money failures, but just sort of—of ineffectual and sad, and—oh, how can I tell you?"

"You mean because we stay here in Tarleton?"

"Yes, Clark; and because you like it and never want to change things or think or go ahead."

He nodded and she reached over and pressed his hand.

"Clark," she said softly, "I wouldn't change you for the world. You're sweet the way you are. The things that'll make you fail I'll love always—the living in the past, the lazy days and nights you have, and all your carelessness and generosity."

"But you're goin' away?"

"Yes—because I couldn't ever marry you. You've a place in my heart no one else ever could have, but tied down here I'd get restless. I'd feel I was—wastin' myself. There's two sides to me, you see. There's the sleepy old side you love; an' there's a sort of energy—the feelin' that makes me do wild things. That's the part of me that may be useful somewhere, that'll last when I'm not beautiful any more."

She broke off with characteristic suddenness and sighed, "Oh, sweet cooky!" as her mood changed.

Half closing her eyes and tipping back her head till it rested on the seat-back she let the savory breeze fan her eyes and ripple the fluffy curls of her bobbed hair. They were in the country now, hurrying between tangled growths of bright-green coppice and grass and tall trees that sent sprays of foliage to hang a cool welcome over the road. Here and there they passed a battered negro cabin, its oldest white-haired inhabitant smoking a corncob pipe beside the door, and half a dozen scantily clothed pickaninnies parading tattered dolls on the wild-grown grass in front. Farther out were lazy cotton-fields, where even the workers seemed intangible shadows lent by the sun to the earth, not for toil, but to while away some age-old tradition in the golden September fields. And round the drowsy picturesqueness, over the trees and shacks and muddy rivers, flowed the heat, never hostile, only comforting, like a great warm nourishing bosom for the infant earth.

"Sally Carrol, we're here!"

"Poor chile's soun' asleep."

"Honey, you dead at last outa sheer laziness?"

"Water, Sally Carrol! Cool water waitin' for you!"

Her eyes opened sleepily.

"Hi!" she murmured, smiling.

II

In November Harry Bellamy, tall, broad, and brisk, came down from his Northern city to spend four days. His intention was to settle a matter that had been hanging fire since he and Sally Carrol had met in Asheville, North Carolina, in midsummer. The settlement took only a quiet afternoon and an evening in front of a glowing open fire, for Harry Bellamy had everything she wanted; and, besides, she loved him—loved him with that side of her she kept especially for loving. Sally Carrol had several rather clearly defined sides.

On his last afternoon they walked, and she found their steps tending half-unconsciously toward one of her favorite haunts, the cemetery. When it came in sight, gray-white and golden-green under the cheerful late sun, she paused, irresolute, by the iron gate.

"Are you mournful by nature, Harry?" she asked with a faint smile.

"Mournful? Not I."

"Then let's go in here. It depresses some folks, but I like it."

They passed through the gateway and followed a path that led through a wavy valley of graves—dusty-gray and mouldy for the fifties; quaintly carved with flowers and jars for the seventies; ornate and hideous for the nineties, with fat marble cherubs lying in sodden sleep on stone pillows, and great impossible growths of nameless granite flowers. Occasionally they saw a kneeling figure with tributary flowers, but over most of the graves lay silence and withered leaves with only the fragrance that their own shadowy memories could waken in living minds.

They reached the top of a hill where they were fronted by a tall, round head-stone, freckled with dark spots of damp and half grown over with vines.

"Margery Lee," she read; "1844–1873. Wasn't she nice? She died when she was twenty-nine. Dear Margery Lee," she added softly. "Can't you see her, Harry?"

"Yes, Sally Carrol."

He felt a little hand insert itself into his.

"She was dark, I think; and she always wore her hair with a ribbon in it, and gorgeous hoop-skirts of alice blue and old rose."

"Yes."

"Oh, she was sweet, Harry! And she was the sort of girl born to stand on a wide, pillared porch and welcome folks in. I think perhaps a lot of men went away to war meanin' to come back to her; but maybe none of 'em ever did."

He stooped down close to the stone, hunting for any record of marriage.

"There's nothing here to show."

"Of course not. How could there be anything there better than just 'Margery Lee,' and that eloquent date?"

She drew close to him and an unexpected lump came into his throat as her yellow hair brushed his cheek.

"You see how she was, don't you, Harry?"

"I see," he agreed gently. "I see through your precious eyes. You're beautiful now, so I know she must have been."

Silent and close they stood, and he could feel her shoulders trembling a little. An ambling breeze swept up the hill and stirred the brim of her floppidy hat.

"Let's go down there!"

She was pointing to a flat stretch on the other side of the hill where along the green turf were a thousand grayish-white crosses stretching in endless, ordered rows like the stacked arms of a battalion.

"Those are the Confederate dead," said Sally Carrol simply.

They walked along and read the inscriptions, always only a name and a date, sometimes quite indecipherable.

"The last row is the saddest—see, 'way over there. Every cross has just a date on it, and the word 'Unknown.'"

She looked at him and her eyes brimmed with tears.

"I can't tell you how real it is to me, darling—if you don't know."

"How you feel about it is beautiful to me."

"No, no, it's not me, it's them—that old time that I've tried to have live in me. These were just men, unimportant evidently or they wouldn't have been 'unknown'; but they died for the most beautiful thing in the world—the dead South. You see," she continued, her voice still husky, her eyes glistening with tears, "people have these dreams they fasten onto things, and I've always grown up with that dream. It was so easy because it was all dead and there weren't any disillusions comin' to me. I've tried in a way to live up to those past standards of noblesse oblige—there's just the last remnants of it, you know, like the roses of an old garden dying all round us—streaks of strange courtliness and chivalry in some of these boys an' stories I used to hear from a Confederate soldier who lived next door, and a few old darkies. Oh, Harry, there was something, there was something! I couldn't ever make you understand, but it was there."

"I understand," he assured her again quietly.

Sally Carrol smiled and dried her eyes on the tip of a handkerchief protruding from his breast pocket.

"You don't feel depressed, do you, lover? Even when I cry I'm happy here, and I get a sort of strength from it."

Hand in hand they turned and walked slowly away. Finding soft grass she drew him down to a seat beside her with their backs against the remnants of a low broken wall.

"Wish those three old women would clear out," he complained. "I want to kiss you, Sally Carrol."

"Me, too."

They waited impatiently for the three bent figures to move off, and then she kissed him until the sky seemed to fade out and all her smiles and tears to vanish in an ecstasy of eternal seconds.

Afterward they walked slowly back together, while on the corners twilight played at somnolent black-and-white checkers with the end of day.

"You'll be up about mid-January," he said, "and you've got to stay a month at least. It'll be slick. There's a winter carnival on, and if you've never really seen snow it'll be like fairyland to you. There'll be skating and skiing and tobogganing and sleigh-riding, and all sorts of torchlight parades on snowshoes. They haven't had one for years, so they're going to make it a knock-out."

"Will I be cold, Harry?" she asked suddenly.

"You certainly won't. You may freeze your nose, but you won't be shivery cold. It's hard and dry, you know."

"I guess I'm a summer child. I don't like any cold I've ever seen."

She broke off and they were both silent for a minute.

"Sally Carrol," he said very slowly, "what do you say to—March?"

"I say I love you."

"March?"

"March, Harry."

III

All night in the Pullman it was very cold. She rang for the porter to ask for another blanket, and when he couldn't give her one she tried vainly, by squeezing down into the bottom of her berth and doubling back the bedclothes, to snatch a few hours' sleep. She wanted to look her best in the morning.

She rose at six and sliding uncomfortably into her clothes stumbled up to the diner for a cup of coffee. The snow had filtered into the vestibules and covered the floor with a slippery coating. It was intriguing, this cold, it crept in everywhere. Her breath was quite visible and she blew into the air with a naïve enjoyment. Seated in the diner she stared out the window at white hills and valleys and scattered pines whose every branch was a green platter for a cold feast of snow. Sometimes a solitary farmhouse would fly by, ugly and bleak and lone on the white waste; and with each one she had an instant of chill compassion for the souls shut in there waiting for spring.

As she left the diner and swayed back into the Pullman she experienced a surging rush of energy and wondered if she was feeling the bracing air of which Harry had spoken. This was the North, the North—her land now!

"Then blow, ye winds, heigho!
A-roving I will go,"

she chanted exultantly to herself.

"What's 'at?" inquired the porter politely.

"I said: 'Brush me off.' "

The long wires of the telegraph-poles doubled; two tracks ran up beside the train—three—four; came a succession of white-roofed houses, a glimpse of a trolley-car with frosted windows, streets—more streets—the city.

She stood for a dazed moment in the frosty station before she saw three fur-bundled figures descending upon her.

"There she is!"

"Oh, Sally Carrol!"

Sally Carrol dropped her bag.

"Hi!"

A faintly familiar icy-cold face kissed her, and then she was in a group of faces all apparently emitting great clouds of heavy smoke; she was shaking hands. There were Gordon, a short, eager man of thirty who looked like an amateur knocked-about model for Harry, and his wife, Myra, a listless lady with flaxen hair under a fur automobile cap. Almost immediately Sally Carrol thought of her as vaguely Scandinavian. A cheerful chauffeur adopted her bag, and amid ricochets of half-phrases, exclamations, and perfunctory listless "my dears" from Myra, they swept each other from the station.

Then they were in a sedan bound through a crooked succession of snowy streets where dozens of little boys were hitching sleds behind grocery wagons and automobiles.

"Oh," cried Sally Carrol, "I want to do that! Can we, Harry?"

"That's for kids. But we might——"

"It looks like such a circus!" she said regretfully.

Home was a rambling frame house set on a white lap of snow, and there she met a big, gray-haired man of whom she approved, and a lady who was like an egg, and who kissed her—these were Harry's parents. There was a breathless indescribable hour crammed full of half-sentences, hot water, bacon and eggs and confusion; and after that she was alone with Harry in the library, asking him if she dared smoke.

It was a large room with a Madonna over the fireplace and rows upon rows of books in covers of light gold and dark gold and shiny red. All the chairs had little lace squares where one's head should rest, the couch was just comfortable, the books looked as if they had been read—some—and Sally Carrol had an instantaneous vision of the battered old library at home, with her father's huge medical books, and the oil-paintings of her three great-uncles, and the old couch that had been mended up for forty-five years and was still luxurious to dream in. This room struck her as being neither attractive nor particularly otherwise. It was simply a room with a lot of fairly expensive things in it that all looked about fifteen years old.

"What do you think of it up here?" demanded Harry eagerly. "Does it surprise you? Is it what you expected, I mean?"

"You are, Harry," she said quietly, and reached out her arms to him.

But after a brief kiss he seemed anxious to extort enthusiasm from her.

"The town, I mean. Do you like it? Can you feel the pep in the air?"

"Oh, Harry," she laughed, "you'll have to give me time. You can't just fling questions at me."

She puffed at her cigarette with a sigh of contentment.

"One thing I want to ask you," he began rather apologetically; "you Southerners put quite an emphasis on family, and all that—not that it isn't quite all right, but you'll find it a little different here. I mean—you'll notice a lot of things that'll seem to you sort of vulgar display at first, Sally Carrol; but just remember that this is a three-generation town. Everybody has a father, and about half of us have grandfathers. Back of that we don't go."

"Of course," she murmured.

"Our grandfathers, you see, founded the place, and a lot of them had to take some pretty queer jobs while they were doing the founding. For instance, there's one woman who at present is about the social model for the town; well, her father was the first public ash man—things like that."

"Why," said Sally Carrol, puzzled, "did you s'pose I was goin' to make remarks about people?"

"Not at all," interrupted Harry; "and I'm not apologizing for any one either. It's just that—well, a Southern girl came up here last summer and said some unfortunate things, and—oh, I just thought I'd tell you."

Sally Carrol felt suddenly indignant—as though she had been unjustly spanked—but Harry evidently considered the subject closed, for he went on with a great surge of enthusiasm.

"It's carnival time, you know. First in ten years. And there's an ice palace they're building now that's the first they've had since eighty-five. Built out of blocks of the clearest ice they could find—on a tremendous scale."

She rose and walking to the window pushed aside the heavy Turkish portières and looked out.

"Oh!" she cried suddenly. "There's two little boys makin' a snow man! Harry, do you reckon I can go out an' help 'em?"

"You dream! Come here and kiss me."

She left the window rather reluctantly.

"I don't guess this is a very kissable climate, is it? I mean, it makes you so you don't want to sit round, doesn't it?"

"We're not going to. I've got a vacation for the first week you're here, and there's a dinner-dance to-night."

"Oh, Harry," she confessed, subsiding in a heap, half in his lap, half in the pillows, "I sure do feel confused. I haven't got an idea whether I'll like it or not, an' I don't know what people expect, or anythin'. You'll have to tell me, honey."

"I'll tell you," he said softly, "if you'll just tell me you're glad to be here."

"Glad—just awful glad!" she whispered, insinuating herself into his arms in her own peculiar way. "Where you are is home for me, Harry."

And as she said this she had the feeling for almost the first time in her life that she was acting a part.

That night, amid the gleaming candles of a dinner-party, where the men seemed to do most of the talking while the girls sat in a haughty and expensive aloofness, even Harry's presence on her left failed to make her feel at home.

"They're a good-looking crowd, don't you think?" he demanded. "Just look round. There's Spud Hubbard, tackle at Princeton last year, and Junie Morton—he and the red-haired fellow next to him were both Yale hockey captains; Junie was in my class. Why, the best athletes in the world come from these States round here. This is a man's country, I tell you. Look at John J. Fishburn!"

"Who's he?" asked Sally Carrol innocently.

"Don't you know?"

"I've heard the name."

"Greatest wheat man in the Northwest, and one of the greatest financiers in the country."

She turned suddenly to a voice on her right.

"I guess they forgot to introduce us. My name's Roger Patton."

"My name is Sally Carrol Happer," she said graciously.

"Yes, I know. Harry told me you were coming."

"You a relative?"

"No, I'm a professor."

"Oh," she laughed.

"At the university. You're from the South, aren't you?"

"Yes; Tarleton, Georgia."

She liked him immediately—a reddish-brown mustache under watery blue eyes that had something in them that these other eyes lacked, some quality of appreciation. They exchanged stray sentences through dinner, and she made up her mind to see him again.

After coffee she was introduced to numerous good-looking young men who danced with conscious precision and seemed to take it for granted that she wanted to talk about nothing except Harry.

"Heavens," she thought, "they talk as if my being engaged made me older than they are—as if I'd tell their mothers on them!"

In the South an engaged girl, even a young married woman, expected the same amount of half-affectionate badinage and flattery that would be accorded a débutante, but here all that seemed banned. One young man, after getting well started on the subject of Sally Carrol's eyes, and how they had allured him ever since she entered the room, went into a violent confusion when he found she was visiting the Bellamys—was Harry's fiancée. He seemed to feel as though he had made some risqué and inexcusable blunder, became immediately formal, and left her at the first opportunity.

She was rather glad when Roger Patton cut in on her and suggested that they sit out a while.

"Well," he inquired, blinking cheerily, "how's Carmen from the South?"

"Mighty fine. How's—how's Dangerous Dan McGrew? Sorry, but he's the only Northerner I know much about."

He seemed to enjoy that.

"Of course," he confessed, "as a professor of literature I'm not supposed to have read Dangerous Dan McGrew."

"Are you a native?"

"No, I'm a Philadelphian. Imported from Harvard to teach French. But I've been here ten years."

"Nine years, three hundred an' sixty-four days longer than me."

"Like it here?"

"Uh-huh. Sure do!"

"Really?"

"Well, why not? Don't I look as if I were havin' a good time?"

"I saw you look out the window a minute ago—and shiver."

"Just my imagination," laughed Sally Carrol. "I'm used to havin' everythin' quiet outside, an' sometimes I look out an' see a flurry of snow, an' it's just as if somethin' dead was movin'."

He nodded appreciatively.

"Ever been North before?"

"Spent two Julys in Asheville, North Carolina."

"Nice-looking crowd, aren't they?" suggested Patton, indicating the swirling floor.

Sally Carrol started. This had been Harry's remark.

"Sure are! They're—canine."

"What?"

She flushed.

"I'm sorry; that sounded worse than I meant it. You see I always think of people as feline or canine, irrespective of sex."

"Which are you?"

"I'm feline. So are you. So are most Southern men an' most of these girls here."

"What's Harry?"

"Harry's canine distinctly. All the men I've met to-night seem to be canine."

"What does 'canine' imply? A certain conscious masculinity as opposed to subtlety?"

"Reckon so. I never analyzed it—only I just look at people an' say 'canine' or 'feline' right off. It's right absurd, I guess."

"Not at all. I'm interested. I used to have a theory about these people. I think they're freezing up."

"What?"

"I think they're growing like Swedes—Ibsenesque, you know. Very gradually getting gloomy and melancholy. It's these long winters. Ever read any Ibsen?"

She shook her head.

"Well, you find in his characters a certain brooding rigidity. They're righteous, narrow, and cheerless, without infinite possibilities for great sorrow or joy."

"Without smiles or tears?"

"Exactly. That's my theory. You see there are thousands of Swedes up here. They come, I imagine, because the climate is very much like their own, and there's been a gradual mingling. There're probably not half a dozen here to-night, but—we've had four Swedish governors. Am I boring you?"

"I'm mighty interested."

"Your future sister-in-law is half Swedish. Personally I like her, but my theory is that Swedes react rather badly on us as a whole. Scandinavians, you know, have the largest suicide rate in the world."

"Why do you live here if it's so depressing?"

"Oh, it doesn't get me. I'm pretty well cloistered, and I suppose books mean more than people to me anyway."

"But writers all speak about the South being tragic. You know—Spanish señoritas, black hair and daggers an' haunting music."

He shook his head.

"No, the Northern races are the tragic races—they don't indulge in the cheering luxury of tears."

Sally Carrol thought of her graveyard. She supposed that that was vaguely what she had meant when she said it didn't depress her.

"The Italians are about the gayest people in the world—but it's a dull subject," he broke off. "Anyway, I want to tell you you're marrying a pretty fine man."

Sally Carrol was moved by an impulse of confidence.

"I know. I'm the sort of person who wants to be taken care of after a certain point, and I feel sure I will be."

"Shall we dance? You know," he continued as they rose, "it's encouraging to find a girl who knows what she's marrying for. Nine-tenths of them think of it as a sort of walking into a moving-picture sunset."

She laughed, and liked him immensely.

Two hours later on the way home she nestled near Harry in the back seat.

"Oh, Harry," she whispered, "it's so co-old!"

"But it's warm in here, darling girl."

"But outside it's cold; and oh, that howling wind!"

She buried her face deep in his fur coat and trembled involuntarily as his cold lips kissed the tip of her ear.

IV

The first week of her visit passed in a whirl. She had her promised toboggan-ride at the back of an automobile through a chill January twilight. Swathed in furs she put in a morning tobogganing on the country-club hill; even tried skiing, to sail through the air for a glorious moment and then land in a tangled laughing bundle on a soft snow-drift. She liked all the winter sports, except an afternoon spent snow-shoeing over a glaring plain under pale yellow sunshine, but she soon realized that these things were for children—that she was being humored and that the enjoyment round her was only a reflection of her own.

At first the Bellamy family puzzled her. The men were reliable and she liked them; to Mr. Bellamy especially, with his iron-gray hair and energetic dignity, she took an immediate fancy, once she found that he was born in Kentucky; this made of him a link between the old life and the new. But toward the women she felt a definite hostility. Myra, her future sister-in-law, seemed the essence of spiritless conventionality. Her conversation was so utterly devoid of personality that Sally Carrol, who came from a country where a certain amount of charm and assurance could be taken for granted in the women, was inclined to despise her.

"If those women aren't beautiful," she thought, "they're nothing. They just fade out when you look at them. They're glorified domestics. Men are the centre of every mixed group."

Lastly there was Mrs. Bellamy, whom Sally Carrol detested. The first day's impression of an egg had been confirmed—an egg with a cracked, veiny voice and such an ungracious dumpiness of carriage that Sally Carrol felt that if she once fell she would surely scramble. In addition, Mrs. Bellamy seemed to typify the town in being innately hostile to strangers. She called Sally Carrol "Sally," and could not be persuaded that the double name was anything more than a tedious ridiculous nickname. To Sally Carrol this shortening of her name was like presenting her to the public half clothed. She loved "Sally Carrol"; she loathed "Sally." She knew also that Harry's mother disapproved of her bobbed hair; and she had never dared smoke down-stairs after that first day when Mrs. Bellamy had come into the library sniffing violently.

Of all the men she met she preferred Roger Patton, who was a frequent visitor at the house. He never again alluded to the Ibsenesque tendency of the populace, but when he came in one day and found her curled upon the sofa bent over "Peer Gynt" he laughed and told her to forget what he'd said—that it was all rot.

And then one afternoon in her second week she and Harry hovered on the edge of a dangerously steep quarrel. She considered that he precipitated it entirely, though the Serbia in the case was an unknown man who had not had his trousers pressed.

They had been walking homeward between mounds of high-piled snow and under a sun which Sally Carrol scarcely recognized. They passed a little girl done up in gray wool until she resembled a small Teddy bear, and Sally Carrol could not resist a gasp of maternal appreciation.

"Look! Harry!"

"What?"

"That little girl—did you see her face?"

"Yes, why?"

"It was red as a little strawberry. Oh, she was cute!"

"Why, your own face is almost as red as that already! Everybody's healthy here. We're out in the cold as soon as we're old enough to walk. Wonderful climate!"

She looked at him and had to agree. He was mighty healthy-looking; so was his brother. And she had noticed the new red in her own cheeks that very morning.

Suddenly their glances were caught and held, and they stared for a moment at the street-corner ahead of them. A man was standing there, his knees bent, his eyes gazing upward with a tense expression as though he were about to make a leap toward the chilly sky. And then they both exploded into a shout of laughter, for coming closer they discovered it had been a ludicrous momentary illusion produced by the extreme bagginess of the man's trousers.

"Reckon that's one on us," she laughed.

"He must be a Southerner, judging by those trousers," suggested Harry mischievously.

"Why, Harry!"

Her surprised look must have irritated him.

"Those damn Southerners!"

Sally Carrol's eyes flashed.

"Don't call 'em that!"

"I'm sorry, dear," said Harry, malignantly apologetic, "but you know what I think of them. They're sort of—sort of degenerates—not at all like the old Southerners. They've lived so long down there with all the colored people that they've gotten lazy and shiftless."

"Hush your mouth, Harry!" she cried angrily. "They're not! They may be lazy—anybody would be in that climate—but they're my best friends, an' I don't want to hear 'em criticised in any such sweepin' way. Some of 'em are the finest men in the world."

"Oh, I know. They're all right when they come North to college, but of all the hangdog, ill-dressed, slovenly lot I ever saw, a bunch of small-town Southerners are the worst!"

Sally Carrol was clinching her gloved hands and biting her lip furiously.

"Why," continued Harry, "there was one in my class at New Haven, and we all thought that at last we'd found the true type of Southern aristocrat, but it turned out that he wasn't an aristocrat at all —just the son of a Northern carpetbagger, who owned about all the cotton round Mobile."

"A Southerner wouldn't talk the way you're talking now," she said evenly.

"They haven't the energy!"

"Or the somethin' else."

"I'm sorry, Sally Carrol, but I've heard you say yourself that you'd never marry——"

"That's quite different. I told you I wouldn't want to tie my life to any of the boys that are round Tarleton now, but I never made any sweepin' generalities."

They walked along in silence.

"I probably spread it on a bit thick, Sally Carrol. I'm sorry."

She nodded but made no answer. Five minutes later as they stood in the hallway she suddenly threw her arms round him.

"Oh, Harry," she cried, her eyes brimming with tears, "let's get married next week. I'm afraid of having fusses like that. I'm afraid, Harry. It wouldn't be that way if we were married."

But Harry, being in the wrong, was still irritated.

"That'd be idiotic. We decided on March."

The tears in Sally Carrol's eyes faded; her expression hardened slightly.

"Very well—I suppose I shouldn't have said that."

Harry melted.

"Dear little nut!" he cried. "Come and kiss me and let's forget."

That very night at the end of a vaudeville performance the orchestra played "Dixie" and Sally Carrol felt something stronger and more enduring than her tears and smiles of the day brim up inside her. She leaned forward gripping the arms of her chair until her face grew crimson.

"Sort of get you, dear?" whispered Harry.

But she did not hear him. To the spirited throb of the violins and the inspiring beat of the kettledrums her own old ghosts were marching by and on into the darkness, and as fifes whistled and sighed in the low encore they seemed so nearly out of sight that she could have waved good-by.

"Away, Away,
 Away down South in Dixie!
Away, away,
 Away down South in Dixie!"

V

It was a particularly cold night. A sudden thaw had nearly cleared the streets the day before, but now they were traversed again with a powdery wraith of loose snow that travelled in wavy lines before the feet of the wind, and filled the lower air with a fine-particled mist. There was no sky—only a dark, ominous tent that draped in the tops of the streets and was in reality a vast approaching army of snowflakes—while over it all, chilling away the comfort from the brown-and-green glow of lighted windows and muffling the steady trot of the horse pulling their sleigh, interminably washed the north wind. It was a dismal town after all, she thought—dismal.

Sometimes at night it had seemed to her as though no one lived here—they had all gone long ago—leaving lighted houses to be covered in time by tombing heaps of sleet. Oh, if there should be snow on her grave! To be beneath great piles of it all winter long, where even her headstone would be a light shadow against light shadows. Her grave—a grave that should be flower-strewn and washed with sun and rain.

She thought again of those isolated country houses that her train had passed, and of the life there the long winter through—the ceaseless glare through the windows, the crust forming on the soft drifts of snow, finally the slow, cheerless melting, and the harsh spring of which Roger Patton had told her. Her spring—to lose it forever—with its lilacs and the lazy sweetness it stirred in her heart. She was laying away that spring—afterward she would lay away that sweetness.

With a gradual insistence the storm broke. Sally Carrol felt a film of flakes melt quickly on her eyelashes, and Harry reached over a furry arm and drew down her complicated flannel cap. Then the small flakes came in skirmish-line, and the horse bent his neck patiently as a transparency of white appeared momentarily on his coat.

"Oh, he's cold, Harry," she said quickly.

"Who? The horse? Oh, no, he isn't. He likes it!"

After another ten minutes they turned a corner and came in sight of their destination. On a tall hill outlined in vivid glaring green against the wintry sky stood the ice palace. It was three stories in the air, with battlements and embrasures and narrow icicled windows, and the innumerable electric lights inside made a gorgeous transparency of the great central hall. Sally Carrol clutched Harry's hand under the fur robe.

"It's beautiful!" he cried excitedly. "My golly, it's beautiful, isn't it! They haven't had one here since eighty-five!"

Somehow the notion of there not having been one since eighty-five oppressed her. Ice was a ghost, and this mansion of it was surely peopled by those shades of the eighties, with pale faces and blurred snow-filled hair.

"Come on, dear," said Harry.

She followed him out of the sleigh and waited while he

hitched the horse. A party of four—Gordon, Myra, Roger Patton, and another girl—drew up beside them with a mighty jingle of bells. There were quite a crowd already, bundled in fur or sheepskin, shouting and calling to each other as they moved through the snow, which was now so thick that people could scarcely be distinguished a few yards away.

"It's a hundred and seventy feet tall," Harry was saying to a muffled figure beside him as they trudged toward the entrance; "covers six thousand square yards."

She caught snatches of conversation: "One main hall"—"walls twenty to forty inches thick"—"and the ice cave has almost a mile of—"—"this Canuck who built it——"

They found their way inside, and dazed by the magic of the great crystal walls Sally Carrol found herself repeating over and over two lines from "Kubla Khan":

"It was a miracle of rare device,
A sunny pleasure-dome with caves of ice!"

In the great glittering cavern with the dark shut out she took a seat on a wooden bench, and the evening's oppression lifted. Harry was right—it was beautiful; and her gaze travelled the smooth surface of the walls, the blocks for which had been selected for their purity and clearness to obtain this opalescent, translucent effect.

"Look! Here we go—oh, boy!" cried Harry.

A band in a far corner struck up "Hail, Hail, the Gang's All Here!" which echoed over to them in wild muddled acoustics, and then the lights suddenly went out; silence seemed to flow down the icy sides and sweep over them. Sally Carrol could still see her white breath in the darkness, and a dim row of pale faces over on the other side.

The music eased to a sighing complaint, and from outside drifted in the full-throated resonant chant of the marching clubs. It grew louder like some pæan of a viking tribe traversing an ancient wild; it swelled—they were coming nearer; then a row of torches appeared, and another and another, and keeping time with their moccasined feet a long column of gray-mackinawed figures swept in, snow-shoes slung at their shoulders, torches soaring and flickering as their voices rose along the great walls.

The gray column ended and another followed, the light streaming luridly this time over red toboggan caps and flaming crimson mackinaws, and as they entered they took up the refrain; then came a long platoon of blue and white, of green, of white, of brown and yellow.

"Those white ones are the Wacouta Club," whispered Harry eagerly. "Those are the men you've met round at dances."

The volume of the voices grew; the great cavern was a phantasmagoria of torches waving in great banks of fire, of colors and the rhythm of soft-leather steps. The leading column turned and halted, platoon deployed in front of platoon until the whole procession made a solid flag of flame, and then from thousands of voices burst a mighty shout that filled the air like a crash of thunder, and sent the torches wavering. It was magnificent, it was tremendous! To Sally Carrol it was the North offering sacrifice on some mighty altar to the gray pagan God of Snow. As the shout died the band struck up again and there came more singing, and then long reverberating cheers by each club. She sat very quiet listening while the staccato cries rent the stillness; and then she started, for there was a volley of explosion, and great clouds of smoke went up here and there through the cavern—the flash-light photographers at work—and the council was over. With the band at their head the clubs formed in column once more, took up their chant, and began to march out.

"Come on!" shouted Harry. "We want to see the labyrinths down-stairs before they turn the lights off!"

They all rose and started toward the chute—Harry and Sally Carrol in the lead, her little mitten buried in his big fur gantlet. At the bottom of the chute was a long empty room of ice, with the ceiling so low that they had to stoop—and their hands were parted. Before she realized what he intended Harry had darted down one of the half-dozen glittering passages that opened into the room and was only a vague receding blot against the green shimmer.

"Harry!" she called.

"Come on!" he cried back.

She looked round the empty chamber; the rest of the party had evidently decided to go home, were already outside somewhere in the blundering snow. She hesitated and then darted in after Harry.

"Harry!" she shouted.

She had reached a turning-point thirty feet down; she heard a faint muffled answer far to the left, and with a touch of panic fled toward it. She passed another turning, two more yawning alleys.

"Harry!"

No answer. She started to run straight forward, and then turned like lightning and sped back the way she had come, enveloped in a sudden icy terror.

She reached a turn—was it here?—took the left and came to what should have been the outlet into the long, low room, but it was only another glittering passage with darkness at the end. She called again, but the walls gave back a flat, lifeless echo with no reverberations. Retracing her steps she turned another corner, this time following a wide passage. It was like the green lane between the parted waters of the Red Sea, like a damp vault connecting empty tombs.

She slipped a little now as she walked, for ice had formed on the bottom of her overshoes; she had to run her gloves along the half-slippery, half-sticky walls to keep her balance.

"Harry!"

Still no answer. The sound she made bounced mockingly down to the end of the passage.

Then on an instant the lights went out, and she was in complete darkness. She gave a small, frightened cry, and sank down into a cold little heap on the ice. She felt her left knee do something as she fell, but she scarcely noticed it as some deep terror far greater than any fear of being lost settled upon her. She was alone with this presence that came out of the North, the dreary loneliness that rose from ice-bound whalers in the Arctic seas, from smokeless, trackless wastes where were strewn the whitened bones of adventure. It was an icy breath of death; it was rolling down low across the land to clutch at her.

With a furious, despairing energy she rose again and started blindly down the darkness. She must get out. She might be lost in here for days, freeze to death and lie embedded in the ice like corpses she had read of, kept perfectly preserved until the melting of a glacier. Harry probably thought she had left with the others—he had gone by now; no one would know until late next day. She reached pitifully for the wall. Forty inches thick, they had said—forty inches thick!

"Oh!"

On both sides of her along the walls she felt things creeping, damp souls that haunted this palace, this town, this North.

"Oh, send somebody—send somebody!" she cried aloud.

Clark Darrow—he would understand; or Joe Ewing; she couldn't be left here to wander forever—to be frozen, heart, body, and soul. This her—this Sally Carrol! Why, she was a happy thing. She was a happy little girl. She liked warmth and summer and Dixie. These things were foreign—foreign.

"You're not crying," something said aloud. "You'll never cry any more. Your tears would just freeze; all tears freeze up here!"

She sprawled full length on the ice.

"Oh, God!" she faltered.

A long single file of minutes went by, and with a great weariness she felt her eyes closing. Then some one seemed to sit down near her and take her face in warm, soft hands. She looked up gratefully.

"Why, it's Margery Lee," she crooned softly to herself. "I knew you'd come." It really was Margery Lee, and she was just as Sally Carrol had known she would be, with a young, white brow, and wide, welcoming eyes, and a hoop-skirt of some soft material that was quite comforting to rest on.

"Margery Lee."

It was getting darker now and darker—all those tombstones ought to be repainted, sure enough, only that would spoil 'em, of course. Still, you ought to be able to see 'em.

Then after a succession of moments that went fast and then slow, but seemed to be ultimately resolving themselves into a multitude of blurred rays converging toward a pale-yellow sun, she heard a great cracking noise break her new-found stillness.

It was the sun, it was a light; a torch, and a torch beyond that, and another one, and voices; a face took flesh below the torch, heavy arms raised her, and she felt something on her cheek—it felt wet. Some one had seized her and was rubbing her face with snow. How ridiculous—with snow!

"Sally Carrol! Sally Carrol!"

It was Dangerous Dan McGrew; and two other faces she didn't know.

"Child, child! We've been looking for you two hours! Harry's half-crazy!"

Things came rushing back into place—the singing, the torches, the great shout of the marching clubs. She squirmed in Patton's arms and gave a long low cry.

"Oh, I want to get out of here! I'm going back home. Take me home"—her voice rose to a scream that sent a chill to Harry's heart as he came racing down the next passage—"to-morrow!" she cried with delirious, unrestrained passion—"To-morrow! To-morrow! To-morrow!"

VI

The wealth of golden sunlight poured a quite enervating yet oddly comforting heat over the house where day long it faced the dusty stretch of road. Two birds were making a great to-do in a cool spot found among the branches of a tree next door, and down the street a colored woman was announcing herself melodiously as a purveyor of strawberries. It was April afternoon.

Sally Carrol Happer, resting her chin on her arm, and her arm on an old window-seat, gazed sleepily down over the spangled dust whence the heat waves were rising for the first time this spring. She was watching a very ancient Ford turn a perilous corner and rattle and groan to a jolting stop at the end of the walk. She made no sound, and in a minute a strident familiar whistle rent the air. Sally Carrol smiled and blinked.

"Good mawnin'."

A head appeared tortuously from under the car-top below.

" 'Tain't mawnin, Sally Carrol."

"Sure enough!" she said in affected surprise. "I guess maybe not."

"What you doin'?"

"Eatin' green peach. 'Spect to die any minute."

Clark twisted himself a last impossible notch to get a view of her face.

"Water's warm as a kettla steam, Sally Carrol. Wanta go swimmin'?"

"Hate to move," sighed Sally Carrol lazily, "but I reckon so."

Head and Shoulders

IN 1915 Horace Tarbox was thirteen years old. In that year he took the examinations for entrance to Princeton University and received the Grade A—excellent—in Cæsar, Cicero, Vergil, Xenophon, Homer, Algebra, Plane Geometry, Solid Geometry, and Chemistry.

Two years later, while George M. Cohan was composing "Over There," Horace was leading the sophomore class by several lengths and digging out theses on "The Syllogism as an Obsolete Scholastic Form," and during the battle of Château-Thierry he was sitting at his desk deciding whether or not to wait until his seventeenth birthday before beginning his series of essays on "The Pragmatic Bias of the New Realists."

After a while some newsboy told him that the war was over, and he was glad, because it meant that Peat Brothers, publishers, would get out their new edition of "Spinoza's Improvement of the Understanding." Wars were all very well in their way, made young men self-reliant or something, but Horace felt that he could never forgive the President for allowing a brass band to play under his window on the night of the false armistice, causing him to leave three important sentences out of his thesis on "German Idealism."

The next year he went up to Yale to take his degree as Master of Arts.

He was seventeen then, tall and slender, with near-sighted gray eyes and an air of keeping himself utterly detached from the mere words he let drop.

"I never feel as though I'm talking to him," expostulated Professor Dillinger to a sympathetic colleague. "He makes me feel as though I were talking to his representative. I always expect him to say: 'Well, I'll ask myself and find out.' "

And then, just as nonchalantly as though Horace Tarbox had been Mr. Beef the butcher or Mr. Hat the haberdasher, life reached in, seized him, handled him, stretched him, and unrolled him like a piece of Irish lace on a Saturday-afternoon bargain-counter.

To move in the literary fashion I should say that this was all because when way back in colonial days the hardy pioneers had come to a bald place in Connecticut and asked of each other, "Now, what shall we build here?" the hardiest one among 'em had answered: "Let's build a town where theatrical managers can try out musical comedies!" How afterward they founded Yale College there, to try the musical comedies on, is a story every one knows. At any rate one December, "Home James" opened at the Shubert, and all the students encored Marcia Meadow, who sang a song about the Blundering Blimp in the first act and did a shaky, shivery, celebrated dance in the last.

Marcia was nineteen. She didn't have wings, but audiences agreed generally that she didn't need them. She was a blonde by natural pigment, and she wore no paint on the streets at high noon. Outside of that she was no better than most women.

It was Charlie Moon who promised her five thousand Pall Malls if she would pay a call on Horace Tarbox, prodigy extraordinary. Charlie was a senior in Sheffield, and he and Horace were first cousins. They liked and pitied each other.

Horace had been particularly busy that night. The failure of the Frenchman Laurier to appreciate the significance of the new realists was preying on his mind. In fact, his only reaction to a low, clear-cut rap at his study was to make him speculate as to whether any rap would have actual existence without an ear there to hear it. He fancied he was verging more and more toward pragmatism. But at that moment, though he did not know it, he was verging with astounding rapidity toward something quite different.

The rap sounded—three seconds leaked by—the rap sounded.

"Come in," muttered Horace automatically.

He heard the door open and then close, but, bent over his book in the big armchair before the fire, he did not look up.

"Leave it on the bed in the other room," he said absently.

"Leave what on the bed in the other room?"

Marcia Meadow had to talk her songs, but her speaking voice was like byplay on a harp.

"The laundry."

"I can't."

Horace stirred impatiently in his chair.

"Why can't you?"

"Why, because I haven't got it."

"Hm!" he replied testily. "Suppose you go back and get it."

Across the fire from Horace was another easy-chair. He was accustomed to change to it in the course of an evening by way of exercise and variety. One chair he called Berkeley, the other he called Hume. He suddenly heard a sound as of a rustling, diaphanous form sinking into Hume. He glanced up.

"Well," said Marcia with the sweet smile she used in Act Two ("Oh, so the Duke liked my dancing!"), "Well, Omar Khayyam, here I am beside you singing in the wilderness."

Horace stared at her dazedly. The momentary suspicion came to him that she existed there only as a phantom of his imagination. Women didn't come into men's rooms and sink into men's Humes. Women brought laundry and took your seat in the street-car and married you later on when you were old enough to know fetters.

This woman had clearly materialized out of Hume. The very froth of her brown gauzy dress was an emanation from Hume's leather arm there! If he looked long enough he would see Hume right through her and then he would be alone again in the room. He passed his fist across his eyes. He really must take up those trapeze exercises again.

"For Pete's sake, don't look so critical!" objected the emanation pleasantly. "I feel as if you were going to wish me away with that patent dome of yours. And then there wouldn't be anything left of me except my shadow in your eyes."

Horace coughed. Coughing was one of his two gestures. When he talked you forgot he had a body at all. It was like hearing a phonograph record by a singer who had been dead a long time.

"What do you want?" he asked.

"I want them letters," whined Marcia melodramatically—"them letters of mine you bought from my grandsire in 1881."

Horace considered.

"I haven't got your letters," he said evenly. "I am only seventeen years old. My father was not born until March 3, 1879. You evidently have me confused with some one else."

"You're only seventeen?" repeated Marcia suspiciously.

"Only seventeen."

"I knew a girl," said Marcia reminiscently, "who went on the ten-twenty-thirty when she was sixteen. She was so stuck on herself that she could never say 'sixteen' without putting the 'only' before it. We got to calling her 'Only Jessie.' And she's just where she was when she started—only worse. 'Only' is a bad habit, Omar—it sounds like an alibi."

"My name is not Omar."

"I know," agreed Marcia, nodding—"your name's Horace. I just call you Omar because you remind me of a smoked cigarette."

"And I haven't your letters. I doubt if I've ever met your grandfather. In fact, I think it very improbable that you yourself were alive in 1881."

Marcia stared at him in wonder.

"Me—1881? Why sure! I was second-line stuff when the Florodora Sextette was still in the convent. I was the original nurse to Mrs. Sol Smith's Juliette. Why, Omar, I was a canteen singer during the War of 1812."

Horace's mind made a sudden successful leap, and he grinned.

"Did Charlie Moon put you up to this?"

Marcia regarded him inscrutably.

"Who's Charlie Moon?"

"Small—wide nostrils—big ears."

She grew several inches and sniffed.

"I'm not in the habit of noticing my friends' nostrils."

"Then it was Charlie?"

Marcia bit her lip—and then yawned.

"Oh, let's change the subject, Omar. I'll pull a snore in this chair in a minute."

"Yes," replied Horace gravely, "Hume has often been considered soporific."

"Who's your friend—and will he die?"

Then of a sudden Horace Tarbox rose slenderly and began to pace the room with his hands in his pockets. This was his other gesture.

"I don't care for this," he said as if he were talking to himself—"at all. Not that I mind your being here—I don't.

You're quite a pretty little thing, but I don't like Charlie Moon's sending you up here. Am I a laboratory experiment on which the janitors as well as the chemists can make experiments? Is my intellectual development humorous in any way? Do I look like the pictures of the little Boston boy in the comic magazines? Has that callow ass, Moon, with his eternal tales about his week in Paris, any right to——"

"No," interrupted Marcia emphatically. "And you're a sweet boy. Come here and kiss me."

Horace stopped quickly in front of her.

"Why do you want me to kiss you?" he asked intently. "Do you just go round kissing people?"

"Why, yes," admitted Marcia, unruffled. "'At's all life is. Just going round kissing people."

"Well," replied Horace emphatically, "I must say your ideas are horribly garbled! In the first place life isn't just that, and in the second place I won't kiss you. It might get to be a habit and I can't get rid of habits. This year I've got in the habit of lolling in bed until seven-thirty."

Marcia nodded understandingly.

"Do you ever have any fun?" she asked.

"What do you mean by fun?"

"See here," said Marcia sternly, "I like you, Omar, but I wish you'd talk as if you had a line on what you were saying. You sound as if you were gargling a lot of words in your mouth and lost a bet every time you spilled a few. I asked you if you ever had any fun."

Horace shook his head.

"Later, perhaps," he answered. "You see I'm a plan. I'm an experiment. I don't say that I don't get tired of it sometimes—I do. Yet—oh, I can't explain! But what you and Charlie Moon call fun wouldn't be fun to me."

"Please explain."

Horace stared at her, started to speak and then, changing his mind, resumed his walk. After an unsuccessful attempt to determine whether or not he was looking at her Marcia smiled at him.

"Please explain."

Horace turned.

"If I do, will you promise to tell Charlie Moon that I wasn't in?"

"Uh-uh."

"Very well, then. Here's my history: I was a 'why' child. I wanted to see the wheels go round. My father was a young economics professor at Princeton. He brought me up on the system of answering every question I asked him to the best of his ability. My response to that gave him the idea of making an experiment in precocity. To aid in the massacre I had ear trouble—seven operations between the ages of nine and twelve. Of course this kept me apart from other boys and made me ripe for forcing. Anyway, while my generation was laboring through Uncle Remus I was honestly enjoying Catullus in the original.

"I passed off my college examinations when I was thirteen because I couldn't help it. My chief associates were professors, and I took a tremendous pride in knowing that I had a fine intelligence, for though I was unusually gifted I was not abnormal in other ways. When I was sixteen I got tired of being a freak; I decided that some one had made a bad mistake. Still as I'd gone that far I concluded to finish it up by taking my degree of Master of Arts. My chief interest in life is the study of modern philosophy. I am a realist of the School of Anton Laurier—with Bergsonian trimmings—and I'll be eighteen years old in two months. That's all."

"Whew!" exclaimed Marcia. "That's enough! You do a neat job with the parts of speech."

"Satisfied?"

"No, you haven't kissed me."

"It's not in my programme," demurred Horace. "Understand that I don't pretend to be above physical things. They have their place, but——"

"Oh, don't be so darned reasonable!"

"I can't help it."

"I hate these slot-machine people."

"I assure you I—" began Horace.

"Oh, shut up!"

"My own rationality——"

"I didn't say anything about your nationality. You're an Amuricun, ar'n't you?"

"Yes."

"Well, that's O.K. with me. I got a notion I want to see you do something that isn't in your highbrow programme. I want to see if a what-ch-call-em with Brazilian trimmings—that thing you said you were—can be a little human."

Horace shook his head again.

"I won't kiss you."

"My life is blighted," muttered Marcia tragically. "I'm a beaten woman. I'll go through life without ever having a kiss with Brazilian trimmings." She sighed. "Anyways, Omar, will you come and see my show?"

"What show?"

"I'm a wicked actress from 'Home James'!"

"Light opera?"

"Yes—at a stretch. One of the characters is a Brazilian rice-planter. That might interest you."

"I saw 'The Bohemian Girl' once," reflected Horace aloud. "I enjoyed it—to some extent."

"Then you'll come?"

"Well, I'm—I'm——"

"Oh, I know—you've got to run down to Brazil for the week-end."

"Not at all. I'd be delighted to come."

Marcia clapped her hands.

"Goodyforyou! I'll mail you a ticket—Thursday night?"

"Why, I——"

"Good! Thursday night it is."

She stood up and walking close to him laid both hands on his shoulders.

"I like you, Omar. I'm sorry I tried to kid you. I thought you'd be sort of frozen, but you're a nice boy."

He eyed her sardonically.

"I'm several thousand generations older than you are."

"You carry your age well."

They shook hands gravely.

"My name's Marcia Meadow," she said emphatically. "'Member it—Marcia Meadow. And I won't tell Charlie Moon you were in."

An instant later as she was skimming down the last flight of stairs three at a time she heard a voice call over the upper banister: "Oh, say——"

She stopped and looked up—made out a vague form leaning over.

"Oh, say!" called the prodigy again. "Can you hear me?"

"Here's your connection, Omar."

"I hope I haven't given you the impression that I consider kissing intrinsically irrational."

"Impression? Why, you didn't even give me the kiss! Never fret—so long."

Two doors near her opened curiously at the sound of a feminine voice. A tentative cough sounded from above. Gathering her skirts, Marcia dived wildly down the last flight, and was swallowed up in the murky Connecticut air outside.

Up-stairs Horace paced the floor of his study. From time to time he glanced toward Berkeley waiting there in suave dark-red respectability, an open book lying suggestively on his cushions. And then he found that his circuit of the floor was bringing him each time nearer to Hume. There was something about Hume that was strangely and inexpressibly different. The diaphanous form still seemed hovering near, and had Horace sat there he would have felt as if he were sitting on a lady's lap. And though Horace couldn't have named the quality of difference, there was such a quality—quite intangible to the speculative mind, but real, nevertheless. Hume was radiating something that in all the two hundred years of his influence he had never radiated before.

Hume was radiating attar of roses.

II

On Thursday night Horace Tarbox sat in an aisle seat in the fifth row and witnessed "Home James." Oddly enough he found that he was enjoying himself. The cynical students near him were annoyed at his audible appreciation of time-honored jokes in the Hammerstein tradition. But Horace was waiting with anxiety for Marcia Meadow singing her song about a Jazz-bound Blundering Blimp. When she did appear, radiant under a floppity flower-faced hat, a warm glow settled over him, and when the song was over he did not join in the storm of applause. He felt somewhat numb.

In the intermission after the second act an usher materialized beside him, demanded to know if he were Mr. Tarbox, and then handed him a note written in a round adolescent hand. Horace read it in some confusion, while the usher lingered with withering patience in the aisle.

"DEAR OMAR: After the show I always grow an awful hunger. If you want to satisfy it for me in the Taft Grill just communicate your answer to the big-timber guide that brought this and oblige.

Your friend,

MARCIA MEADOW."

"Tell her"—he coughed—"tell her that it will be quite all right. I'll meet her in front of the theatre."

The big-timber guide smiled arrogantly.

"I giss she meant for you to come roun' t' the stage door."

"Where—where is it?"

"Ou'side. Tunayulef. Down ee alley."

"What?"

"Ou'side. Turn to y' left! Down ee alley!"

The arrogant person withdrew. A freshman behind Horace snickered.

Then half an hour later, sitting in the Taft Grill opposite the hair that was yellow by natural pigment, the prodigy was saying an odd thing.

"Do you have to do that dance in the last act?" he was asking earnestly—"I mean, would they dismiss you if you refused to do it?"

Marcia grinned.

"It's fun to do it. I like to do it."

And then Horace came out with a *faux pas.*

"I should think you'd detest it," he remarked succinctly. "The people behind me were making remarks about your bosom."

Marcia blushed fiery red.

"I can't help that," she said quickly. "The dance to me is only a sort of acrobatic stunt. Lord, it's hard enough to do! I rub liniment into my shoulders for an hour every night."

"Do you have—fun while you're on the stage?"

"Uh-huh—sure! I got in the habit of having people look at me, Omar, and I like it."

"Hm!" Horace sank into a brownish study.

"How's the Brazilian trimmings?"

"Hm!" repeated Horace, and then after a pause: "Where does the play go from here?"

"New York."

"For how long?"

"All depends. Winter—maybe."

"Oh!"

"Coming up to lay eyes on me, Omar, or aren't you int'rested? Not as nice here, is it, as it was up in your room? I wish we was there now."

"I feel idiotic in this place," confessed Horace, looking round him nervously.

"Too bad! We got along pretty well."

At this he looked suddenly so melancholy that she changed her tone, and reaching over patted his hand.

"Ever take an actress out to supper before?"

"No," said Horace miserably, "and I never will again. I don't know why I came to-night. Here under all these lights and with all these people laughing and chattering I feel completely out of my sphere. I don't know what to talk to you about."

"We'll talk about me. We talked about you last time."

"Very well."

"Well, my name really is Meadow, but my first name isn't Marcia—it's Veronica. I'm nineteen. Question—how did the girl make her leap to the footlights? Answer—she was born in Passaic, New Jersey, and up to a year ago she got the right to breathe by pushing Nabiscoes in Marcel's tea-room in Trenton. She started going with a guy named Robbins, a singer in the Trent House cabaret, and he got her to try a song and dance with him one evening. In a month we were filling the supper-room every night. Then we went to New York with meet-my-friend letters thick as a pile of napkins.

"In two days we'd landed a job at Divinerries', and I learned to shimmy from a kid at the Palais Royal. We stayed at Divinerries' six months until one night Peter Boyce Wendell, the columnist, ate his milk-toast there. Next morning a poem about Marvellous Marcia came out in his newspaper, and within two days I had three vaudeville offers and a chance at the Midnight Frolic. I wrote Wendell a thank-you letter, and he printed it in his column—said that the style was like Carlyle's, only more rugged, and that I ought to quit dancing and do North American literature. This got me a coupla more vaudeville offers and a chance as an ingénue in a regular show. I took it—and here I am, Omar."

When she finished they sat for a moment in silence, she draping the last skeins of a Welsh rabbit on her fork and waiting for him to speak.

"Let's get out of here," he said suddenly.

Marcia's eyes hardened.

"What's the idea? Am I making you sick?"

"No, but I don't like it here. I don't like to be sitting here with you."

Without another word Marcia signalled for the waiter.

"What's the check?" she demanded briskly. "My part—the rabbit and the ginger ale."

Horace watched blankly as the waiter figured it.

"See here," he began, "I intended to pay for yours too. You're my guest."

With a half-sigh Marcia rose from the table and walked from the room. Horace, his face a document in bewilderment, laid a bill down and followed her out, up the stairs and into the lobby. He overtook her in front of the elevator and they faced each other.

"See here," he repeated, "you're my guest. Have I said something to offend you?"

After an instant of wonder Marcia's eyes softened.

"You're a rude fella," she said slowly. "Don't you know you're rude?"

"I can't help it," said Horace with a directness she found quite disarming. "You know I like you."

"You said you didn't like being with me."

"I didn't like it."

"Why not?"

Fire blazed suddenly from the gray forests of his eyes.

"Because I didn't. I've formed the habit of liking you. I've been thinking of nothing much else for two days."

"Well, if you——"

"Wait a minute," he interrupted. "I've got something to say. It's this: in six weeks I'll be eighteen years old. When I'm eighteen years old I'm coming up to New York to see you. Is there some place in New York where we can go and not have a lot of people in the room?"

"Sure!" smiled Marcia. "You can come up to my 'partment. Sleep on the couch, if you want to."

"I can't sleep on couches," he said shortly. "But I want to talk to you."

"Why, sure," repeated Marcia—"in my 'partment."

In his excitement Horace put his hands in his pockets.

"All right—just so I can see you alone. I want to talk to you as we talked up in my room."

"Honey boy," cried Marcia, laughing, "is it that you want to kiss me?"

"Yes," Horace almost shouted. "I'll kiss you if you want me to."

The elevator man was looking at them reproachfully. Marcia edged toward the grated door.

"I'll drop you a post-card," she said.

Horace's eyes were quite wild.

"Send me a post-card! I'll come up any time after January first. I'll be eighteen then."

And as she stepped into the elevator he coughed enigmatically, yet with a vague challenge, at the ceiling, and walked quickly away.

III

He was there again. She saw him when she took her first glance at the restless Manhattan audience—down in the front row with his head bent a bit forward and his gray eyes fixed on her. And she knew that to him they were alone together in a world where the high-rouged row of ballet faces and the massed whines of the violins were as imperceivable as powder on a marble Venus. An instinctive defiance rose within her.

"Silly boy!" she said to herself hurriedly, and she didn't take her encore.

"What do they expect for a hundred a week—perpetual motion?" she grumbled to herself in the wings.

"What's the trouble, Marcia?"

"Guy I don't like down in front."

During the last act as she waited for her specialty she had an odd attack of stage fright. She had never sent Horace the promised post-card. Last night she had pretended not to see him—had hurried from the theatre immediately after her dance to pass a sleepless night in her apartment, thinking—as she had so often in the last month—of his pale, rather intent face, his slim, boyish figure, the merciless, unworldly abstraction that made him charming to her.

And now that he had come she felt vaguely sorry—as though an unwonted responsibility was being forced on her.

"Infant prodigy!" she said aloud.

"What?" demanded the negro comedian standing beside her.

"Nothing—just talking about myself."

On the stage she felt better. This was her dance—and she always felt that the way she did it wasn't suggestive any more than to some men every pretty girl is suggestive. She made it a stunt.

"Uptown, downtown, jelly on a spoon,
After sundown shiver by the moon."

He was not watching her now. She saw that clearly. He was looking very deliberately at a castle on the back drop, wearing that expression he had worn in the Taft Grill. A wave of exasperation swept over her—he was criticising her.

"That's the vibration that thr-ills me,
Funny how affection fi-lls me,
Uptown, downtown——"

Unconquerable revulsion seized her. She was suddenly and horribly conscious of her audience as she had never been since her first appearance. Was that a leer on a pallid face in the front row, a droop of disgust on one young girl's mouth?

These shoulders of hers—these shoulders shaking—were they hers? Were they real? Surely shoulders weren't made for this!

"Then—you'll see at a glance
I'll need some funeral ushers with St. Vitus dance
At the end of the world I'll——"

The bassoon and two cellos crashed into a final chord. She paused and poised a moment on her toes with every muscle tense, her young face looking out dully at the audience in what one young girl afterward called "such a curious, puzzled look," and then without bowing rushed from the stage. Into the dressing-room she sped, kicked out of one dress and into another, and caught a taxi outside.

Her apartment was very warm—small, it was, with a row of professional pictures and sets of Kipling and O. Henry which she had bought once from a blue-eyed agent and read occasionally. And there were several chairs which matched, but were none of them comfortable, and a pink-shaded lamp with blackbirds painted on it and an atmosphere of rather stifled pink throughout. There were nice things in it—nice things unrelentingly hostile to each other, offsprings of a vicarious, impatient taste acting in stray moments. The worst was typified by a great picture framed in oak bark of Passaic as seen from the Erie Railroad—altogether a frantic, oddly extravagant, oddly penurious attempt to make a cheerful room. Marcia knew it was a failure.

Into this room came the prodigy and took her two hands awkwardly.

"I followed you this time," he said.

"Oh!"

"I want you to marry me," he said.

Her arms went out to him. She kissed his mouth with a sort of passionate wholesomeness.

"There!"

"I love you," he said.

She kissed him again and then with a little sigh flung herself into an armchair and half lay there, shaken with absurd laughter.

"Why, you infant prodigy!" she cried.

"Very well, call me that if you want to. I once told you that I was ten thousand years older than you—I am."

She laughed again.

"I don't like to be disapproved of."

"No one's ever going to disapprove of you again."

"Omar," she asked, "why do you want to marry me?"

The prodigy rose and put his hands in his pockets.

"Because I love you, Marcia Meadow."

And then she stopped calling him Omar.

"Dear boy," she said, "you know I sort of love you. There's something about you—I can't tell what—that just puts my heart through the wringer every time I'm round you. But, honey—" She paused.

"But what?"

"But lots of things. But you're only just eighteen, and I'm nearly twenty."

"Nonsense!" he interrupted. "Put it this way—that I'm in my nineteenth year and you're nineteen. That makes us pretty close—without counting that other ten thousand years I mentioned."

Marcia laughed.

"But there are some more 'buts.' Your people——"

"My people!" exclaimed the prodigy ferociously. "My people tried to make a monstrosity out of me." His face grew quite crimson at the enormity of what he was going to say. "My people can go way back and sit down!"

"My heavens!" cried Marcia in alarm. "All that? On tacks, I suppose."

"Tacks—yes," he agreed wildly—"on anything. The more I think of how they allowed me to become a little dried-up mummy——"

"What makes you think you're that?" asked Marcia quietly—"me?"

"Yes. Every person I've met on the streets since I met you has made me jealous because they knew what love was before I did. I used to call it the 'sex impulse.' Heavens!"

"There's more 'buts,'" said Marcia.

"What are they?"

"How could we live?"

"I'll make a living."

"You're in college."

"Do you think I care anything about taking a Master of Arts degree?"

"You want to be Master of Me, hey?"

"Yes! What? I mean, no!"

Marcia laughed, and crossing swiftly over sat in his lap. He put his arm round her wildly and implanted the vestige of a kiss somewhere near her neck.

"There's something white about you," mused Marcia, "but it doesn't sound very logical."

"Oh, don't be so darned reasonable!"

"I can't help it," said Marcia.

"I hate these slot-machine people!"

"But we——"

"Oh, shut up!"

And as Marcia couldn't talk through her ears she had to.

IV

Horace and Marcia were married early in February. The sensation in academic circles both at Yale and Princeton was tremendous. Horace Tarbox, who at fourteen had been played up in the Sunday magazines sections of metropolitan newspapers, was throwing over his career, his chance of being a world authority on American philosophy, by marrying a chorus girl—they made Marcia a chorus girl. But like all modern stories it was a four-and-a-half-day wonder.

They took a flat in Harlem. After two weeks' search, during which his idea of the value of academic knowledge faded unmercifully, Horace took a position as clerk with a South American export company—some one had told him that exporting was the coming thing. Marcia was to stay in her show for a few months—anyway until he got on his feet. He was getting a hundred and twenty-five to start with, and though of course they told him it was only a question of months until he would be earning double that, Marcia refused even to consider giving up the hundred and fifty a week that she was getting at the time.

"We'll call ourselves Head and Shoulders, dear," she said

softly, "and the shoulders'll have to keep shaking a little longer until the old head gets started."

"I hate it," he objected gloomily.

"Well," she replied emphatically, "your salary wouldn't keep us in a tenement. Don't think I want to be public—I don't. I want to be yours. But I'd be a half-wit to sit in one room and count the sunflowers on the wall-paper while I waited for you. When you pull down three hundred a month I'll quit."

And much as it hurt his pride, Horace had to admit that hers was the wiser course.

March mellowed into April. May read a gorgeous riot act to the parks and waters of Manhattan, and they were very happy. Horace, who had no habits whatsoever—he had never had time to form any—proved the most adaptable of husbands, and as Marcia entirely lacked opinions on the subjects that engrossed him there were very few joltings and bumpings. Their minds moved in different spheres. Marcia acted as practical factotum, and Horace lived either in his old world of abstract ideas or in a sort of triumphantly earthy worship and adoration of his wife. She was a continual source of astonishment to him—the freshness and originality of her mind, her dynamic, clear-headed energy, and her unfailing good humor.

And Marcia's co-workers in the nine-o'clock show, whither she had transferred her talents, were impressed with her tremendous pride in her husband's mental powers. Horace they knew only as a very slim, tight-lipped, and immature-looking young man, who waited every night to take her home.

"Horace," said Marcia one evening when she met him as usual at eleven, "you looked like a ghost standing there against the street lights. You losing weight?"

He shook his head vaguely.

"I don't know. They raised me to a hundred and thirty-five dollars to-day, and——"

"I don't care," said Marcia severely. "You're killing yourself working at night. You read those big books on economy——"

"Economics," corrected Horace.

"Well, you read 'em every night long after I'm asleep. And you're getting all stooped over like you were before we were married."

"But, Marcia, I've got to——"

"No, you haven't, dear. I guess I'm running this shop for the present, and I won't let my fella ruin his health and eyes. You got to get some exercise."

"I do. Every morning I——"

"Oh, I know! But those dumb-bells of yours wouldn't give a consumptive two degrees of fever. I mean real exercise. You've got to join a gymnasium. 'Member you told me you were such a trick gymnast once that they tried to get you out for the team in college and they couldn't because you had a standing date with Herb Spencer?"

"I used to enjoy it," mused Horace, "but it would take up too much time now."

"All right," said Marcia. "I'll make a bargain with you. You join a gym and I'll read one of those books from the brown row of 'em."

" 'Pepys' Diary'? Why, that ought to be enjoyable. He's very light."

"Not for me—he isn't. It'll be like digesting plate glass. But you been telling me how much it'd broaden my lookout. Well, you go to a gym three nights a week and I'll take one big dose of Sammy."

Horace hesitated.

"Well——"

"Come on, now! You do some giant swings for me and I'll chase some culture for you."

So Horace finally consented, and all through a baking summer he spent three and sometimes four evenings a week experimenting on the trapeze in Skipper's Gymnasium. And in August he admitted to Marcia that it made him capable of more mental work during the day.

"*Mens sana in corpore sano*," he said.

"Don't believe in it," replied Marcia. "I tried one of those patent medicines once and they're all bunk. You stick to gymnastics."

One night in early September while he was going through one of his contortions on the rings in the nearly deserted room he was addressed by a meditative fat man whom he had noticed watching him for several nights.

"Say, lad, do that stunt you were doin' last night."

Horace grinned at him from his perch.

"I invented it," he said. "I got the idea from the fourth proposition of Euclid."

"What circus he with?"

"He's dead."

"Well, he must of broke his neck doin' that stunt. I set here last night thinkin' sure you was goin' to break yours."

"Like this!" said Horace, and swinging onto the trapeze he did his stunt.

"Don't it kill your neck an' shoulder muscles?"

"It did at first, but inside of a week I wrote the *quod erat demonstrandum* on it."

"Hm!"

Horace swung idly on the trapeze.

"Ever think of takin' it up professionally?" asked the fat man.

"Not I."

"Good money in it if you're willin' to do stunts like 'at an' can get away with it."

"Here's another," chirped Horace eagerly, and the fat man's mouth dropped suddenly agape as he watched this pink-jerseyed Prometheus again defy the gods and Isaac Newton.

The night following this encounter Horace got home from work to find a rather pale Marcia stretched out on the sofa waiting for him.

"I fainted twice to-day," she began without preliminaries.

"What?"

"Yep. You see baby's due in four months now. Doctor says I ought to have quit dancing two weeks ago."

Horace sat down and thought it over.

"I'm glad, of course," he said pensively—"I mean glad that we're going to have a baby. But this means a lot of expense."

"I've got two hundred and fifty in the bank," said Marcia hopefully, "and two weeks' pay coming."

Horace computed quickly.

"Including my salary, that'll give us nearly fourteen hundred for the next six months."

Marcia looked blue.

"That all? Course I can get a job singing somewhere this month. And I can go to work again in March."

"Of course nothing!" said Horace gruffly. "You'll stay right here. Let's see now—there'll be doctor's bills and a nurse, besides the maid. We've got to have some more money."

"Well," said Marcia wearily, "I don't know where it's coming from. It's up to the old head now. Shoulders is out of business."

Horace rose and pulled on his coat.

"Where are you going?"

"I've got an idea," he answered. "I'll be right back."

Ten minutes later as he headed down the street toward Skipper's Gymnasium he felt a placid wonder, quite unmixed with humor, at what he was going to do. How he would have gaped at himself a year before! How every one would have gaped! But when you opened your door at the rap of life you let in many things.

The gymnasium was brightly lit, and when his eyes became accustomed to the glare he found the meditative fat man seated on a pile of canvas mats smoking a big cigar.

"Say," began Horace directly, "were you in earnest last night when you said I could make money on my trapeze stunts?"

"Why, yes," said the fat man in surprise.

"Well, I've been thinking it over, and I believe I'd like to try it. I could work at night and on Saturday afternoons—and regularly if the pay is high enough."

The fat man looked at his watch.

"Well," he said, "Charlie Paulson's the man to see. He'll book you inside of four days, once he sees you work out. He won't be in now, but I'll get hold of him for to-morrow night."

The fat man was as good as his word. Charlie Paulson arrived next night and put in a wondrous hour watching the prodigy swoop through the air in amazing parabolas, and on the night following he brought two large men with him who looked as though they had been born smoking black cigars and talking about money in low, passionate voices. Then on the succeeding Saturday Horace Tarbox's torso made its first professional appearance in a gymnastic exhibition at the Coleman Street Gardens. But though the audience numbered nearly five thousand people, Horace felt no nervousness. From his childhood he had read papers to audiences—learned that trick of detaching himself.

"Marcia," he said cheerfully later that same night, "I think we're out of the woods. Paulson thinks he can get me an opening at the Hippodrome, and that means an all-winter engagement. The Hippodrome, you know, is a big——"

"Yes, I believe I've heard of it," interrupted Marcia, "but I want to know about this stunt you're doing. It isn't any spectacular suicide, is it?"

"It's nothing," said Horace quietly. "But if you can think of any nicer way of a man killing himself than taking a risk for you, why that's the way I want to die."

Marcia reached up and wound both arms tightly round his neck.

"Kiss me," she whispered, "and call me 'dear heart.' I love to hear you say 'dear heart.' And bring me a book to read tomorrow. No more Sam Pepys, but something trick and trashy. I've been wild for something to do all day. I felt like writing letters, but I didn't have anybody to write to."

"Write to me," said Horace. "I'll read them."

"I wish I could," breathed Marcia. "If I knew words enough I could write you the longest love-letter in the world—and never get tired."

But after two more months Marcia grew very tired indeed, and for a row of nights it was a very anxious, weary-looking young athlete who walked out before the Hippodrome crowd. Then there were two days when his place was taken by a young man who wore pale blue instead of white, and got very little applause. But after the two days Horace appeared again, and those who sat close to the stage remarked an expression of beatific happiness on that young acrobat's face, even when he was twisting breathlessly in the air in the middle of his amazing and original shoulder swing. After that performance he laughed at the elevator man and dashed up the stairs to the flat five steps at a time—and then tiptoed very carefully into a quiet room.

"Marcia," he whispered.

"Hello!" She smiled up at him wanly. "Horace, there's something I want you to do. Look in my top bureau drawer and you'll find a big stack of paper. It's a book—sort of—Horace. I wrote it down in these last three months while I've been laid up. I wish you'd take it to that Peter Boyce Wendell who put my letter in his paper. He could tell you whether it'd be a good book. I wrote it just the way I talk, just the way I wrote that letter to him. It's just a story about a lot of things that happened to me. Will you take it to him, Horace?"

"Yes, darling."

He leaned over the bed until his head was beside her on the pillow, and began stroking back her yellow hair.

"Dearest Marcia," he said softly.

"No," she murmured, "call me what I told you to call me."

"Dear heart," he whispered passionately—"dearest, dearest heart."

"What'll we call her?"

They rested a minute in happy, drowsy content, while Horace considered.

"We'll call her Marcia Hume Tarbox," he said at length.

"Why the Hume?"

"Because he's the fellow who first introduced us."

"That so?" she murmured, sleepily surprised. "I thought his name was Moon."

Her eyes closed, and after a moment the slow, lengthening surge of the bedclothes over her breast showed that she was asleep.

Horace tiptoed over to the bureau and opening the top drawer found a heap of closely scrawled, lead-smeared pages. He looked at the first sheet:

SANDRA PEPYS, SYNCOPATED

BY MARCIA TARBOX

He smiled. So Samuel Pepys had made an impression on her after all. He turned a page and began to read. His smile deepened—he read on. Half an hour passed and he became aware that Marcia had waked and was watching him from the bed.

"Honey," came in a whisper.

"What, Marcia?"

"Do you like it?"

Horace coughed.

"I seem to be reading on. It's bright."

"Take it to Peter Boyce Wendell. Tell him you got the highest marks in Princeton once and that you ought to know when a book's good. Tell him this one's a world beater."

"All right, Marcia," said Horace gently.

Her eyes closed again and Horace crossing over kissed her forehead—stood there for a moment with a look of tender pity. Then he left the room.

All that night the sprawly writing on the pages, the constant mistakes in spelling and grammar, and the weird punctuation danced before his eyes. He woke several times in the night, each time full of a welling chaotic sympathy for this desire of Marcia's soul to express itself in words. To him there was something infinitely pathetic about it, and for the first time in months he began to turn over in his mind his own half-forgotten dreams.

He had meant to write a series of books, to popularize the new realism as Schopenhauer had popularized pessimism and William James pragmatism.

But life hadn't come that way. Life took hold of people and forced them into flying rings. He laughed to think of that rap at his door, the diaphanous shadow in Hume, Marcia's threatened kiss.

"And it's still me," he said aloud in wonder as he lay awake in the darkness. "I'm the man who sat in Berkeley with temerity to wonder if that rap would have had actual existence had my ear not been there to hear it. I'm still that man. I could be electrocuted for the crimes he committed.

"Poor gauzy souls trying to express ourselves in something tangible. Marcia with her written book; I with my unwritten ones. Trying to choose our mediums and then taking what we get—and being glad."

V

"Sandra Pepys, Syncopated," with an introduction by Peter Boyce Wendell, the columnist, appeared serially in *Jordan's Magazine*, and came out in book form in March. From its first published instalment it attracted attention far and wide. A trite enough subject—a girl from a small New Jersey town coming to New York to go on the stage—treated simply, with a peculiar vividness of phrasing and a haunting undertone of sadness in the very inadequacy of its vocabulary, it made an irresistible appeal.

Peter Boyce Wendell, who happened at that time to be advocating the enrichment of the American language by the immediate adoption of expressive vernacular words, stood as its sponsor and thundered his indorsement over the placid bromides of the conventional reviewers.

Marcia received three hundred dollars an instalment for the serial publication, which came at an opportune time, for though Horace's monthly salary at the Hippodrome was now more than Marcia's had ever been, young Marcia was emitting shrill cries which they interpreted as a demand for country air. So early April found them installed in a bungalow in Westchester County, with a place for a lawn, a place for a garage, and a place for everything, including a sound-proof impregnable study, in which Marcia faithfully promised Mr. Jordan she would shut herself up when her daughter's demands began to be abated, and compose immortally illiterate literature.

"It's not half bad," thought Horace one night as he was on his way from the station to his house. He was considering several prospects that had opened up, a four months' vaudeville offer in five figures, a chance to go back to Princeton in charge of all gymnasium work. Odd! He had once intended to go back there in charge of all philosophic work, and now he had not even been stirred by the arrival in New York of Anton Laurier, his old idol.

The gravel crunched raucously under his heel. He saw the lights of his sitting-room gleaming and noticed a big car standing in the drive. Probably Mr. Jordan again, come to persuade Marcia to settle down to work.

She had heard the sound of his approach and her form was silhouetted against the lighted door as she came out to meet him.

"There's some Frenchman here," she whispered nervously. "I can't pronounce his name, but he sounds awful deep. You'll have to jaw with him."

"What Frenchman?"

"You can't prove it by me. He drove up an hour ago with Mr. Jordan, and said he wanted to meet Sandra Pepys, and all that sort of thing."

Two men rose from chairs as they went inside.

"Hello, Tarbox," said Jordan. "I've just been bringing together two celebrities. I've brought M'sieur Laurier out with me. M'sieur Laurier, let me present Mr. Tarbox, Mrs. Tarbox's husband."

"Not Anton Laurier!" exclaimed Horace.

"But, yes. I must come. I have to come. I have read the book of Madame, and I have been charmed"—he fumbled in his pocket—"ah, I have read of you too. In this newspaper which I read to-day it has your name."

He finally produced a clipping from a magazine.

"Read it!" he said eagerly. "It has about you too."

Horace's eye skipped down the page.

"A distinct contribution to American dialect literature," it said. "No attempt at literary tone; the book derives its very quality from this fact, as did 'Huckleberry Finn.' "

Horace's eyes caught a passage lower down; he became suddenly aghast—read on hurriedly:

"Marcia Tarbox's connection with the stage is not only as a spectator but as the wife of a performer. She was married last year to Horace Tarbox, who every evening delights the children at the Hippodrome with his wondrous flying-ring performance. It is said that the young couple have dubbed themselves Head and Shoulders, referring doubtless to the fact that Mrs. Tarbox supplies the literary and mental qualities, while the supple and agile shoulders of her husband contribute their share to the family fortunes.

"Mrs. Tarbox seems to merit that much-abused title—'prodigy.' Only twenty——"

Horace stopped reading, and with a very odd expression in his eyes gazed intently at Anton Laurier.

"I want to advise you—" he began hoarsely.

"What?"

"About raps. Don't answer them! Let them alone—have a padded door."

The Cut-Glass Bowl

THERE was a rough stone age and a smooth stone age and a bronze age, and many years afterward a cut-glass age. In the cut-glass age, when young ladies had persuaded young men with long, curly mustaches to marry them, they sat down several months afterward and wrote thank-you notes for all sorts of cut-glass presents—punch-bowls, finger-bowls, dinner-glasses, wine-glasses, ice-cream dishes, bonbon dishes, decanters, and vases—for, though cut glass was nothing new in the nineties, it was then especially busy reflecting the dazzling light of fashion from the Back Bay to the fastnesses of the Middle West.

After the wedding the punch-bowls were arranged on the sideboard with the big bowl in the centre; the glasses were set up in the china-closet; the candlesticks were put at both ends of things—and then the struggle for existence began. The bonbon dish lost its little handle and became a pin-tray upstairs; a promenading cat knocked the little bowl off the sideboard, and the hired girl chipped the middle-sized one with the sugar-dish; then the wine-glasses succumbed to leg fractures, and even the dinner-glasses disappeared one by one like the ten little niggers, the last one ending up, scarred and maimed, as a tooth-brush holder among other shabby genteels on the bathroom shelf. But by the time all this had happened the cut-glass age was over, anyway.

It was well past its first glory on the day the curious Mrs. Roger Fairboalt came to see the beautiful Mrs. Harold Piper.

"My *dear*," said the curious Mrs. Roger Fairboalt, "I *love* your house. I think it's *quite* artistic."

"I'm *so* glad," said the beautiful Mrs. Harold Piper, lights appearing in her young, dark eyes; "and you *must* come often. I'm almost *always* alone in the afternoon."

Mrs. Fairboalt would have liked to remark that she didn't believe this at all and couldn't see how she'd be expected to—it was all over town that Mr. Freddy Gedney had been dropping in on Mrs. Piper five afternoons a week for the past six months. Mrs. Fairboalt was at that ripe age where she distrusted all beautiful women——

"I love the dining-room *most*," she said, "all that *marvellous* china, and that *huge* cut-glass bowl."

Mrs. Piper laughed, so prettily that Mrs. Fairboalt's lingering reservations about the Freddy Gedney story quite vanished.

"Oh, that big bowl!" Mrs. Piper's mouth forming the words was a vivid rose petal. "There's a story about that bowl——"

"Oh——"

"You remember young Carleton Canby? Well, he was very attentive at one time, and the night I told him I was going to marry Harold, seven years ago, in ninety-two, he drew himself way up and said: 'Evylyn, I'm going to give a present that's as hard as you are and as beautiful and as empty and as easy to see through.' He frightened me a little—his eyes were so black. I thought he was going to deed me a haunted house or something that would explode when you opened it. That bowl came, and of course it's beautiful. Its diameter or circumference or something is two and a half feet—or perhaps it's three and a half. Anyway, the sideboard is really too small for it; it sticks way out."

"My *dear*, wasn't that *odd!* And he left town about then, didn't he?" Mrs. Fairboalt was scribbling italicized notes on her memory—"hard, beautiful, empty, and easy to see through."

"Yes, he went West—or South—or somewhere," answered Mrs. Piper, radiating that divine vagueness that helps to lift beauty out of time.

Mrs. Fairboalt drew on her gloves, approving the effect of largeness given by the open sweep from the spacious music-room through the library, disclosing a part of the dining-room beyond. It was really the nicest smaller house in town, and Mrs. Piper had talked of moving to a larger one on Devereaux Avenue. Harold Piper must be *coining* money.

As she turned into the sidewalk under the gathering autumn dusk she assumed that disapproving, faintly unpleasant expression that almost all successful women of forty wear on the street.

If *I* were Harold Piper, she thought, I'd spend a *little* less time on business and a *little* more time at home. Some *friend* should speak to him.

But if Mrs. Fairboalt had considered it a successful afternoon she would have named it a triumph had she waited two minutes longer. For while she was still a black receding figure a hundred yards down the street, a very good-looking distraught young man turned up the walk to the Piper house. Mrs. Piper answered the door-bell herself, and with a rather dismayed expression led him quickly into the library.

"I had to see you," he began wildly; "your note played the devil with me. Did Harold frighten you into this?"

She shook her head.

"I'm through, Fred," she said slowly, and her lips had never looked to him so much like tearings from a rose. "He came home last night sick with it. Jessie Piper's sense of duty was too much for her, so she went down to his office and told him. He was hurt and—oh, I can't help seeing it his way, Fred. He says we've been club gossip all summer and he didn't know it, and now he understands snatches of conversation he's caught and veiled hints people have dropped about me. He's mighty angry, Fred, and he loves me and I love him—rather."

Gedney nodded slowly and half closed his eyes.

"Yes," he said, "yes, my trouble's like yours. I can see other people's points of view too plainly." His gray eyes met her dark ones frankly. "The blessed thing's over. My God, Evylyn, I've been sitting down at the office all day looking at the outside of your letter, and looking at it and looking at it——"

"You've got to go, Fred," she said steadily, and the slight emphasis of hurry in her voice was a new thrust for him. "I gave him my word of honor I wouldn't see you. I know just how far I can go with Harold, and being here with you this evening is one of the things I can't do."

They were still standing, and as she spoke she made a little movement toward the door. Gedney looked at her miserably, trying, here at the end, to treasure up a last picture of her—and then suddenly both of them were stiffened into marble at the sound of steps on the walk outside. Instantly her arm reached out grasping the lapel of his coat—half urged, half swung him through the big door into the dark dining-room.

"I'll make him go up-stairs," she whispered close to his ear; "don't move till you hear him on the stairs. Then go out the front way."

Then he was alone listening as she greeted her husband in the hall.

Harold Piper was thirty-six, nine years older than his wife. He was handsome—with marginal notes: these being eyes that were too close together, and a certain woodenness when his face was in repose. His attitude toward this Gedney matter was typical of all his attitudes. He had told Evylyn that he considered the subject closed and would never reproach her nor allude to it in any form; and he told himself that this was rather a big way of looking at it—that she was not a little impressed. Yet, like all men who are preoccupied with their own broadness, he was exceptionally narrow.

He greeted Evylyn with emphasized cordiality this evening.

"You'll have to hurry and dress, Harold," she said eagerly; "we're going to the Bronsons'."

He nodded.

"It doesn't take me long to dress, dear," and, his words trailing off, he walked on into the library. Evylyn's heart clattered loudly.

"Harold—" she began, with a little catch in her voice, and followed him in. He was lighting a cigarette. "You'll have to hurry, Harold," she finished, standing in the doorway.

"Why?" he asked, a trifle impatiently; "you're not dressed yourself yet, Evie."

He stretched out in a Morris chair and unfolded a newspaper. With a sinking sensation Evylyn saw that this meant at least ten minutes—and Gedney was standing breathless in the next room. Supposing Harold decided that before he went up-stairs he wanted a drink from the decanter on the sideboard. Then it occurred to her to forestall this contingency by bringing him the decanter and a glass. She dreaded calling his attention to the dining-room in any way, but she couldn't risk the other chance.

But at the same moment Harold rose and, throwing his paper down, came toward her.

"Evie, dear," he said, bending and putting his arms about her, "I hope you're not thinking about last night—" She moved close to him, trembling. "I know," he continued, "it was just an imprudent friendship on your part. We all make mistakes."

Evylyn hardly heard him. She was wondering if by sheer clinging to him she could draw him out and up the stairs. She thought of playing sick, asking to be carried up—unfortunately, she knew he would lay her on the couch and bring her whiskey.

Suddenly her nervous tension moved up a last impossible notch. She had heard a very faint but quite unmistakable creak from the floor of the dining-room. Fred was trying to get out the back way.

Then her heart took a flying leap as a hollow ringing note like a gong echoed and re-echoed through the house. Gedney's arm had struck the big cut-glass bowl.

"What's that!" cried Harold. "Who's there?"

She clung to him but he broke away, and the room seemed to crash about her ears. She heard the pantry-door swing open, a scuffle, the rattle of a tin pan, and in wild despair she rushed into the kitchen and pulled up the gas. Her husband's arm slowly unwound from Gedney's neck, and he stood there very still, first in amazement, then with pain dawning in his face.

"My golly!" he said in bewilderment, and then repeated: "My *golly!*"

He turned as if to jump again at Gedney, stopped, his muscles visibly relaxed, and he gave a bitter little laugh.

"You people—you people—" Evylyn's arms were around him and her eyes were pleading with him frantically, but he pushed her away and sank dazed into a kitchen chair, his face like porcelain. "You've been doing things to me, Evylyn. Why, you little devil! You little *devil!*"

She had never felt so sorry for him; she had never loved him so much.

"It wasn't her fault," said Gedney rather humbly. "I just came." But Piper shook his head, and his expression when he stared up was as if some physical accident had jarred his mind into a temporary inability to function. His eyes, grown suddenly pitiful, struck a deep, unsounded chord in Evylyn—and simultaneously a furious anger surged in her. She felt her eyelids burning; she stamped her foot violently; her hands scurried nervously over the table as if searching for a weapon, and then she flung herself wildly at Gedney.

"Get out!" she screamed, dark eyes blazing, little fists beating helplessly on his outstretched arm. "You did this! Get out of here—get out—get *out! Get out!*"

II

Concerning Mrs. Harold Piper at thirty-five, opinion was divided—women said she was still handsome; men said she was pretty no longer. And this was probably because the qualities in her beauty that women had feared and men had followed had vanished. Her eyes were still as large and as dark and as sad, but the mystery had departed; their sadness was no longer eternal, only human, and she had developed a habit, when she was startled or annoyed, of twitching her brows together and blinking several times. Her mouth also had lost: the red had receded and the faint down-turning of its corners when she smiled, that had added to the sadness of the eyes and been vaguely mocking and beautiful, was quite gone. When she smiled now the corners of her lips turned up. Back in the days when she revelled in her own beauty Evylyn had enjoyed that smile of hers—she had accentuated it. When she stopped accentuating it, it faded out and the last of her mystery with it.

Evylyn had ceased accentuating her smile within a month after the Freddy Gedney affair. Externally things had gone on very much as they had before. But in those few minutes during which she had discovered how much she loved her husband Evylyn had realized how indelibly she had hurt him. For a month she struggled against aching silences, wild reproaches and accusations—she pled with him, made quiet, pitiful little love to him, and he laughed at her bitterly—and then she, too, slipped gradually into silence and a shadowy, unpenetrable barrier dropped between them. The surge of love that had risen in her she lavished on Donald, her little boy, realizing him almost wonderingly as a part of her life.

The next year a piling up of mutual interests and responsibilities and some stray flicker from the past brought husband and wife together again—but after a rather pathetic flood of passion Evylyn realized that her great opportunity was gone. There simply wasn't anything left. She might have been youth and love for both—but that time of silence had slowly dried up the springs of affection and her own desire to drink again of them was dead.

She began for the first time to seek women friends, to prefer books she had read before, to sew a little where she could watch her two children to whom she was devoted. She worried about little things—if she saw crumbs on the dinner-table her mind drifted off the conversation: she was receding gradually into middle age.

Her thirty-fifth birthday had been an exceptionally busy one, for they were entertaining on short notice that night, and as she stood in her bedroom window in the late afternoon she discovered that she was quite tired. Ten years before she would have lain down and slept, but now she had a feeling that things needed watching: maids were cleaning down-stairs, bric-à-brac was all over the floor, and there were sure to be grocery-men that had to be talked to imperatively—and then there was a letter to write Donald, who was fourteen and in his first year away at school.

She had nearly decided to lie down, nevertheless, when she heard a sudden familiar signal from little Julie down-stairs. She compressed her lips, her brows twitched together, and she blinked.

"Julie!" she called.

"Ah-h-h-ow!" prolonged Julie plaintively. Then the voice of Hilda, the second maid, floated up the stairs.

"She cut herself a little, Mis' Piper."

Evylyn flew to her sewing-basket, rummaged until she found a torn handkerchief, and hurried down-stairs. In a moment Julie was crying in her arms as she searched for the cut, faint, disparaging evidences of which appeared on Julie's dress!

"My *thu*-umb!" explained Julie. "Oh-h-h-h, t'urts."

"It was the bowl here, the he one," said Hilda apologetically. "It was waitin' on the floor while I polished the sideboard, and Julie come along an' went to foolin' with it. She yust scratch herself."

Evylyn frowned heavily at Hilda, and twisting Julie decisively in her lap, began tearing strips off the handkerchief.

"Now—let's see it, dear."

Julie held it up and Evylyn pounced.

"There!"

Julie surveyed her swathed thumb doubtfully. She crooked it; it waggled. A pleased, interested look appeared in her tear-stained face. She sniffled and waggled it again.

"You *precious!*" cried Evylyn and kissed her, but before she left the room she levelled another frown at Hilda. Careless! Servants all that way nowadays. If she could get a good Irishwoman—but you couldn't any more—and these Swedes——

At five o'clock Harold arrived and, coming up to her room, threatened in a suspiciously jovial tone to kiss her thirty-five times for her birthday. Evylyn resisted.

"You've been drinking," she said shortly, and then added qualitatively, "a little. You know I loathe the smell of it."

"Evie," he said, after a pause, seating himself in a chair by the window, "I can tell you something now. I guess you've known things haven't been going quite right down-town."

She was standing at the window combing her hair, but at these words she turned and looked at him.

"How do you mean? You've always said there was room for more than one wholesale hardware house in town." Her voice expressed some alarm.

"There *was*," said Harold significantly, "but this Clarence Ahearn is a smart man."

"I was surprised when you said he was coming to dinner."

"Evie," he went on, with another slap at his knee, "after January first 'The Clarence Ahearn Company' becomes 'The Ahearn, Piper Company'—and 'Piper Brothers' as a company ceases to exist."

Evylyn was startled. The sound of his name in second place was somehow hostile to her; still he appeared jubilant.

"I don't understand, Harold."

"Well, Evie, Ahearn has been fooling around with Marx. If those two had combined we'd have been the little fellow, struggling along, picking up smaller orders, hanging back on risks. It's a question of capital, Evie, and 'Ahearn and Marx' would have had the business just like 'Ahearn and Piper' is going to now." He paused and coughed and a little cloud of whiskey floated up to her nostrils. "Tell you the truth, Evie, I've suspected that Ahearn's wife had something to do with it. Ambitious little lady, I'm told. Guess she knew the Marxes couldn't help her much here."

"Is she—common?" asked Evie.

"Never met her, I'm sure—but I don't doubt it. Clarence Ahearn's name's been up at the Country Club five months—no action taken." He waved his hand disparagingly. "Ahearn and I had lunch together to-day and just about clinched it, so I thought it'd be nice to have him and his wife up to-night—just have nine, mostly family. After all, it's a big thing for me, and of course we'll have to see something of them, Evie."

"Yes," said Evie thoughtfully, "I suppose we will."

Evylyn was not disturbed over the social end of it—but the idea of "Piper Brothers" becoming "The Ahearn, Piper Company" startled her. It seemed like going down in the world.

Half an hour later, as she began to dress for dinner, she heard his voice from down-stairs.

"Oh, Evie, come down!"

She went out into the hall and called over the banister:

"What is it?"

"I want you to help me make some of that punch before dinner."

Hurriedly rehooking her dress, she descended the stairs and found him grouping the essentials on the dining-room table. She went to the sideboard and, lifting one of the bowls, carried it over.

"Oh, no," he protested, "let's use the big one. There'll be Ahearn and his wife and you and I and Milton, that's five, and Tom and Jessie, that's seven, and your sister and Joe Ambler, that's nine. You don't know how quick that stuff goes when *you* make it."

"We'll use this bowl," she insisted. "It'll hold plenty. You know how Tom is."

Tom Lowrie, husband to Jessie, Harold's first cousin, was

rather inclined to finish anything in a liquid way that he began.

Harold shook his head.

"Don't be foolish. That one holds only about three quarts and there's nine of us, and the servants'll want some—and it isn't strong punch. It's so much more cheerful to have a lot, Evie; we don't have to drink all of it."

"I say the small one."

Again he shook his head obstinately.

"No; be reasonable."

"I *am* reasonable," she said shortly. "I don't want any drunken men in the house."

"Who said you did?"

"Then use the small bowl."

"Now, Evie——"

He grasped the smaller bowl to lift it back. Instantly her hands were on it, holding it down. There was a momentary struggle, and then, with a little exasperated grunt, he raised his side, slipped it from her fingers, and carried it to the sideboard.

She looked at him and tried to make her expression contemptuous, but he only laughed. Acknowledging her defeat but disclaiming all future interest in the punch, she left the room.

III

At seven-thirty, her cheeks glowing and her high-piled hair gleaming with a suspicion of brilliantine, Evylyn descended the stairs. Mrs. Ahearn, a little woman concealing a slight nervousness under red hair and an extreme Empire gown, greeted her volubly. Evylyn disliked her on the spot, but the husband she rather approved of. He had keen blue eyes and a natural gift of pleasing people that might have made him, socially, had he not so obviously committed the blunder of marrying too early in his career.

"I'm glad to know Piper's wife," he said simply. "It looks as though your husband and I are going to see a lot of each other in the future."

She bowed, smiled graciously, and turned to greet the

others: Milton Piper, Harold's quiet, unassertive younger brother; the two Lowries, Jessie and Tom; Irene, her own unmarried sister; and finally Joe Ambler, a confirmed bachelor and Irene's perennial beau.

Harold led the way into dinner.

"We're having a punch evening," he announced jovially—Evylyn saw that he had already sampled his concoction—"so there won't be any cocktails except the punch. It's m' wife's greatest achievement, Mrs. Ahearn; she'll give you the recipe if you want it; but owing to a slight"—he caught his wife's eye and paused—"to a slight indisposition, I'm responsible for this batch. Here's how!"

All through dinner there was punch, and Evylyn, noticing that Ahearn and Milton Piper and all the women were shaking their heads negatively at the maid, knew she had been right about the bowl; it was still half full. She resolved to caution Harold directly afterward, but when the women left the table Mrs. Ahearn cornered her, and she found herself talking cities and dressmakers with a polite show of interest.

"We've moved around a lot," chattered Mrs. Ahearn, her red head nodding violently. "Oh, yes, we've never stayed so long in a town before—but I do hope we're here for good. I like it here; don't you?"

"Well, you see, I've always lived here, so, naturally——"

"Oh, that's true," said Mrs. Ahearn and laughed. "Clarence always used to tell me he had to have a wife he could come home to and say: 'Well, we're going to Chicago to-morrow to live, so pack up.' I got so I never expected to live *any*where." She laughed her little laugh again; Evylyn suspected that it was her society laugh.

"Your husband is a very able man, I imagine."

"Oh, yes," Mrs. Ahearn assured her eagerly. "He's brainy, Clarence is. Ideas and enthusiasm, you know. Finds out what he wants and then goes and gets it."

Evylyn nodded. She was wondering if the men were still drinking punch back in the dining-room. Mrs. Ahearn's history kept unfolding jerkily, but Evylyn had ceased to listen. The first odor of massed cigars began to drift in. It wasn't really a large house, she reflected; on an evening like this the library sometimes grew blue with smoke, and next day one had to leave the windows open for hours to air the heavy staleness out of the curtains. Perhaps this partnership might . . . she began to speculate on a new house . . .

Mrs. Ahearn's voice drifted in on her:

"I really would like the recipe if you have it written down somewhere——"

Then there was a sound of chairs in the dining-room and the men strolled in. Evylyn saw at once that her worst fears were realized. Harold's face was flushed and his words ran together at the ends of sentences, while Tom Lowrie lurched when he walked and narrowly missed Irene's lap when he tried to sink onto the couch beside her. He sat there blinking dazedly at the company. Evylyn found herself blinking back at him, but she saw no humor in it. Joe Ambler was smiling contentedly and purring on his cigar. Only Ahearn and Milton Piper seemed unaffected.

"It's a pretty fine town, Ahearn," said Ambler, "you'll find that."

"I've found it so," said Ahearn pleasantly.

"You find it more, Ahearn," said Harold, nodding emphatically, " 'f I've an'thin' do 'th it."

He soared into a eulogy of the city, and Evylyn wondered uncomfortably if it bored every one as it bored her. Apparently not. They were all listening attentively. Evylyn broke in at the first gap.

"Where've you been living, Mr. Ahearn?" she asked interestedly. Then she remembered that Mrs. Ahearn had told her, but it didn't matter. Harold mustn't talk so much. He was such an *ass* when he'd been drinking. But he plopped directly back in.

"Tell you, Ahearn. Firs' you wanna get a house up here on the hill. Get Stearne house or Ridgeway house. Wanna have it so people say: 'There's Ahearn house.' Solid, you know, tha's effec' it gives."

Evylyn flushed. This didn't sound right at all. Still Ahearn didn't seem to notice anything amiss, only nodded gravely.

"Have you been looking—" But her words trailed off unheard as Harold's voice boomed on.

"Get house—tha's start. Then you get know people. Snobbish town first toward outsider, but not long—not after know you. People like you"—he indicated Ahearn and his wife with a sweeping gesture—"all right. Cordial as an'thin' once get by first barrer-bar-barrer—" He swallowed, and then said "barrier," repeated it masterfully.

Evylyn looked appealingly at her brother-in-law, but before he could intercede a thick mumble had come crowding out of Tom Lowrie, hindered by the dead cigar which he gripped firmly with his teeth.

"Huma uma ho huma ahdy um——"

"What?" demanded Harold earnestly.

Resignedly and with difficulty Tom removed the cigar—that is, he removed part of it, and then blew the remainder with a *whut* sound across the room, where it landed liquidly and limply in Mrs. Ahearn's lap.

"Beg pardon," he mumbled, and rose with the vague intention of going after it. Milton's hand on his coat collapsed him in time, and Mrs. Ahearn not ungracefully flounced the tobacco from her skirt to the floor, never once looking at it.

"I was sayin'," continued Tom thickly, " 'fore 'at happened"—he waved his hand apologetically toward Mrs. Ahearn—"I was sayin' I heard all truth that Country Club matter."

Milton leaned and whispered something to him.

"Lemme 'lone," he said petulantly; "know what I'm doin'. 'At's what they came for."

Evylyn sat there in a panic, trying to make her mouth form words. She saw her sister's sardonic expression and Mrs. Ahearn's face turning a vivid red. Ahearn was looking down at his watch-chain, fingering it.

"I heard who's been keepin' y' out, an' he's not a bit better'n you. I can fix whole damn thing up. Would've before, but I didn't know you. Harol' tol' me you felt bad about the thing——"

Milton Piper rose suddenly and awkwardly to his feet. In a second every one was standing tensely and Milton was saying something very hurriedly about having to go early, and the Ahearns were listening with eager intentness. Then Mrs. Ahearn swallowed and turned with a forced smile toward Jessie. Evylyn saw Tom lurch forward and put his hand on Ahearn's shoulder—and suddenly she was listening to a new, anxious voice at her elbow, and, turning, found Hilda, the second maid.

"Please, Mis' Piper, I tank Yulie got her hand poisoned. It's all swole up and her cheeks is hot and she's moanin' an' groanin'——"

"Julie is?" Evylyn asked sharply. The party suddenly receded. She turned quickly, sought with her eyes for Mrs. Ahearn, slipped toward her.

"If you'll excuse me, Mrs.—" She had momentarily forgotten the name, but she went right on: "My little girl's been taken sick. I'll be down when I can." She turned and ran quickly up the stairs, retaining a confused picture of rays of cigar smoke and a loud discussion in the centre of the room that seemed to be developing into an argument.

Switching on the light in the nursery, she found Julie tossing feverishly and giving out odd little cries. She put her hand against the cheeks. They were burning. With an exclamation she followed the arm down under the cover until she found the hand. Hilda was right. The whole thumb was swollen to the wrist and in the centre was a little inflamed sore. Blood-poisoning! her mind cried in terror. The bandage had come off the cut and she'd gotten something in it. She'd cut it at three o'clock—it was now nearly eleven. Eight hours. Blood-poisoning couldn't possibly develop so soon. She rushed to the 'phone.

Doctor Martin across the street was out. Doctor Foulke, their family physician, didn't answer. She racked her brains and in desperation called her throat specialist, and bit her lip furiously while he looked up the numbers of two physicians. During that interminable moment she thought she heard loud voices down-stairs—but she seemed to be in another world now. After fifteen minutes she located a physician who sounded angry and sulky at being called out of bed. She ran back to the nursery and, looking at the hand, found it was somewhat more swollen.

"Oh, God!" she cried, and kneeling beside the bed began smoothing back Julie's hair over and over. With a vague idea of getting some hot water, she rose and started toward the door, but the lace of her dress caught in the bed-rail and she fell forward on her hands and knees. She struggled up and jerked frantically at the lace. The bed moved and Julie groaned. Then more quietly but with suddenly fumbling fingers she found the pleat in front, tore the whole pannier completely off, and rushed from the room.

Out in the hall she heard a single loud, insistent voice, but as she reached the head of the stairs it ceased and an outer door banged.

The music-room came into view. Only Harold and Milton were there, the former leaning against a chair, his face very pale, his collar open, and his mouth moving loosely.

"What's the matter?"

Milton looked at her anxiously.

"There was a little trouble——"

Then Harold saw her and, straightening up with an effort, began to speak.

" 'Sult m'own cousin m'own house. God damn common nouveau rish. 'Sult m'own cousin——"

"Tom had trouble with Ahearn and Harold interfered," said Milton.

"My Lord, Milton," cried Evylyn, "couldn't you have done something?"

"I tried; I——"

"Julie's sick," she interrupted; "she's poisoned herself. Get him to bed if you can."

Harold looked up.

"Julie sick?"

Paying no attention, Evylyn brushed by through the dining-room, catching sight, with a burst of horror, of the big punch-bowl still on the table, the liquid from melted ice in its bottom. She heard steps on the front stairs—it was Milton helping Harold up—and then a mumble: "Why, Julie's a'righ'."

"Don't let him go into the nursery!" she shouted.

The hours blurred into a nightmare. The doctor arrived just before midnight and within a half-hour had lanced the wound. He left at two after giving her the addresses of two nurses to call up and promising to return at half past six. It was blood-poisoning.

At four, leaving Hilda by the bedside, she went to her room, and slipping with a shudder out of her evening dress, kicked it into a corner. She put on a house dress and returned to the nursery while Hilda went to make coffee.

Not until noon could she bring herself to look into Harold's room, but when she did it was to find him awake and staring very miserably at the ceiling. He turned bloodshot hollow eyes upon her. For a minute she hated him, couldn't speak. A husky voice came from the bed.

"What time is it?"

"Noon."

"I made a damn fool——"

"It doesn't matter," she said sharply. "Julie's got blood-poisoning. They may"—she choked over the words—"they think she'll have to lose her hand."

"What?"

"She cut herself on that—that bowl."

"Last night?"

"Oh, what does it matter?" she cried; "she's got blood-poisoning. Can't you hear?"

He looked at her bewildered—sat half-way up in bed.

"I'll get dressed," he said.

Her anger subsided and a great wave of weariness and pity for him rolled over her. After all, it was his trouble, too.

"Yes," she answered listlessly, "I suppose you'd better."

IV

If Evylyn's beauty had hesitated in her early thirties it came to an abrupt decision just afterward and completely left her. A tentative outlay of wrinkles on her face suddenly deepened and flesh collected rapidly on her legs and hips and arms. Her mannerism of drawing her brows together had become an expression—it was habitual when she was reading or speaking and even while she slept. She was forty-six.

As in most families whose fortunes have gone down rather than up, she and Harold had drifted into a colorless antagonism. In repose they looked at each other with the toleration they might have felt for broken old chairs; Evylyn worried a little when he was sick and did her best to be cheerful under the wearying depression of living with a disappointed man.

Family bridge was over for the evening and she sighed with

relief. She had made more mistakes than usual this evening and she didn't care. Irene shouldn't have made that remark about the infantry being particularly dangerous. There had been no letter for three weeks now, and, while this was nothing out of the ordinary, it never failed to make her nervous; naturally she hadn't known how many clubs were out.

Harold had gone up-stairs, so she stepped out on the porch for a breath of fresh air. There was a bright glamour of moonlight diffusing on the sidewalks and lawns, and with a little half yawn, half laugh, she remembered one long moonlight affair of her youth. It was astonishing to think that life had once been the sum of her current love-affairs. It was now the sum of her current problems.

There was the problem of Julie—Julie was thirteen, and lately she was growing more and more sensitive about her deformity and preferred to stay always in her room reading. A few years before she had been frightened at the idea of going to school, and Evylyn could not bring herself to send her, so she grew up in her mother's shadow, a pitiful little figure with the artificial hand that she made no attempt to use but kept forlornly in her pocket. Lately she had been taking lessons in using it because Evylyn had feared she would cease to lift the arm altogether, but after the lessons, unless she made a move with it in listless obedience to her mother, the little hand would creep back to the pocket of her dress. For a while her dresses were made without pockets, but Julie had moped around the house so miserably at a loss all one month that Evylyn weakened and never tried the experiment again.

The problem of Donald had been different from the start. She had attempted vainly to keep him near her as she had tried to teach Julie to lean less on her—lately the problem of Donald had been snatched out of her hands; his division had been abroad for three months.

She yawned again—life was a thing for youth. What a happy youth she must have had! She remembered her pony, Bijou, and the trip to Europe with her mother when she was eighteen——

"Very, very complicated," she said aloud and severely to the moon, and, stepping inside, was about to close the door when she heard a noise in the library and started.

It was Martha, the middle-aged servant: they kept only one now.

"Why, Martha!" she said in surprise.

Martha turned quickly.

"Oh, I thought you was up-stairs. I was jist——"

"Is anything the matter?"

Martha hesitated.

"No; I—" She stood there fidgeting. "It was a letter, Mrs. Piper, that I put somewhere."

"A letter? Your own letter?" asked Evylyn, switching on the light.

"No, it was to you. 'Twas this afternoon, Mrs. Piper, in the last mail. The postman give it to me and then the back door-bell rang. I had it in my hand, so I must have stuck it somewhere. I thought I'd just slip in now and find it."

"What sort of a letter? From Mr. Donald?"

"No, it was an advertisement, maybe, or a business letter. It was a long, narrow one, I remember."

They began a search through the music-room, looking on trays and mantelpieces, and then through the library, feeling on the tops of rows of books. Martha paused in despair.

"I can't think where. I went straight to the kitchen. The dining-room, maybe." She started hopefully for the dining-room, but turned suddenly at the sound of a gasp behind her. Evylyn had sat down heavily in a Morris chair, her brows drawn very close together, eyes blinking furiously.

"Are you sick?"

For a minute there was no answer. Evylyn sat there very still and Martha could see the very quick rise and fall of her bosom.

"Are you sick?" she repeated.

"No," said Evylyn slowly, "but I know where the letter is. Go 'way, Martha. I know."

Wonderingly, Martha withdrew, and still Evylyn sat there, only the muscles around her eyes moving—contracting and relaxing and contracting again. She knew now where the letter was—she knew as well as if she had put it there herself. And she felt instinctively and unquestionably what the letter was. It was long and narrow like an advertisement, but up in the corner in large letters it said "War Department" and, in smaller letters below, "Official Business." She knew it lay there in the big bowl with her name in ink on the outside and her soul's death within.

Rising uncertainly, she walked toward the dining-room, feeling her way along the bookcases and through the doorway. After a moment she found the light and switched it on.

There was the bowl, reflecting the electric light in crimson squares edged with black and yellow squares edged with blue, ponderous and glittering, grotesquely and triumphantly ominous. She took a step forward and paused again; another step and she would see over the top and into the inside—another step and she would see an edge of white—another step—her hands fell on the rough, cold surface——

In a moment she was tearing it open, fumbling with an obstinate fold, holding it before her while the typewritten page glared out and struck at her. Then it fluttered like a bird to the floor. The house that had seemed whirring, buzzing a moment since, was suddenly very quiet; a breath of air crept in through the open front door carrying the noise of a passing motor; she heard faint sounds from up-stairs and then a grinding racket in the pipe behind the bookcases—her husband turning off a water-tap——

And in that instant it was as if this were not, after all, Donald's hour except in so far as he was a marker in the insidious contest that had gone on in sudden surges and long, listless interludes between Evylyn and this cold, malignant thing of beauty, a gift of enmity from a man whose face she had long since forgotten. With its massive, brooding passivity it lay there in the centre of her house as it had lain for years, throwing out the ice-like beams of a thousand eyes, perverse glitterings merging each into each, never aging, never changing.

Evylyn sat down on the edge of the table and stared at it fascinated. It seemed to be smiling now, a very cruel smile, as if to say:

"You see, this time I didn't have to hurt you directly. I didn't bother. You know it was I who took your son away. You know how cold I am and how hard and how beautiful, because once you were just as cold and hard and beautiful."

The bowl seemed suddenly to turn itself over and then to

distend and swell until it became a great canopy that glittered and trembled over the room, over the house, and, as the walls melted slowly into mist, Evylyn saw that it was still moving out, out and far away from her, shutting off far horizons and suns and moons and stars except as inky blots seen faintly through it. And under it walked all the people, and the light that came through to them was refracted and twisted until shadow seemed light and light seemed shadow—until the whole panorama of the world became changed and distorted under the twinkling heaven of the bowl.

Then there came a far-away, booming voice like a low, clear bell. It came from the centre of the bowl and down the great sides to the ground and then bounced toward her eagerly.

"You see, I am fate," it shouted, "and stronger than your puny plans; and I am how-things-turn-out and I am different from your little dreams, and I am the flight of time and the end of beauty and unfulfilled desire; all the accidents and imperceptions and the little minutes that shape the crucial hours are mine. I am the exception that proves no rules, the limits of your control, the condiment in the dish of life."

The booming sound stopped; the echoes rolled away over the wide land to the edge of the bowl that bounded the world and up the great sides and back to the centre where they hummed for a moment and died. Then the great walls began slowly to bear down upon her, growing smaller and smaller, coming closer and closer as if to crush her; and as she clinched her hands and waited for the swift bruise of the cold glass, the bowl gave a sudden wrench and turned over—and lay there on the sideboard, shining and inscrutable, reflecting in a hundred prisms, myriad, many-colored glints and gleams and crossings and interlacings of light.

The cold wind blew in again through the front door, and with a desperate, frantic energy Evylyn stretched both her arms around the bowl. She must be quick—she must be strong. She tightened her arms until they ached, tauted the thin strips of muscle under her soft flesh, and with a mighty effort raised it and held it. She felt the wind blow cold on her back where her dress had come apart from the strain of her effort, and as she felt it she turned toward it and staggered under the great weight out through the library and on toward the front door. She must be quick—she must be strong. The blood in her arms throbbed dully and her knees kept giving way under her, but the feel of the cool glass was good.

Out the front door she tottered and over to the stone steps, and there, summoning every fibre of her soul and body for a last effort, swung herself half around—for a second, as she tried to loose her hold, her numb fingers clung to the rough surface, and in that second she slipped and, losing balance, toppled forward with a despairing cry, her arms still around the bowl . . . down . . .

Over the way lights went on; far down the block the crash was heard, and pedestrians rushed up wonderingly; up-stairs a tired man awoke from the edge of sleep and a little girl whimpered in a haunted doze. And all over the moonlit sidewalk around the still, black form, hundreds of prisms and cubes and splinters of glass reflected the light in little gleams of blue, and black edged with yellow, and yellow, and crimson edged with black.

Bernice Bobs Her Hair

AFTER DARK on Saturday night one could stand on the first tee of the golf-course and see the country-club windows as a yellow expanse over a very black and wavy ocean. The waves of this ocean, so to speak, were the heads of many curious caddies, a few of the more ingenious chauffeurs, the golf professional's deaf sister—and there were usually several stray, diffident waves who might have rolled inside had they so desired. This was the gallery.

The balcony was inside. It consisted of the circle of wicker chairs that lined the wall of the combination clubroom and ballroom. At these Saturday-night dances it was largely feminine; a great babel of middle-aged ladies with sharp eyes and icy hearts behind lorgnettes and large bosoms. The main function of the balcony was critical. It occasionally showed grudging admiration, but never approval, for it is well known among ladies over thirty-five that when the younger set dance in the summer-time it is with the very worst intentions in the world, and if they are not bombarded with stony eyes stray couples will dance weird barbaric interludes in the corners, and the more popular, more dangerous, girls will sometimes be kissed in the parked limousines of unsuspecting dowagers.

But, after all, this critical circle is not close enough to the stage to see the actors' faces and catch the subtler byplay. It can only frown and lean, ask questions and make satisfactory deductions from its set of postulates, such as the one which states that every young man with a large income leads the life of a hunted partridge. It never really appreciates the drama of the shifting, semicruel world of adolescence. No; boxes, orchestra-circle, principals, and chorus are represented by the medley of faces and voices that sway to the plaintive African rhythm of Dyer's dance orchestra.

From sixteen-year-old Otis Ormonde, who has two more years at Hill School, to G. Reece Stoddard, over whose bureau at home hangs a Harvard law diploma; from little Madeleine Hogue, whose hair still feels strange and uncomfortable on top of her head, to Bessie MacRae, who has been the life of the party a little too long—more than ten years—the medley is not only the centre of the stage but contains the only people capable of getting an unobstructed view of it.

With a flourish and a bang the music stops. The couples exchange artificial, effortless smiles, facetiously repeat "*la*-de-*da-da* dum-*dum*," and then the clatter of young feminine voices soars over the burst of clapping.

A few disappointed stags caught in midfloor as they had been about to cut in subsided listlessly back to the walls, because this was not like the riotous Christmas dances—these summer hops were considered just pleasantly warm and exciting, where even the younger marrieds rose and performed ancient waltzes and terrifying fox trots to the tolerant amusement of their younger brothers and sisters.

Warren McIntyre, who casually attended Yale, being one of the unfortunate stags, felt in his dinner-coat pocket for a cigarette and strolled out onto the wide, semidark veranda, where couples were scattered at tables, filling the lantern-hung night with vague words and hazy laughter. He nodded here and there at the less absorbed and as he passed each couple some half-forgotten fragment of a story played in his mind, for it was not a large city and every one was Who's Who to every one else's past. There, for example, were Jim Strain and Ethel Demorest, who had been privately engaged for three years. Every one knew that as soon as Jim managed to hold a job for more than two months she would marry him. Yet how bored they both looked, and how wearily Ethel regarded Jim sometimes, as if she wondered why she had trained the vines of her affection on such a wind-shaken poplar.

Warren was nineteen and rather pitying with those of his friends who hadn't gone East to college. But, like most boys, he bragged tremendously about the girls of his city when he was away from it. There was Genevieve Ormonde, who regularly made the rounds of dances, house-parties, and football games at Princeton, Yale, Williams, and Cornell; there was black-eyed Roberta Dillon, who was quite as famous to her own generation as Hiram Johnson or Ty Cobb; and, of course, there was Marjorie Harvey, who besides having a fairylike face and a dazzling, bewildering tongue was already justly celebrated for having turned five cart-wheels in succession during the last pump-and-slipper dance at New Haven.

Warren, who had grown up across the street from Marjorie, had long been "crazy about her." Sometimes she seemed to reciprocate his feeling with a faint gratitude, but she had tried him by her infallible test and informed him gravely that she did not love him. Her test was that when she was away from him she forgot him and had affairs with other boys. Warren found this discouraging, especially as Marjorie had been making little trips all summer, and for the first two or three days after each arrival home he saw great heaps of mail on the Harveys' hall table addressed to her in various masculine handwritings. To make matters worse, all during the month of August she had been visited by her cousin Bernice from Eau Claire, and it seemed impossible to see her alone. It was always necessary to hunt round and find some one to take care of Bernice. As August waned this was becoming more and more difficult.

Much as Warren worshipped Marjorie, he had to admit that Cousin Bernice was sorta dopeless. She was pretty, with dark hair and high color, but she was no fun on a party. Every Saturday night he danced a long arduous duty dance with her to please Marjorie, but he had never been anything but bored in her company.

"Warren"—a soft voice at his elbow broke in upon his thoughts, and he turned to see Marjorie, flushed and radiant as usual. She laid a hand on his shoulder and a glow settled almost imperceptibly over him.

"Warren," she whispered, "do something for me—dance with Bernice. She's been stuck with little Otis Ormonde for almost an hour."

Warren's glow faded.

"Why—sure," he answered half-heartedly.

"You don't mind, do you? I'll see that you don't get stuck."

" 'Sall right."

Marjorie smiled—that smile that was thanks enough.

"You're an angel, and I'm obliged loads."

With a sigh the angel glanced round the veranda, but Bernice and Otis were not in sight. He wandered back inside, and there in front of the women's dressing-room he found Otis in the centre of a group of young men who were convulsed with laughter. Otis was brandishing a piece of timber he had picked up, and discoursing volubly.

"She's gone in to fix her hair," he announced wildly. "I'm waiting to dance another hour with her."

Their laughter was renewed.

"Why don't some of you cut in?" cried Otis resentfully. "She likes more variety."

"Why, Otis," suggested a friend, "you've just barely got used to her."

"Why the two-by-four, Otis?" inquired Warren, smiling.

"The two-by-four? Oh, this? This is a club. When she comes out I'll hit her on the head and knock her in again."

Warren collapsed on a settee and howled with glee.

"Never mind, Otis," he articulated finally. "I'm relieving you this time."

Otis simulated a sudden fainting attack and handed the stick to Warren.

"If you need it, old man," he said hoarsely.

No matter how beautiful or brilliant a girl may be, the reputation of not being frequently cut in on makes her position at a dance unfortunate. Perhaps boys prefer her company to that of the butterflies with whom they dance a dozen times an evening, but youth in this jazz-nourished generation is temperamentally restless, and the idea of fox-trotting more than one full fox trot with the same girl is distasteful, not to say odious. When it comes to several dances and the intermissions between she can be quite sure that a young man, once relieved, will never tread on her wayward toes again.

Warren danced the next full dance with Bernice, and finally, thankful for the intermission, he led her to a table on the veranda. There was a moment's silence while she did unimpressive things with her fan.

"It's hotter here than in Eau Claire," she said.

Warren stifled a sigh and nodded. It might be for all he knew or cared. He wondered idly whether she was a poor conversationalist because she got no attention or got no attention because she was a poor conversationalist.

"You going to be here much longer?" he asked, and then turned rather red. She might suspect his reasons for asking.

"Another week," she answered, and stared at him as if to lunge at his next remark when it left his lips.

Warren fidgeted. Then with a sudden charitable impulse he decided to try part of his line on her. He turned and looked at her eyes.

"You've got an awfully kissable mouth," he began quietly.

This was a remark that he sometimes made to girls at college proms when they were talking in just such half dark as this. Bernice distinctly jumped. She turned an ungraceful red and became clumsy with her fan. No one had ever made such a remark to her before.

"Fresh!"—the word had slipped out before she realized it, and she bit her lip. Too late she decided to be amused, and offered him a flustered smile.

Warren was annoyed. Though not accustomed to have that remark taken seriously, still it usually provoked a laugh or a paragraph of sentimental banter. And he hated to be called fresh, except in a joking way. His charitable impulse died and he switched the topic.

"Jim Strain and Ethel Demorest sitting out as usual," he commented.

This was more in Bernice's line, but a faint regret mingled with her relief as the subject changed. Men did not talk to her about kissable mouths, but she knew that they talked in some such way to other girls.

"Oh, yes," she said, and laughed. "I hear they've been mooning round for years without a red penny. Isn't it silly?"

Warren's disgust increased. Jim Strain was a close friend of his brother's, and anyway he considered it bad form to sneer at people for not having money. But Bernice had had no intention of sneering. She was merely nervous.

II

When Marjorie and Bernice reached home at half after midnight they said good night at the top of the stairs. Though cousins, they were not intimates. As a matter of fact Marjorie had no female intimates—she considered girls stupid. Bernice on the contrary all through this parent-arranged visit had rather longed to exchange those confidences flavored with giggles and tears that she considered an indispensable factor in all feminine intercourse. But in this respect she found Marjorie rather cold; felt somehow the same difficulty in talking to her that she had in talking to men. Marjorie never giggled, was never frightened, seldom embarrassed, and in fact had very few of the qualities which Bernice considered appropriately and blessedly feminine.

As Bernice busied herself with tooth-brush and paste this night she wondered for the hundredth time why she never had any attention when she was away from home. That her family were the wealthiest in Eau Claire; that her mother entertained tremendously, gave little dinners for her daughter before all dances and bought her a car of her own to drive round in, never occurred to her as factors in her home-town social success. Like most girls she had been brought up on the warm milk prepared by Annie Fellows Johnston and on novels in which the female was beloved because of certain mysterious womanly qualities, always mentioned but never displayed.

Bernice felt a vague pain that she was not at present engaged in being popular. She did not know that had it not been for Marjorie's campaigning she would have danced the entire evening with one man; but she knew that even in Eau Claire other girls with less position and less pulchritude were given a much bigger rush. She attributed this to something subtly unscrupulous in those girls. It had never worried her, and if it had her mother would have assured her that the other girls cheapened themselves and that men really respected girls like Bernice.

She turned out the light in her bathroom, and on an impulse decided to go in and chat for a moment with her aunt Josephine, whose light was still on. Her soft slippers bore her noiselessly down the carpeted hall, but hearing voices inside she stopped near the partly opened door. Then she caught her own name, and without any definite intention of eavesdropping lingered—and the thread of the conversation going on inside pierced her consciousness sharply as if it had been drawn through with a needle.

"She's absolutely hopeless!" It was Marjorie's voice. "Oh, I know what you're going to say! So many people have told you how pretty and sweet she is, and how she can cook! What of it? She has a bum time. Men don't like her."

"What's a little cheap popularity?"

Mrs. Harvey sounded annoyed.

"It's everything when you're eighteen," said Marjorie emphatically. "I've done my best. I've been polite and I've made men dance with her, but they just won't stand being bored. When I think of that gorgeous coloring wasted on such a ninny, and think what Martha Carey could do with it—oh!"

"There's no courtesy these days."

Mrs. Harvey's voice implied that modern situations were too much for her. When she was a girl all young ladies who belonged to nice families had glorious times.

"Well," said Marjorie, "no girl can permanently bolster up a lame-duck visitor, because these days it's every girl for herself. I've even tried to drop her hints about clothes and things, and she's been furious—given me the funniest looks. She's sensitive enough to know she's not getting away with much, but I'll bet she consoles herself by thinking that she's very virtuous and that I'm too gay and fickle and will come to a bad end. All unpopular girls think that way. Sour grapes! Sarah Hopkins refers to Genevieve and Roberta and me as gardenia girls! I'll bet she'd give ten years of her life and her European education to be a gardenia girl and have three or four men in love with her and be cut in on every few feet at dances."

"It seems to me," interrupted Mrs. Harvey rather wearily, "that you ought to be able to do something for Bernice. I know she's not very vivacious."

Marjorie groaned.

"Vivacious! Good grief! I've never heard her say anything to a boy except that it's hot or the floor's crowded or that she's going to school in New York next year. Sometimes she asks them what kind of car they have and tells them the kind she has. Thrilling!"

There was a short silence, and then Mrs. Harvey took up her refrain:

"All I know is that other girls not half so sweet and attractive get partners. Martha Carey, for instance, is stout and loud, and her mother is distinctly common. Roberta Dillon is so thin this year that she looks as though Arizona were the place for her. She's dancing herself to death."

"But, mother," objected Marjorie impatiently, "Martha is cheerful and awfully witty and an awfully slick girl, and Roberta's a marvellous dancer. She's been popular for ages!"

Mrs. Harvey yawned.

"I think it's that crazy Indian blood in Bernice," continued Marjorie. "Maybe she's a reversion to type. Indian women all just sat round and never said anything."

"Go to bed, you silly child," laughed Mrs. Harvey. "I wouldn't have told you that if I'd thought you were going to remember it. And I think most of your ideas are perfectly idiotic," she finished sleepily.

There was another silence, while Marjorie considered whether or not convincing her mother was worth the trouble. People over forty can seldom be permanently convinced of anything. At eighteen our convictions are hills from which we look; at forty-five they are caves in which we hide.

Having decided this, Marjorie said good night. When she came out into the hall it was quite empty.

III

While Marjorie was breakfasting late next day Bernice came into the room with a rather formal good morning, sat down opposite, stared intently over and slightly moistened her lips.

"What's on your mind?" inquired Marjorie, rather puzzled.

Bernice paused before she threw her hand-grenade.

"I heard what you said about me to your mother last night."

Marjorie was startled, but she showed only a faintly heightened color and her voice was quite even when she spoke.

"Where were you?"

"In the hall. I didn't mean to listen—at first."

After an involuntary look of contempt Marjorie dropped her eyes and became very interested in balancing a stray cornflake on her finger.

"I guess I'd better go back to Eau Claire—if I'm such a nuisance." Bernice's lower lip was trembling violently and she continued on a wavering note: "I've tried to be nice, and—and I've been first neglected and then insulted. No one ever visited me and got such treatment."

Marjorie was silent.

"But I'm in the way, I see. I'm a drag on you. Your friends don't like me." She paused, and then remembered another one of her grievances. "Of course I was furious last week when you tried to hint to me that that dress was unbecoming. Don't you think I know how to dress myself?"

"No," murmured Marjorie less than half-aloud.

"What?"

"I didn't hint anything," said Marjorie succinctly. "I said, as I remember, that it was better to wear a becoming dress three times straight than to alternate it with two frights."

"Do you think that was a very nice thing to say?"

"I wasn't trying to be nice." Then after a pause: "When do you want to go?"

Bernice drew in her breath sharply.

"Oh!" It was a little half-cry.

Marjorie looked up in surprise.

"Didn't you say you were going?"

"Yes, but——"

"Oh, you were only bluffing!"

They stared at each other across the breakfast-table for a moment. Misty waves were passing before Bernice's eyes, while Marjorie's face wore that rather hard expression that she used when slightly intoxicated undergraduates were making love to her.

"So you were bluffing," she repeated as if it were what she might have expected.

Bernice admitted it by bursting into tears. Marjorie's eyes showed boredom.

"You're my cousin," sobbed Bernice. "I'm v-v-visiting you. I was to stay a month, and if I go home my mother will know and she'll wah-wonder——"

Marjorie waited until the shower of broken words collapsed into little sniffles.

"I'll give you my month's allowance," she said coldly, "and

you can spend this last week anywhere you want. There's a very nice hotel——"

Bernice's sobs rose to a flute note, and rising of a sudden she fled from the room.

An hour later, while Marjorie was in the library absorbed in composing one of those non-committal, marvellously elusive letters that only a young girl can write, Bernice reappeared, very red-eyed and consciously calm. She cast no glance at Marjorie but took a book at random from the shelf and sat down as if to read. Marjorie seemed absorbed in her letter and continued writing. When the clock showed noon Bernice closed her book with a snap.

"I suppose I'd better get my railroad ticket."

This was not the beginning of the speech she had rehearsed up-stairs, but as Marjorie was not getting her cues—wasn't urging her to be reasonable; it's all a mistake—it was the best opening she could muster.

"Just wait till I finish this letter," said Marjorie without looking round. "I want to get it off in the next mail."

After another minute, during which her pen scratched busily, she turned round and relaxed with an air of "at your service." Again Bernice had to speak.

"Do you want me to go home?"

"Well," said Marjorie, considering, "I suppose if you're not having a good time you'd better go. No use being miserable."

"Don't you think common kindness——"

"Oh, please don't quote 'Little Women'!" cried Marjorie impatiently. "That's out of style."

"You think so?"

"Heavens, yes! What modern girl could live like those inane females?"

"They were the models for our mothers."

Marjorie laughed.

"Yes, they were—not! Besides, our mothers were all very well in their way, but they know very little about their daughters' problems."

Bernice drew herself up.

"Please don't talk about my mother."

Marjorie laughed.

"I don't think I mentioned her."

Bernice felt that she was being led away from her subject.

"Do you think you've treated me very well?"

"I've done my best. You're rather hard material to work with."

The lids of Bernice's eyes reddened.

"I think you're hard and selfish, and you haven't a feminine quality in you."

"Oh, my Lord!" cried Marjorie in desperation. "You little nut! Girls like you are responsible for all the tiresome colorless marriages; all those ghastly inefficiencies that pass as feminine qualities. What a blow it must be when a man with imagination marries the beautiful bundle of clothes that he's been building ideals round, and finds that she's just a weak, whining, cowardly mass of affectations!"

Bernice's mouth had slipped half open.

"The womanly woman!" continued Marjorie. "Her whole early life is occupied in whining criticisms of girls like me who really do have a good time."

Bernice's jaw descended farther as Marjorie's voice rose.

"There's some excuse for an ugly girl whining. If I'd been irretrievably ugly I'd never have forgiven my parents for bringing me into the world. But you're starting life without any handicap—" Marjorie's little fist clinched. "If you expect me to weep with you you'll be disappointed. Go or stay, just as you like." And picking up her letters she left the room.

Bernice claimed a headache and failed to appear at luncheon. They had a matinée date for the afternoon, but the headache persisting, Marjorie made explanation to a not very downcast boy. But when she returned late in the afternoon she found Bernice with a strangely set face waiting for her in her bedroom.

"I've decided," began Bernice without preliminaries, "that maybe you're right about things—possibly not. But if you'll tell me why your friends aren't—aren't interested in me I'll see if I can do what you want me to."

Marjorie was at the mirror shaking down her hair.

"Do you mean it?"

"Yes."

"Without reservations? Will you do exactly what I say?"

"Well, I——"

"Well nothing! Will you do exactly as I say?"

"If they're sensible things."

"They're not! You're no case for sensible things."

"Are you going to make—to recommend——"

"Yes, everything. If I tell you to take boxing-lessons you'll have to do it. Write home and tell your mother you're going to stay another two weeks."

"If you'll tell me——"

"All right—I'll just give you a few examples now. First, you have no ease of manner. Why? Because you're never sure about your personal appearance. When a girl feels that she's perfectly groomed and dressed she can forget that part of her. That's charm. The more parts of yourself you can afford to forget the more charm you have."

"Don't I look all right?"

"No; for instance, you never take care of your eyebrows. They're black and lustrous, but by leaving them straggly they're a blemish. They'd be beautiful if you'd take care of them in one-tenth the time you take doing nothing. You're going to brush them so that they'll grow straight."

Bernice raised the brows in question.

"Do you mean to say that men notice eyebrows?"

"Yes—subconsciously. And when you go home you ought to have your teeth straightened a little. It's almost imperceptible, still—"

"But I thought," interrupted Bernice in bewilderment, "that you despised little dainty feminine things like that."

"I hate dainty minds," answered Marjorie. "But a girl has to be dainty in person. If she looks like a million dollars she can talk about Russia, ping-pong, or the League of Nations and get away with it."

"What else?"

"Oh, I'm just beginning! There's your dancing."

"Don't I dance all right?"

"No, you don't—you lean on a man; yes, you do—ever so slightly. I noticed it when we were dancing together yesterday. And you dance standing up straight instead of bending over a little. Probably some old lady on the side-line once told you that you looked so dignified that way. But except with a very small girl it's much harder on the man, and he's the one that counts."

"Go on." Bernice's brain was reeling.

"Well, you've got to learn to be nice to men who are sad birds. You look as if you'd been insulted whenever you're thrown with any except the most popular boys. Why, Bernice, I'm cut in on every few feet—and who does most of it? Why, those very sad birds. No girl can afford to neglect them. They're the big part of any crowd. Young boys too shy to talk are the very best conversational practice. Clumsy boys are the best dancing practice. If you can follow them and yet look graceful you can follow a baby tank across a barb-wire skyscraper."

Bernice sighed profoundly, but Marjorie was not through.

"If you go to a dance and really amuse, say, three sad birds that dance with you; if you talk so well to them that they forget they're stuck with you, you've done something. They'll come back next time, and gradually so many sad birds will dance with you that the attractive boys will see there's no danger of being stuck—then they'll dance with you."

"Yes," agreed Bernice faintly. "I think I begin to see."

"And finally," concluded Marjorie, "poise and charm will just come. You'll wake up some morning knowing you've attained it, and men will know it too."

Bernice rose.

"It's been awfully kind of you—but nobody's ever talked to me like this before, and I feel sort of startled."

Marjorie made no answer but gazed pensively at her own image in the mirror.

"You're a peach to help me," continued Bernice.

Still Marjorie did not answer, and Bernice thought she had seemed too grateful.

"I know you don't like sentiment," she said timidly.

Marjorie turned to her quickly.

"Oh, I wasn't thinking about that. I was considering whether we hadn't better bob your hair."

Bernice collapsed backward upon the bed.

IV

On the following Wednesday evening there was a dinner-dance at the country club. When the guests strolled in Bernice found her place-card with a slight feeling of irritation. Though at her right sat G. Reece Stoddard, a most desirable and distinguished young bachelor, the all-important left held only Charley Paulson. Charley lacked height, beauty, and social shrewdness, and in her new enlightenment Bernice decided that his only qualification to be her partner was that he had never been stuck with her. But this feeling of irritation left with the last of the soup-plates, and Marjorie's specific instruction came to her. Swallowing her pride she turned to Charley Paulson and plunged.

"Do you think I ought to bob my hair, Mr. Charley Paulson?"

Charley looked up in surprise.

"Why?"

"Because I'm considering it. It's such a sure and easy way of attracting attention."

Charley smiled pleasantly. He could not know this had been rehearsed. He replied that he didn't know much about bobbed hair. But Bernice was there to tell him.

"I want to be a society vampire, you see," she announced coolly, and went on to inform him that bobbed hair was the necessary prelude. She added that she wanted to ask his advice, because she had heard he was so critical about girls.

Charley, who knew as much about the psychology of women as he did of the mental states of Buddhist contemplatives, felt vaguely flattered.

"So I've decided," she continued, her voice rising slightly, "that early next week I'm going down to the Sevier Hotel barber-shop, sit in the first chair, and get my hair bobbed." She faltered, noticing that the people near her had paused in their conversation and were listening; but after a confused second Marjorie's coaching told, and she finished her paragraph to the vicinity at large. "Of course I'm charging admission, but if you'll all come down and encourage me I'll issue passes for the inside seats."

There was a ripple of appreciative laughter, and under cover of it G. Reece Stoddard leaned over quickly and said close to her ear: "I'll take a box right now."

She met his eyes and smiled as if he had said something surpassingly brilliant.

"Do you believe in bobbed hair?" asked G. Reece in the same undertone.

"I think it's unmoral," affirmed Bernice gravely. "But, of course, you've either got to amuse people or feed 'em or shock 'em." Marjorie had culled this from Oscar Wilde. It was greeted with a ripple of laughter from the men and a series of quick, intent looks from the girls. And then as though she had said nothing of wit or moment Bernice turned again to Charley and spoke confidentially in his ear.

"I want to ask you your opinion of several people. I imagine you're a wonderful judge of character."

Charley thrilled faintly—paid her a subtle compliment by overturning her water.

Two hours later, while Warren McIntyre was standing passively in the stag line abstractedly watching the dancers and wondering whither and with whom Marjorie had disappeared, an unrelated perception began to creep slowly upon him—a perception that Bernice, cousin to Marjorie, had been cut in on several times in the past five minutes. He closed his eyes, opened them and looked again. Several minutes back she had been dancing with a visiting boy, a matter easily accounted for; a visiting boy would know no better. But now she was dancing with some one else, and there was Charley Paulson headed for her with enthusiastic determination in his eye. Funny—Charley seldom danced with more than three girls an evening.

Warren was distinctly surprised when—the exchange having been effected—the man relieved proved to be none other than G. Reece Stoddard himself. And G. Reece seemed not at all jubilant at being relieved. Next time Bernice danced near, Warren regarded her intently. Yes, she was pretty, distinctly pretty; and to-night her face seemed really vivacious. She had that look that no woman, however histrionically proficient, can successfully counterfeit—she looked as if she were having a good time. He liked the way she had her hair arranged, wondered if it was brilliantine that made it glisten so. And that dress was becoming—a dark red that set off her shadowy eyes and high coloring. He remembered that he had thought her pretty when she first came to town, before he had realized that she was dull. Too bad she was dull—dull girls unbearable—certainly pretty though.

His thoughts zigzagged back to Marjorie. This disappearance would be like other disappearances. When she reappeared he would demand where she had been—would be told emphatically that it was none of his business. What a pity she was so sure of him! She basked in the knowledge that no other girl in town interested him; she defied him to fall in love with Genevieve or Roberta.

Warren sighed. The way to Marjorie's affections was a labyrinth indeed. He looked up. Bernice was again dancing with the visiting boy. Half unconsciously he took a step out from the stag line in her direction, and hesitated. Then he said to himself that it was charity. He walked toward her—collided suddenly with G. Reece Stoddard.

"Pardon me," said Warren.

But G. Reece had not stopped to apologize. He had again cut in on Bernice.

That night at one o'clock Marjorie, with one hand on the electric-light switch in the hall, turned to take a last look at Bernice's sparkling eyes.

"So it worked?"

"Oh, Marjorie, yes!" cried Bernice.

"I saw you were having a gay time."

"I did! The only trouble was that about midnight I ran short of talk. I had to repeat myself—with different men of course. I hope they won't compare notes."

"Men don't," said Marjorie, yawning, "and it wouldn't matter if they did—they'd think you were even trickier."

She snapped out the light, and as they started up the stairs Bernice grasped the banister thankfully. For the first time in her life she had been danced tired.

"You see," said Marjorie at the top of the stairs, "one man sees another man cut in and he thinks there must be something there. Well, we'll fix up some new stuff to-morrow. Good night."

"Good night."

As Bernice took down her hair she passed the evening before her in review. She had followed instructions exactly. Even when Charley Paulson cut in for the eighth time she had simulated delight and had apparently been both interested and flattered. She had not talked about the weather or Eau Claire or automobiles or her school, but had confined her conversation to me, you, and us.

But a few minutes before she fell asleep a rebellious thought was churning drowsily in her brain—after all, it was she who had done it. Marjorie, to be sure, had given her her conversation, but then Marjorie got much of her conversation out of things she read. Bernice had bought the red dress, though she had never valued it highly before Marjorie dug it out of her trunk—and her own voice had said the words, her own lips had smiled, her own feet had danced. Marjorie nice girl—vain, though—nice evening—nice boys—like Warren—Warren—Warren—what's-his-name—Warren——

She fell asleep.

V

To Bernice the next week was a revelation. With the feeling that people really enjoyed looking at her and listening to her came the foundation of self-confidence. Of course there were numerous mistakes at first. She did not know, for instance, that Draycott Deyo was studying for the ministry; she was unaware that he had cut in on her because he thought she was a quiet, reserved girl. Had she known these things she would not have treated him to the line which began "Hello, Shell Shock!" and continued with the bathtub story—"It takes a frightful lot of energy to fix my hair in the summer—there's so much of it—so I always fix it first and powder my face and put on my hat; then I get into the bathtub, and dress afterward. Don't you think that's the best plan?"

Though Draycott Deyo was in the throes of difficulties concerning baptism by immersion and might possibly have seen a connection, it must be admitted that he did not. He considered feminine bathing an immoral subject, and gave her some of his ideas on the depravity of modern society.

But to offset that unfortunate occurrence Bernice had

several signal successes to her credit. Little Otis Ormonde pleaded off from a trip East and elected instead to follow her with a puppylike devotion, to the amusement of his crowd and to the irritation of G. Reece Stoddard, several of whose afternoon calls Otis completely ruined by the disgusting tenderness of the glances he bent on Bernice. He even told her the story of the two-by-four and the dressing-room to show her how frightfully mistaken he and every one else had been in their first judgment of her. Bernice laughed off that incident with a slight sinking sensation.

Of all Bernice's conversation perhaps the best known and most universally approved was the line about the bobbing of her hair.

"Oh, Bernice, when you goin' to get the hair bobbed?"

"Day after to-morrow maybe," she would reply, laughing. "Will you come and see me? Because I'm counting on you, you know."

"Will we? You know! But you better hurry up."

Bernice, whose tonsorial intentions were strictly dishonorable, would laugh again.

"Pretty soon now. You'd be surprised."

But perhaps the most significant symbol of her success was the gray car of the hypercritical Warren McIntyre, parked daily in front of the Harvey house. At first the parlor-maid was distinctly startled when he asked for Bernice instead of Marjorie; after a week of it she told the cook that Miss Bernice had gotta holda Miss Marjorie's best fella.

And Miss Bernice had. Perhaps it began with Warren's desire to rouse jealousy in Marjorie perhaps it was the familiar though unrecognized strain of Marjorie in Bernice's conversation; perhaps it was both of these and something of sincere attraction besides. But somehow the collective mind of the younger set knew within a week that Marjorie's most reliable beau had made an amazing face-about and was giving an indisputable rush to Marjorie's guest. The question of the moment was how Marjorie would take it. Warren called Bernice on the 'phone twice a day, sent her notes, and they were frequently seen together in his roadster, obviously engrossed in one of those tense, significant conversations as to whether or not he was sincere.

Marjorie on being twitted only laughed. She said she was mighty glad that Warren had at last found some one who appreciated him. So the younger set laughed, too, and guessed that Marjorie didn't care and let it go at that.

One afternoon when there were only three days left of her visit Bernice was waiting in the hall for Warren, with whom she was going to a bridge party. She was in rather a blissful mood, and when Marjorie—also bound for the party—appeared beside her and began casually to adjust her hat in the mirror, Bernice was utterly unprepared for anything in the nature of a clash. Marjorie did her work very coldly and succinctly in three sentences.

"You may as well get Warren out of your head," she said coldly.

"What?" Bernice was utterly astounded.

"You may as well stop making a fool of yourself over Warren McIntyre. He doesn't care a snap of his fingers about you."

For a tense moment they regarded each other—Marjorie scornful, aloof; Bernice astounded, half-angry, half-afraid. Then two cars drove up in front of the house and there was a riotous honking. Both of them gasped faintly, turned, and side by side hurried out.

All through the bridge party Bernice strove in vain to master a rising uneasiness. She had offended Marjorie, the sphinx of sphinxes. With the most wholesome and innocent intentions in the world she had stolen Marjorie's property. She felt suddenly and horribly guilty. After the bridge game, when they sat in an informal circle and the conversation became general, the storm gradually broke. Little Otis Ormonde inadvertently precipitated it.

"When you going back to kindergarten, Otis?" some one had asked.

"Me? Day Bernice gets her hair bobbed."

"Then your education's over," said Marjorie quickly. "That's only a bluff of hers. I should think you'd have realized."

"That a fact?" demanded Otis, giving Bernice a reproachful glance.

Bernice's ears burned as she tried to think up an effectual

come-back. In the face of this direct attack her imagination was paralyzed.

"There's a lot of bluffs in the world," continued Marjorie quite pleasantly. "I should think you'd be young enough to know that, Otis."

"Well," said Otis, "maybe so. But gee! With a line like Bernice's——"

"Really?" yawned Marjorie. "What's her latest bon mot?"

No one seemed to know. In fact, Bernice, having trifled with her muse's beau, had said nothing memorable of late.

"Was that really all a line?" asked Roberta curiously.

Bernice hesitated. She felt that wit in some form was demanded of her, but under her cousin's suddenly frigid eyes she was completely incapacitated.

"I don't know," she stalled.

"Splush!" said Marjorie. "Admit it!"

Bernice saw that Warren's eyes had left a ukulele he had been tinkering with and were fixed on her questioningly.

"Oh, I don't know!" she repeated steadily. Her cheeks were glowing.

"Splush!" remarked Marjorie again.

"Come through, Bernice," urged Otis. "Tell her where to get off."

Bernice looked round again—she seemed unable to get away from Warren's eyes.

"I like bobbed hair," she said hurriedly, as if he had asked her a question, "and I intend to bob mine."

"When?" demanded Marjorie.

"Any time."

"No time like the present," suggested Roberta.

Otis jumped to his feet.

"Good stuff!" he cried. "We'll have a summer bobbing party. Sevier Hotel barber-shop, I think you said."

In an instant all were on their feet. Bernice's heart throbbed violently.

"What?" she gasped.

Out of the group came Marjorie's voice, very clear and contemptuous.

"Don't worry—she'll back out!"

"Come on, Bernice!" cried Otis, starting toward the door.

Four eyes—Warren's and Marjorie's—stared at her, challenged her, defied her. For another second she wavered wildly.

"All right," she said swiftly, "I don't care if I do."

An eternity of minutes later, riding down-town through the late afternoon beside Warren, the others following in Roberta's car close behind, Bernice had all the sensations of Marie Antoinette bound for the guillotine in a tumbrel. Vaguely she wondered why she did not cry out that it was all a mistake. It was all she could do to keep from clutching her hair with both hands to protect it from the suddenly hostile world. Yet she did neither. Even the thought of her mother was no deterrent now. This was the test supreme of her sportsmanship; her right to walk unchallenged in the starry heaven of popular girls.

Warren was moodily silent, and when they came to the hotel he drew up at the curb and nodded to Bernice to precede him out. Roberta's car emptied a laughing crowd into the shop, which presented two bold plate-glass windows to the street.

Bernice stood on the curb and looked at the sign, Sevier Barber-Shop. It was a guillotine indeed, and the hangman was the first barber, who, attired in a white coat and smoking a cigarette, leaned nonchalantly against the first chair. He must have heard of her; he must have been waiting all week, smoking eternal cigarettes beside that portentous, too-often-mentioned first chair. Would they blindfold her? No, but they would tie a white cloth round her neck lest any of her blood—nonsense—hair—should get on her clothes.

"All right, Bernice," said Warren quickly.

With her chin in the air she crossed the sidewalk, pushed open the swinging screen-door, and giving not a glance to the uproarious, riotous row that occupied the waiting bench, went up to the first barber.

"I want you to bob my hair."

The first barber's mouth slid somewhat open. His cigarette dropped to the floor.

"Huh?"

"My hair—bob it!"

Refusing further preliminaries, Bernice took her seat on

high. A man in the chair next to her turned on his side and gave her a glance, half lather, half amazement. One barber started and spoiled little Willy Schuneman's monthly haircut. Mr. O'Reilly in the last chair grunted and swore musically in ancient Gaelic as a razor bit into his cheek. Two bootblacks became wide-eyed and rushed for her feet. No, Bernice didn't care for a shine.

Outside a passer-by stopped and stared; a couple joined him; half a dozen small boys' noses sprang into life, flattened against the glass; and snatches of conversation borne on the summer breeze drifted in through the screen-door.

"Lookada long hair on a kid!"

"Where'd yuh get 'at stuff? 'At's a bearded lady he just finished shavin'."

But Bernice saw nothing, heard nothing. Her only living sense told her that this man in the white coat had removed one tortoise-shell comb and then another; that his fingers were fumbling clumsily with unfamiliar hairpins; that this hair, this wonderful hair of hers, was going—she would never again feel its long voluptuous pull as it hung in a dark-brown glory down her back. For a second she was near breaking down, and then the picture before her swam mechanically into her vision—Marjorie's mouth curling in a faint ironic smile as if to say:

"Give up and get down! You tried to buck me and I called your bluff. You see you haven't got a prayer."

And some last energy rose up in Bernice, for she clinched her hands under the white cloth, and there was a curious narrowing of her eyes that Marjorie remarked on to some one long afterward.

Twenty minutes later the barber swung her round to face the mirror, and she flinched at the full extent of the damage that had been wrought. Her hair was not curly, and now it lay in lank lifeless blocks on both sides of her suddenly pale face. It was ugly as sin—she had known it would be ugly as sin. Her face's chief charm had been a Madonna-like simplicity. Now that was gone and she was—well, frightfully mediocre—not stagy; only ridiculous, like a Greenwich Villager who had left her spectacles at home.

As she climbed down from the chair she tried to smile—

failed miserably. She saw two of the girls exchange glances; noticed Marjorie's mouth curved in attenuated mockery—and that Warren's eyes were suddenly very cold.

"You see"—her words fell into an awkward pause—"I've done it."

"Yes, you've—done it," admitted Warren.

"Do you like it?"

There was a half-hearted "Sure" from two or three voices, another awkward pause, and then Marjorie turned swiftly and with serpentlike intensity to Warren.

"Would you mind running me down to the cleaners?" she asked. "I've simply got to get a dress there before supper. Roberta's driving right home and she can take the others."

Warren stared abstractedly at some infinite speck out the window. Then for an instant his eyes rested coldly on Bernice before they turned to Marjorie.

"Be glad to," he said slowly.

VI

Bernice did not fully realize the outrageous trap that had been set for her until she met her aunt's amazed glance just before dinner.

"Why, Bernice!"

"I've bobbed it, Aunt Josephine."

"Why, child!"

"Do you like it?"

"Why, Ber-nice!"

"I suppose I've shocked you."

"No, but what'll Mrs. Deyo think to-morrow night? Bernice, you should have waited until after the Deyos' dance—you should have waited if you wanted to do that."

"It was sudden, Aunt Josephine. Anyway, why does it matter to Mrs. Deyo particularly?"

"Why, child," cried Mrs. Harvey, "in her paper on 'The Foibles of the Younger Generation' that she read at the last meeting of the Thursday Club she devoted fifteen minutes to bobbed hair. It's her pet abomination. And the dance is for you and Marjorie!"

"I'm sorry."

"Oh, Bernice, what'll your mother say? She'll think I let you do it."

"I'm sorry."

Dinner was an agony. She had made a hasty attempt with a curling-iron, and burned her finger and much hair. She could see that her aunt was both worried and grieved, and her uncle kept saying, "Well, I'll be darned!" over and over in a hurt and faintly hostile tone. And Marjorie sat very quietly, intrenched behind a faint smile, a faintly mocking smile.

Somehow she got through the evening. Three boys called; Marjorie disappeared with one of them, and Bernice made a listless unsuccessful attempt to entertain the two others—sighed thankfully as she climbed the stairs to her room at half past ten. What a day!

When she had undressed for the night the door opened and Marjorie came in.

"Bernice," she said, "I'm awfully sorry about the Deyo dance. I'll give you my word of honor I'd forgotten all about it."

" 'Sall right," said Bernice shortly. Standing before the mirror she passed her comb slowly through her short hair.

"I'll take you down-town to-morrow," continued Marjorie, "and the hairdresser'll fix it so you'll look slick. I didn't imagine you'd go through with it. I'm really mighty sorry."

"Oh, 'sall right!"

"Still it's your last night, so I suppose it won't matter much."

Then Bernice winced as Marjorie tossed her own hair over her shoulders and began to twist it slowly into two long blond braids until in her cream-colored negligée she looked like a delicate painting of some Saxon princess. Fascinated, Bernice watched the braids grow. Heavy and luxurious they were, moving under the supple fingers like restive snakes—and to Bernice remained this relic and the curling-iron and a to-morrow full of eyes. She could see G. Reece Stoddard, who liked her, assuming his Harvard manner and telling his dinner partner that Bernice shouldn't have been allowed to go to the movies so much; she could see Draycott Deyo exchanging glances with his mother and then being conscientiously charitable to her. But then perhaps by to-morrow Mrs.

Deyo would have heard the news; would send round an icy little note requesting that she fail to appear—and behind her back they would all laugh and know that Marjorie had made a fool of her; that her chance at beauty had been sacrificed to the jealous whim of a selfish girl. She sat down suddenly before the mirror, biting the inside of her cheek.

"I like it," she said with an effort. "I think it'll be becoming."

Marjorie smiled.

"It looks all right. For heaven's sake, don't let it worry you!"

"I won't."

"Good night, Bernice."

But as the door closed something snapped within Bernice. She sprang dynamically to her feet, clinching her hands, then swiftly and noiselessly crossed over to her bed and from underneath it dragged out her suitcase. Into it she tossed toilet articles and a change of clothing. Then she turned to her trunk and quickly dumped in two drawerfuls of lingerie and summer dresses. She moved quietly, but with deadly efficiency, and in three-quarters of an hour her trunk was locked and strapped and she was fully dressed in a becoming new travelling suit that Marjorie had helped her pick out.

Sitting down at her desk she wrote a short note to Mrs. Harvey, in which she briefly outlined her reasons for going. She sealed it, addressed it, and laid it on her pillow. She glanced at her watch. The train left at one, and she knew that if she walked down to the Marborough Hotel two blocks away she could easily get a taxicab.

Suddenly she drew in her breath sharply and an expression flashed into her eyes that a practised character reader might have connected vaguely with the set look she had worn in the barber's chair—somehow a development of it. It was quite a new look for Bernice—and it carried consequences.

She went stealthily to the bureau, picked up an article that lay there, and turning out all the lights stood quietly until her eyes became accustomed to the darkness. Softly she pushed open the door to Marjorie's room. She heard the quiet, even breathing of an untroubled conscience asleep.

She was by the bedside now, very deliberate and calm. She

acted swiftly. Bending over she found one of the braids of Marjorie's hair, followed it up with her hand to the point nearest the head, and then holding it a little slack so that the sleeper would feel no pull, she reached down with the shears and severed it. With the pigtail in her hand she held her breath. Marjorie had muttered something in her sleep. Bernice deftly amputated the other braid, paused for an instant, and then flitted swiftly and silently back to her own room.

Down-stairs she opened the big front door, closed it carefully behind her, and feeling oddly happy and exuberant stepped off the porch into the moonlight, swinging her heavy grip like a shopping-bag. After a minute's brisk walk she discovered that her left hand still held the two blond braids. She laughed unexpectedly—had to shut her mouth hard to keep from emitting an absolute peal. She was passing Warren's house now, and on the impulse she set down her baggage, and swinging the braids like pieces of rope flung them at the wooden porch, where they landed with a slight thud. She laughed again, no longer restraining herself.

"Huh!" she giggled wildly. "Scalp the selfish thing!"

Then picking up her suitcase she set off at a half-run down the moonlit street.

Benediction

THE Baltimore Station was hot and crowded, so Lois was forced to stand by the telegraph desk for interminable, sticky seconds while a clerk with big front teeth counted and recounted a large lady's day message, to determine whether it contained the innocuous forty-nine words or the fatal fifty-one.

Lois, waiting, decided she wasn't quite sure of the address, so she took the letter out of her bag and ran over it again.

"Darling": *it began*—"I understand and I'm happier than life ever meant me to be. If I could give you the things you've always been in tune with—but I can't, Lois; we can't marry and we can't lose each other and let all this glorious love end in nothing.

"Until your letter came, dear, I'd been sitting here in the half dark thinking and thinking where I could go and ever forget you; abroad, perhaps, to drift through Italy or Spain and dream away the pain of having lost you where the crumbling ruins of older, mellower civilizations would mirror only the desolation of my heart—and then your letter came.

"Sweetest, bravest girl, if you'll wire me I'll meet you in Wilmington—till then I'll be here just waiting and hoping for every long dream of you to come true.

"HOWARD."

She had read the letter so many times that she knew it word by word, yet it still startled her. In it she found many faint reflections of the man who wrote it—the mingled sweetness and sadness in his dark eyes, the furtive, restless excitement she felt sometimes when he talked to her, his dreamy sensuousness that lulled her mind to sleep. Lois was nineteen and very romantic and curious and courageous.

The large lady and the clerk having compromised on fifty words, Lois took a blank and wrote her telegram. And there were no overtones to the finality of her decision.

It's just destiny—she thought—it's just the way things work out in this damn world. If cowardice is all that's been holding me back there won't be any more holding back. So we'll just let things take their course, and never be sorry.

The clerk scanned her telegram:

"Arrived Baltimore today spend day with my brother meet me Wilmington three P.M. Wednesday Love

"LOIS."

"Fifty-four cents," said the clerk admiringly.

And never be sorry—thought Lois—and never be sorry——

II

Trees filtering light onto dappled grass. Trees like tall, languid ladies with feather fans coquetting airily with the ugly roof of the monastery. Trees like butlers, bending courteously over placid walks and paths. Trees, trees over the hills on either side and scattering out in clumps and lines and woods all through eastern Maryland, delicate lace on the hems of many yellow fields, dark opaque backgrounds for flowered bushes or wild climbing gardens.

Some of the trees were very gay and young, but the monastery trees were older than the monastery which, by true monastic standards, wasn't very old at all. And, as a matter of fact, it wasn't technically called a monastery, but only a seminary; nevertheless it shall be a monastery here despite its Victorian architecture or its Edward VII additions, or even its Woodrow Wilsonian, patented, last-a-century roofing.

Out behind was the farm where half a dozen lay brothers were sweating lustily as they moved with deadly efficiency around the vegetable-gardens. To the left, behind a row of elms, was an informal baseball diamond where three novices were being batted out by a fourth, amid great chasings and puffings and blowings. And in front as a great mellow bell boomed the half-hour a swarm of black, human leaves were blown over the checker-board of paths under the courteous trees.

Some of these black leaves were very old with cheeks furrowed like the first ripples of a splashed pool. Then there was a scattering of middle-aged leaves whose forms when viewed in profile in their revealing gowns were beginning to be faintly unsymmetrical. These carried thick volumes of Thomas Aquinas and Henry James and Cardinal Mercier and Immanuel Kant and many bulging note-books filled with lecture data.

But most numerous were the young leaves; blond boys of nineteen with very stern, conscientious expressions; men in the late twenties with a keen self-assurance from having taught out in the world for five years—several hundreds of them, from city and town and country in Maryland and Pennsylvania and Virginia and West Virginia and Delaware.

There were many Americans and some Irish and some tough Irish and a few French, and several Italians and Poles, and they walked informally arm in arm with each other in twos and threes or in long rows, almost universally distinguished by the straight mouth and the considerable chin—for this was the Society of Jesus, founded in Spain five hundred years before by a tough-minded soldier who trained men to hold a breach or a salon, preach a sermon or write a treaty, and do it and not argue . . .

Lois got out of a bus into the sunshine down by the outer gate. She was nineteen with yellow hair and eyes that people were tactful enough not to call green. When men of talent saw her in a street-car they often furtively produced little stub-pencils and backs of envelopes and tried to sum up that profile or the thing that the eyebrows did to her eyes. Later they looked at their results and usually tore them up with wondering sighs.

Though Lois was very jauntily attired in an expensively appropriate travelling affair, she did not linger to pat out the dust which covered her clothes, but started up the central walk with curious glances at either side. Her face was very eager and expectant, yet she hadn't at all that glorified expression that girls wear when they arrive for a Senior Prom at Princeton or New Haven; still, as there were no senior proms here, perhaps it didn't matter.

She was wondering what he would look like, whether she'd possibly know him from his picture. In the picture, which hung over her mother's bureau at home, he seemed very young and hollow-cheeked and rather pitiful, with only a well-developed mouth and an ill-fitting probationer's gown to show that he had already made a momentous decision about his life. Of course he had been only nineteen then and now he was thirty-six—didn't look like that at all; in recent snap-shots he was much broader and his hair had grown a little thin—but the impression of her brother she had always retained was that of the big picture. And so she had always been a little sorry for him. What a life for a man! Seventeen years of preparation and he wasn't even a priest yet—wouldn't be for another year.

Lois had an idea that this was all going to be rather solemn if she let it be. But she was going to give her very best imitation of undiluted sunshine, the imitation she could give even when her head was splitting or when her mother had a nervous breakdown or when she was particularly romantic and curious and courageous. This brother of hers undoubtedly needed cheering up, and he was going to be cheered up, whether he liked it or not.

As she drew near the great, homely front door she saw a man break suddenly away from a group and, pulling up the skirts of his gown, run toward her. He was smiling, she noticed, and he looked very big and—and reliable. She stopped and waited, knew that her heart was beating unusually fast.

"Lois!" he cried, and in a second she was in his arms. She was suddenly trembling.

"Lois!" he cried again, "why, this is wonderful! I can't tell you, Lois, how *much* I've looked forward to this. Why, Lois, you're beautiful!"

Lois gasped.

His voice, though restrained, was vibrant with energy and that odd sort of enveloping personality she had thought that she only of the family possessed.

"I'm mighty glad, too—Kieth."

She flushed, but not unhappily, at this first use of his name.

"Lois—Lois—Lois," he repeated in wonder. "Child, we'll go in here a minute, because I want you to meet the rector, and then we'll walk around. I have a thousand things to talk to you about."

His voice became graver. "How's mother?"

She looked at him for a moment and then said something

that she had not intended to say at all, the very sort of thing she had resolved to avoid.

"Oh, Kieth—she's—she's getting worse all the time, every way."

He nodded slowly as if he understood.

"Nervous, well—you can tell me about that later. Now——"

She was in a small study with a large desk, saying something to a little, jovial, white-haired priest who retained her hand for some seconds.

"So this is Lois!"

He said it as if he had heard of her for years.

He entreated her to sit down.

Two other priests arrived enthusiastically and shook hands with her and addressed her as "Kieth's little sister," which she found she didn't mind a bit.

How assured they seemed; she had expected a certain shyness, reserve at least. There were several jokes unintelligible to her, which seemed to delight every one, and the little Father Rector referred to the trio of them as "dim old monks," which she appreciated, because of course they weren't monks at all. She had a lightning impression that they were especially fond of Kieth—the Father Rector had called him "Kieth" and one of the others had kept a hand on his shoulder all through the conversation. Then she was shaking hands again and promising to come back a little later for some ice-cream, and smiling and smiling and being rather absurdly happy . . . she told herself that it was because Kieth was so delighted in showing her off.

Then she and Kieth were strolling along a path, arm in arm, and he was informing her what an absolute jewel the Father Rector was.

"Lois," he broke off suddenly, "I want to tell you before we go any farther how much it means to me to have you come up here. I think it was—mighty sweet of you. I know what a gay time you've been having."

Lois gasped. She was not prepared for this. At first when she had conceived the plan of taking the hot journey down to Baltimore, staying the night with a friend and then coming out to see her brother, she had felt rather consciously virtuous, hoped he wouldn't be priggish or resentful about her not having come before—but walking here with him under the trees seemed such a little thing, and surprisingly a happy thing.

"Why, Kieth," she said quickly, "you know I couldn't have waited a day longer. I saw you when I was five, but of course I didn't remember, and how could I have gone on without practically ever having seen my only brother?"

"It was mighty sweet of you, Lois," he repeated.

Lois blushed—he *did* have personality.

"I want you to tell me all about yourself," he said after a pause. "Of course I have a general idea what you and mother did in Europe those fourteen years, and then we were all so worried, Lois, when you had pneumonia and couldn't come down with mother—let's see, that was two years ago—and then, well, I've seen your name in the papers, but it's all been so unsatisfactory. I haven't known you, Lois."

She found herself analyzing his personality as she analyzed the personality of every man she met. She wondered if the effect of—of intimacy that he gave was bred by his constant repetition of her name. He said it as if he loved the word, as if it had an inherent meaning to him.

"Then you were at school," he continued.

"Yes, at Farmington. Mother wanted me to go to a convent—but I didn't want to."

She cast a side glance at him to see if he would resent this.

But he only nodded slowly.

"Had enough convents abroad, eh?"

"Yes—and Kieth, convents are different there anyway. Here even in the nicest ones there are so many *common* girls."

He nodded again.

"Yes," he agreed, "I suppose there are, and I know how you feel about it. It grated on me here, at first, Lois, though I wouldn't say that to any one but you; we're rather sensitive, you and I, to things like this."

"You mean the men here?"

"Yes, some of them of course were fine, the sort of men I'd always been thrown with, but there were others; a man named Regan, for instance—I hated the fellow, and now he's about the best friend I have. A wonderful character, Lois; you'll meet him later. Sort of man you'd like to have with you in a fight."

Lois was thinking that Kieth was the sort of man she'd like to have with *her* in a fight.

"How did you—how did you first happen to do it?" she asked, rather shyly, "to come here, I mean. Of course mother told me the story about the Pullman car."

"Oh, that—" He looked rather annoyed.

"Tell me that. I'd like to hear you tell it."

"Oh, it's nothing, except what you probably know. It was evening and I'd been riding all day and thinking about—about a hundred things, Lois, and then suddenly I had a sense that some one was sitting across from me, felt that he'd been there for some time, and had a vague idea that he was another traveller. All at once he leaned over toward me and I heard a voice say: 'I want you to be a priest, that's what I want.' Well, I jumped up and cried out, 'Oh, my God, not that!'—made an idiot of myself before about twenty people; you see there wasn't any one sitting there at all. A week after that I went to the Jesuit College in Philadelphia and crawled up the last flight of stairs to the rector's office on my hands and knees."

There was another silence and Lois saw that her brother's eyes wore a far-away look, that he was staring unseeingly out over the sunny fields. She was stirred by the modulations of his voice and the sudden silence that seemed to flow about him when he finished speaking.

She noticed now that his eyes were of the same fibre as hers, with the green left out, and that his mouth was much gentler, really, than in the picture—or was it that the face had grown up to it lately? He was getting a little bald just on top of his head. She wondered if that was from wearing a hat so much. It seemed awful for a man to grow bald and no one to care about it.

"Were you—pious when you were young, Kieth?" she asked. "You know what I mean. Were you religious? If you don't mind these personal questions."

"Yes," he said with his eyes still far away—and she felt that his intense abstraction was as much a part of his personality as his attention. "Yes, I suppose I was, when I was—sober."

Lois thrilled slightly.

"Did you drink?"

He nodded.

"I was on the way to making a bad hash of things." He smiled and, turning his gray eyes on her, changed the subject.

"Child, tell me about mother. I know it's been awfully hard for you there, lately. I know you've had to sacrifice a lot and put up with a great deal, and I want you to know how fine of you I think it is. I feel, Lois, that you're sort of taking the place of both of us there."

Lois thought quickly how little she had sacrificed; how lately she had constantly avoided her nervous, half-invalid mother.

"Youth shouldn't be sacrificed to age, Kieth," she said steadily.

"I know," he sighed, "and you oughtn't to have the weight on your shoulders, child. I wish I were there to help you."

She saw how quickly he had turned her remark and instantly she knew what this quality was that he gave off. He was *sweet*. Her thoughts went off on a side-track and then she broke the silence with an odd remark.

"Sweetness is hard," she said suddenly.

"What?"

"Nothing," she denied in confusion. "I didn't mean to speak aloud. I was thinking of something—of a conversation with a man named Freddy Kebble."

"Maury Kebble's brother?"

"Yes," she said, rather surprised to think of him having known Maury Kebble. Still there was nothing strange about it. "Well, he and I were talking about sweetness a few weeks ago. Oh, I don't know—I said that a man named Howard—that a man I knew was sweet, and he didn't agree with me, and we began talking about what sweetness in a man was. He kept telling me I meant a sort of soppy softness, but I knew I didn't—yet I didn't know exactly how to put it. I see now. I meant just the opposite. I suppose real sweetness is a sort of hardness—and strength."

Kieth nodded.

"I see what you mean. I've known old priests who had it."

"I'm talking about young men," she said, rather defiantly.

"Oh!"

They had reached the now deserted baseball diamond and,

pointing her to a wooden bench, he sprawled full length on the grass.

"Are these *young* men happy here, Kieth?"

"Don't they look happy, Lois?"

"I suppose so, but those *young* ones, those two we just passed—have they—are they——"

"Are they signed up?" he laughed. "No, but they will be next month."

"Permanently?"

"Yes—unless they break down mentally or physically. Of course in a discipline like ours a lot drop out."

"But those *boys*. Are they giving up fine chances outside—like you did?"

He nodded.

"Some of them."

"But, Kieth, they don't know what they're doing. They haven't had any experience of what they're missing."

"No, I suppose not."

"It doesn't seem fair. Life has just sort of scared them at first. Do they all come in so *young*?"

"No, some of them have knocked around, led pretty wild lives—Regan, for instance."

"I should think that sort would be better," she said meditatively, "men that had *seen* life."

"No," said Kieth earnestly, "I'm not sure that knocking about gives a man the sort of experience he can communicate to others. Some of the broadest men I've known have been absolutely rigid about themselves. And reformed libertines are a notoriously intolerant class. Don't you think so, Lois?"

She nodded, still meditative, and he continued:

"It seems to me that when one weak person goes to another, it isn't help they want; it's a sort of companionship in guilt, Lois. After you were born, when mother began to get nervous she used to go and weep with a certain Mrs. Comstock. Lord, it used to make me shiver. She said it comforted her, poor old mother. No, I don't think that to help others you've got to show yourself at all. Real help comes from a stronger person whom you respect. And their sympathy is all the bigger because it's impersonal."

"But people want human sympathy," objected Lois. "They want to feel the other person's been tempted."

"Lois, in their hearts they want to feel that the other person's been weak. That's what they mean by human.

"Here in this old monkery, Lois," he continued with a smile, "they try to get all that self-pity and pride in our own wills out of us right at the first. They put us to scrubbing floors—and other things. It's like that idea of saving your life by losing it. You see we sort of feel that the less human a man is, in your sense of human, the better servant he can be to humanity. We carry it out to the end, too. When one of us dies his family can't even have him then. He's buried here under a plain wooden cross with a thousand others."

His tone changed suddenly and he looked at her with a great brightness in his gray eyes.

"But way back in a man's heart there are some things he can't get rid of—and one of them is that I'm awfully in love with my little sister."

With a sudden impulse she knelt beside him in the grass and, leaning over, kissed his forehead.

"You're hard, Kieth," she said, "and I love you for it—and you're sweet."

III

Back in the reception-room Lois met a half-dozen more of Kieth's particular friends; there was a young man named Jarvis, rather pale and delicate-looking, who, she knew, must be a grandson of old Mrs. Jarvis at home, and she mentally compared this ascetic with a brace of his riotous uncles.

And there was Regan with a scarred face and piercing intent eyes that followed her about the room and often rested on Kieth with something very like worship. She knew then what Kieth had meant about "a good man to have with you in a fight."

He's the missionary type—she thought vaguely—China or something.

"I want Kieth's sister to show us what the shimmy is," demanded one young man with a broad grin.

Lois laughed.

"I'm afraid the Father Rector would send me shimmying out the gate. Besides, I'm not an expert."

"I'm sure it wouldn't be best for Jimmy's soul anyway," said Kieth solemnly. "He's inclined to brood about things like shimmys. They were just starting to do the—maxixe, wasn't it, Jimmy?—when he became a monk, and it haunted him his whole first year. You'd see him when he was peeling potatoes, putting his arm around the bucket and making irreligious motions with his feet."

There was a general laugh in which Lois joined.

"An old lady who comes here to Mass sent Kieth this ice-cream," whispered Jarvis under cover of the laugh, "because she'd heard you were coming. It's pretty good, isn't it?"

There were tears trembling in Lois' eyes.

IV

Then half an hour later over in the chapel things suddenly went all wrong. It was several years since Lois had been at Benediction and at first she was thrilled by the gleaming monstrance with its central spot of white, the air rich and heavy with incense, and the sun shining through the stained-glass window of St. Francis Xavier overhead and falling in warm red tracery on the cassock of the man in front of her, but at the first notes of the *"O Salutaris Hostia"* a heavy weight seemed to descend upon her soul. Kieth was on her right and young Jarvis on her left, and she stole uneasy glances at both of them.

What's the matter with me? she thought impatiently.

She looked again. Was there a certain coldness in both their profiles, that she had not noticed before—a pallor about the mouth and a curious set expression in their eyes? She shivered slightly: they were like dead men.

She felt her soul recede suddenly from Kieth's. This was her brother—this, this unnatural person. She caught herself in the act of a little laugh.

"What is the matter with me?"

She passed her hand over her eyes and the weight increased. The incense sickened her and a stray, ragged note from one of the tenors in the choir grated on her ear like the shriek of a slate-pencil. She fidgeted, and raising her hand to her hair touched her forehead, found moisture on it.

"It's hot in here, hot as the deuce."

Again she repressed a faint laugh, and then in an instant the weight upon her heart suddenly diffused into cold fear. . . . It was that candle on the altar. It was all wrong—wrong. Why didn't somebody see it? There was something *in* it. There was something coming out of it, taking form and shape above it.

She tried to fight down her rising panic, told herself it was the wick. If the wick wasn't straight, candles did something—but they didn't do this! With incalculable rapidity a force was gathering within her, a tremendous, assimilative force, drawing from every sense, every corner of her brain, and as it surged up inside her she felt an enormous, terrified repulsion. She drew her arms in close to her side, away from Kieth and Jarvis.

Something in that candle . . . she was leaning forward—in another moment she felt she would go forward toward it—didn't any one see it? . . . anyone?

"Ugh!"

She felt a space beside her and something told her that Jarvis had gasped and sat down very suddenly . . . then she was kneeling and as the flaming monstrance slowly left the altar in the hands of the priest, she heard a great rushing noise in her ears—the crash of the bells was like hammer-blows . . . and then in a moment that seemed eternal a great torrent rolled over her heart—there was a shouting there and a lashing as of waves . . .

. . . She was calling, felt herself calling for Kieth, her lips mouthing the words that would not come:

"Kieth! Oh, my God! *Kieth!*"

Suddenly she became aware of a new presence, something external, in front of her, consummated and expressed in warm red tracery. Then she knew. It was the window of St. Francis Xavier. Her mind gripped at it, clung to it finally, and she felt herself calling again endlessly, impotently—Kieth—Kieth!

Then out of a great stillness came a voice:

"Blessed be God."

With a gradual rumble sounded the response rolling heavily through the chapel:

"Blessed be God."

The words sang instantly in her heart; the incense lay mystically and sweetly peaceful upon the air, and *the candle on the altar went out.*

"Blessed be His Holy Name."

"Blessed be His Holy Name."

Everything blurred into a swinging mist. With a sound half-gasp, half-cry she rocked on her feet and reeled backward into Kieth's suddenly outstretched arms.

V

"Lie still, child."

She closed her eyes again. She was on the grass outside, pillowed on Kieth's arm, and Regan was dabbing her head with a cold towel.

"I'm all right," she said quietly.

"I know, but just lie still a minute longer. It was too hot in there. Jarvis felt it, too."

She laughed as Regan again touched her gingerly with the towel.

"I'm all right," she repeated.

But though a warm peace was filling her mind and heart she felt oddly broken and chastened, as if some one had held her stripped soul up and laughed.

VI

Half an hour later she walked leaning on Kieth's arm down the long central path toward the gate.

"It's been such a short afternoon," he sighed, "and I'm so sorry you were sick, Lois."

"Kieth, I'm feeling fine now, really; I wish you wouldn't worry."

"Poor old child. I didn't realize that Benediction'd be a long service for you after your hot trip out here and all."

She laughed cheerfully.

"I guess the truth is I'm not much used to Benediction. Mass is the limit of my religious exertions."

She paused and then continued quickly:

"I don't want to shock you, Kieth, but I can't tell you how—how *inconvenient* being a Catholic is. It really doesn't seem to apply any more. As far as morals go, some of the wildest boys I know are Catholics. And the brightest boys—I mean the ones who think and read a lot, don't seem to believe in much of anything any more."

"Tell me about it. The bus won't be here for another half-hour."

They sat down on a bench by the path.

"For instance, Gerald Carter, he's published a novel. He absolutely roars when people mention immortality. And then Howa—well, another man I've known well, lately, who was Phi Beta Kappa at Harvard, says that no intelligent person can believe in Supernatural Christianity. He says Christ was a great socialist, though. Am I shocking you?"

She broke off suddenly.

Kieth smiled.

"You can't shock a monk. He's a professional shock-absorber."

"Well," she continued, "that's about all. It seems so—so *narrow*. Church schools, for instance. There's more freedom about things that Catholic people can't see—like birth control."

Kieth winced, almost imperceptibly, but Lois saw it.

"Oh," she said quickly, "everybody talks about everything now."

"It's probably better that way."

"Oh, yes, much better. Well, that's all, Kieth. I just wanted to tell you why I'm a little—luke-warm, at present."

"I'm not shocked, Lois. I understand better than you think. We all go through those times. But I know it'll come out all right, child. There's that gift of faith that we have, you and I, that'll carry us past the bad spots."

He rose as he spoke and they started again down the path.

"I want you to pray for me sometimes, Lois. I think your prayers would be about what I need. Because we've come very close in these few hours, I think."

Her eyes were suddenly shining.

"Oh, we have, we have!" she cried. "I feel closer to you now than to any one in the world."

He stopped suddenly and indicated the side of the path.

"We might—just a minute——"

It was a pietà, a life-size statue of the Blessed Virgin set within a semicircle of rocks.

Feeling a little self-conscious she dropped on her knees beside him and made an unsuccessful attempt at prayer.

She was only half through when he rose. He took her arm again.

"I wanted to thank Her for letting us have this day together," he said simply.

Lois felt a sudden lump in her throat and she wanted to say something that would tell him how much it had meant to her, too. But she found no words.

"I'll always remember this," he continued, his voice trembling a little—"this summer day with you. It's been just what I expected. You're just what I expected, Lois."

"I'm awfully glad, Kieth."

"You see, when you were little they kept sending me snapshots of you, first as a baby and then as a child in socks playing on the beach with a pail and shovel, and then suddenly as a wistful little girl with wondering, pure eyes—and I used to build dreams about you. A man has to have something living to cling to. I think, Lois, it was your little white soul I tried to keep near me—even when life was at its loudest and every intellectual idea of God seemed the sheerest mockery, and desire and love and a million things came up to me and said: 'Look here at me! See, I'm Life. You're turning your back on it!' All the way through that shadow, Lois, I could always see your baby soul flitting on ahead of me, very frail and clear and wonderful."

Lois was crying softly. They had reached the gate and she rested her elbow on it and dabbed furiously at her eyes.

"And then later, child, when you were sick I knelt all one night and asked God to spare you for me—for I knew then that I wanted more; He had taught me to want more. I wanted to know you moved and breathed in the same world with me. I saw you growing up, that white innocence of yours changing to a flame and burning to give light to other weaker souls. And then I wanted some day to take your children on my knee and hear them call the crabbed old monk Uncle Kieth."

He seemed to be laughing now as he talked.

"Oh, Lois, Lois, I was asking God for more then. I wanted the letters you'd write me and the place I'd have at your table. I wanted an awful lot, Lois, dear."

"You've got me, Kieth," she sobbed, "you know it, say you know it. Oh, I'm acting like a baby but I didn't think you'd be this way, and I—oh, Kieth—Kieth——"

He took her hand and patted it softly.

"Here's the bus. You'll come again, won't you?"

She put her hands on his cheeks, and drawing his head down, pressed her tear-wet face against his.

"Oh, Kieth, brother, some day I'll tell you something——"

He helped her in, saw her take down her handkerchief and smile bravely at him, as the driver flicked his whip and the bus rolled off. Then a thick cloud of dust rose around it and she was gone.

For a few minutes he stood there on the road, his hand on the gate-post, his lips half parted in a smile.

"Lois," he said aloud in a sort of wonder, "Lois, Lois."

Later, some probationers passing noticed him kneeling before the pietà, and coming back after a time found him still there. And he was there until twilight came down and the courteous trees grew garrulous overhead and the crickets took up their burden of song in the dusky grass.

VII

The first clerk in the telegraph booth in the Baltimore Station whistled through his buck teeth at the second clerk:

"S'matter?"

"See that girl—no, the pretty one with the big black dots on her veil. Too late—she's gone. You missed somep'n."

"What about her?"

"Nothing. 'Cept she's damn good-looking. Came in here yesterday and sent a wire to some guy to meet her somewhere. Then a minute ago she came in with a telegram all written out and was standin' there goin' to give it to me when she changed her mind or somep'n and all of a sudden tore it up."

"Hm."

The first clerk came around the counter and picking up the two pieces of paper from the floor put them together idly. The second clerk read them over his shoulder and subconsciously counted the words as he read. There were just thirteen.

"This is in the way of a permanent goodbye. I should suggest Italy.

"LOIS."

"Tore it up, eh?" said the second clerk.

Dalyrimple Goes Wrong

IN the millennium an educational genius will write a book to be given to every young man on the date of his disillusion. This work will have the flavor of Montaigne's essays and Samuel Butler's note-books—and a little of Tolstoi and Marcus Aurelius. It will be neither cheerful nor pleasant but will contain numerous passages of striking humor. Since first-class minds never believe anything very strongly until they've experienced it, its value will be purely relative . . . all people over thirty will refer to it as "depressing."

This prelude belongs to the story of a young man who lived, as you and I do, before the book.

II

The generation which numbered Bryan Dalyrimple drifted out of adolescence to a mighty fanfare of trumpets. Bryan played the star in an affair which included a Lewis gun and a nine-day romp behind the retreating German lines, so luck triumphant or sentiment rampant awarded him a row of medals and on his arrival in the States he was told that he was second in importance only to General Pershing and Sergeant York. This was a lot of fun. The governor of his State, a stray congressman, and a citizens' committee gave him enormous smiles and "By God, Sirs," on the dock at Hoboken; there were newspaper reporters and photographers who said "would you mind" and "if you could just"; and back in his home town there were old ladies, the rims of whose eyes grew red as they talked to him, and girls who hadn't remembered him so well since his father's business went blah! in nineteen-twelve.

But when the shouting died he realized that for a month he had been the house guest of the mayor, that he had only fourteen dollars in the world, and that "the name that will live forever in the annals and legends of this State" was already living there very quietly and obscurely.

One morning he lay late in bed and just outside his door he

heard the up-stairs maid talking to the cook. The up-stairs maid said that Mrs. Hawkins, the mayor's wife, had been trying for a week to hint Dalyrimple out of the house. He left at eleven o'clock in intolerable confusion, asking that his trunk be sent to Mrs. Beebe's boarding-house.

Dalyrimple was twenty-three and he had never worked. His father had given him two years at the State University and passed away about the time of his son's nine-day romp, leaving behind him some mid-Victorian furniture and a thin packet of folded papers that turned out to be grocery bills. Young Dalyrimple had very keen gray eyes, a mind that delighted the army psychological examiners, a trick of having read it—whatever it was—some time before, and a cool hand in a hot situation. But these things did not save him a final, unresigned sigh when he realized that he had to go to work—right away.

It was early afternoon when he walked into the office of Theron G. Macy, who owned the largest wholesale grocery house in town. Plump, prosperous, wearing a pleasant but quite unhumorous smile, Theron G. Macy greeted him warmly.

"Well—how do, Bryan? What's on your mind?"

To Dalyrimple, straining with his admission, his own words, when they came, sounded like an Arab beggar's whine for alms.

"Why—this question of a job." ("This question of a job" seemed somehow more clothed than just "a job.")

"A job?" An almost imperceptible breeze blew across Mr. Macy's expression.

"You see, Mr. Macy," continued Dalyrimple, "I feel I'm wasting time. I want to get started at something. I had several chances about a month ago but they all seem to have—gone——"

"Let's see," interrupted Mr. Macy. "What were they?"

"Well, just at the first the governor said something about a vacancy on his staff. I was sort of counting on that for a while, but I hear he's given it to Allen Gregg, you know, son of G. P. Gregg. He sort of forgot what he said to me—just talking, I guess."

"You ought to push those things."

"Then there was that engineering expedition, but they decided they'd have to have a man who knew hydraulics, so they couldn't use me unless I paid my own way."

"You had just a year at the university?"

"Two. But I didn't take any science or mathematics. Well, the day the battalion paraded, Mr. Peter Jordan said something about a vacancy in his store. I went around there to-day and I found he meant a sort of floor-walker—and then you said something one day"—he paused and waited for the older man to take him up, but noting only a minute wince continued—"about a position, so I thought I'd come and see you."

"There was a position," confessed Mr. Macy reluctantly, "but since then we've filled it." He cleared his throat again. "You've waited quite a while."

"Yes, I suppose I did. Everybody told me there was no hurry—and I'd had these various offers."

Mr. Macy delivered a paragraph on present-day opportunities which Dalyrimple's mind completely skipped.

"Have you had any business experience?"

"I worked on a ranch two summers as a rider."

"Oh, well," Mr. Macy disparaged this neatly, and then continued: "What do you think you're worth?"

"I don't know."

"Well, Bryan, I tell you, I'm willing to strain a point and give you a chance."

Dalyrimple nodded.

"Your salary won't be much. You'll start by learning the stock. Then you'll come in the office for a while. Then you'll go on the road. When could you begin?"

"How about to-morrow?"

"All right. Report to Mr. Hanson in the stock-room. He'll start you off."

He continued to regard Dalyrimple steadily until the latter, realizing that the interview was over, rose awkwardly.

"Well, Mr. Macy, I'm certainly much obliged."

"That's all right. Glad to help you, Bryan."

After an irresolute moment, Dalyrimple found himself in the hall. His forehead was covered with perspiration, and the room had not been hot.

"Why the devil did I thank the son of a gun?" he muttered.

III

Next morning Mr. Hanson informed him coldly of the necessity of punching the time-clock at seven every morning, and delivered him for instruction into the hands of a fellow worker, one Charley Moore.

Charley was twenty-six, with that faint musk of weakness hanging about him that is often mistaken for the scent of evil. It took no psychological examiner to decide that he had drifted into indulgence and laziness as casually as he had drifted into life, and was to drift out. He was pale and his clothes stank of smoke; he enjoyed burlesque shows, billiards, and Robert Service, and was always looking back upon his last intrigue or forward to his next one. In his youth his taste had run to loud ties, but now it seemed to have faded, like his vitality, and was expressed in pale-lilac four-in-hands and indeterminate gray collars. Charley was listlessly struggling that losing struggle against mental, moral, and physical anæmia that takes place ceaselessly on the lower fringe of the middle classes.

The first morning he stretched himself on a row of cereal cartons and carefully went over the limitations of the Theron G. Macy Company.

"It's a piker organization. My Gosh! Lookit what they give me. I'm quittin' in a coupla months. Hell! Me stay with this bunch!"

The Charley Moores are always going to change jobs next month. They do, once or twice in their careers, after which they sit around comparing their last job with the present one, to the infinite disparagement of the latter.

"What do you get?" asked Dalyrimple curiously.

"Me? I get sixty." This rather defiantly.

"Did you start at sixty?"

"Me? No, I started at thirty-five. He told me he'd put me on the road after I learned the stock. That's what he tells 'em all."

"How long've you been here?" asked Dalyrimple with a sinking sensation.

"Me? Four years. My last year, too, you bet your boots."

Dalyrimple rather resented the presence of the store detective as he resented the time-clock, and he came into contact with him almost immediately through the rule against smoking. This rule was a thorn in his side. He was accustomed to his three or four cigarettes in a morning, and after three days without it he followed Charley Moore by a circuitous route up a flight of back stairs to a little balcony where they indulged in peace. But this was not for long. One day in his second week the detective met him in a nook of the stairs, on his descent, and told him sternly that next time he'd be reported to Mr. Macy. Dalyrimple felt like an errant schoolboy.

Unpleasant facts came to his knowledge. There were "cave-dwellers" in the basement who had worked there for ten or fifteen years at sixty dollars a month, rolling barrels and carrying boxes through damp, cement-walled corridors, lost in that echoing half-darkness between seven and five-thirty and, like himself, compelled several times a month to work until nine at night.

At the end of a month he stood in line and received forty dollars. He pawned a cigarette-case and a pair of field-glasses and managed to live—to eat, sleep, and smoke. It was, however, a narrow scrape; as the ways and means of economy were a closed book to him and the second month brought no increase, he voiced his alarm.

"If you've got a drag with old Macy, maybe he'll raise you," was Charley's disheartening reply. "But he didn't raise *me* till I'd been here nearly two years."

"I've got to live," said Dalyrimple simply. "I could get more pay as a laborer on the railroad but, Golly, I want to feel I'm where there's a chance to get ahead."

Charles shook his head sceptically and Mr. Macy's answer next day was equally unsatisfactory.

Dalyrimple had gone to the office just before closing time.

"Mr. Macy, I'd like to speak to you."

"Why—yes." The unhumorous smile appeared. The voice was faintly resentful.

"I want to speak to you in regard to more salary."

Mr. Macy nodded.

"Well," he said doubtfully, "I don't know exactly what you're doing. I'll speak to Mr. Hanson."

He knew exactly what Dalyrimple was doing, and Dalyrimple knew he knew.

"I'm in the stock-room—and, sir, while I'm here I'd like to ask you how much longer I'll have to stay there."

"Why—I'm not sure exactly. Of course it takes some time to learn the stock."

"You told me two months when I started."

"Yes. Well, I'll speak to Mr. Hanson."

Dalyrimple paused irresolute.

"Thank you, sir."

Two days later he again appeared in the office with the result of a count that had been asked for by Mr. Hesse, the bookkeeper. Mr. Hesse was engaged and Dalyrimple, waiting, began idly fingering a ledger on the stenographer's desk.

Half unconsciously he turned a page—he caught sight of his name—it was a salary list:

Dalyrimple
Demming
Donahoe
Everett

His eyes stopped——

Everett $60

So Tom Everett, Macy's weak-chinned nephew, had started at sixty—and in three weeks he had been out of the packing-room and into the office.

So that was it! He was to sit and see man after man pushed over him: sons, cousins, sons of friends, irrespective of their capabilities, while *he* was cast for a pawn, with "going on the road" dangled before his eyes—put off with the stock remark: "I'll see; I'll look into it." At forty, perhaps, he would be a bookkeeper like old Hesse, tired, listless Hesse with dull routine for his stint and a dull background of boarding-house conversation.

This was a moment when a genii should have pressed into his hand the book for disillusioned young men. But the book has not been written.

A great protest swelling into revolt surged up in him. Ideas half forgotten, chaotically perceived and assimilated, filled his mind. Get on—that was the rule of life—and that was all.

How he did it, didn't matter—but to be Hesse or Charley Moore.

"I won't!" he cried aloud.

The bookkeeper and the stenographers looked up in surprise.

"What?"

For a second Dalyrimple stared—then walked up to the desk.

"Here's that data," he said brusquely. "I can't wait any longer."

Mr. Hesse's face expressed surprise.

It didn't matter what he did—just so he got out of this rut. In a dream he stepped from the elevator into the stock-room, and walking to an unused aisle, sat down on a box, covering his face with his hands.

His brain was whirring with the frightful jar of discovering a platitude for himself.

"I've got to get out of this," he said aloud and then repeated, "I've got to get out"—and he didn't mean only out of Macy's wholesale house.

When he left at five-thirty it was pouring rain, but he struck off in the opposite direction from his boarding-house, feeling, in the first cool moisture that oozed soggily through his old suit, an odd exultation and freshness. He wanted a world that was like walking through rain, even though he could not see far ahead of him, but fate had put him in the world of Mr. Macy's fetid storerooms and corridors. At first merely the overwhelming need of change took him, then half-plans began to formulate in his imagination.

"I'll go East—to a big city—meet people—bigger people—people who'll help me. Interesting work somewhere. My God, there *must* be."

With sickening truth it occurred to him that his facility for meeting people was limited. Of all places it was here in his own town that he should be known, was known—famous—before the waters of oblivion had rolled over him.

You had to cut corners, that was all. Pull—relationship—wealthy marriages——

For several miles the continued reiteration of this preoccupied him and then he perceived that the rain had become thicker and more opaque in the heavy gray of twilight and that the houses were falling away. The district of full blocks, then of big houses, then of scattering little ones, passed and great sweeps of misty country opened out on both sides. It was hard walking here. The sidewalk had given place to a dirt road, streaked with furious brown rivulets that splashed and squashed around his shoes.

Cutting corners—the words began to fall apart, forming curious phrasings—little illuminated pieces of themselves. They resolved into sentences, each of which had a strangely familiar ring.

Cutting corners meant rejecting the old childhood principles that success came from faithfulness to duty, that evil was necessarily punished or virtue necessarily rewarded—that honest poverty was happier than corrupt riches.

It meant being hard.

This phrase appealed to him and he repeated it over and over. It had to do somehow with Mr. Macy and Charley Moore—the attitudes, the methods of each of them.

He stopped and felt his clothes. He was drenched to the skin. He looked about him and, selecting a place in the fence where a tree sheltered it, perched himself there.

In my credulous years—he thought—they told me that evil was a sort of dirty hue, just as definite as a soiled collar, but it seems to me that evil is only a manner of hard luck, or heredity-and-environment, or "being found out." It hides in the vacillations of dubs like Charley Moore as certainly as it does in the intolerance of Macy, and if it ever gets much more tangible it becomes merely an arbitrary label to paste on the unpleasant things in other people's lives.

In fact—he concluded—it isn't worth worrying over what's evil and what isn't. Good and evil aren't any standard to me—and they can be a devil of a bad hindrance when I want something. When I want something bad enough, common sense tells me to go and take it—and not get caught.

And then suddenly Dalyrimple knew what he wanted first. He wanted fifteen dollars to pay his overdue board bill.

With a furious energy he jumped from the fence, whipped off his coat, and from its black lining cut with his knife a piece about five inches square. He made two holes near its edge and then fixed it on his face, pulling his hat down to hold it in place. It flapped grotesquely and then dampened and clung to his forehead and cheeks.

Now . . . The twilight had merged to dripping dusk . . . black as pitch. He began to walk quickly back toward town, not waiting to remove the mask but watching the road with difficulty through the jagged eye-holes. He was not conscious of any nervousness . . . the only tension was caused by a desire to do the thing as soon as possible.

He reached the first sidewalk, continued on until he saw a hedge far from any lamp-post, and turned in behind it. Within a minute he heard several series of footsteps—he waited—it was a woman and he held his breath until she passed . . . and then a man, a laborer. The next passer, he felt, would be what he wanted . . . the laborer's footfalls died far up the drenched street . . . other steps grew near, grew suddenly louder.

Dalyrimple braced himself.

"Put up your hands!"

The man stopped, uttered an absurd little grunt, and thrust pudgy arms skyward.

Dalyrimple went through the waistcoat.

"Now, you shrimp," he said, setting his hand suggestively to his own hip pocket, "you run, and stamp—loud! If I hear your feet stop I'll put a shot after you!"

Then he stood there in sudden uncontrollable laughter as audibly frightened footsteps scurried away into the night.

After a moment he thrust the roll of bills into his pocket, snatched off his mask, and running quickly across the street, darted down an alley.

IV

Yet, however Dalyrimple justified himself intellectually, he had many bad moments in the weeks immediately following his decision. The tremendous pressure of sentiment and inherited tradition kept raising riot with his attitude. He felt morally lonely.

The noon after his first venture he ate in a little lunch-room with Charley Moore and, watching him unspread the paper, waited for a remark about the hold-up of the day before. But either the hold-up was not mentioned or Charley wasn't interested. He turned listlessly to the sporting sheet, read Doctor Crane's crop of seasoned bromides, took in an editorial on ambition with his mouth slightly ajar, and then skipped to Mutt and Jeff.

Poor Charley—with his faint aura of evil and his mind that refused to focus, playing a lifeless solitaire with cast-off mischief.

Yet Charley belonged on the other side of the fence. In him could be stirred up all the flamings and denunciations of righteousness; he would weep at a stage heroine's lost virtue, he could become lofty and contemptuous at the idea of dishonor.

On my side, thought Dalyrimple, there aren't any resting-places; a man who's a strong criminal is after the weak criminals as well, so it's all guerilla warfare over here.

What will it all do to me? he thought, with a persistent weariness. Will it take the color out of life with the honor? Will it scatter my courage and dull my mind?—despiritualize me completely—does it mean eventual barrenness, eventual remorse, failure?

With a great surge of anger, he would fling his mind upon the barrier—and stand there with the flashing bayonet of his pride. Other men who broke the laws of justice and charity lied to all the world. He at any rate would not lie to himself. He was more than Byronic now: not the spiritual rebel, Don Juan; not the philosophical rebel, Faust; but a new psychological rebel of his own century—defying the sentimental a priori forms of his own mind——

Happiness was what he wanted—a slowly rising scale of gratifications of the normal appetites—and he had a strong conviction that the materials, if not the inspiration of happiness, could be bought with money.

V

The night came that drew him out upon his second venture, and as he walked the dark street he felt in himself a great resemblance to a cat—a certain supple, swinging litheness.

His muscles were rippling smoothly and sleekly under his spare, healthy flesh—he had an absurd desire to bound along the street, to run dodging among trees, to turn "cart-wheels" over soft grass.

It was not crisp, but in the air lay a faint suggestion of acerbity, inspirational rather than chilling.

"The moon is down—I have not heard the clock!"

He laughed in delight at the line which an early memory had endowed with a hushed, awesome beauty.

He passed a man, and then another a quarter of a mile afterward.

He was on Philmore Street now and it was very dark. He blessed the city council for not having put in new lamp-posts as a recent budget had recommended. Here was the red-brick Sterner residence which marked the beginning of the avenue; here was the Jordon house, the Eisenhaurs', the Dents', the Markhams', the Frasers'; the Hawkins', where he had been a guest; the Willoughbys', the Everetts', colonial and ornate; the little cottage where lived the Watts old maids between the imposing fronts of the Macys' and the Krupstadts'; the Craigs'——

Ah . . . *there!* He paused, wavered violently—far up the street was a blot, a man walking, possibly a policeman. After an eternal second he found himself following the vague, ragged shadow of a lamp-post across a lawn, running bent very low. Then he was standing tense, without breath or need of it, in the shadow of his limestone prey.

Interminably he listened—a mile off a cat howled, a hundred yards away another took up the hymn in a demoniacal snarl, and he felt his heart dip and swoop, acting as shock-absorber for his mind. There were other sounds; the faintest fragment of song far away; strident, gossiping laughter from a back porch diagonally across the alley; and crickets, crickets singing in the patched, patterned, moonlit grass of the yard. Within the house there seemed to lie an ominous silence. He was glad he did not know who lived here.

His slight shiver hardened to steel; the steel softened and his nerves became pliable as leather; gripping his hands he gratefully found them supple, and taking out knife and pliers he went to work on the screen.

So sure was he that he was unobserved that, from the dining-room where in a minute he found himself, he leaned out and carefully pulled the screen up into position, balancing it so it would neither fall by chance nor be a serious obstacle to a sudden exit.

Then he put the open knife in his coat pocket, took out his pocket-flash, and tiptoed around the room.

There was nothing here he could use—the dining-room had never been included in his plans, for the town was too small to permit disposing of silver.

As a matter of fact his plans were of the vaguest. He had found that with a mind like his, lucrative in intelligence, intuition, and lightning decision, it was best to have but the skeleton of a campaign. The machine-gun episode had taught him that. And he was afraid that a method preconceived would give him two points of view in a crisis—and two points of view meant wavering.

He stumbled slightly on a chair, held his breath, listened, went on, found the hall, found the stairs, started up; the seventh stair creaked at his step, the ninth, the fourteenth. He was counting them automatically. At the third creak he paused again for over a minute—and in that minute he felt more alone than he had ever felt before. Between the lines on patrol, even when alone, he had had behind him the moral support of half a billion people; now he was alone, pitted against that same moral pressure—a bandit. He had never felt this fear, yet he had never felt this exultation.

The stairs came to an end, a doorway approached; he went in and listened to regular breathing. His feet were economical of steps and his body swayed sometimes at stretching as he felt over the bureau, pocketing all articles which held promise—he could not have enumerated them ten seconds afterward. He felt on a chair for possible trousers, found soft garments, women's lingerie. The corners of his mouth smiled mechanically.

Another room . . . the same breathing, enlivened by one ghastly snort that sent his heart again on its tour of his breast. Round object—watch; chain; roll of bills; stick-pins; two rings—he remembered that he had got rings from the other bureau. He started out, winced as a faint glow flashed in front of him, facing him. God!—it was the glow of his own wrist-watch on his outstretched arm.

Down the stairs. He skipped two creaking steps but found another. He was all right now, practically safe; as he neared the bottom he felt a slight boredom. He reached the dining-room—considered the silver—again decided against it.

Back in his room at the boarding-house he examined the additions to his personal property:

Sixty-five dollars in bills.

A platinum ring with three medium diamonds, worth, probably, about seven hundred dollars. Diamonds were going up.

A cheap gold-plated ring with the initials O. S. and the date inside—'03—probably a class-ring from school. Worth a few dollars. Unsalable.

A red-cloth case containing a set of false teeth.

A silver watch.

A gold chain worth more than the watch.

An empty ring-box.

A little ivory Chinese god—probably a desk ornament.

A dollar and sixty-two cents in small change.

He put the money under his pillow and the other things in the toe of an infantry boot, stuffing a stocking in on top of them. Then for two hours his mind raced like a high-power engine here and there through his life, past and future, through fear and laughter. With a vague, inopportune wish that he were married, he fell into a deep sleep about half past five.

VI

Though the newspaper account of the burglary failed to mention the false teeth, they worried him considerably. The picture of a human waking in the cool dawn and groping for them in vain, of a soft, toothless breakfast, of a strange, hollow, lisping voice calling the police station, of weary, dispirited visits to the dentist, roused a great fatherly pity in him.

Trying to ascertain whether they belonged to a man or a woman, he took them carefully out of the case and held them up near his mouth. He moved his own jaws experimentally;

he measured with his fingers; but he failed to decide: they might belong either to a large-mouthed woman or a small-mouthed man.

On a warm impulse he wrapped them in brown paper from the bottom of his army trunk, and printed FALSE TEETH on the package in clumsy pencil letters. Then, the next night, he walked down Philmore Street, and shied the package onto the lawn so that it would be near the door. Next day the paper announced that the police had a clew—they knew that the burglar was in town. However, they didn't mention what the clew was.

VII

At the end of a month "Burglar Bill of the Silver District" was the nurse-girl's standby for frightening children. Five burglaries were attributed to him, but though Dalyrimple had only committed three, he considered that majority had it and appropriated the title to himself. He had once been seen—"a large bloated creature with the meanest face you ever laid eyes on." Mrs. Henry Coleman, awaking at two o'clock at the beam of an electric torch flashed in her eye, could not have been expected to recognize Bryan Dalyrimple at whom she had waved flags last Fourth of July, and whom she had described as "not at all the daredevil type, do you think?"

When Dalyrimple kept his imagination at white heat he managed to glorify his own attitude, his emancipation from petty scruples and remorses—but let him once allow his thought to rove unarmored, great unexpected horrors and depressions would overtake him. Then for reassurance he had to go back to think out the whole thing over again. He found that it was on the whole better to give up considering himself as a rebel. It was more consoling to think of every one else as a fool.

His attitude toward Mr. Macy underwent a change. He no longer felt a dim animosity and inferiority in his presence. As his fourth month in the store ended he found himself regarding his employer in a manner that was almost fraternal. He had a vague but very assured conviction that Mr. Macy's innermost soul would have abetted and approved. He no longer worried about his future. He had the intention of accumulating several thousand dollars and then clearing out—going east, back to France, down to South America. Half a dozen times in the last two months he had been about to stop work, but a fear of attracting attention to his being in funds prevented him. So he worked on, no longer in listlessness, but with contemptuous amusement.

VIII

Then with astounding suddenness something happened that changed his plans and put an end to his burglaries.

Mr. Macy sent for him one afternoon and with a great show of jovial mystery asked him if he had an engagement that night. If he hadn't, would he please call on Mr. Alfred J. Fraser at eight o'clock. Dalyrimple's wonder was mingled with uncertainty. He debated with himself whether it were not his cue to take the first train out of town. But an hour's consideration decided him that his fears were unfounded and at eight o'clock he arrived at the big Fraser house in Philmore Avenue.

Mr. Fraser was commonly supposed to be the biggest political influence in the city. His brother was Senator Fraser, his son-in-law was Congressman Demming, and his influence, though not wielded in such a way as to make him an objectionable boss, was strong nevertheless.

He had a great, huge face, deep-set eyes, and a barn-door of an upper lip, the melange approaching a worthy climax in a long professional jaw.

During his conversation with Dalyrimple his expression kept starting toward a smile, reached a cheerful optimism, and then receded back to imperturbability.

"How do you do, sir?" he said, holding out his hand. "Sit down. I suppose you're wondering why I wanted you. Sit down."

Dalyrimple sat down.

"Mr. Dalyrimple, how old are you?"

"I'm twenty-three."

"You're young. But that doesn't mean you're foolish. Mr. Dalyrimple, what I've got to say won't take long. I'm going to make you a proposition. To begin at the beginning, I've been watching you ever since last Fourth of July when you made that speech in response to the loving-cup."

Dalyrimple murmured disparagingly, but Fraser waved him to silence.

"It was a speech I've remembered. It was a brainy speech, straight from the shoulder, and it got to everybody in that crowd. I know. I've watched crowds for years." He cleared his throat, as if tempted to digress on his knowledge of crowds—then continued. "But, Mr. Dalyrimple, I've seen too many young men who promised brilliantly go to pieces, fail through want of steadiness, too many high-power ideas, and not enough willingness to work. So I waited. I wanted to see what you'd do. I wanted to see if you'd go to work, and if you'd stick to what you started."

Dalyrimple felt a glow settle over him.

"So," continued Fraser, "when Theron Macy told me you'd started down at his place, I kept watching you, and I followed your record through him. The first month I was afraid for a while. He told me you were getting restless, too good for your job, hinting around for a raise——"

Dalyrimple started.

"—But he said after that you evidently made up your mind to shut up and stick to it. That's the stuff I like in a young man! That's the stuff that wins out. And don't think I don't understand. I know how much harder it was for you, after all that silly flattery a lot of old women had been giving you. I know what a fight it must have been——"

Dalyrimple's face was burning brightly. He felt young and strangely ingenuous.

"Dalyrimple, you've got brains and you've got the stuff in you—and that's what I want. I'm going to put you into the State Senate."

"The *what*?"

"The State Senate. We want a young man who has got brains, but is solid and not a loafer. And when I say State Senate I don't stop there. We're up against it here, Dalyrimple. We've got to get some young men into politics—you know the old blood that's been running on the party ticket year in and year out."

Dalyrimple licked his lips.

"You'll run me for the State Senate?"

"I'll *put* you in the State Senate."

Mr. Fraser's expression had now reached the point nearest a smile and Dalyrimple in a happy frivolity felt himself urging it mentally on—but it stopped, locked, and slid from him. The barn-door and the jaw were separated by a line straight as a nail. Dalyrimple remembered with an effort that it was a mouth, and talked to it.

"But I'm through," he said. "My notoriety's dead. People are fed up with me."

"Those things," answered Mr. Fraser, "are mechanical. Linotype is a resuscitator of reputations. Wait till you see the *Herald*, beginning next week—that is if you're with us—that is," and his voice hardened slightly, "if you haven't got too many ideas yourself about how things ought to be run."

"No," said Dalyrimple, looking him frankly in the eyes. "You'll have to give me a lot of advice at first."

"Very well. I'll take care of your reputation then. Just keep yourself on the right side of the fence."

Dalyrimple started at this repetition of a phrase he had thought of so much lately. There was a sudden ring at the door-bell.

"That's Macy now," observed Fraser, rising. "I'll go let him in. The servants have gone to bed."

He left Dalyrimple there in a dream. The world was opening up suddenly— The State Senate, the United States Senate—so life was this after all—cutting corners—cutting corners—common sense, that was the rule. No more foolish risks now unless necessity called—but it was being hard that counted— Never to let remorse or self-reproach lose him a night's sleep—let his life be a sword of courage—there was no payment—all that was drivel—drivel. He sprang to his feet with clinched hands in a sort of triumph.

"Well, Bryan," said Mr. Macy stepping through the portières.

The two older men smiled their half-smiles at him.

"Well, Bryan," said Mr. Macy again.

Dalyrimple smiled also.

"How do, Mr. Macy?"

He wondered if some telepathy between them had made this new appreciation possible—some invisible realization. . . .

Mr. Macy held out his hand.

"I'm glad we're to be associated in this scheme—I've been for you all along—especially lately. I'm glad we're to be on the same side of the fence."

"I want to thank you, sir," said Dalyrimple simply. He felt a whimsical moisture gathering back of his eyes.

The Four Fists

At the present time no one I know has the slightest desire to hit Samuel Meredith; possibly this is because a man over fifty is liable to be rather severely cracked at the impact of a hostile fist, but, for my part, I am inclined to think that all his hitable qualities have quite vanished. But it is certain that at various times in his life hitable qualities were in his face, as surely as kissable qualities have ever lurked in a girl's lips.

I'm sure every one has met a man like that, been casually introduced, even made a friend of him, yet felt he was the sort who aroused passionate dislike—expressed by some in the involuntary clinching of fists, and in others by mutterings about "takin' a poke" and "landin' a swift smash in ee eye." In the juxtaposition of Samuel Meredith's features this quality was so strong that it influenced his entire life.

What was it? Not the shape, certainly, for he was a pleasant-looking man from earliest youth: broad-browed, with gray eyes that were frank and friendly. Yet I've heard him tell a room full of reporters angling for a "success" story that he'd be ashamed to tell them the truth, that they wouldn't believe it, that it wasn't one story but four, that the public would not want to read about a man who had been walloped into prominence.

It all started at Phillips Andover Academy when he was fourteen. He had been brought up on a diet of caviar and bell-boys' legs in half the capitals of Europe, and it was pure luck that his mother had nervous prostration and had to delegate his education to less tender, less biassed hands.

At Andover he was given a roommate named Gilly Hood. Gilly was thirteen, undersized, and rather the school pet. From the September day when Mr. Meredith's valet stowed Samuel's clothing in the best bureau and asked, on departing, "hif there was hanything helse, Master Samuel?" Gilly cried out that the faculty had played him false. He felt like an irate frog in whose bowl has been put a goldfish.

"Good gosh!" he complained to his sympathetic contemporaries, "he's a damn stuck-up Willie. He said, 'Are the crowd here gentlemen?' and I said, 'No, they're boys,' and he said age didn't matter, and I said, 'Who said it did?' Let him get fresh with me, the ole pieface!"

For three weeks Gilly endured in silence young Samuel's comments on the clothes and habits of Gilly's personal friends, endured French phrases in conversation, endured a hundred half-feminine meannesses that show what a nervous mother can do to a boy, if she keeps close enough to him—then a storm broke in the aquarium.

Samuel was out. A crowd had gathered to hear Gilly be wrathful about his roommate's latest sins.

"He said, 'Oh, I don't like the windows open at night,' he said, 'except only a little bit,' " complained Gilly.

"Don't let him boss you."

"Boss me? You bet he won't. I open those windows, I guess, but the darn fool won't take turns shuttin' 'em in the morning."

"Make him, Gilly, why don't you?"

"I'm going to." Gilly nodded his head in fierce agreement. "Don't you worry. He needn't think I'm any ole butler."

"Le's see you make him."

At this point the darn fool entered in person and included the crowd in one of his irritating smiles. Two boys said, " 'Lo, Mer'dith"; the others gave him a chilly glance and went on talking to Gilly. But Samuel seemed unsatisfied.

"Would you mind not sitting on my bed?" he suggested politely to two of Gilly's particulars who were perched very much at ease.

"Huh?"

"My bed. Can't you understand English?"

This was adding insult to injury. There were several comments on the bed's sanitary condition and the evidence within it of animal life.

"S'matter with your old bed?" demanded Gilly truculently.

"The bed's all right, but——"

Gilly interrupted this sentence by rising and walking up to Samuel. He paused several inches away and eyed him fiercely.

"You an' your crazy ole bed," he began. "You an' your crazy——"

"Go to it, Gilly," murmured some one.

"Show the darn fool——"

Samuel returned the gaze coolly.

"Well," he said finally, "it's my bed——"

He got no further, for Gilly hauled off and hit him succinctly in the nose.

"Yea! Gilly!"

"Show the big bully!"

"Just let him touch you—he'll see!"

The group closed in on them and for the first time in his life Samuel realized the insuperable inconvenience of being passionately detested. He gazed around helplessly at the glowering, violently hostile faces. He towered a head taller than his roommate, so if he hit back he'd be called a bully and have half a dozen more fights on his hands within five minutes; yet if he didn't he was a coward. For a moment he stood there facing Gilly's blazing eyes, and then, with a sudden choking sound, he forced his way through the ring and rushed from the room.

The month following bracketed the thirty most miserable days of his life. Every waking moment he was under the lashing tongues of his contemporaries; his habits and mannerisms became butts for intolerable witticisms and, of course, the sensitiveness of adolescence was a further thorn. He considered that he was a natural pariah; that the unpopularity at school would follow him through life. When he went home for the Christmas holidays he was so despondent that his father sent him to a nerve specialist. When he returned to Andover he arranged to arrive late so that he could be alone in the bus during the drive from station to school.

Of course when he had learned to keep his mouth shut every one promptly forgot all about him. The next autumn, with his realization that consideration for others was the discreet attitude, he made good use of the clean start given him by the shortness of boyhood memory. By the beginning of his senior year Samuel Meredith was one of the best-liked boys of his class—and no one was any stronger for him than his first friend and constant companion, Gilly Hood.

II

Samuel became the sort of college student who in the early nineties drove tandems and coaches and tallyhos between Princeton and Yale and New York City to show that they appreciated the social importance of football games. He believed passionately in good form—his choosing of gloves, his tying of ties, his holding of reins were imitated by impressionable freshmen. Outside of his own set he was considered rather a snob, but as his set was *the* set, it never worried him. He played football in the autumn, drank high-balls in the winter, and rowed in the spring. Samuel despised all those who were merely sportsmen without being gentlemen, or merely gentlemen without being sportsmen.

He lived in New York and often brought home several of his friends for the week-end. Those were the days of the horse-car and in case of a crush it was, of course, the proper thing for any one of Samuel's set to rise and deliver his seat to a standing lady with a formal bow. One night in Samuel's junior year he boarded a car with two of his intimates. There were three vacant seats. When Samuel sat down he noticed a heavy-eyed laboring man sitting next to him who smelt objectionably of garlic, sagged slightly against Samuel and, spreading a little as a tired man will, took up quite too much room.

The car had gone several blocks when it stopped for a quartet of young girls, and, of course, the three men of the world sprang to their feet and proffered their seats with due observance of form. Unfortunately, the laborer, being unacquainted with the code of neckties and tallyhos, failed to follow their example, and one young lady was left at an embarrassed stance. Fourteen eyes glared reproachfully at the barbarian; seven lips curled slightly; but the object of scorn stared stolidly into the foreground in sturdy unconsciousness of his despicable conduct. Samuel was the most violently affected. He was humiliated that any male should so conduct himself. He spoke aloud.

"There's a lady standing," he said sternly.

That should have been quite enough, but the object of scorn only looked up blankly. The standing girl tittered and exchanged nervous glances with her companions. But Samuel was aroused.

"There's a lady standing," he repeated, rather raspingly. The man seemed to comprehend.

"I pay my fare," he said quietly.

Samuel turned red and his hands clinched, but the conductor was looking their way, so at a warning nod from his friends he subsided into sullen gloom.

They reached their destination and left the car, but so did the laborer, who followed them, swinging his little pail. Seeing his chance, Samuel no longer resisted his aristocratic inclination. He turned around and, launching a full-featured, dime-novel sneer, made a loud remark about the right of the lower animals to ride with human beings.

In a half-second the workman had dropped his pail and let fly at him. Unprepared, Samuel took the blow neatly on the jaw and sprawled full length into the cobblestone gutter.

"Don't laugh at me!" cried his assailant. "I been workin' all day. I'm tired as hell!"

As he spoke the sudden anger died out of his eyes and the mask of weariness dropped again over his face. He turned and picked up his pail. Samuel's friends took a quick step in his direction.

"Wait!" Samuel had risen slowly and was motioning them back. Some time, somewhere, he had been struck like that before. Then he remembered—Gilly Hood. In the silence, as he dusted himself off, the whole scene in the room at Andover was before his eyes—and he knew intuitively that he had been wrong again. This man's strength, his rest, was the protection of his family. He had more use for his seat in the street-car than any young girl.

"It's all right," said Samuel gruffly. "Don't touch him. I've been a damn fool."

Of course it took more than an hour, or a week, for Samuel to rearrange his ideas on the essential importance of good form. At first he simply admitted that his wrongness had made him powerless—as it had made him powerless against Gilly—but eventually his mistake about the workman influenced his entire attitude. Snobbishness is, after all, merely good breeding grown dictatorial; so Samuel's code remained, but the necessity of imposing it upon others had faded out in a certain gutter. Within that year his class had somehow stopped referring to him as a snob.

III

After a few years Samuel's university decided that it had shone long enough in the reflected glory of his neckties, so they declaimed to him in Latin, charged him ten dollars for the paper which proved him irretrievably educated, and sent him into the turmoil with much self-confidence, a few friends, and the proper assortment of harmless bad habits.

His family had by that time started back to shirt-sleeves, through a sudden decline in the sugar-market, and it had already unbuttoned its vest, so to speak, when Samuel went to work. His mind was that exquisite *tabula rasa* that a university education sometimes leaves, but he had both energy and influence, so he used his former ability as a dodging half-back in twisting through Wall Street crowds as runner for a bank.

His diversion was—women. There were half a dozen: two or three débutantes, an actress (in a minor way), a grass-widow, and one sentimental little brunette who was married and lived in a little house in Jersey City.

They had met on a ferry-boat. Samuel was crossing from New York on business (he had been working several years by this time) and he helped her look for a package that she had dropped in the crush.

"Do you come over often?" he inquired casually.

"Just to shop," she said shyly. She had great brown eyes and the pathetic kind of little mouth. "I've only been married three months, and we find it cheaper to live over here."

"Does he—does your husband like your being alone like this?"

she laughed, a cheery young laugh.

"Oh, dear me, no. We were to meet for dinner but I must have misunderstood the place. He'll be awfully worried."

"Well," said Samuel disapprovingly, "he ought to be. If you'll allow me I'll see you home."

She accepted his offer thankfully, so they took the cable-car together. When they walked up the path to her little house they saw a light there; her husband had arrived before her.

"He's frightfully jealous," she announced, laughingly apologetic.

"Very well," answered Samuel, rather stiffly. "I'd better leave you here."

She thanked him and, waving a good night, he left her.

That would have been quite all if they hadn't met on Fifth Avenue one morning a week later. She started and blushed and seemed so glad to see him that they chatted like old friends. She was going to her dressmaker's, eat lunch alone at Taine's, shop all afternoon, and meet her husband on the ferry at five. Samuel told her that her husband was a very lucky man. She blushed again and scurried off.

Samuel whistled all the way back to his office, but about twelve o'clock he began to see that pathetic, appealing little mouth everywhere—and those brown eyes. He fidgeted when he looked at the clock; he thought of the grill down-stairs where he lunched and the heavy male conversation thereof, and opposed to that picture appeared another: a little table at Taine's with the brown eyes and the mouth a few feet away. A few minutes before twelve-thirty he dashed on his hat and rushed for the cable-car.

She was quite surprised to see him.

"Why—hello," she said. Samuel could tell that she was just pleasantly frightened.

"I thought we might lunch together. It's so dull eating with a lot of men."

She hesitated.

"Why, I suppose there's no harm in it. How could there be!"

It occurred to her that her husband should have taken lunch with her—but he was generally so hurried at noon. She told Samuel all about him: he was a little smaller than Samuel, but, oh, *much* better-looking. He was a bookkeeper and not making a lot of money, but they were very happy and expected to be rich within three or four years.

Samuel's grass-widow had been in a quarrelsome mood for three or four weeks, and, through contrast, he took an accentuated pleasure in this meeting; so fresh was she, and earnest, and faintly adventurous. Her name was Marjorie.

They made another engagement; in fact, for a month they lunched together two or three times a week. When she was sure that her husband would work late Samuel took her over to New Jersey on the ferry, leaving her always on the tiny front porch, after she had gone in and lit the gas to use the security of his masculine presence outside. This grew to be a ceremony—and it annoyed him. Whenever the comfortable glow fell out through the front windows, that was his *congé*; yet he never suggested coming in and Marjorie didn't invite him.

Then, when Samuel and Marjorie had reached a stage in which they sometimes touched each other's arms gently, just to show that they were very good friends, Marjorie and her husband had one of those ultrasensitive, supercritical quarrels that couples never indulge in unless they care a great deal about each other. It started with a cold mutton-chop or a leak in the gas-jet—and one day Samuel found her in Taine's, with dark shadows under her brown eyes and a terrifying pout.

By this time Samuel thought he was in love with Marjorie—so he played up the quarrel for all it was worth. He was her best friend and patted her hand—and leaned down close to her brown curls while she whispered in little sobs what her husband had said that morning; and he was a little more than her best friend when he took her over to the ferry in a hansom.

"Marjorie," he said gently, when he left her, as usual, on the porch, "if at any time you want to call on me, remember that I am always waiting, always waiting."

She nodded gravely and put both her hands in his.

"I know," she said. "I know you're my friend, my best friend."

Then she ran into the house and he watched there until the gas went on.

For the next week Samuel was in a nervous turmoil. Some persistently rational strain warned him that at bottom he and Marjorie had little in common, but in such cases there is usually so much mud in the water that one can seldom see to the bottom. Every dream and desire told him that he loved Marjorie, wanted her, had to have her.

The quarrel developed. Marjorie's husband took to staying in New York until late at night, came home several times disagreeably overstimulated, and made her generally miserable. They must have had too much pride to talk it out—for Marjorie's husband was, after all, pretty decent—so it drifted on from one misunderstanding to another. Marjorie kept coming more and more to Samuel; when a woman can accept masculine sympathy it is much more satisfactory to her than crying to another girl. But Marjorie didn't realize how much she had begun to rely on him, how much he was part of her little cosmos.

One night, instead of turning away when Marjorie went in and lit the gas, Samuel went in, too, and they sat together on the sofa in the little parlor. He was very happy. He envied their home, and he felt that the man who neglected such a possession out of stubborn pride was a fool and unworthy of his wife. But when he kissed Marjorie for the first time she cried softly and told him to go. He sailed home on the wings of desperate excitement, quite resolved to fan this spark of romance, no matter how big the blaze or who was burned. At the time he considered that his thoughts were unselfishly of her; in a later perspective he knew that she had meant no more than the white screen in a motion picture: it was just Samuel—blind, desirous.

Next day at Taine's, when they met for lunch, Samuel dropped all pretense and made frank love to her. He had no plans, no definite intentions, except to kiss her lips again, to hold her in his arms and feel that she was very little and pathetic and lovable. . . . He took her home, and this time they kissed until both their hearts beat high—words and phrases formed on his lips.

And then suddenly there were steps on the porch—a hand tried the outside door. Marjorie turned dead-white.

"Wait!" she whispered to Samuel, in a frightened voice, but in angry impatience at the interruption he walked to the front door and threw it open.

Every one has seen such scenes on the stage—seen them so often that when they actually happen people behave very much like actors. Samuel felt that he was playing a part and the lines came quite naturally: he announced that all had a right to lead their own lives and looked at Marjorie's husband menacingly, as if daring him to doubt it. Marjorie's husband spoke of the sanctity of the home, forgetting that it hadn't seemed very holy to him lately; Samuel continued along the line of "the right to happiness"; Marjorie's husband mentioned firearms and the divorce court. Then suddenly he stopped and scrutinized both of them—Marjorie in pitiful collapse on the sofa, Samuel haranguing the furniture in a consciously heroic pose.

"Go up-stairs, Marjorie," he said, in a different tone.

"Stay where you are!" Samuel countered quickly.

Marjorie rose, wavered, and sat down, rose again and moved hesitatingly toward the stairs.

"Come outside," said her husband to Samuel. "I want to talk to you."

Samuel glanced at Marjorie, tried to get some message from her eyes; then he shut his lips and went out.

There was a bright moon and when Marjorie's husband came down the steps Samuel could see plainly that he was suffering—but he felt no pity for him.

They stood and looked at each other, a few feet apart, and the husband cleared his throat as though it were a bit husky.

"That's my wife," he said quietly, and then a wild anger surged up inside him. "Damn you!" he cried—and hit Samuel in the face with all his strength.

In that second, as Samuel slumped to the ground, it flashed to him that he had been hit like that twice before, and simultaneously the incident altered like a dream—he felt suddenly awake. Mechanically he sprang to his feet and squared off. The other man was waiting, fists up, a yard away, but Samuel knew that though physically he had him by several inches and many pounds, he wouldn't hit him. The situation had miraculously and entirely changed—a moment before Samuel had seemed to himself heroic; now he seemed the cad, the outsider, and Marjorie's husband, silhouetted against the lights of the little house, the eternal heroic figure, the defender of his home.

There was a pause and then Samuel turned quickly away and went down the path for the last time.

IV

Of course, after the third blow Samuel put in several weeks at conscientious introspection. The blow years before at Andover had landed on his personal unpleasantness; the workman of his college days had jarred the snobbishness out of his system, and Marjorie's husband had given a severe jolt to his greedy selfishness. It threw women out of his ken until a year later, when he met his future wife; for the only sort of woman worth while seemed to be the one who could be protected as Marjorie's husband had protected her. Samuel could not imagine his grass-widow, Mrs. De Ferriac, causing any very righteous blows on her own account.

His early thirties found him well on his feet. He was associated with old Peter Carhart, who was in those days a national figure. Carhart's physique was like a rough model for a statue of Hercules, and his record was just as solid—a pile made for the pure joy of it, without cheap extortion or shady scandal. He had been a great friend of Samuel's father, but he watched the son for six years before taking him into his own office. Heaven knows how many things he controlled at that time—mines, railroads, banks, whole cities. Samuel was very close to him, knew his likes and dislikes, his prejudices, weaknesses and many strengths.

One day Carhart sent for Samuel and, closing the door of his inner office, offered him a chair and a cigar.

"Everything O.K., Samuel?" he asked.

"Why, yes."

"I've been afraid you're getting a bit stale."

"Stale?" Samuel was puzzled.

"You've done no work outside the office for nearly ten years?"

"But I've had vacations, in the Adiron——"

Carhart waved this aside.

"I mean outside work. Seeing the things move that we've always pulled the strings of here."

"No," admitted Samuel; "I haven't."

"So," he said abruptly, "I'm going to give you an outside job that'll take about a month."

Samuel didn't argue. He rather liked the idea and he made

up his mind that, whatever it was, he would put it through just as Carhart wanted it. That was his employer's greatest hobby, and the men around him were as dumb under direct orders as infantry subalterns.

"You'll go to San Antonio and see Hamil," continued Carhart. "He's got a job on hand and he wants a man to take charge."

Hamil was in charge of the Carhart interests in the Southwest, a man who had grown up in the shadow of his employer, and with whom, though they had never met, Samuel had had much official correspondence.

"When do I leave?"

"You'd better go to-morrow," answered Carhart, glancing at the calendar. "That's the 1st of May. I'll expect your report here on the 1st of June."

Next morning Samuel left for Chicago, and two days later he was facing Hamil across a table in the office of the Merchants' Trust in San Antonio. It didn't take long to get the gist of the thing. It was a big deal in oil which concerned the buying up of seventeen huge adjoining ranches. This buying up had to be done in one week, and it was a pure squeeze. Forces had been set in motion that put the seventeen owners between the devil and the deep sea, and Samuel's part was simply to "handle" the matter from a little village near Pueblo. With tact and efficiency the right man could bring it off without any friction, for it was merely a question of sitting at the wheel and keeping a firm hold. Hamil, with an astuteness many times valuable to his chief, had arranged a situation that would give a much greater clear gain than any dealing in the open market. Samuel shook hands with Hamil, arranged to return in two weeks, and left for San Felipe, New Mexico.

It occurred to him, of course, that Carhart was trying him out. Hamil's report on his handling of this might be a factor in something big for him, but even without that he would have done his best to put the thing through. Ten years in New York hadn't made him sentimental, and he was quite accustomed to finish everything he began—and a little bit more.

All went well at first. There was no enthusiasm, but each one of the seventeen ranchers concerned knew Samuel's business, knew what he had behind him, and that they had as little chance of holding out as flies on a window-pane. Some of them were resigned—some of them cared like the devil, but they'd talked it over, argued it with lawyers and couldn't see any possible loophole. Five of the ranches had oil, the other twelve were part of the chance, but quite as necessary to Hamil's purpose, in any event.

Samuel soon saw that the real leader was an early settler named McIntyre, a man of perhaps fifty, gray-haired, clean-shaven, bronzed by forty New Mexico summers, and with those clear, steady eyes that Texas and New Mexico weather are apt to give. His ranch had not as yet shown oil, but it was in the pool, and if any man hated to lose his land McIntyre did. Every one had rather looked to him at first to avert the big calamity, and he had hunted all over the territory for the legal means with which to do it, but he had failed, and he knew it. He avoided Samuel assiduously, but Samuel was sure that when the day came for the signatures he would appear.

It came—a baking May day, with hot waves rising off the parched land as far as eyes could see, and as Samuel sat stewing in his little improvised office—a few chairs, a bench, and a wooden table—he was glad the thing was almost over. He wanted to get back East the worst way, and join his wife and children for a week at the seashore.

The meeting was set for four o'clock, and he was rather surprised at three-thirty when the door opened and McIntyre came in. Samuel could not help respecting the man's attitude, and feeling a bit sorry for him. McIntyre seemed closely related to the prairies, and Samuel had the little flicker of envy that city people feel toward men who live in the open.

"Afternoon," said McIntyre, standing in the open doorway, with his feet apart and his hands on his hips.

"Hello, Mr. McIntyre." Samuel rose, but omitted the formality of offering his hand. He imagined the rancher cordially loathed him, and he hardly blamed him. McIntyre came in and sat down leisurely.

"You got us," he said suddenly.

This didn't seem to require any answer.

"When I heard Carhart was back of this," he continued, "I gave up."

"Mr. Carhart is—" began Samuel, but McIntyre waved him silent.

"Don't talk about the dirty sneak-thief!"

"Mr. McIntyre," said Samuel briskly, "if this half-hour is to be devoted to that sort of talk——"

"Oh, dry up, young man," McIntyre interrupted, "you can't abuse a man who'd do a thing like this."

Samuel made no answer.

"It's simply a dirty filch. There just *are* skunks like him too big to handle."

"You're being paid liberally," offered Samuel.

"Shut up!" roared McIntyre suddenly. "I want the privilege of talking." He walked to the door and looked out across the land, the sunny, steaming pasturage that began almost at his feet and ended with the gray-green of the distant mountains. When he turned around his mouth was trembling.

"Do you fellows love Wall Street?" he said hoarsely, "or wherever you do your dirty scheming—" He paused. "I suppose you do. No critter gets so low that he doesn't sort of love the place he's worked, where he's sweated out the best he's had in him."

Samuel watched him awkwardly. McIntyre wiped his forehead with a huge blue handkerchief, and continued:

"I reckon this rotten old devil had to have another million. I reckon we're just a few of the poor beggars he's blotted out to buy a couple more carriages or something." He waved his hand toward the door. "I built a house out there when I was seventeen, with these two hands. I took a wife there at twenty-one, added two wings, and with four mangy steers I started out. Forty summers I've saw the sun come up over those mountains and drop down red as blood in the evening, before the heat drifted off and the stars came out. I been happy in that house. My boy was born there and he died there, late one spring, in the hottest part of an afternoon like this. Then the wife and I lived there alone like we'd lived before, and sort of tried to have a home, after all, not a real home but nigh it—cause the boy always seemed around close, somehow, and we expected a lot of nights to see him runnin' up the path to supper." His voice was shaking so he could hardly speak and he turned again to the door, his gray eyes contracted.

"That's my land out there," he said, stretching out his arm, "my land, by God— It's all I got in the world—and ever wanted." He dashed his sleeve across his face, and his tone changed as he turned slowly and faced Samuel. "But I suppose it's got to go when they want it—it's got to go."

Samuel had to talk. He felt that in a minute more he would lose his head. So he began, as level-voiced as he could—in the sort of tone he saved for disagreeable duties.

"It's business, Mr. McIntyre," he said; "it's inside the law. Perhaps we couldn't have bought out two or three of you at any price, but most of you did have a price. Progress demands some things——"

Never had he felt so inadequate, and it was with the greatest relief that he heard hoof-beats a few hundred yards away.

But at his words the grief in McIntyre's eyes had changed to fury.

"You and your dirty gang of crooks!" he cried. "Not one of you has got an honest love for anything on God's earth! You're a herd of money-swine!"

Samuel rose and McIntyre took a step toward him.

"You long-winded dude. You got our land—take that for Peter Carhart!"

He swung from the shoulder quick as lightning and down went Samuel in a heap. Dimly he heard steps in the doorway and knew that some one was holding McIntyre, but there was no need. The rancher had sunk down in his chair, and dropped his head in his hands.

Samuel's brain was whirring. He realized that the fourth fist had hit him, and a great flood of emotion cried out that the law that had inexorably ruled his life was in motion again. In a half-daze he got up and strode from the room.

The next ten minutes were perhaps the hardest of his life. People talk of the courage of convictions, but in actual life a man's duty to his family may make a rigid course seem a selfish indulgence of his own righteousness. Samuel thought mostly of his family, yet he never really wavered. That jolt had brought him to.

When he came back in the room there were a lot of worried faces waiting for him, but he didn't waste any time explaining.

"Gentlemen," he said, "Mr. McIntyre has been kind enough to convince me that in this matter you are absolutely right, and the Peter Carhart interests absolutely wrong. As far as I am concerned you can keep your ranches to the rest of your days."

He pushed his way through an astounded gathering, and within a half-hour he had sent two telegrams that staggered the operator into complete unfitness for business; one was to Hamil in San Antonio; one was to Peter Carhart in New York.

Samuel didn't sleep much that night. He knew that for the first time in his business career he had made a dismal, miserable failure. But some instinct in him, stronger than will, deeper than training, had forced him to do what would probably end his ambitions and his happiness. But it was done and it never occurred to him that he could have acted otherwise.

Next morning two telegrams were waiting for him. The first was from Hamil. It contained three words:

"You blamed idiot!"

The second was from New York:

"Deal off come to New York immediately Carhart."

Within a week things had happened. Hamil quarrelled furiously and violently defended his scheme. He was summoned to New York, and spent a bad half-hour on the carpet in Peter Carhart's office. He broke with the Carhart interests in July, and in August Samuel Meredith, at thirty-five years old, was, to all intents, made Carhart's partner. The fourth fist had done its work.

I suppose that there's a caddish streak in every man that runs crosswise across his character and disposition and general outlook. With some men it's secret and we never know it's there until they strike us in the dark one night. But Samuel's showed when it was in action, and the sight of it made people see red. He was rather lucky in that, because every time his little devil came up it met a reception that sent it scurrying down below in a sickly, feeble condition. It was the same devil, the same streak that made him order Gilly's friends off the bed, that made him go inside Marjorie's house.

If you could run your hand along Samuel Meredith's jaw you'd feel a lump. He admits he's never been sure which fist left it there, but he wouldn't lose it for anything. He says there's no cad like an old cad, and that sometimes just before making a decision, it's a great help to stroke his chin. The reporters call it a nervous characteristic, but it's not that. It's so he can feel again the gorgeous clarity, the lightning sanity of those four fists.

THE BEAUTIFUL AND DAMNED

The victor belongs to the spoils.
—Anthony Patch

TO

SHANE LESLIE, GEORGE JEAN NATHAN
AND MAXWELL PERKINS
IN APPRECIATION OF MUCH LITERARY HELP
AND ENCOURAGEMENT

CONTENTS

BOOK ONE

I. Anthony Patch 439

II. Portrait of a Siren 461

III. The Connoisseur of Kisses 495

BOOK TWO

I. The Radiant Hour 540

II. Symposium 589

III. The Broken Lute 646

BOOK THREE

I. A Matter of Civilization 685

II. A Matter of Æsthetics 723

III. No Matter! 760

BOOK ONE

CHAPTER I

Anthony Patch

IN 1913, when Anthony Patch was twenty-five, two years were already gone since irony, the Holy Ghost of this later day, had, theoretically at least, descended upon him. Irony was the final polish of the shoe, the ultimate dab of the clothes-brush, a sort of intellectual "There!"—yet at the brink of this story he has as yet gone no further than the conscious stage. As you first see him he wonders frequently whether he is not without honor and slightly mad, a shameful and obscene thinness glistening on the surface of the world like oil on a clean pond, these occasions being varied, of course, with those in which he thinks himself rather an exceptional young man, thoroughly sophisticated, well adjusted to his environment, and somewhat more significant than any one else he knows.

This was his healthy state and it made him cheerful, pleasant, and very attractive to intelligent men and to all women. In this state he considered that he would one day accomplish some quiet subtle thing that the elect would deem worthy and, passing on, would join the dimmer stars in a nebulous, indeterminate heaven half-way between death and immortality. Until the time came for this effort he would be Anthony Patch—not a portrait of a man but a distinct and dynamic personality, opinionated, contemptuous, functioning from within outward—a man who was aware that there could be no honor and yet had honor, who knew the sophistry of courage and yet was brave.

A WORTHY MAN AND HIS GIFTED SON

Anthony drew as much consciousness of social security from being the grandson of Adam J. Patch as he would have had from tracing his line over the sea to the crusaders. This is inevitable; Virginians and Bostonians to the contrary notwithstanding, an aristocracy founded sheerly on money postulates wealth in the particular.

Now Adam J. Patch, more familiarly known as "Cross Patch," left his father's farm in Tarrytown early in sixty-one to join a New York cavalry regiment. He came home from the war a major, charged into Wall Street, and amid much fuss, fume, applause, and ill will he gathered to himself some seventy-five million dollars.

This occupied his energies until he was fifty-seven years old. It was then that he determined, after a severe attack of sclerosis, to consecrate the remainder of his life to the moral regeneration of the world. He became a reformer among reformers. Emulating the magnificent efforts of Anthony Comstock, after whom his grandson was named, he levelled a varied assortment of uppercuts and body-blows at liquor, literature, vice, art, patent medicines, and Sunday theatres. His mind, under the influence of that insidious mildew which eventually forms on all but the few, gave itself up furiously to every indignation of the age. From an armchair in the office of his Tarrytown estate he directed against the enormous hypothetical enemy, unrighteousness, a campaign which went on through fifteen years, during which he displayed himself a rabid monomaniac, an unqualified nuisance, and an intolerable bore. The year in which this story opens found him wearying; his campaign had grown desultory; 1861 was creeping up slowly on 1895; his thoughts ran a great deal on the Civil War, somewhat on his dead wife and son, almost infinitesimally on his grandson Anthony.

Early in his career Adam Patch had married an anæmic lady of thirty, Alicia Withers, who brought him one hundred thousand dollars and an impeccable entré into the banking circles of New York. Immediately and rather spunkily she had borne him a son and, as if completely devitalized by the magnificence of this performance, she had thenceforth effaced herself within the shadowy dimensions of the nursery. The boy, Adam Ulysses Patch, became an inveterate joiner of clubs, connoisseur of good form, and driver of tandems—at the astonishing age of twenty-six he began his memoirs under the title "New York Society as I Have Seen It." On the rumor of its conception this work was eagerly bid for among publishers, but as it proved after his death to be immoderately verbose and overpoweringly dull, it never obtained even a private printing.

This Fifth Avenue Chesterfield married at twenty-two. His wife was Henrietta Lebrune, the Boston "Society Contralto," and the single child of the union was, at the request of his grandfather, christened Anthony Comstock Patch. When he went to Harvard, the Comstock dropped out of his name to a nether hell of oblivion and was never heard of thereafter.

Young Anthony had one picture of his father and mother together—so often had it faced his eyes in childhood that it had acquired the impersonality of furniture, but every one who came into his bedroom regarded it with interest. It showed a dandy of the nineties, spare and handsome, standing beside a tall dark lady with a muff and the suggestion of a bustle. Between them was a little boy with long brown curls, dressed in a velvet Lord Fauntleroy suit. This was Anthony at five, the year of his mother's death.

His memories of the Boston Society Contralto were nebulous and musical. She was a lady who sang, sang, sang, in the music-room of their house on Washington Square—sometimes with guests scattered all about her, the men with their arms folded, balanced breathlessly on the edges of sofas, the women with their hands in their laps, occasionally making little whispers to the men and always clapping very briskly and uttering cooing cries after each song—and often she sang to Anthony alone, in Italian or French or in a strange and terrible dialect which she imagined to be the speech of the Southern negro.

His recollections of the gallant Ulysses, the first man in America to roll the lapels of his coat, were much more vivid. After Henrietta Lebrune Patch had "joined another choir," as her widower huskily remarked from time to time, father and son lived up at grampa's in Tarrytown, and Ulysses came daily to Anthony's nursery and expelled pleasant, thick-smelling words for sometimes as much as an hour. He was continually promising Anthony hunting trips and fishing trips and excursions to Atlantic City, "oh, some time soon now"; but none of them ever materialized. One trip they did take; when

Anthony was eleven they went abroad, to England and Switzerland, and there in the best hotel in Lucerne his father died with much sweating and grunting and crying aloud for air. In a panic of despair and terror Anthony was brought back to America, wedded to a vague melancholy that was to stay beside him through the rest of his life.

Past and Person of the Hero

At eleven he had a horror of death. Within six impressionable years his parents had died and his grandmother had faded off almost imperceptibly, until, for the first time since her marriage, her person held for one day an unquestioned supremacy over her own drawing-room. So to Anthony life was a struggle against death, that waited at every corner. It was as a concession to his hypochondriacal imagination that he formed the habit of reading in bed—it soothed him. He read until he was tired and often fell asleep with the lights still on.

His favorite diversion until he was fourteen was his stamp collection; enormous, as nearly exhaustive as a boy's could be—his grandfather considered fatuously that it was teaching him geography. So Anthony kept up a correspondence with a half-dozen "Stamp and Coin" companies and it was rare that the mail failed to bring him new stamp-books or packages of glittering approval sheets—there was a mysterious fascination in transferring his acquisitions interminably from one book to another. His stamps were his greatest happiness and he bestowed impatient frowns on any one who interrupted him at play with them; they devoured his allowance every month, and he lay awake at night musing untiringly on their variety and many-colored splendor.

At sixteen he had lived almost entirely within himself, an inarticulate boy, thoroughly un-American, and politely bewildered by his contemporaries. The two preceding years had been spent in Europe with a private tutor, who persuaded him that Harvard was the thing; it would "open doors," it would be a tremendous tonic, it would give him innumerable self-sacrificing and devoted friends. So he went to Harvard—there was no other logical thing to be done with him.

Oblivious to the social system, he lived for a while alone

and unsought in a high room in Beck Hall—a slim dark boy of medium height with a shy sensitive mouth. His allowance was more than liberal. He laid the foundations for a library by purchasing from a wandering bibliophile first editions of Swinburne, Meredith, and Hardy, and a yellowed illegible autograph letter of Keats's, finding later that he had been amazingly overcharged. He became an exquisite dandy, amassed a rather pathetic collection of silk pajamas, brocaded dressing-gowns, and neckties too flamboyant to wear; in this secret finery he would parade before a mirror in his room or lie stretched in satin along his window-seat looking down on the yard and realizing dimly this clamor, breathless and immediate, in which it seemed he was never to have a part.

Curiously enough he found in senior year that he had acquired a position in his class. He learned that he was looked upon as a rather romantic figure, a scholar, a recluse, a tower of erudition. This amused him but secretly pleased him—he began going out, at first a little and then a great deal. He made the Pudding. He drank—quietly and in the proper tradition. It was said of him that had he not come to college so young he might have "done extremely well." In 1909, when he graduated, he was only twenty years old.

Then abroad again—to Rome this time, where he dallied with architecture and painting in turn, took up the violin, and wrote some ghastly Italian sonnets, supposedly the ruminations of a thirteenth-century monk on the joys of the contemplative life. It became established among his Harvard intimates that he was in Rome, and those of them who were abroad that year looked him up and discovered with him, on many moonlight excursions, much in the city that was older than the Renaissance or indeed than the republic. Maury Noble, from Philadelphia, for instance, remained two months, and together they realized the peculiar charm of Latin women and had a delightful sense of being very young and free in a civilization that was very old and free. Not a few acquaintances of his grandfather's called on him, and had he so desired he might have been *persona grata* with the diplomatic set—indeed, he found that his inclinations tended more and more toward conviviality, but that long adolescent aloofness and consequent shyness still dictated to his conduct.

He returned to America in 1912 because of one of his grandfather's sudden illnesses, and after an excessively tiresome talk with the perpetually convalescent old man he decided to put off until his grandfather's death the idea of living permanently abroad. After a prolonged search he took an apartment on Fifty-second Street and to all appearances settled down.

In 1913 Anthony Patch's adjustment of himself to the universe was in process of consummation. Physically, he had improved since his undergraduate days—he was still too thin but his shoulders had widened and his brunette face had lost the frightened look of his freshman year. He was secretly orderly and in person spick and span—his friends declared that they had never seen his hair rumpled. His nose was too sharp; his mouth was one of those unfortunate mirrors of mood inclined to droop perceptibly in moments of unhappiness, but his blue eyes were charming, whether alert with intelligence or half closed in an expression of melancholy humor.

One of those men devoid of the symmetry of feature essential to the Aryan ideal, he was yet, here and there, considered handsome—moreover, he was very clean, in appearance and in reality, with that especial cleanness borrowed from beauty.

The Reproachless Apartment

Fifth and Sixth Avenues, it seemed to Anthony, were the uprights of a gigantic ladder stretching from Washington Square to Central Park. Coming up-town on top of a bus toward Fifty-second Street invariably gave him the sensation of hoisting himself hand by hand on a series of treacherous rungs, and when the bus jolted to a stop at his own rung he found something akin to relief as he descended the reckless metal steps to the sidewalk.

After that, he had but to walk down Fifty-second Street half a block, pass a stodgy family of brownstone houses—and then in a jiffy he was under the high ceilings of his great front room. This was entirely satisfactory. Here, after all, life began. Here he slept, breakfasted, read, and entertained.

The house itself was of murky material, built in the late

nineties; in response to the steadily growing need of small apartments each floor had been thoroughly remodelled and rented individually. Of the four apartments Anthony's, on the second floor, was the most desirable.

The front room had fine high ceilings and three large windows that loomed down pleasantly upon Fifty-second Street. In its appointments it escaped by a safe margin being of any particular period; it escaped stiffness, stuffiness, bareness, and decadence. It smelt neither of smoke nor of incense—it was tall and faintly blue. There was a deep lounge of the softest brown leather with somnolence drifting about it like a haze. There was a high screen of Chinese lacquer chiefly concerned with geometrical fishermen and huntsmen in black and gold; this made a corner alcove for a voluminous chair guarded by an orange-colored standing lamp. Deep in the fireplace a quartered shield was burned to a murky black.

Passing through the dining-room, which, as Anthony took only breakfast at home, was merely a magnificent potentiality, and down a comparatively long hall, one came to the heart and core of the apartment—Anthony's bedroom and bath.

Both of them were immense. Under the ceilings of the former even the great canopied bed seemed of only average size. On the floor an exotic rug of crimson velvet was soft as fleece on his bare feet. His bathroom, in contrast to the rather portentous character of his bedroom, was gay, bright, extremely habitable and even faintly facetious. Framed around the walls were photographs of four celebrated thespian beauties of the day: Julia Sanderson as "The Sunshine Girl," Ina Claire as "The Quaker Girl," Billie Burke as "The Mind-the-Paint Girl," and Hazel Dawn as "The Pink Lady." Between Billie Burke and Hazel Dawn hung a print representing a great stretch of snow presided over by a cold and formidable sun—this, claimed Anthony, symbolized the cold shower.

The bathtub, equipped with an ingenious book-holder, was low and large. Beside it a wall wardrobe bulged with sufficient linen for three men and with a generation of neckties. There was no skimpy glorified towel of a carpet—instead, a rich rug, like the one in his bedroom a miracle of softness, that seemed almost to massage the wet foot emerging from the tub. . . .

All in all a room to conjure with—it was easy to see that

Anthony dressed there, arranged his immaculate hair there, in fact did everything but sleep and eat there. It was his pride, this bathroom. He felt that if he had a love he would have hung her picture just facing the tub so that, lost in the soothing steamings of the hot water, he might lie and look up at her and muse warmly and sensuously on her beauty.

Nor Does He Spin

The apartment was kept clean by an English servant with the singularly, almost theatrically, appropriate name of Bounds, whose technic was marred only by the fact that he wore a soft collar. Had he been entirely Anthony's Bounds this defect would have been summarily remedied, but he was also the Bounds of two other gentlemen in the neighborhood. From eight until eleven in the morning he was entirely Anthony's. He arrived with the mail and cooked breakfast. At nine-thirty he pulled the edge of Anthony's blanket and spoke a few terse words—Anthony never remembered clearly what they were and rather suspected they were deprecative; then he served breakfast on a card-table in the front room, made the bed and, after asking with some hostility if there was anything else, withdrew.

In the mornings, at least once a week, Anthony went to see his broker. His income was slightly under seven thousand a year, the interest on money inherited from his mother. His grandfather, who had never allowed his own son to graduate from a very liberal allowance, judged that this sum was sufficient for young Anthony's needs. Every Christmas he sent him a five-hundred-dollar bond, which Anthony usually sold, if possible, as he was always a little, not very, hard up.

The visits to his broker varied from semi-social chats to discussions of the safety of eight per cent investments, and Anthony always enjoyed them. The big trust company building seemed to link him definitely to the great fortunes whose solidarity he respected and to assure him that he was adequately chaperoned by the hierarchy of finance. From these hurried men he derived the same sense of safety that he had in contemplating his grandfather's money—even more, for the latter appeared, vaguely, a demand loan made by the world to

Adam Patch's own moral righteousness, while this money down-town seemed rather to have been grasped and held by sheer indomitable strengths and tremendous feats of will; in addition, it seemed more definitely and explicitly—money.

Closely as Anthony trod on the heels of his income, he considered it to be enough. Some golden day, of course, he would have many millions; meanwhile he possessed a *raison d'être* in the theoretical creation of essays on the popes of the Renaissance. This flashes back to the conversation with his grandfather immediately upon his return from Rome.

He had hoped to find his grandfather dead, but had learned by telephoning from the pier that Adam Patch was comparatively well again—the next day he had concealed his disappointment and gone out to Tarrytown. Five miles from the station his taxicab entered an elaborately groomed drive that threaded a veritable maze of walls and wire fences guarding the estate—this, said the public, was because it was definitely known that if the Socialists had their way, one of the first men they'd assassinate would be old Cross Patch.

Anthony was late and the venerable philanthropist was awaiting him in a glass-walled sun-parlor, where he was glancing through the morning papers for the second time. His secretary, Edward Shuttleworth—who before his regeneration had been gambler, saloon-keeper, and general reprobate—ushered Anthony into the room, exhibiting his redeemer and benefactor as though he were displaying a treasure of immense value.

They shook hands gravely. "I'm awfully glad to hear you're better," Anthony said.

The senior Patch, with an air of having seen his grandson only last week, pulled out his watch.

"Train late?" he asked mildly.

It had irritated him to wait for Anthony. He was under the delusion not only that in his youth he had handled his practical affairs with the utmost scrupulousness, even to keeping every engagement on the dot, but also that this was the direct and primary cause of his success.

"It's been late a good deal this month," he remarked with a shade of meek accusation in his voice—and then after a long sigh, "Sit down."

Anthony surveyed his grandfather with that tacit amazement which always attended the sight. That this feeble, unintelligent old man was possessed of such power that, yellow journals to the contrary, the men in the republic whose souls he could not have bought directly or indirectly would scarcely have populated White Plains, seemed as impossible to believe as that he had once been a pink-and-white baby.

The span of his seventy-five years had acted as a magic bellows—the first quarter-century had blown him full with life, and the last had sucked it all back. It had sucked in the cheeks and the chest and the girth of arm and leg. It had tyrannously demanded his teeth, one by one, suspended his small eyes in dark-bluish sacks, tweeked out his hairs, changed him from gray to white in some places, from pink to yellow in others—callously transposing his colors like a child trying over a paint-box. Then through his body and his soul it had attacked his brain. It had sent him night-sweats and tears and unfounded dreads. It had split his intense normality into credulity and suspicion. Out of the coarse material of his enthusiasm it had cut dozens of meek but petulant obsessions; his energy was shrunk to the bad temper of a spoiled child, and for his will to power was substituted a fatuous puerile desire for a land of harps and canticles on earth.

The amenities having been gingerly touched upon, Anthony felt that he was expected to outline his intentions—and simultaneously a glimmer in the old man's eye warned him against broaching, for the present, his desire to live abroad. He wished that Shuttleworth would have tact enough to leave the room—he detested Shuttleworth—but the secretary had settled blandly in a rocker and was dividing between the two Patches the glances of his faded eyes.

"Now that you're here you ought to *do* something," said his grandfather softly, "accomplish something."

Anthony waited for him to speak of "leaving something done when you pass on." Then he made a suggestion:

"I thought—it seemed to me that perhaps I'm best qualified to write——"

Adam Patch winced, visualizing a family poet with long hair and three mistresses.

"—history," finished Anthony.

"History? History of what? The Civil War? The Revolution?"

"Why—no, sir. A history of the Middle Ages." Simultaneously an idea was born for a history of the Renaissance popes, written from some novel angle. Still, he was glad he had said "Middle Ages."

"Middle Ages? Why not your own country? Something you know about?"

"Well, you see I've lived so much abroad——"

"Why you should write about the Middle Ages, I don't know. Dark Ages, we used to call 'em. Nobody knows what happened, and nobody cares, except that they're over now." He continued for some minutes on the uselessness of such information, touching, naturally, on the Spanish Inquisition and the "corruption of the monasteries." Then:

"Do you think you'll be able to do any work in New York—or do you really intend to work at all?" This last with soft, almost imperceptible, cynicism.

"Why, yes, I do, sir."

"When'll you be done?"

"Well, there'll be an outline, you see—and a lot of preliminary reading."

"I should think you'd have done enough of that already."

The conversation worked itself jerkily toward a rather abrupt conclusion, when Anthony rose, looked at his watch, and remarked that he had an engagement with his broker that afternoon. He had intended to stay a few days with his grandfather, but he was tired and irritated from a rough crossing, and quite unwilling to stand a subtle and sanctimonious browbeating. He would come out again in a few days, he said.

Nevertheless, it was due to this encounter that work had come into his life as a permanent idea. During the year that had passed since then, he had made several lists of authorities, he had even experimented with chapter titles and the division of his work into periods, but not one line of actual writing existed at present, or seemed likely ever to exist. He did nothing—and contrary to the most accredited copy-book logic, he managed to divert himself with more than average content.

Afternoon

It was October in 1913, midway in a week of pleasant days, with the sunshine loitering in the cross-streets and the atmosphere so languid as to seem weighted with ghostly falling leaves. It was pleasant to sit lazily by the open window finishing a chapter of "Erewhon." It was pleasant to yawn about five, toss the book on a table, and saunter humming along the hall to his bath.

"To . . . you . . . beaut-if-ul lady,"

he was singing as he turned on the tap.

"I raise . . . my . . . eyes;
To . . . you . . . beaut-if-ul la-a-dy
My . . . heart . . . cries——"

He raised his voice to compete with the flood of water pouring into the tub, and as he looked at the picture of Hazel Dawn upon the wall he put an imaginary violin to his shoulder and softly caressed it with a phantom bow. Through his closed lips he made a humming noise, which he vaguely imagined resembled the sound of a violin. After a moment his hands ceased their gyrations and wandered to his shirt, which he began to unfasten. Stripped, and adopting an athletic posture like the tiger-skin man in the advertisement, he regarded himself with some satisfaction in the mirror, breaking off to dabble a tentative foot in the tub. Readjusting a faucet and indulging in a few preliminary grunts, he slid in.

Once accustomed to the temperature of the water he relaxed into a state of drowsy content. When he finished his bath he would dress leisurely and walk down Fifth Avenue to the Ritz, where he had an appointment for dinner with his two most frequent companions, Dick Caramel and Maury Noble. Afterward he and Maury were going to the theatre—Caramel would probably trot home and work on his book, which ought to be finished pretty soon.

Anthony was glad *he* wasn't going to work on *his* book. The notion of sitting down and conjuring up, not only words in which to clothe thoughts but thoughts worthy of being clothed—the whole thing was absurdly beyond his desires.

Emerging from his bath he polished himself with the meticulous attention of a bootblack. Then he wandered into the bedroom, and whistling the while a weird, uncertain melody, strolled here and there buttoning, adjusting, and enjoying the warmth of the thick carpet on his feet.

He lit a cigarette, tossed the match out the open top of the window, then paused in his tracks with the cigarette two inches from his mouth—which fell faintly ajar. His eyes were focussed upon a spot of brilliant color on the roof of a house farther down the alley.

It was a girl in a red negligé, silk surely, drying her hair by the still hot sun of late afternoon. His whistle died upon the stiff air of the room; he walked cautiously another step nearer the window with a sudden impression that she was beautiful. Sitting on the stone parapet beside her was a cushion the same color as her garment and she was leaning both arms upon it as she looked down into the sunny areaway, where Anthony could hear children playing.

He watched her for several minutes. Something was stirred in him, something not accounted for by the warm smell of the afternoon or the triumphant vividness of red. He felt persistently that the girl was beautiful—then of a sudden he understood: it was her distance, not a rare and precious distance of soul but still distance, if only in terrestrial yards. The autumn air was between them, and the roofs and the blurred voices. Yet for a not altogether explained second, posing perversely in time, his emotion had been nearer to adoration than in the deepest kiss he had ever known.

He finished his dressing, found a black bow tie and adjusted it carefully by the three-sided mirror in the bathroom. Then yielding to an impulse he walked quickly into the bedroom and again looked out the window. The woman was standing up now; she had tossed her hair back and he had a full view of her. She was fat, full thirty-five, utterly undistinguished. Making a clicking noise with his mouth he returned to the bathroom and reparted his hair.

"To . . . you . . . beaut-if-ul lady,"

he sang lightly,

"I raise . . . my . . . eyes——"

Then with a last soothing brush that left an iridescent surface of sheer gloss he left his bathroom and his apartment and walked down Fifth Avenue to the Ritz-Carlton.

Three Men

At seven Anthony and his friend Maury Noble are sitting at a corner table on the cool roof. Maury Noble is like nothing so much as a large slender and imposing cat. His eyes are narrow and full of incessant, protracted blinks. His hair is smooth and flat, as though it has been licked by a possible—and, if so, Herculean—mother-cat. During Anthony's time at Harvard he had been considered the most unique figure in his class, the most brilliant, the most original—smart, quiet and among the saved.

This is the man whom Anthony considers his best friend. This is the only man of all his acquaintance whom he admires and, to a bigger extent than he likes to admit to himself, envies.

They are glad to see each other now—their eyes are full of kindness as each feels the full effect of novelty after a short separation. They are drawing a relaxation from each other's presence, a new serenity; Maury Noble behind that fine and absurdly catlike face is all but purring. And Anthony, nervous as a will-o'-the-wisp, restless—he is at rest now.

They are engaged in one of those easy short-speech conversations that only men under thirty or men under great stress indulge in.

ANTHONY: Seven o'clock. Where's the Caramel? (*Impatiently.*) I wish he'd finish that interminable novel. I've spent more time hungry——

MAURY: He's got a new name for it. "The Demon Lover"—not bad, eh?

ANTHONY: (*Interested*) "The Demon Lover"? Oh "woman wailing"—No—not a bit bad! Not bad at all—d'you think?

MAURY: Rather good. What time did you say?

ANTHONY: Seven.

MAURY: (*His eyes narrowing—not unpleasantly, but to express a faint disapproval*) Drove me crazy the other day.

ANTHONY: How?

MAURY: That habit of taking notes.

ANTHONY: Me, too. Seems I'd said something night before that he considered material but he'd forgotten it—so he had at me. He'd say "Can't you try to concentrate?" And I'd say "You bore me to tears. How do I remember?"

(MAURY *laughs noiselessly, by a sort of bland and appreciative widening of his features.*)

MAURY: Dick doesn't necessarily see more than any one else. He merely can put down a larger proportion of what he sees.

ANTHONY: That rather impressive talent——

MAURY: Oh, yes. Impressive!

ANTHONY: And energy—ambitious, well-directed energy. He's so entertaining—he's so tremendously stimulating and exciting. Often there's something breathless in being with him.

MAURY: Oh, yes.

(*Silence, and then:*)

ANTHONY: (*With his thin, somewhat uncertain face at its most convinced*) But not indomitable energy. Some day, bit by bit, it'll blow away, and his rather impressive talent with it, and leave only a wisp of a man, fretful and egotistic and garrulous.

MAURY: (*With laughter*) Here we sit vowing to each other that little Dick sees less deeply into things than we do. And I'll bet he feels a measure of superiority on his side—creative mind over merely critical mind and all that.

ANTHONY: Oh, yes. But he's wrong. He's inclined to fall for a million silly enthusiasms. If it wasn't that he's absorbed in realism and therefore has to adopt the garments of the cynic he'd be—he'd be credulous as a college religious leader. He's an idealist. Oh, yes. He thinks he's not, because he's rejected Christianity. Remember him in college? Just swallow every writer whole, one after another, ideas, technic, and characters, Chesterton, Shaw, Wells, each one as easily as the last.

MAURY: (*Still considering his own last observation*) I remember.

ANTHONY: It's true. Natural born fetich-worshipper. Take art——

MAURY: Let's order. He'll be——

ANTHONY: Sure. Let's order. I told him——

MAURY: Here he comes. Look—he's going to bump that waiter. (*He lifts his finger as a signal—lifts it as though it were a soft and friendly claw.*) Here y'are, Caramel.

A NEW VOICE: (*Fiercely*) Hello, Maury. Hello, Anthony Comstock Patch. How is old Adam's grandson? Débutantes still after you, eh?

In person RICHARD CARAMEL *is short and fair—he is to be bald at thirty-five. He has yellowish eyes—one of them startlingly clear, the other opaque as a muddy pool—and a bulging brow like a funny-paper baby. He bulges in other places—his paunch bulges, prophetically, his words have an air of bulging from his mouth, even his dinner-coat pockets bulge, as though from contamination, with a dog-eared collection of time-tables, programmes, and miscellaneous scraps—on these he takes his notes with great screwings up of his unmatched yellow eyes and motions of silence with his disengaged left hand.*

When he reaches the table he shakes hands with ANTHONY *and* MAURY. *He is one of those men who invariably shake hands, even with people whom they have seen an hour before.*

ANTHONY: Hello, Caramel. Glad you're here. We needed a comic relief.

MAURY: You're late. Been racing the postman down the block? We've been clawing over your character.

DICK: (*Fixing* ANTHONY *eagerly with the bright eye*) What'd you say? Tell me and I'll write it down. Cut three thousand words out of Part One this afternoon.

MAURY: Noble æsthete. And I poured alcohol into my stomach.

DICK: I don't doubt it. I bet you two have been sitting here for an hour talking about liquor.

ANTHONY: We never pass out, my beardless boy.

MAURY: We never go home with ladies we meet when we're lit.

ANTHONY: All in all our parties are characterized by a certain haughty distinction.

DICK: The particularly silly sort who boast about being "tanks"! Trouble is you're both in the eighteenth century. School of the Old English Squire. Drink quietly until you roll under the table. Never have a good time. Oh, no, that isn't done at all.

ANTHONY: This from Chapter Six, I'll bet.

DICK: Going to the theatre?

MAURY: Yes. We intend to spend the evening doing some deep thinking over of life's problems. The thing is tersely called "The Woman." I presume that she will "pay."

ANTHONY: My God! Is that what it is? Let's go to the Follies again.

MAURY: I'm tired of it. I've seen it three times. (*To* DICK.) The first time, we went out after Act One and found a most amazing bar. When we came back we entered the wrong theatre.

ANTHONY: Had a protracted dispute with a scared young couple we thought were in our seats.

DICK: (*As though talking to himself*) I think—that when I've done another novel and a play, and maybe a book of short stories, I'll do a musical comedy.

MAURY: I know—with intellectual lyrics that no one will listen to. And all the critics will groan and grunt about "Dear old Pinafore." And I shall go on shining as a brilliantly meaningless figure in a meaningless world.

DICK: (*Pompously*) Art isn't meaningless.

MAURY: It is in itself. It isn't in that it tries to make life less so.

ANTHONY: In other words, Dick, you're playing before a grand stand peopled with ghosts.

MAURY: Give a good show anyhow.

ANTHONY: (*To* MAURY) On the contrary, I'd feel that it being a meaningless world, why write? The very attempt to give it purpose is purposeless.

DICK: Well, even admitting all that, be a decent pragmatist and grant a poor man the instinct to live. Would you want every one to accept that sophistic rot?

ANTHONY: Yeah, I suppose so.

MAURY: No, sir! I believe that every one in America but a selected thousand should be compelled to accept a very rigid system of morals—Roman Catholicism, for instance. I don't complain of conventional morality. I complain rather of the mediocre heretics who seize upon the findings of sophistication and adopt the pose of a moral freedom to which they are by no means entitled by their intelligences.

(*Here the soup arrives and what* MAURY *might have gone on to say is lost for all time.*)

NIGHT

Afterward they visited a ticket speculator and, at a price, obtained seats for a new musical comedy called "High Jinks." In the foyer of the theatre they waited a few moments to see the first-night crowd come in. There were opera-cloaks stitched of myriad, many-colored silks and furs; there were jewels dripping from arms and throats and ear-tips of white and rose; there were innumerable broad shimmers down the middles of innumerable silk hats; there were shoes of gold and bronze and red and shining black; there were the high-piled, tight-packed coiffures of many women and the slick, watered hair of well-kept men—most of all there was the ebbing, flowing, chattering, chuckling, foaming, slow-rolling wave effect of this cheerful sea of people as to-night it poured its glittering torrent into the artificial lake of laughter. . . .

After the play they parted—Maury was going to a dance at Sherry's, Anthony homeward and to bed.

He found his way slowly over the jostled evening mass of Times Square, which the chariot-race and its thousand satellites made rarely beautiful and bright and intimate with carnival. Faces swirled about him, a kaleidoscope of girls, ugly, ugly as sin—too fat, too lean, yet floating upon this autumn air as upon their own warm and passionate breaths poured out into the night. Here, for all their vulgarity, he thought, they were faintly and subtly mysterious. He inhaled carefully, swallowing into his lungs perfume and the not unpleasant scent of many cigarettes. He caught the glance of a dark young beauty sitting alone in a closed taxicab. Her eyes in the half-light suggested night and violets, and for a moment he stirred again to that half-forgotten remoteness of the afternoon.

Two young Jewish men passed him, talking in loud voices and craning their necks here and there in fatuous supercilious glances. They were dressed in suits of the exaggerated tightness then semi-fashionable; their turnover collars were notched at the Adam's apple; they wore gray spats and carried gray gloves on their cane handles.

Passed a bewildered old lady borne along like a basket of eggs between two men who exclaimed to her of the wonders of Times Square—explained them so quickly that the old lady, trying to be impartially interested, waved her head here and there like a piece of wind-worried old orange-peel. Anthony heard a snatch of their conversation:

"There's the Astor, mama!"

"Look! See the chariot-race sign——"

"There's where we were to-day. No, *there!*"

"Good gracious! . . ."

"You should worry and grow thin like a dime." He recognized the current witticism of the year as it issued stridently from one of the pairs at his elbow.

"And I says to him, I says——"

The soft rush of taxis by him, and laughter, laughter hoarse as a crow's, incessant and loud, with the rumble of the subways underneath—and over all, the revolutions of light, the growings and recedings of light—light dividing like pearls—forming and reforming in glittering bars and circles and monstrous grotesque figures cut amazingly on the sky.

He turned thankfully down the hush that blew like a dark wind out of a cross-street, passed a bakery-restaurant in whose windows a dozen roast chickens turned over and over on an automatic spit. From the door came a smell that was hot, doughy, and pink. A drug-store next, exhaling medicines, spilt soda-water and a pleasant undertone from the cosmetic counter; then a Chinese laundry, still open, steamy and stifling, smelling folded and vaguely yellow. All these depressed him; reaching Sixth Avenue he stopped at a corner cigar-store and emerged feeling better—the cigar-store was cheerful, humanity in a navy-blue mist, buying a luxury. . . .

Once in his apartment he smoked a last cigarette, sitting in the dark by his open front window. For the first time in over a year he found himself thoroughly enjoying New York.

There was a rare pungency in it certainly, a quality almost Southern. A lonesome town, though. He who had grown up alone had lately learned to avoid solitude. During the past several months he had been careful, when he had no engagement for the evening, to hurry to one of his clubs and find some one. Oh, there was a loneliness here——

His cigarette, its smoke bordering the thin folds of curtain with rims of faint white spray, glowed on until the clock in St. Anne's down the street struck one with a querulous fashionable beauty. The elevated, half a quiet block away, sounded a rumble of drums—and should he lean from his window he would see the train, like an angry eagle, breasting the dark curve at the corner. He was reminded of a fantastic romance he had lately read in which cities had been bombed from aerial trains, and for a moment he fancied that Washington Square had declared war on Central Park and that this was a north-bound menace loaded with battle and sudden death. But as it passed the illusion faded; it diminished to the faintest of drums—then to a far-away droning eagle.

There were the bells and the continued low blur of auto-horns from Fifth Avenue, but his own street was silent and he was safe in here from all the threat of life, for there was his door and the long hall and his guardian bedroom—safe, safe! The arc-light shining into his window seemed for this hour like the moon, only brighter and more beautiful than the moon.

A Flash-Back in Paradise

Beauty, who was born anew every hundred years, sat in a sort of outdoor waiting-room through which blew gusts of white wind and occasionally a breathless hurried star. The stars winked at her intimately as they went by and the winds made a soft incessant flurry in her hair. She was incomprehensible, for, in her, soul and spirit were one—the beauty of her body was the essence of her soul. She was that unity sought for by philosophers through many centuries. In this outdoor waiting-room of winds and stars she had been sitting for a hundred years, at peace in the contemplation of herself.

It became known to her, at length, that she was to be born again. Sighing, she began a long conversation with a voice that was in the white wind, a conversation that took many hours and of which I can give only a fragment here.

BEAUTY: (*Her lips scarcely stirring, her eyes turned, as always, inward upon herself*) Whither shall I journey now?

THE VOICE: To a new country—a land you have never seen before.

BEAUTY: (*Petulantly*) I loathe breaking into these new civilizations. How long a stay this time?

THE VOICE: Fifteen years.

BEAUTY: And what's the name of the place?

THE VOICE: It is the most opulent, most gorgeous land on earth—a land whose wisest are but little wiser than its dullest; a land where the rulers have minds like little children and the law-givers believe in Santa Claus; where ugly women control strong men——

BEAUTY: (*In astonishment*) What?

THE VOICE: (*Very much depressed*) Yes, it is truly a melancholy spectacle. Women with receding chins and shapeless noses go about in broad daylight saying "Do this!" and "Do that!" and all the men, even those of great wealth, obey implicitly their women to whom they refer sonorously either as "Mrs. So-and-so" or as "the wife."

BEAUTY: But this can't be true! I can understand, of course, their obedience to women of charm—but to fat women? to bony women? to women with scrawny cheeks?

THE VOICE: Even so.

BEAUTY: What of me? What chance shall I have?

THE VOICE: It will be "harder going," if I may borrow a phrase.

BEAUTY: (*After a dissatisfied pause*) Why not the old lands, the land of grapes and soft-tongued men or the land of ships and seas?

THE VOICE: It's expected that they'll be very busy shortly.

BEAUTY: Oh!

THE VOICE: Your life on earth will be, as always, the interval between two significant glances in a mundane mirror.

BEAUTY: What will I be? Tell me?

THE VOICE: At first it was thought that you would go this time as an actress in the motion-pictures but, after all, it's not advisable. You will be disguised during your fifteen years as what is called a "susciety gurl."

BEAUTY: What's that?

(*There is a new sound in the wind which must for our purposes be interpreted as* THE VOICE *scratching its head.*)

THE VOICE: (*At length*) It's a sort of bogus aristocrat.

BEAUTY: Bogus? What is bogus?

THE VOICE: That, too, you will discover in this land. You will find much that is bogus. Also, you will do much that is bogus.

BEAUTY: (*Placidly*) It all sounds so vulgar.

THE VOICE: Not half as vulgar as it is. You will be known during your fifteen years as a ragtime kid, a flapper, a jazz-baby, and a baby vamp. You will dance new dances neither more nor less gracefully than you danced the old ones.

BEAUTY: (*In a whisper*) Will I be paid?

THE VOICE: Yes, as usual—in love.

BEAUTY: (*With a faint laugh which disturbs only momentarily the immobility of her lips*) And will I like being called a jazz-baby?

THE VOICE: (*Soberly*) You will love it. . . .

(*The dialogue ends here, with* BEAUTY *still sitting quietly, the stars pausing in an ecstasy of appreciation, the wind, white and gusty, blowing through her hair.*

All this took place seven years before ANTHONY *sat by the front windows of his apartment and listened to the chimes of St. Anne's.*)

CHAPTER II

Portrait of a Siren

CRISPNESS folded down upon New York a month later, bringing November and the three big football games and a great fluttering of furs along Fifth Avenue. It brought, also, a sense of tension to the city, and suppressed excitement. Every morning now there were invitations in Anthony's mail. Three dozen virtuous females of the first layer were proclaiming their fitness, if not their specific willingness, to bear children unto three dozen millionaires. Five dozen virtuous females of the second layer were proclaiming not only this fitness, but in addition a tremendous undaunted ambition toward the first three dozen young men, who were of course invited to each of the ninety-six parties—as were the young lady's group of family friends, acquaintances, college boys, and eager young outsiders. To continue, there was a third layer from the skirts of the city, from Newark and the Jersey suburbs up to bitter Connecticut and the ineligible sections of Long Island—and doubtless contiguous layers down to the city's shoes: Jewesses were coming out into a society of Jewish men and women, from Riverside to the Bronx, and looking forward to a rising young broker or jeweller and a kosher wedding; Irish girls were casting their eyes, with license at last to do so, upon a society of young Tammany politicians, pious undertakers, and grown-up choirboys.

And, naturally, the city caught the contagious air of en[illegible] the working girls, poor ugly souls, wrapping soap in t[illegible]tories and showing finery in the big stores, dream[illegible] that perhaps in the spectacular excitement of this wi[illegible]r they might obtain for themselves the coveted male—as [illegible] a muddled carnival crowd an inefficient pickpocket [illegible] consider his chances increased. And the chimneys [illegible]menced to smoke and the subway's foulness was fre[illegible]d. And the ac[illegible] came out in new plays [illegible]ublishers came out [illegible] came out with new dances. And the [illegible] came out with new schedules containing new mistakes instead of the old ones that the commuters had grown used to. . . .

The City was coming out!

Anthony, walking along Forty-second Street one afternoon under a steel-gray sky, ran unexpectedly into Richard Caramel emerging from the Manhattan Hotel barber-shop. It was a cold day, the first definitely cold day, and Caramel had on one of those knee-length, sheep-lined coats long worn by the working men of the Middle West, that were just coming into fashionable approval. His soft hat was of a discreet dark brown, and from under it his clear eye flamed like a topaz. He stopped Anthony enthusiastically, slapping him on the arms more from a desire to keep himself warm than from playfulness, and, after his inevitable hand-shake, exploded into sound.

"Cold as the devil— Good Lord, I've been working like the deuce all day till my room got so cold I thought I'd get pneumonia. Darn landlady economizing on coal came up when I yelled over the stairs for her for half an hour. Began explaining why and all. God! First she drove me crazy, then I began to think she was sort of a character, and took notes while she talked—so she couldn't see me, you know, just as though I were writing casually——"

He had seized Anthony's arm and was walking him briskly up Madison Avenue.

"Where to?"

"Nowhere in particular."

"Well, then what's the use?" demanded Anthony.

They stopped and stared at each other, and Anthony wondered if the cold made his own face as repellent as Dick Caramel's, whose nose was crimson, whose bulging brow was blue, whose yellow unmatched eyes were red and watery at the rims. After a moment they began walking again.

"Done some good work on my novel." Dick was looking and talking emphatically at the sidewalk. "But I have to get out once in a while." He glanced at Anthony apologetically, as though craving encouragement. "I have to talk. I guess very few people ever really *think*, I mean sit down and ponder and have ideas in sequence. I do my thinking in writing or conversation. You've got to have a start, sort of—something to defend or contradict—don't you think?"

Anthony grunted and withdrew his arm gently.

"I don't mind carrying you, Dick, but with that coat——"

"I mean," continued Richard Caramel gravely, "that on paper your first paragraph contains the idea you're going to damn or enlarge on. In conversation you've got your vis-à-vis's last statement—but when you simply *ponder*, why, your ideas just succeed each other like magic-lantern pictures and each one forces out the last."

They passed Forty-fifth Street and slowed down slightly. Both of them lit cigarettes and blew tremendous clouds of smoke and frosted breath into the air.

"Let's walk up to the Plaza and have an egg-nog," suggested Anthony. "Do you good. Air'll get the rotten nicotine out of your lungs. Come on—I'll let you talk about your book all the way."

"I don't want to if it bores you. I mean you needn't do it as a favor." The words tumbled out in haste, and though he tried to keep his face casual it screwed up uncertainly. Anthony was compelled to protest: "Bore me? I should say not!"

"Got a cousin—" began Dick, but Anthony interrupted by stretching out his arms and breathing forth a low cry of exultation.

"Good weather!" he exclaimed, "isn't it? Makes me feel about ten. I mean it makes me feel as I should have felt when I was ten. Murderous! Oh, God! one minute it's my world, and the next I'm the world's fool. To-day it's my world and everything's easy, easy. Even Nothing is easy!"

"Got a cousin up at the Plaza. Famous girl. We can go up and meet her. She lives there in the winter—has lately anyway—with her mother and father."

"Didn't know you had cousins in New York."

"Her name's Gloria. She's from home—Kansas City. Her mother's a practising Bilphist, and her father's quite dull but a perfect gentleman."

"What are they? Literary material?"

"They try to be. All the old man does is tell me he just met the most wonderful character for a novel. Then he tells me about some idiotic friend of his and [redacted] character for you! Why [redacted] Everybody'd [redacted] he tells me about Japan or Paris, or some other very obvious place, and says: 'Why don't you write a story about that place? That'd be a wonderful setting for a story!' "

"How about the girl?" inquired Anthony casually, "Gloria—Gloria what?"

"Gilbert. Oh, you've heard of her—Gloria Gilbert. Goes to dances at colleges—all that sort of thing."

"I've heard her name."

"Good-looking—in fact damned attractive."

They reached Fiftieth Street and turned over toward the Avenue.

"I don't care for young girls as a rule," said Anthony, frowning.

This was not strictly true. While it seemed to him that the average débutante spent every hour of her day thinking and talking about what the great world had mapped out for her to do during the next hour, any girl who made a living directly on her prettiness interested him enormously.

"Gloria's darn nice—not a brain in her head."

Anthony laughed in a one-syllabled snort.

"By that you mean that she hasn't a line of literary patter."

"No, I don't."

"Dick, you know what passes as brains in a girl for you. Earnest young women who sit with you in a corner and talk earnestly about life. The kind who when they were sixteen argued with grave faces as to whether kissing was right or wrong—and whether it was immoral for freshmen to drink beer."

Richard Caramel was offended. His scowl crinkled like crushed paper.

"No—" he began, but Anthony interrupted ruthlessly.

"Oh, yes; kind who just at present sit in corners and confer on the latest Scandinavian Dante available in English translation."

Dick turned to him, a curious falling in his whole countenance. His question was almost an appeal.

"What's the matter with you and Maury? You talk sometimes as though I were a sort of inferior."

Anthony was confused, but he was also cold and a little uncomfortable, so he took refuge in attack.

"I don't think your brains matter, Dick."

"Of course they matter!" exclaimed Dick angrily. "What do you mean? Why don't they matter?"

"You might know too much for your pen."

"I couldn't possibly."

"I can imagine," insisted Anthony, "a man knowing too much for his talent to express. Like me. Suppose, for instance, I have more wisdom than you, and less talent. It would tend to make me inarticulate. You, on the contrary, have enough water to fill the pail and a big enough pail to hold the water."

"I don't follow you at all," complained Dick in a crestfallen tone. Infinitely dismayed, he seemed to bulge in protest. He was staring intently at Anthony and carroming off a succession of passers-by, who reproached him with fierce, resentful glances.

"I simply mean that a talent like Wells's could carry the intelligence of a Spencer. But an inferior talent can only be graceful when it's carrying inferior ideas. And the more narrowly you can look at a thing the more entertaining you can be about it."

Dick considered, unable to decide the exact degree of criticism intended by Anthony's remarks. But Anthony, with that facility which seemed so frequently to flow from him, continued, his dark eyes gleaming in his thin face, his chin raised, his voice raised, his whole physical being raised:

"Say I am proud and sane and wise—an Athenian among Greeks. Well, I might fail where a lesser man would succeed. He could imitate, he could adorn, he could be enthusiastic, he could be hopefully constructive. But this hypothetical me would be too proud to imitate, too sane to be enthusiastic, too sophisticated to be Utopian, too Grecian to adorn."

"Then you don't think the artist works from his intelligence?"

"No. He goes on improving, if he can, what he imitates in the way of style, and choosing from his own interpretation of the things around him what constitutes material. But after all every writer writes because it's his mode of living. Don't tell me you like this 'Divine function of the Artist' business?"

"I'm not accustomed even to refer to myself as an artist."

"Dick," said Anthony, changing his tone, "I want to beg your pardon."

"Why?"

"For that outburst. I'm honestly sorry. I was talking for effect."

Somewhat mollified, Dick rejoined:

"I've often said you were a Philistine at heart."

It was a crackling dusk when they turned in under the white façade of the Plaza and tasted slowly the foam and yellow thickness of an egg-nog. Anthony looked at his companion. Richard Caramel's nose and brow were slowly approaching a like pigmentation; the red was leaving the one, the blue deserting the other. Glancing in a mirror, Anthony was glad to find that his own skin had not discolored. On the contrary, a faint glow had kindled in his cheeks—he fancied that he had never looked so well.

"Enough for me," said Dick, his tone that of an athlete in training. "I want to go up and see the Gilberts. Won't you come?"

"Why—yes. If you don't dedicate me to the parents and dash off in the corner with Dora."

"Not Dora—Gloria."

A clerk announced them over the phone, and ascending to the tenth floor they followed a winding corridor and knocked at 1088. The door was answered by a middle-aged lady—Mrs. Gilbert herself.

"How do you do?" She spoke in the conventional American lady-lady language. "Well, I'm *aw*fully glad to see you——"

Hasty interjections by Dick, and then:

"Mr. Pats? Well, do come in, and leave your coat there." She pointed to a chair and changed her inflection to a deprecatory laugh full of minute gasps. "This is really lovely—lovely. Why, Richard, you haven't been here for *so* long—no!—no!" The latter monosyllables served half as responses, half as periods, to some vague starts from Dick. "Well, do sit down and tell me what you've been doing."

One crossed and recrossed; one stood and bowed ever so gently; one smiled again and again with helpless stupidity; one wondered if she would ever sit down—at length one slid thankfully into a chair and settled for a pleasant call.

"I suppose it's because you've been busy—as much as anything else," smiled Mrs. Gilbert somewhat ambiguously. The "as much as anything else" she used to balance all her more rickety sentences. She had two other ones: "at least that's the way I look at it" and "pure and simple"—these three, alternated, gave each of her remarks an air of being a general reflection on life, as though she had calculated all causes and, at length, put her finger on the ultimate one.

Richard Caramel's face, Anthony saw, was now quite normal. The brow and cheeks were of a flesh color, the nose politely inconspicuous. He had fixed his aunt with the bright-yellow eye, giving her that acute and exaggerated attention that young males are accustomed to render to all females who are of no further value.

"Are you a writer too, Mr. Pats? . . . Well, perhaps we can all bask in Richard's fame."—Gentle laughter led by Mrs. Gilbert.

"Gloria's out," she said, with an air of laying down an axiom from which she would proceed to derive results. "She's dancing somewhere. Gloria goes, goes, goes. I tell her I don't see how she stands it. She dances all afternoon and all night, until I think she's going to wear herself to a shadow. Her father is very worried about her."

She smiled from one to the other. They both smiled.

She was composed, Anthony perceived, of a succession of semicircles and parabolas, like those figures that gifted folk make on the typewriter: head, arms, bust, hips, thighs, and ankles were in a bewildering tier of roundnesses. Well ordered and clean she was, with hair of an artificially rich gray; her large face sheltered weather-beaten blue eyes and was adorned with just the faintest white mustache.

"I always say," she remarked to Anthony, "that Richard is an ancient soul."

In the tense pause that followed, Anthony considered a pun—something about Dick having been much walked upon.

"We all have souls of different ages," continued Mrs. Gilbert radiantly; "at least that's what I say."

"Perhaps so," agreed Anthony with an air of quickening to a hopeful idea. The voice bubbled on:

"Gloria has very young soul—irresponsible, as much as anything else. She has no sense of responsibility."

"She's sparkling, Aunt Catherine," said Richard pleasantly. "A sense of responsibility would spoil her. She's too pretty."

"Well," confessed Mrs. Gilbert, "all I know is that she goes and goes and goes——"

The number of goings to Gloria's discredit was lost in the rattle of the door-knob as it turned to admit Mr. Gilbert.

He was a short man with a mustache resting like a small white cloud beneath his undistinguished nose. He had reached the stage where his value as a social creature was a black and imponderable negative. His ideas were the popular delusions of twenty years before; his mind steered a wabbly and anæmic course in the wake of the daily newspaper editorials. After graduating from a small but terrifying Western university, he had entered the celluloid business, and as this required only the minute measure of intelligence he brought to it, he did well for several years—in fact until about 1911, when he began exchanging contracts for vague agreements with the moving-picture industry. The moving-picture industry had decided about 1912 to gobble him up, and at this time he was, so to speak, delicately balanced on its tongue. Meanwhile he was supervising manager of the Associated Mid-western Film Materials Company, spending six months of each year in New York and the remainder in Kansas City and St. Louis. He felt credulously that there was a good thing coming to him—and his wife thought so, and his daughter thought so too.

He disapproved of Gloria: she stayed out late, she never ate her meals, she was always in a mix-up—he had irritated her once and she had used toward him words that he had not thought were part of her vocabulary. His wife was easier. After fifteen years of incessant guerilla warfare he had conquered her—it was a war of muddled optimism against organized dulness, and something in the number of "yes's" with which he could poison a conversation had won him the victory.

"Yes-yes-yes-yes," he would say, "yes-yes-yes-yes. Let me

see. That was the summer of—let me see—ninety-one or ninety-two— Yes-yes-yes-yes——"

Fifteen years of yes's had beaten Mrs. Gilbert. Fifteen further years of that incessant unaffirmative affirmative, accompanied by the perpetual flicking of ash-mushrooms from thirty-two thousand cigars, had broken her. To this husband of hers she made the last concession of married life, which is more complete, more irrevocable, than the first—she listened to him. She told herself that the years had brought her tolerance—actually they had slain what measure she had ever possessed of moral courage.

She introduced him to Anthony.

"This is Mr. Pats," she said.

The young man and the old touched flesh; Mr. Gilbert's hand was soft, worn away to the pulpy semblance of a squeezed grapefruit. Then husband and wife exchanged greetings—he told her it had grown colder out; he said he had walked down to a news-stand on Forty-fourth Street for a Kansas City paper. He had intended to ride back in the bus but he had found it too cold, yes, yes, yes, yes, too cold.

Mrs. Gilbert added flavor to his adventure by being impressed with his courage in braving the harsh air.

"Well, you *are* spunky!" she exclaimed admiringly. "You *are* spunky. I wouldn't have gone out for anything."

Mr. Gilbert with true masculine impassivity disregarded the awe he had excited in his wife. He turned to the two young men and triumphantly routed them on the subject of the weather. Richard Caramel was called on to remember the month of November in Kansas. No sooner had the theme been pushed toward him, however, than it was violently fished back to be lingered over, pawed over, elongated, and generally devitalized by its sponsor.

The immemorial thesis that the days somewhere were warm but the nights very pleasant was successfully propounded and they decided the exact distance on an obscure railroad between two points that Dick had inadvertently mentioned. Anthony fixed Mr. Gilbert with a steady stare and went into a trance through which, after a moment, Mrs. Gilbert's smiling voice penetrated:

"It seems as though the cold were damper here—it seems to eat into my bones."

As this remark, adequately yessed, had been on the tip of Mr. Gilbert's tongue, he could not be blamed for rather abruptly changing the subject.

"Where's Gloria?"

"She ought to be here any minute."

"Have you met my daughter, Mr.——?"

"Haven't had the pleasure. I've heard Dick speak of her often."

"She and Richard are cousins."

"Yes?" Anthony smiled with some effort. He was not used to the society of his seniors, and his mouth was stiff from superfluous cheerfulness. It was such a pleasant thought about Gloria and Dick being cousins. He managed within the next minute to throw an agonized glance at his friend.

Richard Caramel was afraid they'd have to toddle off.

Mrs. Gilbert was tremendously sorry.

Mr. Gilbert thought it was too bad.

Mrs. Gilbert had a further idea—something about being glad they'd come, anyhow, even if they'd only seen an old lady 'way too old to flirt with them. Anthony and Dick evidently considered this a sly sally, for they laughed one bar in three-four time.

Would they come again soon?

"Oh, yes."

Gloria would be *aw*fully sorry!

"Good-by——"

"Good-by——"

Smiles!

Smiles!

Bang!

Two disconsolate young men walking down the tenth-floor corridor of the Plaza in the direction of the elevator.

A Lady's Legs

Behind Maury Noble's attractive indolence, his irrelevance and his easy mockery, lay a surprising and relentless maturity of purpose. His intention, as he stated it in college, had been to use three years in travel, three years in utter leisure—and then to become immensely rich as quickly as possible.

His three years of travel were over. He had accomplished the globe with an intensity and curiosity that in any one else would have seemed pedantic, without redeeming spontaneity, almost the self-editing of a human Baedeker; but, in this case, it assumed an air of mysterious purpose and significant design—as though Maury Noble were some predestined anti-Christ, urged by a preordination to go everywhere there was to go along the earth and to see all the billions of humans who bred and wept and slew each other here and there upon it.

Back in America, he was sallying into the search for amusement with the same consistent absorption. He who had never taken more than a few cocktails or a pint of wine at a sitting, taught himself to drink as he would have taught himself Greek—like Greek it would be the gateway to a wealth of new sensations, new psychic states, new reactions in joy or misery.

His habits were a matter for esoteric speculation. He had three rooms in a bachelor apartment on Forty-fourth Street, but he was seldom to be found there. The telephone girl had received the most positive instructions that no one should even have his ear without first giving a name to be passed upon. She had a list of half a dozen people to whom he was never at home, and of the same number to whom he was always at home. Foremost on the latter list were Anthony Patch and Richard Caramel.

Maury's mother lived with her married son in Philadelphia, and there Maury went usually for the week-ends, so one Saturday night when Anthony, prowling the chilly streets in a fit of utter boredom, dropped in at the Molton Arms he was overjoyed to find that Mr. Noble was at home.

His spirits soared faster than the flying elevator. This was so good, so extremely good, to be about to talk to Maury—who would be equally happy at seeing him. They would look at each other with a deep affection just behind their eyes which both would conceal beneath some attenuated raillery. Had it been summer they would have gone out together and indolently sipped two long Tom Collinses, as they wilted their collars and watched the faintly diverting round of some lazy

August cabaret. But it was cold outside, with wind around the edges of the tall buildings and December just up the street, so better far an evening together under the soft lamplight and a drink or two of Bushmill's, or a thimbleful of Maury's Grand Marnier, with the books gleaming like ornaments against the walls, and Maury radiating a divine inertia as he rested, large and catlike, in his favorite chair.

There he was! The room closed about Anthony, warmed him. The glow of that strong persuasive mind, that temperament almost Oriental in its outward impassivity, warmed Anthony's restless soul and brought him a peace that could be likened only to the peace a stupid woman gives. One must understand all—else one must take all for granted. Maury filled the room, tigerlike, godlike. The winds outside were stilled; the brass candlesticks on the mantel glowed like tapers before an altar.

"What keeps you here to-day?" Anthony spread himself over a yielding sofa and made an elbow-rest among the pillows.

"Just been here an hour. Tea dance—and I stayed so late I missed my train to Philadelphia."

"Strange to stay so long," commented Anthony curiously.

"Rather. What'd you do?"

"Geraldine. Little usher at Keith's. I told you about her."

"Oh!"

"Paid me a call about three and stayed till five. Peculiar little soul—she gets me. She's so utterly stupid."

Maury was silent.

"Strange as it may seem," continued Anthony, "so far as I'm concerned, and even so far as I know, Geraldine is a paragon of virtue."

He had known her a month, a girl of nondescript and nomadic habits. Some one had casually passed her on to Anthony, who considered her amusing and rather liked the chaste and fairylike kisses she had given him on the third night of their acquaintance, when they had driven in a taxi through the Park. She had a vague family—a shadowy aunt and uncle who shared with her an apartment in the labyrinthine hundreds. She was company, familiar and faintly intimate and restful. Further than that he did not care to experiment—not from any moral compunction, but from a dread of allowing any entanglement to disturb what he felt was the growing serenity of his life.

"She has two stunts," he informed Maury; "one of them is to get her hair over her eyes some way and then blow it out, and the other is to say 'You cra-a-azy!' when some one makes a remark that's over her head. It fascinates me. I sit there hour after hour, completely intrigued by the maniacal symptoms she finds in my imagination."

Maury stirred in his chair and spoke.

"Remarkable that a person can comprehend so little and yet live in such a complex civilization. A woman like that actually takes the whole universe in the most matter-of-fact way. From the influence of Rousseau to the bearing of the tariff rates on her dinner, the whole phenomenon is utterly strange to her. She's just been carried along from an age of spearheads and plunked down here with the equipment of an archer for going into a pistol duel. You could sweep away the entire crust of history and she'd never know the difference."

"I wish our Richard would write about her."

"Anthony, surely you don't think she's worth writing about."

"As much as anybody," he answered, yawning. "You know I was thinking to-day that I have a great confidence in Dick. So long as he sticks to people and not to ideas, and as long as his inspirations come from life and not from art, and always granting a normal growth, I believe he'll be a big man."

"I should think the appearance of the black note-book would prove that he's going to life."

Anthony raised himself on his elbow and answered eagerly:

"He tries to go to life. So does every author except the very worst, but after all most of them live on predigested food. The incident or character may be from life, but the writer usually interprets it in terms of the last book he read. For instance, suppose he meets a sea-captain and thinks he's an original character. The truth is that he sees the resemblance between the sea-captain and the last sea-captain Dana created, or whoever creates sea-captains, and therefore he knows how to set this sea-captain on paper. Dick, of course, can set down any consciously picturesque, character-like character, but could he accurately transcribe his own sister?"

Then they were off for half an hour on literature.

"A classic," suggested Anthony, "is a successful book that has survived the reaction of the next period or generation. Then it's safe, like a style in architecture or furniture. It's acquired a picturesque dignity to take the place of its fashion. . . ."

After a time the subject temporarily lost its tang. The interest of the two young men was not particularly technical. They were in love with generalities. Anthony had recently discovered Samuel Butler and the brisk aphorisms in the note-book seemed to him the quintessence of criticism. Maury, his whole mind so thoroughly mellowed by the very hardness of his scheme of life, seemed inevitably the wiser of the two, yet in the actual stuff of their intelligences they were not, it seemed, fundamentally different.

They drifted from letters to the curiosities of each other's day.

"Whose tea was it?"

"People named Abercrombie."

"Why'd you stay late? Meet a luscious débutante?"

"Yes."

"Did you really?" Anthony's voice lifted in surprise.

"Not a débutante exactly. Said she came out two winters ago in Kansas City."

"Sort of left-over?"

"No," answered Maury with some amusement, "I think that's the last thing I'd say about her. She seemed—well, somehow the youngest person there."

"Not too young to make you miss a train."

"Young enough. Beautiful child."

Anthony chuckled in his one-syllable snort.

"Oh, Maury, you're in your second childhood. What do you mean by beautiful?"

Maury gazed helplessly into space.

"Well, I can't describe her exactly—except to say that she was beautiful. She was—tremendously alive. She was eating gum-drops."

"What!"

"It was a sort of attenuated vice. She's a nervous kind—said she always ate gum-drops at teas because she had to stand around so long in one place."

"What'd you talk about—Bergson? Bilphism? Whether the one-step is immoral?"

Maury was unruffled; his fur seemed to run all ways.

"As a matter of fact we did talk on Bilphism. Seems her mother's a Bilphist. Mostly, though, we talked about legs."

Anthony rocked in glee.

"My God! Whose legs?"

"Hers. She talked a lot about hers. As though they were a sort of choice bric-à-brac. She aroused a great desire to see them."

"What is she—a dancer?"

"No, I found she was a cousin of Dick's."

Anthony sat upright so suddenly that the pillow he released stood on end like a live thing and dove to the floor.

"Name's Gloria Gilbert?" he cried.

"Yes. Isn't she remarkable?"

"I'm sure I don't know—but for sheer dulness her father——"

"Well," interrupted Maury with implacable conviction, "her family may be as sad as professional mourners but I'm inclined to think that she's a quite authentic and original character. The outer signs of the cut-and-dried Yale prom girl and all that—but different, very emphatically different."

"Go on, go on!" urged Anthony. "Soon as Dick told me she didn't have a brain in her head I knew she must be pretty good."

"Did he say that?"

"Swore to it," said Anthony with another snorting laugh.

"Well, what he means by brains in a woman is——"

"I know," interrupted Anthony eagerly, "he means a smattering of literary misinformation."

"That's it. The kind who believes that the annual moral let-down of the country is a very good thing or the kind who believes it's a very ominous thing. Either pince-nez or postures. Well, this girl talked about legs. She talked about skin too—her own skin. Always her own. She told me the sort of tan she'd like to get in the summer and how closely she usually approximated it."

"You sat enraptured by her low alto?"

"By her low alto! No, by tan! I began thinking about tan.

I began to think what color I turned when I made my last exposure about two years ago. I did use to get a pretty good tan. I used to get a sort of bronze, if I remember rightly."

Anthony retired into the cushions, shaken with laughter.

"She's got you going—oh, Maury! Maury the Connecticut life-saver. The human nutmeg. Extra! Heiress elopes with coast-guard because of his luscious pigmentation! Afterward found to be Tasmanian strain in his family!"

Maury sighed; rising he walked to the window and raised the shade.

"Snowing hard."

Anthony, still laughing quietly to himself, made no answer.

"Another winter." Maury's voice from the window was almost a whisper. "We're growing old, Anthony. I'm twenty-seven, by God! Three years to thirty, and then I'm what an undergraduate calls a middle-aged man."

Anthony was silent for a moment.

"You *are* old, Maury," he agreed at length. "The first signs of a very dissolute and wabbly senescence—you have spent the afternoon talking about tan and a lady's legs."

Maury pulled down the shade with a sudden harsh snap.

"Idiot!" he cried, "that from you! Here I sit, young Anthony, as I'll sit for a generation or more and watch such gay souls as you and Dick and Gloria Gilbert go past me, dancing and singing and loving and hating one another and being moved, being eternally moved. And I am moved only by my lack of emotion. I shall sit and the snow will come—oh, for a Caramel to take notes—and another winter and I shall be thirty and you and Dick and Gloria will go on being eternally moved and dancing by me and singing. But after you've all gone I'll be saying things for new Dicks to write down, and listening to the disillusions and cynicisms and emotions of new Anthonys—yes, and talking to new Glorias about the tans of summers yet to come."

The firelight flurried up on the hearth. Maury left the window, stirred the blaze with a poker, and dropped a log upon the andirons. Then he sat back in his chair and the remnants of his voice faded in the new fire that spit red and yellow along the bark.

"After all, Anthony, it's you who are very romantic and

young. It's you who are infinitely more susceptible and afraid of your calm being broken. It's me who tries again and again to be moved—let myself go a thousand times and I'm always me. Nothing—quite—stirs me.

"Yet," he murmured after another long pause, "there was something about that little girl with her absurd tan that was eternally old—like me."

TURBULENCE

Anthony turned over sleepily in his bed, greeting a patch of cold sun on his counterpane, crisscrossed with the shadows of the leaded window. The room was full of morning. The carved chest in the corner, the ancient and inscrutable wardrobe, stood about the room like dark symbols of the obliviousness of matter; only the rug was beckoning and perishable to his perishable feet, and Bounds, horribly inappropriate in his soft collar, was of stuff as fading as the gauze of frozen breath he uttered. He was close to the bed, his hand still lowered where he had been jerking at the upper blanket, his dark-brown eyes fixed imperturbably upon his master.

"Bows!" muttered the drowsy god. "Thachew, Bows?"

"It's I, sir."

Anthony moved his head, forced his eyes wide, and blinked triumphantly.

"Bounds."

"Yes, sir?"

"Can you get off—yeow-ow-oh-oh-oh God!—" Anthony yawned insufferably and the contents of his brain seemed to fall together in a dense hash. He made a fresh start.

"Can you come around about four and serve some tea and sandwiches or something?"

"Yes, sir."

Anthony considered with chilling lack of inspiration.

"Some sandwiches," he repeated helplessly, "oh, some cheese sandwiches and jelly ones and chicken and olive, I guess. Never mind breakfast."

The strain of invention was too much. He shut his eyes wearily, let his head roll to rest inertly, and quickly relaxed what he had regained of muscular control. Out of a crevice of his mind crept the vague but inevitable spectre of the night before—but it proved in this case to be nothing but a seemingly interminable conversation with Richard Caramel, who had called on him at midnight; they had drunk four bottles of beer and munched dry crusts of bread while Anthony listened to a reading of the first part of "The Demon Lover."

—Came a voice now after many hours. Anthony disregarded it, as sleep closed over him, folded down upon him, crept up into the byways of his mind.

Suddenly he was awake, saying: "What?"

"For how many, sir?" It was still Bounds, standing patient and motionless at the foot of the bed—Bounds who divided his manner among three gentlemen.

"How many what?"

"I think, sir, I'd better know how many are coming. I'll have to plan for the sandwiches, sir."

"Two," muttered Anthony huskily; "lady and a gentleman."

Bounds said, "Thank you, sir," and moved away, bearing with him his humiliating reproachful soft collar, reproachful to each of the three gentlemen, who only demanded of him a third.

After a long time Anthony arose and drew an opalescent dressing-gown of brown and blue over his slim pleasant figure. With a last yawn he went into the bathroom, and turning on the dresser light (the bathroom had no outside exposure) he contemplated himself in the mirror with some interest. A wretched apparition, he thought; he usually thought so in the morning—sleep made his face unnaturally pale. He lit a cigarette and glanced through several letters and the morning Tribune.

An hour later, shaven and dressed, he was sitting at his desk looking at a small piece of paper he had taken out of his wallet. It was scrawled with semilegible memoranda: "See Mr. Howland at five. Get hair-cut. See about Rivers' bill. Go book-store."

—And under the last: "Cash in bank, $690 (crossed out), $612 (crossed out), $607."

Finally, down at the bottom and in a hurried scrawl: "Dick and Gloria Gilbert for tea."

This last item brought him obvious satisfaction. His day, usually a jelly-like creature, a shapeless, spineless thing, had attained Mesozoic structure. It was marching along surely, even jauntily, toward a climax, as a play should, as a day should. He dreaded the moment when the backbone of the day should be broken, when he should have met the girl at last, talked to her, and then bowed her laughter out the door, returning only to the melancholy dregs in the teacups and the gathering staleness of the uneaten sandwiches.

There was a growing lack of color in Anthony's days. He felt it constantly and sometimes traced it to a talk he had had with Maury Noble a month before. That anything so ingenuous, so priggish, as a sense of waste should oppress him was absurd, but there was no denying the fact that some unwelcome survival of a fetich had drawn him three weeks before down to the public library, where, by the token of Richard Caramel's card, he had drawn out half a dozen books on the Italian Renaissance. That these books were still piled on his desk in the original order of carriage, that they were daily increasing his liabilities by twelve cents, was no mitigation of their testimony. They were cloth and morocco witnesses to the fact of his defection. Anthony had had several hours of acute and startling panic.

In justification of his manner of living there was first, of course, The Meaninglessness of Life. As aides and ministers, pages and squires, butlers and lackeys to this great Khan there were a thousand books glowing on his shelves, there was his apartment and all the money that was to be his when the old man up the river should choke on his last morality. From a world fraught with the menace of débutantes and the stupidity of many Geraldines he was thankfully delivered—rather should he emulate the feline immobility of Maury and wear proudly the culminative wisdom of the numbered generations.

Over and against these things was something which his brain persistently analyzed and dealt with as a tiresome complex but which, though logically disposed of and bravely trampled under foot, had sent him out through the soft slush of late November to a library which had none of the books he most wanted. It is fair to analyze Anthony as far as he could analyze himself; further than that it is, of course, presumption. He found in himself a growing horror and loneliness. The idea of eating alone frightened him; in preference he dined often with men he detested. Travel, which had once charmed him, seemed, at length, unendurable, a business of color without substance, a phantom chase after his own dream's shadow.

—If I am essentially weak, he thought, I need work to do, work to do. It worried him to think that he was, after all, a facile mediocrity, with neither the poise of Maury nor the enthusiasm of Dick. It seemed a tragedy to want nothing—and yet he wanted something, something. He knew in flashes what it was—some path of hope to lead him toward what he thought was an imminent and ominous old age.

After cocktails and luncheon at the University Club Anthony felt better. He had run into two men from his class at Harvard, and in contrast to the gray heaviness of their conversation his life assumed color. Both of them were married: one spent his coffee time in sketching an extra-nuptial adventure to the bland and appreciative smiles of the other. Both of them, he thought, were Mr. Gilberts in embryo; the number of their "yes's" would have to be quadrupled, their natures crabbed by twenty years—then they would be no more than obsolete and broken machines, pseudo-wise and valueless, nursed to an utter senility by the women they had broken.

Ah, he was more than that, as he paced the long carpet in the lounge after dinner, pausing at the window to look into the harried street. He was Anthony Patch, brilliant, magnetic, the heir of many years and many men. This was his world now—and that last strong irony he craved lay in the offing.

With a stray boyishness he saw himself a power upon the earth; with his grandfather's money he might build his own pedestal and be a Talleyrand, a Lord Verulam. The clarity of his mind, its sophistication, its versatile intelligence, all at their maturity and dominated by some purpose yet to be born would find him work to do. On this minor his dream faded—work to do: he tried to imagine himself in Congress rooting around in the litter of that incredible pigsty with the narrow and porcine brows he saw pictured sometimes in the rotogravure sections of the Sunday newspapers, those glorified proletarians babbling blandly to the nation the ideas of high-school seniors! Little men with copy-book ambitions who by mediocrity had thought to emerge from mediocrity into the lustreless and unromantic heaven of a government by the people—and the best, the dozen shrewd men at the top, egotistic and cynical, were content to lead this choir of white ties and wire collar-buttons in a discordant and amazing hymn, compounded of a vague confusion between wealth as a reward of virtue and wealth as a proof of vice, and continued cheers for God, the Constitution, and the Rocky Mountains!

Lord Verulam! Talleyrand!

Back in his apartment the grayness returned. His cocktails had died, making him sleepy, somewhat befogged and inclined to be surly. Lord Verulam—he? The very thought was bitter. Anthony Patch with no record of achievement, without courage, without strength to be satisfied with truth when it was given him. Oh, he was a pretentious fool, making careers out of cocktails and meanwhile regretting, weakly and secretly, the collapse of an insufficient and wretched idealism. He had garnished his soul in the subtlest taste and now he longed for the old rubbish. He was empty, it seemed, empty as an old bottle——

The buzzer rang at the door. Anthony sprang up and lifted the tube to his ear. It was Richard Caramel's voice, stilted and facetious:

"Announcing Miss Gloria Gilbert."

THE BEAUTIFUL LADY

"How do you do?" he said, smiling and holding the door ajar.

Dick bowed.

"Gloria, this is Anthony."

"Well!" she cried, holding out a little gloved hand.

Under her fur coat her dress was Alice-blue, with white lace crinkled stiffly about her throat.

"Let me take your things."

Anthony stretched out his arms and the brown mass of fur tumbled into them.

"Thanks."

"What do you think of her, Anthony?" Richard Caramel demanded barbarously. "Isn't she beautiful?"

"Well!" cried the girl defiantly—withal unmoved.

She was dazzling—alight; it was agony to comprehend her beauty in a glance. Her hair, full of a heavenly glamour, was gay against the winter color of the room.

Anthony moved about, magician-like, turning the mushroom lamp into an orange glory. The stirred fire burnished the copper andirons on the hearth——

"I'm a solid block of ice," murmured Gloria casually, glancing around with eyes whose irises were of the most delicate and transparent bluish white. "What a slick fire! We found a place where you could stand on an iron-bar grating, sort of, and it blew warm air up at you—but Dick wouldn't wait there with me. I told him to go on alone and let me be happy."

Conventional enough this. She seemed talking for her own pleasure, without effort. Anthony, sitting at one end of the sofa, examined her profile against the foreground of the lamp: the exquisite regularity of nose and upper lip, the chin, faintly decided, balanced beautifully on a rather short neck. On a photograph she must have been completely classical, almost cold—but the glow of her hair and cheeks, at once flushed and fragile, made her the most living person he had ever seen.

". . . Think you've got the best name I've heard," she was saying, still apparently to herself; her glance rested on him a moment and then flitted past him—to the Italian bracket-lamps clinging like luminous yellow turtles at intervals along the walls, to the books row upon row, then to her cousin on the other side. "Anthony Patch. Only you ought to look sort of like a horse, with a long narrow face—and you ought to be in tatters."

"That's all the Patch part, though. How should Anthony look?"

"You look like Anthony," she assured him seriously—he thought she had scarcely seen him—"rather majestic," she continued, "and solemn."

Anthony indulged in a disconcerted smile.

"Only I like alliterative names," she went on, "all except mine. Mine's too flamboyant. I used to know two girls named

Jinks, though, and just think if they'd been named anything except what they were named—Judy Jinks and Jerry Jinks. Cute, what? Don't you think?" Her childish mouth was parted, awaiting a rejoinder.

"Everybody in the next generation," suggested Dick, "will be named Peter or Barbara—because at present all the piquant literary characters are named Peter or Barbara."

Anthony continued the prophecy:

"Of course Gladys and Eleanor, having graced the last generation of heroines and being at present in their social prime, will be passed on to the next generation of shop-girls——"

"Displacing Ella and Stella," interrupted Dick.

"And Pearl and Jewel," Gloria added cordially, "and Earl and Elmer and Minnie."

"And then I'll come along," remarked Dick, "and picking up the obsolete name, Jewel, I'll attach it to some quaint and attractive character and it'll start its career all over again."

Her voice took up the thread of subject and wove along with faintly upturning, half-humorous intonations for sentence ends—as though defying interruption—and intervals of shadowy laughter. Dick had told her that Anthony's man was named Bounds—she thought that was wonderful! Dick had made some sad pun about Bounds doing patchwork, but if there was one thing worse than a pun, she said, it was a person who, as the inevitable come-back to a pun, gave the perpetrator a mock-reproachful look.

"Where are you from?" inquired Anthony. He knew, but beauty had rendered him thoughtless.

"Kansas City, Missouri."

"They put her out the same time they barred cigarettes."

"Did they bar cigarettes? I see the hand of my holy grandfather."

"He's a reformer or something, isn't he?"

"I blush for him."

"So do I," she confessed. "I detest reformers, especially the sort who try to reform me."

"Are there many of those?"

"Dozens. It's 'Oh, Gloria, if you smoke so many cigarettes you'll lose your pretty complexion!' and 'Oh, Gloria, why don't you marry and settle down?' "

Anthony agreed emphatically while he wondered who had had the temerity to speak thus to such a personage.

"And then," she continued, "there are all the subtle reformers who tell you the wild stories they've heard about you and how they've been sticking up for you."

He saw, at length, that her eyes were gray, very level and cool, and when they rested on him he understood what Maury had meant by saying she was very young and very old. She talked always about herself as a very charming child might talk, and her comments on her tastes and distastes were unaffected and spontaneous.

"I must confess," said Anthony gravely, "that even *I*'ve heard one thing about you."

Alert at once, she sat up straight. Those eyes, with the grayness and eternity of a cliff of soft granite, caught his.

"Tell me. I'll believe it. I always believe anything any one tells me about myself—don't you?"

"Invariably!" agreed the two men in unison.

"Well, tell me."

"I'm not sure that I ought to," teased Anthony, smiling unwillingly. She was so obviously interested, in a state of almost laughable self-absorption.

"He means your nickname," said her cousin.

"What name?" inquired Anthony, politely puzzled.

Instantly she was shy—then she laughed, rolled back against the cushions, and turned her eyes up as she spoke:

"Coast-to-Coast Gloria." Her voice was full of laughter, laughter undefined as the varying shadows playing between fire and lamp upon her hair. "O Lord!"

Still Anthony was puzzled.

"What do you mean?"

"*Me*, I mean. That's what some silly boys coined for *me*."

"Don't you see, Anthony," explained Dick, "traveller of nation-wide notoriety and all that. Isn't that what you've heard? She's been called that for years—since she was seventeen."

Anthony's eyes became sad and humorous.

"Who's this female Methuselah you've brought in here, Caramel?"

She disregarded this, possibly rather resented it, for she switched back to the main topic.

"What *have* you heard of me?"

"Something about your physique."

"Oh," she said, coolly disappointed, "that all?"

"Your tan."

"My tan?" She was puzzled. Her hand rose to her throat, rested there an instant as though the fingers were feeling variants of color.

"Do you remember Maury Noble? Man you met about a month ago. You made a great impression."

She thought a moment.

"I remember—but he didn't call me up."

"He was afraid to, I don't doubt."

It was black dark without now and Anthony wondered that his apartment had ever seemed gray—so warm and friendly were the books and pictures on the walls and the good Bounds offering tea from a respectful shadow and the three nice people giving out waves of interest and laughter back and forth across the happy fire.

Dissatisfaction

On Thursday afternoon Gloria and Anthony had tea together in the grill-room at the Plaza. Her fur-trimmed suit was gray—"because with gray you *have* to wear a lot of paint," she explained—and a small toque sat rakishly on her head, allowing yellow ripples of hair to wave out in jaunty glory. In the higher light it seemed to Anthony that her personality was infinitely softer—she seemed so young, scarcely eighteen; her form under the tight sheath, known then as a hobble-skirt, was amazingly supple and slender, and her hands, neither "artistic" nor stubby, were small as a child's hands should be.

As they entered, the orchestra were sounding the preliminary whimpers to a maxixe, a tune full of castanets and facile faintly languorous violin harmonies, appropriate to the crowded winter grill teeming with an excited college crowd, high-spirited at the approach of the holidays. Carefully, Gloria considered several locations, and rather to Anthony's annoyance paraded him circuitously to a table for two at the far side of the room. Reaching it she again considered. Would she sit on the right or on the left? Her beautiful eyes and lips were very grave as she made her choice, and Anthony thought again how naïve was her every gesture; she took all the things of life for hers to choose from and apportion, as though she were continually picking out presents for herself from an inexhaustible counter.

Abstractedly she watched the dancers for a few moments, commenting murmurously as a couple eddied near.

"There's a pretty girl in blue"—and as Anthony looked obediently—"there! No, behind you—there!"

"Yes," he agreed helplessly.

"You didn't see her."

"I'd rather look at you."

"I know, but she was pretty. Except that she had big ankles."

"Was she?—I mean, did she?" he said indifferently.

A girl's salutation came from a couple dancing close to them.

"Hello, Gloria! O Gloria!"

"Hello there."

"Who's that?" he demanded.

"I don't know. Somebody." She caught sight of another face. "Hello, Muriel!" Then to Anthony: "There's Muriel Kane. Now I think she's attractive, 'cept not very."

Anthony chuckled appreciatively.

"Attractive, 'cept not very," he repeated.

She smiled—was interested immediately.

"Why is that funny?" Her tone was pathetically intent.

"It just was."

"Do you want to dance?"

"Do you?"

"Sort of. But let's sit," she decided.

"And talk about you? You love to talk about you, don't you?"

"Yes." Caught in a vanity, she laughed.

"I imagine your autobiography would be a classic."

"Dick says I haven't got one."

"Dick!" he exclaimed. "What does he know about you?"

"Nothing. But he says the biography of every woman begins with the first kiss that counts, and ends when her last child is laid in her arms."

"He's talking from his book."

"He says unloved women have no biographies—they have histories."

Anthony laughed again.

"Surely you don't claim to be unloved!"

"Well, I suppose not."

"Then why haven't you a biography? Haven't you ever had a kiss that counted?" As the words left his lips he drew in his breath sharply as though to suck them back. This *baby*!

"I don't know what you mean 'counts,' " she objected.

"I wish you'd tell me how old you are."

"Twenty-two," she said, meeting his eyes gravely. "How old did you think?"

"About eighteen."

"I'm going to start being that. I don't like being twenty-two. I hate it more than anything in the world."

"Being twenty-two?"

"No. Getting old and everything. Getting married."

"Don't you ever want to marry?"

"I don't want to have responsibility and a lot of children to take care of."

Evidently she did not doubt that on her lips all things were good. He waited rather breathlessly for her next remark, expecting it to follow up her last. She was smiling, without amusement but pleasantly, and after an interval half a dozen words fell into the space between them:

"I wish I had some gum-drops."

"You shall!" He beckoned to a waiter and sent him to the cigar counter.

"D'you mind? I love gum-drops. Everybody kids me about it because I'm always whacking away at one—whenever my daddy's not around."

"Not at all.—Who are all these children?" he asked suddenly. "Do you know them all?"

"Why—no, but they're from—oh, from everywhere, I suppose. Don't you ever come here?"

"Very seldom. I don't care particularly for 'nice girls.' "

Immediately he had her attention. She turned a definite shoulder to the dancers, relaxed in her chair, and demanded:

"What *do* you do with yourself?"

Thanks to a cocktail Anthony welcomed the question. In a mood to talk, he wanted, moreover, to impress this girl whose interest seemed so tantalizingly elusive—she stopped to browse in unexpected pastures, hurried quickly over the in-obviously obvious. He wanted to pose. He wanted to appear suddenly to her in novel and heroic colors. He wanted to stir her from that casualness she showed toward everything except herself.

"I do nothing," he began, realizing simultaneously that his words were to lack the debonair grace he craved for them. "I do nothing, for there's nothing I can do that's worth doing."

"Well?" He had neither surprised her nor even held her, yet she had certainly understood him, if indeed he had said aught worth understanding.

"Don't you approve of lazy men?"

She nodded.

"I suppose so, if they're gracefully lazy. Is that possible for an American?"

"Why not?" he demanded, discomfited.

But her mind had left the subject and wandered up ten floors.

"My daddy's mad at me," she observed dispassionately.

"Why? But I want to know just why it's impossible for an American to be gracefully idle"—his words gathered conviction—"it astonishes me. It—it—I don't understand why people think that every young man ought to go down-town and work ten hours a day for the best twenty years of his life at dull, unimaginative work, certainly not altruistic work."

He broke off. She watched him inscrutably. He waited for her to agree or disagree, but she did neither.

"Don't you ever form judgments on things?" he asked with some exasperation.

She shook her head and her eyes wandered back to the dancers as she answered:

"I don't know. I don't know anything about—what you should do, or what anybody should do."

She confused him and hindered the flow of his ideas. Self-expression had never seemed at once so desirable and so impossible.

"Well," he admitted apologetically, "neither do I, of course, but——"

"I just think of people," she continued, "whether they seem right where they are and fit into the picture. I don't mind if they don't do anything. I don't see why they should; in fact it always astonishes me when anybody does anything."

"You don't want to do anything?"

"I want to sleep."

For a second he was startled, almost as though she had meant this literally.

"Sleep?"

"Sort of. I want to just be lazy and I want some of the people around me to be doing things, because that makes me feel comfortable and safe—and I want some of them to be doing nothing at all, because they can be graceful and companionable for me. But I never want to change people or get excited over them."

"You're a quaint little determinist," laughed Anthony. "It's your world, isn't it?"

"Well—" she said with a quick upward glance, "isn't it? As long as I'm—young."

She had paused slightly before the last word and Anthony suspected that she had started to say "beautiful." It was undeniably what she had intended.

Her eyes brightened and he waited for her to enlarge on the theme. He had drawn her out, at any rate—he bent forward slightly to catch the words.

But "Let's dance!" was all she said.

Admiration

That winter afternoon at the Plaza was the first of a succession of "dates" Anthony made with her in the blurred and stimulating days before Christmas. Invariably she was busy. What particular strata of the city's social life claimed her he was a long time finding out. It seemed to matter very little. She attended the semi-public charity dances at the big hotels; he saw her several times at dinner-parties in Sherry's, and once as he waited for her to dress, Mrs. Gilbert, apropos of her daughter's habit of "going," rattled off an amazing holiday programme that included half a dozen dances to which Anthony had received cards.

He made engagements with her several times for lunch and tea—the former were hurried and, to him at least, rather unsatisfactory occasions, for she was sleepy-eyed and casual, incapable of concentrating upon anything or of giving consecutive attention to his remarks. When after two of these sallow meals he accused her of tendering him the skin and bones of the day she laughed and gave him a tea-time three days off. This was infinitely more satisfactory.

One Sunday afternoon just before Christmas he called up and found her in the lull directly after some important but mysterious quarrel: she informed him in a tone of mingled wrath and amusement that she had sent a man out of her apartment—here Anthony speculated violently—and that the man had been giving a little dinner for her that very night and that of course she wasn't going. So Anthony took her to supper.

"Let's go to something!" she proposed as they went down in the elevator. "I want to see a show, don't you?"

Inquiry at the hotel ticket-desk disclosed only two Sunday-night "concerts."

"They're always the same," she complained unhappily, "same old Yiddish comedians. Oh, let's go somewhere!"

To conceal a guilty suspicion that he should have arranged a performance of some kind for her approval Anthony affected a knowing cheerfulness.

"We'll go to a good cabaret."

"I've seen every one in town."

"Well, we'll find a new one."

She was in wretched humor; that was evident. Her gray eyes were granite now indeed. When she wasn't speaking she stared straight in front of her as if at some distasteful abstraction in the lobby.

"Well, come on, then."

He followed her, a graceful girl even in her enveloping fur, out to a taxicab, and, with an air of having a definite place in mind, instructed the driver to go over to Broadway and then turn south. He made several casual attempts at conversation but as she adopted an impenetrable armor of silence and answered him in sentences as morose as the cold darkness of the taxicab he gave up, and assuming a like mood fell into a dim gloom.

A dozen blocks down Broadway Anthony's eyes were caught by a large and unfamiliar electric sign spelling "Marathon" in glorious yellow script, adorned with electrical leaves and flowers that alternately vanished and beamed upon the wet and glistening street. He leaned and rapped on the taxi-window and in a moment was receiving information from a colored doorman: Yes, this was a cabaret. Fine cabaret. Bes' showina city!

"Shall we try it?"

With a sigh Gloria tossed her cigarette out the open door and prepared to follow it; then they had passed under the screaming sign, under the wide portal, and up by a stuffy elevator into this unsung palace of pleasure.

The gay habitats of the very rich and the very poor, the very dashing and the very criminal, not to mention the lately exploited very Bohemian, are made known to the awed high-school girls of Augusta, Georgia, and Redwing, Minnesota, not only through the bepictured and entrancing spreads of the Sunday theatrical supplements but through the shocked and alarmful eyes of Mr. Rupert Hughes and other chroniclers of the mad pace of America. But the excursions of Harlem onto Broadway, the deviltries of the dull and the revelries of the respectable are a matter of esoteric knowledge only to the participants themselves.

A tip circulates—and in the place knowingly mentioned, gather the lower moral-classes on Saturday and Sunday nights—the little troubled men who are pictured in the comics as "the Consumer" or "the Public." They have made sure that the place has three qualifications: it is cheap; it imitates with a sort of shoddy and mechanical wistfulness the glittering antics of the great cafés in the theatre district; and—this, above all, important—it is a place where they can "take a nice girl," which means, of course, that every one has become equally harmless, timid, and uninteresting through lack of money and imagination.

There on Sunday nights gather the credulous, sentimental, underpaid, overworked people with hyphenated occupations: book-keepers, ticket-sellers, office-managers, salesmen, and, most of all, clerks—clerks of the express, of the mail, of the grocery, of the brokerage, of the bank. With them are their giggling, over-gestured, pathetically pretentious women, who grow fat with them, bear them too many babies, and float helpless and uncontent in a colorless sea of drudgery and broken hopes.

They name these brummagem cabarets after Pullman cars. The "Marathon"! Not for them the salacious similes borrowed from the cafés of Paris! This is where their docile patrons bring their "nice women," whose starved fancies are only too willing to believe that the scene is comparatively gay and joyous, and even faintly immoral. This is life! Who cares for the morrow?

Abandoned people!

Anthony and Gloria, seated, looked about them. At the next table a party of four were in process of being joined by a party of three, two men and a girl, who were evidently late—and the manner of the girl was a study in national sociology. She was meeting some new men—and she was pretending desperately. By gesture she was pretending and by words and by the scarcely perceptible motionings of her eyelids that she belonged to a class a little superior to the class with which she now had to do, that a while ago she had been, and presently would again be, in a higher, rarer air. She was almost painfully refined—she wore a last year's hat covered with violets no more yearningly pretentious and palpably artificial than herself.

Fascinated, Anthony and Gloria watched the girl sit down and radiate the impression that she was only condescendingly present. For *me*, her eyes said, this is practically a slumming expedition, to be cloaked with belittling laughter and semi-apologetics.

—And the other women passionately poured out the impression that though they were in the crowd they were not of it. This was not the sort of place to which they were accustomed; they had dropped in because it was near by and convenient—every party in the restaurant poured out that impression . . . who knew? They were forever changing class, all of them—the women often marrying above their opportunities, the men striking suddenly a magnificent opulence: a sufficiently preposterous advertising scheme, a celestialized ice-cream cone. Meanwhile, they met here to eat, closing their eyes to the economy displayed in infrequent changings of table-cloths, in the casualness of the cabaret performers, most of all in the colloquial carelessness and familiarity of the waiters. One was sure that these waiters were not impressed by their patrons. One expected that presently they would sit at the tables. . . .

"Do you object to this?" inquired Anthony.

Gloria's face warmed and for the first time that evening she smiled.

"I love it," she said frankly. It was impossible to doubt her. Her gray eyes roved here and there, drowsing, idle or alert, on each group, passing to the next with unconcealed enjoyment, and to Anthony were made plain the different values of her profile, the wonderfully alive expressions of her mouth, and the authentic distinction of face and form and manner that made her like a single flower amidst a collection of cheap bric-à-brac. At her happiness, a gorgeous sentiment welled into his eyes, choked him up, set his nerves a-tingle, and filled his throat with husky and vibrant emotion. There was a hush upon the room. The careless violins and saxophones, the shrill rasping complaint of a child near by, the voice of the violet-hatted girl at the next table, all moved slowly out, receded, and fell away like shadowy reflections on the shining floor—and they two, it seemed to him, were alone and infinitely remote, quiet. Surely the freshness of her cheeks was a gossamer projection from a land of delicate and undiscovered shades; her hand gleaming on the stained table-cloth was a shell from some far and wildly virginal sea. . . .

Then the illusion snapped like a nest of threads; the room grouped itself around him, voices, faces, movement; the garish shimmer of the lights overhead became real, became portentous; breath began, the slow respiration that she and he took in time with this docile hundred, the rise and fall of bosoms, the eternal meaningless play and interplay and tossing and reiterating of word and phrase—all these wrenched his senses open to the suffocating pressure of life—and then her voice came at him, cool as the suspended dream he had left behind.

"I belong here," she murmured, "I'm like these people."

For an instant this seemed a sardonic and unnecessary paradox hurled at him across the impassable distances she created about herself. Her entrancement had increased—her eyes rested upon a Semitic violinist who swayed his shoulders to the rhythm of the year's mellowest fox-trot:

"Something—goes
Ring-a-ting-a-ling-a-ling
Right in-your ear——"

Again she spoke, from the centre of this pervasive illusion of her own. It amazed him. It was like blasphemy from the mouth of a child.

"I'm like they are—like Japanese lanterns and crape paper, and the music of that orchestra."

"You're a young idiot!" he insisted wildly.

She shook her blond head.

"No, I'm not. I *am* like them. . . . You ought to see. . . . You don't know me." She hesitated and her eyes came back to him, rested abruptly on his, as though surprised at the last to see him there. "I've got a streak of what you'd call cheapness. I don't know where I get it but it's—oh, things like this and bright colors and gaudy vulgarity. I seem to belong here. These people could appreciate me and take me for granted, and these men would fall in love with me and admire me, whereas the clever men I meet would just analyze me and tell me I'm this because of this or that because of that."

—Anthony for the moment wanted fiercely to paint her, to set her down *now*, as she was, as, as with each relentless second she could never be again.

"What were you thinking?" she asked.

"Just that I'm not a realist," he said, and then: "No, only the romanticist preserves the things worth preserving."

Out of the deep sophistication of Anthony an understanding formed, nothing atavistic or obscure, indeed scarcely physical at all, an understanding remembered from the romancings of many generations of minds that as she talked and caught his eyes and turned her lovely head, she moved him as he had never been moved before. The sheath that held her soul had assumed significance—that was all. She was a sun, radiant, growing, gathering light and storing it—then after an eternity pouring it forth in a glance, the fragment of a sentence, to that part of him that cherished all beauty and all illusion.

CHAPTER III

The Connoisseur of Kisses

FROM his undergraduate days as editor of The Harvard Crimson Richard Caramel had desired to write. But as a senior he had picked up the glorified illusion that certain men were set aside for "service" and, going into the world, were to accomplish a vague yearnful something which would react either in eternal reward or, at the least, in the personal satisfaction of having striven for the greatest good of the greatest number.

This spirit has long rocked the colleges in America. It begins, as a rule, during the immaturities and facile impressions of freshman year—sometimes back in preparatory school. Prosperous apostles known for their emotional acting go the rounds of the universities and, by frightening the amiable sheep and dulling the quickening of interest and intellectual curiosity which is the purpose of all education, distil a mysterious conviction of sin, harking back to childhood crimes and to the ever-present menace of "women." To these lectures go the wicked youths to cheer and joke and the timid to swallow the tasty pills, which would be harmless if administered to farmers' wives and pious drug-clerks but are rather dangerous medicine for these "future leaders of men."

This octopus was strong enough to wind a sinuous tentacle about Richard Caramel. The year after his graduation it called him into the slums of New York to muck about with bewildered Italians as secretary to an "Alien Young Men's Rescue Association." He labored at it over a year before the monotony began to weary him. The aliens kept coming inexhaustibly—Italians, Poles, Scandinavians, Czechs, Armenians—with the same wrongs, the same exceptionally ugly faces and very much the same smells, though he fancied that these grew more profuse and diverse as the months passed. His eventual conclusions about the expediency of service were vague, but concerning his own relation to it they were abrupt and decisive. Any amiable young man, his head ringing with the latest crusade, could accomplish as much as he could with the débris of Europe—and it was time for him to write.

He had been living in a down-town Y.M.C.A., but when he quit the task of making sow-ear purses out of sows' ears, he moved up-town and went to work immediately as a reporter for The Sun. He kept at this for a year, doing desultory writing on the side, with little success, and then one day an infelicitous incident peremptorily closed his newspaper career. On a February afternoon he was assigned to report a parade of Squadron A. Snow threatening, he went to sleep instead before a hot fire, and when he woke up did a smooth column about the muffled beats of the horses' hoofs in the snow. . . . This he handed in. Next morning a marked copy of the paper was sent down to the City Editor with a scrawled note: "Fire the man who wrote this." It seemed that Squadron A had also seen the snow threatening—and had postponed the parade until another day.

A week later he had begun "The Demon Lover." . . .

In January, the Monday of the months, Richard Caramel's nose was blue constantly, a sardonic blue, vaguely suggestive of the flames licking around a sinner. His book was nearly ready, and as it grew in completeness it seemed to grow also in its demands, sapping him, overpowering him, until he walked haggard and conquered in its shadow. Not only to Anthony and Maury did he pour out his hopes and boasts and indecisions, but to any one who could be prevailed upon to listen. He called on polite but bewildered publishers, he discussed it with his casual vis-à-vis at the Harvard Club; it was even claimed by Anthony that he had been discovered, one Sunday night, debating the transposition of Chapter Two with a literary ticket-collector in the chill and dismal recesses of a Harlem subway-station. And latest among his confidantes was Mrs. Gilbert, who sat with him by the hour and alternated between Bilphism and literature in an intense cross-fire.

"Shakespeare was a Bilphist," she assured him through a fixed smile. "Oh, yes! He was a Bilphist. It's been proved."

At this Dick would look a bit blank.

"If you've read 'Hamlet' you can't help but see."

"Well, he—he lived in a more credulous age—a more religious age."

But she demanded the whole loaf:

"Oh, yes, but you see Bilphism isn't a religion. It's the science of all religions." She smiled defiantly at him. This was the *bon mot* of her belief. There was something in the arrangement of words which grasped her mind so definitely that the statement became superior to any obligation to define itself. It is not unlikely that she would have accepted any idea encased in this radiant formula—which was perhaps not a formula; it was the *reductio ad absurdum* of all formulas.

Then eventually, but gorgeously, would come Dick's turn.

"You've heard of the new poetry movement. You haven't? Well, it's a lot of young poets that are breaking away from the old forms and doing a lot of good. Well, what I was going to say was that my book is going to start a new prose movement, a sort of renaissance."

"I'm sure it will," beamed Mrs. Gilbert. "I'm *sure* it will. I went to Jenny Martin last Tuesday, the palmist, you know, that every one's *mad* about. I told her my nephew was engaged upon a work and she said she knew I'd be glad to hear that his success would be *extraordinary.* But she'd never seen you or known anything about you—not even your *name.*"

Having made the proper noises to express his amazement at this astounding phenomenon, Dick waved her theme by him as though he were an arbitrary traffic policeman, and, so to speak, beckoned forward his own traffic.

"I'm absorbed, Aunt Catherine," he assured her, "I really am. All my friends are joshing me—oh, I see the humor in it and I don't care. I think a person ought to be able to take joshing. But I've got a sort of conviction," he concluded gloomily.

"You're an ancient soul, I always say."

"Maybe I am." Dick had reached the stage where he no longer fought, but submitted. He *must* be an ancient soul, he fancied grotesquely; so old as to be absolutely rotten. However, the reiteration of the phrase still somewhat embarrassed him and sent uncomfortable shivers up his back. He changed the subject.

"Where is my distinguished cousin Gloria?"

"She's on the go somewhere, with some one."

Dick paused, considered, and then, screwing up his face into what was evidently begun as a smile but ended as a terrifying frown, delivered a comment.

"I think my friend Anthony Patch is in love with her."

Mrs. Gilbert started, beamed half a second too late, and breathed her "Really?" in the tone of a detective play-whisper.

"I *think* so," corrected Dick gravely. "She's the first girl I've ever seen him with, so much."

"Well, of course," said Mrs. Gilbert with meticulous carelessness, "Gloria never makes me her confidante. She's very secretive. Between you and me"—she bent forward cautiously, obviously determined that only Heaven and her nephew should share her confession—"between you and me, I'd like to see her settle down."

Dick arose and paced the floor earnestly, a small, active, already rotund young man, his hands thrust unnaturally into his bulging pockets.

"I'm not claiming I'm right, mind you," he assured the infinitely-of-the-hotel steel-engraving which smirked respectably back at him. "I'm saying nothing that I'd want Gloria to know. But I think Mad Anthony is interested—tremendously so. He talks about her constantly. In any one else that'd be a bad sign."

"Gloria is a very young soul—" began Mrs. Gilbert eagerly, but her nephew interrupted with a hurried sentence:

"Gloria'd be a very young nut not to marry him." He stopped and faced her, his expression a battle map of lines and dimples, squeezed and strained to its ultimate show of intensity—this as if to make up by his sincerity for any indiscretion in his words. "Gloria's a wild one, Aunt Catherine. She's uncontrollable. How she's done it I don't know, but lately she's picked up a lot of the funniest friends. She doesn't seem to care. And the men she used to go with around New York were—" He paused for breath.

"Yes-yes-yes," interjected Mrs. Gilbert, with an anæmic attempt to hide the immense interest with which she listened.

"Well," continued Richard Caramel gravely, "there it is. I mean that the men she went with and the people she went with used to be first rate. Now they aren't."

Mrs. Gilbert blinked very fast—her bosom trembled, inflated, remained so for an instant, and with the exhalation her words flowed out in a torrent.

She knew, she cried in a whisper; oh, yes, mothers see these things. But what could she do? He knew Gloria. He'd seen enough of Gloria to know how hopeless it was to try to deal with her. Gloria had been so spoiled—in a rather complete and unusual way. She had been suckled until she was three, for instance, when she could probably have chewed sticks. Perhaps—one never knew—it was this that had given that health and *hardiness* to her whole personality. And then ever since she was twelve years old she'd had boys about her so thick—oh, so thick one couldn't *move*. At sixteen she began going to dances at preparatory schools, and then came the colleges; and everywhere she went, boys, boys, boys. At first, oh, until she was eighteen there had been so many that it never seemed one any more than the others, but then she began to single them out.

She knew there had been a string of affairs spread over about three years, perhaps a dozen of them altogether. Sometimes the men were undergraduates, sometimes just out of college—they lasted on an average of several months each, with short attractions in between. Once or twice they had endured longer and her mother had hoped she would be engaged, but always a new one came—a new one——

The men? Oh, she made them miserable, literally! There was only one who had kept any sort of dignity, and he had been a mere child, young Carter Kirby, of Kansas City, who was so conceited anyway that he just sailed out on his vanity one afternoon and left for Europe next day with his father. The others had been—wretched. They never seemed to know when she was tired of them, and Gloria had seldom been deliberately unkind. They would keep phoning, writing letters to her, trying to see her, making long trips after her around the country. Some of them had confided in Mrs. Gilbert, told her with tears in their eyes that they would never get over Gloria . . . at least two of them had since married, though. . . . But Gloria, it seemed, struck to kill—to this day Mr. Carstairs called up once a week, and sent her flowers which she no longer bothered to refuse.

Several times, twice, at least, Mrs. Gilbert knew it had gone as far as a private engagement—with Tudor Baird and that Holcome boy at Pasadena. She was sure it had, because—this must go no further—she had come in unexpectedly and found Gloria acting, well, very much engaged indeed. She had not spoken to her daughter, of course. She had had a certain sense of delicacy and, besides, each time she had expected an announcement in a few weeks. But the announcement never came; instead, a new man came.

Scenes! Young men walking up and down the library like caged tigers! Young men glaring at each other in the hall as one came and the other left! Young men calling up on the telephone and being hung up upon in desperation! Young men threatening South America! . . . Young men writing the most pathetic letters! (She said nothing to this effect, but Dick fancied that Mrs. Gilbert's eyes had seen some of these letters.)

. . . And Gloria, between tears and laughter, sorry, glad, out of love and in love, miserable, nervous, cool, amidst a great returning of presents, substitution of pictures in immemorial frames, and taking of hot baths and beginning again—with the next.

That state of things continued, assumed an air of permanency. Nothing harmed Gloria or changed her or moved her. And then out of a clear sky one day she informed her mother that undergraduates wearied her. She was absolutely going to no more college dances.

This had begun the change—not so much in her actual habits, for she danced, and had as many "dates" as ever—but they were dates in a different spirit. Previously it had been a sort of pride, a matter of her own vainglory. She had been, probably, the most celebrated and sought-after young beauty in the country. Gloria Gilbert of Kansas City! She had fed on it ruthlessly—enjoying the crowds around her, the manner in which the most desirable men singled her out; enjoying the fierce jealousy of other girls; enjoying the fabulous, not to say scandalous, and, her mother was glad to say, entirely unfounded rumors about her—for instance, that she had gone in the Yale swimming-pool one night in a chiffon evening dress.

And from loving it with a vanity that was almost masculine—it had been in the nature of a triumphant and dazzling career—she became suddenly anæsthetic to it. She retired. She who had dominated countless parties, who had blown fragrantly through many ballrooms to the tender tribute of many eyes, seemed to care no longer. He who fell in love with her now was dismissed utterly, almost angrily. She went listlessly with the most indifferent men. She continually broke engagements, not as in the past from a cool assurance that she was irreproachable, that the man she insulted would return like a domestic animal—but indifferently, without contempt or pride. She rarely stormed at men any more—she yawned at them. She seemed—and it was so strange—she seemed to her mother to be growing cold.

Richard Caramel listened. At first he had remained standing, but as his aunt's discourse waxed in content—it stands here pruned by half, of all side references to the youth of Gloria's soul and to Mrs. Gilbert's own mental distresses—he drew a chair up and attended rigorously as she floated, between tears and plaintive helplessness, down the long story of Gloria's life. When she came to the tale of this last year, a tale of the ends of cigarettes left all over New York in little trays marked "Midnight Frolic" and "Justine Johnson's Little Club," he began nodding his head slowly, then faster and faster, until, as she finished on a staccato note, it was bobbing briskly up and down, absurdly like a doll's wired head, expressing—almost anything.

In a sense Gloria's past was an old story to him. He had followed it with the eyes of a journalist, for he was going to write a book about her some day. But his interests, just at present, were family interests. He wanted to know, in particular, who was this Joseph Bloeckman that he had seen her with several times; and those two girls she was with constantly, "this" Rachael Jerryl and "this" Miss Kane—surely Miss Kane wasn't exactly the sort one would associate with Gloria!

But the moment had passed. Mrs. Gilbert having climbed the hill of exposition was about to glide swiftly down the ski-jump of collapse. Her eyes were like a blue sky seen through two round, red window-casements. The flesh about her mouth was trembling.

And at the moment the door opened, admitting into the room Gloria and the two young ladies lately mentioned.

Two Young Women

"Well!"

"How do you do, Mrs. Gilbert!"

Miss Kane and Miss Jerryl are presented to Mr. Richard Caramel. "This is Dick" (laughter).

"I've heard so much about you," says Miss Kane between a giggle and a shout.

"How do you do," says Miss Jerryl shyly.

Richard Caramel tries to move about as if his figure were better. He is torn between his innate cordiality and the fact that he considers these girls rather common—not at all the Farmover type.

Gloria has disappeared into the bedroom.

"Do sit down," beams Mrs. Gilbert, who is by now quite herself. "Take off your things." Dick is afraid she will make some remark about the age of his soul, but he forgets his qualms in completing a conscientious, novelist's examination of the two young women.

Muriel Kane had originated in a rising family of East Orange. She was short rather than small, and hovered audaciously between plumpness and width. Her hair was black and elaborately arranged. This, in conjunction with her handsome, rather bovine eyes, and her over-red lips, combined to make her resemble Theda Bara, the prominent motion-picture actress. People told her constantly that she was a "vampire," and she believed them. She suspected hopefully that they were afraid of her, and she did her utmost under all circumstances to give the impression of danger. An imaginative man could see the red flag that she constantly carried, waving it wildly, beseechingly—and, alas, to little spectacular avail. She was also tremendously timely: she knew the latest songs, all the latest songs—when one of them was played on the phonograph she would rise to her feet and rock her shoulders back and forth and snap her fingers, and if there was no music she would accompany herself by humming.

Her conversation was also timely: "I don't care," she would

say, "I should worry and lose my figure"—and again: "I can't make my feet behave when I hear that tune. Oh, baby!"

Her finger-nails were too long and ornate, polished to a pink and unnatural fever. Her clothes were too tight, too stylish, too vivid, her eyes too roguish, her smile too coy. She was almost pitifully overemphasized from head to foot.

The other girl was obviously a more subtle personality. She was an exquisitely dressed Jewess with dark hair and a lovely milky pallor. She seemed shy and vague, and these two qualities accentuated a rather delicate charm that floated about her. Her family were "Episcopalians," owned three smart women's shops along Fifth Avenue, and lived in a magnificent apartment on Riverside Drive. It seemed to Dick, after a few moments, that she was attempting to imitate Gloria—he wondered that people invariably chose inimitable people to imitate.

"We had the most *hectic* time!" Muriel was exclaiming enthusiastically. "There was a crazy woman behind us on the bus. She was absitively, posolutely *nutty!* She kept talking to herself about something she'd like to do to somebody or something. I was *pet*rified, but Gloria simply *wouldn't* get off."

Mrs. Gilbert opened her mouth, properly awed.

"Really?"

"Oh, she was crazy. But we should worry, she didn't hurt us. Ugly! Gracious! The man across from us said her face ought to be on a night-nurse in a home for the blind, and we all *howled*, naturally, so the man tried to pick us up."

Presently Gloria emerged from her bedroom and in unison every eye turned on her. The two girls receded into a shadowy background, unperceived, unmissed.

"We've been talking about you," said Dick quickly, "—your mother and I."

"Well," said Gloria.

A pause—Muriel turned to Dick.

"You're a great writer, aren't you?"

"I'm a writer," he confessed sheepishly.

"I always say," said Muriel earnestly, "that if I ever had time to write down all my experiences it'd make a wonderful book."

Rachael giggled sympathetically; Richard Caramel's bow was almost stately. Muriel continued:

"But I don't see how you can sit down and do it. And poetry! Lordy, I can't make two lines rhyme. Well, I should worry!"

Richard Caramel with difficulty restrained a shout of laughter. Gloria was chewing an amazing gum-drop and staring moodily out the window. Mrs. Gilbert cleared her throat and beamed.

"But you see," she said in a sort of universal exposition, "you're not an ancient soul—like Richard."

The Ancient Soul breathed a gasp of relief—it was out at last.

Then as if she had been considering it for five minutes, Gloria made a sudden announcement:

"I'm going to give a party."

"Oh, can I come?" cried Muriel with facetious daring.

"A dinner. Seven people: Muriel and Rachael and I, and you, Dick, and Anthony, and that man named Noble—I liked him—and Bloeckman."

Muriel and Rachael went into soft and purring ecstasies of enthusiasm. Mrs. Gilbert blinked and beamed. With an air of casualness Dick broke in with a question:

"Who is this fellow Bloeckman, Gloria?"

Scenting a faint hostility, Gloria turned to him.

"Joseph Bloeckman? He's the moving-picture man. Vice-president of 'Films Par Excellence.' He and father do a lot of business."

"Oh!"

"Well, will you all come?"

They would all come. A date was arranged within the week. Dick rose, adjusted hat, coat, and muffler, and gave out a general smile.

"By-by," said Muriel, waving her hand gaily, "call me up some time."

Richard Caramel blushed for her.

Deplorable End of the Chevalier O'Keefe

It was Monday and Anthony took Geraldine Burke to luncheon at the Beaux Arts—afterward they went up to his apartment and he wheeled out the little rolling-table that held his supply of liquor, selecting vermuth, gin, and absinthe for a proper stimulant.

Geraldine Burke, usher at Keith's, had been an amusement of several months. She demanded so little that he liked her, for since a lamentable affair with a débutante the preceding summer, when he had discovered that after half a dozen kisses a proposal was expected, he had been wary of girls of his own class. It was only too easy to turn a critical eye on their imperfections: some physical harshness or a general lack of personal delicacy—but a girl who was usher at Keith's was approached with a different attitude. One could tolerate qualities in an intimate valet that would be unforgivable in a mere acquaintance on one's social level.

Geraldine, curled up at the foot of the lounge, considered him with narrow slanting eyes.

"You drink all the time, don't you?" she said suddenly.

"Why, I suppose so," replied Anthony in some surprise. "Don't you?"

"Nope. I go on parties sometimes—you know, about once a week, but I only take two or three drinks. You and your friends keep on drinking all the time. I should think you'd ruin your health."

Anthony was somewhat touched.

"Why, aren't you sweet to worry about me!"

"Well, I do."

"I don't drink so very much," he declared. "Last month I didn't touch a drop for three weeks. And I only get really tight about once a week."

"But you have something to drink every day and you're only twenty-five. Haven't you any ambition? Think what you'll be at forty?"

"I sincerely trust that I won't live that long."

She clicked her tongue with her teeth.

"You cra-azy!" she said as he mixed another cocktail—and then: "Are you any relation to Adam Patch?"

"Yes, he's my grandfather."

"Really?" She was obviously thrilled.

"Absolutely."

"That's funny. My daddy used to work for him."

"He's a queer old man."

"Is he nice?" she demanded.

"Well, in private life he's seldom unnecessarily disagreeable."

"Tell us about him."

"Why," Anthony considered "—he's all shrunken up and he's got the remains of some gray hair that always looks as though the wind were in it. He's very moral."

"He's done a lot of good," said Geraldine with intense gravity.

"Rot!" scoffed Anthony. "He's a pious ass—a chicken-brain."

Her mind left the subject and flitted on.

"Why don't you live with him?"

"Why don't I board in a Methodist parsonage?"

"You cra-azy!"

Again she made a little clicking sound to express disapproval. Anthony thought how moral was this little waif at heart—how completely moral she would still be after the inevitable wave came that would wash her off the sands of respectability.

"Do you hate him?"

"I wonder. I never liked him. You never like people who do things for you."

"Does he hate you?"

"My dear Geraldine," protested Anthony, frowning humorously, "do have another cocktail. I annoy him. If I smoke a cigarette he comes into the room sniffing. He's a prig, a bore, and something of a hypocrite. I probably wouldn't be telling you this if I hadn't had a few drinks, but I don't suppose it matters."

Geraldine was persistently interested. She held her glass, untasted, between finger and thumb and regarded him with eyes in which there was a touch of awe.

"How do you mean a hypocrite?"

"Well," said Anthony impatiently, "maybe he's not. But he doesn't like the things that I like, and so, as far as I'm concerned, he's uninteresting."

"Hm." Her curiosity seemed, at length, satisfied. She sank back into the sofa and sipped her cocktail.

"You're a funny one," she commented thoughtfully. "Does everybody want to marry you because your grandfather is rich?"

"They don't—but I shouldn't blame them if they did. Still, you see, I never intend to marry."

She scorned this.

"You'll fall in love some day. Oh, you will—I know." She nodded wisely.

"It'd be idiotic to be overconfident. That's what ruined the Chevalier O'Keefe."

"Who was he?"

"A creature of my splendid mind. He's my one creation, the Chevalier."

"Cra-a-azy!" she murmured pleasantly, using the clumsy rope-ladder with which she bridged all gaps and climbed after her mental superiors. Subconsciously she felt that it eliminated distances and brought the person whose imagination had eluded her back within range.

"Oh, no!" objected Anthony, "oh, no, Geraldine. You mustn't play the alienist upon the Chevalier. If you feel yourself unable to understand him I won't bring him in. Besides, I should feel a certain uneasiness because of his regrettable reputation."

"I guess I can understand anything that's got any sense to it," answered Geraldine a bit testily.

"In that case there are various episodes in the life of the Chevalier which might prove diverting."

"Well?"

"It was his untimely end that caused me to think of him and made him apropos in the conversation. I hate to introduce him end foremost, but it seems inevitable that the Chevalier must back into your life."

"Well, what about him? Did he die?"

"He did! In this manner. He was an Irishman, Geraldine, a semi-fictional Irishman—the wild sort with a genteel brogue and 'reddish hair.' He was exiled from Erin in the late days of chivalry and, of course, crossed over to France. Now the Chevalier O'Keefe, Geraldine, had, like me, one weakness. He was enormously susceptible to all sorts and conditions of women. Besides being a sentimentalist he was a romantic, a vain fellow, a man of wild passions, a little blind in one eye and almost stone-blind in the other. Now a male roaming the world in this condition is as helpless as a lion without teeth, and in consequence the Chevalier was made utterly miserable for twenty years by a series of women who hated him, used him, bored him, aggravated him, sickened him, spent his money, made a fool of him—in brief, as the world has it, loved him.

"This was bad, Geraldine, and as the Chevalier, save for this one weakness, this exceeding susceptibility, was a man of penetration, he decided that he would rescue himself once and for all from these drains upon him. With this purpose he went to a very famous monastery in Champagne called—well, anachronistically known as St. Voltaire's. It was the rule at St. Voltaire's that no monk could descend to the ground story of the monastery so long as he lived, but should exist engaged in prayer and contemplation in one of the four towers, which were called after the four commandments of the monastery rule: Poverty, Chastity, Obedience, and Silence.

"When the day came that was to witness the Chevalier's farewell to the world he was utterly happy. He gave all his Greek books to his landlady, and his sword he sent in a golden sheath to the King of France, and all his mementos of Ireland he gave to the young Huguenot who sold fish in the street where he lived.

"Then he rode out to St. Voltaire's, slew his horse at the door, and presented the carcass to the monastery cook.

"At five o'clock that night he felt, for the first time, free—forever free from sex. No woman could enter the monastery; no monk could descend below the second story. So as he climbed the winding stair that led to his cell at the very top of the Tower of Chastity he paused for a moment by an open window which looked down fifty feet on to a road below. It was all so beautiful, he thought, this world that he was leaving, the golden shower of sun beating down upon the long fields, the spray of trees in the distance, the vineyards, quiet and green, freshening wide miles before him. He leaned his elbows on the window-casement and gazed at the winding road.

"Now, as it happened, Thérèse, a peasant girl of sixteen from a neighboring village, was at that moment passing along this same road that ran in front of the monastery. Five minutes before, the little piece of ribbon which held up the stocking on her pretty left leg had worn through and broken. Being a girl of rare modesty she had thought to wait until she arrived home before repairing it, but it had bothered her to such an extent that she felt she could endure it no longer. So, as she passed the Tower of Chastity, she stopped and with a pretty gesture lifted her skirt—as little as possible, be it said to her credit—to adjust her garter.

"Up in the tower the newest arrival in the ancient monastery of St. Voltaire, as though pulled forward by a gigantic and irresistible hand, leaned from the window. Further he leaned and further until suddenly one of the stones loosened under his weight, broke from its cement with a soft powdery sound—and, first headlong, then head over heels, finally in a vast and impressive revolution tumbled the Chevalier O'Keefe, bound for the hard earth and eternal damnation.

"Thérèse was so much upset by the occurrence that she ran all the way home and for ten years spent an hour a day in secret prayer for the soul of the monk whose neck and vows were simultaneously broken on that unfortunate Sunday afternoon.

"And the Chevalier O'Keefe, being suspected of suicide, was not buried in consecrated ground, but tumbled into a field near by, where he doubtless improved the quality of the soil for many years afterward. Such was the untimely end of a very brave and gallant gentleman. What do you think, Geraldine?"

But Geraldine, lost long before, could only smile roguishly, wave her first finger at him, and repeat her bridge-all, her explain-all:

"Crazy!" she said, "you cra-a-azy!"

His thin face was kindly, she thought, and his eyes quite gentle. She liked him because he was arrogant without being conceited, and because, unlike the men she met about the theatre, he had a horror of being conspicuous. What an odd, pointless story! But she had enjoyed the part about the stocking!

After the fifth cocktail he kissed her, and between laughter and bantering caresses and a half-stifled flare of passion they passed an hour. At four-thirty she claimed an engagement, and going into the bathroom she rearranged her hair. Refusing to let him order her a taxi she stood for a moment in the doorway.

"You *will* get married," she was insisting, "you wait and see."

Anthony was playing with an ancient tennis-ball, and he bounced it carefully on the floor several times before he answered with a soupçon of acidity:

"You're a little idiot, Geraldine."

She smiled provokingly.

"Oh, I am, am I? Want to bet?"

"That'd be silly too."

"Oh, it would, would it? Well, I'll just bet you'll marry somebody inside of a year."

Anthony bounced the tennis-ball very hard. This was one of his handsome days, she thought; a sort of intensity had displaced the melancholy in his dark eyes.

"Geraldine," he said, at length, "in the first place I have no one I want to marry; in the second place I haven't enough money to support two people; in the third place I am entirely opposed to marriage for people of my type; in the fourth place I have a strong distaste for even the abstract consideration of it."

But Geraldine only narrowed her eyes knowingly, made her clicking sound, and said she must be going. It was late.

"Call me up soon," she reminded him as he kissed her good-by, "you haven't for three weeks, you know."

"I will," he promised fervently.

He shut the door and coming back into the room stood for a moment lost in thought with the tennis-ball still clasped in his hand. There was one of his lonelinesses coming, one of those times when he walked the streets or sat, aimless and depressed, biting a pencil at his desk. It was a self-absorption with no comfort, a demand for expression with no outlet, a sense of time rushing by, ceaselessly and wastefully—assuaged only by that conviction that there was nothing to waste, because all efforts and attainments were equally valueless.

He thought with emotion—aloud, ejaculative, for he was hurt and confused.

"No *idea* of getting married, by *God!*"

Of a sudden he hurled the tennis-ball violently across the room, where it barely missed the lamp, and, rebounding here and there for a moment, lay still upon the floor.

Signlight and Moonlight

For her dinner Gloria had taken a table in the Cascades at the Biltmore, and when the men met in the hall outside a little after eight, "that person Bloeckman" was the target of six masculine eyes. He was a stoutening, ruddy Jew of about thirty-five, with an expressive face under smooth sandy hair—and, no doubt, in most business gatherings his personality would have been considered ingratiating. He sauntered up to the three younger men, who stood in a group smoking as they waited for their hostess, and introduced himself with a little too evident assurance—nevertheless it is to be doubted whether he received the intended impression of faint and ironic chill: there was no hint of understanding in his manner.

"You related to Adam J. Patch?" he inquired of Anthony, emitting two slender strings of smoke from nostrils overwide.

Anthony admitted it with the ghost of a smile.

"He's a fine man," pronounced Bloeckman profoundly. "He's a fine example of an American."

"Yes," agreed Anthony, "he certainly is."

—I detest these underdone men, he thought coldly. Boiled looking! Ought to be shoved back in the oven; just one more minute would do it.

Bloeckman squinted at his watch.

"Time these girls were showing up . . ."

—Anthony waited breathlessly; it came——

". . . but then," with a widening smile, "you know how women are."

The three young men nodded; Bloeckman looked casually about him, his eyes resting critically on the ceiling and then passing lower. His expression combined that of a Middle-Western farmer appraising his wheat-crop and that of an actor wondering whether he is observed—the public manner of all good Americans. As he finished his survey he turned back quickly to the reticent trio, determined to strike to their very heart and core.

"You college men? . . . Harvard, eh. I see the Princeton boys beat you fellows in hockey."

Unfortunate man. He had drawn another blank. They had been three years out and heeded only the big football games. Whether, after the failure of this sally, Mr. Bloeckman would have perceived himself to be in a cynical atmosphere is problematical, for——

Gloria arrived. Muriel arrived. Rachael arrived. After a hurried "Hello, people!" uttered by Gloria and echoed by the other two, the three swept by into the dressing-room.

A moment later Muriel appeared in a state of elaborate undress and *crept* toward them. She was in her element: her ebony hair was slicked straight back on her head; her eyes were artificially darkened; she reeked of insistent perfume. She was got up to the best of her ability as a siren, more popularly a "vamp"—a picker up and thrower away of men, an unscrupulous and fundamentally unmoved toyer with affections. Something in the exhaustiveness of her attempt fascinated Maury at first sight—a woman with wide hips affecting a pantherlike litheness! As they waited the extra three minutes for Gloria, and, by polite assumption, for Rachael, he was unable to take his eyes from her. She would turn her head away, lowering her eyelashes and biting her nether lip in an amazing exhibition of coyness. She would rest her hands on her hips and sway from side to side in tune to the music, saying:

"Did you ever hear such perfect ragtime? I just can't make my shoulders behave when I hear that."

Mr. Bloeckman clapped his hands gallantly.

"You ought to be on the stage."

"I'd like to be!" cried Muriel; "will you back me?"

"I sure will."

With becoming modesty Muriel ceased her motions and turned to Maury, asking what he had "seen" this year. He interpreted this as referring to the dramatic world, and they had a gay and exhilarating exchange of titles, after this manner:

MURIEL: Have you seen "Peg o' My Heart"?

MAURY: No, I haven't.

MURIEL: (*Eagerly*) It's wonderful! You want to see it.
MAURY: Have you seen "Omar, the Tentmaker"?
MURIEL: No, but I hear it's wonderful. I'm very anxious to see it. Have you seen "Fair and Warmer"?
MAURY: (*Hopefully*) Yes.
MURIEL: I don't think it's very good. It's trashy.
MAURY: (*Faintly*) Yes, that's true.
MURIEL: But I went to "Within the Law" last night and I thought it was fine. Have you seen "The Little Café"? . . .

This continued until they ran out of plays. Dick, meanwhile, turned to Mr. Bloeckman, determined to extract what gold he could from this unpromising load.

"I hear all the new novels are sold to the moving pictures as soon as they come out."

"That's true. Of course the main thing in a moving picture is a strong story."

"Yes, I suppose so."

"So many novels are all full of talk and psychology. Of course those aren't as valuable to us. It's impossible to make much of that interesting on the screen."

"You want plots first," said Richard brilliantly.

"Of course. Plots first—" He paused, shifted his gaze. His pause spread, included the others with all the authority of a warning finger. Gloria followed by Rachael was coming out of the dressing-room.

Among other things it developed during dinner that Joseph Bloeckman never danced, but spent the music time watching the others with the bored tolerance of an elder among children. He was a dignified man and a proud one. Born in Munich he had begun his American career as a peanut vender with a travelling circus. At eighteen he was a side-show ballyhoo; later, the manager of the side-show, and, soon after, the proprietor of a second-class vaudeville house. Just when the moving picture had passed out of the stage of a curiosity and become a promising industry he was an ambitious young man of twenty-six with some money to invest, nagging financial ambitions and a good working knowledge of the popular show business. That had been nine years before. The moving-picture industry had borne him up with it where it threw off dozens of men with more financial ability, more imagination, and more practical ideas . . . . and now he sat here and contemplated the immortal Gloria for whom young Stuart Holcome had gone from New York to Pasadena—watched her, and knew that presently she would cease dancing and come back to sit on his left hand.

He hoped she would hurry. The oysters had been standing some minutes.

Meanwhile Anthony, who had been placed on Gloria's left hand, was dancing with her, always in a certain fourth of the floor. This, had there been stags, would have been a delicate tribute to the girl, meaning "Damn you, don't cut in!" It was very consciously intimate.

"Well," he began, looking down at her, "you look mighty sweet to-night."

She met his eyes over the horizontal half foot that separated them.

"Thank you—Anthony."

"In fact you're uncomfortably beautiful," he added. There was no smile this time.

"And you're very charming."

"Isn't this nice?" he laughed. "We actually approve of each other."

"Don't you, usually?" She had caught quickly at his remark, as she always did at any unexplained allusion to herself, however faint.

He lowered his voice, and when he spoke there was in it no more than a wisp of badinage.

"Does a priest approve the Pope?"

"I don't know—but that's probably the vaguest compliment I ever received."

"Perhaps I can muster a few bromides."

"Well, I wouldn't have you strain yourself. Look at Muriel! Right here next to us."

He glanced over his shoulder. Muriel was resting her brilliant cheek against the lapel of Maury Noble's dinner-coat and her powdered left arm was apparently twisted around his head. One was impelled to wonder why she failed to seize the nape of his neck with her hand. Her eyes, turned ceilingward, rolled largely back and forth; her hips swayed, and as she danced she kept up a constant low singing. This at first seemed to be a translation of the song into some foreign tongue but became eventually apparent as an attempt to fill out the metre of the song with the only words she knew—the words of the title—

"He's a rag-picker,
A rag-picker,
A rag-time picking man,
Rag-picking, picking, pick, pick,
Rag-pick, pick, pick."

—and so on, into phrases still more strange and barbaric. When she caught the amused glances of Anthony and Gloria she acknowledged them only with a faint smile and a half-closing of her eyes, to indicate that the music entering into her soul had put her into an ecstatic and exceedingly seductive trance.

The music ended and they returned to their table, whose solitary but dignified occupant arose and tendered each of them a smile so ingratiating that it was as if he were shaking their hands and congratulating them on a brilliant performance.

"Blockhead never will dance! I think he has a wooden leg," remarked Gloria to the table at large. The three young men started and the gentleman referred to winced perceptibly.

This was the one rough spot in the course of Bloeckman's acquaintance with Gloria. She relentlessly punned on his name. First it had been "Block-house," lately, the more invidious "Blockhead." He had requested with a strong undertone of irony that she use his first name, and this she had done obediently several times—then slipping, helpless, repentant but dissolved in laughter, back into "Blockhead."

It was a very sad and thoughtless thing.

"I'm afraid Mr. Bloeckman thinks we're a frivolous crowd," sighed Muriel, waving a balanced oyster in his direction.

"He has that air," murmured Rachael. Anthony tried to remember whether she had said anything before. He thought not. It was her initial remark.

Mr. Bloeckman suddenly cleared his throat and said in a loud, distinct voice:

"On the contrary. When a man speaks he's merely

tradition. He has at best a few thousand years back of him. But woman, why, she is the miraculous mouthpiece of posterity."

In the stunned pause that followed this astounding remark, Anthony choked suddenly on an oyster and hurried his napkin to his face. Rachael and Muriel raised a mild if somewhat surprised laugh, in which Dick and Maury joined, both of them red in the face and restraining uproariousness with the most apparent difficulty.

"—My God!" thought Anthony. "It's a subtitle from one of his movies. The man's memorized it!"

Gloria alone made no sound. She fixed Mr. Bloeckman with a glance of silent reproach.

"Well, for the love of Heaven! Where on earth did you dig that up?"

Bloeckman looked at her uncertainly, not sure of her intention. But in a moment he recovered his poise and assumed the bland and consciously tolerant smile of an intellectual among spoiled and callow youth.

The soup came up from the kitchen—but simultaneously the orchestra leader came up from the bar, where he had absorbed the tone color inherent in a seidel of beer. So the soup was left to cool during the delivery of a ballad entitled "Everything's at Home Except Your Wife."

Then the champagne—and the party assumed more amusing proportions. The men, except Richard Caramel, drank freely; Gloria and Muriel sipped a glass apiece; Rachael Jerryl took none. They sat out the waltzes but danced to everything else—all except Gloria, who seemed to tire after a while and preferred to sit smoking at the table, her eyes now lazy, now eager, according to whether she listened to Bloeckman or watched a pretty woman among the dancers. Several times Anthony wondered what Bloeckman was telling her. He was chewing a cigar back and forth in his mouth, and had expanded after dinner to the extent of violent gestures.

Ten o'clock found Gloria and Anthony beginning a dance. Just as they were out of ear-shot of the table she said in a low voice:

"Dance over by the door. I want to go down to the drugstore."

Obediently Anthony guided her through the crowd in the designated direction; in the hall she left him for a moment, to reappear with a cloak over her arm.

"I want some gum-drops," she said, humorously apologetic; "you can't guess what for this time. It's just that I want to bite my finger-nails, and I will if I don't get some gum-drops." She sighed, and resumed as they stepped into the empty elevator: "I've been biting 'em all day. A bit nervous, you see. Excuse the pun. It was unintentional—the words just arranged themselves. Gloria Gilbert, the female wag."

Reaching the ground floor they naïvely avoided the hotel candy counter, descended the wide front staircase, and walking through several corridors found a drug-store in the Grand Central Station. After an intense examination of the perfume counter she made her purchase. Then on some mutual unmentioned impulse they strolled, arm in arm, not in the direction from which they had come, but out into Forty-third Street.

The night was alive with thaw; it was so nearly warm that a breeze drifting low along the sidewalk brought to Anthony a vision of an unhoped-for hyacinthine spring. Above in the blue oblong of sky, around them in the caress of the drifting air, the illusion of a new season carried relief from the stiff and breathed-over atmosphere they had left, and for a hushed moment the traffic sounds and the murmur of water flowing in the gutters seemed an illusive and rarefied prolongation of that music to which they had lately danced. When Anthony spoke it was with surety that his words came from something breathless and desirous that the night had conceived in their two hearts.

"Let's take a taxi and ride around a bit!" he suggested, without looking at her.

Oh, Gloria, Gloria!

A cab yawned at the curb. As it moved off like a boat on a labyrinthine ocean and lost itself among the inchoate night masses of the great buildings, among the now stilled, now strident, cries and clangings, Anthony put his arm around the girl, drew her over to him and kissed her damp, childish mouth.

She was silent. She turned her face up to him, pale under

the wisps and patches of light that trailed in like moonshine through a foliage. Her eyes were gleaming ripples in the white lake of her face; the shadows of her hair bordered the brow with a persuasive unintimate dusk. No love was there, surely; nor the imprint of any love. Her beauty was cool as this damp breeze, as the moist softness of her own lips.

"You're such a swan in this light," he whispered after a moment. There were silences as murmurous as sound. There were pauses that seemed about to shatter and were only to be snatched back to oblivion by the tightening of his arms about her and the sense that she was resting there as a caught, gossamer feather, drifted in out of the dark. Anthony laughed, noiselessly and exultantly, turning his face up and away from her, half in an overpowering rush of triumph, half lest her sight of him should spoil the splendid immobility of her expression. Such a kiss—it was a flower held against the face, never to be described, scarcely to be remembered; as though her beauty were giving off emanations of itself which settled transiently and already dissolving upon his heart.

. . . The buildings fell away in melted shadows; this was the Park now, and after a long while the great white ghost of the Metropolitan Museum moved majestically past, echoing sonorously to the rush of the cab.

"Why, Gloria! Why, Gloria!"

Her eyes appeared to regard him out of many thousand years: all emotion she might have felt, all words she might have uttered, would have seemed inadequate beside the adequacy of her silence, ineloquent against the eloquence of her beauty—and of her body, close to him, slender and cool.

"Tell him to turn around," she murmured, "and drive pretty fast going back. . . ."

Up in the supper-room the air was hot. The table, littered with napkins and ash-trays, was old and stale. It was between dances as they entered, and Muriel Kane looked up with roguishness extraordinary.

"Well, where have *you* been?"

"To call up mother," answered Gloria coolly. "I promised her I would. Did we miss a dance?"

Then followed an incident that though slight in itself

Anthony had cause to reflect on many years afterward. Joseph Bloeckman, leaning well back in his chair, fixed him with a peculiar glance, in which several emotions were curiously and inextricably mingled. He did not greet Gloria except by rising, and he immediately resumed a conversation with Richard Caramel about the influence of literature on the moving pictures.

Magic

The stark and unexpected miracle of a night fades out with the lingering death of the last stars and the premature birth of the first newsboys. The flame retreats to some remote and platonic fire; the white heat has gone from the iron and the glow from the coal.

Along the shelves of Anthony's library, filling a wall amply, crept a chill and insolent pencil of sunlight touching with frigid disapproval Thérèse of France and Ann the Superwoman, Jenny of the Orient Ballet and Zuleika the Conjurer—and Hoosier Cora—then down a shelf and into the years, resting pityingly on the over-invoked shades of Helen, Thaïs, Salome, and Cleopatra.

Anthony, shaved and bathed, sat in his most deeply cushioned chair and watched it until at the steady rising of the sun it lay glinting for a moment on the silk-ends of the rug—and went out.

It was ten o'clock. The Sunday Times, scattered about his feet, proclaimed by rotogravure and editorial, by social revelation and sporting sheet, that the world had been tremendously engrossed during the past week in the business of moving toward some splendid if somewhat indeterminate goal. For his part Anthony had been once to his grandfather's, twice to his broker's, and three times to his tailor's—and in the last hour of the week's last day he had kissed a very beautiful and charming girl.

When he reached home his imagination had been teeming with high-pitched, unfamiliar dreams. There was suddenly no question on his mind, no eternal problem for a solution and re-solution. He had experienced an emotion that was neither mental nor physical, nor merely a mixture of the two, and the love of life absorbed him for the present to the exclusion of all else. He was content to let the experiment remain isolated and unique.

Almost impersonally he was convinced that no woman he had ever met compared in any way with Gloria. She was deeply herself; she was immeasurably sincere—of these things he was certain. Beside her the two dozen schoolgirls and débutantes, young married women and waifs and strays whom he had known were so many *females*, in the word's most contemptuous sense, breeders and bearers, exuding still that faintly odorous atmosphere of the cave and the nursery.

So far as he could see, she had neither submitted to any will of his nor caressed his vanity—except as her pleasure in his company was a caress. Indeed he had no reason for thinking she had given him aught that she did not give to others. This was as it should be. The idea of an entanglement growing out of the evening was as remote as it would have been repugnant. And she had disclaimed and buried the incident with a decisive untruth. Here were two young people with fancy enough to distinguish a game from its reality—who by the very casualness with which they met and passed on would proclaim themselves unharmed.

Having decided this he went to the phone and called up the Plaza Hotel.

Gloria was out. Her mother knew neither where she had gone nor when she would return.

It was somehow at this point that the first wrongness in the case asserted itself. There was an element of callousness, almost of indecency, in Gloria's absence from home. He suspected that by going out she had intrigued him into a disadvantage. Returning she would find his name, and smile. Most discreetly! He should have waited a few hours in order to drive home the utter inconsequence with which he regarded the incident. What an asinine blunder! She would think he considered himself particularly favored. She would think he was reacting with the most inept intimacy to a quite trivial episode.

He remembered that during the previous month his janitor, to whom he had delivered a rather muddled lecture on the "brother-hoove man," had come up next day and, on the basis of what had happened the night before, seated himself in the window-seat for a cordial and chatty half-hour. Anthony wondered in horror if Gloria would regard him as he had regarded that man. Him—Anthony Patch! Horror!

It never occurred to him that he was a passive thing, acted upon by an influence above and beyond Gloria, that he was merely the sensitive plate on which the photograph was made. Some gargantuan photographer had focussed the camera on Gloria and *snap!*—the poor plate could but develop, confined like all things to its nature.

But Anthony, lying upon his couch and staring at the orange lamp, passed his thin fingers incessantly through his dark hair and made new symbols for the hours. She was in a shop now, it seemed, moving lithely among the velvets and the furs, her own dress making, as she walked, a debonair rustle in that world of silken rustles and cool soprano laughter and scents of many slain but living flowers. The Minnies and Pearls and Jewels and Jennies would gather round her like courtiers, bearing wispy frailties of Georgette crepe, delicate chiffon to echo her cheeks in faint pastel, milky lace to rest in pale disarray against her neck—damask was used but to cover priests and divans in these days, and cloth of Samarand was remembered only by the romantic poets.

She would go elsewhere after a while, tilting her head a hundred ways under a hundred bonnets, seeking in vain for mock cherries to match her lips or plumes that were graceful as her own supple body.

Noon would come—she would hurry along Fifth Avenue, a Nordic Ganymede, her fur coat swinging fashionably with her steps, her cheeks redder by a stroke of the wind's brush, her breath a delightful mist upon the bracing air—and the doors of the Ritz would revolve, the crowd would divide, fifty masculine eyes would start, stare, as she gave back forgotten dreams to the husbands of many obese and comic women.

One o'clock. With her fork she would tantalize the heart of an adoring artichoke, while her escort served himself up in the thick, dripping sentences of an enraptured man.

Four o'clock: her little feet moving to melody, her face distinct in the crowd, her partner happy as a petted puppy and mad as the immemorial hatter. . . . Then—then night would come drifting down and perhaps another damp. The signs would spill their light into the street. Who knew? No wiser than he, they haply sought to recapture that picture done in cream and shadow they had seen on the hushed Avenue the night before. And they might, ah, they might! A thousand taxis would yawn at a thousand corners, and only to him was that kiss forever lost and done. In a thousand guises Thaïs would hail a cab and turn up her face for loving. And her pallor would be virginal and lovely, and her kiss chaste as the moon. . . .

He sprang excitedly to his feet. How inappropriate that she should be out! He had realized at last what he wanted—to kiss her again, to find rest in her great immobility. She was the end of all restlessness, all malcontent.

Anthony dressed and went out, as he should have done long before, and down to Richard Caramel's room to hear the last revision of the last chapter of "The Demon Lover." He did not call Gloria again until six. He did not find her in until eight and—oh, climax of anticlimaxes!—she could give him no engagement until Tuesday afternoon. A broken piece of gutta-percha clattered to the floor as he banged up the phone.

Black Magic

Tuesday was freezing cold. He called at a bleak two o'clock and as they shook hands he wondered confusedly whether he had ever kissed her; it was almost unbelievable—he seriously doubted if she remembered it.

"I called you four times on Sunday," he told her.

"Did you?"

There was surprise in her voice and interest in her expression. Silently he cursed himself for having told her. He might have known her pride did not deal in such petty triumphs. Even then he had not guessed at the truth—that never having had to worry about men she had seldom used the wary subterfuges, the playings out and haulings in, that were the stock in trade of her sisterhood. When she liked a man, that was trick enough. Did she think she loved him—there was an ultimate and fatal thrust. Her charm endlessly preserved itself.

"I was anxious to see you," he said simply. "I want to talk to you—I mean really talk, somewhere where we can be alone. May I?"

"What do you mean?"

He swallowed a sudden lump of panic. He felt that she knew what he wanted.

"I mean, not at a tea-table," he said.

"Well, all right, but not to-day. I want to get some exercise. Let's walk!"

It was bitter and raw. All the evil hate in the mad heart of February was wrought into the forlorn and icy wind that cut its way cruelly across Central Park and down along Fifth Avenue. It was almost impossible to talk, and discomfort made him distracted, so much so that he turned at Sixty-first Street to find that she was no longer beside him. He looked around. She was forty feet in the rear standing motionless, her face half hidden in her fur-coat collar, moved either by anger or laughter—he could not determine which. He started back.

"Don't let me interrupt your walk!" she called.

"I'm mighty sorry," he answered in confusion. "Did I go too fast?"

"I'm cold," she announced. "I want to go home. And you walk too fast."

"I'm very sorry."

Side by side they started for the Plaza. He wished he could see her face.

"Men don't usually get so absorbed in themselves when they're with me."

"I'm sorry."

"That's very interesting."

"It *is* rather too cold to walk," he said, briskly, to hide his annoyance.

She made no answer and he wondered if she would dismiss him at the hotel entrance. She walked in without speaking, however, and to the elevator, throwing him a single remark as she entered it:

"You'd better come up."

He hesitated for the fraction of a moment.

"Perhaps I'd better call some other time."

"Just as you say." Her words were murmured as an aside.

The main concern of life was the adjusting of some stray wisps of hair in the elevator mirror. Her cheeks were brilliant, her eyes sparkled—she had never seemed so lovely, so exquisitely to be desired.

Despising himself, he found that he was walking down the tenth-floor corridor a subservient foot behind her; was in the sitting-room while she disappeared to shed her furs. Something had gone wrong—in his own eyes he had lost a shred of dignity; in an unpremeditated yet significant encounter he had been completely defeated.

However, by the time she reappeared in the sitting-room he had explained himself to himself with sophistic satisfaction. After all he had done the strongest thing, he thought. He had wanted to come up, he had come. Yet what happened later on that afternoon must be traced to the indignity he had experienced in the elevator; the girl was worrying him intolerably, so much so that when she came out he involuntarily drifted into criticism.

"Who's this Bloeckman, Gloria?"

"A business friend of father's."

"Odd sort of fellow!"

"He doesn't like you either," she said with a sudden smile.

Anthony laughed.

"I'm flattered at his notice. He evidently considers me a—" He broke off with "Is he in love with you?"

"I don't know."

"The deuce you don't," he insisted. "Of course he is. I remember the look he gave me when we got back to the table. He'd probably have had me quietly assaulted by a delegation of movie supes if you hadn't invented that phone call."

"He didn't mind. I told him afterward what really happened."

"You told him!"

"He asked me."

"I don't like that very well," he remonstrated.

She laughed again.

"Oh, you don't?"

"What business is it of his?"

"None. That's why I told him."

Anthony in a turmoil bit savagely at his mouth.

"Why should I lie?" she demanded directly. "I'm not ashamed of anything I do. It happened to interest him to know that I kissed you, and I happened to be in a good humor, so I satisfied his curiosity by a simple and precise 'yes.' Being rather a sensible man, after his fashion, he dropped the subject."

"Except to say that he hated me."

"Oh, it worries you? Well, if you must probe this stupendous matter to its depths he didn't say he hated you. I simply know he does."

"It doesn't wor——"

"Oh, let's drop it!" she cried spiritedly. "It's a most uninteresting matter to me."

With a tremendous effort Anthony made his acquiescence a twist of subject, and they drifted into an ancient question-and-answer game concerned with each other's pasts, gradually warming as they discovered the age-old, immemorial resemblances in tastes and ideas. They said things that were more revealing than they intended—but each pretended to accept the other at face, or rather word, value.

The growth of intimacy is like that. First one gives off his best picture, the bright and finished product mended with bluff and falsehood and humor. Then more details are required and one paints a second portrait, and a third—before long the best lines cancel out—and the secret is exposed at last; the planes of the pictures have intermingled and given us away, and though we paint and paint we can no longer sell a picture. We must be satisfied with hoping that such fatuous accounts of ourselves as we make to our wives and children and business associates are accepted as true.

"It seems to me," Anthony was saying earnestly, "that the position of a man with neither necessity nor ambition is unfortunate. Heaven knows it'd be pathetic of me to be sorry for myself—yet, sometimes I envy Dick."

Her silence was encouragement. It was as near as she ever came to an intentional lure.

"—And there used to be dignified occupations for a gentleman who had leisure, things a little more constructive than filling up the landscape with smoke or juggling some one else's money. There's science, of course: sometimes I wish I'd taken a good foundation, say at Boston Tech. But now, by golly, I'd have to sit down for two years and struggle through the fundamentals of physics and chemistry."

She yawned.

"I've told you I don't know what anybody ought to do," she said ungraciously, and at her indifference his rancor was born again.

"Aren't you interested in anything except yourself?"

"Not much."

He glared; his growing enjoyment in the conversation was ripped to shreds. She had been irritable and vindictive all day, and it seemed to him that for this moment he hated her hard selfishness. He stared morosely at the fire.

Then a strange thing happened. She turned to him and smiled, and as he saw her smile every rag of anger and hurt vanity dropped from him—as though his very moods were but the outer ripples of her own, as though emotion rose no longer in his breast unless she saw fit to pull an omnipotent controlling thread.

He moved closer and taking her hand pulled her ever so gently toward him until she half lay against his shoulder. She smiled up at him as he kissed her.

"Gloria," he whispered very softly. Again she had made a magic, subtle and pervading as a spilt perfume, irresistible and sweet.

Afterward, neither the next day nor after many years, could he remember the important things of that afternoon. Had she been moved? In his arms had she spoken a little—or at all? What measure of enjoyment had she taken in his kisses? And had she at any time lost herself ever so little?

Oh, for him there was no doubt. He had risen and paced the floor in sheer ecstasy. That such a girl should be; should poise curled in a corner of the couch like a swallow newly landed from a clean swift flight, watching him with inscrutable eyes. He would stop his pacing and, half shy each time at first, drop his arm around her and find her kiss.

She was fascinating, he told her. He had never met any one like her before. He besought her jauntily but earnestly to send him away; he didn't want to fall in love. He wasn't coming to see her any more—already she had haunted too many of his ways.

What delicious romance! His true reaction was neither fear nor sorrow—only this deep delight in being with her that colored the banality of his words and made the mawkish seem sad and the posturing seem wise. He *would* come back—eternally. He should have known!

"This is all. It's been very rare to have known you, very strange and wonderful. But this wouldn't do—and wouldn't last." As he spoke there was in his heart that tremulousness that we take for sincerity in ourselves.

Afterward he remembered one reply of hers to something he had asked her. He remembered it in this form—perhaps he had unconsciously arranged and polished it:

"A woman should be able to kiss a man beautifully and romantically without any desire to be either his wife or his mistress."

As always when he was with her she seemed to grow gradually older until at the end ruminations too deep for words would be wintering in her eyes.

An hour passed, and the fire leaped up in little ecstasies as though its fading life was sweet. It was five now, and the clock over the mantel became articulate in sound. Then as if a brutish sensibility in him was reminded by those thin, tinny beats that the petals were falling from the flowered afternoon, Anthony pulled her quickly to her feet and held her helpless, without breath, in a kiss that was neither a game nor a tribute.

Her arms fell to her side. In an instant she was free.

"Don't!" she said quietly. "I don't want that."

She sat down on the far side of the lounge and gazed straight before her. A frown had gathered between her eyes. Anthony sank down beside her and closed his hand over hers. It was lifeless and unresponsive.

"Why, Gloria!" He made a motion as if to put his arm about her but she drew away.

"I don't want that," she repeated.

"I'm very sorry," he said, a little impatiently. "I—I didn't know you made such fine distinctions."

She did not answer.

"Won't you kiss me, Gloria?"

"I don't want to." It seemed to him she had not moved for hours.

"A sudden change, isn't it?" Annoyance was growing in his voice.

"Is it?" She appeared uninterested. It was almost as though she were looking at some one else.

"Perhaps I'd better go."

No reply. He rose and regarded her angrily, uncertainly. Again he sat down.

"Gloria, Gloria, won't you kiss me?"

"No." Her lips, parting for the word, had just faintly stirred.

Again he got to his feet, this time with less decision, less confidence.

"Then I'll go."

Silence.

"All right—I'll go."

He was aware of a certain irremediable lack of originality in his remarks. Indeed he felt that the whole atmosphere had grown oppressive. He wished she would speak, rail at him, cry out upon him, anything but this pervasive and chilling silence. He cursed himself for a weak fool; his clearest desire was to move her, to hurt her, to see her wince. Helplessly, involuntarily, he erred again.

"If you're tired of kissing me I'd better go."

He saw her lips curl slightly and his last dignity left him. She spoke, at length:

"I believe you've made that remark several times before."

He looked about him immediately, saw his hat and coat on a chair—blundered into them, during an intolerable moment. Looking again at the couch he perceived that she had not turned, not even moved. With a shaken, immediately regretted "good-by" he went quickly but without dignity from the room.

For over a moment Gloria made no sound. Her lips were still curled; her glance was straight, proud, remote. Then her eyes blurred a little, and she murmured three words half aloud to the death-bound fire:

"Good-by, you ass!" she said.

Panic

The man had had the hardest blow of his life. He knew at last what he wanted, but in finding it out it seemed that he had put it forever beyond his grasp. He reached home in misery, dropped into an armchair without even removing his overcoat, and sat there for over an hour, his mind racing the paths of fruitless and wretched self-absorption. She had sent him away! That was the reiterated burden of his despair. Instead of seizing the girl and holding her by sheer strength until she became passive to his desire, instead of beating down her will by the force of his own, he had walked, defeated and powerless, from her door, with the corners of his mouth drooping and what force there might have been in his grief and rage hidden behind the manner of a whipped schoolboy. At one minute she had liked him tremendously—ah, she had nearly loved him. In the next he had become a thing of indifference to her, an insolent and efficiently humiliated man.

He had no great self-reproach—some, of course, but there were other things dominant in him now, far more urgent. He was not so much in love with Gloria as mad for her. Unless he could have her near him again, kiss her, hold her close and acquiescent, he wanted nothing more from life. By her three minutes of utter unwavering indifference the girl had lifted herself from a high but somehow casual position in his mind, to be instead his complete preoccupation. However much his wild thoughts varied between a passionate desire for her kisses and an equally passionate craving to hurt and mar her, the residue of his mind craved in finer fashion to possess the triumphant soul that had shone through those three minutes. She was beautiful—but especially she was without mercy. He must own that strength that could send him away.

At present no such analysis was possible to Anthony. His clarity of mind, all those endless resources which he thought his irony had brought him were swept aside. Not only for that night but for the days and weeks that followed his books were to be but furniture and his friends only people who lived and walked in a nebulous outer world from which he was trying to escape—that world was cold and full of bleak wind, and for a little while he had seen into a warm house where fires shone.

About midnight he began to realize that he was hungry. He went down into Fifty-second Street, where it was so cold that he could scarcely see; the moisture froze on his lashes and in the corners of his lips. Everywhere dreariness had come down from the north, settling upon the thin and cheerless street, where black bundled figures blacker still against the night, moved stumbling along the sidewalk through the shrieking wind, sliding their feet cautiously ahead as though they were on skis. Anthony turned over toward Sixth Avenue, so absorbed in his thoughts as not to notice that several passers-by had stared at him. His overcoat was wide open, and the wind was biting in, hard and full of merciless death.

. . . After a while a waitress spoke to him, a fat waitress with black-rimmed eye-glasses from which dangled a long black cord.

"Order, please!"

Her voice, he considered, was unnecessarily loud. He looked up resentfully.

"You wanna order or doncha?"

"Of course," he protested.

"Well, I ast you three times. This ain't no restroom."

He glanced at the big clock and discovered with a start that it was after two. He was down around Thirtieth Street somewhere, and after a moment he found and translated the

CHILD'S

in a white semicircle of letters upon the glass front. The place was inhabited sparsely by three or four bleak and half-frozen night-hawks.

"Give me some bacon and eggs and coffee, please."

The waitress bent upon him a last disgusted glance and, looking ludicrously intellectual in her corded glasses, hurried away.

God! Gloria's kisses had been such flowers. He remembered as though it had been years ago the low freshness of her voice, the beautiful lines of her body shining through her clothes, her face lily-colored under the lamps of the street—under the lamps.

Misery struck at him again, piling a sort of terror upon the ache and yearning. He had lost her. It was true—no denying it, no softening it. But a new idea had seared his sky—what of Bloeckman! What would happen now? There was a wealthy man, middle-aged enough to be tolerant with a beautiful wife, to baby her whims and indulge her unreason, to wear her as she perhaps wished to be worn—a bright flower in his buttonhole, safe and secure from the things she feared. He felt that she had been playing with the idea of marrying Bloeckman, and it was well possible that this disappointment in Anthony might throw her on sudden impulse into Bloeckman's arms.

The idea drove him childishly frantic. He wanted to kill Bloeckman and make him suffer for his hideous presumption. He was saying this over and over to himself with his teeth tight shut, and a perfect orgy of hate and fright in his eyes.

But, behind this obscene jealousy, Anthony was in love at last, profoundly and truly in love, as the word goes between man and woman.

His coffee appeared at his elbow and gave off for a certain time a gradually diminishing wisp of steam. The night manager, seated at his desk, glanced at the motionless figure alone at the last table, and then with a sigh moved down upon him just as the hour-hand crossed the figure three on the big clock.

Wisdom

After another day the turmoil subsided and Anthony began to exercise a measure of reason. He was in love—he cried it passionately to himself. The things that a week before would have seemed insuperable obstacles, his limited income, his desire to be irresponsible and independent, had in this forty hours become the merest chaff before the wind of his infatuation. If he did not marry her his life would be a feeble parody on his own adolescence. To be able to face people and to endure the constant reminder of Gloria that all existence had become, it was necessary for him to have hope. So he built hope desperately and tenaciously out of the stuff of his dream, a hope flimsy enough, to be sure, a hope that was cracked and dissipated a dozen times a day, a hope mothered by mockery, but, nevertheless, a hope that would be brawn and sinew to his self-respect.

Out of this developed a spark of wisdom, a true perception of his own from out the effortless past.

"Memory is short," he thought.

So very short. At the crucial point the Trust President is on the stand, a potential criminal needing but one push to be a jailbird, scorned by the upright for leagues around. Let him be acquitted—and in a year all is forgotten. "Yes, he did have some trouble once, just a technicality, I believe." Oh, memory is very short!

Anthony had seen Gloria altogether about a dozen times, say two dozen hours. Supposing he left her alone for a month, made no attempt to see her or speak to her, and avoided every place where she might possibly be. Wasn't it possible, the more possible because she had never loved him, that at the end of that time the rush of events would efface his personality from her conscious mind, and with his personality his offense and humiliation? She would forget, for there would be other men. He winced. The implication struck out at him—other men. Two months—God! Better three weeks, two weeks——

He thought this the second evening after the catastrophe when he was undressing, and at this point he threw himself down on the bed and lay there, trembling very slightly and looking at the top of the canopy.

Two weeks—that was worse than no time at all. In two weeks he would approach her much as he would have to now, without personality or confidence—remaining still the man who had gone too far and then for a period that in time was but a moment but in fact an eternity, whined. No, two weeks was too short a time. Whatever poignancy there had been for her in that afternoon must have time to dull. He must give her a period when the incident should fade, and then a new period when she should gradually begin to think of him, no matter how dimly, with a true perspective that would remember his pleasantness as well as his humiliation.

He fixed, finally, on six weeks as approximately the interval best suited to his purpose, and on a desk calendar he marked the days off, finding that it would fall on the ninth of April. Very well, on that day he would phone and ask her if he might call. Until then—silence.

After his decision a gradual improvement was manifest. He had taken at least a step in the direction to which hope pointed, and he realized that the less he brooded upon her the better he would be able to give the desired impression when they met.

In another hour he fell into a deep sleep.

The Interval

Nevertheless, though, as the days passed, the glory of her hair dimmed perceptibly for him and in a year of separation might have departed completely, the six weeks held many abominable days. He dreaded the sight of Dick and Maury, imagining wildly that they knew all—but when the three met it was Richard Caramel and not Anthony who was the centre of attention; "The Demon Lover" had been accepted for immediate publication. Anthony felt that from now on he moved apart. He no longer craved the warmth and security of Maury's society which had cheered him no further back than November. Only Gloria could give that now and no one else ever again. So Dick's success rejoiced him only casually and worried him not a little. It meant that the world was going ahead—writing and reading and publishing—and living. And he wanted the world to wait motionless and breathless for six weeks—while Gloria forgot.

Two Encounters

His greatest satisfaction was in Geraldine's company. He took her once to dinner and the theatre and entertained her several times in his apartment. When he was with her she absorbed him, not as Gloria had, but quieting those erotic sensibilities in him that worried over Gloria. It didn't matter how he kissed Geraldine. A kiss was a kiss—to be enjoyed to the utmost for its short moment. To Geraldine things belonged in definite pigeonholes: a kiss was one thing, anything further was quite another; a kiss was all right; the other things were "bad."

When half the interval was up two incidents occurred on successive days that upset his increasing calm and caused a temporary relapse.

The first was—he saw Gloria. It was a short meeting. Both bowed. Both spoke, yet neither heard the other. But when it was over Anthony read down a column of The Sun three times in succession without understanding a single sentence.

One would have thought Sixth Avenue a safe street! Having forsworn his barber at the Plaza he went around the corner one morning to be shaved, and while waiting his turn he took off coat and vest, and with his soft collar open at the neck stood near the front of the shop. The day was an oasis in the cold desert of March and the sidewalk was cheerful with a population of strolling sun-worshippers. A stout woman upholstered in velvet, her flabby cheeks too much massaged, swirled by with her poodle straining at its leash—the effect being given of a tug bringing in an ocean liner. Just behind them a man in a striped blue suit, walking slue-footed in white-spatted feet, grinned at the sight and catching Anthony's eye, winked through the glass. Anthony laughed, thrown immediately into that humor in which men and women were graceless and absurd phantasms, grotesquely curved and rounded in a rectangular world of their own building. They inspired the same sensations in him as did those strange and monstrous fish who inhabit the esoteric world of green in the aquarium.

Two more strollers caught his eye casually, a man and a girl—then in a horrified instant the girl resolved herself into Gloria. He stood here powerless; they came nearer and Gloria, glancing in, saw him. Her eyes widened and she smiled politely. Her lips moved. She was less than five feet away.

"How do you do?" he muttered inanely.

Gloria, happy, beautiful, and young—with a man he had never seen before!

It was then that the barber's chair was vacated and he read down the newspaper column three times in succession.

*

The second incident took place the next day. Going into the Manhattan bar about seven he was confronted with Bloeckman. As it happened, the room was nearly deserted, and before the mutual recognition he had stationed himself within a foot of the older man and ordered his drink, so it was inevitable that they should converse.

"Hello, Mr. Patch," said Bloeckman amiably enough.

Anthony took the proffered hand and exchanged a few aphorisms on the fluctuations of the mercury.

"Do you come in here much?" inquired Bloeckman.

"No, very seldom." He omitted to add that the Plaza bar had, until lately, been his favorite.

"Nice bar. One of the best bars in town."

Anthony nodded. Bloeckman emptied his glass and picked up his cane. He was in evening dress.

"Well, I'll be hurrying on. I'm going to dinner with Miss Gilbert."

Death looked suddenly out at him from two blue eyes. Had he announced himself as his vis-à-vis's prospective murderer he could not have struck a more vital blow at Anthony. The younger man must have reddened visibly, for his every nerve was in instant clamor. With tremendous effort he mustered a rigid—oh, so rigid—smile, and said a conventional good-by. But that night he lay awake until after four, half wild with grief and fear and abominable imaginings.

Weakness

And one day in the fifth week he called her up. He had been sitting in his apartment trying to read "L'Éducation Sentimental," and something in the book had sent his thoughts racing in the direction that, set free, they always took, like horses racing for a home stable. With suddenly quickened breath he walked to the telephone. When he gave the number it seemed to him that his voice faltered and broke like a schoolboy's. The Central must have heard the pounding of his heart. The sound of the receiver being taken up at the other end was a crack of doom, and Mrs. Gilbert's voice, soft as maple-syrup running into a glass container, had for him a quality of horror in its single "Hello-o-ah?"

"Miss Gloria's not feeling well. She's lying down, asleep. Who shall I say called?"

"Nobody!" he shouted.

In a wild panic he slammed down the receiver; collapsed into his armchair in the cold sweat of breathless relief.

Serenade

The first thing he said to her was: "Why, you've bobbed your hair!" and she answered: "Yes, isn't it gorgeous?"

It was not fashionable then. It was to be fashionable in five or six years. At that time it was considered extremely daring.

"It's all sunshine outdoors," he said gravely. "Don't you want to take a walk?"

She put on a light coat and a quaintly piquant Napoleon hat of Alice Blue, and they walked along the Avenue and into the Zoo, where they properly admired the grandeur of the elephant and the collar-height of the giraffe, but did not visit the monkey-house because Gloria said that monkeys smelt so bad.

Then they returned toward the Plaza, talking about nothing, but glad for the spring singing in the air and for the warm balm that lay upon the suddenly golden city. To their right was the Park, while at the left a great bulk of granite and marble muttered dully a millionaire's chaotic message to whosoever would listen: something about "I worked and I saved and I was sharper than all Adam and here I sit, by golly, by golly!"

All the newest and most beautiful designs in automobiles were out on Fifth Avenue, and ahead of them the Plaza loomed up rather unusually white and attractive. The supple, indolent Gloria walked a short shadow's length ahead of him, pouring out lazy casual comments that floated a moment on the dazzling air before they reached his ear.

"Oh!" she cried, "I want to go south to Hot Springs! I want to get out in the air and just roll around on the new grass and forget there's ever been any winter."

"Don't you, though!"

"I want to hear a million robins making a frightful racket. I sort of like birds."

"All women *are* birds," he ventured.

"What kind am I?"—quick and eager.

"A swallow, I think, and sometimes a bird of paradise. Most girls are sparrows, of course—see that row of nurse-maids over there? They're sparrows—or are they magpies? And of course you've met canary girls—and robin girls."

"And swan girls and parrot girls. All grown women are hawks, I think, or owls."

"What am I—a buzzard?"

She laughed and shook her head.

"Oh, no, you're not a bird at all, do you think? You're a Russian wolfhound."

Anthony remembered that they were white and always looked unnaturally hungry. But then they were usually photographed with dukes and princesses, so he was properly flattered.

"Dick's a fox-terrier, a trick fox-terrier," she continued.

"And Maury's a cat." Simultaneously it occurred to him how like Bloeckman was to a robust and offensive hog. But he preserved a discreet silence.

Later, as they parted, Anthony asked when he might see her again.

"Don't you ever make long engagements?" he pleaded, "even if it's a week ahead, I think it'd be fun to spend a whole day together, morning and afternoon both."

"It would be, wouldn't it?" She thought for a moment. "Let's do it next Sunday."

"All right. I'll map out a programme that'll take up every minute."

He did. He even figured to a nicety what would happen in the two hours when she would come to his apartment for tea: how the good Bounds would have the windows wide to let in the fresh breeze—but a fire going also lest there be chill in the air—and how there would be clusters of flowers about in big cool bowls that he would buy for the occasion. They would sit on the lounge.

And when the day came they did sit upon the lounge. After a while Anthony kissed her because it came about quite naturally; he found sweetness sleeping still upon her lips, and felt that he had never been away. The fire was bright and the breeze sighing in through the curtains brought a mellow damp, promising May and world of summer. His soul thrilled to remote harmonies; he heard the strum of far guitars and waters lapping on a warm Mediterranean shore—for he was young now as he would never be again, and more triumphant than death.

Six o'clock stole down too soon and rang the querulous melody of St. Anne's chimes on the corner. Through the gathering dusk they strolled to the Avenue, where the crowds, like prisoners released, were walking with elastic step at last after the long winter, and the tops of the busses were thronged with congenial kings and the shops full of fine soft things for the summer, the rare summer, the gay promising summer that seemed for love what the winter was for money. Life was singing for his supper on the corner! Life was handing round cocktails in the street! Old women there were in that crowd who felt that they could have run and won a hundred-yard dash!

In bed that night with the lights out and the cool room swimming with moonlight, Anthony lay awake and played with every minute of the day like a child playing in turn with each one of a pile of long-wanted Christmas toys. He had told her gently, almost in the middle of a kiss, that he loved her, and she had smiled and held him closer and murmured, "I'm glad," looking into his eyes. There had been a new quality in her attitude, a new growth of sheer physical attraction toward him and a strange emotional tenseness, that was enough to make him clinch his hands and draw in his breath at the recollection. He had felt nearer to her than ever before. In a rare delight he cried aloud to the room that he loved her.

He phoned next morning—no hesitation now, no uncertainty—instead a delirious excitement that doubled and trebled when he heard her voice:

"Good morning—Gloria."

"Good morning."

"That's all I called you up to say—dear."

"I'm glad you did."

"I wish I could see you."

"You will, to-morrow night."

"That's a long time, isn't it?"

"Yes—" Her voice was reluctant. His hand tightened on the receiver.

"Couldn't I come to-night?" He dared anything in the glory and revelation of that almost whispered "yes."

"I have a date."

"Oh——"

"But I might—I might be able to break it."

"Oh!"—a sheer cry, a rhapsody. "Gloria?"

"What?"

"I love you."

Another pause and then:

"I—I'm glad."

Happiness, remarked Maury Noble one day, is only the first hour after the alleviation of some especially intense misery. But oh, Anthony's face as he walked down the tenth-floor corridor of the Plaza that night! His dark eyes were gleaming—around his mouth were lines it was a kindness to see. He was handsome then if never before, bound for one of those immortal moments which come so radiantly that their remembered light is enough to see by for years.

He knocked and, at a word, entered. Gloria, dressed in simple pink, starched and fresh as a flower, was across the room, standing very still, and looking at him wide-eyed.

As he closed the door behind him she gave a little cry and moved swiftly over the intervening space, her arms rising in a premature caress as she came near. Together they crushed out the stiff folds of her dress in one triumphant and enduring embrace.

BOOK TWO

CHAPTER I

The Radiant Hour

AFTER a fortnight Anthony and Gloria began to indulge in "practical discussions," as they called those sessions when under the guise of severe realism they walked in an eternal moonlight.

"Not as much as I do you," the critic of belles-lettres would insist. "If you really loved me you'd want every one to know it."

"I do," she protested; "I want to stand on the street corner like a sandwich-man, informing all the passers-by."

"Then tell me all the reasons why you're going to marry me in June."

"Well, because you're so clean. You're sort of blowy clean, like I am. There's two sorts, you know. One's like Dick: he's clean like polished pans. You and I are clean like streams and winds. I can tell whenever I see a person whether he is clean, and if so, which kind of clean he is."

"We're twins."

Ecstatic thought!

"Mother says"—she hesitated uncertainly—"mother says that two souls are sometimes created together and—and in love before they're born."

Bilphism gained its easiest convert. . . . After a while he lifted up his head and laughed soundlessly toward the ceiling. When his eyes came back to her he saw that she was angry.

"Why did you laugh?" she cried, "you've done that twice before. There's nothing funny about our relation to each other. I don't mind playing the fool, and I don't mind having you do it, but I can't stand it when we're together."

"I'm sorry."

"Oh, don't say you're sorry! If you can't think of anything better than that, just keep quiet!"

"I love you."

"I don't care."

There was a pause. Anthony was depressed. . . . At length Gloria murmured:

"I'm sorry I was mean."

"You weren't. I was the one."

Peace was restored—the ensuing moments were so much more sweet and sharp and poignant. They were stars on this stage, each playing to an audience of two: the passion of their pretense created the actuality. Here, finally, was the quintessence of self-expression—yet it was probable that for the most part their love expressed Gloria rather than Anthony. He felt often like a scarcely tolerated guest at a party she was giving.

Telling Mrs. Gilbert had been an embarrassed matter. She sat stuffed into a small chair and listened with an intense and very blinky sort of concentration. She must have known it—for three weeks Gloria had seen no one else—and she must have noticed that this time there was an authentic difference in her daughter's attitude. She had been given special deliveries to post; she had heeded, as all mothers seem to heed, the hither end of telephone conversations, disguised but still rather warm——

—Yet she had delicately professed surprise and declared herself immensely pleased; she doubtless was; so were the geranium-plants blossoming in the window-boxes, and so were the cabbies when the lovers sought the romantic privacy of hansom cabs—quaint device—and the staid bill of fares on which they scribbled "you know I do," pushing it over for the other to see.

But between kisses Anthony and this golden girl quarrelled incessantly.

"Now, Gloria," he would cry, "please let me explain!"

"Don't explain. Kiss me."

"I don't think that's right. If I hurt your feelings we ought to discuss it. I don't like this kiss-and-forget."

"But I don't want to argue. I think it's wonderful that we *can* kiss and forget, and when we can't it'll be time to argue."

At one time some gossamer difference attained such bulk that Anthony arose and punched himself into his overcoat—for a moment it appeared that the scene of the preceding February was to be repeated, but knowing how deeply she was moved he retained his dignity with his pride, and in a moment Gloria was sobbing in his arms, her lovely face miserable as a frightened little girl's.

Meanwhile they kept unfolding to each other, unwillingly, by curious reactions and evasions, by distastes and prejudices and unintended hints of the past. The girl was proudly incapable of jealousy and, because he was extremely jealous, this virtue piqued him. He told her recondite incidents of his own life on purpose to arouse some spark of it, but to no avail. She possessed him now—nor did she desire the dead years.

"Oh, Anthony," she would say, "always when I'm mean to you I'm sorry afterward. I'd give my right hand to save you one little moment's pain."

And in that instant her eyes were brimming and she was not aware that she was voicing an illusion. Yet Anthony knew that there were days when they hurt each other purposely—taking almost a delight in the thrust. Incessantly she puzzled him: one hour so intimate and charming, striving desperately toward an unguessed, transcendent union; the next, silent and cold, apparently unmoved by any consideration of their love or anything he could say. Often he would eventually trace these portentous reticences to some physical discomfort—of these she never complained until they were over—or to some carelessness or presumption in him, or to an unsatisfactory dish at dinner, but even then the means by which she created the infinite distances she spread about herself were a mystery, buried somewhere back in those twenty-two years of unwavering pride.

"Why do you like Muriel?" he demanded one day.

"I don't—very much."

"Then why do you go with her?"

"Just for some one to go with. They're no exertion, those girls. They sort of believe everything I tell 'em—but I rather like Rachael. I think she's cute—and so clean and slick, don't you? I used to have other friends—in Kansas City and at school—casual, all of them, girls who just flitted into my range and out of it for no more reason than that boys took us places together. They didn't interest me after environment stopped throwing us together. Now they're mostly married. What does it matter—they were all just people."

"You like men better, don't you?"

"Oh, much better. I've got a man's mind."

"You've got a mind like mine. Not strongly gendered either way."

Later she told him about the beginnings of her friendship with Bloeckman. One day in Delmonico's, Gloria and Rachael had come upon Bloeckman and Mr. Gilbert having luncheon and curiosity had impelled her to make it a party of four. She had liked him—rather. He was a relief from younger men, satisfied as he was with so little. He humored her and he laughed, whether he understood her or not. She met him several times, despite the open disapproval of her parents, and within a month he had asked her to marry him, tendering her everything from a villa in Italy to a brilliant career on the screen. She had laughed in his face—and he had laughed too.

But he had not given up. To the time of Anthony's arrival in the arena he had been making steady progress. She treated him rather well—except that she had called him always by an invidious nickname—perceiving, meanwhile, that he was figuratively following along beside her as she walked the fence, ready to catch her if she should fall.

The night before the engagement was announced she told Bloeckman. It was a heavy blow. She did not enlighten Anthony as to the details, but she implied that he had not hesitated to argue with her. Anthony gathered that the interview had terminated on a stormy note, with Gloria very cool and unmoved lying in her corner of the sofa and Joseph Bloeckman of "Films Par Excellence" pacing the carpet with eyes narrowed and head bowed. Gloria had been sorry for him but she had judged it best not to show it. In a final burst of kindness she had tried to make him hate her, there at the last. But Anthony, understanding that Gloria's indifference was her strongest appeal, judged how futile this must have been. He wondered, often but quite casually, about Bloeckman—finally he forgot him entirely.

Heyday

One afternoon they found front seats on the sunny roof of a bus and rode for hours from the fading Square up along the sullied river, and then, as the stray beams fled the westward streets, sailed down the turgid Avenue, darkening with ominous bees from the department-stores. The traffic was clotted and gripped in a patternless jam; the busses were packed four deep like platforms above the crowd as they waited for the moan of the traffic whistle.

"Isn't it good!" cried Gloria. "Look!"

A miller's wagon, stark white with flour, driven by a powdery clown, passed in front of them behind a white horse and his black team-mate.

"What a pity!" she complained; "they'd look so beautiful in the dusk, if only both horses were white. I'm mighty happy just this minute, in this city."

Anthony shook his head in disagreement.

"I think the city's a mountebank. Always struggling to approach the tremendous and impressive urbanity ascribed to it. Trying to be romantically metropolitan."

"I don't. I think it is impressive."

"Momentarily. But it's really a transparent, artificial sort of spectacle. It's got its press-agented stars and its flimsy, unenduring stage-settings and, I'll admit, the greatest army of supers ever assembled—" He paused, laughed shortly, and added: "Technically excellent, perhaps, but not convincing."

"I'll bet policemen think people are fools," said Gloria thoughtfully, as she watched a large but cowardly lady being helped across the street. "He always sees them frightened and inefficient and old—they are," she added. And then: "We'd better get off. I told mother I'd have an early supper and go to bed. She says I look tired, damn it."

"I wish we were married," he muttered soberly; "there'll be no good night then and we can do just as we want."

"Won't it be good! I think we ought to travel a lot. I want to go to the Mediterranean and Italy. And I'd like to go on the stage some time—say for about a year."

"You bet. I'll write a play for you."

"Won't that be good! And I'll act in it. And then some

time when we have more money"—old Adam's death was always thus tactfully alluded to—"we'll build a magnificent estate, won't we?"

"Oh, yes, with private swimming-pools."

"Dozens of them. And private rivers. Oh, I wish it were now."

Odd coincidence—he had just been wishing that very thing. They plunged like divers into the dark eddying crowd and emerging in the cool fifties sauntered indolently homeward, infinitely romantic to each other . . . both were walking alone in a dispassionate garden with a ghost found in a dream.

Halcyon days like boats drifting along slow-moving rivers; spring evenings full of a plaintive melancholy that made the past beautiful and bitter, bidding them look back and see that the loves of other summers long gone were dead with the forgotten waltzes of their years. Always the most poignant moments were when some artificial barrier kept them apart: in the theatre their hands would steal together, join, give and return gentle pressures through the long dark; in crowded rooms they would form words with their lips for each other's eyes—not knowing that they were but following in the foot-steps of dusty generations but comprehending dimly that if truth is the end of life happiness is a mode of it, to be cherished in its brief and tremulous moment. And then, one fairy night, May became June. Sixteen days now—fifteen—fourteen——

Three Disgressions

Just before the engagement was announced Anthony had gone up to Tarrytown to see his grandfather, who, a little more wizened and grizzly as time played its ultimate chuckling tricks, greeted the news with profound cynicism.

"Oh, you're going to get married, are you?" He said this with such a dubious mildness and shook his head up and down so many times that Anthony was not a little depressed. While he was unaware of his grandfather's intentions he presumed that a large part of the money would come to him. A good deal would go in charities, of course; a good deal to carry on the business of reform.

"Are you going to work?"

"Why—" temporized Anthony, somewhat disconcerted. "I *am* working. You know——"

"Ah, I mean work," said Adam Patch dispassionately.

"I'm not quite sure yet what I'll do. I'm not exactly a beggar, grampa," he asserted with some spirit.

The old man considered this with eyes half closed. Then almost apologetically he asked:

"How much do you save a year?"

"Nothing so far——"

"And so after just managing to get along on your money you've decided that by some miracle two of you can get along on it."

"Gloria has some money of her own. Enough to buy clothes."

"How much?"

Without considering this question impertinent, Anthony answered it.

"About a hundred a month."

"That's altogether about seventy-five hundred a year." Then he added softly: "It ought to be plenty. If you have any sense it ought to be plenty. But the question is whether you have any or not."

"I suppose it is." It was shameful to be compelled to endure this pious browbeating from the old man, and his next words were stiffened with vanity. "I can manage very well. You seem convinced that I'm utterly worthless. At any rate I came up here simply to tell you that I'm getting married in June. Good-by, sir." With this he turned away and headed for the door, unaware that in that instant his grandfather, for the first time, rather liked him.

"Wait!" called Adam Patch, "I want to talk to you."

Anthony faced about.

"Well, sir?"

"Sit down. Stay all night."

Somewhat mollified, Anthony resumed his seat.

"I'm sorry, sir, but I'm going to see Gloria to-night."

"What's her name?"

"Gloria Gilbert."

"New York girl? Some one you know?"

"She's from the Middle West."

"What business her father in?"

"In a celluloid corporation or trust or something. They're from Kansas City."

"You going to be married out there?"

"Why, no, sir. We thought we'd be married in New York—rather quietly."

"Like to have the wedding out here?"

Anthony hesitated. The suggestion made no appeal to him, but it was certainly the part of wisdom to give the old man, if possible, a proprietary interest in his married life. In addition Anthony was a little touched.

"That's very kind of you, grampa, but wouldn't it be a lot of trouble?"

"Everything's a lot of trouble. Your father was married here—but in the old house."

"Why—I thought he was married in Boston."

Adam Patch considered.

"That's true. He *was* married in Boston."

Anthony felt a moment's embarrassment at having made the correction, and he covered it up with words.

"Well, I'll speak to Gloria about it. Personally I'd like to, but of course it's up to the Gilberts, you see."

His grandfather drew a long sigh, half closed his eyes, and sank back in his chair.

"In a hurry?" he asked in a different tone.

"Not especially."

"I wonder," began Adam Patch, looking out with a mild, kindly glance at the lilac-bushes that rustled against the windows, "I wonder if you ever think about the after-life."

"Why—sometimes."

"I think a great deal about the after-life." His eyes were dim but his voice was confident and clear. "I was sitting here to-day thinking about what's lying in wait for us, and somehow I began to remember an afternoon nearly sixty-five years ago, when I was playing with my little sister Annie, down where that summer-house is now." He pointed out into the long flower-garden, his eyes trembling of tears, his voice shaking.

"I began thinking—and it seemed to me that *you* ought to

think a little more about the after-life. You ought to be—steadier"—he paused and seemed to grope about for the right word—"more industrious—why——"

Then his expression altered, his entire personality seemed to snap together like a trap, and when he continued the softness had gone from his voice.

"—Why, when I was just two years older than you," he rasped with a cunning chuckle, "I sent three members of the firm of Wrenn and Hunt to the poorhouse."

Anthony started with embarrassment.

"Well, good-by," added his grandfather suddenly, "you'll miss your train."

Anthony left the house unusually elated, and strangely sorry for the old man; not because his wealth could buy him "neither youth nor digestion" but because he had asked Anthony to be married there, and because he had forgotten something about his son's wedding that he should have remembered.

Richard Caramel, who was one of the ushers, caused Anthony and Gloria much distress in the last few weeks by continually stealing the rays of their spot-light. "The Demon Lover" had been published in April, and it interrupted the love-affair as it may be said to have interrupted everything its author came in contact with. It was a highly original, rather overwritten piece of sustained description concerned with a Don Juan of the New York slums. As Maury and Anthony had said before, as the more hospitable critics were saying then, there was no writer in America with such power to describe the atavistic and unsubtle reactions of that section of society.

The book hesitated and then suddenly "went." Editions, small at first, then larger, crowded each other week by week. A spokesman of the Salvation Army denounced it as a cynical misrepresentation of all the uplift taking place in the underworld. Clever press-agenting spread the unfounded rumor that "Gypsy" Smith was beginning a libel suit because one of the principal characters was a burlesque of himself. It was barred from the public library of Burlington, Iowa, and a mid-Western columnist announced by innuendo that Richard Caramel was in a sanitarium with delirium tremens.

The author, indeed, spent his days in a state of pleasant madness. The book was in his conversation three-fourths of the time—he wanted to know if one had heard "the latest"; he would go into a store and in a loud voice order books to be charged to him, in order to catch a chance morsel of recognition from clerk or customer. He knew to a town in what sections of the country it was selling best; he knew exactly what he cleared on each edition, and when he met any one who had not read it, or, as it happened only too often, had not heard of it, he succumbed to moody depression.

So it was natural for Anthony and Gloria to decide, in their jealousy, that he was so swollen with conceit as to be a bore. To Dick's great annoyance Gloria publicly boasted that she had never read "The Demon Lover," and didn't intend to until every one stopped talking about it. As a matter of fact, she had no time to read now, for the presents were pouring in—first a scattering, then an avalanche, varying from the bric-à-brac of forgotten family friends to the photographs of forgotten poor relations.

Maury gave them an elaborate "drinking set," which included silver goblets, cocktail-shaker, and bottle-openers. The extortion from Dick was more conventional—a tea-set from Tiffany's. From Joseph Bloeckman came a simple and exquisite travelling clock, with his card. There was even a cigarette-holder from Bounds; this touched Anthony and made him want to weep—indeed, any emotion short of hysteria seemed natural in the half-dozen people who were swept up by this tremendous sacrifice to convention. The room set aside in the Plaza bulged with offerings sent by Harvard friends and by associates of his grandfather, with remembrances of Gloria's Farmover days, and with rather pathetic trophies from her former beaux, which last arrived with esoteric, melancholy messages, written on cards tucked carefully inside, beginning "I little thought when—" or "I'm sure I wish you all the happiness—" or even "When you get this I shall be on my way to——"

The most munificent gift was simultaneously the most disappointing. It was a concession of Adam Patch's—a check for five thousand dollars.

To most of the presents Anthony was cold. It seemed to

him that they would necessitate keeping a chart of the marital status of all their acquaintances during the next half-century. But Gloria exulted in each one, tearing at the tissue-paper and excelsior with the rapaciousness of a dog digging for a bone, breathlessly seizing a ribbon or an edge of metal and finally bringing to light the whole article and holding it up critically, no emotion except rapt interest in her unsmiling face.

"Look, Anthony!"

"Darn nice, isn't it!"

No answer until an hour later when she would give him a careful account of her precise reaction to the gift, whether it would have been improved by being smaller or larger, whether she was surprised at getting it, and, if so, just how much surprised.

Mrs. Gilbert arranged and rearranged a hypothetical house, distributing the gifts among the different rooms, tabulating articles as "second-best clock" or "silver to use *every* day," and embarrassing Anthony and Gloria by semi-facetious references to a room she called the nursery. She was pleased by old Adam's gift and thereafter had it that he was a very ancient soul, "as much as anything else." As Adam Patch never quite decided whether she referred to the advancing senility of his mind or to some private and psychic schema of her own, it cannot be said to have pleased him. Indeed he always spoke of her to Anthony as "that old woman, the mother," as though she were a character in a comedy he had seen staged many times before. Concerning Gloria he was unable to make up his mind. She attracted him but, as she herself told Anthony, he had decided that she was frivolous and was afraid to approve of her.

Five days!—A dancing platform was being erected on the lawn at Tarrytown. Four days!—A special train was chartered to convey the guests to and from New York. Three days!——

The Diary

She was dressed in blue silk pajamas and standing by her bed with her hand on the light to put the room in darkness, when she changed her mind and opening a table-drawer brought out a little black book—a "Line-a-day" diary. This she had kept for seven years. Many of the pencil entries were almost illegible and there were notes and references to nights and afternoons long since forgotten, for it was not an intimate diary, even though it began with the immemorial "I am going to keep a diary for my children." Yet as she thumbed over the pages the eyes of many men seemed to look out at her from their half-obliterated names. With one she had gone to New Haven for the first time—in 1908, when she was sixteen and padded shoulders were fashionable at Yale—she had been flattered because "Touch down" Michaud had "rushed" her all evening. She sighed, remembering the grown-up satin dress she had been so proud of and the orchestra playing "Yama-yama, My Yama Man" and "Jungle-Town." So long ago!—the names: Eltynge Reardon, Jim Parsons, "Curly" McGregor, Kenneth Cowan, "Fish-eye" Fry (whom she had liked for being so ugly), Carter Kirby—he had sent her a present; so had Tudor Baird;—Marty Reffer, the first man she had been in love with for more than a day, and Stuart Holcome, who had run away with her in his automobile and tried to make her marry him by force. And Larry Fenwick, whom she had always admired because he had told her one night that if she wouldn't kiss him she could get out of his car and walk home. What a list!

. . . And, after all, an obsolete list. She was in love now, set for the eternal romance that was to be the synthesis of all romance, yet sad for these men and these moonlights and for the "thrills" she had had—and the kisses. The past—her past, oh, what a joy! She had been exuberantly happy.

Turning over the pages her eyes rested idly on the scattered entries of the past four months. She read the last few carefully.

"*April 1st.*—I know Bill Carstairs hates me because I was so disagreeable, but I hate to be sentimentalized over sometimes. We drove out to the Rockyear Country Club and the most wonderful moon kept shining through the trees. My silver dress is getting tarnished. Funny how one forgets the other nights at Rockyear—with Kenneth Cowan when I loved him so!

"*April 3rd.*—After two hours of Schroeder who, they inform me, has millions, I've decided that this matter of sticking to things wears one out, particularly when the things concerned are men. There's nothing so often overdone and from to-day I swear to be amused. We talked about 'love'—how banal! With how many men have I talked about love?

"*April 11th.*—Patch actually called up to-day! and when he forswore me about a month ago he fairly raged out the door. I'm gradually losing faith in any man being susceptible to fatal injuries.

"*April 20th.*—Spent the day with Anthony. Maybe I'll marry him some time. I kind of like his ideas—he stimulates all the originality in me. Blockhead came around about ten in his new car and took me out Riverside Drive. I liked him to-night: he's so considerate. He knew I didn't want to talk so he was quiet all during the ride.

"*April 21st.*—Woke up thinking of Anthony and sure enough he called and sounded sweet on the phone—so I broke a date for him. To-day I feel I'd break anything for him, including the ten commandments and my neck. He's coming at eight and I shall wear pink and look very fresh and starched——"

She paused here, remembering that after he had gone that night she had undressed with the shivering April air streaming in the windows. Yet it seemed she had not felt the cold, warmed by the profound banalities burning in her heart.

The next entry occurred a few days later:

"*April 24th.*—I want to marry Anthony, because husbands are so often 'husbands' and I must marry a lover.

"There are four general types of husbands.

(1) The husband who always wants to stay in in the evening, has no vices and works for a salary. Totally undesirable!

(2) The atavistic master whose mistress one is, to wait on his pleasure. This sort always considers every pretty woman 'shallow,' a sort of peacock with arrested development.

(3) Next comes the worshipper, the idolater of his wife and all that is his, to the utter oblivion of everything else. This sort demands an emotional actress for a wife. God! it must be an exertion to be thought righteous.

(4) And Anthony—a temporarily passionate lover with wisdom enough to realize when it has flown and that it must fly. And I want to get married to Anthony.

"What grubworms women are to crawl on their bellies through colorless marriages! Marriage was created not to be a background but to need one. Mine is going to be outstanding. It can't, shan't be the setting—it's going to be the performance, the live, lovely, glamourous performance, and the world shall be the scenery. I refuse to dedicate my life to posterity. Surely one owes as much to the current generation as to one's unwanted children. What a fate—to grow rotund and unseemly, to lose my self-love, to think in terms of milk, oatmeal, nurse, diapers. . . . Dear dream children, how much more beautiful you are, dazzling little creatures who flutter (all dream children must flutter) on golden, golden wings——

"Such children, however, poor dear babies, have little in common with the wedded state.

"*June 7th.*—Moral question: Was it wrong to make Bloeckman love me? Because I did really make him. He was almost sweetly sad to-night. How opportune it was that my throat is swollen plunk together and tears were easy to muster. But he's just the past—buried already in my plentiful lavender.

"*June 8th.*—And to-day I've promised not to chew my mouth. Well, I won't, I suppose—but if he'd only asked me not to eat!

"Blowing bubbles—that's what we're doing, Anthony and me. And we blew such beautiful ones to-day, and they'll explode and then we'll blow more and more, I guess—bubbles just as big and just as beautiful, until all the soap and water is used up."

On this note the diary ended. Her eyes wandered up the page, over the June 8th's of 1912, 1910, 1907. The earliest entry was scrawled in the plump, bulbous hand of a sixteen-year-old girl—it was the name, Bob Lamar, and a word she could not decipher. Then she knew what it was—and, knowing, she found her eyes misty with tears. There in a graying blur was the record of her first kiss, faded as its intimate afternoon, on a rainy veranda seven years before. She seemed to remember something one of them had said that day and yet she could not remember. Her tears came faster, until she could scarcely see the page. She was crying, she told herself, because she could remember only the rain and the wet flowers in the yard and the smell of the damp grass.

. . . After a moment she found a pencil and holding it unsteadily drew three parallel lines beneath the last entry. Then she printed FINIS in large capitals, put the book back in the drawer, and crept into bed.

Breath of the Cave

Back in his apartment after the bridal dinner, Anthony snapped out his lights and, feeling impersonal and fragile as a piece of china waiting on a serving-table, got into bed. It was a warm night—a sheet was enough for comfort—and through his wide-open windows came sound, evanescent and summery, alive with remote anticipation. He was thinking that the young years behind him, hollow and colorful, had been lived in facile and vacillating cynicism upon the recorded emotions of men long dust. And there was something beyond that; he knew now. There was the union of his soul with Gloria's, whose radiant fire and freshness was the living material of which the dead beauty of books was made.

From the night into his high-walled room there came, persistently, that evanescent and dissolving sound—something the city was tossing up and calling back again, like a child playing with a ball. In Harlem, the Bronx, Gramercy Park, and along the water-fronts, in little parlors or on pebble-strewn, moon-flooded roofs, a thousand lovers were making this sound, crying little fragments of it into the air. All the city was playing with this sound out there in the blue summer dark, throwing it up and calling it back, promising that, in a little while, life would be beautiful as a story, promising happiness—and by that promise giving it. It gave love hope in its own survival. It could do no more.

It was then that a new note separated itself jarringly from the soft crying of the night. It was a noise from an areaway within a hundred feet from his rear window, the noise of a woman's laughter. It began low, incessant and whining—

some servant-maid with her fellow, he thought—and then it grew in volume and became hysterical, until it reminded him of a girl he had seen overcome with nervous laughter at a vaudeville performance. Then it sank, receded, only to rise again and include words—a coarse joke, some bit of obscure horse-play he could not distinguish. It would break off for a moment and he would just catch the low rumble of a man's voice, then begin again—interminably; at first annoying, then strangely terrible. He shivered, and getting up out of bed went to the window. It had reached a high point, tensed and stifled, almost the quality of a scream—then it ceased and left behind it a silence empty and menacing as the greater silence overhead. Anthony stood by the window a moment longer before he returned to his bed. He found himself upset and shaken. Try as he might to strangle his reaction, some animal quality in that unrestrained laughter had grasped at his imagination, and for the first time in four months aroused his old aversion and horror toward all the business of life. The room had grown smothery. He wanted to be out in some cool and bitter breeze, miles above the cities, and to live serene and detached back in the corners of his mind. Life was that sound out there, that ghastly reiterated female sound.

"Oh, my *God!*" he cried, drawing in his breath sharply.

Burying his face in the pillows he tried in vain to concentrate upon the details of the next day.

Morning

In the gray light he found that it was only five o'clock. He regretted nervously that he had awakened so early—he would appear fagged at the wedding. He envied Gloria who could hide her fatigue with careful pigmentation.

In his bathroom he contemplated himself in the mirror and saw that he was unusually white—half a dozen small imperfections stood out against the morning pallor of his complexion, and overnight he had grown the faint stubble of a beard—the general effect, he fancied, was unprepossessing, haggard, half unwell.

On his dressing-table were spread a number of articles which he told over carefully with suddenly fumbling fingers—

their tickets to California, the book of traveller's checks, his watch, set to the half minute, the key to his apartment, which he must not forget to give to Maury, and, most important of all, the ring. It was of platinum set around with small emeralds; Gloria had insisted on this; she had always wanted an emerald wedding-ring, she said.

It was the third present he had given her; first had come the engagement ring, and then a little gold cigarette-case. He would be giving her many things now—clothes and jewels and friends and excitement. It seemed absurd that from now on he would pay for all her meals. It was going to cost: he wondered if he had not underestimated for this trip, and if he had not better cash a larger check. The question worried him.

Then the breathless impendency of the event swept his mind clear of details. This was the day—unsought, unsuspected six months before, but now breaking in yellow light through his east window, dancing along the carpet as though the sun were smiling at some ancient and reiterated gag of his own.

Anthony laughed in a nervous one-syllable snort.

"By God!" he muttered to himself, "I'm as good as married!"

The Ushers

Six young men in Cross Patch's *library growing more and more cheery under the influence of Mumm's Extra Dry, set surreptitiously in cold pails by the bookcases.*

The First Young Man: By golly! Believe me, in my next book I'm going to do a wedding scene that'll knock 'em cold!

The Second Young Man: Met a débutante th'other day said she thought your book was powerful. As a rule young girls cry for this primitive business.

The Third Young Man: Where's Anthony?

The Fourth Young Man: Walking up and down outside talking to himself.

Second Young Man: Lord! Did you see the minister? Most peculiar looking teeth.

FIFTH YOUNG MAN: Think they're natural. Funny thing people having gold teeth.

SIXTH YOUNG MAN: They say they love 'em. My dentist told me once a woman came to him and insisted on having two of her teeth covered with gold. No reason at all. All right the way they were.

FOURTH YOUNG MAN: Hear you got out a book, Dicky. 'Gratulations!

DICK: (*Stiffly*) Thanks.

FOURTH YOUNG MAN: (*Innocently*) What is it? College stories?

DICK: (*More stiffly*) No. Not college stories.

FOURTH YOUNG MAN: Pity! Hasn't been a good book about Harvard for years.

DICK: (*Touchily*) Why don't you supply the lack?

THIRD YOUNG MAN: I think I saw a squad of guests turn the drive in a Packard just now.

SIXTH YOUNG MAN: Might open a couple more bottles on the strength of that.

THIRD YOUNG MAN: It was the shock of my life when I heard the old man was going to have a wet wedding. Rabid prohibitionist, you know.

FOURTH YOUNG MAN: (*Snapping his fingers excitedly*) By gad! I knew I'd forgotten something. Kept thinking it was my vest.

DICK: What was it?

FOURTH YOUNG MAN: By gad! By gad!

SIXTH YOUNG MAN: Here! Here! Why the tragedy?

SECOND YOUNG MAN: What'd you forget? The way home?

DICK: (*Maliciously*) He forgot the plot for his book of Harvard stories.

FOURTH YOUNG MAN: No, sir, I forgot the present, by George! I forgot to buy old Anthony a present. I kept putting it off and putting it off, and by gad I've forgotten it! What'll they think?

SIXTH YOUNG MAN: (*Facetiously*) That's probably what's been holding up the wedding.

(THE FOURTH YOUNG MAN *looks nervously at his watch. Laughter.*)

FOURTH YOUNG MAN: By gad! What an ass I am!

SECOND YOUNG MAN: What'd you make of the bridesmaid who thinks she's Nora Bayes? Kept telling me she wished this was a ragtime wedding. Name's Haines or Hampton.

DICK: (*Hurriedly spurring his imagination*) Kane, you mean, Muriel Kane. She's a sort of debt of honor, I believe. Once saved Gloria from drowning, or something of the sort.

SECOND YOUNG MAN: I didn't think she could stop that perpetual swaying long enough to swim. Fill up my glass, will you? Old man and I had a long talk about the weather just now.

MAURY: Who? Old Adam?

SECOND YOUNG MAN: No, the bride's father. He must be with a weather bureau.

DICK: He's my uncle, Otis.

OTIS: Well, it's an honorable profession. (*Laughter.*)

SIXTH YOUNG MAN: Bride your cousin, isn't she?

DICK: Yes, Cable, she is.

CABLE: She certainly is a beauty. Not like you, Dicky. Bet she brings old Anthony to terms.

MAURY: Why are all grooms given the title of "old"? I think marriage is an error of youth.

DICK: Maury, the professional cynic.

MAURY: Why, you intellectual faker!

FIFTH YOUNG MAN: Battle of the highbrows here, Otis. Pick up what crumbs you can.

DICK: Faker yourself! What do *you* know?

MAURY: What do *you* know?

DICK: Ask me anything. Any branch of knowledge.

MAURY: All right. What's the fundamental principle of biology?

DICK: You don't know yourself.

MAURY: Don't hedge!

DICK: Well, natural selection?

MAURY: Wrong.

DICK: I give it up.

MAURY: Ontogony recapitulates phyllogony.

FIFTH YOUNG MAN: Take your base!

MAURY: Ask you another. What's the influence of mice on the clover crop? (*Laughter.*)

FOURTH YOUNG MAN: What's the influence of rats on the Decalogue?

MAURY: Shut up, you saphead. There *is* a connection.

DICK: What is it then?

MAURY: (*Pausing a moment in growing disconcertion*) Why, let's see. I seem to have forgotten exactly. Something about the bees eating the clover.

FOURTH YOUNG MAN: And the clover eating the mice! Haw! Haw!

MAURY: (*Frowning*) Let me just think a minute.

DICK: (*Sitting up suddenly*) Listen!

(*A volley of chatter explodes in the adjoining room. The six young men arise, feeling at their neckties.*)

DICK: (*Weightily*) We'd better join the firing-squad. They're going to take the picture, I guess. No, that's afterward.

OTIS: Cable, you take the ragtime bridesmaid.

FOURTH YOUNG MAN: I wish to God I'd sent that present.

MAURY: If you'll give me another minute I'll think of that about the mice.

OTIS: I was usher last month for old Charlie McIntyre and——

(*They move slowly toward the door as the chatter becomes a babel and the practising preliminary to the overture issues in long pious groans from* ADAM PATCH'S *organ.*)

ANTHONY

There were five hundred eyes boring through the back of his cutaway and the sun glinting on the clergyman's inappropriately bourgeois teeth. With difficulty he restrained a laugh. Gloria was saying something in a clear proud voice and he tried to think that the affair was irrevocable, that every second was significant, that his life was being slashed into two periods and that the face of the world was changing before him. He tried to recapture that ecstatic sensation of ten weeks before. All these emotions eluded him, he did not even feel the physical nervousness of that very morning—it was all one gigantic aftermath. And those gold teeth! He wondered if the clergyman were married; he wondered perversely if a clergyman could perform his own marriage service. . . .

But as he took Gloria into his arms he was conscious of a strong reaction. The blood was moving in his veins now. A languorous and pleasant content settled like a weight upon him, bringing responsibility and possession. He was married.

Gloria

So many, such mingled emotions, that no one of them was separable from the others! She could have wept for her mother, who was crying quietly back there ten feet and for the loveliness of the June sunlight flooding in at the windows. She was beyond all conscious perceptions. Only a sense, colored with delirious wild excitement, that the ultimately important was happening—and a trust, fierce and passionate, burning in her like a prayer, that in a moment she would be forever and securely safe.

Late one night they arrived in Santa Barbara, where the night-clerk at the Hotel Lacfadio refused to admit them, on the grounds that they were not married.

The clerk thought that Gloria was beautiful. He did not think that anything so beautiful as Gloria could be moral.

"Con Amore"

That first half-year—the trip West, the long months' loiter along the California coast, and the gray house near Greenwich where they lived until late autumn made the country dreary—those days, those places, saw the enraptured hours. The breathless idyl of their engagement gave way, first, to the intense romance of the more passionate relationship. The breathless idyl left them, fled on to other lovers; they looked around one day and it was gone, how, they scarcely knew. Had either of them lost the other in the days of the idyl, the love lost would have been ever to the loser that dim desire without fulfilment which stands back of all life. But magic must hurry on, and the lovers remain. . . .

The idyl passed, bearing with it its extortion of youth.

Came a day when Gloria found that other men no longer bored her; came a day when Anthony discovered that he could sit again late into the evening, talking with Dick of those tremendous abstractions that had once occupied his world. But, knowing they had had the best of love, they clung to what remained. Love lingered—by way of long conversations at night into those stark hours when the mind thins and sharpens and the borrowings from dreams become the stuff of all life, by way of deep and intimate kindnesses they developed toward each other, by way of their laughing at the same absurdities and thinking the same things noble and the same things sad.

It was, first of all, a time of discovery. The things they found in each other were so diverse, so intermixed and, moreover, so sugared with love as to seem at the time not so much discoveries as isolated phenomena—to be allowed for, and to be forgotten. Anthony found that he was living with a girl of tremendous nervous tension and of the most high-handed selfishness. Gloria knew within a month that her husband was an utter coward toward any one of a million phantasms created by his imagination. Her perception was intermittent, for this cowardice sprang out, became almost obscenely evident, then faded and vanished as though it had been only a creation of her own mind. Her reactions to it were not those attributed to her sex—it roused her neither to disgust nor to a premature feeling of motherhood. Herself almost completely without physical fear, she was unable to understand, and so she made the most of what she felt to be his fear's redeeming feature, which was that though he was a coward under a shock and a coward under a strain—when his imagination was given play—he had yet a sort of dashing recklessness that moved her on its brief occasions almost to admiration, and a pride that usually steadied him when he thought he was observed.

The trait first showed itself in a dozen incidents of little more than nervousness—his warning to a taxi-driver against fast driving, in Chicago; his refusal to take her to a certain tough café she had always wished to visit; these of course admitted the conventional interpretation—that it was of her he had been thinking; nevertheless, their culminative weight disturbed her. But something that occurred in a San Francisco hotel, when they had been married a week, gave the matter certainty.

It was after midnight and pitch dark in their room. Gloria was dozing off and Anthony's even breathing beside her made her suppose that he was asleep, when suddenly she saw him raise himself on his elbow and stare at the window.

"What is it, dearest?" she murmured.

"Nothing"—he had relaxed to his pillow and turned toward her—"nothing, my darling wife."

"Don't say 'wife.' I'm your mistress. Wife's such an ugly word. Your 'permanent mistress' is so much more tangible and desirable. . . . Come into my arms," she added in a rush of tenderness; "I can sleep so well, so well with you in my arms."

Coming into Gloria's arms had a quite definite meaning. It required that he should slide one arm under her shoulder, lock both arms about her, and arrange himself as nearly as possible as a sort of three-sided crib for her luxurious ease. Anthony, who tossed, whose arms went tinglingly to sleep after half an hour of that position, would wait until she was asleep and roll her gently over to her side of the bed—then, left to his own devices, he would curl himself into his usual knots.

Gloria, having attained sentimental comfort, retired into her doze. Five minutes ticked away on Bloeckman's travelling clock; silence lay all about the room, over the unfamiliar, impersonal furniture and the half-oppressive ceiling that melted imperceptibly into invisible walls on both sides. Then there was suddenly a rattling flutter at the window, staccato and loud upon the hushed, pent air.

With a leap Anthony was out of the bed and standing tense beside it.

"Who's there?" he cried in an awful voice.

Gloria lay very still, wide awake now and engrossed not so much in the rattling as in the rigid breathless figure whose voice had reached from the bedside into that ominous dark.

The sound stopped; the room was quiet as before—then Anthony pouring words in at the telephone.

"Some one just tried to get into the room! . . .

"There's some one at the window!" His voice was emphatic now, faintly terrified.

"All right! Hurry!" He hung up the receiver; stood motionless.

. . . . There was a rush and commotion at the door, a knocking—Anthony went to open it upon an excited night-clerk with three bell-boys grouped staring behind him. Between thumb and finger the night-clerk held a wet pen with the threat of a weapon; one of the bell-boys had seized a telephone directory and was looking at it sheepishly. Simultaneously the group was joined by the hastily summoned house-detective, and as one man they surged into the room.

Lights sprang on with a click. Gathering a piece of sheet about her Gloria dove away from sight, shutting her eyes to keep out the horror of this unpremeditated visitation. There was no vestige of an idea in her stricken sensibilities save that her Anthony was at grievous fault.

. . . The night-clerk was speaking from the window, his tone half of the servant, half of the teacher reproving a schoolboy.

"Nobody out there," he declared conclusively; "my golly, nobody *could* be out there. This here's a sheer fall to the street of fifty feet. It was the wind you heard, tugging at the blind."

"Oh."

Then she was sorry for him. She wanted only to comfort him and draw him back tenderly into her arms, to tell them to go away because the thing their presence connotated was odious. Yet she could not raise her head for shame. She heard a broken sentence, apologies, conventions of the employee and one unrestrained snicker from a bell-boy.

"I've been nervous as the devil all evening," Anthony was saying; "somehow that noise just shook me—I was only about half awake."

"Sure, I understand," said the night-clerk with comfortable tact; "been that way myself."

The door closed; the lights snapped out; Anthony crossed the floor quietly and crept into bed. Gloria, feigning to be heavy with sleep, gave a quiet little sigh and slipped into his arms.

"What was it, dear?"

"Nothing," he answered, his voice still shaken; "I thought there was somebody at the window, so I looked out, but I couldn't see any one and the noise kept up, so I phoned down-stairs. Sorry if I disturbed you, but I'm awfully darn nervous to-night."

Catching the lie, she gave an interior start—he had not gone to the window, nor near the window. He had stood by the bed and then sent in his call of fear.

"Oh," she said—and then: "I'm so sleepy."

For an hour they lay awake side by side, Gloria with her eyes shut so tight that blue moons formed and revolved against backgrounds of deepest mauve, Anthony staring blindly into the darkness overhead.

After many weeks it came gradually out into the light, to be laughed and joked at. They made a tradition to fit over it—whenever that overpowering terror of the night attacked Anthony, she would put her arms about him and croon, soft as a song:

"I'll protect my Anthony. Oh, nobody's ever going to harm my Anthony!"

He would laugh as though it were a jest they played for their mutual amusement, but to Gloria it was never quite a jest. It was, at first, a keen disappointment; later, it was one of the times when she controlled her temper.

The management of Gloria's temper, whether it was aroused by a lack of hot water for her bath or by a skirmish with her husband, became almost the primary duty of Anthony's day. It must be done just so—by this much silence, by that much pressure, by this much yielding, by that much force. It was in her angers with their attendant cruelties that her inordinate egotism chiefly displayed itself. Because she was brave, because she was "spoiled," because of her outrageous and commendable independence of judgment, and finally because of her arrogant consciousness that she had never seen a girl as beautiful as herself, Gloria had developed into a consistent, practising Nietzschean. This, of course, with overtones of profound sentiment.

There was, for example, her stomach. She was used to certain dishes, and she had a strong conviction that she could not possibly eat anything else. There must be a lemonade and a tomato sandwich late in the morning, then a light lunch with a stuffed tomato. Not only did she require food from a selection of a dozen dishes, but in addition this food must be prepared in just a certain way. One of the most annoying half hours of the first fortnight occurred in Los Angeles, when an unhappy waiter brought her a tomato stuffed with chicken salad instead of celery.

"We always serve it that way, madame," he quavered to the gray eyes that regarded him wrathfully.

Gloria made no answer, but when the waiter had turned discreetly away she banged both fists upon the table until the china and silver rattled.

"Poor Gloria!" laughed Anthony unwittingly, "you can't get what you want ever, can you?"

"I can't eat *stuff*!" she flared up.

"I'll call back the waiter."

"I don't want you to! He doesn't know anything, the darn *fool*!"

"Well, it isn't the hotel's fault. Either send it back, forget it, or be a sport and eat it."

"Shut up!" she said succinctly.

"Why take it out on me?"

"Oh, I'm *not*," she wailed, "but I simply *can't* eat it."

Anthony subsided helplessly.

"We'll go somewhere else," he suggested.

"I don't *want* to go anywhere else. I'm tired of being trotted around to a dozen cafés and not getting *one thing* fit to eat."

"When did we go around to a dozen cafés?"

"You'd *have* to in *this* town," insisted Gloria with ready sophistry.

Anthony, bewildered, tried another tack.

"Why don't you try to eat it? It can't be as bad as you think."

"Just—because—I—don't—like—chicken!"

She picked up her fork and began poking contemptuously at the tomato, and Anthony expected her to begin flinging the stuffings in all directions. He was sure that she was approximately as angry as she had ever been—for an instant he had detected a spark of hate directed as much toward him as toward any one else—and Gloria angry was, for the present, unapproachable.

Then, surprisingly, he saw that she had tentatively raised the fork to her lips and tasted the chicken salad. Her frown had not abated and he stared at her anxiously, making no comment and daring scarcely to breathe. She tasted another forkful—in another moment she was eating. With difficulty Anthony restrained a chuckle; when at length he spoke his words had no possible connection with chicken salad.

This incident, with variations, ran like a lugubrious fugue through the first year of marriage; always it left Anthony baffled, irritated, and depressed. But another rough brushing of temperaments, a question of laundry-bags, he found even more annoying as it ended inevitably in a decisive defeat for him.

One afternoon in Coronado, where they made the longest stay of their trip, more than three weeks, Gloria was arraying herself brilliantly for tea. Anthony, who had been down-stairs listening to the latest rumor-bulletins of war in Europe, entered the room, kissed the back of her powdered neck, and went to his dresser. After a great pulling out and pushing in of drawers, evidently unsatisfactory, he turned around to the Unfinished Masterpiece.

"Got any handkerchiefs, Gloria?" he asked.

Gloria shook her golden head.

"Not a one. I'm using one of yours."

"The last one, I deduce." He laughed dryly.

"Is it?" She applied an emphatic though very delicate contour to her lips.

"Isn't the laundry back?"

"I don't know."

Anthony hesitated — then, with sudden discernment, opened the closet door. His suspicions were verified. On the hook provided hung the blue bag furnished by the hotel. This was full of his clothes—he had put them there himself. The floor beneath it was littered with an astonishing mass of finery—lingerie, stockings, dresses, nightgowns, and pajamas—most of it scarcely worn but all of it coming indubitably under the general heading of Gloria's laundry.

He stood holding the closet door open.

"Why, Gloria!"

"What?"

The lip line was being erased and corrected according to some mysterious perspective; not a finger trembled as she manipulated the lip-stick, not a glance wavered in his direction. It was a triumph of concentration.

"Haven't you ever sent out the laundry?"

"Is it there?"

"It most certainly is."

"Well, I guess I haven't, then."

"Gloria," began Anthony, sitting down on the bed and trying to catch her mirrored eyes, "you're a nice fellow, you are! I've sent it out every time it's been sent since we left New York, and over a week ago you promised you'd do it for a change. All you'd have to do would be to cram your own junk into that bag and ring for the chambermaid."

"Oh, why fuss about the laundry?" exclaimed Gloria petulantly, "I'll take care of it."

"I haven't fussed about it. I'd just as soon divide the bother with you, but when we run out of handkerchiefs it's darn near time something's done."

Anthony considered that he was being extraordinarily logical. But Gloria, unimpressed, put away her cosmetics and casually offered him her back.

"Hook me up," she suggested; "Anthony, dearest, I forgot all about it. I meant to, honestly, and I will to-day. Don't be cross with your sweetheart."

What could Anthony do then but draw her down upon his knee and kiss a shade of color from her lips.

"But I don't mind," she murmured with a smile, radiant and magnanimous. "You can kiss all the paint off my lips any time you want."

They went down to tea. They bought some handkerchiefs in a notion store near by. All was forgotten.

But two days later Anthony looked in the closet and saw the bag still hung limp upon its hook and that the gay and vivid pile on the floor had increased surprisingly in height.

"Gloria!" he cried.

"Oh—" Her voice was full of real distress. Despairingly Anthony went to the phone and called the chambermaid.

"It seems to me," he said impatiently, "that you expect me to be some sort of French valet to you."

Gloria laughed, so infectiously that Anthony was unwise enough to smile. Unfortunate man! In some intangible manner his smile made her mistress of the situation—with an air of injured righteousness she went emphatically to the closet and began pushing her laundry violently into the bag. Anthony watched her—ashamed of himself.

"There!" she said, implying that her fingers had been worked to the bone by a brutal taskmaster.

He considered, nevertheless, that he had given her an object-lesson and that the matter was closed, but on the contrary it was merely beginning. Laundry pile followed laundry pile—at long intervals; dearth of handkerchief followed dearth of handkerchief—at short ones; not to mention dearth of sock, of shirt, of everything. And Anthony found at length that either he must send it out himself or go through the increasingly unpleasant ordeal of a verbal battle with Gloria.

Gloria and General Lee

On their way East they stopped two days in Washington, strolling about with some hostility in its atmosphere of harsh repellent light, of distance without freedom, of pomp without splendor—it seemed a pasty-pale and self-conscious city. The second day they made an ill-advised trip to General Lee's old home at Arlington.

The bus which bore them was crowded with hot, unprosperous people, and Anthony, intimate to Gloria, felt a storm brewing. It broke at the Zoo, where the party stopped for ten minutes. The Zoo, it seemed, smelt of monkeys. Anthony laughed; Gloria called down the curse of Heaven upon monkeys, including in her malevolence all the passengers of the bus and their perspiring offspring who had hied themselves monkey-ward.

Eventually the bus moved on to Arlington. There it met other busses and immediately a swarm of women and children were leaving a trail of peanut-shells through the halls of

General Lee and crowding at length into the room where he was married. On the wall of this room a pleasing sign announced in large red letters "Ladies' Toilet." At this final blow Gloria broke down.

"I think it's perfectly terrible!" she said furiously, "the idea of letting these people come here! And of encouraging them by making these houses show-places."

"Well," objected Anthony, "if they weren't kept up they'd go to pieces."

"What if they did!" she exclaimed as they sought the wide pillared porch. "Do you think they've left a breath of 1860 here? This has become a thing of 1914."

"Don't you want to preserve old things?"

"But you *can't*, Anthony. Beautiful things grow to a certain height and then they fail and fade off, breathing out memories as they decay. And just as any period decays in our minds, the things of that period should decay too, and in that way they're preserved for a while in the few hearts like mine that react to them. That graveyard at Tarrytown, for instance. The asses who give money to preserve things have spoiled that too. Sleepy Hollow's gone; Washington Irving's dead and his books are rotting in our estimation year by year—then let the graveyard rot too, as it should, as all things should. Trying to preserve a century by keeping its relics up to date is like keeping a dying man alive by stimulants."

"So you think that just as a time goes to pieces its houses ought to go too?"

"Of course! Would you value your Keats letter if the signature was traced over to make it last longer? It's just because I love the past that I want this house to look back on its glamourous moment of youth and beauty, and I want its stairs to creak as if to the foot-steps of women with hoop-skirts and men in boots and spurs. But they've made it into a blondined, rouged-up old woman of sixty. It hasn't any right to look so prosperous. It might care enough for Lee to drop a brick now and then. How many of these—these *animals*"—she waved her hand around—"get anything from this, for all the histories and guide-books and restorations in existence? How many of them who think that, at best, appreciation is talking in undertones and walking on tiptoes would even come here if it was any trouble? I want it to smell of magnolias instead of peanuts and I want my shoes to crunch on the same gravel that Lee's boots crunched on. There's no beauty without poignancy and there's no poignancy without the feeling that it's going, men, names, books, houses—bound for dust—mortal——"

A small boy appeared beside them and, swinging a handful of banana-peels, flung them valiantly in the direction of the Potomac.

Sentiment

Simultaneously with the fall of Liège, Anthony and Gloria arrived in New York. In retrospect the six weeks seemed miraculously happy. They had found to a great extent, as most young couples find in some measure, that they possessed in common many fixed ideas and curiosities and odd quirks of mind; they were essentially companionable.

But it had been a struggle to keep many of their conversations on the level of discussions. Arguments were fatal to Gloria's disposition. She had all her life been associated either with her mental inferiors or with men who, under the almost hostile intimidation of her beauty, had not dared to contradict her; naturally, then, it irritated her when Anthony emerged from the state in which her pronouncements were an infallible and ultimate decision.

He failed to realize, at first, that this was the result partly of her "female" education and partly of her beauty, and he was inclined to include her with her entire sex as curiously and definitely limited. It maddened him to find she had no sense of justice. But he discovered that, when a subject did interest her, her brain tired less quickly than his. What he chiefly missed in her mind was the pedantic teleology—the sense of order and accuracy, the sense of life as a mysteriously correlated piece of patchwork, but he understood after a while that such a quality in her would have been incongruous.

Of the things they possessed in common, greatest of all was their almost uncanny pull at each other's hearts. The day they left the hotel in Coronado she sat down on one of the beds while they were packing, and began to weep bitterly.

"Dearest—" His arms were around her; he pulled her head down upon his shoulder. "What is it, my own Gloria? Tell me."

"We're going away," she sobbed. "Oh, Anthony, it's sort of the first place we've lived together. Our two little beds here—side by side—they'll be always waiting for us, and we're never coming back to 'em any more."

She was tearing at his heart as she always could. Sentiment came over him, rushed into his eyes.

"Gloria, why, we're going on to another room. And two other little beds. We're going to be together all our lives."

Words flooded from her in a low husky voice.

"But it won't be—like our two beds—ever again. Everywhere we go and move on and change, something's lost—something's left behind. You can't ever quite repeat anything, and I've been so yours, here——"

He held her passionately near, discerning far beyond any criticism of her sentiment, a wise grasping of the minute, if only an indulgence of her desire to cry—Gloria the idler, caresser of her own dreams, extracting poignancy from the memorable things of life and youth.

Later in the afternoon when he returned from the station with the tickets he found her asleep on one of the beds, her arm curled about a black object which he could not at first identify. Coming closer he found it was one of his shoes, not a particularly new one, nor clean one, but her face, tear-stained, was pressed against it, and he understood her ancient and most honorable message. There was almost ecstasy in waking her and seeing her smile at him, shy but well aware of her own nicety of imagination.

With no appraisal of the worth or dross of these two things, it seemed to Anthony that they lay somewhere near the heart of love.

The Gray House

It is in the twenties that the actual momentum of life begins to slacken, and it is a simple soul indeed to whom as many things are significant and meaningful at thirty as at ten years before. At thirty an organ-grinder is a more or less moth-eaten man who grinds an organ—and once he was an organ-grinder! The unmistakable stigma of humanity touches all those impersonal and beautiful things that only youth ever grasps in their impersonal glory. A brilliant ball, gay with light romantic laughter, wears through its own silks and satins to show the bare framework of a man-made thing—oh, that eternal hand!—a play, most tragic and most divine, becomes merely a succession of speeches, sweated over by the eternal plagiarist in the clammy hours and acted by men subject to cramps, cowardice, and manly sentiment.

And this time with Gloria and Anthony, this first year of marriage, and the gray house caught them in that stage when the organ-grinder was slowly undergoing his inevitable metamorphosis. She was twenty-three; he was twenty-six.

The gray house was, at first, of sheerly pastoral intent. They lived impatiently in Anthony's apartment for the first fortnight after the return from California, in a stifled atmosphere of open trunks, too many callers, and the eternal laundry-bags. They discussed with their friends the stupendous problem of their future. Dick and Maury would sit with them agreeing solemnly, almost thoughtfully, as Anthony ran through his list of what they "ought" to do, and where they "ought" to live.

"I'd like to take Gloria abroad," he complained, "except for this damn war—and next to that I'd sort of like to have a place in the country, somewhere near New York, of course, where I could write—or whatever I decide to do."

Gloria laughed.

"Isn't he cute?" she required of Maury. " 'Whatever he decides to do!' But what am *I* going to do if he works? Maury, will you take me around if Anthony works?"

"Anyway, I'm not going to work yet," said Anthony quickly.

It was vaguely understood between them that on some misty day he would enter a sort of glorified diplomatic service and be envied by princes and prime ministers for his beautiful wife.

"Well," said Gloria helplessly, "I'm sure I don't know. We talk and talk and never get anywhere, and we ask all our friends and they just answer the way we want 'em to. I wish somebody'd take care of us."

"Why don't you go out to—out to Greenwich or something?" suggested Richard Caramel.

"I'd like that," said Gloria, brightening. "Do you think we could get a house there?"

Dick shrugged his shoulders and Maury laughed.

"You two amuse me," he said. "Of all the unpractical people! As soon as a place is mentioned you expect us to pull great piles of photographs out of our pockets showing the different styles of architecture available in bungalows."

"That's just what I don't want," wailed Gloria, "a hot stuffy bungalow, with a lot of babies next door and their father cutting the grass in his shirt-sleeves——"

"For Heaven's sake, Gloria," interrupted Maury, "nobody wants to lock you up in a bungalow. Who in God's name brought bungalows into the conversation? But you'll never get a place anywhere unless you go out and hunt for it."

"Go where? You say 'go out and hunt for it,' but where?"

With dignity Maury waved his hand paw-like about the room.

"Out anywhere. Out in the country. There're lots of places."

"Thanks."

"Look here!" Richard Caramel brought his yellow eye rakishly into play. "The trouble with you two is that you're all disorganized. Do you know anything about New York State? Shut up, Anthony, I'm talking to Gloria."

"Well," she admitted finally, "I've been to two or three house-parties in Portchester and around in Connecticut—but, of course, that isn't in New York State, is it? And neither is Morristown," she finished with drowsy irrelevance.

There was a shout of laughter.

"Oh, Lord!" cried Dick, " 'neither is Morristown!' No, and neither is Santa Barbara, Gloria. Now listen. To begin with, unless you have a fortune there's no use considering any place like Newport or Southampton or Tuxedo. They're out of the question."

They all agreed to this solemnly.

"And personally I hate New Jersey. Then, of course, there's upper New York, above Tuxedo."

"Too cold," said Gloria briefly. "I was there once in an automobile."

"Well, it seems to me there're a lot of towns like Rye between New York and Greenwich where you could buy a little gray house of some——"

Gloria leaped at the phrase triumphantly. For the first time since their return East she knew what she wanted.

"Oh, *yes!*" she cried. "Oh, *yes!* that's it: a little gray house with sort of white around and a whole lot of swamp-maples just as brown and gold as an October picture in a gallery. Where can we find one?"

"Unfortunately, I've mislaid my list of little gray houses with swamp-maples around them—but I'll try to find it. Meanwhile you take a piece of paper and write down the names of seven possible towns. And every day this week you take a trip to one of those towns."

"Oh, gosh!" protested Gloria, collapsing mentally, "why won't you do it for us? I hate trains."

"Well, hire a car, and——"

Gloria yawned.

"I'm tired of discussing it. Seems to me all we do is talk about where to live."

"My exquisite wife wearies of thought," remarked Anthony ironically. "She must have a tomato sandwich to stimulate her jaded nerves. Let's go out to tea."

As the unfortunate upshot of this conversation, they took Dick's advice literally, and two days later went out to Rye, where they wandered around with an irritated real-estate agent, like bewildered babes in the wood. They were shown houses at a hundred a month which closely adjoined other houses at a hundred a month; they were shown isolated houses to which they invariably took violent dislikes, though they submitted weakly to the agent's desire that they "look at that stove—some stove!" and to a great shaking of door-posts and tapping of walls, intended evidently to show that the house would not immediately collapse, no matter how convincingly it gave that impression. They gazed through windows into interiors furnished either "commercially" with slab-like chairs and unyielding settees, or "home-like" with the melancholy bric-à-brac of other summers—crossed tennis-rackets, fit-form couches, and depressing Gibson girls. With a feeling of guilt they looked at a few really nice houses, aloof, dignified, and cool—at three hundred a month. They went away from Rye thanking the real-estate agent very much indeed.

On the crowded train back to New York the seat behind was occupied by a super-respirating Latin whose last few meals had obviously been composed entirely of garlic. They reached the apartment gratefully, almost hysterically, and Gloria rushed for a hot bath in the reproachless bathroom. So far as the question of a future abode was concerned both of them were incapacitated for a week.

The matter eventually worked itself out with unhoped-for romance. Anthony ran into the living-room one afternoon fairly radiating "the idea."

"I've got it," he was exclaiming as though he had just caught a mouse. "We'll get a car."

"Gee whiz! Haven't we got troubles enough taking care of ourselves?"

"Give me a second to explain, can't you? Just let's leave our stuff with Dick and just pile a couple of suitcases in our car, the one we're going to buy—we'll have to have one in the country anyway—and just start out in the direction of New Haven. You see, as we get out of commuting distance from New York, the rents'll get cheaper, and as soon as we find a house we want we'll just settle down."

By his frequent and soothing interpolation of the word "just" he aroused her lethargic enthusiasm. Strutting violently about the room, he simulated a dynamic and irresistible efficiency. "We'll buy a car to-morrow."

Life, limping after imagination's ten-league boots, saw them out of town a week later in a cheap but sparkling new roadster, saw them through the chaotic unintelligible Bronx, then over a wide murky district which alternated cheerless blue-green wastes with suburbs of tremendous and sordid activity. They left New York at eleven and it was well past a hot and beatific noon when they moved rakishly through Pelham.

"These aren't towns," said Gloria scornfully, "these are just city blocks plumped down coldly into waste acres. I imagine all the men here have their mustaches stained from drinking their coffee too quickly in the morning."

"And play pinochle on the commuting trains."

"What's pinochle?"

"Don't be so literal. How should I know? But it sounds as though they ought to play it."

"I like it. It sounds as if it were something where you sort of cracked your knuckles or something. . . . Let me drive."

Anthony looked at her suspiciously.

"You swear you're a good driver?"

"Since I was fourteen."

He stopped the car cautiously at the side of the road and they changed seats. Then with a horrible grinding noise the car was put in gear, Gloria adding an accompaniment of laughter which seemed to Anthony disquieting and in the worst possible taste.

"Here we go!" she yelled. "Whoo-oop!"

Their heads snapped back like marionettes on a single wire as the car leaped ahead and curved retchingly about a standing milk-wagon, whose driver stood up on his seat and bellowed after them. In the immemorial tradition of the road Anthony retorted with a few brief epigrams as to the grossness of the milk-delivering profession. He cut his remarks short, however, and turned to Gloria with the growing conviction that he had made a grave mistake in relinquishing control and that Gloria was a driver of many eccentricities and of infinite carelessness.

"Remember now!" he warned her nervously, "the man said we oughtn't to go over twenty miles an hour for the first five thousand miles."

She nodded briefly, but evidently intending to accomplish the prohibitive distance as quickly as possible, slightly increased her speed. A moment later he made another attempt.

"See that sign? Do you want to get us pinched?"

"Oh, for Heaven's sake," cried Gloria in exasperation, "you *always* exaggerate things so!"

"Well, I don't want to get arrested."

"Who's arresting you? You're so persistent—just like you were about my cough medicine last night."

"It was for your own good."

"Ha! I might as well be living with mama."

"What a thing to say to me!"

A standing policeman swerved into view, was hastily passed.

"See him?" demanded Anthony.

"Oh, you drive me crazy! He didn't arrest us, did he?"

"When he does it'll be too late," countered Anthony brilliantly.

Her reply was scornful, almost injured.

"Why, this old thing won't *go* over thirty-five."

"It isn't old."

"It is in spirit."

That afternoon the car joined the laundry-bags and Gloria's appetite as one of the trinity of contention. He warned her of railroad-tracks; he pointed out approaching automobiles; finally he insisted on taking the wheel and a furious, insulted Gloria sat silently beside him between the towns of Larchmont and Rye.

But it was due to this furious silence of hers that the gray house materialized from its abstraction, for just beyond Rye he surrendered gloomily to it and re-relinquished the wheel. Mutely he beseeched her and Gloria, instantly cheered, vowed to be more careful. But because a discourteous street-car persisted callously in remaining upon its track Gloria ducked down a side-street—and thereafter that afternoon was never able to find her way back to the Post Road. The street they finally mistook for it lost its Post-Road aspect when it had gone five miles from Cos Cob. Its macadam became gravel, then dirt—moreover, it narrowed and developed a border of maple-trees, through which filtered the westering sun, making its endless experiments with shadow designs upon the long grass.

"We're lost now," complained Anthony.

"Read that sign!"

"Marietta—Five Miles. What's Marietta?"

"Never heard of it, but let's go on. We can't turn here and there's probably a detour back to the Post Road."

The way became scarred with deepening ruts and insidious shoulders of stone. Three farmhouses faced them momentarily, slid by. A town sprang up in a cluster of dull roofs around a white tall steeple.

Then Gloria, hesitating between two approaches, and making her choice too late, drove over a fire-hydrant and ripped the transmission violently from the car.

*

It was dark when the real-estate agent of Marietta showed them the gray house. They came upon it just west of the village, where it rested against a sky that was a warm blue cloak buttoned with tiny stars. The gray house had been there when women who kept cats were probably witches, when Paul Revere made false teeth in Boston preparatory to arousing the great commercial people, when our ancestors were gloriously deserting Washington in droves. Since those days the house had been bolstered up in a feeble corner, considerably repartitioned and newly plastered inside, amplified by a kitchen and added to by a side-porch—but, save for where some jovial oaf had roofed the new kitchen with red tin, Colonial it defiantly remained.

"How did you happen to come to Marietta?" demanded the real-estate agent in a tone that was first cousin to suspicion. He was showing them through four spacious and airy bedrooms.

"We broke down," explained Gloria. "I drove over a fire-hydrant and we had ourselves towed to the garage and then we saw your sign."

The man nodded, unable to follow such a sally of spontaneity. There was something subtly immoral in doing anything without several months' consideration.

They signed a lease that night and, in the agent's car, returned jubilantly to the somnolent and dilapidated Marietta Inn, which was too broken for even the chance immoralities and consequent gaieties of a country roadhouse. Half the night they lay awake planning the things they were to do there. Anthony was going to work at an astounding pace on his history and thus ingratiate himself with his cynical grandfather. . . . When the car was repaired they would explore the country and join the nearest "really nice" club, where Gloria would play golf "or something" while Anthony wrote. This, of course, was Anthony's idea—Gloria was sure she wanted but to read and dream and be fed tomato sandwiches and lemonades by some angelic servant still in a shadowy hinterland. Between paragraphs Anthony would come and kiss her as she lay indolently in the hammock. . . . The hammock! a host of new dreams in tune to its imagined rhythm, while the wind stirred it and waves of sun undulated over the shadows of blown wheat, or the dusty road freckled and darkened with quiet summer rain. . . .

And guests—here they had a long argument, both of them trying to be extraordinarily mature and far-sighted. Anthony claimed that they would need people at least every other week-end "as a sort of change." This provoked an involved and extremely sentimental conversation as to whether Anthony did not consider Gloria change enough. Though he assured her that he did, she insisted upon doubting him. . . . Eventually the conversation assumed its eternal monotone: "What then? Oh, what'll we do then?"

"Well, we'll have a dog," suggested Anthony.

"I don't want one. I want a kitty." She went thoroughly and with great enthusiasm into the history, habits, and tastes of a cat she had once possessed. Anthony considered that it must have been a horrible character with neither personal magnetism nor a loyal heart.

Later they slept, to wake an hour before dawn with the gray house dancing in phantom glory before their dazzled eyes.

The Soul of Gloria

For that autumn the gray house welcomed them with a rush of sentiment that falsified its cynical old age. True, there were the laundry-bags, there was Gloria's appetite, there was Anthony's tendency to brood and his imaginative "nervousness," but there were intervals also of an unhoped-for serenity. Close together on the porch they would wait for the moon to stream across the silver acres of farmland, jump a thick wood and tumble waves of radiance at their feet. In such a moonlight Gloria's face was of a pervading, reminiscent white, and with a modicum of effort they would slip off the blinders of custom and each would find in the other almost the quintessential romance of the vanished June.

One night while her head lay upon his heart and their cigarettes glowed in swerving buttons of light through the dome of darkness over the bed, she spoke for the first time and fragmentarily of the men who had hung for brief moments on her beauty.

"Do you ever think of them?" he asked her.

"Only occasionally—when something happens that recalls a particular man."

"What do you remember—their kisses?"

"All sorts of things. . . . Men are different with women."

"Different in what way?"

"Oh, entirely—and quite inexpressibly. Men who had the most firmly rooted reputation for being this way or that would sometimes be surprisingly inconsistent with me. Brutal men were tender, negligible men were astonishingly loyal and lovable, and, often, honorable men took attitudes that were anything but honorable."

"For instance?"

"Well, there was a boy named Percy Wolcott from Cornell who was quite a hero in college, a great athlete, and saved a lot of people from a fire or something like that. But I soon found he was stupid in a rather dangerous way."

"What way?"

"It seems he had some naïve conception of a woman 'fit to be his wife,' a particular conception that I used to run into a lot and that always drove me wild. He demanded a girl who'd never been kissed and who liked to sew and sit home and pay tribute to his self-esteem. And I'll bet a hat if he's gotten an idiot to sit and be stupid with him he's tearing out on the side with some much speedier lady."

"I'd be sorry for his wife."

"I wouldn't. Think what an ass she'd be not to realize it before she married him. He's the sort whose idea of honoring and respecting a woman would be never to give her any excitement. With the best intentions, he was deep in the dark ages."

"What was his attitude toward you?"

"I'm coming to that. As I told you—or did I tell you?—he was mighty good-looking: big brown honest eyes and one of those smiles that guarantee the heart behind it is twenty-karat gold. Being young and credulous, I thought he had some discretion, so I kissed him fervently one night when we were riding around after a dance at the Homestead at Hot Springs. It had been a wonderful week, I remember—with the most luscious trees spread like green lather, sort of, all over the valley and a mist rising out of them on October mornings like bonfires lit to turn them brown——"

"How about your friend with the ideals?" interrupted Anthony.

"It seems that when he kissed me he began to think that perhaps he could get away with a little more, that I needn't be 'respected' like this Beatrice Fairfax glad-girl of his imagination."

"What'd he do?"

"Not much. I pushed him off a sixteen-foot embankment before he was well started."

"Hurt him?" inquired Anthony with a laugh.

"Broke his arm and sprained his ankle. He told the story all over Hot Springs, and when his arm healed a man named Barley who liked me fought him and broke it over again. Oh, it was all an awful mess. He threatened to sue Barley, and Barley—he was from Georgia—was seen buying a gun in town. But before that mama had dragged me North again, much against my will, so I never did find out all that happened—though I saw Barley once in the Vanderbilt lobby."

Anthony laughed long and loud.

"What a career! I suppose I ought to be furious because you've kissed so many men. I'm not, though."

At this she sat up in bed.

"It's funny, but I'm so sure that those kisses left no mark on me—no taint of promiscuity, I mean—even though a man once told me in all seriousness that he hated to think I'd been a public drinking-glass."

"He had his nerve."

"I just laughed and told him to think of me rather as a loving-cup that goes from hand to hand but should be valued none the less."

"Somehow it doesn't bother me—on the other hand it would, of course, if you'd done any more than kiss them. But I believe *you're* absolutely incapable of jealousy except as hurt vanity. Why don't you care what I've done? Wouldn't you prefer it if I'd been absolutely innocent?"

"It's all in the impression it might have made on you. *My* kisses were because the man was good-looking, or because there was a slick moon, or even because I've felt vaguely sentimental and a little stirred. But that's all—it's had utterly no effect on me. But you'd remember and let memories haunt you and worry you."

"Haven't you ever kissed any one like you've kissed me?"

"No," she answered simply. "As I've told you, men have tried—oh, lots of things. Any pretty girl has that experience. . . . You see," she resumed, "it doesn't matter to me how many women you've stayed with in the past, so long as it was merely a physical satisfaction, but I don't believe I could endure the idea of your ever having lived with another woman for a protracted period or even having wanted to marry some possible girl. It's different somehow. There'd be all the little intimacies remembered—and they'd dull that freshness that after all is the most precious part of love."

Rapturously he pulled her down beside him on the pillow.

"Oh, my darling," he whispered, "as if I remembered anything but your dear kisses."

Then Gloria, in a very mild voice:

"Anthony, did I hear anybody say they were thirsty?"

Anthony laughed abruptly and with a sheepish and amused grin got out of bed.

"With just a *little* piece of ice in the water," she added. "Do you suppose I could have that?"

Gloria used the adjective "little" whenever she asked a favor—it made the favor sound less arduous. But Anthony laughed again—whether she wanted a cake of ice or a marble of it, he must go down-stairs to the kitchen. . . . Her voice followed him through the hall: "And just a *little* cracker with just a *little* marmalade on it. . . ."

"Oh, gosh!" sighed Anthony in rapturous slang, "she's wonderful, that girl! She *has* it!"

"When we have a baby," she began one day—this, it had already been decided, was to be after three years—"I want it to look like you."

"Except its legs," he insinuated slyly.

"Oh, yes, except his legs. He's got to have my legs. But the rest of him can be you."

"My nose?"

Gloria hesitated.

"Well, perhaps my nose. But certainly your eyes—and my mouth, and I guess my shape of the face. I wonder; I think he'd be sort of cute if he had my hair."

"My dear Gloria, you've appropriated the whole baby."

"Well, I didn't mean to," she apologized cheerfully.

"Let him have my neck at least," he urged, regarding himself gravely in the glass. "You've often said you liked my neck because the Adam's apple doesn't show, and, besides, your neck's too short."

"Why, it is *not!*" she cried indignantly, turning to the mirror, "it's just right. I don't believe I've ever seen a better neck."

"It's too short," he repeated teasingly.

"Short?" Her tone expressed exasperated wonder. "Short? You're crazy!" She elongated and contracted it to convince herself of its reptilian sinuousness. "Do you call *that* a short neck?"

"One of the shortest I've ever seen."

For the first time in weeks tears started from Gloria's eyes and the look she gave him had a quality of real pain.

"Oh, Anthony——"

"My Lord, Gloria!" He approached her in bewilderment and took her elbows in his hands. "Don't cry, *please!* Didn't you know I was only kidding? Gloria, look at me! Why, dearest, you've got the longest neck I've ever seen. Honestly."

Her tears dissolved in a twisted smile.

"Well—you shouldn't have said that, then. Let's talk about the b-baby."

Anthony paced the floor and spoke as though rehearsing for a debate.

"To put it briefly, there are two babies we could have, two distinct and logical babies, utterly differentiated. There's the baby that's the combination of the best of both of us. Your body, my eyes, my mind, your intelligence—and then there is the baby which is our worst—my body, your disposition, and my irresolution."

"I like that second baby," she said.

"What I'd really like," continued Anthony, "would be to have two sets of triplets one year apart and then experiment with the six boys——"

"Poor me," she interjected.

"—I'd educate them each in a different country and by a different system and when they were twenty-three I'd call them together and see what they were like."

"Let's have 'em all with my neck," suggested Gloria.

The End of a Chapter

The car was at length repaired and with a deliberate vengeance took up where it left off the business of causing infinite dissension. Who should drive? How fast should Gloria go? These two questions and the eternal recriminations involved ran through the days. They motored to the Post-Road towns, Rye, Portchester, and Greenwich, and called on a dozen friends, mostly Gloria's, who all seemed to be in different stages of having babies and in this respect as well as in others bored her to a point of nervous distraction. For an hour after each visit she would bite her fingers furiously and be inclined to take out her rancor on Anthony.

"I loathe women," she cried in a mild temper. "What on earth can you say to them—except talk 'lady-lady'? I've enthused over a dozen babies that I've wanted only to choke. And every one of those girls is either incipiently jealous and suspicious of her husband if he's charming or beginning to be bored with him if he isn't."

"Don't you ever intend to see any women?"

"I don't know. They never seem clean to me—never—never. Except just a few. Constance Shaw—you know, the Mrs. Merriam who came over to see us last Tuesday—is almost the only one. She's so tall and fresh-looking and stately."

"I don't like them so tall."

Though they went to several dinner-dances at various country clubs, they decided that the autumn was too nearly over for them to "go out" on any scale, even had they been so inclined. He hated golf; Gloria liked it only mildly, and though she enjoyed a violent rush that some undergraduates gave her one night and was glad that Anthony should be proud of her beauty, she also perceived that their hostess for the evening, a Mrs. Granby, was somewhat disquieted by the fact that Anthony's classmate, Alec Granby, joined with enthusiasm in the rush. The Granbys never phoned again, and though Gloria laughed, it piqued her not a little.

"You see," she explained to Anthony, "if I wasn't married it wouldn't worry her—but she's been to the movies in her day and she thinks I may be a vampire. But the point is that placating such people requires an effort that I'm simply unwilling to make. . . . And those cute little freshmen making eyes at me and paying me idiotic compliments! I've grown up, Anthony."

Marietta itself offered little social life. Half a dozen farm-estates formed a hectagon around it, but these belonged to ancient men who displayed themselves only as inert, gray-thatched lumps in the back of limousines on their way to the station, whither they were sometimes accompanied by equally ancient and doubly massive wives. The townspeople were a particularly uninteresting type—unmarried females were predominant for the most part—with school-festival horizons and souls bleak as the forbidding white architecture of the three churches. The only native with whom they came into close contact was the broad-hipped, broad-shouldered Swedish girl who came every day to do their work. She was silent and efficient, and Gloria, after finding her weeping violently into her bowed arms upon the kitchen table, developed an uncanny fear of her and stopped complaining about the food. Because of her untold and esoteric grief the girl stayed on.

Gloria's penchant for premonitions and her bursts of vague supernaturalism were a surprise to Anthony. Either some complex, properly and scientifically inhibited in the early years with her Bilphistic mother, or some inherited hypersensitiveness, made her susceptible to any suggestion of the psychic, and, far from gullible about the motives of people, she was inclined to credit any extraordinary happening attributed to the whimsical perambulations of the buried. The desperate squeakings about the old house on windy nights that to Anthony were burglars with revolvers ready in hand represented to Gloria the auras, evil and restive, of dead generations, expiating the inexpiable upon the ancient and romantic hearth. One night, because of two swift bangs down-stairs, which Anthony fearfully but unavailingly investigated, they lay awake nearly until dawn asking each other examination-paper questions about the history of the world.

In October Muriel came out for a two weeks' visit. Gloria had called her on long-distance, and Miss Kane ended the conversation characteristically by saying "All-ll-ll righty. I'll be there with bells!" She arrived with a dozen popular songs under her arm.

"You ought to have a phonograph out here in the country," she said, "just a little Vic—they don't cost much. Then whenever you're lonesome you can have Caruso or Al Jolson right at your door."

She worried Anthony to distraction by telling him that "he was the first clever man she had ever known and she got so tired of shallow people." He wondered that people fell in love with such women. Yet he supposed that under a certain impassioned glance even she might take on a softness and promise.

But Gloria, violently showing off her love for Anthony, was diverted into a state of purring content.

Finally Richard Caramel arrived for a garrulous and to Gloria painfully literary week-end, during which he discussed himself with Anthony long after she lay in childlike sleep upstairs.

"It's been mighty funny, this success and all," said Dick. "Just before the novel appeared I'd been trying, without success, to sell some short stories. Then, after my book came out, I polished up three and had them accepted by one of the magazines that had rejected them before. I've done a lot of them since; publishers don't pay me for my book till this winter."

"Don't let the victor belong to the spoils."

"You mean write trash?" He considered. "If you mean deliberately injecting a slushy fade-out into each one, I'm not. But I don't suppose I'm being so careful. I'm certainly writing faster and I don't seem to be thinking as much as I used to. Perhaps it's because I don't get any conversation, now that you're married and Maury's gone to Philadelphia. Haven't the old urge and ambition. Early success and all that."

"Doesn't it worry you?"

"Frantically. I get a thing I call sentence-fever that must be like buck-fever—it's a sort of intense literary self-consciousness that comes when I try to force myself. But the really awful days aren't when I think I can't write. They're when I wonder whether any writing is worth while at all—I mean whether I'm not a sort of glorified buffoon."

"I like to hear you talk that way," said Anthony with a touch of his old patronizing insolence. "I was afraid you'd gotten a bit idiotic over your work. Read the damnedest interview you gave out——"

Dick interrupted with an agonized expression.

"Good Lord! Don't mention it. Young lady wrote it—most admiring young lady. Kept telling me my work was 'strong,' and I sort of lost my head and made a lot of strange pronouncements. Some of it was good, though, don't you think?"

"Oh, yes; that part about the wise writer writing for the youth of his generation, the critic of the next, and the schoolmaster of ever afterward."

"Oh, I believe a lot of it," admitted Richard Caramel with a faint beam. "It simply was a mistake to give it out."

In November they moved into Anthony's apartment, from which they sallied triumphantly to the Yale-Harvard and Harvard-Princeton football games, to the St. Nicholas ice-skating rink, to a thorough round of the theatres and to a miscellany of entertainments—from small, staid dances to the great affairs that Gloria loved, held in those few houses where lackeys with powdered wigs scurried around in magnificent Anglomania under the direction of gigantic majordomos. Their intention was to go abroad the first of the year or, at any rate, when the war was over. Anthony had actually completed a Chestertonian essay on the twelfth century by way of introduction to his proposed book and Gloria had done some extensive research work on the question of Russian-sable coats—in fact the winter was approaching quite comfortably, when the Bilphistic demiurge decided suddenly in mid-December that Mrs. Gilbert's soul had aged sufficiently in its present incarnation. In consequence Anthony took a miserable and hysterical Gloria out to Kansas City, where, in the fashion of mankind, they paid the terrible and mind-shaking deference to the dead.

Mr. Gilbert became, for the first and last time in his life, a truly pathetic figure. That woman he had broken to wait upon his body and play congregation to his mind had ironically deserted him—just when he could not much longer have supported her. Never again would he be able so satisfactorily to bore and bully a human soul.

CHAPTER II

Symposium

GLORIA had lulled Anthony's mind to sleep. She, who seemed of all women the wisest and the finest, hung like a brilliant curtain across his doorways, shutting out the light of the sun. In those first years what he believed bore invariably the stamp of Gloria; he saw the sun always through the pattern of the curtain.

It was a sort of lassitude that brought them back to Marietta for another summer. Through a golden enervating spring they had loitered, restive and lazily extravagant, along the California coast, joining other parties intermittently and drifting from Pasadena to Coronado, from Coronado to Santa Barbara, with no purpose more apparent than Gloria's desire to dance by different music or catch some infinitesimal variant among the changing colors of the sea. Out of the Pacific there rose to greet them savage rocklands and equally barbaric hostelries built that at tea-time one might drowse into a languid wicker bazaar glorified by the polo costumes of Southampton and Lake Forest and Newport and Palm Beach. And, as the waves met and splashed and glittered in the most placid of the bays, so they joined this group and that, and with them shifted stations, murmuring ever of those strange unsubstantial gaieties in wait just over the next green and fruitful valley.

A simple healthy leisure class it was—the best of the men not unpleasantly undergraduate—they seemed to be on a perpetual candidates list for some etherealized "Porcellian" or "Skull and Bones" extended out indefinitely into the world; the women, of more than average beauty, fragilely athletic, somewhat idiotic as hostesses but charming and infinitely decorative as guests. Sedately and gracefully they danced the steps of their selection in the balmy tea hours, accomplishing with a certain dignity the movements so horribly burlesqued by clerk and chorus girl the country over. It seemed ironic that in this lone and discredited offspring of the arts Americans should excel, unquestionably.

Having danced and splashed through a lavish spring, Anthony and Gloria found that they had spent too much money and for this must go into retirement for a certain period. There was Anthony's "work," they said. Almost before they knew it they were back in the gray house, more aware now that other lovers had slept there, other names had been called over the banisters, other couples had sat upon the porch steps watching the gray-green fields and the black bulk of woods beyond.

It was the same Anthony, more restless, inclined to quicken only under the stimulus of several high-balls, faintly, almost imperceptibly, apathetic toward Gloria. But Gloria—she would be twenty-four in August and was in an attractive but sincere panic about it. Six years to thirty! Had she been less in love with Anthony her sense of the flight of time would have expressed itself in a reawakened interest in other men, in a deliberate intention of extracting a transient gleam of romance from every potential lover who glanced at her with lowered brows over a shining dinner-table. She said to Anthony one day:

"How I feel is that if I wanted anything I'd take it. That's what I've always thought all my life. But it happens that I want you, and so I just haven't room for any other desires."

They were bound eastward through a parched and lifeless Indiana, and she had looked up from one of her beloved moving-picture magazines to find a casual conversation suddenly turned grave.

Anthony frowned out the car-window. As the track crossed a country road a farmer appeared momentarily in his wagon; he was chewing on a straw and was apparently the same farmer they had passed a dozen times before, sitting in silent and malignant symbolism. As Anthony turned to Gloria his frown intensified.

"You worry me," he objected; "I can imagine *wanting* another woman under certain transitory circumstances, but I can't imagine taking her."

"But I don't feel that way, Anthony. I can't be bothered resisting things I want. My way is not to want them—to want nobody but you."

"Yet when I think that if you just happened to take a fancy to some one——"

"Oh, don't be an idiot!" she exclaimed. "There'd be nothing casual about it. And I can't even imagine the possibility."

This emphatically closed the conversation. Anthony's unfailing appreciation made her happier in his company than in any one's else. She definitely enjoyed him—she loved him. So the summer began very much as had the one before.

There was, however, one radical change in ménage. The icy-hearted Scandinavian, whose austere cooking and sardonic manner of waiting on table had so depressed Gloria, gave way to an exceedingly efficient Japanese whose name was Tanalahaka, but who confessed that he heeded any summons which included the dissyllable "Tana."

Tana was unusually small even for a Japanese, and displayed a somewhat naïve conception of himself as a man of the world. On the day of his arrival from "R. Gugimoniki, Japanese Reliable Employment Agency," he called Anthony into his room to see the treasures of his trunk. These included a large collection of Japanese post-cards, which he was all for explaining to his employer at once, individually and at great length. Among them were half a dozen of pornographic intent and plainly of American origin, though the makers had modestly omitted both their names and the form for mailing. He next brought out some of his own handiwork—a pair of American pants, which he had made himself, and two suits of solid silk underwear. He informed Anthony confidentially as to the purpose for which these latter were reserved. The next exhibit was a rather good copy of an etching of Abraham Lincoln, to whose face he had given an unmistakable Japanese cast. Last came a flute; he had made it himself but it was broken: he was going to fix it soon.

After these polite formalities, which Anthony conjectured must be native to Japan, Tana delivered a long harangue in splintered English on the relation of master and servant from which Anthony gathered that he had worked on large estates but had always quarrelled with the other servants because they were not honest. They had a great time over the word "honest," and in fact became rather irritated with each other, because Anthony persisted stubbornly that Tana was trying to say "hornets," and even went to the extent of buzzing in the manner of a bee and flapping his arms to imitate wings.

After three-quarters of an hour Anthony was released with the warm assurance that they would have other nice chats in which Tana would tell "how we do in my countree."

Such was Tana's garrulous première in the gray house—and he fulfilled its promise. Though he was conscientious and honorable, he was unquestionably a terrific bore. He seemed unable to control his tongue, sometimes continuing from paragraph to paragraph with a look akin to pain in his small brown eyes.

Sunday and Monday afternoons he read the comic sections of the newspapers. One cartoon which contained a facetious Japanese butler diverted him enormously, though he claimed that the protagonist, who to Anthony appeared clearly Oriental, had really an American face. The difficulty with the funny paper was that when, aided by Anthony, he had spelled out the last three pictures and assimilated their context with a concentration surely adequate for Kant's "Critique," he had entirely forgotten what the first pictures were about.

In the middle of June Anthony and Gloria celebrated their first anniversary by having a "date." Anthony knocked at the door and she ran to let him in. Then they sat together on the couch calling over those names they had made for each other, new combinations of endearments ages old. Yet to this "date" was appended no attenuated good night with its ecstasy of regret.

Later in June horror leered out at Gloria, struck at her and frightened her bright soul back half a generation. Then slowly it faded out, faded back into that impenetrable darkness whence it had come—taking relentlessly its modicum of youth.

With an infallible sense of the dramatic it chose a little railroad-station in a wretched village near Portchester. The station platform lay all day bare as a prairie, exposed to the dusty yellow sun and to the glance of that most obnoxious type of countryman who lives near a metropolis and has attained its cheap smartness without its urbanity. A dozen of these yokels, red-eyed, cheerless as scarecrows, saw the incident. Dimly it passed across their confused and uncomprehending minds, taken at its broadest for a coarse joke, at its subtlest for a "shame." Meanwhile there upon the platform a measure of brightness faded from the world.

With Eric Merriam, Anthony had been sitting over a decanter of Scotch all the hot summer afternoon, while Gloria and Constance Merriam swam and sunned themselves at the Beach Club, the latter under a striped parasol-awning, Gloria stretched sensuously upon the soft hot sand, tanning her inevitable legs. Later they had all four played with inconsequential sandwiches; then Gloria had risen, tapping Anthony's knee with her parasol to get his attention.

"We've got to go, dear."

"Now?" He looked at her unwillingly. At that moment nothing seemed of more importance than to idle on that shady porch drinking mellowed Scotch, while his host reminisced interminably on the byplay of some forgotten political campaign.

"We've really got to go," repeated Gloria. "We can get a taxi to the station. . . . Come on, Anthony!" she commanded a bit more imperiously.

"Now see here—" Merriam, his yarn cut off, made conventional objections, meanwhile provocatively filling his guest's glass with a high-ball that should have been sipped through ten minutes. But at Gloria's annoyed "We really *must!*" Anthony drank it off, got to his feet and made an elaborate bow to his hostess.

"It seems we 'must,' " he said, with little grace.

In a minute he was following Gloria down a garden-walk between tall rose-bushes, her parasol brushing gently the June-blooming leaves. Most inconsiderate, he thought, as they reached the road. He felt with injured naïvete that Gloria should not have interrupted such innocent and harmless enjoyment. The whiskey had both soothed and clarified the restless things in his mind. It occurred to him that she had taken this same attitude several times before. Was he always to retreat from pleasant episodes at a touch of her parasol or a flicker of her eye? His unwillingness blurred to ill will, which rose within him like a resistless bubble. He kept silent, perversely inhibiting a desire to reproach her. They found a taxi in front of the Inn; rode silently to the little station. . . .

Then Anthony knew what he wanted—to assert his will

against this cool and impervious girl, to obtain with one magnificent effort a mastery that seemed infinitely desirable.

"Let's go over to see the Barneses," he said without looking at her. "I don't feel like going home."

—Mrs. Barnes, née Rachael Jerryl, had a summer place several miles from Redgate.

"We went there day before yesterday," she answered shortly.

"I'm sure they'd be glad to see us." He felt that that was not a strong enough note, braced himself stubbornly, and added: "I want to see the Barneses. I haven't any desire to go home."

"Well, I haven't any desire to go to the Barneses."

Suddenly they stared at each other.

"Why, Anthony," she said with annoyance, "this is Sunday night and they probably have guests for supper. Why we should go in at this hour——"

"Then why couldn't we have stayed at the Merriams'?" he burst out. "Why go home when we were having a perfectly decent time? They asked us to supper."

"They had to. Give me the money and I'll get the railroad-tickets."

"I certainly will not! I'm in no humor for a ride in that damn hot train."

Gloria stamped her foot on the platform.

"Anthony, you act as if you're tight!"

"On the contrary, I'm perfectly sober."

But his voice had slipped into a husky key and she knew with certainty that this was untrue.

"If you're sober you'll give me the money for the tickets."

But it was too late to talk to him that way. In his mind was but one idea—that Gloria was being selfish, that she was always being selfish and would continue to be unless here and now he asserted himself as her master. This was the occasion of all occasions, since for a whim she had deprived him of a pleasure. His determination solidified, approached momentarily a dull and sullen hate.

"I won't go in the train," he said, his voice trembling a little with anger. "We're going to the Barneses."

"I'm not!" she cried. "If you go I'm going home alone."

"Go on, then."

Without a word she turned toward the ticket-office; simultaneously he remembered that she had some money with her and that this was not the sort of victory he wanted, the sort he must have. He took a step after her and seized her arm.

"See here!" he muttered, "you're *not* going alone!"

"I certainly am—why, Anthony!" This exclamation as she tried to pull away from him and he only tightened his grasp.

He looked at her with narrowed and malicious eyes.

"Let go!" Her cry had a quality of fierceness. "If you have *any* decency you'll let go."

"Why?" He knew why. But he took a confused and not quite confident pride in holding her there.

"I'm going home, do you understand? And you're going to let me go!"

"No, I'm not."

Her eyes were burning now.

"Are you going to make a scene here?"

"I say you're not going! I'm tired of your eternal selfishness!"

"I only want to go home." Two wrathful tears started from her eyes.

"This time you're going to do what *I* say."

Slowly her body straightened: her head went back in a gesture of infinite scorn.

"I hate you!" Her low words were expelled like venom through her clenched teeth. "Oh, *let* me go! Oh, I *hate* you!" She tried to jerk herself away but he only grasped the other arm. "I hate you! I hate you!"

At Gloria's fury his uncertainty returned, but he felt that now he had gone too far to give in. It seemed that he had always given in and that in her heart she had despised him for it. Ah, she might hate him now, but afterward she would admire him for his dominance.

The approaching train gave out a premonitory siren that tumbled melodramatically toward them down the glistening blue tracks. Gloria tugged and strained to free herself, and words older than the Book of Genesis came to her lips.

"Oh, you brute!" she sobbed. "Oh, you brute! Oh, I hate you! Oh, you brute! Oh——"

On the station platform other prospective passengers were beginning to turn and stare; the drone of the train was audible, it increased to a clamor. Gloria's efforts redoubled, then ceased altogether, and she stood there trembling and hot-eyed at this helpless humiliation, as the engine roared and thundered into the station.

Low, below the flood of steam and the grinding of the brakes came her voice:

"Oh, if there was one *man* here you couldn't do this! You couldn't do this! You coward! You coward, oh, you coward!"

Anthony, silent, trembling himself, gripped her rigidly, aware that faces, dozens of them, curiously unmoved, shadows of a dream, were regarding him. Then the bells distilled metallic crashes that were like physical pain, the smoke-stacks volleyed in slow acceleration at the sky, and in a moment of noise and gray gaseous turbulence the line of faces ran by, moved off, became indistinct—until suddenly there was only the sun slanting east across the tracks and a volume of sound decreasing far off like a train made out of tin thunder. He dropped her arms. He had won.

Now, if he wished, he might laugh. The test was done and he had sustained his will with violence. Let leniency walk in the wake of victory.

"We'll hire a car here and drive back to Marietta," he said with fine reserve.

For answer Gloria seized his hand with both of hers and raising it to her mouth bit deeply into his thumb. He scarcely noticed the pain; seeing the blood spurt he absent-mindedly drew out his handkerchief and wrapped the wound. That too was part of the triumph he supposed—it was inevitable that defeat should thus be resented—and as such was beneath notice.

She was sobbing, almost without tears, profoundly and bitterly.

"I won't go! I won't go! You—can't—make—me—go! You've—you've killed any love I ever had for you, and any respect. But all that's left in me would die before I'd move from this place. Oh, if I'd thought *you'd* lay your hands on me——"

"You're going with me," he said brutally, "if I have to carry you."

He turned, beckoned to a taxicab, told the driver to go to Marietta. The man dismounted and swung the door open. Anthony faced his wife and said between his clenched teeth:

"Will you get in?—or will I *put* you in?"

With a subdued cry of infinite pain and despair she yielded herself up and got into the car.

All the long ride, through the increasing dark of twilight, she sat huddled in her side of the car, her silence broken by an occasional dry and solitary sob. Anthony stared out the window, his mind working dully on the slowly changing significance of what had occurred. Something was wrong—that last cry of Gloria's had struck a chord which echoed posthumously and with incongruous disquiet in his heart. He must be right—yet, she seemed such a pathetic little thing now, broken and dispirited, humiliated beyond the measure of her lot to bear. The sleeves of her dress were torn; her parasol was gone, forgotten on the platform. It was a new costume, he remembered, and she had been so proud of it that very morning when they had left the house. . . . He began wondering if any one they knew had seen the incident. And persistently there recurred to him her cry:

"All that's left in me would die——"

This gave him a confused and increasing worry. It fitted so well with the Gloria who lay in the corner—no longer a proud Gloria, nor any Gloria he had known. He asked himself if it were possible. While he did not believe she would cease to love him—this, of course, was unthinkable—it was yet problematical whether Gloria without her arrogance, her independence, her virginal confidence and courage, would be the girl of his glory, the radiant woman who was precious and charming because she was ineffably, triumphantly herself.

He was very drunk even then, so drunk as not to realize his own drunkenness. When they reached the gray house he went to his own room and, his mind still wrestling helplessly and sombrely with what he had done, fell into a deep stupor on his bed.

*

It was after one o'clock and the hall seemed extraordinarily quiet when Gloria, wide-eyed and sleepless, traversed it and pushed open the door of his room. He had been too befuddled to open the windows and the air was stale and thick with whiskey. She stood for a moment by his bed, a slender, exquisitely graceful figure in her boyish silk pajamas—then with abandon she flung herself upon him, half waking him in the frantic emotion of her embrace, dropping her warm tears upon his throat.

"Oh, Anthony!" she cried passionately, "oh, my darling, you don't know what you did!"

Yet in the morning, coming early into her room, he knelt down by her bed and cried like a little boy, as though it was his heart that had been broken.

"It seemed, last night," she said gravely, her fingers playing in his hair, "that all the part of me you loved, the part that was worth knowing, all the pride and fire, was gone. I knew that what was left of me would always love you, but never in quite the same way."

Nevertheless, she was aware even then that she would forget in time and that it is the manner of life seldom to strike but always to wear away. After that morning the incident was never mentioned and its deep wound healed with Anthony's hand—and if there was triumph some darker force than theirs possessed it, possessed the knowledge and the victory.

Nietzschean Incident

Gloria's independence, like all sincere and profound qualities, had begun unconsciously, but, once brought to her attention by Anthony's fascinated discovery of it, it assumed more nearly the proportions of a formal code. From her conversation it might be assumed that all her energy and vitality went into a violent affirmation of the negative principle "Never give a damn."

"Not for anything or anybody," she said, "except myself and, by implication, for Anthony. That's the rule of all life and if it weren't I'd be that way anyhow. Nobody'd do anything for me if it didn't gratify them to, and I'd do as little for them."

She was on the front porch of the nicest lady in Marietta when she said this, and as she finished she gave a curious little cry and sank in a dead faint to the porch floor.

The lady brought her to and drove her home in her car. It had occurred to the estimable Gloria that she was probably with child.

She lay upon the long lounge down-stairs. Day was slipping warmly out the window, touching the late roses on the porch pillars.

"All I think of ever is that I love you," she wailed. "I value my body because you think it's beautiful. And this body of mine—of yours—to have it grow ugly and shapeless? It's simply intolerable. Oh, Anthony, I'm not afraid of the pain."

He consoled her desperately—but in vain. She continued:

"And then afterward I might have wide hips and be pale, with all my freshness gone and no radiance in my hair."

He paced the floor with his hands in his pockets, asking:

"Is it certain?"

"*I* don't know anything. I've always hated obstrics, or whatever you call them. I thought I'd have a child some time. But not now."

"Well, for God's sake don't lie there and go to pieces."

Her sobs lapsed. She drew down a merciful silence from the twilight which filled the room. "Turn on the lights," she pleaded. "These days seem so short—June seemed—to—have—longer days when I was a little girl."

The lights snapped on and it was as though blue drapes of softest silk had been dropped behind the windows and the door. Her pallor, her immobility, without grief now, or joy, awoke his sympathy.

"Do you want me to have it?" she asked listlessly.

"I'm indifferent. That is, I'm neutral. If you have it I'll probably be glad. If you don't—well, that's all right too."

"I wish you'd make up your mind one way or the other!"

"Suppose you make up *your* mind."

She looked at him contemptuously, scorning to answer.

"You'd think you'd been singled out of all the women in the world for this crowning indignity."

"What if I do!" she cried angrily. "It isn't an indignity for them. It's their one excuse for living. It's the one thing they're good for. It *is* an indignity for *me*."

"See here, Gloria, I'm with you whatever you do, but for God's sake be a sport about it."

"Oh, don't *fuss* at me!" she wailed.

They exchanged a mute look of no particular significance but of much stress. Then Anthony took a book from the shelf and dropped into a chair.

Half an hour later her voice came out of the intense stillness that pervaded the room and hung like incense on the air.

"I'll drive over and see Constance Merriam to-morrow."

"All right. And I'll go to Tarrytown and see Grampa."

"—You see," she added, "it isn't that I'm afraid—of this or anything else. I'm being true to me, you know."

"I know," he agreed.

The Practical Men

Adam Patch, in a pious rage against the Germans, subsisted on the war news. Pin maps plastered his walls; atlases were piled deep on tables convenient to his hand together with "Photographic Histories of the World War," official Explain-alls, and the "Personal Impressions" of war correspondents and of Privates X, Y, and Z. Several times during Anthony's visit his grandfather's secretary, Edward Shuttleworth, the one-time "Accomplished Gin-physician" of "Pat's Place" in Hoboken, now shod with righteous indignation, would appear with an extra. The old man attacked each paper with untiring fury, tearing out those columns which appeared to him of sufficient pregnancy for preservation and thrusting them into one of his already bulging files.

"Well, what have you been doing?" he asked Anthony blandly. "Nothing? Well, I thought so. I've been intending to drive over and see you, all summer."

"I've been writing. Don't you remember the essay I sent you—the one I sold to The Florentine last winter?"

"Essay? You never sent *me* any essay."

"Oh, yes, I did. We talked about it."

Adam Patch shook his head mildly.

"Oh, no. You never sent *me* any essay. You may have thought you sent it but it never reached me."

"Why, you read it, Grampa," insisted Anthony, somewhat exasperated, "you read it and disagreed with it."

The old man suddenly remembered, but this was made apparent only by a partial falling open of his mouth, displaying rows of gray gums. Eying Anthony with a green and ancient stare he hesitated between confessing his error and covering it up.

"So you're writing," he said quickly. "Well, why don't you go over and write about these Germans? Write something real, something about what's going on, something people can read."

"Anybody can't be a war correspondent," objected Anthony. "You have to have some newspaper willing to buy your stuff. And I can't spare the money to go over as a free-lance."

"I'll send you over," suggested his grandfather surprisingly. "I'll get you over as an authorized correspondent of any newspaper you pick out."

Anthony recoiled from the idea—almost simultaneously he bounded toward it.

"I—don't—know——"

He would have to leave Gloria, whose whole life yearned toward him and enfolded him. Gloria was in trouble. Oh, the thing wasn't feasible—yet—he saw himself in khaki, leaning, as all war correspondents lean, upon a heavy stick, portfolio at shoulder—trying to look like an Englishman. "I'd like to think it over," he confessed. "It's certainly very kind of you. I'll think it over and I'll let you know."

Thinking it over absorbed him on the journey to New York. He had had one of those sudden flashes of illumination vouchsafed to all men who are dominated by a strong and beloved woman, which show them a world of harder men, more fiercely trained and grappling with the abstractions of thought and war. In that world the arms of Gloria would exist only as the hot embrace of a chance mistress, coolly sought and quickly forgotten. . . .

These unfamiliar phantoms were crowding closely about him when he boarded his train for Marietta, in the Grand

Central Station. The car was crowded; he secured the last vacant seat and it was only after several minutes that he gave even a casual glance to the man beside him. When he did he saw a heavy lay of jaw and nose, a curved chin and small, puffed-under eyes. In a moment he recognized Joseph Bloeckman.

Simultaneously they both half rose, were half embarrassed, and exchanged what amounted to a half handshake. Then, as though to complete the matter, they both half laughed.

"Well," remarked Anthony without inspiration, "I haven't seen you for a long time." Immediately he regretted his words and started to add: "I didn't know you lived out this way." But Bloeckman anticipated him by asking pleasantly:

"How's your wife? . . ."

"She's very well. How've you been?"

"Excellent." His tone amplified the grandeur of the word.

It seemed to Anthony that during the last year Bloeckman had grown tremendously in dignity. The boiled look was gone, he seemed "done" at last. In addition he was no longer overdressed. The inappropriate facetiousness he had affected in ties had given way to a sturdy dark pattern, and his right hand, which had formerly displayed two heavy rings, was now innocent of ornament and even without the raw glow of a manicure.

This dignity appeared also in his personality. The last aura of the successful travelling-man had faded from him, that deliberate ingratiation of which the lowest form is the bawdy joke in the Pullman smoker. One imagined that, having been fawned upon financially, he had attained aloofness; having been snubbed socially, he had acquired reticence. But whatever had given him weight instead of bulk, Anthony no longer felt a correct superiority in his presence.

"D'you remember Caramel, Richard Caramel? I believe you met him one night."

"I remember. He was writing a book."

"Well, he sold it to the movies. Then they had some scenario man named Jordan work on it. Well, Dick subscribes to a clipping bureau and he's furious because about half the movie reviewers speak of the 'power and strength of William Jordan's "Demon Lover."' Didn't mention old Dick at all.

You'd think this fellow Jordan had actually conceived and developed the thing."

Bloeckman nodded comprehensively.

"Most of the contracts state that the original writer's name goes into all the paid publicity. Is Caramel still writing?"

"Oh, yes. Writing hard. Short stories."

"Well, that's fine, that's fine. . . . You on this train often?"

"About once a week. We live in Marietta."

"Is that so? Well, well! I live near Cos Cob myself. Bought a place there only recently. We're only five miles apart."

"You'll have to come and see us." Anthony was surprised at his own courtesy. "I'm sure Gloria'd be delighted to see an old friend. Anybody'll tell you where the house is—it's our second season there."

"Thank you." Then, as though returning a complementary politeness: "How is your grandfather?"

"He's been well. I had lunch with him to-day."

"A great character," said Bloeckman severely. "A fine example of an American."

The Triumph of Lethargy

Anthony found his wife deep in the porch hammock voluptuously engaged with a lemonade and a tomato sandwich and carrying on an apparently cheery conversation with Tana upon one of Tana's complicated themes.

"In my countree," Anthony recognized his invariable preface, "all time—peoples—eat rice—because haven't got. Cannot eat what no have got." Had his nationality not been desperately apparent one would have thought he had acquired his knowledge of his native land from American primary-school geographies.

When the Oriental had been squelched and dismissed to the kitchen, Anthony turned questioningly to Gloria:

"It's all right," she announced, smiling broadly. "And it surprised me more than it does you."

"There's no doubt?"

"None! Couldn't be!"

They rejoiced happily, gay again with reborn irresponsibility.

Then he told her of his opportunity to go abroad, and that he was almost ashamed to reject it.

"What do *you* think? Just tell me frankly."

"Why, Anthony!" Her eyes were startled. "Do you want to go? Without me?"

His face fell—yet he knew, with his wife's question, that it was too late. Her arms, sweet and strangling, were around him, for he had made all such choices back in that room in the Plaza the year before. This was an anachronism from an age of such dreams.

"Gloria," he lied, in a great burst of comprehension, "of course I don't. I was thinking you might go as a nurse or something." He wondered dully if his grandfather would consider this.

As she smiled he realized again how beautiful she was, a gorgeous girl of miraculous freshness and sheerly honorable eyes. She embraced his suggestion with luxurious intensity, holding it aloft like a sun of her own making and basking in its beams. She strung together an amazing synopsis for an extravaganza of martial adventure.

After supper, surfeited with the subject, she yawned. She wanted not to talk but only to read "Penrod," stretched upon the lounge until at midnight she fell asleep. But Anthony, after he had carried her romantically up the stairs, stayed awake to brood upon the day, vaguely angry with her, vaguely dissatisfied.

"What am I going to do?" he began at breakfast. "Here we've been married a year and we've just worried around without even being efficient people of leisure."

"Yes, you ought to do something," she admitted, being in an agreeable and loquacious humor. This was not the first of these discussions, but as they usually developed Anthony in the rôle of protagonist, she had come to avoid them.

"It's not that I have any moral compunctions about work," he continued, "but grampa may die to-morrow and he may live for ten years. Meanwhile we're living above our income and all we've got to show for it is a farmer's car and a few clothes. We keep an apartment that we've only lived in three months and a little old house way off in nowhere. We're frequently bored and yet we won't make any effort to know any one except the same crowd who drift around California all summer wearing sport clothes and waiting for their families to die."

"How you've changed!" remarked Gloria. "Once you told me you didn't see why an American couldn't loaf gracefully."

"Well, damn it, I wasn't married. And the old mind was working at top speed and now it's going round and round like a cog-wheel with nothing to catch it. As a matter of fact I think that if I hadn't met you I *would* have done something. But you make leisure so subtly attractive——"

"Oh, it's all my fault——"

"I didn't mean that, and you know I didn't. But here I'm almost twenty-seven and——"

"Oh," she interrupted in vexation, "you make me tired! Talking as though I were objecting or hindering you!"

"I was just discussing it, Gloria. Can't I discuss——"

"I should think you'd be strong enough to settle——"

"—something with you without——"

"—your own problems without coming to me. You *talk* a lot about going to work. I could use more money very easily, but *I'm* not complaining. Whether you work or not I love you." Her last words were gentle as fine snow upon hard ground. But for the moment neither was attending to the other—they were each engaged in polishing and perfecting his own attitude.

"I have worked—some." This by Anthony was an imprudent bringing up of raw reserves. Gloria laughed, torn between delight and derision; she resented his sophistry as at the same time she admired his nonchalance. She would never blame him for being the ineffectual idler so long as he did it sincerely, from the attitude that nothing much was worth doing.

"Work!" she scoffed. "Oh, you sad bird! You bluffer! Work—that means a great arranging of the desk and the lights, a great sharpening of pencils, and 'Gloria, don't sing!' and 'Please keep that damn Tana away from me,' and 'Let me read you my opening sentence,' and 'I won't be through for a long time, Gloria, so don't stay up for me,' and a tremendous consumption of tea or coffee. And that's all. In just about an hour I hear the old pencil stop scratching and look over. You've got out a book and you're 'looking up' something. Then you're reading. Then yawns—then bed and a great tossing about because you're all full of caffeine and can't sleep. Two weeks later the whole performance over again."

With much difficulty Anthony retained a scanty breech-clout of dignity.

"Now that's a *slight* exaggeration. You know *darn well* I sold an essay to The Florentine—and it attracted a lot of attention considering the circulation of The Florentine. And what's more, Gloria, you know I sat up till five o'clock in the morning finishing it."

She lapsed into silence, giving him rope. And if he had not hanged himself he had certainly come to the end of it.

"At least," he concluded feebly, "I'm perfectly willing to be a war correspondent."

But so was Gloria. They were both willing—anxious; they assured each other of it. The evening ended on a note of tremendous sentiment, the majesty of leisure, the ill health of Adam Patch, love at any cost.

"Anthony!" she called over the banister one afternoon a week later, "there's some one at the door."

Anthony, who had been lolling in the hammock on the sun-speckled south porch, strolled around to the front of the house. A foreign car, large and impressive, crouched like an immense and saturnine bug at the foot of the path. A man in a soft pongee suit, with cap to match, hailed him.

"Hello there, Patch. Ran over to call on you."

It was Bloeckman; as always, infinitesimally improved, of subtler intonation, of more convincing ease.

"I'm awfully glad you did." Anthony raised his voice to a vine-covered window: "Glor-i-*a*! We've got a visitor!"

"I'm in the tub," wailed Gloria politely.

With a smile the two men acknowledged the triumph of her alibi.

"She'll be down. Come round here on the side-porch. Like a drink? Gloria's always in the tub—good third of every day."

"Pity she doesn't live on the Sound."

"Can't afford it."

As coming from Adam Patch's grandson, Bloeckman took

this as a form of pleasantry. After fifteen minutes filled with estimable brilliancies, Gloria appeared, fresh in starched yellow, bringing atmosphere and an increase of vitality.

"I want to be a successful sensation in the movies," she announced. "I hear that Mary Pickford makes a million dollars annually."

"You could, you know," said Bloeckman. "I think you'd film very well."

"Would you let me, Anthony? If I only play unsophisticated rôles?"

As the conversation continued in stilted commas, Anthony wondered that to him and Bloeckman both this girl had once been the most stimulating, the most tonic personality they had ever known—and now the three sat like overoiled machines, without conflict, without fear, without elation, heavily enamelled little figures secure beyond enjoyment in a world where death and war, dull emotion and noble savagery were covering a continent with the smoke of terror.

In a moment he would call Tana and they would pour into themselves a gay and delicate poison which would restore them momentarily to the pleasurable excitement of childhood, when every face in a crowd had carried its suggestion of splendid and significant transactions taking place somewhere to some magnificent and illimitable purpose. . . . Life was no more than this summer afternoon; a faint wind stirring the lace collar of Gloria's dress; the slow baking drowsiness of the veranda. . . . Intolerably unmoved they all seemed, removed from any romantic imminency of action. Even Gloria's beauty needed wild emotions, needed poignancy, needed death. . . .

". . . Any day next week," Bloeckman was saying to Gloria. "Here—take this card. What they do is to give you a test of about three hundred feet of film, and they can tell pretty accurately from that."

"How about Wednesday?"

"Wednesday's fine. Just phone me and I'll go around with you——"

He was on his feet, shaking hands briskly—then his car was a wraith of dust down the road. Anthony turned to his wife in bewilderment.

"Why, Gloria!"

"You don't mind if I have a trial, Anthony. Just a trial? I've got to go to town Wednesday, *any*how."

"But it's so silly! You don't want to go into the movies—moon around a studio all day with a lot of cheap chorus people."

"Lot of mooning around Mary Pickford does!"

"Everybody isn't a Mary Pickford."

"Well, I can't see how you'd object to my *try*ing."

"I do, though. I hate actors."

"Oh, you make me tired. Do you imagine I have a very thrilling time dozing on this damn porch?"

"You wouldn't mind if you loved me."

"Of course I love you," she said impatiently, making out a quick case for herself. "It's just because I do that I hate to see you go to pieces by just lying around and saying you ought to work. Perhaps if I *did* go into this for a while it'd stir you up so you'd do something."

"It's just your craving for excitement, that's all it is."

"Maybe it is! It's a perfectly natural craving, isn't it?"

"Well, I'll tell you one thing. If you go to the movies I'm going to Europe."

"Well, go on then! *I'm* not stopping you!"

To show she was not stopping him she melted into melancholy tears. Together they marshalled the armies of sentiment—words, kisses, endearments, self-reproaches. They attained nothing. Inevitably they attained nothing. Finally, in a burst of gargantuan emotion each of them sat down and wrote a letter. Anthony's was to his grandfather; Gloria's was to Joseph Bloeckman. It was a triumph of lethargy.

One day early in July Anthony, returned from an afternoon in New York, called up-stairs to Gloria. Receiving no answer he guessed she was asleep and so went into the pantry for one of the little sandwiches that were always prepared for them. He found Tana seated at the kitchen-table before a miscellaneous assortment of odds and ends—cigar-boxes, knives, pencils, the tops of cans, and some scraps of paper covered with elaborate figures and diagrams.

"What the devil you doing?" demanded Anthony curiously.

Tana politely grinned.

"I show you," he exclaimed enthusiastically. "I tell——"

"You making a dog-house?"

"No, sa." Tana grinned again. "Make typewutta."

"Typewriter?"

"Yes, sa. I think, oh all time I think, lie in bed think 'bout typewutta."

"So you thought you'd make one, eh?"

"Wait. I tell."

Anthony, munching a sandwich, leaned leisurely against the sink. Tana opened and closed his mouth several times as though testing its capacity for action. Then with a rush he began:

"I been think—typewutta—has, oh, many many many many *thing*. Oh many many many many."

"Many keys. I see."

"No-o? *Yes*—key! Many many many many lettah. Like so a-b-c."

"Yes, you're right."

"Wait. I tell." He screwed his face up in a tremendous effort to express himself: "I been think—many words—end same. Like i-n-g."

"You bet. A whole raft of them."

"So—I make—typewutta—quick. Not so many lettah——"

"That's a great idea, Tana. Save time. You'll make a fortune. Press one key and there's 'ing.' Hope you work it out."

Tana laughed disparagingly.

"Wait. I tell——"

"Where's Mrs. Patch?"

"She out. Wait, I tell—" Again he screwed up his face for action. "*My* typewutta——"

"Where is she?"

"Here—I make." He pointed to the miscellany of junk on the table.

"I mean Mrs. Patch."

"She out." Tana reassured him. "She be back five o'clock, she say."

"Down in the village?"

"No. Went off be-fore lunch. She go Mr. Bloeckman."

Anthony started.

"Went out with Mr. Bloeckman?"

"She be back five."

Without a word Anthony left the kitchen with Tana's disconsolate "I tell" trailing after him. So this was Gloria's idea of excitement, by God! His fists were clenched; within a moment he had worked himself up to a tremendous pitch of indignation. He went to the door and looked out; there was no car in sight and his watch stood at four minutes of five. With furious energy he dashed down to the end of the path—as far as the bend of the road a mile off he could see no car—except—but it was a farmer's flivver. Then, in an undignified pursuit of dignity, he rushed back to the shelter of the house as quickly as he had rushed out.

Pacing up and down the living-room he began an angry rehearsal of the speech he would make to her when she came in——

"So this is love!" he would begin—or no, it sounded too much like the popular phrase "So this is Paris!" He must be dignified, hurt, grieved. Anyhow—"So this is what *you* do when I have to go up and trot all day around the hot city on business. No wonder I can't write! No wonder I don't dare let you out of my sight!" He was expanding now, warming to his subject. "I'll tell you," he continued, "I'll tell you—" He paused, catching a familiar ring in the words—then he realized—it was Tana's "I tell."

Yet Anthony neither laughed nor seemed absurd to himself. To his frantic imagination it was already six—seven—eight, and she was never coming! Bloeckman finding her bored and unhappy had persuaded her to go to California with him. . . .

—There was a great to-do out in front, a joyous "Yoho, Anthony!" and he rose trembling, weakly happy to see her fluttering up the path. Bloeckman was following, cap in hand.

"Dearest!" she cried.

"We've been for the best jaunt—all over New York State."

"I'll have to be starting home," said Bloeckman, almost immediately. "Wish you'd both been here when I came."

"I'm sorry I wasn't," answered Anthony dryly.

When he had departed Anthony hesitated. The fear was gone from his heart, yet he felt that some protest was ethically apropos. Gloria resolved his uncertainty.

"I knew you wouldn't mind. He came just before lunch and said he had to go to Garrison on business and wouldn't I go with him. He looked so lonesome, Anthony. And I drove his car all the way."

Listlessly Anthony dropped into a chair, his mind tired—tired with nothing, tired with everything, with the world's weight he had never chosen to bear. He was ineffectual and vaguely helpless here as he had always been. One of those personalities who, in spite of all their words, are inarticulate, he seemed to have inherited only the vast tradition of human failure—that, and the sense of death.

"I suppose I don't care," he answered.

One must be broad about these things, and Gloria being young, being beautiful, must have reasonable privileges. Yet it wearied him that he failed to understand.

Winter

She rolled over on her back and lay still for a moment in the great bed watching the February sun suffer one last attenuated refinement in its passage through the leaded panes into the room. For a time she had no accurate sense of her whereabouts or of the events of the day before, or the day before that; then, like a suspended pendulum, memory began to beat out its story, releasing with each swing a burdened quota of time until her life was given back to her.

She could hear, now, Anthony's troubled breathing beside her; she could smell whiskey and cigarette-smoke. She noticed that she lacked complete muscular control; when she moved it was not a sinuous motion with the resultant strain distributed easily over her body—it was a tremendous effort of her nervous system as though each time she were hypnotizing herself into performing an impossible action. . . .

She was in the bathroom, brushing her teeth to get rid of that intolerable taste; then back by the bedside listening to the rattle of Bounds's key in the outer door.

"Wake up, Anthony!" she said sharply.

She climbed into bed beside him and closed her eyes.

Almost the last thing she remembered was a conversation with Mr. and Mrs. Lacy. Mrs. Lacy had said, "Sure you don't want us to get you a taxi?" and Anthony had replied that he guessed they could walk over to Fifth all right. Then they had both attempted, imprudently, to bow—and collapsed absurdly into a battalion of empty milk-bottles just outside the door. There must have been two dozen milk-bottles standing open-mouthed in the dark. She could conceive of no plausible explanation of those milk-bottles. Perhaps they had been attracted by the singing in the Lacy house and had hurried over agape with wonder to see the fun. Well, they'd had the worst of it—though it seemed that she and Anthony never would get up, the perverse things rolled so. . . .

Still, they had found a taxi. "My meter's broken and it'll cost you a dollar and a half to get home," said the taxi-driver. "Well," said Anthony, "I'm young Packy McFarland and if you'll come down here I'll beat you till you can't stand up." . . . At that point the man had driven off without them. They must have found another taxi, for they were in the apartment. . . .

"What time is it?" Anthony was sitting up in bed, staring at her with owlish precision.

This was obviously a rhetorical question. Gloria could think of no reason why she should be expected to know the time.

"Golly, I feel like the devil!" muttered Anthony dispassionately. Relaxing, he tumbled back upon his pillow. "Bring on your grim reaper!"

"Anthony, how'd we finally get home last night?"

"Taxi."

"Oh!" Then, after a pause: "Did you put me to bed?"

"I don't know. Seems to me you put *me* to bed. What day is it?"

"Tuesday."

"Tuesday? I hope so. If it's Wednesday, I've got to start work at that idiotic place. Supposed to be down at nine or some such ungodly hour."

"Ask Bounds," suggested Gloria feebly.

"Bounds!" he called.

Sprightly, sober—a voice from a world that it seemed in the past two days they had left forever, Bounds sprang in short steps down the hall and appeared in the half darkness of the door.

"What day, Bounds?"

"February the twenty-second, I think, sir."

"I mean day of the week."

"Tuesday, sir." "Thanks." After a pause: "Are you ready for breakfast, sir?"

"Yes, and Bounds, before you get it, will you make a pitcher of water, and set it here beside the bed? I'm a little thirsty."

"Yes, sir."

Bounds retreated in sober dignity down the hallway.

"Lincoln's birthday," affirmed Anthony without enthusiasm, "or St. Valentine's or somebody's. When did we start on this insane party?"

"Sunday night."

"After prayers?" he suggested sardonically.

"We raced all over town in those hansoms and Maury sat up with his driver, don't you remember? Then we came home and he tried to cook some bacon—came out of the pantry with a few blackened remains, insisting it was 'fried to the proverbial crisp.' "

Both of them laughed, spontaneously but with some difficulty, and lying there side by side reviewed the chain of events that had ended in this rusty and chaotic dawn.

They had been in New York for almost four months, since the country had grown too cool in late October. They had given up California this year, partly because of lack of funds, partly with the idea of going abroad should this interminable war, persisting now into its second year, end during the winter. Of late their income had lost elasticity; no longer did it stretch to cover gay whims and pleasant extravagances, and Anthony had spent many puzzled and unsatisfactory hours over a densely figured pad, making remarkable budgets that left huge margins for "amusements, trips, etc.," and trying to apportion, even approximately, their past expenditures.

He remembered a time when in going on a "party" with his two best friends, he and Maury had invariably paid more than their share of the expenses. They would buy the tickets for the theatre or squabble between themselves for the dinner-check. It had seemed fitting; Dick, with his naïveté and his astonishing fund of information about himself, had been a diverting, almost juvenile, figure—court jester to their royalty. But this was no longer true. It was Dick who always had money; it was Anthony who entertained within limitations—always excepting occasional wild, wine-inspired, check-cashing parties—and it was Anthony who was solemn about it next morning and told the scornful and disgusted Gloria that they'd have to be "more careful next time."

In the two years since the publication of "The Demon Lover," Dick had made over twenty-five thousand dollars, most of it lately, when the reward of the author of fiction had begun to swell unprecedentedly as a result of the voracious hunger of the motion-pictures for plots. He received seven hundred dollars for every story, at that time a large emolument for such a young man—he was not quite thirty—and for every one that contained enough "action" (kissing, shooting, and sacrificing) for the movies, he obtained an additional thousand. His stories varied; there was a measure of vitality and a sort of instinctive technic in all of them, but none attained the personality of "The Demon Lover," and there were several that Anthony considered downright cheap. These, Dick explained severely, were to widen his audience. Wasn't it true that men who had attained real permanence from Shakespeare to Mark Twain had appealed to the many as well as to the elect?

Though Anthony and Maury disagreed, Gloria told him to go ahead and make as much money as he could—that was the only thing that counted anyhow. . . .

Maury, a little stouter, faintly mellower, and more complaisant, had gone to work in Philadelphia. He came to New York once or twice a month and on such occasions the four of them travelled the popular routes from dinner to the theatre, thence to the Frolic or, perhaps, at the urging of the ever-curious Gloria, to one of the cellars of Greenwich Village, notorious through the furious but short-lived vogue of the "new poetry movement."

In January, after many monologues directed at his reticent wife, Anthony determined to "get something to do," for the winter at any rate. He wanted to please his grandfather and even, in a measure, to see how he liked it himself. He discovered during several tentative semi-social calls that employers were not interested in a young man who was only going to "try it for a few months or so." As the grandson of Adam Patch he was received everywhere with marked courtesy, but the old man was a back number now—the heyday of his fame as first an "oppressor" and then an uplifter of the people had been during the twenty years preceding his retirement. Anthony even found several of the younger men who were under the impression that Adam Patch had been dead for some years.

Eventually Anthony went to his grandfather and asked his advice, which turned out to be that he should enter the bond business as a salesman, a tedious suggestion to Anthony, but one that in the end he determined to follow. Sheer money in deft manipulation had fascinations under all circumstances, while almost any side of manufacturing would be insufferably dull. He considered newspaper work but decided that the hours were not ordered for a married man. And he lingered over pleasant fancies of himself either as editor of a brilliant weekly of opinion, an American Mercure de France, or as scintillant producer of satiric comedy and Parisian musical revue. However, the approaches to these latter guilds seemed to be guarded by professional secrets. Men drifted into them by the devious highways of writing and acting. It was palpably impossible to get on a magazine unless you had been on one before.

So in the end he entered, by way of his grandfather's letter, that Sanctum Americanum where sat the president of Wilson, Hiemer and Hardy at his "cleared desk," and issued therefrom employed. He was to begin work on the twenty-third of February.

In tribute to the momentous occasion this two-day revel had been planned, since, he said, after he began working he'd have to get to bed early during the week. Maury Noble had arrived from Philadelphia on a trip that had to do with seeing some man in Wall Street (whom, incidentally, he failed to see), and Richard Caramel had been half persuaded, half tricked into joining them. They had condescended to a wet and fashionable wedding on Monday afternoon, and in the evening had occurred the dénouement: Gloria, going beyond her accustomed limit of four precisely timed cocktails, led them on as gay and joyous a bacchanal as they had ever known, disclosing an astonishing knowledge of ballet steps, and singing songs which she confessed had been taught her by her cook when she was innocent and seventeen. She repeated these by request at intervals throughout the evening with such frank conviviality that Anthony, far from being annoyed, was gratified at this fresh source of entertainment. The occasion was memorable in other ways—a long conversation between Maury and a defunct crab, which he was dragging around on the end of a string, as to whether the crab was fully conversant with the applications of the binomial theorem, and the aforementioned race in two hansom cabs with the sedate and impressive shadows of Fifth Avenue for audience, ending in a labyrinthine escape into the darkness of Central Park. Finally Anthony and Gloria had paid a call on some wild young married people—the Lacys—and collapsed in the empty milk-bottles.

Morning now—theirs to add up the checks cashed here and there in clubs, stores, restaurants. Theirs to air the dank staleness of wine and cigarettes out of the tall blue front room, to pick up the broken glass and brush at the stained fabric of chairs and sofas; to give Bounds suits and dresses for the cleaners; finally, to take their smothery half-feverish bodies and faded depressed spirits out into the chill air of February, that life might go on and Wilson, Hiemer and Hardy obtain the services of a vigorous man at nine next morning.

"Do you remember," called Anthony from the bathroom, "when Maury got out at the corner of One Hundred and Tenth Street and acted as a traffic cop, beckoning cars forward and motioning them back? They must have thought he was a private detective."

After each reminiscence they both laughed inordinately, their overwrought nerves responding as acutely and janglingly to mirth as to depression.

Gloria at the mirror was wondering at the splendid color and freshness of her face—it seemed that she had never looked so well, though her stomach hurt her and her head was aching furiously.

The day passed slowly. Anthony, riding in a taxi to his broker's to borrow money on a bond, found that he had only two dollars in his pocket. The fare would cost all of that, but he felt that on this particular afternoon he could not have endured the subway. When the taximetre reached his limit he must get out and walk.

With this his mind drifted off into one of its characteristic day-dreams. . . . In this dream he discovered that the metre was going too fast—the driver had dishonestly adjusted it. Calmly he reached his destination and then nonchalantly handed the man what he justly owed him. The man showed fight, but almost before his hands were up Anthony had knocked him down with one terrific blow. And when he rose Anthony quickly sidestepped and floored him definitely with a crack in the temple.

. . . He was in court now. The judge had fined him five dollars and he had no money. Would the court take his check? Ah, but the court did not know him. Well, he could identify himself by having them call his apartment.

. . . They did so. Yes, it was Mrs. Anthony Patch speaking—but how did she know that this man was her husband? How could she know? Let the police sergeant ask her if she remembered the milk-bottles . . .

He leaned forward hurriedly and tapped at the glass. The taxi was only at Brooklyn Bridge, but the metre showed a dollar and eighty cents, and Anthony would never have omitted the ten per cent tip.

Later in the afternoon he returned to the apartment. Gloria had also been out—shopping—and was asleep, curled in a corner of the sofa with her purchase locked securely in her arms. Her face was as untroubled as a little girl's, and the bundle that she pressed tightly to her bosom was a child's doll, a profound and infinitely healing balm to her disturbed and childish heart.

Destiny

It was with this party, more especially with Gloria's part in it, that a decided change began to come over their way of living. The magnificent attitude of not giving a damn altered overnight; from being a mere tenet of Gloria's it became the entire solace and justification for what they chose to do and what consequence it brought. Not to be sorry, not to loose one cry of regret, to live according to a clear code of honor toward each other, and to seek the moment's happiness as fervently and persistently as possible.

"No one cares about us but ourselves, Anthony," she said one day. "It'd be ridiculous for me to go about pretending I felt any obligations toward the world, and as for worrying what people think about me, I simply *don't*, that's all. Since I was a little girl in dancing-school I've been criticised by the mothers of all the little girls who weren't as popular as I was, and I've always looked on criticism as a sort of envious tribute."

This was because of a party in the "Boul' Mich' " one night, where Constance Merriam had seen her as one of a highly stimulated party of four. Constance Merriam, "as an old school friend," had gone to the trouble of inviting her to lunch next day in order to inform her how terrible it was.

"I told her I couldn't see it," Gloria told Anthony. "Eric Merriam is a sort of sublimated Percy Wolcott—you remember that man in Hot Springs I told you about—his idea of respecting Constance is to leave her at home with her sewing and her baby and her book, and such innocuous amusements, whenever he's going on a party that promises to be anything but deathly dull."

"Did you tell her that?"

"I certainly did. And I told her that what she really objected to was that I was having a better time than she was."

Anthony applauded her. He was tremendously proud of Gloria, proud that she never failed to eclipse whatever other women might be in the party, proud that men were always glad to revel with her in great rowdy groups, without any attempt to do more than enjoy her beauty and the warmth of her vitality.

These "parties" gradually became their chief source of entertainment. Still in love, still enormously interested in each other, they yet found as spring drew near that staying at home in the evening palled on them; books were unreal; the old magic of being alone had long since vanished—instead they preferred to be bored by a stupid musical comedy, or to go to dinner with the most uninteresting of their acquaintances, so long as there would be enough cocktails to keep the conversation from becoming utterly intolerable. A scattering of younger married people who had been their friends in school or college, as well as a varied assortment of single men, began to think instinctively of them whenever color and excitement were needed, so there was scarcely a day without its phone call, its "Wondered what you were doing this evening." Wives, as a rule, were afraid of Gloria—her facile attainment of the centre of the stage, her innocent but nevertheless disturbing way of becoming a favorite with husbands—these things drove them instinctively into an attitude of profound distrust, heightened by the fact that Gloria was largely unresponsive to any intimacy shown her by a woman.

On the appointed Wednesday in February Anthony had gone to the imposing offices of Wilson, Hiemer and Hardy and listened to many vague instructions delivered by an energetic young man of about his own age, named Kahler, who wore a defiant yellow pompadour, and in announcing himself as an assistant secretary gave the impression that it was a tribute to exceptional ability.

"There's two kinds of men here, you'll find," he said. "There's the man who gets to be an assistant secretary or treasurer, gets his name on our folder here, before he's thirty, and there's the man who gets his name there at forty-five. The man who gets his name there at forty-five stays there the rest of his life."

"How about the man who gets it there at thirty?" inquired Anthony politely.

"Why, he gets up here, you see." He pointed to a list of assistant vice-presidents upon the folder. "Or maybe he gets to be president or secretary or treasurer."

"And what about these over here?"

"Those? Oh, those are the trustees—the men with capital."

"I see."

"Now some people," continued Kahler, "think that whether a man gets started early or late depends on whether he's got a college education. But they're wrong."

"I see."

"I had one; I was Buckleigh, class of nineteen-eleven, but when I came down to the Street I soon found that the things that would help me here weren't the fancy things I learned in college. In fact, I had to get a lot of fancy stuff out of my head."

Anthony could not help wondering what possible "fancy stuff" he had learned at Buckleigh in nineteen-eleven. An irrepressible idea that it was some sort of needlework recurred to him throughout the rest of the conversation.

"See that fellow over there?" Kahler pointed to a youngish-looking man with handsome gray hair, sitting at a desk inside a mahogany railing. "That's Mr. Ellinger, the first vice-president. Been everywhere, seen everything; got a fine education."

In vain did Anthony try to open his mind to the romance of finance; he could think of Mr. Ellinger only as one of the buyers of the handsome leather sets of Thackeray, Balzac, Hugo, and Gibbon that lined the walls of the big bookstores.

Through the damp and uninspiring month of March he was prepared for salesmanship. Lacking enthusiasm he was capable of viewing the turmoil and bustle that surrounded him only as a fruitless circumambient striving toward an incomprehensible goal, tangibly evidenced only by the rival mansions of Mr. Frick and Mr. Carnegie on Fifth Avenue. That these portentous vice-presidents and trustees should be actually the fathers of the "best men" he had known at Harvard seemed to him incongruous.

He ate in an employees' lunch-room up-stairs with an uneasy suspicion that he was being uplifted, wondering through that first week if the dozens of young clerks, some of them alert and immaculate, and just out of college, lived in flamboyant hope of crowding onto that narrow slip of cardboard before the catastrophic thirties. The conversation that interwove with the pattern of the day's work was all much of a piece. One discussed how Mr. Wilson had made his money, what method Mr. Hiemer had employed, and the means resorted to by Mr. Hardy. One related age-old but eternally breathless anecdotes of the fortunes stumbled on precipitously in the Street by a "butcher" or a "bartender," or "a darn *mess*enger boy, by golly!" and then one talked of the current gambles, and whether it was best to go out for a hundred thousand a year or be content with twenty. During the preceding year one of the assistant secretaries had invested all his savings in Bethlehem Steel. The story of his spectacular magnificence, of his haughty resignation in January, and of the triumphal palace he was now building in California, was the favorite office subject. The man's very name had acquired a magic significance, symbolizing as he did the aspirations of all good Americans. Anecdotes were told about him—how one of the vice-presidents had advised him to sell, by golly, but he had hung on, even bought on margin, "and *now* look where he is!"

Such, obviously, was the stuff of life—a dizzy triumph dazzling the eyes of all of them, a gypsy siren to content them with meagre wage and with the arithmetical improbability of their eventual success.

To Anthony the notion became appalling. He felt that to succeed here the idea of success must grasp and limit his mind. It seemed to him that the essential element in these men at the top was their faith that their affairs were the very core of life. All other things being equal, self-assurance and opportunism won out over technical knowledge; it was obvious that the more expert work went on near the bottom—so, with appropriate efficiency, the technical experts were kept there.

His determination to stay in at night during the week did not survive, and a good half of the time he came to work with a splitting, sickish headache and the crowded horror of the morning subway ringing in his ears like an echo of hell.

Then, abruptly, he quit. He had remained in bed all one Monday, and late in the evening, overcome by one of those attacks of moody despair to which he periodically succumbed, he wrote and mailed a letter to Mr. Wilson, confessing that he considered himself ill adapted to the work. Gloria, coming in from the theatre with Richard Caramel, found him on the lounge, silently staring at the high ceiling, more depressed and discouraged than he had been at any time since their marriage.

She wanted him to whine. If he had she would have reproached him bitterly, for she was not a little annoyed, but he only lay there so utterly miserable that she felt sorry for him, and kneeling down she stroked his head, saying how little it mattered, how little anything mattered so long as they loved each other. It was like their first year, and Anthony, reacting to her cool hand, to her voice that was soft as breath itself upon his ear, became almost cheerful, and talked with her of his future plans. He even regretted, silently, before he went to bed that he had so hastily mailed his resignation.

"Even when everything seems rotten you can't trust that judgment," Gloria had said. "It's the sum of all your judgments that counts."

In mid-April came a letter from the real-estate agent in Marietta, encouraging them to take the gray house for another year at a slightly increased rental, and enclosing a lease made out for their signatures. For a week lease and letter lay carelessly neglected on Anthony's desk. They had no intention of returning to Marietta. They were weary of the place, and had been bored most of the preceding summer. Besides, their car had deteriorated to a rattling mass of hypochondriacal metal, and a new one was financially inadvisable.

But because of another wild revel, enduring through four days and participated in, at one time or another, by more than a dozen people, they did sign the lease; to their utter horror they signed it and sent it, and immediately it seemed as though they heard the gray house, drably malevolent at last, licking its white chops and waiting to devour them.

"Anthony, where's that lease?" she called in high alarm one Sunday morning, sick and sober to reality. "Where did you leave it? It was here!"

Then she knew where it was. She remembered the house-party they had planned on the crest of their exuberance; she remembered a room full of men to whose less exhilarated moments she and Anthony were of no importance, and Anthony's boast of the transcendent merit and seclusion of the gray house, that it was so isolated that it didn't matter how much noise went on there. Then Dick, who had visited them, cried enthusiastically that it was the best little house imaginable, and that they were idiotic not to take it for another summer. It had been easy to work themselves up to a sense of how hot and deserted the city was getting, of how cool and ambrosial were the charms of Marietta. Anthony had picked up the lease and waved it wildly, found Gloria happily acquiescent, and with one last burst of garrulous decision during which all the men agreed with solemn handshakes that they would come out for a visit . . .

"Anthony," she cried, "we've signed and sent it!"

"What?"

"The lease!"

"What the devil!"

"Oh, *An*thony!" There was utter misery in her voice. For the summer, for eternity, they had built themselves a prison. It seemed to strike at the last roots of their stability. Anthony thought they might arrange it with the real-estate agent. They could no longer afford the double rent, and going to Marietta meant giving up his apartment, his reproachless apartment with the exquisite bath and the rooms for which he had bought his furniture and hangings—it was the closest to a home that he had ever had—familiar with memories of four colorful years.

But it was not arranged with the real-estate agent, nor was it arranged at all. Dispiritedly, without even any talk of making the best of it, without even Gloria's all-sufficing "I don't care," they went back to the house that they now knew heeded neither youth nor love—only those austere and incommunicable memories that they could never share.

The Sinister Summer

There was a horror in the house that summer. It came with them and settled itself over the place like a sombre pall, pervasive through the lower rooms, gradually spreading and climbing up the narrow stairs until it oppressed their very sleep. Anthony and Gloria grew to hate being there alone. Her bedroom, which had seemed so pink and young and delicate, appropriate to her pastel-shaded lingerie tossed here and there on chair and bed, seemed now to whisper with its rustling curtains:

"Ah, my beautiful young lady, yours is not the first daintiness and delicacy that has faded here under the summer suns . . . generations of unloved women have adorned themselves by that glass for rustic lovers who paid no heed. . . . Youth has come into this room in palest blue and left it in the gray cerements of despair, and through long nights many girls have lain awake where that bed stands pouring out waves of misery into the darkness."

Gloria finally tumbled all her clothes and unguents ingloriously out of it, declaring that she had come to live with Anthony, and making the excuse that one of her screens was rotten and admitted bugs. So her room was abandoned to insensitive guests, and they dressed and slept in her husband's chamber, which Gloria considered somehow "good," as though Anthony's presence there had acted as exterminator of any uneasy shadows of the past that might have hovered about its walls.

The distinction between "good" and "bad," ordered early and summarily out of both their lives, had been reinstated in another form. Gloria insisted that any one invited to the gray house must be "good," which, in the case of a girl, meant that she must be either simple and reproachless or, if otherwise, must possess a certain solidity and strength. Always intensely sceptical of her sex, her judgments were now concerned with the question of whether women were or were not clean. By uncleanliness she meant a variety of things, a lack of pride, a slackness in fibre and, most of all, the unmistakable aura of promiscuity.

"Women soil easily," she said, "far more easily than men. Unless a girl's very young and brave it's almost impossible for her to go down-hill without a certain hysterical animality, the cunning, dirty sort of animality. A man's different—and I suppose that's why one of the commonest characters of romance is a man going gallantly to the devil."

She was disposed to like many men, preferably those who gave her frank homage and unfailing entertainment—but often with a flash of insight she told Anthony that some one of his friends was merely using him, and consequently had best be left alone. Anthony customarily demurred, insisting that the accused was a "good one," but he found that his judgment was more fallible than hers, memorably when, as it happened on several occasions, he was left with a succession of restaurant checks for which to render a solitary account.

More from their fear of solitude than from any desire to go through the fuss and bother of entertaining, they filled the house with guests every week-end, and often on through the week. The week-end parties were much the same. When the three or four men invited had arrived, drinking was more or less in order, followed by a hilarious dinner and a ride to the Cradle Beach Country Club, which they had joined because it was inexpensive, lively if not fashionable, and almost a necessity for just such occasions as these. Moreover, it was of no great moment what one did there, and so long as the Patch party were reasonably inaudible, it mattered little whether or not the social dictators of Cradle Beach saw the gay Gloria imbibing cocktails in the supper-room at frequent intervals during the evening.

Saturday ended, generally, in a glamourous confusion—it proving often necessary to assist a muddled guest to bed. Sunday brought the New York papers and a quiet morning of recuperating on the porch—and Sunday afternoon meant good-by to the one or two guests who must return to the city, and a great revival of drinking among the one or two who remained until next day, concluding in a convivial if not hilarious evening.

The faithful Tana, pedagogue by nature and man of all work by profession, had returned with them. Among their more frequent guests a tradition had sprung up about him. Maury Noble remarked one afternoon that his real name was Tannenbaum, and that he was a German agent kept in this country to disseminate Teutonic propaganda through Westchester County, and, after that, mysterious letters began to arrive from Philadelphia addressed to the bewildered Oriental as "Lt. Emile Tannenbaum," containing a few cryptic messages signed "General Staff," and adorned with an atmospheric double column of facetious Japanese. Anthony always handed them to Tana without a smile; hours afterward the recipient could be found puzzling over them in the kitchen and declaring earnestly that the perpendicular symbols were not Japanese, nor anything resembling Japanese.

Gloria had taken a strong dislike to the man ever since the day when, returning unexpectedly from the village, she had discovered him reclining on Anthony's bed, puzzling out a newspaper. It was the instinct of all servants to be fond of Anthony and to detest Gloria, and Tana was no exception to the rule. But he was thoroughly afraid of her and made plain his aversion only in his moodier moments by subtly addressing Anthony with remarks intended for her ear:

"What Miz Pats want dinner?" he would say, looking at his master. Or else he would comment about the bitter selfishness of "'Merican peoples" in such manner that there was no doubt who were the "peoples" referred to.

But they dared not dismiss him. Such a step would have been abhorrent to their inertia. They endured Tana as they endured ill weather and sickness of the body and the estimable Will of God—as they endured all things, even themselves.

In Darkness

One sultry afternoon late in July Richard Caramel telephoned from New York that he and Maury were coming out, bringing a friend with them. They arrived about five, a little drunk, accompanied by a small, stocky man of thirty-five, whom they introduced as Mr. Joe Hull, one of the best fellows that Anthony and Gloria had ever met.

Joe Hull had a yellow beard continually fighting through his skin and a low voice which varied between basso profundo and a husky whisper. Anthony, carrying Maury's suitcase up-stairs, followed into the room and carefully closed the door.

"Who is this fellow?" he demanded.

Maury chuckled enthusiastically.

"Who, Hull? Oh, *he's* all right. He's a good one."

"Yes, but who is he?"

"Hull? He's just a good fellow. He's a prince." His laughter redoubled, culminating in a succession of pleasant catlike grins. Anthony hesitated between a smile and a frown.

"He looks sort of funny to me. Weird-looking clothes"—he paused—"I've got a sneaking suspicion you two picked him up somewhere last night."

"Ridiculous," declared Maury. "Why, I've known him all my life." However, as he capped this statement with another series of chuckles, Anthony was impelled to remark: "The devil you have!"

Later, just before dinner, while Maury and Dick were conversing uproariously, with Joe Hull listening in silence as he sipped his drink, Gloria drew Anthony into the dining-room:

"I don't like this man Hull," she said. "I wish he'd use Tana's bathtub."

"I can't very well ask him to."

"Well, I don't want him in ours."

"He seems to be a simple soul."

"He's got on white shoes that look like gloves. I can see his toes right through them. Uh! Who is he, anyway?"

"You've got me."

"Well, I think they've got their nerve to bring him out here. This isn't a Sailor's Rescue Home!"

"They were tight when they phoned. Maury said they've been on a party since yesterday afternoon."

Gloria shook her head angrily, and saying no more returned to the porch. Anthony saw that she was trying to forget her uncertainty and devote herself to enjoying the evening.

It had been a tropical day, and even into late twilight the heat-waves emanating from the dry road were quivering faintly like undulating panes of isinglass. The sky was cloudless, but far beyond the woods in the direction of the Sound a faint and persistent rolling had commenced. When Tana announced dinner the men, at a word from Gloria, remained coatless and went inside.

Maury began a song, which they accomplished in harmony during the first course. It had two lines and was sung to a popular air called Daisy Dear. The lines were:

> "The—pan-ic—has—come—over us,
> So *ha-a-as*—the moral de*cline!*"

Each rendition was greeted with bursts of enthusiasm and prolonged applause.

"Cheer up, Gloria!" suggested Maury. "You seem the least bit depressed."

"I'm not," she lied.

"Here, Tannenbaum!" he called over his shoulder. "I've filled you a drink. Come on!"

Gloria tried to stay his arm.

"Please don't, Maury!"

"Why not? Maybe he'll play the flute for us after dinner. Here, Tana."

Tana, grinning, bore the glass away to the kitchen. In a few moments Maury gave him another.

"Cheer up, Gloria!" he cried. "For Heaven's sakes everybody, cheer up Gloria."

"Dearest, have another drink," counselled Anthony.

"Do, please!"

"Cheer up, Gloria," said Joe Hull easily.

Gloria winced at this uncalled-for use of her first name, and glanced around to see if any one else had noticed it. The word coming so glibly from the lips of a man to whom she had taken an inordinate dislike repelled her. A moment later she noticed that Joe Hull had given Tana another drink, and her anger increased, heightened somewhat from the effects of the alcohol.

"—and once," Maury was saying, "Peter Granby and I went into a Turkish bath in Boston, about two o'clock at night. There was no one there but the proprietor, and we jammed him into a closet and locked the door. Then a fella came in and wanted a Turkish bath. Thought we were the rubbers, by golly! Well, we just picked him up and tossed him into the pool with all his clothes on. Then we dragged him out and laid him on a slab and slapped him until he was black and blue. 'Not so rough, fellows!' he'd say in a little squeaky voice, 'please! . . .' "

—Was this Maury? thought Gloria. From any one else the story would have amused her, but from Maury, the infinitely appreciative, the apotheosis of tact and consideration . . .

"The—pan-ic—has—come—over us,
So *ha-a-as*——"

A drum of thunder from outside drowned out the rest of the song; Gloria shivered and tried to empty her glass, but the first taste nauseated her, and she set it down. Dinner was over and they all marched into the big room, bearing several bottles and decanters. Some one had closed the porch door to keep out the wind, and in consequence circular tentacles of cigar-smoke were twisting already upon the heavy air.

"Paging Lieutenant Tannenbaum!" Again it was the changeling Maury. "Bring us the flute!"

Anthony and Maury rushed into the kitchen; Richard Caramel started the phonograph and approached Gloria.

"Dance with your well-known cousin."

"I don't want to dance."

"Then I'm going to carry you around."

As though he were doing something of overpowering importance, he picked her up in his fat little arms and started trotting gravely about the room.

"Set me down, Dick! I'm dizzy!" she insisted.

He dumped her in a bouncing bundle on the couch, and rushed off to the kitchen, shouting "Tana! Tana!"

Then, without warning, she felt other arms around her, felt herself lifted from the lounge. Joe Hull had picked her up and was trying, drunkenly, to imitate Dick.

"Put me down!" she said sharply.

His maudlin laugh, and the sight of that prickly yellow jaw close to her face, stirred her to intolerable disgust.

"At once!"

"The—pan-ic—" he began, but got no further, for Gloria's hand swung around swiftly and caught him in the cheek. At this he all at once let go of her, and she fell to the floor, her shoulder hitting the table a glancing blow in transit. . . .

Then the room seemed full of men and smoke. There was Tana in his white coat reeling about supported by Maury. Into his flute he was blowing a weird blend of sound that was known, cried Anthony, as the Japanese train-song. Joe Hull had found a box of candles and was juggling them, yelling "One down!" every time he missed, and Dick was dancing by himself in a fascinated whirl around and about the room. It appeared to her that everything in the room was staggering in grotesque fourth-dimensional gyrations through intersecting planes of hazy blue.

Outside, the storm had come up amazingly—the lulls within were filled with the scrape of the tall bushes against the house and the roaring of the rain on the tin roof of the kitchen. The lightning was interminable, letting down thick drips of thunder like pig iron from the heart of a white-hot furnace. Gloria could see that the rain was spitting in at three of the windows—but she could not move to shut them. . . .

. . . She was in the hall. She had said good night but no one had heard or heeded her. It seemed for an instant as though something had looked down over the head of the banister, but she could not have gone back into the living-room—better madness than the madness of that clamor. . . . Up-stairs she fumbled for the electric switch and missed it in the darkness; a roomful of lightning showed her the button plainly on the wall. But when the impenetrable black shut down, it again eluded her fumbling fingers, so she slipped off her dress and petticoat and threw herself weakly on the dry side of the half-drenched bed.

She shut her eyes. From down-stairs arose the babel of the drinkers, punctured suddenly by a tinkling shiver of broken glass, and then another, and by a soaring fragment of unsteady, irregular song. . . .

She lay there for something over two hours—so she calculated afterward, sheerly by piecing together the bits of time. She was conscious, even aware, after a long while that the noise down-stairs had lessened, and that the storm was moving off westward, throwing back lingering showers of sound that fell, heavy and lifeless as her soul, into the soggy fields. This was succeeded by a slow, reluctant scattering of the rain and wind, until there was nothing outside her windows but a gentle dripping and the swishing play of a cluster of wet vine against the sill. She was in a state half-way between sleeping and waking, with neither condition predominant . . . and she was harassed by a desire to rid herself of a weight pressing down upon her breast. She felt that if she could cry the weight would be lifted, and forcing the lids of her eyes together she tried to raise a lump in her throat . . . to no avail. . . .

Drip! Drip! Drip! The sound was not unpleasant—like spring, like a cool rain of her childhood, that made cheerful mud in her back yard and watered the tiny garden she had dug with miniature rake and spade and hoe. Drip—dri-ip! It was like days when the rain came out of yellow skies that melted just before twilight and shot one radiant shaft of sunlight diagonally down the heavens into the damp green trees.

So cool, so clear and clean—and her mother there at the centre of the world, at the centre of the rain, safe and dry and strong. She wanted her mother now, and her mother was dead, beyond sight and touch forever. And this weight was pressing on her, pressing on her—oh, it pressed on her so!

She became rigid. Some one had come to the door and was standing regarding her, very quiet except for a slight swaying motion. She could see the outline of his figure distinct against some indistinguishable light. There was no sound anywhere, only a great persuasive silence—even the dripping had ceased . . . only this figure, swaying, swaying in the doorway, an indiscernible and subtly menacing terror, a personality filthy under its varnish, like smallpox spots under a layer of powder. Yet her tired heart, beating until it shook her breasts, made her sure that there was still life in her, desperately shaken, threatened. . . .

The minute or succession of minutes prolonged itself interminably, and a swimming blur began to form before her eyes, which tried with childish persistence to pierce the gloom in the direction of the door. In another instant it seemed that some unimaginable force would shatter her out of existence . . . and then the figure in the doorway—it was Hull, she saw, Hull—turned deliberately and, still slightly swaying, moved back and off, as if absorbed into that incomprehensible light that had given him dimension.

Blood rushed back into her limbs, blood and life together. With a start of energy she sat upright, shifting her body until her feet touched the floor over the side of the bed. She knew what she must do—now, now, before it was too late. She must go out into this cool damp, out, away, to feel the wet swish of the grass around her feet and the fresh moisture on her forehead. Mechanically she struggled into her clothes, groping in the dark of the closet for a hat. She must go from this house where the thing hovered that pressed upon her bosom, or else made itself into stray, swaying figures in the gloom.

In a panic she fumbled clumsily at her coat, found the sleeve just as she heard Anthony's footsteps on the lower stair. She dared not wait; he might not let her go, and even Anthony was part of this weight, part of this evil house and the sombre darkness that was growing up about it. . . .

Through the hall then . . . and down the back stairs, hearing Anthony's voice in the bedroom she had just left——

"Gloria! Gloria!"

But she had reached the kitchen now, passed out through the doorway into the night. A hundred drops, startled by a flare of wind from a dripping tree, scattered on her and she pressed them gladly to her face with hot hands.

"Gloria! Gloria!"

The voice was infinitely remote, muffled and made plaintive by the walls she had just left. She rounded the house and started down the front path toward the road, almost exultant as she turned into it, and followed the carpet of short grass alongside, moving with caution in the intense darkness.

"Gloria!"

She broke into a run, stumbled over the segment of a branch twisted off by the wind. The voice was outside the house now. Anthony, finding the bedroom deserted, had come onto the porch. But this thing was driving her forward; it was back there with Anthony, and she must go on in her flight under this dim and oppressive heaven, forcing herself through the silence ahead as though it were a tangible barrier before her.

She had gone some distance along the barely discernible road, probably half a mile, passed a single deserted barn that loomed up, black and foreboding, the only building of any sort between the gray house and Marietta; then she turned the fork, where the road entered the wood and ran between two high walls of leaves and branches that nearly touched overhead. She noticed suddenly a thin, longitudinal gleam of silver upon the road before her, like a bright sword half embedded in the mud. As she came closer she gave a little cry of satisfaction—it was a wagon-rut full of water, and glancing heavenward she saw a light rift of sky and knew that the moon was out.

"Gloria!"

She started violently. Anthony was not two hundred feet behind her.

"Gloria, wait for me!"

She shut her lips tightly to keep from screaming, and increased her gait. Before she had gone another hundred yards the woods disappeared, rolling back like a dark stocking from the leg of the road. Three minutes' walk ahead of her, suspended in the now high and limitless air, she saw a thin interlacing of attenuated gleams and glitters, centred in a regular undulation on some one invisible point. Abruptly she knew where she would go. That was the great cascade of wires that rose high over the river, like the legs of a gigantic spider whose eye was the little green light in the switch-house, and ran with the railroad-bridge in the direction of the station. The station! There would be the train to take her away.

"Gloria, it's me! It's Anthony! Gloria, I won't try to stop you! For God's sake, where are you?"

She made no answer but began to run, keeping on the high side of the road and leaping the gleaming puddles —dimensionless pools of thin, unsubstantial gold. Turning sharply to the left, she followed a narrow wagon-road, serving to avoid a dark body on the ground. She looked up as an owl hooted mournfully from a solitary tree. Just ahead of her she could see the trestle that led to the railroad-bridge and the steps mounting up to it. The station lay across the river.

Another sound startled her, the melancholy siren of an approaching train, and almost simultaneously, a repeated call, thin now and far away.

"Gloria! Gloria!"

Anthony must have followed the main road. She laughed with a sort of malicious cunning at having eluded him; she could spare the time to wait until the train went by.

The siren soared again, closer at hand, and then, with no anticipatory roar and clamor, a dark and sinuous body curved into view against the shadows far down the high-banked track, and with no sound but the rush of the cleft wind and the clocklike tick of the rails, moved toward the bridge—it was an electric train. Above the engine two vivid blurs of blue light formed incessantly a radiant crackling bar between them, which, like a spluttering flame in a lamp beside a corpse, lit for an instant the successive rows of trees and caused Gloria to draw back instinctively to the far side of the road. The light was tepid—the temperature of warm blood. . . . The clicking blended suddenly with itself in a rush of even sound, and then, elongating in sombre elasticity, the thing roared blindly by her and thundered onto the bridge, racing the lurid shaft of fire it cast into the solemn river alongside. Then it contracted swiftly, sucking in its sound until it left only a reverberant echo, which died upon the farther bank.

Silence crept down again over the wet country; the faint dripping resumed, and suddenly a great shower of drops tumbled upon Gloria, stirring her out of the trance-like torpor which the passage of the train had wrought. She ran swiftly down a descending level to the bank and began climbing the iron stairway to the bridge, remembering that it was something she had always wanted to do, and that she would have the added excitement of traversing the yard-wide plank that ran beside the tracks over the river.

There! This was better. She was at the top now and could see the lands about her as successive sweeps of open country, cold under the moon, coarsely patched and seamed with thin rows and heavy clumps of trees. To her right, half a mile down the river, which trailed away behind the light like the shiny, slimy path of a snail, winked the scattered lights of Marietta. Not two hundred yards away at the end of the bridge squatted the station, marked by a sullen lantern. The oppression was lifted now—the tree-tops below her were rocking the young starlight to a haunted doze. She stretched out her arms with a gesture of freedom. This was what she had wanted, to stand alone where it was high and cool.

"Gloria!"

Like a startled child she scurried along the plank, hopping, skipping, jumping, with an ecstatic sense of her own physical lightness. Let him come now—she no longer feared that, only she must first reach the station, because that was part of the game. She was happy. Her hat, snatched off, was clutched tightly in her hand, and her short curled hair bobbed up and down about her ears. She had thought she would never feel so young again, but this was her night, her world. Triumphantly she laughed as she left the plank, and reaching the wooden platform flung herself down happily beside an iron roof-post.

"Here I am!" she called, gay as the dawn in her elation. "Here I am, Anthony, dear—old, worried Anthony."

"Gloria!" He reached the platform, ran toward her. "Are you all right?" Coming up he knelt and took her in his arms.

"Yes."

"What was the matter? Why did you leave?" he queried anxiously.

"I had to—there was something"—she paused and a flicker of uneasiness lashed at her mind—"there was something sitting on me—here." She put her hand on her breast. "I had to go out and get away from it."

"What do you mean by 'something'?"

"I don't know—that man Hull——"

"Did he bother you?"

"He came to my door, drunk. I think I'd gotten sort of crazy by that time."

"Gloria, dearest——"

Wearily she laid her head upon his shoulder.

"Let's go back," he suggested.

She shivered.

"Uh! No, I couldn't. It'd come and sit on me again." Her voice rose to a cry that hung plaintive on the darkness. "That thing——"

"There—there," he soothed her, pulling her close to him. "We won't do anything you don't want to do. What do you want to do? Just sit here?"

"I want—I want to go away."

"Where?"

"Oh—anywhere."

"By golly, Gloria," he cried, "you're still tight!"

"No, I'm not. I haven't been, all evening. I went up-stairs about, oh, I don't know, about half an hour after dinner . . . Ouch!"

He had inadvertently touched her right shoulder.

"It hurts me. I hurt it some way. I don't know—somebody picked me up and dropped me."

"Gloria, come home. It's late and damp."

"I can't," she wailed. "Oh, Anthony, don't ask me to! I will to-morrow. You go home and I'll wait here for a train. I'll go to a hotel——"

"I'll go with you."

"No, I don't want you with me. I want to be alone. I want

to sleep—oh, I want to sleep. And then to-morrow, when you've got all the smell of whiskey and cigarettes out of the house, and everything straight, and Hull is gone, then I'll come home. If I went now, that thing—oh—!" She covered her eyes with her hand; Anthony saw the futility of trying to persuade her.

"I was all sober when you left," he said. "Dick was asleep on the lounge and Maury and I were having a discussion. That fellow Hull had wandered off somewhere. Then I began to realize I hadn't seen you for several hours, so I went upstairs——"

He broke off as a salutatory "Hello, there!" boomed suddenly out of the darkness. Gloria sprang to her feet and he did likewise.

"It's Maury's voice," she cried excitedly. "If it's Hull with him, keep them away, keep them away!"

"Who's there?" Anthony called.

"Just Dick and Maury," returned two voices reassuringly.

"Where's Hull?"

"He's in bed. Passed out."

Their figures appeared dimly on the platform.

"What the devil are you and Gloria doing here?" inquired Richard Caramel with sleepy bewilderment.

"What are *you* two doing here?"

Maury laughed.

"Damned if I know. We followed you, and had the deuce of a time doing it. I heard you out on the porch yelling for Gloria, so I woke up the Caramel here and got it through his head, with some difficulty, that if there was a search-party we'd better be on it. He slowed me up by sitting down in the road at intervals and asking me what it was all about. We tracked you by the pleasant scent of Canadian Club."

There was a rattle of nervous laughter under the low train-shed.

"How did you track us, really?"

"Well, we followed along down the road and then we suddenly lost you. Seems you turned off at a wagon-trail. After a while somebody hailed us and asked us if we were looking for a young girl. Well, we came up and found it was a little shivering old man, sitting on a fallen tree like somebody in a fairy-tale. 'She turned down here,' he said, 'and most steppud on me, goin' somewhere in an awful hustle, and then a fella in short golfin' pants come runnin' along and went after her. He throwed me this.' The old fellow had a dollar bill he was waving around——"

"Oh, the poor old man!" ejaculated Gloria, moved.

"I threw him another and we went on, though he asked us to stay and tell him what it was all about."

"Poor old man," repeated Gloria dismally.

Dick sat down sleepily on a box.

"And now what?" he inquired in the tone of stoic resignation.

"Gloria's upset," explained Anthony. "She and I are going to the city by the next train."

Maury in the darkness had pulled a time-table from his pocket.

"Strike a match."

A tiny flare leaped out of the opaque background illuminating the four faces, grotesque and unfamiliar here in the open night.

"Let's see. Two, two-thirty—no, that's evening. By gad, you won't get a train till five-thirty."

Anthony hesitated.

"Well," he muttered uncertainly, "we've decided to stay here and wait for it. You two might as well go back and sleep."

"You go, too, Anthony," urged Gloria; "I want you to have some sleep, dear. You've been pale as a ghost all day."

"Why, you little idiot!"

Dick yawned.

"Very well. You stay, we stay."

He walked out from under the shed and surveyed the heavens.

"Rather a nice night, after all. Stars are out and everything. Exceptionally tasty assortment of them."

"Let's see." Gloria moved after him and the other two followed her. "Let's sit out here," she suggested. "I like it much better."

Anthony and Dick converted a long box into a back-rest and found a board dry enough for Gloria to sit on. Anthony dropped down beside her and with some effort Dick hoisted himself onto an apple-barrel near them.

"Tana went to sleep in the porch hammock," he remarked. "We carried him in and left him next to the kitchen-stove to dry. He was drenched to the skin."

"That awful little man!" sighed Gloria.

"How do you do!" The voice, sonorous and funereal, had come from above, and they looked up startled to find that in some manner Maury had climbed to the roof of the shed, where he sat dangling his feet over the edge, outlined as a shadowy and fantastic gargoyle against the now brilliant sky.

"It must be for such occasions as this," he began softly, his words having the effect of floating down from an immense height and settling softly upon his auditors, "that the righteous of the land decorate the railroads with bill-boards asserting in red and yellow that 'Jesus Christ is God,' placing them, appropriately enough, next to announcements that 'Gunter's Whiskey is Good.' "

There was gentle laughter and the three below kept their heads tilted upward.

"I think I shall tell you the story of my education," continued Maury, "under these sardonic constellations."

"Do! Please!"

"Shall I, really?"

They waited expectantly while he directed a ruminative yawn toward the white smiling moon.

"Well," he began, "as an infant I prayed. I stored up prayers against future wickedness. One year I stored up nineteen hundred 'Now I lay me's.' "

"Throw down a cigarette," murmured some one.

A small package reached the platform simultaneously with the stentorian command:

"Silence! I am about to unburden myself of many memorable remarks reserved for the darkness of such earths and the brilliance of such skies."

Below, a lighted match was passed from cigarette to cigarette. The voice resumed:

"I was adept at fooling the deity. I prayed immediately after all crimes until eventually prayer and crime became indistinguishable to me. I believed that because a man cried out

'My God!' when a safe fell on him, it proved that belief was rooted deep in the human breast. Then I went to school. For fourteen years half a hundred earnest men pointed to ancient flint-locks and cried to me: 'There's the real thing. These new rifles are only shallow, superficial imitations.' They damned the books I read and the things I thought by calling them immoral; later the fashion changed, and they damned things by calling them 'clever.'

"And so I turned, canny for my years, from the professors to the poets, listening—to the lyric tenor of Swinburne and the tenor robusto of Shelley, to Shakespeare with his first bass and his fine range, to Tennyson with his second bass and his occasional falsetto, to Milton and Marlowe, bassos profundo. I gave ear to Browning chatting, Byron declaiming, and Wordsworth droning. This, at least, did me no harm. I learned a little of beauty—enough to know that it had nothing to do with truth—and I found, moreover, that there was no great literary tradition; there was only the tradition of the eventful death of every literary tradition. . . .

"Then I grew up, and the beauty of succulent illusions fell away from me. The fibre of my mind coarsened and my eyes grew miserably keen. Life rose around my island like a sea, and presently I was swimming.

"The transition was subtle—the thing had lain in wait for me for some time. It has its insidious, seemingly innocuous trap for every one. With me? No—I didn't try to seduce the janitor's wife—nor did I run through the streets unclothed, proclaiming my virility. It is never quite passion that does the business—it is the dress that passion wears. I became bored—that was all. Boredom, which is another name and a frequent disguise for vitality, became the unconscious motive of all my acts. Beauty was behind me, do you understand?—I was grown." He paused. "End of school and college period. Opening of Part Two."

Three quietly active points of light showed the location of his listeners. Gloria was now half sitting, half lying, in Anthony's lap. His arm was around her so tightly that she could hear the beating of his heart. Richard Caramel, perched on the apple-barrel, from time to time stirred and gave off a faint grunt.

"I grew up then, into this land of jazz, and fell immediately into a state of almost audible confusion. Life stood over me like an immoral schoolmistress, editing my ordered thoughts. But, with a mistaken faith in intelligence, I plodded on. I read Smith, who laughed at charity and insisted that the sneer was the highest form of self-expression—but Smith himself replaced charity as an obscurer of the light. I read Jones, who neatly disposed of individualism—and behold! Jones was still in my way. I did not think—I was a battle-ground for the thoughts of many men; rather was I one of those desirable but impotent countries over which the great powers surge back and forth.

"I reached maturity under the impression that I was gathering the experience to order my life for happiness. Indeed, I accomplished the not unusual feat of solving each question in my mind long before it presented itself to me in life—and of being beaten and bewildered just the same.

"But after a few tastes of this latter dish I had had enough. Here! I said, Experience is not worth the getting. It's not a thing that happens pleasantly to a passive you—it's a wall that an active you runs up against. So I wrapped myself in what I thought was my invulnerable scepticism and decided that my education was complete. But it was too late. Protect myself as I might by making no new ties with tragic and predestined humanity, I was lost with the rest. I had traded the fight against love for the fight against loneliness, the fight against life for the fight against death."

He broke off to give emphasis to his last observation—after a moment he yawned and resumed.

"I suppose that the beginning of the second phase of my education was a ghastly dissatisfaction at being used in spite of myself for some inscrutable purpose of whose ultimate goal I was unaware—if, indeed, there *was* an ultimate goal. It was a difficult choice. The schoolmistress seemed to be saying, 'We're going to play football and nothing but football. If you don't want to play football you can't play at all——"

"What was I to do—the playtime was so short!

"You see, I felt that we were even denied what consolation there might have been in being a figment of a corporate man rising from his knees. Do you think that I leaped at this pessimism, grasped it as a sweetly smug superior thing, no more depressing really than, say, a gray autumn day before a fire?—I don't think I did that. I was a great deal too warm for that, and too alive.

"For it seemed to me that there was no ultimate goal for man. Man was beginning a grotesque and bewildered fight with nature—nature, that by the divine and magnificent accident had brought us to where we could fly in her face. She had invented ways to rid the race of the inferior and thus give the remainder strength to fill her higher—or, let us say, her more amusing—though still unconscious and accidental intentions. And, actuated by the highest gifts of the enlightenment, we were seeking to circumvent her. In this republic I saw the black beginning to mingle with the white—in Europe there was taking place an economic catastrophe to save three or four diseased and wretchedly governed races from the one mastery that might organize them for material prosperity.

"We produce a Christ who can raise up the leper—and presently the breed of the leper is the salt of the earth. If any one can find any lesson in that, let him stand forth."

"There's only one lesson to be learned from life, anyway," interrupted Gloria, not in contradiction but in a sort of melancholy agreement.

"What's that?" demanded Maury sharply.

"That there's no lesson to be learned from life."

After a short silence Maury said:

"Young Gloria, the beautiful and merciless lady, first looked at the world with the fundamental sophistication I have struggled to attain, that Anthony never will attain, that Dick will never fully understand."

There was a disgusted groan from the apple-barrel. Anthony, grown accustomed to the dark, could see plainly the flash of Richard Caramel's yellow eye and the look of resentment on his face as he cried:

"You're crazy! By your own statement I should have attained some experience by trying."

"Trying what?" cried Maury fiercely. "Trying to pierce the darkness of political idealism with some wild, despairing urge toward truth? Sitting day after day supine in a rigid chair and infinitely removed from life staring at the tip of a steeple through the trees, trying to separate, definitely and for all time, the knowable from the unknowable? Trying to take a piece of actuality and give it glamour from your own soul to make for that inexpressible quality it possessed in life and lost in transit to paper or canvas? Struggling in a laboratory through weary years for one iota of relative truth in a mass of wheels or a test-tube——"

"Have you?"

Maury paused, and in his answer, when it came, there was a measure of weariness, a bitter overnote that lingered for a moment in those three minds before it floated up and off like a bubble bound for the moon.

"Not I," he said softly. "I was born tired—but with the quality of mother wit, the gift of women like Gloria—to that, for all my talking and listening, my waiting in vain for the eternal generality that seems to lie just beyond every argument and every speculation, to that I have added not one jot."

In the distance a deep sound that had been audible for some moments identified itself by a plaintive mooing like that of a gigantic cow and by the pearly spot of a headlight apparent half a mile away. It was a steam-driven train this time, rumbling and groaning, and as it tumbled by with a monstrous complaint it sent a shower of sparks and cinders over the platform.

"Not one jot!" Again Maury's voice dropped down to them as from a great height. "What a feeble thing intelligence is, with its short steps, its waverings, its pacings back and forth, its disastrous retreats! Intelligence is a mere instrument of circumstances. There are people who say that intelligence must have built the universe—why, intelligence never built a steam-engine! Circumstances built a steam-engine. Intelligence is little more than a short foot-rule by which we measure the infinite achievements of Circumstances.

"I could quote you the philosophy of the hour—but, for all we know, fifty years may see a complete reversal of this abnegation that's absorbing the intellectuals to-day, the triumph of Christ over Anatole France—" He hesitated, and then added: "But all I know—the tremendous importance of myself to me, and the necessity of acknowledging that importance to myself—these things the wise and lovely Gloria was born knowing, these things and the painful futility of trying to know anything else.

"Well, I started to tell you of my education, didn't I? But I learned nothing, you see, very little even about myself. And if I had I should die with my lips shut and the guard on my fountain-pen—as the wisest men have done since—oh, since the failure of a certain matter—a strange matter, by the way. It concerned some sceptics who thought they were far-sighted, just as you and I. Let me tell you about them by way of an evening prayer before you all drop off to sleep.

"Once upon a time all the men of mind and genius in the world became of one belief—that is to say, of no belief. But it wearied them to think that within a few years after their death many cults and systems and prognostications would be ascribed to them which they had never meditated nor intended. So they said to one another:

"'Let's join together and make a great book that will last forever to mock the credulity of man. Let's persuade our more erotic poets to write about the delights of the flesh, and induce some of our robust journalists to contribute stories of famous amours. We'll include all the most preposterous old wives' tales now current. We'll choose the keenest satirist alive to compile a deity from all the deities worshipped by mankind, a deity who will be more magnificent than any of them, and yet so weakly human that he'll become a byword for laughter the world over—and we'll ascribe to him all sorts of jokes and vanities and rages, in which he'll be supposed to indulge for his own diversion, so that the people will read our book and ponder it, and there'll be no more nonsense in the world.

"'Finally, let us take care that the book possesses all the virtues of style, so that it may last forever as a witness to our profound scepticism and our universal irony.'

"So the men did, and they died.

"But the book lived always, so beautifully had it been written, and so astounding the quality of imagination with which these men of mind and genius had endowed it. They had neglected to give it a name, but after they were dead it became known as the Bible."

When he concluded there was no comment. Some damp languor sleeping on the air of night seemed to have bewitched them all.

"As I said, I started on the story of my education. But my high-balls are dead and the night's almost over, and soon there'll be an awful jabbering going on everywhere, in the trees and the houses, and the two little stores over there behind the station, and there'll be a great running up and down upon the earth for a few hours— Well," he concluded with a laugh, "thank God we four can all pass to our eternal rest knowing we've left the world a little better for having lived in it."

A breeze sprang up, blowing with it faint wisps of life which flattened against the sky.

"Your remarks grow rambling and inconclusive," said Anthony sleepily. "You expected one of those miracles of illumination by which you say your most brilliant and pregnant things in exactly the setting that should provoke the ideal symposium. Meanwhile Gloria has shown her far-sighted detachment by falling asleep—I can tell that by the fact that she has managed to concentrate her entire weight upon my broken body."

"Have I bored you?" inquired Maury, looking down with some concern.

"No, you have disappointed us. You've shot a lot of arrows but did you shoot any birds?"

"I leave the birds to Dick," said Maury hurriedly. "I speak erratically, in disassociated fragments."

"You can get no rise from me," muttered Dick. "My mind is full of any number of material things. I want a warm bath too much to worry about the importance of my work or what proportion of us are pathetic figures."

Dawn made itself felt in a gathering whiteness eastward over the river and an intermittent cheeping in the near-by trees.

"Quarter to five," sighed Dick; "almost another hour to wait. Look! Two gone." He was pointing to Anthony, whose lids had sagged over his eyes. "Sleep of the Patch family——"

But in another five minutes, despite the amplifying cheeps

and chirrups, his own head had fallen forward, nodded down twice, thrice. . . .

Only Maury Noble remained awake, seated upon the station roof, his eyes wide open and fixed with fatigued intensity upon the distant nucleus of morning. He was wondering at the unreality of ideas, at the fading radiance of existence, and at the little absorptions that were creeping avidly into his life, like rats into a ruined house. He was sorry for no one now—on Monday morning there would be his business, and later there would be a girl of another class whose whole life he was; these were the things nearest his heart. In the strangeness of the brightening day it seemed presumptuous that with this feeble, broken instrument of his mind he had ever tried to think.

There was the sun, letting down great glowing masses of heat; there was life, active and snarling, moving about them like a fly swarm—the dark pants of smoke from the engine, a crisp "all aboard!" and a bell ringing. Confusedly Maury saw eyes in the milk-train staring curiously up at him, heard Gloria and Anthony in quick controversy as to whether he should go to the city with her—then another clamor and she was gone and the three men, pale as ghosts, were standing alone upon the platform while a grimy coal-heaver went down the road on top of a motor-truck, carolling hoarsely at the summer morning.

CHAPTER III

The Broken Lute

It is seven-thirty of an August evening. The windows in the living-room of the gray house are wide open, patiently exchanging the tainted inner atmosphere of liquor and smoke for the fresh drowsiness of the late hot dusk. There are dying flower scents upon the air, so thin, so fragile, as to hint already of a summer laid away in time. But August is still proclaimed relentlessly by a thousand crickets around the side-porch, and by one who has broken into the house and concealed himself confidently behind a bookcase, from time to time shrieking of his cleverness and his indomitable will.

The room itself is in messy disorder. On the table is a dish of fruit, which is real but appears artificial. Around it are grouped an ominous assortment of decanters, glasses, and heaped ash-trays, the latter still raising wavy smoke-ladders into the stale air—the effect on the whole needing but a skull to resemble that venerable chromo, once a fixture in every "den," which presents the appendages to the life of pleasure with delightful and awe-inspiring sentiment.

After a while the sprightly solo of the supercricket is interrupted rather than joined by a new sound—the melancholy wail of an erratically fingered flute. It is obvious that the musician is practising rather than performing, for from time to time the gnarled strain breaks off and, after an interval of indistinct mutterings, recommences.

Just prior to the seventh false start a third sound contributes to the subdued discord. It is a taxi outside. A minute's silence, then the taxi again, its boisterous retreat almost obliterating the scrape of footsteps on the cinder walk. The door-bell shrieks alarmingly through the house.

From the kitchen enters a small, fatigued Japanese, hastily buttoning a servant's coat of white duck. He opens the front screen-door and admits a handsome young man of thirty, clad in the sort of well-intentioned clothes peculiar to those who serve mankind. To his whole personality clings a well-intentioned air: his glance about the room is compounded of curiosity and a determined optimism; when he looks at Tana the entire burden of uplifting the godless Oriental is in his eyes. His name is FREDERICK E. PARAMORE. *He was at Harvard with* ANTHONY, *where because of the initials of their surnames they were constantly placed next to each other in classes. A fragmentary acquaintance developed—but since that time they have never met.*

Nevertheless, PARAMORE *enters the room with a certain air of arriving for the evening.*

Tana is answering a question.

TANA: (*Grinning with ingratiation*) Gone to Inn for dinnah. Be back half-hour. Gone since ha' past six.

PARAMORE: (*Regarding the glasses on the table*) Have they company?

TANA: Yes. Company. Mistah Caramel, Mistah and Missays Barnes, Miss Kane, all stay here.

PARAMORE: I see. (*Kindly*) They've been having a spree, I see.

TANA: I no un'stan'.

PARAMORE: They've been having a fling.

TANA: Yes, they have drink. Oh, many, many, many drink.

PARAMORE: (*Receding delicately from the subject*) Didn't I hear the sounds of music as I approached the house?

TANA: (*With a spasmodic giggle*) Yes, I play.

PARAMORE: One of the Japanese instruments.

(*He is quite obviously a subscriber to the "National Geographic Magazine."*)

TANA: I play flu-u-ute, Japanese flu-u-ute.

PARAMORE: What song were you playing? One of your Japanese melodies?

TANA: (*His brow undergoing preposterous contraction*) I play train song. How you call?—*railroad* song. So call in my countree. Like train. It go so-o-o; that mean whistle; train start. Then go so-o-o; that mean train go. Go like that. Vera nice song in my countree. Children song.

PARAMORE: It sounded very nice.

(*It is apparent at this point that only a gigantic effort at control restrains* TANA *from rushing up-stairs for his post-cards, including the six made in America.*)

TANA: I fix high-ball for gentleman?

PARAMORE: No, thanks. I don't use it. (*He smiles.*)

(TANA *withdraws into the kitchen, leaving the intervening door slightly ajar. From the crevice there suddenly issues again the melody of the Japanese train song—this time not a practice, surely, but a performance, a lusty, spirited performance.*

The phone rings. TANA, *absorbed in his harmonics, gives no heed, so* PARAMORE *takes up the receiver.*)

PARAMORE: Hello. . . . Yes. . . . No, he's not here now, but he'll be back any moment. . . . Butterworth? Hello, I didn't quite catch the name. . . . Hello, hello, hello. Hello! . . . Huh!

(*The phone obstinately refuses to yield up any more sound.* PARAMORE *replaces the receiver.*

At this point the taxi motif re-enters, wafting with it a second young man; he carries a suitcase and opens the front door without ringing the bell.)

MAURY: (*In the hall*) Oh, Anthony! Yoho! (*He comes into the large room and sees* PARAMORE) How do?

PARAMORE: (*Gazing at him with gathering intensity*) Is this—is this Maury Noble?

MAURY: That's it. (*He advances, smiling, and holding out his hand*) How are you, old boy? Haven't seen you for years.

(*He has vaguely associated the face with Harvard, but is not even positive about that. The name, if he ever knew it, he has long since forgotten. However, with a fine sensitiveness and an equally commendable charity* PARAMORE *recognizes the fact and tactfully relieves the situation.*)

PARAMORE: You've forgotten Fred Paramore? We were both in old Unc Robert's history class.

MAURY: No, I haven't, Unc—I mean Fred. Fred was—I mean Unc was a great old fellow, wasn't he?

PARAMORE: (*Nodding his head humorously several times*) Great old character. Great old character.

MAURY: (*After a short pause*) Yes—he was. Where's Anthony?

PARAMORE: The Japanese servant told me he was at some inn. Having dinner, I suppose.

MAURY: (*Looking at his watch*) Gone long?

PARAMORE: I guess so. The Japanese told me they'd be back shortly.

MAURY: Suppose we have a drink.

PARAMORE: No, thanks. I don't use it. (*He smiles.*)

MAURY: Mind if I do? (*Yawning as he helps himself from a bottle*) What have you been doing since you left college?

PARAMORE: Oh, many things. I've led a very active life. Knocked about here and there. (*His tone implies anything from lion-stalking to organized crime.*)

MAURY: Oh, been over to Europe?

PARAMORE: No, I haven't—unfortunately.

MAURY: I guess we'll all go over before long.

PARAMORE: Do you really think so?

MAURY: Sure! Country's been fed on sensationalism for more than two years. Everybody getting restless. Want to have some fun.

PARAMORE: Then you don't believe any ideals are at stake?

MAURY: Nothing of much importance. People want excitement every so often.

PARAMORE: (*Intently*) It's very interesting to hear you say that. Now I was talking to a man who'd been over there——

(*During the ensuing testament, left to be filled in by the reader with such phrases as "Saw with his own eyes," "Splendid spirit of France," and "Salvation of civilization,"* MAURY *sits with lowered eyelids, dispassionately bored.*)

MAURY: (*At the first available opportunity*) By the way, do you happen to know that there's a German agent in this very house?

PARAMORE: (*Smiling cautiously*) Are you serious?

MAURY: Absolutely. Feel it my duty to warn you.

PARAMORE: (*Convinced*) A governess?

MAURY: (*In a whisper, indicating the kitchen with his thumb*) *Tana!* That's not his real name. I understand he constantly gets mail addressed to Lieutenant Emile Tannenbaum.

PARAMORE: (*Laughing with hearty tolerance*) You were kidding me.

MAURY: I may be accusing him falsely. But, you haven't told me what you've been doing.

PARAMORE: For one thing—writing.

MAURY: Fiction?

PARAMORE: No. Non-fiction.

MAURY: What's that? A sort of literature that's half fiction and half fact?

PARAMORE: Oh, I've confined myself to fact. I've been doing a good deal of social-service work.

MAURY: Oh!

(*An immediate glow of suspicion leaps into his eyes. It is as though* PARAMORE *had announced himself as an amateur pickpocket.*)

PARAMORE: At present I'm doing service work in Stamford. Only last week some one told me that Anthony Patch lived so near.

(*They are interrupted by a clamor outside, unmistakable as that of two sexes in conversation and laughter. Then there enter the room in a body* ANTHONY, GLORIA, RICHARD CARAMEL, MURIEL KANE, RACHAEL BARNES *and* RODMAN BARNES, *her husband. They surge about* MAURY, *illogically replying* "Fine!" *to his general* "Hello." . . . ANTHONY, *meanwhile, approaches his other guest.*)

ANTHONY: Well, I'll be darned. How are you? Mighty glad to see you.

PARAMORE: It's good to see you, Anthony. I'm stationed in Stamford, so I thought I'd run over. (*Roguishly*) We have to work to beat the devil most of the time, so we're entitled to a few hours' vacation.

(*In an agony of concentration* ANTHONY *tries to recall the name. After a struggle of parturition his memory gives up the fragment* "Fred," *around which he hastily builds the sentence* "Glad you did, Fred!" *Meanwhile the slight hush prefatory to an introduction has fallen upon the company.* MAURY, *who could help, prefers to look on in malicious enjoyment.*)

ANTHONY: (*In desperation*) Ladies and gentlemen, this is—this is Fred.

MURIEL: (*With obliging levity*) Hello, Fred!

(RICHARD CARAMEL *and* PARAMORE *greet each other intimately by their first names, the latter recollecting that* DICK *was one of the men in his class who had never before troubled to speak to him.* DICK *fatuously imagines that* PARAMORE *is some one he has previously met in* ANTHONY'S *house.*

The three young women go up-stairs.)

MAURY: (*In an undertone to* DICK) Haven't seen Muriel since Anthony's wedding.

DICK: She's now in her prime. Her latest is "*I'll* say so!"

(ANTHONY *struggles for a while with* PARAMORE *and at length attempts to make the conversation general by asking every one to have a drink.*)

MAURY: I've done pretty well on this bottle. I've gone from "Proof" down to "Distillery." (*He indicates the words on the label.*)

ANTHONY: (*To* PARAMORE) Never can tell when these two will turn up. Said good-by to them one afternoon at five and darned if they didn't appear about two in the morning. A big hired touring-car from New York drove up to the door and out they stepped, drunk as lords, of course.

(*In an ecstasy of consideration* PARAMORE *regards the cover of a book which he holds in his hand.* MAURY *and* DICK *exchange a glance.*)

DICK: (*Innocently, to* PARAMORE) You work here in town?

PARAMORE: No, I'm in the Laird Street Settlement in Stamford. (*To* ANTHONY) You have no idea of the amount of poverty in these small Connecticut towns. Italians and other immigrants. Catholics mostly, you know, so it's very hard to reach them.

ANTHONY: (*Politely*) Lot of crime?

PARAMORE: Not so much crime as ignorance and dirt.

MAURY: That's my theory: immediate electrocution of all ignorant and dirty people. I'm all for the criminals—give color to life. Trouble is if you started to punish ignorance you'd have to begin in the first families, then you could take up the moving-picture people, and finally Congress and the clergy.

PARAMORE: (*Smiling uneasily*) I was speaking of the more fundamental ignorance—of even our language.

MAURY: (*Thoughtfully*) I suppose it is rather hard. Can't even keep up with the new poetry.

PARAMORE: It's only when the settlement work has gone on for months that one realizes how bad things are. As our secretary said to me, your finger-nails never seem dirty until you wash your hands. Of course we're already attracting much attention.

MAURY: (*Rudely*) As your secretary might say, if you stuff paper into a grate it'll burn brightly for a moment.

(*At this point* GLORIA, *freshly tinted and lustful of admiration and entertainment, rejoins the party, followed by her two friends. For several moments the conversation becomes entirely fragmentary.* GLORIA *calls* ANTHONY *aside.*)

GLORIA: Please don't drink much, Anthony.

ANTHONY: Why?

GLORIA: Because you're so simple when you're drunk.

ANTHONY: Good Lord! What's the matter now?

GLORIA: (*After a pause during which her eyes gaze coolly into his*) Several things. In the first place, why do you insist on paying for everything? Both those men have more money than you!

ANTHONY: Why, Gloria! They're my guests!

GLORIA: That's no reason why you should pay for a bottle of champagne Rachael Barnes smashed. Dick tried to fix that second taxi bill, and you wouldn't let him.

ANTHONY: Why, Gloria——

GLORIA: When we have to keep selling bonds to even pay our bills, it's time to cut down on excess generosities. Moreover, I wouldn't be quite so attentive to Rachael Barnes. Her husband doesn't like it any more than I do!

ANTHONY: Why, Gloria——

GLORIA: (*Mimicking him sharply*) "Why, Gloria!" But that's happened a little too often this summer—with every pretty woman you meet. It's grown to be a sort of habit, and I'm *not* going to stand it! If you can play around, I can, too. (*Then, as an afterthought*) By the way, this Fred person isn't a second Joe Hull, is he?

ANTHONY: Heavens, no! He probably came up to get me to wheedle some money out of grandfather for his flock.

(GLORIA *turns away from a very depressed* ANTHONY *and returns to her guests.*

By nine o'clock these can be divided into two classes—those who have been drinking consistently and those who have taken little or nothing. In the second group are the BARNESES, MURIEL, *and* FREDERICK E. PARAMORE).

MURIEL: I wish I could write. I get these ideas but I never seem to be able to put them in words.

DICK: As Goliath said, he understood how David felt, but he couldn't express himself. The remark was immediately adopted for a motto by the Philistines.

MURIEL: I don't get you. I must be getting stupid in my old age.

GLORIA: (*Weaving unsteadily among the company like an exhilarated angel*) If any one's hungry there's some French pastry on the dining-room table.

MAURY: Can't tolerate those Victorian designs it comes in.

MURIEL: (*Violently amused*) *I'll* say you're tight, Maury.

(*Her bosom is still a pavement that she offers to the hoofs of many passing stallions, hoping that their iron shoes may strike even a spark of romance in the darkness. . . .*

Messrs. BARNES *and* PARAMORE *have been engaged in conversation upon some wholesome subject, a subject so wholesome that* MR. BARNES *has been trying for several moments to creep into the more tainted air around the central lounge. Whether* PARAMORE *is lingering in the gray house out of politeness or curiosity, or in order at some future time to make a sociological report on the decadence of American life, is problematical.*)

MAURY: Fred, I imagined you were very broad-minded.

PARAMORE: I am.

MURIEL: Me, too. I believe one religion's as good as another and everything.

PARAMORE: There's some good in all religions.

MURIEL: I'm a Catholic but, as I always say, I'm not working at it.

PARAMORE: (*With a tremendous burst of tolerance*) The Catholic religion is a very—a very powerful religion.

MAURY: Well, such a broad-minded man should consider

the raised plane of sensation and the stimulated optimism contained in this cocktail.

PARAMORE: (*Taking the drink, rather defiantly*) Thanks, I'll try—one.

MAURY: One? Outrageous! Here we have a class of 'nineteen ten reunion, and you refuse to be even a little pickled. Come on!

"Here's a health to King Charles,
Here's a health to King Charles,
Bring the bowl that you boast——"

(PARAMORE *joins in with a hearty voice.*)

MAURY: Fill the cup, Frederick. You know everything's subordinated to nature's purposes with us, and her purpose with you is to make you a rip-roaring tippler.

PARAMORE: If a fellow can drink like a gentleman——

MAURY: What is a gentleman, anyway?

ANTHONY: A man who never has pins under his coat lapel.

MAURY: Nonsense! A man's social rank is determined by the amount of bread he eats in a sandwich.

DICK: He's a man who prefers the first edition of a book to the last edition of a newspaper.

RACHAEL: A man who never gives an impersonation of a dope-fiend.

MAURY: An American who can fool an English butler into thinking he's one.

MURIEL: A man who comes from a good family and went to Yale or Harvard or Princeton, and has money and dances well, and all that.

MAURY: At last—the perfect definition! Cardinal Newman's is now a back number.

PARAMORE: I think we ought to look on the question more broad-mindedly. Was it Abraham Lincoln who said that a gentleman is one who never inflicts pain?

MAURY: It's attributed, I believe, to General Ludendorff.

PARAMORE: Surely you're joking.

MAURY: Have another drink.

PARAMORE: I oughtn't to. (*Lowering his voice for* MAURY'S *ear alone*) What if I were to tell you this is the third drink I've ever taken in my life?

(DICK *starts the phonograph, which provokes* MURIEL *to rise and sway from side to side, her elbows against her ribs, her forearms perpendicular to her body and out like fins.*)

MURIEL: Oh, let's take up the rugs and dance!

(*This suggestion is received by* ANTHONY *and* GLORIA *with interior groans and sickly smiles of acquiescence.*)

MURIEL: Come on, you lazy-bones. Get up and move the furniture back.

DICK: Wait till I finish my drink.

MAURY: (*Intent on his purpose toward* PARAMORE) I'll tell you what. Let's each fill one glass, drink it off—and then we'll dance.

(*A wave of protest which breaks against the rock of* MAURY'S *insistence.*)

MURIEL: My head is simply going *round* now.

RACHAEL: (*In an undertone to* ANTHONY) Did Gloria tell you to stay away from me?

ANTHONY: (*Confused*) Why, certainly not. Of course not.

(RACHAEL *smiles at him inscrutably. Two years have given her a sort of hard, well-groomed beauty.*)

MAURY: (*Holding up his glass*) Here's to the defeat of democracy and the fall of Christianity.

MURIEL: Now really!

(*She flashes a mock-reproachful glance at* MAURY *and then drinks.*

They all drink, with varying degrees of difficulty.)

MURIEL: Clear the floor!

(*It seems inevitable that this process is to be gone through, so* ANTHONY *and* GLORIA *join in the great moving of tables, piling of chairs, rolling of carpets, and breaking of lamps. When the furniture has been stacked in ugly masses at the sides, there appears a space about eight feet square.*)

MURIEL: Oh, let's have music!

MAURY: Tana will render the love-song of an eye, ear, nose, and throat specialist.

(*Amid some confusion due to the fact that* TANA *has retired for the night, preparations are made for the performance. The pajamaed Japanese, flute in hand, is wrapped in a comforter and placed in a chair atop one of the tables, where he makes a ludicrous and grotesque spectacle.* PARAMORE *is perceptibly drunk and so enraptured with the notion that he increases the effect by simulating funny-paper staggers and even venturing on an occasional hiccough.*)

PARAMORE: (*To* GLORIA) Want to dance with me?

GLORIA: No, sir! Want to do the swan dance. Can you do it?

PARAMORE: Sure. Do them all.

GLORIA: All right. You start from that side of the room and I'll start from this.

MURIEL: Let's go!

(*Then Bedlam creeps screaming out of the bottles:* TANA *plunges into the recondite mazes of the train song, the plaintive "tootle toot-toot" blending its melancholy cadences with the* "Poor Butter-fly (tink-atink), by the blossoms wait-ing" *of the phonograph.* MURIEL *is too weak with laughter to do more than cling desperately to* BARNES, *who, dancing with the ominous rigidity of an army officer, tramps without humor around the small space.* ANTHONY *is trying to hear* RACHAEL'S *whisper—without attracting* GLORIA'S *attention. . . .*

But the grotesque, the unbelievable, the histrionic incident is about to occur, one of those incidents in which life seems set upon the passionate imitation of the lowest forms of literature. PARAMORE *has been trying to emulate* GLORIA, *and as the commotion reaches its height he begins to spin round and round, more and more dizzily—he staggers, recovers, staggers again and then falls in the direction of the hall . . . almost into the arms of old* ADAM PATCH, *whose approach has been rendered inaudible by the pandemonium in the room.*

ADAM PATCH *is very white. He leans upon a stick. The man with him is* EDWARD SHUTTLEWORTH, *and it is he who seizes* PARAMORE *by the shoulder and deflects the course of his fall away from the venerable philanthropist.*

The time required for quiet to descend upon the room like a monstrous pall may be estimated at two minutes, though for a short period after that the phonograph gags and the notes of the Japanese train song dribble from the end of TANA'S *flute. Of the nine people only* BARNES, PARAMORE, *and* TANA *are unaware of the late-comer's identity. Of the nine not one is aware that* ADAM PATCH *has that morning made a contribution of fifty thousand dollars to the cause of national prohibition.*

It is given to PARAMORE *to break the gathering silence; the high tide of his life's depravity is reached in his incredible remark.*)

PARAMORE: (*Crawling rapidly toward the kitchen on his hands and knees*) I'm not a guest here—I work here.

(*Again silence falls—so deep now, so weighted with intolerably contagious apprehension, that* RACHAEL *gives a nervous little giggle, and* DICK *finds himself telling over and over a line from Swinburne, grotesquely appropriate to the scene:*

"One gaunt bleak blossom of scentless breath."

. . . *Out of the hush the voice of* ANTHONY, *sober and strained, saying something to* ADAM PATCH; *then this, too, dies away.*)

SHUTTLEWORTH: (*Passionately*) Your grandfather thought he would motor over to see your house. I phoned from Rye and left a message.

(*A series of little gasps, emanating, apparently, from nowhere, from no one, fall into the next pause.* ANTHONY *is the color of chalk.* GLORIA'S *lips are parted and her level gaze at the old man is tense and frightened. There is not one smile in the room. Not one? Or does* CROSS PATCH'S *drawn mouth tremble slightly open, to expose the even rows of his thin teeth? He speaks—five mild and simple words.*)

ADAM PATCH: We'll go back now, Shuttleworth——

(*And that is all. He turns, and assisted by his cane goes out through the hall, through the front door, and with hellish portentousness his uncertain footsteps crunch on the gravel path under the August moon.*)

Retrospect

In this extremity they were like two goldfish in a bowl from which all the water had been drawn; they could not even swim across to each other.

Gloria would be twenty-six in May. There was nothing, she had said, that she wanted, except to be young and beautiful for a long time, to be gay and happy, and to have money and love. She wanted what most women want, but she wanted it much more fiercely and passionately. She had been married over two years. At first there had been days of serene understanding, rising to ecstasies of proprietorship and pride. Alternating with these periods had occurred sporadic hates, enduring a short hour, and forgetfulnesses lasting no longer than an afternoon. That had been for half a year.

Then the serenity, the content, had become less jubilant, had become gray—very rarely, with the spur of jealousy or forced separation, the ancient ecstasies returned, the apparent communion of soul and soul, the emotional excitement. It was possible for her to hate Anthony for as much as a full day, to be carelessly incensed at him for as long as a week. Recrimination had displaced affection as an indulgence, almost as an entertainment, and there were nights when they would go to sleep trying to remember who was angry and who should be reserved next morning. And as the second year waned there had entered two new elements. Gloria realized that Anthony had become capable of utter indifference toward her, a temporary indifference, more than half lethargic, but one from which she could no longer stir him by a whispered word, or a certain intimate smile. There were days when her caresses affected him as a sort of suffocation. She was conscious of these things; she never entirely admitted them to herself.

It was only recently that she perceived that in spite of her adoration of him, her jealousy, her servitude, her pride, she fundamentally despised him—and her contempt blended indistinguishably with her other emotions. . . . All this was her love—the vital and feminine illusion that had directed itself toward him one April night, many months before.

On Anthony's part she was, in spite of these qualifications, his sole preoccupation. Had he lost her he would have been a broken man, wretchedly and sentimentally absorbed in her memory for the remainder of life. He seldom took pleasure in an entire day spent alone with her—except on occasions he preferred to have a third person with them. There were times when he felt that if he were not left absolutely alone he would go mad—there were a few times when he definitely hated her. In his cups he was capable of short attractions toward other women, the hitherto-suppressed outcroppings of an experimental temperament.

That spring, that summer, they had speculated upon future happiness—how they were to travel from summer land to summer land, returning eventually to a gorgeous estate and possible idyllic children, then entering diplomacy or politics, to accomplish, for a while, beautiful and important things, until finally as a white-haired (beautifully, silkily, white-haired) couple they were to loll about in serene glory, worshipped by the bourgeoisie of the land. . . . These times were to begin "when we get our money"; it was on such dreams rather than on any satisfaction with their increasingly irregular, increasingly dissipated life that their hope rested. On gray mornings when the jests of the night before had shrunk to ribaldries without wit or dignity, they could, after a fashion, bring out this batch of common hopes and count them over, then smile at each other and repeat, by way of clinching the matter, the terse yet sincere Nietzscheanism of Gloria's defiant "I don't care!"

Things had been slipping perceptibly. There was the money question, increasingly annoying, increasingly ominous; there was the realization that liquor had become a practical necessity to their amusement—not an uncommon phenomenon in the British aristocracy of a hundred years ago, but a somewhat alarming one in a civilization steadily becoming more temperate and more circumspect. Moreover, both of them seemed vaguely weaker in fibre, not so much in what they did as in their subtle reactions to the civilization about them. In Gloria had been born something that she had hitherto never needed—the skeleton, incomplete but nevertheless unmistakable, of her ancient abhorrence, a conscience. This admission to herself was coincidental with the slow decline of her physical courage.

Then, on the August morning after Adam Patch's unexpected call, they awoke, nauseated and tired, dispirited with life, capable only of one pervasive emotion—fear.

Panic

"Well?" Anthony sat up in bed and looked down at her. The corners of his lips were drooping with depression, his voice was strained and hollow.

Her reply was to raise her hand to her mouth and begin a slow, precise nibbling at her finger.

"We've done it," he said after a pause; then, as she was still silent, he became exasperated. "Why don't you say something?"

"What on earth do you want me to say?"

"What are you thinking?"

"Nothing."

"Then stop biting your finger!"

Ensued a short confused discussion of whether or not she had been thinking. It seemed essential to Anthony that she should muse aloud upon last night's disaster. Her silence was a method of settling the responsibility on him. For her part she saw no necessity for speech—the moment required that she should gnaw at her finger like a nervous child.

"I've got to fix up this damn mess with my grandfather," he said with uneasy conviction. A faint new-born respect was indicated by his use of "my grandfather" instead of "grampa."

"You can't," she affirmed abruptly. "You can't—*ever*. He'll never forgive you as long as he lives."

"Perhaps not," agreed Anthony miserably. "Still—I might possibly square myself by some sort of reformation and all that sort of thing——"

"He looked sick," she interrupted, "pale as flour."

"He *is* sick. I told you that three months ago."

"I wish he'd died last week!" she said petulantly. "Inconsiderate old fool!"

Neither of them laughed.

"But just let me say," she added quietly, "the next time I see you acting with any woman like you did with Rachael Barnes last night, I'll leave you—*just—like—that!* I'm simply *not* going to stand it!"

Anthony quailed.

"Oh, don't be absurd," he protested. "You know there's no woman in the world for me except you—none, dearest."

His attempt at a tender note failed miserably—the more imminent danger stalked back into the foreground.

"If I went to him," suggested Anthony, "and said with appropriate biblical quotations that I'd walked too long in the way of unrighteousness and at last seen the light—" He broke off and glanced with a whimsical expression at his wife. "I wonder what he'd do?"

"I don't know."

She was speculating as to whether or not their guests would have the acumen to leave directly after breakfast.

Not for a week did Anthony muster the courage to go to Tarrytown. The prospect was revolting and left alone he would have been incapable of making the trip—but if his will had deteriorated in these past three years, so had his power to resist urging. Gloria compelled him to go. It was all very well to wait a week, she said, for that would give his grandfather's violent animosity time to cool—but to wait longer would be an error—it would give it a chance to harden.

He went, in trepidation . . . and vainly. Adam Patch was not well, said Shuttleworth indignantly. Positive instructions had been given that no one was to see him. Before the ex-"gin-physician's" vindictive eye Anthony's front wilted. He walked out to his taxicab with what was almost a slink—recovering only a little of his self-respect as he boarded the train; glad to escape, boylike, to the wonder-palaces of consolation that still rose and glittered in his own mind.

Gloria was scornful when he returned to Marietta. Why had he not forced his way in? That was what she would have done!

Between them they drafted a letter to the old man, and after considerable revision sent it off. It was half an apology, half a manufactured explanation. The letter was not answered.

Came a day in September, a day slashed with alternate sun and rain, sun without warmth, rain without freshness. On that day they left the gray house, which had seen the flower of their love. Four trunks and three monstrous crates were piled in the dismantled room where, two years before, they had sprawled lazily, thinking in terms of dreams, remote, languorous, content. The room echoed with emptiness. Gloria, in a new brown dress edged with fur, sat upon a trunk in silence, and Anthony walked nervously to and fro smoking, as they waited for the truck that would take their things to the city.

"What are those?" she demanded, pointing to some books piled upon one of the crates.

"That's my old stamp collection," he confessed sheepishly. "I forgot to pack it."

"Anthony, it's so silly to carry it around."

"Well, I was looking through it the day we left the apartment last spring, and I decided not to store it."

"Can't you sell it? Haven't we enough junk?"

"I'm sorry," he said humbly.

With a thunderous rattling the truck rolled up to the door. Gloria shook her fist defiantly at the four walls.

"I'm so glad to go!" she cried, "so glad. Oh, my God, how I hate this house!"

So the brilliant and beautiful lady went up with her husband to New York. On the very train that bore them away they quarrelled—her bitter words had the frequency, the regularity, the inevitability of the stations they passed.

"Don't be cross," begged Anthony piteously. "We've got nothing but each other, after all."

"We haven't even that, most of the time," cried Gloria.

"When haven't we?"

"A lot of times—beginning with one occasion on the station platform at Redgate."

"You don't mean to say that——"

"No," she interrupted coolly, "I don't brood over it. It came and went—and when it went it took something with it."

She finished abruptly. Anthony sat in silence, confused, depressed. The drab visions of train-side Mamaroneck, Larchmont, Rye, Pelham Manor, succeeded each other with intervals of bleak and shoddy wastes posing ineffectually as country. He found himself remembering how on one summer morning they two had started from New York in search of happiness. They had never expected to find it, perhaps, yet in itself that quest had been happier than anything he expected forevermore. Life, it seemed, must be a setting up of props around one—otherwise it was disaster. There was no rest, no quiet. He had been futile in longing to drift and dream; no one drifted except to maelstroms, no one dreamed, without his dreams becoming fantastic nightmares of indecision and regret.

Pelham! They had quarrelled in Pelham because Gloria must drive. And when she set her little foot on the accelerator the car had jumped off spunkily, and their two heads had jerked back like marionettes worked by a single string.

The Bronx—the houses gathering and gleaming in the sun, which was falling now through wide refulgent skies and tumbling caravans of light down into the streets. New York, he supposed, was home—the city of luxury and mystery, of preposterous hopes and exotic dreams. Here on the outskirts absurd stucco palaces reared themselves in the cool sunset, poised for an instant in cool unreality, glided off far away, succeeded by the mazed confusion of the Harlem River. The train moved in through the deepening twilight, above and past half a hundred cheerful sweating streets of the upper East Side, each one passing the car-window like the space between the spokes of a gigantic wheel, each one with its vigorous colorful revelation of poor children swarming in feverish activity like vivid ants in alleys of red sand. From the tenement windows leaned rotund, moon-shaped mothers, as constellations of this sordid heaven; women like dark imperfect jewels, women like vegetables, women like great bags of abominably dirty laundry.

"I like these streets," observed Anthony aloud. "I always feel as though it's a performance being staged for me; as though the second I've passed they'll all stop leaping and laughing and, instead, grow very sad, remembering how poor they are, and retreat with bowed heads into their houses. You often get that effect abroad, but seldom in this country."

Down in a tall busy street he read a dozen Jewish names on a line of stores; in the door of each stood a dark little man watching the passers from intent eyes—eyes gleaming with suspicion, with pride, with clarity, with cupidity, with comprehension. New York—he could not dissociate it now from the slow, upward creep of this people—the little stores, growing, expanding, consolidating, moving, watched over with hawk's eyes and a bee's attention to detail—they slathered out on all sides. It was impressive—in perspective it was tremendous.

Gloria's voice broke in with strange appropriateness upon his thoughts.

"I wonder where Bloeckman's been this summer."

The Apartment

After the sureties of youth there sets in a period of intense and intolerable complexity. With the soda-jerker this period is so short as to be almost negligible. Men higher in the scale hold out longer in the attempt to preserve the ultimate niceties of relationship, to retain "impractical" ideas of integrity. But by the late twenties the business has grown too intricate, and what has hitherto been imminent and confusing has become gradually remote and dim. Routine comes down like twilight on a harsh landscape, softening it until it is tolerable. The complexity is too subtle, too varied; the values are changing utterly with each lesion of vitality; it has begun to appear that we can learn nothing from the past with which to face the future—so we cease to be impulsive, convincible men, interested in what is ethically true by fine margins, we substitute rules of conduct for ideas of integrity, we value safety above romance, we become, quite unconsciously, pragmatic. It is left to the few to be persistently concerned with the nuances of relationships—and even this few only in certain hours especially set aside for the task.

Anthony Patch had ceased to be an individual of mental adventure, of curiosity, and had become an individual of bias and prejudice, with a longing to be emotionally undisturbed. This gradual change had taken place through the past several years, accelerated by a succession of anxieties preying on his mind. There was, first of all, the sense of waste, always dormant in his heart, now awakened by the circumstances of his position. In his moments of insecurity he was haunted by the suggestion that life might be, after all, significant. In his early twenties the conviction of the futility of effort, of the wisdom of abnegation, had been confirmed by the philosophies he had admired as well as by his association with Maury Noble, and later with his wife. Yet there had been occasions—just before his first meeting with Gloria, for example, and when his grandfather had suggested that he should go abroad as a war correspondent—upon which his dissatisfaction had driven him almost to a positive step.

One day just before they left Marietta for the last time, in carelessly turning over the pages of a Harvard Alumni Bulletin, he had found a column which told him what his contemporaries had been about in this six years since graduation. Most of them were in business, it was true, and several were converting the heathen of China or America to a nebulous protestantism; but a few, he found, were working constructively at jobs that were neither sinecures nor routines. There was Calvin Boyd, for instance, who, though barely out of medical school, had discovered a new treatment for typhus, had shipped abroad and was mitigating some of the civilization that the Great Powers had brought to Servia; there was Eugene Bronson, whose articles in The New Democracy were stamping him as a man with ideas transcending both vulgar timeliness and popular hysteria; there was a man named Daly who had been suspended from the faculty of a righteous university for preaching Marxian doctrines in the classroom: in art, science, politics, he saw the authentic personalities of his time emerging—there was even Severance, the quarter-back, who had given up his life rather neatly and gracefully with the Foreign Legion on the Aisne.

He laid down the magazine and thought for a while about these diverse men. In the days of his integrity he would have defended his attitude to the last—an Epicurus in Nirvana, he would have cried that to struggle was to believe, to believe was to limit. He would as soon have become a churchgoer because the prospect of immortality gratified him as he would have considered entering the leather business because the intensity of the competition would have kept him from unhappiness. But at present he had no such delicate scruples. This autumn, as his twenty-ninth year began, he was inclined to close his mind to many things, to avoid prying deeply into motives and first causes, and mostly to long passionately for security from the world and from himself. He hated to be alone, as has been said he often dreaded being alone with Gloria.

Because of the chasm which his grandfather's visit had opened before him, and the consequent revulsion from his late mode of life, it was inevitable that he should look around in this suddenly hostile city for the friends and environments that had once seemed the warmest and most secure. His first step was a desperate attempt to get back his old apartment.

In the spring of 1912 he had signed a four-year lease at seventeen hundred a year, with an option of renewal. This lease had expired the previous May. When he had first rented the rooms they had been mere potentialities, scarcely to be discerned as that, but Anthony had seen into these potentialities and arranged in the lease that he and the landlord should each spend a certain amount in improvements. Rents had gone up in the past four years, and last spring when Anthony had waived his option the landlord, a Mr. Sohenberg, had realized that he could get a much bigger price for what was now a prepossessing apartment. Accordingly, when Anthony approached him on the subject in September he was met with Sohenberg's offer of a three-year lease at twenty-five hundred a year. This, it seemed to Anthony, was outrageous. It meant that well over a third of their income would be consumed in rent. In vain he argued that his own money, his own ideas on the repartitioning, had made the rooms attractive.

In vain he offered two thousand dollars—twenty-two hundred, though they could ill afford it: Mr. Sohenberg was obdurate. It seemed that two other gentlemen were considering it; just that sort of an apartment was in demand for the moment, and it would scarcely be business to *give* it to Mr. Patch. Besides, though he had never mentioned it before, several of the other tenants had complained of noise during the previous winter—singing and dancing late at night, that sort of thing.

Internally raging Anthony hurried back to the Ritz to report his discomfiture to Gloria.

"I can just see you," she stormed, "letting him back you down!"

"What could I say?"

"You could have told him what he *was*. I wouldn't have *stood* it. No other man in the world would have stood it! You just let people order you around and cheat you and bully you and take advantage of you as if you were a silly little boy. It's absurd!"

"Oh, for Heaven's sake, don't lose your temper."

"I know, Anthony, but you *are* such an ass!"

"Well, possibly. Anyway, we can't afford that apartment. But we can afford it better than living here at the Ritz."

"You were the one who insisted on coming here."

"Yes, because I knew you'd be miserable in a cheap hotel."

"Of course I would!"

"At any rate we've got to find a place to live."

"How much can we pay?" she demanded.

"Well, we can pay even his price if we sell more bonds, but we agreed last night that until I had gotten something definite to do we——"

"Oh, I know all that. I asked you how much we can pay out of just our income."

"They say you ought not to pay more than a fourth."

"How much is a fourth?"

"One hundred and fifty a month."

"Do you mean to say we've got only six hundred dollars coming in every month?" A subdued note crept into her voice.

"Of course!" he answered angrily. "Do you think we've gone on spending more than twelve thousand a year without cutting way into our capital?"

"I knew we'd sold bonds, but—have we spent that much a year? How did we?" Her awe increased.

"Oh, I'll look in those careful account-books we kept," he remarked ironically, and then added: "Two rents a good part of the time, clothes, travel—why, each of those springs in

California cost about four thousand dollars. That darn car was an expense from start to finish. And parties and amusements and—oh, one thing or another."

They were both excited now and inordinately depressed. The situation seemed worse in the actual telling Gloria than it had when he had first made the discovery himself.

"You've got to make some money," she said suddenly.

"I know it."

"And you've got to make another attempt to see your grandfather."

"I will."

"When?"

"When we get settled."

This eventuality occurred a week later. They rented a small apartment on Fifty-seventh Street at one hundred and fifty a month. It included bedroom, living-room, kitchenette, and bath, in a thin, white-stone apartment-house, and though the rooms were too small to display Anthony's best furniture, they were clean, new, and, in a blonde and sanitary way, not unattractive. Bounds had gone abroad to enlist in the British army, and in his place they tolerated rather than enjoyed the services of a gaunt, big-boned Irishwoman, whom Gloria loathed because she discussed the glories of Sinn Fein as she served breakfast. But they had vowed they would have no more Japanese, and English servants were for the present hard to obtain. Like Bounds, the woman prepared only breakfast. Their other meals they took at restaurants and hotels.

What finally drove Anthony post-haste up to Tarrytown was an announcement in several New York papers that Adam Patch, the multimillionaire, the philanthropist, the venerable uplifter, was seriously ill and not expected to recover.

The Kitten

Anthony could not see him. The doctors' instructions were that he was to talk to no one, said Mr. Shuttleworth—who offered kindly to take any message that Anthony might care to intrust with him, and deliver it to Adam Patch when his condition permitted. But by obvious innuendo he confirmed Anthony's melancholy inference that the prodigal grandson would be particularly unwelcome at the bedside. At one point in the conversation Anthony, with Gloria's positive instructions in mind, made a move as though to brush by the secretary, but Shuttleworth with a smile squared his brawny shoulders, and Anthony saw how futile such an attempt would be.

Miserably intimidated, he returned to New York, where husband and wife passed a restless week. A little incident that occurred one evening indicated to what tension their nerves were drawn.

Walking home along a cross-street after dinner, Anthony noticed a night-bound cat prowling near a railing.

"I always have an instinct to kick a cat," he said idly.

"I like them."

"I yielded to it once."

"When?"

"Oh, years ago; before I met you. One night between the acts of a show. Cold night, like this, and I was a little tight—one of the first times I was ever tight," he added. "The poor little beggar was looking for a place to sleep, I guess, and I was in a mean mood, so it took my fancy to kick it——"

"Oh, the poor kitty!" cried Gloria, sincerely moved.

Inspired with the narrative instinct, Anthony enlarged on the theme.

"It was pretty bad," he admitted. "The poor little beast turned around and looked at me rather plaintively as though hoping I'd pick him up and be kind to him—he was really just a kitten—and before he knew it a big foot launched out at him and caught his little back——"

"Oh!" Gloria's cry was full of anguish.

"It was such a cold night," he continued, perversely, keeping his voice upon a melancholy note. "I guess it expected kindness from somebody, and it got only pain——"

He broke off suddenly—Gloria was sobbing. They had reached home, and when they entered the apartment she threw herself upon the lounge, crying as though he had struck at her very soul.

"Oh, the poor little kitty!" she repeated piteously, "the poor little kitty. So cold——"

"Gloria——"

"Don't come near me! Please, don't come near me. You killed the soft little kitty."

Touched, Anthony knelt beside her.

"Dear," he said. "Oh, Gloria, darling. It isn't true. I invented it—every word of it."

But she would not believe him. There had been something in the details he had chosen to describe that made her cry herself asleep that night, for the kitten, for Anthony, for herself, for the pain and bitterness and cruelty of all the world.

The Passing of an American Moralist

Old Adam died on a midnight of late November with a pious compliment to his God on his thin lips. He, who had been flattered so much, faded out flattering the Omnipotent Abstraction which he fancied he might have angered in the more lascivious moments of his youth. It was announced that he had arranged some sort of an armistice with the deity, the terms of which were not made public, though they were thought to have included a large cash payment. All the newspapers printed his biography, and two of them ran short editorials on his sterling worth, and his part in the drama of industrialism, with which he had grown up. They referred guardedly to the reforms he had sponsored and financed. The memories of Comstock and Cato the Censor were resuscitated and paraded like gaunt ghosts through the columns.

Every newspaper remarked that he was survived by a single grandson, Anthony Comstock Patch, of New York.

The burial took place in the family plot at Tarrytown. Anthony and Gloria rode in the first carriage, too worried to feel grotesque, both trying desperately to glean presage of fortune from the faces of retainers who had been with him at the end.

They waited a frantic week for decency, and then, having received no notification of any kind, Anthony called up his grandfather's lawyer. Mr. Brett was not in—he was expected back in an hour. Anthony left his telephone number.

It was the last day of November, cool and crackling outside, with a lustreless sun peering bleakly in at the windows. While they waited for the call, ostensibly engaged in reading, the atmosphere, within and without, seemed pervaded with a deliberate rendition of the pathetic fallacy. After an interminable while, the bell jingled, and Anthony, starting violently, took up the receiver.

"Hello . . ." His voice was strained and hollow. "Yes—I did leave word. Who is this, please? . . . Yes. . . . Why, it was about the estate. Naturally I'm interested, and I've received no word about the reading of the will—I thought you might not have my address. . . . What? . . . Yes . . ."

Gloria fell on her knees. The intervals between Anthony's speeches were like tourniquets winding on her heart. She found herself helplessly twisting the large buttons from a velvet cushion. Then:

"That's — that's very, very odd — that's very odd — that's very odd. Not even any—ah—mention or any—ah—reason——?"

His voice sounded faint and far away. She uttered a little sound, half gasp, half cry.

"Yes, I'll see. . . . All right, thanks . . . thanks. . . ."

The phone clicked. Her eyes looking along the floor saw his feet cut the pattern of a patch of sunlight on the carpet. She arose and faced him with a gray, level glance just as his arms folded about her.

"My dearest," he whispered huskily. "He did it, God damn him!"

NEXT DAY

"Who are the heirs?" asked Mr. Haight. "You see when you can tell me so little about it——"

Mr. Haight was tall and bent and beetle-browed. He had been recommended to Anthony as an astute and tenacious lawyer.

"I only know vaguely," answered Anthony. "A man named Shuttleworth, who was a sort of pet of his, has the whole thing in charge as administrator or trustee or something—all except the direct bequests to charity and the provisions for servants and for those two cousins in Idaho."

"How distant are the cousins?"

"Oh, third or fourth, anyway. I never even heard of them."

Mr. Haight nodded comprehensively.

"And you want to contest a provision of the will?"

"I guess so," admitted Anthony helplessly. "I want to do what sounds most hopeful—that's what I want you to tell me."

"You want them to refuse probate to the will?"

Anthony shook his head.

"You've got me. I haven't any idea what 'probate' is. I want a share of the estate."

"Suppose you tell me some more details. For instance, do you know why the testator disinherited you?"

"Why—yes," began Anthony. "You see he was always a sucker for moral reform, and all that——"

"I know," interjected Mr. Haight humorlessly.

"—and I don't suppose he ever thought I was much good. I didn't go into business, you see. But I feel certain that up to last summer I was one of the beneficiaries. We had a house out in Marietta, and one night grandfather got the notion he'd come over and see us. It just happened that there was a rather gay party going on and he arrived without any warning. Well, he took one look, he and this fellow Shuttleworth, and then turned around and tore right back to Tarrytown. After that he never answered my letters or even let me see him."

"He was a prohibitionist, wasn't he?"

"He was everything—regular religious maniac."

"How long before his death was the will made that disinherited you?"

"Recently—I mean since August."

"And you think that the direct reason for his not leaving you the majority of the estate was his displeasure with your recent actions?"

"Yes."

Mr. Haight considered. Upon what grounds was Anthony thinking of contesting the will?

"Why, isn't there something about evil influence?"

"Undue influence is one ground—but it's the most difficult. You would have to show that such pressure was brought to bear so that the deceased was in a condition where he disposed of his property contrary to his intentions——"

"Well, suppose this fellow Shuttleworth dragged him over to Marietta just when he thought some sort of a celebration was probably going on?"

"That wouldn't have any bearing on the case. There's a strong division between advice and influence. You'd have to prove that the secretary had a sinister intention. I'd suggest some other grounds. A will is automatically refused probate in case of insanity, drunkenness"—here Anthony smiled—"or feeble-mindedness through premature old age."

"But," objected Anthony, "his private physician, being one of the beneficiaries, would testify that he wasn't feeble-minded. And he wasn't. As a matter of fact he probably did just what he intended to with his money—it was perfectly consistent with everything he'd ever done in his life——"

"Well, you see, feeble-mindedness is a great deal like undue influence—it implies that the property wasn't disposed of as originally intended. The most common ground is duress—physical pressure."

Anthony shook his head.

"Not much chance on that, I'm afraid. Undue influence sounds best to me."

After more discussion, so technical as to be largely unintelligible to Anthony, he retained Mr. Haight as counsel. The lawyer proposed an interview with Shuttleworth, who, jointly with Wilson, Hiemer and Hardy, was executor of the will. Anthony was to come back later in the week.

It transpired that the estate consisted of approximately forty million dollars. The largest bequest to an individual was of one million, to Edward Shuttleworth, who received in addition thirty thousand a year salary as administrator of the thirty-million-dollar trust fund, left to be doled out to various charities and reform societies practically at his own discretion. The remaining nine millions were proportioned among the two cousins in Idaho and about twenty-five other beneficiaries: friends, secretaries, servants, and employees, who had, at one time or another, earned the seal of Adam Patch's approval.

At the end of another fortnight Mr. Haight, on a retainer's fee of fifteen thousand dollars, had begun preparations for contesting the will.

The Winter of Discontent

Before they had been two months in the little apartment on Fifty-seventh Street, it had assumed for both of them the same indefinable but almost material taint that had impregnated the gray house in Marietta. There was the odor of tobacco always—both of them smoked incessantly; it was in their clothes, their blankets, the curtains, and the ash-littered carpets. Added to this was the wretched aura of stale wine, with its inevitable suggestion of beauty gone foul and revelry remembered in disgust. About a particular set of glass goblets on the sideboard the odor was particularly noticeable, and in the main room the mahogany table was ringed with white circles where glasses had been set down upon it. There had been many parties—people broke things; people became sick in Gloria's bathroom; people spilled wine; people made unbelievable messes of the kitchenette.

These things were a regular part of their existence. Despite the resolutions of many Mondays it was tacitly understood as the week-end approached that it should be observed with some sort of unholy excitement. When Saturday came they would not discuss the matter, but would call up this person or that from among their circle of sufficiently irresponsible friends, and suggest a rendezvous. Only after the friends had gathered and Anthony had set out decanters, would he murmur casually: "I guess I'll have just one high-ball myself——"

Then they were off for two days—realizing on a wintry dawn that they had been the noisiest and most conspicuous members of the noisiest and most conspicuous party at the Boul' Mich', or the Club Ramée, or at other resorts much less particular about the hilarity of their clientèle. They would find that they had, somehow, squandered eighty or ninety dollars, how, they never knew; they customarily attributed it to the general penury of the "friends" who had accompanied them.

It began to be not unusual for the more sincere of their friends to remonstrate with them, in the very course of a party, and to predict a sombre end for them in the loss of Gloria's "looks" and Anthony's "constitution." The story of the summarily interrupted revel in Marietta had, of course, leaked out in detail—"Muriel doesn't mean to tell every one she knows," said Gloria to Anthony, "but she thinks every one she tells is the only one she's going to tell"—and, diaphanously veiled, the tale had been given a conspicuous place in Town Tattle. When the terms of Adam Patch's will were made public and the newspapers printed items concerning Anthony's suit, the story was beautifully rounded out—to Anthony's infinite disparagement. They began to hear rumors about themselves from all quarters, rumors founded usually on a soupçon of truth, but overlaid with preposterous and sinister detail.

Outwardly they showed no signs of deterioration. Gloria at twenty-six was still the Gloria of twenty; her complexion a fresh damp setting for her candid eyes; her hair still a childish glory, darkening slowly from corn color to a deep russet gold; her slender body suggesting ever a nymph running and dancing through Orphic groves. Masculine eyes, dozens of them, followed her with a fascinated stare when she walked through a hotel lobby or down the aisle of a theatre. Men asked to be introduced to her, fell into prolonged states of sincere admiration, made definite love to her—for she was still a thing of exquisite and unbelievable beauty. And for his part Anthony had rather gained than lost in appearance; his face had taken on a certain intangible air of tragedy, romantically contrasted with his trim and immaculate person.

Early in the winter, when all conversation turned on the probability of America's going into the war, when Anthony was making a desperate and sincere attempt to write, Muriel Kane arrived in New York and came immediately to see them. Like Gloria, she seemed never to change. She knew the latest slang, danced the latest dances, and talked of the latest songs and plays with all the fervor of her first season as a New York drifter. Her coyness was eternally new, eternally ineffectual; her clothes were extreme; her black hair was bobbed, now, like Gloria's.

"I've come up for the midwinter prom at New Haven," she announced, imparting her delightful secret. Though she must have been older then than any of the boys in college, she managed always to secure some sort of invitation, imagining vaguely that at the next party would occur the flirtation which was to end at the romantic altar.

"Where've you been?" inquired Anthony, unfailingly amused.

"I've been at Hot Springs. It's been slick and peppy this fall—more *men!*"

"Are you in love, Muriel?"

"What do you mean 'love'?" This was the rhetorical question of the year. "I'm going to tell you something," she said, switching the subject abruptly. "I suppose it's none of my business, but I think it's time for you two to settle down."

"Why, we are settled down."

"Yes, you are!" she scoffed archly. "Everywhere I go I hear stories of your escapades. Let me tell you, I have an awful time sticking up for you."

"You needn't bother," said Gloria coldly.

"Now, Gloria," she protested, "you know I'm one of your best friends."

Gloria was silent. Muriel continued:

"It's not so much the idea of a woman drinking, but Gloria's so pretty, and so many people know her by sight all around, that it's naturally conspicuous——"

"What have you heard recently?" demanded Gloria, her dignity going down before her curiosity.

"Well, for instance, that that party in Marietta *killed* Anthony's grandfather."

Instantly husband and wife were tense with annoyance.

"Why, I think that's outrageous."

"That's what they say," persisted Muriel stubbornly.

Anthony paced the room. "It's preposterous!" he declared. "The very people we take on parties shout the story around as a great joke—and eventually it gets back to us in some such form as this."

Gloria began running her finger through a stray reddish curl. Muriel licked her veil as she considered her next remark.

"You ought to have a baby."

Gloria looked up wearily.

"We can't afford it."

"All the people in the slums have them," said Muriel triumphantly.

Anthony and Gloria exchanged a smile. They had reached the stage of violent quarrels that were never made up, quarrels that smouldered and broke out again at intervals or died away from sheer indifference—but this visit of Muriel's drew them temporarily together. When the discomfort under which they were living was remarked upon by a third party, it gave them the impetus to face this hostile world together. It was very seldom, now, that the impulse toward reunion sprang from within.

Anthony found himself associating his own existence with that of the apartment's night elevator man, a pale, scraggly bearded person of about sixty, with an air of being somewhat above his station. It was probably because of this quality that he had secured the position; it made him a pathetic and memorable figure of failure. Anthony recollected, without humor, a hoary jest about the elevator man's career being a matter of ups and downs—it was, at any rate, an enclosed life of infinite dreariness. Each time Anthony stepped into the car he waited breathlessly for the old man's "Well, I guess we're going to have some sunshine to-day." Anthony thought how little rain or sunshine he would enjoy shut into that close little cage in the smoke-colored, windowless hall.

A darkling figure, he attained tragedy in leaving the life that had used him so shabbily. Three young gunmen came in one night, tied him up and left him on a pile of coal in the cellar while they went through the trunk-room. When the janitor found him next morning he had collapsed from chill. He died of pneumonia four days later.

He was replaced by a glib Martinique negro, with an incongruous British accent and a tendency to be surly, whom Anthony detested. The passing of the old man had approximately the same effect on him that the kitten story had had on Gloria. He was reminded of the cruelty of all life and, in consequence, of the increasing bitterness of his own.

He was writing—and in earnest at last. He had gone to Dick and listened for a tense hour to an elucidation of those minutiæ of procedure which hitherto he had rather scornfully looked down upon. He needed money immediately—he was selling bonds every month to pay their bills. Dick was frank and explicit:

"So far as articles on literary subjects in these obscure magazines go, you couldn't make enough to pay your rent. Of course if a man has the gift of humor, or a chance at a big biography, or some specialized knowledge, he may strike it rich. But for you, fiction's the only thing. You say you need money right away?"

"I certainly do."

"Well, it'd be a year and a half before you'd make any money out of a novel. Try some popular short stories. And, by the way, unless they're exceptionally brilliant they have to be cheerful and on the side of the heaviest artillery to make you any money."

Anthony thought of Dick's recent output, which had been appearing in a well-known monthly. It was concerned chiefly with the preposterous actions of a class of sawdust effigies who, one was assured, were New York society people, and it turned, as a rule, upon questions of the heroine's technical purity, with mock-sociological overtones about the "mad antics of the four hundred."

"But your stories—" exclaimed Anthony aloud, almost involuntarily.

"Oh, that's different," Dick asserted astoundingly. "I have a reputation, you see, so I'm expected to deal with strong themes."

Anthony gave an interior start, realizing with this remark how much Richard Caramel had fallen off. Did he actually think that these amazing latter productions were as good as his first novel?

Anthony went back to the apartment and set to work. He found that the business of optimism was no mean task. After half a dozen futile starts he went to the public library and for a week investigated the files of a popular magazine. Then, better equipped, he accomplished his first story, "The Dictaphone of Fate." It was founded upon one of his few remaining impressions of that six weeks in Wall Street the year before. It purported to be the sunny tale of an office boy who, quite by accident, hummed a wonderful melody into the dictaphone. The cylinder was discovered by the boss's brother, a well-known producer of musical comedy—and then immediately lost. The body of the story was concerned with the pursuit of the missing cylinder and the eventual marriage of the noble office boy (now a successful composer) to

Miss Rooney, the virtuous stenographer, who was half Joan of Arc and half Florence Nightingale.

He had gathered that this was what the magazines wanted. He offered, in his protagonists, the customary denizens of the pink-and-blue literary world, immersing them in a saccharine plot that would offend not a single stomach in Marietta. He had it typed in double space—this last as advised by a booklet, "Success as a Writer Made Easy," by R. Meggs Widdlestien, which assured the ambitious plumber of the futility of perspiration, since after a six-lesson course he could make at least a thousand dollars a month.

After reading it to a bored Gloria and coaxing from her the immemorial remark that it was "better than a lot of stuff that gets published," he satirically affixed the nom de plume of "Gilles de Sade," enclosed the proper return envelope, and sent it off.

Following the gigantic labor of conception he decided to wait until he heard from the first story before beginning another. Dick had told him that he might get as much as two hundred dollars. If by any chance it did happen to be unsuited, the editor's letter would, no doubt, give him an idea of what changes should be made.

"It is, without question, the most abominable piece of writing in existence," said Anthony.

The editor quite conceivably agreed with him. He returned the manuscript with a rejection slip. Anthony sent it off elsewhere and began another story. The second one was called "The Little Open Doors"; it was written in three days. It concerned the occult: an estranged couple were brought together by a medium in a vaudeville show.

There were six altogether, six wretched and pitiable efforts to "write down" by a man who had never before made a consistent effort to write at all. Not one of them contained a spark of vitality, and their total yield of grace and felicity was less than that of an average newspaper column. During their circulation they collected, all told, thirty-one rejection slips, headstones for the packages that he would find lying like dead bodies at his door.

In mid-January Gloria's father died, and they went again to Kansas City—a miserable trip, for Gloria brooded interminably, not upon her father's death, but on her mother's. Russel Gilbert's affairs having been cleared up they came into possession of about three thousand dollars, and a great amount of furniture. This was in storage, for he had spent his last days in a small hotel. It was due to his death that Anthony made a new discovery concerning Gloria. On the journey East she disclosed herself, astonishingly, as a Bilphist.

"Why, Gloria," he cried, "you don't mean to tell me you believe that stuff."

"Well," she said defiantly, "why not?"

"Because it's—it's fantastic. You know that in every sense of the word you're an agnostic. You'd laugh at any orthodox form of Christianity—and then you come out with the statement that you believe in some silly rule of reincarnation."

"What if I do? I've heard you and Maury, and every one else for whose intellect I have the slightest respect, agree that life as it appears is utterly meaningless. But it's always seemed to me that if I were unconsciously learning something here it might not be so meaningless."

"You're not learning anything—you're just getting tired. And if you must have a faith to soften things, take up one that appeals to the reason of some one beside a lot of hysterical women. A person like you oughtn't to accept anything unless it's decently demonstrable."

"I don't care about truth. I want some happiness."

"Well, if you've got a decent mind the second has got to be qualified by the first. Any simple soul can delude himself with mental garbage."

"I don't care," she held out stoutly, "and, what's more, I'm not propounding any doctrine."

The argument faded off, but reoccurred to Anthony several times thereafter. It was disturbing to find this old belief, evidently assimilated from her mother, inserting itself again under its immemorial disguise as an innate idea.

They reached New York in March after an expensive and ill-advised week spent in Hot Springs, and Anthony resumed his abortive attempts at fiction. As it became plainer to both of them that escape did not lie in the way of popular literature, there was a further slipping of their mutual confidence and courage. A complicated struggle went on incessantly between them. All efforts to keep down expenses died away from sheer inertia, and by March they were again using any pretext as an excuse for a "party." With an assumption of recklessness Gloria tossed out the suggestion that they should take all their money and go on a real spree while it lasted—anything seemed better than to see it go in unsatisfactory driblets.

"Gloria, you want parties as much as I do."

"It doesn't matter about me. Everything I do is in accordance with my ideas: to use every minute of these years, when I'm young, in having the best time I possibly can."

"How about after that?"

"After that I won't care."

"Yes, you will."

"Well, I may—but I won't be able to do anything about it. And I'll have had my good time."

"You'll be the same then. After a fashion, we *have* had our good time, raised the devil, and we're in the state of paying for it."

Nevertheless, the money kept going. There would be two days of gaiety, two days of moroseness—an endless, almost invariable round. The sharp pull-ups, when they occurred, resulted usually in a spurt of work for Anthony, while Gloria, nervous and bored, remained in bed or else chewed abstractedly at her fingers. After a day or so of this, they would make an engagement, and then—Oh, what did it matter? This night, this glow, the cessation of anxiety and the sense that if living was not purposeful it was, at any rate, essentially romantic! Wine gave a sort of gallantry to their own failure.

Meanwhile the suit progressed slowly, with interminable examinations of witnesses and marshallings of evidence. The preliminary proceedings of settling the estate were finished. Mr. Haight saw no reason why the case should not come up for trial before summer.

Bloeckman appeared in New York late in March; he had been in England for nearly a year on matters concerned with "Films Par Excellence." The process of general refinement was still in progress—always he dressed a little better, his intonation was mellower, and in his manner there was perceptibly more assurance that the fine things of the world were his by a natural and inalienable right. He called at the apartment, remained only an hour, during which he talked chiefly of the war, and left telling them he was coming again. On his second visit Anthony was not at home, but an absorbed and excited Gloria greeted her husband later in the afternoon.

"Anthony," she began, "would you still object if I went in the movies?"

His whole heart hardened against the idea. As she seemed to recede from him, if only in threat, her presence became again not so much precious as desperately necessary.

"Oh, Gloria——!"

"Blockhead said he'd put me in—only if I'm ever going to do anything I'll have to start now. They only want young women. Think of the money, Anthony!"

"For you—yes. But how about me?"

"Don't you know that anything I have is yours too?"

"It's such a hell of a career!" he burst out, the moral, the infinitely circumspect Anthony, "and such a hell of a bunch. And I'm so utterly tired of that fellow Bloeckman coming here and interfering. I hate theatrical things."

"It isn't theatrical! It's utterly different."

"What am I supposed to do? Chase you all over the country? Live on your money?"

"Then make some yourself."

The conversation developed into one of the most violent quarrels they had ever had. After the ensuing reconciliation and the inevitable period of moral inertia, she realized that he had taken the life out of the project. Neither of them ever mentioned the probability that Bloeckman was by no means disinterested, but they both knew that it lay back of Anthony's objection.

In April war was declared with Germany. Wilson and his cabinet—a cabinet that in its lack of distinction was strangely reminiscent of the twelve apostles—let loose the carefully starved dogs of war, and the press began to whoop hysterically against the sinister morals, sinister philosophy, and sinister music produced by the Teutonic temperament. Those who fancied themselves particularly broad-minded made the exquisite distinction that it was only the German Government which aroused them to hysteria; the rest were worked up to a condition of retching indecency. Any song which contained the word "mother" and the word "kaiser" was assured of a tremendous success. At last every one had something to talk about—and almost every one fully enjoyed it, as though they had been cast for parts in a sombre and romantic play.

Anthony, Maury, and Dick sent in their applications for officers' training-camps and the two latter went about feeling strangely exalted and reproachless; they chattered to each other, like college boys, of war's being the one excuse for, and justification of, the aristocrat, and conjured up an impossible caste of officers, to be composed, it appeared, chiefly of the more attractive alumni of three or four Eastern colleges. It seemed to Gloria that in this huge red light streaming across the nation even Anthony took on a new glamour.

The Tenth Infantry, arriving in New York from Panama, were escorted from saloon to saloon by patriotic citizens, to their great bewilderment. West Pointers began to be noticed for the first time in years, and the general impression was that everything was glorious, but not half so glorious as it was going to be pretty soon, and that everybody was a fine fellow, and every race a great race—always excepting the Germans—and in every strata of society outcasts and scapegoats had but to appear in uniform to be forgiven, cheered, and wept over by relatives, ex-friends, and utter strangers.

Unfortunately, a small and precise doctor decided that there was something the matter with Anthony's blood-pressure. He could not conscientiously pass him for an officers' training-camp.

The Broken Lute

Their third anniversary passed, uncelebrated, unnoticed. The season warmed in thaw, melted into hotter summer, simmered and boiled away. In July the will was offered for probate, and upon the contestation was assigned by the surrogate to trial term for trial. The matter was prolonged into September—there was difficulty in empanelling an unbiassed jury because of the moral sentiments involved. To Anthony's disappointment a verdict was finally returned in favor of the testator, whereupon Mr. Haight caused a notice of appeal to be served upon Edward Shuttleworth.

As the summer waned Anthony and Gloria talked of the things they were to do when the money was theirs, and of the places they were to go to after the war, when they would "agree on things again," for both of them looked forward to a time when love, springing like the phœnix from its own ashes, should be born again in its mysterious and unfathomable haunts.

He was drafted early in the fall, and the examining doctor made no mention of low blood-pressure. It was all very purposeless and sad when Anthony told Gloria one night that he wanted, above all things, to be killed. But, as always, they were sorry for each other for the wrong things at the wrong times. . . .

They decided that for the present she was not to go with him to the Southern camp where his contingent was ordered. She would remain in New York to "use the apartment," to save money, and to watch the progress of the case—which was pending now in the Appellate Division, of which the calendar, Mr. Haight told them, was far behind.

Almost their last conversation was a senseless quarrel about the proper division of the income—at a word either would have given it all to the other. It was typical of the muddle and confusion of their lives that on the October night when Anthony reported at the Grand Central Station for the journey to camp, she arrived only in time to catch his eye over the anxious heads of a gathered crowd. Through the dark light of the enclosed train-sheds their glances stretched across a hysterical area, foul with yellow sobbing and the smells of poor women. They must have pondered upon what they had done to one another, and each must have accused himself of drawing this sombre pattern through which they were tracing tragically and obscurely. At the last they were too far away for either to see the other's tears.

BOOK THREE

CHAPTER I

A Matter of Civilization

AT a frantic command from some invisible source, Anthony groped his way inside. He was thinking that for the first time in more than three years he was to remain longer than a night away from Gloria. The finality of it appealed to him drearily. It was his clean and lovely girl that he was leaving.

They had arrived, he thought, at the most practical financial settlement: she was to have three hundred and seventy-five dollars a month—not too much considering that over half of that would go in rent—and he was taking fifty to supplement his pay. He saw no need for more: food, clothes, and quarters would be provided—there were no social obligations for a private.

The car was crowded and already thick with breath. It was one of the type known as "tourist" cars, a sort of brummagem Pullman, with a bare floor, and straw seats that needed cleaning. Nevertheless, Anthony greeted it with relief. He had vaguely expected that the trip South would be made in a freight-car, in one end of which would stand eight horses and in the other forty men. He had heard the "hommes 40, chevaux 8" story so often that it had become confused and ominous.

As he rocked down the aisle with his barrack-bag slung at his shoulder like a monstrous blue sausage, he saw no vacant seats, but after a moment his eye fell on a single space at present occupied by the feet of a short swarthy Sicilian, who, with his hat drawn over his eyes, hunched defiantly in the corner. As Anthony stopped beside him he stared up with a scowl, evidently intended to be intimidating; he must have adopted it as a defense against this entire gigantic equation. At Anthony's sharp "That seat taken?" he very slowly lifted the feet as though they were a breakable package, and placed them with some care upon the floor. His eyes remained on Anthony, who meanwhile sat down and unbuttoned the uniform coat issued him at Camp Upton the day before. It chafed him under the arms.

Before Anthony could scrutinize the other occupants of the section a young second lieutenant blew in at the upper end of the car and wafted airily down the aisle, announcing in a voice of appalling acerbity:

"There will be no smoking in this car! No smoking! Don't smoke, men, in this car!"

As he sailed out at the other end a dozen little clouds of expostulation arose on all sides.

"Oh, cripe!"

"Jeese!"

"No *smokin'*?"

"Hey, come back here, fella!"

"What's 'ee idea?"

Two or three cigarettes were shot out through the open windows. Others were retained inside, though kept sketchily away from view. From here and there in accents of bravado, of mockery, of submissive humor, a few remarks were dropped that soon melted into the listless and pervasive silence.

The fourth occupant of Anthony's section spoke up suddenly.

"G'by, liberty," he said sullenly. "G'by, everything except bein' an officer's dog."

Anthony looked at him. He was a tall Irishman with an expression moulded of indifference and utter disdain. His eyes fell on Anthony, as though he expected an answer, and then upon the others. Receiving only a defiant stare from the Italian he groaned and spat noisily on the floor by way of a dignified transition back into taciturnity.

A few minutes later the door opened again and the second lieutenant was borne in upon his customary official zephyr, this time singing out a different tiding:

"All right, men, smoke if you want to! My mistake, men! It's all right, men! Go on and smoke—my mistake!"

This time Anthony had a good look at him. He was young, thin, already faded; he was like his own mustache; he was like a great piece of shiny straw. His chin receded, faintly; this was offset by a magnificent and unconvincing scowl, a scowl that

Anthony was to connect with the faces of many young officers during the ensuing year.

Immediately every one smoked—whether they had previously desired to or not. Anthony's cigarette contributed to the hazy oxidation which seemed to roll back and forth in opalescent clouds with every motion of the train. The conversation, which had lapsed between the two impressive visits of the young officer, now revived tepidly; the men across the aisle began making clumsy experiments with their straw seats' capacity for comparative comfort; two card-games, half-heartedly begun, soon drew several spectators to sitting positions on the arms of seats. In a few minutes Anthony became aware of a persistently obnoxious sound—the small, defiant Sicilian had fallen audibly asleep. It was wearisome to contemplate that animate protoplasm, reasonable by courtesy only, shut up in a car by an incomprehensible civilization, taken somewhere, to do a vague something without aim or significance or consequence. Anthony sighed, opened a newspaper which he had no recollection of buying, and began to read by the dim yellow light.

Ten o'clock bumped stuffily into eleven; the hours clogged and caught and slowed down. Amazingly the train halted along the dark countryside, from time to time indulging in short, deceitful movements backward or forward, and whistling harsh pæans into the high October night. Having read his newspaper through, editorials, cartoons, and war-poems, his eye fell on a half-column headed *Shakespeareville, Kansas.* It seemed that the Shakespeareville Chamber of Commerce had recently held an enthusiastic debate as to whether the American soldiers should be known as "Sammies" or "Battling Christians." The thought gagged him. He dropped the newspaper, yawned, and let his mind drift off at a tangent. He wondered why Gloria had been late. It seemed so long ago already—he had a pang of illusive loneliness. He tried to imagine from what angle she would regard her new position, what place in her considerations he would continue to hold. The thought acted as a further depressant—he opened his paper and began to read again.

The members of the Chamber of Commerce in Shakespeareville had decided upon "Liberty Lads."

For two nights and two days they rattled southward, making mysterious inexplicable stops in what were apparently arid wastes, and then rushing through large cities with a pompous air of hurry. The whimsicalities of this train foreshadowed for Anthony the whimsicalities of all army administration.

In the arid wastes they were served from the baggage-car with beans and bacon that at first he was unable to eat—he dined scantily on some milk chocolate distributed by a village canteen. But on the second day the baggage-car's output began to appear surprisingly palatable. On the third morning the rumor was passed along that within the hour they would arrive at their destination, Camp Hooker.

It had become intolerably hot in the car, and the men were all in shirt-sleeves. The sun came in through the windows, a tired and ancient sun, yellow as parchment and stretched out of shape in transit. It tried to enter in triumphant squares and produced only warped splotches—but it was appallingly steady; so much so that it disturbed Anthony not to be the pivot of all the inconsequential sawmills and trees and telegraph-poles that were turning around him so fast. Outside it played its heavy tremolo over olive roads and fallow cotton-fields, back of which ran a ragged line of woods broken with eminences of gray rock. The foreground was dotted sparsely with wretched, ill-patched shanties, among which there would flash by, now and then, a specimen of the languid yokelry of South Carolina, or else a strolling darky with sullen and bewildered eyes.

Then the woods moved off and they rolled into a broad space like the baked top of a gigantic cake, sugared with an infinity of tents arranged in geometric figures over its surface. The train came to an uncertain stop, and the sun and the poles and the trees faded, and his universe rocked itself slowly back to its old usualness, with Anthony Patch in the centre. As the men, weary and perspiring, crowded out of the car, he smelt that unforgettable aroma that impregnates all permanent camps—the odor of garbage.

Camp Hooker was an astonishing and spectacular growth, suggesting "A Mining Town in 1870—The Second Week." It was a thing of wooden shacks and whitish-gray tents, connected by a pattern of roads, with hard tan drill-grounds fringed with trees. Here and there stood green Y.M.C.A. houses, unpromising oases, with their muggy odor of wet flannels and closed telephone-booths—and across from each of them there was usually a canteen, swarming with life, presided over indolently by an officer who, with the aid of a side-car, usually managed to make his detail a pleasant and chatty sinecure.

Up and down the dusty roads sped the soldiers of the quartermaster corps, also in side-cars. Up and down drove the generals in their government automobiles, stopping now and then to bring unalert details to attention, to frown heavily upon captains marching at the heads of companies, to set the pompous pace in that gorgeous game of showing off which was taking place triumphantly over the entire area.

The first week after the arrival of Anthony's draft was filled with a series of interminable inoculations and physical examinations, and with the preliminary drilling. The days left him desperately tired. He had been issued the wrong-size shoes by a popular, easy-going supply-sergeant, and in consequence his feet were so swollen that the last hours of the afternoon were an acute torture. For the first time in his life he could throw himself down on his cot between dinner and afternoon drill-call, and seeming to sink with each moment deeper into a bottomless bed, drop off immediately to sleep, while the noise and laughter around him faded to a pleasant drone of drowsy summer sound. In the morning he awoke stiff and aching, hollow as a ghost, and hurried forth to meet the other ghostly figures who swarmed in the wan company streets, while a harsh bugle shrieked and spluttered at the gray heavens.

He was in a skeleton infantry company of about a hundred men. After the invariable breakfast of fatty bacon, cold toast, and cereal, the entire hundred would rush for the latrines, which, however well policed, seemed always intolerable, like the lavatories in cheap hotels. Out on the field, then, in ragged order—the lame man on his left grotesquely marring Anthony's listless efforts to keep in step, the platoon sergeants either showing off violently to impress the officers and recruits, or else quietly lurking in close to the line of march, avoiding both labor and unnecessary visibility.

When they reached the field, work began immediately—they peeled off their shirts for calisthenics. This was the only part of the day that Anthony enjoyed. Lieutenant Kretching, who presided at the antics, was sinewy and muscular, and Anthony followed his movements faithfully, with a feeling that he was doing something of positive value to himself. The other officers and sergeants walked about among the men with the malice of schoolboys, grouping here and there around some unfortunate who lacked muscular control, giving him confused instructions and commands. When they discovered a particularly forlorn, ill-nourished specimen, they would linger the full half-hour making cutting remarks and snickering among themselves.

One little officer named Hopkins, who had been a sergeant in the regular army, was particularly annoying. He took the war as a gift of revenge from the high gods to himself, and the constant burden of his harangues was that these rookies did not appreciate the full gravity and responsibility of "the service." He considered that by a combination of foresight and dauntless efficiency he had raised himself to his current magnificence. He aped the particular tyrannies of every officer under whom he had served in times gone by. His frown was frozen on his brow—before giving a private a pass to go to town he would ponderously weigh the effect of such an absence upon the company, the army, and the welfare of the military profession the world over.

Lieutenant Kretching, blond, dull and phlegmatic, introduced Anthony ponderously to the problems of attention, right face, about face, and at ease. His principal defect was his forgetfulness. He often kept the company straining and aching at attention for five minutes while he stood out in front and explained a new movement—as a result only the men in the centre knew what it was all about—those on both flanks had been too emphatically impressed with the necessity of staring straight ahead.

The drill continued until noon. It consisted of stressing a succession of infinitely remote details, and though Anthony perceived that this was consistent with the logic of war, it none the less irritated him. That the same faulty blood-pressure which would have been indecent in an officer did not interfere with the duties of a private was a preposterous incongruity. Sometimes, after listening to a sustained invective concerned with a dull and, on the face of it, absurd subject known as military "courtesy," he suspected that the dim purpose of the war was to let the regular army officers—men with the mentality and aspirations of schoolboys—have their fling with some real slaughter. He was being grotesquely sacrificed to the twenty-year patience of a Hopkins!

Of his three tent-mates—a flat-faced, conscientious objector from Tennessee, a big, scared Pole, and the disdainful Celt whom he had sat beside on the train—the two former spent the evenings in writing eternal letters home, while the Irishman sat in the tent-door whistling over and over to himself half a dozen shrill and monotonous bird-calls. It was rather to avoid an hour of their company than with any hope of diversion that, when the quarantine was lifted at the end of the week, he went into town. He caught one of the swarm of jitneys that overran the camp each evening, and in half an hour was set down in front of the Stonewall Hotel on the hot and drowsy main street.

Under the gathering twilight the town was unexpectedly attractive. The sidewalks were peopled by vividly dressed, overpainted girls, who chattered volubly in low, lazy voices, by dozens of taxi-drivers who assailed passing officers with "Take y' anywheh, *Lieu*tenant," and by an intermittent procession of ragged, shuffling, subservient negroes. Anthony, loitering along through the warm dusk, felt for the first time in years the slow, erotic breath of the South, imminent in the hot softness of the air, in the pervasive lull of thought and time.

He had gone about a block when he was arrested suddenly by a harsh command at his elbow.

"Haven't you been taught to salute officers?"

He looked dumbly at the man who addressed him, a stout, black-haired captain, who fixed him menacingly with brown pop-eyes.

"*Come to attention!*" The words were literally thundered. A few pedestrians near by stopped and stared. A soft-eyed girl in a lilac dress tittered to her companion.

Anthony came to attention.

"What's your regiment and company?"

Anthony told him.

"After this when you pass an officer on the street you straighten up and salute!"

"All right!"

"Say 'Yes, sir!' "

"Yes, sir."

The stout officer grunted, turned sharply, and marched down the street. After a moment Anthony moved on; the town was no longer indolent and exotic; the magic was suddenly gone out of the dusk. His eyes were turned precipitately inward upon the indignity of his position. He hated that officer, every officer—life was unendurable.

After he had gone half a block he realized that the girl in the lilac dress who had giggled at his discomfiture was walking with her friend about ten paces ahead of him. Several times she had turned and stared at Anthony, with cheerful laughter in the large eyes that seemed the same color as her gown.

At the corner she and her companion visibly slackened their pace—he must make his choice between joining them and passing obliviously by. He passed, hesitated, then slowed down. In a moment the pair were abreast of him again, dissolved in laughter now—not such strident mirth as he would have expected in the North from actresses in this familiar comedy, but a soft, low rippling, like the overflow from some subtle joke, into which he had inadvertently blundered.

"How do you do?" he said.

Her eyes were soft as shadows. Were they violet, or was it their blue darkness mingling with the gray hues of dusk?

"Pleasant evening," ventured Anthony uncertainly.

"Sure is," said the second girl.

"Hasn't been a very pleasant evening for you," sighed the girl in lilac. Her voice seemed as much a part of the night as the drowsy breeze stirring the wide brim of her hat.

"He had to have a chance to show off," said Anthony with a scornful laugh.

"Reckon so," she agreed.

They turned the corner and moved lackadaisically up a side street, as if following a drifting cable to which they were attached. In this town it seemed entirely natural to turn corners like that, it seemed natural to be bound nowhere in particular, to be thinking nothing. . . . The side street was dark, a sudden offshoot into a district of wild-rose hedges and little quiet houses set far back from the street.

"Where're you going?" he inquired politely.

"Just goin'." The answer was an apology, a question, an explanation.

"Can I stroll along with you?"

"Reckon so."

It was an advantage that her accent was different. He could not have determined the social status of a Southerner from her talk—in New York a girl of a lower class would have been raucous, unendurable—except through the rosy spectacles of intoxication.

Dark was creeping down. Talking little—Anthony in careless, casual questions, the other two with provincial economy of phrase and burden—they sauntered past another corner, and another. In the middle of a block they stopped beneath a lamp-post.

"I live near here," explained the other girl.

"I live around the block," said the girl in lilac.

"Can I see you home?"

"To the corner, if you want to."

The other girl took a few steps backward. Anthony removed his hat.

"You're supposed to salute," said the girl in lilac with a laugh. "All the soldiers salute."

"I'll learn," he responded soberly.

The other girl said, "Well—" hesitated, then added, "call me up to-morrow, Dot," and retreated from the yellow circle of the street-lamp. Then, in silence, Anthony and the girl in lilac walked the three blocks to the small rickety house which was her home. Outside the wooden gate she hesitated.

"Well—thanks."

"Must you go in so soon?"

"I ought to."

"Can't you stroll around a little longer?"

She regarded him dispassionately.

"I don't even know you."

Anthony laughed.

"It's not too late."

"I reckon I better go in."

"I thought we might walk down and see a movie."

"I'd like to."

"Then I could bring you home. I'd have just enough time. I've got to be in camp by eleven."

It was so dark that he could scarcely see her now. She was a dress swayed infinitesimally by the wind, two limpid, reckless eyes . . .

"Why don't you come—Dot? Don't you like movies? Better come."

She shook her head.

"I oughtn't to."

He liked her, realizing that she was temporizing for the effect on him. He came closer and took her hand.

"If we get back by ten, can't you? Just to the movies?"

"Well—I reckon so——"

Hand in hand they walked back toward down-town, along a hazy, dusky street where a negro newsboy was calling an extra in the cadence of the local venders' tradition, a cadence that was as musical as song.

Dot

Anthony's affair with Dorothy Raycroft was an inevitable result of his increasing carelessness about himself. He did not go to her desiring to possess the desirable, nor did he fall before a personality more vital, more compelling than his own, as he had done with Gloria four years before. He merely slid into the matter through his inability to make definite judgments. He could say "No!" neither to man nor woman; borrower and temptress alike found him tender-minded and pliable. Indeed he seldom made decisions at all, and when he did they were but half-hysterical resolves formed in the panic of some aghast and irreparable awakening.

The particular weakness he indulged on this occasion was his need of excitement and stimulus from without. He felt that for the first time in four years he could express and interpret himself anew. The girl promised rest; the hours in her company each evening alleviated the morbid and inevitably futile poundings of his imagination. He had become a coward in earnest—completely the slave of a hundred disordered and prowling thoughts which were released by the collapse of the authentic devotion to Gloria that had been the chief jailer of his insufficiency.

On that first night, as they stood by the gate, he kissed Dorothy and made an engagement to meet her the following Saturday. Then he went out to camp, and with the light burning lawlessly in his tent, he wrote a long letter to Gloria, a glowing letter, full of the sentimental dark, full of the remembered breath of flowers, full of a true and exceeding tenderness—these things he had learned again for a moment in a kiss given and taken under a rich warm moonlight just an hour before.

When Saturday night came he found Dot waiting at the entrance of the Bijou Moving Picture Theatre. She was dressed as on the preceding Wednesday in her lilac gown of frailest organdy, but it had evidently been washed and starched since then, for it was fresh and unrumpled. Daylight confirmed the impression he had received that in a sketchy, faulty way she was lovely. She was clean, her features were small, irregular, but eloquent and appropriate to each other. She was a dark, unenduring little flower—yet he thought he detected in her some quality of spiritual reticence, of strength drawn from her passive acceptance of all things. In this he was mistaken.

Dorothy Raycroft was nineteen. Her father had kept a small, unprosperous corner store, and she had graduated from high school in the lowest fourth of her class two days before he died. At high school she had enjoyed a rather unsavory reputation. As a matter of fact her behavior at the class picnic, where the rumors started, had been merely indiscreet—she had retained her technical purity until over a year later. The boy had been a clerk in a store on Jackson Street, and on the day after the incident he departed unexpectedly to New York. He had been intending to leave for some time, but had tarried for the consummation of his amorous enterprise.

After a while she confided the adventure to a girl friend, and later, as she watched her friend disappear down the sleepy street of dusty sunshine, she knew in a flash of intuition that her story was going out into the world. Yet after telling it she felt much better, and a little bitter, and made as near an approach to character as she was capable of by walking in another direction and meeting another man with the honest intention of gratifying herself again. As a rule things happened to Dot. She was not weak, because there was nothing in her to tell her she was being weak. She was not strong, because she never knew that some of the things she did were brave. She neither defied nor conformed nor compromised.

She had no sense of humor, but, to take its place, a happy disposition that made her laugh at the proper times when she was with men. She had no definite intentions—sometimes she regretted vaguely that her reputation precluded what chance she had ever had for security. There had been no open discovery: her mother was interested only in starting her off on time each morning for the jewelry-store where she earned fourteen dollars a week. But some of the boys she had known in high school now looked the other way when they were walking with "nice girls," and these incidents hurt her feelings. When they occurred she went home and cried.

Besides the Jackson Street clerk there had been two other men, of whom the first was a naval officer, who passed through town during the early days of the war. He had stayed over a night to make a connection, and was leaning idly against one of the pillars of the Stonewall Hotel when she passed by. He remained in town four days. She thought she loved him—lavished on him that first hysteria of passion that would have gone to the pusillanimous clerk. The naval officer's uniform—there were few of them in those days—had made the magic. He left with vague promises on his lips, and, once on the train, rejoiced that he had not told her his real name.

Her resultant depression had thrown her into the arms of Cyrus Fielding, the son of a local clothier, who had hailed her from his roadster one day as she passed along the sidewalk. She had always known him by name. Had she been born to a higher stratum he would have known her before. She had descended a little lower—so he met her after all. After a month he had gone away to training-camp, a little afraid of the intimacy, a little relieved in perceiving that she had not cared deeply for him, and that she was not the sort who would ever make trouble. Dot romanticized this affair and conceded to her vanity that the war had taken these men away from her. She told herself that she could have married the naval officer. Nevertheless, it worried her that within eight months there had been three men in her life. She thought with more fear than wonder in her heart that she would soon be like those "bad girls" on Jackson Street at whom she and her gum-chewing, giggling friends had stared with fascinated glances three years before.

For a while she attempted to be more careful. She let men "pick her up"; she let them kiss her, and even allowed certain other liberties to be forced upon her, but she did not add to her trio. After several months the strength of her resolution—or rather the poignant expediency of her fears—was worn away. She grew restless drowsing there out of life and time while the summer months faded. The soldiers she met were either obviously below her or, less obviously, above her—in which case they desired only to use her; they were Yankees, harsh and ungracious; they swarmed in large crowds. . . . And then she met Anthony.

On that first evening he had been little more than a pleasantly unhappy face, a voice, the means with which to pass an hour, but when she kept her engagement with him on Saturday she regarded him with consideration. She liked him. Unknowingly she saw her own tragedies mirrored in his face.

Again they went to the movies, again they wandered along the shadowy, scented streets, hand in hand this time, speaking a little in hushed voices. They passed through the gate—up toward the little porch——

"I can stay a while, can't I?"

"Sh!" she whispered, "we've got to be very quiet. Mother sits up reading Snappy Stories." In confirmation he heard the faint crackling inside as a page was turned. The open-shutter slits emitted horizontal rods of light that fell in thin parallels across Dorothy's skirt. The street was silent save for a group on the steps of a house across the way, who, from time to time, raised their voices in a soft, bantering song.

"—*When you wa-ake*
You shall ha-ave
All the pretty little hawsiz——"

Then, as though it had been waiting on a near-by roof for their arrival, the moon came slanting suddenly through the vines and turned the girl's face to the color of white roses.

Anthony had a start of memory, so vivid that before his closed eyes there formed a picture, distinct as a flashback on a screen—a spring night of thaw set out of time in a half-forgotten winter five years before—another face, radiant, flower-like, upturned to lights as transforming as the stars——

Ah, *la belle dame sans merci* who lived in his heart, made known to him in transitory fading splendor by dark eyes in the Ritz-Carlton, by a shadowy glance from a passing carriage in the Bois de Boulogne! But those nights were only part of a song, a remembered glory—here again were the faint winds, the illusions, the eternal present with its promise of romance.

"Oh," she whispered, "do you love me? Do you love me?"

The spell was broken—the drifted fragments of the stars became only light, the singing down the street diminished to a monotone, to the whimper of locusts in the grass. With almost a sigh he kissed her fervent mouth, while her arms crept up about his shoulders.

The Man-at-Arms

As the weeks dried up and blew away, the range of Anthony's travels extended until he grew to comprehend the camp and its environment. For the first time in his life he was in constant personal contact with the waiters to whom he had given tips, the chauffeurs who had touched their hats to him, the carpenters, plumbers, barbers, and farmers who had previously been remarkable only in the subservience of their professional genuflections. During his first two months in camp he did not hold ten minutes' consecutive conversation with a single man.

On the service record his occupation stood as "student"; on the original questionnaire he had prematurely written "author"; but when men in his company asked his business he commonly gave it as bank clerk—had he told the truth, that he did no work, they would have been suspicious of him as a member of the leisure class.

His platoon sergeant, Pop Donnelly, was a scraggly "old soldier," worn thin with drink. In the past he had spent unnumbered weeks in the guard-house, but recently, thanks to the drill-master famine, he had been elevated to his present pinnacle. His complexion was full of shell-holes—it bore an unmistakable resemblance to those aerial photographs of "the battle-field at Blank." Once a week he got drunk down-town on white liquor, returned quietly to camp and collapsed upon his bunk, joining the company at reveille looking more than ever like a white mask of death.

He nursed the astounding delusion that he was astutely "slipping it over" on the government—he had spent eighteen years in its service at a minute wage, and he was soon to retire (here he usually winked) on the impressive income of fifty-five dollars a month. He looked upon it as a gorgeous joke that he had played upon the dozens who had bullied and scorned him since he was a Georgia country boy of nineteen.

At present there were but two lieutenants—Hopkins and the popular Kretching. The latter was considered a good fellow and a fine leader, until a year later, when he disappeared with a mess fund of eleven hundred dollars and, like so many leaders, proved exceedingly difficult to follow.

Eventually there was Captain Dunning, god of this brief but self-sufficing microcosm. He was a reserve officer, nervous, energetic, and enthusiastic. This latter quality, indeed, often took material form and was visible as fine froth in the corners of his mouth. Like most executives he saw his charges strictly from the front, and to his hopeful eyes his command seemed just such an excellent unit as such an excellent war deserved. For all his anxiety and absorption he was having the time of his life.

Baptiste, the little Sicilian of the train, fell foul of him the second week of drill. The captain had several times ordered the men to be clean-shaven when they fell in each morning. One day there was disclosed an alarming breech of this rule, surely a case of Teutonic connivance—during the night four men had grown hair upon their faces. The fact that three of the four understood a minimum of English made a practical object-lesson only the more necessary, so Captain Dunning resolutely sent a volunteer barber back to the company street for a razor. Whereupon for the safety of democracy a half-ounce of hair was scraped dry from the cheeks of three Italians and one Pole.

Outside the world of the company there appeared, from time to time, the colonel, a heavy man with snarling teeth, who circumnavigated the battalion drill-field upon a handsome black horse. He was a West Pointer, and, mimetically, a gentleman. He had a dowdy wife and a dowdy mind, and spent much of his time in town taking advantage of the army's lately exalted social position. Last of all was the general, who traversed the roads of the camp preceded by his flag—a figure so austere, so removed, so magnificent, as to be scarcely comprehensible.

December. Cool winds at night now, and damp, chilly mornings on the drill-grounds. As the heat faded, Anthony found himself increasingly glad to be alive. Renewed strangely through his body, he worried little and existed in the present with a sort of animal content. It was not that Gloria or the life that Gloria represented was less often in his thoughts—it was simply that she became, day by day, less real, less vivid. For a week they had corresponded passionately, almost hysterically—then by an unwritten agreement they had ceased to write more than twice, and then once, a week. She was bored, she said; if his brigade was to be there a long time she was coming down to join him. Mr. Haight was going to be able to submit a stronger brief than he had expected, but doubted that the appealed case would come up until late spring. Muriel was in the city doing Red Cross work, and they went out together rather often. What would Anthony think if *she* went into the Red Cross? Trouble was she had heard that she might have to bathe negroes in alcohol, and after that she hadn't felt so patriotic. The city was full of soldiers and she'd seen a lot of boys she hadn't laid eyes on for years. . . .

Anthony did not want her to come South. He told himself that this was for many reasons—he needed a rest from her and she from him. She would be bored beyond measure in town, and she would be able to see Anthony for only a few hours each day. But in his heart he feared that it was because he was attracted to Dorothy. As a matter of fact he lived in terror that Gloria should learn by some chance or intention of the relation he had formed. By the end of a fortnight the entanglement began to give him moments of misery at his own faithlessness. Nevertheless, as each day ended he was unable to withstand the lure that would draw him irresistibly out of his tent and over to the telephone at the Y.M.C.A.

"Dot."

"Yes?"

"I may be able to get in to-night."

"I'm so glad."

"Do you want to listen to my splendid eloquence for a few starry hours?"

"Oh, you funny—" For an instant he had a memory of five years before—of Geraldine. Then——

"I'll arrive about eight."

At seven he would be in a jitney bound for the city, where hundreds of little Southern girls were waiting on moonlit porches for their lovers. He would be excited already for her warm retarded kisses, for the amazed quietude of the glances she gave him—glances nearer to worship than any he had ever inspired. Gloria and he had been equals, giving without thought of thanks or obligation. To this girl his very caresses were an inestimable boon. Crying quietly she had confessed to him that he was not the first man in her life; there had been one other—he gathered that the affair had no sooner commenced than it had been over.

Indeed, so far as she was concerned, she spoke the truth. She had forgotten the clerk, the naval officer, the clothier's son, forgotten her vividness of emotion, which is true forgetting. She knew that in some opaque and shadowy existence some one had taken her—it was as though it had occurred in sleep.

Almost every night Anthony came to town. It was too cool now for the porch, so her mother surrendered to them the tiny sitting-room, with its dozens of cheaply framed chromos, its yard upon yard of decorative fringe, and its thick atmosphere of several decades in the proximity of the kitchen. They would build a fire—then, happily, inexhaustibly, she would go about the business of love. Each evening at ten she would walk with him to the door, her black hair in disarray, her face pale without cosmetics, paler still under the whiteness of the moon. As a rule it would be bright and silver outside; now and then there was a slow warm rain, too indolent, almost, to reach the ground.

"Say you love me," she would whisper.

"Why, of course, you sweet baby."

"Am I a baby?" This almost wistfully.

"Just a little baby."

She knew vaguely of Gloria. It gave her pain to think of it, so she imagined her to be haughty and proud and cold. She had decided that Gloria must be older than Anthony, and that there was no love between husband and wife. Sometimes she let herself dream that after the war Anthony would get a divorce and they would be married—but she never mentioned this to Anthony, she scarcely knew why. She shared his company's idea that he was a sort of bank clerk—she thought that he was respectable and poor. She would say:

"If I had some money, darlin', I'd give ev'y bit of it to you. . . . I'd like to have about fifty thousand dollars."

"I suppose that'd be plenty," agreed Anthony.

—In her letter that day Gloria had written: "I suppose if we *could* settle for a million it would be better to tell Mr. Haight to go ahead and settle. But it'd seem a pity. . . ."

. . . "We could have an automobile," exclaimed Dot, in a final burst of triumph.

An Impressive Occasion

Captain Dunning prided himself on being a great reader of character. Half an hour after meeting a man he was accustomed to place him in one of a number of astonishing categories—fine man, good man, smart fellow, theorizer, poet, and "worthless." One day early in February he caused Anthony to be summoned to his presence in the orderly tent.

"Patch," he said sententiously, "I've had my eye on you for several weeks."

Anthony stood erect and motionless.

"And I think you've got the makings of a good soldier."

He waited for the warm glow, which this would naturally arouse, to cool—and then continued:

"This is no child's play," he said, narrowing his brows.

Anthony agreed with a melancholy "No, sir."

"It's a man's game—and we need leaders." Then the climax, swift, sure, and electric: "Patch, I'm going to make you a corporal."

At this point Anthony should have staggered slightly backward, overwhelmed. He was to be one of the quarter million selected for that consummate trust. He was going to be able to shout the technical phrase, "Follow me!" to seven other frightened men.

"You seem to be a man of some education," said Captain Dunning.

"Yes, sir."

"That's good, that's good. Education's a great thing, but don't let it go to your head. Keep on the way you're doing and you'll be a good soldier."

With these parting words lingering in his ears, Corporal Patch saluted, executed a right about face, and left the tent.

Though the conversation amused Anthony, it did generate the idea that life would be more amusing as a sergeant or, should he find a less-exacting medical examiner, as an officer. He was little interested in the work, which seemed to belie the army's boasted gallantry. At the inspections one did not dress up to look well, one dressed up to keep from looking badly.

But as winter wore away—the short, snowless winter marked by damp nights and cool, rainy days—he marvelled at how quickly the system had grasped him. He was a soldier—all who were not soldiers were civilians. The world was divided primarily into those two classifications.

It occurred to him that all strongly accentuated classes, such as the military, divided men into two kinds: their own kind—and those without. To the clergyman there were clergy and laity, to the Catholic there were Catholics and non-Catholics, to the negro there were blacks and whites, to the prisoner there were the imprisoned and the free, and to the sick man there were the sick and the well. . . . So, without thinking of it once in his lifetime, he had been a civilian, a layman, a non-Catholic, a Gentile, white, free, and well. . . .

As the American troops were poured into the French and British trenches he began to find the names of many Harvard men among the casualties recorded in the Army and Navy Journal. But for all the sweat and blood the situation appeared unchanged, and he saw no prospect of the war's ending in the perceptible future. In the old chronicles the right wing of one army always defeated the left wing of the other, the left wing being, meanwhile, vanquished by the enemy's right. After that the mercenaries fled. It had been so simple, in those days, almost as if prearranged. . . .

Gloria wrote that she was reading a great deal. What a mess they had made of their affairs, she said. She had so little to do now that she spent her time imagining how differently things might have turned out. Her whole environment appeared insecure—and a few years back she had seemed to hold all the strings in her own little hand. . . .

In June her letters grew hurried and less frequent. She suddenly ceased to write about coming South.

Defeat

March in the country around was rare with jasmine and jonquils and patches of violets in the warming grass. Afterward he remembered especially one afternoon of such a fresh and magic glamour that as he stood in the rifle-pit marking targets he recited "Atalanta in Calydon" to an uncomprehending Pole, his voice mingling with the rip, sing, and splatter of the bullets overhead.

"When the hounds of spring . . ."

Spang!

"Are on winter's traces . . ."

Whirr-r-r-r! . . .

"The mother of months . . ."

"*Hey!* Come to! Mark three-e-e! . . ."

In town the streets were in a sleepy dream again, and together Anthony and Dot idled in their own tracks of the previous autumn until he began to feel a drowsy attachment for this South—a South, it seemed, more of Algiers than of Italy, with faded aspirations pointing back over innumerable generations to some warm, primitive Nirvana, without hope or care. Here there was an inflection of cordiality, of comprehension, in every voice. "Life plays the same lovely and agonizing joke on all of us," they seemed to say in their plaintive pleasant cadence, in the rising inflection terminating on an unresolved minor.

He liked his barber-shop, where he was "Hi, corporal!" to a pale, emaciated young man, who shaved him and pushed a cool vibrating machine endlessly over his insatiable head. He liked "Johnston's Gardens" where they danced, where a tragic negro made yearning, aching music on a saxophone until the garish hall became an enchanted jungle of barbaric rhythms and smoky laughter, where to forget the uneventful passage of time upon Dorothy's soft sighs and tender whisperings was the consummation of all aspiration, of all content.

There was an undertone of sadness in her character, a conscious evasion of all except the pleasurable minutiæ of life. Her violet eyes would remain for hours apparently insensate as, thoughtless and reckless, she basked like a cat in the sun. He wondered what the tired, spiritless mother thought of them, and whether in her moments of uttermost cynicism she ever guessed at their relationship.

On Sunday afternoons they walked along the countryside, resting at intervals on the dry moss in the out-skirts of a wood. Here the birds had gathered and the clusters of violets and white dogwood; here the hoar trees shone crystalline and cool, oblivious to the intoxicating heat that waited outside; here he would talk, intermittently, in a sleepy monologue, in a conversation of no significance, of no replies.

July came scorching down. Captain Dunning was ordered to detail one of his men to learn blacksmithing. The regiment was filling up to war strength, and he needed most of his veterans for drill-masters, so he selected the little Italian, Baptiste, whom he could most easily spare. Little Baptiste had never had anything to do with horses. His fear made matters worse. He reappeared in the orderly room one day and told Captain Dunning that he wanted to die if he couldn't be relieved. The horses kicked at him, he said; he was no good at the work. Finally he fell on his knees and besought Captain Dunning, in a mixture of broken English and scriptural Italian, to get him out of it. He had not slept for three days; monstrous stallions reared and cavorted through his dreams.

Captain Dunning reproved the company clerk (who had burst out laughing), and told Baptiste he would do what he could. But when he thought it over he decided that he couldn't spare a better man. Little Baptiste went from bad to worse. The horses seemed to divine his fear and take every advantage of it. Two weeks later a great black mare crushed his skull in with her hoofs while he was trying to lead her from her stall.

In mid-July came rumors, and then orders, that concerned a change of camp. The brigade was to move to an empty cantonment, a hundred miles farther south, there to be expanded into a division. At first the men thought they were departing for the trenches, and all evening little groups jabbered in the company street, shouting to each other in swaggering exclamations: "Su-u-ure we are!" When the truth leaked out, it was rejected indignantly as a blind to conceal their real destination. They revelled in their own importance. That night they told their girls in town that they were "going to get the Germans." Anthony circulated for a while among the groups—then, stopping a jitney, rode down to tell Dot that he was going away.

She was waiting on the dark veranda in a cheap white dress that accentuated the youth and softness of her face.

"Oh," she whispered, "I've wanted you so, honey. All this day."

"I have something to tell you."

She drew him down beside her on the swinging seat, not noticing his ominous tone.

"Tell me."

"We're leaving next week."

Her arms seeking his shoulders remained poised upon the dark air, her chin tipped up. When she spoke the softness was gone from her voice.

"Leaving for France?"

"No. Less luck than that. Leaving for some darn camp in Mississippi."

She shut her eyes and he could see that the lids were trembling.

"Dear little Dot, life is so damned hard."

She was crying upon his shoulder.

"So damned hard, so damned hard," he repeated aimlessly; "it just hurts people and hurts people, until finally it hurts them so that they can't be hurt ever any more. That's the last and worst thing it does."

Frantic, wild with anguish, she strained him to her breast.

"Oh, God!" she whispered brokenly, "you can't go way from me. I'd die."

He was finding it impossible to pass off his departure as a common, impersonal blow. He was too near to her to do more than repeat "Poor little Dot. Poor little Dot."

"And then what?" she demanded wearily.

"What do you mean?"

"You're my whole life, that's all. I'd die for you right now if you said so. I'd get a knife and kill myself. You can't leave me here."

Her tone frightened him.

"These things happen," he said evenly.

"Then I'm going with you." Tears were streaming down her cheeks. Her mouth was trembling in an ecstasy of grief and fear.

"Sweet," he muttered sentimentally, "sweet little girl. Don't you see we'd just be putting off what's bound to happen? I'll be going to France in a few months——"

She leaned away from him and clinching her fists lifted her face toward the sky.

"I want to die," she said, as if moulding each word carefully in her heart.

"Dot," he whispered uncomfortably, "you'll forget. Things are sweeter when they're lost. I know—because once I wanted something and got it. It was the only thing I ever wanted badly, Dot. And when I got it it turned to dust in my hands."

"All right."

Absorbed in himself, he continued:

"I've often thought that if I hadn't got what I wanted things might have been different with me. I might have found something in my mind and enjoyed putting it in circulation. I might have been content with the work of it, and had some sweet vanity out of the success. I suppose that at one time I could have had anything I wanted, within reason, but that was the only thing I ever wanted with any fervor. God! And that taught me you can't have *any*thing, you can't have anything at *all*. Because desire just cheats you. It's like a sunbeam skipping here and there about a room. It stops and gilds some inconsequential object, and we poor fools try to grasp it—but when we do the sunbeam moves on to something else, and you've got the inconsequential part, but the glitter that made you want it is gone—" He broke off uneasily. She had risen and was standing, dry-eyed, picking little leaves from a dark vine.

"Dot——"

"Go way," she said coldly.

"What? Why?"

"I don't want just words. If that's all you have for me you'd better go."

"Why, Dot——"

"What's death to me is just a lot of words to you. You put 'em together so pretty."

"I'm sorry. I was talking about you, Dot."

"Go way from here."

He approached her with arms outstretched, but she held him away.

"You don't want me to go with you," she said evenly; "maybe you're going to meet that—that girl—" She could not bring herself to say wife. "How do I know? Well, then, I reckon you're not my fellow any more. So go way."

For a moment, while conflicting warnings and desires prompted Anthony, it seemed one of those rare times when he would take a step prompted from within. He hesitated. Then a wave of weariness broke against him. It was too late—everything was too late. For years now he had dreamed the world away, basing his decisions upon emotions unstable as water. The little girl in the white dress dominated him, as she approached beauty in the hard symmetry of her desire. The fire blazing in her dark and injured heart seemed to glow around her like a flame. With some profound and uncharted pride she had made herself remote and so achieved her purpose.

"I didn't—mean to seem so callous, Dot."

"It don't matter."

The fire rolled over Anthony. Something wrenched at his bowels, and he stood there helpless and beaten.

"Come with me, Dot—little loving Dot. Oh, come with me. I couldn't leave you now——"

With a sob she wound her arms around him and let him support her weight while the moon, at its perennial labor of covering the bad complexion of the world, showered its illicit honey over the drowsy street.

The Catastrophe

Early September in Camp Boone, Mississippi. The darkness, alive with insects, beat in upon the mosquito-netting, beneath the shelter of which Anthony was trying to write a letter. An intermittent chatter over a poker game was going on in the next tent, and outside a man was strolling up the company street singing a current bit of doggerel about "K-K-K-Katy."

With an effort Anthony hoisted himself to his elbow and, pencil in hand, looked down at his blank sheet of paper. Then, omitting any heading, he began:

I can't imagine what the matter is, Gloria. I haven't had a line from you for two weeks and it's only natural to be worried——

He threw this away with a disturbed grunt and began again:

I don't know what to think, Gloria. Your last letter, short, cold, without a word of affection or even a decent account of what you've been doing, came two weeks ago. It's only natural that I should wonder. If your love for me isn't absolutely dead it seems that you'd at least keep me from worry——

Again he crumpled the page and tossed it angrily through a tear in the tent wall, realizing simultaneously that he would have to pick it up in the morning. He felt disinclined to try again. He could get no warmth into the lines—only a persistent jealousy and suspicion. Since midsummer these discrepancies in Gloria's correspondence had grown more and more noticeable. At first he had scarcely perceived them. He was so inured to the perfunctory "dearest" and "darlings" scattered through her letters that he was oblivious to their presence or absence. But in this last fortnight he had become increasingly aware that there was something amiss.

He had sent her a night-letter saying that he had passed his examinations for an officers' training-camp, and expected to leave for Georgia shortly. She had not answered. He had wired again—when he received no word he imagined that she might be out of town. But it occurred and recurred to him that she was not out of town, and a series of distraught imaginings began to plague him. Supposing Gloria, bored and restless, had found some one, even as he had. The thought terrified him with its possibility—it was chiefly because he had been so sure of her personal integrity that he had considered her so sparingly during the year. And now, as a doubt was born, the old angers, the rages of possession, swarmed back a thousandfold. What more natural than that she should be in love again?

He remembered the Gloria who promised that should she ever want anything, she would take it, insisting that since she would act entirely for her own satisfaction she could go through such an affair unsmirched—it was only the effect on a person's mind that counted, anyhow, she said, and her reaction would be the masculine one, of satiation and faint dislike.

But that had been when they were first married. Later, with the discovery that she could be jealous of Anthony, she had, outwardly at least, changed her mind. There were no other men in the world for her. This he had known only too surely. Perceiving that a certain fastidiousness would restrain her, he had grown lax in preserving the completeness of her love—which, after all, was the keystone of the entire structure.

Meanwhile all through the summer he had been maintaining Dot in a boarding-house down-town. To do this it had been necessary to write to his broker for money. Dot had covered her journey south by leaving her house a day before the brigade broke camp, informing her mother in a note that she had gone to New York. On the evening following Anthony had called as though to see her. Mrs. Raycroft was in a state of collapse and there was a policeman in the parlor. A questionnaire had ensued, from which Anthony had extricated himself with some difficulty.

In September, with his suspicions of Gloria, the company of Dot had become tedious, then almost intolerable. He was nervous and irritable from lack of sleep; his heart was sick and afraid. Three days ago he had gone to Captain Dunning and asked for a furlough, only to be met with benignant procrastination. The division was starting overseas, while Anthony was going to an officers' training-camp; what furloughs could be given must go to the men who were leaving the country.

Upon this refusal Anthony had started to the telegraph office intending to wire Gloria to come South—he reached the door and receded despairingly, seeing the utter impracticability of such a move. Then he had spent the evening quarrelling irritably with Dot, and returned to camp morose and angry with the world. There had been a disagreeable scene, in the midst of which he had precipitately departed. What was to be done with her did not seem to concern him vitally at present—he was completely absorbed in the disheartening silence of his wife. . . .

The flap of the tent made a sudden triangle back upon itself, and a dark head appeared against the night.

"Sergeant Patch?" The accent was Italian, and Anthony saw by the belt that the man was a headquarters orderly.

"Want me?"

"Lady call up headquarters ten minutes ago. Say she have speak with you. Ver' important."

Anthony swept aside the mosquito-netting and stood up. It might be a wire from Gloria telephoned over.

"She say to get you. She call again ten o'clock."

"All right, thanks." He picked up his hat and in a moment was striding beside the orderly through the hot, almost suffocating, darkness. Over in the headquarters shack he saluted a dozing night-service officer.

"Sit down and wait," suggested the lieutenant nonchalantly. "Girl seemed awful anxious to speak to you."

Anthony's hopes fell away.

"Thank you very much, sir." And as the phone squeaked on the side-wall he knew who was calling.

"This is Dot," came an unsteady voice, "I've got to see you."

"Dot, I told you I couldn't get down for several days."

"I've got to see you to-night. It's important."

"It's too late," he said coldly; "it's ten o'clock, and I have to be in camp at eleven."

"All right." There was so much wretchedness compressed into the two words that Anthony felt a measure of compunction.

"What's the matter?"

"I want to tell you good-by."

"Oh, don't be a little idiot!" he exclaimed. But his spirits rose. What luck if she should leave town this very night! What a burden from his soul. But he said: "You can't possibly leave before to-morrow."

Out of the corner of his eye he saw the night-service officer regarding him quizzically. Then, startlingly, came Dot's next words:

"I don't mean 'leave' that way."

Anthony's hand clutched the receiver fiercely. He felt his nerves turning cold as if the heat was leaving his body.

"What?"

Then quickly in a wild broken voice he heard:

"Good-by—oh, good-by!"

Cul-*lup!* She had hung up the receiver. With a sound that was half a gasp, half a cry, Anthony hurried from the headquarters building. Outside, under the stars that dripped like silver tassels through the trees of the little grove, he stood motionless, hesitating. Had she meant to kill herself?—oh, the little fool! He was filled with bitter hate toward her. In this dénouement he found it impossible to realize that he had ever begun such an entanglement, such a mess, a sordid mélange of worry and pain.

He found himself walking slowly away, repeating over and over that it was futile to worry. He had best go back to his tent and sleep. He needed sleep. God! Would he ever sleep again? His mind was in a vast clamor and confusion; as he reached the road he turned around in a panic and began running, not toward his company but away from it. Men were returning now—he could find a taxicab. After a minute two yellow eyes appeared around a bend. Desperately he ran toward them.

"Jitney! Jitney!" . . . It was an empty Ford. . . . "I want to go to town."

"Cost you a dollar."

"All right. If you'll just hurry——"

After an interminable time he ran up the steps of a dark ramshackle little house, and through the door, almost knocking over an immense negress who was walking, candle in hand, along the hall.

"Where's my wife?" he cried wildly.

"She gone to bed."

Up the stairs three at a time, down the creaking passage. The room was dark and silent, and with trembling fingers he struck a match. Two wide eyes looked up at him from a wretched ball of clothes on the bed.

"Ah, I knew you'd come," she murmured brokenly.

Anthony grew cold with anger.

"So it was just a plan to get me down here, get me in trouble!" he said. "God damn it, you've shouted 'wolf' once too often!"

She regarded him pitifully.

"I had to see you. I couldn't have lived. Oh, I had to see you——"

He sat down on the side of the bed and slowly shook his head.

"You're no good," he said decisively, talking unconsciously as Gloria might have talked to him. "This sort of thing isn't fair to me, you know."

"Come closer." Whatever he might say Dot was happy now. He cared for her. She had brought him to her side.

"Oh, God," said Anthony hopelessly. As weariness rolled along its inevitable wave his anger subsided, receded, vanished. He collapsed suddenly, fell sobbing beside her on the bed.

"Oh, my darling," she begged him, "don't cry! Oh, don't cry!"

She took his head upon her breast and soothed him, mingled her happy tears with the bitterness of his. Her hand played gently with his dark hair.

"I'm such a little fool," she murmured brokenly, "but I love you, and when you're cold to me it seems as if it isn't worth while to go on livin'."

After all, this was peace—the quiet room with the mingled scent of women's powder and perfume, Dot's hand soft as a warm wind upon his hair, the rise and fall of her bosom as she took breath—for a moment it was as though it were Gloria there, as though he were at rest in some sweeter and safer home than he had ever known.

An hour passed. A clock began to chime in the hall. He jumped to his feet and looked at the phosphorescent hands of his wrist-watch. It was twelve o'clock.

He had trouble in finding a taxi that would take him out at that hour. As he urged the driver faster along the road he speculated on the best method of entering camp. He had been late several times recently, and he knew that were he caught again his name would probably be stricken from the list of officer candidates. He wondered if he had not better dismiss the taxi and take a chance on passing the sentry in the dark. Still, officers often rode past the sentries after midnight. . . .

"Halt!" The monosyllable came from the yellow glare that the headlights dropped upon the changing road. The taxi-driver threw out his clutch and a sentry walked up, carrying his rifle at the port. With him, by an ill chance, was the officer of the guard.

"Out late, sergeant."

"Yes, sir. Got delayed."

"Too bad. Have to take your name."

As the officer waited, note-book and pencil in hand, something not fully intended crowded to Anthony's lips, something born of panic, of muddle, of despair.

"Sergeant R. A. Foley," he answered breathlessly.

"And the outfit?"

"Company Q, Eighty-third Infantry."

"All right. You'll have to walk from here, sergeant."

Anthony saluted, quickly paid his taxi-driver, and set off for a run toward the regiment he had named. When he was out of sight he changed his course, and with his heart beating wildly, hurried to his company, feeling that he had made a fatal error of judgment.

Two days later the officer who had been in command of the guard recognized him in a barber-shop down-town. In charge of a military policeman he was taken back to the camp, where he was reduced to the ranks without trial, and confined for a month to the limits of his company street.

With this blow a spell of utter depression overtook him, and within a week he was again caught down-town, wandering around in a drunken daze, with a pint of bootleg whiskey in his hip pocket. It was because of a sort of craziness in his behavior at the trial that his sentence to the guard-house was for only three weeks.

Nightmare

Early in his confinement the conviction took root in him that he was going mad. It was as though there were a quantity of dark yet vivid personalities in his mind, some of them familiar, some of them strange and terrible, held in check by a little monitor, who sat aloft somewhere and looked on. The thing that worried him was that the monitor was sick, and holding out with difficulty. Should he give up, should he falter for a moment, out would rush these intolerable things—only Anthony could know what a state of blackness there would be if the worst of him could roam his consciousness unchecked.

The heat of the day had changed, somehow, until it was a burnished darkness crushing down upon a devastated land. Over his head the blue circles of ominous uncharted suns, of unnumbered centres of fire, revolved interminably before his eyes as though he were lying constantly exposed to the hot light and in a state of feverish coma. At seven in the morning something phantasmal, something almost absurdly unreal that he knew was his mortal body, went out with seven other prisoners and two guards to work on the camp roads. One day they loaded and unloaded quantities of gravel, spread it, raked it—the next day they worked with huge barrels of red-hot tar, flooding the gravel with black, shining pools of molten heat. At night, locked up in the guard-house, he would lie without thought, without courage to compass thought, staring at the irregular beams of the ceiling overhead until about three o'clock, when he would slip into a broken, troubled sleep.

During the work hours he labored with uneasy haste, attempting, as the day bore toward the sultry Mississippi sunset, to tire himself physically so that in the evening he might sleep deeply from utter exhaustion. . . . Then one afternoon in the second week he had a feeling that two eyes were watching him from a place a few feet beyond one of the guards. This aroused him to a sort of terror. He turned his back on the eyes and shovelled feverishly, until it became necessary for him to face about and go for more gravel. Then they entered his vision again, and his already taut nerves tightened up to the breaking-point. The eyes were leering at him. Out of a hot silence he heard his name called in a tragic voice, and the earth tipped absurdly back and forth to a babel of shouting and confusion.

When next he became conscious he was back in the guard-house, and the other prisoners were throwing him curious glances. The eyes returned no more. It was many days before he realized that the voice must have been Dot's, that she had called out to him and made some sort of disturbance. He decided this just previous to the expiration of his sentence, when the cloud that oppressed him had lifted, leaving him in a deep, dispirited lethargy. As the conscious mediator, the monitor who kept that fearsome ménage of horror, grew stronger, Anthony became physically weaker. He was scarcely able to get through the two days of toil, and when he was released, one rainy afternoon, and returned to his company, he reached his tent only to fall into a heavy doze, from which he awoke before dawn, aching and unrefreshed. Beside his cot were two letters that had been awaiting him in the orderly tent for some time. The first was from Gloria; it was short and cool:

The case is coming to trial late in November. Can you possibly get leave?

I've tried to write you again and again but it just seems to make things worse. I want to see you about several matters, but you know that you have once prevented me from coming and I am disinclined to try again. In view of a number of things it seems necessary that we have a conference. I'm very glad about your appointment.

GLORIA.

He was too tired to try to understand—or to care. Her phrases, her intentions, were all very far away in an incomprehensible past. At the second letter he scarcely glanced; it was from Dot—an incoherent, tear-swollen scrawl, a flood of protest, endearment, and grief. After a page he let it slip from his inert hand and drowsed back into a nebulous hinterland of his own. At drill-call he awoke with a high fever and fainted when he tried to leave his tent—at noon he was sent to the base hospital with influenza.

He was aware that this sickness was providential. It saved him from a hysterical relapse—and he recovered in time to entrain on a damp November day for New York, and for the interminable massacre beyond.

When the regiment reached Camp Mills, Long Island, Anthony's single idea was to get into the city and see Gloria as soon as possible. It was now evident that an armistice would be signed within the week, but rumor had it that in any case troops would continue to be shipped to France until the last moment. Anthony was appalled at the notion of the long voyage, of a tedious debarkation at a French port, and of being kept abroad for a year, possibly, to replace the troops who had seen actual fighting.

His intention had been to obtain a two-day furlough, but Camp Mills proved to be under a strict influenza quarantine—it was impossible for even an officer to leave except on official business. For a private it was out of the question.

The camp itself was a dreary muddle, cold, wind-swept, and filthy, with the accumulated dirt incident to the passage through of many divisions. Their train came in at seven one night, and they waited in line until one while a military tangle was straightened out somewhere ahead. Officers ran up and down ceaselessly, calling orders and making a great uproar. It turned out that the trouble was due to the colonel, who was in a righteous temper because he was a West Pointer, and the war was going to stop before he could get overseas. Had the militant governments realized the number of broken hearts among the older West Pointers during that week, they would indubitably have prolonged the slaughter another month. The thing was pitiable!

Gazing out at the bleak expanse of tents extending for miles over a trodden welter of slush and snow, Anthony saw the impracticability of trudging to a telephone that night. He would call her at the first opportunity in the morning.

Aroused in the chill and bitter dawn he stood at reveille and listened to a passionate harangue from Captain Dunning:

"You men may think the war is over. Well, let me tell you, it isn't! Those fellows aren't going to sign the armistice. It's another trick, and we'd be crazy to let anything slacken up here in the company, because, let me tell you, we're going to sail from here within a week, and when we do we're going to see some real fighting." He paused that they might get the full effect of his pronouncement. And then: "If you think the war's over, just talk to any one who's been in it and see if *they* think the Germans are all in. They don't. Nobody does. I've talked to the people that *know*, and they say there'll be, anyways, a year longer of war. *They* don't think it's over. So you men better not get any foolish ideas that it is."

Doubly stressing this final admonition, he ordered the company dismissed.

At noon Anthony set off at a run for the nearest canteen telephone. As he approached what corresponded to the down-town of the camp, he noticed that many other soldiers were running also, that a man near him had suddenly leaped into the air and clicked his heels together. The tendency to run became general, and from little excited groups here and there came the sounds of cheering. He stopped and listened—over the cold country whistles were blowing and the chimes of the Garden City churches broke suddenly into reverberatory sound.

Anthony began to run again. The cries were clear and distinct now as they rose with clouds of frosted breath into the chilly air:

"*Germany's surrendered! Germany's surrendered!*"

THE FALSE ARMISTICE

That evening in the opaque gloom of six o'clock Anthony slipped between two freight-cars, and once over the railroad, followed the track along to Garden City, where he caught an electric train for New York. He stood some chance of apprehension—he knew that the military police were often sent through the cars to ask for passes, but he imagined that tonight the vigilance would be relaxed. But, in any event, he would have tried to slip through, for he had been unable to locate Gloria by telephone, and another day of suspense would have been intolerable.

After inexplicable stops and waits that reminded him of the night he had left New York, over a year before, they drew into the Pennsylvania Station, and he followed the familiar way to the taxi-stand, finding it grotesque and oddly stimulating to give his own address.

Broadway was a riot of light, thronged as he had never seen it with a carnival crowd which swept its glittering way through scraps of paper, piled ankle-deep on the sidewalks. Here and there, elevated upon benches and boxes, soldiers addressed the heedless mass, each face in which was clear cut and distinct under the white glare overhead. Anthony picked out half a dozen figures—a drunken sailor, tipped backward and supported by two other gobs, was waving his hat and emitting a wild series of roars; a wounded soldier, crutch in hand, was borne along in an eddy on the shoulders of some shrieking civilians; a dark-haired girl sat cross-legged and meditative on top of a parked taxicab. Here surely the victory had come in time, the climax had been scheduled with the uttermost celestial foresight. The great rich nation had made triumphant war, suffered enough for poignancy but not enough for bitterness—hence the carnival, the feasting, the triumph. Under these bright lights glittered the faces of peoples whose glory had long since passed away, whose very civilizations were dead—men whose ancestors had heard the news of victory in Babylon, in Nineveh, in Bagdad, in Tyre, a hundred generations before; men whose ancestors had seen a flower-decked, slave-adorned cortege drift with its wake of captives down the avenues of Imperial Rome. . . .

Past the Rialto, the glittering front of the Astor, the jewelled magnificence of Times Square . . . a gorgeous alley of incandescence ahead. . . . Then—was it years later?—he was paying the taxi-driver in front of a white building on Fifty-seventh Street. He was in the hall—ah, there was the negro boy from Martinique, lazy, indolent, unchanged.

"Is Mrs. Patch in?"

"I have just came on, sah," the man announced with his incongruous British accent.

"Take me up——"

Then the slow drone of the elevator, the three steps to the door, which swung open at the impetus of his knock.

"Gloria!" His voice was trembling. No answer. A faint string of smoke was rising from a cigarette-tray—a number of Vanity Fair sat astraddle on the table.

"Gloria!"

He ran into the bedroom, the bath. She was not there. A negligée of robin's-egg blue laid out upon the bed diffused a faint perfume, illusive and familiar. On a chair were a pair of stockings and a street dress; an open powder-box yawned upon the bureau. She must just have gone out.

The telephone rang abruptly and he started—answered it with all the sensations of an impostor.

"Hello. Is Mrs. Patch there?"

"No, I'm looking for her myself. Who is this?"

"This is Mr. Crawford."

"This is Mr. Patch speaking. I've just arrived unexpectedly, and I don't know where to find her."

"Oh." Mr. Crawford sounded a bit taken aback. "Why, I imagine she's at the Armistice Ball. I know she intended going, but I didn't think she'd leave so early."

"Where's the Armistice Ball?"

"At the Astor."

"Thanks."

Anthony hung up sharply and rose. Who was Mr. Crawford? And who was it that was taking her to the ball? How long had this been going on? All these questions asked and answered themselves a dozen times, a dozen ways. His very proximity to her drove him half frantic.

In a frenzy of suspicion he rushed here and there about the

apartment, hunting for some sign of masculine occupation, opening the bathroom cupboard, searching feverishly through the bureau drawers. Then he found something that made him stop suddenly and sit down on one of the twin beds, the corners of his mouth drooping as though he were about to weep. There in a corner of her drawer, tied with a frail blue ribbon, were all the letters and telegrams he had written her during the year past. He was suffused with happy and sentimental shame.

"I'm not fit to touch her," he cried aloud to the four walls. "I'm not fit to touch her little hand."

Nevertheless, he went out to look for her.

In the Astor lobby he was engulfed immediately in a crowd so thick as to make progress almost impossible. He asked the direction of the ballroom from half a dozen people before he could get a sober and intelligible answer. Eventually, after a last long wait, he checked his military overcoat in the hall.

It was only nine but the dance was in full blast. The panorama was incredible. Women, women everywhere—girls gay with wine singing shrilly above the clamor of the dazzling confetti-covered throng; girls set off by the uniforms of a dozen nations; fat females collapsing without dignity upon the floor and retaining self-respect by shouting "Hurraw for the Allies!"; three women with white hair dancing hand in hand around a sailor, who revolved in a dizzying spin upon the floor, clasping to his heart an empty bottle of champagne.

Breathlessly Anthony scanned the dancers, scanned the muddled lines trailing in single file in and out among the tables, scanned the horn-blowing, kissing, coughing, laughing, drinking parties under the great full-bosomed flags which leaned in glowing color over the pageantry and the sound.

Then he saw Gloria. She was sitting at a table for two directly across the room. Her dress was black, and above it her animated face, tinted with the most glamourous rose, made, he thought, a spot of poignant beauty on the room. His heart leaped as though to a new music. He jostled his way toward her and called her name just as the gray eyes looked up and found him. For that instant as their bodies met and melted, the world, the revel, the tumbling whimper of the music faded to an ecstatic monotone hushed as a song of bees.

"Oh, my Gloria!" he cried.

Her kiss was a cool rill flowing from her heart.

CHAPTER II

A Matter of Æsthetics

On the night when Anthony had left for Camp Hooker one year before, all that was left of the beautiful Gloria Gilbert—her shell, her young and lovely body—moved up the broad marble steps of the Grand Central Station with the rhythm of the engine beating in her ears like a dream, and out onto Vanderbilt Avenue, where the huge bulk of the Biltmore overhung the street and, down at its low, gleaming entrance, sucked in the many-colored opera-cloaks of gorgeously dressed girls. For a moment she paused by the taxi-stand and watched them—wondering that but a few years before she had been of their number, ever setting out for a radiant Somewhere, always just about to have that ultimate passionate adventure for which the girls' cloaks were delicate and beautifully furred, for which their cheeks were painted and their hearts higher than the transitory dome of pleasure that would engulf them, coiffure, cloak, and all.

It was growing colder and the men passing had flipped up the collars of their overcoats. This change was kind to her. It would have been kinder still had everything changed, weather, streets, and people, and had she been whisked away, to wake in some high, fresh-scented room, alone, and statuesque within and without, as in her virginal and colorful past.

Inside the taxicab she wept impotent tears. That she had not been happy with Anthony for over a year mattered little. Recently his presence had been no more than what it would awake in her of that memorable June. The Anthony of late, irritable, weak, and poor, could do no less than make her irritable in turn—and bored with everything except the fact that in a highly imaginative and eloquent youth they had come together in an ecstatic revel of emotion. Because of this mutually vivid memory she would have done more for Anthony than for any other human—so when she got into the taxicab she wept passionately, and wanted to call his name aloud.

Miserable, lonesome as a forgotten child, she sat in the quiet apartment and wrote him a letter full of confused sentiment:

. . . I can almost look down the tracks and see you going but without you, dearest, dearest, I can't see or hear or feel or think. Being apart—whatever has happened or will happen to us—is like begging for mercy from a storm, Anthony; it's like growing old. I want to kiss you so—in the back of your neck where your old black hair starts. Because I love you and whatever we do or say to each other, or have done, or have said, you've got to feel how much I do, how inanimate I am when you're gone. I can't even hate the damnable presence of PEOPLE, *those people in the station who haven't any right to live—I can't resent them even though they're dirtying up our world, because I'm engrossed in wanting you so.*

If you hated me, if you were covered with sores like a leper, if you ran away with another woman or starved me or beat me—how absurd this sounds—I'd still want you, I'd still love you. I KNOW, *my darling.*

It's late—I have all the windows open and the air outside is just as soft as spring, yet, somehow, much more young and frail than spring. Why do they make spring a young girl, why does that illusion dance and yodel its way for three months through the world's preposterous barrenness. Spring is a lean old plough-horse with its ribs showing—it's a pile of refuse in a field, parched by the sun and the rain to an ominous cleanliness.

In a few hours you'll wake up, my darling—and you'll be miserable, and disgusted with life. You'll be in Delaware or Carolina or somewhere and so unimportant. I don't believe there's any one alive who can contemplate themselves as an impermanent institution, as a luxury or an unnecessary evil. Very few of the people who accentuate the futility of life remark the futility of themselves. Perhaps they think that in proclaiming the evil of living they somehow salvage their own worth from the ruin—but they don't, even you and I. . . .

. . . Still I can see you. There's blue haze about the trees where you'll be passing, too beautiful to be predominant. No, the fallow squares of earth will be most frequent—they'll be along beside the track like dirty coarse brown sheets drying in the sun,

alive, mechanical, abominable. Nature, slovenly old hag, has been sleeping in them with every old farmer or negro or immigrant who happened to covet her. . . .

So you see that now you're gone I've written a letter all full of contempt and despair. And that just means that I love you, Anthony, with all there is to love with in your

GLORIA.

When she had addressed the letter she went to her twin bed and lay down upon it, clasping Anthony's pillow in her arms as though by sheer force of emotion she could metamorphize it into his warm and living body. Two o'clock saw her dry-eyed, staring with steady persistent grief into the darkness, remembering, remembering unmercifully, blaming herself for a hundred fancied unkindnesses, making a likeness of Anthony akin to some martyred and transfigured Christ. For a time she thought of him as he, in his more sentimental moments, probably thought of himself.

At five she was still awake. A mysterious grinding noise that went on every morning across the areaway told her the hour. She heard an alarm-clock ring, and saw a light make a yellow square on an illusory blank wall opposite. With the half-formed resolution of following him South immediately, her sorrow grew remote and unreal, and moved off from her as the dark moved westward. She fell asleep.

When she awoke the sight of the empty bed beside her brought a renewal of misery, dispelled shortly, however, by the inevitable callousness of the bright morning. Though she was not conscious of it, there was relief in eating breakfast without Anthony's tired and worried face opposite her. Now that she was alone she lost all desire to complain about the food. She would change her breakfasts, she thought—have a lemonade and a tomato sandwich instead of the sempiternal bacon and eggs and toast.

Nevertheless, at noon when she had called up several of her acquaintances, including the martial Muriel, and found each one engaged for lunch, she gave way to a quiet pity for herself and her loneliness. Curled on the bed with pencil and paper she wrote Anthony another letter.

Late in the afternoon arrived a special delivery, mailed from some small New Jersey town, and the familiarity of the phrasing, the almost audible undertone of worry and discontent, were so familiar that they comforted her. Who knew? Perhaps army discipline would harden Anthony and accustom him to the idea of work. She had immutable faith that the war would be over before he was called upon to fight, and meanwhile the suit would be won, and they could begin again, this time on a different basis. The first thing different would be that she would have a child. It was unbearable that she should be so utterly alone.

It was a week before she could stay in the apartment with the probability of remaining dry-eyed. There seemed little in the city that was amusing. Muriel had been shifted to a hospital in New Jersey, from which she took a metropolitan holiday only every other week, and with this defection Gloria grew to realize how few were the friends she had made in all these years of New York. The men she knew were in the army. "Men she knew"?—she had conceded vaguely to herself that all the men who had ever been in love with her were her friends. Each one of them had at a certain considerable time professed to value her favor above anything in life. But now—where were they? At least two were dead, half a dozen or more were married, the rest scattered from France to the Philippines. She wondered whether any of them thought of her, and how often, and in what respect. Most of them must still picture the little girl of seventeen or so, the adolescent siren of nine years before.

The girls, too, were gone far afield. She had never been popular in school. She had been too beautiful, too lazy, not sufficiently conscious of being a Farmover girl and a "Future Wife and Mother" in perpetual capital letters. And girls who had never been kissed hinted, with shocked expressions on their plain but not particularly wholesome faces, that Gloria had. Then these girls had gone east or west or south, married and become "people," prophesying, if they prophesied about Gloria, that she would come to a bad end—not knowing that no endings were bad, and that they, like her, were by no means the mistresses of their destinies.

Gloria told over to herself the people who had visited them in the gray house at Marietta. It had seemed at the time that they were always having company—she had indulged in an unspoken conviction that each guest was ever afterward slightly indebted to her. They owed her a sort of moral ten dollars apiece, and should she ever be in need she might, so to speak, borrow from them this visionary currency. But they were gone, scattered like chaff, mysteriously and subtly vanished in essence or in fact.

By Christmas Gloria's conviction that she should join Anthony had returned, no longer as a sudden emotion, but as a recurrent need. She decided to write him word of her coming, but postponed the announcement upon the advice of Mr. Haight, who expected almost weekly that the case was coming up for trial.

One day, early in January, as she was walking on Fifth Avenue, bright now with uniforms and hung with the flags of the virtuous nations, she met Rachael Barnes, whom she had not seen for nearly a year. Even Rachael, whom she had grown to dislike, was a relief from ennui, and together they went to the Ritz for tea.

After a second cocktail they became enthusiastic. They liked each other. They talked about their husbands, Rachael in that tone of public vainglory, with private reservations, in which wives are wont to speak.

"Rodman's abroad in the Quartermaster Corps. He's a captain. He was bound he would go, and he didn't think he could get into anything else."

"Anthony's in the Infantry." The words in their relation to the cocktail gave Gloria a sort of glow. With each sip she approached a warm and comforting patriotism.

"By the way," said Rachael half an hour later, as they were leaving, "can't you come up to dinner to-morrow night? I'm having two awfully sweet officers who are just going overseas. I think we ought to do all we can to make it attractive for them."

Gloria accepted gladly. She took down the address—recognizing by its number a fashionable apartment building on Park Avenue.

"It's been awfully good to have seen you, Rachael."

"It's been wonderful. I've wanted to."

With these three sentences a certain night in Marietta two

summers before, when Anthony and Rachael had been unnecessarily attentive to each other, was forgiven—Gloria forgave Rachael, Rachael forgave Gloria. Also it was forgiven that Rachael had been witness to the greatest disaster in the lives of Mr. and Mrs. Anthony Patch——

Compromising with events time moves along.

The Wiles of Captain Collins

The two officers were captains of the popular craft, machine gunnery. At dinner they referred to themselves with conscious boredom as members of the "Suicide Club"—in those days every recondite branch of the service referred to itself as the Suicide Club. One of the captains—Rachael's captain, Gloria observed—was a tall horsy man of thirty with a pleasant mustache and ugly teeth. The other, Captain Collins, was chubby, pink-faced, and inclined to laugh with abandon every time he caught Gloria's eye. He took an immediate fancy to her, and throughout dinner showered her with inane compliments. With her second glass of champagne Gloria decided that for the first time in months she was thoroughly enjoying herself.

After dinner it was suggested that they all go somewhere and dance. The two officers supplied themselves with bottles of liquor from Rachael's sideboard—a law forbade service to the military—and so equipped they went through innumerable fox-trots in several glittering caravanseries along Broadway, faithfully alternating partners—while Gloria became more and more uproarious and more and more amusing to the pink-faced captain, who seldom bothered to remove his genial smile at all.

At eleven o'clock to her great surprise she was in the minority for staying out. The others wanted to return to Rachael's apartment—to get some more liquor, they said. Gloria argued persistently that Captain Collins's flask was half full—she had just seen it—then catching Rachael's eye she received an unmistakable wink. She deduced, confusedly, that her hostess wanted to get rid of the officers and assented to being bundled into a taxicab outside.

Captain Wolf sat on the left with Rachael on his knees.

Captain Collins sat in the middle, and as he settled himself he slipped his arm about Gloria's shoulder. It rested there lifelessly for a moment and then tightened like a vise. He leaned over her.

"You're awfully pretty," he whispered.

"Thank you kindly, sir." She was neither pleased nor annoyed. Before Anthony came so many arms had done likewise that it had become little more than a gesture, sentimental but without significance.

Up in Rachael's long front room a low fire and two lamps shaded with orange silk gave all the light, so that the corners were full of deep and somnolent shadows. The hostess, moving about in a dark-figured gown of loose chiffon, seemed to accentuate the already sensuous atmosphere. For a while they were all four together, tasting the sandwiches that waited on the tea-table—then Gloria found herself alone with Captain Collins on the fireside lounge; Rachael and Captain Wolf had withdrawn to the other side of the room, where they were conversing in subdued voices.

"I wish you weren't married," said Collins, his face a ludicrous travesty of "in all seriousness."

"Why?" She held out her glass to be filled with a high-ball.

"Don't drink any more," he urged her, frowning.

"Why not?"

"You'd be nicer—if you didn't."

Gloria caught suddenly the intended suggestion of the remark, the atmosphere he was attempting to create. She wanted to laugh—yet she realized that there was nothing to laugh at. She had been enjoying the evening, and she had no desire to go home—at the same time it hurt her pride to be flirted with on just that level.

"Pour me another drink," she insisted.

"Please——"

"Oh, don't be ridiculous!" she cried in exasperation.

"Very well." He yielded with ill grace.

Then his arm was about her again, and again she made no protest. But when his pink cheek came close she leaned away.

"You're awfully sweet," he said with an aimless air.

She began to sing softly, wishing now that he would take down his arm. Suddenly her eye fell on an intimate scene across the room—Rachael and Captain Wolf were engrossed in a long kiss. Gloria shivered slightly—she knew not why. . . . Pink face approached again.

"You shouldn't look at them," he whispered. Almost immediately his other arm was around her . . . his breath was on her cheek. Again absurdity triumphed over disgust, and her laugh was a weapon that needed no edge of words.

"Oh, I thought you were a sport," he was saying.

"What's a sport?"

"Why, a person that likes to—to enjoy life."

"Is kissing you generally considered a joyful affair?"

They were interrupted as Rachael and Captain Wolf appeared suddenly before them.

"It's late, Gloria," said Rachael—she was flushed and her hair was dishevelled. "You'd better stay here all night."

For an instant Gloria thought the officers were being dismissed. Then she understood, and, understanding, got to her feet as casually as she was able.

Uncomprehendingly Rachael continued:

"You can have the room just off this one. I can lend you everything you need."

Collins's eyes implored her like a dog's; Captain Wolf's arm had settled familiarly around Rachael's waist; they were waiting.

But the lure of promiscuity, colorful, various, labyrinthine, and ever a little odorous and stale, had no call or promise for Gloria. Had she so desired she would have remained, without hesitation, without regret; as it was she could face coolly the six hostile and offended eyes that followed her out into the hall with forced politeness and hollow words.

"*He* wasn't even sport enough to try to take me home," she thought in the taxi, and then with a quick surge of resentment: "How *utter*ly common!"

GALLANTRY

In February she had an experience of quite a different sort. Tudor Baird, an ancient flame, a young man whom at one time she had fully intended to marry, came to New York by way of the Aviation Corps, and called upon her. They went several times to the theatre, and within a week, to her great enjoyment, he was as much in love with her as ever. Quite deliberately she brought it about, realizing too late that she had done a mischief. He reached the point of sitting with her in miserable silence whenever they went out together.

A Scroll and Keys man at Yale, he possessed the correct reticences of a "good egg," the correct notions of chivalry and *noblesse oblige*—and, of course but unfortunately, the correct biases and the correct lack of ideas—all those traits which Anthony had taught her to despise, but which, nevertheless, she rather admired. Unlike the majority of his type, she found that he was not a bore. He was handsome, witty in a light way, and when she was with him she felt that because of some quality he possessed—call it stupidity, loyalty, sentimentality, or something not quite as definite as any of the three—he would have done anything in his power to please her.

He told her this among other things, very correctly and with a ponderous manliness that masked a real suffering. Loving him not at all she grew sorry for him and kissed him sentimentally one night because he was so charming, a relic of a vanishing generation which lived a priggish and graceful illusion and was being replaced by less gallant fools. Afterward she was glad she had kissed him, for next day when his plane fell fifteen hundred feet at Mineola a piece of a gasolene engine smashed through his heart.

Gloria Alone

When Mr. Haight told her that the trial would not take place until autumn she decided that without telling Anthony she would go into the movies. When he saw her successful, both histrionically and financially, when he saw that she could have her will of Joseph Bloeckman, yielding nothing in return, he would lose his silly prejudices. She lay awake half one night planning her career and enjoying her successes in anticipation, and the next morning she called up "Films Par Excellence." Mr. Bloeckman was in Europe.

But the idea had gripped her so strongly this time that she decided to go the rounds of the moving-picture employment agencies. As so often had been the case, her sense of smell worked against her good intentions. The employment agency smelt as though it had been dead a very long time. She waited five minutes inspecting her unprepossessing competitors—then she walked briskly out into the farthest recesses of Central Park and remained so long that she caught a cold. She was trying to air the employment agency out of her walking suit.

In the spring she began to gather from Anthony's letters—not from any one in particular but from their culminative effect—that he did not want her to come South. Curiously repeated excuses that seemed to haunt him by their very insufficiency occurred with Freudian regularity. He set them down in each letter as though he feared he had forgotten them the last time, as though it were desperately necessary to impress her with them. And the dilutions of his letters with affectionate diminutives began to be mechanical and unspontaneous—almost as though, having completed the letter, he had looked it over and literally stuck them in, like epigrams in an Oscar Wilde play. She jumped to the solution, rejected it, was angry and depressed by turns—finally she shut her mind to it proudly, and allowed an increasing coolness to creep into her end of the correspondence.

Of late she had found a good deal to occupy her attention. Several aviators whom she had met through Tudor Baird came into New York to see her and two other ancient beaux turned up, stationed at Camp Dix. As these men were ordered overseas they, so to speak, handed her down to their friends. But after another rather disagreeable experience with a potential Captain Collins she made it plain that when any one was introduced to her he should be under no misapprehensions as to her status and personal intentions.

When summer came she learned, like Anthony, to watch the officers' casualty list, taking a sort of melancholy pleasure in hearing of the death of some one with whom she had once danced a german and in identifying by name the younger brothers of former suitors—thinking, as the drive toward Paris progressed, that here at length went the world to inevitable and well-merited destruction.

She was twenty-seven. Her birthday fled by scarcely noticed.

Years before it had frightened her when she became twenty, to some extent when she reached twenty-six—but now she looked in the glass with calm self-approval seeing the British freshness of her complexion and her figure boyish and slim as of old.

She tried not to think of Anthony. It was as though she were writing to a stranger. She told her friends that he had been made a corporal and was annoyed when they were politely unimpressed. One night she wept because she was sorry for him—had he been even slightly responsive she would have gone to him without hesitation on the first train—whatever he was doing he needed to be taken care of spiritually, and she felt that now she would be able to do even that. Recently, without his continual drain upon her moral strength she found herself wonderfully revived. Before he left she had been inclined through sheer association to brood on her wasted opportunities—now she returned to her normal state of mind, strong, disdainful, existing each day for each day's worth. She bought a doll and dressed it; one week she wept over "Ethan Frome"; the next she revelled in some novels of Galsworthy's, whom she liked for his power of recreating, by spring in darkness, that illusion of young romantic love to which women look forever forward and forever back.

In October Anthony's letters multiplied, became almost frantic—then suddenly ceased. For a worried month it needed all her powers of control to refrain from leaving immediately for Mississippi. Then a telegram told her that he had been in the hospital and that she could expect him in New York within ten days. Like a figure in a dream he came back into her life across the ballroom on that November evening—and all through long hours that held familiar gladness she took him close to her breast, nursing an illusion of happiness and security she had not thought that she would know again.

Discomfiture of the Generals

After a week Anthony's regiment went back to the Mississippi camp to be discharged. The officers shut themselves up in the compartments on the Pullman cars and drank the whiskey they had bought in New York, and in the coaches the soldiers got as drunk as possible also—and pretended whenever the train stopped at a village that they were just returned from France, where they had practically put an end to the German army. As they all wore overseas caps and claimed that they had not had time to have their gold service stripes sewed on, the yokelry of the seaboard were much impressed and asked them how they liked the trenches—to which they replied "Oh, *boy!*" with great smacking of tongues and shaking of heads. Some one took a piece of chalk and scrawled on the side of the train, "We won the war—now we're going home," and the officers laughed and let it stay. They were all getting what swagger they could out of this ignominious return.

As they rumbled on toward camp, Anthony was uneasy lest he should find Dot awaiting him patiently at the station. To his relief he neither saw nor heard anything of her and thinking that were she still in town she would certainly attempt to communicate with him, he concluded that she had gone—whither he neither knew nor cared. He wanted only to return to Gloria—Gloria reborn and wonderfully alive. When eventually he was discharged he left his company on the rear of a great truck with a crowd who had given tolerant, almost sentimental, cheers for their officers, especially for Captain Dunning. The captain, on his part, had addressed them with tears in his eyes as to the pleasure, etc., and the work, etc., and time not wasted, etc., and duty, etc. It was very dull and human; having given ear to it Anthony, whose mind was freshened by his week in New York, renewed his deep loathing for the military profession and all it connoted. In their childish hearts two out of every three professional officers considered that wars were made for armies and not armies for wars. He rejoiced to see general and field-officers riding desolately about the barren camp deprived of their commands. He rejoiced to hear the men in his company laugh scornfully at the inducements tendered them to remain in the army. They were to attend "schools." He knew what these "schools" were.

Two days later he was with Gloria in New York.

Another Winter

Late one February afternoon Anthony came into the apartment and groping through the little hall, pitch-dark in the winter dusk, found Gloria sitting by the window. She turned as he came in.

"What did Mr. Haight have to say?" she asked listlessly.

"Nothing," he answered, "usual thing. Next month, perhaps."

She looked at him closely; her ear attuned to his voice caught the slightest thickness in the dissyllable.

"You've been drinking," she remarked dispassionately.

"Couple glasses."

"Oh."

He yawned in the armchair and there was a moment's silence between them. Then she demanded suddenly:

"Did you go to Mr. Haight? Tell me the truth."

"No." He smiled weakly. "As a matter of fact I didn't have time."

"I thought you didn't go. . . . He sent for you."

"I don't give a damn. I'm sick of waiting around his office. You'd think he was doing *me* a favor." He glanced at Gloria as though expecting moral support, but she had turned back to her contemplation of the dubious and unprepossessing out-of-doors.

"I feel rather weary of life to-day," he offered tentatively. Still she was silent. "I met a fellow and we talked in the Biltmore bar."

The dusk had suddenly deepened but neither of them made any move to turn on the lights. Lost in heaven knew what contemplation, they sat there until a flurry of snow drew a languid sigh from Gloria.

"What've you been doing?" he asked, finding the silence oppressive.

"Reading a magazine—all full of idiotic articles by prosperous authors about how terrible it is for poor people to buy silk shirts. And while I was reading it I could think of nothing except how I wanted a gray squirrel coat—and how we can't afford one."

"Yes, we can."

"Oh, no."

"Oh, yes! If you want a fur coat you can have one."

Her voice coming through the dark held an implication of scorn.

"You mean we can sell another bond?"

"If necessary. I don't want you to go without things. We have spent a lot, though, since I've been back."

"Oh, shut up!" she said in irritation.

"Why?"

"Because I'm sick and tired of hearing you talk about what we've spent or what we've done. You came back two months ago and we've been on some sort of a party practically every night since. We've both wanted to go out, and we've gone. Well, you haven't heard me complain, have you? But all you do is whine, whine, whine. I don't care any more what we do or what becomes of us and at least I'm consistent. But I will *not* tolerate your complaining and calamity-howling——"

"You're not very pleasant yourself sometimes, you know."

"I'm under no obligations to be. You're not making any attempt to make things different."

"But I am——"

"Huh! Seems to me I've heard that before. This morning you weren't going to touch another thing to drink until you'd gotten a position. And you didn't even have the spunk to go to Mr. Haight when he sent for you about the suit."

Anthony got to his feet and switched on the lights.

"See here!" he cried, blinking, "I'm getting sick of that sharp tongue of yours."

"Well, what are you going to do about it?"

"Do you think *I'm* particularly happy?" he continued, ignoring her question. "Do you think I don't know we're not living as we ought to?"

In an instant Gloria stood trembling beside him.

"I won't *stand* it!" she burst out. "I won't be lectured to. You and your suffering! You're just a pitiful weakling and you always have been!"

They faced one another idiotically, each of them unable to impress the other, each of them tremendously, achingly, bored. Then she went into the bedroom and shut the door behind her.

His return had brought into the foreground all their pre-bellum exasperations. Prices had risen alarmingly and in perverse ratio their income had shrunk to a little over half of its original size. There had been the large retainer's fee to Mr. Haight; there were stocks bought at one hundred, now down to thirty and forty and other investments that were not paying at all. During the previous spring Gloria had been given the alternative of leaving the apartment or of signing a year's lease at two hundred and twenty-five a month. She had signed it. Inevitably as the necessity for economy had increased they found themselves as a pair quite unable to save. The old policy of prevarication was resorted to. Weary of their incapabilities they chattered of what they would do—oh—to-morrow, of how they would "stop going on parties" and of how Anthony would go to work. But when dark came down Gloria, accustomed to an engagement every night, would feel the ancient restlessness creeping over her. She would stand in the doorway of the bedroom, chewing furiously at her fingers and sometimes meeting Anthony's eyes as he glanced up from his book. Then the telephone, and her nerves would relax, she would answer it with ill-concealed eagerness. Some one was coming up "for just a few minutes"—and oh, the weariness of pretense, the appearance of the wine-table, the revival of their jaded spirits—and the awakening, like the mid-point of a sleepless night in which they moved.

As the winter passed with the march of the returning troops along Fifth Avenue they became more and more aware that since Anthony's return their relations had entirely changed. After that reflowering of tenderness and passion each of them had returned into some solitary dream unshared by the other and what endearments passed between them passed, it seemed, from empty heart to empty heart, echoing hollowly the departure of what they knew at last was gone.

Anthony had again made the rounds of the metropolitan newspapers and had again been refused encouragement by a motley of office boys, telephone girls, and city editors. The word was: "We're keeping any vacancies open for our own men who are still in France." Then, late in March, his eye fell on an advertisement in the morning paper and in consequence he found at last the semblance of an occupation.

YOU CAN SELL! ! !
Why not earn while you learn?
Our salesmen make $50–$200 weekly.

There followed an address on Madison Avenue, and instructions to appear at one o'clock that afternoon. Gloria, glancing over his shoulder after one of their usual late breakfasts, saw him regarding it idly.

"Why don't you try it?" she suggested.

"Oh—it's one of these crazy schemes."

"It might not be. At least it'd be experience."

At her urging he went at one o'clock to the appointed address, where he found himself one of a dense miscellany of men waiting in front of the door. They ranged from a messenger-boy evidently misusing his company's time to an immemorial individual with a gnarled body and a gnarled cane. Some of the men were seedy, with sunken cheeks and puffy pink eyes—others were young, possibly still in high school. After a jostled fifteen minutes during which they all eyed one another with apathetic suspicion there appeared a smart young shepherd clad in a "waist-line" suit and wearing the manner of an assistant rector who herded them up-stairs into a large room, which resembled a schoolroom and contained innumerable desks. Here the prospective salesmen sat down—and again waited. After an interval a platform at the end of the hall was clouded with half a dozen sober but sprightly men who, with one exception, took seats in a semicircle facing the audience.

The exception was the man who seemed the soberest, the most sprightly and the youngest of the lot, and who advanced to the front of the platform. The audience scrutinized him hopefully. He was rather small and rather pretty, with the commercial rather than the thespian sort of prettiness. He had straight blond bushy brows and eyes that were almost preposterously honest, and as he reached the edge of his rostrum he seemed to throw these eyes out into the audience, simultaneously extending his arm with two fingers outstretched. Then while he rocked himself to a state of balance an expectant silence settled over the hall. With perfect assurance the young man had taken his listeners in hand and his words when they came were steady and confident and of the school of "straight from the shoulder."

"Men!"—he began, and paused. The word died with a prolonged echo at the end of the hall, the faces regarding him, hopefully, cynically, wearily, were alike arrested, engrossed. Six hundred eyes were turned slightly upward. With an even graceless flow that reminded Anthony of the rolling of bowling-balls he launched himself into the sea of exposition.

"This bright and sunny morning you picked up your favorite newspaper and you found an advertisement which made the plain, unadorned statement that *you* could sell. That was all it said—it didn't say 'what,' it didn't say 'how,' it didn't say 'why.' It just made one single solitary assertion that *you* and *you* and *you*"—business of pointing—"could sell. Now my job isn't to make a success of you, because every man is born a success, he makes himself a failure; it's not to teach you how to talk, because each man is a natural orator and only makes himself a clam; my business is to tell you one thing in a way that will make you *know* it—it's to tell you that *you* and *you* and *you* have the heritage of money and prosperity waiting for you to come and claim it."

At this point an Irishman of saturnine appearance rose from his desk near the rear of the hall and went out.

"That man thinks he'll go look for it in the beer parlor around the corner. (Laughter.) He won't find it there. Once upon a time I looked for it there myself (laughter), but that was before I did what every one of you men no matter how young or how old, how poor or how rich (a faint ripple of satirical laughter), can do. It was before I found—my*self*!

"Now I wonder if any of you men know what a 'Heart Talk' is. A 'Heart Talk' is a little book in which I started, about five years ago, to write down what I had discovered were the principal reasons for a man's failure and the principal reasons for a man's success—from John D. Rockerfeller back to John D. Napoleon (laughter), and before that, back in the days when Abel sold his birthright for a mess of pottage. There are now one hundred of these 'Heart Talks.' Those of you who are sincere, who are interested in our proposition, above all who are dissatisfied with the way things are breaking for you at present will be handed one to take home with you as you go out yonder door this afternoon.

"Now in my own pocket I have four letters just received concerning 'Heart Talks.' These letters have names signed to them that are familiar in every household in the U.S.A. Listen to this one from Detroit:

DEAR MR. CARLETON:

I want to order three thousand more copies of "Heart Talks" for distribution among my salesmen. They have done more for getting work out of the men than any bonus proposition ever considered. I read them myself constantly, and I desire to heartily congratulate you on getting at the roots of the biggest problem that faces our generation to-day—the problem of salesmanship. The rock bottom on which the country is founded is the problem of salesmanship. With many felicitations I am

Yours very cordially,
HENRY W. TERRAL.

He brought the name out in three long booming triumphancies—pausing for it to produce its magical effect. Then he read two more letters, one from a manufacturer of vacuum cleaners and one from the president of the Great Northern Doily Company.

"And now," he continued, "I'm going to tell you in a few words what the proposition is that's going to *make* those of you who go into it in the right spirit. Simply put, it's this: 'Heart Talks' have been incorporated as a company. We're going to put these little pamphlets into the hands of every big business organization, every salesman, and every man who *knows*—I don't say 'thinks,' I say '*knows*'—that he can sell! We are offering some of the stock of the 'Heart Talks' concern upon the market, and in order that the distribution may be as wide as possible, and in order also that we can furnish a living, concrete, flesh-and-blood example of what salesmanship is, or rather what it may be, we're going to give those of you who are the real thing a chance to sell that stock. Now, I don't care what you've tried to sell before or how you've tried to sell it. It don't matter how old you are or how young you are. I only want to know two things—first, do you *want* success, and, second, will you work for it?

"My name is Sammy Carleton. Not 'Mr.' Carleton, but just plain Sammy. I'm a regular no-nonsense man with no fancy frills about me. I want you to call me Sammy.

"Now this is all I'm going to say to you to-day. To-morrow I want those of you who have thought it over and have read the copy of 'Heart Talks' which will be given to you at the door, to come back to this same room at this same time, then we'll go into the proposition further and I'll explain to you what I've found the principles of success to be. I'm going to make you *feel* that *you* and *you* and *you* can sell!"

Mr. Carleton's voice echoed for a moment through the hall and then died away. To the stamping of many feet Anthony was pushed and jostled with the crowd out of the room.

Further Adventures with "Heart Talks"

With an accompaniment of ironic laughter Anthony told Gloria the story of his commercial adventure. But she listened without amusement.

"You're going to give up again?" she demanded coldly.

"Why—you don't expect me to——"

"I never expected anything of you."

He hesitated.

"Well—I can't see the slightest benefit in laughing myself sick over this sort of affair. If there's anything older than the old story, it's the new twist."

It required an astonishing amount of moral energy on Gloria's part to intimidate him into returning, and when he reported next day, somewhat depressed from his perusal of the senile bromides skittishly set forth in "Heart Talks on Ambition," he found only fifty of the original three hundred awaiting the appearance of the vital and compelling Sammy Carleton. Mr. Carleton's powers of vitality and compulsion were this time exercised in elucidating that magnificent piece of speculation—how to sell. It seemed that the approved method was to state one's proposition and then to say not "And now, will you buy?"—this was not the way—oh, no!—the way was to state one's proposition and then, having reduced one's adversary to a state of exhaustion, to deliver oneself of the categorical imperative: "Now see here! You've taken up my time explaining this matter to you. You've admitted my points—all I want to ask is how many do you want?"

As Mr. Carleton piled assertion upon assertion Anthony began to feel a sort of disgusted confidence in him. The man appeared to know what he was talking about. Obviously prosperous, he had risen to the position of instructing others. It did not occur to Anthony that the type of man who attains commercial success seldom knows how or why, and, as in his grandfather's case, when he ascribes reasons, the reasons are generally inaccurate and absurd.

Anthony noted that of the numerous old men who had answered the original advertisement, only two had returned, and that among the thirty odd who assembled on the third day to get actual selling instructions from Mr. Carleton, only one gray head was in evidence. These thirty were eager converts; with their mouths they followed the working of Mr. Carleton's mouth; they swayed in their seats with enthusiasm, and in the intervals of his talk they spoke to each other in tense approving whispers. Yet of the chosen few who, in the words of Mr. Carleton, "were determined to get those deserts that rightly and truly belonged to them," less than half a dozen combined even a modicum of personal appearance with that great gift of being a "pusher." But they were told that they were all natural pushers—it was merely necessary that they should believe with a sort of savage passion in what they were selling. He even urged each one to buy some stock himself, if possible, in order to increase his own sincerity.

On the fifth day then, Anthony sallied into the street with all the sensations of a man wanted by the police. Acting according to instructions he selected a tall office-building in order that he might ride to the top story and work downward, stopping in every office that had a name on the door. But at the last minute he hesitated. Perhaps it would be more practicable to acclimate himself to the chilly atmosphere which he felt was awaiting him by trying a few offices on, say, Madison Avenue. He went into an arcade that seemed only semi-prosperous, and seeing a sign which read Percy B. Weatherbee,

Architect, he opened the door heroically and entered. A starchy young woman looked up questioningly.

"Can I see Mr. Weatherbee?" He wondered if his voice sounded tremulous.

She laid her hand tentatively on the telephone-receiver.

"What's the name, please?"

"He wouldn't—ah—know me. He wouldn't know my name."

"What's your business with him? You an insurance agent?"

"Oh, no, nothing like that!" denied Anthony hurriedly. "Oh, no. It's a—it's a personal matter." He wondered if he should have said this. It had all sounded so simple when Mr. Carleton had enjoined his flock: "Don't allow yourself to be kept out! Show them you've made up your mind to talk to them, and they'll listen."

The girl succumbed to Anthony's pleasant, melancholy face, and in a moment the door to the inner room opened and admitted a tall, splay-footed man with slicked hair. He approached Anthony with ill-concealed impatience.

"You wanted to see me on a personal matter?"

Anthony quailed.

"I wanted to talk to you," he said defiantly.

"About what?"

"It'll take some time to explain."

"Well, what's it about?" Mr. Weatherbee's voice indicated rising irritation.

Then Anthony, straining at each word, each syllable, began:

"I don't know whether or not you've ever heard of a series of pamphlets called 'Heart Talks'——"

"Good grief!" cried Percy B. Weatherbee, Architect, "are you trying to touch my heart?"

"No, it's business. 'Heart Talks' have been incorporated and we're putting some shares on the market——"

His voice faded slowly off, harassed by a fixed and contemptuous stare from his unwilling prey. For another minute he struggled on, increasingly sensitive, entangled in his own words. His confidence oozed from him in great retching emanations that seemed to be sections of his own body. Almost mercifully Percy B. Weatherbee, Architect, terminated the interview:

"Good grief!" he exploded in disgust, "and you call that a *personal* matter!" He whipped about and strode into his private office, banging the door behind him. Not daring to look at the stenographer, Anthony in some shameful and mysterious way got himself from the room. Perspiring profusely he stood in the hall wondering why they didn't come and arrest him; in every hurried look he discerned infallibly a glance of scorn.

After an hour and with the help of two strong whiskies he brought himself up to another attempt. He walked into a plumber's shop, but when he mentioned his business the plumber began pulling on his coat in a great hurry, gruffly announcing that he had to go to lunch. Anthony remarked politely that it was futile to try to sell a man anything when he was hungry, and the plumber heartily agreed.

This episode encouraged Anthony; he tried to think that had the plumber not been bound for lunch he would at least have listened.

Passing by a few glittering and formidable bazaars he entered a grocery-store. A talkative proprietor told him that before buying any stocks he was going to see how the armistice affected the market. To Anthony this seemed almost unfair. In Mr. Carleton's salesman's Utopia the only reason prospective buyers ever gave for not purchasing stock was that they doubted it to be a promising investment. Obviously a man in that state was almost ludicrously easy game, to be brought down merely by the judicious application of the correct selling points. But these men—why, actually they weren't considering buying anything at all.

Anthony took several more drinks before he approached his fourth man, a real-estate agent; nevertheless, he was floored with a coup as decisive as a syllogism. The real-estate agent said that he had three brothers in the investment business. Viewing himself as a breaker-up of homes Anthony apologized and went out.

After another drink he conceived the brilliant plan of selling the stock to the bartenders along Lexington Avenue. This occupied several hours, for it was necessary to take a few drinks in each place in order to get the proprietor in the proper frame of mind to talk business. But the bartenders one and all contended that if they had any money to buy bonds they would not be bartenders. It was as though they had all convened and decided upon that rejoinder. As he approached a dark and soggy five o'clock he found that they were developing a still more annoying tendency to turn him off with a jest.

At five, then, with a tremendous effort at concentration he decided that he must put more variety into his canvassing. He selected a medium-sized delicatessen store, and went in. He felt, illuminatingly, that the thing to do was to cast a spell not only over the store-keeper but over all the customers as well—and perhaps through the psychology of the herd instinct they would buy as an astounded and immediately convinced whole.

"Af'ernoon," he began in a loud thick voice. "Ga l'il prop'sition."

If he had wanted silence he obtained it. A sort of awe descended upon the half-dozen women marketing and upon the gray-haired ancient who in cap and apron was slicing chicken.

Anthony pulled a batch of papers from his flapping brief case and waved them cheerfully.

"Buy a bon'," he suggested, "good as liberty bon'!" The phrase pleased him and he elaborated upon it. "Better'n liberty bon'. Every one these bon's worth *two* liberty bon's." His mind made a hiatus and skipped to his peroration, which he delivered with appropriate gestures, these being somewhat marred by the necessity of clinging to the counter with one or both hands. "Now see here. You taken up my time. I don't want know *why* you won't buy. I just want you say *why*. Want you say *how many!*"

At this point they should have approached him with check-books and fountain-pens in hand. Realizing that they must have missed a cue Anthony, with the instincts of an actor, went back and repeated his finale.

"Now see here! You taken up my time. You followed prop'-sition. You agreed 'th reasonin'? Now, all I want from *you* is, how many lib'ty bon's?"

"See here!" broke in a new voice. A portly man whose face was adorned with symmetrical scrolls of yellow hair had come out of a glass cage in the rear of the store and was bearing down upon Anthony. "See here, you!"

"How many?" repeated the salesman sternly. "You taken up my time——"

"Hey, you!" cried the proprietor, "I'll have you taken up by the police."

"You mos' cert'nly won't!" returned Anthony with fine defiance. "All I want know is how many."

From here and there in the store went up little clouds of comment and expostulation.

"How terrible!"

"He's a raving maniac."

"He's disgracefully drunk."

The proprietor grasped Anthony's arm sharply.

"Get out, or I'll call a policeman."

Some relics of rationality moved Anthony to nod and replace his bonds clumsily in the case.

"How many?" he reiterated doubtfully.

"The whole force if necessary!" thundered his adversary, his yellow mustache trembling fiercely.

"Sell 'em all a bon'."

With this Anthony turned, bowed gravely to his late auditors, and wabbled from the store. He found a taxicab at the corner and rode home to the apartment. There he fell sound asleep on the sofa, and so Gloria found him, his breath filling the air with an unpleasant pungency, his hand still clutching his open brief case.

Except when Anthony was drinking, his range of sensation had become less than that of a healthy old man and when prohibition came in July he found that, among those who could afford it, there was more drinking than ever before. One's host now brought out a bottle upon the slightest pretext. The tendency to display liquor was a manifestation of the same instinct that led a man to deck his wife with jewels. To have liquor was a boast, almost a badge of respectability.

In the mornings Anthony awoke tired, nervous, and worried. Halcyon summer twilights and the purple chill of morning alike left him unresponsive. Only for a brief moment every day in the warmth and renewed life of a first high-ball did his mind turn to those opalescent dreams of future pleasure—the mutual heritage of the happy and the damned. But this was only for a little while. As he grew drunker the dreams faded and he became a confused spectre, moving in odd crannies of his own mind, full of unexpected devices, harshly contemptuous at best and reaching sodden and dispirited depths. One night in June he had quarrelled violently with Maury over a matter of the utmost triviality. He remembered dimly next morning that it had been about a broken pint bottle of champagne. Maury had told him to sober up and Anthony's feelings had been hurt, so with an attempted gesture of dignity he had risen from the table and seizing Gloria's arm half led, half shamed her into a taxicab outside, leaving Maury with three dinners ordered and tickets for the opera.

This sort of semi-tragic fiasco had become so usual that when they occurred he was no longer stirred into making amends. If Gloria protested—and of late she was more likely to sink into a contemptuous silence—he would either engage in a bitter defense of himself or else stalk dismally from the apartment. Never since the incident on the station platform at Redgate had he laid his hands on her in anger—though he was withheld often only by some instinct that itself made him tremble with rage. Just as he still cared more for her than for any other creature, so did he more intensely and frequently hate her.

So far, the judges of the Appellate Division had failed to hand down a decision, but after another postponement they finally affirmed the decree of the lower court—two justices dissenting. A notice of appeal was served upon Edward Shuttleworth. The case was going to the court of last resort, and they were in for another interminable wait. Six months, perhaps a year. It had grown enormously unreal to them, remote and uncertain as heaven.

Throughout the previous winter one small matter had been a subtle and omnipresent irritant—the question of Gloria's gray fur coat. At that time women enveloped in long squirrel wraps could be seen every few yards along Fifth Avenue. The women were converted to the shape of tops. They seemed porcine and obscene; they resembled kept women in the concealing richness, the feminine animality of the garment. Yet—Gloria wanted a gray squirrel coat.

Discussing the matter—or, rather, arguing it, for even more

than in the first year of their marriage did every discussion take the form of bitter debate full of such phrases as "most certainly," "utterly outrageous," "it's so, nevertheless," and the ultra-emphatic "regardless"—they concluded that they could not afford it. And so gradually it began to stand as a symbol of their growing financial anxiety.

To Gloria the shrinkage of their income was a remarkable phenomenon, without explanation or precedent—that it could happen at all within the space of five years seemed almost an intended cruelty, conceived and executed by a sardonic God. When they were married seventy-five hundred a year had seemed ample for a young couple, especially when augmented by the expectation of many millions. Gloria had failed to realize that it was decreasing not only in amount but in purchasing power until the payment of Mr. Haight's retaining fee of fifteen thousand dollars made the fact suddenly and startlingly obvious. When Anthony was drafted they had calculated their income at over four hundred a month, with the dollar even then decreasing in value, but on his return to New York they discovered an even more alarming condition of affairs. They were receiving only forty-five hundred a year from their investments. And though the suit over the will moved ahead of them like a persistent mirage and the financial danger-mark loomed up in the near distance they found, nevertheless, that living within their income was impossible.

So Gloria went without the squirrel coat and every day upon Fifth Avenue she was a little conscious of her well-worn, half-length leopard skin, now hopelessly old-fashioned. Every other month they sold a bond, yet when the bills were paid it left only enough to be gulped down hungrily by their current expenses. Anthony's calculations showed that their capital would last about seven years longer. So Gloria's heart was very bitter, for in one week, on a prolonged hysterical party during which Anthony whimsically divested himself of coat, vest, and shirt in a theatre and was assisted out by a posse of ushers, they spent twice what the gray squirrel coat would have cost.

It was November, Indian summer rather, and a warm, warm night—which was unnecessary, for the work of the summer was done. Babe Ruth had smashed the home-run record for the first time and Jack Dempsey had broken Jess Willard's cheek-bone out in Ohio. Over in Europe the usual number of children had swollen stomachs from starvation, and the diplomats were at their customary business of making the world safe for new wars. In New York City the proletariat were being "disciplined," and the odds on Harvard were generally quoted at five to three. Peace had come down in earnest, the beginning of new days.

Up in the bedroom of the apartment on Fifty-seventh Street Gloria lay upon her bed and tossed from side to side, sitting up at intervals to throw off a superfluous cover and once asking Anthony, who was lying awake beside her, to bring her a glass of ice-water. "Be sure and put ice in it," she said with insistence; "it isn't cold enough the way it comes from the faucet."

Looking through the frail curtains she could see the rounded moon over the roofs and beyond it on the sky the yellow glow from Times Square—and watching the two incongruous lights, her mind worked over an emotion, or rather an interwoven complex of emotions, that had occupied it through the day, and the day before that and back to the last time when she could remember having thought clearly and consecutively about anything—which must have been while Anthony was in the army.

She would be twenty-nine in February. The month assumed an ominous and inescapable significance—making her wonder, through these nebulous half-fevered hours whether after all she had not wasted her faintly tired beauty, whether there was such a thing as use for any quality bounded by a harsh and inevitable mortality.

Years before, when she was twenty-one, she had written in her diary: "Beauty is only to be admired, only to be loved—to be harvested carefully and then flung at a chosen lover like a gift of roses. It seems to me, so far as I can judge clearly at all, that my beauty should be used like that. . . ."

And now, all this November day, all this desolate day, under a sky dirty and white, Gloria had been thinking that perhaps she had been wrong. To preserve the integrity of her first gift she had looked no more for love. When the first flame and ecstasy had grown dim, sunk down, departed, she had begun preserving—what? It puzzled her that she no longer knew just what she was preserving—a sentimental memory or some profound and fundamental concept of honor. She was doubting now whether there had been any moral issue involved in her way of life—to walk unworried and unregretful along the gayest of all possible lanes and to keep her pride by being always herself and doing what it seemed beautiful that she should do. From the first little boy in an Eton collar whose "girl" she had been, down to the latest casual man whose eyes had grown alert and appreciative as they rested upon her, there was needed only that matchless candor she could throw into a look or clothe with an inconsequent clause—for she had talked always in broken clauses—to weave about her immeasurable illusions, immeasurable distances, immeasurable light. To create souls in men, to create fine happiness and fine despair she must remain deeply proud—proud to be inviolate, proud also to be melting, to be passionate and possessed.

She knew that in her breast she had never wanted children. The reality, the earthiness, the intolerable sentiment of child-bearing, the menace to her beauty—had appalled her. She wanted to exist only as a conscious flower, prolonging and preserving itself. Her sentimentality could cling fiercely to her own illusions, but her ironic soul whispered that motherhood was also the privilege of the female baboon. So her dreams were of ghostly children only—the early, the perfect symbols of her early and perfect love for Anthony.

In the end then, her beauty was all that never failed her. She had never seen beauty like her own. What it meant ethically or æsthetically faded before the gorgeous concreteness of her pink-and-white feet, the clean perfectness of her body, and the baby mouth that was like the material symbol of a kiss.

She would be twenty-nine in February. As the long night waned she grew supremely conscious that she and beauty were going to make use of these next three months. At first she was not sure for what, but the problem resolved itself gradually into the old lure of the screen. She was in earnest now. No material want could have moved her as this fear moved her. No matter for Anthony, Anthony the poor in spirit, the weak and broken man with bloodshot eyes, for whom she still had moments of tenderness. No matter. She would be twenty-nine in February—a hundred days, so many days; she would go to Bloeckman to-morrow.

With the decision came relief. It cheered her that in some manner the illusion of beauty could be sustained, or preserved perhaps in celluloid after the reality had vanished. Well—to-morrow.

The next day she felt weak and ill. She tried to go out, and saved herself from collapse only by clinging to a mail-box near the front door. The Martinique elevator boy helped her up-stairs, and she waited on the bed for Anthony's return without energy to unhook her brassière.

For five days she was down with influenza, which, just as the month turned the corner into winter, ripened into double pneumonia. In the feverish perambulations of her mind she prowled through a house of bleak unlighted rooms hunting for her mother. All she wanted was to be a little girl, to be efficiently taken care of by some yielding yet superior power, stupider and steadier than herself. It seemed that the only lover she had ever wanted was a lover in a dream.

"Odi Profanum Vulgus"

One day in the midst of Gloria's illness there occurred a curious incident that puzzled Miss McGovern, the trained nurse, for some time afterward. It was noon, but the room in which the patient lay was dark and quiet. Miss McGovern was standing near the bed mixing some medicine, when Mrs. Patch, who had apparently been sound asleep, sat up and began to speak vehemently:

"Millions of people," she said, "swarming like rats, chattering like apes, smelling like all hell . . . monkeys! Or lice, I suppose. For one really exquisite palace . . . on Long Island, say—or even in Greenwich . . . for one palace full of pictures from the Old World and exquisite things—with avenues of trees and green lawns and a view of the blue sea, and lovely people about in slick dresses . . . I'd sacrifice a hundred thousand of them, a million of them." She raised her hand feebly and snapped her fingers. "I care nothing for them—understand me?"

The look she bent upon Miss McGovern at the conclusion of this speech was curiously elfin, curiously intent. Then she gave a short little laugh polished with scorn, and tumbling backward fell off again to sleep.

Miss McGovern was bewildered. She wondered what were the hundred thousand things that Mrs. Patch would sacrifice for her palace. Dollars, she supposed—yet it had not sounded exactly like dollars.

The Movies

It was February, seven days before her birthday, and the great snow that had filled up the cross streets as dirt fills the cracks in a floor had turned to slush and was being escorted to the gutters by the hoses of the street-cleaning department. The wind, none the less bitter for being casual, whipped in through the open windows of the living-room bearing with it the dismal secrets of the areaway and clearing the Patch apartment of stale smoke in its cheerless circulation.

Gloria, wrapped in a warm kimona, came into the chilly room and taking up the telephone-receiver called Joseph Bloeckman.

"Do you mean Mr. Joseph *Black*?" demanded the telephone girl at "Films Par Excellence."

"Bloeckman, Joseph Bloeckman. B-l-o——"

"Mr. Joseph Bloeckman has changed his name to Black. Do you want him?"

"Why—yes." She remembered nervously that she had once called him "Blockhead" to his face.

His office was reached by courtesy of two additional female voices; the last was a secretary who took her name. Only with the flow through the transmitter of his own familiar but faintly impersonal tone did she realize that it had been three years since they had met. And he had changed his name to Black.

"Can you see me?" she suggested lightly. "It's on a business matter, really. I'm going into the movies at last—if I can."

"I'm awfully glad. I've always thought you'd like it."

"Do you think you can get me a trial?" she demanded with

the arrogance peculiar to all beautiful women, to all women who have ever at any time considered themselves beautiful.

He assured her that it was merely a question of when she wanted the trial. Any time? Well, he'd phone later in the day and let her know a convenient hour. The conversation closed with conventional padding on both sides. Then from three o'clock to five she sat close to the telephone—with no result.

But next morning came a note that contented and excited her:

My dear Gloria:

Just by luck a matter came to my attention that I think will be just suited to you. I would like to see you start with something that would bring you notice. At the same time if a very beautiful girl of your sort is put directly into a picture next to one of the rather shop-worn stars with which every company is afflicted, tongues would very likely wag. But there is a "flapper" part in a Percy B. Debris production that I think would be just suited to you and would bring you notice. Willa Sable plays opposite Gaston Mears in a sort of character part and your part I believe would be her younger sister.

Anyway Percy B. Debris who is directing the picture says if you'll come to the studios day after to-morrow (Thursday) he will run off a test. If ten o'clock is suited to you I will meet you there at that time.

With all good wishes

Ever Faithfully

JOSEPH BLACK.

Gloria had decided that Anthony was to know nothing of this until she had obtained a definite position, and accordingly she was dressed and out of the apartment next morning before he awoke. Her mirror had given her, she thought, much the same account as ever. She wondered if there were any lingering traces of her sickness. She was still slightly under weight, and she had fancied, a few days before, that her cheeks were a trifle thinner—but she felt that those were merely transitory conditions and that on this particular day she looked as fresh as ever. She had bought and charged a new hat, and as the day was warm she had left the leopard-skin coat at home.

At the "Films Par Excellence" studios she was announced over the telephone and told that Mr. Black would be down directly. She looked around her. Two girls were being shown about by a little fat man in a slash-pocket coat, and one of them had indicated a stack of thin parcels, piled breast-high against the wall, and extending along for twenty feet.

"That's studio mail," explained the fat man. "Pictures of the stars who are with 'Films Par Excellence.' "

"Oh."

"Each one's autographed by Florence Kelley or Gaston Mears or Mack Dodge—" He winked confidentially. "At least when Minnie McGlook out in Sauk Center gets the picture she wrote for, she *thinks* it's autographed."

"Just a stamp?"

"Sure. It'd take 'em a good eight-hour day to autograph half of 'em. They say Mary Pickford's studio mail costs her fifty thousand a year."

"Say!"

"Sure. Fifty thousand. But it's the best kinda advertising there is——"

They drifted out of earshot and almost immediately Bloeckman appeared—Bloeckman, a dark suave gentleman, gracefully engaged in the middle forties, who greeted her with courteous warmth and told her she had not changed a bit in three years. He led the way into a great hall, as large as an armory and broken intermittently with busy sets and blinding rows of unfamiliar light. Each piece of scenery was marked in large white letters "Gaston Mears Company," "Mack Dodge Company," or simply "Films Par Excellence."

"Ever been in a studio before?"

"Never have."

She liked it. There was no heavy closeness of grease-paint, no scent of soiled and tawdry costumes which years before had revolted her behind the scenes of a musical comedy. This work was done in the clean mornings; the appurtenances seemed rich and gorgeous and new. On a set that was joyous with Manchu hangings a perfect Chinaman was going through a scene according to megaphone directions as the great glittering machine ground out its ancient moral tale for the edification of the national mind.

A red-headed man approached them and spoke with familiar deference to Bloeckman, who answered:

"Hello, Debris. Want you to meet Mrs. Patch. . . . Mrs. Patch wants to go into pictures, as I explained to you. . . . All right, now, where do we go?"

Mr. Debris—the great Percy B. Debris, thought Gloria—showed them to a set which represented the interior of an office. Some chairs were drawn up around the camera, which stood in front of it, and the three of them sat down.

"Ever been in a studio before?" asked Mr. Debris, giving her a glance that was surely the quintessence of keenness. "No? Well, I'll explain exactly what's going to happen. We're going to take what we call a test in order to see how your features photograph and whether you've got natural stage presence and how you respond to coaching. There's no need to be nervous over it. I'll just have the camera-man take a few hundred feet in an episode I've got marked here in the scenario. We can tell pretty much what we want to from that."

He produced a typewritten continuity and explained to her the episode she was to enact. It developed that one Barbara Wainwright had been secretly married to the junior partner of the firm whose office was there represented. Entering the deserted office one day by accident she was naturally interested in seeing where her husband worked. The telephone rang and after some hesitation she answered it. She learned that her husband had been struck by an automobile and instantly killed. She was overcome. At first she was unable to realize the truth, but finally she succeeded in comprehending it, and went into a dead faint on the floor.

"Now that's all we want," concluded Mr. Debris. "I'm going to stand here and tell you approximately what to do, and you're to act as though I wasn't here, and just go on do it your own way. You needn't be afraid we're going to judge this too severely. We simply want to get a general idea of your screen personality."

"I see."

"You'll find make-up in the room in back of the set. Go light on it. Very little red."

"I see," repeated Gloria, nodding. She touched her lips nervously with the tip of her tongue.

The Test

As she came into the set through the real wooden door and closed it carefully behind her, she found herself inconveniently dissatisfied with her clothes. She should have bought a "misses' " dress for the occasion—she could still wear them, and it might have been a good investment if it had accentuated her airy youth.

Her mind snapped sharply into the momentous present as Mr. Debris's voice came from the glare of the white lights in front.

"You look around for your husband. . . . Now—you don't see him . . . you're curious about the office. . . ."

She became conscious of the regular sound of the camera. It worried her. She glanced toward it involuntarily and wondered if she had made up her face correctly. Then, with a definite effort she forced herself to act—and she had never felt that the gestures of her body were so banal, so awkward, so bereft of grace or distinction. She strolled around the office, picking up articles here and there and looking at them inanely. Then she scrutinized the ceiling, the floor, and thoroughly inspected an inconsequential lead-pencil on the desk. Finally, because she could think of nothing else to do, and less than nothing to express, she forced a smile.

"All right. Now the phone rings. Ting-a-ling-a-ling! Hesitate, and then answer it."

She hesitated—and then, too quickly, she thought, picked up the receiver.

"Hello."

Her voice was hollow and unreal. The words rang in the empty set like the ineffectualities of a ghost. The absurdities of their requirements appalled her— Did they expect that on an instant's notice she could put herself in the place of this preposterous and unexplained character?

". . . No . . . no. . . . Not yet! Now listen: 'John Sumner has just been knocked over by an automobile and instantly killed!' "

Gloria let her baby mouth drop slowly open. Then:

"Now hang up! With a bang!"

She obeyed, clung to the table with her eyes wide and staring.

At length she was feeling slightly encouraged and her confidence increased.

"My God!" she cried. Her voice was good, she thought. "Oh, my God!"

"Now faint."

She collapsed forward to her knees and throwing her body outward on the ground lay without breathing.

"All right!" called Mr. Debris. "That's enough, thank you. That's plenty. Get up—that's enough."

Gloria arose, mustering her dignity and brushing off her skirt.

"Awful!" she remarked with a cool laugh, though her heart was bumping tumultuously. "Terrible, wasn't it?"

"Did you mind it?" said Mr. Debris, smiling blandly. "Did it seem hard? I can't tell anything about it until I have it run off."

"Of course not," she agreed, trying to attach some sort of meaning to his remark—and failing. It was just the sort of thing he would have said had he been trying not to encourage her.

A few moments later she left the studio. Bloeckman had promised that she should hear the result of the test within the next few days. Too proud to force any definite comment she felt a baffling uncertainty and only now when the step had at last been taken did she realize how the possibility of a successful screen career had played in the back of her mind for the past three years. That night she tried to tell over to herself the elements that might decide for or against her. Whether or not she had used enough make-up worried her, and as the part was that of a girl of twenty, she wondered if she had not been just a little too grave. About her acting she was least of all satisfied. Her entrance had been abominable—in fact not until she reached the phone had she displayed a shred of poise—and then the test had been over. If they had only realized! She wished that she could try it again. A mad plan to call up in the morning and ask for a new trial took possession of her, and as suddenly faded. It seemed neither politic nor polite to ask another favor of Bloeckman.

The third day of waiting found her in a highly nervous condition. She had bitten the insides of her mouth until they were raw and smarting, and burnt unbearably when she washed them with listerine. She had quarrelled so persistently with Anthony that he had left the apartment in a cold fury. But because he was intimidated by her exceptional frigidity, he called up an hour afterward, apologized and said he was having dinner at the Amsterdam Club, the only one in which he still retained membership.

It was after one o'clock and she had breakfasted at eleven, so, deciding to forego luncheon, she started for a walk in the Park. At three there would be a mail. She would be back by three.

It was an afternoon of premature spring. Water was drying on the walks and in the Park little girls were gravely wheeling white doll-buggies up and down under the thin trees while behind them followed bored nursery-maids in two's, discussing with each other those tremendous secrets that are peculiar to nursery-maids.

Two o'clock by her little gold watch. She should have a new watch, one made in a platinum oblong and incrusted with diamonds—but those cost even more than squirrel coats and of course they were out of her reach now, like everything else—unless perhaps the right letter was awaiting her . . . in about an hour . . . fifty-eight minutes exactly. Ten to get there left forty-eight . . . forty-seven now . . .

Little girls soberly wheeling their buggies along the damp sunny walks. The nursery-maids chattering in pairs about their inscrutable secrets. Here and there a raggedy man seated upon newspapers spread on a drying bench, related not to the radiant and delightful afternoon but to the dirty snow that slept exhausted in obscure corners, waiting for extermination. . . .

Ages later, coming into the dim hall she saw the Martinique elevator boy standing incongruously in the light of the stained-glass window.

"Is there any mail for us?" she asked.

"Up-stays, madame."

The switchboard squawked abominably and Gloria waited while he ministered to the telephone. She sickened as the elevator groaned its way up—the floors passed like the slow lapse of centuries, each one ominous, accusing, significant.

The letter, a white leprous spot, lay upon the dirty tiles of the hall. . . .

My dear Gloria:

We had the test run off yesterday afternoon, and Mr. Debris seemed to think that for the part he had in mind he needed a younger woman. He said that the acting was not bad, and that there was a small character part supposed to be a very haughty rich widow that he thought you might——

Desolately Gloria raised her glance until it fell out across the areaway. But she found she could not see the opposite wall, for her gray eyes were full of tears. She walked into the bedroom, the letter crinkled tightly in her hand, and sank down upon her knees before the long mirror on the wardrobe floor. This was her twenty-ninth birthday, and the world was melting away before her eyes. She tried to think that it had been the make-up, but her emotions were too profound, too overwhelming for any consolation that the thought conveyed.

She strained to see until she could feel the flesh on her temples pull forward. Yes—the cheeks were ever so faintly thin, the corners of the eyes were lined with tiny wrinkles. The eyes were different. Why, they were different! . . . And then suddenly she knew how tired her eyes were.

"Oh, my pretty face," she whispered, passionately grieving. "Oh, my pretty face! Oh, I don't want to live without my pretty face! Oh, what's *happened*?"

Then she slid toward the mirror and, as in the test, sprawled face downward upon the floor—and lay there sobbing. It was the first awkward movement she had ever made.

CHAPTER III

No Matter!

WITHIN another year Anthony and Gloria had become like players who had lost their costumes, lacking the pride to continue on the note of tragedy—so that when Mrs. and Miss Hulme of Kansas City cut them dead in the Plaza one evening, it was only that Mrs. and Miss Hulme, like most people, abominated mirrors of their atavistic selves.

Their new apartment, for which they paid eighty-five dollars a month, was situated on Claremont Avenue, which is two blocks from the Hudson in the dim hundreds. They had lived there a month when Muriel Kane came to see them late one afternoon.

It was a reproachless twilight on the summer side of spring. Anthony lay upon the lounge looking up One Hundred and Twenty-seventh Street toward the river, near which he could just see a single patch of vivid green trees that guaranteed the brummagem umbrageousness of Riverside Drive. Across the water were the Palisades, crowned by the ugly framework of the amusement park—yet soon it would be dusk and those same iron cobwebs would be a glory against the heavens, an enchanted palace set over the smooth radiance of a tropical canal.

The streets near the apartment, Anthony had found, were streets where children played—streets a little nicer than those he had been used to pass on his way to Marietta, but of the same general sort, with an occasional hand-organ or hurdy-gurdy, and in the cool of the evening many pairs of young girls walking down to the corner drug-store for ice-cream soda and dreaming unlimited dreams under the low heavens.

Dusk in the streets now, and children playing, shouting up incoherent ecstatic words that faded out close to the open window—and Muriel, who had come to find Gloria, chattering to him from an opaque gloom over across the room.

"Light the lamp, why don't we?" she suggested. "It's getting *ghost*ly in here."

With a tired movement he arose and obeyed; the gray window-panes vanished. He stretched himself. He was heavier now, his stomach was a limp weight against his belt; his flesh had softened and expanded. He was thirty-two and his mind was a bleak and disordered wreck.

"Have a little drink, Muriel?"

"Not me, thanks. I don't use it any more. What're you doing these days, Anthony?" she asked curiously.

"Well, I've been pretty busy with this lawsuit," he answered indifferently. "It's gone to the Court of Appeals—ought to be settled up one way or another by autumn. There's been some objection as to whether the Court of Appeals has jurisdiction over the matter."

Muriel made a clicking sound with her tongue and cocked her head on one side.

"Well, you tell 'em! I never heard of anything taking so long."

"Oh, they all do," he replied listlessly; "all will cases. They say it's exceptional to have one settled under four or five years."

"Oh . . ." Muriel daringly changed her tack, "why don't you go to work, you la-azy!"

"At what?" he demanded abruptly.

"Why, at anything, I suppose. You're still a young man."

"If that's encouragement, I'm much obliged," he answered dryly—and then with sudden weariness: "Does it bother you particularly that I don't want to work?"

"It doesn't bother me—but, it does bother a lot of people who claim——"

"Oh, God!" he said brokenly, "it seems to me that for three years I've heard nothing about myself but wild stories and virtuous admonitions. I'm tired of it. If you don't want to see us, let us alone. I don't bother my former 'friends.' But I need no charity calls, and no criticism disguised as good advice—" Then he added apologetically: "I'm sorry—but really, Muriel, you mustn't talk like a lady slum-worker even if you are visiting the lower middle classes." He turned his bloodshot eyes on her reproachfully—eyes that had once been a deep, clear blue, that were weak now, strained, and half-ruined from reading when he was drunk.

"Why do you say such awful things?" she protested. "You talk as if you and Gloria were in the middle classes."

"Why pretend we're not? I hate people who claim to be great aristocrats when they can't even keep up the appearances of it."

"Do you think a person has to have money to be aristocratic?"

Muriel . . . the horrified democrat . . . . !

"Why, of course. Aristocracy's only an admission that certain traits which we call fine—courage and honor and beauty and all that sort of thing—can best be developed in a favorable environment, where you don't have the warpings of ignorance and necessity."

Muriel bit her lower lip and waved her head from side to side.

"Well, all *I* say is that if a person comes from a good family they're always nice people. That's the trouble with you and Gloria. You think that just because things aren't going your way right now all your old friends are trying to avoid you. You're too sensitive——"

"As a matter of fact," said Anthony, "you know nothing at all about it. With me it's simply a matter of pride, and for once Gloria's reasonable enough to agree that we oughtn't go where we're not wanted. And people don't want us. We're too much the ideal bad examples."

"Nonsense! You can't park your pessimism in my little sun-parlor. I think you ought to forget all those morbid speculations and go to work."

"Here I am, thirty-two. Suppose I did start in at some idiotic business. Perhaps in two years I might rise to fifty dollars a week—with luck. That's *if* I could get a job at all; there's an awful lot of unemployment. Well, suppose I made fifty a week. Do you think I'd be any happier? Do you think that if I don't get this money of my grandfather's life will be *endurable*?"

Muriel smiled complacently.

"Well," she said, "that may be clever but it isn't common sense."

A few minutes later Gloria came in seeming to bring with her into the room some dark color, indeterminate and rare. In a taciturn way she was happy to see Muriel. She greeted Anthony with a casual "Hi!"

"I've been talking philosophy with your husband," cried the irrepressible Miss Kane.

"We took up some fundamental concepts," said Anthony, a faint smile disturbing his pale cheeks, paler still under two days' growth of beard.

Oblivious to his irony Muriel rehashed her contention. When she had done, Gloria said quietly:

"Anthony's right. It's no fun to go around when you have the sense that people are looking at you in a certain way."

He broke in plaintively:

"Don't you think that when even Maury Noble, who was my best friend, won't come to see us it's high time to stop calling people up?" Tears were standing in his eyes.

"That was your fault about Maury Noble," said Gloria coolly.

"It wasn't."

"It most certainly was."

Muriel intervened quickly:

"I met a girl who knew Maury, the other day, and she says he doesn't drink any more. He's getting pretty cagey."

"Doesn't?"

"Practically not at all. He's making *piles* of money. He's sort of changed since the war. He's going to marry a girl in Philadelphia who has millions, Ceci Larrabee—anyhow, that's what Town Tattle said."

"He's thirty-three," said Anthony, thinking aloud. "But it's odd to imagine his getting married. I used to think he was so brilliant."

"He was," murmured Gloria, "in a way."

"But brilliant people don't settle down in business—or do they? Or what do they do? Or what becomes of everybody you used to know and have so much in common with?"

"You drift apart," suggested Muriel with the appropriate dreamy look.

"They change," said Gloria. "All the qualities that they don't use in their daily lives get cobwebbed up."

"The last thing he said to me," recollected Anthony, "was that he was going to work so as to forget that there was nothing worth working for."

Muriel caught at this quickly.

"That's what *you* ought to do," she exclaimed triumphantly. "Of course I shouldn't think anybody would want to work for nothing. But it'd give you something to do. What do you do with yourselves, anyway? Nobody ever sees you at Montmartre or—or anywhere. Are you economizing?"

Gloria laughed scornfully, glancing at Anthony from the corners of her eyes.

"Well," he demanded, "what are you laughing at?"

"You know what I'm laughing at," she answered coldly.

"At that case of whiskey?"

"Yes"—she turned to Muriel—"he paid seventy-five dollars for a case of whiskey yesterday."

"What if I did? It's cheaper that way than if you get it by the bottle. You needn't pretend that you won't drink any of it."

"At least I don't drink in the daytime."

"That's a fine distinction!" he cried, springing to his feet in a weak rage. "What's more, I'll be damned if you can hurl that at me every few minutes!"

"It's true."

"It is *not!* And I'm getting sick of this eternal business of criticising me before visitors!" He had worked himself up to such a state that his arms and shoulders were visibly trembling. "You'd think everything was my fault. You'd think you hadn't encouraged me to spend money—and spent a lot more on yourself than I ever did by a long shot."

Now Gloria rose to her feet.

"I *won't* let you talk to me that way!"

"All right, then; by Heaven, you don't have to!"

In a sort of rush he left the room. The two women heard his steps in the hall and then the front door banged. Gloria sank back into her chair. Her face was lovely in the lamplight, composed, inscrutable.

"Oh—!" cried Muriel in distress. "Oh, what *is* the matter?"

"Nothing particularly. He's just drunk."

"Drunk? Why, he's perfectly sober. He talked——"

Gloria shook her head.

"Oh, no, he doesn't show it any more unless he can hardly stand up, and he talks all right until he gets excited. He talks much better than he does when he's sober. But he's been sitting here all day drinking—except for the time it took him to walk to the corner for a newspaper."

"Oh, how terrible!" Muriel was sincerely moved. Her eyes filled with tears. "Has this happened much?"

"Drinking, you mean?"

"No, this—leaving you?"

"Oh, yes. Frequently. He'll come in about midnight—and weep and ask me to forgive him."

"And do you?"

"I don't know. We just go on."

The two women sat there in the lamplight and looked at each other, each in a different way helpless before this thing. Gloria was still pretty, as pretty as she would ever be again—her cheeks were flushed and she was wearing a new dress that she had bought—imprudently—for fifty dollars. She had hoped she could persuade Anthony to take her out to-night, to a restaurant or even to one of the great, gorgeous moving-picture palaces where there would be a few people to look at her, at whom she could bear to look in turn. She wanted this because she knew her cheeks were flushed and because her dress was new and becomingly fragile. Only very occasionally, now, did they receive any invitations. But she did not tell these things to Muriel.

"Gloria, dear, I wish we could have dinner together, but I promised a man—and it's seven-thirty already. I've got to *tear*."

"Oh, I couldn't, anyway. In the first place I've been ill all day. I couldn't eat a thing."

After she had walked with Muriel to the door, Gloria came back into the room, turned out the lamp, and leaning her elbows on the window-sill looked out at Palisades Park, where the brilliant revolving circle of the Ferris wheel was like a trembling mirror catching the yellow reflection of the moon. The street was quiet now; the children had gone in—over the way she could see a family at dinner. Pointlessly, ridiculously, they rose and walked about the table; seen thus, all that they did appeared incongruous—it was as though they were being jiggled carelessly and to no purpose by invisible overhead wires.

She looked at her watch—it was eight o'clock. She had been pleased for a part of the day—the early afternoon—in walking along that Broadway of Harlem, One Hundred and Twenty-fifth Street, with her nostrils alert to many odors, and her mind excited by the extraordinary beauty of some Italian children. It affected her curiously—as Fifth Avenue had affected her once, in the days when, with the placid confidence of beauty, she had known that it was all hers, every shop and all it held, every adult toy glittering in a window, all hers for the asking. Here on One Hundred and Twenty-fifth Street there were Salvation Army bands and spectrum-shawled old ladies on door-steps and sugary, sticky candy in the grimy hands of shiny-haired children—and the late sun striking down on the sides of the tall tenements. All very rich and racy and savory, like a dish by a provident French chef that one could not help enjoying, even though one knew that the ingredients were probably left-overs. . . .

Gloria shuddered suddenly as a river siren came moaning over the dusky roofs, and leaning back in till the ghostly curtains fell from her shoulder, she turned on the electric lamp. It was growing late. She knew there was some change in her purse, and she considered whether she would go down and have some coffee and rolls where the liberated subway made a roaring cave of Manhattan Street or eat the devilled ham and bread in the kitchen. Her purse decided for her. It contained a nickel and two pennies.

After an hour the silence of the room had grown unbearable, and she found that her eyes were wandering from her magazine to the ceiling, toward which she stared without thought. Suddenly she stood up, hesitated for a moment, biting at her finger—then she went to the pantry, took down a bottle of whiskey from the shelf and poured herself a drink. She filled up the glass with ginger ale, and returning to her chair finished an article in the magazine. It concerned the last revolutionary widow, who, when a young girl, had married an ancient veteran of the Continental Army and who had died in

1906. It seemed strange and oddly romantic to Gloria that she and this woman had been contemporaries.

She turned a page and learned that a candidate for Congress was being accused of atheism by an opponent. Gloria's surprise vanished when she found that the charges were false. The candidate had merely denied the miracle of the loaves and fishes. He admitted, under pressure, that he gave full credence to the stroll upon the water.

Finishing her first drink, Gloria got herself a second. After slipping on a negligée and making herself comfortable on the lounge, she became conscious that she was miserable and that the tears were rolling down her cheeks. She wondered if they were tears of self-pity, and tried resolutely not to cry, but this existence without hope, without happiness, oppressed her, and she kept shaking her head from side to side, her mouth drawn down tremulously in the corners, as though she were denying an assertion made by some one, somewhere. She did not know that this gesture of hers was years older than history, that, for a hundred generations of men, intolerable and persistent grief has offered that gesture, of denial, of protest, of bewilderment, to something more profound, more powerful than the God made in the image of man, and before which that God, did he exist, would be equally impotent. It is a truth set at the heart of tragedy that this force never explains, never answers—this force intangible as air, more definite than death.

Richard Caramel

Early in the summer Anthony resigned from his last club, the Amsterdam. He had come to visit it hardly twice a year, and the dues were a recurrent burden. He had joined it on his return from Italy because it had been his grandfather's club and his father's, and because it was a club that, given the opportunity, one indisputably joined—but as a matter of fact he had preferred the Harvard Club, largely because of Dick and Maury. However, with the decline of his fortunes, it had seemed an increasingly desirable bauble to cling to. . . . It was relinquished at the last, with some regret. . . .

His companions numbered now a curious dozen. Several of them he had met in a place called "Sammy's," on Forty-third Street, where, if one knocked on the door and were favorably passed on from behind a grating, one could sit around a great round table drinking fairly good whiskey. It was here that he encountered a man named Parker Allison, who had been exactly the wrong sort of rounder at Harvard, and who was running through a large "yeast" fortune as rapidly as possible. Parker Allison's notion of distinction consisted in driving a noisy red-and-yellow racing-car up Broadway with two glittering, hard-eyed girls beside him. He was the sort who dined with two girls rather than with one—his imagination was almost incapable of sustaining a dialogue.

Besides Allison there was Pete Lytell, who wore a gray derby on the side of his head. He always had money and he was customarily cheerful, so Anthony held aimless, long-winded conversation with him through many afternoons of the summer and fall. Lytell, he found, not only talked but reasoned in phrases. His philosophy was a series of them, assimilated here and there through an active, thoughtless life. He had phrases about Socialism—the immemorial ones; he had phrases pertaining to the existence of a personal deity—something about one time when he had been in a railroad accident; and he had phrases about the Irish problem, the sort of woman he respected, and the futility of prohibition. The only time his conversation ever rose superior to these muddled clauses, with which he interpreted the most rococo happenings in a life that had been more than usually eventful, was when he got down to the detailed discussion of his most animal existence: he knew, to a subtlety, the foods, the liquor, and the women that he preferred.

He was at once the commonest and the most remarkable product of civilization. He was nine out of ten people that one passes on a city street—and he was a hairless ape with two dozen tricks. He was the hero of a thousand romances of life and art—and he was a virtual moron, performing staidly yet absurdly a series of complicated and infinitely astounding epics over a span of threescore years.

With such men as these two Anthony Patch drank and discussed and drank and argued. He liked them because they knew nothing about him, because they lived in the obvious and had not the faintest conception of the inevitable continuity of life. They sat not before a motion-picture with consecutive reels, but at a musty old-fashioned travelogue with all values stark and hence all implications confused. Yet they themselves were not confused, because there was nothing in them to be confused—they changed phrases from month to month as they changed neckties.

Anthony, the courteous, the subtle, the perspicacious, was drunk each day—in Sammy's with these men, in the apartment over a book, some book he knew, and, very rarely, with Gloria, who, in his eyes, had begun to develop the unmistakable outlines of a quarrelsome and unreasonable woman. She was not the Gloria of old, certainly—the Gloria who, had she been sick, would have preferred to inflict misery upon every one around her rather than confess that she needed sympathy or assistance. She was not above whining now; she was not above being sorry for herself. Each night when she prepared for bed she smeared her face with some new unguent which she hoped illogically would give back the glow and freshness to her vanishing beauty. When Anthony was drunk he taunted her about this. When he was sober he was polite to her, on occasions even tender; he seemed to show for short hours a trace of that old quality of understanding too well to blame—that quality which was the best of him and had worked swiftly and ceaselessly toward his ruin.

But he hated to be sober. It made him conscious of the people around him, of that air of struggle, of greedy ambition, of hope more sordid than despair, of incessant passage up or down, which in every metropolis is most in evidence through the unstable middle class. Unable to live with the rich he thought that his next choice would have been to live with the very poor. Anything was better than this cup of perspiration and tears.

The sense of the enormous panorama of life, never strong in Anthony, had become dim almost to extinction. At long intervals now some incident, some gesture of Gloria's, would take his fancy—but the gray veils had come down in earnest upon him. As he grew older those things faded—after that there was wine.

There was a kindliness about intoxication—there was that indescribable gloss and glamour it gave, like the memories of ephemeral and faded evenings. After a few high-balls there was magic in the tall glowing Arabian night of the Bush Terminal Building—its summit a peak of sheer grandeur, gold and dreaming against the inaccessible sky. And Wall Street, the crass, the banal—again it was the triumph of gold, a gorgeous sentient spectacle; it was where the great kings kept the money for their wars. . . .

. . . The fruit of youth or of the grape, the transitory magic of the brief passage from darkness to darkness—the old illusion that truth and beauty were in some way entwined.

As he stood in front of Delmonico's lighting a cigarette one night he saw two hansoms drawn up close to the curb, waiting for a chance drunken fare. The outmoded cabs were worn and dirty—the cracked patent leather wrinkled like an old man's face, the cushions faded to a brownish lavender; the very horses were ancient and weary, and so were the white-haired men who sat aloft, cracking their whips with a grotesque affectation of gallantry. A relic of vanished gaiety!

Anthony Patch walked away in a sudden fit of depression, pondering the bitterness of such survivals. There was nothing, it seemed, that grew stale so soon as pleasure.

On Forty-second Street one afternoon he met Richard Caramel for the first time in many months, a prosperous, fattening Richard Caramel, whose face was filling out to match the Bostonian brow.

"Just got in this week from the coast. Was going to call you up, but I didn't know your new address."

"We've moved."

Richard Caramel noticed that Anthony was wearing a soiled shirt, that his cuffs were slightly but perceptibly frayed, that his eyes were set in half-moons the color of cigar-smoke.

"So I gathered," he said, fixing his friend with his bright-yellow eye. "But where and how is Gloria? My God, Anthony, I've been hearing the dog-gonedest stories about you two even out in California—and when I get back to New York I find you've sunk absolutely out of sight. Why don't you pull yourself together?"

"Now, listen," chattered Anthony unsteadily, "I can't stand a long lecture. We've lost money in a dozen ways, and naturally people have talked—on account of the lawsuit, but the thing's coming to a final decision this winter, surely——"

"You're talking so fast that I can't understand you," interrupted Dick calmly.

"Well, I've said all I'm going to say," snapped Anthony. "Come and see us if you like—or don't!"

With this he turned and started to walk off in the crowd, but Dick overtook him immediately and grasped his arm.

"Say, Anthony, don't fly off the handle so easily! You know Gloria's my cousin, and you're one of my oldest friends, so it's natural for me to be interested when I hear that you're going to the dogs—and taking her with you."

"I don't want to be preached to."

"Well, then, all right— How about coming up to my apartment and having a drink? I've just got settled. I've bought three cases of Gordon gin from a revenue officer."

As they walked along he continued in a burst of exasperation:

"And how about your grandfather's money—you going to get it?"

"Well," answered Anthony resentfully, "that old fool Haight seems hopeful, especially because people are tired of reformers right now—you know it might make a slight difference, for instance, if some judge thought that Adam Patch made it harder for him to get liquor."

"You can't do without money," said Dick sententiously. "Have you tried to write any—lately?"

Anthony shook his head silently.

"That's funny," said Dick. "I always thought that you and Maury would write some day, and now he's grown to be a sort of tight-fisted aristocrat, and you're——"

"I'm the bad example."

"I wonder why?"

"You probably think you know," suggested Anthony, with an effort at concentration. "The failure and the success both believe in their hearts that they have accurately balanced points of view, the success because he's succeeded, and the failure because he's failed. The successful man tells his son to profit by his father's good fortune, and the failure tells *his* son to profit by his father's mistakes."

"I don't agree with you," said the author of "A Shave-tail in France." "I used to listen to you and Maury when we were young, and I used to be impressed because you were so consistently cynical, but now—well, after all, by God, which of us three has taken to the—to the intellectual life? I don't want to sound vainglorious, but—it's me, and I've always believed that moral values existed, and I always will."

"Well," objected Anthony, who was rather enjoying himself, "even granting that, you know that in practice life never presents problems as clear cut, does it?"

"It does to me. There's nothing I'd violate certain principles for."

"But how do you know when you're violating them? You have to guess at things just like most people do. You have to apportion the values when you look back. You finish up the portrait then—paint in the details and shadows."

Dick shook his head with a lofty stubbornness.

"Same old futile cynic," he said. "It's just a mode of being sorry for yourself. You don't do anything—so nothing matters."

"Oh, I'm quite capable of self-pity," admitted Anthony, "nor am I claiming that I'm getting as much fun out of life as you are."

"You say—at least you used to—that happiness is the only thing worth while in life. Do you think you're any happier for being a pessimist?"

Anthony grunted savagely. His pleasure in the conversation began to wane. He was nervous and craving for a drink.

"My golly!" he cried, "where do you live? I can't keep walking forever."

"Your endurance is all mental, eh?" returned Dick sharply. "Well, I live right here."

He turned in at the apartment-house on Forty-ninth Street, and a few minutes later they were in a large new room with an open fireplace and four walls lined with books. A colored butler served them gin rickeys, and an hour vanished politely with the mellow shortening of their drinks and the glow of a light mid-autumn fire.

"The arts are very old," said Anthony after a while. With a few glasses the tension of his nerves relaxed and he found that he could think again.

"Which art?"

"All of them. Poetry is dying first. It'll be absorbed into prose sooner or later. For instance, the beautiful word, the colored and glittering word, and the beautiful simile belong in prose now. To get attention poetry has got to strain for the unusual word, the harsh, earthy word that's never been beautiful before. Beauty, as the sum of several beautiful parts, reached its apotheosis in Swinburne. It can't go any further—except in the novel, perhaps."

Dick interrupted him impatiently:

"You know these new novels make me tired. My God! Everywhere I go some silly girl asks me if I've read 'This Side of Paradise.' Are our girls really like that? If it's true to life, which I don't believe, the next generation is going to the dogs. I'm sick of all this shoddy realism. I think there's a place for the romanticist in literature."

Anthony tried to remember what he had read lately of Richard Caramel's. There was "A Shave-tail in France," a novel called "The Land of Strong Men," and several dozen short stories, which were even worse. It had become the custom among young and clever reviewers to mention Richard Caramel with a smile of scorn. "Mr." Richard Caramel, they called him. His corpse was dragged obscenely through every literary supplement. He was accused of making a great fortune by writing trash for the movies. As the fashion in books shifted he was becoming almost a byword of contempt.

While Anthony was thinking this, Dick had got to his feet and seemed to be hesitating at an avowal.

"I've gathered quite a few books," he said suddenly.

"So I see."

"I've made an exhaustive collection of good American stuff, old and new. I don't mean the usual Longfellow-Whittier thing—in fact, most of it's modern."

He stepped to one of the walls and, seeing that it was expected of him, Anthony arose and followed.

"Look!"

Under a printed tag *Americana* he displayed six long rows of books, beautifully bound and, obviously, carefully chosen.

"And here are the contemporary novelists."

Then Anthony saw the joker. Wedged in between Mark Twain and Dreiser were eight strange and inappropriate volumes, the works of Richard Caramel—"The Demon Lover," true enough . . . but also seven others that were execrably awful, without sincerity or grace.

Unwillingly Anthony glanced at Dick's face and caught a slight uncertainty there.

"I've put my own books in, of course," said Richard Caramel hastily, "though one or two of them are uneven—I'm afraid I wrote a little too fast when I had that magazine contract. But I don't believe in false modesty. Of course some of the critics haven't paid so much attention to me since I've been established—but, after all, it's not the critics that count. They're just sheep."

For the first time in so long that he could scarcely remember, Anthony felt a touch of the old pleasant contempt for his friend. Richard Caramel continued:

"My publishers, you know, have been advertising me as the Thackeray of America—because of my New York novel."

"Yes," Anthony managed to muster, "I suppose there's a good deal in what you say."

He knew that his contempt was unreasonable. He knew that he would have changed places with Dick unhesitatingly. He himself had tried his best to write with his tongue in his cheek. Ah, well, then—can a man disparage his life-work so readily? . . .

—And that night while Richard Caramel was hard at toil, with great hittings of the wrong keys and screwings up of his weary, unmatched eyes, laboring over his trash far into those cheerless hours when the fire dies down, and the head is swimming from the effect of prolonged concentration—Anthony, abominably drunk, was sprawled across the back seat of a taxi on his way to the flat on Claremont Avenue.

The Beating

As winter approached it seemed that a sort of madness seized upon Anthony. He awoke in the morning so nervous that Gloria could feel him trembling in the bed before he could muster enough vitality to stumble into the pantry for a drink. He was intolerable now except under the influence of liquor, and as he seemed to decay and coarsen under her eyes, Gloria's soul and body shrank away from him; when he stayed out all night, as he did several times, she not only failed to be sorry but even felt a measure of dismal relief. Next day he would be faintly repentant, and would remark in a gruff, hang-dog fashion that he guessed he was drinking a little too much.

For hours at a time he would sit in the great armchair that had been in his apartment, lost in a sort of stupor—even his interest in reading his favorite books seemed to have departed, and though an incessant bickering went on between husband and wife, the one subject upon which they ever really conversed was the progress of the will case. What Gloria hoped in the tenebrous depths of her soul, what she expected that great gift of money to bring about, is difficult to imagine. She was being bent by her environment into a grotesque similitude of a housewife. She who until three years before had never made coffee, prepared sometimes three meals a day. She walked a great deal in the afternoons, and in the evenings she read—books, magazines, anything she found at hand. If now she wished for a child, even a child of the Anthony who sought her bed blind drunk, she neither said so nor gave any show or sign of interest in children. It is doubtful if she could have made it clear to any one what it was she wanted, or indeed what there was to want—a lonely, lovely woman, thirty now, retrenched behind some impregnable inhibition born and coexistent with her beauty.

One afternoon when the snow was dirty again along Riverside Drive, Gloria, who had been to the grocer's, entered the apartment to find Anthony pacing the floor in a state of aggravated nervousness. The feverish eyes he turned on her were traced with tiny pink lines that reminded her of rivers on a map. For a moment she received the impression that he was suddenly and definitely old.

"Have you any money?" he inquired of her precipitately.

"What? What do you mean?"

"Just what I said. Money! Money! Can't you speak English?"

She paid no attention but brushed by him and into the pantry to put the bacon and eggs in the ice-box. When his drinking had been unusually excessive he was invariably in a whining mood. This time he followed her and, standing in the pantry door, persisted in his question.

"You heard what I said. Have you any money?"

She turned about from the ice-box and faced him.

"Why, Anthony, you must be crazy! You know I haven't any money—except a dollar in change."

He executed an abrupt about-face and returned to the living-room, where he renewed his pacing. It was evident that he had something portentous on his mind—he quite obviously wanted to be asked what was the matter. Joining him a moment later she sat upon the long lounge and began taking down her hair. It was no longer bobbed, and it had changed in the last year from a rich gold dusted with red to an unresplendent light brown. She had brought some shampoo soap and meant to wash it now; she had considered putting a bottle of peroxide into the rinsing water.

"—Well?" she implied silently.

"That darn bank!" he quavered. "They've had my account for over ten years—ten *years*. Well, it seems they've got some autocratic rule that you have to keep over five hundred dollars there or they won't carry you. They wrote me a letter a few months ago and told me I'd been running too low. Once I gave out two bum checks—remember? that night in Reisenweber's?—but I made them good the very next day. Well, I promised old Halloran—he's the manager, the greedy Mick—that I'd watch out. And I thought I was going all right; I kept up the stubs in my check-book pretty regular. Well, I went in there to-day to cash a check, and Halloran came up and told me they'd have to close my account. Too many bad checks, he said, and I never had more than five hundred to my credit—and that only for a day or so at a time. And by God! What do you think he said then?"

"What?"

"He said this was a good time to do it because I didn't have a damn penny in there!"

"You didn't?"

"That's what he told me. Seems I'd given these Bedros people a check for sixty for that last case of liquor—and I only had forty-five dollars in the bank. Well, the Bedros people deposited fifteen dollars to my account and drew the whole thing out."

In her ignorance Gloria conjured up a spectre of imprisonment and disgrace.

"Oh, they won't do anything," he assured her. "Bootlegging's too risky a business. They'll send me a bill for fifteen dollars and I'll pay it."

"Oh." She considered a moment. "—Well, we can sell another bond."

He laughed sarcastically.

"Oh, yes, that's always easy. When the few bonds we have that are paying any interest at all are only worth between fifty and eighty cents on the dollar. We lose about half the bond every time we sell."

"What else can we do?"

"Oh, we'll sell something—as usual. We've got paper worth eighty thousand dollars at par." Again he laughed unpleasantly. "Bring about thirty thousand on the open market."

"I distrusted those ten per cent investments."

"The deuce you did!" he said. "You pretended you did, so you could claw at me if they went to pieces, but you wanted to take a chance as much as I did."

She was silent for a moment as if considering, then:

"Anthony," she cried suddenly, "two hundred a month is worse than nothing. Let's sell all the bonds and put the thirty thousand dollars in the bank—and if we lose the case we can live in Italy for three years, and then just die." In her excitement as she talked she was aware of a faint flush of sentiment, the first she had felt in many days.

"Three years," he said nervously, "three years! You're crazy. Mr. Haight'll take more than that if we lose. Do you think he's working for charity?"

"I forgot that."

"—And here it is Saturday," he continued, "and I've only

got a dollar and some change, and we've got to live till Monday, when I can get to my broker's. . . . And not a drink in the house," he added as a significant after-thought.

"Can't you call up Dick?"

"I did. His man says he's gone down to Princeton to address a literary club or some such thing. Won't be back till Monday."

"Well, let's see— Don't you know some friend you might go to?"

"I tried a couple of fellows. Couldn't find anybody in. I wish I'd sold that Keats letter like I started to last week."

"How about those men you play cards with in that Sammy place?"

"Do you think I'd ask *them*?" His voice rang with righteous horror. Gloria winced. He would rather contemplate her active discomfort than feel his own skin crawl at asking an inappropriate favor. "I thought of Muriel," he suggested.

"She's in California."

"Well, how about some of those men who gave you such a good time while I was in the army? You'd think they might be glad to do a little favor for you."

She looked at him contemptuously, but he took no notice.

"Or how about your old friend Rachael—or Constance Merriam?"

"Constance Merriam's been dead a year, and I wouldn't ask Rachael."

"Well, how about that gentleman who was so anxious to help you once that he could hardly restrain himself, Bloeckman?"

"Oh—!" He had hurt her at last, and he was not too obtuse or too careless to perceive it.

"Why not him?" he insisted callously.

"Because—he doesn't like me any more," she said with difficulty, and then as he did not answer but only regarded her cynically: "If you want to know why, I'll tell you. A year ago I went to Bloeckman—he's changed his name to Black—and asked him to put me into pictures."

"You went to Bloeckman?"

"Yes."

"Why didn't you tell me?" he demanded incredulously, the smile fading from his face.

"Because you were probably off drinking somewhere. He had them give me a test, and they decided that I wasn't young enough for anything except a character part."

"A character part?"

"The 'woman of thirty' sort of thing. I wasn't thirty, and I didn't think I—looked thirty."

"Why, damn him!" cried Anthony, championing her violently with a curious perverseness of emotion, "why——"

"Well, that's why I can't go to him."

"Why, the insolence!" insisted Anthony nervously, "the insolence!"

"Anthony, that doesn't matter now; the thing is we've got to live over Sunday and there's nothing in the house but a loaf of bread and a half-pound of bacon and two eggs for breakfast." She handed him the contents of her purse. "There's seventy, eighty, a dollar fifteen. With what you have that makes about two and a half altogether, doesn't it? Anthony, we can get along on that. We can buy lots of food with that—more than we can possibly eat."

Jingling the change in his hand he shook his head.

"No. I've got to have a drink. I'm so darn nervous that I'm shivering." A thought struck him. "Perhaps Sammy'd cash a check. And then Monday I could rush down to the bank with the money."

"But they've closed your account."

"That's right, that's right—I'd forgotten. I'll tell you what: I'll go down to Sammy's and I'll find somebody there who'll lend me something. I hate like the devil to ask them, though. . . ." He snapped his fingers suddenly. "I know what I'll do. I'll hock my watch. I can get twenty dollars on it, and get it back Monday for sixty cents extra. It's been hocked before—when I was at Cambridge."

He had put on his overcoat, and with a brief good-by he started down the hall toward the outer door.

Gloria got to her feet. It had suddenly occurred to her where he would probably go first.

"Anthony!" she called after him, "hadn't you better leave two dollars with me? You'll only need car-fare."

The outer door slammed—he had pretended not to hear her. She stood for a moment looking after him; then she went into the bathroom among her tragic unguents and began preparations for washing her hair.

Down at Sammy's he found Parker Allison and Pete Lytell sitting alone at a table, drinking whiskey sours. It was just after six o'clock, and Sammy, or Samuele Bendiri, as he had been christened, was sweeping an accumulation of cigarette butts and broken glass into a corner.

"Hi, Tony!" called Parker Allison to Anthony. Sometimes he addressed him as Tony, at other times it was Dan. To him all Anthonys must sail under one of these diminutives.

"Sit down. What'll you have?"

On the subway Anthony had counted his money and found that he had almost four dollars. He could pay for two rounds at fifty cents a drink—which meant that he would have six drinks. Then he would go over to Sixth Avenue and get twenty dollars and a pawn-ticket in exchange for his watch.

"Well, roughnecks," he said jovially, "how's the life of crime?"

"Pretty good," said Allison. He winked at Pete Lytell. "Too bad you're a married man. We've got some pretty good stuff lined up for about eleven o'clock, when the shows let out. Oh, boy! Yes, sir—too bad he's married—isn't it, Pete?"

" 'Sa shame."

At half past seven, when they had completed the six rounds, Anthony found that his intentions were giving audience to his desires. He was happy and cheerful now—thoroughly enjoying himself. It seemed to him that the story which Pete had just finished telling was unusually and profoundly humorous—and he decided, as he did every day at about this point, that they were "damn good fellows, by golly!" who would do a lot more for him than any one else he knew. The pawnshops would remain open until late Saturday nights, and he felt that if he took just one more drink he would attain a gorgeous rose-colored exhilaration.

Artfully, he fished in his vest pockets, brought up his two quarters, and stared at them as though in surprise.

"Well, I'll be darned," he protested in an aggrieved tone, "here I've come out without my pocketbook."

"Need some cash?" asked Lytell easily.

"I left my money on the dresser at home. And I wanted to buy you another drink."

"Oh—knock it." Lytell waved the suggestion away disparagingly. "I guess we can blow a good fella to all the drinks he wants. What'll you have—same?"

"I tell you," suggested Parker Allison, "suppose we send Sammy across the street for some sandwiches and eat dinner here."

The other two agreed.

"Good idea."

"Hey, Sammy, wantcha do somep'm for us. . . ."

Just after nine o'clock Anthony staggered to his feet and, bidding them a thick good night, walked unsteadily to the door, handing Sammy one of his two quarters as he passed out. Once in the street he hesitated uncertainly and then started in the direction of Sixth Avenue, where he remembered to have frequently passed several loan-offices. He went by a news-stand and two drug-stores—and then he realized that he was standing in front of the place which he sought, and that it was shut and barred. Unperturbed he continued; another one, half a block down, was also closed—so were two more across the street, and a fifth in the square below. Seeing a faint light in the last one, he began to knock on the glass door; he desisted only when a watchman appeared in the back of the shop and motioned him angrily to move on. With growing discouragement, with growing befuddlement, he crossed the street and walked back toward Forty-third. On the corner near Sammy's he paused undecided—if he went back to the apartment, as he felt his body required, he would lay himself open to bitter reproach; yet, now that the pawnshops were closed, he had no notion where to get the money. He decided finally that he might ask Parker Allison, after all—but he approached Sammy's only to find the door locked and the lights out. He looked at his watch; nine-thirty. He began walking.

Ten minutes later he stopped aimlessly at the corner of Forty-third Street and Madison Avenue, diagonally across from the bright but nearly deserted entrance to the Biltmore Hotel. Here he stood for a moment, and then sat down heavily on a damp board amid some débris of construction work. He rested there for almost half an hour, his mind a shifting pattern of surface thoughts, chiefest among which were that he must obtain some money and get home before he became too sodden to find his way.

Then, glancing over toward the Biltmore, he saw a man standing directly under the overhead glow of the porte-cochère lamps beside a woman in an ermine coat. As Anthony watched, the couple moved forward and signalled to a taxi. Anthony perceived by the infallible identification that lurks in the walk of a friend that it was Maury Noble.

He rose to his feet.

"Maury!" he shouted.

Maury looked in his direction, then turned back to the girl just as the taxi came up into place. With the chaotic idea of borrowing ten dollars, Anthony began to run as fast as he could across Madison Avenue and along Forty-third Street.

As he came up Maury was standing beside the yawning door of the taxicab. His companion turned and looked curiously at Anthony.

"Hello, Maury!" he said, holding out his hand. "How are you?"

"Fine, thank you."

Their hands dropped and Anthony hesitated. Maury made no move to introduce him, but only stood there regarding him with an inscrutable feline silence.

"I wanted to see you—" began Anthony uncertainly. He did not feel that he could ask for a loan with the girl not four feet away, so he broke off and made a perceptible motion of his head as if to beckon Maury to one side.

"I'm in rather a big hurry, Anthony."

"I know—but can you, can you—" Again he hesitated.

"I'll see you some other time," said Maury.

"It's important."

"I'm sorry, Anthony."

Before Anthony could make up his mind to blurt out his request, Maury had turned coolly to the girl, helped her into the car and, with a polite "good evening," stepped in after her. As he nodded from the window it seemed to Anthony that his expression had not changed by a shade or a hair.

Then with a fretful clatter the taxi moved off, and Anthony was left standing there alone under the lights.

Anthony went on into the Biltmore, for no reason in particular except that the entrance was at hand, and ascending the wide stair found a seat in an alcove. He was furiously aware that he had been snubbed; he was as hurt and angry as it was possible for him to be when in that condition. Nevertheless, he was stubbornly preoccupied with the necessity of obtaining some money before he went home, and once again he told over on his fingers the acquaintances he might conceivably call on in this emergency. He thought, eventually, that he might approach Mr. Howland, his broker, at his home.

After a long wait he found that Mr. Howland was out. He returned to the operator, leaning over her desk and fingering his quarter as though loath to leave unsatisfied.

"Call Mr. Bloeckman," he said suddenly. His own words surprised him. The name had come from some crossing of two suggestions in his mind.

"What's the number, please?"

Scarcely conscious of what he did, Anthony looked up Joseph Bloeckman in the telephone directory. He could find no such person, and was about to close the book when it flashed into his mind that Gloria had mentioned a change of name. It was the matter of a minute to find Joseph Black—then he waited in the booth while central called the number.

"Hello-o. Mr. Bloeckman—I mean Mr. Black in?"

"No, he's out this evening. Is there any message?" The intonation was cockney; it reminded him of the rich vocal deferences of Bounds.

"Where is he?"

"Why, ah, who is this, please, sir?"

"This Mr. Patch. Matter of vi'al importance."

"Why, he's with a party at the Boul' Mich', sir."

"Thanks."

Anthony got his five cents change and started for the Boul' Mich', a popular dancing resort on Forty-fifth Street. It was nearly ten but the streets were dark and sparsely peopled until the theatres should eject their spawn an hour later. Anthony knew the Boul' Mich', for he had been there with Gloria during the year before, and he remembered the existence of a rule that patrons must be in evening dress. Well, he would not go up-stairs—he would send a boy up for Bloeckman and wait for him in the lower hall. For a moment he did not doubt that the whole project was entirely natural and graceful. To his distorted imagination Bloeckman had become simply one of his old friends.

The entrance-hall of the Boul' Mich' was warm. There were high yellow lights over a thick green carpet, from the centre of which a white stairway rose to the dancing floor.

Anthony spoke to the hallboy:

"I want to see Mr. Bloeckman—Mr. Black," he said. "He's up-stairs—have him paged."

The boy shook his head.

" 'Sagainsa rules to have him paged. You know what table he's at?"

"No. But I've got see him."

"Wait an' I'll getcha waiter."

After a short interval a head waiter appeared, bearing a card on which were charted the table reservations. He darted a cynical look at Anthony—which, however, failed of its target. Together they bent over the cardboard and found the table without difficulty—a party of eight, Mr. Black's own.

"Tell him Mr. Patch. Very, very important."

Again he waited, leaning against the banister and listening to the confused harmonies of "Jazz-mad" which came floating down the stairs. A check-girl near him was singing:

"Out in—the shimmee sanitarium
The jazz-mad nuts reside.
Out in—the shimmee sanitarium
I left my blushing bride.
She went and shook herself insane,
So let her shiver back again——"

Then he saw Bloeckman descending the staircase, and took a step forward to meet him and shake hands.

"You wanted to see me?" said the older man coolly.

"Yes," answered Anthony, nodding, "personal matter. Can you jus' step over here?"

Regarding him narrowly Bloeckman followed Anthony to a half bend made by the staircase where they were beyond observation or earshot of any one entering or leaving the restaurant.

"Well?" he inquired.

"Wanted talk to you."

"What about?"

Anthony only laughed—a silly laugh; he intended it to sound casual.

"What do you want to talk to me about?" repeated Bloeckman.

"Wha's hurry, old man?" He tried to lay his hand in a friendly gesture upon Bloeckman's shoulder, but the latter drew away slightly. "How've been?"

"Very well, thanks. . . . See here, Mr. Patch, I've got a party up-stairs. They'll think it's rude if I stay away too long. What was it you wanted to see me about?"

For the second time that evening Anthony's mind made an abrupt jump, and what he said was not at all what he had intended to say.

"Un'erstand you kep' my wife out of the movies."

"What?" Bloeckman's ruddy face darkened in parallel planes of shadows.

"You heard me."

"Look here, Mr. Patch," said Bloeckman, evenly and without changing his expression, "you're drunk. You're disgustingly and insultingly drunk."

"Not too drunk talk to you," insisted Anthony with a leer. "Firs' place, my wife wants nothin' whatever do with you. Never did. Un'erstand me?"

"Be quiet!" said the older man angrily. "I should think you'd respect your wife enough not to bring her into the conversation under these circumstances."

"Never you min' how I expect my wife. One thing—you leave her alone. You go to hell!"

"See here—I think you're a little crazy!" exclaimed Bloeckman. He took two paces forward as though to pass by, but Anthony stepped in his way.

"Not so fas', you Goddam Jew."

For a moment they stood regarding each other, Anthony swaying gently from side to side, Bloeckman almost trembling with fury.

"Be careful!" he cried in a strained voice.

Anthony might have remembered then a certain look Bloeckman had given him in the Biltmore Hotel years before. But he remembered nothing, nothing——

"I'll say it again, you God——"

Then Bloeckman struck out, with all the strength in the arm of a well-conditioned man of forty-five, struck out and caught Anthony squarely in the mouth. Anthony cracked up against the staircase, recovered himself and made a wild drunken swing at his opponent, but Bloeckman, who took exercise every day and knew something of sparring, blocked it with ease and struck him twice in the face with two swift smashing jabs. Anthony gave a little grunt and toppled over onto the green-plush carpet, finding, as he fell, that his mouth was full of blood and seemed oddly loose in front. He struggled to his feet, panting and spitting, and then as he started toward Bloeckman, who stood a few feet away, his fists clenched but not up, two waiters who had appeared from nowhere seized his arms and held him, helpless. In back of them a dozen people had miraculously gathered.

"I'll kill him," cried Anthony, pitching and straining from side to side. "Let me kill——"

"Throw him out!" ordered Bloeckman excitedly, just as a small man with a pockmarked face pushed his way hurriedly through the spectators.

"Any trouble, Mr. Black?"

"This bum tried to blackmail me!" said Bloeckman, and then, his voice rising to a faintly shrill note of pride: "He got what was coming to him!"

The little man turned to a waiter.

"Call a policeman!" he commanded.

"Oh, no," said Bloeckman quickly. "I can't be bothered. Just throw him out in the street. . . . Ugh! What an outrage!" He turned and with conscious dignity walked toward the wash-room just as six brawny hands seized upon Anthony and dragged him toward the door. The "bum" was propelled violently to the sidewalk, where he landed on his hands and knees with a grotesque slapping sound and rolled over slowly onto his side.

The shock stunned him. He lay there for a moment in

acute distributed pain. Then his discomfort became centralized in his stomach, and he regained consciousness to discover that a large foot was prodding him.

"You've got to move on, y' bum! Move on!"

It was the bulky doorman speaking. A town car had stopped at the curb and its occupants had disembarked—that is, two of the women were standing on the dashboard, waiting in offended delicacy until this obscene obstacle should be removed from their path.

"Move on! Or else I'll *throw* y'on!"

"Here—I'll get him."

This was a new voice; Anthony imagined that it was somehow more tolerant, better disposed than the first. Again arms were about him, half lifting, half dragging him into a welcome shadow four doors up the street and propping him against the stone front of a millinery shop.

"Much obliged," muttered Anthony feebly. Some one pushed his soft hat down upon his head and he winced.

"Just sit still, buddy, and you'll feel better. Those guys sure give you a bump."

"I'm going back and kill that dirty—" He tried to get to his feet but collapsed backward against the wall.

"You can't do nothin' now," came the voice. "Get 'em some other time. I'm tellin' you straight, ain't I? I'm helpin' you."

Anthony nodded.

"An' you better go home. You dropped a tooth to-night, buddy. You know that?"

Anthony explored his mouth with his tongue, verifying the statement. Then with an effort he raised his hand and located the gap.

"I'm agoin' to get you home, friend. Whereabouts do you live——"

"Oh, by God! By God!" interrupted Anthony, clenching his fists passionately. "I'll show the dirty bunch. You help me show 'em and I'll fix it with you. My grandfather's Adam Patch, of Tarrytown——"

"Who?"

"Adam Patch, by God!"

"You wanna go all the way to Tarrytown?"

"No."

"Well, you tell me where to go, friend, and I'll get a cab."

Anthony made out that his Samaritan was a short, broad-shouldered individual, somewhat the worse for wear.

"Where d'you live, hey?"

Sodden and shaken as he was, Anthony felt that his address would be poor collateral for his wild boast about his grandfather.

"Get me a cab," he commanded, feeling in his pockets.

A taxi drove up. Again Anthony essayed to rise, but his ankle swung loose, as though it were in two sections. The Samaritan must needs help him in—and climb in after him.

"See here, fella," said he, "you're soused and you're bunged up, and you won't be able to get in your house 'less somebody carries you in, so I'm going with you, and I know you'll make it all right with me. Where d'you live?"

With some reluctance Anthony gave his address. Then, as the cab moved off, he leaned his head against the man's shoulder and went into a shadowy, painful torpor. When he awoke, the man had lifted him from the cab in front of the apartment on Claremont Avenue and was trying to set him on his feet.

"Can y' walk?"

"Yes—sort of. You better not come in with me." Again he felt helplessly in his pockets. "Say," he continued, apologetically, swaying dangerously on his feet, "I'm afraid I haven't got a cent."

"Huh?"

"I'm cleaned out."

"Sa-a-ay! Didn't I hear you promise you'd fix it with me? Who's goin' to pay the taxi bill?" He turned to the driver for confirmation. "Didn't you hear him say he'd fix it? All that about his grandfather?"

"Matter of fact," muttered Anthony imprudently, "it was you did all the talking; however, if you come round, to-morrow——"

At this point the taxi-driver leaned from his cab and said ferociously:

"Ah, poke him one, the dirty cheap skate. If he wasn't a bum they wouldn'ta throwed him out."

In answer to this suggestion the fist of the Samaritan shot out like a battering-ram and sent Anthony crashing down against the stone steps of the apartment-house, where he lay without movement, while the tall buildings rocked to and fro above him. . . .

After a long while he awoke and was conscious that it had grown much colder. He tried to move himself but his muscles refused to function. He was curiously anxious to know the time, but he reached for his watch, only to find the pocket empty. Involuntarily his lips formed an immemorial phrase:

"What a night!"

Strangely enough, he was almost sober. Without moving his head he looked up to where the moon was anchored in mid-sky, shedding light down into Claremont Avenue as into the bottom of a deep and uncharted abyss. There was no sign or sound of life save for the continuous buzzing in his own ears, but after a moment Anthony himself broke the silence with a distinct and peculiar murmur. It was the sound that he had consistently attempted to make back there in the Boul' Mich', when he had been face to face with Bloeckman—the unmistakable sound of ironic laughter. And on his torn and bleeding lips it was like a pitiful retching of the soul.

Three weeks later the trial came to an end. The seemingly endless spool of legal red tape having unrolled over a period of four and a half years, suddenly snapped off. Anthony and Gloria and, on the other side, Edward Shuttleworth and a platoon of beneficiaries testified and lied and ill-behaved generally in varying degrees of greed and desperation. Anthony awoke one morning in March realizing that the verdict was to be given at four that afternoon, and at the thought he got up out of his bed and began to dress. With his extreme nervousness there was mingled an unjustified optimism as to the outcome. He believed that the decision of the lower court would be reversed, if only because of the reaction, due to excessive prohibition, that had recently set in against reforms and reformers. He counted more on the personal attacks that they had levelled at Shuttleworth than on the more sheerly legal aspects of the proceedings.

Dressed, he poured himself a drink of whiskey and then

went into Gloria's room, where he found her already wide awake. She had been in bed for a week, humoring herself, Anthony fancied, though the doctor had said that she had best not be disturbed.

"Good morning," she murmured, without smiling. Her eyes seemed unusually large and dark.

"How do you feel?" he asked grudgingly. "Better?"

"Yes."

"Much?"

"Yes."

"Do you feel well enough to go down to court with me this afternoon?"

She nodded.

"Yes. I want to. Dick said yesterday that if the weather was nice he was coming up in his car and take me for a ride in Central Park—and look, the room's all full of sunshine."

Anthony glanced mechanically out the window and then sat down upon the bed.

"God, I'm nervous!" he exclaimed.

"Please don't sit there," she said quickly.

"Why not?"

"You smell of whiskey. I can't stand it."

He got up absent-mindedly and left the room. A little later she called to him and he went out and brought her some potato salad and cold chicken from the delicatessen.

At two o'clock Richard Caramel's car arrived at the door and, when he phoned up, Anthony took Gloria down in the elevator and walked with her to the curb.

She told her cousin that it was sweet of him to take her riding. "Don't be simple," Dick replied disparagingly. "It's nothing."

But he did not mean that it was nothing and this was a curious thing. Richard Caramel had forgiven many people for many offenses. But he had never forgiven his cousin, Gloria Gilbert, for a statement she had made just prior to her wedding, seven years before. She had said that she did not intend to read his book.

Richard Caramel remembered this—he had remembered it well for seven years.

"What time will I expect you back?" asked Anthony.

"We won't come back," she answered, "we'll meet you down there at four."

"All right," he muttered, "I'll meet you."

Up-stairs he found a letter waiting for him. It was a mimeographed notice urging "the boys" in condescendingly colloquial language to pay the dues of the American Legion. He threw it impatiently into the waste-basket and sat down with his elbows on the window-sill, looking down blindly into the sunny street.

Italy—if the verdict was in their favor it meant Italy. The word had become a sort of talisman to him, a land where the intolerable anxieties of life would fall away like an old garment. They would go to the watering-places first and among the bright and colorful crowds forget the gray appendages of despair. Marvellously renewed, he would walk again in the Piazza di Spogna at twilight, moving in that drifting flotsam of dark women and ragged beggars, of austere, barefooted friars. The thought of Italian women stirred him faintly—when his purse hung heavy again even romance might fly back to perch upon it—the romance of blue canals in Venice, of the golden green hills of Fiesole after rain, and of women, women who changed, dissolved, melted into other women and receded from his life, but who were always beautiful and always young.

But it seemed to him that there should be a difference in his attitude. All the distress that he had ever known, the sorrow and the pain, had been because of women. It was something that in different ways they did to him, unconsciously, almost casually—perhaps finding him tender-minded and afraid, they killed the things in him that menaced their absolute sway.

Turning about from the window he faced his reflection in the mirror, contemplating dejectedly the wan, pasty face, the eyes with their crisscross of lines like shreds of dried blood, the stooped and flabby figure whose very sag was a document in lethargy. He was thirty-three—he looked forty. Well, things would be different.

The door-bell rang abruptly and he started as though he had been dealt a blow. Recovering himself, he went into the hall and opened the outer door. It was Dot.

THE ENCOUNTER

He retreated before her into the living-room, comprehending only a word here and there in the slow flood of sentences that poured from her steadily, one after the other, in a persistent monotone. She was decently and shabbily dressed—a somehow pitiable little hat adorned with pink and blue flowers covered and hid her dark hair. He gathered from her words that several days before she had seen an item in the paper concerning the lawsuit, and had obtained his address from the clerk of the Appellate Division. She had called up the apartment and had been told that Anthony was out by a woman to whom she had refused to give her name.

In the living-room he stood by the door regarding her with a sort of stupefied horror as she rattled on. . . . His predominant sensation was that all the civilization and convention around him was curiously unreal. . . . She was in a milliner's shop on Sixth Avenue, she said. It was a lonesome life. She had been sick for a long while after he left for Camp Mills; her mother had come down and taken her home again to Carolina. . . . She had come to New York with the idea of finding Anthony.

She was appallingly in earnest. Her violet eyes were red with tears; her soft intonation was ragged with little gasping sobs.

That was all. She had never changed. She wanted him now, and if she couldn't have him she must die. . . .

"You'll have to get out," he said at length, speaking with tortuous intensity. "Haven't I enough to worry me now without you coming here? My *God!* You'll have to get *out!*"

Sobbing, she sat down in a chair.

"I love you," she cried; "I don't care what you say to me! I love you."

"I don't care!" he almost shrieked; "get out—oh, get out! Haven't you done me harm enough? Haven't—you—done—*enough?*"

"Hit me!" she implored him—wildly, stupidly. "Oh, hit me, and I'll kiss the hand you hit me with!"

His voice rose until it was pitched almost at a scream. "I'll kill you!" he cried. "If you don't get out I'll kill you, I'll kill you!"

There was madness in his eyes now, but, unintimidated, Dot rose and took a step toward him.

"Anthony! Anthony!——"

He made a little clicking sound with his teeth and drew back as though to spring at her—then, changing his purpose, he looked wildly about him on the floor and wall.

"I'll kill you!" he was muttering in short, broken gasps. "I'll *kill* you!" He seemed to bite at the word as though to force it into materialization. Alarmed at last she made no further movement forward, but meeting his frantic eyes took a step back toward the door. Anthony began to race here and there on his side of the room, still giving out his single cursing cry. Then he found what he had been seeking—a stiff oaken chair that stood beside the table. Uttering a harsh, broken shout, he seized it, swung it above his head and let it go with all his raging strength straight at the white, frightened face across the room . . . Then a thick, impenetrable darkness came down upon him and blotted out thought, rage, and madness together—with almost a tangible snapping sound the face of the world changed before his eyes. . . .

Gloria and Dick came in at five and called his name. There was no answer—they went into the living-room and found a chair with its back smashed lying in the doorway, and they noticed that all about the room there was a sort of disorder—the rugs had slid, the pictures and bric-à-brac were upset upon the centre-table. The air was sickly sweet with cheap perfume.

They found Anthony sitting in a patch of sunshine on the floor of his bedroom. Before him, open, were spread his three big stamp-books, and when they entered he was running his hands through a great pile of stamps that he had dumped from the back of one of them. Looking up and seeing Dick and Gloria he put his head critically on one side and motioned them back.

"Anthony!" cried Gloria tensely, "we've won! They reversed the decision!"

"Don't come in," he murmured wanly, "you'll muss them.

I'm sorting, and I know you'll step in them. Everything always gets mussed."

"What are you doing?" demanded Dick in astonishment. "Going back to childhood? Don't you realize you've won the suit? They've reversed the decision of the lower courts. You're worth thirty millions!"

Anthony only looked at him reproachfully.

"Shut the door when you go out." He spoke like a pert child.

With a faint horror dawning in her eyes, Gloria gazed at him——

"Anthony!" she cried, "what is it? What's the matter? Why didn't you come—why, what *is* it?"

"See here," said Anthony softly, "you two get out—now, both of you. Or else I'll tell my grandfather."

He held up a handful of stamps and let them come drifting down about him like leaves, varicolored and bright, turning and fluttering gaudily upon the sunny air: stamps of England and Ecuador, Venezuela and Spain—Italy. . . .

Together with the Sparrows

That exquisite heavenly irony which has tabulated the demise of so many generations of sparrows doubtless records the subtlest verbal inflections of the passengers of such ships as *The Berengaria*. And doubtless it was listening when the young man in the plaid cap crossed the deck quickly and spoke to the pretty girl in yellow.

"That's him," he said, pointing to a bundled figure seated in a wheel-chair near the rail. "That's Anthony Patch. First time he's been on deck."

"Oh—that's him?"

"Yes. He's been a little crazy, they say, ever since he got his money, four or five months ago. You see, the other fellow, Shuttleworth, the religious fellow, the one that didn't get the money, he locked himself up in a room in a hotel and shot himself——"

"Oh, he *did*——"

"But I guess Anthony Patch don't care much. He got his thirty million. And he's got his private physician along in case he doesn't feel just right about it. Has *she* been on deck?" he asked.

The pretty girl in yellow looked around cautiously.

"She was here a minute ago. She had on a Russian-sable coat that must have cost a small fortune." She frowned and then added decisively: "I can't stand her, you know. She seems sort of—sort of dyed and *unclean*, if you know what I mean. Some people just have that look about them whether they are or not."

"Sure, I know," agreed the man with the plaid cap. "She's not bad-looking, though." He paused. "Wonder what he's thinking about—his money, I guess, or maybe he's got remorse about that fellow Shuttleworth."

"Probably. . . ."

But the man in the plaid cap was quite wrong. Anthony Patch, sitting near the rail and looking out at the sea, was not thinking of his money, for he had seldom in his life been really preoccupied with material vainglory, nor of Edward Shuttleworth, for it is best to look on the sunny side of these things. No—he was concerned with a series of reminiscences, much as a general might look back upon a successful campaign and analyze his victories. He was thinking of the hardships, the insufferable tribulations he had gone through. They had tried to penalize him for the mistakes of his youth. He had been exposed to ruthless misery, his very craving for romance had been punished, his friends had deserted him—even Gloria had turned against him. He had been alone, alone—facing it all.

Only a few months before people had been urging him to give in, to submit to mediocrity, to go to work. But he had known that he was justified in his way of life—and he had stuck it out stanchly. Why, the very friends who had been most unkind had come to respect him, to know he had been right all along. Had not the Lacys and the Merediths and the Cartwright-Smiths called on Gloria and him at the Ritz-Carlton just a week before they sailed?

Great tears stood in his eyes, and his voice was tremulous as he whispered to himself.

"I showed them," he was saying. "It was a hard fight, but I didn't give up and I came through!"

TALES OF THE JAZZ AGE

QUITE INAPPROPRIATELY

TO MY MOTHER

A TABLE OF CONTENTS

MY LAST FLAPPERS

THE JELLY-BEAN . . . . *Page 803*

This is a Southern story, with the scene laid in the small city of Tarleton, Georgia. I have a profound affection for Tarleton, but somehow whenever I write a story about it I receive letters from all over the South denouncing me in no uncertain terms. "The Jelly-Bean," published in "The Metropolitan," drew its full share of these admonitory notes.

It was written under strange circumstances shortly after my first novel was published, and, moreover, it was the first story in which I had a collaborator. For, finding that I was unable to manage the crap-shooting episode, I turned it over to my wife, who, as a Southern girl, was presumably an expert on the technique and terminology of that great sectional pastime.

THE CAMEL'S BACK . . . . *Page 823*

I suppose that of all the stories I have ever written this one cost me the least travail and perhaps gave me the most amusement. As to the labor involved, it was written during one day in the city of New Orleans, with the express purpose of buying a platinum and diamond wrist watch which cost six hundred dollars. I began it at seven in the morning and finished it at two o'clock the same night. It was published in the "Saturday Evening Post" in 1920, and later included in the O. Henry Memorial Collection for the same year. I like it least of all the stories in this volume.

My amusement was derived from the fact that the camel part of the story is literally true; in fact, I have a standing engagement with the gentleman involved to attend the next fancy-dress party to which we are mutually invited, attired as the latter part of the camel—this as a sort of atonement for being his historian.

MAY DAY . . . . *Page 850*

This somewhat unpleasant tale, published as a novelette in the "Smart Set" in July, 1920, relates a series of events which took place in the spring of the previous year. Each of the three events made a great impression upon me. In life they were unrelated, except by the general hysteria of that spring which inaugurated the Age of Jazz, but in my story I have tried, unsuccessfully I fear, to weave them into a pattern—a pattern which would give the effect of those months in New York as they appeared to at least one member of what was then the younger generation.

PORCELAIN AND PINK . . . . Page 903

"And do you write for any other magazines?" inquired the young lady.

"Oh, yes," I assured her. "I've had some stories and plays in the 'Smart Set,' for instance——"

The young lady shivered.

"The 'Smart Set'!" she exclaimed. "How can you? Why, they publish stuff about girls in blue bathtubs, and silly things like that!"

And I had the magnificent joy of telling her that she was referring to "Porcelain and Pink," which had appeared there several months before.

FANTASIES

THE DIAMOND AS BIG AS THE RITZ . . . . Page 913

These next stories are written in what, were I of imposing stature, I should call my "second manner." "The Diamond as Big as the Ritz," which appeared last summer in the "Smart Set," was designed utterly for my own amusement. I was in that familiar mood characterized by a perfect craving for luxury, and the story began as an attempt to feed that craving on imaginary foods.

One well-known critic has been pleased to like this extravaganza better than anything I have written. Personally I prefer "The Off Shore Pirate." But, to tamper slightly with Lincoln: If you like this sort of thing, this, possibly, is the sort of thing you'll like.

THE CURIOUS CASE OF BENJAMIN BUTTON . . . . Page 954

This story was inspired by a remark of Mark Twain's to the effect that it was a pity that the best part of life came at the beginning and the worst part at the end. By trying the experiment upon only one man in a perfectly normal world I have scarcely given his idea a fair trial. Several weeks after completing it, I discovered an almost identical plot in Samuel Butler's "Note-books."

The story was published in "Collier's" last summer and provoked this startling letter from an anonymous admirer in Cincinnati:

"Sir—

I have read the story Benjamin Button in Colliers and I wish to say that as a short story writer you would make a good lunatic I have seen many peices of cheese in my life but of all the peices of cheese I have ever seen you are the biggest peice. I hate to waste a peice of stationary on you but I will."

TARQUIN OF CHEAPSIDE . . . . Page 980

Written almost six years ago, this story is a product of undergraduate days at Princeton. Considerably revised, it was published in the "Smart Set" in 1921. At the time of its conception I had but one idea—to be a poet—and the fact that I was interested in the ring of every phrase, that I dreaded the obvious in prose if not in plot, shows throughout. Probably the peculiar affection I feel for it depends more upon its age than upon any intrinsic merit.

O RUSSET WITCH! . . . . Page 988

When this was written I had just completed the first draft of my second novel, and a natural reaction made me revel in a story wherein none of the characters need be taken seriously. And I'm afraid that I was somewhat carried away by the feeling that there was no ordered scheme to which I must conform. After due consideration, however, I have decided to let it stand as it is, although the reader may find himself somewhat puzzled at the time element. I had best say that however the years may have dealt with Merlin Grainger, I myself was thinking always in the present.

It was published in the "Metropolitan."

UNCLASSIFIED MASTERPIECES

THE LEES OF HAPPINESS . . . . Page 1019

Of this story I can say that it came to me in an irresistible form, crying to be written. It will be accused perhaps of being a mere piece of sentimentality, but, as I saw it, it was a great deal more. If, therefore, it lacks the ring of sincerity, or even of tragedy, the fault rests not with the theme but with my handling of it.

It appeared in the "Chicago Tribune," and later obtained, I believe, the quadruple gold laurel leaf or some such encomium from one of the anthologists who at present swarm among us. The gentleman I refer to runs as a rule to stark melodramas with a volcano or the ghost of John Paul Jones in the rôle of Nemesis, melodramas carefully disguised by early paragraphs in Jamesian manner which hint dark and subtle complexities to follow. On this order:

"The case of Shaw McPhee, curiously enough, had no bearing on the almost incredible attitude of Martin Sulo. This is parenthetical and, to at least three observers, whose names for the present I must conceal, it seems improbable, etc., etc., etc.," until the poor rat of fiction is at least forced out into the open and the melodrama begins.

MR. ICKY . . . . Page 1041

This has the distinction of being the only magazine piece ever written in a New York hotel. The business was done in a bedroom in the Knickerbocker, and shortly afterward that memorable hostelry closed its doors forever.

When a fitting period of mourning had elapsed it was published in the "Smart Set."

JEMINA . . . . Page 1049

Written, like "Tarquin of Cheapside," while I was at Princeton, this sketch was published years later in "Vanity Fair." For its technique I must apologize to Mr. Stephen Leacock.

I have laughed over it a great deal, especially when I first wrote it, but I can laugh over it no longer. Still, as other people tell me it is amusing, I include it here. It seems to me worth preserving a few years—at least until the ennui of changing fashions suppresses me, my books, and it together.

With due apologies for this impossible Table of Contents, I tender these tales of the Jazz Age into the hands of those who read as they run and run as they read.

MY LAST FLAPPERS

The Jelly-Bean

JIM POWELL was a Jelly-bean. Much as I desire to make him an appealing character, I feel that it would be unscrupulous to deceive you on that point. He was a bred-in-the-bone, dyed-in-the-wool, ninety-nine three-quarters per cent Jelly-bean and he grew lazily all during Jelly-bean season, which is every season, down in the land of the Jelly-beans well below the Mason-Dixon line.

Now if you call a Memphis man a Jelly-bean he will quite possibly pull a long sinewy rope from his hip pocket and hang you to a convenient telegraph-pole. If you call a New Orleans man a Jelly-bean he will probably grin and ask you who is taking your girl to the Mardi Gras ball. The particular Jelly-bean patch which produced the protagonist of this history lies somewhere between the two—a little city of forty thousand that has dozed sleepily for forty thousand years in southern Georgia, occasionally stirring in its slumbers and muttering something about a war that took place sometime, somewhere, and that everyone else has forgotten long ago.

Jim was a Jelly-bean. I write that again because it has such a pleasant sound—rather like the beginning of a fairy story—as if Jim were nice. It somehow gives me a picture of him with a round, appetizing face and all sorts of leaves and vegetables growing out of his cap. But Jim was long and thin and bent at the waist from stooping over pool-tables, and he was what might have been known in the indiscriminating North as a corner loafer. "Jelly-bean" is the name throughout the undissolved Confederacy for one who spends his life conjugating the verb to idle in the first person singular—I am idling, I have idled, I will idle.

Jim was born in a white house on a green corner. It had four weather-beaten pillars in front and a great amount of lattice-work in the rear that made a cheerful criss-cross background for a flowery sun-drenched lawn. Originally the dwellers in the white house had owned the ground next door and next door to that and next door to that, but this had been so long ago that even Jim's father scarcely remembered it. He had, in fact, thought it a matter of so little moment that when he was dying from a pistol wound got in a brawl he neglected even to tell little Jim, who was five years old and miserably frightened. The white house became a boarding-house run by a tight-lipped lady from Macon, whom Jim called Aunt Mamie and detested with all his soul.

He became fifteen, went to high school, wore his hair in black snarls, and was afraid of girls. He hated his home where four women and one old man prolonged an interminable chatter from summer to summer about what lots the Powell place had originally included and what sort of flowers would be out next. Sometimes the parents of little girls in town, remembering Jim's mother and fancying a resemblance in the dark eyes and hair, invited him to parties, but parties made him shy and he much preferred sitting on a disconnected axle in Tilly's Garage, rolling the bones or exploring his mouth endlessly with a long straw. For pocket money, he picked up odd jobs, and it was due to this that he stopped going to parties. At his third party little Marjorie Haight had whispered indiscreetly and within hearing distance that he was a boy who brought the groceries sometimes. So instead of the two-step and polka, Jim had learned to throw any number he desired on the dice and had listened to spicy tales of all the shootings that had occurred in the surrounding country during the past fifty years.

He became eighteen. The war broke out and he enlisted as a gob and polished brass in the Charleston Navy-yard for a year. Then, by way of variety, he went North and polished brass in the Brooklyn Navy-yard for a year.

When the war was over he came home. He was twenty-one, his trousers were too short and too tight. His buttoned shoes were long and narrow. His tie was an alarming conspiracy of purple and pink marvellously scrolled, and over it were two blue eyes faded like a piece of very good old cloth long exposed to the sun.

In the twilight of one April evening when a soft gray had

drifted down along the cottonfields and over the sultry town, he was a vague figure leaning against a board fence, whistling and gazing at the moon's rim above the lights of Jackson Street. His mind was working persistently on a problem that had held his attention for an hour. The Jelly-bean had been invited to a party.

Back in the days when all the boys had detested all the girls, Clark Darrow and Jim had sat side by side in school. But, while Jim's social aspirations had died in the oily air of the garage, Clark had alternately fallen in and out of love, gone to college, taken to drink, given it up, and, in short, become one of the best beaux of the town. Nevertheless Clark and Jim had retained a friendship that, though casual, was perfectly definite. That afternoon Clark's ancient Ford had slowed up beside Jim, who was on the sidewalk and, out of a clear sky, Clark had invited him to a party at the country club. The impulse that made him do this was no stranger than the impulse which made Jim accept. The latter was probably an unconscious ennui, a half-frightened sense of adventure. And now Jim was soberly thinking it over.

He began to sing, drumming his long foot idly on a stone block in the sidewalk till it wobbled up and down in time to the low throaty tune:

"One mile from Home in Jelly-bean town,
Lives Jeanne, the Jelly-bean Queen.
She loves her dice and treats 'em nice;
No dice would treat her mean."

He broke off and agitated the sidewalk to a bumpy gallop.

"Daggone!" he muttered, half aloud.

They would all be there—the old crowd, the crowd to which, by right of the white house, sold long since, and the portrait of the officer in gray over the mantel, Jim should have belonged. But that crowd had grown up together into a tight little set as gradually as the girls' dresses had lengthened inch by inch, as definitely as the boys' trousers had dropped suddenly to their ankles. And to that society of first names and dead puppy-loves Jim was an outsider—a running mate of poor whites. Most of the men knew him, condescendingly; he tipped his hat to three or four girls. That was all.

When the dusk had thickened into a blue setting for the moon, he walked through the hot, pleasantly pungent town to Jackson Street. The stores were closing and the last shoppers were drifting homeward, as if borne on the dreamy revolution of a slow merry-go-round. A street-fair farther down made a brilliant alley of varicolored booths and contributed a blend of music to the night—an oriental dance on a calliope, a melancholy bugle in front of a freak show, a cheerful rendition of "Back Home in Tennessee" on a hand-organ.

The Jelly-bean stopped in a store and bought a collar. Then he sauntered along toward Soda Sam's, where he found the usual three or four cars of a summer evening parked in front and the little darkies running back and forth with sundaes and lemonades.

"Hello, Jim."

It was a voice at his elbow—Joe Ewing sitting in an automobile with Marylyn Wade. Nancy Lamar and a strange man were in the back seat.

The Jelly-bean tipped his hat quickly.

"Hi, Ben—" then, after an almost imperceptible pause—"How y' all?"

Passing, he ambled on toward the garage where he had a room up-stairs. His "How y' all" had been said to Nancy Lamar, to whom he had not spoken in fifteen years.

Nancy had a mouth like a remembered kiss and shadowy eyes and blue-black hair inherited from her mother who had been born in Budapest. Jim passed her often in the street, walking small-boy fashion with her hands in her pockets and he knew that with her inseparable Sally Carrol Hopper she had left a trail of broken hearts from Atlanta to New Orleans.

For a few fleeting moments Jim wished he could dance. Then he laughed and as he reached his door began to sing softly to himself:

"Her Jelly Roll can twist your soul,
Her eyes are big and brown,
She's the Queen of the Queens of the Jelly-beans—
My Jeanne of Jelly-bean Town."

II

At nine-thirty Jim and Clark met in front of Soda Sam's and started for the Country Club in Clark's Ford.

"Jim," asked Clark casually, as they rattled through the jasmine-scented night, "how do you keep alive?"

The Jelly-bean paused, considered.

"Well," he said finally, "I got a room over Tilly's garage. I help him some with the cars in the afternoon an' he gives it to me free. Sometimes I drive one of his taxies and pick up a little thataway. I get fed up doin' that regular though."

"That all?"

"Well, when there's a lot of work I help him by the day—Saturdays usually—and then there's one main source of revenue I don't generally mention. Maybe you don't recollect I'm about the champion crap-shooter of this town. They make me shoot from a cup now because once I get the feel of a pair of dice they just roll for me."

Clark grinned appreciatively.

"I never could learn to set 'em so's they'd do what I wanted. Wish you'd shoot with Nancy Lamar some day and take all her money away from her. She will roll 'em with the boys and she loses more than her daddy can afford to give her. I happen to know she sold a good ring last month to pay a debt."

The Jelly-bean was non-committal.

"The white house on Elm Street still belong to you?"

Jim shook his head.

"Sold. Got a pretty good price, seein' it wasn't in a good part of town no more. Lawyer told me to put it into Liberty bonds. But Aunt Mamie got so she didn't have no sense, so it takes all the interest to keep her up at Great Farms Sanitarium.

"Hm."

"I got an old uncle up-state an' I reckin I kin go up there if ever I get sure enough pore. Nice farm, but not enough niggers around to work it. He's asked me to come up and help him, but I don't guess I'd take much to it. Too doggone lonesome——" He broke off suddenly. "Clark, I want to tell you I'm much obliged to you for askin' me out, but I'd be a lot happier if you'd just stop the car right here an' let me walk back into town."

"Shucks!" Clark grunted. "Do you good to step out. You don't have to dance—just get out there on the floor and shake."

"Hold on," exclaimed Jim uneasily, "Don't you go leadin' me up to any girls and leavin' me there so I'll have to dance with 'em."

Clark laughed.

" 'Cause," continued Jim desperately, "without you swear you won't do that I'm agoin' to get out right here an' my good legs goin' carry me back to Jackson Street."

They agreed after some argument that Jim, unmolested by females, was to view the spectacle from a secluded settee in the corner where Clark would join him whenever he wasn't dancing.

So ten o'clock found the Jelly-bean with his legs crossed and his arms conservatively folded, trying to look casually at home and politely uninterested in the dancers. At heart he was torn between overwhelming self-consciousness and an intense curiosity as to all that went on around him. He saw the girls emerge one by one from the dressing-room, stretching and pluming themselves like bright birds, smiling over their powdered shoulders at the chaperones, casting a quick glance around to take in the room and, simultaneously, the room's reaction to their entrance—and then, again like birds, alighting and nestling in the sober arms of their waiting escorts. Sally Carrol Hopper, blonde and lazy-eyed, appeared clad in her favorite pink and blinking like an awakened rose. Marjorie Haight, Marylyn Wade, Harriet Cary, all the girls he had seen loitering down Jackson Street by noon, now, curled and brilliantined and delicately tinted for the overhead lights, were miraculously strange Dresden figures of pink and blue and red and gold, fresh from the shop and not yet fully dried.

He had been there half an hour, totally uncheered by Clark's jovial visits which were each one accompanied by a "Hello, old boy, how you making out?" and a slap at his knee. A dozen males had spoken to him or stopped for a moment beside him, but he knew that they were each one surprised at finding him there and fancied that one or two were even slightly resentful. But at half past ten his embarrassment suddenly left him and a pull of breathless interest took him completely out of himself—Nancy Lamar had come out of the dressing-room.

She was dressed in yellow organdie, a costume of a hundred cool corners, with three tiers of ruffles and a big bow in back until she shed black and yellow around her in a sort of phosphorescent lustre. The Jelly-bean's eyes opened wide and a lump arose in his throat. For a minute she stood beside the door until her partner hurried up. Jim recognized him as the stranger who had been with her in Joe Ewing's car that afternoon. He saw her set her arms akimbo and say something in a low voice, and laugh. The man laughed too and Jim experienced the quick pang of a weird new kind of pain. Some ray had passed between the pair, a shaft of beauty from that sun that had warmed him a moment since. The Jelly-bean felt suddenly like a weed in a shadow.

A minute later Clark approached him, bright-eyed and glowing.

"Hi, old man," he cried with some lack of originality. "How you making out?"

Jim replied that he was making out as well as could be expected.

"You come along with me," commanded Clark. "I've got something that'll put an edge on the evening."

Jim followed him awkwardly across the floor and up the stairs to the locker-room where Clark produced a flask of nameless yellow liquid.

"Good old corn."

Ginger ale arrived on a tray. Such potent nectar as "good old corn" needed some disguise beyond seltzer.

"Say, boy," exclaimed Clark breathlessly, "doesn't Nancy Lamar look beautiful?"

Jim nodded.

"Mighty beautiful," he agreed.

"She's all dolled up to a fare-you-well to-night," continued Clark. "Notice that fellow she's with?"

"Big fella? White pants?"

"Yeah. Well, that's Ogden Merritt from Savannah. Old man

Merritt makes the Merritt safety razors. This fella's crazy about her. Been chasing after her all year.

"She's a wild baby," continued Clark, "but I like her. So does everybody. But she sure does do crazy stunts. She usually gets out alive, but she's got scars all over her reputation from one thing or another she's done."

"That so?" Jim passed over his glass. "That's good corn."

"Not so bad. Oh, she's a wild one. Shoots craps, say, boy! And she do like her high-balls. Promised I'd give her one later on."

"She in love with this—Merritt?"

"Damned if I know. Seems like all the best girls around here marry fellas and go off somewhere."

He poured himself one more drink and carefully corked the bottle.

"Listen, Jim, I got to go dance and I'd be much obliged if you just stick this corn right on your hip as long as you're not dancing. If a man notices I've had a drink he'll come up and ask me and before I know it it's all gone and somebody else is having my good time."

So Nancy Lamar was going to marry. This toast of a town was to become the private property of an individual in white trousers—and all because white trousers' father had made a better razor than his neighbor. As they descended the stairs Jim found the idea inexplicably depressing. For the first time in his life he felt a vague and romantic yearning. A picture of her began to form in his imagination—Nancy walking boylike and debonnaire along the street, taking an orange as tithe from a worshipful fruit-dealer, charging a dope on a mythical account at Soda Sam's, assembling a convoy of beaux and then driving off in triumphal state for an afternoon of splashing and singing.

The Jelly-bean walked out on the porch to a deserted corner, dark between the moon on the lawn and the single lighted door of the ballroom. There he found a chair and, lighting a cigarette, drifted into the thoughtless reverie that was his usual mood. Yet now it was a reverie made sensuous by the night and by the hot smell of damp powder puffs, tucked in the fronts of low dresses and distilling a thousand rich scents to float out through the open door. The music itself, blurred by a loud trombone, became hot and shadowy, a languorous overtone to the scraping of many shoes and slippers.

Suddenly the square of yellow light that fell through the door was obscured by a dark figure. A girl had come out of the dressing-room and was standing on the porch not more than ten feet away. Jim heard a low-breathed "doggone" and then she turned and saw him. It was Nancy Lamar.

Jim rose to his feet.

"Howdy?"

"Hello—" she paused, hesitated and then approached. "Oh, it's—Jim Powell."

He bowed slightly, tried to think of a casual remark.

"Do you suppose," she began quickly, "I mean—do you know anything about gum?"

"What?"

"I've got gum on my shoe. Some utter ass left his or her gum on the floor and of course I stepped in it."

Jim blushed, inappropriately.

"Do you know how to get it off?" she demanded petulantly. "I've tried a knife. I've tried every damn thing in the dressing-room. I've tried soap and water—and even perfume and I've ruined my powder-puff trying to make it stick to that."

Jim considered the question in some agitation.

"Why—I think maybe gasolene——"

The words had scarcely left his lips when she grasped his hand and pulled him at a run off the low veranda, over a flower bed and at a gallop toward a group of cars parked in the moonlight by the first hole of the golf course.

"Turn on the gasolene," she commanded breathlessly.

"What?"

"For the gum of course. I've got to get it off. I can't dance with gum on."

Obediently Jim turned to the cars and began inspecting them with a view to obtaining the desired solvent. Had she demanded a cylinder he would have done his best to wrench one out.

"Here," he said after a moment's search. "Here's one that's easy. Got a handkerchief?"

"It's up-stairs wet. I used it for the soap and water."

Jim laboriously explored his pockets.

"Don't believe I got one either."

"Doggone it! Well, we can turn it on and let it run on the ground."

He turned the spout; a dripping began.

"More!"

He turned it on fuller. The dripping became a flow and formed an oily pool that glistened brightly, reflecting a dozen tremulous moons on its quivering bosom.

"Ah," she sighed contentedly, "let it all out. The only thing to do is to wade in it."

In desperation he turned on the tap full and the pool suddenly widened sending tiny rivers and trickles in all directions.

"That's fine. That's something like."

Raising her skirts she stepped gracefully in.

"I know this'll take it off," she murmured.

Jim smiled.

"There's lots more cars."

She stepped daintily out of the gasolene and began scraping her slippers, side and bottom, on the running-board of the automobile. The Jelly-bean contained himself no longer. He bent double with explosive laughter and after a second she joined in.

"You're here with Clark Darrow, aren't you?" she asked as they walked back toward the veranda.

"Yes."

"You know where he is now?"

"Out dancin', I reckin."

"The deuce. He promised me a highball."

"Well," said Jim, "I guess that'll be all right. I got his bottle right here in my pocket."

She smiled at him radiantly.

"I guess maybe you'll need ginger ale though," he added.

"Not me. Just the bottle."

"Sure enough?"

She laughed scornfully.

"Try me. I can drink anything any man can. Let's sit down."

She perched herself on the side of a table and he dropped into one of the wicker chairs beside her. Taking out the cork she held the flask to her lips and took a long drink. He watched her fascinated.

"Like it?"

She shook her head breathlessly.

"No, but I like the way it makes me feel. I think most people are that way."

Jim agreed.

"My daddy liked it too well. It got him."

"American men," said Nancy gravely, "don't know how to drink."

"What?" Jim was startled.

"In fact," she went on carelessly, "they don't know how to do anything very well. The one thing I regret in my life is that I wasn't born in England."

"In England?"

"Yes. It's the one regret of my life that I wasn't."

"Do you like it over there?"

"Yes. Immensely. I've never been there in person, but I've met a lot of Englishmen who were over here in the army, Oxford and Cambridge men—you know, that's like Sewanee and University of Georgia are here—and of course I've read a lot of English novels."

Jim was interested, amazed.

"D' you ever hear of Lady Diana Manners?" she asked earnestly.

No, Jim had not.

"Well, she's what I'd like to be. Dark, you know, like me, and wild as sin. She's the girl who rode her horse up the steps of some cathedral or church or something and all the novelists made their heroines do it afterwards."

Jim nodded politely. He was out of his depths.

"Pass the bottle," suggested Nancy. "I'm going to take another little one. A little drink wouldn't hurt a baby.

"You see," she continued, again breathless after a draught. "People over there have style. Nobody has style here. I mean the boys here aren't really worth dressing up for or doing sensational things for. Don't you know?"

"I suppose so—I mean I suppose not," murmured Jim.

"And I'd like to do 'em an' all. I'm really the only girl in town that has style."

She stretched out her arms and yawned pleasantly.

"Pretty evening."

"Sure is," agreed Jim.

"Like to have boat," she suggested dreamily. "Like to sail out on a silver lake, say the Thames, for instance. Have champagne and caviare sandwiches along. Have about eight people. And one of the men would jump overboard to amuse the party and get drowned like a man did with Lady Diana Manners once."

"Did he do it to please her?"

"Didn't mean drown himself to please her. He just meant to jump overboard and make everybody laugh."

"I reckin they just died laughin' when he drowned."

"Oh, I suppose they laughed a little," she admitted. "I imagine she did, anyway. She's pretty hard, I guess—like I am."

"You hard?"

"Like nails." She yawned again and added, "Give me a little more from that bottle."

Jim hesitated but she held out her hand defiantly.

"Don't treat me like a girl," she warned him. "I'm not like any girl *you* ever saw." She considered. "Still, perhaps you're right. You got—you got old head on young shoulders."

She jumped to her feet and moved toward the door. The Jelly-bean rose also.

"Good-bye," she said politely, "good-bye. Thanks, Jelly-bean."

Then she stepped inside and left him wide-eyed upon the porch.

III

At twelve o'clock a procession of cloaks issued single file from the women's dressing-room and, each one pairing with a coated beau like dancers meeting in a cotillion figure, drifted through the door with sleepy happy laughter—through the door into the dark where autos backed and snorted and parties called to one another and gathered around the water-cooler.

Jim, sitting in his corner, rose to look for Clark. They had met at eleven; then Clark had gone in to dance. So, seeking him, Jim wandered into the soft-drink stand that had once been a bar. The room was deserted except for a sleepy negro dozing behind the counter and two boys lazily fingering a pair of dice at one of the tables. Jim was about to leave when he saw Clark coming in. At the same moment Clark looked up.

"Hi, Jim!" he commanded. "C'mon over and help us with this bottle. I guess there's not much left, but there's one all around."

Nancy, the man from Savannah, Marylyn Wade, and Joe Ewing were lolling and laughing in the doorway. Nancy caught Jim's eye and winked at him humorously.

They drifted over to a table and arranging themselves around it waited for the waiter to bring ginger ale. Jim, faintly ill at ease, turned his eyes on Nancy, who had drifted into a nickel crap game with the two boys at the next table.

"Bring them over here," suggested Clark.

Joe looked around.

"We don't want to draw a crowd. It's against club rules."

"Nobody's around," insisted Clark, "except Mr. Taylor. He's walking up and down like a wild-man trying to find out who let all the gasolene out of his car."

There was a general laugh.

"I bet a million Nancy got something on her shoe again. You can't park when she's around."

"O Nancy, Mr. Taylor's looking for you!"

Nancy's cheeks were glowing with excitement over the game. "I haven't seen his silly little flivver in two weeks."

Jim felt a sudden silence. He turned and saw an individual of uncertain age standing in the doorway.

Clark's voice punctuated the embarrassment.

"Won't you join us, Mr. Taylor?"

"Thanks."

Mr. Taylor spread his unwelcome presence over a chair. "Have to, I guess. I'm waiting till they dig me up some gasolene. Somebody got funny with my car."

His eyes narrowed and he looked quickly from one to the other. Jim wondered what he had heard from the doorway—tried to remember what had been said.

"I'm right to-night," Nancy sang out, "and my four bits is in the ring."

"Faded!" snapped Taylor suddenly.

"Why, Mr. Taylor, I didn't know you shot craps!" Nancy was overjoyed to find that he had seated himself and instantly covered her bet. They had openly disliked each other since the night she had definitely discouraged a series of rather pointed advances.

"All right, babies, do it for your mamma. Just one little seven." Nancy was *cooing* to the dice. She rattled them with a brave underhand flourish, and rolled them out on the table.

"Ah-h! I suspected it. And now again with the dollar up."

Five passes to her credit found Taylor a bad loser. She was making it personal, and after each success Jim watched triumph flutter across her face. She was doubling with each throw—such luck could scarcely last.

"Better go easy," he cautioned her timidly.

"Ah, but watch this one," she whispered. It was eight on the dice and she called her number.

"Little Ada, this time we're going South."

Ada from Decatur rolled over the table. Nancy was flushed and half-hysterical, but her luck was holding. She drove the pot up and up, refusing to drag. Taylor was drumming with his fingers on the table, but he was in to stay.

Then Nancy tried for a ten and lost the dice. Taylor seized them avidly. He shot in silence, and in the hush of excitement the clatter of one pass after another on the table was the only sound.

Now Nancy had the dice again, but her luck had broken. An hour passed. Back and forth it went. Taylor had been at it again—and again and again. They were even at last—Nancy lost her ultimate five dollars.

"Will you take my check," she said quickly, "for fifty, and we'll shoot it all?" Her voice was a little unsteady and her hand shook as she reached to the money.

Clark exchanged an uncertain but alarmed glance with Joe Ewing. Taylor shot again. He had Nancy's check.

"How 'bout another?" she said wildly. "Jes' any bank'll do—money everywhere as a matter of fact."

Jim understood—the "good old corn" he had given her—

the "good old corn" she had taken since. He wished he dared interfere—a girl of that age and position would hardly have two bank accounts. When the clock struck two he contained himself no longer.

"May I—can't you let me roll 'em for you?" he suggested, his low, lazy voice a little strained.

Suddenly sleepy and listless, Nancy flung the dice down before him.

"All right—old boy! As Lady Diana Manners says, 'Shoot 'em, Jelly-bean'—My luck's gone."

"Mr. Taylor," said Jim, carelessly, "we'll shoot for one of those there checks against the cash."

Half an hour later Nancy swayed forward and clapped him on the back.

"Stole my luck, you did." She was nodding her head sagely.

Jim swept up the last check and putting it with the others tore them into confetti and scattered them on the floor. Someone started singing, and Nancy kicking her chair backward rose to her feet.

"Ladies and gentlemen," she announced. "Ladies—that's you Marylyn. I want to tell the world that Mr. Jim Powell, who is a well-known Jelly-bean of this city, is an exception to a great rule—'lucky in dice—unlucky in love.' He's lucky in dice, and as matter fact I—I *love* him. Ladies and gentlemen, Nancy Lamar, famous dark-haired beauty often featured in the *Herald* as one th' most popular members of younger set as other girls are often featured in this particular case. Wish to announce—wish to announce, anyway, Gentlemen——" She tipped suddenly. Clark caught her and restored her balance.

"My error," she laughed, "she stoops to—stoops to—anyways——We'll drink to Jelly-bean . . . Mr. Jim Powell, King of the Jelly-beans."

And a few minutes later as Jim waited hat in hand for Clark in the darkness of that same corner of the porch where she had come searching for gasolene, she appeared suddenly beside him.

"Jelly-bean," she said, "are you here, Jelly-bean? I think—" and her slight unsteadiness seemed part of an enchanted dream—"I think you deserve one of my sweetest kisses for that, Jelly-bean."

For an instant her arms were around his neck—her lips were pressed to his.

"I'm a wild part of the world, Jelly-bean, but you did me a good turn."

Then she was gone, down the porch, over the cricket-loud lawn. Jim saw Merritt come out the front door and say something to her angrily—saw her laugh and, turning away, walk with averted eyes to his car. Marylyn and Joe followed, singing a drowsy song about a Jazz baby.

Clark came out and joined Jim on the steps. "All pretty lit, I guess," he yawned. "Merritt's in a mean mood. He's certainly off Nancy."

Over east along the golf course a faint rug of gray spread itself across the feet of the night. The party in the car began to chant a chorus as the engine warmed up.

"Good-night everybody," called Clark.

"Good-night, Clark."

"Good-night."

There was a pause, and then a soft, happy voice added,

"Good-night, Jelly-bean."

The car drove off to a burst of singing. A rooster on a farm across the way took up a solitary mournful crow, and behind them a last negro waiter turned out the porch light. Jim and Clark strolled over toward the Ford, their shoes crunching raucously on the gravel drive.

"Oh, boy!" sighed Clark softly, "how you can set those dice!"

It was still too dark for him to see the flush on Jim's thin cheeks—or to know that it was a flush of unfamiliar shame.

IV

Over Tilly's garage a bleak room echoed all day to the rumble and snorting down-stairs and the singing of the negro washers as they turned the hose on the cars outside. It was a cheerless square of a room, punctuated with a bed and a battered table on which lay half a dozen books—Joe Miller's "Slow Train thru Arkansas," "Lucille," in an old edition very much annotated in an old-fashioned hand; "The Eyes of the World," by Harold Bell Wright, and an ancient prayer-book of the Church of England with the name Alice Powell and the date 1831 written on the fly-leaf.

The East, gray when the Jelly-bean entered the garage, became a rich and vivid blue as he turned on his solitary electric light. He snapped it out again, and going to the window rested his elbows on the sill and stared into the deepening morning. With the awakening of his emotions, his first perception was a sense of futility, a dull ache at the utter grayness of his life. A wall had sprung up suddenly around him hedging him in, a wall as definite and tangible as the white wall of his bare room. And with his perception of this wall all that had been the romance of his existence, the casualness, the light-hearted improvidence, the miraculous open-handedness of life faded out. The Jelly-bean strolling up Jackson Street humming a lazy song, known at every shop and street stand, cropful of easy greeting and local wit, sad sometimes for only the sake of sadness and the flight of time—that Jelly-bean was suddenly vanished. The very name was a reproach, a triviality. With a flood of insight he knew that Merritt must despise him, that even Nancy's kiss in the dawn would have awakened not jealousy but only a contempt for Nancy's so lowering herself. And on his part the Jelly-bean had used for her a dingy subterfuge learned from the garage. He had been her moral laundry; the stains were his.

As the gray became blue, brightened and filled the room, he crossed to his bed and threw himself down on it, gripping the edges fiercely.

"I love her," he cried aloud, "God!"

As he said this something gave way within him like a lump melting in his throat. The air cleared and became radiant with dawn, and turning over on his face he began to sob dully into the pillow.

In the sunshine of three o'clock Clark Darrow chugging painfully along Jackson Street was hailed by the Jelly-bean, who stood on the curb with his fingers in his vest pockets.

"Hi!" called Clark, bringing his Ford to an astonishing stop alongside. "Just get up?"

The Jelly-bean shook his head.

"Never did go to bed. Felt sorta restless, so I took a long

walk this morning out in the country. Just got into town this minute."

"Should think you *would* feel restless. I been feeling thataway all day——"

"I'm thinkin' of leavin' town," continued the Jelly-bean, absorbed by his own thoughts. "Been thinkin' of goin' up on the farm, and takin' a little that work off Uncle Dun. Reckin I been bummin' too long."

Clark was silent and the Jelly-bean continued:

"I reckin maybe after Aunt Mamie dies I could sink that money of mine in the farm and make somethin' out of it. All my people originally came from that part up there. Had a big place."

Clark looked at him curiously.

"That's funny," he said. "This—this sort of affected me the same way."

The Jelly-bean hesitated.

"I don't know," he began slowly, "somethin' about—about that girl last night talkin' about a lady named Diana Manners—an English lady, sorta got me thinkin'!" He drew himself up and looked oddly at Clark. "I had a family once," he said defiantly.

Clark nodded.

"I know."

"And I'm the last of 'em," continued the Jelly-bean, his voice rising slightly, "and I ain't worth shucks. Name they call me by means jelly—weak and wobbly like. People who weren't nothin' when my folks was a lot turn up their noses when they pass me on the street."

Again Clark was silent.

"So I'm through. I'm goin' to-day. And when I come back to this town it's going to be like a gentleman."

Clark took out his handkerchief and wiped his damp brow.

"Reckon you're not the only one it shook up," he admitted gloomily. "All this thing of girls going round like they do is going to stop right quick. Too bad, too, but everybody'll have to see it thataway."

"Do you mean," demanded Jim in surprise, "that all that's leaked out?"

"Leaked out? How on earth could they keep it secret. It'll

be announced in the papers to-night. Doctor Lamar's got to save his name somehow."

Jim put his hands on the sides of the car and tightened his long fingers on the metal.

"Do you mean Taylor investigated those checks?"

It was Clark's turn to be surprised.

"Haven't you heard what happened?"

Jim's startled eyes were answer enough.

"Why," announced Clark dramatically, "those four got another bottle of corn, got tight and decided to shock the town—so Nancy and that fella Merritt were married in Rockville at seven o'clock this morning."

A tiny indentation appeared in the metal under the Jelly-bean's fingers.

"Married?"

"Sure enough. Nancy sobered up and rushed back into town, crying and frightened to death—claimed it'd all been a mistake. First Doctor Lamar went wild and was going to kill Merritt, but finally they got it patched up some way, and Nancy and Merritt went to Savannah on the two-thirty train."

Jim closed his eyes and with an effort overcame a sudden sickness.

"It's too bad," said Clark philosophically. "I don't mean the wedding—reckon that's all right, though I don't guess Nancy cared a darn about him. But it's a crime for a nice girl like that to hurt her family that way."

The Jelly-bean let go the car and turned away. Again something was going on inside him, some inexplicable but almost chemical change.

"Where you going?" asked Clark.

The Jelly-bean turned and looked dully back over his shoulder.

"Got to go," he muttered. "Been up too long; feelin' right sick."

"Oh."

The street was hot at three and hotter still at four, the April dust seeming to enmesh the sun and give it forth again as a world-old joke forever played on an eternity of afternoons. But at half past four a first layer of quiet fell and the shades lengthened under the awnings and heavy foliaged trees. In this heat nothing mattered. All life was weather, a waiting through the hot where events had no significance for the cool that was soft and caressing like a woman's hand on a tired forehead. Down in Georgia there is a feeling—perhaps inarticulate—that this is the greatest wisdom of the South—so after a while the Jelly-bean turned into a pool-hall on Jackson Street where he was sure to find a congenial crowd who would make all the old jokes—the ones he knew.

The Camel's Back

THE glazed eye of the tired reader resting for a second on the above title will presume it to be merely metaphorical. Stories about the cup and the lip and the bad penny and the new broom rarely have anything to do with cups or lips or pennies or brooms. This story is the exception. It has to do with a material, visible and large-as-life camel's back.

Starting from the neck we shall work toward the tail. I want you to meet Mr. Perry Parkhurst, twenty-eight, lawyer, native of Toledo. Perry has nice teeth, a Harvard diploma, parts his hair in the middle. You have met him before—in Cleveland, Portland, St. Paul, Indianapolis, Kansas City, and so forth. Baker Brothers, New York, pause on their semi-annual trip through the West to clothe him; Montmorency & Co. dispatch a young man post-haste every three months to see that he has the correct number of little punctures on his shoes. He has a domestic roadster now, will have a French roadster if he lives long enough, and doubtless a Chinese tank if it comes into fashion. He looks like the advertisement of the young man rubbing his sunset-colored chest with liniment and goes East every other year to his class reunion.

I want you to meet his Love. Her name is Betty Medill, and she would take well in the movies. Her father gives her three hundred a month to dress on, and she has tawny eyes and hair and feather fans of five colors. I shall also introduce her father, Cyrus Medill. Though he is to all appearances flesh and blood, he is, strange to say, commonly known in Toledo as the Aluminum Man. But when he sits in his club window with two or three Iron Men, and the White Pine Man, and the Brass Man, they look very much as you and I do, only more so, if you know what I mean.

Now during the Christmas holidays of 1919 there took place in Toledo, counting only the people with the italicized *the*, forty-one dinner parties, sixteen dances, six luncheons, male and female, twelve teas, four stag dinners, two weddings, and thirteen bridge parties. It was the cumulative effect of all this that moved Perry Parkhurst on the twenty-ninth day of December to a decision.

This Medill girl would marry him and she wouldn't marry him. She was having such a good time that she hated to take such a definite step. Meanwhile, their secret engagement had got so long that it seemed as if any day it might break off of its own weight. A little man named Warburton, who knew it all, persuaded Perry to superman her, to get a marriage license and go up to the Medill house and tell her she'd have to marry him at once or call it off forever. So he presented himself, his heart, his license, and his ultimatum, and within five minutes they were in the midst of a violent quarrel, a burst of sporadic open fighting such as occurs near the end of all long wars and engagements. It brought about one of those ghastly lapses in which two people who are in love pull up sharp, look at each other coolly and think it's all been a mistake. Afterward they usually kiss wholesomely and assure the other person it was all their fault. Say it all was my fault! Say it was! I want to hear you say it!

But while reconciliation was trembling in the air, while each was, in a measure, stalling it off, so that they might the more voluptuously and sentimentally enjoy it when it came, they were permanently interrupted by a twenty-minute phone call for Betty from a garrulous aunt. At the end of eighteen minutes Perry Parkhurst, urged on by pride and suspicion and injured dignity, put on his long fur coat, picked up his light brown soft hat, and stalked out the door.

"It's all over," he muttered brokenly as he tried to jam his car into first. "It's all over—if I have to choke you for an hour, damn you!" This last to the car, which had been standing some time and was quite cold.

He drove downtown—that is, he got into a snow rut that led him downtown. He sat slouched down very low in his seat, much too dispirited to care where he went.

In front of the Clarendon Hotel he was hailed from the sidewalk by a bad man named Baily, who had big teeth and lived at the hotel and had never been in love.

"Perry," said the bad man softly when the roadster drew up beside him at the curb, "I've got six quarts of the dog-gonedest still champagne you ever tasted. A third of it's yours, Perry, if you'll come up-stairs and help Martin Macy and me drink it."

"Baily," said Perry tensely, "I'll drink your champagne. I'll drink every drop of it. I don't care if it kills me."

"Shut up, you nut!" said the bad man gently. "They don't put wood alcohol in champagne. This is the stuff that proves the world is more than six thousand years old. It's so ancient that the cork is petrified. You have to pull it with a stone drill."

"Take me up-stairs," said Perry moodily. "If that cork sees my heart it'll fall out from pure mortification."

The room up-stairs was full of those innocent hotel pictures of little girls eating apples and sitting in swings and talking to dogs. The other decorations were neckties and a pink man reading a pink paper devoted to ladies in pink tights.

"When you have to go into the highways and byways——" said the pink man, looking reproachfully at Baily and Perry.

"Hello, Martin Macy," said Perry shortly, "where's this stone-age champagne?"

"What's the rush? This isn't an operation, understand. This is a party."

Perry sat down dully and looked disapprovingly at all the neckties.

Baily leisurely opened the door of a wardrobe and brought out six handsome bottles.

"Take off that darn fur coat!" said Martin Macy to Perry. "Or maybe you'd like to have us open all the windows."

"Give me champagne," said Perry.

"Going to the Townsends' circus ball to-night?"

"Am not!"

" 'Vited?"

"Uh-huh."

"Why not go?"

"Oh, I'm sick of parties," exclaimed Perry. "I'm sick of 'em. I've been to so many that I'm sick of 'em."

"Maybe you're going to the Howard Tates' party?"

"No, I tell you; I'm sick of 'em."

"Well," said Macy consolingly, "the Tates' is just for college kids anyways."

"I tell you——"

"I thought you'd be going to one of 'em anyways. I see by the papers you haven't missed a one this Christmas."

"Hm," grunted Perry morosely.

He would never go to any more parties. Classical phrases played in his mind—that side of his life was closed, closed. Now when a man says "closed, closed" like that, you can be pretty sure that some woman has double-closed him, so to speak. Perry was also thinking that other classical thought, about how cowardly suicide is. A noble thought that one—warm and inspiring. Think of all the fine men we should lose if suicide were not so cowardly!

An hour later was six o'clock, and Perry had lost all resemblance to the young man in the liniment advertisement. He looked like a rough draft for a riotous cartoon. They were singing—an impromptu song of Baily's improvisation:

"One Lump Perry, the parlor snake,
Famous through the city for the way he drinks his tea;
Plays with it, toys with it,
Makes no noise with it,
Balanced on a napkin on his well-trained knee——"

"Trouble is," said Perry, who had just banged his hair with Baily's comb and was tying an orange tie round it to get the effect of Julius Cæsar, "that you fellas can't sing worth a damn. Soon's I leave th' air and start singin' tenor you start singin' tenor too."

" 'M a natural tenor," said Macy gravely. "Voice lacks cultivation, tha's all. Gotta natural voice, m'aunt used say. Naturally good singer."

"Singers, singers, all good singers," remarked Baily, who was at the telephone. "No, not the cabaret; I want night egg. I mean some dog-gone clerk 'at's got food—food! I want——"

"Julius Cæsar," announced Perry, turning round from the mirror. "Man of iron will and stern 'termination."

"Shut up!" yelled Baily. "Say, iss Mr. Baily. Sen' up enormous supper. Use y'own judgment. Right away."

He connected the receiver and the hook with some difficulty, and then with his lips closed and an expression of solemn intensity in his eyes went to the lower drawer of his dresser and pulled it open.

"Lookit!" he commanded. In his hands he held a truncated garment of pink gingham.

"Pants," he exclaimed gravely. "Lookit!"

This was a pink blouse, a red tie, and a Buster Brown collar.

"Lookit!" he repeated. "Costume for the Townsends' circus ball. I'm li'l' boy carries water for the elephants."

Perry was impressed in spite of himself.

"I'm going to be Julius Cæsar," he announced after a moment of concentration.

"Thought you weren't going!" said Macy.

"Me? Sure, I'm goin'. Never miss a party. Good for the nerves—like celery."

"Cæsar!" scoffed Baily. "Can't be Cæsar! He is not about a circus. Cæsar's Shakespeare. Go as a clown."

Perry shook his head.

"Nope; Cæsar."

"Cæsar?"

"Sure. Chariot."

Light dawned on Baily.

"That's right. Good idea."

Perry looked round the room searchingly.

"You lend me a bathrobe and this tie," he said finally.

Baily considered.

"No good."

"Sure, tha's all I need. Cæsar was a savage. They can't kick if I come as Cæsar, if he was a savage."

"No," said Baily, shaking his head slowly. "Get a costume over at a costumer's. Over at Nolak's."

"Closed up."

"Find out."

After a puzzling five minutes at the phone a small, weary voice managed to convince Perry that it was Mr. Nolak speaking, and that they would remain open until eight because of the Townsends' ball. Thus assured, Perry ate a great amount of filet mignon and drank his third of the last bottle of champagne. At eight-fifteen the man in the tall hat who stands in front of the Clarendon found him trying to start his roadster.

"Froze up," said Perry wisely. "The cold froze it. The cold air."

"Froze, eh?"

"Yes. Cold air froze it."

"Can't start it?"

"Nope. Let it stand here till summer. One those hot ole August days'll thaw it out awright."

"Goin' let it stand?"

"Sure. Let 'er stand. Take a hot thief to steal it. Gemme taxi."

The man in the tall hat summoned a taxi.

"Where to, mister?"

"Go to Nolak's—costume fella."

II

Mrs. Nolak was short and ineffectual looking, and on the cessation of the world war had belonged for a while to one of the new nationalities. Owing to unsettled European conditions she had never since been quite sure what she was. The shop in which she and her husband performed their daily stint was dim and ghostly, and peopled with suits of armor and Chinese mandarins, and enormous papier-mâché birds suspended from the ceiling. In a vague background many rows of masks glared eyelessly at the visitor, and there were glass cases full of crowns and scepters, and jewels and enormous stomachers, and paints, and crape hair, and wigs of all colors.

When Perry ambled into the shop Mrs. Nolak was folding up the last troubles of a strenuous day, so she thought, in a drawer full of pink silk stockings.

"Something for you?" she queried pessimistically.

"Want costume of Julius Hur, the charioteer."

Mrs. Nolak was sorry, but every stitch of charioteer had been rented long ago. Was it for the Townsends' circus ball?

It was.

"Sorry," she said, "but I don't think there's anything left that's really circus."

This was an obstacle.

"Hm," said Perry. An idea struck him suddenly. "If you've got a piece of canvas I could go's a tent."

"Sorry, but we haven't anything like that. A hardware store is where you'd have to go to. We have some very nice Confederate soldiers."

"No. No soldiers."

"And I have a very handsome king."

He shook his head.

"Several of the gentlemen," she continued hopefully, "are wearing stovepipe hats and swallow-tail coats and going as ringmasters—but we're all out of tall hats. I can let you have some crape hair for a mustache."

"Want somep'n 'stinctive."

"Something—let's see. Well, we have a lion's head, and a goose, and a camel——"

"Camel?" The idea seized Perry's imagination, gripped it fiercely.

"Yes, but it needs two people."

"Camel. That's the idea. Lemme see it."

The camel was produced from his resting place on a top shelf. At first glance he appeared to consist entirely of a very gaunt, cadaverous head and a sizable hump, but on being spread out he was found to possess a dark brown, unwholesome-looking body made of thick, cottony cloth.

"You see it takes two people," explained Mrs. Nolak, holding the camel in frank admiration. "If you have a friend he could be part of it. You see there's sorta pants for two people. One pair is for the fella in front, and the other pair for the fella in back. The fella in front does the lookin' out through these here eyes, an' the fella in back he's just gotta stoop over an' folla the front fella round."

"Put it on," commanded Perry.

Obediently Mrs. Nolak put her tabby-cat face inside the camel's head and turned it from side to side ferociously.

Perry was fascinated.

"What noise does a camel make?"

"What?" asked Mrs. Nolak as her face emerged, somewhat smudgy. "Oh, what noise? Why, he sorta brays."

"Lemme see it in a mirror."

Before a wide mirror Perry tried on the head and turned from side to side appraisingly. In the dim light the effect was distinctly pleasing. The camel's face was a study in pessimism, decorated with numerous abrasions, and it must be admitted that his coat was in that state of general negligence peculiar to camels—in fact, he needed to be cleaned and pressed—but distinctive he certainly was. He was majestic. He would have attracted attention in any gathering, if only by his melancholy cast of feature and the look of hunger lurking round his shadowy eyes.

"You see you have to have two people," said Mrs. Nolak again.

Perry tentatively gathered up the body and legs and wrapped them about him, tying the hind legs as a girdle round his waist. The effect on the whole was bad. It was even irreverent—like one of those mediæval pictures of a monk changed into a beast by the ministrations of Satan. At the very best the ensemble resembled a humpbacked cow sitting on her haunches among blankets.

"Don't look like anything at all," objected Perry gloomily.

"No," said Mrs. Nolak; "you see you got to have two people."

A solution flashed upon Perry.

"You got a date to-night?"

"Oh, I couldn't possibly——"

"Oh, come on," said Perry encouragingly. "Sure you can! Here! Be good sport, and climb into these hind legs."

With difficulty he located them, and extended their yawning depths ingratiatingly. But Mrs. Nolak seemed loath. She backed perversely away.

"Oh, no——"

"C'm on! You can be the front if you want to. Or we'll flip a coin."

"Oh, no——"

"Make it worth your while."

Mrs. Nolak set her lips firmly together.

"Now you just stop!" she said with no coyness implied. "None of the gentlemen ever acted up this way before. My husband——"

"You got a husband?" demanded Perry. "Where is he?"

"He's home."

"Wha's telephone number?"

After considerable parley he obtained the telephone number

pertaining to the Nolak penates and got into communication with that small, weary voice he had heard once before that day. But Mr. Nolak, though taken off his guard and somewhat confused by Perry's brilliant flow of logic, stuck staunchly to his point. He refused firmly, but with dignity, to help out Mr. Parkhurst in the capacity of back part of a camel.

Having rung off, or rather having been rung off on, Perry sat down on a three-legged stool to think it over. He named over to himself those friends on whom he might call, and then his mind paused as Betty Medill's name hazily and sorrowfully occurred to him. He had a sentimental thought. He would ask her. Their love affair was over, but she could not refuse this last request. Surely it was not much to ask—to help him keep up his end of social obligation for one short night. And if she insisted, she could be the front part of the camel and he would go as the back. His magnanimity pleased him. His mind even turned to rosy-colored dreams of a tender reconciliation inside the camel—there hidden away from all the world. . . .

"Now you'd better decide right off."

The bourgeois voice of Mrs. Nolak broke in upon his mellow fancies and roused him to action. He went to the phone and called up the Medill house. Miss Betty was out; had gone out to dinner.

Then, when all seemed lost, the camel's back wandered curiously into the store. He was a dilapidated individual with a cold in his head and a general trend about him of downwardness. His cap was pulled down low on his head, and his chin was pulled down low on his chest, his coat hung down to his shoes, he looked rundown, down at the heels, and—Salvation Army to the contrary—down and out. He said that he was the taxicab-driver that the gentleman had hired at the Clarendon Hotel. He had been instructed to wait outside, but he had waited some time, and a suspicion had grown upon him that the gentleman had gone out the back way with purpose to defraud him—gentlemen sometimes did—so he had come in. He sank down onto the three-legged stool.

"Wanta go to a party?" demanded Perry sternly.

"I gotta work," answered the taxi-driver lugubriously. "I gotta keep my job."

"It's a very good party."

" 'S a very good job."

"Come on!" urged Perry. "Be a good fella. See—it's pretty!" He held the camel up and the taxi-driver looked at it cynically.

"Huh!"

Perry searched feverishly among the folds of the cloth.

"See!" he cried enthusiastically, holding up a selection of folds. "This is your part. You don't even have to talk. All you have to do is to walk—and sit down occasionally. You do all the sitting down. Think of it. I'm on my feet all the time and *you* can sit down some of the time. The only time *I* can sit down is when we're lying down, and you can sit down when —oh, any time. See?"

"What's 'at thing?" demanded the individual dubiously. "A shroud?"

"Not at all," said Perry indignantly. "It's a camel."

"Huh?"

Then Perry mentioned a sum of money, and the conversation left the land of grunts and assumed a practical tinge. Perry and the taxi-driver tried on the camel in front of the mirror.

"You can't see it," explained Perry, peering anxiously out through the eyeholes, "but honestly, ole man, you look sim'ly great! Honestly!"

A grunt from the hump acknowledged this somewhat dubious compliment.

"Honestly, you look great!" repeated Perry enthusiastically. "Move round a little."

The hind legs moved forward, giving the effect of a huge cat-camel hunching his back preparatory to a spring.

"No; move sideways."

The camel's hips went neatly out of joint; a hula dancer would have writhed in envy.

"Good, isn't it?" demanded Perry, turning to Mrs. Nolak for approval.

"It looks lovely," agreed Mrs. Nolak.

"We'll take it," said Perry.

The bundle was stowed under Perry's arm and they left the shop.

"Go to the party!" he commanded as he took his seat in the back.

"What party?"

"Fanzy-dress party."

"Where'bouts is it?"

This presented a new problem. Perry tried to remember, but the names of all those who had given parties during the holidays danced confusedly before his eyes. He could ask Mrs. Nolak, but on looking out the window he saw that the shop was dark. Mrs. Nolak had already faded out, a little black smudge far down the snowy street.

"Drive uptown," directed Perry with fine confidence. "If you see a party, stop. Otherwise I'll tell you when we get there."

He fell into a hazy daydream and his thoughts wandered again to Betty—he imagined vaguely that they had had a disagreement because she refused to go to the party as the back part of the camel. He was just slipping off into a chilly doze when he was wakened by the taxi-driver opening the door and shaking him by the arm.

"Here we are, maybe."

Perry looked out sleepily. A striped awning led from the curb up to a spreading gray stone house, from which issued the low drummy whine of expensive jazz. He recognized the Howard Tate house.

"Sure," he said emphatically; " 'at's it! Tate's party tonight. Sure, everybody's goin'."

"Say," said the individual anxiously after another look at the awning, "you sure these people ain't gonna romp on me for comin' here?"

Perry drew himself up with dignity.

" 'F anybody says anything to you, just tell 'em you're part of my costume."

The visualization of himself as a thing rather than a person seemed to reassure the individual.

"All right," he said reluctantly.

Perry stepped out under the shelter of the awning and began unrolling the camel.

"Let's go," he commanded.

Several minutes later a melancholy, hungry-looking camel,

emitting clouds of smoke from his mouth and from the tip of his noble hump, might have been seen crossing the threshold of the Howard Tate residence, passing a startled footman without so much as a snort, and heading directly for the main stairs that led up to the ballroom. The beast walked with a peculiar gait which varied between an uncertain lockstep and a stampede—but can best be described by the word "halting." The camel had a halting gait—and as he walked he alternately elongated and contracted like a gigantic concertina.

III

The Howard Tates are, as every one who lives in Toledo knows, the most formidable people in town. Mrs. Howard Tate was a Chicago Todd before she became a Toledo Tate, and the family generally affect that conscious simplicity which has begun to be the earmark of American aristocracy. The Tates have reached the stage where they talk about pigs and farms and look at you icy-eyed if you are not amused. They have begun to prefer retainers rather than friends as dinner guests, spend a lot of money in a quiet way, and, having lost all sense of competition, are in process of growing quite dull.

The dance this evening was for little Millicent Tate, and though all ages were represented, the dancers were mostly from school and college—the younger married crowd was at the Townsends' circus ball up at the Tallyho Club. Mrs. Tate was standing just inside the ballroom, following Millicent round with her eyes, and beaming whenever she caught her eye. Beside her were two middle-aged sycophants, who were saying what a perfectly exquisite child Millicent was. It was at this moment that Mrs. Tate was grasped firmly by the skirt and her youngest daughter, Emily, aged eleven, hurled herself with an "Oof!" into her mother's arms.

"Why, Emily, what's the trouble?"

"Mamma," said Emily, wild-eyed but voluble, "there's something out on the stairs."

"What?"

"There's a thing out on the stairs, mamma. I think it's a big dog, mamma, but it doesn't look like a dog."

"What do you mean, Emily?"

The sycophants waved their heads sympathetically.

"Mamma, it looks like a—like a camel."

Mrs. Tate laughed.

"You saw a mean old shadow, dear, that's all."

"No, I didn't. No, it was some kind of thing, mamma—big. I was going down-stairs to see if there were any more people, and this dog or something, he was coming up-stairs. Kinda funny, mamma, like he was lame. And then he saw me and gave a sort of growl, and then he slipped at the top of the landing, and I ran."

Mrs. Tate's laugh faded.

"The child must have seen something," she said.

The sycophants agreed that the child must have seen something—and suddenly all three women took an instinctive step away from the door as the sounds of muffled steps were audible just outside.

And then three startled gasps rang out as a dark brown form rounded the corner, and they saw what was apparently a huge beast looking down at them hungrily.

"Oof!" cried Mrs. Tate.

"O-o-oh!" cried the ladies in a chorus.

The camel suddenly humped his back, and the gasps turned to shrieks.

"Oh—look!"

"What is it?"

The dancing stopped, but the dancers hurrying over got quite a different impression of the invader; in fact, the young people immediately suspected that it was a stunt, a hired entertainer come to amuse the party. The boys in long trousers looked at it rather disdainfully, and sauntered over with their hands in their pockets, feeling that their intelligence was being insulted. But the girls uttered little shouts of glee.

"It's a camel!"

"Well, if he isn't the funniest!"

The camel stood there uncertainly, swaying slightly from side to side, and seeming to take in the room in a careful, appraising glance; then as if he had come to an abrupt decision he turned and ambled swiftly out the door.

Mr. Howard Tate had just come out of the library on the

lower floor, and was standing chatting with a young man in the hall. Suddenly they heard the noise of shouting up-stairs, and almost immediately a succession of bumping sounds, followed by the precipitous appearance at the foot of the stairway of a large brown beast that seemed to be going somewhere in a great hurry.

"Now what the devil!" said Mr. Tate, starting.

The beast picked itself up not without dignity and, affecting an air of extreme nonchalance, as if he had just remembered an important engagement, started at a mixed gait toward the front door. In fact, his front legs began casually to run.

"See here now," said Mr. Tate sternly. "Here! Grab it, Butterfield! Grab it!"

The young man enveloped the rear of the camel in a pair of compelling arms, and, realizing that further locomotion was impossible, the front end submitted to capture and stood resignedly in a state of some agitation. By this time a flood of young people was pouring down-stairs, and Mr. Tate, suspecting everything from an ingenious burglar to an escaped lunatic, gave crisp directions to the young man:

"Hold him! Lead him in here; we'll soon see."

The camel consented to be led into the library, and Mr. Tate, after locking the door, took a revolver from a table drawer and instructed the young man to take the thing's head off. Then he gasped and returned the revolver to its hiding-place.

"Well, Perry Parkhurst!" he exclaimed in amazement.

"Got the wrong party, Mr. Tate," said Perry sheepishly. "Hope I didn't scare you."

"Well—you gave us a thrill, Perry." Realization dawned on him. "You're bound for the Townsends' circus ball."

"That's the general idea."

"Let me introduce Mr. Butterfield, Mr. Parkhurst." Then turning to Perry: "Butterfield is staying with us for a few days."

"I got a little mixed up," mumbled Perry. "I'm very sorry."

"Perfectly all right; most natural mistake in the world. I've got a clown rig and I'm going down there myself after a while." He turned to Butterfield. "Better change your mind and come down with us."

The young man demurred. He was going to bed.

"Have a drink, Perry?" suggested Mr. Tate.

"Thanks, I will."

"And, say," continued Tate quickly, "I'd forgotten all about your—friend here." He indicated the rear part of the camel. "I didn't mean to seem discourteous. Is it any one I know? Bring him out."

"It's not a friend," explained Perry hurriedly. "I just rented him."

"Does he drink?"

"Do you?" demanded Perry, twisting himself tortuously round.

There was a faint sound of assent.

"Sure he does!" said Mr. Tate heartily. "A really efficient camel ought to be able to drink enough so it'd last him three days."

"Tell you," said Perry anxiously, "he isn't exactly dressed up enough to come out. If you give me the bottle I can hand it back to him and he can take his inside."

From under the cloth was audible the enthusiastic smacking sound inspired by this suggestion. When a butler had appeared with bottles, glasses, and siphon one of the bottles was handed back; thereafter the silent partner could be heard imbibing long potations at frequent intervals.

Thus passed a benign hour. At ten o'clock Mr. Tate decided that they'd better be starting. He donned his clown's costume; Perry replaced the camel's head, and side by side they traversed on foot the single block between the Tate house and the Tallyho Club.

The circus ball was in full swing. A great tent fly had been put up inside the ballroom and round the walls had been built rows of booths representing the various attractions of a circus side show, but these were now vacated and over the floor swarmed a shouting, laughing medley of youth and color—clowns, bearded ladies, acrobats, bareback riders, ringmasters, tattooed men, and charioteers. The Townsends had determined to assure their party of success, so a great quantity of liquor had been surreptitiously brought over from their house and was now flowing freely. A green ribbon ran along the wall completely round the ballroom, with pointing arrows alongside and signs which instructed the uninitiated to "Follow the green line!" The green line led down to the bar, where waited pure punch and wicked punch and plain dark-green bottles.

On the wall above the bar was another arrow, red and very wavy, and under it the slogan: "Now follow this!"

But even amid the luxury of costume and high spirits represented there, the entrance of the camel created something of a stir, and Perry was immediately surrounded by a curious, laughing crowd attempting to penetrate the identity of this beast that stood by the wide doorway eying the dancers with his hungry, melancholy gaze.

And then Perry saw Betty standing in front of a booth, talking to a comic policeman. She was dressed in the costume of an Egyptian snake-charmer: her tawny hair was braided and drawn through brass rings, the effect crowned with a glittering Oriental tiara. Her fair face was stained to a warm olive glow and on her arms and the half moon of her back writhed painted serpents with single eyes of venomous green. Her feet were in sandals and her skirt was slit to the knees, so that when she walked one caught a glimpse of other slim serpents painted just above her bare ankles. Wound about her neck was a glittering cobra. Altogether a charming costume—one that caused the more nervous among the older women to shrink away from her when she passed, and the more troublesome ones to make great talk about "shouldn't be allowed" and "perfectly disgraceful."

But Perry, peering through the uncertain eyes of the camel, saw only her face, radiant, animated, and glowing with excitement, and her arms and shoulders, whose mobile, expressive gestures made her always the outstanding figure in any group. He was fascinated and his fascination exercised a sobering effect on him. With a growing clarity the events of the day came back—rage rose within him, and with a half-formed intention of taking her away from the crowd he started toward her—or rather he elongated slightly, for he had neglected to issue the preparatory command necessary to locomotion.

But at this point fickle Kismet, who for a day had played with him bitterly and sardonically, decided to reward him in full for the amusement he had afforded her. Kismet turned the tawny eyes of the snake-charmer to the camel. Kismet led her to lean toward the man beside her and say, "Who's that? That camel?"

"Darned if I know."

But a little man named Warburton, who knew it all, found it necessary to hazard an opinion:

"It came in with Mr. Tate. I think part of it's probably Warren Butterfield, the architect from New York, who's visiting the Tates."

Something stirred in Betty Medill—that age-old interest of the provincial girl in the visiting man.

"Oh," she said casually after a slight pause.

At the end of the next dance Betty and her partner finished up within a few feet of the camel. With the informal audacity that was the key-note of the evening she reached out and gently rubbed the camel's nose.

"Hello, old camel."

The camel stirred uneasily.

"You 'fraid of me?" said Betty, lifting her eyebrows in reproof. "Don't be. You see I'm a snake-charmer, but I'm pretty good at camels too."

The camel bowed very low and some one made the obvious remark about beauty and the beast.

Mrs. Townsend approached the group.

"Well, Mr. Butterfield," she said helpfully, "I wouldn't have recognized you."

Perry bowed again and smiled gleefully behind his mask.

"And who is this with you?" she inquired.

"Oh," said Perry, his voice muffled by the thick cloth and quite unrecognizable, "he isn't a fellow, Mrs. Townsend. He's just part of my costume."

Mrs. Townsend laughed and moved away. Perry turned again to Betty.

"So," he thought, "this is how much she cares! On the very day of our final rupture she starts a flirtation with another man—an absolute stranger."

On an impulse he gave her a soft nudge with his shoulder and waved his head suggestively toward the hall, making it clear that he desired her to leave her partner and accompany him.

"By-by, Rus," she called to her partner. "This old camel's got me. Where we going, Prince of Beasts?"

The noble animal made no rejoinder, but stalked gravely along in the direction of a secluded nook on the side stairs.

There she seated herself, and the camel, after some seconds of confusion which included gruff orders and sounds of a heated dispute going on in his interior, placed himself beside her—his hind legs stretching out uncomfortably across two steps.

"Well, old egg," said Betty cheerfully, "how do you like our happy party?"

The old egg indicated that he liked it by rolling his head ecstatically and executing a gleeful kick with his hoofs.

"This is the first time that I ever had a tête-à-tête with a man's valet 'round"—she pointed to the hind legs—"or whatever that is."

"Oh," mumbled Perry, "he's deaf and blind."

"I should think you'd feel rather handicapped—you can't very well toddle, even if you want to."

The camel hung his head lugubriously.

"I wish you'd say something," continued Betty sweetly. "Say you like me, camel. Say you think I'm beautiful. Say you'd like to belong to a pretty snake-charmer."

The camel would.

"Will you dance with me, camel?"

The camel would try.

Betty devoted half an hour to the camel. She devoted at least half an hour to all visiting men. It was usually sufficient. When she approached a new man the current débutantes were accustomed to scatter right and left like a close column deploying before a machine-gun. And so to Perry Parkhurst was awarded the unique privilege of seeing his love as others saw her. He was flirted with violently!

IV

This paradise of frail foundation was broken into by the sounds of a general ingress to the ballroom; the cotillion was beginning. Betty and the camel joined the crowd, her brown hand resting lightly on his shoulder, defiantly symbolizing her complete adoption of him.

When they entered the couples were already seating themselves at tables round the walls, and Mrs. Townsend, resplendent as a super bareback rider with rather too rotund calves, was standing in the centre with the ringmaster in charge of arrangements. At a signal to the band every one rose and began to dance.

"Isn't it just slick!" sighed Betty. "Do you think you can possibly dance?"

Perry nodded enthusiastically. He felt suddenly exuberant. After all, he was here incognito talking to his love—he could wink patronizingly at the world.

So Perry danced the cotillion. I say danced, but that is stretching the word far beyond the wildest dreams of the jazziest terpsichorean. He suffered his partner to put her hands on his helpless shoulders and pull him here and there over the floor while he hung his huge head docilely over her shoulder and made futile dummy motions with his feet. His hind legs danced in a manner all their own, chiefly by hopping first on one foot and then on the other. Never being sure whether dancing was going on or not, the hind legs played safe by going through a series of steps whenever the music started playing. So the spectacle was frequently presented of the front part of the camel standing at ease and the rear keeping up a constant energetic motion calculated to rouse a sympathetic perspiration in any soft-hearted observer.

He was frequently favored. He danced first with a tall lady covered with straw who announced jovially that she was a bale of hay and coyly begged him not to eat her.

"I'd like to; you're so sweet," said the camel gallantly.

Each time the ringmaster shouted his call of "Men up!" he lumbered ferociously for Betty with the cardboard wienerwurst or the photograph of the bearded lady or whatever the favor chanced to be. Sometimes he reached her first, but usually his rushes were unsuccessful and resulted in intense interior arguments.

"For Heaven's sake," Perry would snarl fiercely between his clenched teeth, "get a little pep! I could have gotten her that time if you'd picked your feet up."

"Well, gimme a little warnin'!"

"I did, darn you."

"I can't see a dog-gone thing in here."

"All you have to do is follow me. It's just like dragging a load of sand round to walk with you."

"Maybe you wanta try back here."

"You shut up! If these people found you in this room they'd give you the worst beating you ever had. They'd take your taxi license away from you!"

Perry surprised himself by the ease with which he made this monstrous threat, but it seemed to have a soporific influence on his companion, for he gave out an "aw gwan" and subsided into abashed silence.

The ringmaster mounted to the top of the piano and waved his hand for silence.

"Prizes!" he cried. "Gather round!"

"Yea! Prizes!"

Self-consciously the circle swayed forward. The rather pretty girl who had mustered the nerve to come as a bearded lady trembled with excitement, thinking to be rewarded for an evening's hideousness. The man who had spent the afternoon having tattoo marks painted on him skulked on the edge of the crowd, blushing furiously when any one told him he was sure to get it.

"Lady and gent performers of this circus," announced the ringmaster jovially, "I am sure we will all agree that a good time has been had by all. We will now bestow honor where honor is due by bestowing the prizes. Mrs. Townsend has asked me to bestow the prizes. Now, fellow performers, the first prize is for that lady who has displayed this evening the most striking, becoming"—at this point the bearded lady sighed resignedly—"and original costume." Here the bale of hay pricked up her ears. "Now I am sure that the decision which has been agreed upon will be unanimous with all here present. The first prize goes to Miss Betty Medill, the charming Egyptian snake-charmer."

There was a burst of applause, chiefly masculine, and Miss Betty Medill, blushing beautifully through her olive paint, was passed up to receive her award. With a tender glance the ringmaster handed down to her a huge bouquet of orchids.

"And now," he continued, looking round him, "the other prize is for that man who has the most amusing and original costume. This prize goes without dispute to a guest in our midst, a gentleman who is visiting here but whose stay we all hope will be long and merry—in short, to the noble camel who has entertained us all by his hungry look and his brilliant dancing throughout the evening."

He ceased and there was a violent clapping and yea-ing, for it was a popular choice. The prize, a large box of cigars, was put aside for the camel, as he was anatomically unable to accept it in person.

"And now," continued the ringmaster, "we will wind up the cotillion with the marriage of Mirth to Folly!

"Form for the grand wedding march, the beautiful snake-charmer and the noble camel in front!"

Betty skipped forward cheerily and wound an olive arm round the camel's neck. Behind them formed the procession of little boys, little girls, country jakes, fat ladies, thin men, sword-swallowers, wild men of Borneo, and armless wonders, many of them well in their cups, all of them excited and happy and dazzled by the flow of light and color round them, and by the familiar faces, strangely unfamiliar under bizarre wigs and barbaric paint. The voluptuous chords of the wedding march done in blasphemous syncopation issued in a delirious blend from the trombones and saxophones—and the march began.

"Aren't you glad, camel?" demanded Betty sweetly as they stepped off. "Aren't you glad we're going to be married and you're going to belong to the nice snake-charmer ever afterward?"

The camel's front legs pranced, expressing excessive joy.

"Minister! Minister! Where's the minister?" cried voices out of the revel. "Who's going to be the clergyman?"

The head of Jumbo, obese negro, waiter at the Tallyho Club for many years, appeared rashly through a half-opened pantry door.

"Oh, Jumbo!"

"Get old Jumbo. He's the fella!"

"Come on, Jumbo. How 'bout marrying us a couple?"

"Yea!"

Jumbo was seized by four comedians, stripped of his apron,

and escorted to a raised daïs at the head of the ball. There his collar was removed and replaced back side forward with ecclesiastical effect. The parade separated into two lines, leaving an aisle for the bride and groom.

"Lawdy, man," roared Jumbo, "Ah got ole Bible 'n' ev'ythin', sho nuff."

He produced a battered Bible from an interior pocket.

"Yea! Jumbo's got a Bible!"

"Razor, too, I'll bet!"

Together the snake-charmer and the camel ascended the cheering aisle and stopped in front of Jumbo.

"Where's yo license, camel?"

A man near by prodded Perry.

"Give him a piece of paper. Anything'll do."

Perry fumbled confusedly in his pocket, found a folded paper, and pushed it out through the camel's mouth. Holding it upside down Jumbo pretended to scan it earnestly.

"Dis yeah's a special camel's license," he said. "Get you ring ready, camel."

Inside the camel Perry turned round and addressed his worse half.

"Gimme a ring, for Heaven's sake!"

"I ain't got none," protested a weary voice.

"You have. I saw it."

"I ain't goin' to take it offen my hand."

"If you don't I'll kill you."

There was a gasp and Perry felt a huge affair of rhinestone and brass inserted into his hand.

Again he was nudged from the outside.

"Speak up!"

"I do!" cried Perry quickly.

He heard Betty's responses given in a debonair tone, and even in this burlesque the sound thrilled him.

Then he had pushed the rhinestone through a tear in the camel's coat and was slipping it on her finger, muttering ancient and historic words after Jumbo. He didn't want any one to know about this ever. His one idea was to slip away without having to disclose his identity, for Mr. Tate had so far kept his secret well. A dignified young man, Perry—and this might injure his infant law practice.

"Embrace the bride!"

"Unmask, camel, and kiss her!"

Instinctively his heart beat high as Betty turned to him laughingly and began to stroke the card-board muzzle. He felt his self-control giving way, he longed to surround her with his arms and declare his identity and kiss those lips that smiled only a foot away—when suddenly the laughter and applause round them died off and a curious hush fell over the hall. Perry and Betty looked up in surprise. Jumbo had given vent to a huge "Hello!" in such a startled voice that all eyes were bent on him.

"Hello!" he said again. He had turned round the camel's marriage license, which he had been holding upside down, produced spectacles, and was studying it agonizingly.

"Why," he exclaimed, and in the pervading silence his words were heard plainly by every one in the room, "this yeah's a sho-nuff marriage permit."

"What?"

"Huh?"

"Say it again, Jumbo!"

"Sure you can read?"

Jumbo waved them to silence and Perry's blood burned to fire in his veins as he realized the break he had made.

"Yassuh!" repeated Jumbo. "This yeah's a sho-nuff license, and the pa'ties concerned one of 'em is dis yeah young lady, Miz Betty Medill, and th' other's Mistah Perry Pa'khurst."

There was a general gasp, and a low rumble broke out as all eyes fell on the camel. Betty shrank away from him quickly, her tawny eyes giving out sparks of fury.

"Is you Mistah Pa'khurst, you camel?"

Perry made no answer. The crowd pressed up closer and stared at him. He stood frozen rigid with embarrassment, his cardboard face still hungry and sardonic as he regarded the ominous Jumbo.

"Y'all bettah speak up!" said Jumbo slowly, "this yeah's a mighty serious mattah. Outside mah duties at this club ah happens to be a sho-nuff minister in the Firs' Cullud Baptis' Church. It done look to me as though y'all is gone an' got married."

V

The scene that followed will go down forever in the annals of the Tallyho Club. Stout matrons fainted, one hundred per cent Americans swore, wild-eyed débutantes babbled in lightning groups instantly formed and instantly dissolved, and a great buzz of chatter, virulent yet oddly subdued, hummed through the chaotic ballroom. Feverish youths swore they would kill Perry or Jumbo or themselves or some one, and the Baptis' preacheh was besieged by a tempestuous covey of clamorous amateur lawyers, asking questions, making threats, demanding precedents, ordering the bonds annulled, and especially trying to ferret out any hint of prearrangement in what had occurred.

In the corner Mrs. Townsend was crying softly on the shoulder of Mr. Howard Tate, who was trying vainly to comfort her; they were exchanging "all my fault's" volubly and voluminously. Outside on a snow-covered walk Mr. Cyrus Medill, the Aluminum Man, was being paced slowly up and down between two brawny charioteers, giving vent now to a string of unrepeatables, now to wild pleadings that they'd just let him get at Jumbo. He was facetiously attired for the evening as a wild man of Borneo, and the most exacting stage-manager would have acknowledged any improvement in casting the part to be quite impossible.

Meanwhile the two principals held the real centre of the stage. Betty Medill—or was it Betty Parkhurst?—storming furiously, was surrounded by the plainer girls—the prettier ones were too busy talking about her to pay much attention to her—and over on the other side of the hall stood the camel, still intact except for his headpiece, which dangled pathetically on his chest. Perry was earnestly engaged in making protestations of his innocence to a ring of angry, puzzled men. Every few minutes, just as he had apparently proved his case, some one would mention the marriage certificate, and the inquisition would begin again.

A girl named Marion Cloud, considered the second best belle of Toledo, changed the gist of the situation by a remark she made to Betty.

"Well," she said maliciously, "it'll all blow over, dear. The courts will annul it without question."

Betty's angry tears dried miraculously in her eyes, her lips shut tight together, and she looked stonily at Marion. Then she rose and, scattering her sympathizers right and left, walked directly across the room to Perry, who stared at her in terror. Again silence crept down upon the room.

"Will you have the decency to grant me five minutes' conversation—or wasn't that included in your plans?"

He nodded, his mouth unable to form words.

Indicating coldly that he was to follow her she walked out into the hall with her chin uptilted and headed for the privacy of one of the little card-rooms.

Perry started after her, but was brought to a jerky halt by the failure of his hind legs to function.

"You stay here!" he commanded savagely.

"I can't," whined a voice from the hump, "unless you get out first and let me get out."

Perry hesitated, but unable any longer to tolerate the eyes of the curious crowd he muttered a command and the camel moved carefully from the room on its four legs.

Betty was waiting for him.

"Well," she began furiously, "you see what you've done! You and that crazy license! I told you you shouldn't have gotten it!"

"My dear girl, I——"

"Don't say 'dear girl' to me! Save that for your real wife if you ever get one after this disgraceful performance. And don't try to pretend it wasn't all arranged. You know you gave that colored waiter money! You know you did! Do you mean to say you didn't try to marry me?"

"No—of course——"

"Yes, you'd better admit it! You tried it, and now what are you going to do? Do you know my father's nearly crazy? It'll serve you right if he tries to kill you. He'll take his gun and put some cold steel in you. Even if this wed—this *thing* can be annulled it'll hang over me all the rest of my life!"

Perry could not resist quoting softly: " 'Oh, camel,

wouldn't you like to belong to the pretty snake-charmer for all your——' "

"Shut up!" cried Betty.

There was a pause.

"Betty," said Perry finally, "there's only one thing to do that will really get us out clear. That's for you to marry me."

"Marry you!"

"Yes. Really it's the only——"

"You shut up! I wouldn't marry you if—if——"

"I know. If I were the last man on earth. But if you care anything about your reputation——"

"Reputation!" she cried. "You're a nice one to think about my reputation *now*. Why didn't you think about my reputation before you hired that horrible Jumbo to—to——"

Perry tossed up his hands hopelessly.

"Very well. I'll do anything you want. Lord knows I renounce all claims!"

"But," said a new voice, "I don't."

Perry and Betty started, and she put her hand to her heart.

"For Heaven's sake, what was that?"

"It's me," said the camel's back.

In a minute Perry had whipped off the camel's skin, and a lax, limp object, his clothes hanging on him damply, his hand clenched tightly on an almost empty bottle, stood defiantly before them.

"Oh," cried Betty, "you brought that object in here to frighten me! You told me he was deaf—that awful person!"

The camel's back sat down on a chair with a sigh of satisfaction.

"Don't talk 'at way about me, lady. I ain't no person. I'm your husband."

"Husband!"

The cry was wrung simultaneously from Betty and Perry.

"Why, sure. I'm as much your husband as that gink is. The smoke didn't marry you to the camel's front. He married you to the whole camel. Why, that's my ring you got on your finger!"

With a little yelp she snatched the ring from her finger and flung it passionately at the floor.

"What's all this?" demanded Perry dazedly.

"Jes' that you better fix me an' fix me right. If you don't I'm a-gonna have the same claim you got to bein' married to her!"

"That's bigamy," said Perry, turning gravely to Betty.

Then came the supreme moment of Perry's evening, the ultimate chance on which he risked his fortunes. He rose and looked first at Betty, where she sat weakly, aghast at this new complication, and then at the individual who swayed from side to side on his chair, uncertainly, menacingly.

"Very well," said Perry slowly to the individual, "you can have her. Betty, I'm going to prove to you that as far as I'm concerned our marriage was entirely accidental. I'm going to renounce utterly my rights to have you as my wife, and give you to—to the man whose ring you wear—your lawful husband."

There was a pause and four horror-stricken eyes were turned on him.

"Good-by, Betty," he said brokenly. "Don't forget me in your new-found happiness. I'm going to leave for the Far West on the morning train. Think of me kindly, Betty."

With a last glance at them he turned and his head rested on his chest as his hand touched the door-knob.

"Good-by," he repeated. He turned the door-knob.

But at this sound the snakes and silk and tawny hair precipitated themselves violently toward him.

"Oh, Perry, don't leave me! Perry, Perry, take me with you!"

Her tears flowed damply on his neck. Calmly he folded his arms about her.

"I don't care," she cried. "I love you and if you can wake up a minister at this hour and have it done over again I'll go West with you."

Over her shoulder the front part of the camel looked at the back part of the camel—and they exchanged a particularly subtle, esoteric sort of wink that only true camels can understand.

May Day

THERE had been a war fought and won and the great city of the conquering people was crossed with triumphal arches and vivid with thrown flowers of white, red, and rose. All through the long spring days the returning soldiers marched up the chief highway behind the strump of drums and the joyous, resonant wind of the brasses, while merchants and clerks left their bickerings and figurings and, crowding to the windows, turned their white-bunched faces gravely upon the passing battalions.

Never had there been such splendor in the great city, for the victorious war had brought plenty in its train, and the merchants had flocked thither from the South and West with their households to taste of all the luscious feasts and witness the lavish entertainments prepared—and to buy for their women furs against the next winter and bags of golden mesh and varicolored slippers of silk and silver and rose satin and cloth of gold.

So gaily and noisily were the peace and prosperity impending hymned by the scribes and poets of the conquering people that more and more spenders had gathered from the provinces to drink the wine of excitement, and faster and faster did the merchants dispose of their trinkets and slippers until they sent up a mighty cry for more trinkets and more slippers in order that they might give in barter what was demanded of them. Some even of them flung up their hands helplessly, shouting:

"Alas! I have no more slippers! and alas! I have no more trinkets! May Heaven help me, for I know not what I shall do!"

But no one listened to their great outcry, for the throngs were far too busy—day by day, the foot-soldiers trod jauntily the highway and all exulted because the young men returning were pure and brave, sound of tooth and pink of cheek, and the young women of the land were virgins and comely both of face and of figure.

So during all this time there were many adventures that happened in the great city, and, of these, several—or perhaps one—are here set down.

I

At nine o'clock on the morning of the first of May, 1919, a young man spoke to the room clerk at the Biltmore Hotel, asking if Mr. Philip Dean were registered there, and if so, could he be connected with Mr. Dean's rooms. The inquirer was dressed in a well-cut, shabby suit. He was small, slender, and darkly handsome; his eyes were framed above with unusually long eyelashes and below with the blue semicircle of ill health, this latter effect heightened by an unnatural glow which colored his face like a low, incessant fever.

Mr. Dean was staying there. The young man was directed to a telephone at the side.

After a second his connection was made; a sleepy voice hello'd from somewhere above.

"Mr. Dean?"—this very eagerly—"it's Gordon, Phil. It's Gordon Sterrett. I'm down-stairs. I heard you were in New York and I had a hunch you'd be here."

The sleepy voice became gradually enthusiastic. Well, how was Gordy, old boy! Well, he certainly was surprised and tickled! Would Gordy come right up, for Pete's sake!

A few minutes later Philip Dean, dressed in blue silk pajamas, opened his door and the two young men greeted each other with a half-embarrassed exuberance. They were both about twenty-four, Yale graduates of the year before the war; but there the resemblance stopped abruptly. Dean was blond, ruddy, and rugged under his thin pajamas. Everything about him radiated fitness and bodily comfort. He smiled frequently, showing large and prominent teeth.

"I was going to look you up," he cried enthusiastically. "I'm taking a couple of weeks off. If you'll sit down a sec I'll be right with you. Going to take a shower."

As he vanished into the bathroom his visitor's dark eyes roved nervously around the room, resting for a moment on a great English travelling bag in the corner and on a family of thick silk shirts littered on the chairs amid impressive neckties and soft woollen socks.

Gordon rose and, picking up one of the shirts, gave it a minute examination. It was of very heavy silk, yellow, with a pale blue stripe—and there were nearly a dozen of them. He stared involuntarily at his own shirt-cuffs—they were ragged and linty at the edges and soiled to a faint gray. Dropping the silk shirt, he held his coat-sleeves down and worked the frayed shirt-cuffs up till they were out of sight. Then he went to the mirror and looked at himself with listless, unhappy interest. His tie, of former glory, was faded and thumb-creased—it served no longer to hide the jagged buttonholes of his collar. He thought, quite without amusement, that only three years before he had received a scattering vote in the senior elections at college for being the best-dressed man in his class.

Dean emerged from the bathroom polishing his body.

"Saw an old friend of yours last night," he remarked. "Passed her in the lobby and couldn't think of her name to save my neck. That girl you brought up to New Haven senior year."

Gordon started.

"Edith Bradin? That whom you mean?"

" 'At's the one. Damn good looking. She's still sort of a pretty doll—you know what I mean: as if you touched her she'd smear."

He surveyed his shining self complacently in the mirror, smiled faintly, exposing a section of teeth.

"She must be twenty-three anyway," he continued.

"Twenty-two last month," said Gordon absently.

"What? Oh, last month. Well, I imagine she's down for the Gamma Psi dance. Did you know we're having a Yale Gamma Psi dance to-night at Delmonico's? You better come up, Gordy. Half of New Haven'll probably be there. I can get you an invitation."

Draping himself reluctantly in fresh underwear, Dean lit a cigarette and sat down by the open window, inspecting his calves and knees under the morning sunshine which poured into the room.

"Sit down, Gordy," he suggested, "and tell me all about

what you've been doing and what you're doing now and everything."

Gordon collapsed unexpectedly upon the bed; lay there inert and spiritless. His mouth, which habitually dropped a little open when his face was in repose, became suddenly helpless and pathetic.

"What's the matter?" asked Dean quickly.

"Oh, God!"

"What's the matter?"

"Every God damn thing in the world," he said miserably. "I've absolutely gone to pieces, Phil. I'm all in."

"Huh?"

"I'm all in." His voice was shaking.

Dean scrutinized him more closely with appraising blue eyes.

"You certainly look all shot."

"I am. I've made a hell of a mess of everything." He paused. "I'd better start at the beginning—or will it bore you?"

"Not at all; go on." There was, however, a hesitant note in Dean's voice. This trip East had been planned for a holiday—to find Gordon Sterrett in trouble exasperated him a little.

"Go on," he repeated, and then added half under his breath, "Get it over with."

"Well," began Gordon unsteadily, "I got back from France in February, went home to Harrisburg for a month, and then came down to New York to get a job. I got one—with an export company. They fired me yesterday."

"Fired you?"

"I'm coming to that, Phil. I want to tell you frankly. You're about the only man I can turn to in a matter like this. You won't mind if I just tell you frankly, will you, Phil?"

Dean stiffened a bit more. The pats he was bestowing on his knees grew perfunctory. He felt vaguely that he was being unfairly saddled with responsibility; he was not even sure he wanted to be told. Though never surprised at finding Gordon Sterrett in mild difficulty, there was something in this present misery that repelled him and hardened him, even though it excited his curiosity.

"Go on."

"It's a girl."

"Hm." Dean resolved that nothing was going to spoil his trip. If Gordon was going to be depressing, then he'd have to see less of Gordon.

"Her name is Jewel Hudson," went on the distressed voice from the bed. "She used to be 'pure,' I guess, up to about a year ago. Lived here in New York—poor family. Her people are dead now and she lives with an old aunt. You see it was just about the time I met her that everybody began to come back from France in droves—and all I did was to welcome the newly arrived and go on parties with 'em. That's the way it started, Phil, just from being glad to see everybody and having them glad to see me."

"You ought to've had more sense."

"I know," Gordon paused, and then continued listlessly. "I'm on my own now, you know, and Phil, I can't stand being poor. Then came this darn girl. She sort of fell in love with me for a while and, though I never intended to get so involved, I'd always seem to run into her somewhere. You can imagine the sort of work I was doing for those exporting people—of course, I always intended to draw; do illustrating for magazines; there's a pile of money in it."

"Why didn't you? You've got to buckle down if you want to make good," suggested Dean with cold formalism.

"I tried, a little, but my stuff's crude. I've got talent, Phil; I can draw—but I just don't know how. I ought to go to art school and I can't afford it. Well, things came to a crisis about a week ago. Just as I was down to about my last dollar this girl began bothering me. She wants some money; claims she can make trouble for me if she doesn't get it."

"Can she?"

"I'm afraid she can. That's one reason I lost my job—she kept calling up the office all the time, and that was sort of the last straw down there. She's got a letter all written to send to my family. Oh, she's got me, all right. I've got to have some money for her."

There was an awkward pause. Gordon lay very still, his hands clenched by his side.

"I'm all in," he continued, his voice trembling. "I'm half crazy, Phil. If I hadn't known you were coming East, I think

I'd have killed myself. I want you to lend me three hundred dollars."

Dean's hands, which had been patting his bare ankles, were suddenly quiet—and the curious uncertainty playing between the two became taut and strained.

After a second Gordon continued:

"I've bled the family until I'm ashamed to ask for another nickel."

Still Dean made no answer.

"Jewel says she's got to have two hundred dollars."

"Tell her where she can go."

"Yes, that sounds easy, but she's got a couple of drunken letters I wrote her. Unfortunately she's not at all the flabby sort of person you'd expect."

Dean made an expression of distaste.

"I can't stand that sort of woman. You ought to have kept away."

"I know," admitted Gordon wearily.

"You've got to look at things as they are. If you haven't got money you've got to work and stay away from women."

"That's easy for you to say," began Gordon, his eyes narrowing. "You've got all the money in the world."

"I most certainly have not. My family keep darn close tab on what I spend. Just because I have a little leeway I have to be extra careful not to abuse it."

He raised the blind and let in a further flood of sunshine.

"I'm no prig, Lord knows," he went on deliberately. "I like pleasure—and I like a lot of it on a vacation like this, but you're—you're in awful shape. I never heard you talk just this way before. You seem to be sort of bankrupt—morally as well as financially."

"Don't they usually go together?"

Dean shook his head impatiently.

"There's a regular aura about you that I don't understand. It's a sort of evil."

"It's an air of worry and poverty and sleepless nights," said Gordon, rather defiantly.

"I don't know."

"Oh, I admit I'm depressing. I depress myself. But, my God, Phil, a week's rest and a new suit and some ready money and I'd be like—like I was. Phil, I can draw like a streak, and you know it. But half the time I haven't had the money to buy decent drawing materials—and I can't draw when I'm tired and discouraged and all in. With a little ready money I can take a few weeks off and get started."

"How do I know you wouldn't use it on some other woman?"

"Why rub it in?" said Gordon quietly.

"I'm not rubbing it in. I hate to see you this way."

"Will you lend me the money, Phil?"

"I can't decide right off. That's a lot of money and it'll be darn inconvenient for me."

"It'll be hell for me if you can't—I know I'm whining, and it's all my own fault but—that doesn't change it."

"When could you pay it back?"

This was encouraging. Gordon considered. It was probably wisest to be frank.

"Of course, I could promise to send it back next month, but—I'd better say three months. Just as soon as I start to sell drawings."

"How do I know you'll sell any drawings?"

A new hardness in Dean's voice sent a faint chill of doubt over Gordon. Was it possible that he wouldn't get the money?

"I supposed you had a little confidence in me."

"I did have—but when I see you like this I begin to wonder."

"Do you suppose if I wasn't at the end of my rope I'd come to you like this? Do you think I'm enjoying it?" He broke off and bit his lip, feeling that he had better subdue the rising anger in his voice. After all, he was the suppliant.

"You seem to manage it pretty easily," said Dean angrily. "You put me in the position where, if I don't lend it to you, I'm a sucker—oh, yes, you do. And let me tell you it's no easy thing for me to get hold of three hundred dollars. My income isn't so big but that a slice like that won't play the deuce with it."

He left his chair and began to dress, choosing his clothes carefully. Gordon stretched out his arms and clenched the edges of the bed, fighting back a desire to cry out. His head was splitting and whirring, his mouth was dry and bitter and he could feel the fever in his blood resolving itself into innumerable regular counts like a slow dripping from a roof.

Dean tied his tie precisely, brushed his eyebrows, and removed a piece of tobacco from his teeth with solemnity. Next he filled his cigarette case, tossed the empty box thoughtfully into the waste basket, and settled the case in his vest pocket.

"Had breakfast?" he demanded.

"No; I don't eat it any more."

"Well, we'll go out and have some. We'll decide about that money later. I'm sick of the subject. I came East to have a good time.

"Let's go over to the Yale Club," he continued moodily, and then added with an implied reproof: "You've given up your job. You've got nothing else to do."

"I'd have a lot to do if I had a little money," said Gordon pointedly.

"Oh, for Heaven's sake drop the subject for a while! No point in glooming on my whole trip. Here, here's some money."

He took a five-dollar bill from his wallet and tossed it over to Gordon, who folded it carefully and put it in his pocket. There was an added spot of color in his cheeks, an added glow that was not fever. For an instant before they turned to go out their eyes met and in that instant each found something that made him lower his own glance quickly. For in that instant they quite suddenly and definitely hated each other.

II

Fifth Avenue and Forty-fourth Street swarmed with the noon crowd. The wealthy, happy sun glittered in transient gold through the thick windows of the smart shops, lighting upon mesh bags and purses and strings of pearls in gray velvet cases; upon gaudy feather fans of many colors; upon the laces and silks of expensive dresses; upon the bad paintings and the fine period furniture in the elaborate show rooms of interior decorators.

Working-girls, in pairs and groups and swarms, loitered by these windows, choosing their future boudoirs from some resplendent display which included even a man's silk pajamas laid domestically across the bed. They stood in front of the jewelry stores and picked out their engagement rings, and their wedding rings and their platinum wrist watches, and then drifted on to inspect the feather fans and opera cloaks; meanwhile digesting the sandwiches and sundaes they had eaten for lunch.

All through the crowd were men in uniform, sailors from the great fleet anchored in the Hudson, soldiers with divisional insignia from Massachusetts to California, wanting fearfully to be noticed, and finding the great city thoroughly fed up with soldiers unless they were nicely massed into pretty formations and uncomfortable under the weight of a pack and rifle.

Through this medley Dean and Gordon wandered; the former interested, made alert by the display of humanity at its frothiest and gaudiest; the latter reminded of how often he had been one of the crowd, tired, casually fed, overworked, and dissipated. To Dean the struggle was significant, young, cheerful; to Gordon it was dismal, meaningless, endless.

In the Yale Club they met a group of their former classmates who greeted the visiting Dean vociferously. Sitting in a semicircle of lounges and great chairs, they had a highball all around.

Gordon found the conversation tiresome and interminable. They lunched together *en masse*, warmed with liquor as the afternoon began. They were all going to the Gamma Psi dance that night—it promised to be the best party since the war.

"Edith Bradin's coming," said some one to Gordon. "Didn't she used to be an old flame of yours? Aren't you both from Harrisburg?"

"Yes." He tried to change the subject. "I see her brother occasionally. He's sort of a socialistic nut. Runs a paper or something here in New York."

"Not like his gay sister, eh?" continued his eager informant. "Well, she's coming to-night with a junior named Peter Himmel."

Gordon was to meet Jewel Hudson at eight o'clock—he had promised to have some money for her. Several times he glanced nervously at his wrist watch. At four, to his relief,

Dean rose and announced that he was going over to Rivers Brothers to buy some collars and ties. But as they left the Club another of the party joined them, to Gordon's great dismay. Dean was in a jovial mood now, happy, expectant of the evening's party, faintly hilarious. Over in Rivers' he chose a dozen neckties, selecting each one after long consultations with the other man. Did he think narrow ties were coming back? And wasn't it a shame that Rivers couldn't get any more Welsh Margotson collars? There never was a collar like the "Covington."

Gordon was in something of a panic. He wanted the money immediately. And he was now inspired also with a vague idea of attending the Gamma Psi dance. He wanted to see Edith—Edith whom he hadn't met since one romantic night at the Harrisburg Country Club just before he went to France. The affair had died, drowned in the turmoil of the war and quite forgotten in the arabesque of these three months, but a picture of her, poignant, debonnaire, immersed in her own inconsequential chatter, recurred to him unexpectedly and brought a hundred memories with it. It was Edith's face that he had cherished through college with a sort of detached yet affectionate admiration. He had loved to draw her—around his room had been a dozen sketches of her—playing golf, swimming—he could draw her pert, arresting profile with his eyes shut.

They left Rivers' at five-thirty and paused for a moment on the sidewalk.

"Well," said Dean genially, "I'm all set now. Think I'll go back to the hotel and get a shave, haircut, and massage."

"Good enough," said the other man, "I think I'll join you."

Gordon wondered if he was to be beaten after all. With difficulty he restrained himself from turning to the man and snarling out, "Go on away, damn you!" In despair he suspected that perhaps Dean had spoken to him, was keeping him along in order to avoid a dispute about the money.

They went into the Biltmore—a Biltmore alive with girls—mostly from the West and South, the stellar débutantes of many cities gathered for the dance of a famous fraternity of a famous university. But to Gordon they were faces in a dream.

He gathered together his forces for a last appeal, was about to come out with he knew not what, when Dean suddenly excused himself to the other man and taking Gordon's arm led him aside.

"Gordy," he said quickly, "I've thought the whole thing over carefully and I've decided that I can't lend you that money. I'd like to oblige you, but I don't feel I ought to—it'd put a crimp in me for a month."

Gordon, watching him dully, wondered why he had never before noticed how much those upper teeth projected.

"—I'm mighty sorry, Gordon," continued Dean, "but that's the way it is."

He took out his wallet and deliberately counted out seventy-five dollars in bills.

"Here," he said, holding them out, "here's seventy-five; that makes eighty all together. That's all the actual cash I have with me, besides what I'll actually spend on the trip."

Gordon raised his clenched hand automatically, opened it as though it were a tongs he was holding, and clenched it again on the money.

"I'll see you at the dance," continued Dean. "I've got to get along to the barber shop."

"So-long," said Gordon in a strained and husky voice.

"So-long."

Dean began to smile, but seemed to change his mind. He nodded briskly and disappeared.

But Gordon stood there, his handsome face awry with distress, the roll of bills clenched tightly in his hand. Then, blinded by sudden tears, he stumbled clumsily down the Biltmore steps.

III

About nine o'clock of the same night two human beings came out of a cheap restaurant in Sixth Avenue. They were ugly, ill-nourished, devoid of all except the very lowest form of intelligence, and without even that animal exuberance that in itself brings color into life; they were lately vermin-ridden, cold, and hungry in a dirty town of a strange land; they were poor, friendless; tossed as driftwood from their births, they would be tossed as driftwood to their deaths. They were dressed in the uniform of the United States Army, and on the shoulder of each was the insignia of a drafted division from New Jersey, landed three days before.

The taller of the two was named Carrol Key, a name hinting that in his veins, however thinly diluted by generations of degeneration, ran blood of some potentiality. But one could stare endlessly at the long, chinless face, the dull, watery eyes, and high cheek-bones, without finding a suggestion of either ancestral worth or native resourcefulness.

His companion was swart and bandy-legged, with rat-eyes and a much-broken hooked nose. His defiant air was obviously a pretense, a weapon of protection borrowed from that world of snarl and snap, of physical bluff and physical menace, in which he had always lived. His name was Gus Rose.

Leaving the café they sauntered down Sixth Avenue, wielding toothpicks with great gusto and complete detachment.

"Where to?" asked Rose, in a tone which implied that he would not be surprised if Key suggested the South Sea Islands.

"What you say we see if we can getta holda some liquor?" Prohibition was not yet. The ginger in the suggestion was caused by the law forbidding the selling of liquor to soldiers.

Rose agreed enthusiastically.

"I got an idea," continued Key, after a moment's thought, "I got a brother somewhere."

"In New York?"

"Yeah. He's an old fella." He meant that he was an elder brother. "He's a waiter in a hash joint."

"Maybe he can get us some."

"I'll say he can!"

"B'lieve me, I'm goin' to get this darn uniform off me tomorra. Never get me in it again, neither. I'm goin' to get me some regular clothes."

"Say, maybe I'm not."

As their combined finances were something less than five dollars, this intention can be taken largely as a pleasant game of words, harmless and consoling. It seemed to please both of them, however, for they reinforced it with chuckling and mention of personages high in biblical circles, adding such further emphasis as "Oh, boy!" "You know!" and "I'll say so!" repeated many times over.

The entire mental pabulum of these two men consisted of an offended nasal comment extended through the years upon the institution—army, business, or poorhouse—which kept them alive, and toward their immediate superior in that institution. Until that very morning the institution had been the "government" and the immediate superior had been the "Cap'n"—from these two they had glided out and were now in the vaguely uncomfortable state before they should adopt their next bondage. They were uncertain, resentful, and somewhat ill at ease. This they hid by pretending an elaborate relief at being out of the army, and by assuring each other that military discipline should never again rule their stubborn, liberty-loving wills. Yet, as a matter of fact, they would have felt more at home in a prison than in this new-found and unquestionable freedom.

Suddenly Key increased his gait. Rose, looking up and following his glance, discovered a crowd that was collecting fifty yards down the street. Key chuckled and began to run in the direction of the crowd; Rose thereupon also chuckled and his short bandy legs twinkled beside the long, awkward strides of his companion.

Reaching the outskirts of the crowd they immediately became an indistinguishable part of it. It was composed of ragged civilians somewhat the worse for liquor, and of soldiers representing many divisions and many stages of sobriety, all clustered around a gesticulating little Jew with long black whiskers, who was waving his arms and delivering an excited but succinct harangue. Key and Rose, having wedged themselves into the approximate parquet, scrutinized him with acute suspicion, as his words penetrated their common consciousness.

"—What have you got outa the war?" he was crying fiercely. "Look arounja, look arounja! Are you rich? Have you got a lot of money offered you?—no; you're lucky if you're alive and got both your legs; you're lucky if you came back an' find your wife ain't gone off with some other fella that had the money to buy himself out of the war! That's when you're lucky! Who got anything out of it except J. P. Morgan an' John D. Rockerfeller?"

At this point the little Jew's oration was interrupted by the hostile impact of a fist upon the point of his bearded chin and he toppled backward to a sprawl on the pavement.

"God damn Bolsheviki!" cried the big soldier-blacksmith who had delivered the blow. There was a rumble of approval, the crowd closed in nearer.

The Jew staggered to his feet, and immediately went down again before a half-dozen reaching-in fists. This time he stayed down, breathing heavily, blood oozing from his lip where it was cut within and without.

There was a riot of voices, and in a minute Rose and Key found themselves flowing with the jumbled crowd down Sixth Avenue under the leadership of a thin civilian in a slouch hat and the brawny soldier who had summarily ended the oration. The crowd had marvellously swollen to formidable proportions and a stream of more non-committal citizens followed it along the sidewalks lending their moral support by intermittent huzzas.

"Where we goin'?" yelled Key to the man nearest him.

His neighbor pointed up to the leader in the slouch hat.

"That guy knows where there's a lot of 'em! We're goin' to show 'em!"

"We're goin' to show 'em!" whispered Key delightedly to Rose, who repeated the phrase rapturously to a man on the other side.

Down Sixth Avenue swept the procession, joined here and there by soldiers and marines, and now and then by civilians, who came up with the inevitable cry that they were just out of the army themselves, as if presenting it as a card of admission to a newly formed Sporting and Amusement Club.

Then the procession swerved down a cross street and headed for Fifth Avenue and the word filtered here and there that they were bound for a Red meeting at Tolliver Hall.

"Where is it?"

The question went up the line and a moment later the answer floated back. Tolliver Hall was down on Tenth Street. There was a bunch of other sojers who was goin' to break it up and was down there now!

But Tenth Street had a faraway sound and at the word a general groan went up and a score of the procession dropped out. Among these were Rose and Key, who slowed down to a saunter and let the more enthusiastic sweep on by.

"I'd rather get some liquor," said Key as they halted and made their way to the sidewalk amid cries of "Shell hole!" and "Quitters!"

"Does your brother work around here?" asked Rose, assuming the air of one passing from the superficial to the eternal.

"He oughta," replied Key. "I ain't seen him for a coupla years. I been out to Pennsylvania since. Maybe he don't work at night anyhow. It's right along here. He can get us some o'right if he ain't gone."

They found the place after a few minutes' patrol of the street—a shoddy tablecloth restaurant between Fifth Avenue and Broadway. Here Key went inside to inquire for his brother George, while Rose waited on the sidewalk.

"He ain't here no more," said Key emerging. "He's a waiter up to Delmonico's."

Rose nodded wisely, as if he'd expected as much. One should not be surprised at a capable man changing jobs occasionally. He knew a waiter once—there ensued a long conversation as they walked as to whether waiters made more in actual wages than in tips—it was decided that it depended on the social tone of the joint wherein the waiter labored. After having given each other vivid pictures of millionaires dining at Delmonico's and throwing away fifty-dollar bills after their first quart of champagne, both men thought privately of becoming waiters. In fact, Key's narrow brow was secreting a resolution to ask his brother to get him a job.

"A waiter can drink up all the champagne those fellas leave in bottles," suggested Rose with some relish, and then added as an afterthought, "Oh, boy!"

By the time they reached Delmonico's it was half past ten, and they were surprised to see a stream of taxis driving up to the door one after the other and emitting marvelous, hatless young ladies, each one attended by a stiff young gentleman in evening clothes.

"It's a party," said Rose with some awe. "Maybe we better not go in. He'll be busy."

"No, he won't. He'll be o'right."

After some hesitation they entered what appeared to them to be the least elaborate door and, indecision falling upon them immediately, stationed themselves nervously in an inconspicuous corner of the small dining-room in which they found themselves. They took off their caps and held them in their hands. A cloud of gloom fell upon them and both started when a door at one end of the room crashed open, emitting a comet-like waiter who streaked across the floor and vanished through another door on the other side.

There had been three of these lightning passages before the seekers mustered the acumen to hail a waiter. He turned, looked at them suspiciously, and then approached with soft, catlike steps, as if prepared at any moment to turn and flee.

"Say," began Key, "say, do you know my brother? He's a waiter here."

"His name is Key," annotated Rose.

Yes, the waiter knew Key. He was up-stairs, he thought. There was a big dance going on in the main ballroom. He'd tell him.

Ten minutes later George Key appeared and greeted his brother with the utmost suspicion; his first and most natural thought being that he was going to be asked for money.

George was tall and weak chinned, but there his resemblance to his brother ceased. The waiter's eyes were not dull, they were alert and twinkling, and his manner was suave, indoor, and faintly superior. They exchanged formalities. George was married and had three children. He seemed fairly interested, but not impressed by the news that Carrol had been abroad in the army. This disappointed Carrol.

"George," said the younger brother, these amenities having been disposed of, "we want to get some booze, and they won't sell us none. Can you get us some?"

George considered.

"Sure. Maybe I can. It may be half an hour, though."

"All right," agreed Carrol, "we'll wait."

At this Rose started to sit down in a convenient chair, but was hailed to his feet by the indignant George.

"Hey! Watch out, you! Can't sit down here! This room's all set for a twelve o'clock banquet."

"I ain't goin' to hurt it," said Rose resentfully. "I been through the delouser."

"Never mind," said George sternly, "if the head waiter seen me here talkin' he'd romp all over me."

"Oh."

The mention of the head waiter was full explanation to the other two; they fingered their overseas caps nervously and waited for a suggestion.

"I tell you," said George, after a pause, "I got a place you can wait; you just come here with me."

They followed him out the far door, through a deserted pantry and up a pair of dark winding stairs, emerging finally into a small room chiefly furnished by piles of pails and stacks of scrubbing brushes, and illuminated by a single dim electric light. There he left them, after soliciting two dollars and agreeing to return in half an hour with a quart of whiskey.

"George is makin' money, I bet," said Key gloomily as he seated himself on an inverted pail. "I bet he's making fifty dollars a week."

Rose nodded his head and spat.

"I bet he is, too."

"What'd he say the dance was of?"

"A lot of college fellas. Yale College."

They both nodded solemnly at each other.

"Wonder where that crowda sojers is now?"

"I don't know. I know that's too damn long to walk for me."

"Me too. You don't catch me walkin' that far."

Ten minutes later restlessness seized them.

"I'm goin' to see what's out here," said Rose, stepping cautiously toward the other door.

It was a swinging door of green baize and he pushed it open a cautious inch.

"See anything?"

For answer Rose drew in his breath sharply.

"Doggone! Here's some liquor I'll say!"

"Liquor?"

Key joined Rose at the door, and looked eagerly.

"I'll tell the world that's liquor," he said, after a moment of concentrated gazing.

It was a room about twice as large as the one they were in—and in it was prepared a radiant feast of spirits. There were long walls of alternating bottles set along two white covered tables; whiskey, gin, brandy, French and Italian vermouths, and orange juice, not to mention an array of syphons and two great empty punch bowls. The room was as yet uninhabited.

"It's for this dance they're just starting," whispered Key; "hear the violins playin'? Say, boy, I wouldn't mind havin' a dance."

They closed the door softly and exchanged a glance of mutual comprehension. There was no need of feeling each other out.

"I'd like to get my hands on a coupla those bottles," said Rose emphatically.

"Me too."

"Do you suppose we'd get seen?"

Key considered.

"Maybe we better wait till they start drinkin' 'em. They got 'em all laid out now, and they know how many of them there are."

They debated this point for several minutes. Rose was all for getting his hands on a bottle now and tucking it under his coat before any one came into the room. Key, however, advocated caution. He was afraid he might get his brother in trouble. If they waited till some of the bottles were opened it'd be all right to take one, and everybody'd think it was one of the college fellas.

While they were still engaged in argument George Key hurried through the room and, barely grunting at them, disappeared by way of the green baize door. A minute later they heard several corks pop, and then the sound of cracking ice and splashing liquid. George was mixing the punch.

The soldiers exchanged delighted grins.

"Oh, boy!" whispered Rose.

George reappeared.

"Just keep low, boys," he said quickly. "I'll have your stuff for you in five minutes."

He disappeared through the door by which he had come.

As soon as his footsteps receded down the stairs, Rose, after a cautious look, darted into the room of delights and reappeared with a bottle in his hand.

"Here's what I say," he said, as they sat radiantly digesting their first drink. "We'll wait till he comes up, and we'll ask him if we can't just stay here and drink what he brings us—see. We'll tell him we haven't got any place to drink it—see. Then we can sneak in there whenever there ain't nobody in that there room and tuck a bottle under our coats. We'll have enough to last us a coupla days—see?"

"Sure," agreed Key enthusiastically. "Oh, boy! And if we want to we can sell it to sojers any time we want to."

They were silent for a moment thinking rosily of this idea. Then Key reached up and unhooked the collar of his O. D. coat.

"It's hot in here, ain't it?"

Rose agreed earnestly.

"Hot as hell."

IV

She was still quite angry when she came out of the dressing-room and crossed the intervening parlor of politeness that opened onto the hall—angry not so much at the actual happening which was, after all, the merest commonplace of her social existence, but because it had occurred on this particular night. She had no quarrel with herself. She had acted with the correct mixture of dignity and reticent pity which she always employed. She had succinctly and deftly snubbed him.

It had happened when their taxi was leaving the Biltmore—hadn't gone half a block. He had lifted his right arm awkwardly—she was on his right side—and attempted to settle it snugly around the crimson fur-trimmed opera cloak she wore. This in itself had been a mistake. It was inevitably more graceful for a young man attempting to embrace a young lady of whose acquiescence he was not certain, to first put his far arm around her. It avoided that awkward movement of raising the near arm.

His second *faux pas* was unconscious. She had spent the

afternoon at the hairdresser's; the idea of any calamity overtaking her hair was extremely repugnant—yet as Peter made his unfortunate attempt the point of his elbow had just faintly brushed it. That was his second *faux pas.* Two were quite enough.

He had begun to murmur. At the first murmur she had decided that he was nothing but a college boy—Edith was twenty-two, and anyhow, this dance, first of its kind since the war, was reminding her, with the accelerating rhythm of its associations, of something else—of another dance and another man, a man for whom her feelings had been little more than a sad-eyed, adolescent mooniness. Edith Bradin was falling in love with her recollection of Gordon Sterrett.

So she came out of the dressing-room at Delmonico's and stood for a second in the doorway looking over the shoulders of a black dress in front of her at the groups of Yale men who flitted like dignified black moths around the head of the stairs. From the room she had left drifted out the heavy fragrance left by the passage to and fro of many scented young beauties—rich perfumes and the fragile memory-laden dust of fragrant powders. This odor drifting out acquired the tang of cigarette smoke in the hall, and then settled sensuously down the stairs and permeated the ballroom where the Gamma Psi dance was to be held. It was an odor she knew well, exciting, stimulating, restlessly sweet—the odor of a fashionable dance.

She thought of her own appearance. Her bare arms and shoulders were powdered to a creamy white. She knew they looked very soft and would gleam like milk against the black backs that were to silhouette them to-night. The hairdressing had been a success; her reddish mass of hair was piled and crushed and creased to an arrogant marvel of mobile curves. Her lips were finely made of deep carmine; the irises of her eyes were delicate, breakable blue, like china eyes. She was a complete, infinitely delicate, quite perfect thing of beauty, flowing in an even line from a complex coiffure to two small slim feet.

She thought of what she would say to-night at this revel, faintly prestiged already by the sounds of high and low laughter and slippered footsteps, and movements of couples up and down the stairs. She would talk the language she had talked for many years—her line—made up of the current expressions, bits of journalese and college slang strung together into an intrinsic whole, careless, faintly provocative, delicately sentimental. She smiled faintly as she heard a girl sitting on the stairs near her say: "You don't know the half of it, dearie!"

And as she smiled her anger melted for a moment, and closing her eyes she drew in a deep breath of pleasure. She dropped her arms to her side until they were faintly touching the sleek sheath that covered and suggested her figure. She had never felt her own softness so much nor so enjoyed the whiteness of her own arms.

"I smell sweet," she said to herself simply, and then came another thought—"I'm made for love."

She liked the sound of this and thought it again; then in inevitable succession came her new-born riot of dreams about Gordon. The twist of her imagination which, two months before, had disclosed to her her unguessed desire to see him again, seemed now to have been leading up to this dance, this hour.

For all her sleek beauty, Edith was a grave, slow-thinking girl. There was a streak in her of that same desire to ponder, of that adolescent idealism that had turned her brother socialist and pacifist. Henry Bradin had left Cornell, where he had been an instructor in economics, and had come to New York to pour the latest cures for incurable evils into the columns of a radical weekly newspaper.

Edith, less fatuously, would have been content to cure Gordon Sterrett. There was a quality of weakness in Gordon that she wanted to take care of; there was a helplessness in him that she wanted to protect. And she wanted someone she had known a long while, someone who had loved her a long while. She was a little tired; she wanted to get married. Out of a pile of letters, half a dozen pictures and as many memories, and this weariness, she had decided that next time she saw Gordon their relations were going to be changed. She would say something that would change them. There was this evening. This was her evening. All evenings were her evenings.

Then her thoughts were interrupted by a solemn undergraduate with a hurt look and an air of strained formality who presented himself before her and bowed unusually low. It was the man she had come with, Peter Himmel. He was tall and humorous, with horned-rimmed glasses and an air of attractive whimsicality. She suddenly rather disliked him—probably because he had not succeeded in kissing her.

"Well," she began, "are you still furious at me?"

"Not at all."

She stepped forward and took his arm.

"I'm sorry," she said softly. "I don't know why I snapped out that way. I'm in a bum humor to-night for some strange reason. I'm sorry."

"S'all right," he mumbled, "don't mention it."

He felt disagreeably embarrassed. Was she rubbing in the fact of his late failure?

"It was a mistake," she continued, on the same consciously gentle key. "We'll both forget it." For this he hated her.

A few minutes later they drifted out on the floor while the dozen swaying, sighing members of the specially hired jazz orchestra informed the crowded ballroom that "if a saxophone and me are left alone why then two is com-pan-ee!"

A man with a mustache cut in.

"Hello," he began reprovingly. "You don't remember me."

"I can't just think of your name," she said lightly—"and I know you so well."

"I met you up at—" His voice trailed disconsolately off as a man with very fair hair cut in. Edith murmured a conventional "Thanks, loads—cut in later," to the *inconnu.*

The very fair man insisted on shaking hands enthusiastically. She placed him as one of the numerous Jims of her acquaintance—last name a mystery. She remembered even that he had a peculiar rhythm in dancing and found as they started that she was right.

"Going to be here long?" he breathed confidentially.

She leaned back and looked up at him.

"Couple of weeks."

"Where are you?"

"Biltmore. Call me up some day."

"I mean it," he assured her. "I will. We'll go to tea."

"So do I—Do."

A dark man cut in with intense formality.

"You don't remember me, do you?" he said gravely.

"I should say I do. Your name's Harlan."

"No-ope. Barlow."

"Well, I knew there were two syllables anyway. You're the boy that played the ukulele so well up at Howard Marshall's house party."

"I played—but not——"

A man with prominent teeth cut in. Edith inhaled a slight cloud of whiskey. She liked men to have had something to drink; they were so much more cheerful, and appreciative and complimentary—much easier to talk to.

"My name's Dean, Philip Dean," he said cheerfully. "You don't remember me, I know, but you used to come up to New Haven with a fellow I roomed with senior year, Gordon Sterrett."

Edith looked up quickly.

"Yes, I went up with him twice—to the Pump and Slipper and the Junior prom."

"You've seen him, of course," said Dean carelessly. "He's here to-night. I saw him just a minute ago."

Edith started. Yet she had felt quite sure he would be here.

"Why, no, I haven't——"

A fat man with red hair cut in.

"Hello, Edith," he began.

"Why—hello there——"

She slipped, stumbled lightly.

"I'm sorry, dear," she murmured mechanically.

She had seen Gordon—Gordon very white and listless, leaning against the side of a doorway, smoking and looking into the ballroom. Edith could see that his face was thin and wan—that the hand he raised to his lips with a cigarette was trembling. They were dancing quite close to him now.

"—They invite so darn many extra fellas that you—" the short man was saying.

"Hello, Gordon," called Edith over her partner's shoulder. Her heart was pounding wildly.

His large dark eyes were fixed on her. He took a step in her direction. Her partner turned her away—she heard his voice bleating——

"—but half the stags get lit and leave before long, so——"

Then a low tone at her side.

"May I, please?"

She was dancing suddenly with Gordon; one of his arms was around her; she felt it tighten spasmodically; felt his hand on her back with the fingers spread. Her hand holding the little lace handkerchief was crushed in his.

"Why Gordon," she began breathlessly.

"Hello, Edith."

She slipped again—was tossed forward by her recovery until her face touched the black cloth of his dinner coat. She loved him—she knew she loved him—then for a minute there was silence while a strange feeling of uneasiness crept over her. Something was wrong.

Of a sudden her heart wrenched, and turned over as she realized what it was. He was pitiful and wretched, a little drunk, and miserably tired.

"Oh——" she cried involuntarily.

His eyes looked down at her. She saw suddenly that they were blood-streaked and rolling uncontrollably.

"Gordon," she murmured, "we'll sit down; I want to sit down."

They were nearly in mid-floor, but she had seen two men start toward her from opposite sides of the room, so she halted, seized Gordon's limp hand and led him bumping through the crowd, her mouth tight shut, her face a little pale under her rouge, her eyes trembling with tears.

She found a place high up on the soft-carpeted stairs, and he sat down heavily beside her.

"Well," he began, staring at her unsteadily, "I certainly am glad to see you, Edith."

She looked at him without answering. The effect of this on her was immeasurable. For years she had seen men in various stages of intoxication, from uncles all the way down to chauffeurs, and her feelings had varied from amusement to disgust, but here for the first time she was seized with a new feeling—an unutterable horror.

"Gordon," she said accusingly and almost crying, "you look like the devil."

He nodded. "I've had trouble, Edith."

"Trouble?"

"All sorts of trouble. Don't you say anything to the family, but I'm all gone to pieces. I'm a mess, Edith."

His lower lip was sagging. He seemed scarcely to see her.

"Can't you—can't you," she hesitated, "can't you tell me about it, Gordon? You know I'm always interested in you."

She bit her lip—she had intended to say something stronger, but found at the end that she couldn't bring it out.

Gordon shook his head dully. "I can't tell you. You're a good woman. I can't tell a good woman the story."

"Rot," she said, defiantly. "I think it's a perfect insult to call any one a good woman in that way. It's a slam. You've been drinking, Gordon."

"Thanks." He inclined his head gravely. "Thanks for the information."

"Why do you drink?"

"Because I'm so damn miserable."

"Do you think drinking's going to make it any better?"

"What you doing—trying to reform me?"

"No; I'm trying to help you, Gordon. Can't you tell me about it?"

"I'm in an awful mess. Best thing you can do is to pretend not to know me."

"Why, Gordon?"

"I'm sorry I cut in on you—its unfair to you. You're pure woman—and all that sort of thing. Here, I'll get some one else to dance with you."

He rose clumsily to his feet, but she reached up and pulled him down beside her on the stairs.

"Here, Gordon. You're ridiculous. You're hurting me. You're acting like a—like a crazy man——"

"I admit it. I'm a little crazy. Something's wrong with me, Edith. There's something left me. It doesn't matter."

"It does, tell me."

"Just that. I was always queer—little bit different from other boys. All right in college, but now it's all wrong. Things have been snapping inside me for four months like little hooks on a dress, and it's about to come off when a few more hooks go. I'm very gradually going loony."

He turned his eyes full on her and began to laugh, and she shrank away from him.

"What *is* the matter?"

"Just me," he repeated. "I'm going loony. This whole place is like a dream to me—this Delmonico's——"

As he talked she saw he had changed utterly. He wasn't at all light and gay and careless—a great lethargy and discouragement had come over him. Revulsion seized her, followed by a faint, surprising boredom. His voice seemed to come out of a great void.

"Edith," he said, "I used to think I was clever, talented, an artist. Now I know I'm nothing. Can't draw, Edith. Don't know why I'm telling you this."

She nodded absently.

"I can't draw, I can't do anything. I'm poor as a church mouse." He laughed, bitterly and rather too loud. "I've become a damn beggar, a leech on my friends. I'm a failure. I'm poor as hell."

Her distaste was growing. She barely nodded this time, waiting for her first possible cue to rise.

Suddenly Gordon's eyes filled with tears.

"Edith," he said, turning to her with what was evidently a strong effort at self-control, "I can't tell you what it means to me to know there's one person left who's interested in me."

He reached out and patted her hand, and involuntarily she drew it away.

"It's mighty fine of you," he repeated.

"Well," she said slowly, looking him in the eye, "any one's always glad to see an old friend—but I'm sorry to see you like this, Gordon."

There was a pause while they looked at each other, and the momentary eagerness in his eyes wavered. She rose and stood looking at him, her face quite expressionless.

"Shall we dance?" she suggested, coolly.

—Love is fragile—she was thinking—but perhaps the pieces are saved, the things that hovered on lips, that might have been said. The new love words, the tendernesses learned, are treasured up for the next lover.

V

Peter Himmel, escort to the lovely Edith, was unaccustomed to being snubbed; having been snubbed, he was hurt and embarrassed, and ashamed of himself. For a matter of two months he had been on special delivery terms with Edith Bradin, and knowing that the one excuse and explanation of the special delivery letter is its value in sentimental correspondence, he had believed himself quite sure of his ground. He searched in vain for any reason why she should have taken this attitude in the matter of a simple kiss.

Therefore when he was cut in on by the man with the mustache he went out into the hall and, making up a sentence, said it over to himself several times. Considerably deleted, this was it:

"Well, if any girl ever led a man on and then jolted him, she did—and she has no kick coming if I go out and get beautifully boiled."

So he walked through the supper room into a small room adjoining it, which he had located earlier in the evening. It was a room in which there were several large bowls of punch flanked by many bottles. He took a seat beside the table which held the bottles.

At the second highball, boredom, disgust, the monotony of time, the turbidity of events, sank into a vague background before which glittering cobwebs formed. Things became reconciled to themselves, things lay quietly on their shelves; the troubles of the day arranged themselves in trim formation and at his curt wish of dismissal, marched off and disappeared. And with the departure of worry came brilliant, permeating symbolism. Edith became a flighty, negligible girl, not to be worried over; rather to be laughed at. She fitted like a figure of his own dream into the surface world forming about him. He himself became in a measure symbolic, a type of the continent bacchanal, the brilliant dreamer at play.

Then the symbolic mood faded and as he sipped his third highball his imagination yielded to the warm glow and he lapsed into a state similar to floating on his back in pleasant water. It was at this point that he noticed that a green baize door near him was open about two inches, and that through the aperture a pair of eyes were watching him intently.

"Hm," murmured Peter calmly.

The green door closed—and then opened again—a bare half inch this time.

"Peek-a-boo," murmured Peter.

The door remained stationary and then he became aware of a series of tense intermittent whispers.

"One guy."

"What's he doin'?"

"He's sittin' lookin'."

"He better beat it off. We gotta get another li'l' bottle."

Peter listened while the words filtered into his consciousness.

"Now this," he thought, "is most remarkable."

He was excited. He was jubilant. He felt that he had stumbled upon a mystery. Affecting an elaborate carelessness he arose and walked around the table—then, turning quickly, pulled open the green door, precipitating Private Rose into the room.

Peter bowed.

"How do you do?" he said.

Private Rose set one foot slightly in front of the other, poised for fight, flight, or compromise.

"How do you do?" repeated Peter politely.

"I'm o'right."

"Can I offer you a drink?"

Private Rose looked at him searchingly, suspecting possible sarcasm.

"O'right," he said finally.

Peter indicated a chair.

"Sit down."

"I got a friend," said Rose, "I got a friend in there." He pointed to the green door.

"By all means let's have him in."

Peter crossed over, opened the door and welcomed in Private Key, very suspicious and uncertain and guilty. Chairs were found and the three took their seats around the punch bowl. Peter gave them each a highball and offered them a cigarette from his case. They accepted both with some diffidence.

"Now," continued Peter easily, "may I ask why you gentlemen prefer to lounge away your leisure hours in a room which is chiefly furnished, as far as I can see, with scrubbing brushes. And when the human race has progressed to the stage where seventeen thousand chairs are manufactured on every day except Sunday—" he paused. Rose and Key regarded him vacantly. "Will you tell me," went on Peter, "why you choose to rest yourselves on articles intended for the transportation of water from one place to another?"

At this point Rose contributed a grunt to the conversation.

"And lastly," finished Peter, "will you tell me why, when you are in a building beautifully hung with enormous candelabra, you prefer to spend these evening hours under one anemic electric light?"

Rose looked at Key; Key looked at Rose. They laughed; they laughed uproariously; they found it was impossible to look at each other without laughing. But they were not laughing with this man—they were laughing at him. To them a man who talked after this fashion was either raving drunk or raving crazy.

"You are Yale men, I presume," said Peter, finishing his highball and preparing another.

They laughed again.

"Na-ah."

"So? I thought perhaps you might be members of that lowly section of the university known as the Sheffield Scientific School."

"Na-ah."

"Hm. Well, that's too bad. No doubt you are Harvard men, anxious to preserve your incognito in this—this paradise of violet blue, as the newspapers say."

"Na-ah," said Key scornfully, "we was just waitin' for somebody."

"Ah," exclaimed Peter, rising and filling their glasses, "very interestin'. Had a date with a scrublady, eh?"

They both denied this indignantly.

"It's all right," Peter reassured them, "don't apologize. A scrublady's as good as any lady in the world. Kipling says 'Any lady and Judy O'Grady under the skin.' "

"Sure," said Key, winking broadly at Rose.

"My case, for instance," continued Peter, finishing his glass. "I got a girl up here that's spoiled. Spoildest darn girl I ever saw. Refused to kiss me; no reason whatsoever. Led me on deliberately to think sure I want to kiss you and then plunk! Threw me over! What's the younger generation comin' to?"

"Say tha's hard luck," said Key—"that's awful hard luck."

"Oh, boy!" said Rose.

"Have another?" said Peter.

"We got in a sort of fight for a while," said Key after a pause, "but it was too far away."

"A fight?—tha's stuff!" said Peter, seating himself unsteadily. "Fight 'em all! I was in the army."

"This was with a Bolshevik fella."

"Tha's stuff!" exclaimed Peter, enthusiastic. "That's what I say! Kill the Bolshevik! Exterminate 'em!"

"We're Americuns," said Rose, implying a sturdy, defiant patriotism.

"Sure," said Peter. "Greatest race in the world! We're all Americuns! Have another."

They had another.

VI

At one o'clock a special orchestra, special even in a day of special orchestras, arrived at Delmonico's, and its members, seating themselves arrogantly around the piano, took up the burden of providing music for the Gamma Psi Fraternity. They were headed by a famous flute-player, distinguished throughout New York for his feat of standing on his head and shimmying with his shoulders while he played the latest jazz on his flute. During his performance the lights were extinguished except for the spotlight on the flute-player and another roving beam that threw flickering shadows and changing kaleidoscopic colors over the massed dancers.

Edith had danced herself into that tired, dreamy state habitual only with débutantes, a state equivalent to the glow of a noble soul after several long highballs. Her mind floated vaguely on the bosom of her music; her partners changed with the unreality of phantoms under the colorful shifting dusk, and to her present coma it seemed as if days had passed since the dance began. She had talked on many fragmentary subjects with many men. She had been kissed once and made love to six times. Earlier in the evening different undergraduates had danced with her, but now, like all the more popular girls there, she had her own entourage—that is, half a dozen gallants had singled her out or were alternating her charms with those of some other chosen beauty; they cut in on her in regular, inevitable succession.

Several times she had seen Gordon—he had been sitting a long time on the stairway with his palm to his head, his dull eyes fixed at an infinite speck on the floor before him, very depressed, he looked, and quite drunk—but Edith each time had averted her glance hurriedly. All that seemed long ago; her mind was passive now, her senses were lulled to trance-like sleep; only her feet danced and her voice talked on in hazy sentimental banter.

But Edith was not nearly so tired as to be incapable of moral indignation when Peter Himmel cut in on her, sublimely and happily drunk. She gasped and looked up at him.

"Why, *Peter!*"

"I'm a li'l' stewed, Edith."

"Why, Peter, you're a *peach*, you are! Don't you think it's a bum way of doing—when you're with me?"

Then she smiled unwillingly, for he was looking at her with owlish sentimentality varied with a silly spasmodic smile.

"Darlin' Edith," he began earnestly, "you know I love you, don't you?"

"You tell it well."

"I love you—and I merely wanted you to kiss me," he added sadly.

His embarrassment, his shame, were both gone. She was a mos' beautiful girl in whole worl'. Mos' beautiful eyes, like stars above. He wanted to 'pologize—firs', for presuming try to kiss her; second, for drinking—but he'd been so discouraged 'cause he had thought she was mad at him——

The red-fat man cut in, and looking up at Edith smiled radiantly.

"Did you bring any one?" she asked.

No. The red-fat man was a stag.

"Well, would you mind—would it be an awful bother for you to—to take me home to-night?" (This extreme diffidence was a charming affectation on Edith's part—she knew that the red-fat man would immediately dissolve into a paroxysm of delight.)

"Bother? Why, good Lord, I'd be darn glad to! You know I'd be darn glad to."

"Thanks *loads!* You're awfully sweet."

She glanced at her wrist-watch. It was half-past one. And, as she said "half-past one" to herself, it floated vaguely into her mind that her brother had told her at luncheon that he worked in the office of his newspaper until after one-thirty every evening.

Edith turned suddenly to her current partner.

"What street is Delmonico's on, anyway?"

"Street? Oh, why Fifth Avenue, of course."

"I mean, what cross street?"

"Why—let's see—it's on Forty-fourth Street."

This verified what she had thought. Henry's office must be across the street and just around the corner, and it occurred to her immediately that she might slip over for a moment and surprise him, float in on him, a shimmering marvel in her new crimson opera cloak and "cheer him up." It was exactly the sort of thing Edith revelled in doing—an unconventional, jaunty thing. The idea reached out and gripped at her imagination—after an instant's hesitation she had decided.

"My hair is just about to tumble entirely down," she said pleasantly to her partner; "would you mind if I go and fix it?"

"Not at all."

"You're a peach."

A few minutes later, wrapped in her crimson opera cloak, she flitted down a side-stairs, her cheeks glowing with excitement at her little adventure. She ran by a couple who stood at the door—a weak-chinned waiter and an over-rouged young lady, in hot dispute—and opening the outer door stepped into the warm May night.

VII

The over-rouged young lady followed her with a brief, bitter glance—then turned again to the weak-chinned waiter and took up her argument.

"You better go up and tell him I'm here," she said defiantly, "or I'll go up myself."

"No, you don't!" said George sternly.

The girl smiled sardonically.

"Oh, I don't, don't I? Well, let me tell you I know more college fellas and more of 'em know me, and are glad to take me out on a party, than you ever saw in your whole life."

"Maybe so——"

"Maybe so," she interrupted. "Oh, it's all right for any of 'em like that one that just ran out—God knows where *she* went—it's all right for them that are asked here to come or go as they like—but when I want to see a friend they have some cheap, ham-slinging, bring-me-a-doughnut waiter to stand here and keep me out."

"See here," said the elder Key indignantly, "I can't lose my job. Maybe this fella you're talkin' about doesn't want to see you."

"Oh, he wants to see me all right."

"Anyways, how could I find him in all that crowd?"

"Oh, he'll be there," she asserted confidently. "You just ask anybody for Gordon Sterrett and they'll point him out to you. They all know each other, those fellas."

She produced a mesh bag, and taking out a dollar bill handed it to George.

"Here," she said, "here's a bribe. You find him and give him my message. You tell him if he isn't here in five minutes I'm coming up."

George shook his head pessimistically, considered the question for a moment, wavered violently, and then withdrew.

In less than the allotted time Gordon came down-stairs. He was drunker than he had been earlier in the evening and in a different way. The liquor seemed to have hardened on him like a crust. He was heavy and lurching—almost incoherent when he talked.

"'Lo, Jewel," he said thickly. "Came right away. Jewel, I couldn't get that money. Tried my best."

"Money nothing!" she snapped. "You haven't been near me for ten days. What's the matter?"

He shook his head slowly.

"Been very low, Jewel. Been sick."

"Why didn't you tell me if you were sick. I don't care about the money that bad. I didn't start bothering you about it at all until you began neglecting me."

Again he shook his head.

"Haven't been neglecting you. Not at all."

"Haven't! You haven't been near me for three weeks, unless you been so drunk you didn't know what you were doing."

"Been sick, Jewel," he repeated, turning his eyes upon her wearily.

"You're well enough to come and play with your society friends here all right. You told me you'd meet me for dinner, and you said you'd have some money for me. You didn't even bother to ring me up."

"I couldn't get any money."

"Haven't I just been saying that doesn't matter? I wanted to see *you*, Gordon, but you seem to prefer your somebody else."

He denied this bitterly.

"Then get your hat and come along," she suggested.

Gordon hesitated—and she came suddenly close to him and slipped her arms around his neck.

"Come on with me, Gordon," she said in a half whisper. "We'll go over to Devineries' and have a drink, and then we can go up to my apartment."

"I can't, Jewel,——"

"You can," she said intensely.

"I'm sick as a dog!"

"Well, then, you oughtn't to stay here and dance."

With a glance around him in which relief and despair were mingled, Gordon hesitated; then she suddenly pulled him to her and kissed him with soft, pulpy lips.

"All right," he said heavily. "I'll get my hat."

VIII

When Edith came out into the clear blue of the May night she found the Avenue deserted. The windows of the big shops were dark; over their doors were drawn great iron masks until they were only shadowy tombs of the late day's splendor. Glancing down toward Forty-second Street she saw a commingled blur of lights from the all-night restaurants. Over on Sixth Avenue the elevated, a flare of fire, roared across the street between the glimmering parallels of light at the station and streaked along into the crisp dark. But at Forty-fourth Street it was very quiet.

Pulling her cloak close about her Edith darted across the Avenue. She started nervously as a solitary man passed her and said in a hoarse whisper—"Where bound, kiddo?" She was reminded of a night in her childhood when she had walked around the block in her pajamas and a dog had howled at her from a mystery-big back yard.

In a minute she had reached her destination, a two-story, comparatively old building on Forty-fourth, in the upper window of which she thankfully detected a wisp of light. It was bright enough outside for her to make out the sign beside the window—the *New York Trumpet*. She stepped inside a dark hall and after a second saw the stairs in the corner.

Then she was in a long, low room furnished with many desks and hung on all sides with file copies of newspapers. There were only two occupants. They were sitting at different ends of the room, each wearing a green eye-shade and writing by a solitary desk light.

For a moment she stood uncertainly in the doorway, and then both men turned around simultaneously and she recognized her brother.

"Why, Edith!" He rose quickly and approached her in surprise, removing his eye-shade. He was tall, lean, and dark, with black, piercing eyes under very thick glasses. They were far-away eyes that seemed always fixed just over the head of the person to whom he was talking.

He put his hands on her arms and kissed her cheek.

"What is it?" he repeated in some alarm.

"I was at a dance across at Delmonico's, Henry," she said excitedly, "and I couldn't resist tearing over to see you."

"I'm glad you did." His alertness gave way quickly to a habitual vagueness. "You oughtn't to be out alone at night though, ought you?"

The man at the other end of the room had been looking at them curiously, but at Henry's beckoning gesture he approached. He was loosely fat with little twinkling eyes, and, having removed his collar and tie, he gave the impression of a Middle-Western farmer on a Sunday afternoon.

"This is my sister," said Henry. "She dropped in to see me."

"How do you do?" said the fat man, smiling. "My name's Bartholomew, Miss Bradin. I know your brother has forgotten it long ago."

Edith laughed politely.

"Well," he continued, "not exactly gorgeous quarters we have here, are they?"

Edith looked around the room.

"They seem very nice," she replied. "Where do you keep the bombs?"

"The bombs?" repeated Bartholomew, laughing. "That's pretty good—the bombs. Did you hear her, Henry? She wants to know where we keep the bombs. Say, that's pretty good."

Edith swung herself onto a vacant desk and sat dangling her feet over the edge. Her brother took a seat beside her.

"Well," he asked, absent-mindedly, "how do you like New York this trip?"

"Not bad. I'll be over at the Biltmore with the Hoyts until Sunday. Can't you come to luncheon to-morrow?"

He thought a moment.

"I'm especially busy," he objected, "and I hate women in groups."

"All right," she agreed, unruffled. "Let's you and me have luncheon together."

"Very well."

"I'll call for you at twelve."

Bartholomew was obviously anxious to return to his desk, but apparently considered that it would be rude to leave without some parting pleasantry.

"Well"—he began awkwardly.

They both turned to him.

"Well, we—we had an exciting time earlier in the evening."

The two men exchanged glances.

"You should have come earlier," continued Bartholomew, somewhat encouraged. "We had a regular vaudeville."

"Did you really?"

"A serenade," said Henry. "A lot of soldiers gathered down there in the street and began to yell at the sign."

"Why?" she demanded.

"Just a crowd," said Henry, abstractedly. "All crowds have to howl. They didn't have anybody with much initiative in the lead, or they'd probably have forced their way in here and smashed things up."

"Yes," said Bartholomew, turning again to Edith, "you should have been here."

He seemed to consider this a sufficient cue for withdrawal, for he turned abruptly and went back to his desk.

"Are the soldiers all set against the Socialists?" demanded Edith of her brother. "I mean do they attack you violently and all that?"

Henry replaced his eye-shade and yawned.

"The human race has come a long way," he said casually, "but most of us are throw-backs; the soldiers don't know what they want, or what they hate, or what they like. They're used to acting in large bodies, and they seem to have to make demonstrations. So it happens to be against us. There've been riots all over the city to-night. It's May Day, you see."

"Was the disturbance here pretty serious?"

"Not a bit," he said scornfully. "About twenty-five of them stopped in the street about nine o'clock, and began to bellow at the moon."

"Oh"—She changed the subject. "You're glad to see me, Henry?"

"Why, sure."

"You don't seem to be."

"I am."

"I suppose you think I'm a—a waster. Sort of the World's Worst Butterfly."

Henry laughed.

"Not at all. Have a good time while you're young. Why? Do I seem like the priggish and earnest youth?"

"No—" She paused, "—but somehow I began thinking how absolutely different the party I'm on is from—from all your purposes. It seems sort of—of incongruous, doesn't it?—me being at a party like that, and you over here working for a thing that'll make that sort of party impossible ever any more, if your ideas work."

"I don't think of it that way. You're young, and you're acting just as you were brought up to act. Go ahead—have a good time!"

Her feet, which had been idly swinging, stopped and her voice dropped a note.

"I wish you'd—you'd come back to Harrisburg and have a good time. Do you feel sure that you're on the right track——"

"You're wearing beautiful stockings," he interrupted. "What on earth are they?"

"They're embroidered," she replied, glancing down. "Aren't they cunning?" She raised her skirts and uncovered slim, silk-sheathed calves. "Or do you disapprove of silk stockings?"

He seemed slightly exasperated, bent his dark eyes on her piercingly.

"Are you trying to make me out as criticizing you in any way, Edith?"

"Not at all——"

She paused. Bartholomew had uttered a grunt. She turned and saw that he had left his desk and was standing at the window.

"What is it?" demanded Henry.

"People," said Bartholomew, and then after an instant: "Whole jam of them. They're coming from Sixth Avenue."

"People?"

The fat man pressed his nose to the pane.

"Soldiers, by God!" he said emphatically. "I had an idea they'd come back."

Edith jumped to her feet, and running over joined Bartholomew at the window.

"There's a lot of them!" she cried excitedly. "Come here, Henry!"

Henry readjusted his shade, but kept his seat.

"Hadn't we better turn out the lights?" suggested Bartholomew.

"No. They'll go away in a minute."

"They're not," said Edith, peering from the window. "They're not even thinking of going away. There's more of them coming. Look—there's a whole crowd turning the corner of Sixth Avenue."

By the yellow glow and blue shadows of the street lamp she could see that the sidewalk was crowded with men. They were mostly in uniform, some sober, some enthusiastically drunk, and over the whole swept an incoherent clamor and shouting.

Henry rose, and going to the window exposed himself as a long silhouette against the office lights. Immediately the shouting became a steady yell, and a rattling fusillade of small missiles, corners of tobacco plugs, cigarette-boxes, and even pennies beat against the window. The sounds of the racket now began floating up the stairs as the folding doors revolved.

"They're coming up!" cried Bartholomew.

Edith turned anxiously to Henry.

"They're coming up, Henry."

From down-stairs in the lower hall their cries were now quite audible.

"—God damn Socialists!"

"Pro-Germans! Boche-lovers!"

"Second floor, front! Come on!"

"We'll get the sons——"

The next five minutes passed in a dream. Edith was conscious that the clamor burst suddenly upon the three of them like a cloud of rain, that there was a thunder of many feet on the stairs, that Henry had seized her arm and drawn her back toward the rear of the office. Then the door opened and an overflow of men were forced into the room—not the leaders, but simply those who happened to be in front.

"Hello, Bo!"

"Up late, ain't you?"

"You an' your girl. Damn *you*!"

She noticed that two very drunken soldiers had been forced to the front, where they wobbled fatuously—one of them was short and dark, the other was tall and weak of chin.

Henry stepped forward and raised his hand.

"Friends!" he said.

The clamor faded into a momentary stillness, punctuated with mutterings.

"Friends!" he repeated, his far-away eyes fixed over the heads of the crowd, "you're injuring no one but yourselves by breaking in here to-night. Do we look like rich men? Do we look like Germans? I ask you in all fairness——"

"Pipe down!"

"I'll say you do!"

"Say, who's your lady friend, buddy?"

A man in civilian clothes, who had been pawing over a table, suddenly held up a newspaper.

"Here it is!" he shouted. "They wanted the Germans to win the war!"

A new overflow from the stairs was shouldered in and of a sudden the room was full of men all closing around the pale little group at the back. Edith saw that the tall soldier with the weak chin was still in front. The short dark one had disappeared.

She edged slightly backward, stood close to the open window, through which came a clear breath of cool night air.

Then the room was a riot. She realized that the soldiers were surging forward, glimpsed the fat man swinging a chair over his head—instantly the lights went out, and she felt the push of warm bodies under rough cloth, and her ears were full of shouting and trampling and hard breathing.

A figure flashed by her out of nowhere, tottered, was edged sideways, and of a sudden disappeared helplessly out through the open window with a frightened, fragmentary cry that died staccato on the bosom of the clamor. By the faint light streaming from the building backing on the area Edith had a quick impression that it had been the tall soldier with the weak chin.

Anger rose astonishingly in her. She swung her arms wildly, edged blindly toward the thickest of the scuffling. She heard grunts, curses, the muffled impact of fists.

"Henry!" she called frantically, "Henry!"

Then, it was minutes later, she felt suddenly that there were other figures in the room. She heard a voice, deep, bullying, authoritative; she saw yellow rays of light sweeping here and there in the fracas. The cries became more scattered. The scuffling increased and then stopped.

Suddenly the lights were on and the room was full of policemen, clubbing left and right. The deep voice boomed out:

"Here now! Here now! Here now!"

And then:

"Quiet down and get out! Here now!"

The room seemed to empty like a wash-bowl. A policeman fast-grappled in the corner released his hold on his soldier antagonist and started him with a shove toward the door. The deep voice continued. Edith perceived now that it came from a bull-necked police captain standing near the door.

"Here now! This is no way! One of your own sojers got shoved out of the back window an' killed hisself!"

"Henry!" called Edith, "Henry!"

She beat wildly with her fists on the back of the man in front of her; she brushed between two others; fought, shrieked, and beat her way to a very pale figure sitting on the floor close to a desk.

"Henry," she cried passionately, "what's the matter? What's the matter? Did they hurt you?"

His eyes were shut. He groaned and then looking up said disgustedly——

"They broke my leg. My God, the fools!"

"Here now!" called the police captain. "Here now! Here now!"

IX

"Childs', Fifty-ninth Street," at eight o'clock of any morning differs from its sisters by less than the width of their marble tables or the degree of polish on the frying-pans. You will see there a crowd of poor people with sleep in the corners of their eyes, trying to look straight before them at their food so as not to see the other poor people. But Childs', Fifty-ninth, four hours earlier is quite unlike any Childs' restaurant from Portland, Oregon, to Portland, Maine. Within its pale but sanitary walls one finds a noisy medley of chorus girls, college boys, débutantes, rakes, *filles de joie*—a not unrepresentative mixture of the gayest of Broadway, and even of Fifth Avenue.

In the early morning of May the second it was unusually full. Over the marble-topped tables were bent the excited faces of flappers whose fathers owned individual villages. They were eating buckwheat cakes and scrambled eggs with relish and gusto, an accomplishment that it would have been utterly impossible for them to repeat in the same place four hours later.

Almost the entire crowd were from the Gamma Psi dance at Delmonico's except for several chorus girls from a midnight revue who sat at a side table and wished they'd taken off a little more make-up after the show. Here and there a drab, mouse-like figure, desperately out of place, watched the butterflies with a weary, puzzled curiosity. But the drab figure was the exception. This was the morning after May Day, and celebration was still in the air.

Gus Rose, sober but a little dazed, must be classed as one of the drab figures. How he had got himself from Forty-fourth Street to Fifty-ninth Street after the riot was only a hazy half-memory. He had seen the body of Carrol Key put in an ambulance and driven off, and then he had started up town with two or three soldiers. Somewhere between Forty-fourth Street and Fifty-ninth Street the other soldiers had met some women and disappeared. Rose had wandered to Columbus Circle and chosen the gleaming lights of Childs' to minister to his craving for coffee and doughnuts. He walked in and sat down.

All around him floated airy, inconsequential chatter and high-pitched laughter. At first he failed to understand, but after a puzzled five minutes he realized that this was the aftermath of some gay party. Here and there a restless, hilarious young man wandered fraternally and familiarly between the tables, shaking hands indiscriminately and pausing occasionally for a facetious chat, while excited waiters, bearing cakes and eggs aloft, swore at him silently, and bumped him out of the way. To Rose, seated at the most inconspicuous and least crowded table, the whole scene was a colorful circus of beauty and riotous pleasure.

He became gradually aware, after a few moments, that the couple seated diagonally across from him, with their backs to the crowd, were not the least interesting pair in the room. The man was drunk. He wore a dinner coat with a dishevelled tie and shirt swollen by spillings of water and wine. His eyes, dim and blood-shot, roved unnaturally from side to side. His breath came short between his lips.

"He's been on a spree!" thought Rose.

The woman was almost if not quite sober. She was pretty, with dark eyes and feverish high color, and she kept her active eyes fixed on her companion with the alertness of a hawk. From time to time she would lean and whisper intently to him, and he would answer by inclining his head heavily or by a particularly ghoulish and repellent wink.

Rose scrutinized them dumbly for some minutes, until the woman gave him a quick, resentful look; then he shifted his gaze to two of the most conspicuously hilarious of the promenaders who were on a protracted circuit of the tables. To his surprise he recognized in one of them the young man by whom he had been so ludicrously entertained at Delmonico's. This started him thinking of Key with a vague sentimentality, not unmixed with awe. Key was dead. He had fallen thirty-five feet and split his skull like a cracked cocoanut.

"He was a darn good guy," thought Rose mournfully. "He was a darn good guy, o'right. That was awful hard luck about him."

The two promenaders approached and started down between Rose's table and the next, addressing friends and strangers alike with jovial familiarity. Suddenly Rose saw the fair-haired one with the prominent teeth stop, look unsteadily at the man and girl opposite, and then begin to move his head disapprovingly from side to side.

The man with the blood-shot eyes looked up.

"Gordy," said the promenader with the prominent teeth, "Gordy."

"Hello," said the man with the stained shirt thickly.

Prominent Teeth shook his finger pessimistically at the pair, giving the woman a glance of aloof condemnation.

"What'd I tell you Gordy?"

Gordon stirred in his seat.

"Go to hell!" he said.

Dean continued to stand there shaking his finger. The woman began to get angry.

"You go way!" she cried fiercely. "You're drunk, that's what you are!"

"So's he," suggested Dean, staying the motion of his finger and pointing it at Gordon.

Peter Himmel ambled up, owlish now and oratorically inclined.

"Here now," he began as if called upon to deal with some petty dispute between children. "Wha's all trouble?"

"You take your friend away," said Jewel tartly. "He's bothering us."

"What's at?"

"You heard me!" she said shrilly. "I said to take your drunken friend away."

Her rising voice rang out above the clatter of the restaurant and a waiter came hurrying up.

"You gotta be more quiet!"

"That fella's drunk," she cried. "He's insulting us."

"Ah-ha, Gordy," persisted the accused. "What'd I tell you." He turned to the waiter. "Gordy an' I friends. Been tryin' help him, haven't I, Gordy?"

Gordy looked up.

"Help me? Hell, no!"

Jewel rose suddenly, and seizing Gordon's arm assisted him to his feet.

"Come on, Gordy!" she said, leaning toward him and speaking in a half whisper. "Let's us get out of here. This fella's got a mean drunk on."

Gordon allowed himself to be urged to his feet and started toward the door. Jewel turned for a second and addressed the provoker of their flight.

"I know all about *you*!" she said fiercely. "Nice friend, you are, I'll say. He told me about you."

Then she seized Gordon's arm, and together they made their way through the curious crowd, paid their check, and went out.

"You'll have to sit down," said the waiter to Peter after they had gone.

"What's 'at? Sit down?"

"Yes—or get out."

Peter turned to Dean.

"Come on," he suggested. "Let's beat up this waiter."

"All right."

They advanced toward him, their faces grown stern. The waiter retreated.

Peter suddenly reached over to a plate on the table beside him and picking up a handful of hash tossed it into the air. It descended as a languid parabola in snowflake effect on the heads of those near by.

"Hey! Ease up!"

"Put him out!"

"Sit down, Peter!"

"Cut out that stuff!"

Peter laughed and bowed.

"Thank you for your kind applause, ladies and gents. If some one will lend me some more hash and a tall hat we will go on with the act."

The bouncer bustled up.

"You've gotta get out!" he said to Peter.

"Hell, no!"

"He's my friend!" put in Dean indignantly.

A crowd of waiters were gathering. "Put him out!"

"Better go, Peter."

There was a short struggle and the two were edged and pushed toward the door.

"I got a hat and a coat here!" cried Peter.

"Well, go get 'em and be spry about it!"

The bouncer released his hold on Peter, who, adopting a ludicrous air of extreme cunning, rushed immediately around to the other table, where he burst into derisive laughter and thumbed his nose at the exasperated waiters.

"Think I just better wait a l'il' longer," he announced.

The chase began. Four waiters were sent around one way and four another. Dean caught hold of two of them by the coat, and another struggle took place before the pursuit of Peter could be resumed; he was finally pinioned after overturning a sugar-bowl and several cups of coffee. A fresh argument ensued at the cashier's desk, where Peter attempted to buy another dish of hash to take with him and throw at policemen.

But the commotion upon his exit proper was dwarfed by another phenomenon which drew admiring glances and a prolonged involuntary "Oh-h-h!" from every person in the restaurant.

The great plate-glass front had turned to a deep creamy blue, the color of a Maxfield Parrish moonlight—a blue that seemed to press close upon the pane as if to crowd its way into the restaurant. Dawn had come up in Columbus Circle, magical, breathless dawn, silhouetting the great statue of the immortal Christopher, and mingling in a curious and uncanny manner with the fading yellow electric light inside.

X

Mr. In and Mr. Out are not listed by the census-taker. You will search for them in vain through the social register or the births, marriages, and deaths, or the grocer's credit list. Oblivion has swallowed them and the testimony that they ever existed at all is vague and shadowy, and inadmissible in a court of law. Yet I have it upon the best authority that for a brief space Mr. In and Mr. Out lived, breathed, answered to their names and radiated vivid personalities of their own.

During the brief span of their lives they walked in their native garments down the great highway of a great nation; were laughed at, sworn at, chased, and fled from. Then they passed and were heard of no more.

They were already taking form dimly, when a taxicab with the top open breezed down Broadway in the faintest glimmer of May dawn. In this car sat the souls of Mr. In and Mr. Out discussing with amazement the blue light that had so precipitately colored the sky behind the statue of Christopher Columbus, discussing with bewilderment the old, gray faces of the early risers which skimmed palely along the street like blown bits of paper on a gray lake. They were agreed on all things, from the absurdity of the bouncer in Childs' to the absurdity of the business of life. They were dizzy with the extreme maudlin happiness that the morning had awakened in their glowing souls. Indeed, so fresh and vigorous was their pleasure in living that they felt it should be expressed by loud cries.

"Ye-ow-ow!" hooted Peter, making a megaphone with his hands—and Dean joined in with a call that, though equally significant and symbolic, derived its resonance from its very inarticulateness.

"Yo-ho! Yea! Yoho! Yo-buba!"

Fifty-third Street was a bus with a dark, bobbed-hair beauty atop; Fifty-second was a street cleaner who dodged, escaped, and sent up a yell of, "Look where you're aimin'!" in a pained and grieved voice. At Fiftieth Street a group of men on a very white sidewalk in front of a very white building turned to stare after them, and shouted:

"Some party, boys!"

At Forty-ninth Street Peter turned to Dean. "Beautiful morning," he said gravely, squinting up his owlish eyes.

"Probably is."

"Go get some breakfast, hey?"

Dean agreed—with additions.

"Breakfast and liquor."

"Breakfast and liquor," repeated Peter, and they looked at each other, nodding. "That's logical."

Then they both burst into loud laughter.

"Breakfast and liquor! Oh, gosh!"

"No such thing," announced Peter.

"Don't serve it? Ne'mind. We force 'em serve it. Bring pressure bear."

"Bring logic bear."

The taxi cut suddenly off Broadway, sailed along a cross street, and stopped in front of a heavy tomb-like building in Fifth Avenue.

"What's idea?"

The taxi-driver informed them that this was Delmonico's.

This was somewhat puzzling. They were forced to devote several minutes to intense concentration, for if such an order had been given there must have been a reason for it.

"Somep'm 'bouta coat," suggested the taxi-man.

That was it. Peter's overcoat and hat. He had left them at Delmonico's. Having decided this, they disembarked from the taxi and strolled toward the entrance arm in arm.

"Hey!" said the taxi-driver.

"Huh?"

"You better pay me."

They shook their heads in shocked negation.

"Later, not now—we give orders, you wait."

The taxi-driver objected; he wanted his money now. With the scornful condescension of men exercising tremendous self-control they paid him.

Inside Peter groped in vain through a dim, deserted check-room in search of his coat and derby.

"Gone, I guess. Somebody stole it."

"Some Sheff student."

"All probability."

"Never mind," said Dean, nobly. "I'll leave mine here too—then we'll both be dressed the same."

He removed his overcoat and hat and was hanging them up when his roving glance was caught and held magnetically by two large squares of cardboard tacked to the two coat-room doors. The one on the left-hand door bore the word "In" in big black letters, and the one on the right-hand door flaunted the equally emphatic word "Out."

"Look!" he exclaimed happily——

Peter's eyes followed his pointing finger.

"What?"

"Look at the signs. Let's take 'em."

"Good idea."

"Probably pair very rare an' valuable signs. Probably come in handy."

Peter removed the left-hand sign from the door and endeavored to conceal it about his person. The sign being of considerable proportions, this was a matter of some difficulty. An idea flung itself at him, and with an air of dignified mystery he turned his back. After an instant he wheeled dramatically around, and stretching out his arms displayed himself to the admiring Dean. He had inserted the sign in his vest, completely covering his shirt front. In effect, the word "In" had been painted upon his shirt in large black letters.

"Yoho!" cheered Dean. "Mister In."

He inserted his own sign in like manner.

"Mister Out!" he announced triumphantly. "Mr. In meet Mr. Out."

They advanced and shook hands. Again laughter overcame them and they rocked in a shaken spasm of mirth.

"Yoho!"

"We probably get a flock of breakfast."

"We'll go—go to the Commodore."

Arm in arm they sallied out the door, and turning east in Forty-fourth Street set out for the Commodore.

As they came out a short dark soldier, very pale and tired, who had been wandering listlessly along the sidewalk, turned to look at them.

He started over as though to address them, but as they immediately bent on him glances of withering unrecognition, he waited until they had started unsteadily down the street, and then followed at about forty paces, chuckling to himself and saying "Oh, boy!" over and over under his breath, in delighted, anticipatory tones.

Mr. In and Mr. Out were meanwhile exchanging pleasantries concerning their future plans.

"We want liquor; we want breakfast. Neither without the other. One and indivisible."

"We want both 'em!"

"Both 'em!"

It was quite light now, and passers-by began to bend curious eyes on the pair. Obviously they were engaged in a discussion, which afforded each of them intense amusement, for occasionally a fit of laughter would seize upon them so violently that, still with their arms interlocked, they would bend nearly double.

Reaching the Commodore, they exchanged a few spicy epigrams with the sleepy-eyed doorman, navigated the revolving door with some difficulty, and then made their way through a thinly populated but startled lobby to the dining-room, where a puzzled waiter showed them an obscure table in a corner. They studied the bill of fare helplessly, telling over the items to each other in puzzled mumbles.

"Don't see any liquor here," said Peter reproachfully.

The waiter became audible but unintelligible.

"Repeat," continued Peter, with patient tolerance, "that there seems to be unexplained and quite distasteful lack of liquor upon bill of fare."

"Here!" said Dean confidently, "let me handle him." He turned to the waiter—"Bring us—bring us—" he scanned the bill of fare anxiously. "Bring us a quart of champagne and a—a—probably ham sandwich."

The waiter looked doubtful.

"Bring it!" roared Mr. In and Mr. Out in chorus.

The waiter coughed and disappeared. There was a short wait during which they were subjected without their knowledge to a careful scrutiny by the head-waiter. Then the champagne arrived, and at the sight of it Mr. In and Mr. Out became jubilant.

"Imagine their objecting to us having champagne for breakfast—jus' imagine."

They both concentrated upon the vision of such an awesome possibility, but the feat was too much for them. It was impossible for their joint imaginations to conjure up a world where any one might object to any one else having champagne for breakfast. The waiter drew the cork with an enormous *pop*—and their glasses immediately foamed with pale yellow froth.

"Here's health, Mr. In."

"Here's same to you, Mr. Out."

The waiter withdrew; the minutes passed; the champagne became low in the bottle.

"It's—it's mortifying," said Dean suddenly.

"Wha's mortifying?"

"The idea their objecting us having champagne breakfast."

"Mortifying?" Peter considered. "Yes, tha's word—mortifying."

Again they collapsed into laughter, howled, swayed, rocked back and forth in their chairs, repeating the word "mortifying" over and over to each other—each repetition seeming to make it only more brilliantly absurd.

After a few more gorgeous minutes they decided on another quart. Their anxious waiter consulted his immediate superior, and this discreet person gave implicit instructions that no more champagne should be served. Their check was brought.

Five minutes later, arm in arm, they left the Commodore and made their way through a curious, staring crowd along

Forty-second Street, and up Vanderbilt Avenue to the Biltmore. There, with sudden cunning, they rose to the occasion and traversed the lobby, walking fast and standing unnaturally erect.

Once in the dining-room they repeated their performance. They were torn between intermittent convulsive laughter and sudden spasmodic discussions of politics, college, and the sunny state of their dispositions. Their watches told them that it was now nine o'clock, and a dim idea was born in them that they were on a memorable party, something that they would remember always. They lingered over the second bottle. Either of them had only to mention the word "mortifying" to send them both into riotous gasps. The dining-room was whirring and shifting now; a curious lightness permeated and rarefied the heavy air.

They paid their check and walked out into the lobby.

It was at this moment that the exterior doors revolved for the thousandth time that morning, and admitted into the lobby a very pale young beauty with dark circles under her eyes, attired in a much-rumpled evening dress. She was accompanied by a plain stout man, obviously not an appropriate escort.

At the top of the stairs this couple encountered Mr. In and Mr. Out.

"Edith," began Mr. In, stepping toward her hilariously and making a sweeping bow, "darling, good morning."

The stout man glanced questioningly at Edith, as if merely asking her permission to throw this man summarily out of the way.

" 'Scuse familiarity," added Peter, as an afterthought. "Edith, good-morning."

He seized Dean's elbow and impelled him into the foreground.

"Meet Mr. In, Edith, my bes' frien'. Inseparable. Mr. In and Mr. Out."

Mr. Out advanced and bowed; in fact, he advanced so far and bowed so low that he tipped slightly forward and only kept his balance by placing a hand lightly on Edith's shoulder.

"I'm Mr. Out, Edith," he mumbled pleasantly, "S'misterin Misterout."

"'Smisterinanout," said Peter proudly.

But Edith stared straight by them, her eyes fixed on some infinite speck in the gallery above her. She nodded slightly to the stout man, who advanced bull-like and with a sturdy brisk gesture pushed Mr. In and Mr. Out to either side. Through this alley he and Edith walked.

But ten paces farther on Edith stopped again—stopped and pointed to a short, dark soldier who was eying the crowd in general, and the tableau of Mr. In and Mr. Out in particular, with a sort of puzzled, spell-bound awe.

"There," cried Edith. "See there!"

Her voice rose, became somewhat shrill. Her pointing finger shook slightly.

"There's the soldier who broke my brother's leg."

There were a dozen exclamations; a man in a cutaway coat left his place near the desk and advanced alertly; the stout person made a sort of lightning-like spring toward the short, dark soldier, and then the lobby closed around the little group and blotted them from the sight of Mr. In and Mr. Out.

But to Mr. In and Mr. Out this event was merely a particolored iridescent segment of a whirring, spinning world.

They heard loud voices; they saw the stout man spring; the picture suddenly blurred.

Then they were in an elevator bound skyward.

"What floor, please?" said the elevator man.

"Any floor," said Mr. In.

"Top floor," said Mr. Out.

"This is the top floor," said the elevator man.

"Have another floor put on," said Mr. Out.

"Higher," said Mr. In.

"Heaven," said Mr. Out.

XI

In a bedroom of a small hotel just off Sixth Avenue Gordon Sterrett awoke with a pain in the back of his head and a sick throbbing in all his veins. He looked at the dusky gray shadows in the corners of the room and at a raw place on a large leather chair in the corner where it had long been in use. He saw clothes, dishevelled, rumpled clothes on the floor and he smelt stale cigarette smoke and stale liquor. The windows were tight shut. Outside the bright sunlight had thrown a dust-filled beam across the sill—a beam broken by the head of the wide wooden bed in which he had slept. He lay very quiet—comatose, drugged, his eyes wide, his mind clicking wildly like an unoiled machine.

It must have been thirty seconds after he perceived the sunbeam with the dust on it and the rip on the large leather chair that he had the sense of life close beside him, and it was another thirty seconds after that before he realized that he was irrevocably married to Jewel Hudson.

He went out half an hour later and bought a revolver at a sporting goods store. Then he took a taxi to the room where he had been living on East Twenty-seventh Street, and, leaning across the table that held his drawing materials, fired a cartridge into his head just behind the temple.

Porcelain and Pink

A room in the down-stairs of a summer cottage. High around the wall runs an art frieze of a fisherman with a pile of nets at his feet and a ship on a crimson ocean, a fisherman with a pile of nets at his feet and a ship on a crimson ocean, a fisherman with a pile of nets at his feet and so on. In one place on the frieze there is an overlapping—here we have half a fisherman with half a pile of nets at his foot, crowded damply against half a ship on half a crimson ocean. The frieze is not in the plot, but frankly it fascinates me. I could continue indefinitely, but I am distracted by one of the two objects in the room—a blue porcelain bath-tub. It has character, this bath-tub. It is not one of the new racing bodies, but is small with a high tonneau and looks as if it were going to jump; discouraged, however, by the shortness of its legs, it has submitted to its environment and to its coat of sky-blue paint. But it grumpily refuses to allow any patron completely to stretch his legs—which brings us neatly to the second object in the room:

It is a girl—clearly an appendage to the bath-tub, only her head and throat—beautiful girls have throats instead of necks—and a suggestion of shoulder appearing above the side. For the first ten minutes of the play the audience is engrossed in wondering if she really is playing the game fairly and hasn't any clothes on or whether it is being cheated and she is dressed.

The girl's name is JULIE MARVIS. *From the proud way she sits up in the bath-tub we deduce that she is not very tall and that she carries herself well. When she smiles, her upper lip rolls a little and reminds you of an Easter Bunny. She is within whispering distance of twenty years old.*

One thing more—above and to the right of the bath-tub is a window. It is narrow and has a wide sill; it lets in much sunshine, but effectually prevents any one who looks in from seeing the bath-tub. You begin to suspect the plot?

We open, conventionally enough, with a song, but, as the startled gasp of the audience quite drowns out the first half, we will give only the last of it:

JULIE: (*In an airy sophrano-enthusiastico*)

When Cæsar did the Chicago
He was a graceful child,
Those sacred chickens
Just raised the dickens
The Vestal Virgins went wild.
Whenever the Nervii got nervy
He gave them an awful razz
They shook in their shoes
With the Consular blues
The Imperial Roman Jazz

(*During the wild applause that follows* JULIE *modestly moves her arms and makes waves on the surface of the water—at least we suppose she does. Then the door on the left opens and* LOIS MARVIS *enters, dressed but carrying garments and towels.* LOIS *is a year older than* JULIE *and is nearly her double in face and voice, but in her clothes and expression are the marks of the conservative. Yes, you've guessed it. Mistaken identity is the old, rusty pivot upon which the plot turns.*)

LOIS: (*Starting*) Oh, 'scuse me. I didn't know you were here.

JULIE: Oh, hello. I'm giving a little concert——

LOIS: (*Interrupting*) Why didn't you lock the door?

JULIE: Didn't I?

LOIS: Of course you didn't. Do you think I just walked through it?

JULIE: I thought you picked the lock, dearest.

LOIS: You're *so* careless.

JULIE: No. I'm happy as a garbage-man's dog and I'm giving a little concert.

LOIS: (*Severely*) Grow up!

JULIE: (*Waving a pink arm around the room*) The walls reflect the sound, you see. That's why there's something very beautiful about singing in a bath-tub. It gives an effect of surpassing loveliness. Can I render you a selection?

LOIS: I wish you'd hurry out of the tub.

JULIE: (*Shaking her head thoughtfully*) Can't be hurried. This is my kingdom at present, Godliness.

LOIS: Why the mellow name?

JULIE: Because you're next to Cleanliness. Don't throw anything please!

LOIS: How long will you be?

JULIE: (*After some consideration*) Not less than fifteen nor more than twenty-five minutes.

LOIS: As a favor to me will you make it ten?

JULIE: (*Reminiscing*) Oh, Godliness, do you remember a day in the chill of last January when one Julie, famous for her Easter-rabbit smile, was going out and there was scarcely any hot water and young Julie had just filled the tub for her own little self when the wicked sister came and did bathe herself therein, forcing the young Julie to perform her ablutions with cold cream—which is expensive and a darn lot of trouble?

LOIS: (*Impatiently*) Then you won't hurry?

JULIE: Why should I?

LOIS: I've got a date.

JULIE: Here at the house?

LOIS: None of your business.

(JULIE *shrugs the visible tips of her shoulders and stirs the water into ripples.*)

JULIE: So be it.

LOIS: Oh, for Heaven's sake, yes! I have a date here at the house—in a way.

JULIE: In a way?

LOIS: He isn't coming in. He's calling for me and we're walking.

JULIE: (*Raising her eyebrows*) Oh, the plot clears. It's that literary Mr. Calkins. I thought you promised mother you wouldn't invite him in.

LOIS: (*Desperately*) She's so idiotic. She detests him because he's just got a divorce. Of course she's had more experience than I have, but——

JULIE: (*Wisely*) Don't let her kid you! Experience is the biggest gold brick in the world. All older people have it for sale.

LOIS: I like him. We talk literature.

JULIE: Oh, so that's why I've noticed all these weighty books around the house lately.

LOIS: He lends them to me.

JULIE: Well, you've got to play his game. When in Rome do as the Romans would like to do. But I'm through with books. I'm all educated.

LOIS: You're very inconsistent—last summer you read every day.

JULIE: If I were consistent I'd still be living on warm milk out of a bottle.

LOIS: Yes, and probably my bottle. But I like Mr. Calkins.

JULIE: I never met him.

LOIS: Well, will you hurry up?

JULIE: Yes. (*After a pause*) I wait till the water gets tepid and then I let in more hot.

LOIS: (*Sarcastically*) How interesting!

JULIE: 'Member when we used to play "soapo"?

LOIS: Yes—and ten years old. I'm really quite surprised that you don't play it still.

JULIE: I do. I'm going to in a minute.

LOIS: Silly game.

JULIE: (*Warmly*) No, it isn't. It's good for the nerves. I'll bet you've forgotten how to play it.

LOIS: (*Defiantly*) No, I haven't. You—you get the tub all full of soapsuds and then you get up on the edge and slide down.

JULIE: (*Shaking her head scornfully*) Huh! That's only part of it. You've got to slide down without touching your hands or feet——

LOIS: (*Impatiently*) Oh, Lord! What do I care? I wish we'd either stop coming here in the summer or else get a house with two bath-tubs.

JULIE: You can buy yourself a little tin one, or use the hose——

LOIS: Oh, shut up!

JULIE: (*Irrelevantly*) Leave the towel.

LOIS: What?

JULIE: Leave the towel when you go.

LOIS: This towel?

JULIE: (*Sweetly*) Yes, I forgot my towel.

LOIS: (*Looking around for the first time*) Why, you idiot! You haven't even a kimono.

JULIE: (*Also looking around*) Why, so I haven't.

LOIS: (*Suspicion growing on her*) How did you get here?

JULIE: (*Laughing*) I guess I—I guess I whisked here. You know—a white form whisking down the stairs and——

LOIS: (*Scandalized*) Why, you little wretch. Haven't you any pride or self-respect?

JULIE: Lots of both. I think that proves it. I looked very well. I really am rather cute in my natural state.

LOIS: Well, you——

JULIE: (*Thinking aloud*) I wish people didn't wear any clothes. I guess I ought to have been a pagan or a native or something.

LOIS: You're a——

JULIE: I dreamt last night that one Sunday in church a small boy brought in a magnet that attracted cloth. He attracted the clothes right off of everybody; put them in an awful state; people were crying and shrieking and carrying on as if they'd just discovered their skins for the first time. Only *I* didn't care. So I just laughed. I had to pass the collection plate because nobody else would.

LOIS: (*Who has turned a deaf ear to this speech*) Do you mean to tell me that if I hadn't come you'd have run back to your room—un—unclothed?

JULIE: *Au naturel* is so much nicer.

LOIS: Suppose there had been some one in the living-room.

JULIE: There never has been yet.

LOIS: Yet! Good grief! How long——

JULIE: Besides, I usually have a towel.

LOIS: (*Completely overcome*) Golly! You ought to be spanked. I hope you get caught. I hope there's a dozen ministers in the living-room when you come out—and their wives and their daughters.

JULIE: There wouldn't be room for them in the living-room, answered Clean Kate of the Laundry District.

LOIS: All right. You've made your own—bath-tub; you can lie in it.

(LOIS *starts determinedly for the door.*)

JULIE: (*In alarm*) Hey! Hey! I don't care about the k'mono, but I want the towel. I can't dry myself on a piece of soap and a wet wash-rag.

LOIS: (*Obstinately*) I won't humor such a creature. You'll have to dry yourself the best way you can. You can roll on the floor like the animals do that don't wear any clothes.

JULIE: (*Complacent again*) All right. Get out!

LOIS: (*Haughtily*) Huh!

(JULIE *turns on the cold water and with her finger directs a parabolic stream at* LOIS. LOIS *retires quickly, slamming the door after her.* JULIE *laughs and turns off the water*)

JULIE: (*Singing*)

When the Arrow-collar man
  Meets the D'jer-kiss girl
On the smokeless Sante Fé
  Her Pebeco smile
  Her Lucile style
De dum da-de-dum one day——

(*She changes to a whistle and leans forward to turn on the taps, but is startled by three loud banging noises in the pipes. Silence for a moment—then she puts her mouth down near the spigot as if it were a telephone*)

JULIE: Hello! (*No answer*) Are you a plumber? (*No answer*) Are you the water department? (*One loud, hollow bang*) What do you want? (*No answer*) I believe you're a ghost. Are you? (*No answer*) Well, then, stop banging. (*She reaches out and turns on the warm tap. No water flows. Again she puts her mouth down close to the spigot*) If you're the plumber that's a mean trick. Turn it on for a fellow. (*Two loud, hollow bangs*) Don't argue! I want water—water! *Water!*

(*A young man's head appears in the window—a head decorated with a slim mustache and sympathetic eyes. These last stare, and though they can see nothing but many fishermen with nets and much crimson ocean, they decide him to speak*)

THE YOUNG MAN: Some one fainted?

JULIE: (*Starting up, all ears immediately*) Jumping cats!

THE YOUNG MAN: (*Helpfully*) Water's no good for fits.

JULIE: Fits! Who said anything about fits!

THE YOUNG MAN: You said something about a cat jumping.

JULIE: (*Decidedly*) I did not!

THE YOUNG MAN: Well, we can talk it over later. Are you ready to go out? Or do you still feel that if you go with me just now everybody will gossip?

JULIE: (*Smiling*) Gossip! Would they? It'd be more than gossip—it'd be a regular scandal.

THE YOUNG MAN: Here, you're going it a little strong. Your family might be somewhat disgruntled—but to the pure all things are suggestive. No one else would even give it a thought, except a few old women. Come on.

JULIE: You don't know what you ask.

THE YOUNG MAN: Do you imagine we'd have a crowd following us?

JULIE: A crowd? There'd be a special, all-steel, buffet train leaving New York hourly.

THE YOUNG MAN: Say, are you house-cleaning?

JULIE: Why?

THE YOUNG MAN: I see all the pictures are off the walls.

JULIE: Why, we never have pictures in this room.

THE YOUNG MAN: Odd. I never heard of a room without pictures or tapestry or panelling or something.

JULIE: There's not even any furniture in here.

THE YOUNG MAN: What a strange house!

JULIE: It depends on the angle you see it from.

THE YOUNG MAN: (*Sentimentally*) It's so nice talking to you like this—when you're merely a voice. I'm rather glad I can't see you.

JULIE: (*Gratefully*) So am I.

THE YOUNG MAN: What color are you wearing?

JULIE: (*After a critical survey of her shoulders*) Why, I guess it's a sort of pinkish white.

THE YOUNG MAN: Is it becoming to you?

JULIE: Very. It's—it's old. I've had it for a long while.

THE YOUNG MAN: I thought you hated old clothes.

JULIE: I do—but this was a birthday present and I sort of have to wear it.

THE YOUNG MAN: Pinkish white. Well, I'll bet it's divine. Is it in style?

JULIE: Quite. It's very simple, standard model.

THE YOUNG MAN: What a voice you have! How it echoes! Sometimes I shut my eyes and seem to see you in a far desert island calling for me. And I plunge toward you through the surf, hearing you call as you stand there, water stretching on both sides of you——

(*The soap slips from the side of the tub and splashes in. The young man blinks*)

THE YOUNG MAN: What was that? Did I dream it?

JULIE: Yes. You're—you're very poetic, aren't you?

THE YOUNG MAN: (*Dreamily*) No. I do prose. I do verse only when I am stirred.

JULIE: (*Murmuring*) Stirred by a spoon——

THE YOUNG MAN: I have always loved poetry. I can remember to this day the first poem I ever learned by heart. It was "Evangeline."

JULIE: That's a fib.

THE YOUNG MAN: Did I say "Evangeline"? I meant "The Skeleton in Armor."

JULIE: I'm a low-brow. But I can remember my first poem. It had one verse:

Parker and Davis
Sittin' on a fence
Tryne to make a dollar
Outa fif-teen cents.

THE YOUNG MAN: (*Eagerly*) Are you growing fond of literature?

JULIE: If it's not too ancient or complicated or depressing. Same way with people. I usually like 'em if they're not too ancient or complicated or depressing.

THE YOUNG MAN: Of course I've read enormously. You told me last night that you were very fond of Walter Scott.

JULIE: (*Considering*) Scott? Let's see. Yes, I've read "Ivanhoe" and "The Last of the Mohicans."

THE YOUNG MAN: That's by Cooper.

JULIE: (*Angrily*) "Ivanhoe" is? You're crazy! I guess I know. I read it.

THE YOUNG MAN: "The Last of the Mohicans" is by Cooper.

JULIE: What do I care! I like O. Henry. I don't see how he ever wrote those stories. Most of them he wrote in prison. "The Ballad of Reading Gaol" he made up in prison.

THE YOUNG MAN: (*Biting his lip*) Literature—literature! How much it has meant to me!

JULIE: Well, as Gaby Deslys said to Mr. Bergson, with my looks and your brains there's nothing we couldn't do.

THE YOUNG MAN: (*Laughing*) You certainly are hard to keep up with. One day you're awfully pleasant and the next you're in a mood. If I didn't understand your temperament so well——

JULIE: (*Impatiently*) Oh, you're one of these amateur character-readers, are you? Size people up in five minutes and then look wise whenever they're mentioned. I hate that sort of thing.

THE YOUNG MAN: I don't boast of sizing you up. You're most mysterious, I'll admit.

JULIE: There's only two mysterious people in history.

THE YOUNG MAN: Who are they?

JULIE: The Man with the Iron Mask and the fella who says "ug uh-glug uh-glug uh-glug" when the line is busy.

THE YOUNG MAN: You *are* mysterious. I love you. You're beautiful, intelligent, and virtuous, and that's the rarest known combination.

JULIE: You're a historian. Tell me if there are any bath-tubs in history. I think they've been frightfully neglected.

THE YOUNG MAN: Bath-tubs! Let's see. Well, Agamemnon was stabbed in his bath-tub. And Charlotte Corday stabbed Marat in his bath-tub.

JULIE: (*Sighing*) Way back there! Nothing new besides the sun, is there? Why only yesterday I picked up a musical-comedy score that must have been at least twenty years old; and there on the cover it said "The Shimmies of Normandy," but shimmie was spelt the old way, with a "C."

THE YOUNG MAN: I loathe these modern dances. Oh, Lois, I wish I could see you. Come to the window.

(*There is a loud bang in the water-pipe and suddenly the flow starts from the open taps. Julie turns them off quickly*)

THE YOUNG MAN: (*Puzzled*) What on earth was that?

JULIE: (*Ingeniously*) I heard something, too.

THE YOUNG MAN: Sounded like running water.

JULIE: Didn't it? Strange like it. As a matter of fact I was filling the gold-fish bowl.

THE YOUNG MAN: (*Still puzzled*) What was that banging noise?

JULIE: One of the fish snapping his golden jaws.

THE YOUNG MAN: (*With sudden resolution*) Lois, I love you. I am not a mundane man but I am a forger——

JULIE: (*Interested at once*) Oh, how fascinating.

THE YOUNG MAN: —a forger ahead. Lois, I want you.

JULIE: (*Skeptically*) Huh! What you really want is for the world to come to attention and stand there till you give "Rest!"

THE YOUNG MAN: Lois I—Lois I——

(*He stops as* LOIS *opens the door, comes in, and bangs it behind her. She looks peevishly at* JULIE *and then suddenly catches sight of the young man in the window*)

LOIS: (*In horror*) Mr. Calkins!

THE YOUNG MAN: (*Surprised*) Why I thought you said you were wearing pinkish white!

(*After one despairing stare* LOIS *shrieks, throws up her hands in surrender, and sinks to the floor.*)

THE YOUNG MAN: (*In great alarm*) Good Lord! She's fainted! I'll be right in.

(JULIE'S *eyes light on the towel which has slipped from* LOIS'S *inert hand.*)

JULIE: In that case I'll be right out.

(*She puts her hands on the side of the tub to lift herself out and a murmur, half gasp, half sigh, ripples from the audience.*

A Belasco midnight comes quickly down and blots out the stage.)

CURTAIN.

FANTASIES

The Diamond as Big as the Ritz

JOHN T. UNGER came from a family that had been well known in Hades—a small town on the Mississippi River—for several generations. John's father had held the amateur golf championship through many a heated contest; Mrs. Unger was known "from hot-box to hot-bed," as the local phrase went, for her political addresses; and young John T. Unger, who had just turned sixteen, had danced all the latest dances from New York before he put on long trousers. And now, for a certain time, he was to be away from home. That respect for a New England education which is the bane of all provincial places, which drains them yearly of their most promising young men, had seized upon his parents. Nothing would suit them but that he should go to St. Midas' School near Boston—Hades was too small to hold their darling and gifted son.

Now in Hades—as you know if you ever have been there—the names of the more fashionable preparatory schools and colleges mean very little. The inhabitants have been so long out of the world that, though they make a show of keeping up to date in dress and manners and literature, they depend to a great extent on hearsay, and a function that in Hades would be considered elaborate would doubtless be hailed by a Chicago beef-princess as "perhaps a little tacky."

John T. Unger was on the eve of departure. Mrs. Unger, with maternal fatuity, packed his trunks full of linen suits and electric fans, and Mr. Unger presented his son with an asbestos pocket-book stuffed with money.

"Remember, you are always welcome here," he said. "You can be sure, boy, that we'll keep the home fires burning."

"I know," answered John huskily.

"Don't forget who you are and where you come from," continued his father proudly, "and you can do nothing to harm you. You are an Unger—from Hades."

So the old man and the young shook hands and John walked away with tears streaming from his eyes. Ten minutes later he had passed outside the city limits, and he stopped to glance back for the last time. Over the gates the old-fashioned Victorian motto seemed strangely attractive to him. His father had tried time and time again to have it changed to something with a little more push and verve about it, such as "Hades—Your Opportunity," or else a plain "Welcome" sign set over a hearty handshake pricked out in electric lights. The old motto was a little depressing, Mr. Unger had thought—but now. . . .

So John took his look and then set his face resolutely toward his destination. And, as he turned away, the lights of Hades against the sky seemed full of a warm and passionate beauty.

St. Midas' School is half an hour from Boston in a Rolls-Pierce motor-car. The actual distance will never be known, for no one, except John T. Unger, had ever arrived there save in a Rolls-Pierce and probably no one ever will again. St. Midas' is the most expensive and the most exclusive boys' preparatory school in the world.

John's first two years there passed pleasantly. The fathers of all the boys were money-kings and John spent his summers visiting at fashionable resorts. While he was very fond of all the boys he visited, their fathers struck him as being much of a piece, and in his boyish way he often wondered at their exceeding sameness. When he told them where his home was they would ask jovially, "Pretty hot down there?" and John would muster a faint smile and answer, "It certainly is." His response would have been heartier had they not all made this joke—at best varying it with, "Is it hot enough for you down there?" which he hated just as much.

In the middle of his second year at school, a quiet, handsome boy named Percy Washington had been put in John's form. The newcomer was pleasant in his manner and exceedingly well dressed even for St. Midas', but for some reason he kept aloof from the other boys. The only person with whom he was intimate was John T. Unger, but even to John he was entirely uncommunicative concerning his home or his family. That he was wealthy went without saying, but beyond a few such deductions John knew little of his friend, so it promised rich confectionery for his curiosity when Percy invited him to spend the summer at his home "in the West." He accepted, without hesitation.

It was only when they were in the train that Percy became, for the first time, rather communicative. One day while they were eating lunch in the dining-car and discussing the imperfect characters of several of the boys at school, Percy suddenly changed his tone and made an abrupt remark.

"My father," he said, "is by far the richest man in the world."

"Oh," said John, politely. He could think of no answer to make to this confidence. He considered "That's very nice," but it sounded hollow and was on the point of saying, "Really?" but refrained since it would seem to question Percy's statement. And such an astounding statement could scarcely be questioned.

"By far the richest," repeated Percy.

"I was reading in the *World Almanac*," began John, "that there was one man in America with an income of over five million a year and four men with incomes of over three million a year, and——"

"Oh, they're nothing." Percy's mouth was a half-moon of scorn. "Catch-penny capitalists, financial small-fry, petty merchants and money-lenders. My father could buy them out and not know he'd done it."

"But how does he——"

"Why haven't they put down *his* income tax? Because he doesn't pay any. At least he pays a little one—but he doesn't pay any on his *real* income."

"He must be very rich," said John simply. "I'm glad. I like very rich people.

"The richer a fella is, the better I like him." There was a look of passionate frankness upon his dark face. "I visited the Schnlitzer-Murphys last Easter. Vivian Schnlitzer-Murphy had rubies as big as hen's eggs, and sapphires that were like globes with lights inside them——"

"I love jewels," agreed Percy enthusiastically. "Of course I wouldn't want any one at school to know about it, but I've got quite a collection myself. I used to collect them instead of stamps."

"And diamonds," continued John eagerly. "The Schnlitzer-Murphys had diamonds as big as walnuts——"

"That's nothing." Percy had leaned forward and dropped his voice to a low whisper. "That's nothing at all. My father has a diamond bigger than the Ritz-Carlton Hotel."

II

The Montana sunset lay between two mountains like a gigantic bruise from which dark arteries spread themselves over a poisoned sky. An immense distance under the sky crouched the village of Fish, minute, dismal, and forgotten. There were twelve men, so it was said, in the village of Fish, twelve sombre and inexplicable souls who sucked a lean milk from the almost literally bare rock upon which a mysterious populatory force had begotten them. They had become a race apart, these twelve men of Fish, like some species developed by an early whim of nature, which on second thought had abandoned them to struggle and extermination.

Out of the blue-black bruise in the distance crept a long line of moving lights upon the desolation of the land, and the twelve men of Fish gathered like ghosts at the shanty depot to watch the passing of the seven o'clock train, the Transcontinental Express from Chicago. Six times or so a year the Transcontinental Express, through some inconceivable jurisdiction, stopped at the village of Fish, and when this occurred a figure or so would disembark, mount into a buggy that always appeared from out of the dusk, and drive off toward the bruised sunset. The observation of this pointless and preposterous phenomenon had become a sort of cult among the men of Fish. To observe, that was all; there remained in them none of the vital quality of illusion which would make them wonder or speculate, else a religion might have grown up around these mysterious visitations. But the men of Fish were beyond all religion—the barest and most savage tenets of even Christianity could gain no foothold on that barren rock—so there was no altar, no priest, no sacrifice; only each night at seven the silent concourse by the shanty depot, a congregation who lifted up a prayer of dim, anæmic wonder.

On this June night, the Great Brakeman, whom, had they

deified any one, they might well have chosen as their celestial protagonist, had ordained that the seven o'clock train should leave its human (or inhuman) deposit at Fish. At two minutes after seven Percy Washington and John T. Unger disembarked, hurried past the spellbound, the agape, the fearsome eyes of the twelve men of Fish, mounted into a buggy which had obviously appeared from nowhere, and drove away.

After half an hour, when the twilight had coagulated into dark, the silent negro who was driving the buggy hailed an opaque body somewhere ahead of them in the gloom. In response to his cry, it turned upon them a luminous disk which regarded them like a malignant eye out of the unfathomable night. As they came closer, John saw that it was the tail-light of an immense automobile, larger and more magnificent than any he had ever seen. Its body was of gleaming metal richer than nickel and lighter than silver, and the hubs of the wheels were studded with iridescent geometric figures of green and yellow—John did not dare to guess whether they were glass or jewel.

Two negroes, dressed in glittering livery such as one sees in pictures of royal processions in London, were standing at attention beside the car and as the two young men dismounted from the buggy they were greeted in some language which the guest could not understand, but which seemed to be an extreme form of the Southern negro's dialect.

"Get in," said Percy to his friend, as their trunks were tossed to the ebony roof of the limousine. "Sorry we had to bring you this far in that buggy, but of course it wouldn't do for the people on the train or those God-forsaken fellas in Fish to see this automobile."

"Gosh! What a car!" This ejaculation was provoked by its interior. John saw that the upholstery consisted of a thousand minute and exquisite tapestries of silk, woven with jewels and embroideries, and set upon a background of cloth of gold. The two armchair seats in which the boys luxuriated were covered with stuff that resembled duvetyn, but seemed woven in numberless colors of the ends of ostrich feathers.

"What a car!" cried John again, in amazement.

"This thing?" Percy laughed. "Why, it's just an old junk we use for a station wagon."

By this time they were gliding along through the darkness toward the break between the two mountains.

"We'll be there in an hour and a half," said Percy, looking at the clock. "I may as well tell you it's not going to be like anything you ever saw before."

If the car was any indication of what John would see, he was prepared to be astonished indeed. The simple piety prevalent in Hades has the earnest worship of and respect for riches as the first article of its creed—had John felt otherwise than radiantly humble before them, his parents would have turned away in horror at the blasphemy.

They had now reached and were entering the break between the two mountains and almost immediately the way became much rougher.

"If the moon shone down here, you'd see that we're in a big gulch," said Percy, trying to peer out of the window. He spoke a few words into the mouthpiece and immediately the footman turned on a search-light and swept the hillsides with an immense beam.

"Rocky, you see. An ordinary car would be knocked to pieces in half an hour. In fact, it'd take a tank to navigate it unless you knew the way. You notice we're going uphill now."

They were obviously ascending, and within a few minutes the car was crossing a high rise, where they caught a glimpse of a pale moon newly risen in the distance. The car stopped suddenly and several figures took shape out of the dark beside it—these were negroes also. Again the two young men were saluted in the same dimly recognizable dialect; then the negroes set to work and four immense cables dangling from overhead were attached with hooks to the hubs of the great jeweled wheels. At a resounding "Hey-yah!" John felt the car being lifted slowly from the ground—up and up—clear of the tallest rocks on both sides—then higher, until he could see a wavy, moonlit valley stretched out before him in sharp contrast to the quagmire of rocks that they had just left. Only on one side was there still rock—and then suddenly there was no rock beside them or anywhere around.

It was apparent that they had surmounted some immense knife-blade of stone, projecting perpendicularly into the air.

In a moment they were going down again, and finally with a soft bump they were landed upon the smooth earth.

"The worst is over," said Percy, squinting out the window. "It's only five miles from here, and our own road—tapestry brick—all the way. This belongs to us. This is where the United States ends, father says."

"Are we in Canada?"

"We are not. We're in the middle of the Montana Rockies. But you are now on the only five square miles of land in the country that's never been surveyed."

"Why hasn't it? Did they forget it?"

"No," said Percy, grinning, "they tried to do it three times. The first time my grandfather corrupted a whole department of the State survey; the second time he had the official maps of the United States tinkered with—that held them for fifteen years. The last time was harder. My father fixed it so that their compasses were in the strongest magnetic field ever artificially set up. He had a whole set of surveying instruments made with a slight defection that would allow for this territory not to appear, and he substituted them for the ones that were to be used. Then he had a river deflected and he had what looked like a village built up on its banks—so that they'd see it, and think it was a town ten miles farther up the valley. There's only one thing my father's afraid of," he concluded, "only one thing in the world that could be used to find us out."

"What's that?"

Percy sank his voice to a whisper.

"Aeroplanes," he breathed. "We've got half a dozen anti-aircraft guns and we've arranged it so far—but there've been a few deaths and a great many prisoners. Not that we mind *that*, you know, father and I, but it upsets mother and the girls, and there's always the chance that some time we won't be able to arrange it."

Shreds and tatters of chinchilla, courtesy clouds in the green moon's heaven, were passing the green moon like precious Eastern stuffs paraded for the inspection of some Tartar Khan. It seemed to John that it was day, and that he was looking at some lads sailing above him in the air, showering down tracts and patent medicine circulars, with their messages of hope for despairing, rock-bound hamlets. It seemed to him that he could see them look down out of the clouds and stare—and stare at whatever there was to stare at in this place whither he was bound— What then? Were they induced to land by some insidious device there to be immured far from patent medicines and from tracts until the judgment day—or, should they fail to fall into the trap, did a quick puff of smoke and the sharp round of a splitting shell bring them drooping to earth—and "upset" Percy's mother and sisters. John shook his head and the wraith of a hollow laugh issued silently from his parted lips. What desperate transaction lay hidden here? What a moral expedient of a bizarre Crœsus? What terrible and golden mystery? . . .

The chinchilla clouds had drifted past now and outside the Montana night was bright as day. The tapestry brick of the road was smooth to the tread of the great tires as they rounded a still, moonlit lake; they passed into darkness for a moment, a pine grove, pungent and cool, then they came out into a broad avenue of lawn and John's exclamation of pleasure was simultaneous with Percy's taciturn "We're home."

Full in the light of the stars, an exquisite château rose from the borders of the lake, climbed in marble radiance half the height of an adjoining mountain, then melted in grace, in perfect symmetry, in translucent feminine languor, into the massed darkness of a forest of pine. The many towers, the slender tracery of the sloping parapets, the chiselled wonder of a thousand yellow windows with their oblongs and hectagons and triangles of golden light, the shattered softness of the intersecting planes of star-shine and blue shade, all trembled on John's spirit like a chord of music. On one of the towers, the tallest, the blackest at its base, an arrangement of exterior lights at the top made a sort of floating fairyland—and as John gazed up in warm enchantment the faint acciaccare sound of violins drifted down in a rococo harmony that was like nothing he had ever heard before. Then in a moment the car stopped before wide, high marble steps around which the night air was fragrant with a host of flowers. At the top of the steps two great doors swung silently open and amber light flooded out upon the darkness, silhouetting the figure of an exquisite lady with black, high-piled hair, who held out her arms toward them.

"Mother," Percy was saying, "this is my friend, John Unger, from Hades."

Afterward John remembered that first night as a daze of many colors, of quick sensory impressions, of music soft as a voice in love, and of the beauty of things, lights and shadows, and motions and faces. There was a white-haired man who stood drinking a many-hued cordial from a crystal thimble set on a golden stem. There was a girl with a flowery face, dressed like Titania with braided sapphires in her hair. There was a room where the solid, soft gold of the walls yielded to the pressure of his hand, and a room that was like a platonic conception of the ultimate prison—ceiling, floor, and all, it was lined with an unbroken mass of diamonds, diamonds of every size and shape, until, lit with tall violet lamps in the corners, it dazzled the eyes with a whiteness that could be compared only with itself, beyond human wish or dream.

Through a maze of these rooms the two boys wandered. Sometimes the floor under their feet would flame in brilliant patterns from lighting below, patterns of barbaric clashing colors, of pastel delicacy, of sheer whiteness, or of subtle and intricate mosaic, surely from some mosque on the Adriatic Sea. Sometimes beneath layers of thick crystal he would see blue or green water swirling, inhabited by vivid fish and growths of rainbow foliage. Then they would be treading on furs of every texture and color or along corridors of palest ivory, unbroken as though carved complete from the gigantic tusks of dinosaurs extinct before the age of man. . . .

Then a hazily remembered transition, and they were at dinner—where each plate was of two almost imperceptible layers of solid diamond between which was curiously worked a filigree of emerald design, a shaving sliced from green air. Music, plangent and unobtrusive, drifted down through far corridors—his chair, feathered and curved insidiously to his back, seemed to engulf and overpower him as he drank his first glass of port. He tried drowsily to answer a question that had been asked him, but the honeyed luxury that clasped his body added to the illusion of sleep—jewels, fabrics, wines, and metals blurred before his eyes into a sweet mist. . . .

"Yes," he replied with a polite effort, "it certainly is hot enough for me down there."

He managed to add a ghostly laugh; then, without movement, without resistance, he seemed to float off and away, leaving an iced dessert that was pink as a dream. . . . He fell asleep.

When he awoke he knew that several hours had passed. He was in a great quiet room with ebony walls and a dull illumination that was too faint, too subtle, to be called a light. His young host was standing over him.

"You fell asleep at dinner," Percy was saying. "I nearly did, too—it was such a treat to be comfortable again after this year of school. Servants undressed and bathed you while you were sleeping."

"Is this a bed or a cloud?" sighed John. "Percy, Percy—before you go, I want to apologize."

"For what?"

"For doubting you when you said you had a diamond as big as the Ritz-Carlton Hotel."

Percy smiled.

"I thought you didn't believe me. It's that mountain, you know."

"What mountain?"

"The mountain the château rests on. It's not very big, for a mountain. But except about fifty feet of sod and gravel on top it's solid diamond. *One* diamond, one cubic mile without a flaw. Aren't you listening? Say——"

But John T. Unger had again fallen asleep.

III

Morning. As he awoke he perceived drowsily that the room had at the same moment become dense with sunlight. The ebony panels of one wall had slid aside on a sort of track, leaving his chamber half open to the day. A large negro in a white uniform stood beside his bed.

"Good-evening," muttered John, summoning his brains from the wild places.

"Good-morning, sir. Are you ready for your bath, sir? Oh, don't get up—I'll put you in, if you'll just unbutton your pajamas—there. Thank you, sir."

John lay quietly as his pajamas were removed—he was amused and delighted; he expected to be lifted like a child by this black Gargantua who was tending him, but nothing of the sort happened; instead he felt the bed tilt up slowly on its side—he began to roll, startled at first, in the direction of the wall, but when he reached the wall its drapery gave way, and sliding two yards farther down a fleecy incline he plumped gently into water the same temperature as his body.

He looked about him. The runway or rollway on which he had arrived had folded gently back into place. He had been projected into another chamber and was sitting in a sunken bath with his head just above the level of the floor. All about him, lining the walls of the room and the sides and bottom of the bath itself, was a blue aquarium, and gazing through the crystal surface on which he sat, he could see fish swimming among amber lights and even gliding without curiosity past his outstretched toes, which were separated from them only by the thickness of the crystal. From overhead, sunlight came down through sea-green glass.

"I suppose, sir, that you'd like hot rosewater and soapsuds this morning, sir—and perhaps cold salt water to finish."

The negro was standing beside him.

"Yes," agreed John, smiling inanely, "as you please." Any idea of ordering this bath according to his own meagre standards of living would have been priggish and not a little wicked.

The negro pressed a button and a warm rain began to fall, apparently from overhead, but really, so John discovered after a moment, from a fountain arrangement near by. The water turned to a pale rose color and jets of liquid soap spurted into it from four miniature walrus heads at the corners of the bath. In a moment a dozen little paddle-wheels, fixed to the sides, had churned the mixture into a radiant rainbow of pink foam which enveloped him softly with its delicious lightness, and burst in shining, rosy bubbles here and there about him.

"Shall I turn on the moving-picture machine, sir?" suggested the negro deferentially. "There's a good one-reel comedy in this machine to-day, or I can put in a serious piece in a moment, if you prefer it."

"No, thanks," answered John, politely but firmly. He was enjoying his bath too much to desire any distraction. But distraction came. In a moment he was listening intently to the sound of flutes from just outside, flutes dripping a melody that was like a waterfall, cool and green as the room itself, accompanying a frothy piccolo, in play more fragile than the lace of suds that covered and charmed him.

After a cold salt-water bracer and a cold fresh finish, he stepped out and into a fleecy robe, and upon a couch covered with the same material he was rubbed with oil, alcohol, and spice. Later he sat in a voluptuous chair while he was shaved and his hair was trimmed.

"Mr. Percy is waiting in your sitting-room," said the negro, when these operations were finished. "My name is Gygsum, Mr. Unger, sir. I am to see to Mr. Unger every morning."

John walked out into the brisk sunshine of his living-room, where he found breakfast waiting for him and Percy, gorgeous in white kid knickerbockers, smoking in an easy chair.

IV

This is a story of the Washington family as Percy sketched it for John during breakfast.

The father of the present Mr. Washington had been a Virginian, a direct descendant of George Washington, and Lord Baltimore. At the close of the Civil War he was a twenty-five-year-old Colonel with a played-out plantation and about a thousand dollars in gold.

Fitz-Norman Culpepper Washington, for that was the young Colonel's name, decided to present the Virginia estate to his younger brother and go West. He selected two dozen of the most faithful blacks, who, of course, worshipped him, and bought twenty-five tickets to the West, where he intended to take out land in their names and start a sheep and cattle ranch.

When he had been in Montana for less than a month and things were going very poorly indeed, he stumbled on his great discovery. He had lost his way when riding in the hills, and after a day without food he began to grow hungry. As he was without his rifle, he was forced to pursue a squirrel, and in the course of the pursuit he noticed that it was carrying something shiny in its mouth. Just before it vanished into its hole—for Providence did not intend that this squirrel should alleviate his hunger—it dropped its burden. Sitting down to consider the situation Fitz-Norman's eye was caught by a gleam in the grass beside him. In ten seconds he had completely lost his appetite and gained one hundred thousand dollars. The squirrel, which had refused with annoying persistence to become food, had made him a present of a large and perfect diamond.

Late that night he found his way to camp and twelve hours later all the males among his darkies were back by the squirrel hole digging furiously at the side of the mountain. He told them he had discovered a rhinestone mine, and, as only one or two of them had ever seen even a small diamond before, they believed him, without question. When the magnitude of his discovery became apparent to him, he found himself in a quandary. The mountain was *a* diamond—it was literally nothing else but solid diamond. He filled four saddle bags full of glittering samples and started on horseback for St. Paul. There he managed to dispose of half a dozen small stones—when he tried a larger one a storekeeper fainted and Fitz-Norman was arrested as a public disturber. He escaped from jail and caught the train for New York, where he sold a few medium-sized diamonds and received in exchange about two hundred thousand dollars in gold. But he did not dare to produce any exceptional gems—in fact, he left New York just in time. Tremendous excitement had been created in jewelry circles, not so much by the size of his diamonds as by their appearance in the city from mysterious sources. Wild rumors became current that a diamond mine had been discovered in the Catskills, on the Jersey coast, on Long Island, beneath Washington Square. Excursion trains, packed with men carrying picks and shovels, began to leave New York hourly, bound for various neighboring El Dorados. But by that time young Fitz-Norman was on his way back to Montana.

By the end of a fortnight he had estimated that the diamond in the mountain was approximately equal in quantity to all the rest of the diamonds known to exist in the world. There was no valuing it by any regular computation, however, for it was *one solid diamond*—and if it were offered for sale not only would the bottom fall out of the market, but also, if the value should vary with its size in the usual arithmetical progression, there would not be enough gold in the world to buy a tenth part of it. And what could any one do with a diamond that size?

It was an amazing predicament. He was, in one sense, the richest man that ever lived—and yet was he worth anything at all? If his secret should transpire there was no telling to what measures the Government might resort in order to prevent a panic, in gold as well as in jewels. They might take over the claim immediately and institute a monopoly.

There was no alternative—he must market his mountain in secret. He sent South for his younger brother and put him in charge of his colored following—darkies who had never realized that slavery was abolished. To make sure of this, he read them a proclamation that he had composed, which announced that General Forrest had reorganized the shattered Southern armies and defeated the North in one pitched battle. The negroes believed him implicitly. They passed a vote declaring it a good thing and held revival services immediately.

Fitz-Norman himself set out for foreign parts with one hundred thousand dollars and two trunks filled with rough diamonds of all sizes. He sailed for Russia in a Chinese junk and six months after his departure from Montana he was in St. Petersburg. He took obscure lodgings and called immediately upon the court jeweller, announcing that he had a diamond for the Czar. He remained in St. Petersburg for two weeks, in constant danger of being murdered, living from lodging to lodging, and afraid to visit his trunks more than three or four times during the whole fortnight.

On his promise to return in a year with larger and finer stones, he was allowed to leave for India. Before he left, however, the Court Treasurers had deposited to his credit, in American banks, the sum of fifteen million dollars—under four different aliases.

He returned to America in 1868, having been gone a little over two years. He had visited the capitals of twenty-two countries and talked with five emperors, eleven kings, three princes, a shah, a khan, and a sultan. At that time Fitz-Norman estimated his own wealth at one billion dollars. One fact worked consistently against the disclosure of his secret. No one of his larger diamonds remained in the public eye for a week before being invested with a history of enough fatalities, amours, revolutions, and wars to have occupied it from the days of the first Babylonian Empire.

From 1870 until his death in 1900, the history of Fitz-Norman Washington was a long epic in gold. There were side issues, of course—he evaded the surveys, he married a Virginia lady, by whom he had a single son, and he was compelled, due to a series of unfortunate complications, to murder his brother, whose unfortunate habit of drinking himself into an indiscreet stupor had several times endangered their safety. But very few other murders stained these happy years of progress and expansion.

Just before he died he changed his policy, and with all but a few million dollars of his outside wealth bought up rare minerals in bulk, which he deposited in the safety vaults of banks all over the world, marked as bric-à-brac. His son, Braddock Tarleton Washington, followed this policy on an even more tensive scale. The minerals were converted into the rarest of all elements—radium—so that the equivalent of a billion dollars in gold could be placed in a receptacle no bigger than a cigar box.

When Fitz-Norman had been dead three years his son, Braddock, decided that the business had gone far enough. The amount of wealth that he and his father had taken out of the mountain was beyond all exact computation. He kept a note-book in cipher in which he set down the approximate quantity of radium in each of the thousand banks he patronized, and recorded the alias under which it was held. Then he did a very simple thing—he sealed up the mine.

He sealed up the mine. What had been taken out of it would support all the Washingtons yet to be born in unparalleled luxury for generations. His one care must be the protection of his secret, lest in the possible panic attendant on its discovery he should be reduced with all the property-holders in the world to utter poverty.

This was the family among whom John T. Unger was staying. This was the story he heard in his silver-walled living-room the morning after his arrival.

V

After breakfast, John found his way out the great marble entrance, and looked curiously at the scene before him. The whole valley, from the diamond mountain to the steep granite cliff five miles away, still gave off a breath of golden haze which hovered idly above the fine sweep of lawns and lakes and gardens. Here and there clusters of elms made delicate groves of shade, contrasting strangely with the tough masses of pine forest that held the hills in a grip of dark-blue green. Even as John looked he saw three fawns in single file patter out from one clump about a half mile away and disappear with awkward gayety into the black-ribbed half-light of another. John would not have been surprised to see a goat-foot piping his way among the trees or to catch a glimpse of pink nymph-skin and flying yellow hair between the greenest of the green leaves.

In some such cool hope he descended the marble steps, disturbing faintly the sleep of two silky Russian wolfhounds at the bottom, and set off along a walk of white and blue brick that seemed to lead in no particular direction.

He was enjoying himself as much as he was able. It is youth's felicity as well as its insufficiency that it can never live in the present, but must always be measuring up the day against its own radiantly imagined future—flowers and gold, girls and stars, they are only prefigurations and prophecies of that incomparable, unattainable young dream.

John rounded a soft corner where the massed rose-bushes filled the air with heavy scent, and struck off across a park toward a patch of moss under some trees. He had never lain upon moss, and he wanted to see whether it was really soft enough to justify the use of its name as an adjective. Then he saw a girl coming toward him over the grass. She was the most beautiful person he had ever seen.

She was dressed in a white little gown that came just below her knees, and a wreath of mignonettes clasped with blue slices of sapphire bound up her hair. Her pink bare feet scattered the dew before them as she came. She was younger than John—not more than sixteen.

"Hello," she cried softly, "I'm Kismine."

She was much more than that to John already. He advanced toward her, scarcely moving as he drew near lest he should tread on her bare toes.

"You haven't met me," said her soft voice. Her blue eyes added, "Oh, but you've missed a great deal!" . . . "You met my sister, Jasmine, last night. I was sick with lettuce poisoning," went on her soft voice, and her eyes continued, "and when I'm sick I'm sweet—and when I'm well."

"You have made an enormous impression on me," said John's eyes, "and I'm not so slow myself"—"How do you do?" said his voice. "I hope you're better this morning."—"You darling," added his eyes tremulously.

John observed that they had been walking along the path. On her suggestion they sat down together upon the moss, the softness of which he failed to determine.

He was critical about women. A single defect—a thick ankle, a hoarse voice, a glass eye—was enough to make him utterly indifferent. And here for the first time in his life he was beside a girl who seemed to him the incarnation of physical perfection.

"Are you from the East?" asked Kismine with charming interest.

"No," answered John simply. "I'm from Hades."

Either she had never heard of Hades, or she could think of no pleasant comment to make upon it, for she did not discuss it further.

"I'm going East to school this fall," she said. "D'you think I'll like it? I'm going to New York to Miss Bulge's. It's very strict, but you see over the week-ends I'm going to live at home with the family in our New York house, because father heard that the girls had to go walking two by two."

"Your father wants you to be proud," observed John.

"We are," she answered, her eyes shining with dignity. "None of us has ever been punished. Father said we never should be. Once when my sister Jasmine was a little girl she pushed him down-stairs and he just got up and limped away.

"Mother was—well, a little startled," continued Kismine, "when she heard that you were from—from where you *are* from, you know. She said that when she was a young girl—but then, you see, she's a Spaniard and old-fashioned."

"Do you spend much time out here?" asked John, to conceal the fact that he was somewhat hurt by this remark. It seemed an unkind allusion to his provincialism.

"Percy and Jasmine and I are here every summer, but next summer Jasmine is going to Newport. She's coming out in London a year from this fall. She'll be presented at court."

"Do you know," began John hesitantly, "you're much more sophisticated than I thought you were when I first saw you?"

"Oh, no, I'm not," she exclaimed hurriedly. "Oh, I wouldn't think of being. I think that sophisticated young people are *terribly* common, don't you? I'm not at all, really. If you say I am, I'm going to cry."

She was so distressed that her lip was trembling. John was impelled to protest:

"I didn't mean that; I only said it to tease you."

"Because I wouldn't mind if I *were*," she persisted, "but I'm *not*. I'm very innocent and girlish. I never smoke, or drink, or read anything except poetry. I know scarcely any mathematics or chemistry. I dress *very* simply—in fact, I scarcely dress at all. I think sophisticated is the last thing you can say about me. I believe that girls ought to enjoy their youths in a wholesome way."

"I do, too," said John heartily.

Kismine was cheerful again. She smiled at him, and a still-born tear dripped from the corner of one blue eye.

"I like you," she whispered, intimately. "Are you going to spend all your time with Percy while you're here, or will you be nice to me? Just think—I'm absolutely fresh ground. I've never had a boy in love with me in all my life. I've never been allowed even to *see* boys alone—except Percy. I came all the way out here into this grove hoping to run into you, where the family wouldn't be around."

Deeply flattered, John bowed from the hips as he had been taught at dancing school in Hades.

"We'd better go now," said Kismine sweetly. "I have to be

with mother at eleven. You haven't asked me to kiss you once. I thought boys always did that nowadays."

John drew himself up proudly.

"Some of them do," he answered, "but not me. Girls don't do that sort of thing—in Hades."

Side by side they walked back toward the house.

VI

John stood facing Mr. Braddock Washington in the full sunlight. The elder man was about forty with a proud, vacuous face, intelligent eyes, and a robust figure. In the mornings he smelt of horses—the best horses. He carried a plain walking-stick of gray birch with a single large opal for a grip. He and Percy were showing John around.

"The slaves' quarters are there." His walking-stick indicated a cloister of marble on their left that ran in graceful Gothic along the side of the mountain. "In my youth I was distracted for a while from the business of life by a period of absurd idealism. During that time they lived in luxury. For instance, I equipped every one of their rooms with a tile bath."

"I suppose," ventured John, with an ingratiating laugh, "that they used the bathtubs to keep coal in. Mr. Schnlitzer-Murphy told me that once he——"

"The opinions of Mr. Schnlitzer-Murphy are of little importance, I should imagine," interrupted Braddock Washington, coldly. "My slaves did not keep coal in their bathtubs. They had orders to bathe every day, and they did. If they hadn't I might have ordered a sulphuric acid shampoo. I discontinued the baths for quite another reason. Several of them caught cold and died. Water is not good for certain races—except as a beverage."

John laughed, and then decided to nod his head in sober agreement. Braddock Washington made him uncomfortable.

"All these negroes are descendants of the ones my father brought North with him. There are about two hundred and fifty now. You notice that they've lived so long apart from the world that their original dialect has become an almost indistinguishable patois. We bring a few of them up to speak English—my secretary and two or three of the house servants.

"This is the golf course," he continued, as they strolled along the velvet winter grass. "It's all a green, you see—no fairway, no rough, no hazards."

He smiled pleasantly at John.

"Many men in the cage, father?" asked Percy suddenly.

Braddock Washington stumbled, and let forth an involuntary curse.

"One less than there should be," he ejaculated darkly—and then added after a moment, "We've had difficulties."

"Mother was telling me," exclaimed Percy, "that Italian teacher——"

"A ghastly error," said Braddock Washington angrily. "But of course there's a good chance that we may have got him. Perhaps he fell somewhere in the woods or stumbled over a cliff. And then there's always the probability that if he did get away his story wouldn't be believed. Nevertheless, I've had two dozen men looking for him in different towns around here."

"And no luck?"

"Some. Fourteen of them reported to my agent that they'd each killed a man answering to that description, but of course it was probably only the reward they were after——"

He broke off. They had come to a large cavity in the earth about the circumference of a merry-go-round and covered by a strong iron grating. Braddock Washington beckoned to John, and pointed his cane down through the grating. John stepped to the edge and gazed. Immediately his ears were assailed by a wild clamor from below.

"Come on down to Hell!"

"Hello, kiddo, how's the air up there?"

"Hey! Throw us a rope!"

"Got an old doughnut, Buddy, or a couple of second-hand sandwiches?"

"Say, fella, if you'll push down that guy you're with, we'll show you a quick disappearance scene."

"Paste him one for me, will you?"

It was too dark to see clearly into the pit below, but John could tell from the coarse optimism and rugged vitality of the remarks and voices that they proceeded from middle-class Americans of the more spirited type. Then Mr. Washington put out his cane and touched a button in the grass, and the scene below sprang into light.

"These are some adventurous mariners who had the misfortune to discover El Dorado," he remarked.

Below them there had appeared a large hollow in the earth shaped like the interior of a bowl. The sides were steep and apparently of polished glass, and on its slightly concave surface stood about two dozen men clad in the half costume, half uniform, of aviators. Their up-turned faces, lit with wrath, with malice, with despair, with cynical humor, were covered by long growths of beard, but with the exception of a few who had pined perceptibly away, they seemed to be a well-fed, healthy lot.

Braddock Washington drew a garden chair to the edge of the pit and sat down.

"Well, how are you, boys?" he inquired genially.

A chorus of execration in which all joined except a few too dispirited to cry out, rose up into the sunny air, but Braddock Washington heard it with unruffled composure. When its last echo had died away he spoke again.

"Have you thought up a way out of your difficulty?"

From here and there among them a remark floated up.

"We decided to stay here for love!"

"Bring us up there and we'll find us a way!"

Braddock Washington waited until they were again quiet. Then he said:

"I've told you the situation. I don't want you here. I wish to heaven I'd never seen you. Your own curiosity got you here, and any time that you can think of a way out which protects me and my interests I'll be glad to consider it. But so long as you confine your efforts to digging tunnels—yes, I know about the new one you've started—you won't get very far. This isn't as hard on you as you make it out, with all your howling for the loved ones at home. If you were the type who worried much about the loved ones at home, you'd never have taken up aviation."

A tall man moved apart from the others, and held up his hand to call his captor's attention to what he was about to say.

"Let me ask you a few questions!" he cried. "You pretend to be a fair-minded man."

"How absurd. How could a man of *my* position be fair-minded toward *you*? You might as well speak of a Spaniard being fair-minded toward a piece of steak."

At this harsh observation the faces of the two dozen steaks fell, but the tall man continued:

"All right!" he cried. "We've argued this out before. You're not a humanitarian and you're not fair-minded, but you're human—at least you say you are—and you ought to be able to put yourself in our place for long enough to think how—how—how——"

"How what?" demanded Washington, coldly.

"—how unnecessary——"

"Not to me."

"Well,—how cruel——"

"We've covered that. Cruelty doesn't exist where self-preservation is involved. You've been soldiers; you know that. Try another."

"Well, then, how stupid."

"There," admitted Washington, "I grant you that. But try to think of an alternative. I've offered to have all or any of you painlessly executed if you wish. I've offered to have your wives, sweethearts, children, and mothers kidnapped and brought out here. I'll enlarge your place down there and feed and clothe you the rest of your lives. If there was some method of producing permanent amnesia I'd have all of you operated on and released immediately, somewhere outside of my preserves. But that's as far as my ideas go."

"How about trusting us not to peach on you?" cried some one.

"You don't proffer that suggestion seriously," said Washington, with an expression of scorn. "I did take out one man to teach my daughter Italian. Last week he got away."

A wild yell of jubilation went up suddenly from two dozen throats and a pandemonium of joy ensued. The prisoners clog-danced and cheered and yodeled and wrestled with one another in a sudden uprush of animal spirits. They even ran up the glass sides of the bowl as far as they could, and slid back to the bottom upon the natural cushions of their bodies. The tall man started a song in which they all joined——

"Oh, we'll hang the kaiser
On a sour apple tree——"

Braddock Washington sat in inscrutable silence until the song was over.

"You see," he remarked, when he could gain a modicum of attention. "I bear you no ill-will. I like to see you enjoying yourselves. That's why I didn't tell you the whole story at once. The man—what was his name? Critchtichiello?—was shot by some of my agents in fourteen different places."

Not guessing that the places referred to were cities, the tumult of rejoicing subsided immediately.

"Nevertheless," cried Washington with a touch of anger, "he tried to run away. Do you expect me to take chances with any of you after an experience like that?"

Again a series of ejaculations went up.

"Sure!"

"Would your daughter like to learn Chinese?"

"Hey, I can speak Italian! My mother was a wop."

"Maybe she'd like t'learna speak N'Yawk!"

"If she's the little one with the big blue eyes I can teach her a lot of things better than Italian."

"I know some Irish songs—and I could hammer brass once't."

Mr. Washington reached forward suddenly with his cane and pushed the button in the grass so that the picture below went out instantly, and there remained only that great dark mouth covered dismally with the black teeth of the grating.

"Hey!" called a single voice from below, "you ain't goin' away without givin' us your blessing?"

But Mr. Washington, followed by the two boys, was already strolling on toward the ninth hole of the golf course, as though the pit and its contents were no more than a hazard over which his facile iron had triumphed with ease.

VII

July under the lee of the diamond mountain was a month of blanket nights and of warm, glowing days. John and

Kismine were in love. He did not know that the little gold football (inscribed with the legend *Pro deo et patria et St. Mida*) which he had given her rested on a platinum chain next to her bosom. But it did. And she for her part was not aware that a large sapphire which had dropped one day from her simple coiffure was stowed away tenderly in John's jewel box.

Late one afternoon when the ruby and ermine music room was quiet, they spent an hour there together. He held her hand and she gave him such a look that he whispered her name aloud. She bent toward him—then hesitated.

"Did you say 'Kismine'?" she asked softly, "or——"

She had wanted to be sure. She thought she might have misunderstood.

Neither of them had ever kissed before, but in the course of an hour it seemed to make little difference.

The afternoon drifted away. That night when a last breath of music drifted down from the highest tower, they each lay awake, happily dreaming over the separate minutes of the day. They had decided to be married as soon as possible.

VIII

Every day Mr. Washington and the two young men went hunting or fishing in the deep forests or played golf around the somnolent course—games which John diplomatically allowed his host to win—or swam in the mountain coolness of the lake. John found Mr. Washington a somewhat exacting personality—utterly uninterested in any ideas or opinions except his own. Mrs. Washington was aloof and reserved at all times. She was apparently indifferent to her two daughters, and entirely absorbed in her son Percy, with whom she held interminable conversations in rapid Spanish at dinner.

Jasmine, the elder daughter, resembled Kismine in appearance—except that she was somewhat bow-legged, and terminated in large hands and feet—but was utterly unlike her in temperament. Her favorite books had to do with poor girls who kept house for widowed fathers. John learned from Kismine that Jasmine had never recovered from the shock and disappointment caused her by the termination of the World

War, just as she was about to start for Europe as a canteen expert. She had even pined away for a time, and Braddock Washington had taken steps to promote a new war in the Balkans—but she had seen a photograph of some wounded Serbian soldiers and lost interest in the whole proceedings. But Percy and Kismine seemed to have inherited the arrogant attitude in all its harsh magnificence from their father. A chaste and consistent selfishness ran like a pattern through their every idea.

John was enchanted by the wonders of the château and the valley. Braddock Washington, so Percy told him, had caused to be kidnapped a landscape gardener, an architect, a designer of stage settings, and a French decadent poet left over from the last century. He had put his entire force of negroes at their disposal, guaranteed to supply them with any materials that the world could offer, and left them to work out some ideas of their own. But one by one they had shown their uselessness. The decadent poet had at once begun bewailing his separation from the boulevards in spring—he made some vague remarks about spices, apes, and ivories, but said nothing that was of any practical value. The stage designer on his part wanted to make the whole valley a series of tricks and sensational effects—a state of things that the Washingtons would soon have grown tired of. And as for the architect and the landscape gardener, they thought only in terms of convention. They must make this like this and that like that.

But they had, at least, solved the problem of what was to be done with them—they all went mad early one morning after spending the night in a single room trying to agree upon the location of a fountain, and were now confined comfortably in an insane asylum at Westport, Connecticut.

"But," inquired John curiously, "who did plan all your wonderful reception rooms and halls, and approaches and bathrooms——?"

"Well," answered Percy, "I blush to tell you, but it was a moving-picture fella. He was the only man we found who was used to playing with an unlimited amount of money, though he did tuck his napkin in his collar and couldn't read or write."

As August drew to a close John began to regret that he

must soon go back to school. He and Kismine had decided to elope the following June.

"It would be nicer to be married here," Kismine confessed, "but of course I could never get father's permission to marry you at all. Next to that I'd rather elope. It's terrible for wealthy people to be married in America at present—they always have to send out bulletins to the press saying that they're going to be married in remnants, when what they mean is just a peck of old second-hand pearls and some used lace worn once by the Empress Eugénie."

"I know," agreed John fervently. "When I was visiting the Schnlitzer-Murphys, the eldest daughter, Gwendolyn, married a man whose father owns half of West Virginia. She wrote home saying what a tough struggle she was carrying on on his salary as a bank clerk—and then she ended up by saying that 'Thank God, I have four good maids anyhow, and that helps a little.' "

"It's absurd," commented Kismine. "Think of the millions and millions of people in the world, laborers and all, who get along with only two maids."

One afternoon late in August a chance remark of Kismine's changed the face of the entire situation, and threw John into a state of terror.

They were in their favorite grove, and between kisses John was indulging in some romantic forebodings which he fancied added poignancy to their relations.

"Sometimes I think we'll never marry," he said sadly. "You're too wealthy, too magnificent. No one as rich as you are can be like other girls. I should marry the daughter of some well-to-do wholesale hardware man from Omaha or Sioux City, and be content with her half-million."

"I knew the daughter of a wholesale hardware man once," remarked Kismine. "I don't think you'd have been contented with her. She was a friend of my sister's. She visited here."

"Oh, then you've had other guests?" exclaimed John in surprise.

Kismine seemed to regret her words.

"Oh, yes," she said hurriedly, "we've had a few."

"But aren't you—wasn't your father afraid they'd talk outside?"

"Oh, to some extent, to some extent," she answered. "Let's talk about something pleasanter."

But John's curiosity was aroused.

"Something pleasanter!" he demanded. "What's unpleasant about that? Weren't they nice girls?"

To his great surprise Kismine began to weep.

"Yes—th—that's the—the whole t-trouble. I grew qu-quite attached to some of them. So did Jasmine, but she kept in-v-viting them anyway. I couldn't under*stand* it."

A dark suspicion was born in John's heart.

"Do you mean that they *told*, and your father had them—removed?"

"Worse than that," she muttered brokenly. "Father took no chances—and Jasmine kept writing them to come, and they had *such* a good time!"

She was overcome by a paroxysm of grief.

Stunned with the horror of this revelation, John sat there open-mouthed, feeling the nerves of his body twitter like so many sparrows perched upon his spinal column.

"Now, I've told you, and I shouldn't have," she said, calming suddenly and drying her dark blue eyes.

"Do you mean to say that your father had them *murdered* before they left?"

She nodded.

"In August usually—or early in September. It's only natural for us to get all the pleasure out of them that we can first."

"How abominable! How—why, I must be going crazy! Did you really admit that——"

"I did," interrupted Kismine, shrugging her shoulders. "We can't very well imprison them like those aviators, where they'd be a continual reproach to us every day. And it's always been made easier for Jasmine and me, because father had it done sooner than we expected. In that way we avoided any farewell scene——"

"So you murdered them! Uh!" cried John.

"It was done very nicely. They were drugged while they were asleep—and their families were always told that they died of scarlet fever in Butte."

"But—I fail to understand why you kept on inviting them!"

"I didn't," burst out Kismine. "I never invited one. Jasmine did. And they always had a very good time. She'd give them the nicest presents toward the last. I shall probably have visitors too—I'll harden up to it. We can't let such an inevitable thing as death stand in the way of enjoying life while we have it. Think how lonesome it'd be out here if we never had *any* one. Why, father and mother have sacrificed some of their best friends just as we have."

"And so," cried John accusingly, "and so you were letting me make love to you and pretending to return it, and talking about marriage, all the time knowing perfectly well that I'd never get out of here alive——"

"No," she protested passionately. "Not any more. I did at first. You were here. I couldn't help that, and I thought your last days might as well be pleasant for both of us. But then I fell in love with you, and—and I'm honestly sorry you're going to—going to be put away—though I'd rather you'd be put away than ever kiss another girl."

"Oh, you would, would you?" cried John ferociously.

"Much rather. Besides, I've always heard that a girl can have more fun with a man whom she knows she can never marry. Oh, why did I tell you? I've probably spoiled your whole good time now, and we were really enjoying things when you didn't know it. I knew it would make things sort of depressing for you."

"Oh, you did, did you?" John's voice trembled with anger. "I've heard about enough of this. If you haven't any more pride and decency than to have an affair with a fellow that you know isn't much better than a corpse, I don't want to have any more to do with you!"

"You're not a corpse!" she protested in horror. "You're not a corpse! I won't have you saying that I kissed a corpse!"

"I said nothing of the sort!"

"You did! You said I kissed a corpse!"

"I didn't!"

Their voices had risen, but upon a sudden interruption they both subsided into immediate silence. Footsteps were coming along the path in their direction, and a moment later the rose bushes were parted displaying Braddock Washington, whose intelligent eyes set in his good-looking vacuous face were peering in at them.

"Who kissed a corpse?" he demanded in obvious disapproval.

"Nobody," answered Kismine quickly. "We were just joking."

"What are you two doing here, anyhow?" he demanded gruffly. "Kismine, you ought to be—to be reading or playing golf with your sister. Go read! Go play golf! Don't let me find you here when I come back!"

Then he bowed at John and went up the path.

"See?" said Kismine crossly, when he was out of hearing. "You've spoiled it all. We can never meet any more. He won't let me meet you. He'd have you poisoned if he thought we were in love."

"We're not, any more!" cried John fiercely, "so he can set his mind at rest upon that. Moreover, don't fool yourself that I'm going to stay around here. Inside of six hours I'll be over those mountains, if I have to gnaw a passage through them, and on my way East."

They had both got to their feet, and at this remark Kismine came close and put her arm through his.

"I'm going, too."

"You must be crazy——"

"Of course I'm going," she interrupted impatiently.

"You most certainly are not. You——"

"Very well," she said quietly, "we'll catch up with father now and talk it over with him."

Defeated, John mustered a sickly smile.

"Very well, dearest," he agreed, with pale and unconvincing affection, "we'll go together."

His love for her returned and settled placidly on his heart. She was his—she would go with him to share his dangers. He put his arms about her and kissed her fervently. After all she loved him; she had saved him, in fact.

Discussing the matter, they walked slowly back toward the château. They decided that since Braddock Washington had seen them together they had best depart the next night. Nevertheless, John's lips were unusually dry at dinner, and he nervously emptied a great spoonful of peacock soup into his left lung. He had to be carried into the turquoise and sable card-room and pounded on the back by one of the under-butlers, which Percy considered a great joke.

IX

Long after midnight John's body gave a nervous jerk, and he sat suddenly upright, staring into the veils of somnolence that draped the room. Through the squares of blue darkness that were his open windows, he had heard a faint far-away sound that died upon a bed of wind before identifying itself on his memory, clouded with uneasy dreams. But the sharp noise that had succeeded it was nearer, was just outside the room—the click of a turned knob, a footstep, a whisper, he could not tell; a hard lump gathered in the pit of his stomach, and his whole body ached in the moment that he strained agonizingly to hear. Then one of the veils seemed to dissolve, and he saw a vague figure standing by the door, a figure only faintly limned and blocked in upon the darkness, mingled so with the folds of the drapery as to seem distorted, like a reflection seen in a dirty pane of glass.

With a sudden movement of fright or resolution John pressed the button by his bedside, and the next moment he was sitting in the green sunken bath of the adjoining room, waked into alertness by the shock of the cold water which half filled it.

He sprang out, and, his wet pajamas scattering a heavy trickle of water behind him, ran for the aquamarine door which he knew led out onto the ivory landing of the second floor. The door opened noiselessly. A single crimson lamp burning in a great dome above lit the magnificent sweep of the carved stairways with a poignant beauty. For a moment John hesitated, appalled by the silent splendor massed about him, seeming to envelop in its gigantic folds and contours the solitary drenched little figure shivering upon the ivory landing. Then simultaneously two things happened. The door of his own sitting-room swung open, precipitating three naked negroes into the hall—and, as John swayed in wild terror toward the stairway, another door slid back in the wall on the other side of the corridor, and John saw Braddock Washington standing in the lighted lift, wearing a fur coat and a pair of riding boots which reached to his knees and displayed, above, the glow of his rose-colored pajamas.

On the instant the three negroes—John had never seen any of them before, and it flashed through his mind that they must be the professional executioners—paused in their movement toward John, and turned expectantly to the man in the lift, who burst out with an imperious command:

"Get in here! All three of you! Quick as hell!"

Then, within the instant, the three negroes darted into the cage, the oblong of light was blotted out as the lift door slid shut, and John was again alone in the hall. He slumped weakly down against an ivory stair.

It was apparent that something portentous had occurred, something which, for the moment at least, had postponed his own petty disaster. What was it? Had the negroes risen in revolt? Had the aviators forced aside the iron bars of the grating? Or had the men of Fish stumbled blindly through the hills and gazed with bleak, joyless eyes upon the gaudy valley? John did not know. He heard a faint whir of air as the lift whizzed up again, and then, a moment later, as it descended. It was probable that Percy was hurrying to his father's assistance, and it occurred to John that this was his opportunity to join Kismine and plan an immediate escape. He waited until the lift had been silent for several minutes; shivering a little with the night cool that whipped in through his wet pajamas, he returned to his room and dressed himself quickly. Then he mounted a long flight of stairs and turned down the corridor carpeted with Russian sable which led to Kismine's suite.

The door of her sitting-room was open and the lamps were lighted. Kismine, in an angora kimono, stood near the window of the room in a listening attitude, and as John entered noiselessly she turned toward him.

"Oh, it's you!" she whispered, crossing the room to him. "Did you hear them?"

"I heard your father's slaves in my——"

"No," she interrupted excitedly. "Aeroplanes!"

"Aeroplanes? Perhaps that was the sound that woke me."

"There're at least a dozen. I saw one a few moments ago

dead against the moon. The guard back by the cliff fired his rifle and that's what roused father. We're going to open on them right away."

"Are they here on purpose?"

"Yes—it's that Italian who got away——"

Simultaneously with her last word, a succession of sharp cracks tumbled in through the open window. Kismine uttered a little cry, took a penny with fumbling fingers from a box on her dresser, and ran to one of the electric lights. In an instant the entire château was in darkness—she had blown out the fuse.

"Come on!" she cried to him. "We'll go up to the roof garden, and watch it from there!"

Drawing a cape about her, she took his hand, and they found their way out the door. It was only a step to the tower lift, and as she pressed the button that shot them upward he put his arms around her in the darkness and kissed her mouth. Romance had come to John Unger at last. A minute later they had stepped out upon the star-white platform. Above, under the misty moon, sliding in and out of the patches of cloud that eddied below it, floated a dozen dark-winged bodies in a constant circling course. From here and there in the valley flashes of fire leaped toward them, followed by sharp detonations. Kismine clapped her hands with pleasure, which, a moment later, turned to dismay as the aeroplanes at some prearranged signal, began to release their bombs and the whole of the valley became a panorama of deep reverberate sound and lurid light.

Before long the aim of the attackers became concentrated upon the points where the anti-aircraft guns were situated, and one of them was almost immediately reduced to a giant cinder to lie smouldering in a park of rose bushes.

"Kismine," begged John, "you'll be glad when I tell you that this attack came on the eve of my murder. If I hadn't heard that guard shoot off his gun back by the pass I should now be stone dead——"

"I can't hear you!" cried Kismine, intent on the scene before her. "You'll have to talk louder!"

"I simply said," shouted John, "that we'd better get out before they begin to shell the château!"

Suddenly the whole portico of the negro quarters cracked asunder, a geyser of flame shot up from under the colonnades, and great fragments of jagged marble were hurled as far as the borders of the lake.

"There go fifty thousand dollars' worth of slaves," cried Kismine, "at prewar prices. So few Americans have any respect for property."

John renewed his efforts to compel her to leave. The aim of the aeroplanes was becoming more precise minute by minute, and only two of the anti-aircraft guns were still retaliating. It was obvious that the garrison, encircled with fire, could not hold out much longer.

"Come on!" cried John, pulling Kismine's arm, "we've got to go. Do you realize that those aviators will kill you without question if they find you?"

She consented reluctantly.

"We'll have to wake Jasmine!" she said, as they hurried toward the lift. Then she added in a sort of childish delight: "We'll be poor, won't we? Like people in books. And I'll be an orphan and utterly free. Free and poor! What fun!" She stopped and raised her lips to him in a delighted kiss.

"It's impossible to be both together," said John grimly. "People have found that out. And I should choose to be free as preferable of the two. As an extra caution you'd better dump the contents of your jewel box into your pockets."

Ten minutes later the two girls met John in the dark corridor and they descended to the main floor of the château. Passing for the last time through the magnificence of the splendid halls, they stood for a moment out on the terrace, watching the burning negro quarters and the flaming embers of two planes which had fallen on the other side of the lake. A solitary gun was still keeping up a sturdy popping, and the attackers seemed timorous about descending lower, but sent their thunderous fireworks in a circle around it, until any chance shot might annihilate its Ethiopian crew.

John and the two sisters passed down the marble steps, turned sharply to the left, and began to ascend a narrow path that wound like a garter about the diamond mountain. Kismine knew a heavily wooded spot half-way up where they could lie concealed and yet be able to observe the wild night in the valley—finally to make an escape, when it should be necessary, along a secret path laid in a rocky gully.

X

It was three o'clock when they attained their destination. The obliging and phlegmatic Jasmine fell off to sleep immediately, leaning against the trunk of a large tree, while John and Kismine sat, his arm around her, and watched the desperate ebb and flow of the dying battle among the ruins of a vista that had been a garden spot that morning. Shortly after four o'clock the last remaining gun gave out a clanging sound and went out of action in a swift tongue of red smoke. Though the moon was down, they saw that the flying bodies were circling closer to the earth. When the planes had made certain that the beleaguered possessed no further resources, they would land and the dark and glittering reign of the Washingtons would be over.

With the cessation of the firing the valley grew quiet. The embers of the two aeroplanes glowed like the eyes of some monster crouching in the grass. The château stood dark and silent, beautiful without light as it had been beautiful in the sun, while the woody rattles of Nemesis filled the air above with a growing and receding complaint. Then John perceived that Kismine, like her sister, had fallen sound asleep.

It was long after four when he became aware of footsteps along the path they had lately followed, and he waited in breathless silence until the persons to whom they belonged had passed the vantage-point he occupied. There was a faint stir in the air now that was not of human origin, and the dew was cold; he knew that the dawn would break soon. John waited until the steps had gone a safe distance up the mountain and were inaudible. Then he followed. About half-way to the steep summit the trees fell away and a hard saddle of rock spread itself over the diamond beneath. Just before he reached this point he slowed down his pace, warned by an animal sense that there was life just ahead of him. Coming to a high boulder, he lifted his head gradually above its edge. His curiosity was rewarded; this is what he saw:

Braddock Washington was standing there motionless, silhouetted against the gray sky without sound or sign of life. As the dawn came up out of the east, lending a cold green color to the earth, it brought the solitary figure into insignificant contrast with the new day.

While John watched, his host remained for a few moments absorbed in some inscrutable contemplation; then he signalled to the two negroes who crouched at his feet to lift the burden which lay between them. As they struggled upright, the first yellow beam of the sun struck through the innumerable prisms of an immense and exquisitely chiselled diamond—and a white radiance was kindled that glowed upon the air like a fragment of the morning star. The bearers staggered beneath its weight for a moment—then their rippling muscles caught and hardened under the wet shine of the skins and the three figures were again motionless in their defiant impotency before the heavens.

After a while the white man lifted his head and slowly raised his arms in a gesture of attention, as one who would call a great crowd to hear—but there was no crowd, only the vast silence of the mountain and the sky, broken by faint bird voices down among the trees. The figure on the saddle of rock began to speak ponderously and with an inextinguishable pride.

"You out there—" he cried in a trembling voice. "You—there—!" He paused, his arms still uplifted, his head held attentively as though he were expecting an answer. John strained his eyes to see whether there might be men coming down the mountain, but the mountain was bare of human life. There was only sky and a mocking flute of wind along the tree-tops. Could Washington be praying? For a moment John wondered. Then the illusion passed—there was something in the man's whole attitude antithetical to prayer.

"Oh, you above there!"

The voice was become strong and confident. This was no forlorn supplication. If anything, there was in it a quality of monstrous condescension.

"You there——"

Words, too quickly uttered to be understood, flowing one into the other. . . . John listened breathlessly, catching a phrase here and there, while the voice broke off, resumed, broke off again—now strong and argumentative, now colored with a slow, puzzled impatience. Then a conviction commenced to dawn on the single listener, and as realization crept over him a spray of quick blood rushed through his arteries. Braddock Washington was offering a bribe to God!

That was it—there was no doubt. The diamond in the arms of his slaves was some advance sample, a promise of more to follow.

That, John perceived after a time, was the thread running through his sentences. Prometheus Enriched was calling to witness forgotten sacrifices, forgotten rituals, prayers obsolete before the birth of Christ. For a while his discourse took the form of reminding God of this gift or that which Divinity had deigned to accept from men—great churches if he would rescue cities from the plague, gifts of myrrh and gold, of human lives and beautiful women and captive armies, of children and queens, of beasts of the forest and field, sheep and goats, harvests and cities, whole conquered lands that had been offered up in lust or blood for His appeasal, buying a meed's worth of alleviation from the Divine wrath—and now he, Braddock Washington, Emperor of Diamonds, king and priest of the age of gold, arbiter of splendor and luxury, would offer up a treasure such as princes before him had never dreamed of, offer it up not in suppliance, but in pride.

He would give to God, he continued, getting down to specifications, the greatest diamond in the world. This diamond would be cut with many more thousand facets than there were leaves on a tree, and yet the whole diamond would be shaped with the perfection of a stone no bigger than a fly. Many men would work upon it for many years. It would be set in a great dome of beaten gold, wonderfully carved and equipped with gates of opal and crusted sapphire. In the middle would be hollowed out a chapel presided over by an altar of iridescent, decomposing, ever-changing radium which would burn out the eyes of any worshipper who lifted up his head from prayer—and on this altar there would be slain for the amusement of the Divine Benefactor any victim He should choose, even though it should be the greatest and most powerful man alive.

In return he asked only a simple thing, a thing that for God would be absurdly easy—only that matters should be as they were yesterday at this hour and that they should so remain. So very simple! Let but the heavens open, swallowing these men and their aeroplanes—and then close again. Let him have his slaves once more, restored to life and well.

There was no one else with whom he had ever needed to treat or bargain.

He doubted only whether he had made his bribe big enough. God had His price, of course. God was made in man's image, so it had been said: He must have His price. And the price would be rare—no cathedral whose building consumed many years, no pyramid constructed by ten thousand workmen, would be like this cathedral, this pyramid.

He paused here. That was his proposition. Everything would be up to specifications and there was nothing vulgar in his assertion that it would be cheap at the price. He implied that Providence could take it or leave it.

As he approached the end his sentences became broken, became short and uncertain, and his body seemed tense, seemed strained to catch the slightest pressure or whisper of life in the spaces around him. His hair had turned gradually white as he talked, and now he lifted his head high to the heavens like a prophet of old—magnificently mad.

Then, as John stared in giddy fascination, it seemed to him that a curious phenomenon took place somewhere around him. It was as though the sky had darkened for an instant, as though there had been a sudden murmur in a gust of wind, a sound of far-away trumpets, a sighing like the rustle of a great silken robe—for a time the whole of nature round about partook of this darkness; the birds' song ceased; the trees were still, and far over the mountain there was a mutter of dull, menacing thunder.

That was all. The wind died along the tall grasses of the valley. The dawn and the day resumed their place in a time, and the risen sun sent hot waves of yellow mist that made its path bright before it. The leaves laughed in the sun, and their laughter shook the trees until each bough was like a girl's school in fairyland. God had refused to accept the bribe.

For another moment John watched the triumph of the day. Then, turning, he saw a flutter of brown down by the lake, then another flutter, then another, like the dance of golden angels alighting from the clouds. The aeroplanes had come to earth.

John slid off the boulder and ran down the side of the mountain to the clump of trees, where the two girls were awake and waiting for him. Kismine sprang to her feet, the jewels in her pockets jingling, a question on her parted lips, but instinct told John that there was no time for words. They must get off the mountain without losing a moment. He seized a hand of each, and in silence they threaded the tree-trunks, washed with light now and with the rising mist. Behind them from the valley came no sound at all, except the complaint of the peacocks far away and the pleasant undertone of morning.

When they had gone about half a mile, they avoided the park land and entered a narrow path that led over the next rise of ground. At the highest point of this they paused and turned around. Their eyes rested upon the mountainside they had just left—oppressed by some dark sense of tragic impendency.

Clear against the sky a broken, white-haired man was slowly descending the steep slope, followed by two gigantic and emotionless negroes, who carried a burden between them which still flashed and glittered in the sun. Half-way down two other figures joined them—John could see that they were Mrs. Washington and her son, upon whose arm she leaned. The aviators had clambered from their machines to the sweeping lawn in front of the château, and with rifles in hand were starting up the diamond mountain in skirmishing formation.

But the little group of five which had formed farther up and was engrossing all the watchers' attention had stopped upon a ledge of rock. The negroes stooped and pulled up what appeared to be a trap-door in the side of the mountain. Into this they all disappeared, the white-haired man first, then his wife and son, finally the two negroes, the glittering tips of whose jeweled head-dresses caught the sun for a moment before the trap-door descended and engulfed them all.

Kismine clutched John's arm.

"Oh," she cried wildly, "where are they going? What are they going to do?"

"It must be some underground way of escape——"

A little scream from the two girls interrupted his sentence.

"Don't you see?" sobbed Kismine hysterically. "The mountain is wired!"

Even as she spoke John put up his hands to shield his sight. Before their eyes the whole surface of the mountain had changed suddenly to a dazzling burning yellow, which showed up through the jacket of turf as light shows through a human hand. For a moment the intolerable glow continued, and then like an extinguished filament it disappeared, revealing a black waste from which blue smoke arose slowly, carrying off with it what remained of vegetation and of human flesh. Of the aviators there was left neither blood nor bone—they were consumed as completely as the five souls who had gone inside.

Simultaneously, and with an immense concussion, the château literally threw itself into the air, bursting into flaming fragments as it rose, and then tumbling back upon itself in a smoking pile that lay projecting half into the water of the lake. There was no fire—what smoke there was drifted off mingling with the sunshine, and for a few minutes longer a powdery dust of marble drifted from the great featureless pile that had once been the house of jewels. There was no more sound and the three people were alone in the valley.

XI

At sunset John and his two companions reached the high cliff which had marked the boundaries of the Washingtons' dominion, and looking back found the valley tranquil and lovely in the dusk. They sat down to finish the food which Jasmine had brought with her in a basket.

"There!" she said, as she spread the table-cloth and put the sandwiches in a neat pile upon it. "Don't they look tempting? I always think that food tastes better outdoors."

"With that remark," remarked Kismine, "Jasmine enters the middle class."

"Now," said John eagerly, "turn out your pocket and let's see what jewels you brought along. If you made a good selection we three ought to live comfortably all the rest of our lives."

Obediently Kismine put her hand in her pocket and tossed two handfuls of glittering stones before him.

"Not so bad," cried John, enthusiastically. "They aren't very big, but—Hello!" His expression changed as he held one of them up to the declining sun. "Why, these aren't diamonds! There's something the matter!"

"By golly!" exclaimed Kismine, with a startled look. "What an idiot I am!"

"Why, these are rhinestones!" cried John.

"I know." She broke into a laugh. "I opened the wrong drawer. They belonged on the dress of a girl who visited Jasmine. I got her to give them to me in exchange for diamonds. I'd never seen anything but precious stones before."

"And this is what you brought?"

"I'm afraid so." She fingered the brilliants wistfully. "I think I like these better. I'm a little tired of diamonds."

"Very well," said John gloomily. "We'll have to live in Hades. And you will grow old telling incredulous women that you got the wrong drawer. Unfortunately your father's bankbooks were consumed with him."

"Well, what's the matter with Hades?"

"If I come home with a wife at my age my father is just as liable as not to cut me off with a hot coal, as they say down there."

Jasmine spoke up.

"I love washing," she said quietly. "I have always washed my own handkerchiefs. I'll take in laundry and support you both."

"Do they have washwomen in Hades?" asked Kismine innocently.

"Of course," answered John. "It's just like anywhere else."

"I thought—perhaps it was too hot to wear any clothes."

John laughed.

"Just try it!" he suggested. "They'll run you out before you're half started."

"Will father be there?" she asked.

John turned to her in astonishment.

"Your father is dead," he replied somberly. "Why should he

go to Hades? You have it confused with another place that was abolished long ago."

After supper they folded up the table-cloth and spread their blankets for the night.

"What a dream it was," Kismine sighed, gazing up at the stars. "How strange it seems to be here with one dress and a penniless fiancé!

"Under the stars," she repeated. "I never noticed the stars before. I always thought of them as great big diamonds that belonged to some one. Now they frighten me. They make me feel that it was all a dream, all my youth."

"It *was* a dream," said John quietly. "Everybody's youth is a dream, a form of chemical madness."

"How pleasant then to be insane!"

"So I'm told," said John gloomily. "I don't know any longer. At any rate, let us love for a while, for a year or so, you and me. That's a form of divine drunkenness that we can all try. There are only diamonds in the whole world, diamonds and perhaps the shabby gift of disillusion. Well, I have that last and I will make the usual nothing of it." He shivered. "Turn up your coat collar, little girl, the night's full of chill and you'll get pneumonia. His was a great sin who first invented consciousness. Let us lose it for a few hours."

So wrapping himself in his blanket he fell off to sleep.

The Curious Case of Benjamin Button

AS LONG AGO as 1860 it was the proper thing to be born at home. At present, so I am told, the high gods of medicine have decreed that the first cries of the young shall be uttered upon the anesthetic air of a hospital, preferably a fashionable one. So young Mr. and Mrs. Roger Button were fifty years ahead of style when they decided, one day in the summer of 1860, that their first baby should be born in a hospital. Whether this anachronism had any bearing upon the astonishing history I am about to set down will never be known.

I shall tell you what occurred, and let you judge for yourself.

The Roger Buttons held an enviable position, both social and financial, in ante-bellum Baltimore. They were related to the This Family and the That Family, which, as every Southerner knew, entitled them to membership in that enormous peerage which largely populated the Confederacy. This was their first experience with the charming old custom of having babies—Mr. Button was naturally nervous. He hoped it would be a boy so that he could be sent to Yale College in Connecticut, at which institution Mr. Button himself had been known for four years by the somewhat obvious nickname of "Cuff."

On the September morning consecrated to the enormous event he arose nervously at six o'clock, dressed himself, adjusted an impeccable stock, and hurried forth through the streets of Baltimore to the hospital, to determine whether the darkness of the night had borne in new life upon its bosom.

When he was approximately a hundred yards from the Maryland Private Hospital for Ladies and Gentlemen he saw Doctor Keene, the family physician, descending the front steps, rubbing his hands together with a washing movement—as all doctors are required to do by the unwritten ethics of their profession.

Mr. Roger Button, the president of Roger Button & Co., Wholesale Hardware, began to run toward Doctor Keene with much less dignity than was expected from a Southern gentleman of that picturesque period. "Doctor Keene!" he called. "Oh, Doctor Keene!"

The doctor heard him, faced around, and stood waiting, a curious expression settling on his harsh, medicinal face as Mr. Button drew near.

"What happened?" demanded Mr. Button, as he came up in a gasping rush. "What was it? How is she? A boy? Who is it? What——"

"Talk sense!" said Doctor Keene sharply. He appeared somewhat irritated.

"Is the child born?" begged Mr. Button.

Doctor Keene frowned. "Why, yes, I suppose so—after a fashion." Again he threw a curious glance at Mr. Button.

"Is my wife all right?"

"Yes."

"Is it a boy or a girl?"

"Here now!" cried Doctor Keene in a perfect passion of irritation, "I'll ask you to go and see for yourself. Outrageous!" He snapped the last word out in almost one syllable, then he turned away muttering: "Do you imagine a case like this will help my professional reputation? One more would ruin me—ruin anybody."

"What's the matter?" demanded Mr. Button, appalled. "Triplets?"

"No, not triplets!" answered the doctor cuttingly. "What's more, you can go and see for yourself. And get another doctor. I brought you into the world, young man, and I've been physician to your family for forty years, but I'm through with you! I don't want to see you or any of your relatives ever again! Good-by!"

Then he turned sharply, and without another word climbed into his phaeton, which was waiting at the curbstone, and drove severely away.

Mr. Button stood there upon the sidewalk, stupefied and trembling from head to foot. What horrible mishap had occurred? He had suddenly lost all desire to go into the Maryland Private Hospital for Ladies and Gentlemen—it was with the greatest difficulty that, a moment later, he forced himself to mount the steps and enter the front door.

A nurse was sitting behind a desk in the opaque gloom

of the hall. Swallowing his shame, Mr. Button approached her.

"Good-morning," she remarked, looking up at him pleasantly.

"Good-morning. I—I am Mr. Button."

At this a look of utter terror spread itself over the girl's face. She rose to her feet and seemed about to fly from the hall, restraining herself only with the most apparent difficulty.

"I want to see my child," said Mr. Button.

The nurse gave a little scream. "Oh—of course!" she cried hysterically. "Up-stairs. Right up-stairs. Go—*up!*"

She pointed the direction, and Mr. Button, bathed in a cool perspiration, turned falteringly, and began to mount to the second floor. In the upper hall he addressed another nurse who approached him, basin in hand. "I'm Mr. Button," he managed to articulate. "I want to see my——"

Clank! The basin clattered to the floor and rolled in the direction of the stairs. Clank! Clank! It began a methodical descent as if sharing in the general terror which this gentleman provoked.

"I want to see my child!" Mr. Button almost shrieked. He was on the verge of collapse.

Clank! The basin had reached the first floor. The nurse regained control of herself, and threw Mr. Button a look of hearty contempt.

"All *right*, Mr. Button," she agreed in a hushed voice. "Very *well!* But if you *knew* what state it's put us all in this morning! It's perfectly outrageous! The hospital will never have the ghost of a reputation after——"

"Hurry!" he cried hoarsely. "I can't stand this!"

"Come this way, then, Mr. Button."

He dragged himself after her. At the end of a long hall they reached a room from which proceeded a variety of howls—indeed, a room which, in later parlance, would have been known as the "crying-room." They entered. Ranged around the walls were half a dozen white-enameled rolling cribs, each with a tag tied at the head.

"Well," gasped Mr. Button, "which is mine?"

"There!" said the nurse.

Mr. Button's eyes followed her pointing finger, and this is

what he saw. Wrapped in a voluminous white blanket, and partially crammed into one of the cribs, there sat an old man apparently about seventy years of age. His sparse hair was almost white, and from his chin dripped a long smoke-colored beard, which waved absurdly back and forth, fanned by the breeze coming in at the window. He looked up at Mr. Button with dim, faded eyes in which lurked a puzzled question.

"Am I mad?" thundered Mr. Button, his terror resolving into rage. "Is this some ghastly hospital joke?"

"It doesn't seem like a joke to us," replied the nurse severely. "And I don't know whether you're mad or not—but that is most certainly your child."

The cool perspiration redoubled on Mr. Button's forehead. He closed his eyes, and then, opening them, looked again. There was no mistake—he was gazing at a man of threescore and ten—a *baby* of threescore and ten, a baby whose feet hung over the sides of the crib in which it was reposing.

The old man looked placidly from one to the other for a moment, and then suddenly spoke in a cracked and ancient voice. "Are you my father?" he demanded.

Mr. Button and the nurse started violently.

"Because if you are," went on the old man querulously, "I wish you'd get me out of this place—or, at least, get them to put a comfortable rocker in here."

"Where in God's name did you come from? Who are you?" burst out Mr. Button frantically.

"I can't tell you *exactly* who I am," replied the querulous whine, "because I've only been born a few hours—but my last name is certainly Button."

"You lie! You're an impostor!"

The old man turned wearily to the nurse. "Nice way to welcome a new-born child," he complained in a weak voice. "Tell him he's wrong, why don't you?"

"You're wrong, Mr. Button," said the nurse severely. "This is your child, and you'll have to make the best of it. We're going to ask you to take him home with you as soon as possible—some time to-day."

"Home?" repeated Mr. Button incredulously.

"Yes, we can't have him here. We really can't, you know?"

"I'm right glad of it," whined the old man. "This is a fine

place to keep a youngster of quiet tastes. With all this yelling and howling, I haven't been able to get a wink of sleep. I asked for something to eat"—here his voice rose to a shrill note of protest—"and they brought me a bottle of milk!"

Mr. Button sank down upon a chair near his son and concealed his face in his hands. "My heavens!" he murmured, in an ecstasy of horror. "What will people say? What must I do?"

"You'll have to take him home," insisted the nurse—"immediately!"

A grotesque picture formed itself with dreadful clarity before the eyes of the tortured man—a picture of himself walking through the crowded streets of the city with this appalling apparition stalking by his side. "I can't. I can't," he moaned.

People would stop to speak to him, and what was he going to say? He would have to introduce this—this septuagenarian: "This is my son, born early this morning." And then the old man would gather his blanket around him and they would plod on, past the bustling stores, the slave market—for a dark instant Mr. Button wished passionately that his son was black—past the luxurious houses of the residential district, past the home for the aged. . . .

"Come! Pull yourself together," commanded the nurse.

"See here," the old man announced suddenly, "if you think I'm going to walk home in this blanket, you're entirely mistaken."

"Babies always have blankets."

With a malicious crackle the old man held up a small white swaddling garment. "Look!" he quavered. "*This* is what they had ready for me."

"Babies always wear those," said the nurse primly.

"Well," said the old man, "this baby's not going to wear anything in about two minutes. This blanket itches. They might at least have given me a sheet."

"Keep it on! Keep it on!" said Mr. Button hurriedly. He turned to the nurse. "What'll I do?"

"Go down town and buy your son some clothes."

Mr. Button's son's voice followed him down into the hall: "And a cane, father. I want to have a cane."

Mr. Button banged the outer door savagely. . . .

II

"Good-morning," Mr. Button said, nervously, to the clerk in the Chesapeake Dry Goods Company. "I want to buy some clothes for my child."

"How old is your child, sir?"

"About six hours," answered Mr. Button, without due consideration.

"Babies' supply department in the rear."

"Why, I don't think—I'm not sure that's what I want. It's—he's an unusually large-size child. Exceptionally—ah—large."

"They have the largest child's sizes."

"Where is the boys' department?" inquired Mr. Button, shifting his ground desperately. He felt that the clerk must surely scent his shameful secret.

"Right here."

"Well—" He hesitated. The notion of dressing his son in men's clothes was repugnant to him. If, say, he could only find a *very* large boy's suit, he might cut off that long and awful beard, dye the white hair brown, and thus manage to conceal the worst, and to retain something of his own self-respect—not to mention his position in Baltimore society.

But a frantic inspection of the boys' department revealed no suits to fit the new-born Button. He blamed the store, of course—in such cases it is the thing to blame the store.

"How old did you say that boy of yours was?" demanded the clerk curiously.

"He's—sixteen."

"Oh, I beg your pardon. I thought you said six *hours*. You'll find the youths' department in the next aisle."

Mr. Button turned miserably away. Then he stopped, brightened, and pointed his finger toward a dressed dummy in the window display. "There!" he exclaimed. "I'll take that suit, out there on the dummy."

The clerk stared. "Why," he protested, "that's not a child's suit. At least it *is*, but it's for fancy dress. You could wear it yourself!"

"Wrap it up," insisted his customer nervously. "That's what I want."

The astonished clerk obeyed.

Back at the hospital Mr. Button entered the nursery and almost threw the package at his son. "Here's your clothes," he snapped out.

The old man untied the package and viewed the contents with a quizzical eye.

"They look sort of funny to me," he complained. "I don't want to be made a monkey of——"

"You've made a monkey of me!" retorted Mr. Button fiercely. "Never you mind how funny you look. Put them on—or I'll—or I'll *spank* you." He swallowed uneasily at the penultimate word, feeling nevertheless that it was the proper thing to say.

"All right, father"—this with a grotesque simulation of filial respect—"you've lived longer; you know best. Just as you say."

As before, the sound of the word "father" caused Mr. Button to start violently.

"And hurry."

"I'm hurrying, father."

When his son was dressed Mr. Button regarded him with depression. The costume consisted of dotted socks, pink pants, and a belted blouse with a wide white collar. Over the latter waved the long whitish beard, drooping almost to the waist. The effect was not good.

"Wait!"

Mr. Button seized a hospital shears and with three quick snaps amputated a large section of the beard. But even with this improvement the ensemble fell far short of perfection. The remaining brush of scraggly hair, the watery eyes, the ancient teeth, seemed oddly out of tone with the gayety of the costume. Mr. Button, however, was obdurate—he held out his hand. "Come along!" he said sternly.

His son took the hand trustingly. "What are you going to call me, dad?" he quavered as they walked from the nursery—"just 'baby' for a while? till you think of a better name?"

Mr. Button grunted. "I don't know," he answered harshly. "I think we'll call you Methuselah."

III

Even after the new addition to the Button family had had his hair cut short and then dyed to a sparse unnatural black, had had his face shaved so close that it glistened, and had been attired in small-boy clothes made to order by a flabbergasted tailor, it was impossible for Mr. Button to ignore the fact that his son was a poor excuse for a first family baby. Despite his aged stoop, Benjamin Button—for it was by this name they called him instead of by the appropriate but invidious Methuselah—was five feet eight inches tall. His clothes did not conceal this, nor did the clipping and dyeing of his eyebrows disguise the fact that the eyes underneath were faded and watery and tired. In fact, the baby-nurse who had been engaged in advance left the house after one look, in a state of considerable indignation.

But Mr. Button persisted in his unwavering purpose. Benjamin was a baby, and a baby he should remain. At first he declared that if Benjamin didn't like warm milk he could go without food altogether, but he was finally prevailed upon to allow his son bread and butter, and even oatmeal by way of a compromise. One day he brought home a rattle and, giving it to Benjamin, insisted in no uncertain terms that he should "play with it," whereupon the old man took it with a weary expression and could be heard jingling it obediently at intervals throughout the day.

There can be no doubt, though, that the rattle bored him, and that he found other and more soothing amusements when he was left alone. For instance, Mr. Button discovered one day that during the preceding week he had smoked more cigars than ever before—a phenomenon which was explained a few days later when, entering the nursery unexpectedly, he found the room full of faint blue haze and Benjamin, with a guilty expression on his face, trying to conceal the butt of a dark Havana. This, of course, called for a severe spanking, but Mr. Button found that he could not bring himself to administer it. He merely warned his son that he would "stunt his growth."

Nevertheless he persisted in his attitude. He brought home

lead soldiers, he brought toy trains, he brought large pleasant animals made of cotton, and, to perfect the illusion which he was creating—for himself at least—he passionately demanded of the clerk in the toy-store whether "the paint would come off the pink duck if the baby put it in his mouth." But, despite all his father's efforts, Benjamin refused to be interested. He would steal down the back stairs and return to the nursery with a volume of the "Encyclopædia Britannica," over which he would pore through an afternoon, while his cotton cows and his Noah's ark were left neglected on the floor. Against such a stubbornness Mr. Button's efforts were of little avail.

The sensation created in Baltimore was, at first, prodigious. What the mishap would have cost the Buttons and their kinsfolk socially cannot be determined, for the outbreak of the Civil War drew the city's attention to other things. A few people who were unfailingly polite racked their brains for compliments to give to the parents—and finally hit upon the ingenious device of declaring that the baby resembled his grandfather, a fact which, due to the standard state of decay common to all men of seventy, could not be denied. Mr. and Mrs. Roger Button were not pleased, and Benjamin's grandfather was furiously insulted.

Benjamin, once he left the hospital, took life as he found it. Several small boys were brought to see him, and he spent a stiff-jointed afternoon trying to work up an interest in tops and marbles—he even managed, quite accidentally, to break a kitchen window with a stone from a sling shot, a feat which secretly delighted his father.

Thereafter Benjamin contrived to break something every day, but he did these things only because they were expected of him, and because he was by nature obliging.

When his grandfather's initial antagonism wore off, Benjamin and that gentleman took enormous pleasure in one another's company. They would sit for hours, these two so far apart in age and experience, and, like old cronies, discuss with tireless monotony the slow events of the day. Benjamin felt more at ease in his grandfather's presence than in his parents'—they seemed always somewhat in awe of him and, despite the dictatorial authority they exercised over him, frequently addressed him as "Mr."

He was as puzzled as any one else at the apparently advanced age of his mind and body at birth. He read up on it in the medical journal, but found that no such case had been previously recorded. At his father's urging he made an honest attempt to play with other boys, and frequently he joined in the milder games—football shook him up too much, and he feared that in case of a fracture his ancient bones would refuse to knit.

When he was five he was sent to kindergarten, where he was initiated into the art of pasting green paper on orange paper, of weaving colored maps and manufacturing eternal cardboard necklaces. He was inclined to drowse off to sleep in the middle of these tasks, a habit which both irritated and frightened his young teacher. To his relief she complained to his parents, and he was removed from the school. The Roger Buttons told their friends that they felt he was too young.

By the time he was twelve years old his parents had grown used to him. Indeed, so strong is the force of custom that they no longer felt that he was different from any other child—except when some curious anomaly reminded them of the fact. But one day a few weeks after his twelfth birthday, while looking in the mirror, Benjamin made, or thought he made, an astonishing discovery. Did his eyes deceive him, or had his hair turned in the dozen years of his life from white to iron-gray under its concealing dye? Was the network of wrinkles on his face becoming less pronounced? Was his skin healthier and firmer, with even a touch of ruddy winter color? He could not tell. He knew that he no longer stooped and that his physical condition had improved since the early days of his life.

"Can it be——?" he thought to himself, or, rather, scarcely dared to think.

He went to his father. "I am grown," he announced determinedly. "I want to put on long trousers."

His father hesitated. "Well," he said finally, "I don't know. Fourteen is the age for putting on long trousers—and you are only twelve."

"But you'll have to admit," protested Benjamin, "that I'm big for my age."

His father looked at him with illusory speculation. "Oh,

I'm not so sure of that," he said. "I was as big as you when I was twelve."

This was not true—it was all part of Roger Button's silent agreement with himself to believe in his son's normality.

Finally a compromise was reached. Benjamin was to continue to dye his hair. He was to make a better attempt to play with boys of his own age. He was not to wear his spectacles or carry a cane in the street. In return for these concessions he was allowed his first suit of long trousers. . . .

IV

Of the life of Benjamin Button between his twelfth and twenty-first year I intend to say little. Suffice to record that they were years of normal ungrowth. When Benjamin was eighteen he was erect as a man of fifty; he had more hair and it was of a dark gray; his step was firm, his voice had lost its cracked quaver and descended to a healthy baritone. So his father sent him up to Connecticut to take examinations for entrance to Yale College. Benjamin passed his examination and became a member of the freshman class.

On the third day following his matriculation he received a notification from Mr. Hart, the college registrar, to call at his office and arrange his schedule. Benjamin, glancing in the mirror, decided that his hair needed a new application of its brown dye, but an anxious inspection of his bureau drawer disclosed that the dye bottle was not there. Then he remembered—he had emptied it the day before and thrown it away.

He was in a dilemma. He was due at the registrar's in five minutes. There seemed to be no help for it—he must go as he was. He did.

"Good-morning," said the registrar politely. "You've come to inquire about your son."

"Why, as a matter of fact, my name's Button—" began Benjamin, but Mr. Hart cut him off.

"I'm very glad to meet you, Mr. Button. I'm expecting your son here any minute."

"That's me!" burst out Benjamin. "I'm a freshman."

"What!"

"I'm a freshman."

"Surely you're joking."

"Not at all."

The registrar frowned and glanced at a card before him. "Why, I have Mr. Benjamin Button's age down here as eighteen."

"That's my age," asserted Benjamin, flushing slightly.

The registrar eyed him wearily. "Now surely, Mr. Button, you don't expect me to believe that."

Benjamin smiled wearily. "I am eighteen," he repeated.

The registrar pointed sternly to the door. "Get out," he said. "Get out of college and get out of town. You are a dangerous lunatic."

"I am eighteen."

Mr. Hart opened the door. "The idea!" he shouted. "A man of your age trying to enter here as a freshman. Eighteen years old, are you? Well, I'll give you eighteen minutes to get out of town."

Benjamin Button walked with dignity from the room, and half a dozen undergraduates, who were waiting in the hall, followed him curiously with their eyes. When he had gone a little way he turned around, faced the infuriated registrar, who was still standing in the doorway, and repeated in a firm voice: "I am eighteen years old."

To a chorus of titters which went up from the group of undergraduates, Benjamin walked away.

But he was not fated to escape so easily. On his melancholy walk to the railroad station he found that he was being followed by a group, then by a swarm, and finally by a dense mass of undergraduates. The word had gone around that a lunatic had passed the entrance examinations for Yale and attempted to palm himself off as a youth of eighteen. A fever of excitement permeated the college. Men ran hatless out of classes, the football team abandoned its practice and joined the mob, professors' wives with bonnets awry and bustles out of position, ran shouting after the procession, from which proceeded a continual succession of remarks aimed at the tender sensibilities of Benjamin Button.

"He must be the Wandering Jew!"

"He ought to go to prep school at his age!"

"Look at the infant prodigy!"

"He thought this was the old men's home."

"Go up to Harvard!"

Benjamin increased his gait, and soon he was running. He would show them! He *would* go to Harvard, and then they would regret these ill-considered taunts!

Safely on board the train for Baltimore, he put his head from the window. "You'll regret this!" he shouted.

"Ha-ha!" the undergraduates laughed. "Ha-ha-ha!" It was the biggest mistake that Yale College had ever made. . . .

V

In 1880 Benjamin Button was twenty years old, and he signalized his birthday by going to work for his father in Roger Button & Co., Wholesale Hardware. It was in that same year that he began "going out socially"—that is, his father insisted on taking him to several fashionable dances. Roger Button was now fifty, and he and his son were more and more companionable—in fact, since Benjamin had ceased to dye his hair (which was still grayish) they appeared about the same age, and could have passed for brothers.

One night in August they got into the phaeton attired in their full-dress suits and drove out to a dance at the Shevlins' country house, situated just outside of Baltimore. It was a gorgeous evening. A full moon drenched the road to the lustreless color of platinum, and late-blooming harvest flowers breathed into the motionless air aromas that were like low, half-heard laughter. The open country, carpeted for rods around with bright wheat, was translucent as in the day. It was almost impossible not to be affected by the sheer beauty of the sky—almost.

"There's a great future in the dry-goods business," Roger Button was saying. He was not a spiritual man—his esthetic sense was rudimentary.

"Old fellows like me can't learn new tricks," he observed profoundly. "It's you youngsters with energy and vitality that have the great future before you."

Far up the road the lights of the Shevlins' country house drifted into view, and presently there was a sighing sound that crept persistently toward them—it might have been the fine plaint of violins or the rustle of the silver wheat under the moon.

They pulled up behind a handsome brougham whose passengers were disembarking at the door. A lady got out, then an elderly gentleman, then another young lady, beautiful as sin. Benjamin started; an almost chemical change seemed to dissolve and recompose the very elements of his body. A rigor passed over him, blood rose into his cheeks, his forehead, and there was a steady thumping in his ears. It was first love.

The girl was slender and frail, with hair that was ashen under the moon and honey-colored under the sputtering gaslamps of the porch. Over her shoulders was thrown a Spanish mantilla of softest yellow, butterflied in black; her feet were glittering buttons at the hem of her bustled dress.

Roger Button leaned over to his son. "That," he said, "is young Hildegarde Moncrief, the daughter of General Moncrief."

Benjamin nodded coldly. "Pretty little thing," he said indifferently. But when the negro boy had led the buggy away, he added: "Dad, you might introduce me to her."

They approached a group of which Miss Moncrief was the centre. Reared in the old tradition, she courtesied low before Benjamin. Yes, he might have a dance. He thanked her and walked away—staggered away.

The interval until the time for his turn should arrive dragged itself out interminably. He stood close to the wall, silent, inscrutable, watching with murderous eyes the young bloods of Baltimore as they eddied around Hildegarde Moncrief, passionate admiration in their faces. How obnoxious they seemed to Benjamin; how intolerably rosy! Their curling brown whiskers aroused in him a feeling equivalent to indigestion.

But when his own time came, and he drifted with her out upon the changing floor to the music of the latest waltz from Paris, his jealousies and anxieties melted from him like a mantle of snow. Blind with enchantment, he felt that life was just beginning.

"You and your brother got here just as we did, didn't you?" asked Hildegarde, looking up at him with eyes that were like bright blue enamel.

Benjamin hesitated. If she took him for his father's brother, would it be best to enlighten her? He remembered his experience at Yale, so he decided against it. It would be rude to contradict a lady; it would be criminal to mar this exquisite occasion with the grotesque story of his origin. Later, perhaps. So he nodded, smiled, listened, was happy.

"I like men of your age," Hildegarde told him. "Young boys are so idiotic. They tell me how much champagne they drink at college, and how much money they lose playing cards. Men of your age know how to appreciate women."

Benjamin felt himself on the verge of a proposal—with an effort he choked back the impulse.

"You're just the romantic age," she continued—"fifty. Twenty-five is too worldly-wise; thirty is apt to be pale from overwork; forty is the age of long stories that take a whole cigar to tell; sixty is—oh, sixty is too near seventy; but fifty is the mellow age. I love fifty."

Fifty seemed to Benjamin a glorious age. He longed passionately to be fifty.

"I've always said," went on Hildegarde, "that I'd rather marry a man of fifty and be taken care of than marry a man of thirty and take care of *him*."

For Benjamin the rest of the evening was bathed in a honey-colored mist. Hildegarde gave him two more dances, and they discovered that they were marvellously in accord on all the questions of the day. She was to go driving with him on the following Sunday, and then they would discuss all these questions further.

Going home in the phaeton just before the crack of dawn, when the first bees were humming and the fading moon glimmered in the cool dew, Benjamin knew vaguely that his father was discussing wholesale hardware.

". . . . And what do you think should merit our biggest attention after hammers and nails?" the elder Button was saying.

"Love," replied Benjamin absent-mindedly.

"Lugs?" exclaimed Roger Button. "Why, I've just covered the question of lugs."

Benjamin regarded him with dazed eyes just as the eastern sky was suddenly cracked with light, and an oriole yawned piercingly in the quickening trees. . . .

VI

When, six months later, the engagement of Miss Hildegarde Moncrief to Mr. Benjamin Button was made known (I say "made known," for General Moncrief declared he would rather fall upon his sword than announce it), the excitement in Baltimore society reached a feverish pitch. The almost forgotten story of Benjamin's birth was remembered and sent out upon the winds of scandal in picaresque and incredible forms. It was said that Benjamin was really the father of Roger Button, that he was his brother who had been in prison for forty years, that he was John Wilkes Booth in disguise—and, finally, that he had two small conical horns sprouting from his head.

The Sunday supplements of the New York papers played up the case with fascinating sketches which showed the head of Benjamin Button attached to a fish, to a snake, and, finally, to a body of solid brass. He became known, journalistically, as the Mystery Man of Maryland. But the true story, as is usually the case, had a very small circulation.

However, every one agreed with General Moncrief that it was "criminal" for a lovely girl who could have married any beau in Baltimore to throw herself into the arms of a man who was assuredly fifty. In vain Mr. Roger Button published his son's birth certificate in large type in the Baltimore *Blaze*. No one believed it. You had only to look at Benjamin and see.

On the part of the two people most concerned there was no wavering. So many of the stories about her fiancé were false that Hildegarde refused stubbornly to believe even the true one. In vain General Moncrief pointed out to her the high mortality among men of fifty—or, at least, among men who looked fifty; in vain he told her of the instability of the wholesale hardware business. Hildegarde had chosen to marry for mellowness—and marry she did. . . .

VII

In one particular, at least, the friends of Hildegarde Moncrief were mistaken. The wholesale hardware business prospered amazingly. In the fifteen years between Benjamin

Button's marriage in 1880 and his father's retirement in 1895, the family fortune was doubled—and this was due largely to the younger member of the firm.

Needless to say, Baltimore eventually received the couple to its bosom. Even old General Moncrief became reconciled to his son-in-law when Benjamin gave him the money to bring out his "History of the Civil War" in twenty volumes, which had been refused by nine prominent publishers.

In Benjamin himself fifteen years had wrought many changes. It seemed to him that the blood flowed with new vigor through his veins. It began to be a pleasure to rise in the morning, to walk with an active step along the busy, sunny street, to work untiringly with his shipments of hammers and his cargoes of nails. It was in 1890 that he executed his famous business coup: he brought up the suggestion that *all nails used in nailing up the boxes in which nails are shipped are the property of the shippee*, a proposal which became a statute, was approved by Chief Justice Fossile, and saved Roger Button and Company, Wholesale Hardware, more than *six hundred nails every year.*

In addition, Benjamin discovered that he was becoming more and more attracted by the gay side of life. It was typical of his growing enthusiasm for pleasure that he was the first man in the city of Baltimore to own and run an automobile. Meeting him on the street, his contemporaries would stare enviously at the picture he made of health and vitality.

"He seems to grow younger every year," they would remark. And if old Roger Button, now sixty-five years old, had failed at first to give a proper welcome to his son he atoned at last by bestowing on him what amounted to adulation.

And here we come to an unpleasant subject which it will be well to pass over as quickly as possible. There was only one thing that worried Benjamin Button: his wife had ceased to attract him.

At that time Hildegarde was a woman of thirty-five, with a son, Roscoe, fourteen years old. In the early days of their marriage Benjamin had worshipped her. But, as the years passed, her honey-colored hair became an unexciting brown, the blue enamel of her eyes assumed the aspect of cheap crockery—moreover, and most of all, she had become too settled in her ways, too placid, too content, too anemic in her excitements, and too sober in her taste. As a bride it had been she who had "dragged" Benjamin to dances and dinners—now conditions were reversed. She went out socially with him, but without enthusiasm, devoured already by that eternal inertia which comes to live with each of us one day and stays with us to the end.

Benjamin's discontent waxed stronger. At the outbreak of the Spanish-American War in 1898 his home had for him so little charm that he decided to join the army. With his business influence he obtained a commission as captain, and proved so adaptable to the work that he was made a major, and finally a lieutenant-colonel just in time to participate in the celebrated charge up San Juan Hill. He was slightly wounded, and received a medal.

Benjamin had become so attached to the activity and excitement of army life that he regretted to give it up, but his business required attention, so he resigned his commission and came home. He was met at the station by a brass band and escorted to his house.

VIII

Hildegarde, waving a large silk flag, greeted him on the porch, and even as he kissed her he felt with a sinking of the heart that these three years had taken their toll. She was a woman of forty now, with a faint skirmish line of gray hairs in her head. The sight depressed him.

Up in his room he saw his reflection in the familiar mirror—he went closer and examined his own face with anxiety, comparing it after a moment with a photograph of himself in uniform taken just before the war.

"Good Lord!" he said aloud. The process was continuing. There was no doubt of it—he looked now like a man of thirty. Instead of being delighted, he was uneasy—he was growing younger. He had hitherto hoped that once he reached a bodily age equivalent to his age in years, the grotesque phenomenon which had marked his birth would cease to function. He shuddered. His destiny seemed to him awful, incredible.

When he came down-stairs Hildegarde was waiting for him. She appeared annoyed, and he wondered if she had at last discovered that there was something amiss. It was with an effort to relieve the tension between them that he broached the matter at dinner in what he considered a delicate way.

"Well," he remarked lightly, "everybody says I look younger than ever."

Hildegarde regarded him with scorn. She sniffed. "Do you think it's anything to boast about?"

"I'm not boasting," he asserted uncomfortably.

She sniffed again. "The idea," she said, and after a moment: "I should think you'd have enough pride to stop it."

"How can I?" he demanded.

"I'm not going to argue with you," she retorted. "But there's a right way of doing things and a wrong way. If you've made up your mind to be different from everybody else, I don't suppose I can stop you, but I really don't think it's very considerate."

"But, Hildegarde, I can't help it."

"You can too. You're simply stubborn. You think you don't want to be like any one else. You always have been that way, and you always will be. But just think how it would be if every one else looked at things as you do—what would the world be like?"

As this was an inane and unanswerable argument Benjamin made no reply, and from that time on a chasm began to widen between them. He wondered what possible fascination she had ever exercised over him.

To add to the breach, he found, as the new century gathered headway, that his thirst for gayety grew stronger. Never a party of any kind in the city of Baltimore but he was there, dancing with the prettiest of the young married women, chatting with the most popular of the débutantes, and finding their company charming, while his wife, a dowager of evil omen, sat among the chaperons, now in haughty disapproval, and now following him with solemn, puzzled, and reproachful eyes.

"Look!" people would remark. "What a pity! A young fellow that age tied to a woman of forty-five. He must be twenty years younger than his wife." They had forgotten—as people inevitably forget—that back in 1880 their mammas and papas had also remarked about this same ill-matched pair.

Benjamin's growing unhappiness at home was compensated for by his many new interests. He took up golf and made a great success of it. He went in for dancing: in 1906 he was an expert at "The Boston," and in 1908 he was considered proficient at the "Maxixe," while in 1909 his "Castle Walk" was the envy of every young man in town.

His social activities, of course, interfered to some extent with his business, but then he had worked hard at wholesale hardware for twenty-five years and felt that he could soon hand it on to his son, Roscoe, who had recently graduated from Harvard.

He and his son were, in fact, often mistaken for each other. This pleased Benjamin—he soon forgot the insidious fear which had come over him on his return from the Spanish-American War, and grew to take a naïve pleasure in his appearance. There was only one fly in the delicious ointment—he hated to appear in public with his wife. Hildegarde was almost fifty, and the sight of her made him feel absurd. . . .

IX

One September day in 1910—a few years after Roger Button & Co., Wholesale Hardware, had been handed over to young Roscoe Button—a man, apparently about twenty years old, entered himself as a freshman at Harvard University in Cambridge. He did not make the mistake of announcing that he would never see fifty again nor did he mention the fact that his son had been graduated from the same institution ten years before.

He was admitted, and almost immediately attained a prominent position in the class, partly because he seemed a little older than the other freshmen, whose average age was about eighteen.

But his success was largely due to the fact that in the football game with Yale he played so brilliantly, with so much dash and with such a cold, remorseless anger that he scored seven touchdowns and fourteen field goals for Harvard, and caused one entire eleven of Yale men to be carried singly from the field, unconscious. He was the most celebrated man in college.

Strange to say, in his third or junior year he was scarcely able to "make" the team. The coaches said that he had lost weight, and it seemed to the more observant among them that he was not quite as tall as before. He made no touchdowns—indeed, he was retained on the team chiefly in hope that his enormous reputation would bring terror and disorganization to the Yale team.

In his senior year he did not make the team at all. He had grown so slight and frail that one day he was taken by some sophomores for a freshman, an incident which humiliated him terribly. He became known as something of a prodigy—a senior who was surely no more than sixteen—and he was often shocked at the worldliness of some of his classmates. His studies seemed harder to him—he felt that they were too advanced. He had heard his classmates speak of St. Midas', the famous preparatory school, at which so many of them had prepared for college, and he determined after his graduation to enter himself at St. Midas', where the sheltered life among boys his own size would be more congenial to him.

Upon his graduation in 1914 he went home to Baltimore with his Harvard diploma in his pocket. Hildegarde was now residing in Italy, so Benjamin went to live with his son, Roscoe. But though he was welcomed in a general way, there was obviously no heartiness in Roscoe's feeling toward him—there was even perceptible a tendency on his son's part to think that Benjamin, as he moped about the house in adolescent mooniness, was somewhat in the way. Roscie was married now and prominent in Baltimore life, and he wanted no scandal to creep out in connection with his family.

Benjamin, no longer persona grata with the débutantes and younger college set, found himself left much alone, except for the companionship of three or four fifteen-year-old boys in the neighborhood. His idea of going to St. Midas' school recurred to him.

"Say," he said to Roscoe one day, "I've told you over and over that I want to go to prep school."

"Well, go, then," replied Roscoe shortly. The matter was distasteful to him, and he wished to avoid a discussion.

"I can't go alone," said Benjamin helplessly. "You'll have to enter me and take me up there."

"I haven't got time," declared Roscoe abruptly. His eyes narrowed and he looked uneasily at his father. "As a matter of fact," he added, "you'd better not go on with this business much longer. You better pull up short. You better—you better"—he paused and his face crimsoned as he sought for words—"you better turn right around and start back the other way. This has gone too far to be a joke. It isn't funny any longer. You—you behave yourself!"

Benjamin looked at him, on the verge of tears.

"And another thing," continued Roscoe, "when visitors are in the house I want you to call me 'Uncle'—not 'Roscoe,' but 'Uncle,' do you understand? It looks absurd for a boy of fifteen to call me by my first name. Perhaps you'd better call me 'Uncle' *all* the time, so you'll get used to it."

With a harsh look at his father, Roscoe turned away. . . .

X

At the termination of this interview, Benjamin wandered dismally up-stairs and stared at himself in the mirror. He had not shaved for three months, but he could find nothing on his face but a faint white down with which it seemed unnecessary to meddle. When he had first come home from Harvard, Roscoe had approached him with the proposition that he should wear eye-glasses and imitation whiskers glued to his cheeks, and it had seemed for a moment that the farce of his early years was to be repeated. But whiskers had itched and made him ashamed. He wept and Roscoe had reluctantly relented.

Benjamin opened a book of boys' stories, "The Boy Scouts in Bimini Bay," and began to read. But he found himself thinking persistently about the war. America had joined the Allied cause during the preceding month, and Benjamin wanted to enlist, but, alas, sixteen was the minimum age, and he did not look that old. His true age, which was fifty-seven, would have disqualified him, anyway.

There was a knock at his door, and the butler appeared with a letter bearing a large official legend in the corner and addressed to Mr. Benjamin Button. Benjamin tore it open eagerly, and read the enclosure with delight. It informed him that many reserve officers who had served in the Spanish-American War were being called back into service with a higher rank, and it enclosed his commission as brigadier-general in the United States army with orders to report immediately.

Benjamin jumped to his feet fairly quivering with enthusiasm. This was what he had wanted. He seized his cap and ten minutes later he had entered a large tailoring establishment on Charles Street, and asked in his uncertain treble to be measured for a uniform.

"Want to play soldier, sonny?" demanded a clerk, casually.

Benjamin flushed. "Say! Never mind what I want!" he retorted angrily. "My name's Button and I live on Mt. Vernon Place, so you know I'm good for it."

"Well," admitted the clerk, hesitantly, "if you're not, I guess your daddy is, all right."

Benjamin was measured, and a week later his uniform was completed. He had difficulty in obtaining the proper general's insignia because the dealer kept insisting to Benjamin that a nice Y.W.C.A. badge would look just as well and be much more fun to play with.

Saying nothing to Roscoe, he left the house one night and proceeded by train to Camp Mosby, in South Carolina, where he was to command an infantry brigade. On a sultry April day he approached the entrance to the camp, paid off the taxicab which had brought him from the station, and turned to the sentry on guard.

"Get some one to handle my luggage!" he said briskly.

The sentry eyed him reproachfully. "Say," he remarked, "where you goin' with the general's duds, sonny?"

Benjamin, veteran of the Spanish-American War, whirled upon him with fire in his eye, but with, alas, a changing treble voice.

"Come to attention!" he tried to thunder; he paused for breath—then suddenly he saw the sentry snap his heels together and bring his rifle to the present. Benjamin concealed a smile of gratification, but when he glanced around his smile faded. It was not he who had inspired obedience, but an imposing artillery colonel who was approaching on horseback.

"Colonel!" called Benjamin shrilly.

The colonel came up, drew rein, and looked coolly down at him with a twinkle in his eyes. "Whose little boy are you?" he demanded kindly.

"I'll soon darn well show you whose little boy I am!" retorted Benjamin in a ferocious voice. "Get down off that horse!"

The colonel roared with laughter.

"You want him, eh, general?"

"Here!" cried Benjamin desperately. "Read this." And he thrust his commission toward the colonel.

The colonel read it, his eyes popping from their sockets.

"Where'd you get this?" he demanded, slipping the document into his own pocket.

"I got it from the Government, as you'll soon find out!"

"You come along with me," said the colonel with a peculiar look. "We'll go up to headquarters and talk this over. Come along."

The colonel turned and began walking his horse in the direction of headquarters. There was nothing for Benjamin to do but follow with as much dignity as possible—meanwhile promising himself a stern revenge.

But this revenge did not materialize. Two days later, however, his son Roscoe materialized from Baltimore, hot and cross from a hasty trip, and escorted the weeping general, *sans* uniform, back to his home.

XI

In 1920 Roscoe Button's first child was born. During the attendant festivities, however, no one thought it "the thing" to mention that the little grubby boy, apparently about ten years of age who played around the house with lead soldiers and a miniature circus, was the new baby's own grandfather.

No one disliked the little boy whose fresh, cheerful face was crossed with just a hint of sadness, but to Roscoe Button his presence was a source of torment. In the idiom of his generation Roscoe did not consider the matter "efficient." It seemed to him that his father, in refusing to look sixty, had not behaved like a "red-blooded he-man"—this was Roscoe's favorite expression—but in a curious and perverse manner. Indeed, to think about the matter for as much as a half an hour drove him to the edge of insanity. Roscoe believed that "live wires" should keep young, but carrying it out on such a scale was—was—was inefficient. And there Roscoe rested.

Five years later Roscoe's little boy had grown old enough to play childish games with little Benjamin under the supervision of the same nurse. Roscoe took them both to kindergarten on the same day and Benjamin found that playing with little strips of colored paper, making mats and chains and curious and beautiful designs, was the most fascinating game in the world. Once he was bad and had to stand in the corner—then he cried—but for the most part there were gay hours in the cheerful room, with the sunlight coming in the windows and Miss Bailey's kind hand resting for a moment now and then in his tousled hair.

Roscoe's son moved up into the first grade after a year, but Benjamin stayed on in the kindergarten. He was very happy. Sometimes when other tots talked about what they would do when they grew up a shadow would cross his little face as if in a dim, childish way he realized that those were things in which he was never to share.

The days flowed on in monotonous content. He went back a third year to the kindergarten, but he was too little now to understand what the bright shining strips of paper were for. He cried because the other boys were bigger than he and he was afraid of them. The teacher talked to him, but though he tried to understand he could not understand at all.

He was taken from the kindergarten. His nurse, Nana, in her starched gingham dress, became the centre of his tiny world. On bright days they walked in the park; Nana would point at a great gray monster and say "elephant," and Benjamin would say it after her, and when he was being undressed for bed that night he would say it over and over aloud to her: "Elyphant, elyphant, elyphant." Sometimes Nana let him jump on the bed, which was fun, because if you sat down exactly right it would bounce you up on your feet again, and if you said "Ah" for a long time while you jumped you got a very pleasing broken vocal effect.

He loved to take a big cane from the hatrack and go around hitting chairs and tables with it and saying: "Fight, fight, fight." When there were people there the old ladies would cluck at him, which interested him, and the young ladies would try to kiss him, which he submitted to with mild boredom. And when the long day was done at five o'clock he would go up-stairs with Nana and be fed oatmeal and nice soft mushy foods with a spoon.

There were no troublesome memories in his childish sleep; no token came to him of his brave days at college, of the glittering years when he flustered the hearts of many girls. There were only the white, safe walls of his crib and Nana and a man who came to see him sometimes, and a great big orange ball that Nana pointed at just before his twilight bed hour and called "sun." When the sun went his eyes were sleepy—there were no dreams, no dreams to haunt him.

The past—the wild charge at the head of his men up San Juan Hill; the first years of his marriage when he worked late into the summer dusk down in the busy city for young Hildegarde whom he loved; the days before that when he sat smoking far into the night in the gloomy old Button house on Monroe Street with his grandfather—all these had faded like unsubstantial dreams from his mind as though they had never been.

He did not remember. He did not remember clearly whether the milk was warm or cool at his last feeding or how the days passed—there was only his crib and Nana's familiar presence. And then he remembered nothing. When he was hungry he cried—that was all. Through the noons and nights he breathed and over him there were soft mumblings and murmurings that he scarcely heard, and faintly differentiated smells, and light and darkness.

Then it was all dark, and his white crib and the dim faces that moved above him, and the warm sweet aroma of the milk, faded out altogether from his mind.

Tarquin of Cheapside

RUNNING footsteps—light, soft-soled shoes made of curious leathery cloth brought from Ceylon setting the pace; thick flowing boots, two pairs, dark blue and gilt, reflecting the moonlight in blunt gleams and splotches, following a stone's throw behind.

Soft Shoes flashes through a patch of moonlight, then darts into a blind labyrinth of alleys and becomes only an intermittent scuffle ahead somewhere in the enfolding darkness. In go Flowing Boots, with short swords lurching and long plumes awry, finding a breath to curse God and the black lanes of London.

Soft Shoes leaps a shadowy gate and crackles through a hedgerow. Flowing Boots leap the gate and crackles through the hedgerow—and there, startlingly, is the watch ahead—two murderous pikemen of ferocious cast of mouth acquired in Holland and the Spanish marches.

But there is no cry for help. The pursued does not fall panting at the feet of the watch, clutching a purse; neither do the pursuers raise a hue and cry. Soft Shoes goes by in a rush of swift air. The watch curse and hesitate, glance after the fugitive, and then spread their pikes grimly across the road and wait for Flowing Boots. Darkness, like a great hand, cuts off the even flow of the moon.

The hand moves off the moon whose pale caress finds again the eaves and lintels, and the watch, wounded and tumbled in the dust. Up the street one of Flowing Boots leaves a black trail of spots until he binds himself, clumsily as he runs, with fine lace caught from his throat.

It was no affair for the watch: Satan was at large tonight and Satan seemed to be he who appeared dimly in front, heel over gate, knee over fence. Moreover, the adversary was obviously travelling near home or at least in that section of London consecrated to his coarser whims, for the street narrowed like a road in a picture and the houses bent over further and further, cooping in natural ambushes suitable for murder and its histrionic sister, sudden death.

Down long and sinuous lanes twisted the hunted and the harriers, always in and out of the moon in a perpetual queen's move over a checker-board of glints and patches. Ahead, the quarry, minus his leather jerkin now and half blinded by drips of sweat, had taken to scanning his ground desperately on both sides. As a result he suddenly slowed short, and retracing his steps a bit scooted up an alley so dark that it seemed that here sun and moon had been in eclipse since the last glacier slipped roaring over the earth. Two hundred yards down he stopped and crammed himself into a niche in the wall where he huddled and panted silently, a grotesque god without bulk or outline in the gloom.

Flowing Boots, two pairs, drew near, came up, went by, halted twenty yards beyond him, and spoke in deep-lunged, scanty whispers:

"I was attune to that scuffle; it stopped."

"Within twenty paces."

"He's hid."

"Stay together now and we'll cut him up."

The voice faded into a low crunch of a boot, nor did Soft Shoes wait to hear more—he sprang in three leaps across the alley, where he bounded up, flapped for a moment on the top of the wall like a huge bird, and disappeared, gulped down by the hungry night at a mouthful.

II

"He read at wine, he read in bed,
He read aloud, had he the breath,
His every thought was with the dead,
And so he read himself to death."

Any visitor to the old James the First graveyard near Peat's Hill may spell out this bit of doggerel, undoubtedly one of the worst recorded of an Elizabethan, on the tomb of Wessel Caxter.

This death of his, says the antiquary, occurred when he was thirty-seven, but as this story is concerned with the night of a certain chase through darkness, we find him still alive, still reading. His eyes were somewhat dim, his stomach somewhat obvious—he was a misbuilt man and indolent—oh, Heavens! But an era is an era, and in the reign of Elizabeth, by the grace of Luther, Queen of England, no man could help but catch the spirit of enthusiasm. Every loft in Cheapside published its *Magnum Folium* (or magazine) of the new blank verse; the Cheapside Players would produce anything on sight as long as it "got away from those reactionary miracle plays," and the English Bible had run through seven "very large" printings in as many months.

So Wessel Caxter (who in his youth had gone to sea) was now a reader of all on which he could lay his hands—he read manuscripts in holy friendship; he dined rotten poets; he loitered about the shops where the *Magna Folia* were printed, and he listened tolerantly while the young playwrights wrangled and bickered among themselves, and behind each other's backs made bitter and malicious charges of plagiarism or anything else they could think of.

To-night he had a book, a piece of work which, though inordinately versed, contained, he thought, some rather excellent political satire. "The Faerie Queene" by Edmund Spenser lay before him under the tremulous candle-light. He had ploughed through a canto; he was beginning another:

The Legend of Britomartis or of Chastity
It falls me here to write of Chastity.
The fayrest vertue, far above the rest. . . .

A sudden rush of feet on the stairs, a rusty swing-open of the thin door, and a man thrust himself into the room, a man without a jerkin, panting, sobbing, on the verge of collapse.

"Wessel," words choked him, "stick me away somewhere, love of Our Lady!"

Caxter rose, carefully closing his book, and bolted the door in some concern.

"I'm pursued," cried out Soft Shoes. "I vow there's two short-witted blades trying to make me into mincemeat and near succeeding. They saw me hop the back wall!"

"It would need," said Wessel, looking at him curiously, "several battalions armed with blunderbusses, and two or three Armadas, to keep you reasonably secure from the revenges of the world."

Soft Shoes smiled with satisfaction. His sobbing gasps were giving way to quick, precise breathing; his hunted air had faded to a faintly perturbed irony.

"I feel little surprise," continued Wessel.

"They were two such dreary apes."

"Making a total of three."

"Only two unless you stick me away. Man, man, come alive; they'll be on the stairs in a spark's age."

Wessel took a dismantled pike-staff from the corner, and raising it to the high ceiling, dislodged a rough trap-door opening into a garret above.

"There's no ladder."

He moved a bench under the trap, upon which Soft Shoes mounted, crouched, hesitated, crouched again, and then leaped amazingly upward. He caught at the edge of the aperture and swung back and forth for a moment, shifting his hold; finally doubled up and disappeared into the darkness above. There was a scurry, a migration of rats, as the trap-door was replaced; . . . silence.

Wessel returned to his reading-table, opened to the Legend of Britomartis or of Chastity—and waited. Almost a minute later there was a scramble on the stairs and an intolerable hammering at the door. Wessel sighed and, picking up his candle, rose.

"Who's there?"

"Open the door!"

"Who's there?"

An aching blow frightened the frail wood, splintered it around the edge. Wessel opened it a scarce three inches, and held the candle high. His was to play the timorous, the super-respectable citizen, disgracefully disturbed.

"One small hour of the night for rest. Is that too much to ask from every brawler and——"

"Quiet, gossip! Have you seen a perspiring fellow?"

The shadows of two gallants fell in immense wavering outlines over the narrow stairs; by the light Wessel scrutinized them closely. Gentlemen, they were, hastily but richly dressed—one of them wounded severely in the hand, both radiating a sort of furious horror. Waving aside Wessel's ready miscomprehension, they pushed by him into the room and with their swords went through the business of poking carefully into all suspected dark spots in the room, further extending their search to Wessel's bedchamber.

"Is he hid here?" demanded the wounded man fiercely.

"Is who here?"

"Any man but you."

"Only two others that I know of."

For a second Wessel feared that he had been too damned funny, for the gallants made as though to prick him through.

"I heard a man on the stairs," he said hastily, "full five minutes ago, it was. He most certainly failed to come up."

He went on to explain his absorption in "The Faerie Queene" but, for the moment at least, his visitors, like the great saints, were anæsthetic to culture.

"What's been done?" inquired Wessel.

"Violence!" said the man with the wounded hand. Wessel noticed that his eyes were quite wild. "My own sister. Oh, Christ in heaven, give us this man!"

Wessel winced.

"Who is the man?"

"God's word! We know not even that. What's that trap up there?" he added suddenly.

"It's nailed down. It's not been used for years." He thought of the pole in the corner and quailed in his belly, but the utter despair of the two men dulled their astuteness.

"It would take a ladder for any one not a tumbler," said the wounded man listlessly.

His companion broke into hysterical laughter.

"A tumbler. Oh, a tumbler. Oh——"

Wessel stared at them in wonder.

"That appeals to my most tragic humor," cried the man, "that no one—oh, no one—could get up there but a tumbler."

The gallant with the wounded hand snapped his good fingers impatiently.

"We must go next door—and then on——"

Helplessly they went as two walking under a dark and storm-swept sky.

Wessel closed and bolted the door and stood a moment by it, frowning in pity.

A low-breathed "Ha!" made him look up. Soft Shoes had already raised the trap and was looking down into the room, his rather elfish face squeezed into a grimace, half of distaste, half of sardonic amusement.

"They take off their heads with their helmets," he remarked in a whisper, "but as for you and me, Wessel, we are two cunning men."

"Now you be cursed," cried Wessel vehemently. "I knew you for a dog, but when I hear even the half of a tale like this, I know you for such a dirty cur that I am minded to club your skull."

Soft Shoes stared at him, blinking.

"At all events," he replied finally, "I find dignity impossible in this position."

With this he let his body through the trap, hung for an instant, and dropped the seven feet to the floor.

"There was a rat considered my ear with the air of a gourmet," he continued, dusting his hands on his breeches. "I told him in the rat's peculiar idiom that I was deadly poison, so he took himself off."

"Let's hear of this night's lechery!" insisted Wessel angrily.

Soft Shoes touched his thumb to his nose and wiggled the fingers derisively at Wessel.

"Street gamin!" muttered Wessel.

"Have you any paper?" demanded Soft Shoes irrelevantly, and then rudely added, "or can you write?"

"Why should I give you paper?"

"You wanted to hear of the night's entertainment. So you shall, and you give me pen, ink, a sheaf of paper, and a room to myself."

Wessel hesitated.

"Get out!" he said finally.

"As you will. Yet you have missed a most intriguing story."

Wessel wavered—he was soft as taffy, that man—gave in. Soft Shoes went into the adjoining room with the begrudged writing materials and precisely closed the door. Wessel grunted and returned to "The Faerie Queene"; so silence came once more upon the house.

III

Three o'clock went into four. The room paled, the dark outside was shot through with damp and chill, and Wessel, cupping his brain in his hands, bent low over his table, tracing through the pattern of knights and fairies and the harrowing distresses of many girls. There were dragons chortling along the narrow street outside; when the sleepy armorer's boy began his work at half-past five the heavy clink and chank of plate and linked mail swelled to the echo of a marching cavalcade.

A fog shut down at the first flare of dawn, and the room was grayish yellow at six when Wessel tiptoed to his cupboard bedchamber and pulled open the door. His guest turned on him a face pale as parchment in which two distraught eyes burned like great red letters. He had drawn a chair close to Wessel's *prie-dieu* which he was using as a desk; and on it was an amazing stack of closely written pages. With a long sigh Wessel withdrew and returned to his siren, calling himself fool for not claiming his bed here at dawn.

The clump of boots outside, the croaking of old beldames from attic to attic, the dull murmur of morning, unnerved him, and, dozing, he slumped in his chair, his brain, overladen with sound and color, working intolerably over the imagery that stacked it. In this restless dream of his he was one of a thousand groaning bodies crushed near the sun, a helpless bridge for the strong-eyed Apollo. The dream tore at him, scraped along his mind like a ragged knife. When a hot hand touched his shoulder, he awoke with what was nearly a scream to find the fog thick in the room and his guest, a gray ghost of misty stuff, beside him with a pile of paper in his hand.

"It should be a most intriguing tale, I believe, though it requires some going over. May I ask you to lock it away, and in God's name let me sleep?"

He waited for no answer, but thrust the pile at Wessel, and literally poured himself like stuff from a suddenly inverted bottle upon a couch in the corner; slept, with his breathing regular, but his brow wrinkled in a curious and somewhat uncanny manner.

Wessel yawned sleepily and, glancing at the scrawled, uncertain first page, he began reading aloud very softly:

The Rape of Lucrece

"From the besieged Ardea all in post,
Borne by the trustless wings of false desire,
Lust-breathing Tarquin leaves the Roman host——"

"O Russet Witch!"

MERLIN GRAINGER was employed by the Moonlight Quill Bookshop, which you may have visited, just around the corner from the Ritz-Carlton on Forty-seventh Street. The Moonlight Quill is, or rather was, a very romantic little store, considered radical and admitted dark. It was spotted interiorly with red and orange posters of breathless exotic intent, and lit no less by the shiny reflecting bindings of special editions than by the great squat lamp of crimson satin that, lighted through all the day, swung overhead. It was truly a mellow bookshop. The words "Moonlight Quill" were worked over the door in a sort of serpentine embroidery. The windows seemed always full of something that had passed the literary censors with little to spare; volumes with covers of deep orange which offer their titles on little white paper squares. And over all there was the smell of the musk, which the clever, inscrutable Mr. Moonlight Quill ordered to be sprinkled about—the smell half of a curiosity shop in Dickens' London and half of a coffee-house on the warm shores of the Bosphorus.

From nine until five-thirty Merlin Grainger asked bored old ladies in black and young men with dark circles under their eyes if they "cared for this fellow" or were interested in first editions. Did they buy novels with Arabs on the cover, or books which gave Shakespeare's newest sonnets as dictated psychically to Miss Sutton of South Dakota? he sniffed. As a matter of fact, his own taste ran to these latter, but as an employee at the Moonlight Quill he assumed for the working day the attitude of a disillusioned connoisseur.

After he had crawled over the window display to pull down the front shade at five-thirty every afternoon, and said goodbye to the mysterious Mr. Moonlight Quill and the lady clerk, Miss McCracken, and the lady stenographer, Miss Masters, he went home to the girl, Caroline. He did not eat supper with Caroline. It is unbelievable that Caroline would have considered eating off his bureau with the collar buttons dangerously near the cottage cheese, and the ends of Merlin's necktie just missing his glass of milk—he had never asked her to eat with him. He ate alone. He went into Braegdort's delicatessen on Sixth Avenue and bought a box of crackers, a tube of anchovy paste, and some oranges, or else a little jar of sausages and some potato salad and a bottled soft drink, and with these in a brown package he went to his room at Fifty-something West Fifty-eighth Street and ate his supper and saw Caroline.

Caroline was a very young and gay person who lived with some older lady and was possibly nineteen. She was like a ghost in that she never existed until evening. She sprang into life when the lights went on in her apartment at about six, and she disappeared, at the latest, about midnight. Her apartment was a nice one, in a nice building with a white stone front, opposite the south side of Central Park. The back of her apartment faced the single window of the single room occupied by the single Mr. Grainger.

He called her Caroline because there was a picture that looked like her on the jacket of a book of that name down at the Moonlight Quill.

Now, Merlin Grainger was a thin young man of twenty-five, with dark hair and no mustache or beard or anything like that, but Caroline was dazzling and light, with a shimmering morass of russet waves to take the place of hair, and the sort of features that remind you of kisses—the sort of features you thought belonged to your first love, but know, when you come across an old picture, didn't. She dressed in pink or blue usually, but of late she had sometimes put on a slender black gown that was evidently her especial pride, for whenever she wore it she would stand regarding a certain place on the wall, which Merlin thought must be a mirror. She sat usually in the profile chair near the window, but sometimes honored the *chaise longue* by the lamp, and often she leaned 'way back and smoked a cigarette with posturings of her arms and hands that Merlin considered very graceful.

At another time she had come to the window and stood in it magnificently, and looked out because the moon had lost its way and was dripping the strangest and most transforming brilliance into the areaway between, turning the motif of ash-cans and clothes-lines into a vivid impressionism of silver casks and gigantic gossamer cobwebs. Merlin was sitting in plain sight, eating cottage cheese with sugar and milk on it; and so quickly did he reach out for the window cord that he tipped the cottage cheese into his lap with his free hand—and the milk was cold and the sugar made spots on his trousers, and he was sure that she had seen him after all.

Sometimes there were callers—men in dinner coats, who stood and bowed, hat in hand and coat on arm, as they talked to Caroline; then bowed some more and followed her out of the light, obviously bound for a play or for a dance. Other young men came and sat and smoked cigarettes, and seemed trying to tell Caroline something—she sitting either in the profile chair and watching them with eager intentness or else in the *chaise longue* by the lamp, looking very lovely and youthfully inscrutable indeed.

Merlin enjoyed these calls. Of some of the men he approved. Others won only his grudging toleration, one or two he loathed—especially the most frequent caller, a man with black hair and a black goatee and a pitch-dark soul, who seemed to Merlin vaguely familiar, but whom he was never quite able to recognize.

Now, Merlin's whole life was not "bound up with this romance he had constructed"; it was not "the happiest hour of his day." He never arrived in time to rescue Caroline from "clutches"; nor did he even marry her. A much stranger thing happened than any of these, and it is this strange thing that will presently be set down here. It began one October afternoon when she walked briskly into the mellow interior of the Moonlight Quill.

It was a dark afternoon, threatening rain and the end of the world, and done in that particularly gloomy gray in which only New York afternoons indulge. A breeze was crying down the streets, whisking along battered newspapers and pieces of things, and little lights were pricking out all the windows—it was so desolate that one was sorry for the tops of sky-scrapers lost up there in the dark green and gray heaven, and felt that now surely the farce was to close, and presently all the buildings would collapse like card houses, and pile up in a dusty, sardonic heap upon all the millions who presumed to wind in and out of them.

At least these were the sort of musings that lay heavily upon the soul of Merlin Grainger, as he stood by the window putting a dozen books back in a row, after a cyclonic visit by a lady with ermine trimmings. He looked out of the window full of the most distressing thoughts—of the early novels of H. G. Wells, of the book of Genesis, of how Thomas Edison had said that in thirty years there would be no dwelling-houses upon the island, but only a vast and turbulent bazaar; and then he set the last book right side up, turned—and Caroline walked coolly into the shop.

She was dressed in a jaunty but conventional walking costume—he remembered this when he thought about it later. Her skirt was plaid, pleated like a concertina; her jacket was a soft but brisk tan; her shoes and spats were brown and her hat, small and trim, completed her like the top of a very expensive and beautifully filled candy box.

Merlin, breathless and startled, advanced nervously toward her.

"Good-afternoon—" he said, and then stopped—why, he did not know, except that it came to him that something very portentous in his life was about to occur, and that it would need no furbishing but silence, and the proper amount of expectant attention. And in that minute before the thing began to happen he had the sense of a breathless second hanging suspended in time: he saw through the glass partition that bounded off the little office the malevolent conical head of his employer, Mr. Moonlight Quill, bent over his correspondence. He saw Miss McCracken and Miss Masters as two patches of hair drooping over piles of paper; he saw the crimson lamp overhead, and noticed with a touch of pleasure how really pleasant and romantic it made the book-store seem.

Then the thing happened, or rather it began to happen. Caroline picked up a volume of poems lying loose upon a pile, fingered it absently with her slender white hand, and suddenly, with an easy gesture, tossed it upward toward the ceiling, where it disappeared in the crimson lamp and lodged there, seen through the illuminated silk as a dark, bulging rectangle. This pleased her—she broke into young, contagious laughter, in which Merlin found himself presently joining.

"It stayed up!" she cried merrily. "It stayed up, didn't it?" To both of them this seemed the height of brilliant absurdity.

Their laughter mingled, filled the bookshop, and Merlin was glad to find that her voice was rich and full of sorcery.

"Try another," he found himself suggesting—"try a red one."

At this her laughter increased, and she had to rest her hands upon the stack to steady herself.

"Try another," she managed to articulate between spasms of mirth. "Oh, golly, try another!"

"Try two."

"Yes, try two. Oh, I'll choke if I don't stop laughing. Here it goes."

Suiting her action to the word, she picked up a red book and sent it in a gentle hyperbola toward the ceiling, where it sank into the lamp beside the first. It was a few minutes before either of them could do more than rock back and forth in helpless glee; but then by mutual agreement they took up the sport anew, this time in unison. Merlin seized a large, specially bound French classic and whirled it upward. Applauding his own accuracy, he took a best-seller in one hand and a book on barnacles in the other, and waited breathlessly while she made her shot. Then the business waxed fast and furious—sometimes they alternated, and, watching, he found how supple she was in every movement; sometimes one of them made shot after shot, picking up the nearest book, sending it off, merely taking time to follow it with a glance before reaching for another. Within three minutes they had cleared a little place on the table, and the lamp of crimson satin was so bulging with books that it was near breaking.

"Silly game, basket-ball," she cried scornfully as a book left her hand. "High-school girls play it in hideous bloomers."

"Idiotic," he agreed.

She paused in the act of tossing a book, and replaced it suddenly in its position on the table.

"I think we've got room to sit down now," she said gravely.

They had; they had cleared an ample space for two. With a faint touch of nervousness Merlin glanced toward Mr. Moonlight Quill's glass partition, but the three heads were still bent earnestly over their work, and it was evident that they had not seen what had gone on in the shop. So when Caroline put her hands on the table and hoisted herself up

Merlin calmly imitated her, and they sat side by side looking very earnestly at each other.

"I had to see you," she began, with a rather pathetic expression in her brown eyes.

"I know."

"It was that last time," she continued, her voice trembling a little, though she tried to keep it steady. "I was frightened. I don't like you to eat off the dresser. I'm so afraid you'll—you'll swallow a collar button."

"I did once—almost," he confessed reluctantly, "but it's not so easy, you know. I mean you can swallow the flat part easy enough or else the other part—that is, separately—but for a whole collar button you'd have to have a specially made throat." He was astonishing himself by the debonnaire appropriateness of his remarks. Words seemed for the first time in his life to run at him shrieking to be used, gathering themselves into carefully arranged squads and platoons, and being presented to him by punctilious adjutants of paragraphs.

"That's what scared me," she said. "I knew you had to have a specially made throat—and I knew, at least I felt sure, that you didn't have one."

He nodded frankly.

"I haven't. It costs money to have one—more money unfortunately than I possess."

He felt no shame in saying this—rather a delight in making the admission—he knew that nothing he could say or do would be beyond her comprehension; least of all his poverty, and the practical impossibility of ever extricating himself from it.

Caroline looked down at her wrist watch, and with a little cry slid from the table to her feet.

"It's after five," she cried. "I didn't realize. I have to be at the Ritz at five-thirty. Let's hurry and get this done. I've got a bet on it."

With one accord they set to work. Caroline began the matter by seizing a book on insects and sending it whizzing, and finally crashing through the glass partition that housed Mr. Moonlight Quill. The proprietor glanced up with a wild look, brushed a few pieces of glass from his desk, and went on with his letters. Miss McCracken gave no sign of having heard—

only Miss Masters started and gave a little frightened scream before she bent to her task again.

But to Merlin and Caroline it didn't matter. In a perfect orgy of energy they were hurling book after book in all directions, until sometimes three or four were in the air at once, smashing against shelves, cracking the glass of pictures on the walls, falling in bruised and torn heaps upon the floor. It was fortunate that no customers happened to come in, for it is certain they would never have come in again—the noise was too tremendous, a noise of smashing and ripping and tearing, mixed now and then with the tinkling of glass, the quick breathing of the two throwers, and the intermittent outbursts of laughter to which both of them periodically surrendered.

At five-thirty Caroline tossed a last book at the lamp, and so gave the final impetus to the load it carried. The weakened silk tore and dropped its cargo in one vast splattering of white and color to the already littered floor. Then with a sigh of relief she turned to Merlin and held out her hand.

"Good-by," she said simply.

"Are you going?" He knew she was. His question was simply a lingering wile to detain her and extract for another moment that dazzling essence of light he drew from her presence, to continue his enormous satisfaction in her features, which were like kisses and, he thought, like the features of a girl he had known back in 1910. For a minute he pressed the softness of her hand—then she smiled and withdrew it and, before he could spring to open the door, she had done it herself and was gone out into the turbid and ominous twilight that brooded narrowly over Forty-seventh Street.

I would like to tell you how Merlin, having seen how beauty regards the wisdom of the years, walked into the little partition of Mr. Moonlight Quill and gave up his job then and there; thence issuing out into the street a much finer and nobler and increasingly ironic man. But the truth is much more commonplace. Merlin Grainger stood up and surveyed the wreck of the bookshop, the ruined volumes, the torn silk remnants of the once beautiful crimson lamp, the crystalline sprinkling of broken glass which lay in iridescent dust over the whole interior—and then he went to a corner where a broom was kept and began cleaning up and rearranging and, as far as he was able, restoring the shop to its former condition. He found that, though some few of the books were uninjured, most of them had suffered in varying extents. The backs were off some, the pages were torn from others, still others were just slightly cracked in the front, which, as all careless book returners know, makes a book unsalable, and therefore second-hand.

Nevertheless by six o'clock he had done much to repair the damage. He had returned the books to their original places, swept the floor, and put new lights in the sockets overhead. The red shade itself was ruined beyond redemption, and Merlin thought in some trepidation that the money to replace it might have to come out of his salary. At six, therefore, having done the best he could, he crawled over the front window display to pull down the blind. As he was treading delicately back, he saw Mr. Moonlight Quill rise from his desk, put on his overcoat and hat, and emerge into the shop. He nodded mysteriously at Merlin and went toward the door. With his hand on the knob he paused, turned around, and in a voice curiously compounded of ferocity and uncertainty, he said:

"If that girl comes in here again, you tell her to behave."

With that he opened the door, drowning Merlin's meek "Yessir" in its creak, and went out.

Merlin stood there for a moment, deciding wisely not to worry about what was for the present only a possible futurity, and then he went into the back of the shop and invited Miss Masters to have supper with him at Pulpat's French Restaurant, where one could still obtain red wine at dinner, despite the Great Federal Government. Miss Masters accepted.

"Wine makes me feel all tingly," she said.

Merlin laughed inwardly as he compared her to Caroline, or rather as he didn't compare her. There was no comparison.

II

Mr. Moonlight Quill, mysterious, exotic, and oriental in temperament was, nevertheless, a man of decision. And it was with decision that he approached the problem of his wrecked shop. Unless he should make an outlay equal to the original cost of his entire stock—a step which for certain private reasons he did not wish to take—it would be impossible for him to continue in business with the Moonlight Quill as before. There was but one thing to do. He promptly turned his establishment from an up-to-the-minute book-store into a second-hand bookshop. The damaged books were marked down from twenty-five to fifty per cent, the name over the door whose serpentine embroidery had once shone so insolently bright, was allowed to grow dim and take on the indescribably vague color of old paint, and, having a strong penchant for ceremonial, the proprietor even went so far as to buy two skull-caps of shoddy red felt, one for himself and one for his clerk, Merlin Grainger. Moreover, he let his goatee grow until it resembled the tail-feathers of an ancient sparrow and substituted for a once dapper business suit a reverence-inspiring affair of shiny alpaca.

In fact, within a year after Caroline's catastrophic visit to the bookshop the only thing in it that preserved any semblance of being up to date was Miss Masters. Miss McCracken had followed in the footsteps of Mr. Moonlight Quill and become an intolerable dowd.

For Merlin too, from a feeling compounded of loyalty and listlessness, had let his exterior take on the semblance of a deserted garden. He accepted the red felt skull-cap as a symbol of his decay. Always a young man known as a "pusher," he had been, since the day of his graduation from the manual training department of a New York High School, an inveterate brusher of clothes, hair, teeth, and even eyebrows, and had learned the value of laying all his clean socks toe upon toe and heel upon heel in a certain drawer of his bureau, which would be known as the sock drawer.

These things, he felt, had won him his place in the greatest splendor of the Moonlight Quill. It was due to them that he was not still making "chests useful for keeping things," as he was taught with breathless practicality in High School, and selling them to whoever had use of such chests—possibly undertakers. Nevertheless when the progressive Moonlight Quill became the retrogressive Moonlight Quill he preferred to sink with it, and so took to letting his suits gather undisturbed the wispy burdens of the air and to throwing his socks indiscriminately into the shirt drawer, the underwear drawer, and even into no drawer at all. It was not uncommon in his new carelessness to let many of his clean clothes go directly back to the laundry without having ever been worn, a common eccentricity of impoverished bachelors. And this in the face of his favorite magazines, which at that time were fairly staggering with articles by successful authors against the frightful impudence of the condemned poor, such as the buying of wearable shirts and nice cuts of meat, and the fact that they preferred good investments in personal jewelry to respectable ones in four per cent saving-banks.

It was indeed a strange state of affairs and a sorry one for many worthy and God-fearing men. For the first time in the history of the Republic almost any negro north of Georgia could change a one-dollar bill. But as at that time the cent was rapidly approaching the purchasing power of the Chinese ubu and was only a thing you got back occasionally after paying for a soft drink, and could use merely in getting your correct weight, this was perhaps not so strange a phenomenon as it at first seems. It was too curious a state of things, however, for Merlin Grainger to take the step that he did take—the hazardous, almost involuntary step of proposing to Miss Masters. Stranger still that she accepted him.

It was at Pulpat's on Saturday night and over a $1.75 bottle of water diluted with *vin ordinaire* that the proposal occurred.

"Wine makes me feel all tingly, doesn't it you?" chattered Miss Masters gaily.

"Yes," answered Merlin absently; and then, after a long and pregnant pause: "Miss Masters—Olive—I want to say something to you if you'll listen to me."

The tingliness of Miss Masters (who knew what was coming) increased until it seemed that she would shortly be electrocuted by her own nervous reactions. But her "Yes, Merlin," came without a sign or flicker of interior disturbance. Merlin swallowed a stray bit of air that he found in his mouth.

"I have no fortune," he said with the manner of making an announcement. "I have no fortune at all."

Their eyes met, locked, became wistful, and dreamy and beautiful.

"Olive," he told her, "I love you."

"I love you too, Merlin," she answered simply. "Shall we have another bottle of wine?"

"Yes," he cried, his heart beating at a great rate. "Do you mean——"

"To drink to our engagement," she interrupted bravely. "May it be a short one!"

"No!" he almost shouted, bringing his fist fiercely down upon the table. "May it last forever!"

"What?"

"I mean—oh, I see what you mean. You're right. May it be a short one." He laughed and added, "My error."

After the wine arrived they discussed the matter thoroughly.

"We'll have to take a small apartment at first," he said, "and I believe, yes, by golly, I know there's a small one in the house where I live, a big room and a sort of a dressing-room-kitchenette and the use of a bath on the same floor."

She clapped her hands happily, and he thought how pretty she was really, that is, the upper part of her face—from the bridge of the nose down she was somewhat out of true. She continued enthusiastically:

"And as soon as we can afford it we'll take a real swell apartment, with an elevator and a telephone girl."

"And after that a place in the country—and a car."

"I can't imagine nothing more fun. Can you?"

Merlin fell silent a moment. He was thinking that he would have to give up his room, the fourth floor rear. Yet it mattered very little now. During the past year and a half—in fact, from the very date of Caroline's visit to the Moonlight Quill—he had never seen her. For a week after that visit her lights had failed to go on—darkness brooded out into the areaway, seemed to grope blindly in at his expectant, uncurtained window. Then the lights had appeared at last, and instead of Caroline and her callers they showed a stodgy family—a little man with a bristly mustache and a full-bosomed woman who spent her evenings patting her hips and rearranging bric-à-brac. After two days of them Merlin had callously pulled down his shade.

No, Merlin could think of nothing more fun than rising in

the world with Olive. There would be a cottage in a suburb, a cottage painted blue, just one class below the sort of cottages that are of white stucco with a green roof. In the grass around the cottage would be rusty trowels and a broken green bench and a baby-carriage with a wicker body that sagged to the left. And around the grass and the baby-carriage and the cottage itself, around his whole world there would be the arms of Olive, a little stouter, the arms of her neo-Olivian period, when, as she walked, her cheeks would tremble up and down ever so slightly from too much face-massaging. He could hear her voice now, two spoons' length away:

"I knew you were going to say this to-night, Merlin. I could see——"

She could see. Ah—suddenly he wondered how much she could see. Could she see that the girl who had come in with a party of three men and sat down at the next table was Caroline? Ah, could she see that? Could she see that the men brought with them liquor far more potent than Pulpat's red ink condensed threefold . . . ?

Merlin stared breathlessly, half-hearing through an auditory ether Olive's low, soft monologue, as like a persistent honey-bee she sucked sweetness from her memorable hour. Merlin was listening to the clinking of ice and the fine laughter of all four at some pleasantry—and that laughter of Caroline's that he knew so well stirred him, lifted him, called his heart imperiously over to her table, whither it obediently went. He could see her quite plainly, and he fancied that in the last year and a half she had changed, if ever so slightly. Was it the light or were her cheeks a little thinner and her eyes less fresh, if more liquid, than of old? Yet the shadows were still purple in her russet hair; her mouth hinted yet of kisses, as did the profile that came sometimes between his eyes and a row of books, when it was twilight in the bookshop where the crimson lamp presided no more.

And she had been drinking. The threefold flush in her cheeks was compounded of youth and wine and fine cosmetic—that he could tell. She was making great amusement for the young man on her left and the portly person on her right, and even for the old fellow opposite her, for the latter from time to time uttered the shocked and mildly reproachful cackles of another generation. Merlin caught the words of a song she was intermittently singing——

> "*Just snap your fingers at care,*
> *Don't cross the bridge 'til you're there——*"

The portly person filled her glass with chill amber. A waiter after several trips about the table, and many helpless glances at Caroline, who was maintaining a cheerful, futile questionnaire as to the succulence of this dish or that, managed to obtain the semblance of an order and hurried away. . . .

Olive was speaking to Merlin——

"When, then?" she asked, her voice faintly shaded with disappointment. He realized that he had just answered no to some question she had asked him.

"Oh, sometime."

"Don't you—care?"

A rather pathetic poignancy in her question brought his eyes back to her.

"As soon as possible, dear," he replied with surprising tenderness. "In two months—in June."

"So soon?" Her delightful excitement quite took her breath away.

"Oh, yes, I think we'd better say June. No use waiting."

Olive began to pretend that two months was really too short a time for her to make preparations. Wasn't he a bad boy! Wasn't he impatient, though! Well, she'd show him he mustn't be too quick with *her*. Indeed he was so sudden she didn't exactly know whether she ought to marry him at all.

"June," he repeated sternly.

Olive sighed and smiled and drank her coffee, her little finger lifted high above the others in true refined fashion. A stray thought came to Merlin that he would like to buy five rings and throw at it.

"By gosh!" he exclaimed aloud. Soon he *would* be putting rings on one of her fingers.

His eyes swung sharply to the right. The party of four had become so riotous that the head-waiter had approached and spoken to them. Caroline was arguing with this head-waiter in a raised voice, a voice so clear and young that it seemed as though the whole restaurant would listen—the whole restaurant except Olive Masters, self-absorbed in her new secret.

"How do you do?" Caroline was saying. "Probably the handsomest head-waiter in captivity. Too much noise? Very unfortunate. Something'll have to be done about it. Gerald"—she addressed the man on her right—"the head-waiter says there's too much noise. Appeals to us to have it stopped. What'll I say?"

"Sh!" remonstrated Gerald, with laughter. "Sh!" and Merlin heard him add in an undertone: "All the bourgeoisie will be aroused. This is where the floorwalkers learn French."

Caroline sat up straight in sudden alertness.

"Where's a floorwalker?" she cried. "Show me a floorwalker." This seemed to amuse the party, for they all, including Caroline, burst into renewed laughter. The head-waiter, after a last conscientious but despairing admonition, became Gallic with his shoulders and retired into the background.

Pulpat's, as every one knows, has the unvarying respectability of the table d'hôte. It is not a gay place in the conventional sense. One comes, drinks the red wine, talks perhaps a little more and a little louder than usual under the low, smoky ceilings, and then goes home. It closes up at nine-thirty, tight as a drum; the policeman is paid off and given an extra bottle of wine for the missis, the coat-room girl hands her tips to the collector, and then darkness crushes the little round tables out of sight and life. But excitement was prepared for Pulpat's this evening—excitement of no mean variety. A girl with russet, purple-shadowed hair mounted to her table-top and began to dance thereon.

"*Sacré nom de Dieu!* Come down off there!" cried the head-waiter. "Stop that music!"

But the musicians were already playing so loud that they could pretend not to hear his order; having once been young, they played louder and gayer than ever, and Caroline danced with grace and vivacity, her pink, filmy dress swirling about her, her agile arms playing in supple, tenuous gestures along the smoky air.

A group of Frenchmen at a table near by broke into cries of applause, in which other parties joined—in a moment the room was full of clapping and shouting; half the diners were on their feet, crowding up, and on the outskirts the hastily summoned proprietor was giving indistinct vocal evidences of his desire to put an end to this thing as quickly as possible.

". . . Merlin!" cried Olive, awake, aroused at last; "she's such a wicked girl! Let's get out—now!"

The fascinated Merlin protested feebly that the check was not paid.

"It's all right. Lay five dollars on the table. I despise that girl. I can't *bear* to look at her." She was on her feet now, tugging at Merlin's arm.

Helplessly, listlessly, and then with what amounted to downright unwillingness, Merlin rose, followed Olive dumbly as she picked her way through the delirious clamor, now approaching its height and threatening to become a wild and memorable riot. Submissively he took his coat and stumbled up half a dozen steps into the moist April air outside, his ears still ringing with the sound of light feet on the table and of laughter all about and over the little world of the café. In silence they walked along toward Fifth Avenue and a bus.

It was not until next day that she told him about the wedding—how she had moved the date forward: it was much better that they should be married on the first of May.

III

And married they were, in a somewhat stuffy manner, under the chandelier of the flat where Olive lived with her mother. After marriage came elation, and then, gradually, the growth of weariness. Responsibility descended upon Merlin, the responsibility of making his thirty dollars a week and her twenty suffice to keep them respectably fat and to hide with decent garments the evidence that they were.

It was decided after several weeks of disastrous and well-nigh humiliating experiments with restaurants that they would join the great army of the delicatessen-fed, so he took up his old way of life again, in that he stopped every evening at Braegdort's delicatessen and bought potatoes in salad, ham in slices, and sometimes even stuffed tomatoes in bursts of extravagance.

Then he would trudge homeward, enter the dark hallway,

and climb three rickety flights of stairs covered by an ancient carpet of long obliterated design. The hall had an ancient smell—of the vegetables of 1880, of the furniture polish in vogue when "Adam-and-Eve" Bryan ran against William McKinley, of portières an ounce heavier with dust, from worn-out shoes and lint from dresses turned long since into patch-work quilts. This smell would pursue him up the stairs, revivified and made poignant at each landing by the aura of contemporary cooking, then, as he began the next flight, diminishing into the odor of the dead routine of dead generations.

Eventually would occur the door of his room, which slipped open with indecent willingness and closed with almost a sniff upon his "Hello, dear! Got a treat for you to-night."

Olive, who always rode home on the bus to "get a morsel of air," would be making the bed and hanging up things. At his call she would come up to him and give him a quick kiss with wide-open eyes, while he held her upright like a ladder, his hands on her two arms, as though she were a thing without equilibrium, and would, once he relinquished hold, fall stiffly backward to the floor. This is the kiss that comes in with the second year of marriage, succeeding the bridegroom kiss (which is rather stagey at best, say those who know about such things, and apt to be copied from passionate movies).

Then came supper, and after that they went out for a walk, up two blocks and through Central Park, or sometimes to a moving picture, which taught them patiently that they were the sort of people for whom life was ordered, and that something very grand and brave and beautiful would soon happen to them if they were docile and obedient to their rightful superiors and kept away from pleasure.

Such was their day for three years. Then change came into their lives: Olive had a baby, and as a result Merlin had a new influx of material resources. In the third week of Olive's confinement, after an hour of nervous rehearsing, he went into the office of Mr. Moonlight Quill and demanded an enormous increase in salary.

"I've been here ten years," he said; "since I was nineteen. I've always tried to do my best in the interests of the business."

Mr. Moonlight Quill said that he would think it over. Next morning he announced, to Merlin's great delight, that he was going to put into effect a project long premeditated—he was going to retire from active work in the bookshop, confining himself to periodic visits and leaving Merlin as manager with a salary of fifty dollars a week and a one-tenth interest in the business. When the old man finished, Merlin's cheeks were glowing and his eyes full of tears. He seized his employer's hand and shook it violently, saying over and over again:

"It's very nice of you, sir. It's very white of you. It's very, very nice of you."

So after ten years of faithful work in the store he had won out at last. Looking back, he saw his own progress toward this hill of elation no longer as a sometimes sordid and always gray decade of worry and failing enthusiasm and failing dreams, years when the moonlight had grown duller in the areaway and the youth had faded out of Olive's face, but as a glorious and triumphant climb over obstacles which he had determinedly surmounted by unconquerable will-power. The optimistic self-delusion that had kept him from misery was seen now in the golden garments of stern resolution. Half a dozen times he had taken steps to leave the Moonlight Quill and soar upward, but through sheer faint-heartedness he had stayed on. Strangely enough he now thought that those were times when he had exerted tremendous persistence and had "determined" to fight it out where he was.

At any rate, let us not for this moment begrudge Merlin his new and magnificent view of himself. He had arrived. At thirty he had reached a post of importance. He left the shop that evening fairly radiant, invested every penny in his pocket in the most tremendous feast that Braegdort's delicatessen offered, and staggered homeward with the great news and four gigantic paper bags. The fact that Olive was too sick to eat, that he made himself faintly but unmistakably ill by a struggle with four stuffed tomatoes, and that most of the food deteriorated rapidly in an iceless ice-box all next day did not mar the occasion. For the first time since the week of his marriage Merlin Grainger lived under a sky of unclouded tranquillity.

The baby boy was christened Arthur, and life became dignified, significant, and, at length, centered. Merlin and Olive resigned themselves to a somewhat secondary place in their own cosmos; but what they lost in personality they regained in a sort of primordial pride. The country house did not come, but a month in an Asbury Park boarding-house each summer filled the gap; and during Merlin's two weeks' holiday this excursion assumed the air of a really merry jaunt—especially when, with the baby asleep in a wide room opening technically on the sea, Merlin strolled with Olive along the thronged board-walk puffing at his cigar and trying to look like twenty thousand a year.

With some alarm at the slowing up of the days and the accelerating of the years, Merlin became thirty-one, thirty-two—then almost with a rush arrived at that age which, with all its washing and panning, can only muster a bare handful of the precious stuff of youth: he became thirty-five. And one day on Fifth Avenue he saw Caroline.

It was Sunday, a radiant, flowerful Easter morning and the avenue was a pageant of lilies and cutaways and happy April-colored bonnets. Twelve o'clock: the great churches were letting out their people—St. Simon's, St. Hilda's, the Church of the Epistles, opened their doors like wide mouths until the people pouring forth surely resembled happy laughter as they met and strolled and chattered, or else waved white bouquets at waiting chauffeurs.

In front of the Church of the Epistles stood its twelve vestrymen, carrying out the time-honored custom of giving away Easter eggs full of face-powder to the church-going débutantes of the year. Around them delightedly danced the two thousand miraculously groomed children of the very rich, correctly cute and curled, shining like sparkling little jewels upon their mothers' fingers. Speaks the sentimentalist for the children of the poor? Ah, but the children of the rich, laundered, sweet-smelling, complexioned of the country, and, above all, with soft, in-door voices.

Little Arthur was five, child of the middle class. Undistinguished, unnoticed, with a nose that forever marred what Grecian yearnings his features might have had, he held tightly to his mother's warm, sticky hand, and, with Merlin on his other side, moved upon the home-coming throng. At Fifty-third Street, where there were two churches, the congestion was at its thickest, its richest. Their progress was of necessity retarded to such an extent that even little Arthur had not the slightest difficulty in keeping up. Then it was that Merlin perceived an open landaulet of deepest crimson, with handsome nickel trimmings, glide slowly up to the curb and come to a stop. In it sat Caroline.

She was dressed in black, a tight-fitting gown trimmed with lavender, flowered at the waist with a corsage of orchids. Merlin started and then gazed at her fearfully. For the first time in the eight years since his marriage he was encountering the girl again. But a girl no longer. Her figure was slim as ever—or perhaps not quite, for a certain boyish swagger, a sort of insolent adolescence, had gone the way of the first blooming of her cheeks. But she was beautiful; dignity was there now, and the charming lines of a fortuitous nine-and-twenty; and she sat in the car with such perfect appropriateness and self-possession that it made him breathless to watch her.

Suddenly she smiled—the smile of old, bright as that very Easter and its flowers, mellower than ever—yet somehow with not quite the radiance and infinite promise of that first smile back there in the bookshop nine years before. It was a steelier smile, disillusioned and sad.

But it was soft enough and smile enough to make a pair of young men in cutaway coats hurry over, to pull their high hats off their wetted, iridescent hair; to bring them, flustered and bowing, to the edge of her landaulet, where her lavender gloves gently touched their gray ones. And these two were presently joined by another, and then two more, until there was a rapidly swelling crowd around the landaulet. Merlin would hear a young man beside him say to his perhaps well-favored companion:

"If you'll just pardon me a moment, there's some one I *have* to speak to. Walk right ahead. I'll catch up."

Within three minutes every inch of the landaulet, front, back, and side, was occupied by a man—a man trying to construct a sentence clever enough to find its way to Caroline through the stream of conversation. Luckily for Merlin a portion of little Arthur's clothing had chosen the opportunity to threaten a collapse, and Olive had hurriedly rushed him over against a building for some extemporaneous repair work, so Merlin was able to watch, unhindered, the salon in the street.

The crowd swelled. A row formed in back of the first, two more behind that. In the midst, an orchid rising from a black bouquet, sat Caroline enthroned in her obliterated car, nodding and crying salutations and smiling with such true happiness that, of a sudden, a new relay of gentlemen had left their wives and consorts and were striding toward her.

The crowd, now phalanx deep, began to be augmented by the merely curious; men of all ages who could not possibly have known Caroline jostled over and melted into the circle of ever-increasing diameter, until the lady in lavender was the centre of a vast impromptu auditorium.

All about her were faces—clean-shaven, bewhiskered, old, young, ageless, and now, here and there, a woman. The mass was rapidly spreading to the opposite curb, and, as St. Anthony's around the corner let out its box-holders, it overflowed to the sidewalk and crushed up against the iron picket-fence of a millionaire across the street. The motors speeding along the avenue were compelled to stop, and in a jiffy were piled three, five, and six deep at the edge of the crowd; autobusses, top-heavy turtles of traffic, plunged into the jam, their passengers crowding to the edges of the roofs in wild excitement and peering down into the centre of the mass, which presently could hardly be seen from the mass's edge.

The crush had become terrific. No fashionable audience at a Yale-Princeton football game, no damp mob at a world's series, could be compared with the panoply that talked, stared, laughed, and honked about the lady in black and lavender. It was stupendous; it was terrible. A quarter mile down the block a half-frantic policeman called his precinct; on the same corner a frightened civilian crashed in the glass of a fire-alarm and sent in a wild pæan for all the fire-engines of the city; up in an apartment high in one of the tall buildings a hysterical old maid telephoned in turn for the prohibition enforcement agent, the special deputies on Bolshevism, and the maternity ward of Bellevue Hospital.

The noise increased. The first fire-engine arrived, filling the Sunday air with smoke, clanging and crying a brazen, metallic message down the high, resounding walls. In the notion that some terrible calamity had overtaken the city, two excited deacons ordered special services immediately and set tolling the great bells of St. Hilda's and St. Anthony's, presently joined by the jealous gongs of St. Simon's and the Church of the Epistles. Even far off in the Hudson and the East River the sounds of the commotion were heard, and the ferry-boats and tugs and ocean liners set up sirens and whistles that sailed in melancholy cadence, now varied, now reiterated, across the whole diagonal width of the city from Riverside Drive to the gray water-fronts of the lower East Side. . . .

In the centre of her landaulet sat the lady in black and lavender, chatting pleasantly first with one, then with another of that fortunate few in cutaways who had found their way to speaking distance in the first rush. After a while she glanced around her and beside her with a look of growing annoyance.

She yawned and asked the man nearest her if he couldn't run in somewhere and get her a glass of water. The man apologized in some embarrassment. He could not have moved hand or foot. He could not have scratched his own ear. . . .

As the first blast of the river sirens keened along the air, Olive fastened the last safety-pin in little Arthur's rompers and looked up. Merlin saw her start, stiffen slowly like hardening stucco, and then give a little gasp of surprise and disapproval.

"That woman," she cried suddenly. "Oh!"

She flashed a glance at Merlin that mingled reproach and pain, and without another word gathered up little Arthur with one hand, grasped her husband by the other, and darted amazingly in a winding, bumping canter through the crowd. Somehow people gave way before her; somehow she managed to retain her grasp on her son and husband; somehow she managed to emerge two blocks up, battered and dishevelled, into an open space, and, without slowing up her pace, darted down a side-street. Then at last, when uproar had died away into a dim and distant clamor, did she come to a walk and set little Arthur upon his feet.

"And on Sunday, too! Hasn't she disgraced herself enough?" This was her only comment. She said it to Arthur, as she seemed to address her remarks to Arthur throughout the remainder of the day. For some curious and esoteric reason she had never once looked at her husband during the entire retreat.

IV

The years between thirty-five and sixty-five revolve before the passive mind as one unexplained, confusing merry-go-round. True, they are a merry-go-round of ill-gaited and wind-broken horses, painted first in pastel colors, then in dull grays and browns, but perplexing and intolerably dizzy the thing is, as never were the merry-go-rounds of childhood or adolescence, as never, surely, were the certain-coursed, dynamic roller-coasters of youth. For most men and women these thirty years are taken up with a gradual withdrawal from life, a retreat first from a front with many shelters, those myriad amusements and curiosities of youth, to a line with less, when we peel down our ambitions to one ambition, our recreations to one recreation, our friends to a few to whom we are anæsthetic; ending up at last in a solitary, desolate strong point that is not strong, where the shells now whistle abominably, now are but half-heard as, by turns frightened and tired, we sit waiting for death.

At forty, then, Merlin was no different from himself at thirty-five; a larger paunch, a gray twinkling near his ears, a more certain lack of vivacity in his walk. His forty-five differed from his forty by a like margin, unless one mention a slight deafness in his left ear. But at fifty-five the process had become a chemical change of immense rapidity. Yearly he was more and more an "old man" to his family—senile almost, so far as his wife was concerned. He was by this time complete owner of the bookshop. The mysterious Mr. Moonlight Quill, dead some five years and not survived by his wife, had deeded the whole stock and store to him, and there he still spent his days, conversant now by name with almost all that man has recorded for three thousand years, a human catalogue, an authority upon tooling and binding, upon folios and first editions, an accurate inventory of a thousand authors whom he could never have understood and had certainly never read.

At sixty-five he distinctly doddered. He had assumed the melancholy habits of the aged so often portrayed by the second old man in standard Victorian comedies. He consumed vast warehouses of time searching for mislaid spectacles. He "nagged" his wife and was nagged in turn. He told the same jokes three or four times a year at the family table, and gave his son weird, impossible directions as to his conduct in life. Mentally and materially he was so entirely different from the Merlin Grainger of twenty-five that it seemed incongruous that he should bear the same name.

He worked still in the bookshop with the assistance of a youth, whom, of course, he considered very idle, indeed, and a new young woman, Miss Gaffney. Miss McCracken, ancient and unvenerable as himself, still kept the accounts. Young Arthur was gone into Wall Street to sell bonds, as all the young men seemed to be doing in that day. This, of course, was as it should be. Let old Merlin get what magic he could from his books—the place of young King Arthur was in the counting-house.

One afternoon at four when he had slipped noiselessly up to the front of the store on his soft-soled slippers, led by a newly formed habit, of which, to be fair, he was rather ashamed, of spying upon the young man clerk, he looked casually out of the front window, straining his faded eyesight to reach the street. A limousine, large, portentous, impressive, had drawn to the curb, and the chauffeur, after dismounting and holding some sort of conversation with persons in the interior of the car, turned about and advanced in a bewildered fashion toward the entrance of the Moonlight Quill. He opened the door, shuffled in, and, glancing uncertainly at the old man in the skull-cap, addressed him in a thick, murky voice, as though his words came through a fog.

"Do you—do you sell additions?"

Merlin nodded.

"The arithmetic books are in the back of the store."

The chauffeur took off his cap and scratched a close-cropped, fuzzy head.

"Oh, naw. This I want's a detecatif story." He jerked a thumb back toward the limousine. "She seen it in the paper. Firs' addition."

Merlin's interest quickened. Here was possibly a big sale.

"Oh, editions. Yes, we've advertised some firsts, but—detective stories, I—don't—believe—What was the title?"

"I forget. About a crime."

"About a crime. I have—well, I have 'The Crimes of the Borgias'—full morocco, London 1769, beautifully——"

"Naw," interrupted the chauffeur, "this was one fella did this crime. She seen you had it for sale in the paper." He rejected several possible titles with the air of connoisseur.

" 'Silver Bones,' " he announced suddenly out of a slight pause.

"What?" demanded Merlin, suspecting that the stiffness of his sinews were being commented on.

"Silver Bones. That was the guy that done the crime."

"Silver Bones?"

"Silver Bones. Indian, maybe."

Merlin stroked his grizzly cheeks.

"Gees, Mister," went on the prospective purchaser, "if you wanna save me an awful bawlin' out jes' try an' think. The old lady goes wile if everything don't run smooth."

But Merlin's musings on the subject of Silver Bones were as futile as his obliging search through the shelves, and five minutes later a very dejected charioteer wound his way back to his mistress. Through the glass Merlin could see the visible symbols of a tremendous uproar going on in the interior of the limousine. The chauffeur made wild, appealing gestures of his innocence, evidently to no avail, for when he turned around and climbed back into the driver's seat his expression was not a little dejected.

Then the door of the limousine opened and gave forth a pale and slender young man of about twenty, dressed in the attenuation of fashion and carrying a wisp of a cane. He entered the shop, walked past Merlin, and proceeded to take out a cigarette and light it. Merlin approached him.

"Anything I can do for you, sir?"

"Old boy," said the youth coolly, "there are several things. You can first let me smoke my ciggy in here out of sight of that old lady in the limousine, who happens to be my grandmother. Her knowledge as to whether I smoke it or not before my majority happens to be a matter of five thousand dollars to me. The second thing is that you should look up your first edition of the 'Crime of Sylvester Bonnard' that you advertised in last Sunday's *Times.* My grandmother there happens to want to take it off your hands."

Detecatif story! Crime of somebody! Silver Bones! All was explained. With a faint deprecatory chuckle, as if to say that he would have enjoyed this had life put him in the habit of enjoying anything, Merlin doddered away to the back of his shop where his treasures were kept, to get this latest investment which he had picked up rather cheaply at the sale of a big collection.

When he returned with it the young man was drawing on his cigarette and blowing out quantities of smoke with immense satisfaction.

"My God!" he said. "She keeps me so close to her the entire day running idiotic errands that this happens to be my first puff in six hours. What's the world coming to, I ask you, when a feeble old lady in the milk-toast era can dictate to a man as to his personal vices? I happen to be unwilling to be so dictated to. Let's see the book."

Merlin passed it to him tenderly and the young man, after opening it with a carelessness that gave a momentary jump to the book-dealer's heart, ran through the pages with his thumb.

"No illustrations, eh?" he commented. "Well, old boy, what's it worth? Speak up! We're willing to give you a fair price, though why I don't know."

"One hundred dollars," said Merlin with a frown.

The young man gave a startled whistle.

"Whew! Come on. You're not dealing with somebody from the cornbelt. I happen to be a city-bred man and my grandmother happens to be a city-bred woman, though I'll admit it'd take a special tax appropriation to keep her in repair. We'll give you twenty-five dollars, and let me tell you that's liberal. We've got books in our attic, up in our attic with my old playthings, that were written before the old boy that wrote this was born."

Merlin stiffened, expressing a rigid and meticulous horror.

"Did your grandmother give you twenty-five dollars to buy this with?"

"She did not. She gave me fifty, but she expects change. I know that old lady."

"You tell her," said Merlin with dignity, "that she has missed a very great bargain."

"Give you forty," urged the young man. "Come on now—be reasonable and don't try to hold us up——"

Merlin had wheeled around with the precious volume under his arm and was about to return it to its special drawer in his office when there was a sudden interruption. With unheard-of magnificence the front door burst rather than swung open, and admitted into the dark interior a regal apparition in black silk and fur which bore rapidly down upon him. The cigarette leaped from the fingers of the urban young man and he gave breath to an inadvertent "Damn!"—but it was upon Merlin that the entrance seemed to have the most remarkable and incongruous effect—so strong an effect that the greatest treasure of his shop slipped from his hand and joined the cigarette on the floor. Before him stood Caroline.

She was an old woman, an old woman remarkably preserved, unusually handsome, unusually erect, but still an old woman. Her hair was a soft, beautiful white, elaborately dressed and jewelled; her face, faintly rouged à la grande dame, showed webs of wrinkles at the edges of her eyes and two deeper lines in the form of stanchions connected her nose with the corners of her mouth. Her eyes were dim, ill natured, and querulous.

But it was Caroline without a doubt: Caroline's features though in decay; Caroline's figure, if brittle and stiff in movement; Caroline's manner, unmistakably compounded of a delightful insolence and an enviable self assurance; and, most of all, Caroline's voice, broken and shaky, yet with a ring in it that still could and did make chauffeurs want to drive laundry wagons and cause cigarettes to fall from the fingers of urban grandsons.

She stood and sniffed. Her eyes found the cigarette upon the floor.

"What's that?" she cried. The words were not a question—they were an entire litany of suspicion, accusation, confirmation, and decision. She tarried over them scarcely an instant.

"Stand up!" she said to her grandson, "stand up and blow that nicotine out of your lungs!"

The young man looked at her in trepidation.

"Blow!" she commanded.

He pursed his lips feebly and blew into the air.

"Blow!" she repeated, more peremptorily than before.

He blew again, helplessly, ridiculously.

"Do you realize," she went on briskly, "that you've forfeited five thousand dollars in five minutes?"

Merlin momentarily expected the young man to fall pleading upon his knees, but such is the nobility of human nature that he remained standing—even blew again into the air, partly from nervousness, partly, no doubt, with some vague hope of reingratiating himself.

"Young ass!" cried Caroline. "Once more, just once more and you leave college and go to work."

This threat had such an overwhelming effect upon the young man that he took on an even paler pallor than was natural to him. But Caroline was not through.

"Do you think I don't know what you and your brothers, yes, and your asinine father too, think of me? Well, I do. You think I'm senile. You think I'm soft. I'm not!" She struck herself with her fist as though to prove that she was a mass of muscle and sinew. "And I'll have more brains left when you've got me laid out in the drawing-room some sunny day than you and the rest of them were born with."

"But Grandmother——"

"Be quiet. You, a thin little stick of a boy, who if it weren't for my money might have risen to be a journeyman barber out in the Bronx—Let me see your hands. Ugh! The hands of a barber—*you* presume to be smart with *me*, who once had three counts and a bona-fide duke, not to mention half a dozen papal titles pursue me from the city of Rome to the city of New York." She paused, took breath. "Stand up! Blow!"

The young man obediently blew. Simultaneously the door opened and an excited gentleman of middle age who wore a coat and hat trimmed with fur, and seemed, moreover, to be trimmed with the same sort of fur himself on upper lip and chin, rushed into the store and up to Caroline.

"Found you at last," he cried. "Been looking for you all

over town. Tried your house on the 'phone and your secretary told me he thought you'd gone to a book-shop called the Moonlight——"

Caroline turned to him irritably.

"Do I employ you for your reminiscences?" she snapped. "Are you my tutor or my broker?"

"Your broker," confessed the fur-trimmed man, taken somewhat aback. "I beg your pardon. I came about that phonograph stock. I can sell for a hundred and five."

"Then do it."

"Very well. I thought I'd better——"

"Go sell it. I'm talking to my grandson."

"Very well. I——"

"Good-by."

"Good-by, Madame." The fur-trimmed man made a slight bow and hurried in some confusion from the shop.

"As for you," said Caroline, turning to her grandson, "you stay just where you are and be quiet."

She turned to Merlin and included his entire length in a not unfriendly survey. Then she smiled and he found himself smiling too. In an instant they had both broken into a cracked but none the less spontaneous chuckle. She seized his arm and hurried him to the other side of the store. There they stopped, faced each other, and gave vent to another long fit of senile glee.

"It's the only way," she gasped in a sort of triumphant malignity. "The only thing that keeps old folks like me happy is the sense that they can make other people step around. To be old and rich and have poor descendants is almost as much fun as to be young and beautiful and have ugly sisters."

"Oh, yes," chuckled Merlin. "I know. I envy you."

She nodded, blinking.

"The last time I was in here, forty years ago," she said, "you were a young man very anxious to kick up your heels."

"I was," he confessed.

"My visit must have meant a good deal to you."

"You have all along," he exclaimed. "I thought—I used to think at first that you were a real person—human, I mean."

She laughed.

"Many men have thought me inhuman."

"But now," continued Merlin excitedly, "I understand. Understanding is allowed to us old people—after nothing much matters. I see now that on a certain night when you danced upon a table-top you were nothing but my romantic yearning for a beautiful and perverse woman."

Her old eyes were far away, her voice no more than the echo of a forgotten dream.

"How I danced that night! I remember."

"You were making an attempt at me. Olive's arms were closing about me and you warned me to be free and keep my measure of youth and irresponsibility. But it seemed like an effect gotten up at the last moment. It came too late."

"You are very old," she said inscrutably. "I did not realize."

"Also I have not forgotten what you did to me when I was thirty-five. You shook me with that traffic tie-up. It was a magnificent effort. The beauty and power you radiated! You became personified even to my wife, and she feared you. For weeks I wanted to slip out of the house at dark and forget the stuffiness of life with music and cocktails and a girl to make me young. But then—I no longer knew how."

"And now you are so very old."

With a sort of awe she moved back and away from him.

"Yes, leave me!" he cried. "You are old also; the spirit withers with the skin. Have you come here only to tell me something I had best forget: that to be old and poor is perhaps more wretched than to be old and rich; to remind me that *my* son hurls my gray failure in my face?"

"Give me my book," she commanded harshly. "Be quick, old man!"

Merlin looked at her once more and then patiently obeyed. He picked up the book and handed it to her, shaking his head when she offered him a bill.

"Why go through the farce of paying me? Once you made me wreck these very premises."

"I did," she said in anger, "and I'm glad. Perhaps there had been enough done to ruin *me*."

She gave him a glance, half disdain, half ill-concealed uneasiness, and with a brisk word to her urban grandson moved toward the door.

Then she was gone—out of his shop—out of his life. The

door clicked. With a sigh he turned and walked brokenly back toward the glass partition that enclosed the yellowed accounts of many years as well as the mellowed, wrinkled Miss McCracken.

Merlin regarded her parched, cobwebbed face with an odd sort of pity. She, at any rate, had had less from life than he. No rebellious, romantic spirit cropping out unbidden had, in its memorable moments, given her life a zest and a glory.

Then Miss McCracken looked up and spoke to him:

"Still a spunky old piece, isn't she?"

Merlin started.

"Who?"

"Old Alicia Dare. Mrs. Thomas Allerdyce she is now, of course; has been these thirty years."

"What? I don't understand you." Merlin sat down suddenly in his swivel chair; his eyes were wide.

"Why, surely, Mr. Grainger, you can't tell me that you've forgotten her, when for ten years she was the most notorious character in New York. Why, one time when she was the corespondent in the Throckmorton divorce case she attracted so much attention on Fifth Avenue that there was a traffic tie-up. Didn't you read about it in the papers."

"I never used to read the papers." His ancient brain was whirring.

"Well, you can't have forgotten the time she came in here and ruined the business. Let me tell you I came near asking Mr. Moonlight Quill for my salary, and clearing out."

"Do you mean that—that you *saw* her?"

"Saw her! How could I help it with the racket that went on. Heaven knows Mr. Moonlight Quill didn't like it either, but of course *he* didn't say anything. He was daffy about her and she could twist him around her little finger. The second he opposed one of her whims she'd threaten to tell his wife on him. Served him right. The idea of that man falling for a pretty adventuress! Of course he was never rich enough for *her*, even though the shop paid well in those days."

"But when I saw her," stammered Merlin, "that is, when I *thought* I saw her, she lived with her mother."

"Mother, trash!" said Miss McCracken indignantly. "She had a woman there she called 'Aunty' who was no more related to her than I am. Oh, she was a bad one—but clever. Right after the Throckmorton divorce case she married Thomas Allerdyce, and made herself secure for life."

"Who was she?" cried Merlin. "For God's sake what was she—a witch?"

"Why, she was Alicia Dare, the dancer, of course. In those days you couldn't pick up a paper without finding her picture."

Merlin sat very quiet, his brain suddenly fatigued and stilled. He was an old man now indeed, so old that it was impossible for him to dream of ever having been young, so old that the glamour was gone out of the world, passing not into the faces of children and into the persistent comforts of warmth and life, but passing out of the range of sight and feeling. He was never to smile again or to sit in a long reverie when spring evenings wafted the cries of children in at his window until gradually they became the friends of his boyhood out there, urging him to come and play before the last dark came down. He was too old now even for memories.

That night he sat at supper with his wife and son, who had used him for their blind purposes. Olive said:

"Don't sit there like a death's-head. Say something."

"Let him sit quiet," growled Arthur. "If you encourage him he'll tell us a story we've heard a hundred times before."

Merlin went up-stairs very quietly at nine o'clock. When he was in his room and had closed the door tight he stood by it for a moment, his thin limbs trembling. He knew now that he had always been a fool.

"O Russet Witch!"

But it was too late. He had angered Providence by resisting too many temptations. There was nothing left but heaven, where he would meet only those who, like him, had wasted earth.

UNCLASSIFIED MASTERPIECES

The Lees of Happiness

IF YOU should look through the files of old magazines for the first years of the present century you would find, sandwiched in between the stories of Richard Harding Davis and Frank Norris and others long since dead, the work of one Jeffrey Curtain: a novel or two, and perhaps three or four dozen short stories. You could, if you were interested, follow them along until, say, 1908, when they suddenly disappeared.

When you had read them all you would have been quite sure that here were no masterpieces—here were passably amusing stories, a bit out of date now, but doubtless the sort that would then have whiled away a dreary half hour in a dental office. The man who did them was of good intelligence, talented, glib, probably young. In the samples of his work you found there would have been nothing to stir you to more than a faint interest in the whims of life—no deep interior laughs, no sense of futility or hint of tragedy.

After reading them you would yawn and put the number back in the files, and perhaps, if you were in some library reading-room, you would decide that by way of variety you would look at a newspaper of the period and see whether the Japs had taken Port Arthur. But if by any chance the newspaper you had chosen was the right one and had crackled open at the theatrical page, your eyes would have been arrested and held, and for at least a minute you would have forgotten Port Arthur as quickly as you forgot Château Thierry. For you would, by this fortunate chance, be looking at the portrait of an exquisite woman.

Those were the days of "Florodora" and of sextets, of pinched-in waists and blown-out sleeves, of almost bustles and absolute ballet skirts, but here, without doubt, disguised as she might be by the unaccustomed stiffness and old fashion of her costume, was a butterfly of butterflies. Here was the gayety of the period—the soft wine of eyes, the songs that flurried hearts, the toasts and the bouquets, the dances and the dinners. Here was a Venus of the hansom cab, the Gibson girl in her glorious prime. Here was . . .

. . . here was, you find by looking at the name beneath, one Roxanne Milbank, who had been chorus girl and understudy in "The Daisy Chain," but who, by reason of an excellent performance when the star was indisposed, had gained a leading part.

You would look again—and wonder. Why you had never heard of her. Why did her name not linger in popular songs and vaudeville jokes and cigar bands, and the memory of that gay old uncle of yours along with Lillian Russell and Stella Mayhew and Anna Held? Roxanne Milbank—whither had she gone? What dark trap-door had opened suddenly and swallowed her up? Her name was certainly not in last Sunday's supplement on that list of actresses married to English noblemen. No doubt she was dead—poor beautiful young lady—and quite forgotten.

I am hoping too much. I am having you stumble on Jeffrey Curtain's stories and Roxanne Milbank's picture. It would be incredible that you should find a newspaper item six months later, a single item two inches by four, which informed the public of the marriage, very quietly, of Miss Roxanne Milbank, who had been on tour with "The Daisy Chain," to Mr. Jeffrey Curtain, the popular author. "Mrs. Curtain," it added dispassionately, "will retire from the stage."

It was a marriage of love. He was sufficiently spoiled to be charming; she was ingenuous enough to be irresistible. Like two floating logs they met in a head-on rush, caught, and sped along together. Yet had Jeffrey Curtain kept at scrivening for twoscore years he could not have put a quirk into one of his stories weirder than the quirk that came into his own life. Had Roxanne Milbank played three dozen parts and filled five thousand houses she could never have had a rôle with more happiness and more despair than were in the fate prepared for Roxanne Curtain.

For a year they lived in hotels, travelled to California, to Alaska, to Florida, to Mexico, loved and quarrelled gently, and gloried in the golden triflings of his wit with her beauty—they were young and gravely passionate; they demanded everything and then yielded everything again in ecstasies of unselfishness and pride. She loved the swift tones of his voice and his frantic, unfounded jealousy. He loved her dark radiance, the white irises of her eyes, the warm, lustrous enthusiasm of her smile.

"Don't you like her?" he would demand rather excitedly and shyly. "Isn't she wonderful? Did you ever see——"

"Yes," they would answer, grinning. "She's a wonder. You're lucky."

The year passed. They tired of hotels. They bought an old house and twenty acres near the town of Marlowe, half an hour from Chicago; bought a little car, and moved out riotously with a pioneering hallucination that would have confounded Balboa.

"Your room will be here!" they cried in turn.

—And then:

"And my room here!"

"And the nursery here when we have children."

"And we'll build a sleeping porch—oh, next year."

They moved out in April. In July Jeffrey's closest friend, Harry Cromwell, came to spend a week—they met him at the end of the long lawn and hurried him proudly to the house.

Harry was married also. His wife had had a baby some six months before and was still recuperating at her mother's in New York. Roxanne had gathered from Jeffrey that Harry's wife was not as attractive as Harry—Jeffrey had met her once and considered her—"shallow." But Harry had been married nearly two years and was apparently happy, so Jeffrey guessed that she was probably all right . . .

"I'm making biscuits," chattered Roxanne gravely. "Can your wife make biscuits? The cook is showing me how. I think every woman should know how to make biscuits. It sounds so utterly disarming. A woman who can make biscuits can surely do no——"

"You'll have to come out here and live," said Jeffrey. "Get a place out in the country like us, for you and Kitty."

"You don't know Kitty. She hates the country. She's got to have her theatres and vaudevilles."

"Bring her out," repeated Jeffrey. "We'll have a colony. There's an awfully nice crowd here already. Bring her out!"

They were at the porch steps now and Roxanne made a brisk gesture toward a dilapidated structure on the right.

"The garage," she announced. "It will also be Jeffrey's writing-room within the month. Meanwhile dinner is at seven. Meanwhile to that I will mix a cocktail."

The two men ascended to the second floor—that is, they ascended half-way, for at the first landing Jeffrey dropped his guest's suitcase and in a cross between a query and a cry exclaimed:

"For God's sake, Harry, how do you like her?"

"We will go up-stairs," answered his guest, "and we will shut the door."

Half an hour later as they were sitting together in the library Roxanne reissued from the kitchen, bearing before her a pan of biscuits. Jeffrey and Harry rose.

"They're beautiful, dear," said the husband, intensely.

"Exquisite," murmured Harry.

Roxanne beamed.

"Taste one. I couldn't bear to touch them before you'd seen them all and I can't bear to take them back until I find what they taste like."

"Like manna, darling."

Simultaneously the two men raised the biscuits to their lips, nibbled tentatively. Simultaneously they tried to change the subject. But Roxanne, undeceived, set down the pan and seized a biscuit. After a second her comment rang out with lugubrious finality:

"Absolutely bum!"

"Really——"

"Why, I didn't notice——"

Roxanne roared.

"Oh, I'm useless," she cried laughing. "Turn me out, Jeffrey—I'm a parasite; I'm no good——"

Jeffrey put his arm around her.

"Darling, I'll eat your biscuits."

"They're beautiful, anyway," insisted Roxanne.

"They're—they're decorative," suggested Harry.

Jeffrey took him up wildly.

"That's the word. They're decorative; they're masterpieces. We'll use them."

He rushed to the kitchen and returned with a hammer and a handful of nails.

"We'll use them, by golly, Roxanne! We'll make a frieze out of them."

"Don't!" wailed Roxanne. "Our beautiful house."

"Never mind. We're going to have the library repapered in October. Don't you remember?"

"Well——"

Bang! The first biscuit was impaled to the wall, where it quivered for a moment like a live thing.

Bang! . . .

When Roxanne returned with a second round of cocktails the biscuits were in a perpendicular row, twelve of them, like a collection of primitive spear-heads.

"Roxanne," exclaimed Jeffrey, "you're an artist! Cook?—nonsense! You shall illustrate my books!"

During dinner the twilight faltered into dusk, and later it was a starry dark outside, filled and permeated with the frail gorgeousness of Roxanne's white dress and her tremulous, low laugh.

—Such a little girl she is, thought Harry. Not as old as Kitty.

He compared the two. Kitty—nervous without being sensitive, temperamental without temperament, a woman who seemed to flit and never light—and Roxanne, who was as young as spring night, and summed up in her own adolescent laughter.

—A good match for Jeffrey, he thought again. Two very young people, the sort who'll stay very young until they suddenly find themselves old.

Harry thought these things between his constant thoughts about Kitty. He was depressed about Kitty. It seemed to him that she was well enough to come back to Chicago and bring his little son. He was thinking vaguely of Kitty when he said good-night to his friend's wife and his friend at the foot of the stairs.

"You're our first real house guest," called Roxanne after him. "Aren't you thrilled and proud?"

When he was out of sight around the stair corner she turned to Jeffrey, who was standing beside her resting his hand on the end of the banister.

"Are you tired, my dearest?"

Jeffrey rubbed the centre of his forehead with his fingers.

"A little. How did you know?"

"Oh, how could I help knowing about you?"

"It's a headache," he said moodily. "Splitting. I'll take some aspirin."

She reached over and snapped out the light, and with his arm tight about her waist they walked up the stairs together.

II

Harry's week passed. They drove about the dreaming lanes or idled in cheerful inanity upon lake or lawn. In the evening Roxanne, sitting inside, played to them while the ashes whitened on the glowing ends of their cigars. Then came a telegram from Kitty saying that she wanted Harry to come East and get her, so Roxanne and Jeffrey were left alone in that privacy of which they never seemed to tire.

"Alone" thrilled them again. They wandered about the house, each feeling intimately the presence of the other; they sat on the same side of the table like honeymooners; they were intensely absorbed, intensely happy.

The town of Marlowe, though a comparatively old settlement, had only recently acquired a "society." Five or six years before, alarmed at the smoky swelling of Chicago, two or three young married couples, "bungalow people," had moved out; their friends had followed. The Jeffrey Curtains found an already formed "set" prepared to welcome them; a country club, ballroom, and golf links yawned for them, and there were bridge parties, and poker parties, and parties where they drank beer, and parties where they drank nothing at all.

It was at a poker party that they found themselves a week after Harry's departure. There were two tables, and a good proportion of the young wives were smoking and shouting their bets, and being very daringly mannish for those days.

Roxanne had left the game early and taken to perambulation; she wandered into the pantry and found herself some grape juice—beer gave her a headache—and then passed from table to table, looking over shoulders at the hands, keeping an eye on Jeffrey and being pleasantly unexcited and content.

Jeffrey, with intense concentration, was raising a pile of chips of all colors, and Roxanne knew by the deepened wrinkle between his eyes that he was interested. She liked to see him interested in small things.

She crossed over quietly and sat down on the arm of his chair.

She sat there five minutes, listening to the sharp intermittent comments of the men and the chatter of the women, which rose from the table like soft smoke—and yet scarcely hearing either. Then quite innocently she reached out her hand, intending to place it on Jeffrey's shoulder—as it touched him he started of a sudden, gave a short grunt, and, sweeping back his arm furiously, caught her a glancing blow on her elbow.

There was a general gasp. Roxanne regained her balance, gave a little cry, and rose quickly to her feet. It had been the greatest shock of her life. This, from Jeffrey, the heart of kindness, of consideration—this instinctively brutal gesture.

The gasp became a silence. A dozen eyes were turned on Jeffrey, who looked up as though seeing Roxanne for the first time. An expression of bewilderment settled on his face.

"Why—Roxanne——" he said haltingly.

Into a dozen minds entered a quick suspicion, a rumor of scandal. Could it be that behind the scenes with this couple, apparently so in love, lurked some curious antipathy? Why else this streak of fire across such a cloudless heaven?

"Jeffrey!"—Roxanne's voice was pleading—startled and horrified, she yet knew that it was a mistake. Not once did it occur to her to blame him or to resent it. Her word was a trembling supplication—"Tell me, Jeffrey," it said, "tell Roxanne, your own Roxanne."

"Why, Roxanne—" began Jeffrey again. The bewildered look changed to pain. He was clearly as startled as she. "I didn't intend that," he went on; "you startled me. You—I felt as if some one were attacking me. I—how—why, how idiotic!"

"Jeffrey!" Again the word was a prayer, incense offered up to a high God through this new and unfathomable darkness.

They were both on their feet, they were saying good-by, faltering, apologizing, explaining. There was no attempt to pass it off easily. That way lay sacrilege. Jeffrey had not been feeling well, they said. He had become nervous. Back of both their minds was the unexplained horror of that blow—the marvel that there had been for an instant something between them—his anger and her fear—and now to both a sorrow, momentary, no doubt, but to be bridged at once, at once, while there was yet time. Was that swift water lashing under their feet—the fierce glint of some uncharted chasm?

Out in their car under the harvest moon he talked brokenly. It was just—incomprehensible to him, he said. He had been thinking of the poker game—absorbed—and the touch on his shoulder had seemed like an attack. An attack! He clung to that word, flung it up as a shield. He had hated what touched him. With the impact of his hand it had gone, that—nervousness. That was all he knew.

Both their eyes filled with tears and they whispered love there under the broad night as the serene streets of Marlowe sped by. Later, when they went to bed, they were quite calm. Jeffrey was to take a week off all work—was simply to loll, and sleep, and go on long walks until this nervousness left him. When they had decided this safety settled down upon Roxanne. The pillows underhead became soft and friendly; the bed on which they lay seemed wide, and white, and sturdy beneath the radiance that streamed in at the window.

Five days later, in the first cool of late afternoon, Jeffrey picked up an oak chair and sent it crashing through his own front window. Then he lay down on the couch like a child, weeping piteously and begging to die. A blood clot the size of a marble had broken in his brain.

III

There is a sort of waking nightmare that sets in sometimes when one has missed a sleep or two, a feeling that comes with extreme fatigue and a new sun, that the quality of the life around has changed. It is a fully articulate conviction that somehow the existence one is then leading is a branch shoot of life and is related to life only as a moving picture or a mirror—that the people, and streets, and houses are only projections from a very dim and chaotic past. It was in such a state that Roxanne found herself during the first months of

Jeffrey's illness. She slept only when she was utterly exhausted; she awoke under a cloud. The long, sober-voiced consultations, the faint aura of medicine in the halls, the sudden tiptoeing in a house that had echoed to many cheerful footsteps, and, most of all, Jeffrey's white face amid the pillows of the bed they had shared—these things subdued her and made her indelibly older. The doctors held out hope, but that was all. A long rest, they said, and quiet. So responsibility came to Roxanne. It was she who paid the bills, pored over his bank-book, corresponded with his publishers. She was in the kitchen constantly. She learned from the nurse how to prepare his meals and after the first month took complete charge of the sick-room. She had had to let the nurse go for reasons of economy. One of the two colored girls left at the same time. Roxanne was realizing that they had been living from short story to short story.

The most frequent visitor was Harry Cromwell. He had been shocked and depressed by the news, and though his wife was now living with him in Chicago he found time to come out several times a month. Roxanne found his sympathy welcome—there was some quality of suffering in the man, some inherent pitifulness that made her comfortable when he was near. Roxanne's nature had suddenly deepened. She felt sometimes that with Jeffrey she was losing her children also, those children that now most of all she needed and should have had.

It was six months after Jeffrey's collapse and when the nightmare had faded, leaving not the old world but a new one, grayer and colder, that she went to see Harry's wife. Finding herself in Chicago with an extra hour before train time, she decided out of courtesy to call.

As she stepped inside the door she had an immediate impression that the apartment was very like some place she had seen before—and almost instantly she remembered a round-the-corner bakery of her childhood, a bakery full of rows and rows of pink frosted cakes—a stuffy pink, pink as a food, pink triumphant, vulgar, and odious.

And this apartment was like that. It was pink. It smelled pink!

Mrs. Cromwell, attired in a wrapper of pink and black,

opened the door. Her hair was yellow, heightened, Roxanne imagined, by a dash of peroxide in the rinsing water every week. Her eyes were a thin waxen blue—she was pretty and too consciously graceful. Her cordiality was strident and intimate, hostility melted so quickly to hospitality that it seemed they were both merely in the face and voice—never touching nor touched by the deep core of egotism beneath.

But to Roxanne these things were secondary; her eyes were caught and held in uncanny fascination by the wrapper. It was vilely unclean. From its lowest hem up four inches it was sheerly dirty with the blue dust of the floor; for the next three inches it was gray—then it shaded off into its natural color, which was—pink. It was dirty at the sleeves, too, and at the collar—and when the woman turned to lead the way into the parlor, Roxanne was sure that her neck was dirty.

A one-sided rattle of conversation began. Mrs. Cromwell became explicit about her likes and dislikes, her head, her stomach, her teeth, her apartment—avoiding with a sort of insolent meticulousness any inclusion of Roxanne with life, as if presuming that Roxanne, having been dealt a blow, wished life to be carefully skirted.

Roxanne smiled. That kimono! That neck!

After five minutes a little boy toddled into the parlor—a dirty little boy clad in dirty pink rompers. His face was smudgy—Roxanne wanted to take him into her lap and wipe his nose; other parts in the vicinity of his head needed attention, his tiny shoes were kicked out at the toes. Unspeakable!

"What a darling little boy!" exclaimed Roxanne, smiling radiantly. "Come here to me."

Mrs. Cromwell looked coldly at her son.

"He *will* get dirty. Look at that face!" She held her head on one side and regarded it critically.

"Isn't he a *darling*?" repeated Roxanne.

"Look at his rompers," frowned Mrs. Cromwell.

"He needs a change, don't you, George?"

George stared at her curiously. To his mind the word rompers connotated a garment extraneously smeared, as this one.

"I tried to make him look respectable this morning," complained Mrs. Cromwell as one whose patience had been sorely tried, "and I found he didn't have any more rompers—so rather than have him go round without any I put him back in those—and his face——"

"How many pairs has he?" Roxanne's voice was pleasantly curious. "How many feather fans have you?" she might have asked.

"Oh,——" Mrs. Cromwell considered, wrinkling her pretty brow. "Five, I think. Plenty, I know."

"You can get them for fifty cents a pair."

Mrs. Cromwell's eyes showed surprise—and the faintest superiority. The price of rompers!

"Can you really? I had no idea. He ought to have plenty, but I haven't had a minute all week to send the laundry out." Then, dismissing the subject as irrelevant—"I must show you some things——"

They rose and Roxanne followed her past an open bathroom door whose garment-littered floor showed indeed that the laundry hadn't been sent out for some time, into another room that was, so to speak, the quintessence of pinkness. This was Mrs. Cromwell's room.

Here the hostess opened a closet door and displayed before Roxanne's eyes an amazing collection of lingerie. There were dozens of filmy marvels of lace and silk, all clean, unruffled, seemingly not yet touched. On hangers beside them were three new evening dresses.

"I have some beautiful things," said Mrs. Cromwell, "but not much of a chance to wear them. Harry doesn't care about going out." Spite crept into her voice. "He's perfectly content to let me play nursemaid and housekeeper all day and loving wife in the evening."

Roxanne smiled again.

"You've got some beautiful clothes here."

"Yes, I have. Let me show you——"

"Beautiful," repeated Roxanne, interrupting, "but I'll have to run if I'm going to catch my train."

She felt that her hands were trembling. She wanted to put them on this woman and shake her—shake her. She wanted her locked up somewhere and set to scrubbing floors.

"Beautiful," she repeated, "and I just came in for a moment."

"Well, I'm sorry Harry isn't here."

They moved toward the door.

"—and, oh," said Roxanne with an effort—yet her voice was still gentle and her lips were smiling—"I think it's Argile's where you can get those rompers. Good-by."

It was not until she had reached the station and bought her ticket to Marlowe that Roxanne realized it was the first five minutes in six months that her mind had been off Jeffrey.

IV

A week later Harry appeared at Marlowe, arrived unexpectedly at five o'clock, and coming up the walk sank into a porch chair in a state of exhaustion. Roxanne herself had had a busy day and was worn out. The doctors were coming at five-thirty, bringing a celebrated nerve specialist from New York. She was excited and thoroughly depressed, but Harry's eyes made her sit down beside him.

"What's the matter?"

"Nothing, Roxanne," he denied. "I came to see how Jeff was doing. Don't you bother about me."

"Harry," insisted Roxanne, "there's something the matter."

"Nothing," he repeated. "How's Jeff?"

Anxiety darkened her face.

"He's a little worse, Harry. Doctor Jewett has come on from New York. They thought he could tell me something definite. He's going to try and find whether this paralysis has anything to do with the original blood clot."

Harry rose.

"Oh, I'm sorry," he said jerkily. "I didn't know you expected a consultation. I wouldn't have come. I thought I'd just rock on your porch for an hour——"

"Sit down," she commanded.

Harry hesitated.

"Sit down, Harry, dear boy." Her kindness flooded out now—enveloped him. "I know there's something the matter. You're white as a sheet. I'm going to get you a cool bottle of beer."

All at once he collapsed into his chair and covered his face with his hands.

"I can't make her happy," he said slowly. "I've tried and I've tried. This morning we had some words about breakfast—I'd been getting my breakfast down town—and—well, just after I went to the office she left the house, went East to her mother's with George and a suitcase full of lace underwear."

"Harry!"

"And I don't know——"

There was a crunch on the gravel, a car turning into the drive. Roxanne uttered a little cry.

"It's Doctor Jewett."

"Oh, I'll——"

"You'll wait, won't you?" she interrupted abstractedly. He saw that his problem had already died on the troubled surface of her mind.

There was an embarrassing minute of vague, elided introductions and then Harry followed the party inside and watched them disappear up the stairs. He went into the library and sat down on the big sofa.

For an hour he watched the sun creep up the patterned folds of the chintz curtains. In the deep quiet a trapped wasp buzzing on the inside of the window pane assumed the proportions of a clamor. From time to time another buzzing drifted down from up-stairs, resembling several more larger wasps caught on larger window-panes. He heard low footfalls, the clink of bottles, the clamor of pouring water.

What had he and Roxanne done that life should deal these crashing blows to them? Up-stairs there was taking place a living inquest on the soul of his friend; he was sitting here in a quiet room listening to the plaint of a wasp, just as when he was a boy he had been compelled by a strict aunt to sit hour-long on a chair and atone for some misbehavior. But who had put him here? What ferocious aunt had leaned out of the sky to make him atone for—what?

About Kitty he felt a great hopelessness. She was too expensive—that was the irremediable difficulty. Suddenly he hated her. He wanted to throw her down and kick at her—to tell her she was a cheat and a leech—that she was dirty. Moreover, she must give him his boy.

He rose and began pacing up and down the room. Simultaneously he heard some one begin walking along the hallway up-stairs in exact time with him. He found himself wondering if they would walk in time until the person reached the end of the hall.

Kitty had gone to her mother. God help her, what a mother to go to! He tried to imagine the meeting: the abused wife collapsing upon the mother's breast. He could not. That Kitty was capable of any deep grief was unbelievable. He had gradually grown to think of her as something unapproachable and callous. She would get a divorce, of course, and eventually she would marry again. He began to consider this. Whom would she marry? He laughed bitterly, stopped; a picture flashed before him—of Kitty's arms around some man whose face he could not see, of Kitty's lips pressed close to other lips in what was surely passion.

"God!" he cried aloud. "God! God! God!"

Then the pictures came thick and fast. The Kitty of this morning faded; the soiled kimono rolled up and disappeared; the pouts, and rages, and tears all were washed away. Again she was Kitty Carr—Kitty Carr with yellow hair and great baby eyes. Ah, she had loved him, she had loved him.

After a while he perceived that something was amiss with him, something that had nothing to do with Kitty or Jeff, something of a different genre. Amazingly it burst on him at last; he was hungry. Simple enough! He would go into the kitchen in a moment and ask the colored cook for a sandwich. After that he must go back to the city.

He paused at the wall, jerked at something round, and, fingering it absently, put it to his mouth and tasted it as a baby tastes a bright toy. His teeth closed on it—Ah!

She'd left that damn kimono, that dirty pink kimono. She might have had the decency to take it with her, he thought. It would hang in the house like the corpse of their sick alliance. He would try to throw it away, but he would never be able to bring himself to move it. It would be like Kitty, soft and pliable, withal impervious. You couldn't move Kitty; you couldn't reach Kitty. There was nothing there to reach. He understood that perfectly—he had understood it all along.

He reached to the wall for another biscuit and with an effort pulled it out, nail and all. He carefully removed the nail from the centre, wondering idly if he had eaten the nail with the first biscuit. Preposterous! He would have remembered—it was a huge nail. He felt his stomach. He must be very hungry. He considered—remembered—yesterday he had had no dinner. It was the girl's day out and Kitty had lain in her room eating chocolate drops. She had said she felt "smothery" and couldn't bear having him near her. He had given George a bath and put him to bed, and then lain down on the couch intending to rest a minute before getting his own dinner. There he had fallen asleep and awakened about eleven, to find that there was nothing in the ice-box except a spoonful of potato salad. This he had eaten, together with some chocolate drops that he found on Kitty's bureau. This morning he had breakfasted hurriedly down town before going to the office. But at noon, beginning to worry about Kitty, he had decided to go home and take her out to lunch. After that there had been the note on his pillow. The pile of lingerie in the closet was gone—and she had left instructions for sending her trunk.

He had never been so hungry, he thought.

At five o'clock, when the visiting nurse tiptoed downstairs, he was sitting on the sofa staring at the carpet.

"Mr. Cromwell?"

"Yes?"

"Oh, Mrs. Curtain won't be able to see you at dinner. She's not well. She told me to tell you that the cook will fix you something and that there's a spare bedroom."

"She's sick, you say?"

"She's lying down in her room. The consultation is just over."

"Did they—did they decide anything?"

"Yes," said the nurse softly. "Doctor Jewett says there's no hope. Mr. Curtain may live indefinitely, but he'll never see again or move again or think. He'll just breathe."

"Just breathe?"

"Yes."

For the first time the nurse noted that beside the writing-desk where she remembered that she had seen a line of a dozen curious round objects she had vaguely imagined to be some exotic form of decoration, there was now only one.

Where the others had been, there was now a series of little nail-holes.

Harry followed her glance dazedly and then rose to his feet.

"I don't believe I'll stay. I believe there's a train."

She nodded. Harry picked up his hat.

"Good-by," she said pleasantly.

"Good-by," he answered, as though talking to himself and, evidently moved by some involuntary necessity, he paused on his way to the door and she saw him pluck the last object from the wall and drop it into his pocket.

Then he opened the screen door and, descending the porch steps, passed out of her sight.

V

After a while the coat of clean white paint on the Jeffrey Curtain house made a definite compromise with the suns of many Julys and showed its good faith by turning gray. It scaled—huge peelings of very brittle old paint leaned over backward like aged men practising grotesque gymnastics and finally dropped to a moldy death in the overgrown grass beneath. The paint on the front pillars became streaky; the white ball was knocked off the left-hand door-post; the green blinds darkened, then lost all pretense of color.

It began to be a house that was avoided by the tender-minded—some church bought a lot diagonally opposite for a graveyard, and this, combined with "the place where Mrs Curtain stays with that living corpse," was enough to throw a ghostly aura over that quarter of the road. Not that she was left alone. Men and women came to see her, met her down town, where she went to do her marketing, brought her home in their cars—and came in for a moment to talk and to rest, in the glamour that still played in her smile. But men who did not know her no longer followed her with admiring glances in the street; a diaphanous veil had come down over her beauty, destroying its vividness, yet bringing neither wrinkles nor fat.

She acquired a character in the village—a group of little stories were told of her: how when the country was frozen over one winter so that no wagons nor automobiles could travel, she taught herself to skate so that she could make quick time to the grocer and druggist, and not leave Jeffrey alone for long. It was said that every night since his paralysis she slept in a small bed beside his bed, holding his hand.

Jeffrey Curtain was spoken of as though he were already dead. As the years dropped by those who had known him died or moved away—there were but half a dozen of the old crowd who had drunk cocktails together, called each other's wives by their first names, and thought that Jeff was about the wittiest and most talented fellow that Marlowe had ever known. Now, to the casual visitor, he was merely the reason that Mrs. Curtain excused herself sometimes and hurried upstairs; he was a groan or a sharp cry borne to the silent parlor on the heavy air of a Sunday afternoon.

He could not move; he was stone blind, dumb, and totally unconscious. All day he lay in his bed, except for a shift to his wheel-chair every morning while she straightened the room. His paralysis was creeping slowly toward his heart. At first—for the first year—Roxanne had received the faintest answering pressure sometimes when she held his hand—then it had gone, ceased one evening and never come back, and through two nights Roxanne lay wide-eyed, staring into the dark and wondering what had gone, what fraction of his soul had taken flight, what last grain of comprehension those shattered broken nerves still carried to the brain.

After that hope died. Had it not been for her unceasing care the last spark would have gone long before. Every morning she shaved and bathed him, shifted him with her own hands from bed to chair and back to bed. She was in his room constantly, bearing medicine, straightening a pillow, talking to him almost as one talks to a nearly human dog, without hope of response or appreciation, but with the dim persuasion of habit, a prayer when faith has gone.

Not a few people, one celebrated nerve specialist among them, gave her a plain impression that it was futile to exercise so much care, that if Jeffrey had been conscious he would have wished to die, that if his spirit were hovering in some wider air it would agree to no such sacrifice from her, it would fret only for the prison of its body to give it full release.

"But you see," she replied, shaking her head gently, "when I married Jeffrey it was—until I ceased to love him."

"But," was protested, in effect, "you can't love that."

"I can love what it once was. What else is there for me to do?"

The specialist shrugged his shoulders and went away to say that Mrs. Curtain was a remarkable woman and just about as sweet as an angel—but, he added, it was a terrible pity.

"There must be some man, or a dozen, just crazy to take care of her. . . ."

Casually—there were. Here and there some one began in hope—and ended in reverence. There was no love in the woman except, strangely enough, for life, for the people in the world, from the tramp to whom she gave food she could ill afford to the butcher who sold her a cheap cut of steak across the meaty board. The other phase was sealed up somewhere in that expressionless mummy who lay with his face turned ever toward the light as mechanically as a compass needle and waited dumbly for the last wave to wash over his heart.

After eleven years he died in the middle of a May night, when the scent of the syringa hung upon the window-sill and a breeze wafted in the shrillings of the frogs and cicadas outside. Roxanne awoke at two, and realized with a start she was alone in the house at last.

VI

After that she sat on her weather-beaten porch through many afternoons, gazing down across the fields that undulated in a slow descent to the white and green town. She was wondering what she would do with her life. She was thirty-six—handsome, strong, and free. The years had eaten up Jeffrey's insurance; she had reluctantly parted with the acres to right and left of her, and had even placed a small mortgage on the house.

With her husband's death had come a great physical restlessness. She missed having to care for him in the morning, she missed her rush to town, and the brief and therefore accentuated neighborly meetings in the butcher's and grocer's;

she missed the cooking for two, the preparation of delicate liquid food for him. One day, consumed with energy, she went out and spaded up the whole garden, a thing that had not been done for years.

And she was alone at night in the room that had seen the glory of her marriage and then the pain. To meet Jeff again she went back in spirit to that wonderful year, that intense, passionate absorption and companionship, rather than looked forward to a problematical meeting hereafter; she awoke often to lie and wish for that presence beside her—inanimate yet breathing—still Jeff.

One afternoon six months after his death she was sitting on the porch, in a black dress which took away the faintest suggestion of plumpness from her figure. It was Indian summer—golden brown all about her; a hush broken by the sighing of leaves; westward a four o'clock sun dripping streaks of red and yellow over a flaming sky. Most of the birds had gone—only a sparrow that had built itself a nest on the cornice of a pillar kept up an intermittent cheeping varied by occasional fluttering sallies overhead. Roxanne moved her chair to where she could watch him and her mind idled drowsily on the bosom of the afternoon.

Harry Cromwell was coming out from Chicago to dinner. Since his divorce over eight years before he had been a frequent visitor. They had kept up what amounted to a tradition between them: when he arrived they would go to look at Jeff; Harry would sit down on the edge of the bed and in a hearty voice ask:

"Well, Jeff, old man, how do you feel to-day?"

Roxanne, standing beside, would look intently at Jeff, dreaming that some shadowy recognition of this former friend had passed across that broken mind—but the head, pale, carven, would only move slowly in its sole gesture toward the light as if something behind the blind eyes were groping for another light long since gone out.

These visits stretched over eight years—at Easter, Christmas, Thanksgiving, and on many a Sunday Harry had arrived, paid his call on Jeff, and then talked for a long while with Roxanne on the porch. He was devoted to her. He made no pretense of hiding, no attempt to deepen, this relation.

She was his best friend as the mass of flesh on the bed there had been his best friend. She was peace, she was rest; she was the past. Of his own tragedy she alone knew.

He had been at the funeral, but since then the company for which he worked had shifted him to the East and only a business trip had brought him to the vicinity of Chicago. Roxanne had written him to come when he could—after a night in the city he had caught a train out.

They shook hands and he helped her move two rockers together.

"How's George?"

"He's fine, Roxanne. Seems to like school."

"Of course it was the only thing to do, to send him."

"Of course——"

"You miss him horribly, Harry?"

"Yes—I do miss him. He's a funny boy——"

He talked a lot about George. Roxanne was interested. Harry must bring him out on his next vacation. She had only seen him once in her life—a child in dirty rompers.

She left him with the newspaper while she prepared dinner—she had four chops to-night and some late vegetables from her own garden. She put it all on and then called him, and sitting down together they continued their talk about George.

"If I had a child—" she would say.

Afterward, Harry having given her what slender advice he could about investments, they walked through the garden, pausing here and there to recognize what had once been a cement bench or where the tennis court had lain . . .

"Do you remember——"

Then they were off on a flood of reminiscences: the day they had taken all the snap-shots and Jeff had been photographed astride the calf; and the sketch Harry had made of Jeff and Roxanne, lying sprawled in the grass, their heads almost touching. There was to have been a covered lattice connecting the barn-studio with the house, so that Jeff could get there on wet days—the lattice had been started, but nothing remained except a broken triangular piece that still adhered to the house and resembled a battered chicken coop.

"And those mint juleps!"

"And Jeff's note-book! Do you remember how we'd laugh, Harry, when we'd get it out of his pocket and read aloud a page of material. And how frantic he used to get?"

"Wild! He was such a kid about his writing."

They were both silent a moment, and then Harry said:

"We were to have a place out here, too. Do you remember? We were to buy the adjoining twenty acres. And the parties we were going to have!"

Again there was a pause, broken this time by a low question from Roxanne.

"Do you ever hear of her, Harry?"

"Why—yes," he admitted placidly. "She's in Seattle. She's married again to a man named Horton, a sort of lumber king. He's a great deal older than she is, I believe."

"And she's behaving?"

"Yes—that is, I've heard so. She has everything, you see. Nothing much to do except dress up for this fellow at dinner-time."

"I see."

Without effort he changed the subject.

"Are you going to keep the house?"

"I think so," she said, nodding. "I've lived here so long, Harry, it'd seem terrible to move. I thought of trained nursing, but of course that'd mean leaving. I've about decided to be a boarding-house lady."

"Live in one?"

"No. Keep one. Is there such an anomaly as a boarding-house lady? Anyway I'd have a negress and keep about eight people in the summer and two or three, if I can get them, in the winter. Of course I'll have to have the house repainted and gone over inside."

Harry considered.

"Roxanne, why—naturally you know best what you can do, but it does seem a shock, Roxanne. You came here as a bride."

"Perhaps," she said, "that's why I don't mind remaining here as a boarding-house lady."

"I remember a certain batch of biscuits."

"Oh, those biscuits," she cried. "Still, from all I heard about the way you devoured them, they couldn't have been so bad. I was *so* low that day, yet somehow I laughed when the nurse told me about those biscuits."

"I noticed that the twelve nail-holes are still in the library wall where Jeff drove them."

"Yes."

It was getting very dark now, a crispness settled in the air; a little gust of wind sent down a last spray of leaves. Roxanne shivered slightly.

"We'd better go in."

He looked at his watch.

"It's late. I've got to be leaving. I go East to-morrow.

"Must you?"

They lingered for a moment just below the stoop, watching a moon that seemed full of snow float out of the distance where the lake lay. Summer was gone and now Indian summer. The grass was cold and there was no mist and no dew. After he left she would go in and light the gas and close the shutters, and he would go down the path and on to the village. To these two life had come quickly and gone, leaving not bitterness, but pity; not disillusion, but only pain. There was already enough moonlight when they shook hands for each to see the gathered kindness in the other's eyes.

Mr. Icky

The Quintessence of Quaintness in One Act

The Scene is the Exterior of a Cottage in West Issacshire on a desperately Arcadian afternoon in August. Mr. Icky, *quaintly dressed in the costume of an Elizabethan peasant, is pottering and doddering among the pots and dods. He is an old man, well past the prime of life, no longer young. From the fact that there is a burr in his speech and that he has absent-mindedly put on his coat wrongside out, we surmise that he is either above or below the ordinary superficialities of life.*

Near him on the grass lies Peter, *a little boy.* Peter, *of course, has his chin on his palm like the pictures of the young Sir Walter Raleigh. He has a complete set of features, including serious, sombre, even funereal, gray eyes—and radiates that alluring air of never having eaten food. This air can best be radiated during the afterglow of a beef dinner. He is looking at* Mr. Icky, *fascinated.*

Silence. . . . The song of birds.

Peter: Often at night I sit at my window and regard the stars. Sometimes I think they're my stars. . . . (*Gravely*) *I think I shall be a star some day. . . .*

Mr. Icky: (*Whimsically*) Yes, yes . . . yes. . . .

Peter: I know them all: Venus, Mars, Neptune, Gloria Swanson.

Mr. Icky: I don't take no stock in astronomy. . . . I've been thinking o' Lunnon, laddie. And calling to mind my daughter, who has gone for to be a typewriter. . . . (*He sighs.*)

Peter: I liked Ulsa, Mr. Icky; she was so plump, so round, so buxom.

Mr. Icky: Not worth the paper she was padded with, laddie. (*He stumbles over a pile of pots and dods.*)

Peter: How is your asthma, Mr. Icky?

Mr. Icky: Worse, thank God! . . . (*Gloomily.*) I'm a hundred years old. . . . I'm getting brittle.

PETER: I suppose life has been pretty tame since you gave up petty arson.

MR. ICKY: Yes . . . yes. . . . You see, Peter, laddie, when I was fifty I reformed once—in prison.

PETER: You went wrong again?

MR. ICKY: Worse than that. The week before my term expired they insisted on transferring to me the glands of a healthy young prisoner they were executing.

PETER: And it renovated you?

MR. ICKY: Renovated me! It put the Old Nick back into me! This young criminal was evidently a suburban burglar and a kleptomaniac. What was a little playful arson in comparison!

PETER: (*Awed*) How ghastly! Science is the bunk.

MR. ICKY: (*Sighing*) I got him pretty well subdued now. 'Tisn't every one who has to tire out two sets o' glands in his lifetime. I wouldn't take another set for all the animal spirits in an orphan asylum.

PETER: (*Considering*) I shouldn't think you'd object to a nice quiet old clergyman's set.

MR. ICKY: Clergymen haven't got glands—they have souls.

(*There is a low, sonorous honking off stage to indicate that a large motor-car has stopped in the immediate vicinity. Then a young man handsomely attired in a dress-suit and a patent-leather silk hat comes onto the stage. He is very mundane. His contrast to the spirituality of the other two is observable as far back as the first row of the balcony. This is* RODNEY DIVINE.)

DIVINE: I am looking for Ulsa Icky.

(MR. ICKY *rises and stands tremulously between two dods.*)

MR. ICKY: My daughter is in Lunnon.

DIVINE: She has left London. She is coming here. I have followed her.

(*He reaches into the little mother-of-pearl satchel that hangs at his side for cigarettes. He selects one and scratching a match touches it to the cigarette. The cigarette instantly lights.*)

DIVINE: I shall wait.

(*He waits. Several hours pass. There is no sound except an occasional cackle or hiss from the dods as they*

MR. ICKY: Come! Who is this Frank? Who is this Jack?

DIVINE: (*Morosely*) Gotch.

ULSA: Dempsey.

DIVINE: We were arguing that if they were deadly enemies and locked in a room together which one would come out alive. Now I claimed that Jack Dempsey would take one——

ULSA: (*Angrily*) Rot! He wouldn't have a——

DIVINE: (*Quickly*) You win.

ULSA: Then I love you again.

MR. ICKY: So I'm going to lose my little daughter. . . .

ULSA: You've still got a houseful of children.

(CHARLES, ULSA'S *brother, coming out of the cottage. He is dressed as if to go to sea; a coil of rope is slung about his shoulder and an anchor is hanging from his neck.*)

CHARLES: (*Not seeing them*) I'm going to sea! I'm going to sea!

(*His voice is triumphant.*)

MR. ICKY: (*Sadly*) You went to seed long ago.

CHARLES: I've been reading "Conrad."

PETER: (*Dreamily*) "Conrad," ah! "Two Years Before the Mast," by Henry James.

CHARLES: What?

PETER: Walter Pater's version of "Robinson Crusoe."

CHARLES: (*To his feyther*) I can't stay here and rot with you. I want to live my life. I want to hunt eels.

MR. ICKY: I will be here . . . when you come back. . . .

CHARLES: (*Contemptuously*) Why, the worms are licking their chops already when they hear your name.

(*It will be noticed that some of the characters have not spoken for some time. It will improve the technique if they can be rendering a spirited saxophone number.*)

MR. ICKY: (*Mournfully*) These vales, these hills, these McCormick harvesters—they mean nothing to my children. I understand.

CHARLES: (*More gently*) Then you'll think of me kindly, feyther. To understand is to forgive.

MR. ICKY: No . . . no. . . . We never forgive those we can understand. . . . We can only forgive those who wound us for no reason at all. . . .

CHARLES: (*Impatiently*) I'm so beastly sick of your human nature line. And, anyway, I hate the hours around here.

(*Several dozen more of* MR. ICKY'S *children trip out of the house, trip over the grass, and trip over the pots and dods. They are muttering "We are going away," and "We are leaving you."*)

MR. ICKY: (*His heart breaking*) They're all deserting me. I've been too kind. Spare the rod and spoil the fun. Oh, for the glands of a Bismarck.

(*There is a honking outside—probably* DIVINE'S *chauffeur growing impatient for his master.*)

MR. ICKY: (*In misery*) They do not love the soil! They have been faithless to the Great Potato Tradition! (*He picks up a handful of soil passionately and rubs it on his bald head. Hair sprouts.*) Oh, Wordsworth, Wordsworth, how true you spoke!

"No motion has she now, no force;
She does not hear or feel;
Roll'd round on earth's diurnal course
In some one's Oldsmobile."

(*They all groan and shouting "Life" and "Jazz" move slowly toward the wings*)

CHARLES: Back to the soil, yes! I've been trying to turn my back to the soil for ten years!

ANOTHER CHILD: The farmers may be the backbone of the country, but who wants to be a backbone?

ANOTHER CHILD: I care not who hoes the lettuce of my country if I can eat the salad!

ALL: Life! Psychic Research! Jazz!

MR. ICKY: (*Struggling with himself*) I must be quaint. That's all there is. It's not life that counts, it's the quaintness you bring to it. . . .

ALL: We're going to slide down the Riviera. We've got tickets for Piccadilly Circus. Life! Jazz!

MR. ICKY: Wait. Let me read to you from the Bible. Let me open it at random. One always finds something that bears on the situation.

(*He finds a Bible lying in one of the dods and opening it at random begins to read.*)

"Anab and Istemo and Anim, Goson and Olon and Gilo, eleven cities and their villages. Arab, and Ruma, and Esaau——"

CHARLES: (*Cruelly*) Buy ten more rings and try again.

MR. ICKY: (*Trying again*) "How beautiful art thou my love, how beautiful art thou! Thy eyes are dove's eyes, besides what is hid within. Thy hair is as flocks of goats which come up from Mount Galaad—" Hm! Rather a coarse passage. . . .

(*His children laugh at him rudely, shouting "Jazz!" and "All life is primarily suggestive!"*)

MR. ICKY: (*Despondently*) It won't work to-day. (*Hopefully*) Maybe it's damp. (*He feels it*) Yes, it's damp. . . . There was water in the dod. . . . It won't work.

ALL: It's damp! It won't work! Jazz!

ONE OF THE CHILDREN: Come, we must catch the six-thirty.

(*Any other cue may be inserted here.*)

MR. ICKY: Good-by. . . .

(*They all go out.* MR. ICKY *is left alone. He sighs and walking over to the cottage steps, lies down, and closes his eyes.*

Twilight has come down and the stage is flooded with such light as never was on land or sea. There is no sound except a sheep-herder's wife in the distance playing an aria from Beethoven's Tenth Symphony, on a mouth-organ. The great white and gray moths swoop down and light on the old man until he is completely covered by them. But he does not stir.

The curtain goes up and down several times to denote the lapse of several minutes. A good comedy effect can be obtained by having MR. ICKY *cling to the curtain and go up and down with it. Fireflies or fairies on wires can also be introduced at this point.*

Then PETER *appears, a look of almost imbecile sweetness on his face. In his hand he clutches something and from time to time glances at it in a transport of ecstasy. After a struggle with himself he lays it on the old man's body and then quietly withdraws.*

The moths chatter among themselves and then scurry away in sudden fright. And as night deepens there still sparkles there, small, white and round, breathing a subtle perfume to the West Issacshire breeze, PETER'S *gift of love—a moth-ball.*

(*The play can end at this point or can go on indefinitely.*)

Jemina, the Mountain Girl

This don't pretend to be "Literature." This is just a tale for red-blooded folks who want a *story* and not just a lot of "psychological" stuff or "analysis." Boy, you'll love it! Read it here, see it in the movies, play it on the phonograph, run it through the sewing-machine.

A Wild Thing

It was night in the mountains of Kentucky. Wild hills rose on all sides. Swift mountain streams flowed rapidly up and down the mountains.

Jemina Tantrum was down at the stream, brewing whiskey at the family still.

She was a typical mountain girl.

Her feet were bare. Her hands, large and powerful, hung down below her knees. Her face showed the ravages of work. Although but sixteen, she had for over a dozen years been supporting her aged pappy and mappy by brewing mountain whiskey.

From time to time she would pause in her task, and, filling a dipper full of the pure, invigorating liquid, would drain it off—then pursue her work with renewed vigor.

She would place the rye in the vat, thresh it out with her feet and, in twenty minutes, the completed product would be turned out.

A sudden cry made her pause in the act of draining a dipper and look up.

"Hello," said a voice. It came from a man clad in hunting boots reaching to his neck, who had emerged from the wood.

"Hi, thar," she answered sullenly.

"Can you tell me the way to the Tantrums' cabin?"

"Are you uns from the settlements down thar?"

She pointed her hand down to the bottom of the hill, where Louisville lay. She had never been there; but once, before she was born, her great-grandfather, old Gore Tantrum, had gone into the settlements in the company of two marshals, and had never come back. So the Tantrums, from generation to generation, had learned to dread civilization.

The man was amused. He laughed a light tinkling laugh, the laugh of a Philadelphian. Something in the ring of it thrilled her. She drank off another dipper of whiskey.

"Where is Mr. Tantrum, little girl?" he asked, not without kindness.

She raised her foot and pointed her big toe toward the woods.

"Thar in the cabing behind those thar pines. Old Tantrum air my old man."

The man from the settlements thanked her and strode off. He was fairly vibrant with youth and personality. As he walked along he whistled and sang and turned handsprings and flapjacks, breathing in the fresh, cool air of the mountains.

The air around the still was like wine.

Jemina Tantrum watched him entranced. No one like him had ever come into her life before.

She sat down on the grass and counted her toes. She counted eleven. She had learned arithmetic in the mountain school.

A Mountain Feud

Ten years before a lady from the settlements had opened a school on the mountain. Jemina had no money, but she had paid her way in whiskey, bringing a pailful to school every morning and leaving it on Miss Lafarge's desk. Miss Lafarge had died of delirium tremens after a year's teaching, and so Jemina's education had stopped.

Across the still stream still another still was standing. It was that of the Doldrums. The Doldrums and the Tantrums never exchanged calls.

They hated each other.

Fifty years before old Jem Doldrum and old Jem Tantrum had quarrelled in the Tantrum cabin over a game of slapjack. Jem Doldrum had thrown the king of hearts in Jem Tantrum's face, and old Tantrum, enraged, had felled the old Doldrum with the nine of diamonds. Other Doldrums and Tantrums had joined in and the little cabin was soon filled with flying cards. Harstrum Doldrum, one of the younger

Doldrums, lay stretched on the floor writhing in agony, the ace of hearts crammed down his throat. Jem Tantrum, standing in the doorway, ran through suit after suit, his face alight with fiendish hatred. Old Mappy Tantrum stood on the table wetting down the Doldrums with hot whiskey. Old Heck Doldrum, having finally run out of trumps, was backed out of the cabin, striking left and right with his tobacco pouch, and gathering around him the rest of his clan. Then they mounted their steers and galloped furiously home.

That night old man Doldrum and his sons, vowing vengeance, had returned, put a ticktock on the Tantrum window, stuck a pin in the doorbell, and beaten a retreat.

A week later the Tantrums had put Cod Liver Oil in the Doldrums' still, and so, from year to year, the feud had continued, first one family being entirely wiped out, then the other.

The Birth of Love

Every day little Jemina worked the still on her side of the stream, and Boscoe Doldrum worked the still on his side.

Sometimes, with automatic inherited hatred, the feudists would throw whiskey at each other, and Jemina would come home smelling like a French table d'hôte.

But now Jemina was too thoughtful to look across the stream.

How wonderful the stranger had been and how oddly he was dressed! In her innocent way she had never believed that there were any civilized settlements at all, and she had put the belief in them down to the credulity of the mountain people.

She turned to go up to the cabin, and, as she turned something struck her in the neck. It was a sponge, thrown by Boscoe Doldrum—a sponge soaked in whiskey from his still on the other side of the stream.

"Hi, thar, Boscoe Doldrum," she shouted in her deep bass voice.

"Yo! Jemina Tantrum. Gosh ding yo'!" he returned.

She continued her way to the cabin.

The stranger was talking to her father. Gold had been discovered on the Tantrum land, and the stranger, Edgar Edison, was trying to buy the land for a song. He was considering what song to offer.

She sat upon her hands and watched him.

He was wonderful. When he talked his lips moved.

She sat upon the stove and watched him.

Suddenly there came a blood-curdling scream. The Tantrums rushed to the windows.

It was the Doldrums.

They had hitched their steers to trees and concealed themselves behind the bushes and flowers, and soon a perfect rattle of stones and bricks beat against the windows, bending them inward.

"Father! father!" shrieked Jemina.

Her father took down his slingshot from his slingshot rack on the wall and ran his hand lovingly over the elastic band. He stepped to a loophole. Old Mappy Tantrum stepped to the coalhole.

A Mountain Battle

The stranger was aroused at last. Furious to get at the Doldrums, he tried to escape from the house by crawling up the chimney. Then he thought there might be a door under the bed, but Jemina told him there was not. He hunted for doors under the beds and sofas, but each time Jemina pulled him out and told him there were no doors there. Furious with anger, he beat upon the door and hollered at the Doldrums. They did not answer him, but kept up their fusillade of bricks and stones against the window. Old Pappy Tantrum knew that as soon as they were able to effect an aperture they would pour in and the fight would be over.

Then old Heck Doldrum, foaming at the mouth and expectorating on the ground, left and right, led the attack.

The terrific slingshots of Pappy Tantrum had not been without their effect. A master shot had disabled one Doldrum, and another Doldrum, shot almost incessantly through the abdomen, fought feebly on.

Nearer and nearer they approached the house.

"We must fly," shouted the stranger to Jemina. "I will sacrifice myself and bear you away."

"No," shouted Pappy Tantrum, his face begrimed. "You stay here and fit on. I will bar Jemina away. I will bar Mappy away. I will bar myself away."

The man from the settlements, pale and trembling with anger, turned to Ham Tantrum, who stood at the door throwing loophole after loophole at the advancing Doldrums.

"Will you cover the retreat?"

But Ham said that he too had Tantrums to bear away, but that he would leave himself here to help the stranger cover the retreat, if he could think of a way of doing it.

Soon smoke began to filter through the floor and ceiling. Shem Doldrum had come up and touched a match to old Japhet Tantrum's breath as he leaned from a loophole, and the alcoholic flames shot up on all sides.

The whiskey in the bathtub caught fire. The walls began to fall in.

Jemina and the man from the settlements looked at each other.

"Jemina," he whispered.

"Stranger," she answered.

"We will die together," he said. "If we had lived I would have taken you to the city and married you. With your ability to hold liquor, your social success would have been assured."

She caressed him idly for a moment, counting her toes softly to herself. The smoke grew thicker. Her left leg was on fire.

She was a human alcohol lamp.

Their lips met in one long kiss and then a wall fell on them and blotted them out.

"As One."

When the Doldrums burst through the ring of flame, they found them dead where they had fallen, their arms about each other.

Old Jem Doldrum was moved.

He took off his hat.

He filled it with whiskey and drank it off.

"They air dead," he said slowly, "they hankered after each other. The fit is over now. We must not part them."

So they threw them together into the stream and the two splashes they made were as one.

CHRONOLOGY

NOTE ON THE TEXTS

NOTES

Chronology

1896 Born September 24 at his parents' home at 481 Laurel Avenue, in St. Paul, Minnesota, first surviving child of Mollie McQuillan Fitzgerald and Edward Fitzgerald. Named Francis Scott Key Fitzgerald after the author of "The Star-Spangled Banner," his father's second cousin three times removed. (Mother, born 1860 in St. Paul, is the eldest of five children of successful grocery wholesaler who at his death in 1877 left an estate of over $250,000 and a large Victorian home on Summit Avenue, St. Paul's most fashionable street. Father, born in 1853 in Rockville, Maryland, is a furniture manufacturer. They had two daughters who died, aged three and one, earlier in 1896.)

1898 When furniture business fails, family moves to Buffalo, New York, where father takes a job as a wholesale grocery salesman for Proctor & Gamble.

1901 Father transferred by Proctor & Gamble to Syracuse, New York, and family moves in January. Sister Annabel born in July.

1902 Enrolls in Miss Goodyear's School in September.

1903 Family moves back to Buffalo. Attends school at Holy Angels Convent.

1905 Transfers to Miss Naden's private Catholic school. Reads *The Scottish Chiefs, Ivanhoe,* and the adventure novels of G. A. Henty.

1908 Father loses his job at Proctor & Gamble in March and in July family moves back to St. Paul, where at first they live with the McQuillans and then in a series of rented homes, eventually settling at 599 Summit Avenue. Enters St. Paul Academy in September.

1909 Publishes first story, "The Mystery of the Raymond Mortgage," in *Now and Then,* the St. Paul Academy school paper, in October.

1910 Publishes two more stories in the *Now and Then,* "Reade, Substitute Right Half" (February) and "A Debt of Honor" (March).

1911 Publishes story "The Room with the Green Blinds" in the June *Now and Then.* In August, writes and plays the lead in a play, *The Girl from Lazy J,* for the Elizabethan Dramatic Club, local amateur theatrical group. Because of poor grades at St. Paul Academy, is sent in September to boarding school at the Newman School in Hackensack, New Jersey, where his boastful and domineering personality makes him unpopular. Takes frequent trips to New York City and attends theater often, seeing Ina Claire in *The Quaker Girl* and Gertrude Bryant in *Little Boy Blue.* Publishes poem "Football" in Christmas issue of the school magazine, the *Newman News.*

1912–13 Writes another play, *The Captured Shadow,* which is produced by the Elizabethan Dramatic Club in the summer of 1912. Publishes three stories in the *Newman News* during the 1912–13 school year. Meets Father Cyril Sigourney Webster Fay, prominent Catholic priest, who becomes a mentor. During a visit to Father Fay in Washington, meets Henry Adams and Irish writer Shane Leslie. Despite failing four courses in two years at the Newman School, Fitzgerald takes entrance examination for Princeton University in May 1913. Writes play *Coward* for Elizabethan Dramatic Club in July. Grandmother McQuillan dies in August, leaving his mother enough money for his college tuition. Enters Princeton in September as member of Class of 1917.

1914 Meets John Peale Bishop and Edmund Wilson, fellow students at Princeton. In January his book and lyrics for *Fie! Fie! Fi-Fi!* win the competition for the 1914–15 Triangle Club show. Contributes to the *Princeton Tiger,* the college humor magazine. Reads and admires the social reform writings of H. G. Wells and George Bernard Shaw and Compton Mackenzie's novel *Sinister Street.* Writes fourth and last play for the Elizabethan Dramatic Club, *Assorted Spirits,* during summer. Returns to Princeton in September but is ineligible for extracurricular activities because of poor grades and cannot act in *Fie! Fie! Fi-Fi!* during the fall semester.

1915 Meets Ginevra King, 16-year-old from socially prominent Lake Forest, Illinois, family, while home for Christmas vacation. Falls in love with her and writes to her almost daily after he returns to Princeton. Elected secretary of the Triangle Club in February after his grades improve; later in the term is selected for the Cottage Club and for the editorial board of the *Tiger*. Story "Shadow Laurels" is published in the *Nassau Literary Magazine* (the *Lit*) in April, followed in June by "The Ordeal." Writes the lyrics (Edmund Wilson writes the book) for *The Evil Eye*, the 1915 Triangle Club show. Takes Ginevra King to the Princeton prom in June. In the fall, his low grades again make him ineligible for campus activities. Takes French literature course taught by Christian Gauss and begins lifelong friendship with Gauss, who later becomes Dean of the College. Continues to write for the *Tiger*. In November, falls ill and leaves college for the remainder of the semester to recuperate (illness is diagnosed as malaria, but may have been mild case of tuberculosis).

1916 Spends the spring in St. Paul on a leave of absence from Princeton; publishes poem "To My Unused Greek Book" in the *Lit*. Continues courtship of Ginevra King, whom he visits in Lake Forest in August. Returns to Princeton in September to repeat his junior year and writes the lyrics for the Triangle Club show, *Safety First*, in which he is again ineligible to perform. Attends Princeton-Yale football game with King in November.

1917 Courtship of Ginevra King ends in January. Publishes play "The Debutante," whose title character is modeled on King, in the *Lit*. During spring semester, his writing appears another 12 times in the *Lit* (four stories, three poems, and five reviews of books by Shane Leslie, E. F. Benson, H. G. Wells, and Booth Tarkington). In May, a month after the U.S. enters World War I, signs up for three weeks of intensive military training and takes exam for infantry commission. During summer in St. Paul, reads William James, Schopenhauer, and Bergson. While waiting for his commission, returns to Princeton in September and rooms with John Biggs Jr., editor of the *Tiger*, and continues to contribute to both the *Tiger* and the *Lit*. Receives commission as second lieutenant in the infantry and in November reports for training to Fort

Leavenworth, Kansas. Expecting that he will eventually be killed in combat, begins writing a novel.

1918 On leave from the army in February, finishes novel, "The Romantic Egotist," at the Cottage Club in Princeton and sends it to Shane Leslie, who has agreed to recommend it to his publisher, Charles Scribner's Sons. Reports in March to 45th Infantry Regiment at Camp Zachary Taylor, near Louisville; in April, regiment is transferred to Camp Gordon in Georgia, and in June, to Camp Sheridan, outside Montgomery, Alabama. In July, at a dance at the Country Club of Montgomery, meets Zelda Sayre, 18-year-old daughter of a justice of the Alabama Supreme Court. Scribners rejects "The Romantic Egotist" in August; Fitzgerald submits a revised version, which is rejected in October. War ends on November 11, as Fitzgerald is waiting to embark for France with his regiment. Continues courtship of Zelda Sayre, who is reluctant to commit to marriage because of his lack of income and prospects.

1919 Father Fay dies on January 10. Fitzgerald is discharged from the army, moves to New York in February, and takes job at Barron Collier advertising agency writing trolley-car ads. Writes fiction and poetry at night, accumulating 112 rejection slips. *The Smart Set* accepts "Babes in the Woods," revised version of story published in 1917 issue of the *Lit,* paying him $30 (story appears in September). Sends Zelda his mother's engagement ring in March, but cannot convince her to marry him during visits to Montgomery, April–June. During his last visit, Zelda breaks off the engagement. Quits job and returns to parents' house in St. Paul, determined to rewrite novel and get it accepted for publication. Sends novel, now titled *This Side of Paradise,* to editor Maxwell Perkins at Scribners in September. Perkins writes on September 16 that firm has accepted it: "The book is so different that it is hard to prophesy how it will sell but we are all for taking a chance and supporting it with vigor." Revises several of his rejected stories; four are accepted by *The Smart Set,* two by *Scribner's Magazine,* and one by *The Saturday Evening Post.* Earns $879 from his writing by the end of the year. During a trip to New York in November, engages Harold Ober as his agent. Visits Zelda in Montgomery.

1920 With Harold Ober's assistance, begins to sell stories regularly to *The Saturday Evening Post,* which pays $400 each for them; by February, they have bought six. Reads Samuel Butler's *Notebooks* and H. L. Mencken's essays. Spends January in New Orleans writing stories and reading proofs of his novel, then moves back to New York in February. Sells story "Head and Shoulders" to Metro Films for $2,500. *This Side of Paradise* is published March 26; it sells 3,000 copies in three days, and makes its author a celebrity. Marries Zelda in vestry of New York's St. Patrick's Cathedral on April 3. Develops friendships with Mencken and George Jean Nathan, editors of *The Smart Set.* Reads Mark Twain. In May, *Metropolitan Magazine* takes option on his stories at $900 per story and, eventually, publishes four. Rents house in Westport, Connecticut, and in July takes car trip to Montgomery. Scribners publishes *Flappers and Philosophers,* collection of eight stories, September 10. Rents apartment on West 59th Street in New York in October and works on second novel.

1921 Zelda discovers she is pregnant in February. In May, they sail for Europe, visiting England, where they have tea with John Galsworthy, Paris, Venice, Florence, and Rome, returning in July to the U.S., where they live in St. Paul. Second novel, *The Beautiful and Damned,* begins to run serially in *Metropolitan Magazine* in September. Daughter Frances Scott (Scottie) Fitzgerald is born on October 26.

1922 *The Beautiful and Damned* published by Scribners March 4; it receives mixed reviews and sells 40,000 copies in a year. Begins work on play. Moves to Great Neck, Long Island, where he begins close friendships with Ring Lardner and John Dos Passos. *Tales of the Jazz Age,* short-story collection, published by Scribners on September 22. Reads Dostoevsky and Dickens.

1923 Sells first option on his stories to Hearst organization for $1,500 per story. Receives $10,000 for film rights to *This Side of Paradise.* Play *The Vegetable* is published by Scribners on April 27. Begins work on third novel. *The Vegetable* opens for pre-Broadway tryout in Atlantic City, New Jersey, on November 19, is received badly, and closes almost immediately, leaving its author in debt. Starts selling stories to *The Saturday Evening Post* for $1,250 each. Earns $28,759.78 from his writing for the year, but spends more.

1924 Sails for France in May to complete novel, settling on the Riviera. Zelda becomes romantically involved with French naval aviator Edouard Jozan in July; although the relationship ends quickly, Fitzgerald later writes, "I knew something had happened that could never be repaired." Meets Gerald and Sara Murphy during the summer. In October, recommends the work of Ernest Hemingway to Perkins and Scribners. After sending manuscript of new novel to Scribners in late October, goes to Rome and Capri for winter. Drinks heavily and quarrels constantly with Zelda.

1925 Extensively revises novel in galley proof in January and February, changing title to *The Great Gatsby.* Moves to Paris in April. *The Great Gatsby* is published by Scribners on April 10, receives mostly favorable reviews, but sales are disappointing. Meets Hemingway for first time at the Dingo bar in Montparnasse and subsequently takes trip to Lyon with him. Has tea with Edith Wharton at her home outside Paris in July. Through Hemingway, meets Gertrude Stein, Robert McAlmon (founder of Contact Editions publishers), and Sylvia Beach (owner of Shakespeare & Co. bookstore in Paris). Spends part of summer ("1000 parties and no work") on the Riviera, where his friends include writers Dos Passos, Max Eastman, Archibald MacLeish, and Floyd Dell and movie star Rudolph Valentino. Returns to Paris in September and spends a great deal of time with Hemingway.

1926 *All the Sad Young Men,* short-story collection, is published by Scribners on February 26. Returns to the Riviera in March and begins work on new novel. Encourages Scribners to publish Hemingway's novels *The Torrents of Spring* and *The Sun Also Rises.* Reads draft of *The Sun Also Rises* in July and convinces Hemingway to eliminate the first two chapters. Returns to U.S. in December, spending Christmas in Montgomery.

1927 Spends first two months of year in Hollywood, under contract to United Artists to write flapper comedy for Constance Talmadge; script, "Lipstick," is eventually rejected. Meets and is infatuated with 17-year-old Hollywood starlet Lois Moran; also meets producer Irving Thalberg, Lillian Gish, John Barrymore, and Richard Barthelmess. With help of Princeton roommate John Bigg Jr., rents Ellerslie, Greek Revival–style mansion outside Wilmington, Delaware. Zelda begins ballet lessons with director of Philadelphia Opera Ballet and also writes magazine articles. Fitzgerald's income from writing for year totals $29,757.87, a new high.

1928 Goes to Paris for the summer in April. Zelda continues ballet studies there with Lubov Egorova. Writes nine Basil Duke Lee stories for *The Saturday Evening Post,* which earn him $31,500. Meets James Joyce at dinner given by Sylvia Beach in June. Later in summer, meets Thornton Wilder and heavyweight boxing champion Gene Tunney, who are on a walking tour of Europe together. Returns to U.S. in October and resumes work on novel. Attends Princeton-Yale football game in Princeton on November 19 with Hemingway and his wife, Pauline.

1929 Gives up lease on Ellerslie in spring and returns to Europe, renting apartment in Paris in April. Zelda resumes ballet lessons with Egorova and also publishes series of short stories in *College Humor.* Fitzgerald reads typescript of Hemingway's novel *A Farewell to Arms* in June and offers suggestions for revisions, all of which Hemingway ridicules but some of which he takes. Rents villa in Cannes from July to September. Now is paid $4,000 per story by *The Saturday Evening Post.* Returns to Paris in October and lives in rented apartment. Works on novel, while Zelda continues her ballet lessons and writing.

1930 Travels with Zelda to North Africa in February. Her behavior shows signs of extreme stress, and on April 23, she enters Malmaison clinic outside Paris. Discharges herself on May 11 to resume ballet lessons, then attempts suicide and enters Val-Mont clinic in Glion, Switzerland, on May 22. After being diagnosed as schizophrenic by Dr. Oscar Forel, she is transferred in June to Forel's Les Rives de

Prangins clinic on Lake Geneva. Fitzgerald spends summer traveling between Paris and Switzerland. Meets Thomas Wolfe in Paris and later spends time with him in Switzerland. In order to pay for Zelda's treatment, writes and sells stories to *The Saturday Evening Post,* earning $32,000 for the year from eight stories, among them "Babylon Revisited," published in December. Spends fall at Hotel de la Paix in Lausanne and has brief affair with Englishwoman Bijou O'Conor.

1931 Father dies in January in Washington and Fitzgerald goes home for funeral. After visits to Montgomery and New York, returns to Europe and finds Zelda's condition improved; she becomes an outpatient and is allowed to take trips to Paris and the Austrian Tyrol, then is discharged from Prangins on September 15. Sails for U.S. with Zelda on September 19, and settles in Montgomery. Goes to Hollywood in November after being offered $1,200 a week by M-G-M to work on a Jean Harlow movie, leaving Zelda in Montgomery to be with her ailing father, who dies on November 17. Returns to Montgomery for Christmas.

1932 Takes Zelda in January on vacation to Florida and she works on a novel. Zelda has relapse on trip back to Montgomery, and enters Henry Phipps Psychiatric Clinic in Baltimore on February 12. Fitzgerald remains in Montgomery to work on his novel. Zelda finishes her novel while at the Phipps Clinic and, after Fitzgerald comes to Baltimore to help her revise it, Scribners accepts it. Rents La Paix, Victorian-style house on the Turnbull estate in Towson, just outside Baltimore, in May. Zelda is discharged from Phipps on June 26. In August, Fitzgerald spends time at Johns Hopkins Hospital with what is diagnosed as typhoid fever (will eventually be hospitalized there eight more times between 1933 and 1937 for alcoholism and chronic inactive fibroid tuberculosis). Zelda's novel *Save Me the Waltz* is published October 7; it receives bad reviews and sells very poorly. Resumes serious work on his novel, while Zelda paints and writes play, *Scandalabra.*

1933 *Scandalabra* is produced by the Junior Vagabonds, Baltimore amateur little theater, in the spring. In September,

Ring Lardner dies and Fitzgerald writes tribute for *The New Republic*. Sends new novel, *Tender Is the Night,* to Scribners in late October.

1934 *Tender Is the Night* appears in *Scribner's Magazine,* January–April, and is published on April 12, receiving largely favorable reviews and selling well. While working on revising the book in New York in January and February, spends time with John O'Hara and with Dorothy Parker. Zelda reenters Phipps Clinic on February 12 and later is transferred to Craig House in Beacon, New York ("I left my capacity for hoping on the little roads that led to Zelda's sanitarium"). Fitzgerald arranges showing of her paintings at art gallery in New York in March and April, and she is permitted to attend opening. When her condition deteriorates, Zelda is admitted to the Sheppard and Enoch Pratt Hospital outside Baltimore on May 19. Fitzgerald begins to sell stories and articles to recently established magazine *Esquire,* which pays $250 per piece.

1935 Travels to Tryon, North Carolina, in February in attempt to improve his health. *Taps at Reveille,* short-story collection, published by Scribners on March 10. Spends summer in Asheville, North Carolina, at the Grove Park Inn, where he has affair with Beatrice Dance, who is married. Returns to Baltimore in September and lives in rented apartment. Spends winter in Hendersonville, North Carolina.

1936 Writes three confessional articles, "The Crack-Up," "Pasting It Together," and "Handle With Care," which appear in *Esquire,* February–April, and arouse considerable consternation among his friends. Zelda is transferred to Highland Hospital in Asheville on April 6, and Fitzgerald spends summer at Grove Park Inn to be near her. Mother dies in August, but Fitzgerald is unable to attend funeral. Daughter enters Ethel Walker School in Simsbury, Connecticut, in September. On his 40th birthday in September is interviewed by Michel Mok of the New York *Post.* Subsequent article is headlined "Scott Fitzgerald, 40, Engulfed in Despair"; after it appears, Fitzgerald attempts suicide with overdose of morphine. Through Perkins, meets Marjorie Kinnan Rawlings when she comes to Asheville. Spends Christmas holidays in Johns

Hopkins Hospital recovering from influenza and heavy drinking.

1937 Spends first months of year at Oak Hall Hotel in Tryon, North Carolina. Has great difficulty selling stories; his debts exceed $40,000, with $12,000 owed to his agent, Harold Ober. Hired as a screenwriter by M-G-M in July for six months at $1,000 per week. Rents small apartment at Garden of Allah, 8152 Sunset Boulevard, in Hollywood. Meets Sheilah Graham, 28-year-old Englishwoman who writes a Hollywood gossip column, at a party soon after his arrival, and they begin an affair. Works on film adaptation of Erich Maria Remarque's novel *Three Comrades.* Though it is extensively altered by producer Joseph Mankiewicz, his work on it contributes to renewal of his M-G-M contract (will be only screenplay for which he receives on-screen credit).

1938 Visits Zelda in January and takes her to Florida and Montgomery. Returns to Hollywood, and works from February to May on "Infidelity," movie for Joan Crawford which is never produced. During daughter's spring vacation, takes her and Zelda to Virginia Beach and Norfolk, Virginia, but gets drunk and behaves badly. Moves to house at 114 Malibu Beach in April. Daughter is accepted at Vassar College. Fitzgerald works from May to October on screenplay of Claire Booth Luce's play *The Women* but is eventually replaced. Moves to Encino in November and rents small house on Belly Acres estate of actor Edward Everett Horton. Hires Frances Kroll as his secretary. Plans educational curriculum, "College of One," for Sheilah Graham, a two-year course in the arts and humanities which he participates in by tutoring her as well as assigning readings. Begins work in November on *Madame Curie,* film for Greta Garbo.

1939 Plans for *Madame Curie* are shelved in January, and after he is loaned to David O. Selznick to work very briefly on *Gone With the Wind,* Fitzgerald learns that M-G-M is dropping its option after eighteen months. Becomes freelance screenwriter and socializes in Hollywood with, among others, Nathanael West and S. J. Perelman. Hired by producer Walter Wanger of United Artists to collaborate with recent Dartmouth graduate Budd Schulberg on screenplay of *Winter Carnival;* they take a disastrous trip to Dartmouth College in February, during which Fitzgerald is drunk the entire time, and they are both fired. Goes on trip to Cuba with Zelda in April, and is so drunk and ill that she has to take him to New York, where he is hospitalized before returning to California. Begins work on a novel about Hollywood, with main character, Monroe Stahr, based on Irving Thalberg (never completed, it is edited by Edmund Wilson and published posthumously in 1941 as *The Last Tycoon*). Receives intermittent but brief screenwriting assignments but falls deeper in debt, eventually severing ties with long-time agent Harold Ober because Ober refuses to lend him any more money; becomes his own agent.

1940 Begins to publish series of stories in *Esquire* about Pat Hobby, a hack Hollywood writer, for which he receives $250 per story; ultimately, *Esquire* publishes 17 Pat Hobby stories, one in each monthly number between January 1940 and July 1941. Writes "Cosmopolitan," screen adaptation of his story "Babylon Revisited," but it is never used. Moves in May to apartment at 1403 Laurel Avenue in Hollywood, a block from Sheilah Graham's apartment, and works intensively on his novel through the summer and fall. Suffers heart attack in late November and is ordered to rest in bed. Moves to Sheilah Graham's apartment, where he dies, apparently of a second heart attack, on December 21. With Zelda's approval, decision is made to bury Fitzgerald with his father's family in Rockville, Maryland, but he is refused burial at St. Mary's Church cemetery because he was not a practicing Catholic at his death. Buried December 27 at Rockville Union Cemetery.

Note on the Texts

This volume contains the first four books of F. Scott Fitzgerald: *This Side of Paradise* (1920), *Flappers and Philosophers* (1920), *The Beautiful and Damned* (1922), and *Tales of the Jazz Age* (1922). Fitzgerald did not significantly revise these works after their initial publication in book form, but changes were made, usually to correct errors, after the first printings of *This Side of Paradise*, *Flappers and Philosophers*, and *Tales of the Jazz Age*. These changes were sanctioned by Fitzgerald. Therefore, the texts presented here come from the printings that contain the final revisions authorized by Fitzgerald.

Fitzgerald began work on a novel entitled "The Romantic Egotist" in the fall of 1917 while awaiting his commission as an officer in the U.S. Army. He wrote most of the manuscript at Fort Leavenworth, Kansas, sending chapters as he finished them to a typist in Princeton. In March 1918 he gave the typescript to Shane Leslie, the Irish novelist, who forwarded it to his publisher, Charles Scribner's Sons, with his recommendation for its publication. Scribners did not accept the novel but encouraged Fitzgerald to revise and resubmit it. He submitted a new version of "The Romantic Egotist" to Scribners in September 1918, but it was also rejected.

After his discharge from the army in February 1919, Fitzgerald returned to his family's home in St. Paul, Minnesota, and again revised "The Romantic Egotist." He entirely rewrote much of the novel, especially its first third, and incorporated into it material he had published while a student at Princeton, including the short story "Eleanor" and the play "The Debutante." Fitzgerald also placed typescript pages from earlier versions of "The Romantic Egotist," with handwritten corrections, into his new draft, producing discrepancies that eventually found their way into print. In August 1919 Fitzgerald finished a new draft of the novel, now titled *This Side of Paradise*, and gave it to Katherine Tighe, a friend from St. Paul, for editorial advice. Tighe corrected spelling and grammatical errors and recommended cuts and revisions in the work, some of which Fitzgerald followed; he then had the entire manuscript retyped. After making additional revisions, Fitzgerald sent the new typescript to Scribners on September 4, 1919, and was informed two weeks later that the novel had been accepted for publication. *This Side of Paradise* was published on March 26, 1920.

Although Fitzgerald read and made minor changes to the galleys, he failed (as did the editors at Scribners) to correct numerous spelling and grammatical errors and factual discrepancies. As a result, the first printing contained many errors, some of which were corrected in the fourth and seventh printings. W. Collins & Sons made additional corrections in the edition of the novel published in London in 1921 but edited the book in conformity with British conventions of spelling, punctuation, and usage, introducing readings that lack Fitzgerald's authority. The text presented here is that of the 1921 Scribners seventh printing of *This Side of Paradise.*

The eight stories collected in *Flappers and Philosophers* had appeared previously in periodical publications: "The Offshore Pirate" (*The Saturday Evening Post*, May 1, 1920), "The Ice Palace" (*The Saturday Evening Post*, May 22, 1920), "Head and Shoulders" (*The Saturday Evening Post*, February 19, 1920), "The Cut-Glass Bowl" (*Scribner's Magazine*, May 1920), "Bernice Bobs Her Hair" (*The Saturday Evening Post*, May 1, 1920), "Benediction" (*The Smart Set*, February 1920), "Dalyrimple Goes Wrong" (*The Smart Set*, February 1920), and "The Four Fists" (*Scribner's Magazine*, June 1920). The stories were revised, sometimes heavily, for their publication in book form. *Flappers and Philosophers* was published by Scribners on September 10, 1920. One change was made in the fourth printing. At 354.9 in this volume, "panoply" was emended to "panorama," a change authorized by Fitzgerald. The text presented here is the 1920 Scribners fourth printing of *Flappers and Philosophers.*

Fitzgerald began writing a novel in the summer of 1920 with the working title "The Flight of the Rocket." In February 1921 he gave a finished draft of the novel to Edmund Wilson for editorial advice, and in April, shortly before leaving for Europe, Fitzgerald sent a typescript of the novel, now titled *The Beautiful and Damned*, to Harold Ober, his agent. Ober sold the serial rights for the novel to *Metropolitan Magazine*, where it appeared (in a version cut and revised by the magazine editor) in seven installments between September 1921 and March 1922. The novel was also accepted by Scribners, and after Fitzgerald returned to St. Paul in September 1921 he made further changes to *The Beautiful and Damned* in the Scribners proofs. Neither the marked proofs nor the setting typescript are known to be extant, so it is difficult to determine the extent of Fitzgerald's revisions at this stage of composition. Comparison of the published novel with a manuscript with typed insertions, now at the Princeton University Library, reveals that Fitzgerald made numerous small changes and shifted the position of several passages in the novel. The last two paragraphs of the *Metropolitan Magazine* version were cut after Zelda Fitzgerald raised objections to them; in a telegram to his editor, Maxwell Perkins, Fitzgerald wrote that Zelda "thinks new ending is a piece of morality" and asked for his advice. Perkins agreed that the ending was better without the two paragraphs, and Fitzgerald omitted them from the book version of the novel. *The Beautiful and Damned* was published by Charles Scribner's Sons on March 3, 1922. The text printed here is from the 1922 Scribners first printing of *The Beautiful and Damned.*

The eleven stories collected in *Tales of the Jazz Age* had been previously published in magazines. The first American periodical publication for each of the stories is listed below:

The Jelly Bean. *Metropolitan Magazine*, October 1920.

The Camel's Back. *The Saturday Evening Post*, April 24, 1920.

May Day. *The Smart Set*, July 1920.

Porcelain and Pink. *The Smart Set*, January 1920, as "Porcelain and Pink (A One-Act Play)."

The Diamond as Big as the Ritz. *The Smart Set*, June 1922.

The Curious Case of Benjamin Button. *Collier's*, May 27, 1922.

Tarquin of Cheapside. *The Smart Set*, February 1921.

"O Russet Witch!" *Metropolitan Magazine*, February 1921, as "His Russet Witch."

The Lees of Happiness. *Chicago Sunday Tribune*, December 12, 1920.

Mr. Icky. *The Smart Set*, March 1920, as "Mister Icky The Quintessence of Quaintness in One Act."

Jemina. *Vanity Fair*, January 1921, as "Jemina, the Mountain Girl (One of Those Family Feud Stories of the Blue Ridge Mountains with Apologies to Stephen Leacock)."

Tales of the Jazz Age was published on September 22, 1922. The text presented here comes from the 1922 first printing of the Scribners edition.

This volume presents the texts of the original printings chosen for inclusion here, but it does not attempt to reproduce features of their typographic design, such as display capitalization of chapter openings. The texts are presented without change, except for the correction of typographical errors. Spelling, punctuation, and capitalization are often expressive features and are not altered, even when inconsistent or irregular. The following is a list of typographical errors corrected, cited by page and line number: 8.33, Ashville; 42.1, flambuoyant; 42.9, tetotalling; 86.37, master; 108.36, "What!"; 109.2, "Why!"; 129.5, unconfinable; 129.33, Cecelia; 150.35, *finished*; 162.7, juvenalia; 162.19, unforgetable; 175.24, clinched; 184.34, rendevouz; 190.6, Juvenalia; 190.32, Juvenalia; 258.5, desk; 298.5, you?'; 404.36, chaoticly; 409.10, of mile; 537.23, 'Don't; 553.17, Such; 573.34, Southhampton; 589.20, Southhampton; 639.13, Marlow; 688.35, unforgetable; 813.17, there."; 820.21, Clark,; 834.2–3, threshhold; 872.4, party.; 883.33, hat.; 902.11, before that; 918.11, blashemy; 921.20, wandred; 934.10, how——; 934.35, yodled; 937.13, state; 959.10, Ecceptionally; 985.31, an you; 1011.36, seveereal.

Notes

In the notes below, the reference numbers denote page and line of this volume (the line count includes chapter headings). No note is made for material included in standard desk-reference books such as Webster's *Collegiate*, *Biographical*, and *Geographical* dictionaries. Biblical quotations are keyed to the King James Version. Quotations from Shakespeare are keyed to *The Riverside Shakespeare*, ed. G. Blakemore Evans (Boston: Houghton Mifflin, 1974). For further biographical information than is contained in the chronology, see Matthew J. Bruccoli, *Some Sort of Epic Grandeur: The Life of F. Scott Fitzgerald*, revised edition (New York: Carroll and Graf, 1991); André Le Vot, *F. Scott Fitzgerald: A Biography*, translated by William Byron (Garden City, N.Y.: Doubleday, 1983); James R. Mellow, *Invented Lives: F. Scott and Zelda Fitzgerald* (Boston: Houghton Mifflin, 1984); Jeffrey Meyers, *Scott Fitzgerald: A Biography* (New York: HarperCollins, 1994); Arthur Mizener, *The Far Side of Paradise: A Biography of F. Scott Fitzgerald* (Boston: Houghton, Mifflin, 1965); and Andrew Turnbull, *Scott Fitzgerald* (New York: Ballantine, 1971).

THIS SIDE OF PARADISE

1.2–4 *Well . . . Brooke*] The final lines of Brooke's 1915 poem "Tiare Tahiti."

1.5–7 *Experience . . . Wilde*] *Lady Windermere's Fan* (1893), Act III.

5.29 Queen Margherita] Margherita di Savoia (1851–1926), Queen (1878–1900) and Queen Dowager (1900–26) of Italy.

6.23–24 "Do and Dare," or "Frank on the Mississippi"] *Do and Dare*, novel (1884) by Horatio Alger, Jr.; *Frank on the Lower Mississippi* (1867), novel by Harry Castlemon, pseudonym for Charles Austin Fosdick.

7.8 "Fêtes Galantes"] Poetry collection (1869) by Paul Verlaine.

12.32 "trade-lasts"] Compliments given with the expectation of receiving one in return.

16.36 "Arsene Lupin."] *Arsène Lupin*, play by Francis de Croisset and Maurice Leblanc, featuring the gentleman criminal created by Leblanc; first performed in the United States in 1909.

17.10 McGovern of Minnesota] John Francis McGovern, first University of Minnesota football player to be named to the first-string All-America team (in 1909).

17.13–14 Three-fingered Brown . . . Christie Mathewson] Mordecai Brown (1876–1948), pitcher for St. Louis Cardinals and Chicago Cubs; Christy Mathewson (1880–1925), pitcher for New York Giants.

17.15–19 "For the Honor . . . Chum,"] *For the Honor of the School* (1900), boys' book by R. H. Barbour; *The Common Law* (1911), novel by Robert W. Chambers; *Sapho* (1884), novel by Alphonse Daudet; "The Shooting of Dan McGrew" (1907), poem by Robert W. Service; *The Broad Highway* (1910), novel by Jeffery Farnol; *Three Weeks* (1907), novel by Elinor Glyn; *Mary Ware* (1908), novel by Annie Fellows Johnston.

17.20 *Jim-Jam Jems*] Mass-circulation pocket-sized magazine.

17.21–23 Henty biasses . . . Rineheart] G. A. Henty's (1832–1902) many boys' adventure novels included *Under Drake's Flag* (1883), *With Clive in India* (1884), and *With Roberts to Pretoria* (1902); the American mystery writer Mary Roberts Rinehart (1876–1956) was the author of many novels including *The Circular Staircase* (1908) and *The Man in Lower Ten* (1909).

26.8–9 "The Beloved Vagabond" . . . "Sir Nigel,"] Historical novels by W. J. Locke (1900) and Arthur Conan Doyle (1906).

28.25–26 "The White Company."] Historical novel (1891) by Arthur Conan Doyle.

28.33–34 chariot-race sign on Broadway] A large electric advertising sign that depicted, with simulated movement, the climactic scene of Lew Wallace's novel *Ben-Hur.*

29.2 "The Little Millionaire"] Play (1911) by George M. Cohan.

30.24 Roland and Horatius, Sir Nigel and Ted Coy] Respectively, legendary knight of Charlemagne commemorated in the medieval French epic *La Chanson de Roland*; legendary Roman hero who in the 6th century B.C. held a bridge against invading Etruscans; the hero of Arthur Conan Doyle's novel of the same name; and football star for Yale.

31.36–38 "The Gentleman . . . Thursday,"] *The Gentleman from Indiana*, novel (1899) by Booth Tarkington; *New Arabian Nights*, short story collection (1882) by Robert Louis Stevenson; *The Morals of Marcus Ordeyne*, novel (1905) by W. J. Locke; *The Man Who Was Thursday*, novel (1908) by G. K. Chesterton.

31.39 "Stover at Yale"] Boys' novel (1912) by O. M. Johnson, depicting the college adventures of "Dink" Stover.

32.1–2 Robert Chambers . . . Oppenheim] Robert W. Chambers (1865–1933), best-selling novelist whose books included *The King in Yellow*

(1895) and *Ashes of Empire* (1897); David Graham Phillips (1867–1911), muckraking journalist and novelist; E. Phillips Oppenheim (1866–1946), whose novels of mystery and espionage included *The Mysterious Mr. Sabin* (1901) and *The Double Traitor* (1920).

32.24 Harstrum's] The Harström School in Norwalk, Connecticut, a remedial school which prepared students for admission to Yale.

32.24 Sheff] Sheffield Scientific School at Yale.

32.30 locomotor ataxia] A syphillis of the spinal cord which results in loss of muscular control and paralysis.

38.8 "By the Sea"] "By the Beautiful Sea" (1914), song by Harold R. Atteridge and Harry Carroll.

44.10 Golden Treasury] *Golden Treasury of the Best Songs and Lyrical Poems of the English Language* (first edition, 1861), anthology of English poetry edited by Francis Turner Palgrave.

46.25 Stephen Phillips] English poet (1868–1915) known for his verse dramas.

46.27 "Come into the Garden, Maude,"] Tennyson's lyrics, from his poem *Maud*, were set to music by Michael William Balfe in 1857.

47.32 'Patience,'] Operetta (1881) by Gilbert and Sullivan which presents a satirical portrait of Wilde.

48.8–9 "Mystic . . . Merci"] "Dolores," poem (1866) by Swinburne; "La Belle Dame sans Merci," poem (1819) by John Keats.

48.16 Robert Hugh Benson] English novelist (1871–1914) who converted to Roman Catholicism; his works included *The Light Invisible* (1903) and *The Lord of the World* (1907).

49.1 'Hearts and Flowers'] Song (1899) by Mary D. Brine and Theodore Moses Tobani.

49.21–24 "*Asleep or waking . . . for a fleck*] Swinburne, "Laus Veneris," lines 1–4.

49.27 "Poems and Ballades"] *Poems and Ballads* (1866), poetry collection by Swinburne.

54.37 Midnight Frolic] Roof garden above New York's New Amsterdam Theatre, owned and operated by theater impresario Florenz Ziegfeld.

56.16 "Thais"] Opera (1894) by Jules Massenet, from Anatole France's 1890 novel.

63.33 "Babes in the Woods"] Song (1915) by Schuyler Greene and Jerome Kern.

68.17–25 "*Oh, winter's rains . . . flower of——*"] Cf. Swinburne, *Atalanta in Calydon*, Chorus, stanza 4.

72.8 "*Beaches . . . came.*"] Kipling, "Lukannon," in *The Jungle Book* (1894).

75.12-14 "Love Moon" . . . "Good-by, Boys, I'm Through,"] "Love Moon" (1914), song by Anne Caldwell and Ivan Caryll; "Good-bye, Boys" (1913), song by Andrew B. Sterling, William Dillon, and Harry von Tilzer.

77.23 'silver-snarling trumpets.'] Cf. Keats, *The Eve of St. Agnes*, line 31.

82.29 "All the perfumes . . . this little hand."] Cf. *Macbeth*, V.i.

85.36–39 "*Each life unfulfilled . . . been happy.*"] Cf. "Youth and Art" (1864).

86.10 conditioned men] Princeton students in academic trouble.

93.8 Lafayette Esquadrille] The Lafayette Escadrille, a French fighter squadron made up of American volunteers that began flying missions in May 1916, 11 months before the U.S. entered World War I. In February 1918 it became the 103rd Pursuit Squadron of the U.S. army air corps.

96.17 John Fox, Jr.] American journalist and novelist (1863–1919), whose books included *The Little Shepherd of Kingdom Come* (1903) and *The Trail of the Lonesome Pine* (1908).

96.18–19 "What Every . . . Yukon"] *What Every Woman Knows* (1918), play by J. M. Barrie; *The Spell of the Yukon* (1915), poetry collection by Robert W. Service.

98.29 *General Booth*] William Booth (1829–1912), founder in 1878 of the Salvation Army.

107.31 "The New Machiavelli,"] Novel (1911) by H. G. Wells.

108.20–21 "None . . . Magnificent"] *None Other Gods* (1911), novel by Robert Hugh Benson; *Sinister Street* (1913), novel by Compton Mackenzie; *The Research Magnificent* (1915), novel by H. G. Wells.

111.16–17 Edward Carpenter] English writer and social reformer (1844–1929).

112.17–18 Ralph Adams Cram] American architect (1863–1942) who served as supervising architect at Princeton University.

119.10 Philadelphian Society] Collegiate religious organization.

120.19 'He who is not with me is against me.'] Matthew 12:30.

124.31 Amelia-like] The reference is to Amelia Osborne in Thackeray's *Vanity Fair* (1848).

133.31 Stephen] Cf. Acts 6–7.

134.22 Peter the Hermit] French priest and military officer (1050–1115) who proposed the First Crusade to Pope Urban II.

137.7–8 "Poor Butterfly"] Song (1916) by John L. Golden and Raymond Hubbell.

138.19 Messalina] Valeria Messalina, third wife of Roman emperor Claudius, notorious for her loose morals.

143.37 Donald Hankey] After Hankey, a British soldier, was killed in action in 1916, his writings were collected in *A Student in Arms* (1917).

145.11–12 *"Cherry Ripe,"*] Sir John Everett Millais' popular painting of a young girl.

161.3 "Kiss Me Again."] Song (1905) by Henry Blossom and Victor Herbert, which enjoyed a popular revival in 1915.

164.26–27 Annette Kellerman] Annette Kellermann (1887–1975), Australian swimmer who beame a stage and screen actress and was known as the "Million Dollar Mermaid."

165.17 "Et tu, Brutus."] *Dear Brutus* (1917), fantasy play by J. M. Barrie.

169.18–23 "For this is wisdom . . . let go."] Cf. Laurence Hope, "The Teak Forest."

176.2 "Claire de Lune"] Poem by Paul Verlaine, collected in *Fêtes Galantes* (1869).

176.11 "The Jest."] Play (1919) by the Italian playwright Sem Benelli, produced successfully on Broadway.

180.36–37 "After you've gone"] Song (1918) by Henry Creamer and Turner Layton.

182.9 "Joan . . . Fire"] *Joan and Peter: The Story of an Education* (1918) and *The Undying Fire* (1919), novels by H. G. Wells.

182.11–12 novels . . . Gerhardt."] By Frank Norris, Harold Frederic, and Theodore Dresier, respectively.

183.2 Irish President] Eamon de Valera, president of the Sinn Fein party, visited the United States in 1919 to enlist support for the Irish republican cause.

184.7–8 Edward Carson and Justice Cohalan] Carson (1854–1935), Irish Protestant politician who led opposition to Irish home rule; Daniel Florence Cohalon, New York State Supreme Court justice who had advocated German air raids on England in support of the Irish revolution.

184.30 Montespan's wraith] Madame de Montespan, mistress of Louis XIV, tried to poison her court rivals and was accused of participating in the Black Mass.

186.10 Guynemer] George Marie Guynemer (1894–1917), French aviator of World War I who shot down more than 50 enemy planes.

186.22 Wood] Leonard Wood (1890–1927), military doctor who served as military governor of Cuba and as army chief of staff.

188.31–32 Gouverneur Morris] American writer (1876–1953), author of novels including *The Pagan's Progress* (1904) and *When My Ship Comes In* (1915).

189.3 Rupert Hughes] American novelist (1872–1956) whose works included *What Will People Say?* (1914) and *Cup of Fury* (1919).

189.34-39 Eunice . . . Iris] Eunice Tietjens (1884–1944), an editor of *Poetry* whose books included *Profiles of China* (1917); Clara Shanafelt, an occasional early contributor to *Poetry*; James Oppenheim (1882–1932), editor of *The Seven Arts* and author of *Monday Morning* (1909) and *Songs for the New Age* (1914); Maxwell Bodenheim (1893–1954), poet and novelist whose books of verse included *Minna and Myself* (1918) and *Introducing Irony* (1922); Richard Glaenzer (1876–1937), author of *Beggar and King* (1917); Scharmel Iris, author of *Lyrics of a Lad* (1914).

195.12–17, 24–29 "*Les sanglots . . . pleure. . . .*"] From Verlaine, "Chanson d'automne," in *Poèmes saturniens* (1866): "The long sobs of the violins of autumn wound my heart with a monotonous langour. Stifling and wan, when the hour sounds, I remember the old days and I weep."

198.20–25 'And now . . . was born.'] Cf. Poe, "Ulalume: A Ballad."

200.36–37 "Bind on . . . thy feet——"] Cf. Swinburne, *Atalanta in Calydon.*

215.15–16 Mann Act] Passed in 1910, the act made it a federal offense to aid or participate in the transportation of women or girls for immoral purposes in interstate or foreign commerce.

230.37 Bernhardi] Friedrich von Bernhardi (1849–1930), Prussian general and military writer who in *Germany and the Next War* (1911) asserted Germany's right to make war.

230.38 Bethmann-Hollweg] Theobald von Bethmann-Hollweg (1856–1921), German chancellor who encouraged his country's participation in World War I.

239.29 Burlesons] Albert Sidney Burleson (1863–1937), American politician; as Postmaster General during World War I, he sought to ban from the mails all materials criticizing government policy.

245.18 Lewis gunner] A Lewis gun was a light machine gun used by British and American forces in World War I.

FLAPPERS AND PHILOSOPHERS

256.35–36 statue of France Aroused] *Marne Battle Memorial* by Frederick MacMonnies, initiated in 1916, completed in 1932.

296.28 Dangerous Dan McGrew] Character in "The Shooting of Dan McGrew" (1907), poem by Robert W. Service.

310.10–11 battle of Château-Thierry] In early June 1918, American troops helped stop a major German offensive in heavy fighting around Château Thierry, a town on the Marne River 40 miles east of Paris.

313.18 Florodora Sextette] The actresses Daisy Greene, Marjorie Relyea, Vaughn Texsmith, Margaret Walker, Agnes Wayburn, and Marie L. Wilson, who sang the hit song "Tell Me Pretty Maiden" in the Broadway musical comedy *Florodora* (1900).

313.19 Mrs. Sol Smith's Juliette] Elizabeth Smith (1812?–87), wife of American theater impresario Sol Smith, sometimes played Juliet to his Romeo.

316.19 'The Bohemian Girl'] Light opera (1843) by Michael William Balfe.

327.32 *Mens sana in corpore sano*] "A sound mind in a sound body." From Juvenal, *Satires*, 10.356.

330.8 Hippodrome] The largest theater in New York in its day, seating over 5,000 and noted for its lavish spectacles; it opened in 1905 on Sixth Avenue between 43rd and 44th Street.

361.18 Annie Fellows Johnston] Children's author (1863–1931) whose works included *The Little Colonel* (1895).

370.8–9 you've either got . . . Wilde] Cf. Wilde's *A Woman of No Importance*, Act III: "To get into the best society, one has either to feed people, amuse people, or shock people—that is all!"

384.3 Cardinal Mercier] Desiré Joseph Mercier (1851–1926), founder of the Institut Superieur de Philosophie in Louvain, Belgium, in 1889; he was made a cardinal in 1907.

392.5 maxixe] Brazilian dance resembling the two-step which became popular in the United States in 1914.

392.23 "*O Salutaris Hostia*"] Hymn played during the benediction ceremony at Mass.

399.16 Lewis gun] See note 245.18.

408.4 Doctor Crane's . . . bromides] Frank Crane (1861–1928) wrote a widely syndicated inspirational newspaper column, 1909–28.

409.7 "The moon . . . clock!"] Cf. *Macbeth*, II.1.2.

THE BEAUTIFUL AND DAMNED

443.19 the Pudding] The Hasty Pudding, a Harvard club.

450.6 "Erewhon"] Satirical utopian novel (1872) by Samuel Butler.

450.9–13 "To . . . cries——"] Cf. "My Beautiful Lady, or, The Kiss Waltz," song by C.M.S. McLellan and Ivan Caryll, from the 1911 musical *The Pink Lady*.

450.15–16 Hazel Dawn] American actress (1891–1988) who starred in *The Pink Lady* (1911) and *The Debutante* (1914).

452.32–33 "Demon Lover" . . . "woman wailing"] Cf. Samuel Taylor Coleridge, "Kubla Khan" (1798).

455.10 "The Woman."] Melodrama (1911) by William C. De Mille.

456.10 "High Jinks."] *High Jinks: A Musical Farce in Three Acts* (1913), with music by Rudolf Friml and book and lyrics by Otto Harbach and Leo Ditrichstein.

461.35 the Castles] The dance team Vernon and Irene Castle, who starred in Broadway musicals such as *The Summer Widowers* (1913) and *Watch Your Step* (1914) and popularized dances including the turkey trot, the one-step, and the Castle walk.

480.33 Lord Verulam] Francis Bacon.

491.21 Rupert Hughes] See note 189.3.

494.4–6 "Something . . . ear——"] Cf. "Ring-A-Ting-A-Ling on the Telephone" (1912), song by Jean Schwartz and William Jerome.

512.39 "Peg o' My Heart"] Long-running comedy (1912) by J. Hartley Manners.

513.2–9 "Omar . . . Café"] *Omar, the Tentmaker* (1914), play by Richard Walton Tully; *Fair and Warmer* (1915), farce by Avery Hopwood; *Within the Law* (1912), play by Bayard Veiller; *The Little Café*, musical (1913) by Ivan Caryll and C.M.S. McLellan.

515.5–9 "He's a rag-picker . . . pick, pick."] Cf. "He's a Rag Picker" (1914), song by Irving Berlin.

516.24 "Everything's . . . Wife."] Song (1912) by Ivan Caryll and C.M.S. McLellan, from *Oh! Oh! Delphine!*

519.16–18 Thérèse of France . . . Hoosier Cora] The heroine of Emile Zola's *Thérèse Raquin* (1867); Ann Whitefield in Shaw's *Man and Superman* (1903); possibly Lady Randolph (Jennie) Churchill, who after visiting Asia in 1894 wanted to stage a ballet featuring Asian dancers in London; the heroine of Max Beerbohm's *Zuleika Dobson* (1911); Cora Wheeler in Booth Tarkington's play *Clarence* (1919).

524.30 movie supes] Extras.

535.28–29 "L'Éducation Sentimental,"] Novel (1870) by Flaubert.

548.36 "Gypsy" Smith] Rodney "Gypsy" Smith (1860–1947), English evangelist.

551.14 "Yama-yama . . . Town"] "The Yama Yama Man" (1908), song by George Collin Davis and Karl Hoschna; "Jungle Town" (1908), song by Walter G. Samuels, Jack Scholl, and Leonard Whitcup.

558.2 Nora Bayes] American singer and songwriter (1880–1928), known for her renditions of "Down Where the Wurzberger Flows" and "Shine On, Harvest Moon."

570.11 Fall of Liège] The Germans captured the Belgian fortresses around Liège between August 5 and 17, 1914.

574.39 Gibson girls] Image of a fashionable young woman of the upper classes, based on the popular drawings of illustrator Charles Dana Gibson (1867–1944).

581.7 Beatrice Fairfax] Pseudonym for authors of popular newspaper advice column.

604.22 "Penrod,"] Booth Tarkington's 1912 novel, named for its 12-year-old hero.

612.14 Packy McFarland] Patrick Francis McFarland (1888–1936), lightweight boxer.

656.17–18 "Poor Butter-fly . . . wait-ing"] Cf. "Poor Butterfly" (1916), song by John L. Golden and Raymond Hubbell.

657.21 "One gaunt bleak . . . breath."] Cf. Swinburne, "A Forsaken Garden" (1876).

685.22 "hommes 40, chevaux 8"] "Forty men, eight horses": the carrying capacity of the boxcars used for troop transport by the French Army in World War I.

697.35 Snappy Stories] Pulp magazine which featured popular fiction, cartoons, and reviews.

698.1–3 "—*When you wa-ake . . . little hawsiz——*"] Refrain from "All the Pretty Little Horses," southern lullaby.

704.26 "Atalanta in Calydon"] Swinburne's verse drama, published in 1865.

709.21 "K-K-K-Katy."] Song (1918) by Geoffrey O'Hara.

751.21 "ODI PROFANUM VULGUS"] "I hate the common herd": Horace, *Odes*, III.i.

TALES OF THE JAZZ AGE

806.9 "Back Home in Tennessee"] "Just Try To Picture Me (Back Home in Tennessee)" (1915), song by William Jerome and Walter Donaldson.

813.24 Lady Diana Manners] Diana Cooper (1893–1986), English stage actress and daughter of the Duke of Rutland; she starred in *The Miracle* and was married to politician Alfred Duff Cooper.

818.35–38 Joe Miller's . . . Wright] *On a Slow Train Through Arkansaw* (1903), joke book by Thomas W. Jackson; *Lucile* (1860), novel in rhyming couplets by Bulwer-Lytton (1831–1891), under the pseudonym Owen Meredith; *The Eyes of the World* (1914), popular novel set in the American Southwest by Harold Bell Wright (1872–1944).

828.25 stomachers] Waistcoats.

831.1 penates] Guardian deities of the household in Roman mythology.

868.15 O. D.] Olive drab.

878.22–23 Sheffield Science School] At Yale.

878.34–35 'Any lady . . . skin.'] Cf. "The Ladies": "For the Colonel's Lady an' Judy O'Grady / Are sisters under their skins!"

910.20–21 "Evangeline" . . . Armor."] *Evangeline: A Tale of Acadie* (1847), long narrative poem by Longfellow; "The Skeleton in Armor," poem by Longfellow collected in *Ballads and Other Poems* (1842).

911.4 "The Ballad of Reading Gaol"] The poem was written by Oscar Wilde just after his release from prison in 1898.

911.7 Gaby Deslys] Madeline Claire (1884?–1920), French dancer and actress famous for her jewelry and her liaisons with royalty.

911.34 "The Shimmies of Normandy,"] *The Chimes of Normandy* (1877), French comic opera by Robert Planquets (1848–1903), originally staged in Paris as *Les Cloches de Corneville.*

917.36 duvetyn] Napped fabric, usually cotton, wool, or silk.

936.2–3 *Pro deo . . . St. Mida*] For God and country and Saint Midas.

971.14 charge up San Juan Hill] On July 1, 1898, American troops assaulted and captured the San Juan heights east of Santiago, Cuba.

982.24–26 THE LEGEND . . . *far above the rest* . . . .] Cf. the opening of Spenser, *The Faerie Queene*, Book III.

987.4–7 "*From the besieged . . . Roman host*——] Cf. Shakespeare, *The Rape of Lucrece*, lines 1–3.

1003.4 "Adam-and-Eve" Bryan] William Jennings Bryan, so called because of his public attacks on Darwin's theory of evolution.

1012.2 'Crime of Sylvester Bonnard'] *Le Crime de Sylvestre Bonnard, Membre de l'Institut* (1881), novel by Anatole France.

1019.22–23 whether the Japs had taken Port Arthur] The Russian garrison at Port Arthur (Lüshun) in Manchuria surrendered to the Japanese on January 2, 1905, after a siege lasting over six months.

1019.27 Château Thierry] See note 310.10–11.

1019.30 "Florodora"] See note 313.18.

1020.2–3 Gibson girl] See note 574.39.

1020.12–13 Lillian . . . Held?] Lillian Russell (1861–1922), long-time musical theater star whose shows included *The Grand Duchess* (1889) and *The Tzigane* (1895); Stella Mayhew (1875–1934), vaudeville and Broadway singer who starred in *Sewanee River*; Anna Held (1873–1918), star of *La Poupee* (1897) and *The Parisian Model* (1906).

1044.40 John Drinkwater] English poet, playwright, and actor (1882–1937), author of the play *Abraham Lincoln* (1918).

1045.2 Gotch] Frank Gotch (1878–1917), American professional wrestler who was world champion from 1904 to 1917.

1045.20 "Conrad."] Probably a reference to Leonard Merrick's popular novel *Conrad In Search of His Youth* (1903).

1046.17–20 "*No motion . . . some one's Oldsmobile.*"] Parody of William Wordsworth's "A Slumber Did My Spirit Steal" (1799).

1047.1-3 "Anab and Istemo . . . and Esaau——"] Cf. Joshua 15:50–52.

1047.5-8 "How beautiful art thou . . . Mount Galaad—"] Cf. Song of Solomon 4:1.

Library of Congress Cataloging-in-Publication Data

Fitzgerald, F. Scott (Francis Scott), 1896–1940.
[Selections. 2000]
Novels and stories, 1920–1922 / F. Scott Fitzgerald.
p. cm. — (The Library of America 117)
Includes bibliographical references.
ISBN 1–883011–84–1 (alk. paper)
1. United States—Social life and customs—20th century—Fiction.
I. Title: This side of paradise. II. Title: Flappers and philosophers.
III. Title: The beautiful and damned. IV. Title: Tales of the Jazz Age.
V. Title VI. Series.

PS3511.I9 A6 2000
813′.52—dc21

00–024287
CIP

THE LIBRARY OF AMERICA SERIES

The Library of America helps to preserve our nation's literary heritage by publishing, and keeping permanently in print, authoritative editions of America's best and most significant writing. An independent nonprofit organization, it was founded in 1979 with seed money from the National Endowment for the Humanities and the Ford Foundation.

1. Herman Melville, *Typee, Omoo, Mardi* (1982)
2. Nathaniel Hawthorne, *Tales and Sketches* (1982)
3. Walt Whitman, *Poetry and Prose* (1982)
4. Harriet Beecher Stowe, *Three Novels* (1982)
5. Mark Twain, *Mississippi Writings* (1982)
6. Jack London, *Novels and Stories* (1982)
7. Jack London, *Novels and Social Writings* (1982)
8. William Dean Howells, *Novels 1875–1886* (1982)
9. Herman Melville, *Redburn, White-Jacket, Moby-Dick* (1983)
10. Nathaniel Hawthorne, *Collected Novels* (1983)
11. Francis Parkman, *France and England in North America*, vol. I (1983)
12. Francis Parkman, *France and England in North America*, vol. II (1983)
13. Henry James, *Novels 1871–1880* (1983)
14. Henry Adams, *Novels, Mont Saint Michel, The Education* (1983)
15. Ralph Waldo Emerson, *Essays and Lectures* (1983)
16. Washington Irving, *History, Tales and Sketches* (1983)
17. Thomas Jefferson, *Writings* (1984)
18. Stephen Crane, *Prose and Poetry* (1984)
19. Edgar Allan Poe, *Poetry and Tales* (1984)
20. Edgar Allan Poe, *Essays and Reviews* (1984)
21. Mark Twain, *The Innocents Abroad, Roughing It* (1984)
22. Henry James, *Essays, American & English Writers* (1984)
23. Henry James, *European Writers & The Prefaces* (1984)
24. Herman Melville, *Pierre, Israel Potter, The Confidence-Man, Tales & Billy Budd* (1985)
25. William Faulkner, *Novels 1930–1935* (1985)
26. James Fenimore Cooper, *The Leatherstocking Tales*, vol. I (1985)
27. James Fenimore Cooper, *The Leatherstocking Tales*, vol. II (1985)
28. Henry David Thoreau, *A Week, Walden, The Maine Woods, Cape Cod* (1985)
29. Henry James, *Novels 1881–1886* (1985)
30. Edith Wharton, *Novels* (1986)
31. Henry Adams, *History of the United States during the Administrations of Jefferson* (1986)
32. Henry Adams, *History of the United States during the Administrations of Madison* (1986)
33. Frank Norris, *Novels and Essays* (1986)
34. W. E. B. Du Bois, *Writings* (1986)
35. Willa Cather, *Early Novels and Stories* (1987)
36. Theodore Dreiser, *Sister Carrie, Jennie Gerhardt, Twelve Men* (1987)
37. Benjamin Franklin, *Writings* (1987)
38. William James, *Writings 1902–1910* (1987)
39. Flannery O'Connor, *Collected Works* (1988)
40. Eugene O'Neill, *Complete Plays 1913–1920* (1988)
41. Eugene O'Neill, *Complete Plays 1920–1931* (1988)
42. Eugene O'Neill, *Complete Plays 1932–1943* (1988)
43. Henry James, *Novels 1886–1890* (1989)
44. William Dean Howells, *Novels 1886–1888* (1989)
45. Abraham Lincoln, *Speeches and Writings 1832–1858* (1989)
46. Abraham Lincoln, *Speeches and Writings 1859–1865* (1989)
47. Edith Wharton, *Novellas and Other Writings* (1990)
48. William Faulkner, *Novels 1936–1940* (1990)
49. Willa Cather, *Later Novels* (1990)
50. Ulysses S. Grant, *Personal Memoirs and Selected Letters* (1990)

51. William Tecumseh Sherman, *Memoirs* (1990)
52. Washington Irving, *Bracebridge Hall, Tales of a Traveller, The Alhambra* (1991)
53. Francis Parkman, *The Oregon Trail, The Conspiracy of Pontiac* (1991)
54. James Fenimore Cooper, *Sea Tales: The Pilot, The Red Rover* (1991)
55. Richard Wright, *Early Works* (1991)
56. Richard Wright, *Later Works* (1991)
57. Willa Cather, *Stories, Poems, and Other Writings* (1992)
58. William James, *Writings 1878–1899* (1992)
59. Sinclair Lewis, *Main Street & Babbitt* (1992)
60. Mark Twain, *Collected Tales, Sketches, Speeches, & Essays 1852–1890* (1992)
61. Mark Twain, *Collected Tales, Sketches, Speeches, & Essays 1891–1910* (1992)
62. *The Debate on the Constitution: Part One* (1993)
63. *The Debate on the Constitution: Part Two* (1993)
64. Henry James, *Collected Travel Writings: Great Britain & America* (1993)
65. Henry James, *Collected Travel Writings: The Continent* (1993)
66. *American Poetry: The Nineteenth Century*, Vol. 1 (1993)
67. *American Poetry: The Nineteenth Century*, Vol. 2 (1993)
68. Frederick Douglass, *Autobiographies*, (1994)
69. Sarah Orne Jewett, *Novels and Stories* (1994)
70. Ralph Waldo Emerson, *Collected Poems and Translations* (1994)
71. Mark Twain, *Historical Romances* (1994)
72. John Steinbeck, *Novels and Stories 1932–1937* (1994)
73. William Faulkner, *Novels 1942–1954* (1994)
74. Zora Neale Hurston, *Novels and Stories* (1995)
75. Zora Neale Hurston, *Folklore, Memoirs, and Other Writings* (1995)
76. Thomas Paine, *Collected Writings* (1995)
77. *Reporting World War II: American Journalism 1938–1944* (1995)
78. *Reporting World War II: American Journalism 1944–1946* (1995)
79. Raymond Chandler, *Stories and Early Novels* (1995)
80. Raymond Chandler, *Later Novels and Other Writings* (1995)
81. Robert Frost, *Collected Poems, Prose, & Plays* (1995)
82. Henry James, *Complete Stories 1892–1898* (1996)
83. Henry James, *Complete Stories 1898–1910* (1996)
84. William Bartram, *Travels and Other Writings* (1996)
85. John Dos Passos, *U.S.A.* (1996)
86. John Steinbeck, *The Grapes of Wrath and Other Writings 1936–1941* (1996)
87. Vladimir Nabokov, *Novels and Memoirs 1941–1951* (1996)
88. Vladimir Nabokov, *Novels 1955–1962* (1996)
89. Vladimir Nabokov, *Novels 1969–1974* (1996)
90. James Thurber, *Writings and Drawings* (1996)
91. George Washington, *Writings* (1997)
92. John Muir, *Nature Writings* (1997)
93. Nathanael West, *Novels and Other Writings* (1997)
94. *Crime Novels: America Noir of the 1930s and 40s* (1997)
95. *Crime Novels: America Noir of the 1950s* (1997)
96. Wallace Stevens, *Collected Poetry and Prose* (1997)
97. James Baldwin, *Early Novels and Stories* (1998)
98. James Baldwin, *Collected Essays* (1998)
99. Gertrude Stein, *Writings 1903–1932* (1998)
100. Gertrude Stein, *Writings 1932–1946* (1998)
101. Eudora Welty, *Complete Novels* (1998)
102. Eudora Welty, *Stories, Essays, & Memoir* (1998)
103. Charles Brockden Brown, *Three Gothic Novels* (1998)
104. *Reporting Vietnam: American Journalism 1959–1969* (1998)
105. *Reporting Vietnam: American Journalism 1969–1975* (1998)
106. Henry James, *Complete Stories 1874–1884* (1999)
107. Henry James, *Complete Stories 1884–1891* (1999)

108. *American Sermons: The Pilgrims to Martin Luther King Jr.* (1999)
109. James Madison, *Writings* (1999)
110. Dashiell Hammett, *Complete Novels* (1999)
111. Henry James, *Complete Stories 1864–1874* (1999)
112. William Faulkner, *Novels 1957–1962* (1999)
113. John James Audubon, *Writings & Drawings* (1999)
114. *Slave Narratives* (2000)
115. *American Poetry: The Twentieth Century,* Vol. 1 (2000)
116. *American Poetry: The Twentieth Century,* Vol. 2 (2000)
117. F. Scott Fitzgerald, *Novels and Stories 1920–1922* (2000)
118. Henry Wadsworth Longfellow, *Poems and Other Writings* (2000)
119. Tennessee Williams, *Plays 1937–1955* (2000)
120. Tennessee Williams, *Plays 1957–1980* (2000)

This book is set in 10 point Linotron Galliard, a face designed for photocomposition by Matthew Carter and based on the sixteenth-century face Granjon. The paper is acid-free Ecusta Nyalite and meets the requirements for permanence of the American National Standards Institute. The binding material is Brillianta, a woven rayon cloth made by Van Heek-Scholco Textielfabrieken, Holland. The composition is by The Clarinda Company. Printing and binding by R.R.Donnelley & Sons Company. Designed by Bruce Campbell.